PRAISE FOR ANNE PERRY
AND HER VICTORIAN NOVELS

"Anne Perry has made this particular era her own literary preserve." —*The San Diego Union-Tribune*

"Beguiling . . . The period detail remains fascinating, and [Anne Perry's] grasp of Victorian character and conscience still astonishes."
—Cleveland *Plain Dealer*

"The most adroit sleight-of-hand practitioner since Agatha Christie." —*Chicago Sun-Times*

"Few mystery writers this side of Arthur Conan Doyle can evoke Victorian London with such relish for detail and mood." —*San Francisco Chronicle*

"[A] master of crime fiction who rarely fails to deliver a strong story and colorful cast of characters."
—Baltimore *Sun*

"The pages fly. . . . Once again we're in the capable hands of Anne Perry, reigning monarch of the Victorian mystery."
—*People* (Page-turner of the Week)

"Anne Perry's historical mysteries suggestively peel away layer after layer of Victorian respectability until the underlying social evils of a gilded era are exposed in all their naked truth."
—*The New York Times Book Review*

BY ANNE PERRY

*Published by The Random House
Publishing Group*

THE
WILLIAM MONK MYSTERIES

The First Three Novels

THE FACE OF A STRANGER

A DANGEROUS MOURNING

DEFEND AND BETRAY

ANNE PERRY

Ballantine Books ⬚ New York

2005 Ballantine Books Trade Paperback Edition

Published in the United States by Ballantine Books, an imprint of The Random House Publishing Group, a division of Random House, Inc., New York.

Ballantine and colophon are registered trademarks of Random House, Inc.

Originally published as three separate works entitled *The Face of a Stranger, A Dangerous Mourning,* and *Defend and Betray* by Ballantine Books in 1990, 1991, and 1992 in hardcover.

ISBN 978-0-345-48093-4

Printed in the United States of America

www.ballantinebooks.com

9   8   7   6   5   4   3   2

THE
WILLIAM MONK
MYSTERIES

THE FACE OF A STRANGER

To Christine M. J. Lynch,
in gratitude for old friendship renewed

1

H*E OPENED HIS EYES* and saw nothing but a pale grayness above him, uniform, like a winter sky, threatening and heavy. He blinked and looked again. He was lying flat on his back; the grayness was a ceiling, dirty with the grime and trapped fumes of years.

He moved slightly. The bed he was lying on was hard and short. He made an effort to sit up and found it acutely painful. Inside his chest a fierce pain stabbed him, and his left arm was heavily bandaged and aching. As soon as he was half up his head thumped as if his pulse were a hammer behind his eyes.

There was another wooden cot just like his own a few feet away, and a pasty-faced man lay on it, moving restlessly, gray blanket mangled and sweat staining his shirt. Beyond him was another, blood-soaked bandages swathing the legs; and beyond that another, and so on down the great room to the black-bellied stove at the far end and the smoke-scored ceiling above it.

Panic exploded inside him, hot prickling through his skin. He was in a workhouse! God in heaven, how had he come to this?

But it was broad daylight! Awkwardly, shifting his position, he stared around the room. There were people in

1

all the cots; they lined the walls, and every last one was occupied. No workhouse in the country allowed that! They should be up and laboring, for the good of their souls, if not for the workhouse purse. Not even children were granted the sin of idleness.

Of course; it was a hospital. It must be! Very carefully he lay down again, relief overwhelming him as his head touched the bran pillow. He had no recollection of how he had come to be in such a place, no memory of having hurt himself—and yet he was undoubtedly injured, his arm was stiff and clumsy, he was aware now of a deep ache in the bone. And his chest hurt him sharply every time he breathed in. There was a thunderstorm raging inside his head. What had happened to him? It must have been a major accident: a collapsing wall, a violent throw from a horse, a fall from a height? But no impression came back, not even a memory of fear.

He was still struggling to recall something when a grinning face appeared above him and a voice spoke cheerfully.

"Now then, you awake again, are you?"

He stared upwards, focusing on the moon face. It was broad and blunt with a chapped skin and a smile that stretched wide over broken teeth.

He tried to clear his head.

"Again?" he said confusedly. The past lay behind him in dreamless sleep like a white corridor without a beginning.

"You're a right one, you are." The voice sighed good-humoredly. "You dunno nuffin' from one day ter the next, do yer? It wouldn't surprise me none if yer didn't remember yer own name! 'Ow are yer then? 'Ow's yer arm?"

"My name?" There was nothing there, nothing at all.

"Yeah." The voice was cheerful and patient. "Wot's yer name, then?"

He must know his name. Of course he must! It was . . . Blank seconds ticked by.

"Well then?" the voice pressed.

2

He struggled. Nothing came except a white panic, like a snowstorm in the brain, whirling and dangerous, and without focus.

"Yer've fergot!" The voice was stoic and resigned. "I thought so. Well the Peelers was 'ere, day afore yesterday; an' they said as you was 'Monk'—'William Monk.' Now wot 'a you gorn an' done that the Peelers is after yer?" He pushed helpfully at the pillow with enormous hands and then straightened the blanket. "You like a nice 'ot drink then, or suffink? Proper parky it is, even in 'ere. July—an it feels like ruddy November! I'll get yer a nice 'ot drink o' gruel, 'ow's that then? Raining a flood outside, it is. Ye're best off in 'ere."

"William Monk?" he repeated the name.

"That's right, leastways that's wot the Peelers says. Feller called Runcorn, 'e was; Mr. Runcorn, a hinspector, no less!" He raised scruffy eyebrows. "Wot yer done, then? You one o' them Swell Mob wot goes around pinchin' gennlemen's wallets and gold watches?" There was no criticism in his round, benign eyes. "That's wot yer looked like when they brought yer in 'ere, proper natty dressed yer was, hunderneath the mud and torn-up stuff, like, and all that blood."

Monk said nothing. His head reeled, pounding in an effort to perceive anything in the mists, even one clear, tangible memory. But even the name had no real significance. "William" had a vague familiarity but it was a common enough name. Everyone must know dozens of Williams.

"So yer don't remember," the man went on, his face friendly and faintly amused. He had seen all manner of human frailty and there was nothing so fearful or so eccentric it disturbed his composure. He had seen men die of the pox and the plague, or climb the wall in terror of things that were not there. A grown man who could not remember yesterday was a curiosity, but nothing to marvel at. "Or else yer ain't saying," he went on. "Don't blame yer." He shrugged. "Don't do ter give the Peelers nothin'

3

as yer don't 'ave ter. Now d'yer feel like a spot of 'ot gruel? Nice and thick, it is, bin sitting on that there stove a fair while. Put a bit of 'eart inter yer."

Monk was hungry, and even under the blanket he realized he was cold.

"Yes please," he accepted.

"Right-oh then, gruel it is. I suppose I'll be a'tellin' yer yer name termorrer jus' the same, an' yer'll look at me all gormless again." He shook his head. "Either yer 'it yer 'ead summink 'orrible, or ye're scared o' yer wits o' them Peelers. Wot yer done? You pinched the crown jools?" And he went off chuckling with laughter to himself, up to the black-bellied stove at the far end of the ward.

Police! Was he a thief? The thought was repellent, not only because of the fear attached to it but for itself, what it made of him. And yet he had no idea if it might be true.

Who was he? What manner of man? Had he been hurt doing something brave, rash? Or chased down like an animal for some crime? Or was he merely unfortunate, a victim, in the wrong place at the wrong time?

He racked his mind and found nothing, not a shred of thought or sensation. He must live somewhere, know people with faces, voices, emotions. And there was nothing! For all that his memory held, he could have sprung into existence here in the hard cot in this bleak hospital ward.

But he was known to someone! The police.

The man returned with the gruel and carefully fed it to Monk, a spoonful at a time. It was thin and tasteless, but he was grateful for it. Afterwards he lay back again, and struggle as he might, even fear could not keep him from deep, apparently dreamless sleep.

When he woke the following morning at least two things were perfectly clear this time: his name, and where he was. He could remember the meager happenings of the previous day quite sharply: the nurse, the hot gruel, the

4

man in the next cot turning and groaning, the gray-white ceiling, the feel of the blankets, and the pain in his chest.

He had little idea of time, but he judged it to be somewhere in the mid-afternoon when the policeman came. He was a big man, or he appeared so in the caped coat and top hat of Peel's Metropolitan Police Force. He had a bony face, long nose and wide mouth, a good brow, but deep-set eyes too small to tell the color of easily; a pleasant enough countenance, and intelligent, but showing small signs of temper between the brows and about the lips. He stopped at Monk's cot.

"Well, do you know me this time, then?" he asked cheerfully.

Monk did not shake his head; it hurt too much.

"No," he said simply.

The man mastered his irritation and something that might even have been disappointment. He looked Monk up and down closely, narrowing one eye in a nervous gesture as if he would concentrate his vision.

"You look better today," he pronounced.

Was that the truth; did he look better? Or did Runcorn merely want to encourage him? For that matter, what did he look like? He had no idea. Was he dark or fair, ugly or pleasing? Was he well built, or ungainly? He could not even see his hands, let alone his body beneath the blankets. He would not look now—he must wait till Runcorn was gone.

"Don't remember anything, I suppose?" Runcorn continued. "Don't remember what happened to you?"

"No." Monk was fighting with a cloud totally without shape. Did this man know him, or merely of him? Was he a public figure Monk ought to recognize? Or did he pursue him for some dutiful and anonymous purpose? Might he only be looking for information, or could he tell Monk something about himself more than a bare name, put flesh and memory to the bleak fact of his presence?

Monk was lying on the cot clothed up to his chin, and yet he felt mentally naked, vulnerable as the exposed and

5

ridiculous are. His instinct was to hide, to conceal his weakness. And yet he must know. There must be dozens, perhaps scores of people in the world who knew him, and he knew nothing. It was a total and paralyzing disadvantage. He did not even know who loved or hated him, whom he had wronged, or helped. His need was like that of a man who starves for food, and yet is terrified that in any mouthful may lurk poison.

He looked back at the policeman. Runcorn, the nurse had said his name was. He must commit himself to something.

"Did I have an accident?" he asked.

"Looked like it," Runcorn replied matter-of-factly. "Hansom was turned over, right mess. You must have hit something at a hell of a lick. Horse frightened out of its wits." He shook his head and pulled the corners of his mouth down. "Cabby killed outright, poor devil. Hit his head on the curb. You were inside, so I suppose you were partly protected. Had a swine of a job to get you out. Dead weight. Never realized you were such a solid feller. Don't remember it, I suppose? Not even the fright?" Again his left eye narrowed a little.

"No." No images came to Monk's mind, no memory of speed, or impact, not even pain.

"Don't remember what you were doing?" Runcorn went on, without any real hope in his voice. "What case you were on?"

Monk seized on a brilliant hope, a thing with shape; he was almost too afraid to ask, in case it crumbled at his touch. He stared at Runcorn. He must know this man, personally, perhaps even daily. And yet nothing in him woke the slightest recall.

"Well, man?" Runcorn demanded. "Do you remember? You weren't anywhere we sent you! What the devil were you doing? You must have discovered something yourself. Can you remember what it was?"

The blank was impenetrable.

Monk moved his head fractionally in negation, but the

6

bright bubble inside him stayed. He was a Peeler himself, that was why they knew him! He was not a thief—not a fugitive.

Runcorn leaned forward a little, watching him keenly, seeing the light in his face.

"You do remember something!" he said triumphantly. "Come on, man—what is it?"

Monk could not explain that it was not memory that changed him, but a dissolving of fear in one of the sharpest forms it had taken. The entire, suffocating blanket was still there, but characterless now, without specific menace.

Runcorn was still waiting, staring at him intently.

"No," Monk said slowly. "Not yet."

Runcorn straightened up. He sighed, trying to control himself. "It'll come."

"How long have I been here?" Monk asked. "I've lost count of time." It sounded reasonable enough; anyone ill might do that.

"Over three weeks—it's the thirty-first of July—1856," he added with a touch of sarcasm.

Dear God! Over three weeks, and all he could remember was yesterday. He shut his eyes; it was infinitely worse than that—a whole lifetime of how many years? And all he could remember was yesterday! How old was he? How many years were lost? Panic boiled up inside him again and for a moment he could have screamed, Help me, somebody, who am I? Give me back my life, my self!

But men did not scream in public, even in private they did not cry out. The sweat stood cold on his skin and he lay rigid, hands clenched by his sides. Runcorn would take it for pain, ordinary physical pain. He must keep up the appearance. He must not let Runcorn think he had forgotten how to do his job. Without a job the workhouse would be a reality—grinding, hopeless, day after day of obedient, servile, pointless labor.

He forced himself back to the present.

"Over three weeks?"

"Yes," Runcorn replied. Then he coughed and cleared

7

his throat. Perhaps he was embarrassed. What does one say to a man who cannot remember you, who cannot even remember himself? Monk felt for him.

"It'll come back," Runcorn repeated. "When you're up again; when you get back on the job. You want a break to get well, that's what you need, a break till you get your strength. Take a week or two. Bound to. Come back to the station when you're fit to work. It'll all come clear then, I dare say."

"Yes," Monk agreed, more for Runcorn's sake than his own. He did not believe it.

Monk left the hospital three days later. He was strong enough to walk, and no one stayed in such places longer than they had to. It was not only financial consideration, but the sheer danger. More people died of cross-infection than of any illness or injury that brought them there in the first place. This much was imparted to him in a cheerfully resigned manner by the nurse who had originally told him his name.

It was easy to believe. In the short days he could remember he had seen doctors move from one bloody or festering wound to another, from fever patient to vomiting and flux, then to open sores, and back again. Soiled bandages lay on the floor; there was little laundry done, although no doubt they did the best they could on the pittance they had.

And to be fair, they did their utmost never knowingly to admit patients suffering from typhoid, cholera or smallpox; and if they did discover these illnesses afterwards, they rectified their error. Those poor souls had to be quarantined in their own houses and left to die, or recover if God were willing. There they would be of least peril to the community. Everyone was familiar with the black flag hanging limply at the ends of a street.

Runcorn had left for him his Peeler's coat and tall hat, carefully dusted off and mended after the accident. At least they fitted him, apart from being a trifle loose because of

8

the weight he had lost lying on his back since the injury. But that would return. He was a strong man, tall and lean muscled, but the nurse had shaved him so he had not yet seen his face. He had felt it, touching with his fingertips when no one was watching him. It was strong boned, and his mouth seemed wide, that was all he knew; and his hands were smooth and uncalloused by labor, with a scattering of dark hairs on the backs.

Apparently he had had a few coins in his pocket when they brought him in, and these were handed to him as he left. Someone else must have paid for his treatment—presumably his police salary had been sufficient? Now he stood on the steps with eight shillings and eleven pence, a cotton handkerchief and an envelope with his name and "27 Grafton Street" written on it. It contained a receipt from his tailor.

He looked around him and recognized nothing. It was a bright day with fast-scudding clouds and a warm wind. Fifty yards away there was an intersection, and a small boy was wielding a broom, keeping the crossing clear of horse manure and other rubbish. A carriage swirled past, drawn by two high-stepping bays.

Monk stepped down, still feeling weak, and made his way to the main road. It took him five minutes to see a vacant hansom, hail it and give the cabby the address. He sat back inside and watched as streets and squares flickered by, other vehicles, carriages, some with liveried footmen, more hansoms, brewers' drays, costermongers' carts. He saw peddlers and vendors, a man selling fresh eels, another with hot pies, plum duff—it sounded good, he was hungry, but he had no idea how much the fare would be, so he did not dare stop.

A newspaper boy was shouting something, but they passed him too quickly to hear above the horse's hooves. A one-legged man sold matches.

There was a familiarity about the streets, but it was at the back of his mind. He could not have named a single one, simply that they did not seem alien.

9

Tottenham Court Road. It was very busy: carriages, drays, carts, women in wide skirts stepping over refuse in the gutter, two soldiers laughing and a little drunk, red coats a splash of color, a flower seller and two washerwomen.

The cab swung left into Grafton Street and stopped.

" 'Ere y'are, sir, Number Twenty-seven."

"Thank you." Monk climbed out awkwardly; he was still stiff and unpleasantly weak. Even that small exertion had tired him. He had no idea how much money to offer. He held out a florin, two sixpences, a penny and a halfpenny in his hand.

The cabby hesitated, then took one of the sixpences and the halfpenny, tipped his hat and slapped the reins across his horse's rump, leaving Monk standing on the pavement. He hesitated, now that the moment was come, overtaken with fear. He had not even the slightest idea what he should find—or whom.

Two men passed, looking at him curiously. They must suppose him lost. He felt foolish, embarrassed. Who would answer his knock? Should he know them? If he lived here, they must know him. How well? Were they friends, or merely landlords? It was preposterous, but he did not even know if he had a family!

But if he had, surely they would have visited him. Runcorn had come, so they would have been told where he was. Or had he been the kind of man who inspires no love, only professional courtesy? Was that why Runcorn had called, because it was his job?

Had he been a good policeman, efficient at his work? Was he liked? It was ridiculous—pathetic.

He shook himself. This was childish. If he had family, a wife or brother or sister, Runcorn would have told him. He must discover each thing as he could; if he was fit to be employed by the Peelers, then he was a detective. He would learn each piece till he had enough to cobble together a whole, the pattern of his life. The first step was

10

to knock on this door, dark brown and closed in front of him.

He lifted his hand and rapped sharply. It was long, desperate minutes with the questions roaring in his mind before it was opened by a broad, middle-aged woman in an apron. Her hair was scraped back untidily, but it was thick and clean and her scrubbed face was generous.

"Well I never!" she said impulsively. "Save my soul, if it in't Mr. Monk back again! I was only saying to Mr. Worley this very morning, as 'ow if you didn't come back again soon I'd 'ave ter let yer rooms; much as it'd go against me ter do it. But a body 'as ter live. Mind that Mr. Runcorn did come around an' say as yer'd 'ad a haccident and bin terrible 'urt and was in one 'o them 'orstipitals." She put her hand to her head in despair. "Gawd save us from such places. Ye're the first man I've seen as 'as come out o' there on 'is own two feet. To tell you the truth, I was expectin' every day to 'ave some messenger boy come and say as you was dead." She screwed up her face and looked at him carefully. "Mind yer does still look proper poorly. Come in and I'll make yer a good meal. Yer must be starved, I'll dare swear yer 'aven't 'ad a decent dish since yer left 'ere! It were as cold as a workhouse master's 'eart the day yer went!" And she whisked her enormous skirts around and led him inside.

He followed her through the paneled hallway hung with sentimental pictures and up the stairs to a large landing. She produced a bunch of keys from her girdle and opened one of the doors.

"I suppose you gorn and lorst your own key, or you wouldn't 'ave knocked; that stands ter reason, don't it?"

"I had my own key?" he asked before realizing how it betrayed him.

"Gawd save us, o' course yer did!" she said in surprise. "Yer don't think I'm goin' ter get up and down at all hours o' the night ter let yer in and out, do yer? A Christian body needs 'er sleep. 'Eathen hours yer keeps, an' no mistake. Comes o' chasin' after 'eathen folk, I expec'."

She turned to look at him. " 'Ere, yer does look ill. Yer must 'ave bin 'it summink terrible. You go in there an' sit down, an' I'll bring yer a good 'ot meal an' a drink. Do you the world o' good, that will." She snorted and straightened her apron fiercely. "I always thought them 'orstipitals din't look after yer proper. I'll wager as 'alf o' them wot dies in there dies o' starvation." And with indignation at the thought twitching in every muscle under her black taffeta, she swept out of the room, leaving the door open behind her.

Monk walked over and closed it, then turned to face the room. It was large, dark brown paneling and green wallpaper. The furniture was well used. A heavy oak table with four matching chairs stood in the center, Jacobean with carved legs and decorated claw feet. The sideboard against the far wall was similar, although what purpose it served he did not know; there was no china on it, and when he opened the drawers, no cutlery. However the lower drawers did contain table linen and napkins, freshly laundered and in good repair. There was also an oak desk with two small, flat drawers. Against the near wall, by the door, there was a handsome bookcase full of volumes. Part of the furniture? Or his own? Later he would look at the titles.

The windows were draped rather than hung with fringed plush curtains of a mid shade of green. The gas brackets on the walls were ornate, with pieces missing. The leather easy chair had faded patches on the arms, and the pile on the cushions was flat. The carpet's colors had long since dimmed to muted plums, navies and forest greens—a pleasant background. There were several pictures of a self-indulgent tone, and a motto over the mantelpiece with the dire warning GOD SEES ALL.

Were they his? Surely not; the emotions jarred on him and he found himself pulling a face at the mawkishness of the subjects, even feeling a touch of contempt.

It was a comfortable room, well lived in, but peculiarly impersonal, without photographs or mementos, no mark of his own taste. His eyes went around it again and again, but nothing was familiar, nothing brought even a pinprick of memory.

He tried the bedroom beyond. It was the same: comfortable, old, shabby. A large bed stood in the center, made up ready with clean sheets, crisp white bolster, and wine-colored eiderdown, flounced at the edges. On the heavy dresser there was a rather pleasant china washbowl and a jug for water. A handsome silver-backed hairbrush lay on the tallboy.

He touched the surfaces. His hands came away clean. Mrs. Worley was at least a good housekeeper.

He was about to open the drawers and look further when there was a sharp rap on the outer door and Mrs. Worley returned, carrying a tray with a steaming plate piled with steak and kidney pudding, boiled cabbage, carrots and beans, and another dish with pie and custard.

"There yer are," she said with satisfaction, setting it down on the table. He was relieved to see knife, fork and spoon with it, and a glass of cider. "You eat that, and yer'll feel better!"

"Thank you, Mrs. Worley." His gratitude was genuine; he had not had a good meal since . . . ?

"It's my duty, Mr. Monk, as a Christian woman," she replied with a little shake of her head. "And yer always paid me prompt, I'll say that for yer—never argued ner was a day late, fer ought else! Now you eat that up, then go ter bed. Yer look proper done in. I don't know what yer bin doin', an' I don't want ter. Prob'ly in't fit fer a body to know anyway."

"What shall I do with the . . ." He looked at the tray.

"Put it outside the door like yer always does!" she said with raised eyebrows. Then she looked at him more closely and sighed. "An' if yer gets took poorly in the night, yer'd best shout out, an I'll come an' see to yer."

"It won't be necessary—I shall be perfectly well."

She sniffed and let out a little gasp, heavy with disbelief, then bustled out, closing the door behind her with a

13

loud click. He realized immediately how ungracious he had been. She had offered to get up in the night to help him if he needed it, and all he had done was assure her she was not needed. And she had not looked surprised, or hurt. Was he always this discourteous? He paid—she said he paid promptly and without quibble. Was that all there was between them, no kindness, no feeling, just a lodger who was financially reliable, and a landlady who did her Christian duty by him, because that was her nature?

It was not an attractive picture.

He turned his attention to the food. It was plain, but of excellent flavor, and she was certainly not ungenerous with her portions. It flickered through his mind with some anxiety to wonder how much he paid for these amenities, and if he could much longer afford them while he was unable to work. The sooner he recovered his strength, and enough of his wits to resume his duties for the police, the better. He could hardly ask her for credit, particularly after her remarks, and his manners. Please heaven he did not owe her already for the time he was in the hospital!

When he had finished the meal he placed the tray outside on the landing table where she could collect it. He went back into the room, closed the door and sat in one of the armchairs, intending to look through the desk in the window corner, but in weariness, and the comfort of the cushions, he fell asleep.

When he woke, cold now and stiff, his side aching, it was dark, and he fumbled to light the gas. He was still tired, and would willingly have gone to bed, but he knew that the temptation of the desk, and the fear of it, would trouble even the most exhausted sleep.

He lit the lamp above it and pulled open the top. There was a flat surface with inkstand, a leather writing block and a dozen small closed drawers.

He started at the top left-hand side, and worked through them all. He must be a methodical man. There were receipted bills; a few newspaper clippings, entirely of crimes,

14

usually violent, and describing brilliant police work in solving them; three railway timetables; business letters; and a note from a tailor.

A tailor. So that was where his money went—vain beggar. He must take a look through his wardrobe and see what his taste was. Expensive, according to the bill in his hand. A policeman who wanted to look like a gentleman! He laughed sharply: a ratcatcher with pretensions—was that what he was? A somewhat ridiculous figure. The thought hurt and he pushed it away with a black humor.

In other drawers there were envelopes, notepaper, good quality—vanity again! Whom did he write to? There was also sealing wax, string, a paper knife and scissors, a number of minor items of convenience. It was not until the tenth drawer that he found the personal correspondence. They were all in the same hand, to judge from the formation of the letters a young person, or someone of slight education. Only one person wrote to him—or only one whose letters he had considered worth keeping. He opened the first, angry with himself that his hands were shaking.

It was very simple, beginning "Dear William," full of homely news, and ending "your loving sister, Beth."

He put it down, the round characters burning in front of him, dizzy and overwhelmed with excitement and relief, and perhaps a shadow of disappointment he forced away. He had a sister, there was someone who knew him, had always known him; more than that, who cared. He picked up the letter again quickly, almost tearing it in his clumsiness to reread it. It was gentle, frank, and yes, it was affectionate; it must be, one did not speak so openly to someone one did not trust, and care for.

And yet there was nothing in it that was any kind of reply, no reference to anything he had written to her. Surely he did write? He could not have treated such a woman with cavalier disregard.

What kind of a man was he? If he had ignored her, not written, then there must be a reason. How could he ex-

15

plain himself, justify anything, when he could not remember? It was like being accused, standing in the dock with no defense.

It was long, painful moments before he thought to look for the address. When he did it came as a sharp, bewildering surprise—it was in Northumberland. He repeated it over and over to himself, aloud. It sounded familiar, but he could not place it. He had to go to the bookcase and search for an atlas to look it up. Even so he could not see it for several minutes. It was very small, a name in fine letters on the coast, a fishing village.

A fishing village! What was his sister doing there? Had she married and gone there? The surname on the envelope was Bannerman. Or had he been born there, and then come south to London? He laughed sharply. Was that the key to his pretension? He was a provincial fisherman's son, with eyes on passing himself off as something better?

When? When had he come?

He realized with a shock he did not know how old he was. He still had not looked at himself in the glass. Why not? Was he afraid of it? What did it matter how a man looked? And yet he was trembling.

He swallowed hard and picked up the oil lamp from the desk. He walked slowly into the bedroom and put the lamp on the dresser. There must be a glass there, at least big enough to shave himself.

It was on a swivel; that was why he had not noticed it before, his eye had been on the silver brush. He set the lamp down and slowly tipped the glass.

The face he saw was dark and very strong, broad, slightly aquiline nose, wide mouth, rather thin upper lip, lower lip fuller, with an old scar just below it, eyes intense luminous gray in the flickering light. It was a powerful face, but not an easy one. If there was humor it would be harsh, of wit rather than laughter. He could have been anything between thirty-five and forty-five.

He picked up the lamp and walked back to the main room, finding the way blindly, his inner eye still seeing

16

the face that had stared back at him from the dim glass. It was not that it displeased him especially, but it was the face of a stranger, and not one easy to know.

The following day he made his decision. He would travel north to see his sister. She would at least be able to tell him his childhood, his family. And to judge from her letters, and the recent date of the last, she still held him in affection, whether he deserved it or not. He wrote in the morning telling her simply that he had had an accident but was considerably recovered now, and intended to visit her when he was well enough to make the journey, which he expected to be no more than another day or two at the outside.

Among the other things in the desk drawer he found a modest sum of money. Apparently he was not extravagant except at the tailor, the clothes in his wardrobe were impeccably cut and of first-quality fabric, and possibly the bookshop—if the contents of the case were his. Other than that he had saved regularly, but if for any particular purpose there was no note of it, and it hardly mattered now. He gave Mrs. Worley what she asked for a further month's rent on account—minus the food he would not consume while he was away—and informed her he was going to visit his sister in Northumberland.

"Very good idea." She nodded her head sagaciously. "More'n time you paid her a visit, if yer ask me. Not that yer did, o' course! I'm not one to interfere"—she drew in her breath—"but yer in't bin orf ter see 'er since I known yer—an that's some years now. An' the poor soul writes to yer reg'lar—although w'en yer writes back I'm blessed if I know!"

She put the money in her pocket and looked at him closely.

"Well, you look after yerself—eat proper and don't go doin' any daft caperin's around chasin' folk. Let ruffians alone an' mind for yerself for a space." And with that parting advice she smoothed her apron again and turned

17

away, her boot heels clicking down the corridor towards the kitchen.

It was August fourth when he boarded the train in London and settled himself for the long journey.

Northumberland was vast and bleak, wind roaring over treeless, heather-darkened moors, but there was a simplicity about its tumultuous skies and clean earth that pleased him enormously. Was it familiar to him, memories stirring from childhood, or only beauty that would have woken the same emotion in him had it been as unknown as the plains of the moon? He stood a long time at the station, bag in his hand, staring out at the hills before he finally made move to begin. He would have to find a conveyance of some kind: he was eleven miles from the sea and the hamlet he wanted. In normal health he might well have walked it, but he was still weak. His rib ached when he breathed deeply, and he had not yet the full use of his broken arm.

It was not more than a pony cart, and he had paid handsomely for it, he thought. But he was glad enough to have the driver take him to his sister's house, which he asked for by name, and deposit him and his bag on the narrow street in front of the door. As the wheels rattled away over the cobbles he conquered his thoughts, the apprehension and the sense of an irretrievable step, and knocked loudly.

He was about to knock again when the door swung open and a pretty, fresh-faced woman stood on the step. She was bordering on the plump and had strong dark hair and features reminiscent of his own only in the broad brow and some echo of cheekbones. Her eyes were blue and her nose had the strength without the arrogance, and her mouth was far softer. All this flashed into his mind, with the realization that she must be Beth, his sister. She would find him inexplicable, and probably be hurt, if he did not know her.

"Beth." He held out his hands.

Her face broke into a broad smile of delight.

"William! I hardly knew you, you've changed so much!

18

We got your letter—you said an accident—are you hurt badly? We didn't expect you so soon—" She blushed. "Not that you aren't very welcome, of course." Her accent was broad Northumberland, and he found it surprisingly pleasing to the ear. Was that familiarity again, or only the music of it after London?

"William?" She was staring at him. "Come inside—you must be tired out, and hungry." She made as if to pull him physically into the house.

He followed her, smiling in a sudden relief. She knew him; apparently she held no grudge for his long absence or the letters he had not written. There was a naturalness about her that made long explanations unnecessary. And he realized he was indeed hungry.

The kitchen was small but scrubbed clean; in fact the table was almost white. It woke no chord of memory in him at all. There were warm smells of bread and baked fish and salt wind from the sea. For the first time since waking in the hospital, he found himself beginning to relax, to ease the knots out.

Gradually, over bread and soup, he told her the facts he knew of the accident, inventing details where the story was so bare as to seem evasive. She listened while she continued to stir her cooking on the stove, warm the flatiron and then began on a series of small children's clothes and a man's Sunday white shirt. If it was strange to her, or less than credible, she gave no outward sign. Perhaps the whole world of London was beyond her knowledge anyway, and inhabited by people who lived incomprehensible lives which could not be hoped to make sense to ordinary people.

It was the late summer dusk when her husband came in, a broad, fair man with wind-scoured face and mild features. His gray eyes still seemed tuned to the sea. He greeted Monk with friendly surprise, but no sense of dismay or of having been disturbed in his feelings, or the peace of his home.

No one asked Monk for explanations, even the three shy

19

children returned from chores and play, and since he had none to give, the matter was passed over. It was a strange mark of the distance between them, which he observed with a wry pain, that apparently he had never shared enough of himself with his only family that they noticed the omission.

Day succeeded day, sometimes golden bright, sun hot when the wind was offshore and the sand soft under his feet. Other times it swung east off the North Sea and blew with sharp chill and the breath of storm. Monk walked along the beach, feeling it rip at him, beating his face, tearing at his hair, and the very size of it was at once frightening and comforting. It had nothing to do with people; it was impersonal, indiscriminate.

He had been there a week, and was feeling the strength of life come back to him, when the alarm was called. It was nearly midnight and the wind screaming around the stone corners of the houses when the shouts came and the hammering on the door.

Rob Bannerman was up within minutes, oilskins and seaboots on still almost in his sleep. Monk stood on the landing in bewilderment, confused; at first no explanation came to his mind as to the emergency. It was not until he saw Beth's face when she ran to the window, and he followed her and saw below them the dancing lanterns and the gleam of light on moving figures, oilskins shining in the rain, that he realized what it was. Instinctively he put his arm around Beth, and she moved fractionally closer to him, but her body was stiff. Under her breath she was praying, and there were tears in her voice.

Rob was already out of the house. He had spoken to neither of them, not even hesitated beyond touching Beth's hand as he passed her.

It was a wreck, some ship driven by the screaming winds onto the outstretched fingers of rock, with God knew how many souls clinging to the sundering planks, water already swirling around their waists.

After the first moment of shock, Beth ran upstairs again

20

to dress, calling to Monk to do the same, then everything was a matter of finding blankets, heating soup, rebuilding fires ready to help the survivors—if, please God, there were any.

The work went on all night, the lifeboats going backwards and forwards, men roped together. Thirty-five people were pulled out of the sea, ten were lost. Survivors were all brought back to the few homes in the village. Beth's kitchen was full of white-faced shivering people and she and Monk plied them with hot soup and what comforting words they could think of.

Nothing was stinted. Beth emptied out every last morsel of food without a thought as to what her own family might eat tomorrow. Every stitch of dry clothing was brought out and offered.

One woman sat in the corner too numb with grief for her lost husband even to weep. Beth looked at her with a compassion that made her beautiful. In a moment between tasks Monk saw her bend and take the woman's hands, holding them between her own to press some warmth into them, speaking to her gently as if she had been a child.

Monk felt a sudden ache of loneliness, of being an outsider whose involvement in this passion of suffering and pity was only chance. He contributed nothing but physical help; he could not even remember whether he had ever done it before, whether these were his people or not. Had he ever risked his life without grudge or question as Rob Bannerman did? He hungered with a terrible need for some part in the beauty of it. Had he ever had courage, generosity? Was there anything in his past to be proud of, to cling to?

There was no one he could ask—

The moment passed and the urgency of the present need overtook him again. He bent to pick up a child shaking with terror and cold, and wrapped it in a warm blanket, holding it close to his own body, stroking it with soft, repetitive words as he might a frightened animal.

By dawn it was over. The seas were still running high

and hard, but Rob was back, too tired to speak and too weary with loss of those the sea had taken. He simply took off his wet clothes in the kitchen and climbed up to bed.

A week later Monk was fully recovered physically; only dreams troubled him, vague nightmares of fear, sharp pain and a sense of being violently struck and losing his balance, then a suffocation. He woke gasping, his heart racing and sweat on his skin, his breath rasping, but nothing was left except the fear, no thread to unravel towards recollection. The need to return to London became more pressing. He had found his distant past, his beginnings, but memory was virgin blank and Beth could tell him nothing whatsoever of his life since leaving, when she was still little more than a child. Apparently he had not written of it, only trivialities, items of ordinary news such as one might read in the journals or newspapers, and small matters of his welfare and concern for hers. This was the first time he had visited her in eight years, something he was not proud to learn. He seemed a cold man, obsessed with his own ambition. Had that compelled him to work so hard, or had he been so poor? He would like to think there was some excuse, but to judge from the money in his desk at Grafton Street, it had not lately been finance.

He racked his brains to recall any emotion, any flash of memory as to what sort of man he was, what he had valued, what sought. Nothing came, no explanations for his self-absorption.

He said good-bye to her and Rob, thanking them rather awkwardly for their kindness, surprising and embarrassing them, and because of it, himself too; but he meant it so deeply. Because they were strangers to him, he felt as if they had taken him in, a stranger, and offered him acceptance, even trust. They looked confused, Beth coloring shyly. But he did not try to explain; he did not have words, nor did he wish them to know.

* * *

London seemed enormous, dirty and indifferent when he got off the train and walked out of the ornate, smoke-grimed station. He took a hansom to Grafton Street, announced his return to Mrs. Worley, then went upstairs and changed his clothes from those worn and crumpled by his journey. He took himself to the police station Runcorn had named when speaking to the nurse. With the experience of Beth and Northumberland behind him he began to feel a little confidence. It was still another essay into the unknown, but with each step accomplished without unpleasant surprise, his apprehension lessened.

When he climbed out of the cab and paid the driver he stood on the pavement. The police station was as unfamiliar as everything else—not strange, simply without any spark of familiarity at all. He opened the doors and went inside, saw the sergeant at the duty desk and wondered how many hundreds of times before he had done exactly this.

" 'Arternoon, Mr. Monk.'' The man looked up with slight surprise, and no pleasure. "Nasty haccident. Better now, are yer, sir?''

There was a chill in his voice, a wariness. Monk looked at him. He was perhaps forty, round-faced, mild and perhaps a trifle indecisive, a man who could be easily befriended, and easily crushed. Monk felt a stirring of shame, and knew no reason for it whatever, except the caution in the man's eyes. He was expecting Monk to say something to which he would not be able to reply with assurance. He was a subordinate, and slower with words, and he knew it.

"Yes I am, thank you.'' Monk could not remember the man's name to use it. He felt contempt for himself—what kind of a man embarrasses someone who cannot retaliate? Why? Was there some long history of incompetence or deceit that would explain such a thing?

"You'll be wantin' Mr. Runcorn, sir.'' The sergeant seemed to notice no change in Monk, and to be keen to speed him on his way.

"Yes, if he's in—please?''

23

The sergeant stepped aside a little and allowed Monk through the counter.

Monk stopped, feeling ridiculous. He had no idea which way to go, and he would raise suspicion if he went the wrong way. He had a hot, prickly sensation that there would be little allowance made for him—he was not liked.

"You o'right, sir?" the sergeant said anxiously.

"Yes—yes I am. Is Mr. Runcorn still"—he took a glance around and made a guess—"at the top of the stairs?"

"Yes sir, right w'ere 'e always was!"

"Thank you." And he set off up the steps rapidly, feeling a fool.

Runcorn was in the first room on the corridor. Monk knocked and went in. It was dark and littered with papers and cabinets and baskets for filing, but comfortable, in spite of a certain institutional bareness. Gas lamps hissed gently on the walls. Runcorn himself was sitting behind a large desk, chewing a pencil.

"Ah!" he said with satisfaction when Monk came in. "Fit for work, are you? About time. Best thing, work. Good for a man to work. Well, sit down then, sit down. Think better sitting down."

Monk obeyed, his muscles tight with tension. He imagined his breathing was so loud it must be audible above the gas.

"Good. Good," Runcorn went on. "Lot of cases, as always; I'll wager there's more stolen in some quarters of this city than is ever bought or sold honestly." He pushed away a pile of papers and set his pen in its stand. "And the Swell Mob's been getting worse. All these enormous crinolines. Crinolines were made to steal from, so many petticoats on no one can feel a dip. But that's not what I had in mind for you. Give you a good one to get your teeth into." He smiled mirthlessly.

Monk waited.

"Nasty murder." He leaned back in his chair and looked directly at Monk. "Haven't managed to do any-

24

thing about it, though heaven knows we've tried. Had Lamb in charge. Poor fellow's sick and taken to his bed. Put you on the case; see what you can do. Make a good job of it. We've got to turn up some kind of result.''

"Who was killed?" Monk asked. "And when?"

"Feller called Joscelin Grey, younger brother of Lord Shelburne, so you can see it's rather important we tidy it up." His eyes never left Monk's face. "When? Well that's the worst part of it—rather a while ago, and we haven't turned up a damned thing. Nearly six weeks now—about when you had your accident, in fact, come to think of it, exactly then. Nasty night, thunderstorm and pouring with rain. Probably some ruffian followed him home, but made a very nasty job of it, bashed the poor feller about to an awful state. Newspapers in an outrage, naturally, crying for justice, and what's the world coming to, where are the police, and so on. We'll give you everything poor Lamb had, of course, and a good man to work with, name of Evan, John Evan; worked with Lamb till he took ill. See what you can do, anyway. Give them something!''

"Yes sir." Monk stood up. "Where is Mr. Evan?"

"Out somewhere; trail's pretty cold. Start tomorrow morning, bright and early. Too late now. Go home and get some rest. Last night of freedom, eh? Make the best of it; tomorrow I'll have you working like one of those railway diggers!''

"Yes sir." Monk excused himself and walked out. It was already darkening in the street and the wind was laden with the smell of coming rain. But he knew where he was going, and he knew what he would do tomorrow, and it would be with identity—and purpose.

2

MONK ARRIVED EARLY to meet John Evan and find out what Lamb had so far learned of the murder of Lord Shelburne's brother, Joscelin Grey.

He still had some sense of apprehension; his discoveries about himself had been commonplace, such small things as one might learn of anyone, likes and dislikes, vanities—his wardrobe had plainly shown him those—discourtesies, such as had made the desk sergeant nervous of him. But the remembered warmth of Northumberland was still with him and it was enough to buoy up his spirits. And he must work! The money would not last much longer.

John Evan was a tall young man, and lean almost to the point of appearing frail, but Monk judged from the way he stood that it was a deception; he might well be wiry under that rather elegant jacket, and the air with which he wore his clothes was a natural grace rather than effeminacy. His face was sensitive, all eyes and nose, and his hair waved back from his brow thick and honey brown. Above all he appeared intelligent, which was both necessary to Monk and frightening. He was not yet ready for a companion of such quick sight, or subtlety of perception.

But he had no choice in the matter. Runcorn introduced Evan, banged a pile of papers on the wide, scratched wooden table in Monk's office, a good-sized room crammed with filing drawers and bookcases and with one sash window overlooking an alley. The carpet was a domestic castoff, but better than the bare wood, and there were two leather-seated chairs. Runcorn went out, leaving them alone.

Evan hesitated for a moment, apparently not wishing to usurp authority, then as Monk did not move, he put out a long finger and touched the top of the pile of papers.

"Those are all the statements from the witnesses, sir. Not very helpful, I'm afraid."

Monk said the first thing that came to him.

"Were you with Mr. Lamb when they were taken?"

"Yes sir, all except the street sweeper; Mr. Lamb saw him while I went after the cabby."

"Cabby?" For a moment Monk had a wild hope that the assailant had been seen, was known, that it was merely his whereabouts that were needed. Then the thought died immediately. It would hardly have taken them six weeks if it were so simple. And more than that, there had been in Runcorn's face a challenge, even a kind of perverse satisfaction.

"The cabby that brought Major Grey home, sir," Evan said, demolishing the hope apologetically.

"Oh." Monk was about to ask him if there was anything useful in the man's statement, then realized how inefficient he would appear. He had all the papers in front of him. He picked up the first, and Evan waited silently by the window while he read.

It was in neat, very legible writing, and headed at the top was the statement of Mary Ann Brown, seller of ribbons and laces in the street. Monk imagined the grammar to have been altered somewhat from the original, and a few aspirates put in, but the flavor was clear enough.

"I was standing in my usual place in Doughty Street near Mecklenburg Square, like as I always do, on the corner, knowing as how there is ladies living in many of them buildings, especially ladies as has their own maids what does sewing for them, and the like."

Question from Mr. Lamb: "So you were there at six o'clock in the evening?"

"I suppose I must have been, though I carsen't tell the time, and I don't have no watch. But I see'd the gentleman arrive what was killed. Something terrible, that is, when even the gentry's not safe."

"You saw Major Grey arrive?"

"Yes sir. What a gentleman he looked, all happy and jaunty, like."

"Was he alone?"

"Yes sir, he was."

"Did he go straight in? After paying the cabby, of course."

"Yes sir, he did."

"What time did you leave Mecklenburg Square?"

"Don't rightly know, not for sure. But I heard the church clock at St. Mark's strike the quarter just afore I got there."

"Home?"

"Yes sir."

"And how far is your home from Mecklenburg Square?"

"About a mile, I reckon."

"Where do you live?"

"Off the Pentonville Road, sir."

"Half an hour's walk?"

"Bless you, no sir, more like quarter. A sight too wet to be hanging around, it was. Besides, girls as hang around that time of an evening gets themselves misunderstood, or worse."

"Quite. So you left Mecklenburg Square about seven o'clock."

"Reckon so."

"Did you see anyone else go into Number Six, after Mr. Grey?"

"Yes sir, one other gentleman in a black coat with a big fur collar."

There was a note in brackets after the last statement to say it had been established that this person was a resident of the apartments, and no suspicion attached to him.

The name of Mary Ann Brown was written in the same hand at the bottom, and a rough cross placed beside it.

Monk put it down. It was a statement of only negative value; it made it highly unlikely that Joscelin Grey had been followed home by his murderer. But then the crime had happened in July, when it was light till nine in the evening. A man with murder, or even robbery, on his mind would not wish to be seen so close to his victim.

By the window Evan stood still, watching him, ignoring the clatter in the street beyond, a drayman shouting as he backed his horse, a coster calling his wares and the hiss and rattle of carriage wheels.

Monk picked up the next statement, in the name of Alfred Cressent, a boy of eleven who swept a crossing at the corner of Mecklenburg Square and Doughty Street, keeping it clear of horse droppings principally, and any other litter that might be let fall.

His contribution was much the same, except that he had not left Doughty Street until roughly half an hour after the ribbon girl.

The cabby claimed to have picked Grey up at a regimental club a little before six o'clock, and driven him straight to Mecklenburg Square. His fare had done no more than pass the time of day with him, some trivial comment about the weather, which had been extraordinarily unpleasant, and wished him a good night upon leaving. He could recall nothing more, and to the best of his knowledge they had not been followed or especially remarked by anyone. He had seen no unusual or suspicious characters in the neighborhood of Guilford Street or Mecklenburg Square, either on the way there or on his departure, only the usual peddlers, street sweepers, flower sellers and a few gentlemen of unobtrusive appearance who might have been clerks returning home after a long day's work, or pickpockets awaiting a victim, or any of a hundred other things. This statement also was of no real help.

Monk put it on top of the other two, then looked up and found Evan's gaze still on him, shyness tinged with a faint, self-deprecating humor. Instinctively he liked Evan—or could it be just loneliness, because he had no friend, no human companionship deeper than the courtesies of office or the impersonal kindness of Mrs. Worley fulfilling her "Christian duty." Had he had friends before, or wanted them? If so, where were they? Why had no one welcomed him back? Not even a letter. The answer was unpleasant, and obvious: he had not earned such a thing. He was clever, ambitious—a rather superior ratcatcher. Not appealing. But he must not let Evan see his weakness. He must appear professional, in command.

"Are they all like this?" he asked.

"Pretty much," Evan replied, standing more upright now that he was spoken to. "Nobody saw or heard anything that has led us even to a time or a description. For that matter, not even a definitive motive."

Monk was surprised; it brought his mind back to the business. He must not let it wander. It would be hard enough to appear efficient without woolgathering.

"Not robbery?" he asked.

Evan shook his head and shrugged very slightly. Without effort he had the elegance Monk strove for, and Runcorn missed absolutely.

"Not unless he was frightened off," he answered. "There was money in Grey's wallet, and several small, easily portable ornaments of value around the room. One fact that might be worth something, though: he had no watch on. Gentlemen of his sort usually have rather good watches, engraved, that sort of thing. And he did have a watch chain."

Monk sat on the edge of the table.

"Could he have pawned it?" he asked. "Did anyone see him with a watch?" It was an intelligent question, and

30

it came to him instinctively. Even well-to-do men sometimes ran short of ready money, or dressed and dined beyond their means and were temporarily embarrassed. How had he known to ask that? Perhaps his skill was so deep it was not dependent on memory?

Evan flushed faintly and his hazel eyes looked suddenly awkward.

"I'm afraid we didn't find out, sir. I mean, the people we asked didn't seem to recall clearly; some said they remembered something about a watch, others that they didn't. We couldn't get a description of one. We wondered if he might have pawned it too; but we didn't find a ticket, and we tried the local pawnshops."

"Nothing?"

Evan shook his head. "Nothing at all, sir."

"So we wouldn't know it, even if it turned up?" Monk said disappointedly, jerking his hand at the door. "Some miserable devil could walk in here sporting it, and we should be none the wiser. Still, I daresay if the killer took it, he will have thrown it into the river when the hue and cry went up anyway. If he didn't he's too daft to be out on his own." He twisted around to look at the pile of papers again and riffled through them untidily. "What else is there?"

The next was the account of the neighbor opposite, one Albert Scarsdale, very bare and prickly. Obviously he had resented the inconsideration, the appalling bad taste of Grey in getting himself murdered in Mecklenburg Square, and felt the less he said about it himself the sooner it would be forgotten, and the sooner he might dissociate himself from the whole sordid affair.

He admitted he thought he had heard someone in the hallway between his apartment and that of Grey at about eight o'clock, and possibly again at about quarter to ten. He could not possibly say whether it was two separate visitors or one arriving and then later leaving; in fact he was not sure beyond doubt that it had not been a stray animal, a cat, or the porter making a round—from his

31

choice of words he regarded the two as roughly equal. It might even have been an errand boy who had lost his way, or any of a dozen other things. He had been occupied with his own interests, and had seen and heard nothing of remark. The statement was signed and affirmed as being true with an ornate and ill-natured signature.

Monk looked across at Evan, still waiting by the window.

"Mr. Scarsdale sounds like an officious and unhelpful little beggar," he observed dryly.

"Very, sir," Evan agreed, his eyes shining but no smile touching his lips. "I imagine it's the scandal in the buildings; attracts notice from the wrong kind of people, and very bad for the social reputation."

"Something less than a gentleman." Monk made an immediate and cruel judgment.

Evan pretended not to understand him, although it was a patent lie.

"Less than a gentleman, sir?" His face puckered.

Monk spoke before he had time to think, or wonder why he was so sure.

"Certainly. Someone secure in his social status would not be affected by a scandal whose proximity was only a geographical accident, and nothing to do with him personally. Unless, of course, he knew Grey well?"

"No sir," Evan said, but his eyes showed his total comprehension. Obviously Scarsdale still smarted under Grey's contempt, and Monk could imagine it vividly. "No, he disclaimed all personal acquaintance with him. And either that's a lie or else it's very odd. If he were the gentleman he pretends to be, he would surely know Grey, at least to speak to. They were immediate neighbors, after all."

Monk did not want to court disappointment.

"It may be no more than social pretension, but worth inquiring into." He looked at the papers again. "What else is there?" He glanced up at Evan. "Who found him, by the way?"

Evan came over and sorted out two more reports from the bottom of the pile. He handed them to Monk.

"Cleaning woman and the porter, sir. Their accounts agree, except that the porter says a bit more, because naturally we asked him about the evening as well."

Monk was temporarily lost. "As well?"

Evan flushed faintly with irritation at his own lack of clarity.

"He wasn't found until the following morning, when the woman who cleans and cooks for him arrived and couldn't get in. He wouldn't give her a key, apparently didn't trust her; he let her in himself, and if he wasn't there then she just went away and came another time. Usually he leaves some message with the porter."

"I see. Did he go away often? I assume we know where to?" There was an instinctive edge of authority to his voice now, and impatience.

"Occasional weekend, so far as the porter knows; sometimes longer, a week or two at a country house, in the season," Evan answered.

"So what happened when Mrs.—what's her name?—arrived?"

Evan stood almost to attention. "Huggins. She knocked as usual, and when she got no answer after the third attempt, she went down to see the porter, Grimwade, to find out if there was a message. Grimwade told her he'd seen Grey arrive home the evening before, and he hadn't gone out yet, and to go back and try again. Perhaps Grey had been in the bathroom, or unusually soundly asleep, and no doubt he'd be standing at the top of the stairs by now, wanting his breakfast."

"But of course he wasn't," Monk said unnecessarily.

"No. Mrs. Huggins came back a few minutes later all fussed and excited—these women love a little drama—and demanded that Grimwade do something about it. To her endless satisfaction"—Evan smiled bleakly—"she said that he'd be lying there murdered in his own blood, and they should do something immediately, and call the police. She must have told me that a dozen times." He pulled a small face. "She's now convinced she has the second sight, and I spent a quarter of an hour persuading her that she should stick to cleaning and not give it up in favor of fortune-telling—although she's already a heroine, of sorts, in the local newspaper—and no doubt the local pub!"

Monk found himself smiling too.

"One more saved from a career in the fairground stalls—and still in the service of the gentry," he said. "Heroine for a day—and free gin every time she retells it for the next six months. Did Grimwade go back with her?"

"Yes, with a master key, of course."

"And what did they find, exactly?" This was perhaps the most important single thing: the precise facts of the discovery of the body.

Evan concentrated till Monk was not sure if he was remembering the witness's words or his own sight of the rooms.

"The small outer hall was perfectly orderly," Evan began. "Usual things you might expect to see, stand for coats and things, and hats, rather a nice stand for sticks, umbrellas and so forth, box for boots, a small table for calling cards, nothing else. Everything was neat and tidy. The door from that led directly into the sitting room; and the bedroom and utilities were off that." A shadow passed over his extraordinary face. He relaxed a little and half unconsciously leaned against the window frame.

"That next room was a different matter altogether. The curtains were drawn and the gas was still burning, even though it was daylight outside. Grey himself was lying half on the floor and half on the big chair, head downward. There was a lot of blood, and he was in a pretty dreadful state." His eyes did not waver, but it was with an effort, and Monk could see it. "I must admit," he continued, "I've seen a few deaths, but this was the most brutal, by a long way. The man had been beaten to death with something quite thin—I mean not a bludgeon—hit a great many times. There had pretty obviously been a fight. A small table had been knocked over and one leg broken off, several ornaments were on the floor and one of the heavy stuffed chairs was on its back, the one he was half on." Evan was frowning at the memory, and his skin was pale. "The other rooms hadn't been touched." He moved his hands in a gesture of negation. "It was quite a while before we could get Mrs. Huggins into a sane state of mind, and then persuade her to look at the kitchen and bedroom; but eventually she did, and said they were just as she had left them the previous day."

Monk breathed in deeply, thinking. He must say something intelligent, not some fatuous comment on the obvious. Evan was watching him, waiting. He found himself self-conscious.

"So it would appear he had a visitor some time in the evening," he said more tentatively than he had wished. "Who quarreled with him, or else simply attacked him. There was a violent fight, and Grey lost."

"More or less," Evan agreed, straightening up again. "At least we don't have anything else to go on. We don't even know if it was a stranger, or someone he knew."

"No sign of a forced entry?"

"No sir. Anyway, no burglar is likely to force an entry into a house when all the lights are still on."

"No." Monk cursed himself for an idiotic question. Was he always such a fool? There was no surprise in Evan's face. Good manners? Or fear of angering a superior not noted for tolerance? "No, of course not," he said aloud. "I suppose he wouldn't have been surprised by Grey, and then lit the lights to fool us?"

"Unlikely sir. If he were that coolheaded, he surely would have taken some of the valuables? At least the money in Grey's wallet, which would be untraceable."

Monk had no answer for that. He sighed and sat down behind the desk. He did not bother to invite Evan to sit also. He read the rest of the porter's statement.

Lamb had asked exhaustively about all visitors the previous evening, if there had been any errand boys, messengers, even a stray animal. Grimwade was affronted at the very suggestion. Certainly not: errand boys were always escorted to the appropriate place, or if possible their errands taken over by Grimwade himself. No stray animal had ever tainted the buildings with its presence—dirty things, stray animals, and apt to soil the place. What did the police think he was—were they trying to insult him?

Monk wondered what Lamb had replied. He would certainly have had a pointed answer to the man on the relative merits of stray animals and stray humans! A couple of acid retorts rose to his mind even now.

Grimwade swore there had been two visitors and only two. He was perfectly sure no others had passed his window. The first was a lady, at about eight o'clock, and he would sooner not say upon whom she called; a question of private affairs must be treated with discretion, but she had not visited Mr. Grey, of that he was perfectly certain. Anyway, she was a very slight creature, and could not possibly have inflicted the injuries suffered by the dead man. The second visitor was a man who called upon a Mr. Yeats, a longtime resident, and Grimwade had escorted him as far as the appropriate landing himself and seen him received.

Whoever had murdered Grey had obviously either used one of the other visitors as a decoy or else had already been in the building in some guise in which he had so far been overlooked. So much was logic.

Monk put the paper down. They would have to question Grimwade more closely, explore even the minutest possibilities; there might be something.

Evan sat down on the window ledge.

Mrs. Huggins's statement was exactly as Evan had said, if a good deal more verbose. Monk read it only because he wanted time to think.

Afterwards he picked up the last one, the medical report. It was the one he found most unpleasant, but maybe also the most necessary. It was written in a small, precise hand, very round. It made him imagine a small doctor

36

with round spectacles and very clean fingers. It did not occur to him until afterwards to wonder if he had ever known such a person, and if it was the first wisp of memory returning.

The account was clinical in the extreme, discussing the corpse as if Joscelin Grey were a species rather than an individual, a human being full of passions and cares, hopes and humors who had been suddenly and violently cut off from life, and who must have experienced terror and extreme pain in the few minutes that were being examined so unemotionally.

The body had been looked at a little after nine thirty A.M. It was that of a man in his early thirties, of slender build but well nourished, and not apparently suffering from any illness or disability apart from a fairly recent wound in the upper part of the right leg, which might have caused him to limp. The doctor judged it to be a shallow wound, such as he had seen in many ex-soldiers, and to be five or six months old. The body had been dead between eight and twelve hours; he could not be more precise than that.

The cause of death was obvious for anyone to see: a succession of violent and powerful blows about the head and shoulders with some long, thin instrument. A heavy cane or stick seemed the most likely.

Monk put down the report, sobered by the details of death. The bare language, shorn of all emotion, perversely brought the very feeling of it closer. His imagination saw it sharply, even smelled it, conjuring up the sour odor and the buzz of flies. Had he dealt with many murders? He could hardly ask.

"Very unpleasant," he said without looking up at Evan.

"Very," Evan agreed, nodding. "Newspapers made rather a lot of it at the time. Been going on at us for not having found the murderer. Apart from the fact that it's made a lot of people nervous, Mecklenburg Square is a pretty good area, and if one isn't safe there, where is one safe? Added to that, Joscelin Grey was a well-liked, pretty harmless young ex-officer, and of extremely good family.

37

He served in the Crimea and was invalided out. He had rather a good record, saw the Charge of the Light Brigade, badly wounded at Sebastopol.'' Evan's face pinched a little with a mixture of embarrassment and perhaps pity. ''A lot of people feel his country has let him down, so to speak, first by allowing this to happen to him, and then by not even catching the man who did it.'' He looked across at Monk, apologizing for the injustice, and because he understood it. ''I know that's unfair, but a spot of crusading sells newspapers; always helps to have a cause, you know! And of course the running patterers have composed a lot of songs about it—returning hero and all that!''

Monk's mouth turned down at the corners.

''Have they been hitting hard?''

''Rather,'' Evan admitted with a little shrug. ''And we haven't a blind thing to go on. We've been over and over every bit of evidence there is, and there's simply nothing to connect him to anyone. Any ruffian could have come in from the street if he dodged the porter. Nobody saw or heard anything useful, and we are right where we started.'' He got up gloomily and came over to the table.

''I suppose you'd better see the physical evidence, not that there is much. And then I daresay you'd like to see the flat, at least get a feeling for the scene?''

Monk stood up also.

''Yes I would. You never know, something might suggest itself.'' Although he could imagine nothing. If Lamb had not succeeded, and this keen, delicate young junior, what was he going to find? He felt failure begin to circle around him, dark and enclosing. Had Runcorn given him this knowing he would fail? Was it a discreet and efficient way of getting rid of him without being seen to be callous? How did he even know for sure that Runcorn was not an old enemy? Had he done him some wrong long ago? The possibility was cold and real. The shadowy outline of himself that had appeared so far was devoid of any quick acts of compassion, any sudden gentlenesses or warmth to seize hold of and to like. He was discovering himself as a stranger might, and what he saw so far did not excite his admiration. He liked Evan far more than he liked himself.

He had imagined he had hidden his complete loss of memory, but perhaps it was obvious, perhaps Runcorn had seen it and taken this chance to even some old score? God, how he wished he knew what kind of man he was, had been. Who loved him, who hated him—and who had what cause? Had he ever loved a woman, or any woman loved him? He did not even know that!

Evan was walking quickly ahead of him, his long legs carrying him at a surprisingly fast pace. Everything in Monk wanted to trust him, and yet he was almost paralyzed by his ignorance. Every foothold he trod on dissolved into quicksand under his weight. He knew nothing. Everything was surmise, constantly shifting guesses.

He behaved automatically, having nothing but instinct and ingrained habit to rely on.

The physical evidence was astonishingly bare, set out like luggage in a lost-and-found office, ownerless; pathetic and rather embarrassing remnants of someone else's life, robbed now of their purpose and meaning—a little like his own belongings in Grafton Street, objects whose history and emotion were obliterated.

He stopped beside Evan and picked up a pile of clothes. The trousers were dark, well cut from expensive material, now spotted with blood. The boots were highly polished and only slightly worn on the soles. Personal linen was obviously changed very recently; shirt was expensive; cravat silk, the neck and front heavily stained. The jacket was tailored to high fashion, but ruined with blood, and a ragged tear in the sleeve. They told him nothing except a hazard at the size and build of Joscelin Grey, and an admiration for his pocket and his taste. There was nothing to be deduced from the bloodstains, since they already knew what the injuries had been.

He put them down and turned to Evan, who was watching him.

"Not very helpful, is it, sir?" Evan looked at them with

a mixture of unhappiness and distaste. There was something in his face that might have been real pity. Perhaps he was too sensitive to be a police officer.

"No, not very," Monk agreed dryly. "What else was there?"

"The weapon, sir." Evan reached out and picked up a heavy ebony stick with a silver head. It too was encrusted with blood and hair.

Monk winced. If he had seen such grisly things before, his immunity to them had gone with his memory.

"Nasty." Evan's mouth turned down, his hazel eyes on Monk's face.

Monk was conscious of him, and abashed. Was the distaste, the pity, for him? Was Evan wondering why a senior officer should be so squeamish? He conquered his revulsion with an effort and took the stick. It was unusually heavy.

"War wound," Evan observed, still watching him. "From what witnesses say, he actually walked with it: I mean it wasn't an ornament."

"Right leg." Monk recalled the medical report. "Accounts for the weight." He put the stick down. "Nothing else?"

"Couple of broken glasses, sir, and a decanter broken too. Must have been on the table that was knocked over, from the way it was lying; and a couple of ornaments. There's a drawing of the way the room was, in Mr. Lamb's file, sir. Not that I know of anything it can tell us. But Mr. Lamb spent hours poring over it."

Monk felt a quick stab of compassion for Lamb, then for himself. He wished for a moment that he could change places with Evan, leave the decisions, the judgments to someone else, and disclaim the failure. He hated failure! He realized now what a driving, burning desire he had to solve this crime—to win—to wipe that smile off Runcorn's face.

"Oh—money, sir." Evan pulled out a cardboard box and opened it. He picked up a fine pigskin wallet and, separately, several gold sovereigns, a couple of cards from a club and an exclusive dining room. There were about a dozen cards of his own, engraved "Major the Honorable Joscelin Grey, Six, Mecklenburg Square, London."

"Is that all?" Monk asked.

"Yes sir, the money is twelve pounds seven shillings and sixpence altogether. If he were a thief, it's odd he didn't take that."

"Perhaps he was frightened—he may have been hurt himself." It was the only thing he could think of. He motioned Evan to put the box away. "I suppose we'd better go and have a look at Mecklenburg Square."

"Yes sir." Evan straightened up to obey. "It's about half an hour's walk. Are you well enough for it yet?"

"A couple of miles? For heaven's sake, man, it was my arm I broke, not both my legs!" He reached sharply for his jacket and hat.

Evan had been a little optimistic. Against the wind and stepping carefully to avoid peddlers and groups of fellow travelers on the footpath, and traffic and horse dung in the streets, it was a good forty minutes before they reached Mecklenburg Square, walked around the gardens and stopped outside Number 6. The boy sweeping the crossing was busy on the corner of Doughty Street, and Monk wondered if it was the same one who had been there on that evening in July. He felt a rush of pity for the child, out in all weather, often with sleet or snow driving down the funnel of the high buildings, dodging in among the carriages and drays, shoveling droppings. What an abysmal way to earn your keep. Then he was angry with himself—that was stupid and sentimental nonsense. He must deal with reality. He squared his chest and marched into the foyer. The porter was standing by a small office doorway, no more than a cubbyhole.

"Yes sir?" He moved forward courteously, but at the same time blocking their further progress.

"Grimwade?" Monk asked him.

"Yes sir?" The man was obviously surprised and embarrassed. "I'm sorry, sir, I can't say as I remember you. I'm not usually bad about faces—" He let it hang, hoping Monk would help him. He glanced across at Evan, and a flicker of memory lit in his face.

"Police," Monk said simply. "We'd like to take another look at Major Grey's flat. You have the key?"

The man's relief was very mixed.

"Oh yes, sir, and we ain't let nobody in. Lock's still as Mr. Lamb left it."

"Good, thank you." Monk had been preparing to show some proof of his identity, but the porter was apparently quite satisfied with his recognition of Evan, and turned back to his cubbyhole to fetch the key.

He came with it a moment later and led them upstairs with the solemnity due the presence of the dead, especially those who had died violently. Monk had the momentarily unpleasant impression that they would find Joscelin Grey's corpse still lying there, untouched and waiting for them.

It was ridiculous, and he shook it off fiercely. It was beginning to assume the repetitive quality of a nightmare, as if events could happen more than once.

"Here we are, sir." Evan was standing at the door, the porter's key in his hand. "There's a back door as well, of course, from the kitchen, but it opens onto the same landing, about twelve yards along, for services, errands, and the like."

Monk recalled his attention.

"But one would still have to pass the porter at the gate?"

"Oh yes, sir. I suppose there's not much point in having a porter if there's a way in without passing him. Then any beggar or peddler could bother you." He pulled an extraordinary face as he pondered the habits of his betters. "Or creditors!" he added lugubriously.

"Quite." Monk was sardonic.

Evan turned and put the key in the lock. He seemed reluctant, as if a memory of the violence he had seen there still clung to the place, repelling him. Or was Monk projecting his own fancies onto someone else?

42

The hallway inside was exactly as Evan had described it: neat, blue Georgian with white paint and trims, very clean and elegant. He saw the hat stand with its place for sticks and umbrellas, the table for calling cards and so forth. Evan was ahead of him, his back stiff, opening the door to the main room.

Monk walked in behind him. He was not sure what he was expecting to see; his body was tight also, as if waiting for an attack, for something startling and ugly on the senses.

The decoration was elegant, and had originally been expensive, but in the flat light, without gas or fire, it looked bleak and commonplace enough. The Wedgwood-blue walls seemed at a glance immaculate, the white trims without scar, but there was a fine rime of dust over the polished wood of the chiffonier and the desk and a film dulling colors of the carpet. His eyes traveled automatically to the window first, then around the other furniture—ornate side table with piecrust edges, a jardiniere with a Japanese bowl on it, a mahogany bookcase—till he came to the overturned heavy chair, the broken table, companion to the other, the pale inner wood a sharp scar against its mellowed satin skin. It looked like an animal with legs in the air.

Then he saw the bloodstain on the floor. There was not a lot of it, not widespread at all, but very dark, almost black. Grey must have bled a lot in that one place. He looked away from it, and noticed then that much of what seemed pattern on the carpet was probably lighter, spattered blood. On the far wall there was a picture crooked, and when he walked over to it and looked more carefully, he saw a bruise in the plaster, and the paint was faintly scarred. It was a bad watercolor of the Bay of Naples, all harsh blues with a conical Mount Vesuvius in the background.

"It must have been a considerable fight," he said quietly.

"Yes sir," Evan agreed. He was standing in the middle

43

of the floor, not sure what to do. "There were several bruises on the body, arms and shoulders, and one knuckle was skinned. I should say he put up a good fight."

Monk looked at him, frowning.

"I don't remember that in the medical report."

"I think it just said 'evidences of a struggle,' sir. But that's pretty obvious from the room here, anyway." His eyes glanced around at it as he spoke. "There's blood on that chair as well." He pointed to the heavy stuffed one lying on its back. "That's where he was, with his head on the floor. We're looking for a violent man, sir." He shivered slightly.

"Yes." Monk stared around, trying to visualize what must have happened in this room nearly six weeks ago, the fear and the impact of flesh on flesh, shadows moving, shadows because he did not know them, furniture crashing over, glass splintering. Then suddenly it became real, a flash sharper and more savage than anything his imagination had called up, red moments of rage and terror, the thrashing stick; then it was gone again, leaving him trembling and his stomach sick. What in God's name had happened in this room that the echo of it still hung here, like an agonized ghost, or a beast of prey?

He turned and walked out, oblivious of Evan behind him, fumbling for the door. He had to get out of here, into the commonplace and grubby street, the sound of voices, the demanding present. He was not even sure if Evan followed him.

44

3

As soon as Monk was out in the street he felt better, but he could not completely shake the impression that had come to him so violently. For an instant it had been real enough to bring his body out in hot, drenching sweat, and then leave him shivering and nauseous at the sheer bestiality of it.

He put up his hand shakily and felt his wet cheek. There was a hard, angular rain driving on the wind.

He turned to see Evan behind him. But if Evan had felt that savage presence, there was no sign of it in his face. He was puzzled, a little concerned, but Monk could read no more in him than that.

"A violent man." Monk repeated Evan's words through stiff lips.

"Yes sir," Evan said solemnly, catching up to him. He started to say something, then changed his mind. "Where are you going to begin, sir?" he asked instead.

It was a moment before Monk could collect his thoughts to reply. They were walking along Doughty Street to Guilford Street.

"Recheck the statements," he answered, stopping on the corner curb as a hansom sped past them, its wheels spraying filth. "That's the only place I know to begin. I'll

45

do the least promising first. The street sweeper boy is there.'' He indicated the child a few yards from them, busy shoveling dung and at the same time seizing a penny that had been thrown him. ''Is he the same one?''

''I think so, sir; I can't see his face from here.'' That was something of a euphemism; the child's features were hidden by dirt and the hazards of his occupation, and the top half of his head was covered by an enormous cloth cap, to protect him from the rain.

Monk and Evan stepped out onto the street towards him.

''Well?'' Monk asked when they reached the boy.

Evan nodded.

Monk fished for a coin; he felt obliged to recompense the child for the earnings he might lose in the time forfeited. He came up with twopence and offered it.

''Alfred, I am a policeman. I want to talk to you about the gentleman who was killed in Number Six in the square.''

The boy took the twopence.

''Yeah guv, I dunno anyfink what I din't tell ve ovver rozzer as asked me.'' He sniffed and looked up hopefully. A man with twopence to spend was worth pleasing.

''Maybe not,'' Monk conceded, ''but I'd like to talk to you anyway.'' A tradesman's cart clattered by them towards Grey's Inn Road, splashing them with mud and leaving a couple of cabbage leaves almost at their feet. ''Can we go to the footpath?'' Monk inquired, hiding his distaste. His good boots were getting soiled and his trouser legs were wet.

The boy nodded, then acknowledging their lack of skill in dodging wheels and hooves with the professional's condescension for the amateur, he steered them to the curb again.

''Yers guv?'' he asked hopefully, pocketing the twopence somewhere inside the folds of his several jackets and sniffing hard. He refrained from wiping his hand across his face in deference to their superior status.

46

"You saw Major Grey come home the day he was killed?" Monk asked with appropriate gravity.

"Yers guv, and vere weren't nob'dy followin' 'im, as fer as I could see."

"Was the street busy?"

"No, wicked night, it were, for July, raining summink 'orrible. Nob'dy much abaht, an' everyone goin' as fast as veir legs'd carry 'em."

"How long have you been at this crossing?"

"Couple o' years." His faint fair eyebrows rose with surprise; obviously it was a question he had not expected.

"So you must know most of the people who live around here?" Monk pursued.

"Yers, reckon as I do." His eyes sparked with sudden sharp comprehension. "Yer means did I see anyone as don't belong?"

Monk nodded in appreciation of his sagacity. "Precisely."

" 'E were bashed ter deaf, weren't 'e?"

"Yes." Monk winced inwardly at the appropriateness of the phrase.

"Ven yer in't lookin' fer a woman?"

"No," Monk agreed. Then it flashed through his mind that a man might dress as a woman, if perhaps it were not some stranger who had murdered Grey, but a person known to him, someone who had built up over the years the kind of hatred that had seemed to linger in that room. "Unless it were a large woman," he added, "and very strong, perhaps."

The boy hid a smirk. "Woman as I saw was on the little side. Most women as makes veir way vat fashion gotta look fetchin' like, or leastways summink as a woman oughter. Don't see no great big scrubbers 'round 'ere, an' no dollymops." He sniffed again and pulled his mouth down fiercely to express his disapproval. "Only the class for gennelmen as 'as money like wot vey got 'ere." He gestured towards the elaborate house fronts behind him towards the square.

47

"I see." Monk hid a brief amusement. "And you saw some woman of that type going into Number Six that evening?" It was probably not worth anything, but every clue must be followed at this stage.

"No one as don't go vere reg'lar, guv."

"What time?"

"Jus' as I were goin' 'ome."

"About half past seven?"

"S' right."

"How about earlier?"

"Only wot goes inter Number Six, like?"

"Yes."

He shut his eyes in deep concentration, trying to be obliging; there might be another twopence. "One of ve gennelmen wot lives in Number Six came 'ome wiv another gent, little feller wiv one o' vem collars wot looks like fur, but all curly."

"Astrakhan?" Monk offered.

"I dunno wot yer calls it. Anyway, 'e went in abaht six, an' I never sawed 'im come aht. Vat any 'elp to yer, guv?"

"It might be. Thank you very much." Monk spoke to him with all seriousness, gave him another penny, to Evan's surprise, and watched him step blithely off into the thoroughfare, dodging in between traffic, and take up his duties again.

Evan's face was brooding, thoughtful, but whether on the boy's answers or his means of livelihood, Monk did not ask.

"The ribbon seller's not here today." Evan looked up and down the Guilford Street footpath. "Who do you want to try next?"

Monk thought for a moment. "How do we find the cabby? I presume we have an address for him?"

"Yes sir, but I doubt he'd be there now."

Monk turned to face the drizzling east wind. "Not unless he's ill," he agreed. "Good evening for trade. No one will walk in this weather if they can ride." He was pleased with that—it sounded intelligent, and it was the merest common sense. "We'll send a message and have him call at the police station. I don't suppose he can add anything to what he's already said anyway." He smiled sarcastically. "Unless, of course, he killed Grey himself!"

Evan stared at him, his eyes wide, unsure for an instant whether he was joking or not. Then Monk suddenly found he was not sure himself. There was no reason to believe the cabby. Perhaps there had been heated words between them, some stupid quarrel, possibly over nothing more important than the fare. Maybe the man had followed Grey upstairs, carrying a case or a parcel for him, seen the flat, the warmth, the space, the ornaments, and in a fit of envy become abusive. He may even have been drunk; he would not be the first cabby to bolster himself against cold, rain and long hours a little too generously. God help them, enough of them died of bronchitis or consumption anyway.

Evan was still looking at him, not entirely sure.

Monk spoke his last thoughts aloud.

"We must check with the porter that Grey actually entered alone. He might easily have overlooked a cabby carrying baggage, invisible, like a postman; we become so used to them, the eye sees but the mind doesn't register."

"It's possible." Belief was strengthening in Evan's voice. "He could have set up the mark for someone else, noted addresses or wealthy fares, likely-looking victims for someone. Could be a well-paying sideline?"

"Could indeed." Monk was getting chilled standing on the curb. "Not as good as a sweep's boy for scouting the inside of a house, but better for knowing when the victim is out. If that was his idea, he certainly mistook Grey." He shivered. "Perhaps we'd better call on him rather than send a message; it might make him nervous. It's late; we'll have a bit of lunch at the local public house, and see what the gossip is. Then you can go back to the station this afternoon and find out if anything is known about this cabby, what sort of reputation he has—if we know him, for example, and who his associates are. I'll try the porter again, and if possible some of the neighbors."

49

The local tavern turned out to be a pleasant, noisy place which served them ale and a sandwich with civility, but something of a wary eye, knowing them to be strangers and perhaps guessing from their clothes that they were police. One or two ribald comments were offered, but apparently Grey had not patronized the place and there was no particular sympathy for him, only the communal interest in the macabre that murder always wakens.

Afterwards Evan went back to the police station, and Monk returned to Mecklenburg Square, and Grimwade. He began at the beginning.

"Yes sir," Grimwade said patiently. "Major Grey came in about quarter after six, or a bit before, and 'e looked 'is usual self to me."

"He came by cab?" Monk wanted to be sure he had not led the man, suggested the answer he wanted.

"Yes sir."

"How do you know? Did you see the cab?"

"Yes sir, I did." Grimwade wavered between nervousness and affront. "Stopped right by the door 'ere; not a night to walk a step as you didn't 'ave to."

"Did you see the cabby?"

" 'Ere, I don't understand what you're getting after." Now the affront was definitely warning.

"Did you see him?" Monk repeated.

Grimwade screwed up his face. "Don't recall as I did," he conceded.

"Did he get down off the box, help Major Grey with a parcel, or a case or anything?"

"Not as I remember; no, 'e didn't."

"Are you sure?"

"Yes I am sure. 'E never got through that door."

That theory at least was gone. He should have been too old at this to be disappointed, but he had no experience to call on. It seemed to come to him easily enough, but possibly most of it was common sense.

"He went upstairs alone?" He tried a last time, to remove every vestige of doubt.

50

"Yes sir, 'e did."

"Did he speak to you?"

"Nothing special, as I can think of. I don't remember nothin', so I reckon it can't 'ave bin. 'E never said nothin' about bein' afraid, or as 'e was expecting anyone."

"But there were visitors to the buildings that afternoon and evening?"

"Nobody as would be a-murderin' anyone."

"Indeed?" Monk raised his eyebrows. "You're not suggesting Major Grey did that to himself in some kind of bizarre accident, are you? Or of course there is the other alternative—that the murderer was someone already here?"

Grimwade's face changed rapidly from resignation through extreme offense to blank horror. He stared at Monk, but no words came to his brain.

"You have another idea? I thought not—neither have I." Monk sighed. "So let us think again. You said there were two visitors after Major Grey came in: one woman at about seven o'clock, and a man later on at about quarter to ten. Now, who did the woman come to see, Mr. Grimwade, and what did she look like? And please, no cosmetic alterations for the sake of discretion!"

"No wot?"

"Tell me the truth, man!" Monk snapped. "It could become very embarrassing for your tenants if we have to investigate it for ourselves."

Grimwade glared at him, but he took the point perfectly.

"A local lady of pleasure, sir; called Mollie Ruggles," he said between his teeth. " 'Andsome piece, with red 'air. I know where she lives, but I expec' you understand it would come real gratifyin' if you could see your way clear to bein' discreet about 'oo told yer she was 'ere?" His expression was comical in its effort to expunge his dislike and look appealing.

Monk hid a sour amusement—it would only alienate the man.

"I will," he agreed. It would be in his own interest

51

also. Prostitutes could be useful informants, if well treated. "Who did she come to see?"

"Mr. Taylor, sir; 'e lives in flat number five. She comes to see 'im quite reg'lar."

"And it was definitely her?"

"Yes sir."

"Did you take her to Mr. Taylor's door?"

"Oh no, sir. Reckon as she knows 'er way by now. And Mr. Taylor—well . . ." He hunched his shoulders. "It wouldn't be tactful, now would it, sir? Not as I suppose you 'as ter be tactful, in your callin'!" he added meaningfully.

"No." Monk smiled slightly. "So you didn't leave your position when she came?"

"No sir."

"Any other women come, Mr. Grimwade?" He looked at him very directly.

Grimwade avoided his eyes.

"Do I have to make my own inquiries?" Monk threatened. "And leave detectives here to follow people?"

Grimwade was shocked. His head came up sharply.

"You wouldn't do that, sir! They're gentlemen as lives 'ere! They'd leave. They won't put up with that kind o' thing!"

"Then don't make it necessary."

"You're an 'ard man, Mr. Monk." But there was a grudging respect behind the grievance in his voice. That was small victory in itself.

"I want to find the man who killed Major Grey," Monk answered him. "Someone came into these buildings, found his way upstairs into that flat and beat Major Grey with a stick, over and over until he was dead, and then went on beating him afterwards." He saw Grimwade wincing, and felt the revulsion himself. He remembered the horror he had felt when actually standing in the room. Did walls retain memory? Could violence or hatred remain in the air after a deed was finished, and touch the sensitive, the imaginative with a shadow of the horror?

No, that was ridiculous. It was not the imaginative, but the nightmare-ridden who felt such things. He was letting his own fear, the horror of his still occasionally recurring dreams and the hollowness of his past extend into the present and warp his judgment. Let a little more time pass, a little more identity build, learn to know himself, and he would grow firmer memories in reality. His sanity would come back; he would have a past to root himself in, other emotions, and people.

Or could it be—could it possibly be that it was some sort of mixed, dreamlike, distorted recollection coming back to him? Could he be recalling snatches of the pain and fear he must have felt when the coach turned over on him, throwing him down, imprisoning him, the scream of terror as the horse fell, the cab driver flung headlong, crushed to death on the stones of the street? He must have known violent fear, and in the instant before unconsciousness, have felt sharp, even blinding pain as his bones broke. Was that what he had sensed? Had it been nothing to do with Grey at all, but his own memory returning, just a flash, a sensation, the fierceness of the feeling long before the clarity of actual perception came back?

He must learn more of himself, what he had been doing that night, where he was going, or had come from. What manner of man had he been, whom had he cared for, whom wronged, or whom owed? What had mattered to him? Every man had relationships, every man had feelings, even hungers; every man who was alive at all stirred some sort of passions in others. There must be people somewhere who had feelings about him—more than professional rivalry and resentment—surely? He could not have been so negative, of so little purpose that his whole life had left no mark on another soul.

As soon as he was off duty, he must leave Grey, stop building the pattern piece by piece of his life, and take up the few clues to his own, place them together with whatever skill he possessed.

Grimwade was still waiting for him, watching curiously, knowing that he had temporarily lost his attention.

Monk looked back at him.

"Well, Mr. Grimwade?" he said with sudden softness. "What other women?"

Grimwade mistook the lowering tone for a further threat.

"One to see Mr. Scarsdale, sir; although 'e paid me 'andsome not to say so."

"What time was it?"

"About eight o'clock."

Scarsdale had said he had heard someone at eight. Was it his own visitor he was talking about, trying to play safe, in case someone else had seen her too?

"Did you go up with her?" He looked at Grimwade.

"No sir, on account o' she'd bin 'ere before, an' knew 'er way, like. An' I knew as she was expected." He gave a slight leer, knowingly, as man to man.

Monk acknowledged it. "And the one at quarter to ten?" he asked. "The visitor for Mr. Yeats, I think you said? Had he been here before too?"

"No sir. I went up with 'im, 'cos 'e didn't know Mr. Yeats very well an' 'adn't called 'ere before. I said that to Mr. Lamb."

"Indeed." Monk forbore from criticizing him over the omission of Scarsdale's woman. He would defeat his own purpose if he antagonized him any further. "So you went up with this man?"

"Yes sir." Grimwade was firm. "Saw Mr. Yeats open the door to 'im."

"What did he look like, this man?"

Grimwade screwed up his eyes. "Oh, big man, 'e was, solid and—'ere!" His face dropped. "You don't think it was 'im wot done it, do yer?" He breathed out slowly, his eyes wide. "Gor'—it must 'a' bin. When I thinks of it now!"

"It might have," Monk agreed cautiously. "It's possible. Would you know him if you saw him again?"

Grimwade's face fell. "Ah, there you 'ave me, sir; I

54

don't think as I would. Yer see, I didn't see 'im close, like, when 'e was down 'ere. An' on the stairs I only looked where I was goin', it bein' dark. 'E 'ad one o' them 'eavy coats on, as it was a rotten night an' rainin' somethin' wicked. A natural night for anyone to 'ave 'is coat turned up an' 'is 'at drawn down. I reckon 'e were dark, that's about all I could say fer sure, an' if 'e 'ad a beard, it weren't much of a one."

"He was probably clean-shaven, and probably dark." Monk tried to keep the disappointment out of his voice. He must not let irritation push the man into saying something to please him, something less than true.

" 'E were big, sir," Grimwade said hopefully. "An' 'e were tall, must 'ave bin six feet. That lets out a lot o' people, don't it?"

"Yes, yes it does," Monk agreed. "When did he leave?"

"I saw 'im out o' the corner o' me eye, sir. 'E went past me window at about 'alf past ten, or a little afore."

"Out of the corner of your eye? You're sure it was him?"

" 'Ad ter be; 'e didn't leave before, ner after, an' 'e looked the same. Same coat, and 'at, same size, same 'eight. Weren't no one else like that lives 'ere."

"Did you speak to him?"

"No, 'e looked like 'e was in a bit of an 'urry. Maybe 'e wanted ter get 'ome. It were a beastly rotten night, like I said, sir; not fit fer man ner beast."

"Yes I know. Thank you, Mr. Grimwade. If you remember anything more, tell me, or leave a message for me at the police station. Good day."

"Good day, sir," Grimwade said with intense relief.

Monk decided to wait for Scarsdale, first to tax him with his lie about the woman, then to try and learn something more about Joscelin Grey. He realized with faint surprise that he knew almost nothing about him, except the manner of his death. Grey's life was as blank an outline as his own, a shadow man, circumscribed by a few

55

physical facts, without color or substance that could have induced love or hate. And surely there had been hate in whoever had beaten Grey to death, and then gone on hitting and hitting him long after there was any purpose? Was there something in Grey, innocently or knowingly, that had generated such a passion, or was he merely the catalyst of something he knew nothing of—and its victim?

He went back outside into the square and found a seat from which he could see the entrance of Number 6.

It was more than an hour before Scarsdale arrived, and already beginning to get darker and colder, but Monk was compelled by the importance it had for him to wait.

He saw him arrive on foot, and followed a few paces after him, inquiring from Grimwade in the hall if it was indeed Scarsdale.

"Yes sir," Grimwade said reluctantly, but Monk was not interested in the porter's misfortunes.

"D' yer need me ter take yer up?"

"No thank you; I'll find it." And he took the stairs two at a time and arrived on the landing just as the door was closing. He strode across from the stair head and knocked briskly. There was a second's hesitation, then the door opened. He explained his identity and his errand tersely.

Scarsdale was not pleased to see him. He was a small, wiry man whose handsomest feature was his fair mustache, not matched by slightly receding hair and undistinguished features. He was smartly, rather fussily dressed.

"I'm sorry, I can't see you this evening," he said brusquely. "I have to change to go out for dinner. Call again tomorrow, or the next day."

Monk was the bigger man, and in no mood to be summarily dismissed.

"I have other people to call on tomorrow," he said, placing himself half in Scarsdale's way. "I need certain information from you now."

"Well I haven't any—" Scarsdale began, retreating as if to close the door.

Monk stepped forward. "For example, the name of the

young woman who visited you the evening Major Grey was killed, and why you lied to us about her.''

It had the result Monk had wished. Scarsdale stopped dead. He fumbled for words, trying to decide whether to bluff it out or attempt a little late conciliation. Monk watched him with contempt.

"I—er,'' Scarsdale began. "I—think you have misunderstood—er . . .'' He still had not made the decision.

Monk's face tightened. "Perhaps you would prefer to discuss it somewhere more discreet than the hallway?'' He looked towards the stairs, and the landing where other doorways led off—including Grey's.

"Yes—yes I suppose so.'' Scarsdale was now acutely uncomfortable, a fine beading of sweat on his brow. "Although I really cannot tell you anything germane to the issue, you know.'' He backed into his own entranceway and Monk followed. "The young lady who visited me has no connection with poor Grey, and she neither saw nor heard anyone else!''

Monk closed the main door, then followed him into the sitting room.

"Then you asked her, sir?'' He allowed his face to register interest.

"Yes, of course I did!'' Scarsdale was beginning to regain his composure, now that he was among his own possessions. The gas was lit and turned up; it glowed gently on polished leather, old Turkey carpet and silver-framed photographs. He was a gentleman, facing a mere member of Peel's police. "Naturally, if there had been anything that could have assisted you in your work, I should have told you.'' He used the word *work* with a vague condescension, a mark of the gulf between them. He did not invite Monk to sit, and remained standing himself, rather awkwardly between the sideboard and the sofa.

"And this young lady, of course, is well known to you?'' Monk did not try to keep his own sarcastic contempt out of his voice.

Scarsdale was confused, not sure whether to affect insult

or to prevaricate because he could think of nothing suitably crushing. He chose the latter.

"I beg your pardon?" he said stiffly.

"You can vouch for her truthfulness," Monk elaborated, his eyes meeting Scarsdale's with a bitter smile. "Apart from her . . . *work*"—he deliberately chose the same word—"she is a person of perfect probity?"

Scarsdale colored heavily and Monk realized he had lost any chance of cooperation from him.

"You exceed your authority!" Scarsdale snapped. "And you are impertinent. My private affairs are no concern of yours. Watch your tongue, or I shall be obliged to complain to your superiors." He looked at Monk and decided this was not a good idea. "The woman in question has no reason to lie," he said stiffly. "She came up alone and left alone, and saw no one at either time, except Grimwade, the porter; and you can ascertain that from him. No one enters these buildings without his permission, you know." He sniffed very slightly. "This is not a common rooming house!" His eyes glanced for a second at the handsome furnishings, then back at Monk.

"Then it follows that Grimwade must have seen the murderer," Monk replied, keeping his eyes on Scarsdale's face.

Scarsdale saw the imputation, and paled; he was arrogant, and perhaps bigoted, but he was not stupid.

Monk took what he believed might well be his best chance.

"You are a gentleman of similar social standing"—he winced inwardly at his own hypocrisy—"and an immediate neighbor of Major Grey's; you must be able to tell me something about him personally. I know nothing."

Scarsdale was happy enough to change the subject, and in spite of his irritation, flattered.

"Yes, of course," he agreed quickly. "Nothing at all?"

"Nothing at all," Monk conceded.

"He was a younger brother of Lord Shelburne, you know?" Scarsdale's eyes widened, and at last he walked to the center of the room and sat down on a hard-backed, carved chair. He waved his arm vaguely, giving Monk permission to do so too.

"Indeed?" Monk chose another hard-backed chair so as not to be below Scarsdale.

"Oh yes, a very old family," Scarsdale said with relish. "The Dowager Lady Shelburne, his mother, of course, was the eldest daughter of the Duke of Ruthven, at least I think it was he; certainly the duke of somewhere."

"Joscelin Grey," Monk reminded him.

"Oh. Very pleasant fellow; officer in the Crimea, forgotten which regiment, but a very distinguished record." He nodded vigorously. "Wounded at Sebastopol, I think he said, then invalided out. Walked with a limp, poor devil. Not that it was disfiguring. Very good-looking fellow, great charm, very well liked, you know."

"A wealthy family?"

"Shelburne?" Scarsdale was faintly amused by Monk's ignorance and his confidence was beginning to return. "Of course. But I suppose you know, or perhaps you don't." He looked Monk up and down disparagingly. "But naturally all the money went to the eldest son, the present Lord Shelburne. Always happens that way, everything to the eldest, along with the title. Keeps the estates whole, otherwise everything would be in bits and pieces, d'you understand? All the power of the land gone!"

Monk controlled his sense of being patronized; he was perfectly aware of the laws of primogeniture.

"Yes, thank you. Where did Joscelin Grey's money come from?"

Scarsdale waved his hands, which were small, with wide knuckles and very short nails. "Oh business interests, I presume. I don't believe he had a great deal, but he didn't appear in any want. Always dressed well. Tell a lot from a fellow's clothes, you know." Again he looked at Monk with a faint curl of his lip, then saw the quality of Monk's jacket and the portion of his shirt that was visible, and changed his mind, his eyes registering confusion.

59

"And as far as you know he was neither married nor betrothed?" Monk kept a stiff face and hid at least most of his satisfaction.

Scarsdale was surprised at his inefficiency.

"Surely you know that?"

"Yes, we know there was no official arrangement," Monk said, hastening to cover his mistake. "But you are in a position to know if there was any other relationship, anyone in whom he—had an interest?"

Scarsdale's rather full mouth turned down at the corners.

"If you mean an arrangement of convenience, not that I am aware of. But then a man of breeding does not inquire into the personal tastes—or accommodations—of another gentleman."

"No, I didn't mean a financial matter," Monk answered with the shadow of a sneer. "I meant some lady he might have—admired—or even been courting."

Scarsdale colored angrily. "Not as far as I know."

"Was he a gambler?"

"I have no idea. I don't gamble myself, except with friends, of course, and Grey was not among them. I haven't heard anything, if that's what you mean."

Monk realized he would get no more this evening, and he was tired. His own mystery was heavy at the back of his mind. Odd, how emptiness could be so intrusive. He rose to his feet.

"Thank you, Mr. Scarsdale. If you should hear anything to throw light on Major Grey's last few days, or who might have wished him harm, I am sure you will let us know. The sooner we apprehend this man, the safer it will be for everyone."

Scarsdale rose also, his face tightening at the subtle and unpleasant reminder that it had happened just across the hall from his own flat, threatening his security even as he stood there.

"Yes, naturally," he said a little sharply. "Now if you

will be good enough to permit me to change—I have a dinner engagement, you know.''

Monk arrived at the police station to find Evan waiting for him. He was surprised at the sharpness of his pleasure at seeing him. Had he always been a lonely person, or was this just the isolation from memory, from all that might have been love or warmth in himself? Surely there was a friend somewhere—someone with whom he had shared pleasure and pain, at least common experience? Had there been no woman—in the past, if not now—some stored-up memory of tenderness, of laughter or tears? If not he must have been a cold fish. Was there perhaps some tragedy? Or some wrong?

The nothingness was crowding in on him, threatening to engulf the precarious present. He had not even the comfort of habit.

Evan's acute face, all eyes and nose, was infinitely welcome.

''Find out anything, sir?'' He stood up from the wooden chair in which he had been sitting.

''Not a lot,'' Monk answered with a voice that was suddenly louder, firmer than the words warranted. ''I don't see much chance of anyone having got in unseen, except the man who visited Yeats at about quarter to ten. Grimwade says he was a biggish man, muffled up, which is reasonable on a night like that. He says he saw him leave at roughly half past ten. Took him upstairs, but didn't see him closely, and wouldn't recognize him again.''

Evan's face was a mixture of excitement and frustration.

''Damn!'' he exploded. ''Could be almost anyone then!'' He looked at Monk quickly. ''But at least we have a fair idea how he got in. That's a great step forward; congratulations, sir!''

Monk felt a quick renewal of his spirits. He knew it was not justified; the step was actually very small. He sat down in the chair behind the desk.

61

"About six feet," he reiterated. "Dark and probably clean-shaven. I suppose that does narrow it a little."

"Oh it narrows it quite a lot, sir," Evan said eagerly, resuming his own seat. "At least we know that it wasn't a chance thief. If he called on Yeats, or said he did, he had planned it, and taken the trouble to scout the building. He knew who else lived there. And of course there's Yeats himself. Did you see him?"

"No, he wasn't in, and anyway I'd rather find out a little about him before I face him with it."

"Yes, yes of course. If he knew anything, he's bound to deny it, I suppose." But the anticipation was building in Evan's face, his voice; even his body was tightening under the elegant coat as if he expected some sudden action here in the police station. "The cabby was no good, by the way. Perfectly respectable fellow, worked this area for twenty years, got a wife and seven or eight children. Never been any complaints against him."

"Yes," Monk agreed. "Grimwade said he hadn't gone into the building, in fact doesn't think he even got off the box."

"What do you want me to do about this Yeats?" Evan asked, a very slight smile curling his lips. "Sunday tomorrow, a bit hard to turn up much then."

Monk had forgotten.

"You're right. Leave it till Monday. He's been there for nearly seven weeks; it's hardly a hot trail."

Evan's smile broadened rapidly.

"Thank you, sir. I did have other ideas for Sunday." He stood up. "Have a good weekend, sir. Good night."

Monk watched him go with a sense of loss. It was foolish. Of course Evan would have friends, even family, and interests, perhaps a woman. He had never thought of that before. Somehow it added to his own sense of isolation. What did he normally do with his own time? Had he friends outside duty, some pursuit or pastime he enjoyed? There had to be more than this single-minded, ambitious man he had found so far.

He was still searching his imagination uselessly when there was a knock on the door, hasty, but not assertive, as though the person would have been pleased enough had there been no answer and he could have left again.

"Come in!" Monk said loudly.

The door opened and a stout young man came in. He wore a constable's uniform. His eyes were anxious, his rather homely face pink.

"Yes?" Monk inquired.

The young man cleared his throat. "Mr. Monk, sir?"

"Yes?" Monk said again. Should he know this man? From his wary expression there was some history in their past which had been important at least to him. He stood in the middle of the floor, fidgeting his weight from one foot to the other. Monk's wordless stare was making him worse.

"Can I do something for you?" Monk tried to sound reassuring. "Have you something to report?" He wished he could remember the man's name.

"No sir—I mean yes sir, I 'ave something to ask you." He took a deep breath. "There's a report of a watch turned up at a pawnbroker's wot I done this arternoon, sir, an'—an' I thought as it might be summink ter do with your gennelman as was murdered—seein' as 'e didn't 'ave no watch, just a chain, like? Sir." He held a piece of paper with copperplate handwriting on it as if it might explode.

Monk took it and glanced at it. It was the description of a gentleman's gold pocket watch with the initials J.G. inscribed ornately on the cover. There was nothing written inside.

He looked up at the constable.

"Thank you," he said with a smile. "It might well be—right initials. What do you know about it?"

The constable blushed scarlet. "Nuffink much, Mr. Monk. 'E swears blind as it was one of 'is reg'lars as brought it in. But you can't believe anyfink 'e says 'cause 'e would say that, wouldn't 'e? He don't want ter be mixed up in no murder."

63

Monk glanced at the paper again. The pawnbroker's name and address were there and he could follow up on it any time he chose.

"No, he'd doubtless lie," he agreed. "But we might learn something all the same, if we can prove this was Grey's watch. Thank you—very observant of you. May I keep it?"

"Yes sir. We don't need it; we 'as lots more agin 'im." Now his furious pink color was obviously pleasure, and considerable surprise. He still stood rooted to the spot.

"Was there anything else?" Monk raised his eyebrows.

"No sir! No there in't. Thank you, sir." And the constable turned on his heel and marched out, tripping on the doorsill as he went and rocketing out into the passage.

Almost immediately the door was opened again by a wiry sergeant with a black mustache.

"You o'right, sir?" he asked, seeing Monk's frown.

"Yes. What's the matter with—er." He waved his hand towards the departing figure of the constable, wishing desperately that he knew the man's name.

" 'Arrison?"

"Yes."

"Nothin'—just afeared of you, that's all. Which in't 'ardly surprisin', seein' as 'ow you tore 'im off such a strip in front o' the 'ole station, w'en that macer slipped through 'is fingers—which weren't 'ardly 'is fault, seein' as the feller were a downright contortionist. 'Arder to 'old then a greased pig, 'e were. An' if we'd broke 'is neck we'd be the ones for the 'igh jump before breakfast!"

Monk was confused. He did not know what to say. Had he been unjust to the man, or was there cause for whatever he had said? On the face of it, it sounded as if he had been gratuitously cruel, but he was hearing only one side of the story—there was no one to defend him, to explain, to give his reasons and say what he knew and perhaps they did not.

And rack and tear as he might, there was nothing in his

64

mind, not even Harrison's face—let alone some shred about the incident.

He felt a fool sitting staring up at the critical eyes of the sergeant, who plainly disliked him, for what he felt was fair cause.

Monk ached to explain himself! Even more he wanted to know for his own understanding. How many incidents would come up like this, things he had done that seemed ugly from the outside, to someone who did not know his side of the story?

"Mr. Monk, sir?"

Monk recalled his attention quickly. "Yes, Sergeant?"

"Thought you might like to know as we got the magsman wot snuffed ol' Billy Marlowe. They'll swing 'im for sure. Right villain."

"Oh—thank you. Well done." He had no idea what the sergeant was talking about, but obviously he was expected to. "Very well done," he added.

"Thank you, sir." The sergeant straightened up, then turned and left, closing the door behind him with a sharp snick.

Monk bent to his work again.

An hour later he left the police station and walked slowly along the dark, wet pavements and found the way back to Grafton Street.

Mrs. Worley's rooms were at least becoming familiar. He knew where to find things, and better than that, they offered privacy: no one would disturb him, intrude on his time to think, to try again to find some thread.

After his meal of mutton stew and dumplings, which were hot and filling, if a little heavy, he thanked Mrs. Worley when she collected the tray, saw her down the stairs, and then began once more to go through the desk. The bills were of little use; he could hardly go to his tailor and say "What kind of man am I? What do I care about? Do you like, or dislike me, and why?" One small comfort he could draw from his accounts was that he appeared to have been prompt in paying them; there were no demand notices, and the receipts were all dated within a few days of presentation. He was learning something, a crumb: he was methodical.

The personal letters from Beth told him much of her: of simplicity, an unforced affection, a life of small detail. She said nothing of hardships or of bitter winters, nothing even of wrecks or the lifeboatmen. Her concern for him was based on her feelings, and seemed to be without knowledge; she simply translated her own affections and interests to his life, and assumed his feelings were the same. He knew without needing deeper evidence that it was because he had told her nothing; perhaps he had not even written regularly. It was an unpleasant thought, and he was harshly ashamed of it. He must write to her soon, compose a letter which would seem rational, and yet perhaps elicit some answer from her which would tell him more.

The following morning he woke late to find Mrs. Worley knocking on the door. He let her in and she put his breakfast on the table with a sigh and a shake of her head. He was obliged to eat it before dressing or it would have grown cold. Afterwards he resumed the search, and again it was fruitless for any sharpening of identity, anything of the man behind the immaculate, rather expensive possessions. They told him nothing except that he had good taste, if a little predictable—perhaps that he liked to be admired? But what was admiration worth if it was for the cost and discretion of one's belongings? A shallow man? Vain? Or a man seeking security he did not feel, making his place in a world that he did not believe accepted him?

The apartment itself was impersonal, with traditional furniture, sentimental pictures. Surely Mrs. Worley's taste rather than his own?

After luncheon he was reduced to the last places to seek: the pockets of his other clothes, jackets hanging in the cupboard. In the best of them, a well-cut, rather formal coat, he found a piece of paper, and on unfolding it carefully, saw that it was a printed sheet for a service of Evensong at a church he did not know.

Perhaps it was close by. He felt a quickening of hope. Maybe he was a member of the congregation. The minister would know him. He might have friends there, a belief, even an office or a calling of some sort. He folded up the paper again carefully and put it in the desk, then went into the bedroom to wash and shave again, and change into his best clothes, and the coat from which the sheet had come. By five o'clock he was ready, and he went downstairs to ask Mrs. Worley where St. Marylebone Church might be.

His disappointment was shattering when she showed complete ignorance. Temper boiled inside him at the frustration. She must know. But her placid, blunt face was expressionless.

He was about to argue, to shout at her that she must know, when he realized how foolish it would be. He would only anger her, drive from himself a friend he sorely needed.

She was staring at him, her face puckered.

"My, you are in a state. Let me ask Mr. Worley for yer; he's a rare fine understanding o' the city. O' course I expect it's on the Marylebone Road, but ezac'ly where I'm sure I wouldn't know. It's a long street, that is."

"Thank you," he said carefully, feeling foolish. "It's rather important."

"Going to a wedding, are yer?" She looked at his carefully brushed dark coat. "What you want is a good cabby, what knows 'is way, and'll get you there nice and prompt, like."

It was an obvious answer, and he wondered why he had not thought of it himself. He thanked her, and when Mr. Worley had been asked, and given his opinion that it might be opposite York Gate, he went out to look for a cab.

Evensong had already begun when he hurried up the steps and into the vestry. He could hear the voices lifted rather thinly in the first hymn. It sounded dutiful rather than joyous. Was he a religious man; or, it would be truer to ask, had he been? He felt no sense of comfort or reverence now, except for the simple beauty of the stonework.

He went in as quickly as he could, walking almost on the sides of his polished boots to make no noise. One or two heads turned, sharp with criticism. He ignored them and slid into a back pew, fumbling for a hymnbook.

Nothing sounded familiar; he followed the hymn because the tune was trite, full of musical clichés. He knelt when everyone else knelt, and rose as they rose. He missed the responses.

When the minister stepped into the pulpit to speak, Monk stared at him, searching his face for some flicker of memory. Could he go to this man and confide in him the truth, ask him to tell him everything he knew? The voice droned on in one platitude after another; his intention was benign, but so tied in words as to be almost incomprehensible. Monk sank deeper and deeper into a feeling of helplessness. The man did not seem able to remember his own train of thought from one sentence to the next, let alone the nature and passions of his flock.

When the last amen had been sung, Monk watched the people file out, hoping someone would touch his memory, or better still, actually speak to him.

He was about to give up even that when he saw a young woman in black, slender and of medium height, dark hair drawn softly back from a face almost luminous, dark eyes and fragile skin, mouth too generous and too big for it. It was not a weak face, and yet it was one that could have moved easily to laughter, or tragedy. There was a grace in the way she walked that compelled him to watch her.

As she drew level she became aware of him and turned. Her eyes widened and she hesitated. She drew in her breath as if to speak.

He waited, hope surging up inside him, and a ridiculous excitement, as if some exquisite realization were about to come.

Then the moment vanished; she seemed to regain a

68

mastery of herself, her chin lifted a little, and she picked up her skirt unnecessarily and continued on her way.

He went after her, but she was lost in a group of people, two of whom, also dressed in black, were obviously accompanying her. One was a tall, fair man in his mid-thirties with smooth hair and a long-nosed, serious face; the other was a woman of unusual uprightness of carriage and features of remarkable character. The three of them walked towards the street and waiting vehicles and none of them turned their heads again.

Monk rode home in a rage of confusion, fear, and wild, disturbing hope.

4

BUT WHEN MONK ARRIVED on Monday morning, breathless and a little late, he was unable to begin investigation on Yeats and his visitor. Runcorn was in his room, pacing the floor and waving a piece of blue notepaper in his hand. He stopped and spun around the moment he heard Monk's feet.

"Ah!" He brandished the paper with a look of bright, shimmering anger, his left eye narrowed almost shut.

The good-morning greeting died on Monk's tongue.

"Letter from upstairs." Runcorn held up the blue paper. "The powers that be are after us again. The Dowager Lady Shelburne has written to Sir Willoughby Gentry, and confided to the said member of Parliament"—he gave every vowel its full value in his volume of scorn for that body—"that she is not happy with the utter lack of success the Metropolitan Police Force is having in apprehending the vile maniac who so foully murdered her son in his own house. No excuses are acceptable for our dilatory and lackadaisical attitude, our total lack of culprits to hand." His face purpled in his offense at the injustice of it, but there was no misery in him, only a feeding rage. "What the hell are you doing, Monk? You're supposed to be such a damn good detective, you've got your eyes on a super-

70

intendency—the commissionership, for all I know! So what do we tell this—this ladyship?''

Monk took a deep breath. He was more stunned by Runcorn's reference to himself, to his ambition, than anything in the letter. Was he an overweeningly ambitious man? There was no time for self-defense now; Runcorn was standing in front of him commanding an answer.

''Lamb's done all the groundwork, sir.'' He gave Lamb the praise that was due him. ''He's investigated all he could, questioned all the other residents, street peddlers, locals, anyone who might have seen or known anything.'' He could see from Runcorn's face that he was achieving nothing, but he persisted. ''Unfortunately it was a particularly foul night and everyone was in a hurry, heads down and collars up against the rain. Because it was so wet no one hung around, and with the overcast it was dark earlier than usual.''

Runcorn was fidgeting with impatience.

''Lamb spent a lot of time checking out the villains we know,'' Monk continued. ''He's written up in his report that he's spoken to every snout and informer in the area. Not a peep. No one knows anything; or if they do, they're not saying. Lamb was of the opinion they were telling the truth. I don't know what else he could have done.'' His experience offered nothing, but neither could his intelligence suggest any omission. All his sympathy was with Lamb.

''Constable Harrison found a watch with the initials J.G. on it in a pawnbroker's—but we don't know it was Grey's.''

''No,'' Runcorn agreed fiercely, running his finger with distaste along the deckle edge of the notepaper. It was a luxury he could not afford. ''Indeed you don't! So what are you doing, then? Take it to Shelburne Hall—get it identified.''

''Harrison's on his way.''

''Can't you at least find out how the bloody man got in?''

''I think so,'' Monk said levelly. ''There was a visitor

for one of the other residents, a Mr. Yeats. He came in at nine forty-five and left at roughly ten thirty. He was a biggish man, dark, well muffled. He's the only person unaccounted for; the others were women. I don't want to leap to conclusions too soon, but it looks as if he could be the murderer. Otherwise I don't know any way a stranger could have got in. Grimwade locks up at midnight, or earlier if all the residents are in, and after that even they have to ring the bell and get him up.''

Runcorn put the letter carefully on Monk's desk.

"And what time did he lock up that night?" he asked.

"Eleven," Monk replied. "No one was out."

"What did Lamb say about this man who visited Yeats?" Runcorn screwed up his face.

"Not much. Apparently he only spoke to Yeats once, and then he spent most of the time trying to find out something about Grey. Maybe he didn't realize the importance of the visitor at that time. Grimwade said he took him up to Yeats's door and Yeats met him. Lamb was still looking for a thief off the street then—"

"Then!" Runcorn leapt on the word, sharp, eager. "So what are you looking for now?"

Monk realized what he had said, and that he meant it. He frowned, and answered as carefully as he could.

"I think I'm looking for someone who knew him, and hated him; someone who intended to kill him."

"Well for God's sake don't say so to the Dowager Lady Shelburne!" Runcorn said dangerously.

"I'm hardly likely to be speaking to her," Monk answered with more than a trace of sarcasm.

"Oh yes you are!" There was a ring of triumph in Runcorn's voice and his big face was glowing with color. "You are going down to Shelburne today to assure Her Ladyship that we are doing everything humanly possible to apprehend the murderer, and that after intensive effort and brilliant work, we at last have a lead to discovering this monster." His lip curled very faintly. "You're generally so blunt, damn near rude, in spite of your fancy airs, she

72

won't take you for a liar." Suddenly his tone altered again and became soft. "Anyway, why do you think it was someone who knew him? Maniacs can kill with a hell of a mess; madmen strike over and over again, hate for no reason."

"Possibly." Monk stared back at him, matching dislike for dislike. "But they don't scout out the names of other residents, call upon them, and then go and kill someone else. If he was merely a homicidal lunatic, why didn't he kill Yeats? Why go and look for Grey?"

Runcorn's eyes were wide; he resented it, but he took the point.

"Find out everything you can about this Yeats," he ordered. "Discreetly, mind! I don't want him scared away!"

"What about Lady Shelburne?" Monk affected innocence.

"Go and see her. Try to be civil, Monk—make an effort! Evan can chase after Yeats, and tell you whatever he finds when you get back. Take the train. You'll be in Shelburne a day or two. Her Ladyship won't be surprised to see you, after the rumpus she's raised. She demanded a report on progress, in person. You can put up at the inn. Well, off you go then. Don't stand there like an ornament, man!"

Monk took the train on the Great Northern line from the King's Cross Station. He ran across the platform and jumped in, slamming the carriage door just as the engine belched forth a cloud of steam, gave a piercing shriek and jolted forward. It was an exciting sensation, a surge of power, immense, controlled noise, and then gathering speed as they emerged from the cavern of the station buildings out into the sharp late-afternoon sunlight.

Monk settled himself into a vacant seat opposite a large woman in black bombazine with a fur tippet around her neck (in spite of the season) and a black hat on at a fierce angle. She had a packet of sandwiches, which she opened immediately and began to eat. A little man with large spectacles eyed them hopefully, but said nothing. Another man in striped trousers studiously read his *Times*.

They roared and hissed their way past tenements, houses and factories, hospitals, churches, public halls and offices, gradually thinning, more interspersed with stretches of green, until at last the city fell away and Monk stared with genuine pleasure at the beauty of soft countryside spread wide in the lushness of full summer. Huge boughs clouded green over fields heavy with ripening crops and thick hedgerows starred with late wild roses. Coppices of trees huddled in folds of the slow hills, and villages were easily marked by the tapering spires of churches, or the occasional squarer Norman tower.

Shelburne came too quickly, while he was still drinking in the loveliness of it. He grabbed his valise off the rack and opened the door hastily, excusing himself past the fat woman in the bombazine and incurring her silent displeasure. On the platform he inquired of the lone attendant where Shelburne Hall lay, and was told it was less than a mile. The man waved his arm to indicate the direction, then sniffed and added, "But the village be two mile in t'opposite way, and doubtless that be w'ere you're a-goin'."

"No thank you," Monk replied. "I have business at the hall."

The man shrugged. "If'n you say so, sir. Then you'd best take the road left an' keep walking."

Monk thanked him again and set out.

It took him only fifteen minutes to walk from the station entrance to the drive gates. It was a truly magnificent estate, an early Georgian mansion three stories high, with a handsome frontage, now covered in places by vines and creepers, and approached by a sweeping carriageway under beech trees and cedars that dotted a parkland which seemed to stretch towards distant fields, and presumably the home farm.

Monk stood in the gateway and looked for several minutes. The grace of proportion, the way it ornamented rather

74

than intruded upon the landscape, were all not only extremely pleasing but also perhaps indicative of something in the nature of the people who had been born here and grown up in such a place.

Finally he began walking up the considerable distance to the house itself, a further third of a mile, and went around past the outhouses and stables to the servants' entrance. He was received by a rather impatient footman.

"We don't buy at the door," he said coldly, looking at Monk's case.

"I don't sell," Monk replied with more tartness than he had intended. "I am from the Metropolitan Police. Lady Shelburne wished a report on the progress we have made in investigating the death of Major Grey. I have come to give that report."

The footman's eyebrows went up.

"Indeed? That would be the Dowager Lady Shelburne. Is she expecting you?"

"Not that I know of. Perhaps you would tell her I am here."

"I suppose you'd better come in." He opened the door somewhat reluctantly. Monk stepped in, then without further explanation the man disappeared, leaving Monk in the back hallway. It was a smaller, barer and more utilitarian version of the front hall, only without pictures, having only the functional furniture necessary for servants' use. Presumably he had gone to consult some higher authority, perhaps even that autocrat of below-stairs—and sometimes above—the butler. It was several minutes before he returned, and motioned Monk to go with him.

"Lady Shelburne will see you in half an hour." He left Monk in a small parlor adjacent to the housekeeper's room, a suitable place for such persons as policemen; not precisely servants or tradesmen, and most certainly not to be considered as of quality.

Monk walked slowly around the room after the footman had gone, looking at the worn furniture, brown upholstered chairs with bow legs and an oak sideboard

75

and table. The walls were papered and fading, the pictures anonymous and rather puritan reminders of rank and the virtues of duty. He preferred the wet grass and heavy trees sloping down to ornamental water beyond the window.

He wondered what manner of woman she was who could control her curiosity for thirty long minutes rather than let her dignity falter in front of a social inferior. Lamb had said nothing about her. Was it likely he had not even seen her? The more he considered it, the more certain he became. Lady Shelburne would not direct her inquiries through a mere employee, and there had been no cause to question her in anything.

But Monk wanted to question her; if Grey had been killed by a man who hated him, not a maniac in the sense of someone without reason, only insofar as he had allowed a passion to outgrow control until it had finally exploded in murder, then it was imperative Monk learn to know Grey better. Intentionally or not, Grey's mother would surely betray something of him, some honesty through the memories and the grief, that would give color to the outline.

He had had time to think a lot about Grey and formulate questions in his mind by the time the footman returned and conducted him through the green baize door and across the corridor to Lady Fabia's sitting room. It was decorated discreetly with deep pink velvet and rosewood furniture. Lady Fabia herself was seated on a Louis Quinze sofa and when Monk saw her all his preconceptions fled his tongue. She was not very big, but as hard and fragile as porcelain, her coloring perfect, not a blemish on her skin, not a soft, fair hair out of place. Her features were regular, her blue eyes wide, only a slightly jutting chin spoiled the delicacy of her face. And she was perhaps too thin; slenderness had given way to angularity. She was dressed in violet and black, as became someone in mourning, although on her it looked more like something to be ob-

76

served for one's own dignity than any sign of distress. There was nothing frail in her manner.

"Good morning," she said briskly, dismissing the footman with a wave of her hand. She did not regard Monk with any particular interest and her eyes barely glanced at his face. "You may sit if you wish. I am told you have come to report to me the progress you have made in discovering and apprehending the murderer of my son. Pray proceed."

Opposite him Lady Fabia sat, her back ramrod-straight from years of obedience to governesses, walking as a child with a book on her head for deportment, and riding upright in a sidesaddle in the park or to hounds. There was little Monk could do but obey, sitting reluctantly on one of the ornate chairs and feeling self-conscious.

"Well?" she demanded when he remained silent. "The watch your constable brought was not my son's."

Monk was stung by her tone, by her almost unthinking assumption of superiority. In the past he must have been used to this, but he could not remember; and now it stung with the shallow sharpness of gravel rash, not a wound but a blistering abrasion. A memory of Beth's gentleness came to his mind. She would not have resented this. What was the difference between them? Why did he not have her soft Northumbrian accent? Had he eradicated it intentionally, washing out his origins in an attempt to appear some kind of gentleman? The thought made him blush for its stupidity.

Lady Shelburne was staring at him.

"We have established the only time a man could have gained entry to the buildings," he replied, still stiff with his own sense of pride. "And we have a description of the only man who did so." He looked straight into her chilly and rather surprised blue eyes. "He was roughly six feet tall, of solid build, as far as can be judged under a greatcoat. He was dark-complexioned and clean-shaven. He went ostensibly to visit a Mr. Yeats, who also lives in the building. We have not yet spoken to Mr. Yeats—"

77

"Why not?"

"Because you required that I come and report our progress to you, ma'am."

Her eyebrows rose in incredulity, touched with contempt. The sarcasm passed her by entirely.

"Surely you cannot be the only man directed to conduct such an important case? My son was a brave and distinguished soldier who risked his life for his country. Is this the best with which you can repay him?"

"London is full of crimes, ma'am; and every man or woman murdered is a loss to someone."

"You can hardly equate the death of a marquis's son with that of some thief or indigent in the street!" she snapped back.

"Nobody has more than one life to lose, ma'am; and all are equal before the law, or they should be."

"Nonsense! Some men are leaders, and contribute to society; most do not. My son was one of those who did."

"Some have nothing to—" he began.

"Then that is their own fault!" she interrupted. "But I do not wish to hear your philosophies. I am sorry for those in the gutter, for whatever reason, but they really do not interest me. What are you doing about apprehending this madman who killed my son? Who is he?"

"We don't know—"

"Then what are you doing to find out?" If she had any feelings under her exquisite exterior, like generations of her kind she had been bred to conceal them, never to indulge herself in weakness or vulgarity. Courage and good taste were her household gods and no sacrifice to them was questioned, nor too great, made daily and without fuss.

Monk ignored Runcorn's admonition, and wondered in passing how often he had done so in the past. There had been a certain asperity in Runcorn's tone this morning which surpassed simply frustration with the case, or Lady Shelburne's letter.

78

"We believe it was someone who knew Major Grey," he answered her. "And planned to kill him."

"Nonsense!" Her response was immediate. "Why should anyone who knew my son have wished to kill him? He was a man of the greatest charm; everyone liked him, even those who barely knew him." She stood up and walked over towards the window, her back half to him. "Perhaps that is difficult for you to understand; but you never met him. Lovel, my eldest son, has the sobriety, the sense of responsibility, and something of a gift to manage men; Menard is excellent with facts and figures. He can make anything profitable; but it was Joscelin who had the charm, Joscelin who could make one laugh." There was a catch in her voice now, the sound of real grief. "Menard cannot sing as Joscelin could; and Lovel has no imagination. He will make an excellent master of Shelburne. He will govern it well and be just to everyone, as just as it is wise to be—but my God"—there was sudden heat in her voice, almost passion—"compared with Joscelin, he is such a bore!"

Suddenly Monk was touched by the sense of loss that came through her words, the loneliness, the feeling that something irrecoverably pleasing had gone from her life and part of her could only look backwards from now on.

"I'm sorry," he said, and he meant it deeply. "I know it cannot bring him back, but we will find the man, and he will be punished."

"Hanged," she said tonelessly. "Taken out one morning and his neck broken on the rope."

"Yes."

"That is of little use to me." She turned back to him. "But it is better than nothing. See to it that it is done."

It was dismissal, but he was not yet ready to go. There were things he needed to know. He stood up.

"I mean to, ma'am; but I still need your help—"

"Mine?" Her voice expressed surprise, and disapproval.

"Yes ma'am. If I am to learn who hated Major Grey

79

enough to kill him"—he caught her expression—"for whatever reason. The finest people, ma'am, can inspire envy, or greed, jealousy over a woman, a debt of honor that cannot be paid—"

"Yes, you make your point." She blinked and the muscles in her thin neck tightened. "What is your name?"

"William Monk."

"Indeed. And what is it you wish to know about my son, Mr. Monk?"

"To start with, I would like to meet the rest of the family."

Her eyebrows rose in faint, dry amusement.

"You think I am biased, Mr. Monk, that I have told you something less than the truth?"

"We frequently show only our most flattering sides to those we care for most, and who care for us," he replied quietly.

"How perceptive of you." Her voice was stinging. He tried to guess what well-covered pain was behind those words.

"When may I speak to Lord Shelburne?" he asked. "And anyone else who knew Major Grey well?"

"If you consider it necessary, I suppose you had better." She went back to the door. "Wait here, and I shall ask him to see you, when it is convenient." She pulled the door open and walked through without looking back at him.

He sat down, half facing the window. Outside a woman in a plain stuff dress walked past, a basket on her arm. For a wild moment memory surged back to him. He saw in his mind a child as well, a girl with dark hair, and he knew the cobbled street beyond the trees, going down to the water. There was something missing; he struggled for it, and then knew it was wind, and the scream of gulls. It was a memory of happiness, of complete safety. Childhood—perhaps his mother, and Beth?

Then it was gone. He fought to add to it, focus it more sharply and see the details again, but nothing else came.

He was an adult back in Shelburne, with the murder of Joscelin Grey.

He waited for another quarter of an hour before the door opened again and Lord Shelburne came in. He was about thirty-eight or forty, heavier of build than Joscelin Grey, to judge by the description and the clothes; but Monk wondered if Joscelin had also had that air of confidence and slight, even unintentional superiority. He was darker than his mother and the balance of his face was different, sensible, without a jot of humor in the mouth.

Monk rose to his feet as a matter of courtesy—and hated himself for doing it.

"You're the police fellow?" Shelburne said with a slight frown. He remained standing, so Monk was obliged to also. "Well, what is it you want? I really can't imagine how anything I can tell you about my brother could help you find the lunatic who broke in and killed him, poor devil."

"No one broke in, sir," Monk corrected him. "Whoever it was, Major Grey gave entrance to him himself."

"Really?" The level brows rose a fraction. "I find that very unlikely."

"Then you are not acquainted with the facts, sir." Monk was irked by the condescension and the arrogance of a man who presumed to know Monk's job better than he did, simply because he was a gentleman. Had he always found it so hard to bear? Had he been quick-tempered? Runcorn had said something about lack of diplomacy, but he could not remember what it was now. His mind flew back to the church the day before, to the woman who had hesitated as she passed him down the aisle. He could see her face as sharply here at Shelburne as he had then; the rustle of taffeta, the faint, almost imaginary perfume, the widening of her eyes. It was a memory that made his heart beat faster and excitement catch in his throat.

"I know my brother was beaten to death by a lunatic." Shelburne's voice cut across him, scattering his thoughts. "And you haven't caught him yet. Those are facts!"

Monk forced his attention to the present.

"With respect, sir." He tried to choose his words with tact. "We know that he was beaten to death. We do not know by whom, or why; but there were no marks of forced entry, and the only person unaccounted for who could possibly have entered the building appears to have visited someone else. Whoever attacked Major Grey took great care about the way he did it, and so far as we know, did not steal anything."

"And you deduce from that that it was someone he knew?" Shelburne was skeptical.

"That, and the violence of the crime," Monk agreed, standing across the room from him so he could see Shelburne's face in the light. "A simple burglar does not go on hitting his victim long after he is quite obviously dead."

Shelburne winced. "Unless he is a madman! Which was rather my point. You are dealing with a madman, Mr.—er." He could not recall Monk's name and did not wait for it to be offered. It was unimportant. "I think there's scant chance of your catching him now. You would probably be better employed stopping muggings, or pickpockets, or whatever it is you usually do."

Monk swallowed his temper with difficulty. "Lady Shelburne seems to disagree with you."

Lovel Grey was unaware of having been rude; one could not be rude to a policeman.

"Mama?" His face flickered for an instant with unaccustomed emotion, which quickly vanished and left his features smooth again. "Oh, well; women feel these things. I am afraid she has taken Joscelin's death very hard, worse than if he'd been killed in the Crimea." It appeared to surprise him slightly.

"It's natural," Monk persisted, trying a different approach. "I believe he was a very charming person—and well liked?"

Shelburne was leaning against the mantelpiece and his boots shone in the sun falling wide through the French window. Irritably he kicked them against the brass fender.

"Joscelin? Yes, I suppose he was. Cheerful sort of fellow, always smiling. Gifted with music, and telling stories, that kind of thing. I know my wife was very fond of him. Great pity, and so pointless, just some bloody madman." He shook his head. "Hard on Mother."

"Did he come down here often?" Monk sensed a vein more promising.

"Oh, every couple of months or so. Why?" He looked up. "Surely you don't think someone followed him from here?"

"Every possibility is worth looking into, sir." Monk leaned his weight a little against the sideboard. "Was he here shortly before he was killed?"

"Yes, as a matter of fact he was; couple of weeks, or less. But I think you are mistaken. Everyone here had known him for years, and they all liked him." A shadow crossed his face. "Matter of fact, I think he was pretty well the servants' favorite. Always had a pleasant word, you know; remembered people's names, even though he hadn't lived here for years."

Monk imagined it: the solid, plodding older brother, worthy but boring; the middle brother still an outline only; and the youngest, trying hard and finding that charm could bring him what birth did not, making people laugh, unbending the formality, affecting an interest in the servants' lives and families, winning small treats for himself that his brothers did not—and his mother's love.

"People can hide hatred, sir," Monk said aloud. "And they usually do, if they have murder in mind."

"I suppose they must," Lovel conceded, straightening up and standing with his back to the empty fireplace. "Still, I think you're on the wrong path. Look for some lunatic in London, some violent burglar; there must be loads of them. Don't you have contacts, people who inform to the police? Why don't you try them?"

"We have, sir—exhaustively. Mr. Lamb, my predecessor, spent weeks combing every possibility in that direction. It was the first place to look." He changed the subject suddenly, hoping to catch him less guarded. "How did Major Grey finance himself, sir? We haven't uncovered any business interest yet."

"What on earth do you want to know that for?" Lovel was startled. "You cannot imagine he had the sort of business rivals who would beat him to death with a stick! That's ludicrous!"

"Someone did."

He wrinkled his face with distaste. "I had not forgotten that! I really don't know what his business interests were. He had a small allowance from the estate, naturally."

"How much, sir?"

"I hardly think that needs to concern you." Now the irritation was back; his affairs had been trespassed upon by a policeman. Again his boot kicked absently at the fender behind him.

"Of course it concerns me, sir." Monk had command of his temper now. He was in control of the conversation, and he had a direction to pursue. "Your brother was murdered, probably by someone who knew him. Money may well come into it; it is one of the commonest motives for murder."

Lovel looked at him without replying.

Monk waited.

"Yes, I suppose it is," Lovel said at last. "Four hundred pounds a year—and of course there was his army pension."

To Monk it sounded a generous amount; one could run a very good establishment and keep a wife and family, with two maids, for less than a thousand pounds. But possibly Joscelin Grey's tastes had been a good deal more extravagant: clothes, clubs, horses, gambling, perhaps women, or at least presents for women. They had not so far explored his social circle, still believing it to have been an intruder from the streets, and Grey a victim of ill fortune rather than someone of his own acquaintance.

"Thank you," he replied to Lord Shelburne. "You know of no other?"

"My brother did not discuss his financial affairs with me."

"You say your wife was fond of him? Would it be possible for me to speak to Lady Shelburne, please? He may have said something to her the last time he was here that could help us."

"Hardly, or she would have told me; and naturally I should have told you, or whoever is in authority."

"Something that meant nothing to Lady Shelburne might have meaning for me," Monk pointed out. "Anyway, it is worth trying."

Lovel moved to the center of the room as if somehow he would crowd Monk to the door. "I don't think so. And she has already suffered a severe shock; I don't see any purpose in distressing her any further with sordid details."

"I was going to ask her about Major Grey's personality, sir," Monk said with the shadow of irony in his voice. "His friends and his interests, nothing further. Or was she so attached to him that would distress her too much?"

"I don't care for your impertinence!" Lovel said sharply. "Of course she wasn't. I just don't want to rake the thing over any further. It is not very pleasant to have a member of one's family beaten to death!"

Monk faced him squarely. There was not more than a yard between them.

"Of course not, but that surely is all the more reason why we must find the man."

"If you insist." With ill humor he ordered Monk to follow him, and led him out of the very feminine sitting room along a short corridor into the main hall. Monk glanced around as much as was possible in the brief time as Shelburne paced ahead of him towards one of the several fine doorways. The walls were paneled to shoulder height in wood, the floor parqueted and scattered with Chinese carpets of cut pile and beautiful pastel shades, and the whole was dominated by a magnificent staircase dividing halfway up and sweeping to left and right at either end of a railed landing. There were pictures in ornate gold frames on all sides, but he had no time to look at them.

Shelburne opened the withdrawing room door and waited impatiently while Monk followed him in, then closed it. The room was long and faced south, with French windows looking onto a lawn bordered with herbaceous flowers in brilliant bloom. Rosamond Shelburne was sitting on a brocaded chaise longue, embroidery hoop in her hand. She looked up when they came in. She was at first glance not unlike her mother-in-law: she had the same fair hair and good brow, the same shape of eye, although hers were dark brown, and there was a different balance to her features, the resolution was not yet hard, there was humor, a width of imagination waiting to be given flight. She was dressed soberly, as befitted one who had recently lost a brother-in-law, but the wide skirt was the color of wine in shadow, and only her beads were black.

"I am sorry, my dear." Shelburne glanced pointedly at Monk. "But this man is from the police, and he thinks you may be able to tell him something about Joscelin that will help." He strode past her and stopped by the first window, glancing at the sun across the grass.

Rosamond's fair skin colored very slightly and she avoided Monk's eyes.

"Indeed?" she said politely. "I know very little of Joscelin's London life, Mr. —?"

"Monk, ma'am," he answered. "But I understand Major Grey had an affection for you, and perhaps he may have spoken of some friend, or an acquaintance who might lead us to another, and so on?"

"Oh." She put her needle and frame down; it was a tracery of roses around a text. "I see. I am afraid I cannot think of anything. But please be seated, and I will do my best to help."

Monk accepted and questioned her gently, not because he expected to learn a great deal from her directly, but because indirectly he watched her, listening to the intonations of her voice, and the fingers turning in her lap.

Slowly he discovered a picture of Joscelin Grey.

"He seemed very young when I came here after my marriage," Rosamond said with a smile, looking beyond Monk and out of the window. "Of course that was before he went to the Crimea. He was an officer then; he had just bought his commission and he was so"—she searched for just the right word—"so jaunty! I remember that day he came in in his uniform, scarlet tunic and gold braid, boots gleaming. One could not help feeling happy for him." Her voice dropped. "It all seemed like an adventure then."

"And after?" Monk prompted, watching the delicate shadows in her face, the search for something glimpsed but not understood except by a leap of instinct.

"He was wounded, you know?" She looked at him, frowning.

"Yes," he said.

"Twice—and ill too." She searched his eyes to see if he knew more than she, and there was nothing in his memory to draw on. "He suffered very much," she continued. "He was thrown from his horse in the charge at Balaclava and sustained a sword wound in his leg at Sebastopol. He refused to speak much to us about being in hospital at Scutari; he said it was too terrible to relate and would distress us beyond bearing." The embroidery slipped on the smooth nap of her skirt and rolled away on the floor. She made no effort to pick it up.

"He was changed?" Monk prompted.

She smiled slowly. She had a lovely mouth, sweeter and more sensitive than her mother-in-law's. "Yes—but he did not lose his humor, he could still laugh and enjoy beautiful things. He gave me a musical box for my birthday." Her smile widened at the thought of it. "It had an enamel top with a rose painted on it. It played 'Fur Elise'—Beethoven, you know—"

"Really, my dear!" Lovel's voice cut across her as he turned from where he had been standing by the window. "The man is here on police business. He doesn't know or care about Beethoven and Joscelin's music box. Please try

87

to concentrate on something relevant—in the remote like-lihood there is anything. He wants to know if Joscelin offended someone—owed them money—God knows what!"

Her face altered so slightly it could have been a change in the light, had not the sky beyond the windows been a steady cloudless blue. Suddenly she looked tired.

"I know Joscelin found finances a little difficult from time to time," she answered quietly. "But I do not know of any particulars, or whom he owed."

"He would hardly have discussed such a thing with my wife." Lovel swung around sharply. "If he wanted to borrow he would come to me—but he had more sense than to try. He had a very generous allowance as it was."

Monk glanced frantically at the splendid room, the swagged velvet curtains, and the garden and parkland beyond, and forbore from making any remark as to generosity. He looked back at Rosamond.

"You never assisted him, ma'am?"

Rosamond hesitated.

"With what?" Lovel asked, raising his eyebrows.

"A gift?" Monk suggested, struggling to be tactful. "Perhaps a small loan to meet a sudden embarrassment?"

"I can only assume you are trying to cause mischief," Lovel said acidly. "Which is despicable, and if you persist I shall have you removed from the case."

Monk was taken aback; he had not deliberately intended offense, simply to uncover a truth. Such sensibilities were peripheral, and he thought a rather silly indulgence now.

Lovel saw his irritation and mistook it for a failure to understand. "Mr. Monk, a married woman does not own anything to dispose of—to a brother-in-law or anyone else."

Monk blushed for making a fool of himself, and for the patronage in Lovel's manner. When reminded, of course he knew the law. Even Rosamond's personal jewelry was not hers in law. If Lovel said she was not to give it away, then she could not. Not that he had any doubt, from the catch in her speech and the flicker of her eyes, that she had done so.

He had no desire to betray her; the knowledge was all he wanted. He bit back the reply he wished to make.

"I did not intend to suggest anything done without your permission, my lord, simply a gesture of kindness on Lady Shelburne's part."

Lovel opened his mouth to retort, then changed his mind and looked out of the window again, his face tight, his shoulders broad and stiff.

"Did the war affect Major Grey deeply?" Monk turned back to Rosamond.

"Oh yes!" For a moment there was intense feeling in her, then she recalled the circumstances and struggled to control herself. Had she not been as schooled in the privileges and the duties of a lady she would have wept. "Yes," she said again. "Yes, although he mastered it with great courage. It was not many months before he began to be his old self—most of the time. He would play the piano, and sing for us sometimes." Her eyes looked beyond Monk to some past place in her own mind. "And he still told us funny stories and made us laugh. But there were occasions when he would think of the men who died, and I suppose his own suffering as well."

Monk was gathering an increasingly sharp picture of Joscelin Grey: a dashing young officer, easy mannered, perhaps a trifle callow; then through experience of war with its blood and pain, and for him an entirely new kind of responsibility, returning home determined to resume as much of the old life as possible; a youngest son with little money but great charm, and a degree of courage.

He had not seemed like a man to make enemies through wronging anyone—but it did not need a leap of imagination to conceive that he might have earned a jealousy powerful enough to have ended in murder. All that was needed for that might lie within this lovely room with its tapestries and its view of the parkland.

"Thank you, Lady Shelburne," he said formally. "You

89

have given me a much clearer picture of him than I had. I am most grateful." He turned to Lovel. "Thank you, my lord. If I might speak with Mr. Menard Grey—"

"He is out," Lovel replied flatly. "He went to see one of the tenant farmers, and I don't know which so there is no point in your traipsing around looking. Anyway, you are looking for who murdered Joscelin, not writing an obituary!"

"I don't think the obituary is finished until it contains the answer," Monk replied, meeting his eyes with a straight, challenging stare.

"Then get on with it!" Lovel snapped. "Don't stand here in the sun—get out and do something useful."

Monk left without speaking and closed the withdrawing room door behind him. In the hall a footman was awaiting discreetly to show him out—or perhaps to make sure that he left without pocketing the silver card tray on the hall table, or the ivory-handled letter opener.

The weather had changed dramatically; from nowhere a swift overcast had brought a squall, the first heavy drops beginning even as he left.

He was outside, walking towards the main drive through the clearing rain, when quite by chance he met the last member of the family. He saw her coming towards him briskly, whisking her skirts out of the way of a stray bramble trailing onto the narrower path. She was reminiscent of Fabia Shelburne in age and dress, but without the brittle glamour. This woman's nose was longer, her hair wilder, and she could never have been a beauty, even forty years ago.

"Good afternoon." He lifted his hat in a small gesture of politeness.

She stopped in her stride and looked at him curiously. "Good afternoon. You are a stranger. What are you doing here? Are you lost?"

"No, thank you ma'am. I am from the Metropolitan Police. I came to report our progress on the murder of Major Grey."

90

Her eyes narrowed and he was not sure whether it was amusement or something else.

"You look a well-set-up young man to be carrying messages. I suppose you came to see Fabia?"

He had no idea who she was, and for a moment he was at a loss for a civil reply.

She understood instantly.

"I'm Callandra Daviot; the late Lord Shelburne was my brother."

"Then Major Grey was your nephew, Lady Callandra?" He spoke her correct title without thinking, and only realized it afterwards, and wondered what experience or interest had taught him. Now he was only concerned for another opinion of Joscelin Grey.

"Naturally," she agreed. "How can that help you?"

"You must have known him."

Her rather wild eyebrows rose slightly.

"Of course. Possibly a little better than Fabia. Why?"

"You were very close to him?" he said quickly.

"On the contrary, I was some distance removed." Now he was quite certain there was a dry humor in her eyes.

"And saw the clearer for it?" He finished her implication.

"I believe so. Do you require to stand here under the trees, young man? I am being steadily dripped on."

He shook his head, and turned to accompany her back along the way he had come.

"It is unfortunate that Joscelin was murdered," she continued. "It would have been much better if he could have died at Sebastopol—better for Fabia anyway. What do you want of me? I was not especially fond of Joscelin, nor he of me. I knew none of his business, and have no useful ideas as to who might have wished him such intense harm."

"You were not fond of him yourself?" Monk said curiously. "Everyone says he was charming."

"So he was," she agreed, walking with large strides not towards the main entrance of the house but along a

91

graveled path in the direction of the stables, and he had no choice but to go also or be left behind. "I do not care a great deal for charm." She looked directly at him, and he found himself warming to her dry honesty. "Perhaps because I never possessed it," she continued. "But it always seems chameleon to me, and I cannot be sure what color the animal underneath might be really. Now will you please either return to the house, or go wherever it is you are going. I have no inclination to get any wetter than I already am, and it is going to rain again. I do not intend to stand in the stable yard talking polite nonsense that cannot possibly assist you."

He smiled broadly and bowed his head in a small salute. Lady Callandra was the only person in Shelburne he liked instinctively.

"Of course, ma'am; thank you for your . . ." He hesitated, not wanting to be so obvious as to say "honesty."

". . . time. I wish you a good day."

She looked at him wryly and with a little nod and strode past and into the harness room calling loudly for the head groom.

Monk walked back along the driveway again—as she had surmised, through a considerable shower—and out past the gates. He followed the road for the three miles to the village. Newly washed by rain, in the brilliant bursts of sun it was so lovely it caught a longing in him as if once it was out of his sight he would never recall it clearly enough. Here and there a coppice showed dark green, billowing over the sweep of grass and mounded against the sky, and beyond the distant stone walls wheat fields shone dark gold with the wind rippling like waves through their heavy heads.

It took him a little short of an hour and he found the peace of it turning his mind from the temporary matter of who murdered Joscelin Grey to the deeper question as to what manner of man he himself was. Here no one knew him; at least for tonight he would be able to start anew, no previous act could mar it, or help. Perhaps he would learn something of the inner man, unfiltered by expectations. What did he believe, what did he truly value? What drove him from day to day—except ambition, and personal vanity?

He stayed overnight in the village public hostelry, and asked some discreet questions of certain locals in the morning, without significantly adding to his picture of Joscelin Grey, but he found a very considerable respect for both Grey's brothers, in their different ways. They were not liked—that was too close a relationship with men whose lives and stations were so different—but they were trusted. They fitted into expectations of their kind, small courtesies were observed, a mutual code was kept.

Of Joscelin it was different. Affection was possible. Everyone had found him more than civil, remembering as many of the generosities as were consistent with his position as a son of the house. If some had thought or felt otherwise they were not saying so to an outsider like Monk. And he had been a soldier; a certain honor was due the dead.

Monk enjoyed being polite, even gracious. No one was afraid of him—guarded certainly, he was still a Peeler—but there was no personal awe, and they were as keen as he to find who had murdered their hero.

He took luncheon in the taproom with several local worthies and contrived to fall into conversation. By the door with the sunlight streaming in, with cider, apple pie and cheese, opinions began to flow fast and free. Monk became involved, and before long his tongue got the better of him, clear, sarcastic and funny. It was only afterwards as he was walking away that he realized that it was also at times unkind.

He left in the early afternoon for the small, silent station, and took a clattering, steam-belching journey back to London.

He arrived a little after four, and went by hansom straight to the police station.

"Well?" Runcorn inquired with lifted eyebrows. "Did

you manage to mollify Her Ladyship? I'm sure you conducted yourself like a gentleman?''

Monk heard that slight edge to Runcorn's voice again, and the flavor of resentment. What for? He struggled desperately to recall any wisp of memory, even a guess as to what he might have done to occasion it. Surely not mere abrasiveness of manner? He had not been so stupid as to be positively rude to a superior? But nothing came. It mattered—it mattered acutely: Runcorn held the key to his employment, the only sure thing in his life now, in fact the very means of it. Without work he was not only completely anonymous, but within a few weeks he would be a pauper. Then there would be only the same bitter choice for him as for every other pauper: beggary, with its threat of starvation or imprisonment as a vagrant; or the workhouse. And God knew, there were those who thought the workhouse the greater evil.

"I believe Her Ladyship understood that we are doing all we can," he answered. "And that we had to exhaust the more likely-seeming possibilities first, like a thief off the streets. She understands that now we must consider that it may have been someone who knew him."

Runcorn grunted. "Asked her about him, did you? What sort of feller he was?"

"Yes sir. Naturally she was biased—"

"Naturally," Runcorn agreed tartly, shooting his eyebrows up. "But you ought to be bright enough to see past that."

Monk ignored the implication. "He seems to have been her favorite son," he replied. "Considerably the most likable. Everyone else gave the same opinion, even in the village. Discount some of that as speaking no ill of the dead." He smiled twistedly. "Or of the son of the big house. Even so, you're still left with a man of unusual charm, a good war record, and no especial vices or weaknesses, except that he found it hard to manage on his allowance, bit of a temper now and then, and a mocking wit when he chose; but generous, remembered birthdays

94

and servants' names—knew how to amuse. It begins to look as if jealousy could have been a motive."

Runcorn sighed.

"Messy," he said decidedly, his left eye narrowing again. "Never like having to dig into family relationships, and the higher you go the nastier you get." He pulled his coat a little straighter without thinking, but it still did not sit elegantly. "That's your society for you; cover their tracks better than any of your average criminals, when they really try. Don't often make a mistake, that lot, but oh my grandfather, when they do!" He poked his finger in the air towards Monk. "Take my word for it, if there's something nasty there, it'll get a lot worse before it gets any better. You may fancy the higher classes, my boy, but they play very dirty when they protect their own; you believe it!"

Monk could think of no answer. He wished he could remember the things he had said and done to prompt Runcorn to these flavors, nuances of disapproval. Was he a brazen social climber? The thought was repugnant, even pathetic in a way, trying to appear something you are not, in order to impress people who don't care for you in the slightest, and can most certainly detect your origins even before you open your mouth!

But did not most men seek to improve themselves, given opportunity? But had he been overambitious, and foolish enough to show it?

The thing lying at the back of his mind, troubling him all the time, was why he had not been back to see Beth in eight years. She seemed the only family he had, and yet he had virtually ignored her. Why?

Runcorn was staring at him.

"Well?" he demanded.

"Yes sir." He snapped to attention. "I agree, sir. I think there may be something very unpleasant indeed. One has to hate very much to beat a man to death as Grey was beaten. I imagine if it is something to do with the family, they will do everything they can to hush it up. In fact the

95

eldest son, the present Lord Shelburne, didn't seem very eager for me to probe it. He tried to guide me back to the idea that it was a casual thief, or a lunatic."

"And Her Ladyship?"

"She wants us to continue."

"Then she's fortunate, isn't she?" Runcorn nodded his head with his lips twisted. "Because that is precisely what you are going to do!"

Monk recognized a dismissal.

"Yes sir; I'll start with Yeats." He excused himself and went to his own room.

Evan was sitting at the table, busy writing. He looked up with a quick smile when Monk came in. Monk found himself overwhelmingly glad to see him. He realized he had already begun to think of Evan as a friend as much as a colleague.

"How was Shelburne?" Evan asked.

"Very splendid," he replied. "And very formal. What about Mr. Yeats?"

"Very respectable." Evan's mouth twitched in a brief and suppressed amusement. "And very ordinary. No one is saying anything to his discredit. In fact no one is saying anything much at all; they have trouble in recalling precisely who he is."

Monk dismissed Yeats from his mind, and spoke of the thing which was more pressing to him.

"Runcorn seems to think it will become unpleasant, and he's expecting rather a lot from us—"

"Naturally." Evan looked at him, his eyes perfectly clear. "That's why he rushed you into it, even though you're hardly back from being ill. It's always sticky when we have to deal with the aristocracy; and let's face it, a policeman is usually treated pretty much as the social equal of a parlor maid and about as desirable to be close to as the drains; necessary in an imperfect society, but not fit to have in the withdrawing room."

At another time Monk would have laughed, but now it was too painful, and too urgent.

"Why me?" he pressed.

Evan was frankly puzzled. He hid what looked like embarrassment with formality.

"Sir?"

"Why me?" Monk repeated a little more harshly. He could hear the rising pitch in his own voice, and could not govern it.

Evan lowered his eyes awkwardly.

"Do you want an honest answer to that, sir; although you must know it as well as I do?"

"Yes I do! Please?"

Evan faced him, his eyes hot and troubled. "Because you are the best detective in the station, and the most ambitious. Because you know how to dress and to speak; you'll be equal to the Shelburnes, if anyone is." He hesitated, biting his lip, then plunged on. "And—and if you come unstuck either by making a mess of it and failing to find the murderer, or rubbing up against Her Ladyship and she complains about you, there are a good few who won't mind if you're demoted. And of course worse still, if it turns out to be one of the family—and you have to arrest him—"

Monk stared at him, but Evan did not look away. Monk felt the heat of shock ripple through him.

"Including Runcorn?" he said very quietly.

"I think so."

"And you?"

Evan was transparently surprised. "No, not me," he said simply. He made no protestations, and Monk believed him.

"Good." He drew a deep breath. "Well, we'll go and see Mr. Yeats tomorrow."

"Yes sir." Evan was smiling, the shadow gone. "I'll be here at eight."

Monk winced inwardly at the time, but he had to agree. He said good-night and turned to go home.

But out in the street he started walking the other way, not consciously thinking until he realized he was moving in the general direction of St. Marylebone Church. It was over two miles away, and he was tired. He had already walked a long way in Shelburne, and his legs were aching, his feet sore. He hailed a cab and when the driver asked him, he gave the address of the church.

It was very quiet inside with only the dimmest of light through the fast-graying windows. Candelabra shed little yellow arcs.

Why the church? He had all the peace and silence he needed in his own rooms, and he certainly had no conscious thought of God. He sat down in one of the pews.

Why had he come here? No matter how much he had dedicated himself to his job, his ambition, he must know someone, have a friend, or even an enemy. His life must have impinged on someone else's—beside Runcorn.

He had been sitting in the dark without count of time, struggling to remember anything at all—a face, a name, even a feeling, something of childhood, like the momentary glimpse at Shelburne—when he saw the girl in black again, standing a few feet away.

He was startled. She seemed so vivid, familiar. Or was it only that she seemed to him to be lovely, evocative of something he wanted to feel, wanted to remember?

But she was not beautiful, not really. Her mouth was too big, her eyes too deep. She was looking at him.

Suddenly he was frightened. Ought he to know her? Was he being unbearably rude in not speaking? But he could know any number of people, of any walk of life! She could be a bishop's daughter, or a prostitute!

No, never with that face.

Don't be ridiculous, harlots could have faces with just that warmth, those luminous eyes; at least they could while they were still young, and nature had not yet written itself on the outside.

Without realizing it, he was still looking at her.

"Good evening, Mr. Monk," she said slowly, a faint embarrassment making her blink.

He rose to his feet. "Good evening, ma'am." He had

no idea of her name, and now he was terrified, wishing he had never come. What should he say? How well did she know him? He could feel the sweat prickly on his body, his tongue dry, his thoughts in a stultified, wordless mass.

"You have not spoken for such a long time," she went on. "I had begun to fear you had discovered something you did not dare to tell me."

Discovered! Was she connected with some case? It must be old; he had been working on Joscelin Grey since he came back, and before that the accident. He fished for something that would not commit him and yet still make sense.

"No, I'm afraid I haven't discovered anything else." His voice was dry, artificial to his own ears. Please God he did not sound so foolish to her!

"Oh." She looked down. It seemed for a moment as if she could not think of anything else to say, then she lifted her head again and met his eyes very squarely. He could only think how dark they were—not brown, but a multitude of shadows. "You may tell me the truth, Mr. Monk, whatever it is. Even if he killed himself, and for whatever reason, I would rather know."

"It is the truth," he said simply. "I had an accident about seven weeks ago. I was in a cab that overturned and I broke my arm and ribs and cracked my head. I can't even remember it. I was in hospital for nearly a month, and then went north to my sister's to regain my strength. I'm afraid I haven't done anything about it since then."

"Oh dear." Her face was tight with concern. "I am sorry. Are you all right now? Are you sure you are better?"

She sounded as if it mattered to her. He found himself warmed ridiculously by it. He forced from his mind the idea that she was merely compassionate, or well-mannered.

"Yes, yes thank you; although there are blanks in my memory." Why had he told her that? To explain his behavior—in case it hurt her? He was taking too much upon himself. Why should she care, more than courtesy required? He remembered Sunday now; she had worn black then too, but expensive black, silk and fashionable. The man accompanying her had been dressed as Monk could not afford to be. Her husband? The thought was acutely depressing, even painful. He did not even think of the other woman.

"Oh." Again she was lost for words.

He was fumbling, trying to find a clue, sharply conscious of her presence; even faintly, although she was several feet away, of her perfume. Or was it imagination?

"What was the last thing I told you?" he asked. "I mean—" He did not know what he meant.

But she answered with only the merest hesitation.

"Not a great deal. You said Papa had certainly discovered that the business was fraudulent but you did not know yet whether he had faced the other partners with it or not. You had seen someone, although you did not name him, but a certain Mr. Robinson disappeared every time you went after him." Her face tightened. "You did not know whether Papa could have been murdered by them, to keep his silence, or if he took his own life, for shame. Perhaps I was wrong to ask you to discover. It just seemed so dreadful that he should choose that way rather than fight them, show them for what they are. It's no crime to be deceived!" There was a spark of anger in her now, as though she were fighting to keep control of herself. "I wanted to believe he would have stayed alive, and fought them, faced his friends, even those who lost money, rather than—" She stopped, otherwise she would have wept. She stood quite still, swallowing hard.

"I'm sorry," he said very quietly. He wanted to touch her, but he was hurtfully aware of the difference between them. It would be a familiarity and would break the moment's trust, the illusion of closeness.

She waited a moment longer, as if for something which did not come; then she abandoned it.

100

"Thank you. I am sure you have done everything you could. Perhaps I saw what I wished to see."

There was a movement up the aisle, towards the door of the church, and the vicar came down, looking vague, and behind him the same woman with the highly individual face whom Monk had seen on the first occasion in the church. She also was dressed in dark, plain clothes, and her thick hair with a very slight wave was pulled back in a manner that owed more to expediency than fashion.

"Mrs. Latterly, is that you?" the vicar asked uncertainly, peering forward. "Why my dear, what are you doing here all by yourself? You mustn't brood, you know. Oh!" He saw Monk. "I beg your pardon. I did not realize you had company."

"This is Mr. Monk," she said, explaining him. "From the police. He was kind enough to help us when Papa . . . died."

The vicar looked at Monk with disapproval.

"Indeed. I do think, my dear child, that it would be wiser for all of us if you were to let the matter rest. Observe mourning, of course, but let your poor father-in-law rest in peace." He crossed the air absently. "Yes—in peace."

Monk stood up. Mrs. Latterly; so she was married—or a widow? He was being absurd.

"If I learn anything more, Mrs. Latterly"—his voice was tight, almost choking—"do you wish me to inform you?" He did not want to lose her, to have her disappear into the past with everything else. He might not discover anything, but he must know where she was, have a reason to see her.

She looked at him for a long moment, undecided, fighting with herself. Then she spoke carefully.

"Yes please, if you will be so kind, but please remember your promise! Good night." She swiveled around, her skirts brushing Monk's feet. "Good night, Vicar. Come, Hester, it is time we returned home; Charles will be expecting us for dinner." And she walked slowly up towards the door. Monk watched her go arm in arm with the other woman as if she had taken the light away with her.

Outside in the sharper evening air Hester Latterly turned to her sister-in-law.

"I think it is past time you explained yourself, Imogen," she said quietly, but with an edge of urgency in her voice. "Just who is that man?"

"He is with the police," Imogen replied, walking briskly towards their carriage, which was waiting at the curbside. The coachman climbed down, opened the door and handed them in, Imogen first, then Hester. Both took his courtesy for granted and Hester arranged her skirts merely sufficiently to be comfortable, Imogen to avoid crushing the fabric.

"What do you mean, 'with'?" Hester demanded as the carriage moved forward. "One does not accompany the police; you make it sound like a social event! 'Miss Smith is with Mr. Jones this evening.' "

"Don't be pedantic," Imogen criticized. "Actually you can say it of a maid as well—'Tilly is with the Robinsons at present'!"

Hester's eyebrows shot up. "Indeed! And is that man presently playing footman to the police?"

Imogen remained silent.

"I'm sorry," Hester said at length. "But I know there is something distressing you, and I feel so helpless because I don't know what it is."

Imogen put out her hand and held Hester's tightly.

"Nothing," she said in a voice so low it could only just be heard above the rattle of the carriage and the dull thud of hooves and the noises of the street. "It is only Papa's death, and all that followed. None of us are over the shock of it yet, and I do appreciate your leaving everything and coming home as you did."

"I never thought of doing less," Hester said honestly, although her work in the Crimean hospitals had changed her beyond anything Imogen or Charles could begin to

102

understand. It had been a hard duty to leave the nursing service and the white-hot spirit to improve, reform and heal that had moved not only Miss Nightingale but so many other women as well. But the death of first her father, then within a few short weeks her mother also, had made it an undeniable duty that she should return home and be there to mourn, and to assist her brother and his wife in all the affairs that there were to be attended to. Naturally Charles had seen to all the business and the finances, but there had been the house to close up, servants to dismiss, endless letters to write, clothes to dispose of to the poor, bequests of a personal nature to be remembered, and the endless social facade to be kept up. It would have been desperately unfair to expect Imogen to bear the burden and that responsibility alone. Hester had given no second thought as to whether she should come, simply excused herself, packed her few belongings and embarked.

It had been an extraordinary contrast after the desperate years in the Crimea with the unspeakable suffering she had seen, the agony of wounds, bodies torn by shot and sword; and to her even more harrowing, those wasted by disease, the racking pain and nausea of cholera, typhus and dysentery, the cold and the starvation; and driving her almost beyond herself with fury, the staggering incompetence.

She, like the other handful of women, had worked herself close to exhaustion, cleaning up human waste where there were no sanitary facilities, excrement from the helpless running on the floor and dripping through to the packed and wretched huddled in the cellars below. She had nursed men delirious with fever, gangrenous from amputations of limbs lost to everything from musket shot, cannon shot, sword thrust, even frostbite on the exposed and fearful bivouacs of the winter encampments where men and horses had perished by the thousands. She had delivered babies of the hungry and neglected army wives, buried many of them, then comforted the bereaved.

And when she could bear the pity no longer she had expended her last energy in fury, fighting the endless, id-

103

iotic inadequacy of the command, who seemed to her not to have the faintest grasp of ordinary sense, let alone management ability.

She had lost a brother, and many friends, chief among them Alan Russell, a brilliant war correspondent who had written home to the newspapers some of the unpalatable truths about one of the bravest and foolhardiest campaigns ever fought. He had shared many of them with her, allowing her to read them before they were posted.

Indeed in the weakness of fever he had dictated his last letter to her and she had sent it. When he died in the hospital at Scutari she had in a rash moment of deep emotion written a dispatch herself, and signed his name to it as if he were still alive.

It had been accepted and printed. From knowledge gleaned from other injured and feverish men she had learned their accounts of battle, siege and trench warfare, crazy charges and long weeks of boredom, and other dispatches had followed, all with Alan's name on them. In the general confusion no one realized.

Now she was home in the orderly, dignified, very sober grief of her brother's household mourning both her parents, wearing black as if this were the only loss and there were nothing else to do but conduct a gentle life of embroidery, letter writing and discreet good works with local charities. And of course obey Charles's continuous and rather pompous orders as to what must be done, and how, and when. It was almost beyond bearing. It was as if she were in suspended animation. She had grown used to having authority, making decisions and being in the heart of emotion, even if overtired, bitterly frustrated, full of anger and pity, desperately needed.

Now Charles was driven frantic because he could not understand her or comprehend the change in her from the brooding, intellectual girl he knew before, nor could he foresee any respectable man offering for her in marriage. He found the thought of having her living under his roof for the rest of her life well nigh insufferable.

104

The prospect did not please Hester either, but then she had no intention of allowing it to come to pass. As long as Imogen needed her she would remain, then she would consider her future and its possibilities.

However, as she sat in the carriage beside Imogen while they rattled through the dusk streets she had a powerful conviction that there was much troubling her sister-in-law and it was something that, for whatever reasons, Imogen was keeping secret, telling neither Charles nor Hester, and bearing the weight of it alone. It was more than grief, it was something that lay not only in the past but in the future also.

5

Monk and Evan saw Grimwade only briefly, then went straight up to visit Yeats. It was a little after eight in the morning and they hoped to catch him at breakfast, or possibly even before.

Yeats opened the door himself; he was a small man of about forty, a trifle plump, with a mild face and thinning hair which fell forward over his brow. He was startled and there was still a piece of toast and orange preserve in his hand. He stared at Monk with some alarm.

"Good morning, Mr. Yeats," Monk said firmly. "We are from the police; we would like to speak to you about the murder of Major Joscelin Grey. May we come in please?" He did not step forward, but his height seemed to press over Yeats and vaguely threaten him, and he used it deliberately.

"Y-yes, y-yes of course," Yeats stuttered, backing away, still clutching the toast. "But I assure you I d-don't know anything I haven't already t-told you. Not you—at least—a Mr. Lamb who was—a—"

"Yes I know." Monk followed him in. He knew he was being oppressive, but he could not afford to be gentle. Yeats must have seen the murderer face-to-face, possibly even been in collusion with him, willingly or unwillingly.

106

"But we have learned quite a few new facts," he went on, "since Mr. Lamb was taken ill and I have been put on the case."

"Oh?" Yeats dropped the toast and bent to pick it up, ignoring the preserve on the carpet. It was a smaller room than Joscelin Grey's and overpoweringly furnished in heavy oak covered in photographs and embroidered linen. There were antimacassars on both the chairs.

"Have you—" Yeats said nervously. "Have you? I still don't think I can—er—could—"

"Perhaps if you were to allow a few questions, Mr. Yeats." Monk did not want him so frightened as to be incapable of thought or memory.

"Well—if you think so. Yes—yes, if . . ." He backed away and sat down sharply on the chair closest to the table.

Monk sat also and was conscious of Evan behind him doing the same on a ladder-back chair by the wall. He wondered fleetingly what Evan was thinking, if he found him harsh, overconscious of his own ambition, his need to succeed. Yeats could so easily be no more than he seemed, a frightened little man whom mischance had placed at the pivot of a murder.

Monk began quietly, thinking with an instant's self-mockery that he might be moderating his tone not to reassure Yeats but to earn Evan's approval. What had led him to such isolation that Evan's opinion mattered so much to him? Had he been too absorbed in learning, climbing, polishing himself, to afford friendship, much less love? Indeed, had anything at all engaged his higher emotions?

Yeats was watching him like a rabbit seeing a stoat, and too horrified to move.

"You yourself had a visitor that night," Monk told him quite gently. "Who was he?"

"I don't know!" Yeats's voice was high, almost a squeak. "I don't know who he was! I told Mr. Lamb that! He came here by mistake; he didn't even really want me!"

107

Monk found himself holding up his hand, trying to calm him as one would with an overexcited child, or an animal.

"But you saw him, Mr. Yeats." He kept his voice low. "No doubt you have some memory of his appearance, perhaps his voice? He must have spoken to you?" Whether Yeats was lying or not, he would achieve nothing by attacking his statement now; Yeats would only entrench himself more and more deeply into his ignorance.

Yeats blinked.

"I-I really can hardly say, Mr.—Mr.—"

"Monk—I'm sorry," he said, apologizing for not having introduced himself. "And my colleague is Mr. Evan. Was he a large man, or small?"

"Oh large, very large," Yeats said instantly. "Big as you are, and looked heavy; of course he had a thick coat on, it was a very bad night—wet—terribly."

"Yes, yes I remember. Was he taller than I am, do you think?" Monk stood up helpfully.

Yeats stared up at him. "No, no, I don't think so. About the same, as well as I can recall. But it was some time ago now." He shook his head unhappily.

Monk seated himself again, aware of Evan discreetly taking notes.

"He really was here only a moment or two," Yeats protested, still holding the toast, now beginning to break and drop crumbs on his trousers. "He just saw me, asked a question as to my business, then realized I was not the person he sought, and left again. That is really all there was." He brushed ineffectively at his trousers. "You must believe me, if I could help, I would. Poor Major Grey, such an appalling death." He shivered. "Such a charming young man. Life plays some dreadful tricks, does it not?"

Monk felt a quick flicker of excitement inside himself.

"You knew Major Grey?" He kept his voice almost casual.

"Oh not very well, no, no!" Yeats protested, shunning any thought of social arrogance—or involvement. "Only to pass the time of day, you understand? But he was very

108

civil, always had a pleasant word, not like some of these young men of fashion. And he didn't affect to have forgotten one's name."

"And what is your business, Mr. Yeats? I don't think you said."

"Oh perhaps not." The toast shed more pieces in his hand, but now he was oblivious of it. "I deal in rare stamps and coins."

"And this visitor, was he also a dealer?"

Yeats looked surprised.

"He did not say, but I should imagine not. It is a small business, you know; one gets to meet most of those who are interested, at one time or another."

"He was English then?"

"I beg your pardon?"

"He was not a foreigner, whom you would not expect to have known, even had he been in the business?"

"Oh, I see." Yeats's brow cleared. "Yes, yes he was English."

"And who was he looking for, if not for you, Mr. Yeats?"

"I-I-really cannot say." He waved his hand in the air. "He asked if I were a collector of maps; I told him I was not. He said he had been misinformed, and he left immediately."

"I think not, Mr. Yeats. I think he then went to call on Major Grey, and within the next three quarters of an hour, beat him to death."

"Oh my dear God!" Yeats's bones buckled inside him and he slid backwards and down into his chair. Behind Monk, Evan moved as if to help, then changed his mind and sat down again.

"That surprises you?" Monk inquired.

Yeats was gasping, beyond speech.

"Are you sure this man was not known to you?" Monk persisted, giving him no time to regather his thoughts. This was the time to press.

109

"Yes, yes I am. Quite unknown." He covered his face with his hands. "Oh my dear heaven!"

Monk stared at Yeats. The man was useless now, either reduced to abject horror, or else very skillfully affecting to be. He turned and looked at Evan. Evan's face was stiff with embarrassment, possibly for their presence and their part in the man's wretchedness, possibly merely at being witness to it.

Monk stood up and heard his own voice far away. He knew he was risking a mistake, and that he was doing it because of Evan.

"Thank you, Mr. Yeats. I'm sorry for distressing you. Just one more thing: was this man carrying a stick?"

Yeats looked up, his face sickly pale; his voice was no more than a whisper.

"Yes, quite a handsome one; I noticed it."

"Heavy or light?"

"Oh heavy, quite heavy. Oh no!" He shut his eyes, screwing them up to hide even his imagination.

"There is no need for you to be frightened, Mr. Yeats," Evan said from behind. "We believe he was someone who knew Major Grey personally, not a chance lunatic. There is no reason to suppose he would have harmed you. I daresay he was looking for Major Grey in the first place and found the wrong door."

It was not until they were outside that Monk realized Evan must have said it purely to comfort the little man. It could not have been true. The visitor had asked for Yeats by name. He looked sideways at Evan, now walking silently beside him in the drizzling rain. He made no remark on it.

Grimwade had proved no further help. He had not seen the man come down after leaving Yeats's door, nor seen him go to Joscelin Grey's. He had taken the opportunity to attend the call of nature, and then had seen the man leave at a quarter past ten, three quarters of an hour later.

"There's only one conclusion," Evan said unhappily, striding along with his head down. "He must have left

110

Yeats's door and gone straight along the hallway to Grey, spent half an hour or so with him, then killed him, and left when Grimwade saw him go.''

"Which doesn't tell us who he was," Monk said, stepping across a puddle and passing a cripple selling bootlaces. A rag and bone cart trundled by, its driver calling out almost unintelligibly in a singsong voice. "I keep coming back to the one thing," Monk resumed. "Why did anyone hate Joscelin Grey so much? There was a passion of hate in that room. Someone hated him so uncontrollably he couldn't stop beating him even after he was dead.''

Evan shivered and the rain ran off his nose and chin. He pulled his collar up closer around his ears and his face was pale.

"Mr. Runcorn was right," he said miserably. "It's going to be extremely nasty. You have to know someone very well to hate them as much as that.''

"Or have been mortally wronged," Monk added. "But you're probably right; it'll be in the family, these things usually are. Either that, or a lover somewhere.''

Evan looked shocked. "You mean Grey was—?''

"No." Monk smiled with a sharp downward twist. "That wasn't what I meant, although I suppose it's possible; in fact it's distinctly possible. But I was thinking of a woman, with a husband perhaps.''

Evan's faced relaxed a fraction.

"I suppose it's too violent for a simple debt, gambling or something?" he said without much hope.

Monk thought for a moment.

"Could be blackmail," he suggested with genuine belief. The idea had only just occurred to him seriously, but he liked it.

Evan frowned. They were walking south along Grey's Inn Road.

"Do you think so?" He looked sideways at Monk. "Doesn't ring right to me. And we haven't found any unaccounted income yet. Of course, we haven't really

111

looked. And blackmail victims can be driven to a very deep hatred indeed, for which I cannot entirely blame them. When a man has been tormented, stripped of all he has, and then is still threatened with ruin, there comes a point when reason breaks."

"We'll have to check on the social company he kept," Monk replied. "Who might have made mistakes damaging enough to be blackmailed over, to the degree that ended in murder."

"Perhaps if he was homosexual?" Evan suggested it with returning distaste, and Monk knew he did not believe his own word. "He might have had a lover who would pay to keep him quiet—and if pushed too far, kill him?"

"Very nasty." Monk stared at the wet pavement. "Runcorn was right." And thought of Runcorn set his mind on a different track.

He sent Evan to question all the local tradesmen, people at the club Grey had been at the evening he was killed, anything to learn about his associates.

Evan began at the wine merchant's whose name they had found on a bill head in Grey's apartments. He was a fat man with a drooping mustache and an unctuous manner. He expressed desolation over the loss of Major Grey. What a terrible misfortune. What an ironic stroke of fate that such a fine officer should survive the war, only to be struck down by a madman in his own home. What a tragedy. He did not know what to say—and he said it at considerable length while Evan struggled to get a word in and ask some useful question.

When at last he did, the answer was what he had guessed it would be. Major Grey—the Honorable Joscelin Grey—was a most valued customer. He had excellent taste—but what else would you expect from such a gentleman? He knew French wine, and he knew German wine. He liked the best. He was provided with it from this establishment. His accounts? No, not always up to date—but paid in due course. The nobility were that way with money—one had to learn to accommodate it. He could add nothing—but nothing at all. Was Mr. Evan interested in wine? He could recommend an excellent Bordeaux.

No, Mr. Evan, reluctantly, was not interested in wine; he was a country parson's son, well educated in the gentilities of life, but with a pocket too short to indulge in more than the necessities, and a few good clothes, which would stand him in better stead than even the best of wines. None of which he explained to the merchant.

Next he tried the local eating establishments, beginning with the chophouse and working down to the public alehouse, which also served an excellent stew with spotted dick pudding, full of currants, as Evan could attest.

"Major Grey?" the landlord said ruminatively. "Yer mean 'im as was murdered? 'Course I knowed 'im. Come in 'ere reg'lar, 'e did."

Evan did not know whether to believe him or not. It could well be true; the food was cheap and filling and the atmosphere not unpleasant to a man who had served in the army, two years of it in the battlefields of the Crimea. On the other hand it could be a boost to his business— already healthy—to say that a famous victim of murder had dined here. There was a grisly curiosity in many people which would give the place an added interest to them.

"What did he look like?" Evan asked.

" 'Ere!" The landlord looked at him suspiciously. "You on the case—or not, then? Doncher know?"

"I never met him alive," Evan replied reasonably. "It makes a lot of difference, you know."

The landlord sucked his teeth. " 'Course it do—sorry, guv, a daft question. 'E were tall, an' not far from your build, kind o' slight—but 'e were real natty wiv it! Looked like a gennelman, even afore 'e opened 'is mouf. Yer can tell. Fair 'air, 'e 'ad; an' a smile as was summat luv'ly."

"Charming," Evan said, more as an observation than a question.

"Not 'alf," the landlord agreed.

"Popular?" Evan pursued.

113

"Yeah. Used ter tell a lot o' stories. People like that—passes the time."

"Generous?" Evan asked.

"Gen'rous?" The landlord's eyebrows rose. "No—not gen'rous. More like 'e took more'n 'e gave. Reckon as 'e din't 'ave that much. An' folk liked ter treat 'im—like I said, 'e were right entertainin'. Flash sometimes. Come in 'ere of an occasion an' treat everyone 'andsome—but not often, like—mebbe once a monf."

"Regularly?"

"Wotcher mean?"

"At a set time in the month?"

"Oh no—could be any time, twice a monf, or not fer two monfs."

Gambler, Evan thought to himself. "Thank you," he said aloud. "Thank you very much." And he finished the cider and placed sixpence on the table and left, going out reluctantly into the fading drizzle.

He spent the rest of the afternoon going to bootmakers, hatters, shirtmakers and tailors, from whom he learned precisely what he expected—nothing that his common sense had not already told him.

He bought a fresh eel pie from a vendor on Guilford Street outside the Foundling Hospital, then took a hansom all the way to St. James's, and got out at Boodles, where Joscelin Grey had been a member.

Here his questions had to be a lot more discreet. It was one of the foremost gentlemen's clubs in London, and servants did not gossip about members if they wished to retain their very agreeable and lucrative positions. All he acquired in an hour and a half of roundabout questions was confirmation that Major Grey was indeed a member, that he came quite regularly when he was in town, that of course, like other gentlemen, he gambled, and it was possible his debts were settled over a period of time, but most assuredly they were settled. No gentleman welshed on his debts of honor—tradesmen possibly, but never other gentlemen. Such a question did not arise.

Might Mr. Evan speak with any of Major Grey's associates?

Unless Mr. Evan had a warrant such a thing was out of the question. Did Mr. Evan have such a warrant?

No Mr. Evan did not.

He returned little wiser, but with several thoughts running through his head.

When Evan had gone, Monk walked briskly back to the police station and went to his own room. He pulled out the records of all his old cases, and read. It gave him little cause for comfort.

If his fears for this case proved to be real—a society scandal, sexual perversion, blackmail and murder—then his own path as detective in charge lay between the perils of a very conspicuous and well-publicized failure and the even more dangerous task of probing to uncover the tragedies that had precipitated the final explosion. And a man who would beat to death a lover, turned blackmailer, to keep his secret, would hardly hesitate to ruin a mere policeman. "Nasty" was an understatement.

Had Runcorn done this on purpose? As he looked through the record of his own career, one success after another, he wondered what the price had been; who else had paid it, apart from himself? He had obviously devoted everything to work, to improving his skill, his knowledge, his manners, his dress and his speech. Looking at it as a stranger might, his ambition was painfully obvious: the long hours, the meticulous attention to detail, the flashes of sheer intuitive brilliance, the judgment of other men and their abilities—and weaknesses, always using the right man for any task, then when it was completed, choosing another. His only loyalty seemed to be the pursuit of justice. Could he have imagined it had all gone unnoticed by Runcorn, who lay in its path?

His rise from country boy from a Northumbrian fishing village to inspector in the Metropolitan Police had been little short of meteoric. In twelve years he had achieved

115

more than most men in twenty. He was treading hard on Runcorn's heels; at this present rate of progress he could shortly hope for another promotion, to Runcorn's place—or better.

Perhaps it all depended on the Grey case?

He could not have risen so far, and so fast, without treading on a good many people as he passed. There was a growing fear in him that he might not even have cared. He had read through the cases, very briefly. He had made a god of truth, and—where the law was equivocal, or silent—of what he had believed to be justice. But if there was anything of compassion and genuine feeling for the victims, he had so far failed to find it. His anger was impersonal: against the forces of society that produced poverty and bred helplessness and crime; against the monstrosity of the rookery slums, the sweatshops, extortion, violence, prostitution and infant mortality.

He admired the man he saw reflected in the records, admired his skill and his brain, his energy and tenacity, even his courage; but he could not like him. There was no warmth, no vulnerability, nothing of human hopes or fears, none of the idiosyncracies that betray the dreams of the heart. The nearest he saw to passion was the ruthlessness with which he pursued injustice; but from the bare written words, it seemed to him that it was the wrong itself he hated, and the wronged were not people but the by-products of the crime.

Why was Evan so keen to work with him? To learn? He felt a quick stab of shame at the thought of what he might teach him; and he did not want Evan turned into a copy of himself. People change, all the time; every day one is a little different from yesterday, a little added, a little forgotten. Could he learn something of Evan's feeling instead and teach him excellence without his accompanying ambition?

It was easy to believe Runcorn's feelings for him were ambivalent, at best. What had he done to him, over the years of climbing; what comparisons presented to supe-

116

riors? What small slights made without sensitivity—had he ever even thought of Runcorn as a man rather than an obstacle between him and the next step up the ladder?

He could hardly blame Runcorn if now he took this perfect opportunity to present him with a case he had to lose; either in failure to solve, or in too much solving, and the uncovering of scandals for which society, and therefore the commissioner of police, would never excuse him.

Monk stared at the paper files. The man in them was a stranger to him, as one-dimensional as Joscelin Grey; in fact more so, because he had spoken to people who cared for Grey, had found charm in him, with whom he had shared laughter and common memories, who missed him with a hollowness of pain.

His own memories were gone, even of Beth, except for the one brief snatch of childhood that had flickered for a moment at Shelburne. But surely more would return, if he did not try to force them and simply let them come?

And the woman in the church, Mrs. Latterly; why had he not remembered her? He had only seen her twice since the accident, and yet her face seemed always at the back of his mind with a sweetness that never quite let him go. Had he spent much time on the case, perhaps questioned her often? It would be ridiculous to have imagined anything personal—the gulf between them was impassable, and if he had entertained ideas, then his ambition was indeed overweening, and indefensible. He blushed hot at the imagination of what he might have betrayed to her in his speech, or his manner. And the vicar had addressed her as "Mrs."—was she wearing black for her father-in-law, or was she a widow? When he saw her again he must correct it, make it plain he dreamed no such effrontery.

But before then he had to discover what on earth the case was about, beyond that her father-in-law had died recently.

He searched all his papers, all the files and everything in his desk, and found nothing with the name Latterly on it. A wretched thought occurred to him, and now an obvious one—the case had been handed on to someone else. Of course it would be, when he had been ill. Runcorn would hardly abandon it, especially if there really was a question of suspicious death involved.

Then why had the new person in charge not spoken to Mrs. Latterly—or more likely her husband, if he were alive? Perhaps he was not. Maybe that was the reason it was she who had asked? He put the files away and went to Runcorn's office. He was startled in passing an outside window to notice that it was now nearly dusk.

Runcorn was still in his office, but on the point of leaving. He did not seem in the least surprised to see Monk.

"Back to your usual hours again?" he said dryly. "No wonder you never married; you've taken a job to wife. Well, cold comfort it'll get you on a winter night," he added with satisfaction. "What is it?"

"Latterly." Monk was irritated by the reminder of what he could now see of himself. Before the accident it must have been there, all his characteristics, habits, but then he was too close to see them. Now he observed them dispassionately, as if they belonged to someone else.

"What?" Runcorn was staring at him, his brow furrowed into lines of incomprehension, his nervous gesture of the left eye more pronounced.

"Latterly," Monk repeated. "I presume you gave the case to someone else when I was ill?"

"Never heard of it," Runcorn said sharply.

"I was working on the case of a man called Latterly. He either committed suicide, or was murdered—"

Runcorn stood up and went to the coat stand and took his serviceable, unimaginative coat off the hook.

"Oh, that case. You said it was suicide and closed it, weeks before the accident. What's the matter with you? Are you losing your memory?"

"No I am not losing my memory!" Monk snapped, feeling a tide of heat rising up inside him. Please heaven it did not show in his face. "But the papers are gone from

118

my files. I presumed something must have occurred to reopen the case and you had given it to someone."

"Oh." Runcorn scowled, proceeding to put on his coat and gloves. "Well, nothing has occurred, and the file is closed. I haven't given it to anyone else. Perhaps you didn't write up anything more? Now will you forget about Latterly, who presumably killed himself, poor devil, and get back to Grey, who most assuredly did not. Have you got anything further? Come on, Monk—you're usually better than this! Anything from this fellow Yeats?"

"No sir, nothing helpful." Monk was stung and his voice betrayed it.

Runcorn turned from the hat stand and smiled fully at him, his eyes bright.

"Then you'd better abandon that and step up your inquiries into Grey's family and friends, hadn't you?" he said with ill-concealed satisfaction. "Especially women friends. There may be a jealous husband somewhere. Looks like that kind of hatred to me. Take my word, there's something very nasty at the bottom of this." He tilted his hat slightly on his head, but it simply looked askew rather than rakish. "And you, Monk, are just the man to uncover it. You'd better go and try Shelburne again!" And with that parting shot, ringing with jubilation, he swung his scarf around his neck and went out.

Monk did not go to Shelburne the next day, or even that week. He knew he would have to, but he intended when he went to be as well armed as possible, both for the best chance of success in discovering the murderer of Joscelin Grey, whom he wanted with an intense and driving sense of justice, and—fast becoming almost as important—to avoid all he could of offense in probing the very private lives of the Shelburnes, or whoever else might have been aroused to such a rage, over whatever jealousies, passions or perversions. Monk knew that the powerful were no less frail than the rest of men, but they were usually far fiercer in covering those frailties from the mockery and the delight

119

of the vulgar. It was not a matter of memory so much as instinct, the same way he knew how to shave, or to tie his cravat.

Instead he set out with Evan the following morning to go back to Mecklenburg Square, this time not to find traces of an intruder but to learn anything he could about Grey himself. Although they walked with scant conversation, each deep in his own thoughts, he was glad not to be alone. Grey's flat oppressed him and he could never free his mind from the violence that had happened there. It was not the blood, or even the death that clung to him, but the hate. He must have seen death before, dozens, if not scores of times, and he could not possibly have been troubled by it like this each time. It must usually have been casual death, pathetic or brainless murder, the utter selfishness of the mugger who wants and takes, or murder by the thief who finds his escape blocked. But in the death of Grey there was a quite different passion, something intimate, a bond of hatred between the killer and the killed.

He was cold in the room, even though the rest of the building was warm. The light through the high windows was colorless as if it would drain rather than illuminate. The furniture seemed oppressive and shabby, too big for the place, although in truth it was exactly like any other. He looked at Evan to see if he felt it also, but Evan's sensitive face was puckered over with the distaste of searching another man's letters, as he opened the desk and began to go through the drawers.

Monk walked past him into the bedroom, a little stale smelling from closed windows. There was a faint film of dust, as last time. He searched cupboards and clothes drawers, dressers, the tallboy. Grey had an excellent wardrobe; not very extensive, but a beautiful cut and quality. He had certainly possessed good taste, if not the purse to indulge it to the full. There were several sets of cuff links, all gold backed, one with his family crest engraved, two with his own initials. There were three stickpins, one with a fair-sized pearl, and a set of silver-backed brushes, a

120

pigskin toilet kit. Certainly no burglar had come this far. There were many fine pocket handkerchiefs, monogrammed, silk and linen shirts, cravats, socks, clean underwear. He was surprised and somewhat disconcerted to find he knew to within a few shillings the price one would pay for each article, and wondered what aspirations had led him to such knowledge.

He had hoped to find letters in the top drawers, perhaps those too personal to mix with bills and casual correspondence in the desk, but there was nothing, and eventually he went back to the main room. Evan was still at the desk, standing motionless. The place was totally silent, as though both of them were aware that it was a dead man's room, and felt intrusive.

Far down in the street there was a rumble of wheels, the sharper sound of hooves, and a street seller's cry which sounded like "Ole clo'—ole clo'!"

"Well?" He found his voice sunk to a near whisper.

Evan looked up, startled. His face was tight.

"Rather a lot of letters here, sir. I'm not sure really what to make of them. There are several from his sister-in-law, Rosamond Grey; a rather sharp one from his brother Lovel—that's Lord Shelburne, isn't it? A very recent note from his mother, but only one, so it looks as if he didn't keep hers. There are several from a Dawlish family, just prior to his death; among them an invitation to stay at their home for a week. They seem to have been friendly." He puckered his mouth slightly. "One is from Miss Amanda Dawlish, sounds quite eager. In fact there are a number of invitations, all for dates after his death. Apparently he didn't keep old ones. And I'm afraid there's no diary. Funny." He looked up at Monk. "You'd think a man like that would have a social diary, wouldn't you?"

"Yes you would!" Monk moved forward. "Perhaps the murderer took it. You're quite sure?"

"Not in the desk." Evan shook his head. "And I've checked for hidden drawers. But why would anyone hide a social diary anyway?"

"No idea," Monk said honestly, taking a step nearer to the desk and peering at it. "Unless it was the murderer who took it. Perhaps his name figures heavily. We'll have to try these Dawlishes. Is there an address on the letters?"

"Oh yes, I've made a note of it."

"Good. What else?"

"Several bills. He wasn't very prompt in paying up, but I knew that already from talking to the tradesmen. Three from his tailor, four or five from a shirtmaker, the one I visited, two from the wine merchant, a rather terse letter from the family solicitor in reply to a request for an increased allowance."

"In the negative, I take it?"

"Very much so."

"Anything from clubs, gambling and so on?"

"No, but then one doesn't usually commit gambling debts to paper, even at Boodles, unless you are the one who is collecting, of course." Then he smiled suddenly. "Not that I can afford to know—except by hearsay!"

Monk relaxed a little. "Quite," he agreed. "Any other letters?"

"One pretty cool one from a Charles Latterly, doesn't say much—"

"Latterly?" Monk froze.

"Yes. You know him?" Evan was watching him.

Monk took a deep breath and controlled himself with an effort. Mrs. Latterly at St. Marylebone had said "Charles," and he had feared it might have been her husband.

"I was working on a Latterly case some time ago," he said, struggling to keep his voice level. "It's probably coincidence. I was looking for the file on Latterly yesterday and I couldn't find it."

"Was he someone who could have been connected with Grey, some scandal to hush up, or—"

"No!" He spoke more harshly than he had intended to, betraying his feelings. He moderated his tone. "No, not at all. Poor man is dead anyway. Died before Grey did."

122

"Oh." Evan turned back to the desk. "That's about all, I'm afraid. Still, we should be able to find a lot of people who knew him from these, and they'll lead us to more."

"Yes, yes quite. I'll take Latterly's address, all the same."

"Oh, right." Evan fished among the letters and passed him one.

Monk read it. It was very cool, as Evan had said, but not impolite, and there was nothing in it to suggest positive dislike, only a relationship which was not now to be continued. Monk read it three times, but could see nothing further in it. He copied down the address, and returned the letter to Evan.

They finished searching the apartment, and then with careful notes went outside again, passing Grimwade in the hall.

"Lunch," Monk said briskly, wanting to be among people, hear laughter and speech and see men who knew nothing about murder and violent, obscene secrets, men engrossed in the trivial pleasures and irritations of daily life.

"Right." Evan fell in step beside him. "There's a good public house about half a mile from here where they serve the most excellent dumplings. That is—" he stopped suddenly. "It's very ordinary—don't know if you—"

"Fine," Monk agreed. "Sounds just what we need. I'm frozen after being in that place. I don't know why, but it seems cold, even inside."

Evan hunched his shoulders and smiled a little sheepishly. "It might be imagination, but it always chills me. I'm not used to murder yet. I suppose you're above that kind of emotionalism, but I haven't got that far—"

"Don't!" Monk spoke more violently than he had meant to. "Don't get used to it!" He was betraying his own rawness, his sudden sensitivity, but he did not care. "I mean," he said more softly, aware that he had startled Evan by his vehemence, "keep your brain clear, by all means, but don't let it cease to shock you. Don't be a

123

detective before you're a man." Now that he had said it it sounded sententious and extremely trite. He was embarrassed.

Evan did not seem to notice.

"I've a long way to go before I'm efficient enough to do that, sir. I confess, even that room up there makes me feel a little sick. This is the first murder like this I've been on." He sounded self-conscious and very young. "Of course I've seen bodies before, but usually accidents, or paupers who died in the street. There are quite a few of them in the winter. That's why I'm so pleased to be on this case with you. I couldn't learn from anyone better."

Monk felt himself color with pleasure—and shame, because he did not deserve it. He could not think of anything at all to say, and he strode ahead through the thickening rain searching for words, and not finding them. Evan walked beside him, apparently not needing an answer.

The following Monday Monk and Evan got off the train at Shelburne and set out towards Shelburne Hall. It was one of the summer days when the wind is fresh from the east, sharp as a slap in the face, and the sky is clear and cloudless. The trees were huge green billows resting on the bosom of the earth, gently, incessantly moving, whispering. There had been rain overnight, and under the shadows the smell of damp earth was sweet where their feet disturbed it.

They walked in silence, each enjoying it in his own way. Monk was not aware of any particular thoughts, except perhaps a sense of pleasure in the sheer distance of the sky, the width across the fields. Suddenly memory flooded back vividly, and he saw Northumberland again: broad, bleak hills, north wind shivering in the grass. The milky sky was mackerel shredded out to sea, and white gulls floated on the currents, screaming.

He could remember his mother, dark like Beth, standing in the kitchen, and the smell of yeast and flour. She had been proud of him, proud that he could read and write.

He must have been very young then. He remembered a room with sun in it, the vicar's wife teaching him letters, Beth in a smock staring at him in awe. She could not read. He could almost feel himself teaching her, years after, slowly, outline by outline. Her writing still carried echoes of those hours, careful, conscious of the skill and its long learning. She had loved him so much, admired him without question. Then the memory disappeared and it was as if someone had drenched him in cold water, leaving him startled and shivering. It was the most acute and powerful memory he had recaptured and its sharpness left him stunned. He did not notice Evan's eyes on him, or the quick glance away as he strove to avoid what he realized would be intrusion.

Shelburne Hall was in sight across the smooth earth, less than a thousand yards away, framed in trees.

"Do you want me to say anything, or just listen?" Evan asked. "It might be better if I listened."

Monk realized with a start that Evan was nervous. Perhaps he had never spoken to a woman of title before, much less questioned her on personal and painful matters. He might not even have seen such a place, except from the distance. He wondered where his own assurance came from, and why he had not ever thought of it before. Runcorn was right, he was ambitious, even arrogant—and insensitive.

"Perhaps if you try the servants," he replied. "Servants notice a lot of things. Sometimes they see a side of their masters that their lordships manage to hide from their equals."

"I'll try the valet," Evan suggested. "I should imagine you are peculiarly vulnerable in the bath, or in your underwear." He grinned suddenly at the thought, and perhaps in some amusement at the physical helplessness of his social superiors to need assistance in such common matters. It offset his own fear of proving inadequate to the situation.

Lady Fabia Shelburne was somewhat surprised to see

125

Monk again, and kept him waiting nearly half an hour, this time in the butler's pantry with the silver polish, a locked desk for the wine book and the cellar keys, and a comfortable armchair by a small grate. Apparently the housekeeper's sitting room was already in use. He was annoyed at the casual insolence of it, and yet part of him was obliged to admire her self-control. She had no idea why he had come. He might even have been able to tell her who had murdered her son, and why.

When he was sent for and conducted to the rosewood sitting room, which seemed to be peculiarly hers, she was cool and gracious, as if he had only just arrived and she had no more than a courteous interest in what he might say.

At her invitation he sat down opposite her on the same deep rose-pink chair as before.

"Well, Mr. Monk?" she inquired with slightly raised eyebrows. "Is there something further you want to say to me?"

"Yes ma'am, if you please. We are even more of the opinion that whoever killed Major Grey did so for some personal reason, and that he was not a chance victim. Therefore we need to know everything further we can about him, his social connections—"

Her eyes widened. "If you imagine his social connections are of a type to indulge in murder, Mr. Monk, then you are extraordinarily ignorant of society."

"I am afraid, ma'am, that most people are capable of murder, if they are hard-pressed enough, and threatened in what they most value—"

"I think not." Her voice indicated the close of the subject and she turned her head a little away from him.

"Let us hope they are rare, ma'am." He controlled his impulse to anger with difficulty. "But it would appear there is at least one, and I am sure you wish to find him, possibly even more than I do."

"You are very slick with words, young man." It was

126

grudgingly given, even something of a criticism. "What is it you imagine I can tell you?"

"A list of his closest friends," he answered. "Family friends, any invitations you may know of that he accepted in the last few months, especially for weeks or weekends away. Perhaps any lady in whom he may have been interested." He saw a slight twitch of distaste cross her immaculate features. "I believe he was extremely charming." He added the flattery in which he felt was her only weakness.

"He was." There was a small movement in her lips, a change in her eyes as for a moment grief overtook her. It was several seconds till she smoothed it out again and was as perfect as before.

Monk waited in silence, for the first time aware of the force of her pain.

"Then possibly some lady was more attracted to him than was acceptable to her other admirers, or even her husband?" he suggested at last, and in a considerably softer tone, although his resolve to find the murderer of Joscelin Grey was if anything hardened even further, and it allowed of no exceptions, no omissions for hurt.

She considered this thought for a moment before deciding to accept it. He imagined she was seeing her son again as he had been in life, elegant, laughing, direct of gaze.

"It might have been," she conceded. "It could be that some young person was indiscreet, and provoked jealousy."

"Perhaps someone who had a little too much to drink?" He pursued it with a tact that did not come to him naturally. "And saw in it more than there was?"

"A gentleman knows how to conduct himself." She looked at Monk with a slight turn downwards at the corners of her mouth. The word *gentleman* was not lost on him. "Even when he has had too much to drink. But unfortunately some people are not as discriminating in their choice of guests as they should be."

"If you would give me some names and addresses,

127

ma'am; I shall conduct my inquiries as cautiously as I can, and naturally shall not mention your name. I imagine all persons of good conscience will be as keen to discover who murdered Major Grey as you are yourself."

It was a well-placed argument, and she acknowledged it with a momentary glance directly into his eyes.

"Quite," she agreed. "If you have a notebook I shall oblige you." She reached across to the rosewood table almost at her side and opened a drawer. She took out a leather-bound and gold-tooled address book.

He made ready and was well started when Lovel Grey came in, again dressed in casual clothes—this time breeches and a Norfolk jacket of well-worn tweed. His face darkened when he saw Monk.

"I really think, Mr. Monk, that if you have something to report, you may do so to me!" he said with extreme irritation. "If you have not, then your presence here serves no purpose, and you are distressing my mother. I am surprised you should come again."

Monk stood up instinctively, annoyed with himself for the necessity.

"I came, my lord, because I needed some further information, which Lady Shelburne has been kind enough to give me." He could feel the color hot in his face.

"There is nothing we can tell you that could be of the least relevance," Lovel snapped. "For heaven's sake, man, can't you do your job without rushing out here every few days?" He moved restlessly, fidgeting with the crop in his hand. "We cannot help you! If you are beaten, admit it! Some crimes are never solved, especially where madmen are concerned."

Monk was trying to compose a civil reply when Lady Shelburne herself intervened in a small, tight voice.

"That may be so, Lovel, but not in this case. Joscelin was killed by someone who knew him, however distasteful that may be to us. Naturally it is also possible it was someone known here. It is far more discreet of Mr. Monk to

128

ask us than to go around inquiring of the whole neighborhood.''

"Good God!" Lovel's face fell. ''You cannot be serious. To allow him to do that would be monstrous. We'd be ruined.''

"Nonsense!" She closed her address book with a snap and replaced it in the drawer. ''We do not ruin so easily. There have been Shelburnes on the land for five hundred years, and will continue to be. However I have no intention of allowing Mr. Monk to do any such thing.'' She looked at Monk coldly. ''That is why I am providing him with a list myself, and suitable questions to ask—and to avoid.''

"There is no need to do either.'' Lovel turned furiously from his mother to Monk and back again, his color high. "Whoever killed Joscelin must have been one of his London acquaintances—if indeed it really was someone he knew at all, which I still doubt. In spite of what you say, I believe it was purely chance he was the victim, and not someone else. I daresay he was seen at a club, or some such place, by someone who saw he had money and hoped to rob him.''

"It was not robbery, sir,'' Monk said firmly. ''There were all sorts of valuable items quite visible and untouched in his rooms, even the money in his wallet was still there.''

"And how do you know how much he had in his wallet?'' Lovel demanded. ''He may have had hundreds!''

"Thieves do not usually count out change and return it to you,'' Monk replied, moderating the natural sarcasm in his voice only slightly.

Lovel was too angry to stop. ''And have you some reason to suppose this was a 'usual' thief? I did not know you had proceeded so far. In fact I did not know you had proceeded at all.''

"Most unusual, thank heaven.'' Monk ignored the jibe. "Thieves seldom kill. Did Major Grey often walk about with hundreds of pounds in his pocket?''

Lovel's face was scarlet. He threw the crop across the room, intending it to land on the sofa, but it fell beyond and rattled to the floor. He ignored it. "No of course not!" he shouted. "But then this was a unique occasion. He was not simply robbed and left lying, he was beaten to death, if you remember."

Lady Fabia's face pinched with misery and disgust.

"Really, Lovel, the man is doing his best, for whatever that is worth. There is no need to be offensive."

Suddenly his tone changed. "You are upset, Mama; and it's quite natural that you should be. Please leave this to me. If I think there is anything to tell Mr. Monk, I shall do so. Why don't you go into the withdrawing room and have tea with Rosamond?"

"Don't patronize me, Lovel!" she snapped, rising to her feet. "I am not too upset to conduct myself properly, and to help the police find the man who murdered my son."

"There is nothing whatsoever we can do, Mama!" He was fast losing his temper again. "Least of all assist them to pester half the country for personal information about poor Joscelin's life and friends."

"It was one of poor Joscelin's 'friends' who beat him to death!" Her cheeks were ashen white and a lesser woman might well have fainted before now, but she stood ramrod stiff, her white hands clenched.

"Rubbish!" Lovel dismissed it instantly. "It was probably someone he played at cards and who simply couldn't take losing. Joscelin gambled a damned sight more than he led you to believe. Some people play for stakes they can't afford, and then when they're beaten, they lose control of themselves and go temporarily off their heads." He breathed in and out hard. "Gaming clubs are not always as discriminating as they should be as to whom they allow in. That is quite probably what happened to Joscelin. Do you seriously imagine anyone at Shelburne would know anything about it?"

"It is also possible it was someone who was jealous

130

over a woman," she answered icily. "Joscelin was very charming, you know."

Lovel flushed and the whole skin of his face appeared to tighten.

"So I have frequently been reminded," he said in a soft, dangerous little voice. "But not everyone was as susceptible to it as you, Mama. It is a very superficial quality."

She stared at him with something that bordered on contempt.

"You never understood charm, Lovel, which is your great misfortune. Perhaps you would be good enough to order extra tea in the withdrawing room." Deliberately she ignored her son and contravened propriety, as if to annoy him. "Will you join us, Mr. Monk? Perhaps my daughter-in-law may be able to suggest something. She was accustomed to attend many of the same functions as Joscelin, and women are frequently more observant of other women, especially where"—she hesitated—"affairs of the emotions are concerned."

Without waiting for his reply she assumed his compliance and, still ignoring Lovel, turned to the door and stopped. Lovel wavered for only the barest second, then he came forward obediently and opened the door for her. She swept through without looking again at either of them.

In the withdrawing room the atmosphere was stiff. Rosamond had difficulty hiding her amazement at being expected to take tea with a policeman as if he were a gentleman; and even the maid with the extra cups and muffins seemed uncomfortable. Apparently the belowstairs gossip had already told her who Monk was. Monk silently thought of Evan, and wondered if he had made any progress.

When the maid had handed everyone their cups and plates and was gone Lady Fabia began in a level, quiet voice, avoiding Lovel's eyes.

"Rosamond, my dear, the police require to know everything they can about Joscelin's social activities in the

131

last few months before he died. You attended most of the same functions, and are thus more aware of any relationships than I. For example, who might have shown more interest in him than was prudent?''

''I?'' Rosamond was either profoundly surprised or a better actress than Monk had judged her to be on their earlier meeting.

''Yes you, my dear.'' Lady Fabia passed her the muffins, which she ignored. ''I am talking to you. I shall, of course, also ask Ursula.''

''Who is Ursula?'' Monk interrupted.

''Miss Ursula Wadham; she is betrothed to my second son, Menard. You may safely leave it to me to glean from her any information that would be of use.'' She dismissed Monk and turned back to Rosamond. ''Well?''

''I don't recall Joscelin having any . . . relationship in— in particular.'' Rosamond sounded rather awkward, as if the subject disturbed her. Watching her, Monk wondered for a moment if she had been in love with Joscelin herself, if perhaps that was why Lovel was so reluctant to have the matter pursued.

Could it even have gone further than a mere attraction?

''That is not what I asked,'' Lady Fabia said with thin patience. ''I asked you if anyone else had shown any interest in Joscelin, albeit a one-sided one?''

Rosamond's head came up. For a moment Monk thought she was about to resist her mother-in-law, then the moment died.

''Norah Partridge was very fond of him,'' she replied slowly, measuring her words. ''But that is hardly new; and I cannot see Sir John taking it badly enough to go all the way up to London and commit murder. I do believe he is fond of Norah, but not enough for that.''

''Then you are more observant than I thought,'' Lady Fabia said with acid surprise. ''But without much understanding of men, my dear. It is not necessary to want something yourself in order profoundly to resent someone else's having the ability to take it away from you; especially if they have the tactlessness to do it publicly." She swiveled to Monk. He was not offered the muffins. "There is somewhere for you to begin. I doubt John Partridge would be moved to murder—or that he would use a stick if he were." Her face flickered with pain again. "But Norah had other admirers. She is a somewhat extravagant creature, and not possessed of much judgment."

"Thank you, ma'am. If you think of anything further?"

For another hour they raked over past romances, affairs and supposed affairs, and Monk half listened. He was not interested in the facts so much as the nuances behind their expression. Joscelin had obviously been his mother's favorite, and if the absent Menard was like his elder brother, it was easy to understand why. But whatever her feelings, the laws of primogeniture ruled that not only the title and the lands, but also the money to support them and the way of life that went with them, must pass to Lovel, the firstborn.

Lovel himself contributed nothing, and Rosamond only enough to satisfy her mother-in-law, of whom she seemed in awe far more than of her husband.

Monk did not see Lady Callandra Daviot, rather to his disappointment. He would have liked her candor on the subject, although he was not sure she would have expressed herself as freely in front of the grieving family as she had in the garden in the rain.

He thanked them and excused himself in time to find Evan and walk down to the village for a pint of cider before the train back to London.

"Well?" Monk asked as soon as they were out of sight of the house.

"Ah." Evan could scarcely suppress his enthusiasm; his stride was surprisingly long, his lean body taut with energy, and he splashed through puddles on the road with complete disregard for his soaking boots. "It's fascinating. I've never been inside a really big house before, I mean inside to know it. My father was a clergyman, you know, and I went along to the manor house sometimes when I was a child—but it was nothing like this. Good Lord, those servants see things that would paralyze me with shame—I mean the family treat them as if they were deaf and blind."

"They don't think of them as people," Monk replied. "At least not people in the same sense as themselves. They are two different worlds, and they don't impinge, except physically. Therefore their opinions don't matter. Did you learn anything else?" He smiled slightly at Evan's innocence.

Evan grinned. "I'll say, although of course they wouldn't intentionally tell a policeman, or anyone else, anything they thought confidential about the family. It would be more than their livelihood was worth. Very closemouthed, they thought they were."

"So how did you learn?" Monk asked curiously, looking at Evan's innocent, imaginative features.

Evan blushed very slightly. "Threw myself on Cook's mercy." He looked down at the ground, but did not decrease his pace in the slightest. "Slandered my landlady appallingly, I'm afraid. Spoke very unkindly about her cooking—oh, and I stood outside for some time before going in, so my hands were cold—" He glanced up at Monk, then away again. "Very motherly sort, Lady Shelburne's cook." He smiled rather smugly. "Daresay I did a lot better than you did."

"I didn't eat at all," Monk said tartly.

"I'm sorry." Evan did not sound it.

"And what did your dramatic debut earn you, apart from luncheon?" Monk asked. "I presume you overheard a good deal—while you were busy being pathetic and eating them out of house and home?"

"Oh yes—did you know that Rosamond comes from a well-to-do family, but a bit come-lately? And she fell for Joscelin first, but her mother insisted she marry the eldest brother, who also offered for her. And she was a good, obedient girl and did as she was told. At least that is what I read between the lines of what the tweeny was saying to

134

the laundry maid—before the parlor maid came in and stopped them gossiping and they were packed off to their duties.''

Monk whistled through his teeth.

''And,'' Evan went on before he could speak, ''they had no children for the first few years, then one son, heir to the title, about a year and a half ago. Someone particularly spiteful is said to have observed that he has the typical Shelburne looks, but more like Joscelin than Lovel—so the second footman heard said in the public house. Blue eyes—you see, Lord Shelburne is dark—so is she—at least her eyes are—''

Monk stopped in the road, staring at him.

''Are you sure?''

''I'm sure that's what they say, and Lord Shelburne must have heard it—at last—'' He looked appalled. ''Oh God! That's what Runcorn meant, isn't it? Very nasty, very nasty indeed.'' He was comical in his dismay, suddenly the enthusiasm gone out of him. ''What on earth are we going to do? I can imagine how Lady Fabia will react if you try opening that one up!''

''So can I,'' Monk said grimly. ''And I don't know what we are going to do.''

135

6

Hester Latterly stood in the small withdrawing room of her brother's house in Thanet Street, a little off the Marylebone Road, and stared out of the window at the carriages passing. It was a smaller house, far less attractive than the family home on Regent Square. But after her father's death that house had had to be sold. She had always imagined that Charles and Imogen would move out of this house and back to Regent Square in such an event, but apparently the funds were needed to settle affairs, and there was nothing above that for any inheritance for any of them. Hence she was now residing with Charles and Imogen, and would be obliged to do so until she should make some arrangements of her own. What they might be now occupied her thoughts.

Her choice was narrow. Disposal of her parents' possessions had been completed, all the necessary letters written and servants given excellent references. Most had fortunately found new positions. It remained for Hester herself to make a decision. Of course Charles had said she was more than welcome to remain as long as she wished—indefinitely, if she chose. The thought was appalling. A permanent guest, neither use nor ornament, intruding on what should be a private house for husband and wife, and in time their children. Aunts were all very well, but not for breakfast, luncheon and dinner every day of the week.

Life had to offer more than that.

Naturally Charles had spoken of marriage, but to be frank, as the situation surely warranted, Hester was very few people's idea of a good match. She was pleasing enough in feature, if a little tall—she looked over the heads of rather too many men for her own comfort, or theirs. But she had no dowry and no expectations at all. Her family was well-bred, but of no connection to any of the great houses; in fact genteel enough to have aspirations, and to have taught its daughters no useful arts, but not privileged enough for birth alone to be sufficient attraction.

All of which might have been overcome if her personality were as charming as Imogen's—but it was not. Where Imogen was gentle, gracious, full of tact and discretion, Hester was abrasive, contemptuous of hypocrisy and impatient of dithering or incompetence and disinclined to suffer foolishness with any grace at all. She was also fonder of reading and study than was attractive in a woman, and not free of the intellectual arrogance of one to whom thought comes easily.

It was not entirely her fault, which mitigated blame but did not improve her chances of gaining or keeping an admirer. She had been among the first to leave England and sail, in appalling conditions, to the Crimea and offer her help to Florence Nightingale in the troop hospital in Scutari.

She could remember quite clearly her first sight of the city, which she had expected to be ravaged by war, and how her breath had caught in her throat with delight at the vividness of the white walls and the copper domes green against the blue sky.

Of course afterwards it had been totally different. She had witnessed such wretchedness and waste there, exacerbated by incompetence that beggared the imagination, and her courage had sustained her, her selflessness never

137

looked for reward, her patience for the truly afflicted never flagged. And at the same time the sight of such terrible suffering had made her rougher to lesser pain than was just. Each person's pain is severe to him at the time, and the thought that there might be vastly worse occurs to very few. Hester did not stop to consider this, except when it was forced upon her, and such was most people's abhorrence of candor on unpleasant subjects that very few did.

She was highly intelligent, with a gift for logical thought which many people found disturbing—especially men, who did not expect it or like it in a woman. That gift had enabled her to be invaluable in the administration of hospitals for the critically injured or desperately ill—but there was no place for it in the domestic homes of gentlemen in England. She could have run an entire castle and marshaled the forces to defend it, and had time to spare. Unfortunately no one desired a castle run—and no one attacked them anymore.

And she was approaching thirty.

The realistic choices lay between nursing at a practical level, at which she was now skilled, although more with injury than the diseases that occur most commonly in a temperate climate like that of England, and, on the other hand, a post in the administration of hospitals, junior as that was likely to be; women were not doctors, and not generally considered for more senior posts. But much had changed in the war, and the work to be done, the reforms that might be achieved, excited her more than she cared to admit, since the possibilities of participating were so slight.

And there was also the call of journalism, although it would hardly bring her the income necessary to provide a living. But it need not be entirely abandoned—?

She really wished for advice. Charles would disapprove of the whole idea, as he had of her going to the Crimea in the first place. He would be concerned for her safety, her reputation, her honor—and anything else general and unspecified that might cause her harm. Poor Charles, he was a very conventional soul. How they could ever be siblings she had no idea.

And there was little use asking Imogen. She had no knowledge from which to speak; and lately she seemed to have half her mind on some turmoil of her own. Hester had tried to discover without prying offensively, and succeeded in learning nothing at all, except close to a certainty that whatever it was Charles knew even less of it than she.

As she stared out through the window into the street her thoughts turned to her mentor and friend of pre-Crimean days, Lady Callandra Daviot. She would give sound advice both as to knowledge of what might be achieved and how to go about it, and what might be dared and, if reached, would make her happy. Callandra had never given a fig for doing what was told her was suitable, and she did not assume a person wanted what society said they ought to want.

She had always said that Hester was welcome to visit her either in her London house or at Shelburne Hall at any time she wished. She had her own rooms there and was free to entertain as pleased her. Hester had already written to both addresses and asked if she might come. Today she had received a reply most decidedly in the affirmative.

The door opened behind her and she heard Charles's step. She turned, the letter still in her hand.

"Charles, I have decided to go and spend a few days, perhaps a week or so, with Lady Callandra Daviot."

"Do I know her?" he said immediately, his eyes widening a fraction.

"I should think it unlikely," she replied. "She is in her late fifties, and does not mix a great deal socially."

"Are you considering becoming her companion?" His eye was to the practical. "I don't think you are suited to the position, Hester. With all the kindness in the world, I have to say you are not a congenial person for an elderly lady of a retiring nature. You are extremely bossy—and you have very little sympathy with the ordinary pains of

139

day-to-day life. And you have never yet succeeded in keeping even your silliest opinions to yourself."

"I have never tried!" she said tartly, a little stung by his wording, even though she knew he meant it for her well-being.

He smiled with a slightly twisted humor. "I am aware of that, my dear. Had you tried, even you must have done better!"

"I have no intention of becoming a companion to anyone," she pointed out. It was on the tip of her tongue to add that, had she such a thing in mind, Lady Callandra would be her first choice; but perhaps if she did that, Charles would question Callandra's suitability as a person to visit. "She is the widow of Colonel Daviot, who was a surgeon in the army. I thought I should seek her advice as to what position I might be best suited for."

He was surprised. "Do you really think she would have any useful idea? It seems to me unlikely. However do go, by all means, if you wish. You have certainly been a most marvelous help to us here, and we are deeply grateful. You came at a moment's notice, leaving all your friends behind, and gave your time and your affections to us when we were sorely in need."

"It was a family tragedy." For once her candor was also gracious. "I should not have wished to be anywhere else. But yes, Lady Callandra has considerable experience and I should value her opinion. If it is agreeable to you, I shall leave tomorrow early."

"Certainly—" He hesitated, looking a trifle uncomfortable. "Er—"

"What is it?"

"Do you—er—have sufficient means?"

She smiled. "Yes, thank you—for the time being."

He looked relieved. She knew he was not naturally generous, but neither was he grudging with his own family. His reluctance was another reinforcement of the observations she had made that there had been a considerable tightening of circumstances in the last four or five months.

140

There had been other small things: the household had not the complement of servants she remembered prior to her leaving for the Crimea; now there were only the cook, one kitchen maid, one scullery maid, one housemaid and a parlor maid who doubled as lady's maid for Imogen. The butler was the only male indoor servant; no footman, not even a bootboy. The scullery maid did the shoes.

Imogen had not refurbished her summer wardrobe with the usual generosity, and at least one pair of Charles's boots had been repaired. The silver tray in the hall for receiving calling cards was no longer there.

It was most assuredly time she considered her own position, and the necessity of earning her own way. Some academic pursuit had been a suggestion; she found study absorbing, but the tutorial positions open to women were few, and the restrictions of the life did not appeal to her. She read for pleasure.

When Charles had gone she went upstairs and found Imogen in the linen room inspecting pillow covers and sheets. Caring for them was a large task, even for so modest a household, especially without the services of a laundry maid.

"Excuse me." She began immediately to assist, looking at embroidered edges for tears or where the stitching was coming away. "I have decided to go and visit Lady Callandra Daviot, in the country, for a short while. I think she can advise me on what I should do next—" She saw Imogen's look of surprise, and clarified her statement. "At least she will know the possibilities open to me better than I."

"Oh." Imogen's face showed a mixture of pleasure and disappointment and it was not necessary for her to explain. She understood that Hester must come to a decision, but also she would miss her company. Since their first meeting they had become close friends and their differences in nature had been complementary rather than irritating. "Then you had better take Gwen. You can't stay with the aristocracy without a lady's maid."

141

"Certainly I can," Hester contradicted decisively. "I don't have one, so I shall be obliged to. It will do me no harm whatsoever, and Lady Callandra will be the last one to mind."

Imogen looked dubious. "And how will you dress for dinner?"

"For goodness sake! I can dress myself!"

Imogen's face twitched very slightly. "Yes my dear, I have seen! And I am sure it is admirable for nursing the sick, and fighting stubborn authorities in the army—"

"Imogen!"

"And what about your hair?" Imogen pressed. "You are likely to arrive at table looking as if you had come sideways through a high wind to get there!"

"Imogen!" Hester threw a bundle of towels at her, one knocking a front lock of her hair askew and the rest scattering on the floor.

Imogen threw a sheet back, achieving the same result. They looked at each other's wild appearance and began to laugh. Within moments both were gasping for breath and sitting on the floor in mounds of skirts with previously crisp laundry lying around them in heaps.

The door opened and Charles stood on the threshold looking bemused and a trifle alarmed.

"What on earth is wrong?" he demanded, at first taking their sobs for distress. "Are you ill? What has happened?" Then he saw it was amusement and looked even more confounded, and as neither of them stopped or took any sensible notice of him, he became annoyed.

"Imogen! Control yourself!" he said sharply. "What is the matter with you?"

Imogen still laughed helplessly.

"Hester!" Charles was growing pink in the face. "Hester, stop it! Stop it at once!"

Hester looked at him and found it funnier still.

Charles sniffed, dismissed it as women's weakness and therefore inexplicable, and left, shutting the door hard so none of the servants should witness such a ridiculous scene.

Hester was perfectly accustomed to travel, and the journey from London to Shelburne was barely worth comment compared with the fearful passage by sea across the Bay of Biscay and through the Mediterranean to the Bosporus and up the Black Sea to Sebastopol. Troopships replete with terrified horses, overcrowded, and with the merest of accommodations, were things beyond the imagination of most Englishmen, let alone women. A simple train journey through the summer countryside was a positive pleasure, and the warm, quiet and sweet-scented mile in the dog cart at the far end before she reached the hall was a glory to the senses.

She arrived at the magnificent front entrance with its Doric columns and portico. The driver had no time to hand her down because she had grown unaccustomed to such courtesies and scrambled to the ground herself while he was still tying the reins. With a frown he unloaded her box and at the same moment a footman opened the door and held it for her to pass through. Another footman carried in the box and disappeared somewhere upstairs with it.

Fabia Shelburne was in the withdrawing room where Hester was shown. It was a room of considerable beauty, and at this height of the year, with the French windows open onto the garden and the scent of roses drifting on a warm breeze, the soft green of the rolling parkland beyond, the marble-surrounded fireplace seemed unnecessary, and the paintings keyholes to another and unnecessary world.

Lady Fabia did not rise, but smiled as Hester was shown in.

"Welcome to Shelburne Hall, Miss Latterly. I hope your journey was not too fatiguing. Why my dear, you seem very blown about! I am afraid it is very windy beyond the garden. I trust it has not distressed you. When you have

143

composed yourself and taken off your traveling clothes, perhaps you would care to join us for afternoon tea? Cook is particularly adept at making crumpets.'' She smiled, a cool, well-practiced gesture. "I expect you are hungry, and it will be an excellent opportunity for us to become acquainted with each other. Lady Callandra will be down, no doubt, and my daughter-in-law, Lady Shelburne. I do not believe you have met?''

"No, Lady Fabia, but it is a pleasure I look forward to.'' She had observed Fabia's deep violet gown, less somber than black but still frequently associated with mourning. Apart from that Callandra had told her of Joscelin Grey's death, although not in detail. "May I express my deepest sympathy for the loss of your son. I have a little understanding of how you feel.''

Fabia's eyebrows rose. "Have you!'' she said with disbelief.

Hester was stung. Did this woman imagine she was the only person who had been bereaved? How self-absorbed grief could be.

"Yes,'' she replied perfectly levelly. "I lost my eldest brother in the Crimea, and a few months ago my father and mother within three weeks of each other.''

"Oh—'' For once Fabia was at a loss for words. She had supposed Hester's sober dress merely a traveling convenience. Her own mourning consumed her to the exclusion of anyone else's. "I am sorry.''

Hester smiled; when she truly meant it it had great warmth.

"Thank you,'' she accepted. "Now if you permit I will accept your excellent idea and change into something suitable before joining you for tea. You are quite right; the very thought of crumpets makes me realize I am very hungry.''

The bedroom they had given her was in the west wing, where Callandra had had a bedroom and sitting room of her own since she had moved out of the nursery. She and her elder brothers had grown up at Shelburne Hall. She had left it to marry thirty years ago, but still visited frequently, and in her widowhood had been extended the courtesy of retaining the accommodation and the hospitality that went with it.

Hester's room was large and a little somber, being hung with muted tapestries on one entire wall and papered in a shade that was undecided between green and gray. The only relief was a delightful painting of two dogs, framed in gold leaf which caught the light. The windows faced westward, and on so fine a day the evening sky was a glory between the great beech trees close to the house, and beyond was a view of an immaculately set-out walled herb garden with fruit trees carefully lined against it. On the far side the heavy boughs of the orchard hid the parkland beyond.

There was hot water ready in a large blue-and-white china jug, and a matching basin beside it, with fresh towels, and she wasted no time in taking off her heavy, dusty skirts, washing her face and neck, and then putting the basin on the floor and easing her hot, aching feet into it.

She was thus employed, indulging in the pure physical pleasure of it, when there was a knock on the door.

"Who is it?" she said in alarm. She was wearing only a camisole and pantaloons and was at a considerable disadvantage. And since she already had water and towels she was not expecting a maid.

"Callandra," came the reply.

"Oh—" Perhaps it was foolish to try to impress Callandra Daviot with something she could not maintain. "Come in!"

Callandra opened the door and stood with a smile of delight in her face.

"My dear Hester! How truly pleased I am to see you. You look as if you have not changed in the slightest—at the core at least." She closed the door behind her and came in, sitting down on one of the upholstered bedroom chairs. She was not and never had been a beautiful woman; she was too broad in the hip, too long in the nose, and

145

her eyes were not exactly the same color. But there was humor and intelligence in her face, and a remarkable strength of will. Hester had never known anyone she had liked better, and the mere sight of her was enough to lift the spirits and fill the heart with confidence.

"Perhaps not." She wriggled her toes in the now cool water. The sensation was delicious. "But a great deal has happened: my circumstances have altered."

"So you wrote to me. I am extremely sorry about your parents—please know that I feel for you deeply."

Hester did not want to talk of it; the pain was still very sharp. Imogen had written and told her of her father's death, although not a great deal of the circumstances, except that he had been shot in what might have been an accident with a pair of dueling pistols he kept, or that he might have surprised an intruder, although since it had happened in the late afternoon it was unlikely, and the police had implied but not insisted that suicide was probable. In consideration to the family, the verdict had been left open. Suicide was not only a crime against the law but a sin against the Church which would exclude him from being buried in hallowed ground and be a burden of shame the family would carry indefinitely.

Nothing appeared to have been taken, and no robber was ever apprehended. The police did not pursue the case.

Within a week another letter had arrived, actually posted two weeks later, to say that her mother had died also. No one had said that it was of heartbreak, but such words were not needed.

"Thank you," Hester acknowledged with a small smile.

Callandra looked at her for a moment, then was sensitive enough to see the hurt in her and understand that probing would only injure further, discussion was no longer any part of the healing. Instead she changed the subject to the practical.

"What are you considering doing now? For heaven's sake don't rush into a marriage!"

146

Hester was a trifle surprised at such unorthodox advice, but she replied with self-deprecatory frankness.

"I have no opportunity to do such a thing. I am nearly thirty, of an uncompromising disposition, too tall, and have no money and no connections. Any man wishing to marry me would be highly suspect as to his motives or his judgment."

"The world is not short of men with either shortcoming," Callandra replied with an answering smile. "As you yourself have frequently written me. The army at least abounds with men whose motives you suspect and whose judgment you abhor."

Hester pulled a face. "Touché," she conceded. "But all the same they have enough wits where their personal interest is concerned." Her memory flickered briefly to an army surgeon in the hospital. She saw again his weary face, his sudden smile, and the beauty of his hands as he worked. One dreadful morning during the siege she had accompanied him to the redan. She could smell the gunpowder and the corpses and feel the bitter cold again as if it were only a moment ago. The closeness had been so intense it had made up for everything else—and then the sick feeling in her stomach when he had spoken for the first time of his wife. She should have known—she should have thought of it—but she had not.

"I should have to be either beautiful or unusually helpless, or preferably both, in order to have them flocking to my door. And as you know, I am neither."

Callandra looked at her closely. "Do I detect a note of self-pity, Hester?"

Hester felt the color hot up her cheeks, betraying her so no answer was necessary.

"You will have to learn to conquer that," Callandra observed, settling herself a little deeper in the chair. Her voice was quite gentle; there was no criticism in it, simply a statement of fact. "Too many women waste their lives grieving because they do not have something other people tell them they should want. Nearly all married women will

147

tell you it is a blessed state, and you are to be pitied for not being in it. That is arrant nonsense. Whether you are happy or not depends to some degree upon outward circumstances, but mostly it depends how you choose to look at things yourself, whether you measure what you have or what you have not.''

Hester frowned, uncertain as to how much she understood, or believed, what Callandra was saying.

Callandra was a trifle impatient. She jerked forward, frowning. "My dear girl, do you really imagine every woman with a smile on her face is really happy? No person of a healthy mentality desires to be pitied, and the simplest way to avoid it is to keep your troubles to yourself and wear a complacent expression. Most of the world will then assume that you are as self-satisfied as you seem. Before you pity yourself, take a great deal closer look at others, and then decide with whom you would, or could, change places, and what sacrifice of your nature you would be prepared to make in order to do so. Knowing you as I do, I think precious little.''

Hester absorbed this thought in silence, turning it over in her mind. Absently she pulled her feet out of the basin at last and began to dry them on the towel.

Callandra stood up. "You will join us in the withdrawing room for tea? It is usually very good as I remember; there is nothing wrong with your appetite. Then later we shall discuss what possibilities there are for you to exercise your talents. There is so much to be done; great reforms are long overdue in all manner of things, and your experience and your emotion should not go to waste.''

"Thank you.'' Hester suddenly felt much better. Her feet were refreshed and clean, she was extremely hungry, and although the future was a mist with no form to it as yet, it had in half an hour grown from gray to a new brightness. "I most certainly shall.''

Callandra looked at Hester's hair. "I shall send you my maid. Her name is Effie, and she is better than my appearance would lead you to believe.'' And with that she went cheerfully out of the door, humming to herself in a rich contralto voice, and Hester could hear her rather firm tread along the landing.

Afternoon tea was taken by the ladies alone. Rosamond appeared from the boudoir, a sitting room especially for female members of the household, where she had been writing letters. Fabia presided, although of course there was the parlor maid to pass the cups and the sandwiches of cucumber, hothouse grown, and later the crumpets and cakes.

The conversation was extremely civilized to the point of being almost meaningless for any exchange of opinion or emotion. They spoke of fashion, what color and what line flattered whom, what might be the season's special feature, would it be a lower waist, or perhaps a greater use of lace, or indeed more or different buttons? Would hats be larger or smaller? Was it good taste to wear green, and did it really become anyone; was it not inclined to make one sallow? A good complexion was so important!

What soap was best for retaining the blush of youth? Were Dr. So-and-so's pills really helpful for female complaints? Mrs. Wellings had it that they were little less than miraculous! But then Mrs. Wellings was much given to exaggeration. She would do anything short of standing on her head in order to attract attention.

Frequently Hester caught Callandra's eyes, and had to look away in case she should giggle and betray an unseemly and very discourteous levity. She might be taken for mocking her hostess, which would be unforgivable— and true.

Dinner was a quite different affair. Effie turned out to be a very agreeable country girl with a cloud of naturally wavy auburn hair many a mistress would have swapped her dowry for and a quick and garrulous tongue. She had hardly been in the room five minutes, whisking through clothes, pinning here, flouncing there, rearranging everything with a skill that left Hester breathless, before she had recounted the amazing news that the police had been at the hall, about the poor major's death up in London, twice now. They had sent two men, one a very grim creature, with a dark visage and manner grand enough to frighten the children, who had spoken with the mistress and taken tea in the withdrawing room as if he thought himself quite the gentleman.

The other, however, was as charming as you could wish, and so terribly elegant—although what a clergyman's son was doing in such an occupation no one could imagine! Such a personable young man should have done something decent, like taking the cloth himself, or tutoring boys of good family, or any other respectable calling.

"But there you are!" she said, seizing the hairbrush and beginning on Hester's hair with determination. "Some of the nicest people do the oddest things, I always say. But Cook took a proper fancy to him. Oh dear!" She looked at the back of Hester's head critically. "You really shouldn't wear your hair like that, ma'am; if you don't mind me saying." She brushed swiftly, piled, stuck pins and looked again. "There now—very fine hair you have, when it's done right. You should have a word with your maid at home, miss—she's not doing right by you—if you'll excuse me saying so. I hope that gives satisfaction?"

"Oh indeed!" Hester assured her with amazement. "You are quite excellent."

Effie colored with pleasure. "Lady Callandra says I talk too much," she essayed modestly.

Hester smiled. "Definitely," she agreed. "So do I. Thank you for your help—please tell Lady Callandra I am very grateful."

"Yes ma'am." And with a half-curtsy Effie grabbed her pincushion and flew out of the door, forgetting to close it behind her, and Hester heard her feet along the passage.

She really looked very striking; the rather severe style she had worn for convenience since embarking on her nursing career had been dramatically softened and filled out. Her gown had been masterfully adapted to be less modest and considerably fuller over a borrowed petticoat, unknown to its owner, and thus height was turned from a disadvantage into a considerable asset. Now that it was time she swept down the main staircase feeling very pleased with herself indeed.

Both Lovel and Menard Grey were at home for the evening, and she was introduced to them in the withdrawing room before going in to the dining room and being seated at the long, highly polished table, which was set for six but could easily have accommodated twelve. There were two joins in it where additional leaves could be inserted so it might have sat twenty-four.

Hester's eye swept over it quickly and noticed the crisp linen napkins, all embroidered with the family crest, the gleaming silver similarly adorned, the cruet sets, the crystal goblets reflecting the myriad lights of the chandelier, a tower of glass like a miniature iceberg alight. There were flowers from the conservatory and from the garden, skillfully arranged in three flat vases up the center of the table, and the whole glittered and gleamed like a display of art.

This time the conversation was centered on the estate, and matters of more political interest. Apparently Lovel had been in the nearest market town all day discussing some matter of land, and Menard had been to one of the tenant farms regarding the sale of a breeding ram, and of course the beginning of harvest.

The meal was served efficiently by the footmen and parlor maid and no one paid them the slightest attention.

They were halfway through the remove, a roast saddle of mutton, when Menard, a handsome man in his early thirties, finally addressed Hester directly. He had similar dark brown hair to his elder brother, and a ruddy complexion from much time spent in the open. He rode to hounds with great pleasure, and considerable daring, and shot pheasant in season. He smiled from enjoyment, but seldom from perception of wit.

151

"How agreeable of you to come and visit Aunt Callandra, Miss Latterly. I hope you will be able to stay with us for a while?"

"Thank you, Mr. Grey," she said graciously. "That is very kind of you. It is a quite beautiful place, and I am sure I shall enjoy myself."

"Have you known Aunt Callandra long?" He was making polite conversation and she knew precisely the pattern it would take.

"Some five or six years. She has given me excellent advice from time to time."

Lady Fabia frowned. The pairing of Callandra and good advice was obviously foreign to her. "Indeed?" she murmured disbelievingly. "With regard to what, pray?"

"What I should do with my time and abilities," Hester replied.

Rosamond looked puzzled. "Do?" she said quietly. "I don't think I understand." She looked at Lovel, then at her mother-in-law. Her fair face and remarkable brown eyes were full of interest and confusion.

"It is necessary that I provide for myself, Lady Shelburne," Hester explained with a smile. Suddenly Callandra's words about happiness came back to her with a force of meaning.

"I'm sorry," Rosamond murmured, and looked down at her plate, obviously feeling she had said something indelicate.

"Not at all," Hester assured her quickly. "I have already had some truly inspiring experiences, and hope to have more." She was about to add that it is a marvelous feeling to be of use, then realized how cruel it would be, and swallowed the words somewhat awkwardly over a mouthful of mutton and sauce.

"Inspiring?" Lovel frowned. "Are you a religious, Miss Latterly?"

Callandra coughed profusely into her napkin; apparently she had swallowed something awry. Fabia passed her a glass of water. Hester averted her eyes.

"No, Lord Shelburne," she said with as much composure as she could. "I have been nursing in the Crimea."

There was a stunned silence all around, not even the clink of silver on porcelain.

"My brother-in-law, Major Joscelin Grey, served in the Crimea," Rosamond said into the void. Her voice was soft and sad. "He died shortly after he returned home."

"That is something of a euphemism," Lovel added, his face hardening. "He was murdered in his flat in London, as no doubt you will hear. The police have been inquiring into it, even out here! But they have not arrested anyone yet."

"I am terribly sorry!" Hester meant it with genuine shock. She had nursed a Joscelin Grey in the hospital in Scutari, only briefly; his injury was serious enough, but not compared with the worst, and those who also suffered from disease. She recalled him: he had been young and fair-haired with a wide, easy smile and a natural grace. "I remember him—" Now Effie's words came back to her with clarity.

Rosamond dropped her fork, the color rushing to her cheeks, then ebbing away again leaving her ash-white. Fabia closed her eyes and took in a very long, deep breath and let it go soundlessly.

Lovel stared at his plate. Only Menard was looking at her, and rather than surprise or grief there was an expression in his face which appeared to be wariness, and a kind of closed, careful pain.

"How remarkable," he said slowly. "Still, I suppose you saw hundreds of soldiers, if not thousands. Our losses were staggering, so I am told."

"They were," she agreed grimly. "Far more than is generally understood, over eighteen thousand, and many of them needlessly—eight-ninths died not in battle but of wounds or disease afterwards."

"Do you remember Joscelin?" Rosamond said eagerly, totally ignoring the horrific figures. "He was injured in the leg. Even afterwards he was compelled to walk with a limp—indeed he often used a stick to support himself.''

"He only used it when he was tired!'' Fabia said sharply.

"He used it when he wanted sympathy,'' Menard said half under his breath.

"That is unworthy!'' Fabia's voice was dangerously soft, laden with warning, and her blue eyes rested on her second son with chill disfavor. "I shall consider that you did not say it.''

"We observe the convention that we speak no ill of the dead,'' Menard said with irony unusual in him. "Which limits conversation considerably.''

Rosamond stared at her plate. "I never understand your humor, Menard,'' she complained.

"That is because he is very seldom intentionally funny,'' Fabia snapped.

"Whereas Joscelin was always amusing.'' Menard was angry and no longer made any pretense at hiding it. "It is marvelous what a little laughter can do—entertain you enough and you will turn a blind eye on anything!''

"I loved Joscelin.'' Fabia met his eyes with a stony glare. "I enjoyed his company. So did a great many others. I love you also, but you bore me to tears.''

"You are happy enough to enjoy the profits of my work!'' His face was burning and his eyes bright with fury. "I preserve the estate's finances and see that it is properly managed, while Lovel keeps up the family name, sits in the House of Lords or does whatever else peers of the realm do—and Joscelin never did a damn thing but lounge around in clubs and drawing rooms gambling it away!''

The blood drained from Fabia's skin leaving her grasping her knife and fork as if they were lifelines.

"And you still resent that?'' Her voice was little more than a whisper. "He fought in the war, risked his life serving his Queen and country in terrible conditions, saw

154

blood and slaughter. And when he came home wounded, you grudged him a little entertainment with his friends?''

Menard drew in his breath to retort, then saw the pain in his mother's face, deeper than her anger and underlying everything else, and held his tongue.

"I was embarrassed by some of his losses," he said softly. "That is all."

Hester glanced at Callandra, and saw a mixture of anger, pity and respect in her highly expressive features, although which emotion was for whom she did not know. She thought perhaps the respect was for Menard.

Lovel smiled very bleakly. "I am afraid you may find the police are still around here, Miss Latterly. They have sent a very ill-mannered fellow, something of an upstart, although I daresay he is better bred than most policemen. But he does not seem to have much idea of what he is doing, and asks some very impertinent questions. If he should return during your stay and give you the slightest trouble, tell him to be off, and let me know."

"By all means," Hester agreed. To the best of her knowledge she had never conversed with a policeman, and she had no interest in doing so now. "It must all be most distressing for you."

"Indeed," Fabia agreed. "But an unpleasantness we have no alternative but to endure. It appears more than possible poor Joscelin was murdered by someone he knew."

Hester could think of no appropriate reply, nothing that was not either wounding or completely senseless.

"Thank you for your counsel," she said to Menard, then lowered her eyes and continued with her meal.

After the fruit had been passed the women withdrew and Lovel and Menard drank port for half an hour or so, then Lovel put on his smoking jacket and retired to the smoking room to indulge, and Menard went to the library. No one remained up beyond ten o'clock, each making some excuse why they had found the day tiring and wished to sleep.

155

Breakfast was the usual generous meal: porridge, bacon, eggs, deviled kidneys, chops, kedgeree, smoked haddock, toast, butter, sweet preserves, apricot compote, marmalade, honey, tea and coffee. Hester ate lightly; the very thought of partaking of all of it made her feel bloated. Both Rosamond and Fabia ate in their rooms, Menard had already dined and left and Callandra had not arisen. Lovel was her only companion.

"Good morning, Miss Latterly. I hope you slept well?"

"Excellently, thank you, Lord Shelburne." She helped herself from the heated dishes on the sideboard and sat down. "I hope you are well also?"

"What? Oh—yes thank you. Always well." He proceeded with his heaped meal and it was several minutes before he looked up at her again. "By the way, I hope you will be generous enough to disregard a great deal of what Menard said at dinner yesterday? We all take grief in different ways. Menard lost his closest friend also—fellow he was at school and Cambridge with. Took it terribly hard. But he was really very fond of Joscelin, you know, just that as immediately elder brother he had—er—" He searched for the right words to explain his thoughts, and failed to find them. "He—er—had—"

"Responsibilities to care for him?" she suggested.

Gratitude shone in his face. "Exactly. Sometimes I daresay Joscelin gambled more than he should, and it was Menard who—er . . ."

"I understand," she said, more to put him out of his embarrassment and end the painful conversation than because she believed him.

Later in a fine, blustery morning, walking under the trees with Callandra, she learned a good deal more.

"Stuff and nonsense," Callandra said sharply. "Joscelin was a cheat. Always was, even in the nursery. I shouldn't be at all surprised if he never grew out of it, and

156

Menard had to pick up after him to avoid a scandal. Very sensitive to the family name, Menard."

"Is Lord Shelburne not also?" Hester was surprised.

"I don't think Lovel has the imagination to realize that a Grey could cheat," Callandra answered frankly. "I think the whole thing would be beyond him to conceive. Gentlemen do not cheat; Joscelin was his brother—and so of course a gentleman—therefore he could not cheat. All very simple."

"You were not especially fond of Joscelin?" Hester searched her face.

Callandra smiled. "Not especially, although I admit he was very witty at times, and we can forgive a great deal of one who makes us laugh. And he played beautifully, and we can also overlook a lot in one who creates glorious sound—or perhaps I should say re-creates it. He did not compose, so far as I know."

They walked a hundred yards in silence except for the roar and rustle of the wind in giant oaks. It sounded like the torrent of a stream falling, or an incessant sea breaking on rocks. It was one of the pleasantest sounds Hester had ever heard, and the bright, sweet air was a sort of cleansing of her whole spirit.

"Well?" Callandra said at last. "What are your choices, Hester? I am quite sure you can find an excellent position if you wish to continue nursing, either in an army hospital or in one of the London hospitals that may be persuaded to accept women." There was no lift in her voice, no enthusiasm.

"But?" Hester said for her.

Callandra's wide mouth twitched in the ghost of a smile. "But I think you would be wasted in it. You have a gift for administration, and a fighting spirit. You should find some cause and battle to win it. You have learned a great deal about better standards of nursing in the Crimea. Teach them here in England, force people to listen—get rid of cross-infection, insanitary conditions, ignorant nurses, incompetent treatments that any good housekeeper would

157

abhor. You will save more lives, and be a happier woman."

Hester did not mention the dispatches she had sent in Alan Russell's name, but a truth in Callandra's words rested with an unusual warmth in her, a kind of resolution as if discord had been melted into harmony.

"How do I do it?" The writing of articles could wait, find its own avenue. The more she knew, the more she would be able to speak with power and intelligence. Of course she already knew that Miss Nightingale would continue to campaign with every ounce of the passion which all but consumed her nervous strength and physical health for a reformation of the entire Army Medical Corps, but she could not do it alone, or even with all the adulation the country offered her or the friends she had in the seats of power. Vested interests were spread through the corridors of authority like the roots of a tree through the earth. The bonds of habit and security of position were steellike in endurance. Too many people would have to change, and in doing so admit they had been ill-advised, unwise, even incompetent.

"How can I obtain a position?"

"I have friends," Callandra said with quiet confidence. "I shall begin to write letters, very discreetly, either to beg favors, prompt a sense of duty, prick consciences, or else threaten disfavor both public and private, if someone does not help!" There was a light of humor in her eyes, but also a complete intention to do exactly what she had said.

"Thank you," Hester accepted. "I shall endeavor to use my opportunities so as to justify your effort."

"Certainly," Callandra agreed. "If I did not believe so, I should not exert them." And she matched her stride to Hester's and together they walked in the wood under the branches and out across the park.

Two days later General Wadham came to dinner with his daughter Ursula, who had been betrothed for several months to Menard Grey. They arrived early enough to join the family in the withdrawing room for conversation before the meal was announced, and Hester found herself immediately tested in her tact. Ursula was a handsome girl whose mane of hair had a touch of red in its fairness and whose skin had the glow of someone who spends a certain amount of time in the open. Indeed, conversation had not proceeded far before her interest in riding to hounds became apparent. This evening she was dressed in a rich blue which in Hester's opinion was too powerful for her; something more subdued would have flattered her and permitted her natural vitality to show through. As it was she appeared a trifle conspicuous between Fabia's lavender silk and her light hair faded to gray at the front, Rosamond in a blue so dull and dark it made her flawless cheeks like alabaster, and Hester herself in a somber grape color rich and yet not out of keeping with her own recent state of mourning. Actually she thought privately she had never worn a color which flattered her more!

Callandra wore black with touches of white, a striking dress, but somehow not quite the right note of fashion. But then whatever Callandra wore was not going to have panache, only distinction; it was not in her nature to be glamorous.

General Wadham was tall and stout with bristling side whiskers and very pale blue eyes which were either far-sighted or nearsighted, Hester was unsure which, but they certainly did not seem to focus upon her when he addressed her.

"Visiting, Miss—er—Miss—"

"Latterly," she supplied.

"Ah yes—of course—Latterly." He reminded her almost ludicrously of a dozen or so middle-aged soldiers she had seen whom she and Fanny Bolsover had lampooned when they were tired and frightened and had sat up all night with the wounded, then afterwards lain together on a single straw pallet, huddled close for warmth and telling each other silly stories, laughing because it was better than

159

weeping, and making fun of the officers because loyalty and pity and hate were too big to deal with, and they had not the energy or spirit left.

"Friend of Lady Shelburne's, are you?" General Wadham said automatically. "Charming—charming."

Hester felt her irritation rise already.

"No," she contradicted. "I am a friend of Lady Callandra Daviot's. I was fortunate enough to know her some time ago."

"Indeed." He obviously could think of nothing to add to that, and moved on to Rosamond, who was more prepared to make light conversation and fall in with whatever mood he wished.

When dinner was announced there was no gentleman to escort her into the dining room, so she was obliged to go in with Callandra, and at table found herself seated opposite the general.

The first course was served and everyone began to eat, the ladies delicately, the men with appetite. At first conversation was slight, then when the initial hunger had been assuaged and the soup and fish eaten, Ursula began to speak about the hunt, and the relative merits of one horse over another.

Hester did not join in. The only riding she had done had been in the Crimea, and the sight of the horses there injured, diseased and starving had so distressed her she put it from her mind. Indeed so much did she close her attention from their speech that Fabia had addressed her three times before she was startled into realizing it.

"I beg your pardon!" she apologized in some embarrassment.

"I believe you said, Miss Latterly, that you were briefly acquainted with my late son, Major Joscelin Grey?"

"Yes. I regret it was very slight—there were so many wounded." She said it politely, as if she were discussing some ordinary commodity, but her mind went back to the reality of the hospitals when the wounded, the frostbitten and those wasted with cholera, dysentery and starvation

160

were lying so close there was barely room for more, and the rats scuttled, huddled and clung everywhere.

And worse than that she remembered the earthworks in the siege of Sebastopol, the bitter cold, the light of lamps in the mud, her body shaking as she held one high for the surgeon to work, its gleam on the saw blade, the dim shapes of men crowding together for a fraction of body's warmth. She remembered the first time she saw the great figure of Rebecca Box striding forward over the battlefield beyond the trenches to ground lately occupied by Russian troops, and lifting the bodies of the fallen and hoisting them over her shoulder to carry them back. Her strength was surpassed only by her sublime courage. No man fell injured so far forward she would not go out for him and carry him back to hospital hut or tent.

They were staring at her, waiting for her to say something more, some word of praise for him. After all, he had been a soldier—a major in the cavalry.

"I remember he was charming." She refused to lie, even for his family. "He had the most delightful smile."

Fabia relaxed and sat back. "That was Joscelin," she agreed with a misty look in her blue eyes. "Courage and a kind of gaiety, even in the most dreadful circumstances. I can still hardly believe he is gone—I half think he will throw the door open and stride in, apologizing for being late and telling us how hungry he is."

Hester looked at the table piled high with food that would have done half a regiment at the height of the siege. They used the word *hunger* so easily.

General Wadham sat back and wiped his napkin over his lips.

"A fine man," he said quietly. "You must have been very proud of him, my dear. A soldier's life is all too often short, but he carries honor with him, and he will not be forgotten."

The table was silent but for the clink of silver on porcelain. No one could think of any immediate reply. Fabia's face was full of a bleak and terrible grief, an almost dev-

161

astating loneliness. Rosamond stared into space, and Lovel looked quietly wretched, whether for their pain or his own was impossible to know. Was it memory or the present which robbed him?

Menard chewed his food over and over, as if his throat were too tight and his mouth too dry to swallow it.

"Glorious campaign," the general went on presently. "Live in the annals of history. Never be surpassed for courage. Thin Red Line, and all that."

Hester found herself suddenly choked with tears, anger and grief boiling up inside her, and intolerable frustration. She could see the hills beyond the Alma River more sharply than the figures around the table and the winking crystal. She could see the breastwork on the forward ridges as it had been that morning, bristling with enemy guns, the Greater and Lesser Redoubts, the wicker barricades filled with stones. Behind them were Prince Menshikoff's fifty thousand men. She remembered the smell of the breeze off the sea. She had stood with the women who had followed the army and watched Lord Raglan sitting in frock coat and white shirt, his back ramrod stiff in the saddle.

At one o'clock the bugle had sounded and the infantry advanced shoulder to shoulder into the mouths of the Russian guns and were cut down like corn. For ninety minutes they were massacred, then at last the order was given and the Hussars, Lancers and Fusiliers joined in, each in perfect order.

"Look well at that," a major had said to one of the wives, "for the Queen of England would give her eyes to see it."

Everywhere men were falling. The colors carried high were ragged with shot. As one bearer fell another took his place, and in his turn fell and was succeeded. Orders were conflicting, men advanced and retreated over each other. The Grenadiers advanced, a moving wall of bearskins, then the Black Watch of the Highland Brigade.

The Dragoons were held back, never used. Why? When

asked, Lord Raglan had replied that he had been thinking of Agnes!

Hester remembered going over the battlefield afterwards, the ground soaked with blood, seeing mangled bodies, some so terrible the limbs lay yards away. She had done all she could to relieve the suffering, working till exhaustion numbed her beyond feeling and she was dizzy with the sights and sounds of pain. Wounded were piled on carts and trundled to field hospital tents. She had worked all night and all day, exhausted, dry-mouthed with thirst, aching and drenched with horror. Orderlies had tried to stop the bleeding; there was little to do for shock but a few precious drops of brandy. What she would have given then for the contents of Shelburne's cellars.

The dinner table conversation buzzed on around her, cheerful, courteous, and ignorant. The flowers swam in her vision, summer blooms grown by careful gardeners, orchids tended in the glass conservatory. She thought of herself walking in the grass one hot afternoon with letters from home in her pocket, amid the dwarf roses and the blue larkspur that grew again in the field of Balaclava the year after the Charge of the Light Brigade, that idiotic piece of insane bungling and suicidal heroism. She had gone back to the hospital and tried to write and tell them what it was really like, what she was doing and how it felt, the sharing and the good things, the friendships, Fanny Bolsover, laughter, courage. The dry resignation of the men when they were issued green coffee beans, and no means to roast or grind them, had evoked her admiration so deeply it made her throat ache with sudden pride. She could hear the scratching of the quill over the paper now—and the sound as she tore it up.

"Fine man," General Wadham was saying, staring into his claret glass. "One of England's heroes. Lucan and Cardigan are related—I suppose you know? Lucan married one of Lord Cardigan's sisters—what a family." He shook his head in wonder. "What duty!"

"Inspires us all," Ursula agreed with shining eyes.

163

"They hated each other on sight," Hester said before she had time for discretion to guard her tongue.

"I beg your pardon!" The general stared at her coldly, his rather wispy eyebrows raised. His look centered all his incredulity at her impertinence and disapproval of women who spoke when it was not required of them.

Hester was stung by it. He was exactly the sort of blind, arrogant fool who had caused such immeasurable loss on the battlefield through refusal to be informed, rigidity of thought, panic when they found they were wrong, and personal emotion which overrode truth.

"I said that Lord Lucan and Lord Cardigan hated each other from the moment they met," she repeated clearly in the total silence.

"I think you are hardly in a position to judge such a thing, madame." He regarded her with total contempt. She was less than a subaltern, less than a private, for heaven's sake—she was a woman! And she had contradicted him, at least by implication, and at the dinner table.

"I was on the battlefield at the Alma, at Inkermann and at Balaclava, and at the siege of Sebastopol, sir," she answered without dropping her gaze. "Where were you?"

His face flushed scarlet. "Good manners, and regard for our hosts, forbid me from giving you the answer you deserve, madame," he said very stiffly. "Since the meal is finished, perhaps it is time the ladies wished to retire to the withdrawing room?"

Rosamond made as if to rise in obedience, and Ursula laid her napkin beside her plate, although there was still half a pear unfinished on it.

Fabia sat where she was, two spots of color in her cheeks, and very carefully and deliberately Callandra reached for a peach and began to peel it with her fruit knife and fork, a small smile on her face.

No one moved. The silence deepened.

"I believe it is going to be a hard winter," Lovel said at last. "Old Beckinsale was saying he expects to lose half his crop."

164

"He says that every year," Menard grunted and finished the remnant of his wine, throwing it back without savor, merely as if he would not waste it.

"A lot of people say things every year." Callandra cut away a squashy piece of fruit carefully and pushed it to the side of her plate. "It is forty years since we beat Napoleon at Waterloo, and most of us still think we have the same invincible army and we expect to win with the same tactics and the same discipline and courage that defeated half Europe and ended an empire."

"And by God, we shall, madame!" The general slammed down his palm, making the cutlery jump. "The British soldier is the superior of any man alive!"

"I don't doubt it," Callandra agreed. "It is the British general in the field who is a hidebound and incompetent ass."

"Callandra! For God's sake!" Fabia was appalled.

Menard put his hands over his face.

"Perhaps we should have done better had you been there, General Wadham," Callandra continued unabashed, looking at him frankly. "You at least have a very considerable imagination!"

Rosamond shut her eyes and slid down in her seat. Lovel groaned.

Hester choked with laughter, a trifle hysterically, and stuffed her napkin over her mouth to stifle it.

General Wadham made a surprisingly graceful strategic retreat. He decided to accept the remark as a compliment.

"Thank you, madame," he said stiffly. "Perhaps I might have prevented the slaughter of the Light Brigade."

And with that it was left. Fabia, with a little help from Lovel, rose from her seat and excused the ladies, leading them to the withdrawing room, where they discussed such matters as music, fashion, society, forthcoming weddings, both planned and speculated, and were excessively polite to one another.

When the visitors finally took their leave, Fabia turned

165

upon her sister-in-law with a look that should have shriveled her.

"Callandra—I shall never forgive you!"

"Since you have never forgiven me for wearing the exact shade of gown as you when we first met forty years ago," Callandra replied, "I shall just have to bear it with the same fortitude I have shown over all the other episodes since."

"You are impossible. Dear heaven, how I miss Joscelin." She stood up slowly and Hester rose as a matter of courtesy. Fabia walked towards the double doors. "I am going to bed. I shall see you tomorrow." And she went out, leaving them also.

"You are impossible, Aunt Callandra," Rosamond agreed, standing in the middle of the floor and looking confused and unhappy. "I don't know why you say such things."

"I know you don't," Callandra said gently. "That is because you have never been anywhere but Middleton, Shelburne Hall or London society. Hester would say the same, if she were not a guest here—indeed perhaps more. Our military imagination has ossified since Waterloo." She stood up and straightened her skirts. "Victory—albeit one of the greatest in history and turning the tide of nations—has still gone to our heads and we think all we have to do to win is to turn up in our scarlet coats and obey the rules. And only God can measure the suffering and the death that pigheadedness has caused. And we women and politicians sit here safely at home and cheer them on without the slightest idea what the reality of it is."

"Joscelin is dead," Rosamond said bleakly, staring at the closed curtains.

"I know that, my dear," Callandra said from close behind her. "But he did not die in the Crimea."

"He may have died because of it!"

"Indeed he may," Callandra conceded, her face suddenly touched with gentleness. "And I know you were extremely fond of him. He had a capacity for pleasure,

166

both to give and to receive, which unfortunately neither Lovel nor Menard seem to share. I think we have exhausted both ourselves and the subject. Good night, my dear. Weep if you wish; tears too long held in do us no good. Composure is all very well, but there is a time to acknowledge pain also.'' She slipped her arm around the slender shoulders and hugged her briefly, then knowing the gesture would release the hurt as well as comfort, she took Hester by the elbow and conducted her out to leave Rosamond alone.

The following morning Hester overslept and rose with a headache. She did not feel like early breakfast, and still less like facing any of the family across the table. She felt passionately about the vanity and the incompetence she had seen in the army, and the horror at the suffering would never leave her; probably the anger would not either. But she had not behaved very well at dinner; and the memory of it churned around in her mind, trying to fall into a happier picture with less fault attached to herself, and did not improve either her headache or her temper.

She decided to take a brisk walk in the park for as long as her energy lasted. She wrapped up appropriately, and by nine o'clock was striding rapidly over the grass getting her boots wet.

She first saw the figure of the man with considerable irritation, simply because she wished to be alone. He was probably inoffensive, and presumably had as much right to be here as herself—perhaps more? He no doubt served some function. However she felt he intruded, he was another human being in a world of wind and great trees and vast, cloud-racked skies and shivering, singing grass.

When he drew level he stopped and spoke to her. He was dark, with an arrogant face, all lean, smooth bones and clear eyes.

"Good morning, ma'am. I see you are from Shelburne Hall—"

"How observant," she said tartly, gazing around at the

totally empty parkland. There was no other place she could conceivably have come from, unless she had emerged from a hole in the ground.

His face tightened, aware of her sarcasm. "Are you a member of the family?" He was staring at her with some intensity and she found it disconcerting, and bordering on the offensive.

"How is that your concern?" she asked coldly.

The concentration deepened in his eyes, and then suddenly there was a flash of recognition, although for the life of her she could not think of any occasion on which she had seen him before. Curiously he did not refer to it.

"I am inquiring into the murder of Joscelin Grey. I wonder if you had known him."

"Good heavens!" she said involuntarily. Then she collected herself. "I have been accused of tactlessness in my time, but you are certainly in a class of your own." A total lie—Callandra would have left him standing! "It would be quite in your deserving if I told you I had been his fiancée—and fainted on the spot!"

"Then it was a secret engagement," he retorted. "And if you go in for clandestine romance you must expect to have your feelings bruised a few times."

"Which you are obviously well equipped to do!" She stood still with the wind whipping her skirts, still wondering why he had seemed to recognize her.

"Did you know him?" he repeated irritably.

"Yes!"

"For how long?"

"As well as I remember it, about three weeks."

"That's an odd time to know anyone!"

"What would you consider a usual time to know someone?" she demanded.

"It was very brief," he explained with careful condescension. "You can hardly have been a friend of the family. Did you meet him just before he died?"

"No. I met him in Scutari."

"You what?"

168

"Are you hard of hearing? I met him in Scutari!" She remembered the general's patronizing manner and all her memories of condescension flooded back, the army officers who considered women out of place, ornaments to be used for recreation or comfort but not creatures of any sense. Gentlewomen were for cossetting, dominating and protecting from everything, including adventure or decision or freedom of any kind. Common women were whores or drudges and to be used like any other livestock.

"Oh yes," he agreed with a frown. "He was injured. Were you out there with your husband?"

"No I was not!" Why should that question be faintly hurtful? "I went to nurse the injured, to assist Miss Nightingale, and those like her."

His face did not show the admiration and profound sense of respect close to awe that the name usually brought. She was thrown off balance by it. He seemed to be single-minded in his interest in Joscelin Grey.

"You nursed Major Grey?"

"Among others. Do you mind if we proceed to walk? I am getting cold standing here."

"Of course." He turned and fell into step with her and they began along the faint track in the grass towards a copse of oaks. "What were your impressions of him?"

She tried hard to distinguish her memory from the picture she had gathered from his family's words, Rosamond's weeping, Fabia's pride and love, the void he had left in her happiness, perhaps Rosamond's also, his brothers' mixture of exasperation and—what—envy?

"I can recall his leg rather better than his face," she said frankly.

He stared at her with temper rising sharply in his face.

"I am not interested in your female fantasies, madame, or your peculiar sense of humor! This is an investigation into an unusually brutal murder!"

She lost her temper completely.

"You incompetent idiot!" she shouted into the wind. "You grubby-minded, fatuous nincompoop. I was nursing him. I dressed and cleaned his wound—which, in case you have forgotten, was in his leg. His face was uninjured, therefore I did not regard it any more than the faces of the other ten thousand injured and dead I saw. I would not know him again if he came up and spoke to me.''

His face was bleak and furious. "It would be a memorable occasion, madame. He is eight weeks dead—and beaten to a pulp.''

If he had hoped to shock her he failed.

She swallowed hard and held his eyes. "Sounds like the battlefield after Inkermann,'' she said levelly. "Only there at least we knew what had happened to them—even if no one had any idea why.''

"We know what happened to Joscelin Grey—we do not know who did it. Fortunately I am not responsible for explaining the Crimean War—only Joscelin Grey's death.''

"Which seems to be beyond you,'' she said unkindly. "And I can be of no assistance. All I can remember is that he was unusually agreeable, that he bore his injury with as much fortitude as most, and that when he was recovering he spent quite a lot of his time moving from bed to bed encouraging and cheering other men, particularly those closest to death. In fact when I think of it, he was a most admirable man. I had forgotten that until now. He comforted many who were dying, and wrote letters home for them, told their families of their deaths and probably gave them much ease in their distress. It is very hard that he should survive that, and come home to be murdered here.''

"He was killed very violently—there was a passion of hatred in the way he was beaten.'' He was looking at her closely and she was startled by the intelligence in his face; it was uncomfortably intense, and unexpected. "I believe it was someone who knew him. One does not hate a stranger as he was hated.''

She shivered. Horrific as was the battlefield, there was still a world of difference between its mindless carnage and the acutely personal malevolence of Joscelin Grey's death.

"I am sorry," she said more gently, but still with the stiffness he engendered in her. "I know nothing of him that would help you find such a relationship. If I did I should tell you. The hospital kept records; you would be able to find out who else was there at the same time, but no doubt you have already done that—" She saw instantly from the shadow in his face that he had not. Her patience broke. "Then for heaven's sake, what have you been doing for eight weeks?"

"For five of them I was lying injured myself," he snapped back. "Or recovering. You make far too many assumptions, madame. You are arrogant, domineering, ill-tempered and condescending. And you leap to conclusions for which you have no foundation. God! I hate clever women!"

She froze for an instant before the reply was on her lips.

"I love clever men!" Her eyes raked him up and down. "It seems we are both to be disappointed." And with that she picked up her skirts and strode past him and along the path towards the copse, tripping over a bramble across her way. "Drat," she swore furiously. "Hellfire."

171

"GOOD MORNING, Miss Latterly," Fabia said coolly when she came into the sitting room at about quarter past ten the following day. She looked smart and fragile and was already dressed as if to go out. She eyed Hester very briefly, noting her extremely plain muslin gown, and then turned to Rosamond, who was sitting poking apologetically at an embroidery frame. "Good morning, Rosamond. I hope you are well? It is a most pleasant day, and I believe we should take the opportunity to visit some of the less fortunate in the village. We have not been lately, and it is your duty, my dear, even more than it is mine."

The color deepened a trifle in Rosamond's cheeks as she accepted the rebuke. From the quick lift in her chin Hester thought there might be far more behind the motion than was apparent. The family was in mourning, and Fabia had quite obviously felt the loss most keenly, at least to the outward eye. Had Rosamond tried to resume life too quickly for her, and this was Fabia's way of choosing the time?

"Of course, Mama-in-law," Rosamond said without looking up.

"And no doubt Miss Latterly will come with us," Fabia added without consulting her. "We shall leave at eleven.

That will allow you time to dress appropriately. The day is most warm—do not be tempted to forget your position." And with that admonition, delivered with a frozen smile, she turned and left them, stopping by the door for a moment to add, "And we might take luncheon with General Wadham, and Ursula." And then she went out.

Rosamond threw the hoop at her workbasket and it went beyond and skittered across the floor. "Drat," she said quietly under her breath. Then she met Hester's eyes and apologized.

Hester smiled at her. "Please don't," she said candidly. "Playing Lady Bountiful 'round the estates is enough to make anyone resort to language better for the stable, or even the barracks, than the drawing room. A simple 'drat' is very mild."

"Do you miss the Crimea, now you are home?" Rosamond said suddenly, her eyes intent and almost frightened of the answer. "I mean—" She looked away, embarrassed and now finding it hard to speak the words which only a moment before had been so ready.

Hester saw a vision of endless days being polite to Fabia, attending to the trivial household management that she was allowed, never feeling it was her house until Fabia was dead; and perhaps even afterwards Fabia's spirit would haunt the house, her belongings, her choices of furniture, of design, marking it indelibly. There would be morning calls, luncheon with suitable people of like breeding and position, visits to the poor—and in season there would be balls, the races at Ascot, the regatta at Henley, and of course in winter the hunt. None of it would be more than pleasant at best, tedious at worst—but without meaning.

But Rosamond did not deserve a lie, even in her loneliness—nor did she deserve the pain of Hester's view of the truth. It was only her view; for Rosamond it might be different.

"Oh yes, sometimes I do," she said with a small smile. "But we cannot fight wars like that for long. It is very dreadful as well as vivid and real. It is not fun being cold

173

and dirty and so tired you feel as if you've been beaten—
nor is it pleasant to eat army rations. It is one of the finest
things in life to be truly useful—but there are less distressing places to do it, and I am sure I shall find many here
in England.''

"You are very kind," Rosamond said gently, meeting
her eyes again. "I admit I had not imagined you would be
so thoughtful." She rose to her feet. "Now I suppose we
had better change into suitable clothes for calling—have
you something modest and dowdy, but very dignified?"
She stifled a giggle and turned it into a sneeze. "I'm
sorry—what a fearful thing to ask!"

"Yes—most of my wardrobe is like that," Hester replied with an amusing smile. "All dark greens and very
tired-looking blues—like faded ink. Will they do?"

"Perfectly—come!"

Menard drove the three of them in the open trap, bowling
along the carriageway through the park towards the edge
of the home estate and across heavy cornfields towards the
village and the church spire beyond the slow swell of the
hill. He obviously enjoyed managing the horse and did it
with the skill of one who is long practiced. He did not
even try to make conversation, supposing the loveliness of
the land, the sky and the trees would be enough for them,
as it was for him.

Hester sat watching him, leaving Rosamond and Fabia
to converse. She looked at his powerful hands holding the
reins lightly, at the ease of his balance and the obvious
reticence in his expression. The daily round of duties in
the estate was no imprisonment to him; she had seen a
brooding in his face occasionally in the time she had been
at Shelburne, sometimes anger, sometimes a stiffness and
a jumpiness of the muscles which made her think of officers she had seen the night before battle, but it was when
they were all at table, with Fabia's conversation betraying
the ache of loneliness underneath as if Joscelin had been
the only person she had totally and completely loved.

174

The first house they called at was that of a farm laborer on the edge of the village, a tiny cottage, one room downstairs crowded with a sunburned, shabby woman and seven children all sharing a loaf of bread spread with pork drippings. Their thin, dusty legs, barefooted, splayed out beneath simple smocks and they were obviously in from working in the garden or fields. Even the youngest, who looked no more than three or four, had fruit stains on her fingers where she had been harvesting.

Fabia asked questions and passed out practical advice on financial management and how to treat croup which the woman received in polite silence. Hester blushed for the condescension of it, and then realized it had been a way of life with little substantial variation for over a thousand years, and both parties were comfortable with its familiarity; and she had nothing more certain to put in its place.

Rosamond spoke with the eldest girl, and took the wide pink ribbon off her own hat and gave it to her, tying it around the child's hair to her shy delight.

Menard stood patiently by the horse, talking to it in a low voice for a few moments, then falling into a comfortable silence. The sunlight on his face showed the fine lines of anxiety around his eyes and mouth, and the deeper marks of pain. Here in the rich land with its great trees, the wind and the fertile earth he was relaxed, and Hester saw a glimpse of a quite different man from the stolid, resentful second son he appeared at Shelburne Hall. She wondered if Fabia had ever allowed herself to see it. Or was the laughing charm of Joscelin always in its light?

The second call was similar in essence, although the family was composed of an elderly woman with no teeth and an old man who was either drunk or had suffered some seizure which impaired both his speech and his movement.

Fabia spoke to him briskly with words of impersonal encouragement, which he ignored, making a face at her when her back was turned, and the old woman bobbed a curtsy, accepted two jars of lemon curd, and once again they climbed into the trap and were on their way.

Menard left them to go out into the fields, high with ripe corn, the reapers already digging the sickles deep, the sun hot on their backs, arms burned, sweat running freely. There was much talk of weather, time, the quarter of the wind, and when the rain would break. The smell of the grain and the broken straw in the heat was one of the sweetest things Hester had ever known. She stood in the brilliant light with her face lifted to the sky, the heat tingling on her skin, and gazed across the dark gold of the land—and thought of those who had been willing to die for it—and prayed that the heirs to so much treasured it deeply enough, to see it with the body and with the heart as well.

Luncheon was another matter altogether. They were received courteously enough until General Wadham saw Hester, then his florid face stiffened and his manner became exaggeratedly formal.

"Good morning, Miss Latterly. How good of you to call. Ursula will be delighted that you are able to join us for luncheon."

"Thank you, sir," she replied equally gravely. "You are very generous."

Ursula did not look particularly delighted to see them at all, and was unable to hide her chagrin that Menard had seen fit to be out with the harvesters instead of here at the dining room table.

Luncheon was a light meal: poached river fish with caper sauce, cold game pie and vegetables, then a sorbet and a selection of fruit, followed by an excellent Stilton cheese.

General Wadham had obviously neither forgotten nor forgiven his rout by Hester on their previous meeting. His chill, rather glassy eye met hers over the cruet sets a number of times before he actually joined battle in a lull between Fabia's comments on the roses and Ursula's speculations as to whether Mr. Danbury would marry Miss Fothergill or Miss Ames.

"Miss Ames is a fine young woman," the general remarked, looking at Hester. "Most accomplished horsewoman, rides to hounds like a man. Courage. And handsome too, dashed handsome." He looked at Hester's dark green dress sourly. "Grandfather died in the Peninsular War—at Corunna—1810. Don't suppose you were there too, were you, Miss Latterly? Bit before your time, eh?" He smiled, as if he had intended it to be good-natured.

"1809," Hester corrected him. "It was before Talavera and after Vimiero and the Convention of Cintra. Otherwise you are perfectly correct—I was not there."

The general's face was scarlet. He swallowed a fish bone and choked into his napkin.

Fabia, white with fury, passed him a glass of water.

Hester, knowing better, removed it instantly and replaced it with bread.

The general took the bread and the bone was satisfactorily coated with it and passed down his throat.

"Thank you," he said freezingly, and then took the water also.

"I am happy to be of assistance," Hester replied sweetly. "It is most unpleasant to swallow a bone, and so easily done, even in the best of fish—and this is delicious."

Fabia muttered something blasphemous and inaudible under her breath and Rosamond launched into a sudden and overenthusiastic recollection of the Vicar's midsummer garden party.

Afterwards, when Fabia had elected to remain with Ursula and the general, and Rosamond hurried Hester out to the trap to resume their visiting of the poor, she whispered to her rapidly and with a little self-consciousness.

"That was awful. Sometimes you remind me of Joscelin. He used to make me laugh like that."

"I didn't notice you laughing," Hester said honestly,

177

climbing up into the trap after her and forgetting to arrange her skirts.

"Of course not." Rosamond took the reins and slapped the horse forward. "It would never do to be seen. You will come again some time, won't you?"

"I am not at all sure I shall be asked," Hester said ruefully.

"Yes you will—Aunt Callandra will ask you. She likes you very much—and I think sometimes she gets bored with us here. Did you know Colonel Daviot?"

"No." For the first time Hester regretted that she had not. She had seen his portrait, but that was all; he had been a stocky, upright man with a strong-featured face, full of wit and temper. "No, I didn't."

Rosamond urged the horse faster and they careered along the track, the wheels bouncing over the ridges.

"He was very charming," she said, watching ahead. "Sometimes. He had a great laugh when he was happy— he also had a filthy temper and was terribly bossy—even with Aunt Callandra. He was always interfering, telling her how she ought to do everything—when he got the whim for it. Then he would forget about whatever it was, and leave her to clear up the mess."

She reined in the horse a little, getting it under better control.

"But he was very generous," she added. "He never betrayed a friend's confidence. And the best horseman I ever saw—far better than either Menard or Lovel—and far better than General Wadham." Her hair was coming undone in the wind, and she ignored it. She giggled happily. "They couldn't bear each other."

It opened up an understanding of Callandra that Hester had never imagined before—a loneliness, and a freedom which explained why she had never entertained the idea of remarriage. Who could follow such a highly individual man? And perhaps also her independence had become more precious as she became more used to its pleasures. And perhaps also there had been more unhappiness there

178

than Hester had imagined in her swift and rather shallow judgments?

She smiled and made some acknowledgment of having heard Rosamond's remark, then changed the subject. They arrived at the small hamlet where their further visiting was to be conducted, and it was late in the afternoon, hot and vividly blue and gold as they returned through the heavy fields past the reapers, whose backs were still bent, arms bare. Hester was glad of the breeze of their movement and passing beneath the huge shade trees that leaned over the narrow road was a pleasure. There was no sound but the thud of the horse's hooves, the hiss of the wheels and the occasional bird song. The light gleamed pale on the straw stalks where the laborers had already passed, and darker on the ungathered heads. A few faint clouds, frail as spun floss, drifted across the horizon.

Hester looked at Rosamond's hands on the reins and her quiet, tense face, and wondered if she saw the timeless beauty of it, or only the unceasing sameness, but it was a question she could not ask.

Hester spent the evening with Callandra in her rooms and did not dine with the family, but she took breakfast in the main dining room the following morning and Rosamond greeted her with evident pleasure.

"Would you like to see my son?" she invited with a faint blush for her assumption, and her vulnerability.

"Of course I would," Hester answered immediately; it was the only possible thing to say. "I cannot think of anything nicer." Indeed that was probably true. She was not looking forward to her next encounter with Fabia and she certainly did not wish to do any more visiting with General Wadham, any more "good works" among those whom Fabia considered "the deserving poor," nor to walk in the park again where she might meet that peculiarly offensive policeman. His remarks had been impertinent, and really very unjust. "It will make a beautiful beginning to the day," she added.

The nursery was a bright south-facing room full of sunlight and chintz, with a low nursing chair by the window, a rocking chair next to the large, well-railed and guarded fireplace, and at present, since the child was so young, a day crib. The nursery maid, a young girl with a handsome face and skin like cream, was busy feeding the baby, about a year and a half old, with fingers of bread and butter dipped in a chopped and buttered boiled egg. Hester and Rosamond did not interrupt but stood watching.

The baby, a quiff of blond hair along the crown of his head like a little bird's comb, was obviously enjoying himself immensely. He accepted every mouthful with perfect obedience and his cheeks grew fatter and fatter. Then with shining eyes he took a deep breath and blew it all out, to the nursery maid's utter consternation. He laughed so hard his face was bright pink and he fell over sideways in his chair, helpless with delight.

Rosamond was filled with embarrassment, but all Hester could do was laugh with the baby, while the maid dabbed at her once spotless apron with a damp cloth.

"Master Harry, you shouldn't do that!" the maid said as fiercely as she dared, but there was no real anger in her voice, more simple exasperation at having been caught yet again.

"Oh you dreadful child." Rosamond went and picked him up, holding him close to her and laying the pale head with its wave of hair close to her cheek. He was still crowing with joy, and looked over his mother's shoulder at Hester with total confidence that she would love him.

They spent a happy hour in gentle conversation, then left the maid to continue with her duties, and Rosamond showed Hester the main nursery where Lovel, Menard and Joscelin had played as children: the rocking horse, the toy soldiers, the wooden swords, the musical boxes, and the kaleidoscope; and the dolls' houses left by an earlier generation of girls—perhaps Callandra herself?

Next they looked at the schoolroom with its tables and shelves of books. Hester found her hands picking at first

180

idly over old exercises of copperplate writing, a child's early, careful attempts. Then as she progressed to adolescent years and essays she found herself absorbed in reading the maturing hand. It was an essay in light, fluent style, surprisingly sharp for one so young and with a penetrating, often unkind wit. The subject was a family picnic, and she found herself smiling as she read, but there was pain in it, an awareness under the humor of cruelty. She did not need to look at the spine of the book to know it was Joscelin's.

She found one of Lovel's and turned the pages till she discovered an essay of similar length. Rosamond was searching a small desk for a copy of some verses, and there was time to read it carefully. It was utterly unlike, diffident, romantic, seeing beyond the simple woodland of Shelburne a forest where great deeds could be done, an ideal woman wooed and loved with a clean and untroubled emotion so far from the realities of human need and difficulty Hester found her eyes prickling for the disillusion that must come to such a youth.

She closed the pages with their faded ink and looked across at Rosamond, the sunlight on her bent head as she fingered through duty books looking for some special poem that caught her own high dream. Did either she or Lovel see beyond the princesses and the knights in armor the fallible, sometimes weak, sometimes frightened, often foolish people beneath—who needed immeasurably more courage, generosity and power to forgive than the creatures of youth's dreams—and were so much more precious?

She wanted to find the third essay, Menard's—and it took her several minutes to locate a book of his and read it. It was stiff, far less comfortable with words, and all through it there was a passionate love of honor, a loyalty to friendship and a sense of history as an unending cavalcade of the proud and the good, with sudden images borrowed from the tales of King Arthur. It was derivative and stilted, but the sincerity still shone through, and she

181

doubted the man had lost the values of the boy who had written so intensely—and awkwardly.

Rosamond had found her poem at last, and was so absorbed in it that she was unaware of Hester's movement towards her, or that Hester glanced over her shoulder and saw that it was an anonymous love poem, very small and very tender.

Hester looked away and walked to the door. It was not something upon which to intrude.

Rosamond closed the book and followed a moment after, recapturing her previous gaiety with an effort which Hester pretended not to notice.

"Thank you for coming up," she said as they came back into the main landing with its huge jardinieres of flowers. "It was kind of you to be so interested."

"It is not kindness at all," Hester denied quickly. "I think it is a privilege to see into the past as one does in nurseries and old schoolrooms. I thank you for allowing me to come. And of course Harry is delightful! Who could fail to be happy in his presence?"

Rosamond laughed and made a small gesture of denial with her hand, but she was obviously pleased. They made their way downstairs together and into the dining room, where luncheon was already served and Lovel was waiting for them. He stood up as they came in, and took a step towards Rosamond. For a moment he seemed about to speak, then the impulse died.

She waited a moment, her eyes full of hope. Hester hated herself for being there, but to leave now would be absurd; the meal was set and the footman waiting to serve it. She knew Callandra had gone to visit an old acquaintance, because it was on Hester's behalf that she had made the journey, but Fabia was also absent and her place was not set.

Lovel saw her glance.

"Mama is not well," he said with a faint chill. "She has remained in her room."

"I am sorry," Hester said automatically. "I hope it is nothing serious?"

"I hope not," he agreed, and as soon as they were seated, resumed his own seat and indicated that the footman might begin to serve them.

Rosamond nudged Hester under the table with her foot, and Hester gathered that the situation was delicate, and wisely did not pursue it.

The meal was conducted with stilted and trivial conversation, layered with meanings, and Hester thought of the boy's essay, the old poem, and all the levels of dreams and realities where so much fell through between one set of meanings and another, and was lost.

Afterwards she excused herself and went to do what she realized was her duty. She must call on Fabia and apologize for having been rude to General Wadham. He had deserved it, but she was Fabia's guest, and she should not have embarrassed her, regardless of the provocation.

It was best done immediately; the longer she thought about it the harder it would be. She had little patience with minor ailments; she had seen too much desperate disease, and her own health was good enough she did not know from experience how debilitating even a minor pain can be when stretched over time.

She knocked on Fabia's door and waited until she heard the command to enter, then she turned the handle and went in.

It was a less feminine room than she had expected. It was plain light Wedgwood blue and sparsely furnished compared with the usual cluttered style. A single silver vase held summer roses in full bloom on the table by the window; the bed was canopied in white muslin, like the inner curtains. On the farthest wall, where the sun was diffused, hung a fine portrait of a young man in the uniform of a cavalry officer. He was slender and straight, his fair hair falling over a broad brow, pale, intelligent eyes and a mobile mouth, humorous, articulate, and she thought in that fleeting instant, a little weak.

183

Fabia was sitting up in her bed, a blue satin bedjacket covering her shoulders and her hair brushed and knotted loosely so it fell in a faded coil over her breast. She looked thin and much older than Hester was prepared for. Suddenly the apology was not difficult. She could see all the loneliness of years in the pale face, the loss which would never be repaired.

"Yes?" Fabia said with distinct chill.

"I came to apologize, Lady Fabia," Hester replied quietly. "I was very rude to General Wadham yesterday, and as your guest it was inexcusable. I am truly sorry."

Fabia's eyebrows rose in surprise, then she smiled very slightly.

"I accept your apology. I am surprised you had the grace to come—I had not expected it of you. It is not often I misjudge a young woman." Her smile lifted the corners of her mouth fractionally, giving her face a sudden life, echoing the girl she must once have been. "It was most embarrassing for me that General Wadham should be so—so deflated. But it was not entirely without its satisfactions. He is a condescending old fool—and I sometimes get very weary of being patronized."

Hester was too surprised to say anything at all. For the first time since arriving at Shelburne Hall she actually liked Fabia.

"You may sit down," Fabia offered with a gleam of humor in her eyes.

"Thank you." Hester sat on the dressing chair covered with blue velvet, and looked around the room at the other, lesser paintings and the few photographs, stiff and very posed for the long time that the camera required to set the image. There was a picture of Rosamond and Lovel, probably at their wedding. She looked fragile and very happy; he was facing the lens squarely, full of hope.

On the other chest there was an early daguerreotype of a middle-aged man with handsome side-whiskers, black hair and a vain, whimsical face. From the resemblance to Joscelin, Hester assumed it to be the late Lord Shelburne.

There was also a pencil sketch of all three brothers as boys, sentimental, features a little idealized, the way one remembers summers of the past.

"I'm sorry you are feeling unwell," Hester said quietly. "Is there anything I can do for you?"

"I should think it highly unlikely; I am not a casualty of war—at least not in the sense that you are accustomed to," Fabia replied.

Hester did not argue. It rose to the tip of her tongue to say she was accustomed to all sorts of hurt, but then she knew it would be trite—she had not lost a son, and that was the only grief Fabia was concerned with.

"My eldest brother was killed in the Crimea." Hester still found the words hard to say. She could see George in her mind's eye, the way he walked, hear his laughter, then it dissolved and a sharper memory returned of herself and Charles and George as children, and the tears ached in her throat beyond bearing. "And both my parents died shortly after," she said quickly. "Shall we speak of something else?"

For a moment Fabia looked startled. She had forgotten, and now she was faced with a loss as huge as her own.

"My dear—I'm so very sorry. Of course—you did say so. Forgive me. What have you done this morning? Would you care to take the trap out later? It would be no difficulty to arrange it."

"I went to the nursery and met Harry." Hester smiled and blinked. "He's beautiful—" And she proceeded to tell the story.

She remained at Shelburne Hall for several more days, sometimes taking long walks alone in the wind and brilliant air. The parkland had a beauty which pleased her immensely and she felt at peace with it as she had in few other places. She was able to consider the future much more clearly, and Callandra's advice, repeated several times more in their many conversations, seemed increasingly wise the more she thought of it. The tension among

185

the members of the household changed after the dinner with General Wadham. Surface anger was covered with the customary good manners, but she became aware through a multitude of small observations that the unhappiness was a deep and abiding part of the fabric of their lives.

Fabia had a personal courage which might have been at least half the habitual discipline of her upbringing and the pride that would not allow others to see her vulnerability. She was autocratic, to some extent selfish, although she would have been the last to think it of herself. But Hester saw the loneliness in her face in moments when she believed herself unobserved, and at times beneath the old woman so immaculately dressed, a bewilderment which laid bare the child she had once been. Undoubtedly she loved her two surviving sons, but she did not especially like them, and no one could charm her or make her laugh as Joscelin had. They were courteous, but they did not flatter her, they did not bring back with small attentions the great days of her beauty when dozens had courted her and she had been the center of so much. With Joscelin's death her own hunger for living had gone.

Hester spent many hours with Rosamond and became fond of her in a distant, nonconfiding sort of way. Callandra's words about a brave, protective smile came to her sharply on several occasions, most particularly one late afternoon as they sat by the fire and made light, trivial conversation. Ursula Wadham was visiting, full of excitement and plans for the time when she would be married to Menard. She babbled on, facing Rosamond but apparently not seeing anything deeper than the perfect complexion, the carefully dressed hair and the rich afternoon gown. To her Rosamond had everything a woman could desire, a wealthy and titled husband, a strong child, beauty, good health and sufficient talent in the arts of pleasing. What else was there to desire?

Hester listened to Rosamond agreeing to all the plans, how exciting it would be and how happy the future looked, and she saw behind the dark eyes no gleam of confidence and hope, only a sense of loss, a loneliness and a kind of desperate courage that keeps going because it knows no way to stop. She smiled because it brought her peace, it prevented questions and it preserved a shred of pride.

Lovel was busy. At least he had purpose and as long as he was fulfilling it any darker emotion was held at bay. Only at the dinner table when they were all together did the occasional remark betray the underlying knowledge that something had eluded him, some precious element that seemed to be his was not really. He could not have called it fear—he would have hated the word and rejected it with horror—but staring at him across the snow-white linen and the glittering crystal, Hester thought that was what it was. She had seen it so often before, in totally different guises, when the danger was physical, violent and immediate. At first because the threat was so different she thought only of anger, then as it nagged persistently at the back of her mind, unclassified, suddenly she saw its other face, domestic, personal, emotional pain, and she knew it was a jar of familiarity.

With Menard it was also anger, but a sharp awareness, too, of something he saw as injustice; past now in act, but the residue still affecting him. Had he tidied up too often after Joscelin, his mother's favorite, protecting her from the truth that he was a cheat? Or was it himself he protected, and the family name?

Only with Callandra did she feel relaxed, but it did on one occasion cross her mind to wonder whether Callandra's comfort with herself was the result of many years' happiness or the resolution within her nature of its warring elements, not a gift but an art. It was one evening when they had taken a light supper in Callandra's sitting room instead of dinner in the main wing, and Callandra had made some remark about her husband, now long dead. Hester had always assumed the marriage to have been happy, not from anything she knew of it, or of Callandra Daviot, but from the peace within Callandra.

Now she realized how blindly she had leaped to such a shortsighted conclusion.

Callandra must have seen the idea waken in her eyes. She smiled with a touch of wryness, and a gentle humor in her face.

"You have a great deal of courage, Hester, and a hunger for life which is a far richer blessing than you think now—but, my dear, you are sometimes very naive. There are many kinds of misery, and many kinds of fortitude, and you should not allow your awareness of one to build to the value of another. You have an intense desire, a passion, to make people's lives better. Be aware that you can truly help people only by aiding them to become what they are, not what you are. I have heard you say 'If I were you, I would do this—or that.' 'I' am never 'you'—and my solutions may not be yours."

Hester remembered the wretched policeman who had told her she was domineering, overbearing and several other unpleasant things.

Callandra smiled. "Remember, my dear, you are dealing with the world as it is, not as you believe, maybe rightly, that it ought to be. There will be a great many things you can achieve not by attacking them but with a little patience and a modicum of flattery. Stop to consider what it is you really want, rather than pursuing your anger or your vanity to charge in. So often we leap to passionate judgments—when if we but knew the one thing more, they would be so different."

Hester was tempted to laugh, in spite of having heard very clearly what Callandra had said, and perceiving the truth of it.

"I know," Callandra agreed quickly. "I preach much better than I practice. But believe me, when I want something enough, I have the patience to bide my time and think how I can bring it about."

"I'll try," Hester promised, and she did mean it. "That miserable policeman will not be right—I shall not allow him to be right."

"I beg your pardon?"

"I met him when I was out walking," Hester explained. "He said I was overbearing and opinionated, or something like that."

Callandra's eyebrows shot up and she did not even attempt to keep a straight face.

"Did he really? What temerity! And what perception, on such a short acquaintance. And what did you think of him, may I ask?"

"An incompetent and insufferable nincompoop!"

"Which of course you told him?"

Hester glared back at her. "Certainly!"

"Quite so. I think he had more of the right of it than you did. I don't think he is incompetent. He has been given an extremely difficult task. There were a great many people who might have hated Joscelin, and it will be exceedingly difficult for a policeman, with all his disadvantages, to discover which one it was—and even harder, I imagine, to prove it."

"You mean, you think—" Hester left it unsaid, hanging in the air.

"I do," Callandra replied. "Now come, we must settle what you are to do with yourself. I shall write to certain friends I have, and I have little doubt, if you hold a civil tongue in your head, refrain from expressing your opinion of men in general and of Her Majesty's Army's generals in particular, we may obtain for you a position in hospital administration which will not only be satisfying to you but also to those who are unfortunate enough to be ill."

"Thank you." Hester smiled. "I am very grateful." She looked down in her lap for a moment, then up at Callandra and her eyes sparkled. "I really do not mind walking two paces behind a man, you know—if only I can find one who can walk two paces faster than I! It is being tied at the knees by convention I hate—and having to pretend I am lame to suit someone else's vanity."

Callandra shook her head very slowly, amusement and sadness sharp in her face. "I know. Perhaps you will have

189

to fall a few times, and have someone else pick you up, before you will learn a more equable pace. But do not walk slowly simply for company—ever. Not even God would wish you to be unequally yoked and result in destroying both of you—in fact God least of all.''

Hester sat back and smiled, lifting up her knees and hugging them in a most unladylike fashion. "I daresay I shall fall many times—and look excessively foolish—and give rise to a good deal of hilarity among those who dislike me—but that is still better than not trying.''

"Indeed it is," Callandra agreed. "But you would do it anyway.''

8

THE MOST PRODUCTIVE of Joscelin Grey's acquaintances was one of the last that Monk and Evan visited, and not from Lady Fabia's list, but from the letters in the flat. They had spent over a week in the area near Shelburne, discreetly questioning on the pretense of tracing a jewel thief who specialized in country houses. They had learned something of Joscelin Grey, of the kind of life he led, at least while home from London. And Monk had had the unnerving and extremely irritating experience one day while walking across the Shelburne parkland of coming upon the woman who had been with Mrs. Latterly in St. Marylebone Church. Perhaps he should not have been startled—after all, society was very small—but it had taken him aback completely. The whole episode in the church with its powerful emotion had returned in the windy, rain-spattered land with its huge trees, and Shelburne House in the distance.

There was no reason why she should not have visited the family, precisely as he later discovered. She was a Miss Hester Latterly, who had nursed in the Crimea, and was a friend of Lady Callandra Daviot. As she had told him, she had known Joscelin Grey briefly at the time of his injury. It was most natural that once she was home she should give her condolences in person. And also certainly within her nature that she should be outstandingly rude to a policeman.

And give the devil her due, he had been rude back—and gained considerable satisfaction from it. It would all have been of no possible consequence were she not obviously related to the woman in the church whose face so haunted him.

What had they learned? Joscelin Grey was liked, even envied for his ease of manner, his quick smile and a gift for making people laugh; and perhaps even more rather than less, because the amusement had frequently an underlying caustic quality. What had surprised Monk was that he was also, if not pitied, then sympathized with because he was a younger son. The usual careers open to younger sons such as the church and the army were either totally unsuitable to him or else denied him now because of his injury, gained in the service of his country. The heiress he had courted had married his elder brother, and he had not yet found another to replace her, at least not one whose family considered him a suitable match. He was, after all, invalided out of the army, without a merchandisable skill and without financial expectations.

Evan had acquired a rapid education in the manners and morals of his financial betters, and now was feeling both bemused and disillusioned. He sat in the train staring out of the window, and Monk regarded him with a compassion not unmixed with humor. He knew the feeling, although he could not recall experiencing it himself. Was it possible he had never been so young? It was an unpleasant thought that he might always have been cynical, without that particular kind of innocence, even as a child.

Discovering himself step by step, as one might a stranger, was stretching his nerves further than he had been aware of until now. Sometimes he woke in the night, afraid of knowledge, feeling himself full of unknown shames and disappointments. The shapelessness of his doubt was worse than certainty would have been; even certainty of arro-

192

gance, indifference, or of having overridden justice for the sake of ambition.

But the more he pulled and struggled with it, the more stubbornly it resisted; it would come only thread by thread, without cohesion, a fragment at a time. Where had he learned his careful, precise diction? Who had taught him to move and to dress like a gentleman, to be so easy in his manners? Had he merely aped his betters over the years? Something very vague stirred in his mind, a feeling rather than a thought, that there had been someone he admired, someone who had taken time and trouble, a mentor—but no voice, nothing but an impression of working, practicing—and an ideal.

The people from whom they learned more about Joscelin Grey were the Dawlishes. Their house was in Primrose Hill, not far from the Zoological Gardens, and Monk and Evan went to visit them the day after returning from Shelburne. They were admitted by a butler too well trained to show surprise, even at the sight of policemen on the front doorstep. Mrs. Dawlish received them in the morning room. She was a small, mild-featured woman with faded hazel eyes and brown hair which escaped its pins.

"Mr. Monk?" She queried his name because it obviously meant nothing to her.

Monk bowed very slightly.

"Yes ma'am; and Mr. Evan. If Mr. Evan might have your permission to speak to the servants and see if they can be of assistance?"

"I think it unlikely, Mr. Monk." The idea was obviously futile in her estimation. "But as long as he does not distract them from their duties, of course he may."

"Thank you, ma'am." Evan departed with alacrity, leaving Monk still standing.

"About poor Joscelin Grey?" Mrs. Dawlish was puzzled and a little nervous, but apparently not unwilling to help. "What can we tell you? It was a most terrible tragedy. We had not known him very long, you know."

"How long, Mrs. Dawlish?"

"About five weeks before he . . . died." She sat down and he was glad to follow suit. "I believe it cannot have been more."

"But you invited him to stay with you? Do you often do that, on such short acquaintance?"

She shook her head, another strand of hair came undone and she ignored it.

"No, no hardly ever. But of course he was Menard Grey's brother—" Her face was suddenly hurt, as if something had betrayed her inexplicably and without warning, wounding where she had believed herself safe. "And Joscelin was so charming, so very natural," she went on. "And of course he also knew Edward, my eldest son, who was killed at Inkermann."

"I'm sorry."

Her face was very stiff, and for a moment he was afraid she would not be able to control herself. He spoke to cover the silence and her embarrassment.

"You said 'also.' Did Menard Grey know your son?"

"Oh yes," she said quietly. "They were close friends—for years." Her eyes filled with tears. "Since school."

"So you invited Joscelin Grey to stay with you?" He did not wait for her to reply; she was beyond speech. "That's very natural." Then quite a new idea occurred to him with sudden, violent hope. Perhaps the murder was nothing to do with any current scandal, but a legacy from the war, something that had happened on the battlefield? It was possible. He should have thought of it before—they all should.

"Yes," she said very quietly, mastering herself again. "If he knew Edward in the war, we wanted to talk with him, listen to him. You see—here at home, we know so little of what really happened." She took a deep breath. "I am not sure if it helps, indeed in some ways it is harder, but we feel . . . less cut off. I know Edward is dead and it cannot matter to him anymore; it isn't reasonable, but I feel closer to him, however it hurts."

She looked at him with a curious need to be understood.

194

Perhaps she had explained precisely this to other people, and they had tried to dissuade her, not realizing that for her, being excluded from her son's suffering was not a kindness but an added loss.

"Of course," he agreed quietly. His own situation was utterly different, yet any knowledge would surely be better than this uncertainty. "The imagination conjures so many things, and one feels the pain of them all, until one knows."

Her eyes widened in surprise. "You understand? So many friends have tried to persuade me into acceptance, but it gnaws away at the back of my mind, a sort of dreadful doubt. I read the newspapers sometimes"—she blushed—"when my husband is out of the house. But I don't know what to believe of them. Their accounts are—" She sighed, crumpling her handkerchief in her lap, her fingers clinging around it. "Well, they are sometimes a little softened so as not to distress us, or make us feel critical of those in command. And they are sometimes at variance with each other."

"I don't doubt it." He felt an unreasonable anger for the confusion of this woman, and all the silent multitude like her, grieving for their dead and being told that the truth was too harsh for them. Perhaps it was, perhaps many could not have borne it, but they had not been consulted, simply told; as their sons had been told to fight. For what? He had no idea. He had looked at many newspapers in the last few weeks, trying to learn, and he still had only the dimmest notion—something to do with the Turkish Empire and the balance of power.

"Joscelin used to speak to us so—so carefully," she went on softly, watching his face. "He told us a great deal about how he felt, and Edward must have felt the same. I had had no idea it was so very dreadful. One just doesn't know, sitting here in England—" She stared at him anxiously. "It wasn't very glorious, you know—not really. So many men dead, not because the enemy killed them, but from the cold and the disease. He told us about the hospital at Scutari. He was there, you know; with a wound in his leg. He suffered quite appallingly. He told us about seeing men freezing to death in the winter. I had not known the Crimea was cold like that. I suppose it was because it was east from here, and I always think of the East as being hot. He said it was hot in the summer, and dry. Then with winter there was endless rain and snow, and winds that all but cut the flesh. And the disease." Her face pinched. "I thanked God that if Edward had to die, at least it was quickly, of a bullet, or a sword, not cholera. Yes, Joscelin was a great comfort to me, even though I wept as I hadn't done before; not only for Edward, but for all the others, and for the women like me, who lost sons and husbands. Do you understand, Mr. Monk?"

"Yes," he said quickly. "Yes I do. I'm very sorry I have to distress you now by speaking of Major Grey's death. But we must find whoever killed him."

She shuddered.

"How could anyone be so vile? What evil gets into a man that he could beat another to death like that? A fight I deplore, but I can understand it; but to go on, to mutilate a man after he is dead! The newspapers say it was dreadful. Of course my husband does not know I read them—having known the poor man, I felt I had to. Do you understand it, Mr. Monk?"

"No, I don't. In all the crimes I have investigated, I have not seen one like this." He did not know if it was true, but he felt it. "He must have been hated with a passion hard to conceive."

"I cannot imagine it, such a violence of feeling." She closed her eyes and shook her head fractionally. "Such a wish to destroy, to—to disfigure. Poor Joscelin, to have been the victim of such a—a creature. It would frighten me even to think someone could feel such an intensity of hatred for me, even if I were quite sure they could not touch me, and I were innocent of its cause. I wonder if poor Joscelin knew?"

It was a thought that had not occurred to Monk before—

196

had Joscelin Grey had any idea that his killer hated him? Had he known, but merely thought him impotent to act?

"He cannot have feared him," he said aloud. "Or he would hardly have allowed him into his rooms while he was alone."

"Poor man." She hunched her shoulders involuntarily, as if chilled. "It is very frightening to think that someone with that madness in their hearts could walk around, looking like you or me. I wonder if anyone dislikes me intensely and I have no idea of it. I had never entertained such a thought before, but now I cannot help it. I shall be unable to look at people as I used to. Are people often killed by those they know quite well?"

"Yes ma'am, I am afraid so; most often of all by relatives."

"How appalling." Her voice was very soft, her eyes staring at some spot beyond him. "And how very tragic."

"Yes it is." He did not want to seem crass, nor indifferent to her horror, but he had to pursue the business of it. "Did Major Grey ever say anything about threats, or anyone who might be afraid of him—"

She lifted her eyes to look at him; her brow was puckered and another strand of hair escaped the inadequate pins. "Afraid of him? But it was he who was killed!"

"People are like other animals," he replied. "They most often kill when they are afraid themselves."

"I suppose so. I had not thought of that." She shook her head a little, still puzzled. "But Joscelin was the most harmless of people! I never heard him speak as if he bore real ill will towards anyone. Of course he had a sharp wit, but one does not kill over a joke, even if it is a trifle barbed, and possibly even not in the kindest of taste."

"Even so," he pressed, "against whom were these remarks directed?"

She hesitated, not only in an effort to remember, but it seemed the memory was disturbing her.

He waited.

"Mostly against his own family," she said slowly. "At

197

least that was how it sounded to me—and I think to others.
His comments on Menard were not always kind, although
my husband knows more of that than I—I always liked
Menard—but then that was no doubt because he and Edward were so close. Edward loved him dearly. They shared
so much—'' She blinked and screwed up her mild face
even more. "But then Joscelin often spoke harshly of himself also—it is hard to understand.''

"Of himself?" Monk was surprised. "I've been to his
family, naturally, and I can understand a certain resentment. But in what way of himself?''

"Oh, because he had no property, being a third son;
and after his being wounded he limped, you know. So of
course there was no career for him in the army. He appeared to feel he was of little—little standing—that no one
accounted him much. Which was quite untrue, of course.
He was a hero—and much liked by all manner of people!''

"I see.'' Monk was thinking of Rosamond Shelburne,
obliged by her mother to marry the son with the title and
the prospects. Had Joscelin loved her, or was it more an
insult than a wound, a reminder that he was third best?
Had he cared, it could only have hurt him that she had not
the courage to follow her heart and marry as she wished.
Or was the status more important to her, and she had used
Joscelin to reach Lovel? That would perhaps have hurt
differently, with a bitterness that would remain.

Perhaps they would never know the answer to that.

He changed the subject. "Did he at any time mention
what his business interests were? He must have had some
income beyond the allowance from his family.''

"Oh yes,'' she agreed. "He did discuss it with my husband, and he mentioned it to me, although not in any great
detail.''

"And what was it, Mrs. Dawlish?''

"I believe it was some investment, quite a sizable one,
in a company to trade with Egypt.'' The memory of it was
bright in her face for a moment, the enthusiasm and expectation of that time coming back.

"Was Mr. Dawlish involved in this investment?"

"He was considering it; he spoke highly of its possibilities."

"I see. May I call again later when Mr. Dawlish is at home, and learn more details of this company from him?"

"Oh dear." The lightness vanished. "I am afraid I have expressed myself badly. The company is not yet formed. I gathered it was merely a prospect that Joscelin intended to pursue."

Monk considered for a moment. If Grey were only forming a company, and perhaps persuading Dawlish to invest, then what had been his source of income up to that time?

"Thank you." He stood up slowly. "I understand. All the same, I should like to speak to Mr. Dawlish. He may well know something about Mr. Grey's finances. If he were contemplating entering business with him, it would be natural he should inquire."

"Yes, yes of course." She poked ineffectually at her hair. "Perhaps about six o'clock."

Evan's questioning of the half-dozen or so domestic servants yielded nothing except the picture of a very ordinary household, well run by a quiet, sad woman stricken with a grief she bore as bravely as she could, but of which they were all only too aware and each in their own way shared. The butler had a nephew who served as a foot soldier and had returned a cripple. Evan was suddenly sobered by the remembrance of so many other losses, so many people who had to struggle on without the notoriety, or the sympathy, of Joscelin Grey's family.

The sixteen-year-old between-stairs maid had lost an elder brother at Inkermann. They all recalled Major Grey, how charming he was, and that Miss Amanda was very taken with him. They had hoped he would return, and were horrified that he could be so terribly murdered right here in his home. They had an obvious duality of thought that confounded Evan—it shocked them that a gentleman

199

should be so killed, and yet they viewed their own losses as things merely to be borne with quiet dignity.

He came away with an admiration for their stoicism, and an anger that they should accept the difference so easily. Then as he came through the green baize door back into the main hallway, the thought occurred to him that perhaps that was the only way of bearing it—anything else would be too destructive, and in the end only futile.

And he had learned little of Joscelin Grey that he had not already deduced from the other calls.

Dawlish was a stout, expensively dressed man with a high forehead and dark, clever eyes, but at present he was displeased at the prospect of speaking with the police, and appeared distinctly ill at ease. There was no reason to assume it was an unquiet conscience; to have the police at one's house, for any reason, was socially highly undesirable, and judging from the newness of the furniture and the rather formal photographs of the family—Mrs. Dawlish seated in imitation of the Queen—Mr. Dawlish was an ambitious man.

It transpired that he knew remarkably little about the business he had half committed himself to support. His involvement was with Joscelin Grey personally, and it was this which had caused him to promise funds, and the use of his good name. "Charming fellow," he said, half facing Monk as he stood by the parlor fire. "Hard when you're brought up in a family, part of it and all that, then the eldest brother marries and suddenly you're nobody." He shook his head grimly. "Dashed hard to make your way if you're not suited to the church, and invalided out of the army. Only thing really is to marry decently." He looked at Monk to see if he understood. "Don't know why young Joscelin didn't, certainly a handsome enough chap, and pleasing with women. Had all the charm, right words to say, and so on. Amanda thought the world of him." He coughed. "My daughter, you know. Poor girl was very distressed over his death. Dreadful thing! Quite appalling." He stared down at the embers and a sharp sadness filled his eyes and softened the lines around his mouth. "Such a decent man. Expect it in the Crimea, die for your country, and so on; but not this. Lost her first suitor at Sebastopol, poor girl; and of course her brother at Balaclava. That's where he met young Grey." He swallowed hard and looked up at Monk, as if to defy his emotions. "Damned good to him." He took a deep breath and fought to control a conflict of emotions that were obviously acutely painful. "Actually spoke to each other night before the battle. Like to think of that, someone we've met, with Edward the night before he was killed. Been a great source of—" He coughed again and was forced to look away, his eyes brimming. "Comfort to us, my wife and I. Taken it hard, poor woman; only son, you know. Five daughters. And now this."

"I understand Menard Grey was also a close friend of your son's," Monk said, as much to fill the silence as that it might have mattered.

Dawlish stared at the coals. "Prefer not to speak of it," he replied with difficulty, his voice husky. "Thought a lot of him—but he led Edward into bad ways—no doubt about it. It was Joscelin who paid his debts—so he did not die with dishonor."

He swallowed convulsively. "We became fond of Joscelin, even on the few weekends he stayed with us." He lifted the poker out of its rest and jabbed at the fire fiercely. "I hope to heaven you catch the madman who did it."

"We'll do everything we can, sir." Monk wanted to say all sorts of other things to express the pity he felt for so much loss. Thousands of men and horses had died, frozen, starved, or been massacred or wasted by disease on the bitter hillsides of a country they neither knew nor loved. If he had ever known the purpose of the war in the Crimea he had forgotten it now. It could hardly have been a war of defense. Crimea was a thousand miles from England. Presumably from the newspapers it was something to do with the political ramifications of Turkey and its

201

disintegrating empire. It hardly seemed a reason for the wretched, pitiful deaths of so many, and the grief they left behind.

Dawlish was staring at him, waiting for him to say something, expecting a platitude.

"I am sorry your son had to die in such a way." Monk held out his hand automatically. "And so young. But at least Joscelin Grey was able to assure you it was with courage and dignity, and that his suffering was brief."

Dawlish took his hand before he had time to think.

"Thank you." There was a faint flush on his skin and he was obviously moved. He did not even realize until after Monk had gone that he had shaken hands with a policeman as frankly as if he had been a gentleman.

That evening Monk found himself for the first time caring about Grey personally. He sat in his own quiet room with nothing but the faint noises from the street in the distance below. In the small kindnesses to the Dawlishes, in paying a dead man's debts, Grey had developed a solidity far more than in the grief of his mother or the pleasant but rather insubstantial memories of his neighbors. He had become a man with a past of something more than a resentment that his talent was wasted while the lesser gifts of his elder brother were overrewarded, more than the rejected suitor of a weak young woman who preferred the ease of doing as she was told and the comfort of status to the relative struggle of following her own desires. Or perhaps she had not really wanted anything enough to fight for it?

Shelburne was comfortable, physically everything was provided; one did not have to work, morally there were no decisions—if something was unpleasant one did not have to look at it. If there were beggars in the street, mutilated or diseased, one could pass to the other side. There was the government to make the social decisions, and the church to make the moral ones.

Of course society demanded a certain, very rigid code of conduct, of taste, and a very small circle of friends and suitable ways to pass one's time, but for those who had been brought up from childhood to observe it, it was little extra effort.

Small wonder if Joscelin Grey was angry with it, even contemptuous after he had seen the frozen bodies on the heights before Sebastopol, the carnage at Balaclava, the filth, the disease and the agony of Scutari.

In the street below a carriage clattered by and someone shouted and there was a roar of laughter.

Suddenly Monk found himself feeling this same strange, almost impersonal disgust Grey must have suffered coming back to England afterwards, to a family who were strangers insofar as their petty, artificial little world was concerned; who knew only the patriotic placebos they read in the newspapers, and had no wish to look behind them for uglier truths.

He had felt the same himself after visiting the "rookeries," the hell-like, rotting tenements crawling with vermin and disease, sometimes only a few dozen yards from the lighted streets where gentlemen rode in carriages from one sumptuous house to another. He had seen fifteen or twenty people in one room, all ages and sexes together, without heating or sanitation. He had seen child prostitutes of eight or ten years old with eyes tired and old as sin, and bodies riddled with venereal disease; children of five or even less frozen to death in the gutters because they could not beg a night's shelter. Small wonder they stole, or sold for a few pence the only things they possessed, their own bodies.

How did he remember that, when his own father's face was still a blank to him? He must have cared very much, been so shocked by it that it left a scar he could not forget, even now. Was that, at least in part, the fire behind his ambition, the fire behind his relentless drive to improve himself, to copy the mentor whose features he could not recall, whose name, whose station, eluded him? Please God that was so. It made a more tolerable man of him, even one he could begin to accept.

Had Joscelin Grey cared?

Monk intended to avenge him; he would not be merely another unsolved mystery, a man remembered for his death rather than his life.

And he must pursue the Latterly case. He could hardly go back to Mrs. Latterly without knowing at least the outline of the matter he had promised her to solve, however painful the truth. And he did intend to go back to her. Now that he thought about it, he realized he had always intended to visit her again, speak with her, see her face, listen to her voice, watch the way she moved; command her attention, even for so short a time.

There was no use looking among his files again; he had already done that almost page by page. Instead he went directly to Runcorn.

"Morning, Monk." Runcorn was not at his desk but over by the window, and he sounded positively cheerful; his rather sallow face was touched with color as if he had walked briskly in the sun, and his eyes were bright. "How's the Grey case coming along? Got something to tell the newspapers yet? They're still pressing, you know." He sniffed faintly and reached in his pocket for a cigar. "They'll be calling for our blood soon; resignations, and that sort of thing!"

Monk could see his satisfaction in the way he stood, shoulders a little high, chin up, the shine on his shoes gleaming in the light.

"Yes sir, I imagine they will," he conceded. "But as you said over a week ago, it's one of those investigations that is bound to rake up something extremely unpleasant, possibly several things. It would be very rash to say anything before we can prove it."

"Have you got anything at all, Monk?" Runcorn's face hardened, but his sense of anticipation was still there, his scent of blood. "Or are you as lost as Lamb was?"

"It looks at the moment as if it could be in the family, sir," Monk replied as levelly as he could. He had a sick-

204

ening awareness that Runcorn was controlling this, and enjoying it. "There was considerable feeling between the brothers," he went on. "The present Lady Shelburne was courted by Joscelin before she married Lord Shelburne—"

"Hardly a reason to murder him," Runcorn said with contempt. "Would only make sense if it had been Shelburne who was murdered. Doesn't sound as if you have anything there!"

Monk kept his temper. He felt Runcorn trying to irritate him, provoke him into betraying all the pent-up past that lay between them; victory would be sweeter if it were acknowledged, and could be savored in the other's presence. Monk wondered how he could have been so insensitive, so stupid as not to have known it before. Why had he not forestalled it, even avoided it altogether? How had he been so blind then when now it was so glaring? Was it really no more than that he was rediscovering himself, fact by fact, from the outside?

"Not that in itself." He went back to the question, keeping his voice light and calm. "But I think the lady still preferred Joscelin, and her one child, conceived just before Joscelin went to the Crimea, looks a good deal more like him than like his lordship."

Runcorn's face fell, then slowly widened again in a smile, showing all his teeth; the cigar was still unlit in his hand.

"Indeed. Yes. Well, I warned you it would be nasty, didn't I? You'll have to be careful, Monk; make any allegations you can't prove, and the Shelburnes will have you dismissed before you've time to get back to London."

Which is just what you want, Monk thought.

"Precisely sir," he said aloud. "That is why as far as the newspapers are concerned, we are still in the dark. I came because I wanted to ask you about the Latterly case—"

"Latterly! What the hell does that matter? Some poor devil committed suicide." He walked around and sat down at his desk and began fishing for matches. "It's a crime for the church, not for us. Have you got any matches, Monk? We wouldn't have taken any notice of it at all if that wretched woman hadn't raised it. Ah—don't bother, here they are. Let them bury their own dead quietly, no fuss." He struck a light and held it to his cigar, puffing gently. "Man got in over his head with a business deal that went sour. All his friends invested in it on his recommendation, and he couldn't take the shame of it. Took that way out; some say coward's way, some say it's the honorable way." He blew out smoke and stared up at Monk. "Damn silly, I call it. But that class is very jealous of what it thinks is its good name. Some of them will keep servants they can't afford for the sake of appearance, serve six-course meals to guests, and live on bread and dripping the rest of the time. Light a fire when there's company, and perish with cold the rest of the time. Pride is a wicked master, most especially social pride." His eyes flickered with malicious pleasure. "Remember that, Monk."

He looked down at the papers in front of him. "Why on earth are you bothering with Latterly? Get on with Grey; we need to solve it, however painful it may prove. The public won't wait much longer; they're even asking questions in the House of Lords. Did you know that?"

"No sir, but considering how Lady Shelburne feels, I'm not surprised. Do you have a file on the Latterly case, sir?"

"You are a stubborn man, Monk. It's a very dubious quality. I've got your written report that it was a suicide, and nothing to concern us. You don't want that again, do you?"

"Yes sir, I do." Monk took it without looking at it and walked out.

He had to visit the Latterlys' house in the evening, in his own time, since he was not officially working on any case that involved them. He must have been here before; he could not have met with Mrs. Latterly casually, nor expected her to report to the police station. He looked up and down the street, but there was nothing familiar in it.

The only streets he could remember were the cold cobbles of Northumberland, small houses whipped clean by the wind, gray seas and the harbor below and the high moors rising to the sky. He could remember vaguely, once, a visit to Newcastle in the train, the enormous furnaces towering over the rooftops, the plumes of smoke, the excitement running through him in their immense, thrumming power, the knowledge of coal-fired blast furnaces inside; steel hammered and beaten into engines to draw trains over the mountains and plains of the whole Empire. He could still capture just an echo of the thrill that had been high in his throat then, tingling his arms and legs, the awe, the beginning of adventure. He must have been very young.

It had been quite different when he had first come to London. He had been so much older, more than the ten or so years the calendar had turned. His mother was dead; Beth was with an aunt. His father had been lost at sea when Beth was still in arms. Coming to London had been the beginning of something new, and the end of all that belonged to childhood. Beth had seen him off at the station, crying, screwing up her pinafore in her hand, refusing to be comforted. She could not have been more than nine, and he about fifteen. But he could read and write, and the world was his for the labor.

But that was a long time ago. He was well over thirty now, probably over thirty-five. What had he done in more than twenty years? Why had he not returned? That was something else he had yet to learn. His police record was there in his office, and in Runcorn's hate. What about himself, his personal life? Or had he no one, was he only a public man?

And what before the police? His files here went back only twelve years, so there must have been more than eight years before that. Had he spent them all learning, climbing, improving himself with his faceless mentor, his eyes always on the goal? He was appalled at his own ambition, and the strength of his will. It was a little frightening, such single-mindedness.

He was at the Latterlys' door, ridiculously nervous. Would she be in? He had thought about her so often; he realized only now and with a sense of having been foolish, vulnerable, that she had probably not thought of him at all. He might even have to explain who he was. He would seem clumsy, gauche, when he said he had no further news.

He hesitated, unsure whether to knock at all, or to leave, and come again when he had a better excuse. A maid came out into the areaway below him, and in order not to appear a loiterer, he raised his hand and knocked.

The parlor maid came almost immediately. Her eyebrows rose in the very slightest of surprise.

"Good evening, Mr. Monk; will you come in, sir?" It was sufficiently courteous not to be in obvious haste to get him off the doorstep. "The family have dined and are in the withdrawing room, sir. Do you wish me to ask if they will receive you?"

"Yes please. Thank you." Monk gave her his coat and followed her through to a small morning room. After she had gone he paced up and down because he could not bear to be still. He hardly noticed anything about the furniture or the pleasant, rather ordinary paintings and the worn carpet. What was he going to say? He had charged into a world where he did not belong, because of something he dreamed in a woman's face. She probably found him distasteful, and would not have suffered him if she were not so concerned about her father-in-law, hoping he could use his skills to discover something that would ease her grief. Suicide was a terrible shame, and in the eyes of the church financial disgrace would not excuse it. He could still be buried in unconsecrated ground if the conclusion were inevitable.

It was too late to back away now, but it crossed his mind. He even considered concocting an excuse, another reason for calling, something to do with Grey and the letter in his flat, when the parlor maid returned and there was no time.

"Mrs. Latterly will see you, sir, if you come this way."

Obediently, heart thumping and mouth dry, he followed the maid.

The withdrawing room was medium sized, comfortable, and originally furnished with the disregard for money of those who have always possessed it, but the ease, the unostentation of those for whom it has no novelty. Now it was still elegant, but the curtains were a little faded in portions where the sun fell on them, and the fringing on the swags with which they were tied was missing a bobble here and there. The carpet was not of equal quality with the pie-crust tables or the chaise longue. He felt pleasure in the room immediately, and wondered where in his merciless self-improvement he had learned such taste.

His eyes went to Mrs. Latterly beside the fire. She was no longer in black, but dark wine, and it brought a faint flush to her skin. Her throat and shoulders were as delicate and slender as a child's, but there was nothing of the child in her face. She was staring at him with luminous eyes, wide now, and too shadowed to read their expression.

Monk turned quickly to the others. The man, fairer than she and with less generous mouth, must be her husband, and the other woman sitting opposite with the proud face with so much anger and imagination in it he knew immediately; they had met and quarreled at Shelburne Hall—Miss Hester Latterly.

"Good evening, Monk." Charles Latterly did not stand. "You remember my wife?" He gestured vaguely towards Imogen. "And my sister, Miss Hester Latterly. She was in the Crimea when our father died." There was a strong accent of disapproval in his voice and it was apparent that he resented Monk's involvement in the affair.

Monk was assailed by an awful thought—had he somehow disgraced himself, been too brash, too insensitive to their pain and added not only to their loss but the manner of it? Had he said something appallingly thoughtless, or been too familiar? The blood burned up his face and he stumbled into speech to cover the hot silence.

"Good evening, sir." Then he bowed very slightly to Imogen and then to Hester. "Good evening, ma'am; Miss Latterly." He would not mention that they had already met. It was not a fortunate episode.

"What can we do for you?" Charles asked, nodding towards a seat, indicating that Monk might make himself comfortable.

Monk accepted, and another extraordinary thought occurred to him. Imogen had been very discreet, almost furtive in speaking to him in St. Marylebone Church. Was it conceivable neither her husband nor her sister-in-law knew that she had pursued the matter beyond the first, formal acknowledgment of the tragedy and the necessary formalities? If that were so he must not betray her now.

He drew a deep breath, hoping he could make sense, wishing to God he could remember anything at all of what Charles had told him, and what he had learned from Imogen alone. He would have to bluff, pretend there was something new, a connection with the murder of Grey; it was the only other case he was working on, or could remember anything at all about. These people had known him, however slightly. He had been working for them shortly before the accident; surely they could tell him something about himself?

But that was less than half a truth. Why lie to himself? He was here because of Imogen Latterly. It was purposeless, but her face haunted his mind, like a memory from the past of which the precise nature is lost, or a ghost from the imagination, from the realm of daydreams so often repeated it seems they must surely have been real.

They were all looking at him, still waiting.

"It is possible . . ." His voice was rough at first. He cleared his throat. "I have discovered something quite new. But before I tell you I must be perfectly sure, more especially since it concerns other people." That should prevent them, as a matter of good taste, from pressing him. He coughed again. "It is some time since I spoke to you last, and I made no notes, as a point of discretion—"

"Thank you," Charles said slowly. "That was considerate of you." He seemed to find it hard to say the words, as if it irritated him to acknowledge that policemen might possess such delicate virtues.

Hester was staring at him with frank disbelief.

"If I could go over the details we know again?" Monk asked, hoping desperately they would fill in the gaping blanks in his mind; he knew only what Runcorn had told him, and that was in turn only what he had told Runcorn. Heaven knew, that was barely enough to justify spending time on the case.

"Yes, yes of course." Again it was Charles who spoke, but Monk felt the eyes of the women on him also: Imogen anxious, her hands clenched beneath the ample folds of her skirt, her dark eyes wide; Hester was thoughtful, ready to criticize. He must dismiss them both from his mind, concentrate on making sense, picking up the threads from Charles, or he would make a complete fool of himself, and he could not bear that in front of them.

"Your father died in his study," he began. "In his home in Highgate on June fourteenth." That much Runcorn had said.

"Yes." Charles agreed. "It was early evening, before dinner. My wife and I were staying with them at the time. Most of us were upstairs changing."

"Most of you?"

"Perhaps I should say 'both of us.' My mother and I were. My wife was late coming in. She had been over to see Mrs. Standing, the vicar's wife, and as it transpired my father was in his study."

The means of death had been a gunshot. The next question was easy.

"And how many of you heard the report?"

"Well, I suppose we all heard it, but my wife was the

211

only one to realize what it was. She was coming in from the back garden entrance and was in the conservatory."

Monk turned to Imogen.

She was looking at him, a slight frown on her face as if she wanted to say something, but dared not. Her eyes were troubled, full of dark hurt.

"Mrs. Latterly?" He forgot what he had intended to ask her. He was conscious of his hands clenched painfully by his sides and had to ease the fingers out deliberately. They were sticky with sweat.

"Yes, Mr. Monk?" she said quietly.

He scrambled for something sensible to say. His brain was blank. What had he said to her the first time? She had come to him; surely she would have told him everything she knew? He must ask her something quickly. They were all waiting, watching him. Charles Latterly cool, disliking the effrontery, Hester exasperated at his incompetence. He already knew what she thought of his abilities. Attack was the only defense his mind could think of.

"Why do you think, Mrs. Latterly, that you suspected a shot, when no one else did?" His voice was loud in the silence, like the sudden chimes of a clock in an empty room. "Were you afraid even then that your father-in-law contemplated taking his life, or that he was in some danger?"

The color came to her face quickly and there was anger in her eyes.

"Of course not, Mr. Monk; or I should not have left him alone." She swallowed, and her next words were softer. "I knew he was distressed, we all knew that; but I did not imagine it was serious enough to think of shooting himself—nor that he was sufficiently out of control of his feelings or his concentration that he would be in danger of having an accident." It was a brave attempt.

"I think if you have discovered something, Mr. Monk," Hester interrupted stiffly, "you had better ascertain what it is, and then come back and tell us. Your present fumbling around is pointless and unnecessarily distressing.

212

And your suggestion that my sister-in-law knew something that she did not report at the time is offensive." She looked him up and down with some disgust. "Really, is this the best you can do? I don't know how you catch anyone, unless you positively fall over them!"

"Hester!" Imogen spoke quite sharply, although she kept her eyes averted. "It is a question Mr. Monk must ask. It is possible I may have seen or heard something to make me anxious—and only realize it now in retrospect."

Monk felt a quick, foolish surge of pleasure. He had not deserved defending.

"Thank you, ma'am." He tried to smile at her, and felt his lips grimacing. "Did you at that time know the full extent of your father-in-law's financial misfortune?"

"It was not the money that killed him," Imogen replied before Charles could get his own words formed and while Hester was still standing in resigned silence—at least temporarily. "It was the disgrace." She bit her lip on all the distress returned to her. Her voice dropped to little more than a whisper, tight with pity. "You see, he had advised so many of his friends to invest. He had lent his name to it, and they had put in money because they trusted him."

Monk could think of nothing to say, and platitudes offended him in the face of real grief. He longed to be able to comfort her, and knew it was impossible. Was this the emotion that surged through him so intensely—pity? And the desire to protect?

"The whole venture has brought nothing but tragedy," Imogen went on very softly, staring at the ground. "Papa-in-law, then poor Mama, and now Joscelin as well."

For an instant everything seemed suspended, an age between the time she spoke and the moment overwhelming realization of what she had said came to Monk.

"You knew Joscelin Grey?" It was as if another person spoke for him and he was still distant, watching strangers, removed from him, on the other side of a glass.

Imogen frowned a little, confused by his apparent unreason; there was a deep color in her face and she lowered

213

her eyes the moment after she had spoken, avoiding everyone else's, especially her husband's.

"For the love of heaven!" Charles's temper snapped. "Are you completely incompetent, man?"

Monk had no idea what to say. What on earth had Grey to do with it? Had he known him?

What were they thinking of him? How could he possibly make sense of it now? They could only conclude he was mad, or was playing some disgusting joke. It was the worst possible taste—life was not sacred to them, but death most certainly was. He could feel the embarrassment burning in his face, and was as conscious of Imogen as if she were touching him, and of Hester's eyes filled with unutterable contempt.

Again it was Imogen who rescued him.

"Mr. Monk never met Joscelin, Charles," she said quietly. "It is very easy to forget a name when you do not know the person to whom it belongs."

Hester stared from one to the other of them, her clear, intelligent eyes filled with a growing perception that something was profoundly wrong.

"Of course," Imogen said more briskly, covering her feelings. "Mr. Monk did not come until after Papa was dead; there was no occasion." She did not look at her husband, but she was obviously speaking to him. "And if you recall, Joscelin did not return after that."

"You can hardly blame him." Charles's voice contained a sharpening of criticism, an implication that Imogen was somehow being unfair. "He was as distressed as we were. He wrote me a very civil letter, expressing his condolences." He put his hands in his pocket, hard, and hunched his shoulders. "Naturally, he felt it unsuitable to call, in the circumstances. He quite understood our association must end; very delicate of him, I thought." He looked at Imogen with impatience, and ignored Hester altogether.

"That was like him, so very sensitive." Imogen was looking far away. "I do miss him."

Charles swiveled to look at her beside him. He seemed

214

about to say something, and then changed his mind and bit it off. Instead he took his hand out of his pocket and put it around her arm. "So you didn't meet him?" he said to Monk.

Monk was still floundering.

"No." It was the only answer he had left himself room to make. "He was out of town." Surely that at least could have been true?

"Poor Joscelin." Imogen appeared unaware of her husband, or his fingers tightening on her shoulder. "He must have felt dreadful," she went on. "Of course he was not responsible, he was as deceived as any of us, but he was the sort of person who would take it on himself." Her voice was sad, gentle and utterly without criticism.

Monk could only guess, he dared not ask: Grey must somehow have been involved in the business venture in which Latterly Senior lost money, and so ill advised his friends. And it would seem Joscelin had lost money himself, which he could hardly afford; hence perhaps the request to the family estate for an increased allowance? The date on the letter from the solicitor was about right, shortly after Latterly's death. Possibly it was that financial disaster that had prompted Joscelin Grey to gamble rashly, or to descend to blackmail. If he had lost enough in the business he might have been desperate, with creditors pressing, social disgrace imminent. Charm was his only stock in trade; his entertainment value was his passport to hospitality in other people's houses the year round, and his only path to the heiress who might ultimately make him independent, no longer begging from his mother and the brother he scarcely loved.

But who? Who among his acquaintances was vulnerable enough to pay for silence; and desperate, murderous enough to kill for it?

Whose houses had he stayed in? All sorts of indiscretions were committed on long weekends away from the city. Scandal was not a matter of what was done but of what was known to have been done. Had Joscelin stumbled on some well-kept secret adultery?

But adultery was hardly worth killing over, unless there was a child to inherit, or some other domestic crisis, a suit for divorce with all its scandal, and the complete social ostracism that followed. To kill would need a secret far worse, like incest, perversion or impotence. The shame of impotence was mortal, God knew why, but it was the most abhorred of afflictions, something not even whispered of.

Runcorn was right, even to speak of such a possibility would be enough to have him reported to the highest authorities, his career blocked forever, if he were not dismissed out of hand. He could never be forgiven for exposing a man to the ruin which must follow such an abominable scandal.

They were all staring at him. Charles was making no secret of his impatience. Hester was exasperated almost beyond endurance; her fingers were fiddling with the plain cambric handkerchief and her foot tapped rapidly and silently on the floor. Her opinion was in every line of her remarkable face.

"What is it you think you may know, Mr. Monk?" Charles said sharply. "If there is nothing, I would ask that you do not distress us again by raking over what can only be to us a tragedy. Whether my father took his own life or it was an accident while his mind was distracted with distress cannot be proved, and we should be obliged if you allowed those who are charitable enough to allow that it might have been an accident to prevail! My mother died of a broken heart. One of our past friends has been brutally murdered. If we cannot be of assistance to you, I would prefer that you permit us to come to terms with our grief in our own way, and do our best to resume the pattern of our lives again. My wife was quite wrong to have persisted in her hope for some more pleasant alternative, but women are tenderhearted by nature, and she finds it hard to accept a bitter truth."

"All she wished of me was to ascertain that it was indeed the truth," Monk said quickly, instinctively angry that Imogen should be criticized. "I cannot believe that mistaken." He stared with chill, level eyes at Charles.

"That is courteous of you, Mr. Monk." Charles glanced at Imogen condescendingly, to imply that Monk had been humoring her. "But I have no doubt she will come to the same conclusion, in time. Thank you for calling; I am sure you have done what you believed to be your duty."

Monk accepted the dismissal and was in the hall before he realized what he had done. He had been thinking of Imogen, and of Hester's scalding disdain, and he had allowed himself to be awed by the house, by Charles Latterly's self-assurance, his arrogance, and his very natural attempts to conceal a family tragedy and mask it in something less shameful.

He turned on his heel and faced the closed door again. He wanted to ask them about Grey, and he had the excuse for it, indeed he had no excuse not to. He took a step forward, and then felt foolish. He could hardly go back and knock like a servant asking entry. But he could not walk out of the house, knowing they had had a relationship with Joscelin Grey, that Imogen at least had cared for him, and not ask more. He stretched out his hand, then withdrew it again.

The door opened and Imogen came out. She stopped in surprise, a foot from him, her back against the panels. The color came up her face.

"I'm sorry." She took a breath. "I—I did not realize you were still here."

He did not know what to say either; he was idiotically speechless. Seconds ticked by. Eventually it was she who spoke.

"Was there something else, Mr. Monk? Have you found something?" Her voice lifted, all eagerness, hope in her eyes; and he felt sure now that she had come to him alone, trusted him with something she had not confided to her husband or Hester.

"I'm working on the Joscelin Grey case." It was the only thing he could think of to say. He was floundering in a morass of ignorance. If only he could remember!

Her eyes dropped. "Indeed. So that is why you came to see us. I'm sorry, I misunderstood. You—you wish to know something about Major Grey?"

It was far from the truth.

"I—" He drew a deep breath. "I dislike having to disturb you, so soon after—"

Her head came up, her eyes angry. He had no idea why. She was so lovely, so gentle; she woke yearnings in him for something his memory could not grasp: some old sweetness, a time of laughter and trust. How could he be stupid enough to feel this torrent of emotion for a woman who had simply come to him for help because of family tragedy, and almost certainly regarded him in the same light as she would the plumber or the fireman?

"Sorrows do not wait for one another." She was talking to him in a stiff little voice. "I know what the newspapers are saying. What do you wish to know about Major Grey? If we knew anything that was likely to be of help, we should have told you ourselves."

"Yes." He was withered by her anger, confusingly and painfully hurt by it. "Of course you would. I—I was just wondering if there was anything else I should have asked. I don't think there is. Good night, Mrs. Latterly."

"Good night, Mr. Monk." She lifted her head a little higher and he was not quite sure whether he saw her blink to disguise tears. But that was ridiculous—why should she weep now? Disappointment? Frustration? Disillusion in him, because she had hoped and expected better? If only he could remember!

"Parkin, will you show Mr. Monk to the door." And without looking at him again, or waiting for the maid, she walked away, leaving him alone.

9

Monk was obliged to go back to the Grey case, although both Imogen Latterly, with her haunting eyes, and Hester, with her anger and intelligence, intruded into his thoughts. Concentration was almost beyond him, and he had to drive himself even to think of its details and try to make patterns from the amorphous mass of facts and suppositions they had so far.

He sat in his office with Evan, reviewing the growing amount of it, but it was all inconclusive of any fact, negative and not positive. No one had broken in, therefore Grey had admitted his murderer himself; and if he had admitted him, then he had been unaware of any reason to fear him. It was not likely he would invite in a stranger at that time in the evening, so it was more probably someone he knew, and who hated him with an intense but secret violence.

Or did Grey know of the hatred, but feel himself safe from it? Did he believe that person powerless to injure, either for an emotional reason, or a physical? Even that answer was still beyond him.

The description both Yeats and Grimwade had given of the only visitor unaccounted for did not fit Lovel Grey, but it was so indistinct that it hardly mattered. If Rosamond Grey's child was Joscelin's, and not Lovel's, that could be reason enough for murder; especially if Joscelin himself knew it and perhaps had not been averse to keeping Lovel reminded. It would not be the first time a cruel tongue, the mockery at pain or impotence had ended in an uncontrolled rage.

Evan broke into his thoughts, almost as if he had read them.

"Do you suppose Shelburne killed Joscelin himself?" He was frowning, his face anxious, his wide eyes clouded. He had no need to fear for his own career—the establishment, even the Shelburnes, would not blame him for a scandal. Was he afraid for Monk? It was a warm thought.

Monk looked up at him.

"Perhaps not. But if he paid someone else, they would have been cleaner and more efficient about it, and less violent. Professionals don't beat a man to death; they usually either stab him or garrote him, and not in his own house."

Evan's delicate mouth turned down at the corners. "You mean an attack in the street, follow him to a quiet spot—and all over in a moment?"

"Probably; and leave the body in an alley where it won't be found too soon, preferably out of his own area. That way there would be less to connect them with the victim, and less of a risk of their being recognized."

"Perhaps he was in a hurry?" Evan suggested. "Couldn't wait for the right time and place?" He leaned back a little in his chair and tilted the legs.

"What hurry?" Monk shrugged. "No hurry if it was Shelburne, not if it were over Rosamond anyway. Couldn't matter a few days, or even a few weeks."

"No." Evan looked gloomy. He allowed the front legs of the chair to settle again. "I don't know how we begin to prove anything, or even where to look."

"Find out where Shelburne was at the time Grey was killed," Monk answered. "I should have done that before."

"Oh, I asked the servants, in a roundabout way." Evan's face was surprised, and there was a touch of satisfaction in it he could not conceal.

"And?" Monk asked quickly. He would not spoil Evan's pleasure.

"He was away from Shelburne; they were told he came to town for dinner. I followed it up. He was at the dinner all right, and spent the night at his club, off Tavistock Place. It would have been difficult for him to have been in Mecklenburg Square at the right time, because he might easily have been missed, but not at all impossible. If he'd gone along Compton Street, right down Hunter Street, 'round Brunswick Square and Lansdowne Place, past the Foundling Hospital, up Caroline Place—and he was there. Ten minutes at the outside, probably less. He'd have been gone at least three quarters of an hour, counting the fight with Grey—and returning. But he could have done it on foot—easily."

Monk smiled; Evan deserved praise and he was glad to give it.

"Thank you. I ought to have done that myself. It might even have been less time, if the quarrel was an old one—say ten minutes each way, and five minutes for the fight. That's not long for a man to be out of sight at a club."

Evan looked down, a faint color in his face. He was smiling.

"It doesn't get us any further," he pointed out ruefully. "It could have been Shelburne, or it could have been anyone else. I suppose we shall have to investigate every other family he could have blackmailed? That should make us rather less popular than the ratman. Do you think it was Shelburne, sir, and we'll just never prove it?"

Monk stood up.

"I don't know but I'm damned if it'll be for lack of trying." He was thinking of Joscelin Grey in the Crimea, seeing the horror of slow death by starvation, cold and disease, the blinding incompetence of commanders sending men to be blown to bits by enemy guns, the sheer stultifying of it all; feeling fear and physical pain, exhaustion, certainly pity, shown by his brief ministrations to the dying in Scutari—all while Lovel stayed at home in his great hall, marrying Rosamond, adding money to money, comfort to comfort.

Monk strode to the door. Injustice ached in him like a gathering boil, angry and festering. He pulled the handle sharply and jerked it open.

"Sir!" Evan half rose to his feet.

Monk turned.

Evan did not know the words, how to phrase the warning urgent inside him. Monk could see it in his face, the wide hazel eyes, the sensitive mouth.

"Don't look so alarmed," he said quietly, pushing the door to again. "I'm going back to Grey's flat. I remember a photograph of his family there. Shelburne was in it, and Menard Grey. I want to see if Grimwade or Yeats recognize either of them. Do you want to come?"

Evan's face ironed out almost comically with relief. He smiled in spite of himself.

"Yes sir. Yes I would." He reached for his coat and scarf. "Can you do that without letting them know who they are? If they know they were his brothers—I mean—Lord Shelburne—"

Monk looked at him sideways and Evan pulled a small face of apology.

"Yes of course," he muttered, following Monk outside. "Although the Shelburnes will deny it, of course, and they'll still ride us to hell and back if we press a charge!"

Monk knew that, and he had no plan even if anyone in the photograph were recognized, but it was a step forward, and he had to take it.

Grimwade was in his cubbyhole as usual and he greeted them cheerfully.

"Lovely mild day, sir." He squinted towards the street. "Looks as if it could clear up."

"Yes," Monk agreed without thinking. "Very pleasant." He was unaware of being wet. "We're going up to

222

Mr. Grey's rooms again, want to pick up one or two things."

"Well with all of you on the case, I 'spec' you'll get somewhere one of these days." Grimwade nodded, a faint trace of sarcasm in his rather lugubrious face. "You certainly are a busy lot, I'll give yer that."

Monk was halfway up the stairs with the key before the significance of Grimwade's remark came to him. He stopped sharply and Evan trod on his heel.

"Sorry," Evan apologized.

"What did he mean?" Monk turned, frowning. "All of us? There's only you and me—isn't there?"

Evan's eyes shadowed. "So far as I know! Do you think Runcorn has been here?"

Monk stood stiffly to the spot. "Why should he? He doesn't want to be the one to solve this, especially if it is Shelburne. He doesn't want to have anything to do with it."

"Curiosity?" There were other thoughts mirrored in Evan's face, but he did not speak them.

Monk thought the same thing—perhaps Runcorn wanted some proof it was Shelburne, then he would force Monk to find it, and then to make the charge. For a moment they stared at each other, the knowledge silent and complete between them.

"I'll go and find out." Evan turned around and went slowly down again.

It was several minutes before he came back, and Monk stood on the stair waiting, his mind at first searching for a way out, a way to avoid accusing Shelburne himself. Then he was drawn to wonder more about Runcorn. How old was the enmity between them? Was it simply an older man fearing a rival on the ladder of success, a younger, cleverer rival?

Only younger and cleverer? Or also harder, more ruthless in his ambitions, one who took credit for other people's work, who cared more for acclaim than for justice, who sought the public, colorful cases, the ones well reported; even a man who managed to shelve his failures onto other people, a thief of other men's work?

If that were so, then Runcorn's hatred was well earned, and his revenge had a justice to it.

Monk stared up at the old, carefully plastered ceiling. Above it was the room where Grey had been beaten to death. He did not feel ruthless now—only confused, oppressed by the void where memory should be, afraid of what he might find out about his own nature, anxious that he would fail in his job. Surely the crack on the head, however hard, could not have changed him so much? But even if the injury could not, maybe the fear had? He had woken up lost and alone, knowing nothing, having to find himself clue by clue, in what others could tell him, what they thought of him, but never why. He knew nothing of the motives for his acts, the nice rationalizations and excuses he had made to himself at the time. All the emotions that had driven him and blocked out judgment were in that empty region that yawned before the hospital bed and Runcorn's face.

But he had no time to pursue it further. Evan was back, his features screwed up in anxiety.

"It was Runcorn!" Monk leaped to the conclusion, suddenly frightened, like a man faced with physical violence.

Evan shook his head.

"No. It was two men I don't recognize at all from Grimwade's description. But he said they were from the police, and he saw their papers before he let them in."

"Papers?" Monk repeated. There was no point in asking what the men had looked like; he could not remember the men of his own division, let alone those from any other.

"Yes." Evan was obviously still anxious. "He said they had police identification papers, like ours."

"Did he see if they were from our station?"

"Yes sir, they were." His face puckered. "But I can't think who they could be. Anyway, why on earth would Runcorn send anyone else? What for?"

"I suppose it would be too much to ask that they gave names?"

"I'm afraid Grimwade didn't notice."

Monk turned around and went back up the stairs, more worried than he wished Evan to see. On the landing he put the key Grimwade had given him into the lock and swung Grey's door open. The small hallway was just as before, and it gave him an unpleasant jar of familiarity, a sense of foreboding for what was beyond.

Evan was immediately behind him. His face was pale and his eyes shadowed, but Monk knew that his oppression stemmed from Runcorn, and the two men who had been here before them, not any sensitivity to the violence still lingering in the air.

There was no purpose in hesitating anymore. He opened the second door.

There was a long sigh from behind him almost at his shoulder as Evan let out his breath in amazement.

The room was in wild disorder; the desk had been tipped over and all its contents flung into the far corner—by the look of them, the papers a sheet at a time. The chairs were on their sides, one upside down, the seats had been taken out, the stuffed sofa ripped open with a knife. All the pictures lay on the floor, backs levered out.

"Oh my God." Evan was stupefied.

"Not the police, I think," Monk said quietly.

"But they had papers," Evan protested. "Grimwade actually read them."

"Have you never heard of a good screever?"

"Forged?" Evan said wearily. "I suppose Grimwade wouldn't have known the difference."

"If the screever were good enough, I daresay we wouldn't either." Monk pulled a sour expression. Some forgeries of testimonials, letters, bills of sale were good enough to deceive even those they were purported to come from. At the upper end, it was a highly skilled and lucrative trade, at the lower no more than a makeshift way of buying a little time, or fooling the hasty or illiterate.

"Who were they?" Evan went past Monk and stared around the wreckage. "And what on earth did they want here?"

Monk's eyes went to the shelves where the ornaments had been.

"There was a silver sugar scuttle up there," he said as he pointed. "See if it's on the floor under any of that paper." He turned slowly. "And there were a couple of pieces of jade on that table. There were two snuffboxes in that alcove; one of them had an inlaid lid. And try the sideboard; there should be silver in the second drawer."

"What an incredible memory you have; I never noticed them." Evan was impressed and his admiration was obvious in his luminous eyes before he knelt down and began carefully to look under the mess, not moving it except to raise it sufficiently to explore beneath.

Monk was startled himself. He could not remember having looked in such detail at trivialities. Surely he had gone straight to the marks of the struggle, the bloodstains, the disarranged furniture, the bruised paint and the crooked pictures on the walls? He had no recollection now of even noticing the sideboard drawer, and yet his mind's eye could see silver, laid out neatly in green-baize-lined fittings.

Had it been in some other place? Was he confusing this room with another, an elegant sideboard somewhere in his past, belonging to someone else? Perhaps Imogen Latterly?

But he must dismiss Imogen from his mind—however easily, with whatever bitter fragrance, she returned. She was a dream, a creation of his own memories and hungers. He could never have known her well enough to feel anything but a charm, a sense of her distress, her courage in fighting it, the strength of her loyalty.

He forced himself to think of the present; Evan searching in the sideboard, the remark on his memory.

"Training," he replied laconically, although he didn't

226

understand it himself. "You'll develop it. It might not be the second drawer, better look in all of them."

Evan obeyed, and Monk turned back to the pile on the floor and began to pick his way through the mess, looking for something to tell him its purpose, or give any clue as to who could have caused it.

"There's nothing here." Evan closed the drawer, his mouth turned down in a grimace of disgust. "But this is the right place; it's all slotted for them to fit in, and lined with cloth. They went to a lot of trouble for a dozen settings of silver. I suppose they expected to get more. Where did you say the jade was?"

"There." Monk stepped over a pile of papers and cushions to an empty shelf, then wondered with a sense of unease how he knew, when he could have noticed it.

He bent and searched the floor carefully, replacing everything as he found it. Evan was watching him.

"No jade?" he asked.

"No, it's gone." Monk straightened up, his back stiff. "But I find it hard to believe ordinary thieves would go to the trouble, and the expense, of forging police identification papers just for a few pieces of silver and a jade ornament, and I think a couple of snuffboxes." He looked around. "They couldn't take much more without being noticed. Grimwade would certainly have been suspicious if they had taken anything like furniture or pictures."

"Well, I suppose the silver and the jade are worth something?"

"Not much, after the fence has taken his cut." Monk looked at the heap of wreckage on the floor and imagined the frenzy and the noise of such a search. "Hardly worth the risk," he said thoughtfully. "Much easier to have burgled a place in which the police have no interest. No, they wanted something else; the silver and the jade were a bonus. Anyway, what professional thief leaves a chaos like this behind him?"

"You mean it was Shelburne?" Evan's voice was half an octave higher with sheer disbelief.

Monk did not know what he meant.

"I can't think what Shelburne could want," he said, staring around the room again, his mind's eye seeing it as it had been before. "Even if he left something here that belonged to him, there are a dozen reasons he could invent if we'd asked him, with Joscelin dead and not able to argue. He could have left it here, whatever it was, any time, or lent it to Joscelin; or Joscelin could simply have taken it." He stared around the ceiling at the elaborate plaster work of acanthus leaves. "And I can't imagine him employing a couple of men to forge police papers and come here to ransack the place. No, it can't have been Shelburne."

"Then who?"

Monk was frightened because suddenly there was no rationality in it at all. Everything that had seemed to fit ten minutes ago was now senseless, like puzzle parts of two quite different pictures. At the same time he was almost elated—if it were not Shelburne, if it were someone who knew forgers and thieves, then perhaps there was no society scandal or blackmail at all.

"I don't know," he answered Evan with sudden new firmness. "But there's no need to tiptoe in this one to find out. Nobody will lose us our jobs if we ask embarrassing questions of a few screevers, or bribe a nose, or even press a fence a little hard."

Evan's face relaxed into a slow smile and his eyes lit up. Monk guessed that perhaps he had had little taste so far of the color of the underworld, and as yet it still held the glamour of mystery. He would find its tones dark; gray of misery, black of long-used pain and habitual fear; its humor quick and bitter, gallows laughter.

He looked at Evan's keen face, its soft, sensitive lines. He could not explain to him; words are only names for what you already know—and what could Evan know that would prepare him for the hive of human waste that teemed in the shadows of Whitechapel, St. Giles, Bluegate Fields, Seven Dials, or the Devil's Acre? Monk had known hardship himself in childhood; he could remember hunger now—it was coming back to him—and cold, shoes that leaked, clothes that let through the bitter northeast wind, plenty of meals of bread and gravy. He remembered faintly the pain of chilblains, angry itching fire when at last you warmed a little; Beth with chapped lips and white, numb fingers.

But they were not unhappy memories; behind all the small pains there had always been a sense of well-being, a knowledge of eventual safety. They were always clean: clean clothes, however few and however old, clean table, smell of flour and fish, salt wind in the spring and summer when the windows were open.

It was sharper in his mind now; he could recall whole scenes, taste and touch, and always the whine of the wind and the cry of gulls. They had all gone to church on Sundays; he could not bring back everything that had been said, but he could think of snatches of music, solemn and full of the satisfaction of people who believe what they sing, and know they sing it well.

His mother had taught him all his values: honesty, labor and learning. He knew even without her words that she believed it. It was a good memory, and he was more grateful for its return than for any other. It brought with it identity. He could not clearly picture his mother's face; each time he tried it blurred and melted into Beth's, as he had seen her only a few weeks ago, smiling, confident of herself. Perhaps they were not unalike.

Evan was waiting for him, eyes still bright with anticipation of seeing at last the real skill of detection, delving into the heartland of crime.

"Yes." Monk recalled himself. "We shall be free there to pursue as we wish." And no satisfaction for Runcorn, he thought, but he did not add it aloud.

He went back to the door and Evan followed him. There was no point in tidying anything; better to leave it as it was—even that mess might yield a clue, some time.

He was in the hallway, next to the small table, when he

229

noticed the sticks in the stand. He had seen them before, but he had been too preoccupied with the acts of violence in the room beyond to look closely. Anyway, they already had the stick that had been the weapon. Now he saw that there were still four there. Perhaps since Grey had used a stick to walk with, he had become something of a collector. It would not be unnatural; he had been a man to whom appearance mattered: everything about him said as much. Probably he had a stick for morning, another for evening, a casual one, and a rougher one for the country.

Monk's eye was caught by a dark, straight stick, the color of mahogany and with a fine brass band on it embossed like the links of a chain. It was an extraordinary sensation, hot, almost like a dizziness; it prickled in his skin—he knew with total clarity that he had seen that stick before, and seen it several times.

Evan was beside him, waiting, wondering why he had stopped. Monk tried to clear his head, to broaden the image till it included where and when, till he saw the man who held it. But nothing came, only the vivid tingle of familiarity—and fear.

"Sir?" Evan's voice was doubtful. He could see no reason for the sudden paralysis. They were both standing in the hallway, frozen, and the only reason was in Monk's mind. And try as he might, bending all the force of his will on it, still he could see nothing but the stick, no man, not even a hand holding it.

"Have you thought of something, sir?" Evan's voice intruded into the intensity of his thought.

"No." Monk moved at last. "No." He must think of something sensible to say, to explain himself, a reason for his behavior. He found the words with difficulty. "I was just wondering where to start. You say Grimwade didn't get any names from those papers?"

"No; but then they wouldn't use their own names anyway, would they?"

"No, of course not, but it would have helped to know what name the screever used for them." It was a foolish

230

question to have asked, but he must make sense of it. Evan was listening to his every word, as to a teacher. "There are a vast number of screevers in London." He made his voice go on with authority, as if he knew what he was saying, and it mattered. "And I daresay more than one who has forged police papers in the last few weeks."

"Oh—yes, of course," Evan was instantly satisfied. "No, I did ask, before I knew they were burglars, but he didn't notice. He was more interested in the authorization part."

"Oh well." Monk had control of himself again. He opened the door and went out. "I daresay the name of the station will be enough anyway." Evan came out also and he turned and closed the door behind him, locking it.

But when they reached the street Monk changed his mind. He wanted to see Runcorn's face when he heard of the robbery and realized Monk would not be forced to ferret for scandals as the only way to Grey's murderer. There was suddenly and beautifully a new way open to him, where the worst possibility was simple failure; and there was even a chance now of real success, unqualified.

He sent Evan off on a trivial errand, with instructions to meet him again in an hour, and caught a hansom through sunny, noisy streets back to the station. Runcorn was in, and there was a glow of satisfaction on his face when Monk came into his office.

"Morning, Monk," he said cheerfully. "No further, I see?"

Monk let the pleasure sink a little deeper into him, as one hesitates exquisitely in a hot bath, inching into it to savor each additional moment.

"It is a most surprising case," he answered meaninglessly, his eyes meeting Runcorn's, affecting concern.

Runcorn's face clouded, but Monk could feel the pleasure in him as if it were an odor in the room.

"Unfortunately the public does not give us credit for amazement," Runcorn replied, stretching out the anticipation. "Just because they are puzzled that does not, in their view, allow us the same privilege. You're not pressing hard enough, Monk." He frowned very slightly and leaned farther back in his chair, the sunlight in a bar through the window falling in on the side of his head. His voice changed to one of unctuous sympathy. "Are you sure you are fully recovered? You don't seem like your old self. You used not to be so—" He smiled as the word pleased him. "So hesitant. Justice was your first aim, indeed your only aim; I've never known you to balk before, even at the most unpleasant inquiries." There was doubt at the very back of his eyes, and dislike. He was balancing between courage and experience, like a man beginning to ride a bicycle. "You believe that very quality was what raised you so far, and so fast." He stopped, waiting; and Monk had a brief vision of spiders resting in the hearts of their webs, knowing flies would come, sooner or later: the time was a matter of delicacy, but they would come.

He decided to play it out a little longer; he wanted to watch Runcorn himself, let him bring his own feelings into the open, and betray his vulnerability.

"This case is different," he answered hesitantly, still putting the anxiety into his manner. He sat down on the chair opposite the desk. "I can't remember any other like it. One cannot make comparison."

"Murder is murder." Runcorn shook his head a trifle pompously. "Justice does not differentiate; and let me be frank, neither does the public—in fact if anything, they care more about this. It has all the elements the public likes, all the journalists need to whip up passions and make people frightened—and indignant."

Monk decided to split hairs.

"Not really," he demurred. "There is no love story, and the public likes romance above all things. There is no woman."

"No love story?" Runcorn's eyebrows went up. "I never suspected you of cowardice, Monk; and never, ever of stupidity!" His face twitched with an impossible blend of satisfaction and affected concern. "Are you sure you are quite well?'' He leaned forward over the desk again to reinforce the effect. ''You don't get headaches, by any chance, do you? It was a very severe blow you received, you know. In fact, I daresay you don't recall it now, but when I first saw you in the hospital you didn't even recognize me.''

Monk refused to acknowledge the appalling thought that had come to the edge of his mind.

''Romance?'' he asked blankly, as if he had heard nothing after that.

''Joscelin Grey and his sister-in-law!'' Runcorn was watching him closely, pretending to be hazy, his eyes a little veiled, but Monk saw the sharp pinpoints under his heavy lids.

''Does the public know of that?'' Monk equally easily pretended innocence. ''I have not had time to look at newspapers.'' He pushed out his lip in doubt. ''Do you think it was wise to tell them? Lord Shelburne will hardly be pleased!''

The skin across Runcorn's face tightened.

''No of course I didn't tell them yet!'' He barely controlled his voice. ''But it can only be a matter of time. You cannot put it off forever.'' There was a hard gleam in his face, almost an appetite. ''You have most assuredly changed, Monk. You used to be such a fighter. It is almost as if you were a different person, a stranger to yourself. Have you forgotten how you used to be?''

For a moment Monk was unable to answer, unable to do anything but absorb the shock. He should have guessed it. He had been overconfident, stupidly blind to the obvious. Of course Runcorn knew he had lost his memory. If he had not known from the beginning, then he had surely guessed it in Monk's careful maneuvering, his unawareness of their relationship. Runcorn was a professional; he spent his life telling truth from lies, divining motives, uncovering the hidden. What an arrogant fool Monk must have been to imagine he had deceived him. His own stupidity made him flush hot at the embarrassment of it.

Runcorn was watching him, seeing the tide of color in his face. He must control it, find a shield; or better, a weapon. He straightened his body a little more and met Runcorn's eyes.

"A stranger to you perhaps, sir, but not to myself. But then we are few of us as plain as we seem to others. I think I am only less rash than you supposed. And it is as well." He savored the moment, although it had not the sweetness he had expected.

He looked at Runcorn's face squarely. "I came to tell you that Joscelin Grey's flat has been robbed, at least it has been thoroughly searched, even ransacked, by two men posing as police. They seemed to have had quite competently forged papers which they showed to the porter."

Runcorn's face was stiff and there was a mottle of red on his skin. Monk could not resist adding to it.

"Puts a different light on it, doesn't it?" he went on cheerfully, pretending they were both pleased. "I don't see Lord Shelburne hiring an accomplice and posing as a Peeler to search his brother's flat."

A few seconds had given Runcorn time to think.

"Then he must have hired a couple of men. Simple enough!"

But Monk was ready. "If it was something worth such a terrible risk," he countered, "why didn't they get it before? It must have been there two months by now."

"What terrible risk?" Runcorn's voice dropped a little in mockery of the idea. "They passed it off beautifully. And it would have been easy enough to do: just watch the building a little while to make sure the real police were not there, then go in with their false papers, get what they went for, and leave. I daresay they had a crow out in the street."

"I wasn't referring to the risk of their being caught in the act," Monk said scornfully. "I was thinking of the much greater risk, from his point of view, of placing himself in the hands of possible blackmailers."

He felt a surge of pleasure as Runcorn's face betrayed that he hadn't thought of that.

"Do it anonymously." Runcorn dismissed the idea.

Monk smiled at him. "If it was worth paying thieves, and a first-class screever, in order to get it back, it wouldn't take a very bright thief to work out it would be worth raising the price a little before handing it over. Everyone in London knows there was murder done in that room. If whatever he wanted was worth paying thieves and forgers to get back, it must be damning."

Runcorn glared at the table top, and Monk waited.

"So what are you suggesting then?" Runcorn said at last. "Somebody wanted it. Or do you say it was just a casual thief, trying his luck?" His contempt for the idea was heavy in his voice and it curled his lip.

Monk avoided the question.

"I intend to find out what it is," he replied, pushing back his chair and rising. "It may be something we haven't even thought of."

"You'll have to be a damn good detective to do that!" The triumph came back into Runcorn's eyes.

Monk straightened and looked levelly back at him.

"I am," he said without a flicker. "Did you think that had changed?"

When he left Runcorn's office Monk had had no idea even how to begin. He had forgotten all his contacts; now a fence or an informer could pass him in the street and he would not recognize him. He could not ask any of his colleagues. If Runcorn hated him, it was more than likely many of them did too and he had no idea which; and to show such vulnerability would invite a coup de grace. Runcorn knew he had lost his memory, of that he was perfectly sure now, although nothing had been said completely beyond ambiguity. There was a chance, a good chance he could fend off one man until he had regained at least enough mixture of memory and skill to do his job well enough to defy them all. If he solved the Grey case he would be unassailable; then let Runcorn say what he pleased.

But it was an unpleasant knowledge that he was so deeply and consistently hated, and with what he increasingly realized was good reason.

And was he fighting for survival? Or was there also an instinct in him to attack Runcorn; not only to find the truth, to be right, but also to be there before Runcorn was and make sure he knew it? Perhaps if he had been an onlooker at this, watching two other men, at least some of his sympathy would have been with Runcorn. There was a cruelty in himself he was seeing for the first time, a pleasure in winning that he did not admire.

Had he always been like this—or was it born of his fear?

How to start finding the thieves? Much as he liked Evan—and he did like him increasingly every day; the man had enthusiasm and gentleness, humor, and a purity of intention Monk envied—even so, he dare not place himself in Evan's hands by telling him the truth. And if he were honest (there was a little vanity in it also), Evan was the only person, apart from Beth, who seemed unaffectedly to think well of him, even to like him. He could not bear to forfeit that.

So he could not ask Evan to tell him the names of informers and fences. He would just have to find them for himself. But if he had been as good a detective as everything indicated, he must know many. They would recognize him.

He was late and Evan had been waiting for him. He apologized, somewhat to Evan's surprise, and only afterward realized that as a superior it was not expected of him. He must be more careful, especially if he were to conceal his purpose, and his inability, from Evan. He wanted to go to an underworld eating house for luncheon, and hoped that if he left word with the potman someone would approach him. He would have to do it in several places, but within three or four days at most he should find a beginning.

He could not bring back to memory any names or faces, but the smell of the back taverns was sharply familiar. Without thinking, he knew how to behave; to alter color like a chameleon, to drop his shoulders, loosen his gait, keep his eyes down and wary. It is not clothes that make the man; a cardsharp, a dragsman, a superior pickpocket or a thief from the Swell Mob could dress as well as most—indeed the nurse at the hospital had taken him for one of the Swell Mob himself.

Evan, with his fair face and wide, humorous eyes, looked too clean to be dishonest. There was none of the wiliness of a survivor in him; yet some of the best survivors of all were those most skilled in deception and the most innocent of face. The underworld was big enough for any variation of lie and fraud, and no weakness was left unexploited.

They began a little to the west of Mecklenburg Square, going to the King's Cross Road. When the first tavern produced nothing immediate, they moved north to the Pentonville Road, then south and east again into Clerkenwell.

In spite of all that logic could tell him, by the following day Monk was beginning to feel as if he were on a fool's errand, and Runcorn would have the last laugh. Then, in a congested public house by the name of the Grinning Rat, a scruffy little man, smiling, showing yellow teeth, slid into the seat beside them, looking warily at Evan. The room was full of noise, the strong smell of ale, sweat, the dirt of clothes and bodies long unwashed, and the heavy steam of food. The floor was covered with sawdust and there was a constant chink of glass.

" 'Ello, Mr. Monk; I hain't seen you for a long time. W'ere yer bin?''

Monk felt a leap of excitement and studied hard to hide it.

"Had an accident," he answered, keeping his voice level.

The man looked him up and down critically and grunted, dismissing it.

"I 'ears as yer after som'un as'll blow a little?"

"That's right," Monk agreed. He must not be too precipitate, or the price would be high, and he could not afford the time to bargain; he must be right first time, or he would appear green. He knew from the air, the smell of it, that haggling was part of the game.

"Worf anyfink?" the man asked.

"Could be."

"Well," the man said, thinking it over. "Yer always bin fair, that's why I comes to yer 'stead o' some 'o them other jacks. Proper mean, some o' them; yer'd be right ashamed if yer knew." He shook his head and sniffed hard, pulling a face of disgust.

Monk smiled.

"Wotcher want, then?" the man asked.

"Several things." Monk lowered his voice even further, still looking across the table and not at the man. "Some stolen goods—a fence, and a good screever."

The man also looked at the table, studying the stain ring marks of mugs.

"Plenty o' fences, guv; and a fair few screevers. Special goods, these?"

"Not very."

"W'y yer want 'em ven? Som'one done over bad?"

"Yes."

"O'right, so wot are vey ven?"

Monk began to describe them as well as he could; he had only memory to go on.

"Table silver—"

The man looked at him witheringly.

Monk abandoned the silver. "A jade ornament," he continued. "About six inches high, of a dancing lady with her arms up in front of her, bent at the elbows. It was pinky-colored jade—"

"Aw, nar vat's better." The man's voice lifted; Monk avoided looking at his face. "Hain't a lot o' pink jade abaht," he went on. "Anyfink else?"

238

"A silver scuttle, about four or five inches, I think, and a couple of inlaid snuffboxes."

"Wot kind o' snuffboxes, guv: siller, gold, enamel? Yer gotta give me mor'n vat!"

"I can't remember."

"Yer wot? Don't ve geezer wot lorst 'em know?" His face darkened with suspicion and for the first time he looked at Monk. " 'Ere! 'E croaked, or suffink?"

"Yes," Monk said levelly, still staring at the wall. "But no reason to suppose the thief did it. He was dead long before the robbery."

"Yer sure o' vat? 'Ow d'yer know 'e were gorn afore?"

"He was dead two months before." Monk smiled acidly. "Even I couldn't mistake that. His empty house was robbed."

The man thought this over for several minutes before delivering his opinion.

Somewhere over near the bar there was a roar of laughter.

"Robbin' a deadlurk?" he said with heavy condescension. "Bit chancy to find anyfink, in' it? Wot did yer say abaht a screever? Wot yer want a screever fer ven?"

"Because the thieves used forged police papers to get in," Monk replied.

The man's face lit up with delight and he chuckled richly.

"A proper downy geezer, vat one. I like it!" He wiped the back of his hand across his mouth and laughed again. "It'd be a sin ter shop a feller wiv vat kind o' class."

Monk took a gold half sovereign out of his pocket and put it on the table. The man's eyes fastened onto it as if it mesmerized him.

"I want the screever who made those fakements for them," Monk repeated. He put out his hand and took the gold coin back again. He put it into his inside pocket. The man's eyes followed it. "And no sly faking," Monk warned. "I'll feel your hands in my pockets, and you remember that, unless you fancy picking oakum for a while. Not do your sensitive fingers any good, picking oakum!'' He winced inwardly as a flash of memory returned of men's fingers bleeding from the endless unraveling of rope ends, day in, day out, while years of their lives slid by.

The man flinched. "Now vat ain't nice, Mr. Monk. I never took nuffink from yer in me life." He crossed himself hastily and Monk was not sure whether it was a surety of truth or a penance for the lie. "I s'pose yer tried all ve jollyshops?" the man continued, screwing up his face. "Couldn't christen that jade lady."

Evan looked vaguely confused, although Monk was not sure by what.

"Pawnshops," he translated for him. "Naturally thieves remove any identification from most articles, but nothing much you can do to jade without spoiling its value." He took five shillings out of his pocket and gave them to the man. "Come back in two days, and if you've got anything, you'll have earned the half sovereign."

"Right, guv, but not 'ere; vere's a slap bang called ve Purple Duck dahn on Plumber's Row—orf ve Whitechapel Road. Yer go vere." He looked Monk up and down with distaste. "An' come out o' twig, eh; not all square rigged like a prater! And bring the gold, 'cos I'll 'ave suffink. Yer 'ealf, guv, an' yers." He glanced sideways at Evan, then slid off the seat and disappeared into the crowd. Monk felt elated, suddenly singing inside. Even the fast-cooling plum duff was bearable. He smiled broadly across at Evan.

"Come in disguise," he explained. "Not soberly dressed like a fake preacher."

"Oh." Evan relaxed and began to enjoy himself also. "I see." He stared around at the throng of faces, seeing mystery behind the dirt, his imagination painting them with nameless color.

Two days later Monk obediently dressed himself in suitable secondhand clothes; "translators" the informer would have called them. He wished he could remember the man's name, but for all his efforts it remained completely beyond recall, hidden like almost everything else after the age of about seventeen. He had had glimpses of the years up to then, even including his first year or two in London, but although he lay awake, staring into the darkness, letting his mind wander, going over and over all he knew in the hope his brain would jerk into life again and continue forward, nothing more returned.

Now he and Evan were sitting in the saloon in the Purple Duck, Evan's delicate face registering both his distaste and his efforts to conceal it. Looking at him, Monk wondered how often he himself must have been here to be so unoffended by it. It must have become habit, the noise, the smell, the uninhibited closeness, things his subconscious remembered even if his mind did not.

They had to wait nearly an hour before the informer turned up, but he was grinning again, and slid into the seat beside Monk without a word.

Monk was not going to jeopardize the price by seeming too eager.

"Drink?" he offered.

"Nah, just ve guinea," the man replied. "Don' want ter draw attention to meself drinkin' wiv ve likes o' you, if yer'll pardon me. But potmen 'as sharp mem'ries an' loose tongues."

"Quite," Monk agreed. "But you'll earn the guinea before you get it."

"Aw, nah Mr. Monk." He pulled a face of deep offense. " 'Ave I ever shorted yer? Now 'ave I?"

Monk had no idea.

"Did you find my screever?" he asked instead.

"I carsn't find yer jade, nor fer sure, like."

"Did you find the screever?"

"You know Tommy, the shofulman?"

For a moment Monk felt a touch of panic. Evan was watching him, fascinated by the bargaining. Ought he to know Tommy? He knew what a shofulman was, someone who passed forged money.

241

"Tommy?" he blinked.

"Yeah!" the man said impatiently. "Blind Tommy, least 'e pretends 'e's blind. I reckon as 'e 'alf is."

"Where do I find him?" If he could avoid admitting anything, perhaps he could bluff his way through. He must not either show an ignorance of something he would be expected to know or on the other hand collect so little information as to be left helpless.

"You find 'im?" The man smiled condescendingly at the idea. "Yer'll never find 'im on yer own; wouldn't be safe anyhow. 'E's in ve rookeries, an' yer'd get a shiv in yer gizzard sure as 'ell's on fire if yer went in vere on yer tod. I'll take yer."

"Tommy taken up screeving?" Monk concealed his relief by making a general and he hoped meaningless remark.

The little man looked at him with amazement.

" 'Course not! 'E can't even write 'is name, let alone a fakement fer some'un else! But 'e knows a right downy geezer wot does. Reckon 'e's the one as writ yer police papers for yer. 'E's known to do vat kind o' fing."

"Good. Now what about the jade—anything at all?"

The man twisted his rubberlike features into the expression of an affronted rodent.

"Bit 'ard, vat, guv. Know one feller wot got a piece, but 'e swears blind it were a snoozer wot brought it—an' you din't say nuffink abaht no snoozer."

"This was no hotel thief," Monk agreed. "That the only one?"

"Only one as I knows fer sure."

Monk knew the man was lying, although he could not have said how—an accumulation of impressions too subtle to be analyzed.

"I don't believe you, Jake; but you've done well with the screever." He fished in his pocket and brought out the promised gold. "And if it leads to the man I want, there'll be another for you. Now take me to Blind Tommy the shofulman."

242

They all stood up and wormed their way out through the crowd into the street. It was not until they were two hundred yards away that Monk realized, with a shudder of excitement he could not control, that he had called the man by name. It was coming back, more than merely his memory for his own sake, but his skill was returning. He quickened his step and found himself smiling broadly at Evan.

The rookery was monstrous, a rotting pile of tenements crammed one beside the other, piled precariously, timbers awry as the damp warped them and floors and walls were patched and repatched. It was dark even in the late summer afternoon and the humid air was clammy to the skin. It smelled of human waste and the gutters down the overhung alleys ran with filth. The squeaking and slithering of rats was a constant background. Everywhere there were people, huddled in doorways, lying on stones, sometimes six or eight together, some of them alive, some already dead from hunger or disease. Typhoid and pneumonia were endemic in such places and venereal diseases passed from one to another, as did the flies and lice.

Monk looked at a child in the gutter as he passed, perhaps five or six years old, its face gray in the half-light, pinched sharp; it was impossible to tell whether it was male or female. Monk thought with a dull rage that bestial as it was to beat a man to death as Grey had been beaten, it was still a better murder than this child's abject death.

He noticed Evan's face, white in the gloom, eyes like holes in his head. There was nothing he could think of to say—no words that served any purpose. Instead he put out his hand and touched him briefly, an intimacy that came quite naturally in that awful place.

They followed Jake through another alley and then another, up a flight of stairs that threatened to give way beneath them with each step, and at the top at last Jake stopped, his voice hushed as if the despair had reached even him. He spoke as one does in the presence of death.

"One more lot o' steps, Mr. Monk, from 'ere, an' Blind Tommy's be'ind ver door on yer right."

"Thank you. I'll give you your guinea when I've seen him, if he can help."

Jake's face split in a grin.

"I already got it, Mr. Monk." He held up a bright coin. "Fink I fergot 'ow ter do it, did yer? I used ter be a fine wirer, I did, w'en I were younger." He laughed and slipped it into his pocket. "I were taught by the best kidsman in ve business. I'll be seein' yer, Mr. Monk; yer owes me anuvver, if yer gets vem fieves."

Monk smiled in spite of himself. The man was a pickpocket, but he had been taught by one of those who make their own living by teaching children to steal for them, and taking the profits in return for the child's keep. It was an apprenticeship in survival. Perhaps his only alternative had been starvation, like the child they had passed. Only the quick-fingered, the strong and the lucky reached adulthood. Monk could not afford to indulge in judgment, and he was too torn with pity and anger to try.

"It's yours, Jack, if I get them," he promised, then started up the last flight and Evan followed. At the top he opened the door without knocking.

Blind Tommy must have been expecting him. He was a dapper little man, about five feet tall with a sharp, ugly face, and dressed in a manner he himself would have described as "flash." He was apparently no more than shortsighted because he saw Monk immediately and knew who he was.

" 'Evenin', Mr. Monk. I 'ears as yer lookin' fer a screever, a partic'lar one, like?"

"That's right, Tommy. I want one who made some fakements for two rampsmen who robbed a house in Mecklenburg Square. Went in pretending to be Peelers."

Tommy's face lit up with amusement.

"I like that," he admitted. "It's a smart lay, vat is."

"Providing you don't get caught."

"Wot's it worf?" Tommy's eyes narrowed.

"It's murder, Tommy. Whoever did it'll be topped, and whoever helps them stands a good chance of getting the boat."

"Oh Gawd!" Tommy's face paled visibly. "I 'an't no fancy for Horstralia. Boats don't suit me at all, vey don't. Men wasn't meant ter go orf all over like vat! In't nat'ral. An' 'orrible stories I've 'eard about vem parts." He shivered dramatically. "Full o' savages an' creatures wot weren't never made by no Christian Gawd. Fings wif dozens 'o legs, an' fings wi' no legs at all. Ugh!" He rolled his eyes. "Right 'eathen place, it is."

"Then don't run any risk of being sent there," Monk advised without any sympathy. "Find me this screever."

"Are yer sure it's murder?" Tommy was still not entirely convinced. Monk wondered how much it was a matter of loyalties, and how much simply a weighing of one advantage against another.

"Of course I'm sure!" he said with a low, level voice. He knew the threat was implicit in it. "Murder and robbery. Silver and jade stolen. Know anything about a jade dancing lady, pink jade, about six inches high?"

Tommy was defensive, a thin, nasal quality of fear in his tone.

"Fencin's not my life, guv. Don't do none o' vat—don't yer try an' hike vat on me."

"The screever?" Monk said flatly.

"Yeah, well I'll take yer. Anyfink in it fer me?" Hope seldom died. If the fearful reality of the rookery did not kill it, Monk certainly could not.

"If it's the right man," he grunted.

Tommy took them through another labyrinth of alleys and stairways, but Monk wondered how much distance they had actually covered. He had a strong feeling it was more to lose their sense of direction than to travel above a few hundred yards. Eventually they stopped at another large door, and after a sharp knock, Blind Tommy disappeared and the door swung open in front of them.

The room inside was bright and smelled of burning.

245

Monk stepped in, then looked up involuntarily and saw glass skylights. He saw down the walls where there were large windows as well. Of course—light for a forger's careful pen.

The man inside turned to look at the intruders. He was squat, with powerful shoulders and large spatulate hands. His face was pale-skinned but ingrained with the dirt of years, and his colorless hair stuck to his head in thin spikes.

"Well?" he demanded irritably. When he spoke Monk saw his teeth were short and black; Monk fancied he could smell the stale odor of them, even from where he stood.

"You wrote police identification papers for two men, purporting to come from the Lye Street station." He made a statement, not a question. "I don't want you for it; I want the men. It's a case of murder, so you'd do well to stay on the right side of it."

The man leered, his thin lips stretching wide in some private amusement. "You Monk?"

"And if I am?" He was surprised the man had heard of him. Was his reputation so wide? Apparently it was.

"Your case they walked inter, was it?" The man's mirth bubbled over in a silent chuckle, shaking his mass of flesh.

"It's my case now," Monk replied. He did not want to tell the man the robbery and the murder were separate; the threat of hanging was too useful.

"Wotcher want?" the man asked. His voice was hoarse, as if from too much shouting or laughter, yet it was hard imagining him doing either.

"Who are they?" Monk pressed.

"Now Mr. Monk, 'ow should I know?" His massive shoulders were still twitching. "Do I ask people's names?"

"Probably not, but you know who they are. Don't pretend to be stupid; it doesn't suit you."

"I know some people," he conceded in little more than a whisper. " 'Course I do; but not every muck snipe 'oo tries 'is 'and at thievin'."

"Muck snipe?" Monk looked at him with derision. "Since when did you hand out fakements for nothing? You don't do favors for down-and-outs. They paid you, or someone did. If they didn't pay you themselves, tell me who did; that'll do."

The man's narrow eyes widened a fraction. "Oh clever, Mr. Monk, very clever." He clapped his broad, powerful hands together in soundless applause.

"So who paid you?"

"My business is confidential, Mr. Monk. Lose it all if I starts putting the down on people wot comes ter me. It was a moneylender, that's all I'll tell yer."

"Not much call for a screever in Australia." Monk looked at the man's subtle, sensitive fingers. "Hard labor—bad climate."

"Put me on the boat, would yer?" The man's lip curled. "Yer'd 'ave ter catch me first, and yer know as well as I do yer'd never find me." The smile on his face did not alter even a fraction. "An' yer'd be a fool ter look; 'orrible fings 'appen ter a Peeler as gets caught in yer rookeries, if ye word goes aht."

"And horrible things happen to a screever who informs on his clients—if the word goes out," Monk added immediately. "Horrible things—like broken fingers. And what use is a screever without his fingers?"

The man stared at him, suddenly hatred undisguised in his heavy eyes.

"An' w'y should the word go out, Mr. Monk, seein' as 'ow I aven't told yer nuffink?"

In the doorway Evan moved uncomfortably. Monk ignored him.

"Because I shall put it out," he replied, "that you have."

"But you ain't got no one fer yer robbery." The hoarse whisper was level again, the amusement creeping back.

"I'll find someone."

"Takes time, Mr. Monk; and 'ow are yer goin' ter do it if I don't tell yer?"

247

"You are leaping to conclusions, screever," Monk said ruthlessly. "It doesn't have to be the right ones; anyone will do. By the time the word gets back I have the wrong people, it'll be too late to save your fingers. Broken fingers heal hard, and they ache for years, so I'm told."

The man called him something obscene.

"Quite." Monk looked at him with disgust. "So who paid you?"

The man glared at him, hate hot in his face.

"Who paid you?" Monk leaned forward a little.

"Josiah Wigtight, moneylender," the man spat out. "Find 'im in Gun Lane, Whitechapel. Now get out!"

"Moneylender. What sort of people does he lend money to?"

"The sort o' people wot can pay 'im back, o' course, fool!"

"Thank you." Monk smiled and straightened up. "Thank you, screever; your business is secure. You have told us nothing."

The screever swore at him again, but Monk was out of the door and hurrying down the rickety stairs, Evan, anxious and doubtful, at his heel, but Monk offered him no explanation, and did not meet his questioning look.

It was too late to try the moneylender that day, and all he could think of was to get out of the rookeries in one piece before someone stabbed one of them for his clothes, poor as they were, or merely because they were strangers.

He said good-night briefly and watched Evan hesitate, then reply in his quiet voice and turn away in the darkness, an elegant figure, oddly young in the gaslight.

Back at Mrs. Worley's, he ate a hot meal, grateful for it, at once savoring each mouthful and hating it because he could not dismiss from his mind all those who would count it victory merely to have survived the day and eaten enough to sustain life.

None of it was strange to him, as it obviously had been to Evan. He must have been to such places many times before. He had behaved instinctively, altering his stance,

248

knowing how to melt into the background, not to look like a stranger, least of all a figure of authority. The beggars, the sick, the hopeless moved him to excruciating pity, and a deep, abiding anger—but no surprise.

And his mercilessness with the screever had come without calculation, his natural reaction. He knew the rookeries and their denizens. He might even have survived in them himself.

Only afterwards, when the plate was empty, did he lean back in the chair and think of the case.

A moneylender made sense. Joscelin Grey might well have borrowed money when he lost his small possessions in the affair with Latterly, and his family would not help. Had the moneylender meant to injure him a little, to frighten repayment from him, and warn other tardy borrowers, and when Grey had fought back it had gone too far? It was possible. And Yeats's visitor had been a moneylender's ruffian. Yeats and Grimwade had both said he was a big man, lean and strong, as far as they could tell under his clothes.

What a baptism for Evan. He had said nothing about it afterwards. He had not even asked if Monk would really have arrested people he knew to be innocent and then spread the word the screever had betrayed them.

Monk flinched as he remembered what he had said; but it had simply been what instinct directed. It was a streak of ruthlessness in himself he had been unaware of; and it would have shocked him in anyone else. Was that really what he was like? Surely it was only a threat, and he would never have carried it out? Or would he? He remembered the anger that had welled up inside him at the mention of moneylenders, parasites of the desperate poor who clung to respectability, to a few precious standards. Sometimes a man's honesty was his only real possession, his only source of pride and identity in the anonymous, wretched, teeming multitude.

What had Evan thought of him? He cared; it was a miserable thought that Evan would be disillusioned, finding

his methods as ugly as the crime he fought, not understanding he was using words, only words.

Or did Evan know him better than he knew himself?
Evan would know his past. Perhaps in the past the words
had been a warning, and reality had followed.

And what would Imogen Latterly have felt? It was a
preposterous dream. The rookeries were as foreign to her
as the planets in the sky. She would be sick, disgusted
even to see them, let alone to have passed through them
and dealt with their occupants. If she had seen him threaten
the screever, standing in the filthy room, she would not
permit him to enter her house again.

He sat staring up at the ceiling, full of anger and pain.
It was cold comfort to him that tomorrow he would find
the usurer who might have killed Joscelin Grey. He hated
the world he had to deal with; he wanted to belong to the
clean, gracious world where he could speak as an equal
with people like the Latterlys; Charles would not patronize
him, he could converse with Imogen Latterly as a friend,
and quarrel with Hester without the hindrance of social
inferiority. That would be a delicate pleasure. He would
dearly like to put that opinionated young woman in her
place.

But purely because he hated the rookeries so fiercely,
he could not ignore them. He had seen them, known their
squalor and their desperation, and they would not go away.

Well at least he could turn his anger to some purpose;
he would find the violent, greedy man who had paid to
have Joscelin Grey beaten to death. Then he could face
Grey in peace in his imagination—and Runcorn would be
defeated.

10

Monk sent Evan to try pawnshops for the pink jade, and then himself went to look for Josiah Wigtight. He had no trouble finding the address. It was half a mile east of Whitechapel off the Mile End Road. The building was narrow and almost lost between a seedy lawyer's office and a sweatshop where in dim light and heavy, breathless air women worked eighteen hours a day sewing shirts for a handful of pence. Some felt driven to walk the street at night also, for the extra dreadfully and easily earned silver coins that meant food and rent. A few were wives or daughters of the poor, the drunken or the inadequate; many were women who had in the past been in domestic service, and had lost their "character" one way or another—for impertinence, dishonesty, loose morals, or because a mistress found them "uppity," or a master had taken advantage of them and been discovered, and in a number of cases they had become with child, and thus not only unemployable but a disgrace and an affront.

Inside, the office was dim behind drawn blinds and smelled of polish, dust and ancient leather. A black-dressed clerk sat at a high stool in the first room. He looked up as Monk came in.

"Good morning, sir; may we be of assistance to you?"

251

His voice was soft, like mud. "Perhaps you have a little problem?" He rubbed his hands together as though the cold bothered him, although it was summer. "A temporary problem, of course?" He smiled at his own hypocrisy.

"I hope so." Monk smiled back.

The man was skilled at his job. He regarded Monk with caution. His expression had not the nervousness he was accustomed to; if anything it was a little wolfish. Monk realized he had been clumsy. Surely in the past he must have been more skilled, more attuned to the nuances of judgment?

"That rather depends on you," he added to encourage the man, and allay any suspicion he might unwittingly have aroused.

"Indeed," the clerk agreed. "That's what we're in business for: to help gentlemen with a temporary embarrassment of funds. Of course there are conditions, you understand?" He fished out a clean sheet of paper and held his pen ready. "If I could just have the details, sir?"

"My problem is not a shortage of funds," Monk replied with the faintest smile. He hated moneylenders; he hated the relish with which they plied their revolting trade. "At least not pressing enough to come to you. I have a matter of business to discuss with Mr. Wigtight."

"Quite." The man nodded with a smirk of understanding. "Quite so. All matters of business are referred to Mr. Wigtight, ultimately, Mr.—er?" He raised his eyebrows.

"I do not want to borrow any money," Monk said rather more tartly. "Tell Mr. Wigtight it is about something he has mislaid, and very badly wishes to have returned to him."

"Mislaid?" The man screwed up his pallid face. "Mislaid? What are you talking about, sir? Mr. Wigtight does not mislay things." He sniffed in offended disapproval.

Monk leaned forward and put both hands on the counter, and the man was obliged to face him.

"Are you going to show me to Mr. Wigtight?" Monk

said very clearly. "Or do I take my information elsewhere?" He did not want to tell the man who he was, or Wigtight would be forewarned, and he needed the slight advantage of surprise.

"Ah—" The man made up his mind rapidly. "Ah—yes; yes sir. I'll take you to Mr. Wigtight, sir. If you'll come this way." He closed his ledger with a snap and slid it into a drawer. With one eye still on Monk he took a key from his waistcoat pocket and locked the drawer, then straightened up. "Yes sir, this way."

The inner office of Josiah Wigtight was quite a different affair from the drab attempt at anonymous respectability of the entrance. It was frankly lush, everything chosen for comfort, almost hedonism. The big armchairs were covered in velvet and the cushions were deep in both color and texture; the carpet muffled sound and the gas lamps hissing softly on the walls were mantled in rose-colored glass which shed a glow over the room, obscuring outlines and dulling glare. The curtains were heavy and drawn in folds to keep out the intrusion and the reality of daylight. It was not a matter of taste, not even of vulgarity, but purely the uses of pleasure. After a moment or two the effect was curiously soporific. Immediately Monk's respect for Wigtight rose. It was clever.

"Ah." Wigtight breathed out deeply. He was a portly man, swelling out like a giant toad behind his desk, wide mouth split into a smile that died long before it reached his bulbous eyes. "Ah," he repeated. "A matter of business somewhat delicate, Mr.—er?"

"Somewhat," Monk agreed. He decided not to sit down in the soft, dark chair; he was almost afraid it would swallow him, like a mire, smother his judgment. He felt he would be at a disadvantage in it and not able to move if he should need to.

"Sit down, sit down!" Wigtight waved. "Let us talk about it. I'm sure some accommodation can be arrived at."

"I hope so." Monk perched on the arm of the chair. It

253

was uncomfortable, but in this room he preferred to be uncomfortable.

"You are temporarily embarrassed?" Wigtight began. "You wish to take advantage of an excellent investment? You have expectations of a relative, in poor health, who favors you—"

"Thank you, I have employment which is quite sufficient for my needs."

"You are a fortunate man." There was no belief in his smooth, expressionless voice; he had heard every lie and excuse human ingenuity could come up with.

"More fortunate than Joscelin Grey!" Monk said baldly.

Wigtight's face changed in only the minutest of ways— a shadow, no more. Had Monk not been watching for it he would have missed it altogether.

"Joscelin Grey?" Wigtight repeated. Monk could see in his face the indecision whether to deny knowing him or admit it as a matter of common knowledge. He decided the wrong way.

"I know no such person, sir."

"You've never heard of him?" Monk tried not to press too hard. He hated moneylenders with far more anger than reason could tell him of. He meant to trap this soft, fat man in his own words, trap him and watch the bloated body struggle.

But Wigtight sensed a pitfall.

"I hear so many names," he added cautiously.

"Then you had better look in your books," Monk suggested. "And see if his is there, since you don't remember."

"I don't keep books, after debts are paid." Wigtight's wide, pale eyes assumed a blandness. "Matter of discretion, you know. People don't like to be reminded of their hard times."

"How civil of you," Monk said sarcastically. "How about looking through the lists of those who didn't repay you?"

"Mr. Grey is not among them."

"So he paid you." Monk allowed only a little of his triumph to creep through.

"I have not said I lent him anything."

"Then if you lent him nothing, why did you hire two men to deceive their way into his flat and ransack it? And incidentally, to steal his silver and small ornaments?" He saw with delight that Wigtight flinched. "Clumsy, that, Mr. Wigtight. You're hiring a very poor class of ruffian these days. A good man would never have helped himself on the side like that. Dangerous; brings another charge into it—and those goods are so easy to trace."

"You're police!" Wigtight's understanding was sudden and venomous.

"That's right."

"I don't hire thieves." Now Wigtight was hedging, trying to gain time to think, and Monk knew it.

"You hire collectors, who turned out to be thieves as well," Monk said immediately. "The law doesn't see any difference."

"I hire people to do my collecting, of course," Wigtight agreed. "Can't go out into the streets after everybody myself."

"How many do you call on with forged police papers, two months after you've murdered them?"

Every vestige of color drained out of Wigtight's face, leaving it gray, like a cold fish skin. Monk thought for a moment he was having some kind of a fit, and he felt no concern at all.

It was long seconds before Wigtight could speak, and Monk merely waited.

"Murdered!" The word when it came was hollow. "I swear on my mother's grave, I never had anything to do with that. Why should I? Why should I do that? It's insane. You're crazed."

"Because you're a usurer," Monk said bitterly, a well of anger and scalding contempt opening up inside him. "And usurers don't allow people not to pay their debts, with all the interest when they're due." He leaned forward

255

toward the man, threatening by his movement when Wigtight was motionless in the chair. "Bad for business if you let them get away with it," he said almost between his teeth. "Encourages other people to do the same. Where would you be if everyone refused to pay you back? Bleed themselves white to satisfy your interest. Better one goose dead than the whole wretched flock running around free and fat, eh?"

"I never killed him!" Wigtight was frightened, not only by the facts, but by Monk's hatred. He knew unreason when he saw it; and Monk enjoyed his fear.

"But you sent someone—it comes to the same thing," Monk pursued.

"No! It wouldn't make sense!" Wigtight's voice was growing higher, a new, sharp note on it. The panic was sweet to Monk's ear. "All right." Wigtight raised his hands, soft and fat. "I sent them to see if Grey had kept any record of borrowing from me. I knew he'd been murdered and I thought he might have kept the cancelled IOU. I didn't want to have anything to do with him. That's all, I swear!" There was sweat on his face now, glistening in the gaslight. "He paid me back. Mother of God, it was only fifty pounds anyway! Do you think I'd send out men to murder a debtor for fifty pounds? It would be mad, insane. They'd have a hold over me for the rest of my life. They'd bleed me dry—or see me to the gibbet."

Monk stared at him. Painfully the truth of it conquered him. Wigtight was a parasite, but he was not a fool. He would not have hired such clumsy chance help to murder a man for a debt, of whatever size. If he had intended murder he would have been cleverer, more discreet about it. A little violence might well have been fruitful, but not this, and not in Grey's own house.

But he might well have wanted to be sure there was no trace of the association left, purely to avoid inconvenience.

"Why did you leave it so long?" Monk asked, his voice

256

flat again, without the hunting edge. "Why didn't you go and look for the IOU straightaway?"

Wigtight knew he had won. It was there gleaming in his pallid, globular face, like pond slime on a frog.

"At first there were too many real police about," he answered. "Always going in and out." He spread his hands in reasonableness. Monk would have liked to call him a liar, but he could not, not yet. "Couldn't get anyone prepared to take the risk," Wigtight went on. "Pay a man too much for a job, and immediately he begins to wonder if there's more to it than you've told him. Might start thinking I had something to be afraid of. Your lot was looking for thieves, in the beginning. Now it's different; you're asking about business, money—"

"How do you know?" Monk believed him, he was forced to, but he wanted every last ounce of discomfort he could drag out.

"Word gets about; you asked his tailor, his wine merchant, looking into the paying of his bills—"

Monk remembered he had sent Evan to do these things. It would seem the usurer had eyes and ears everywhere. He realized now it was to be expected: that was how he found his customers, he learned weaknesses, sought out vulnerability. God, how he loathed this man and his kind.

"Oh." In spite of himself his face betrayed his defeat. "I shall have to be more discreet with my inquiries."

Wigtight smiled coldly.

"I shouldn't trouble yourself. It will make no difference." He knew his success; it was a taste he was used to, like a ripe Stilton cheese and port after dinner.

There was nothing more to say, and Monk could not stomach more of Wigtight's satisfaction. He left, going out past the oily clerk in the front office; but he was determined to take the first opportunity to charge Josiah Wigtight with something, preferably something earning a good long spell on the prison treadmill. Perhaps it was hate of usury and all its cancerous agonies eating away the hearts of people, or hate for Wigtight particularly, for his fat belly and cold eyes; but more probably it was the bitterness of disappointment because he knew it was not the moneylender who had killed Joscelin Grey.

All of which brought him back again to facing the only other avenue of investigation. Joscelin Grey's friends, the people whose secrets he might have known. He was back to Shelburne again—and Runcorn's triumph.

But before he began on that course to one of its inevitable conclusions—either the arrest of Shelburne, and his own ruin after it; or else the admission that he could not prove his case and must accept failure; and Runcorn could not lose—Monk would follow all the other leads, however faint, beginning with Charles Latterly.

He called in the late afternoon, when he felt it most likely Imogen would be at home, and he could reasonably ask to see Charles.

He was greeted civilly, but no more than that. The parlor maid was too well trained to show surprise. He was kept waiting only a few minutes before being shown into the withdrawing room and its discreet comfort washed over him again.

Charles was standing next to a small table in the window bay.

"Good afternoon, Mr.—er—Monk," he said with distinct chill. "To what do we owe this further attention?"

Monk felt his stomach sink. It was as if the smell of the rookeries still clung to him. Perhaps it was obvious what manner of man he was, where he worked, what he dealt with; and it had been all the time. He had been too busy with his own feelings to be aware of theirs.

"I am still inquiring into the murder of Joscelin Grey," he replied a little stiltedly. He knew both Imogen and Hester were in the room but he refused to look at them. He bowed very slightly, without raising his eyes. He made a similar acknowledgment in their direction.

"Then it's about time you reached some conclusion, isn't it?" Charles raised his eyebrows. "We are very sorry,

258

naturally, since we knew him; but we do not require a day-by-day account of your progress, or lack of it.''

''It's as well,'' Monk answered, stirred to tartness in his hurt, and the consciousness that he did not, and would never, belong in this faded and gracious room with its padded furniture and gleaming walnut. ''Because I could not afford it. It is because you knew Major Grey that I wish to speak to you again.'' He swallowed. ''We naturally first considered the possibility of his having been attacked by some chance thief, then of its being over a matter of debt, perhaps gambling, or borrowing. We have exhausted these avenues now, and are driven back to what has always, regrettably, seemed the most probable—''

''I thought I had explained it to you, Mr. Monk.'' Charles's voice was sharper. ''We do not wish to know! And quite frankly, I will not have my wife or my sister distressed by hearing of it. Perhaps the women of your—'' He searched for the least offensive word. ''Your background—are less sensitive to such things: unfortunately they may be more used to violence and the sordid aspects of life. But my sister and my wife are gentlewomen, and do not even know of such things. I must ask you to respect their feelings.''

Monk could sense the color burning up his face. He ached to be equally rude in return, but his awareness of Imogen, only a few feet from him, was overwhelming. He did not care in the slightest what Hester thought; in fact it would be a positive pleasure to quarrel with her, like the sting in the face of clean, icy water—invigorating.

''I had no intention of distressing anyone unnecessarily, sir.'' He forced the words out, muffled between his teeth. ''And I have not come for your information, but to ask you some further questions. I was merely trying to give you the reason for them, that you might feel freer to answer.''

Charles blinked at him. He was half leaning against the mantel shelf, and he stiffened.

"I know nothing whatsoever about the affair, and naturally neither do my family."

"I am sure we should have helped you if we could," Imogen added. For an instant Monk thought she looked abashed by Charles's so open condescension.

Hester stood up and walked across the room opposite Monk.

"We have not been asked any questions yet," she pointed out to Charles reasonably. "How do we know whether we could answer them or not? And I cannot speak for Imogen, of course, but I am not in the least offended by being asked; indeed if you are capable of considering the murder, then so am I. We surely have a duty."

"My dear Hester, you don't know what you are speaking of." Charles's face was sharp and he put his hand out towards her, but she avoided it. "What unpleasant things may be involved, quite beyond your experience!"

"Balderdash!" she said instantly. "My experience has included a multitude of things you wouldn't have in your nightmares. I've seen men hacked to death by sabers, shot by cannon, frozen, starved, wasted by disease—"

"Hester!" Charles exploded. "For the love of heaven!"

"So don't tell me I cannot survive the drawing room discussion of one wretched murder," she finished.

Charles's face was very pink and he ignored Monk. "Has it not crossed your very unfeminine mind that Imogen has feelings, and has led a considerably more decorous life than you have chosen for yourself?" he demanded. "Really, sometimes you are beyond enduring!"

"Imogen is not nearly as helpless as you seem to imagine," Hester retorted, but there was a faint blush to her cheeks. "Nor, I think, does she wish to conceal truth because it may be unpleasant to discuss. You do her courage little credit."

Monk looked at Charles and was perfectly sure that had they been alone he would have disciplined his sister in whatever manner was open to him—which was probably not a great deal. Personally Monk was very glad it was not his problem.

Imogen took the matter into her own hands. She turned towards Monk.

"You were saying that you were driven to an inevitable conclusion, Mr. Monk. Pray tell us what it is." She stared at him and her eyes were angry, almost defensive. She seemed more inwardly alive and sensitive to hurt than anyone else he had ever seen. For seconds he could not think of words to answer her. The moments hung in the air. Her chin came a little higher, but she did not look away.

"I—" he began, and failed. He tried again. "That— that it was someone he knew who killed him." Then his voice came mechanically. "Someone well known to him, of his own position and social circle."

"Nonsense!" Charles interrupted him sharply, coming into the center of the room as if to confront him physically. "People of Joscelin Grey's circle do not go around murdering people. If that's the best you can do, then you had better give up the case and hand it over to someone more skilled."

"You are being unnecessarily rude, Charles." Imogen's eyes were bright and there was a touch of color in her face. "We have no reason to suppose that Mr. Monk is not skilled at his job, and quite certainly no call to suggest it."

Charles's whole body tightened; the impertinence was intolerable.

"Imogen," he began icily; then remembering the feminine frailty he had asserted, altered his tone. "The matter is naturally upsetting to you; I understand that. Perhaps it would be better if you were to leave us. Retire to your room and rest for a little while. Return when you have composed yourself. Perhaps a tisane?"

"I am not tired, and I do not wish for a tisane. I am perfectly composed, and the police wish to question me." She swung around. "Don't you, Mr. Monk?"

He wished he could remember what he knew of them,

but although he strained till his brain ached, he could recall nothing. All his memories were blurred and colored by the overwhelming emotion she aroused in him, the hunger for something always just out of reach, like a great music that haunts the senses but cannot quite be caught, disturbingly and unforgettably sweet, evocative of a whole life on the brink of remembrance.

But he was behaving like a fool. Her gentleness, something in her face had woken in him the memory of a time when he had loved, of the softer side of himself which he had lost when the carriage had crashed and obliterated the past. There was more in him than the detective, brilliant, ambitious, sharp tongued, solitary. There had been those who loved him, as well as the rivals who hated, the subordinates who feared or admired, the villains who knew his skill, the poor who looked for justice—or vengeance. Imogen reminded him that he had a humanity as well, and it was too precious for him to drown in reason. He had lost his balance, and if he were to survive this nightmare—Runcorn, the murder, his career—he must regain it.

"Since you knew Major Grey," he tried again, "it is possible he may have confided in you any anxieties he may have had for his safety—anyone who disliked him or was harassing him for any reason." He was not being as articulate as he wished, and he cursed himself for it.

"Did he mention any envies or rivalries to you?"

"None at all. Why would anyone he knew kill him?" she asked. "He was very charming; I never knew of him picking a quarrel more serious than a few sharp words. Perhaps his humor was a little unkind, but hardly enough to provoke more than a passing irritation."

"My dear Imogen, they wouldn't!" Charles snapped. "It was robbery; it must have been."

Imogen breathed in and out deeply and ignored her husband, still regarding Monk with solemn eyes, waiting for his reply.

"I believe blackmail," Monk replied. "Or perhaps jealousy over a woman."

262

"Blackmail!" Charles was horrified and his voice was thick with disbelief. "You mean Grey was blackmailing someone? Over what, may I ask?"

"If we knew that, sir, we should almost certainly know who it was," Monk answered. "And it would solve the case."

"Then you know nothing." There was derision back again in Charles's voice.

"On the contrary, we know a great deal. We have a suspect, but before we charge him we must have eliminated all the other possibilities." That was overstating the case dangerously, but Charles's smug face, his patronizing manner roused Monk's temper beyond the point where he had complete control. He wanted to shake him, to force him out of his complacency and his infuriating superiority.

"Then you are making a mistake." Charles looked at him through narrow eyes. "At least it seems most likely you are."

Monk smiled dryly. "I am trying to avoid that, sir, by exploring every alternative first, and by gaining all the information anyone can give. I'm sure you appreciate that!"

From the periphery of his vision Monk could see Hester smile and was distinctly pleased.

Charles grunted.

"We do really wish to help you," Imogen said in the silence. "My husband is only trying to protect us from unpleasantness, which is most delicate of him. But we were exceedingly fond of Joscelin, and we are quite strong enough to tell you anything we can."

" 'Exceedingly fond' is overstating it, my dear," Charles said uncomfortably. "We liked him, and of course we felt an extra affection for him for George's sake."

"George?" Monk frowned, he had not heard George mentioned before.

"My younger brother," Charles supplied.

"He knew Major Grey?" Monk asked keenly. "Then may I speak with him also?"

263

"I am afraid not. But yes, he knew Grey quite well. I believe they were very close, for a while."

"For a while? Did they have some disagreement?"

"No, George is dead."

"Oh." Monk hesitated, abashed. "I am sorry."

"Thank you." Charles coughed and cleared his throat. "We were fond of Grey, but to say we were extremely so is too much. My wife is, I think, quite naturally transferring some of our affection for George to George's friend."

"I see." Monk was not sure what to say. Had Imogen seen in Joscelin only her dead brother-in-law's friend, or had Joscelin himself charmed her with his wit and talent to please? There had been a keenness in her face when she had spoken of him. It reminded him of Rosamond Shelburne: there was the same gentleness in it, the same echo of remembered times of happiness, shared laughter and grace. Had Charles been too blind to see it—or too conceited to understand it for what it was?

An ugly, dangerous thought came to his mind and refused to be ignored. Was the woman not Rosamond, but Imogen Latterly? He wanted intensely to disprove it. But how? If Charles had been somewhere else at the time, provably so, then the whole question was over, dismissed forever.

He stared at Charles's smooth face. He looked irritable, but totally unconscious of any guilt. Monk tried frantically to think of an oblique way to ask him. His brain was like glue, heavy and congealing. Why in God's name did Charles have to be Imogen's husband?

Was there another way? If only he could remember what he knew of them. Was this fear unreasonable, the result of an imagination free of the sanity of memory? Or was it memory slowly returning, in bits and pieces, that woke that very fear?

The stick in Joscelin Grey's hall stand. The image of it was so clear in his head. If only he could enlarge it, see the hand and the arm, the man who held it. That was the knowledge that lay like a sickness in his stomach; he knew

264

the owner of the stick, and he knew with certainty that Lovel Grey was a complete stranger to him. When he had been to Shelburne not one member of the household had greeted him with the slightest flicker of recognition. And why should they pretend? In fact to do so would in itself have been suspicious, since they had no idea he had lost his memory. Lovel Grey could not be the owner of that stick with the brass chain embossed around the top.

But it could be Charles Latterly.

"Have you ever been to Major Grey's flat, Mr. Latterly?" The question was out before he realized it. It was like a die cast, and he did not now want to know the answer. Once begun, he would have to pursue it; even if only for himself he would have to know, always hoping he was wrong, seeking the one more fact to prove himself so.

Charles looked slightly surprised.

"No. Why? Surely you have been there yourself? I cannot tell you anything about it!"

"You have never been there?"

"No, I have told you so. I had no occasion."

"Nor, I take it, have any of your family?" He did not look at either of the women. He knew the question would be regarded as indelicate, if not outrightly impertinent.

"Of course not!" Charles controlled his temper with some difficulty. He seemed about to add something when Imogen interrupted.

"Would you care for us to account for our whereabouts on the day Joscelin was killed, Mr. Monk?"

He looked carefully, but he could see no sarcasm in her. She regarded him with deep, steady eyes.

"Don't be ridiculous!" Charles snapped with mounting fury. "If you cannot treat this matter with proper seriousness, Imogen, then you had better leave us and return to your room."

"I am being perfectly serious," she replied, turning away from Monk. "If it was one of Joscelin's friends who killed him, then there is no reason why we should not be

265

suspected. Surely, Charles, it would be better to clear ourselves by the simple fact of having been elsewhere at the time than it would be to have Mr. Monk satisfy himself we had no reason to, by investigating our affairs?''

Charles paled visibly and looked at Imogen as if she were some venomous creature that had come out of the carpeting and bitten him. Monk felt the tightness in his stomach grip harder.

''I was at dinner with friends,'' Charles said thinly.

Considering he had just supplied what seemed to be an alibi, he looked peculiarly wretched. Monk could not avoid it; he had to press. He stared at Charles's pale face.

''Where was that, sir?''

''Doughty Street.''

Imogen looked at Monk blandly, innocently, but Hester had turned away.

''What number, sir?''

''Can that matter, Mr. Monk?'' Imogen asked innocently.

Hester's head came up, waiting.

Monk found himself explaining to her, guilt surprising him.

''Doughty Street leads into Mecklenburg Square, Mrs. Latterly. It is no more than a two- or three-minute walk from one to the other.''

''Oh.'' Her voice was small and flat. She turned slowly to her husband.

''Twenty-two,'' he said, teeth clenched. ''But I was there all evening, and I had no idea Grey lived anywhere near.''

Again Monk spoke before he permitted himself to think, or he would have hesitated.

''I find that hard to believe, sir, since you wrote to him at that address. We found your letter among his effects.''

''God damn it—I—'' Charles stopped, frozen.

Monk waited. The silence was so intense he imagined he could hear horses' hooves in the next street. He did not look at either of the women.

"I mean—" Charles began, and again stopped.

Monk found himself unable to avoid it any longer. He was embarrassed for them, and desperately sorry. He looked at Imogen, wanting her to know that, even if it meant nothing to her at all.

She was standing very still. Her eyes were so dark he could see nothing in them, but there did not seem to be the hate he feared. For a wild moment he felt that if only he could have talked to her alone he could have explained, made her understand the necessity for all this, the compulsion.

"My friends will swear I was there all evening." Charles's words cut across them. "I'll give you their names. This is ridiculous; I liked Joscelin, and our misfortunes were as much his. There was no reason whatever to wish him harm, and you will find none!"

"If I could have their names, Mr. Latterly?"

Charles's head came up sharply.

"You're not going to go 'round asking them to account for me at the time of a murder, for God's sake! I'll only give you their names—"

"I shall be discreet, sir."

Charles snorted with derision at the idea of so delicate a virtue as discretion in a policeman.

Monk looked at him patiently.

"It will be easier if you give me their names, sir, than if I have to discover them for myself."

"Damn you!" Charles's face was suffused with blood.

"Their names, please sir?"

Charles strode over to one of the small tables and took out a sheet of paper and a pencil. He wrote for several moments before folding it and handing it to Monk.

Monk took it without looking and put it in his pocket.

"Thank you, sir."

"Is that all?"

"No, I'm afraid I would still like to ask you anything further you might know about Major Grey's other friends, anyone with whom he stayed, and could have known well enough to be aware, even accidentally, of some secret damaging to them.''

"Such as what, for God's sake?" Charles looked at him with extreme distaste.

Monk did not wish to be drawn into speaking of the sort of things his imagination feared, especially in Imogen's hearing. In spite of the irrevocable position he was now in, every vestige of good opinion she might keep of him mattered, like fragments of a broken treasure.

"I don't know, sir; and without strong evidence it would be unseemly to suggest anything."

"Unseemly," Charles said sarcastically, his voice grating with the intensity of his emotion. "You mean that matters to you? I'm surprised you know what the word means."

Imogen turned away in embarrassment, and Hester's face froze. She opened her mouth as if to speak, then realized she would be wiser to keep silent.

Charles colored faintly in the silence that followed, but he was incapable of apology.

"He spoke of some people named Dawlish," he said irritably. "And I believe he stayed with Gerry Fortescue once or twice."

Monk took down such details as they could remember of the Dawlishes, the Fortescues and others, but it sounded useless, and he was aware of Charles's heavy disbelief, as if he were humoring an uncaged animal it might be dangerous to annoy. He stayed only to justify himself, because he had said to them that it was his reason for having come.

When he left he imagined he could hear the sigh of relief behind him, and his mind conjured up their quick looks at each other, then the understanding in their eyes, needing no words, that an intruder had gone at last, an extreme unpleasantness was over. All the way along the street his thoughts were in the bright room behind him and on Imogen. He considered what she was doing, what she thought of him, if she saw him as a man at all, or only the inhabiter of an office that had become suddenly more than usually offensive to her.

And yet she had looked so directly at him. That seemed a timeless moment, recurring again and again—or was it simply that he dwelt in it? What had she asked of him originally? What had they said to one another?

What a powerful and ridiculous thing the imagination was—had he not known it so foolish, he could have believed there must have been deep memories between them.

When Monk had gone, Hester, Imogen and Charles were left standing in the withdrawing room, the sun streaming in from the French windows into the small garden, bright through the leaves in the silence.

Charles drew in his breath as if to speak, looked first at his wife, then at Hester, and let out a sigh. He said nothing. His face was tight and unhappy as he walked to the door, excused himself perfunctorily, and went out.

A torrent of thoughts crowded Hester's mind. She disliked Monk, and he angered her, yet the longer she watched him the less did she think he was as incompetent as he had first seemed. His questions were erratic, and he appeared to be no nearer finding Joscelin Grey's killer than he had been when he began; and yet she was keenly aware both of an intelligence and a tenacity in him. He cared about it, more than simply for vanity or ambition. For justice sake he wanted to know and to do something about it.

She would have smiled, did it not wound so deep, but she had also seen in him a startling softness towards Imogen, an admiration and a desire to protect—something which he certainly did not feel for Hester. She had seen that look on several men's faces; Imogen had woken precisely the same emotions in Charles when they first met, and in many men since. Hester never knew if Imogen herself was aware of it or not.

Had she stirred Joscelin Grey as well? Had he fallen in

love with her, the gentleness, those luminous eyes, the quality of innocence which touched everything she did?

Charles was still in love with her. He was quiet, admittedly a trifle pompous, and he had been anxious and shorter tempered than customarily since his father's death; but he was honorable, at times generous, and sometimes fun—at least he had been. Lately he had become more sober, as though a heavy weight could never be totally forgotten.

Was it conceivable that Imogen had found the witty, charming, gallant Joscelin Grey more interesting, even if only briefly? If that had been so, then Charles, for all his seeming self-possession, would have cared deeply, and the hurt might have been something he could not control.

Imogen was keeping a secret. Hester knew her well enough, and liked her, to be aware of the small tensions, the silences where before she would have confided, the placing of a certain guard on her tongue when they were together. It was not Charles she was afraid might notice and suspect; he was not perceptive enough, he did not expect to understand any woman—it was Hester. She was still as affectionate, as generous with small trinkets, the loan of a kerchief or a silk shawl, a word of praise, gratitude for a courtesy—but she was careful, she hesitated before she spoke, she told the exact truth and the impetuosity was gone.

What was the secret? Something in her attitude, an extra awareness, made Hester believe it had to do with Joscelin Grey, because Imogen both pursued and was afraid of the policeman Monk.

"You did not mention before that Joscelin Grey had known George," she said aloud.

Imogen looked out of the window. "Did I not? Well, it was probably a desire not to hurt you, dear. I did not wish to remind you of George, as well as Mama and Papa."

Hester could not argue with that. She did not believe it, but it was exactly the sort of thing Imogen would have done.

"Thank you," she replied. "It was most thoughtful of you, especially since you were so fond of Major Grey."

Imogen smiled, her far-off gaze seeing beyond the dappled light through the window, but to what Hester thought it unfair to guess.

"He was fun," Imogen said slowly. "He was so different from anyone else I know. It was a very dreadful way to die—but I suppose it was quick, and much less painful than many you have seen."

Again Hester did not know what to say.

When Monk returned to the police station Runcorn was waiting for him, sitting at his desk looking at a sheaf of papers. He put them down and pulled a face as Monk came in.

"So your thief was a moneylender," he said dryly. "And the newspapers are not interested in moneylenders, I assure you."

"Then they should be!" Monk snapped back. "They're a filthy infestation, one of the more revolting symptoms of poverty—"

"Oh for heaven's sake, either run for Parliament or be a policeman," Runcorn said with exasperation. "But if you value your job, stop trying to do both at once. And policemen are employed to solve cases, not make moral commentary."

Monk glared at him.

"If we got rid of some of the poverty, and its parasites, we might prevent the crime before it came to the stage of needing a solution," he said with heat that surprised himself. A memory of passion was coming back, even if he could not know anything of its cause.

"Joscelin Grey," Runcorn said flatly. He was not going to be diverted.

"I'm working," Monk replied.

"Then your success has been embarrassingly limited!"

"Can you prove it was Shelburne?" Monk demanded. He knew what Runcorn was trying to do, and he would

271

fight him to the very last step. If Runcorn forced him to arrest Shelburne before he was ready, he would see to it that it was publicly Runcorn's doing.

But Runcorn was not to be drawn.

"It's your job," he said acidly. "I'm not on the case."

"Perhaps you should be." Monk raised his eyebrows as if he were really considering it. "Perhaps you should take over?"

Runcorn's eyes narrowed. "Are you saying you cannot manage?" he asked very softly, a lift at the end of his words. "That it is too big for you?"

Monk called his bluff.

"If it is Shelburne, then perhaps it is. Maybe you should make the arrest; a senior officer, and all that."

Runcorn's face fell blank, and Monk tasted a certain sweetness; but it was only for a moment.

"It seems you've lost your nerve, as well as your memory," Runcorn answered with a faint sneer. "Are you giving up?"

Monk took a deep breath.

"I haven't lost anything," he said deliberately. "And I certainly haven't lost my head. I don't intend to go charging in to arrest a man against whom I have a damn good suspicion, but nothing else. If you want to, then take this case from me, officially, and do it yourself. And God help you when Lady Fabia hears about it. You'll be beyond anyone else's help, I promise you."

"Coward! By God you've changed, Monk."

"If I would have arrested a man without proof before, then I needed to change. Are you taking the case from me?"

"I'll give you another week. I don't think I can persuade the public to give you any more than that."

"Give *us*," Monk corrected him. "As far as they know, we are all working for the same end. Now have you anything helpful to say, like an idea how to prove it was Shelburne, without a witness? Or would you have gone ahead and done it yourself, if you had?"

The implication was not lost on Runcorn. Surprisingly, his face flushed hotly in anger, perhaps even guilt.

"It's your case," he said angrily. "I shan't take it from you till you come and admit you've failed or I'm asked to remove you."

"Good. Then I'll get on with it."

"Do that. Do that, Monk; if you can!"

Outside the sky was leaden and it was raining hard. Monk thought grimly as he walked home that the newspapers were right in their criticism; he knew little more now than he had when Evan had first showed him the material evidence. Shelburne was the only one for whom he knew a motive, and yet that wretched walking stick clung in his mind. It was not the murder weapon, but he knew he had seen it before. It could not be Joscelin Grey's, because Imogen had said quite distinctly that Grey had not been back to the Latterlys' house since her father-in-law's death, and of course Monk had never been to the house before then.

Then whose was it?

Not Shelburne's.

Without realizing it his feet had taken him not towards his own rooms but to Mecklenburg Square.

Grimwade was in the hallway.

"Evenin', Mr. Monk. Bad night, sir. I dunno wot summer's comin' ter—an' that's the truth. 'Ailstones an' all! Lay like snow, it did, in July. An' now this. Cruel to be out in, sir." He regarded Monk's soaking clothes with sympathy. "Can I 'elp yer wif summink, sir?"

"The man who came to see Mr. Yeats—"

"The murderer?" Grimwade shivered but there was a certain melodramatic savoring in his thin face.

"It would seem so," Monk conceded. "Describe him again, will you?"

Grimwade screwed up his eyes and ran his tongue around his lips.

"Well that's 'ard, sir. It's a fair while ago now, an' the more I tries to remember 'im, the fainter 'e gets. 'E were tallish, I know vat, but not outsize, as you might say. 'Ard ter say w'en somebody's away from yer a bit. W'en 'e came in 'e seemed a good couple o' hinches less than you are, although 'e seemed bigger w'en 'e left. Can be deceivin', sir.''

"Well that's something. What sort of coloring had he: fresh, sallow, pale, swarthy?''

"Kind o' fresh, sir. But then that could 'a' bin the cold. Proper wicked night it were, somethin' cruel for July. Shockin' unseasonal. Rainin' 'ard, an' east wind like a knife.''

"And you cannot remember whether he had a beard or not?''

"I think as 'e 'adn't, leastways if 'e 'ad, it were one o' vem very small ones wot can be 'idden by a muffler.''

"And dark hair? Or could it have been brown, or even fair?''

"No sir, it couldn't 'a' bin fair, not yeller, like; but it could 'a' bin brahn. But I do remember as 'e 'ad very gray eyes. I noticed that as 'e were goin' out, very piercin' eyes 'e 'ad, like one o' vem fellers wot puts people inter a trance.''

"Piercing eyes? You're sure?'' Monk said dubiously, skeptical of Grimwade's sense of melodrama in hindsight.

"Yes sir, more I fink of it, more I'm sure. Don't remember 'is face, but I do remember 'is eyes w'en 'e looked at me. Not w'en 'e was comin' in , but w'en 'e was a-goin' out. Funny thing, that. Yer'd fink I'd a noticed vem w'en 'e spoke ter me, but sure as I'm standin' 'ere, I didn't.'' He looked at Monk ingenuously.

"Thank you, Mr. Grimwade. Now I'll see Mr. Yeats, if he's in. If he isn't then I'll wait for him.''

"Oh 'e's in, sir. Bin in a little while. Shall I take you up, or do you remember the way?''

"I remember the way, thank you.'' Monk smiled grimly and started up the stairs. The place was becoming wretchedly familiar to him. He passed Grey's entrance quickly, still conscious of the horror inside, and knocked sharply at Yeats's door, and a moment later it opened and Yeats's worried little face looked up at him.

"Oh!" he said in some alarm. "I—I was going to speak to you. I—I, er—I suppose I should have done it before." He wrung his hands nervously, twisting them in front of him, red knuckled. "But I heard all about the—er—the burglar—from Mr. Grimwade, you know—and I rather thought you'd, er—found the murderer—so—"

"May I come in, Mr. Yeats?" Monk interrupted. It was natural Grimwade should have mentioned the burglar, if only to warn the other tenants, and because one could hardly expect a garrulous and lonely old man to keep to himself such a thrilling and scandalous event, but Monk was irritated by the reminder of its uselessness.

"I'm—I'm sorry," Yeats stammered as Monk moved past him. "I—I do realize I should have said something to you before."

"About what, Mr. Yeats?" Monk exercised his patience with an effort. The poor little man was obviously much upset.

"Why, about my visitor, of course. I was quite sure you knew, when you came to the door." Yeats's voice rose to a squeak in amazement.

"What about him, Mr. Yeats? Have you recalled something further?" Suddenly hope shot up inside him. Could this be the beginning of proof at last?

"Why sir, I discovered who he was."

"What?" Monk did not dare to believe. The room was singing around him, bubbling with excitement. In an instant this funny little man was going to tell him the name of the murderer of Joscelin Grey. It was incredible, dazzling.

"I discovered who he was," Yeats repeated. "I knew I should have told you as soon as I found out, but I thought—"

The moment of paralysis was broken.

"Who?" Monk demanded; he knew his voice was shaking. "Who was it?"

Yeats was startled. He began to stammer again.

"Who was it?" Monk made a desperate effort to control himself, but his own voice was rising to a shout.

"Why—why, sir, it was a man called Bartholomew Stubbs. He is a dealer in old maps, as he said. Is it—is it important, Mr. Monk?"

Monk was stunned.

"Bartholomew Stubbs?" he repeated foolishly.

"Yes sir. I met him again, through a mutual acquaintance. I thought I would ask him." His hands fluttered. "I was quite shockingly nervous, I assure you; but I felt in view of the fate of poor Major Grey that I must approach him. He was most civil. He left here straight after speaking to me at my doorstep. He was at a temperance meeting in Farringdon Road, near the House of Correction, fifteen minutes later. I ascertained that because my friend was there also." He moved from one foot to the other in his agitation. "He distinctly remembers Mr. Stubbs's arrival, because the first speaker had just commenced his address."

Monk stared at him. It was incomprehensible. If Stubbs had left immediately, and it seemed he had, then who was the man Grimwade had seen leaving later?

"Did—did he remain at the temperance meeting all evening?" he asked desperately.

"No sir." Yeats shook his head. "He only went there to meet my friend, who is also a collector, a very learned one—"

"He left!" Monk seized on it.

"Yes sir." Yeats danced around in his anxiety, his hands jerking to and fro. "I am trying to tell you! They left together and went to get some supper—"

"Together?"

"Yes sir. I am afraid, Mr. Monk, Mr. Stubbs could not have been the one to have so dreadfully attacked poor Major Grey."

"No." Monk was too shaken, too overwhelmingly disappointed to move. He did not know where to start again.

"Are you quite well, Mr. Monk?" Yeats asked tentatively. "I am so sorry. Perhaps I really should have told you earlier, but I did not think it would be important, since he was not guilty."

"No—no, never mind," Monk said almost under his breath. "I understand."

"Oh, I'm so glad. I thought perhaps I was in error."

Monk muttered something polite, probably meaningless—he did not want to be unkind to the little man—and made his way out onto the landing again. He was hardly aware of going down the stairs, nor did he register the drenching weight of the rain when he passed Grimwade and went outside into the street with its gaslight and swirling gutters.

He began to walk, blindly, and it was not until he was spattered with mud and a cab wheel missed him by less than a foot that he realized he was on Doughty Street.

" 'Ere!" the cabby shouted at him. "Watch w'ere yer going', guv! Yer want ter get yerself killed?"

Monk stopped, staring up at him. "You occupied?"

"No guv. Yer want ter go somewhere? Mebbe yer'd better, afore yer get someb'dy into a haccident."

"Yes," Monk accepted, still without moving.

"Well come on then," the cabby said sharply, leaning forward to peer at him. "Not a night fer man ner beast ter be out in, it ain't. Mate o' mine were killed on a night like this, poor sod. 'Orse bolted and 'is cab turned over. Killed, 'e were. 'It 'is 'ead on the curb an' 'e died, jes' like that. And 'is fare were all smashed abaht too, but they say as 'e were o'right, in the end. Took 'im orf ter 'orspital, o' course. 'Ere, are yer goin' ter stand there all night, guv? Come on now, either get in, or don't; but make up yer mind!"

"This friend of yours." Monk's voice was distorted, as if from far away. "When was he killed, when was this accident, exactly?"

"July it were, terrible weather fer July. Wicked night.

'Ailstorm wot lay like snow. Swear ter Gawd—I don't know wot the wevver's comin' ter.''

"What date in July?'' Monk's whole body was cold, and idiotically calm.

"Come on now, sir?'' the cabby wheedled, as one does a drunk or a recalcitrant animal. "Get in aht o' the rain. It's shockin' wet aht there. Yer'll catch yer death.''

"What date?''

"I fink as it were the fourf. Why? We ain't goin' ter 'ave no haccident ternight, I promises yer. I'll be as careful as if you was me muvver. Jus' make up yer mind, sir!''

"Did you know him well?''

"Yes sir, 'e were a good mate o' mine. Did yer know 'im too, sir? Yer live 'rahnd 'ere, do yer? 'E used ter work this patch all ve time. Picked up 'is last fare 'ere, right in vis street, accordin' ter 'is paper. Saw 'im vat very night meself, I did. Nah is yer comin', sir, or ain't yer? 'Cos I 'aven't got all night. I reckon w'en yer goes a henjoyin' yerself, yer oughter take someone wiv yer. Yer in't safe.''

On this street. The cabby had picked him, Monk, up on this street, less than a hundred yards from Mecklenburg Square, on the night Joscelin Grey was murdered. What had he been doing here? Why?

"Yer sick, sir?'' The cabby's voice changed; he was suddenly concerned. " 'Ere, yer ain't 'ad one too many?'' He climbed down off his box and opened the cab door.

"No, no I'm quite well.'' Monk stepped up and inside obediently and the cabby muttered something to himself about gentlemen whose families should take better care of them, stepped back up onto the box and slapped the reins over his horse's back.

As soon as they arrived at Grafton Street Monk paid the cabby and hurried inside.

"Mrs. Worley!''

Silence.

"Mrs. Worley!'' His voice was hard, hoarse.

She came out, rubbing her hands dry on her apron.

"Oh my heavens, you are wet. You'd like an 'ot drink.

278

You'll 'ave to change them clothes; you've let yourself get soaked through! What 'ave you bin thinking of?"

"Mrs. Worley."

The tone of his voice stopped her.

"Why, whatever is the matter, Mr. Monk? You look proper poorly."

"I—" The words were slow, distant. "I can't find a stick in my room, Mrs. Worley. Have you seen it?"

"No, Mr. Monk, I 'aven't, although what you're thinking about sticks for on a night like this, I'm sure I don't know. What you need is an umbrella."

"Have you seen it?"

She stood there in front of him, square and motherly. "Not since you 'ad yer haccident, I 'aven't. You mean that dark reddish brown one with the gold chain like 'round the top as yer bought the day afore? Proper 'andsome it were, although wot yer want one like that fer, I'll never know. I do 'ope as you 'aven't gorn and lorst it. If yer did, it must 'a' bin in yer haccident. You 'ad it with yer, 'cos I remember plain as day. Proud of it. Proper dandy, yer was."

There was a roaring in Monk's ears, shapeless and immense. Through the darkness one thought was like a brilliant stab of light, searingly painful. He had been in Grey's flat the night he was killed; he had left his own stick there in the hall stand. He himself was the man with the gray eyes whom Grimwade had seen leaving at half past ten. He must have gone in when Grimwade was showing Bartholomew Stubbs up to Yeats's door.

There was only one conclusion—hideous and senseless—but the only one left. God knew why, but he himself had killed Joscelin Grey.

11

Monk SAT IN THE ARMCHAIR in his room staring at the ceiling. The rain had stopped and the air was warm and clammy, but he was still chilled to the bone.

Why?

Why? It was as inconceivably senseless as a nightmare, and as entanglingly, recurringly inescapable.

He had been in Grey's flat that night, and something had happened after which he had gone in such haste he had left his stick in the stand behind him. The cabby had picked him up from Doughty Street, and then barely a few miles away, met with an accident which had robbed him of his life, and Monk of all memory.

But why should he have killed Grey? In what connection did he even know him? He had not met him at the Latterlys'; Imogen had said so quite clearly. He could imagine no way in which he could have met him socially. If he were involved in any case, then Runcorn would have known; and his own case notes would have shown it.

So why? Why kill him? One did not follow a complete stranger to his house and then beat him to death for no reason. Unless one were insane?

Could that be it—he was mad? His brain had been damaged even before the accident? He had forgotten what he

280

had done because it was another self which had enacted such a hideousness, and the self he was in now knew nothing of it, was unaware even of its lusts and compulsions, its very existence? And there had been feeling—inescapable, consuming, and appalling feeling—a passion of hate. Was it possible?

He must think. Thought was the only possible way of dealing with this, making some sense, finding an escape back into reason and an understandable world again, following and examining it, piece by piece—but he could not believe it. But then perhaps no clever, ambitious man truly believes he is mad? He turned that over in his mind too.

Minutes turned into hours, dragging through the night. At first he paced restlessly, back and forth, back and forth, till his legs ached, then he threw himself into the chair and sat motionless, his hands and feet so cold he lost all sensation in them, and still the nightmare was just as real, and just as senseless. He tormented his memory, scrambling after tiny fragments, retelling himself everything he could remember from the schoolroom onward, but there was nothing of Joscelin Grey, not even his face. There was no reason to it, no pattern, no vestige of anger left, no jealousy, no hatred, no fear—only the evidence. He had been there; he must have gone up when Grimwade had taken Bartholomew Stubbs up to see Yeats and been absent for a moment on his other errand.

He had been in Joscelin Grey's flat for three quarters of an hour, and Grimwade had seen him going out and presumed he was Stubbs leaving, whereas in truth Stubbs must have passed him on the stair, as Stubbs left and he arrived. Grimwade had said that the man leaving had seemed heavier, a little taller, and he had especially noticed his eyes. Monk remembered the eyes he had seen staring back at him from the bedroom mirror when he had first come from the hospital. They were unusual, as Grimwade had said, level, dark, clear gray; clever, almost hypnotic eyes. But he had been trying to find the mind beyond, a flash of the memory—the shade was irrelevant. He had made no connection of thought between his grave police-man's gaze—and the stare of the man that night—any more than had Grimwade.

He had been there, inside Grey's flat; it was incontro-vertible. But he had not followed Grey; he had gone af-terwards, independently, knowing where to find him. So he had known Grey, known where he lived. But why? Why in God's name did he hate him enough to have lost all reason, ignored all his adult life's training and beliefs and beaten the man to death, and gone on beating him when even a madman must have seen he was dead?

He must have known fear before, of the sea when he was young. He could dimly remember its monumental power when the bowels of the deep opened to engulf men, ships, even the shore itself. He could still feel its scream like an echo of all childhood.

And later he must have known fear on the dark streets of London, fear in the rookeries; even now his skin crawled at the memory of the anger and the despair in them, the hunger and the disregard for life in the fight to survive. But he was too proud and too ambitious to be a coward. He had grasped what he wanted without flinching.

But how do you face the unknown darkness, the mon-strosity inside your own brain, your own soul?

He had discovered many things in himself he did not like: insensitivity, overpowerful ambition, a ruthlessness. But they were bearable, things for which he could make amends, improve from now on—indeed he had started.

But why should he have murdered Joscelin Grey? The more he struggled with it the less did it make any sense. Why should he have cared enough? There was nothing in his life, no personal relationship that called up such pas-sion.

And he could not believe he was simply mad. Anyway, he had not attacked a stranger in the street, he had delib-erately sought out Grey, taken trouble to go to his home; and even madmen have some reason, however distorted.

He must find it, for himself—and he must find the reason before Runcorn found it.

Only it would not be Runcorn, it would be Evan.

The cold inside him grew worse. That was one of the most painful realizations of all, the time when Evan must know that it was he who had killed Grey, he was the murderer who had raised such horror in both of them, such revulsion for the mad appetite, the bestiality. They had looked upon the murderer as being another kind of creature, alien, capable of some darkness beyond their comprehension. To Evan it would still be such a creature, less than quite human—whereas to Monk it was not outward and foreign, where he could sometimes forget it, bar it out, but the deformed and obscene within himself.

Tonight he must sleep; the clock on the mantel said thirteen minutes past four. But tomorrow he would begin a new investigation. To save his own mind, he must discover why he had killed Joscelin Grey; and he must discover it before Evan did.

He was not ready to see Evan when he went into his office in the morning, not prepared; but then he would never be.

"Good morning, sir," Evan said cheerfully.

Monk replied, but kept his face turned away, so Evan could not read his expression. He found lying surprisingly hard; and he must lie all the time, every day in every contact from now on.

"I've been thinking, sir." Evan did not appear to notice anything unusual. "We should look into all these other people before we try to charge Lord Shelburne. You know, Joscelin Grey may well have had affairs with other women. We should try the Dawlishes; they had a daughter. And there's Fortescue's wife, and Charles Latterly may have a wife."

Monk froze. He had forgotten that Evan had seen Charles's letter in Grey's desk. He had been supposing blithely that Evan knew nothing of the Latterlys.

Evan's voice cut across him, low and quite gentle. It

sounded as though there were nothing more than concern in it.

"Sir?"

"Yes," Monk agreed quickly. He must keep control, speak sensibly. "Yes I suppose we had better." What a hypocrite he was, sending Evan off to pry the secret hurts out of people in the search for a murderer. What would Evan think, feel, when he discovered that the murderer was Monk?

"Shall I start with Latterly, sir?" Evan was still talking. "We don't know much about him."

"No!"

Evan looked startled.

Monk mastered himself; when he spoke his voice was quite calm again, but still he kept his face away.

"No, I'll try the people here: I want you to go back to Shelburne Hall." He must get Evan out of the city for a while, give himself time. "See if you can learn anything more from the servants," he elaborated. "Become friendly with the upstairs maids, if you can, and the parlor maid. Parlor maids are on in the morning; they observe all sorts of things when people are off their guard. It may be one of the other families, but Shelburne is still the most likely. It can be harder to forgive a brother for cuckolding you than it would be a stranger—it's not just an offense, it's a betrayal—and he's constantly there to remind you of it."

"You think so, sir?" There was a lift of surprise in Evan's voice.

Oh God. Surely Evan could not know, could not suspect anything so soon? Sweat broke out on Monk's body, and chilled instantly, leaving him shivering.

"Isn't that what Mr. Runcorn thinks?" he asked, his voice husky with the effort of seeming casual. What isolation this was. He felt cut off from every human contact by his fearful knowledge.

"Yes sir." He knew Evan was staring at him, puzzled, even anxious. "It is, but he could be wrong. He wants to see you arrest Lord Shelburne—" That was an understanding he had not committed to words before. It was the first time he had acknowledged that he understood Runcorn's envy, or his intention. Monk was startled into looking up, and instantly regretted it. Evan's eyes were anxious and appallingly direct.

"Well he won't—unless I have evidence," Monk said slowly. "So go out to Shelburne Hall and see what you can find. But tread softly, listen rather than speak. Above all, don't make any implications."

Evan hesitated.

Monk said nothing. He did not want conversation.

After a moment Evan left and Monk sat down on his own chair, closing his eyes to shut out the room. It was going to be even harder than it had seemed last night. Evan had believed in him, liked him. Disillusionment so often turned to pity, and then to hate.

And what about Beth? Perhaps far up in Northumberland she need never know. Maybe he could find someone to write to her and say simply that he had died. They would not do it for him; but if he explained, told them of her children, then for her?

"Asleep, Monk? Or dare I hope you are merely thinking?" It was Runcorn's voice, dark with sarcasm.

Monk opened his eyes. He had no career left, no future. But one of the few reliefs it brought was that he need no longer be afraid of Runcorn. Nothing Runcorn could do would matter in the least, compared with what he had already done to himself.

"Thinking," Monk replied coldly. "I find it better to think before I face a witness than after I have got there. Either one stands foolishly silent, or rushes, even more foolishly, into saying something inept, merely to fill the chasm."

"Social arts again?" Runcorn raised his eyebrows. "I would not have thought you would have had time for them now." He was standing in front of Monk, rocking a little on his feet, hands behind his back. Now he brought them forward with a sheaf of daily newspapers displayed bellig-

285

erently. "Have you read the newspapers this morning? There has been a murder in Stepney, a man knifed in the street, and they are saying it is time we did our job, or were replaced by someone who can."

"Why do they presume there is only one person in London capable of knifing a man?" Monk asked bitterly.

"Because they are angry and frightened," Runcorn snapped back. "And they have been let down by the men they trusted to safeguard them. That is why." He slammed the newspapers down on the desk top. "They do not care whether you speak like a gentleman or know which knife and fork to eat with, Mr. Monk; but they care very much whether you are capable of doing your job and catching murderers and taking them off the streets."

"Do you think Lord Shelburne knifed this man in Stepney?" Monk looked straight into Runcorn's eyes. He was pleased to be able to hate someone freely and without feeling any guilt about lying to him.

"Of course I don't." Runcorn's voice was thick with anger. "But I think it past time you stopped giving yourself airs and graces and found enough courage to forget climbing the ladder of your own career for a moment and arrested Shelburne."

"Indeed? Well I don't, because I'm not at all sure that he's guilty," Monk answered him with a straight, hard stare. "If you are sure, then you arrest him!"

"I'll have you for insolence!" Runcorn shouted, leaning forward towards him, fists clenched white. "And I'll make damned sure you never reach senior rank as long as I'm in this station. Do you hear me?"

"Of course I hear you." Monk deliberately kept calm. "Although it was unnecessary for you to say so, your actions have long made it obvious; unless of course you wish to inform the rest of the building? Your voice was certainly loud enough. As for me, I knew your intentions long ago. And now . . ." He stood up and walked past him to the door. "If you have nothing else to say, sir; I have several witnesses to question."

"I'll give you till the end of the week," Runcorn bellowed behind him, his face purple, but Monk was outside and going down the stairs for his hat and coat. The only advantage of disaster was that all lesser ills are swallowed up in it.

By the time he had reached the Latterlys' house and been shown in by the parlor maid, he had made up his mind to do the only thing that might lead him to the truth. Runcorn had given him a week. And Evan would be back long before that. Time was desperately short.

He asked to see Imogen, alone. The maid hesitated, but it was morning and Charles was quite naturally out; and anyway, as a servant she had not the authority to refuse.

He paced backwards and forwards nervously, counting seconds until he heard light, decisive footsteps outside and the door opened. He swung around. It was not Imogen but Hester Latterly who came in.

He felt an immediate rush of disappointment, then something almost resembling relief. The moment was put off; Hester had not been here at the time. Unless Imogen had confided in her she could not help. He would have to return. He needed the truth, and yet it terrified him.

"Good morning, Mr. Monk," she said curiously. "What may we do for you this time?"

"I am afraid you cannot help me," he replied. He did not like her, but it would be pointless and stupid to be rude. "It is Mrs. Latterly I would like to see, since she was here at the time of Major Grey's death. I believe you were still abroad?"

"Yes I was. But I am sorry, Imogen is out all day and I do not expect her return until late this evening." She frowned very slightly and he was uncomfortably aware of her acute perception, the sensitivity with which she was regarding him. Imogen was kinder, immeasurably less abrasive, but there was an intelligence in Hester which might meet his present need more readily.

"I can see that something very serious troubles you,"

287

she said gravely. "Please sit down. If it is to do with Imogen, I would greatly appreciate it if you would confide in me, and I may help the matter to be dealt with with as little pain as possible. She has already suffered a great deal, as has my brother. What have you discovered, Mr. Monk?"

He looked at her levelly, searching the wide, very clear eyes. She was a remarkable woman and her courage must be immense to have defied her family and traveled virtually alone to one of the most dreadful battlefields in the world, and to have risked her own life and health to care for the wounded. She must have very few illusions, and that thought was comforting now. There was an infinity of experience between himself and Imogen: horror, violence, hatred and pain outside her grasp to think of, and which from now on would be his shadow, even his skin. Hester must have seen men in the very extremity of life and death, the nakedness of soul that comes when fear strips everything away and the honesty that loosens the tongue when pretense is futile.

Perhaps after all it was right he should speak to her.

"I have a most profound problem, Miss Latterly," he began. It was easier to talk to her than he had expected. "I have not told you, or anyone else, the entire truth about my investigation of Major Grey's death."

She waited without interruption; surprisingly, she did know when to keep silent.

"I have not lied," he went on. "But I have omitted one of the most important facts."

She was very pale. "About Imogen?"

"No! No. I do not know anything about her, beyond what she told me herself—that she knew and liked Joscelin Grey, and that he called here, as a friend of your brother George. What I did not tell you is about myself."

He saw the flash of concern in her face, but he did not know the reason for it. Was it her nurse's professional training, or some fear for Imogen, something she knew and he did not? But again she did not interrupt.

"The accident I suffered before beginning the Joscelin Grey case is a severe complication which I did not mention." Then for a hideous moment he thought she might imagine he was seeking some kind of sympathy, and he felt the blood burn up his skin. "I lost my memory." He rushed to dispel the idea. "Completely. When I came to my senses in the hospital I could not even think of my own name." How far away that minimal nightmare seemed now! "When I was recovered enough to go back to my rooms they were strange to me, like the rooms of a man I had never met. I knew no one, I could not even think how old I was, or what I looked like. When I saw myself in the mirror I did not recognize myself even then."

There was pity in her face, gentle and quite pure, without a shadow of condescension or setting herself apart. It was far sweeter than anything he had expected.

"I'm deeply sorry," she said quietly. "Now I understand why some of your questions seemed so very odd. You must have had to learn everything over again."

"Miss Latterly—I believe your sister-in-law came to me before, asked me something, confided—perhaps to do with Joscelin Grey—but I cannot remember. If she could tell me everything she knows of me, anything I may have said—"

"How could that help you with Joscelin Grey?" Then suddenly she looked down at the hand in her lap. "You mean you think Imogen may have something to do with his death?" Her head came up sharply, her eyes candid and full of fear. "Do you think Charles may have killed him, Mr. Monk?"

"No—no, I am quite sure he did not." He must lie; the truth was impossible, but he needed her help. "I found old notes of mine, made before the accident, which indicate I knew something important then, but I can't remember it. Please, Miss Latterly—ask her to help me."

Her face was a little bleak, as if she too feared the outcome.

"Of course, Mr. Monk. When she returns I will explain

the necessity to her, and when I have something to tell you I shall come and do so. Where may I find you that we can talk discreetly?''

He was right: she was afraid. She did not wish her family to overhear—perhaps especially Charles. He stared at her, smiling with a bitter humor, and saw it answered in her eyes. They were in an absurd conspiracy, she to protect her family as far as was possible, he to discover the truth about himself, before Evan or Runcorn made it impossible. He must know *why* he had killed Joscelin Grey.

"Send me a message, and I shall meet you in Hyde Park, at the Piccadilly end of the Serpentine. No one will remark two people walking together."

"Very well, Mr. Monk. I shall do what I can."

"Thank you." He rose and took his leave, and she watched his straight, very individual figure as he walked down the steps and out into the street. She would have recognized his stride anywhere; there was an ease in it not unlike a soldier's who was used to the self-discipline of long marches, and yet it was not military.

When he was out of sight she sat down, cold, unhappy, but knowing it was unavoidable she should do exactly as he had asked. Better she should learn the truth first than that it should be dragged out longer, and found by others.

She spent a solitary and miserable evening, dining alone in her room. Until she knew the truth from Imogen she could not bear to risk a long time with Charles, such as at a meal table. It was too likely her thoughts would betray her and end in hurting them both. As a child she had imagined herself to be marvelously subtle and capable of all sorts of deviousness. At about twenty she had mentioned it quite seriously at the dinner table. It was the only occasion she could recall of every member of her family laughing at once. George had begun, his face crinkling into uncontrollable delight and his voice ringing out with hilarity. The very idea was funny. She had the most transparent emotions any of them had seen. Her happiness swept the house in a whirlwind; her misery wrapped it in a purple gloom.

It would be futile, and painful, to try to deceive Charles now.

It was the following afternoon before she had the opportunity to speak alone with Imogen for any length of time. Imogen had been out all morning and came in in a swirl of agitation, swinging her skirts around as she swept into the hallway and deposited a basket full of linen on the settle at the bottom of the stairs and took off her hat.

"Really, I don't know what the vicar's wife is thinking of," she said furiously. "Sometimes I swear that woman believes all the world's ills can be cured with an embroidered homily on good behavior, a clean undershirt and a jar of homemade broth. And Miss Wentworth is the last person on earth to help a young mother with too many children and no maidservant."

"Mrs. Addison?" Hester said immediately.

"Poor creature doesn't know whether she is coming or going," Imogen argued. "Seven children, and she's as thin as a slat and exhausted. I don't think she eats enough to keep a bird alive—giving it all to those hungry little mouths forever asking for more. And what use is Miss Wentworth? She has fits of the vapors every few minutes! I spend half my time picking her up off the floor."

"I'd have fits of the vapors myself if my stays were as tight as hers," Hester said wryly. "Her maid must lace them with one foot on the bedpost. Poor soul. And of course her mother's trying to marry her off to Sydney Abernathy—he has plenty of money and a fancy for wraithlike fragility—it makes him feel masterful."

"I shall have to see if I can find a suitable homily for her on vanity." Imogen ignored the basket and led the way through to the withdrawing room and threw herself into one of the large chairs. "I am hot and tired. Do have Martha bring us some lemonade. Can you reach the bell?"

It was an idle question, since Hester was still standing.

Absently she pulled the end. "It isn't vanity," she said, still referring to Miss Wentworth. "It's survival. What is the poor creature to do if she doesn't marry? Her mother and sisters have convinced her the only alternative is shame, poverty and a lonely and pitiful old age."

"That reminds me," Imogen said, pushing her boots off. "Have you heard from Lady Callandra's hospital yet? I mean the one you want to administer."

"I don't aim quite so high; I merely want to assist," Hester corrected.

"Rubbish!" Imogen stretched her feet luxuriously and sank a little further into the chair. "You want to order around the entire staff."

The maid came in and stood waiting respectfully.

"Lemonade, please, Martha," Imogen ordered. "I'm so hot I could expire. This climate really is ridiculous. One day it rains enough to float an ark, the next we are all suffocated with heat."

"Yes ma'am. Would you like some cucumber sandwiches as well, ma'am?"

"Oh yes. Yes I would—thank you."

"Yes ma'am." And with a whisk of skirts she was gone.

Hester filled the few minutes while the maid was absent with trivial conversation. She had always found it easy to talk to Imogen and their friendship was more like that of sisters than of two women related only by marriage, whose patterns of life were so different. When Martha had brought the sandwiches and lemonade and they were alone, she turned at last to the matter which was pressing so urgently on her mind.

"Imogen, that policeman, Monk, was here again yesterday—"

Imogen's hand stopped in the air, the sandwich ignored, but there was curiosity in her face and a shadow of amusement. There was nothing that looked like fear. But then Imogen, unlike Hester, could conceal her feelings perfectly if she chose.

"Monk? What did he want this time?"

"Why are you smiling?"

"At you, my dear. He annoys you so much, and yet I think part of you quite likes him. You are not dissimilar in some ways, full of impatience at stupidity and anger at injustice, and perfectly prepared to be as rude as you can."

"I am nothing like him whatever," Hester said impatiently. "And this is not a laughing matter." She could feel an irritating warmth creep up in her cheeks. Just once in a while she would like to take more naturally to feminine arts, as Imogen did as easily as breathing. Men did not rush to protect her as they did Imogen; they always assumed she was perfectly competent to take care of herself, and it was a compliment she was growing tired of.

Imogen ate her sandwich, a tiny thing about two inches square.

"Are you going to tell me what he came for, or not?"

"Certainly I am." Hester took a sandwich herself and bit into it; it was lacily thin and the cucumber was crisp and cool. "A few weeks ago he had a very serious accident, about the time Joscelin Grey was killed."

"Oh—I'm sorry. Is he ill now? He seemed perfectly recovered."

"I think his body is quite mended," Hester answered, and seeing the sudden gravity and concern in Imogen's face felt a gentleness herself. "But he was struck very severely on the head, and he cannot remember anything before regaining his senses in a London hospital."

"Not anything." A flicker of amazement crossed Imogen's face. "You mean he didn't remember me—I mean us?"

"He didn't remember himself," Hester said starkly. "He did not know his name or his occupation. He did not recognize his own face when he saw it in the glass."

"How extraordinary—and terrible. I do not always like myself completely—but to lose yourself! I cannot imagine having nothing at all left of all your past—all your experiences, and the reason why you love or hate things."

"Why did you go to him, Imogen?"

293

"What? I mean, I beg your pardon?"

"You heard what I said. When we first saw Monk in St. Marylebone Church you went over to speak to him. You knew him. I assumed at the time that he knew you, but he did not. He did not know anyone."

Imogen looked away, and very carefully took another sandwich.

"I presume it is something Charles does not know about," Hester went on.

"Are you threatening me?" Imogen asked, her enormous eyes quite frank.

"No I am not!" Hester was annoyed, with herself for being clumsy as well as Imogen for thinking such a thing. "I didn't know there was anything to threaten you with. I was going to say that unless it is unavoidable, I shall not tell him. Was it something to do with Joscelin Grey?"

Imogen choked on her sandwich and had to sit forward sharply to avoid suffocating herself altogether.

"No," she said when at last she caught her breath. "No it was not. I can see that perhaps it was foolish, on reflection. But at the time I really hoped—"

"Hoped what? For goodness sake, explain yourself."

Slowly, with a good deal of help, criticism and consolation from Hester, Imogen recounted detail by detail exactly what she had done, what she had told Monk, and why.

Four hours later, in the golden sunlight of early evening, Hester stood in the park by the Serpentine watching the light dimple on the water. A small boy in a blue smock carrying a toy boat under his arm passed by with his nursemaid. She was dressed in a plain stuff dress, had a starched lace cap on her head and walked as uprightly as any soldier on parade. An off-duty bandsman watched her with admiration.

Beyond the grass and trees two ladies of fashion rode along Rotten Row, their horses gleaming, harnesses jingling and hooves falling with a soft thud on the earth.

Carriages rattling along Knightsbridge towards Piccadilly seemed in another world, like toys in the distance.

She heard Monk's step before she saw him. She turned when he was almost upon her. He stopped a yard away; their eyes met. Lengthy politeness would be ridiculous between them. There was no outward sign of fear in him—his gaze was level and unflinching—but she knew the void and the imagination that was there.

She was the first to speak.

"Imogen came to you after my father's death, in the rather fragile hope that you might discover some evidence that it was not suicide. The family was devastated. First George had been killed in the war, then Papa had been shot in what the police were kind enough to say might have been an accident, but appeared to everyone to be suicide. He had lost a great deal of money. Imogen was trying to salvage something out of the chaos—for Charles's sake, and for my mother's." She stopped for a moment, trying to keep her composure, but the pain of it was still very deep.

Monk stood perfectly still, not intruding, for which she was grateful. It seemed he understood she must tell it all without interruption in order to be able to tell it at all.

She let out her breath slowly, and resumed.

"It was too late for Mama. Her whole world had collapsed. Her youngest son dead, financial disgrace, and then her husband's suicide—not only his loss but the shame of the manner of it. She died ten days later—she was simply broken—" Again she was obliged to stop for several minutes. Monk said nothing, but stretched out his hand and held hers, hard, firmly, and the pressure of his fingers was like a lifeline to the shore.

In the distance a dog scampered through the grass, and a small boy chased a penny hoop.

"She came to you without Charles's knowing—he would not have approved. That is why she never mentioned it to you again—and of course she did not know you had forgotten. She says you questioned her about everything that had happened prior to Papa's death, and on successive meetings you asked her about Joscelin Grey. I shall tell you what she told me—"

A couple in immaculate riding habits cantered down the Row. Monk still held her hand.

"My family first met Joscelin Grey in March. They had none of them heard of him before and he called on them quite unexpectedly. He came one evening. You never met him, but he was very charming—even I can remember that from his brief stay in the hospital where I was in Scutari. He went out of his way to befriend other wounded men, and often wrote letters for those too ill to do it for themselves. He often smiled, even laughed and made small jokes. It did a great deal for morale. Of course his wound was not as serious as many, nor did he have cholera or dysentery."

Slowly they began to walk, so as not to draw attention to themselves, close together.

She forced her mind back to that time, the smell, the closeness of pain, the constant tiredness and the pity. She pictured Joscelin Grey as she had last seen him, hobbling away down the steps with a corporal beside him, going down to the harbor to be shipped back to England.

"He was a little above average height," she said aloud. "Slender, fair-haired. I should think he still had quite a limp—I expect he always would have had. He told them his name, and that he was the younger brother of Lord Shelburne, and of course that he had served in the Crimea and been invalided home. He explained his own story, his time in Scutari, and that his injury was the reason he had delayed so long in calling on them."

She looked at Monk's face and saw the unspoken question.

"He said he had known George—before the battle of the Alma, where George was killed. Naturally the whole family made him most welcome, for George's sake, and for his own. Mama was still deeply grieved. One knows with one's mind that if young men go to war there is always a chance they will be killed, but that is nothing like a preparation for the feelings when it happens. Papa had his loss, so Imogen said, but for Mama it was the end of something terribly precious. George was the youngest son and she always had a special feeling for him. He was—" She struggled with memories of childhood like a patch of sunlight in a closed garden. "He looked the most like Papa—he had the same smile, and his hair grew the same way, although it was dark like Mama's. He loved animals. He was an excellent horseman. I suppose it was natural he should join the cavalry.

"Anyway, of course they did not ask Grey a great deal about George the first time he called. It would have been very discourteous, as if they had no regard for his own friendship, so they invited him to return any time he should find himself free to do so, and would wish to—"

"And he did?" Monk spoke for the first time, quietly, just an ordinary question. His face was pinched and there was a darkness in his eyes.

"Yes, several times, and after a while Papa finally thought it acceptable to ask him about George. They had received letters, of course, but George had told them very little of what it was really like." She smiled grimly. "Just as I did not. I wonder now if perhaps we both should have? At least to have told Charles. Now we live in different worlds: And I should be distressing him to no purpose."

She looked beyond Monk to a couple walking arm in arm along the path.

"It hardly matters now. Joscelin Grey came again, and stayed to dinner, and then he began to tell them about the Crimea. Imogen says he was always most delicate; he never used unseemly language, and although Mama was naturally terribly upset, and grieved to hear how wretched the conditions were, he seemed to have a special sense of how much he could say without trespassing beyond sorrow and admiration into genuine horror. He spoke of battles, but he told them nothing of the starvation and the disease. And he always spoke so well of George, it made them all proud to hear.

"Naturally they also asked him about his own exploits. He saw the Charge of the Light Brigade at Balaclava. He said the courage was sublime: never were soldiers braver or more loyal to their duty. But he said the slaughter was the most dreadful thing he had ever seen, because it was so needless. They rode right into the guns; he told them that." She shivered as she remembered the cartloads of dead and wounded, the labor all through the night, the helplessness, all the blood. Had Joscelin Grey felt anything of the overwhelming emotions of anger and pity that she had?

"There was never any chance whatsoever that they could have survived," she said quietly, her voice so low it was almost carried away by the murmur of the wind. "Imogen said he was very angry about it. He said some terrible things about Lord Cardigan. I think that was the moment I most thought I should have liked him."

Deeply as it hurt, Monk also most liked him for it. He had heard of that suicidal charge, and when the brief thrill of admiration had passed, he was left with a towering rage at the monumental incompetence and the waste, the personal vanity, the idiotic jealousies that had uselessly, senselessly squandered so many lives.

For what, in heaven's name, could he have hated Joscelin Grey?

She was talking and he was not listening. Her face was earnest, pinched for the loss and the pain. He wanted to touch her, to tell her simply, elementally, without words that he felt the same.

What sort of revulsion would she feel if she knew it was he who had beaten Joscelin Grey to death in that dreadful room?

"—as they got to know him," she was saying, "they all came to like him better and better for himself. Mama used to look forward to his visits; she would prepare for them days before. Thank heavens she never knew what happened to him.''

He refrained at the last moment, when it was on the tip of his tongue, from asking her when her mother had died. He remembered something about shock, a broken heart.

"Go on," he said instead. "Or is that all about him?"

"No." She shook her head. "No, there is much more. As I said, they were all fond of him; Imogen and Charles also. Imogen used to like to hear about the bravery of the soldiers, and of the hospital in Scutari, I suppose at least in part because of me."

He remembered what he had heard of the military hospital—of Florence Nightingale and her women. The sheer physical labor of it, quite apart from the social stigma. Nurses were traditionally mostly men; the few women were of the strongest, the coarsest, and they did little but clean up the worst of the refuse and waste.

She was speaking again. "It was about four weeks after they first met him that he first mentioned the watch—"

"Watch?" He had heard nothing of a watch, except he recalled they had found no watch on the body. Constable Harrison had found one at a pawnbroker's—which had turned out to be irrelevant.

"It was Joscelin Grey's," she replied. "Apparently it was a gold watch of great personal value to him because he had been given it by his grandfather, who had fought with the Duke of Wellington at Waterloo. It had a dent in it where a ball from a French musket struck it and was deflected, thus saving his grandfather's life. When he had first expressed a desire to be a soldier himself, the old man had given it to him. It was considered something of a talisman. Joscelin Grey said that poor George had been nervous that night, the night before the Battle of the Alma, perhaps something of a premonition, and Joscelin had lent him the watch. Of course George was killed the next day, and so never returned it. Joscelin did not make much of it, but he said that if it had been returned to them with George's effects, he would be most grateful if he might have it again. He described it most minutely, even to the inscription inside."

"And they returned it to him?" he asked.

"No. No, they did not have it. They had no idea what could have happened to it, but it was not among the things that the army sent them from George's body, nor his personal possessions. I can only presume someone must have stolen it. It is the most contemptible of crimes, but it happens. They felt quite dreadful about it, especially Papa."

"And Joscelin Grey?"

"He was distressed, of course, but according to Imogen he did his best to hide it; in fact he hardly mentioned it again."

"And your father?"

Her eyes were staring blindly past him at the wind in the leaves. "Papa could not return the watch, nor could he replace it, since in spite of its monetary value, its personal value was far greater, and it was that which really mattered. So when Joscelin Grey was interested in a certain business venture, Papa felt it was the very least he could do to offer to join him in it. Indeed from what both he and Charles said, it seemed at the time to be, in their judgment, an excellent scheme."

"That was the one in which your father lost his money?"

Her face tightened.

"Yes. He did not lose it all, but a considerable amount. What caused him to take his life, and Imogen has accepted now that he did so, was that he had recommended the scheme to his friends, and some of them had lost far more. That was the shame of it. Of course Joscelin Grey lost much of his own money too, and he was terribly distressed."

"And from that time their friendship ceased?"

"Not immediately. It was a week later, when Papa shot himself. Joscelin Grey sent a letter of condolence, and Charles wrote back, thanking him, and suggesting that they discontinue their acquaintance, in the circumstances."

300

"Yes, I saw the letter. Grey kept it—I don't know why."

"Mama died a few days after that." She went on very quietly. "She simply collapsed, and never got up again. And of course it was not a time for social acquaintance: they were all in mourning." She hesitated a moment. "We still are."

"And it was after your father's death that Imogen came to see me?" he prompted after a moment.

"Yes, but not straightaway. She came the day after they buried Mama. I cannot think there was ever anything you could have done, but she was too upset to be thinking as deeply as she might, and who can blame her? She just found it too hard then to accept what must have been the truth."

They turned and began walking back again.

"So she came to the police station?" he asked.

"Yes."

"And told me everything that you have told me now?"

"Yes. And you asked her all the details of Papa's death: how he died, precisely when, who was in the house, and so on."

"And I noted it?"

"Yes, you said it might have been murder, or an accident, although you doubted it. You said that you would make some investigation."

"Do you know what I did?"

"I asked Imogen, but she did not know, only that you found no evidence that it was other than it seemed, which was that he took his own life while in deep despair. But you said you would continue to investigate it and let her know if you discovered anything further. But you never did, at least not until after we saw you again in the church, more than two months later."

He was disappointed, and becoming frightened as well. There was still no direct connection between himself and Joscelin Grey, still less any reason why he should have hated him. He tried a last time.

"And she does not know what my investigations were? I told her nothing?"

"No." She shook her head. "But I imagine, from the questions you asked her about Papa and the business, such as she knew it, that you inquired into that."

"Did I meet Joscelin Grey?"

"No. You met a Mr. Marner, who was one of the principals. You spoke of him; but you never met Joscelin Grey so far as she knows. In fact the last time she saw you you said quite plainly that you had not. He was also a victim of the same misfortune, and you seemed to consider Mr. Marner the author of it, whether intentionally or not."

It was something, however frail; a place to begin.

"Do you know where I can find Mr. Marner now?"

"No, I am afraid not. I asked Imogen, but she had no knowledge."

"Did she know his Christian name?"

Again she shook her head. "No. You mentioned him only very briefly. I'm sorry. I wish I could help."

"You have helped. At least now I know what I was doing before the accident. It is somewhere to begin." That was a lie, but there was nothing to be gained in the truth.

"Do you think Joscelin Grey was killed over something to do with the business? Could he have known something about this Mr. Marner?" Her face was blank and sad with the sharpness of memory, but she did not evade the thought. "Was the business fraudulent, and he discovered it?"

Again he could only lie.

"I don't know. I'll start again, from the beginning. Do you know what manner of business it was, or at least the names of some of the friends of your father who invested in it? They would be able to give me the details."

She told him several names and he wrote them down, with addresses. He thanked her, feeling a little awkward, wanting her to know, without the embarrassment for both of them of his saying it, that he was grateful—for her candor, her understanding without pity, the moment's truce from all argument or social games.

He hesitated, trying to think of words. She put her hand very lightly on his sleeve and met his eyes for an instant. For a wild moment he thought of friendship, a closeness better than romance, cleaner and more honest; then it disappeared. There was the battered corpse of Joscelin Grey between him and everyone else.

"Thank you," he said calmly. "You have been very helpful. I appreciate your time and your frankness." He smiled very slightly, looking straight into her eyes. "Good afternoon, Miss Latterly."

12

THE NAME MARNER meant nothing to Monk, and the following day, even after he had been to three of the addresses Hester had given him, he still had no more than a name and the nature of the business—importing. It seemed no one else had met the elusive Mr. Marner either. All inquiries and information had come from Latterly, through Joscelin Grey. The business was for the importing of tobacco from the United States of America, and a very profitable retailing of it was promised, in alliance with a certain Turkish house. No one knew more than that; except of course a large quantity of figures which indicated the amount of capital necessary to begin the venture and the projected increase to the fortunes of those who participated.

Monk did not leave the last house until well into the afternoon, but he could not afford time for leisure. He ate briefly, purchasing fresh sandwiches from a street seller, then went to the police station to seek the help of a man he had learned investigated business fraud. He might at least know the name of dealers in tobacco; perhaps he could find the Turkish house in question.

"Marner?" the man repeated agreeably, pushing his

fingers through his scant hair. "Can't say as I've ever heard of him. You don't know his first name, you say?"

"No, but he floated a company for importing tobacco from America, mixing it with Turkish, and selling it at a profit."

The man pulled a face.

"Sounds unpleasant—can't stand Turkish myself—but then I prefer snuff anyway. Marner?" He shook his head. "You don't mean old Zebedee Marner, by any chance? I suppose you've tried him, or you wouldn't ask. Very sly old bird, that. But I never knew him mixed up with importing."

"What does he do?"

The man's eyebrows went up in surprise.

"Losing your grip, Monk? What's the matter with you?" He squinted a little. "You must know Zebedee Marner. Never been able to charge him with anything because he always weasels his way out, but we all know he's behind half the pawnbrokers, sweatshops and brothels in the Limehouse area right down to the Isle of Dogs. Personally I think he takes a percentage from the child prostitutes and the opium as well, although he's far too downy to go anywhere near them himself." He sighed in disgust. "But then, of course, there's a few who wouldn't say as far as that."

Monk hardly dared hope. If this were the same Marner, then here at last was something that could lead to motive. It was back to the underworld, to greed, fraud and vice. Reason why Joscelin Grey should have killed—but why should he have been the victim?

Was there something in all this evidence that could at last convict Zebedee Marner? Was Grey in collusion with Marner? But Grey had lost his own money—or had he?

"Where can I find Marner?" he asked urgently. "I need him, and time is short." There was no time to seek out addresses himself. If this man thought he was peculiar, incompetent at his job, he would just have to think it. Soon it would hardly matter anyway.

305

The man looked at Monk, interest suddenly sharpening in his face, his body coming upright.

"Do you know something about Marner that I don't, Monk? I've been trying to catch that slimy bastard for years. Let me in on it?" His face was eager, a light in his eyes as if he had seen a sudden glimpse of an elusive happiness. "I don't want any of the credit; I won't say anything. I just want to see his face when he's pinched."

Monk understood. He was sorry not to be able to help.

"I don't have anything on Marner," he answered. "I don't even know if the business I'm investigating is fraudulent or not. Someone committed suicide, and I'd like to know the reasons."

"Why?" He was curious and his puzzlement was obvious. He cocked his head a little to one side. "What do you care about a suicide? I thought you were on the Grey case. Don't tell me Runcorn's let you off it—without an arrest?"

So even this man knew of Runcorn's feelings about him. Did everyone? No wonder Runcorn knew he had lost his memory! He must have laughed at Monk's confusion, his fumbling.

"No." He pulled a wry face. "No, it's all part of the same thing. Grey was involved in the business."

"Importing?" His voice rose an octave. "Don't tell me he was killed over a shipment of tobacco!"

"Not over tobacco; but there was a lot of money invested, and apparently the company failed."

"Oh yes? That's a new departure for Marner—"

"If it's the same man," Monk said cautiously. "I don't know that it is. I don't know anything about him but his name, and only part of that. Where do I find him?"

"Thirteen Gun Lane, Limehouse." He hesitated. "If you get anything, Monk, will you tell me, as long as it isn't the actual murder? Is that what you're after?"

"No. No, I just want some information. If I find evidence of fraud I'll bring it back for you." He smiled bleakly. "You have my word."

The man's face eased into a smile. "Thank you."

Monk went early in the morning and was in Limehouse by nine o'clock. He would have been there sooner had there been any purpose. He had spent much of the time since he woke at six planning what he would say.

It was a long way from Grafton Street and he took a hansom eastward through Clerkenwell, Whitechapel and down towards the cramped and crowded docks and Limehouse. It was a still morning and the sun was gleaming on the river, making white sparkles on the water between the black barges coming up from the Pool of London. Across on the far side were Bermondsey—the Venice of the Drains—and Rotherhithe, and ahead of him the Surrey Docks, and along the shining Reach the Isle of Dogs, and on the far side Deptford and then the beautiful Greenwich with its green park and trees and the exquisite architecture of the naval college.

But his duty lay in the squalid alleys of Limehouse with beggars, usurers and thieves of every degree—and Zebedee Marner.

Gun Lane was a byway off the West India Dock Road, and he found Number 13 without difficulty. He passed an evil-looking idler on the pavement and another lounging in the doorway, but neither troubled him, perhaps considering him unlikely to give to a beggar and too crisp of gait to be wise to rob. There was other, easier prey. He despised them, and understood them at the same time.

Good fortune was with him: Zebedee Marner was in, and after a discreet inquiry, the clerk showed Monk into the upper office.

"Good morning, Mr.—Monk." Marner sat behind a large, important desk, his white hair curled over his ears and his white hands spread on the leather-inlaid surface in front of him. "What can I do for you?"

"You come recommended as a man of many businesses, Mr. Marner," Monk started smoothly, gliding over the hatred in his voice. "With a knowledge of all kinds of things."

"And so I am, Mr. Monk, so I am. Have you money to invest?"

"What could you offer me?"

"All manner of things. How much money?" Marner was watching him narrowly, but it was well disguised as a casual cheerfulness.

"I am interested also in safety, rather than quick profit," Monk said, ignoring the question. "I wouldn't care to lose what I have."

"Of course not, who would?" Marner spread his hands wide and shrugged expressively, but his eyes were fixed and blinkless as a snake's. "You want your money invested safely?"

"Oh, quite definitely," Monk agreed. "And since I know of many other gentlemen who are also interested in investment, I should wish to be certain that any recommendation I made was secure."

Marner's eyes flickered, then the lids came down to hide his thoughts. "Excellent," he said calmly. "I quite understand, Mr. Monk. Have you considered importing and exporting? Very nourishing trade; never fails."

"So I've heard." Monk nodded. "But is it safe?"

"Some is, some isn't. It is the skill of people like me to know the difference." His eyes were wide again, his hands folded across his paunch. "That is why you came here, instead of investing it yourself."

"Tobacco?"

Marner's face did not change in the slightest.

"An excellent commodity." He nodded. "Excellent. I cannot see gentlemen giving up their pleasures, whatever the economic turns of life. As long as there are gentlemen, there will be a market for tobacco. And unless our climate changes beyond our wit to imagine"—he grinned and his body rocked with silent mirth at his own humor—"we will be unable to grow it, so must need import it. Have you any special company in mind?"

"Are you familiar with the market?" Monk asked, swallowing hard to contain his loathing of this man sitting here like a fat white spider in his well-furnished office, safe in his gray web of lies and facades. Only the poor flies like Latterly got caught—and perhaps Joscelin Grey.

"Of course," Marner replied complacently. "I know it well."

"You have dealt in it?"

"I have, frequently. I assure you, Mr. Monk, I know very well what I am doing."

"You would not be taken unaware and find yourself faced with a collapse?"

"Most certainly not." Marner looked at him as if he had let fall some vulgarity at the table.

"You are sure?" Monk pressed him.

"I am more than sure, my dear sir." Now he was quite pained. "I am positive."

"Good." Monk at last allowed the venom to flood into his voice. "That is what I thought. Then you will no doubt be able to tell me how the disaster occurred that ruined Major Joscelin Grey's investment in the same commodity. You were connected with it."

Marner's face paled and for a moment he was confused to find words.

"I—er—assure you, you need have no anxiety as to its happening again," he said, avoiding Monk's eyes, then looking very directly at him, to cover the lie of intent.

"That is good," Monk answered him coolly. "But hardly of more than the barest comfort now. It has cost two lives already. Was there much of your own money lost, Mr. Marner?"

"Much of mine?" Marner looked startled.

"I understand Major Grey lost a considerable sum?"

"Oh—no. No, you are misinformed." Marner shook his head and his white hair bounced over his ears. "The company did not precisely fail. Oh dear me no. It simply transferred its operation; it was taken over. If you are not

309

a man of affairs, you could not be expected to understand. Business is highly complicated these days, Mr. Monk."

"It would seem so. And you say Major Grey did not lose a great deal of his own money? Can you substantiate that in any way?"

"I could, of course." The smug veils came over Marner's eyes again. "But Major Grey's affairs are his own, of course, and I should not discuss his affairs with you, any more than I should dream of discussing yours with him. The essence of good business is discretion, sir." He smiled, pleased with himself, his composure at least in part regained.

"Naturally," Monk agreed. "But I am from the police, and am investigating Major Grey's murder, therefore I am in a different category from the merely inquisitive." He lowered his voice and it became peculiarly menacing. He saw Marner's face tighten. "And as a law-abiding man," he continued, "I am sure you will be only too happy to give me every assistance you can. I should like to see your records in the matter. Precisely how much did Major Grey lose, Mr. Marner, to the guinea, if you please?"

Marner's chin came up sharply; his eyes were hot and offended.

"The police? You said you wanted to make an investment."

"No, I did not say that—you assumed it. How much did Joscelin Grey lose, Mr. Marner?"

"Oh, well, to the guinea, Mr. Monk, he—he did not lose any."

"But the company dissolved."

"Yes—yes, that is true; it was most unfortunate. But Major Grey withdrew his own investment at the last moment, just before the—the takeover."

Monk remembered the policeman from whom he had learned Marner's address. If he had been after Marner for years, let him have the satisfaction of taking him now.

"Oh." Monk sat back, altering his whole attitude, almost smiling. "So he was not really concerned in the loss?"

"No, not at all."

Monk stood up.

"Then it hardly constitutes a part of his murder. I'm sorry to have wasted your time, Mr. Marner. And I thank you for your cooperation. You do, of course, have some papers to prove this, just for my superiors?"

"Yes. Yes, I have." Marner relaxed visibly. "If you care to wait for a moment—" He stood up from his desk and went to a large cabinet of files. He pulled a drawer and took out a small notebook ruled in ledger fashion. He put it, open, on the desk in front of Monk.

Monk picked it up, glanced at it, read the entry where Grey had withdrawn his money, and snapped it shut.

"Thank you." He put the book in the inside pocket of his coat and stood up.

Marner's hand came forward for the return of the book. He realized he was not going to get it, debated in his mind whether to demand it or not, and decided it would raise more interest in the subject than he could yet afford. He forced a smile, a sickly thing in his great white face.

"Always happy to be of service, sir. Where should we be without the police? So much crime these days, so much violence."

"Indeed," Monk agreed. "And so much theft that breeds violence. Good day, Mr. Marner."

Outside he walked briskly along Gun Lane and back towards the West India Dock Road, but he was thinking hard. If this evidence was correct, and not fiddled with by Zebedee Marner, then the hitherto relatively honest Joscelin Grey had almost certainly been forewarned in time to escape at the last moment himself, leaving Latterly and his friends to bear the loss. Dishonest, but not precisely illegal. It would be interesting to know who had shares in the company that took over the tobacco importing, and if Grey was one of them.

Had he uncovered this much before? Marner had shown

311

no signs of recognition. He had behaved as if the whole question were entirely new to him. In fact it must be, or Monk would never have been able to deceive him into imagining him an investor.

But even if Zebedee Marner had never seen him before, it was not impossible he had known all this before Grey's death, because then he had had his memory, known his contacts, who to ask, who to bribe, who could be threatened, and with what.

But there was no way yet to find out. On the West India Dock Road he found a hansom and sank back for the long ride, thinking.

At the police station he went to the man who had given him Zebedee Marner's address and told him of his visit, gave him the ledger and showed him what he thought the fraud would be. The man positively bubbled with delight, like someone who contemplates a rich feast only hours away. Monk had a brief, fierce glow of satisfaction.

It did not last.

Runcorn was waiting for him in his own office.

"No arrest yet?" he said with black relish. "No one charged?"

Monk did not bother to reply.

"Monk!" Runcorn slammed his fist on the table.

"Yes sir?"

"You sent John Evan out to Shelburne to question the staff?"

"Yes I did. Isn't that what you wanted?" He raised sarcastic eyebrows. "Evidence against Shelburne?"

"You won't get it out there. We know what his motive was. What we need is evidence of opportunity, someone who saw him here."

"I'll start looking," Monk said with bitter irony. Inside himself he was laughing, and Runcorn knew it, but he had not the faintest idea why, and it infuriated him.

"You should have been looking for the last month!" he shouted. "What in hell is the matter with you, Monk? You were always a hard, arrogant devil, with airs beyond your

312

station, but you were a good policeman. But now you're a fool. This crack on the head seems to have impaired your brain. Perhaps you should have some more sick leave?''

"I am perfectly well." Misery was black inside Monk; he wanted to frighten this man who hated him so much and was going to have the last victory. "But maybe you ought to take over this case? You are right, I am getting nowhere with it." He looked straight back at Runcorn with wide eyes. "The powers that be want a result—you should do the job yourself."

Runcorn's face set. "You must take me for a fool. I've sent for Evan. He'll be back tomorrow." He held up his thick finger, wagging it in Monk's face. "Arrest Shelburne this week, or I will take you off it." He turned and strode out, leaving the door squealing on its hinges.

Monk stared after him. So he had sent for Evan to return. Time was even shorter than he had feared. Before much longer Evan must come to the same conclusion as he had, and that would be the end.

In fact Evan came back the next day, and Monk met him for luncheon. They sat together in a steamy public house. It was heavy and damp with the odor of massed bodies, sawdust, spilled ale and nameless vegetables stewed into soup.

"Anything?" Monk asked as a matter of form. It would have seemed remarkable had he not.

"Lots of indication," Evan replied with a frown. "But I wonder sometimes if I see it only because I'm looking for it."

"You mean invent it for yourself?"

Evan's eyes came up quickly and met Monk's. They were devastatingly clear.

"You don't honestly believe he did it, do you, sir?"

How could he know so quickly? Rapidly Monk flew in his mind through all the possible things he might say. Would Evan know a lie? Had he seen all the lies already?

Was he clever enough, subtle enough, to be leading Monk gently into trapping himself? Was it conceivable the whole police department knew, and were simply waiting for him to uncover his own proof, his own condemnation? For a moment fear engulfed him and the cheerful rattle of the alehouse became a din like bedlam— witless, formless and persecutory. They all knew; they were merely waiting for him to know, to betray himself, and then the mystery would end. They would come out in the open, with laughter, handcuffs, questions, congratulations at another murder solved; there would be a trial, a brief imprisonment, and then the tight, strong rope, a quick pain—and nothing.

But why? Why had he killed Joscelin Grey? Surely not because Grey had escaped the crash of the tobacco company—probably even profited from it?

"Sir? Sir, are you all right?" It was Evan's voice cutting across his panic, Evan's face peering at him anxiously. "You look a little pale, sir. Are you sure you are all right?"

Monk forced himself to sit upright and meet Evan's eyes. If he were to be given one wish now, it would be that Evan would not have to know. Imogen Latterly had never really been more than a dream, a reminder of the softer self, the part of him that could be wounded and could care for something better than ambition—but Evan had been a friend. Maybe there had been others, but he could not remember them now.

"Yes," he said carefully. "Yes, thank you. I was just thinking. No, you are right; I am not at all sure it was Shelburne."

Evan leaned forward a little, his face eager.

"I'm glad you say that, sir. Don't let Mr. Runcorn push you." His long fingers were playing with the bread, too excited to eat. "I think it's someone here in London. In fact I have been looking at Mr. Lamb's notes again, and ours, and the more I read them the more I think it could have something to do with money, with business.

"Joscelin Grey seems to have lived fairly comfortably,

314

better than the allowance from his family supported." He put down his spoon and abandoned all pretense of the meal. "So either he was blackmailing someone, or else he gambled very successfully, or, most likely of all, he had some business we know nothing about. And if it were honest, we ought to have found some record of it, and the other people concerned should have come forward. Similarly, if he borrowed money, the lenders would have put in some claim against the estate."

"Unless they were sharks," Monk said automatically, his mind cold with fear, watching Evan draw closer and closer to the thread that must lead him to the truth. Any moment now and his fine, sensitive hands would grasp it.

"But if they were sharks," Evan said quickly, his eyes alight, "they would not have lent to someone like Grey. Sharks are exceedingly careful about their investments. That much I've learned. They don't lend a second sum out before they have the first back, and with interest, or a mortgage on property." A lock of his heavy hair fell forward over his brow and he ignored it. "Which brings us back to the same question: Where did Grey get the repayment, not to mention the interest? He was the third brother, remember, and he had no property of his own. No sir, he had some business, I'm sure of it. And I have some thoughts where to start looking for it."

He was coming closer with every new idea.

Monk said nothing; his mind was racing for a thought, any thought to put Evan off. He could not avoid it forever, the time would come; but before that he must know why. There was something vital so close, a finger's length out of his reach.

"Do you not agree, sir?" Evan was disappointed; his eyes were shadowed with it. Or was it disappointment that Monk had lied?

Monk jerked himself back, dismissing his pain. He must think clearly just a little longer.

"I was turning it over," he said, trying to keep the desperation out of his voice. "Yes, I think you may very well be right. Dawlish spoke of a business venture. I don't recall how much I told you of it; I gathered it had not yet begun, but there may easily have been others already involved." How he hated lying. Especially to Evan—this betrayal was the worst of all. He could not bear to think what Evan would feel when he knew. "It would be a good thing if we investigated it far more thoroughly."

Evan's face lit up again.

"Excellent. You know I really believe we could yet catch Joscelin Grey's murderer. I think we are near it; it will only take just one or two more clues and it will all fall into place."

Did he know how appallingly near he was to the truth?

"Possibly," Monk agreed, keeping his voice level with an effort. He looked down at the plate in front of him, anything to avoid Evan's eyes. "You will still have to be discreet, though. Dawlish is a man of considerable standing."

"Oh I will, sir, I will. Anyway, I do not especially suspect him. What about the letter we saw from Charles Latterly? That was pretty chilly, I thought. And I found out quite a lot more about him." He took a spoonful of his stew at last. "Did you know his father committed suicide just a few weeks before Grey was killed? Dawlish is a business affair in the future, but Latterly could have been one from the past. Don't you think so, sir?" He was ignoring the taste and texture of the food, almost swallowing it whole in his preoccupation. "Perhaps there was something not quite right there, and the elder Mr. Latterly took his life when he was implicated, and young Mr. Charles Latterly, the one who sent the letter, was the one who killed Grey in revenge?"

Monk took a deep breath. He must have just a little more time.

"That letter sounded too controlled for a man passionate enough to kill in revenge," he said carefully, beginning to eat his own stew. "But I will look into it. You try Dawlish, and you might try the Fortescues as well. We

316

don't know very much about their connection either." He could not let Evan pursue Charles for his, Monk's, crime; also the truth was too close for Charles to deny it easily. He had no liking for him, but there was something of honor left to cling to—and he was Hester's brother.

"Yes," he added, "try the Fortescues as well."

In the afternoon when Evan set off full of enthusiasm after Dawlish and Fortescue, Monk went back to the police station and again sought out the man who had given him Marner's address. The man's face lit up as soon as Monk came in.

"Ah, Monk, I owe you something. Good old Zebedee at last." He waved a book in the air triumphantly. "Went down to his place on the strength of the ledger you brought, and searched the whole building. The rackets he was running." He positively chortled with delight and hiccupped very slightly. "Swindling left and right, taking a rake-off from half the crime and vice in Limehouse—and the Isle of Dogs. God knows how many thousands of pounds must have gone through his hands, the old blackguard."

Monk was pleased; it was one career other than his own he had helped.

"Good," he said sincerely. "I always like to imagine that particular kind of bloodsucker running his belly off in the treadmills for a few years."

The other man grinned.

"Me too, and that one especially. By the way, the tobacco importing company was a sham. Did you know that?" He hiccupped again and excused himself. "There was a company, but there was never any practical chance it could have done any trading, let alone make a profit. Your fellow Grey took his money out at precisely the right moment. If he wasn't dead I should be wishing I could charge him as well."

Charge Grey? Monk froze. The room vanished except for a little whirling light in front of him, and the man's face.

317

"Wishing? Why only wishing?" He hardly dared ask. Hope hurt like a physical thing.

"Because there's no proof," the man replied, oblivious of Monk's ecstasy. "He did nothing actually illegal. But I'm as sure as I am that Hell's hot, he was part of it; just too damned clever to step over the law. But he set it up—and brought in the money."

"But he was taken in the fraud," Monk protested, afraid to believe. He wanted to grab the man and shake him; he resisted only with difficulty. "You're sure beyond doubt?"

"Of course I am." The other raised his eyebrows. "I may not be as brilliant a detective as you are, Monk, but I know my job. And I certainly know a fraud when I see one. Your friend Grey was one of the best, and very tidy about it." He hitched himself more comfortably in his seat. "Not much money, not enough to cause suspicion, just a small profit, and no guilt attached to him. If he made a habit of it he must have done quite nicely. Although how he got all those people to trust him with their money I don't know. You should see the names of some of those who invested."

"Yes," Monk said slowly. "I also should like to know how he persuaded them. I think I want to know that almost as much as I want to know anything." His brain was racing, casting for clues, threads anywhere. "Any other names in that ledger, any partners of Marner's?"

"Employees—just the clerk in the outer office."

"No partners; were there no partners? Anyone else who might know the business about Grey? Who got most of the money, if Grey didn't?"

The man hiccupped gently and sighed. "A rather nebulous 'Mr. Robinson,' and a lot of money went on keeping it secret, and tidy, covering tracks. No proof so far that this Robinson actually knew exactly what was going on. We've got a watch on him, but nothing good enough to arrest him yet."

"Where is he?" He had to find out if he had seen this

318

Robinson before, the first time he had investigated Grey. If Marner did not know him, then perhaps Robinson did?

The man wrote an address on a slip of paper and handed it to him.

Monk took it: it was just above the Elephant Stairs in Rotherhithe, across the river. He folded it and put it in his pocket.

"I won't spoil your case," he promised. "I only want to ask him one question, and it's to do with Grey, not the tobacco fraud."

"It's all right," the other man said, sighing happily. "Murder is always more important than fraud, at least it is when it's a lord's son that's been killed." He sighed and hiccupped together. "Of course if he'd been some poor shopkeeper or chambermaid it would be different. Depends who's been robbed, or who's been killed, doesn't it?"

Monk gave a hard little grimace for the injustice of it, then thanked him and left.

Robinson was not at the Elephant Stairs, and it took Monk all afternoon to find him, eventually running him down in a gin mill in Seven Dials, but he learned everything he wanted to know almost before Robinson spoke. The man's face tightened as soon as Monk came in and a cautious look came into his eyes.

"Good day, Mr. Monk; I didn't expect to see you again. What is it this time?"

Monk felt the excitement shiver through him. He swallowed hard.

"Still the same thing—"

Robinson's voice was low and sibilant, and there was a timber in it that struck Monk with an almost electric familiarity. The sweat tingled on his skin. It was real memory, actual sight and feelings coming back at last. He stared hard at the man.

Robinson's narrow, wedge-shaped face was stiff.

"I've already told you everything I know, Mr. Monk. Anyway, what does it matter now Joscelin Grey is dead?"

319

"And you told me everything you knew before? You swear it?"

Robinson snorted with a faint contempt.

"Yes I swear it," he said wearily. "Now will you please go away? You're known around 'ere. It don't do me no good to 'ave the police nosing around and asking questions. People think I 'ave something to 'ide."

Monk did not bother to argue with him. The fraud detective would catch up with him soon enough.

"Good," he said simply. "Then I don't need to trouble you again." He went out into the hot, gray street milling with peddlers and waifs, his feet hardly feeling the pavement beneath. So he had known about Grey before he had been to see him, before he had killed him.

But why was it he had hated Grey so much? Marner was the principal, the brains behind the fraud, and the greatest beneficiary. And it seemed he had made no move against Marner.

He needed to think about it, sort out his ideas, decide where at least to look for the last missing piece.

It was hot and close, the air heavy with the humidity coming up from the river, and his mind was tired, staggering, spinning with the burden of what he had learned. He needed food and something to drink away this terrible thirst, to wash the stench of the rookeries from his mouth.

Without realizing it he had walked to the door of an eating house. He pushed it open and the fresh smell of sawdust and apple cider engulfed him. Automatically he made his way to the counter. He did not want ale, but fresh bread and sharp, homemade pickle. He could smell them, pungent and a little sweet.

The potman smiled at him and fetched the crusty bread, crumbling Wensleydale cheese, and juicy onions. He passed over the plate.

" 'Aven't seen yer for a w'ile, sir," he said cheerfully. "I s'pose you was too late to find that fellow you was looking for?"

Monk took the plate in stiff hands, awkwardly. He could

320

not draw his eyes from the man's face. Memory was coming back; he knew he knew him.

"Fellow?" he said huskily.

"Yes." The potman smiled. "Major Grey; you was looking for 'im last time you was 'ere. It was the same night 'e was murdered, so I don't s'pose you ever found 'im."

Something was just beyond Monk's memory, the last piece, tantalizing, the shape of it almost recognizable at last.

"You knew him?" he said slowly, still holding the plate in his hands.

"Bless you, 'course I knew 'im, sir. I told you that." He frowned. " 'Ere, don't you remember?"

"No." Monk shook his head. It was too late now to lie. "I had an accident that night. I don't remember what you said. I'm sorry. Can you tell me again?"

The man shook his head and continued wiping a glass. "Too late now, sir. Major Grey was murdered that night. You'll not see 'im now. Don't you read the newspapers?"

"But you knew him," Monk repeated. "Where? In the army? You called him 'Major'!"

"That's right. Served in the army with 'im, I did, till I got invalided out."

"Tell me about him! Tell me everything you told me that night!"

"I'm busy right now, sir. I got to serve or I'll not make me livin'," the man protested. "Come back later, eh?"

Monk fished in his pocket and brought out all the money he had, every last coin. He put it on the counter.

"No, I need it now."

The man looked at the money, shining in the light. He met Monk's eyes, saw the urgency in them, understood something of importance. He slid his hand over the money and put it rapidly in the pocket under his apron before picking up the cloth again.

"You asked me what I knew of Major Grey, sir. I told you when I first met 'im and where—in the army in the

321

Crimea. 'E were a major, and I were just a private o' course. But I served under 'im for a long time. 'E were a good enough officer, not specially good nor specially bad; just like most. 'E were brave enough, as fair as most to 'is men. Good to 'is 'orses, but then most well-bred gents is."

The man blinked. "You didn't seem terribly interested in that," he went on, still absently working on the glass. "You listened, but it didn't seem to weigh much with you. Then you asked me about the Battle o' the Alma, where some Lieutenant Latterly 'ad died; an' I told you as we wasn't at the Battle o' the Alma, so I couldn't tell you about this Lieutenant Latterly—"

"But Major Grey spent the last night before the battle with Lieutenant Latterly." Monk grabbed at his arm. "He lent him his watch. Latterly was afraid; it was a lucky piece, a talisman. It had belonged to his grandfather at Waterloo."

"No sir, I can't say about any Lieutenant Latterly, but Major Grey weren't nowhere near the Battle o' the Alma, and 'e never 'ad no special watch."

"Are you sure?" Monk was gripping the man's wrist, unaware of hurting him.

"O' course I'm sure, sir." The man eased his hand. "I was there. An' 'is watch were an ordinary gold plate one, and as new as 'is uniform. It weren't no more at Waterloo than 'e were."

"And an officer called Dawlish?"

The potman frowned, rubbing his wrist. "Dawlish? I don't remember you asking me about 'im."

"I probably didn't. But do you remember him?"

"No sir, I don't recall an officer o' that name."

"But you are sure of the Battle of the Alma?"

"Yes sir, I'd swear before God positive. If you'd been in the Crimea, sir, you'd not forget what battle you was at, and what you wasn't. I reckon that's about the worst war there's ever been, for cold and muck and men dyin'."

"Thank you."

322

"Don't you want your bread an' cheese, sir? That pickle's 'omemade special. You should eat it. You look right peaked, you do."

Monk took it, thanked him automatically, and sat down at one of the tables. He ate without tasting and then walked out into the first spots of rain. He could remember doing this before, remember the slow building anger. It had all been a lie, a brutal and carefully calculated lie to earn first acceptance from the Latterlys, then their friendship, and finally to deceive them into a sufficient sense of obligation, over the lost watch, to repay him by supporting his business scheme. Grey had used his skill to play like an instrument first their grief, then their debt. Perhaps he had even done the same with the Dawlishes.

The rage was gathering up inside him again. It was coming back exactly as it had before. He was walking faster and faster, the rain beating in his face now. He was unaware of it. He splashed through the swimming gutters into the street to hail a cab. He gave the address in Mecklenburg Square, as he knew he had done before.

When he got out he went into the building. Grimwade handed him the key this time; the first time there had been no one there.

He went upstairs. It seemed new, strange, as if he were reliving the first time when it was unknown to him. He got to the top and hesitated at the door. Then he had knocked. Now he slipped the key into the lock. It swung open quite easily and he went in. Before Joscelin Grey had come to the door, dressed in pale dove, his fair face handsome, smiling, just a little surprised. He could see it now as if it had been only a few minutes ago.

Grey had asked him in, quite casually, unperturbed. He had put his stick in the hall stand, his mahogany stick with the brass chain embossed in the handle. It was still there. Then he had followed Grey into the main room. Grey had been very composed, a slight smile on his face. Monk had told him what he had come for: about the tobacco business, the failure, Latterly's death, the fact that Grey had lied, that he had never known George Latterly, and there had been no watch.

He could see Grey now as he had turned from the sideboard, holding out a drink for Monk, taking one himself. He had smiled again, more widely.

"My dear fellow, a harmless little lie." His voice had been light, very easy, very calm. "I told them what an excellent fellow poor George was, how brave, how charming, how well loved. It was what they wanted to hear. What does it matter whether it was true or not?"

"It was a lie," Monk had shouted back. "You didn't even know George Latterly. You did it purely for money."

Grey had grinned.

"So I did, and what's more, I shall do it again, and again. I have an endless stream of gold watches, or whatever; and there's not a thing you can do about it, policeman. I shall go on as long as anyone is left who remembers the Crimea—which will be a hell of a long time—and shall damned well never run out of the dead!"

Monk had stared at him, helpless, anger raging inside him till he could have wept like an impotent child.

"I didn't know Latterly," Grey had gone on. "I got his name from the casualty lists. They're absolutely full of names, you've no idea. Although actually I got some of the better ones from the poor devils themselves—saw them die in Scutari, riddled with disease, bleeding and spewing all over the place. I wrote their last letters for them. Poor George might have been a raving coward, for all I know. But what good does it do to tell his family that? I've no idea what he was like, but it doesn't take much wit to work out what they wanted to hear! Poor little Imogen adored him, and who can blame her? Charles is a hell of a bore; reminds me a bit of my eldest brother, another pompous fool." His fair face had become momentarily ugly with envy. A look of malice and pleasure had slid into it. He looked at Monk up and down knowingly.

"And who wouldn't have told the lovely Imogen whatever she would listen to? I told her all about that extraor-

324

dinary creature, Florence Nightingale. I painted up the heroism a bit, certainly, gave her all the glory of 'angels of mercy' holding lamps by the dying through the night. You should have seen her face." He had laughed; then seeing something in Monk, a vulnerability, perhaps a memory or a dream, and understanding its depth in a flash: "Ah yes, Imogen." He sighed. "Got to know her very well." His smile was half a leer. "Love the way she walks, all eager, full of promise, and hope." He had looked at Monk and the slow smile spread to his eyes till the light in them was as old as appetite and knowledge itself. He had tittered slightly. "I do believe you're taken with Imogen yourself.

"You clod, she'd no more touch you than carry out her own refuse.

"She's in love with Florence Nightingale and the glory of the Crimea!" His eyes met Monk's, glittering bright. "I could have had her any time, all eager and quivering." His lip curled and he had almost laughed as he looked at Monk. "I'm a soldier; I've seen reality, blood and passion, fought for Queen and country. I've seen the Charge of the Light Brigade, lain in hospital at Scutari among the dying. What do you imagine she thinks of grubby little London policemen who spend their time sniffing about in human filth after the beggars and the degenerate? You're a scavenger, a cleaner up of other people's dirt—one of life's necessities, like the drains." He took a long gulp of his brandy and looked at Monk over the top of the glass.

"Perhaps when they've got over that old idiot getting hysterical and shooting himself, I shall go back and do just that. Can't remember when I've fancied a woman more."

It had been then, with that leer on his mouth, that Monk had taken his own glass and thrown the brandy across Grey's face. He could remember the blinding anger as if it were a dream he had only just woken from. He could still taste the heat and the gall of it on his tongue.

The liquid had hit Grey in his open eyes and burned

him, seared his pride beyond bearing. He was a gentleman, one already robbed by birth of fortune, and now this oaf of a policeman, jumped above himself, had insulted him in his own house. His features had altered into a snarl of fury and he had picked up his own heavy stick and struck Monk across the shoulders with it. He had aimed at his head, but Monk had almost felt it before it came, and moved.

They had closed in a struggle. It should have been self-defense, but it was far more than that. Monk had been glad of it—he had wanted to smash that leering face, beat it in, undo all that he had said, wipe from him the thoughts he had had of Imogen, expunge some of the wrong to her family. But above all towering in his head and burning in his soul, he wanted to beat him so hard he would never feed on the gullible and the bereaved again, telling them lies of invented debt and robbing the dead of the only heritage they had left, the truth of memory in those who had loved them.

Grey had fought back; for a man invalided out of the army he had been surprisingly strong. They had been locked together struggling for the stick, crashing into furniture, upsetting chairs. The very violence of it was a catharsis, and all the pent-up fear, the nightmare of rage and the agonizing pity poured forth and he barely felt the pain of blows, even the breaking of his ribs when Grey caught him a tremendous crack on the chest with his stick.

But Monk's weight and strength told, and perhaps his rage was even stronger than Grey's fear and all his held-in anger of years of being slighted and passed over.

Monk could remember quite clearly now the moment when he had wrested the heavy stick out of Grey's hands and struck at him with it, trying to destroy the hideousness, the blasphemy he saw, the obscenity the law was helpless to curb.

Then he had stopped, breathless and terrified by his own violence and the storm of his hatred. Grey was splayed out on the floor, swearing like a trooper.

Monk had turned and gone out, leaving the door swinging behind him, blundering down the stairs, turning his coat collar up and pulling his scarf up to hide the abrasion on his face where Grey had hit him. He had passed Grimwade in the hall. He remembered a bell ringing and Grimwade leaving his position and starting upstairs.

Outside the weather was fearful. As soon as he had opened the door the wind had blown it against him so hard it had knocked him backwards. He had put his head down and plunged out, the rain engulfing him, beating in his face cold and hard. He had his back to the light, going into the darkness between one lamp and the next.

There was a man coming towards him, towards the light and the door still open in the wind—for a moment he saw his face before he turned and went in. It was Menard Grey.

Now it all made obvious and tragic sense—it was not George Latterly's death, or the abuse of it, which had spurred Joscelin Grey's murder, it was Edward Dawlish's—and Joscelin's own betrayal of every ideal his brother believed.

And then the joy vanished just as suddenly as it had come, the relief evaporated, leaving him shivering cold. How could he prove it? It was his word against Menard's. Grimwade had been up the stairs answering the bell, and seen nothing. Menard had gone in the door Monk had left open in the gale. There was nothing material, no evidence—only Monk's memory of Menard's face for a moment in the gaslight.

They would hang him. He could imagine the trial now, himself standing in the dock, the ridiculousness of trying to explain what manner of man Joscelin Grey had been, and that it was not Monk, but Joscelin's own brother Menard who had killed him. He could see the disbelief in their faces, and the contempt for a man who would try to escape justice by making such a charge.

Despair closed around him like the blackness of the night, eating away strength, crushing with the sheer weight of it. And he began to be afraid. There would be the few short weeks in the stone cell, the stolid warders, at once pitying and contemptuous, then the last meal, the priest, and the short walk to the scaffold, the smell of rope, the pain, the fighting for breath—and oblivion.

He was still drowned and paralyzed by it when he heard the sound on the stairs. The latch turned and Evan stood in the doorway. It was the worst moment of all. There was no point in lying, Evan's face was full of knowledge, and pain. And anyway, he did not want to.

"How did you know?" Monk said quietly.

Evan came in and closed the door. "You sent me after Dawlish. I found an officer who'd served with Edward Dawlish. He didn't gamble, and Joscelin Grey never paid any debts for him. Everything he knew about him he learned from Menard. He took a hell of a chance lying to the family like that—but it worked. They'd have backed him financially, if he hadn't died. They blamed Menard for Edward's fall from honor, and forbade him in the house. A nice touch on Joscelin's part."

Monk stared at him. It made perfect sense. And yet it would never even raise a reasonable doubt in a juror's mind.

"I think that is where Grey's money came from—cheating the families of the dead," Evan continued. "You were so concerned about the Latterly case, it wasn't a great leap of the imagination to assume he cheated them too—and that is why Charles Latterly's father shot himself." His eyes were soft and intense with distress. "Did you come this far the first time too—before the accident?"

So he knew about the memory also. Perhaps it was all far more obvious than he believed; the fumbling for words, the unfamiliarity with streets, public houses, old haunts— even Runcorn's hatred of him. It did not matter anymore.

"Yes." Monk spoke very slowly, as if letting the words fall one by one would make them believable. "But I did not kill Joscelin Grey. I fought with him, I probably hurt him—he certainly hurt me—but he was alive and swearing at me when I left." He searched Evan's countenance fea-

328

ture by feature. "I saw Menard Grey go in as I turned in the street. He was facing the light and I was going away from it. The outer door was still open in the wind."

A desperate, painful relief flooded Evan's face, and he looked bony and young, and very tired. "So it was Menard who killed him." It was a statement.

"Yes." A blossom of gratitude opened wide inside Monk, filling him with sweetness. Even without hope, it was to be treasured immeasurably. "But there is no proof."

"But—" Evan began to argue, then the words died on his lips as he realized the truth of it. In all their searches they had found nothing. Menard had motive, but so had Charles Latterly, or Mr. Dawlish, or any other family Joscelin had cheated, any friend he had dishonored—or Lovel Grey, whom he might have betrayed in the cruelest way of all—or Monk himself. And Monk had been there. Now that they knew it, they also knew how easily provable it was, simply find the shop where he had bought that highly distinctive stick—such a piece of vanity. Mrs. Worley would remember it, and its subsequent absence. Lamb would recall seeing it in Grey's flat the morning after the murder. Imogen Latterly would have to admit Monk had been working on the case of her father's death.

The darkness was growing closer, tighter around them, the light guttering.

"We'll have to get Menard to confess," Evan said at last.

Monk laughed harshly. "And how do you propose we should do that? There's no evidence, and he knows it. No one would take my word against his that I saw him, and kept silent about it till now. It will look like a rather shabby and very stupid attempt to shift the blame from myself."

That was true, and Evan racked his mind in vain for a rebuttal. Monk was still sitting in the big chair, limp and exhausted with emotions from terror through joy and back to fear and despair again.

"Go home," Evan said gently. "You can't stay here.

There may be—'' Then the idea came to him with a flutter of hope, growing and rising. There was one person who might help. It was a chance, but there was nothing left to lose. "Yes," he repeated. "Go home—I'll be there soon. I've just got an errand. Someone to see—'' And he swung on his heel and went out of the door, leaving it ajar behind him.

He ran down the stairs two at a time—he never knew afterwards how he did not break his neck—shot past Grimwade, and plunged out into the rain. He ran all the way along the pavement of Mecklenburg Square along Doughty Street and accosted a hansom as it passed him, driver's coat collar up around his neck and stovepipe hat jammed forward over his brow.

"I ain't on duty, guv!" the driver said crossly. "Finished, I am. Goin' 'ome ter me supper."

Evan ignored him and climbed in, shouting the Latterlys' address in Thanet Street at him.

"I told you, I ain't goin' nowhere!" the cabby repeated, louder this time. " 'Ceptin 'ome fer me supper. You'll 'ave ter get someone else!"

"You're taking me to Thanet Street!" Evan shouted back at him. "Police! Now get on with it, or I'll have your badge!"

"Bleedin' rozzers," the cabby muttered sullenly, but he realized he had a madman in the back, and it would be quicker in the long run to do what he said. He lifted the reins and slapped them on the horse's soaking back, and they set off at a brisk trot.

At Thanet Street Evan scrambled out and commanded the cabby to wait, on pain of his livelihood.

Hester was at home when Evan was shown in by a startled maid. He was streaming water everywhere and his extraordinary, ugly, beautiful face was white. His hair was plastered crazily across his brow and he stared at her with anguished eyes.

She had seen hope and despair too often not to recognize both.

"Can you come with me!" he said urgently. "Please? I'll explain as we go. Miss Latterly—I—"

"Yes." She did not need time to decide. To refuse was an impossibility. And she must leave before Charles or Imogen came from the withdrawing room, impelled by curiosity, and discovered the drenched and frantic policeman in the hall. She could not even go back for her cloak—what use would it be in this downpour anyway? "Yes—I'll come now." She walked past him and out of the front door. The wall of rain hit her in the face and she ignored it, continuing across the pavement, over the bubbling gutter and up into the hansom before either Evan or the driver had time to hand her up.

Evan scrambled behind her and slammed the door, shouting his instructions to drive to Grafton Street. Since the cabby had not yet been paid, he had little alternative.

"What has happened, Mr. Evan?" Hester asked as soon as they were moving. "I can see that it is something very terrible. Have you discovered who murdered Joscelin Grey?"

There was no point in hesitating now; the die was cast.

"Yes, Miss Latterly. Mr. Monk retraced all the steps of his first investigation—with your help." He took a deep breath. He was cold now that the moment came; he was wet to the skin and shaking. "Joscelin Grey made his living by finding the families of men killed in the Crimea, pretending he had known the dead soldier and befriended him—either lending him money, paying the debts he left, or giving him some precious personal belonging, like the watch he claimed to have lent your brother, then when the family could not give it back to him—which they never could, since it did not exist—they felt in his debt, which he used to obtain invitations, influence, financial or social backing. Usually it was only a few hundred guineas, or to be a guest at their expense. In your father's case it was to his ruin and death. Either way Grey did not give a damn what happened to his victims, and he had every intention of continuing."

"What a vile crime," she said quietly. "He was totally

331

despicable. I am glad that he is dead—and perhaps sorry for whoever killed him. You have not said who it was?" Suddenly she was cold also. "Mr. Evan—?"

"Yes ma'am—Mr. Monk went to his flat in Mecklenburg Square and faced him with it. They fought—Mr. Monk beat him, but he was definitely alive and not mortally hurt when Mr. Monk left. But as Monk reached the street he saw someone else arrive, and go towards the door which was still swinging open in the wind."

He saw Hester's face pale in the glare of the streetlamps through the carriage window.

"Who?"

"Menard Grey," he replied, waiting in the dark again to judge from her voice, or her silence, if she believed it. "Probably because Joscelin dishonored the memory of his friend Edward Dawlish, and deceived Edward's father into giving him hospitality, as he did your father—and the money would have followed."

She said nothing for several minutes. They swayed and rattled through the intermittent darkness, the rain battering on the roof and streaming past in torrents, yellow where the gaslight caught it.

"How very sad," she said at last, and her voice was tight with emotion as though the pity caused a physical pain in her throat. "Poor Menard. I suppose you are going to arrest him? Why have you brought me? I can do nothing."

"We can't arrest him," he answered quietly. "There is no proof."

"There—" She swiveled around in her seat; he felt her rather than saw her. "Then what are you going to do? They'll think it was Monk. They'll charge him—they'll—" She swallowed. "They'll hang him."

"I know. We must make Menard confess. I thought you might know how we could do that? You know the Greys far better than we could, from the outside. And Joscelin was responsible for your father's death—and your mother's, indirectly."

Again she sat silent for so long he was afraid he had

offended her, or reminded her of grief so deep she was unable to do anything but nurse its pain inside her. They were drawing close to Grafton Street, and soon they must leave the cab and face Monk with some resolution—or admit failure. Then he would be faced with the task he dreaded so much the thought of it made him sick. He must either tell Runcorn the truth, that Monk fought with Joscelin Grey the night of his death—or else deliberately conceal the fact and lay himself open to certain dismissal from the police force—and the possible charge of accessory to murder.

They were in the Tottenham Court Road, lamps gleaming on the wet pavements, gutters awash. There was no time left.

"Miss Latterly."

"Yes. Yes," she said firmly. "I will come with you to Shelburne Hall. I have thought about it, and the only way I can see success is if you tell Lady Fabia the truth about Joscelin. I will corroborate it. My family were his victims as well, and she will have to believe me, because I have no interest in lying. It does not absolve my father's suicide in the eyes of the church." She hesitated only an instant. "Then if you proceed to tell her about Edward Dawlish as well, I think Menard may be persuaded to confess. He may see no other avenue open to him, once his mother realizes that he killed Joscelin—which she will. It will devastate her—it may destroy her." Her voice was very low. "And they may hang Menard. But we cannot permit the law to hang Mr. Monk instead, merely because the truth is a tragedy that will wound perhaps beyond bearing. Joscelin Grey was a man who did much evil. We cannot protect his mother either from her part in it, or from the pain of knowing."

"You'll come to Shelburne tomorrow?" He had to hear her say it again. "You are prepared to tell her your own family's suffering at Joscelin's hands?"

"Yes. And how Joscelin obtained the names of the dying in Scutari, as I now realize, so he could use them to cheat their families. At what time will you depart?''

Again relief swept over him, and an awe for her that she could so commit herself without equivocation. But then to go out to the Crimea to nurse she must be a woman of courage beyond the ordinary imagination, and to remain there, of a strength of purpose that neither danger nor pain could bend.

''I don't know,'' he said a trifle foolishly. ''There was little purpose in going at all unless you were prepared to come. Lady Shelburne would hardly believe us without further substantiation from beyond police testimony. Shall we say the first train after eight o'clock in the morning?'' Then he remembered he was asking a lady of some gentility. ''Is that too early?''

''Certainly not.'' Had he been able to see her face there might have been the faintest of smiles on it.

''Thank you. Then do you wish to take this hansom back home again, and I shall alight here and go and tell Mr. Monk?''

''That would be the most practical thing,'' she agreed. ''I shall see you at the railway station in the morning.''

He wanted to say something more, but all that came to his mind was either repetitious or vaguely condescending. He simply thanked her again and climbed out into the cold and teeming rain. It was only when the cab had disappeared into the darkness and he was halfway up the stairs to Monk's rooms that he realized with acute embarrassment that he had left her to pay the cabby.

The journey to Shelburne was made at first with heated conversation and then in silence, apart from the small politenesses of travel. Monk was furious that Hester was present. He refrained from ordering her home again only because the train was already moving when she entered the carriage from the corridor, bidding them good-morning and seating herself opposite.

''I asked Miss Latterly to come,'' Evan explained without a blush, "because her additional testimony will carry great weight with Lady Fabia, who may well not believe us, since we have an obvious interest in claiming Joscelin was a cad. Miss Latterly's experience, and that of her family, is something she cannot so easily deny." He did not make the mistake of claiming that Hester had any moral right to be there because of her own loss, or her part in the solution. Monk wished he had, so he could lose his temper and accuse him of irrelevance. The argument he had presented was extremely reasonable—in fact he was right. Hester's corroboration would be very likely to tip the balance of decision, which otherwise the Greys together might rebut.

"I trust you will speak only when asked?" Monk said to her coldly. "This is a police operation, and a very delicate one." That she of all people should be the one whose assistance he needed at this point was galling in the extreme, and yet it was undeniable. She was in many ways everything he loathed in a woman, the antithesis of the gentleness that still lingered with such sweetness in his memory; and yet she had rare courage, and a force of character which would equal Fabia Grey's any day.

"Certainly, Mr. Monk," she replied with her chin high and her eyes unflinching, and he knew in that instant that she had expected precisely this reception, and come to the carriage late intentionally to circumvent the possibility of being ordered home. Although of course it was highly debatable as to whether she would have gone. And Evan would never countenance leaving her on the station platform at Shelburne. And Monk did care what Evan felt.

He sat and stared across at Hester, wishing he could think of something else crushing to say.

She smiled at him, clear-eyed and agreeable. It was not so much friendliness as triumph.

They continued the rest of the journey with civility, and gradually each became consumed in private thoughts, and a dread of the task ahead.

When they arrived at Shelburne they alighted onto the

335

platform. The weather was heavy and dark with the presage of winter. It had stopped raining, but a cold wind stirred in gusts and chilled the skin even through heavy coats.

They were obliged to wait some fifteen minutes before a trap arrived, which they hired to take them to the hall. This journey, too, they made huddled together and without speaking. They were all oppressed by what was to come, and the trivialities of conversation would have been grotesque.

They were admitted reluctantly by the footman, but no persuasion would cause him to show them into the withdrawing room. Instead they were left together in the morning room, neither cheered nor warmed by the fire smoldering in the grate, and required to wait until Her Ladyship should decide whether she would receive them or not.

After twenty-five minutes the footman returned and conducted them to the boudoir, where Fabia was seated on her favorite settee, looking pale and somewhat strained, but perfectly composed.

"Good morning, Mr. Monk. Constable." She nodded at Evan. Her eyebrows rose and her eyes became icier. "Good morning, Miss Latterly. I assume you can explain your presence here in such curious company?"

Hester took the bull by the horns before Monk had time to form a reply.

"Yes, Lady Fabia. I have come to inform you of the truth about my family's tragedy—and yours."

"You have my condolences, Miss Latterly." Fabia looked at her with pity and distaste. "But I have no desire to know the details of your loss, nor do I wish to discuss my bereavement with you. It is a private matter. I imagine your intention is good, but it is entirely misplaced. Good day to you. The footman will see you to the door."

Monk felt the first flicker of anger stir, in spite of the consuming disillusion he knew this woman was shortly going to feel. Her willful blindness was monumental, her ability to disregard other people total.

Hester's face set hard with resolve, as granite hard as Fabia's own.

"It is the same tragedy, Lady Fabia. And I do not discuss it out of good intentions, but because it is a truth we are all obliged to face. It gives me no pleasure at all, but neither do I plan to run away from it—"

Fabia's chin came up and the thin muscles tightened in her neck, suddenly looking scraggy, as if age had descended on her in the brief moments since they entered the room.

"I have never run from a truth in my life, Miss Latterly, and I do not care for your impertinence in suggesting I might. You forget yourself."

"I would prefer to forget everything and go home." A ghost of a smile crossed Hester's face and vanished. "But I cannot. I think it would be better if Lord Shelburne and Mr. Menard Grey were to be present, rather than repeat the story for them later. There may be questions they wish to ask—Major Grey was their brother and they have some rights in knowing how and why he died."

Fabia sat motionless, her face rigid, her hands poised halfway towards the bell pull. She had not invited any of them to be seated, in fact she was on the point of asking again that they leave. Now, with the mention of Joscelin's murderer, everything was changed. There was not the slightest sound in the room except the ticking of the ormolu clock on the mantelpiece.

"You know who killed Joscelin?" She looked at Monk, ignoring Hester.

"Yes ma'am, we do." He found his mouth dry and the pulse beating violently in his head. Was it fear, or pity—or both?

Fabia stared at him, demanding he explain everything for her, then slowly the challenge died. She saw something in his face which she could not overcome, a knowledge and a finality which touched her with the first breath of a chill, nameless fear. She pulled the bell, and when the maid came, told her to send both Menard and Lovel to her immediately. No mention was made of Rosamond.

She was not a Grey by blood, and apparently Fabia did not consider she had any place in this revelation.

They waited in silence, each in their separate worlds of misery and apprehension. Lovel came first, looking irritably from Fabia to Monk, and with surprise at Hester. He had obviously been interrupted while doing something he considered of far greater urgency.

"What is it?" he said, frowning at his mother. "Has something further been discovered?"

"Mr. Monk says he knows at last who killed Joscelin," she answered with masklike calm.

"Who?"

"He has not told me. He is waiting for Menard."

Lovel turned to Hester, his face puckered with confusion. "Miss Latterly?"

"The truth involves the death of my father also, Lord Shelburne," she explained gravely. "There are parts of it which I can tell you, so you understand it all."

The first shadow of anxiety touched him, but before he could press her further Menard came in, glanced from one to another of them, and paled.

"Monk finally knows who killed Joscelin," Lovel explained. "Now for heaven's sake, get on with it. I presume you have arrested him?"

"It is in hand, sir." Monk found himself more polite to them all than previously. It was a form of distancing himself, almost a sort of verbal defense.

"Then what is it you want of us?" Lovel demanded.

It was like plunging into a deep well of ice.

"Major Grey made his living out of his experience in the Crimean War—" Monk began. Why was he so mealymouthed? He was dressing it in sickening euphemisms.

"My son did not 'make his living' as you put it!" Fabia snapped. "He was a gentleman—there was no necessity. He had an allowance from the family estates."

"Which didn't begin to cover the expenses of the way he liked to live," Menard said savagely. "If you'd ever looked at him closely, even once, you would have known that."

"I did know it." Lovel glared at his brother. "I assumed he was successful at cards."

"He was—sometimes. At other times he'd lose—heavily—more than he had. He'd go on playing, hoping to get it back, ignoring the debts—until I paid them, to save the family honor."

"Liar," Fabia said with withering disgust. "You were always jealous of him, even as a child. He was braver, kinder and infinitely more charming than you." For a moment a brief glow of memory superseded the present and softened all the lines of anger in her face—then the rage returned deeper than before. "And you couldn't forgive him for it."

Dull color burned up Menard's face and he winced as if he had been struck. But he did not retaliate. There was still in his eyes, in the turn of his lips, a pity for her which concealed the bitter truth.

Monk hated it. Futilely he tried again to think of any way he could to avoid exposing Menard even now.

The door opened and Callandra Daviot came in, meeting Hester's eyes, seeing the intense relief in them, then the contempt in Fabia's eyes and the anguish in Menard's.

"This is a family concern," Fabia said, dismissing her. "You need not trouble yourself with it."

Callandra walked past Hester and sat down.

"In case you have forgotten, Fabia, I was born a Grey. Something which you were not. I see the police are here. Presumably they have learned more about Joscelin's death—possibly even who was responsible. What are you doing here, Hester?"

Again Hester took the initiative. Her face was bleak and she stood with her shoulders stiff as if she were bracing herself against a blow.

"I came because I know a great deal about Joscelin's death, which you may not believe from anyone else."

"Then why have you concealed it until now," Fabia said with heavy disbelief. "I think you are indulging in a most vulgar intrusion, Miss Latterly, which I can only presume is a result of that same willful nature which drove you to go traipsing off to the Crimea. No wonder you are unmarried.''

Hester had been called worse things than vulgar, and by people for whose opinion she cared a great deal more than she did for Fabia Grey's.

''Because I did not know it had any relevance before,'' she said levelly. ''Now I do. Joscelin came to visit my parents after my brother was lost in the Crimea. He told them he had lent George a gold watch the night before his death. He asked for its return, assuming it was found among George's effects.'' Her voice dropped a fraction and her back became even stiffer. ''There was no watch in George's effects, and my father was so embarrassed he did what he could to make amends to Joscelin—with hospitality, money to invest in Joscelin's business enterprise, not only his own but his friends' also. The business failed and my father's money, and all that of his friends, was lost. He could not bear the shame of it, and he took his own life. My mother died of grief a short while later.''

''I am truly sorry for your parents' death,'' Lovel interrupted, looking first at Fabia, then at Hester again. ''But how can all this have anything to do with Joscelin's murder? It seems an ordinary enough matter—an honorable man making a simple compensation to clear his dead son's debt to a brother officer.''

Hester's voice shook and at last her control seemed in danger of breaking.

''There was no watch. Joscelin never knew George—any more than he knew a dozen others whose names he picked from the casualty lists, or whom he watched die in Scutari—I saw him do it—only then I didn't know why.''

Fabia was white-lipped. ''That is a most scandalous lie—and beneath contempt. If you were a man I should have you horsewhipped.''

''Mother!'' Lovel protested, but she ignored him.

''Joscelin was a beautiful man—brave and talented and full of charm and wit,'' she plunged on, her voice thick with emotion, the joy of the past, and the anguish. ''Everyone loved him—except those few who were eaten with envy.'' Her eyes darted at Menard with something close to hatred. "Little men who couldn't bear to see anyone succeed beyond their own petty efforts.'' Her mouth trembled. "Lovel, because Rosamond loved Joscelin; he could make her laugh—and dream.'' Her voice hardened. "And Menard, who couldn't live with the fact that I loved Joscelin more than I loved anyone else in the world, and I always did.''

She shuddered and her body seemed to shrink into itself as if withdrawing from something vile. "Now this woman has come here with her warped and fabricated story, and you stand there and listen to it. If you were men worthy of the name, you would throw her out and damn it for the slander it is. But it seems I must do it myself. No one has any sense of the family honor but me.'' She put her hands on the arm of her chair as if to rise to her feet.

"You'll have no one thrown out until I say so,'' Lovel said with a tight, calm voice, suddenly cutting like steel across her emotion. "It is not you who have defended the family honor; all you've defended is Joscelin—whether he deserved it or not. It was Menard who paid his debts and cleaned up the trail of cheating and welching he left behind—''

"Nonsense. Whose word do you have for that? Menard's?'' She spat the name. "He is calling Joscelin a cheat, no one else. And he wouldn't dare, if Joscelin were alive. He only has the courage to do it now because he thinks you will back him, and there is no one here to call him the pathetic, treacherous liar he is.''

Menard stood motionless, the final blow visible in the agony of his face. She had hurt him, and he had defended Joscelin for her sake for the last time.

Callandra stood up.

"You are wrong, Fabia, as you have been wrong all the time. Miss Latterly here, for one, will testify that Joscelin was a cheat who made money deceiving the bereaved who were too hurt and bewildered to see him for what he was. Menard was always a better man, but you were too fond of flattery to see it. Perhaps you were the one Joscelin deceived most of all—first, last and always." She did not flinch now, even from Fabia's stricken face as she caught sight at last of a fearful truth. "But you wanted to be deceived. He told you what you wished to hear; he told you you were beautiful, charming, gay—all the things a man loves in a woman. He learned his art in your gullibility, your willingness to be entertained, to laugh and to be the center of all the life and love in Shelburne. He said all that not because he thought for a moment it was true, but because he knew you would love him for saying it—and you did, blindly and indiscriminately, to the exclusion of everyone else. That is your tragedy, as well as his."

Fabia seemed to wither as they watched her.

"You never liked Joscelin," she said in a last, frantic attempt to defend her world, her dreams, all the past that was golden and lovely to her, everything that gave her meaning as it crumbled in front of her—not only what Joscelin had been, but what she herself had been. "You are a wicked woman."

"No, Fabia," Callandra replied. "I am a very sad one." She turned to Hester. "I assume it is not your brother who killed Joscelin, or you would not have come here to tell us this way. We would have believed the police, and the details would not have been necessary." With immeasurable sorrow she looked across at Menard. "You paid his debts. What else did you do?"

There was an aching silence in the room.

Monk could feel his heart beating as if it had the force to shake his whole body. They were poised on the edge of truth, and yet it was still so far away. It could be lost again by a single slip; they could plunge away into an abyss of fear, whispered doubts, always seeing suspicions, double meanings, hearing the footstep behind and the hand on the shoulder.

Against his will, he looked across at Hester, and saw that she was looking at him, the same thoughts plain in her eyes. He turned his head quickly back to Menard, who was ashen-faced.

"What else did you do?" Callandra repeated. "You knew what Joscelin was—"

"I paid his debts." Menard's voice was no more than a whisper.

"Gambling debts," she agreed. "What about his debts of honor, Menard? What about his terrible debts to men like Hester's father and brother—did you pay them as well?"

"I—I didn't know about the Latterlys," Menard stammered.

Callandra's face was tight with grief.

"Don't equivocate, Menard. You may not have known the Latterlys by name, but you knew what Joscelin was doing. You knew he got money from somewhere, because you knew how much he had to gamble with. Don't tell us you didn't learn where it came from. I know you better than that. You would not have rested in that ignorance— you knew what a fraud and a cheat Joscelin was, and you knew there was no honest way for him to come by so much. Menard—" Her face was gentle, full of pity. "You have behaved with such honor so far—don't soil it now by lying. There is no point, and no escape."

He winced as if she had struck him, and for a second Monk thought he was going to collapse. Then he straightened up and faced her, as though she had been a long-awaited execution squad—and death was not now the worst fear.

"Was it Edward Dawlish?" Now her voice also was barely above a whisper. "I remember how you cared for each other as boys, and your grief when he was killed. Why did his father quarrel with you?"

Menard did not evade the truth, but he spoke not to Callandra but to his mother, his voice low and hard, a lifetime of seeking and being rejected naked in it finally.

"Because Joscelin told him I had led Edward into gambling beyond his means, and that in the Crimea he had got in over his head with his brother officers, and would have died in debt—except that Joscelin settled it all for him."

343

There was a rich irony in that, and it was lost on no one. Even Fabia flinched in a death's-head acknowledgment of its cruel absurdity.

"For his family's sake," Menard continued, his voice husky, his eyes on Callandra. "Since I was the one who had led him to ruin."

He gulped. "Of course there was no debt. Joscelin never even served in the same area as Edward—I found that out afterwards. It was all another of his lies—to get money." He looked at Hester. "It was not as bad as your loss. At least Dawlish didn't kill himself. I am truly sorry about your family."

"He didn't lose any money." Monk spoke at last. "He didn't have time. You killed Joscelin before he could take it. But he had asked."

There was utter silence. Callandra put both her hands to her face. Lovel was stunned, unable to comprehend. Fabia was a broken woman. She no longer cared. What happened to Menard was immaterial. Joscelin, her beloved Joscelin, had been murdered in front of her in a new and infinitely more dreadful way. They had robbed her not only of the present and the future, but all the warm, sweet, precious past. It had all gone; there was nothing left but a handful of bitter ash.

They all waited, each in a separate world in the moments between hope and the finality of despair. Only Fabia had already been dealt the ultimate blow.

Monk found the nails of his hands cutting his palms, so tightly were his fists clenched. It could all still slip away from him. Menard could deny it, and there would be no proof sufficient. Runcorn would have only the bare facts, and come after Monk, and what was there to protect him?

The silence was like a slow pain, growing with each second.

Menard looked at his mother and she saw the movement of his head, and turned her face away, slowly and deliberately.

"Yes," Menard said at last. "Yes I did. He was despica-

344

ble. It wasn't only what he had done to Edward Dawlish, or me, but what he was going to go on doing. He had to be stopped—before it became public, and the name of Grey was a byword for a man who cheats the families of his dead comrades-in-arms, a more subtle and painful version of those who crawl over the battlefield the morning after and rob the corpses of the fallen.''

Callandra walked over to him and put her hand on his arm.

"We will get the best legal defense available,'' she said very quietly. "You had a great deal of provocation. I think they will not find murder.''

"We will not." Fabia's voice was a mere crackle, almost a sob, and she looked at Menard with terrible hatred.

"I will," Callandra corrected. "I have quite sufficient means." She turned back to Menard again. "I will not leave you alone, my dear. I imagine you will have to go with Mr. Monk now—but I will do all that is necessary, I promise you.''

Menard held her hand for a moment; something crossed his lips that was almost a smile. Then he turned to Monk.

"I am ready."

Evan was standing by the door with the manacles in his pocket. Monk shook his head, and Menard walked out slowly between them. The last thing Monk heard was Hester's voice as she stood next to Callandra.

"I will testify for him. When the jury hears what Joscelin did to my family, they may understand—''

Monk caught Evan's eye and felt a lift of hope. If Hester Latterly fought for Menard, the battle could not easily be lost. His hand held Menard's arm—but gently.

A DANGEROUS MOURNING

To John and Mary MacKenzie,
and my friends in Alness,
for making me welcome

1

"GOOD MORNING, Monk," Runcorn said with satisfaction spreading over his strong, narrow features. His wing collar was a trifle askew and apparently pinched him now and again. "Go over to Queen Anne Street. Sir Basil Moidore." He said the name as though it were long familiar to him, and watched Monk's face to see if he registered ignorance. He saw nothing, and continued rather more waspishly. "Sir Basil's widowed daughter, Octavia Haslett, was found stabbed to death. Looks like a burglar was rifling her jewelry and she woke and caught him." His smile tightened. "You're supposed to be the best detective we've got—go and see if you can do better with this than you did with the Grey case!"

Monk knew precisely what he meant. Don't upset the family; they are quality, and we are very definitely not. Be properly respectful, not only in what you say, how you stand, or whether you meet their eyes, but more importantly in what you discover.

Since he had no choice, Monk accepted with a look of bland unconcern, as if he had not understood the implications.

"Yes sir. What number in Queen Anne Street?"

"Number Ten. Take Evan with you. I daresay by the time you get there, there'll be some medical opinion as to the time of her death and kind of weapon used. Well, don't stand there, man! Get on with it!"

Monk turned on his heel without allowing time for Runcorn to add any more, and strode out, saying "Yes sir" almost

1

under his breath. He closed the door with a sharpness very close to a slam.

Evan was coming up the stairs towards him, his sensitive, mobile face expectant.

"Murder in Queen Anne Street." Monk's irritation eased away. He liked Evan more than anyone else he could remember, and since his memory extended only as far back as the morning he had woken in the hospital four months ago, mistaking it at first for the poorhouse, that friendship was unusually precious to him. He also trusted Evan, one of only two people who knew the utter blank of his life. The other person, Hester Latterly, he could hardly think of as a friend. She was a brave, intelligent, opinionated and profoundly irritating woman who had been of great assistance in the Grey case. Her father had been one of the victims, and she had returned from her nursing post in the Crimea, although the war was actually over at that point, in order to sustain her family in its grief. It was hardly likely Monk would meet her again, except perhaps when they both came to testify at the trial of Menard Grey, which suited Monk. He found her abrasive and not femininely pleasing, nothing like her sister-in-law, whose face still returned to his mind with such elusive sweetness.

Evan turned and fell into step behind him as they went down the stairs, through the duty room and out into the street. It was late November and a bright, blustery day. The wind caught at the wide skirts of the women, and a man ducked sideways and held on to his top hat with difficulty as a carriage bowled past him and he avoided the mud and ordure thrown up by its wheels. Evan hailed a hansom cab, a new invention nine years ago, and much more convenient than the old-fashioned coaches.

"Queen Anne Street," he ordered the driver, and as soon as he and Monk were seated the cab sped forward, across Tottenham Court Road, and east to Portland Place, Langham Place and then a dogleg into Chandos Street and Queen Anne Street. On the journey Monk told Evan what Runcorn had said.

"Who is Sir Basil Moidore?" Evan asked innocently.

"No idea," Monk admitted. "He didn't tell me." He grunted. "Either he doesn't know himself or he's leaving us to find out, probably by making a mistake."

Evan smiled. He was quite aware of the ill feeling between

2

Monk and his superior, and of most of the reasons behind it. Monk was not easy to work with; he was opinionated, ambitious, intuitive, quick-tongued and acerbic of wit. On the other hand, he cared passionately about real injustice, as he saw it, and minded little whom he offended in order to set it right. He tolerated fools ungraciously, and fools, in his view, included Runcorn, an opinion of which he had made little secret in the past.

Runcorn was also ambitious, but his goals were different; he wanted social acceptability, praise from his superiors, and above all safety. His few victories over Monk were sweet to him, and to be savored.

They were in Queen Anne Street, elegant and discreet houses with gracious facades, high windows and imposing entrances. They alighted, Evan paid the cabby, and they presented themselves at the servants' door of Number 10. It rankled to go climbing down the areaway steps rather than up and in through the front portico, but it was far less humiliating than going to the front and being turned away by a liveried footman, looking down his nose, and dispatched to the back to ask again.

"Yes?" the bootboy said soberly, his face pasty white and his apron crooked.

"Inspector Monk and Sergeant Evan, to see Lord Moidore," Monk replied quietly. Whatever his feeling for Runcorn, or his general intolerance of fools, he had a deep pity for bereavement and the confusion and shock of sudden death.

"Oh—" The bootboy looked startled, as if their presence had turned a nightmare into truth. "Oh—yes. Yer'd better come in." He pulled the door wide and stepped back, turning into the kitchen to call for help, his voice plaintive and desperate. "Mr. Phillips! Mr. Phillips—the p'lice is 'ere!"

The butler appeared from the far end of the huge kitchen. He was lean and a trifle stooped, but he had the autocratic face of a man used to command—and receiving obedience without question. He regarded Monk with both anxiety and distaste, and some surprise at Monk's well-cut suit, carefully laundered shirt, and polished, fine leather boots. Monk's appearance did not coincide with his idea of a policeman's social position, which was beneath that of a peddler or a costermonger. Then he looked at Evan, with his long, curved nose and imaginative eyes and mouth, and felt no better. It made him uncomfortable when people did not fit into their prescribed niches in the order of things. It was confusing.

"Sir Basil will see you in the library," he said stiffly. "If you will come this way." And without waiting to see if they did, he walked very uprightly out of the kitchen, ignoring the cook seated in a wooden rocking chair. They continued into the passageway beyond, past the cellar door, his own pantry, the still room, the outer door to the laundry, the housekeeper's sitting room, and then through the green baize door into the main house.

The hall floor was wood parquet, scattered with magnificent Persian carpets, and the walls were half paneled and hung with excellent landscapes. Monk had a flicker of memory from some distant time, perhaps a burglary detail, and the word *Flemish* came to mind. There was still so much that was closed in that part of him before the accident, and only flashes came back, like movement caught out of the corner of the eye, when one turns just too late to see.

But now he must follow the butler, and train all his attention on learning the facts of this case. He must succeed, and without allowing anyone else to realize how much he was stumbling, guessing, piecing together from fragments out of what they thought was his store of knowledge. They must not guess he was working with the underworld connections any good detective has. His reputation was high; people expected brilliance from him. He could see that in their eyes, hear it in their words, the casual praise given as if they were merely remarking the obvious. He also knew he had made too many enemies to afford mistakes. He heard it between the words and in the inflections of a comment, the barb and then the nervousness, the look away. Only gradually was he discovering what he had done in the years before to earn their fear, their envy or their dislike. A piece at a time he found evidence of his own extraordinary skill, the instinct, the relentless pursuit of truth, the long hours, the driving ambition, the intolerance of laziness, weakness in others, failure in himself. And of course, in spite of all his disadvantages since the accident, he had solved the extremely difficult Grey case.

They were at the library. Phillips opened the door and announced them, then stepped back to allow them in.

4

The room was traditional, lined with shelves. One large bay window let in the light, and green carpet and furnishings made it restful, almost gave an impression of a garden.

But there was no time now to examine it. Basil Moidore stood in the center of the floor. He was a tall man, loose boned, unathletic, but not yet running to fat, and he held himself very erect. He could never have been handsome; his features were too mobile, his mouth too large, the lines around it deeply etched and reflecting appetite and temper more than wit. His eyes were startlingly dark, not fine, but very penetrating and highly intelligent. His thick, straight hair was thickly peppered with gray.

Now he was both angry and extremely distressed. His skin was pale and he clenched and unclenched his hands nervously.

"Good morning, sir." Monk introduced himself and Evan. He hated speaking to the newly bereaved—and there was something peculiarly appalling about seeing one's child dead—but he was used to it. No loss of memory wiped out the familiarity of pain, and seeing it naked in others.

"Good morning, Inspector," Moidore said automatically. "I'm damned if I know what you can do, but I suppose you'd better try. Some ruffian broke in during the night and murdered my daughter. I don't know what else we can tell you."

"May we see the room where it happened, sir?" Monk asked quietly. "Has the doctor come yet?"

Sir Basil's heavy eyebrows rose in surprise. "Yes—but I don't know what damned good the man can do now."

"He can establish the time and manner of death, sir."

"She was stabbed some time during the night. It won't require a doctor to tell you that." Sir Basil drew in a deep breath and let it out slowly. His gaze wandered around the room, unable to sustain any interest in Monk. The inspector and Evan were only functionaries incidental to the tragedy, and he was too shocked for his mind to concentrate on a single thought. Little things intruded, silly things; a picture crooked on the wall, the sun on the title of a book, the vase of late chrysanthemums on the small table. Monk saw it in his face and understood.

"One of the servants will show us." Monk excused himself and Evan and turned to leave.

"Oh . . . yes. And anything else you need," Basil acknowledged.

"I suppose you didn't hear anything in the night, sir?" Evan asked from the doorway.

Sir Basil frowned. "What? No, of course not, or I'd have mentioned it." And even before Evan turned away the man's attention had left them and was on the leaves wind whipped against the window.

In the hall, Phillips the butler was waiting for them. He led them silently up the wide, curved staircase to the landing, carpeted in reds and blues and set with several tables around the walls. It stretched to right and left fifty feet or more to oriel windows at either end. They were led to the left and stopped outside the third door.

"In there, sir, is Miss Octavia's room," Phillips said very quietly. "Ring if you require anything."

Monk opened the door and went in, Evan close behind him. The room had a high, ornately plastered ceiling with pendant chandeliers. The floral curtains were drawn to let in the light. There were three well-upholstered chairs, a dressing table with a three-mirror looking glass, and a large four-poster bed draped in the same pink-and-green floral print as the curtains. Across the bed lay the body of a young woman, wearing only an ivory silk nightgown, a dark crimson stain slashing down from the middle of her chest almost to her knees. Her arms were thrown wide and her heavy brown hair was loose over her shoulders.

Monk was surprised to see beside her a slender man of just average height whose clever face was now very grave and pinched in thought. The sun through the window caught his fair hair, thickly curled and sprinkled with white.

"Police?" he asked, looking Monk up and down. "Dr. Faverell," he said as introduction. "The duty constable called me when the footman called him—about eight o'clock."

"Monk," Monk replied. "And Sergeant Evan. What can you tell us?"

Evan shut the door behind them and moved closer to the bed, his young face twisted with pity.

"She died some time during the night," Faverell replied bleakly. "From the stiffness of the body I should say at least seven hours ago." He took his watch out of his pocket and glanced at it. "It's now ten past nine. That makes it well be-

6

fore, say, three A.M. at the very outside. One deep, rather ragged wound, very deep. Poor creature must have lost consciousness immediately and died within two or three minutes.''

"Are you the family physician?'' Monk asked.

"No. I live 'round the corner in Harley Street. Local constable knew my address.''

Monk moved closer to the bed, and Faverell stepped aside for him. The inspector leaned over and looked at the body. Her face had a slightly surprised look, as if the reality of death had been unexpected, but even through the pallor there was a kind of loveliness left. The bones were broad across the brow and cheek, the eye sockets were large with delicately marked brows, the lips full. It was a face of deep emotion, and yet femininely soft, a woman he might have liked. There was something in the curve of her lips that reminded him for a moment of someone else, but he could not recall who.

His eyes moved down and saw under the torn fabric of her nightgown the scratches on her throat and shoulder with smears of blood on them. There was another long rent in the silk from hem to groin, although it was folded over, as if to preserve decency. He looked at her hands, lifting them gently, but her nails were perfect and there was no skin or blood under them. If she had fought, she had not marked her attacker.

He looked more carefully for bruises. There should be some purpling of the skin, even if she had died only a few moments after being hurt. He searched her arms first, the most natural place for injury in a struggle, but there was nothing. He could find no mark on the legs or body either.

"She's been moved," he said after a few moments, seeing the pattern of the stains to the end of her garments, and only smears on the sheets beneath her where there should have been a deep pool. "Did you move her?''

"No.'' Faverell shook his head. "I only opened the curtain.'' He looked around the floor. There were dark roses on the carpet. "There.'' He pointed. "That might be blood, and there's a tear on that chair. I suppose the poor woman put up a fight.''

Monk looked around also. Several things on the dressing table were crooked, but it was hard to tell what would have been the natural design. However a cut glass dish was broken,

7

and there were dried rose leaves scattered over the carpet underneath it. He had not noticed them before in the pattern of the flowers woven in.

Evan walked towards the window.

"It's unlatched," he said, moving it experimentally.

"I closed it," the doctor put in. "It was open when I came, and damned cold. Took it into account for the rigor, though, so don't bother to ask me. Maid said it was open when she came with Mrs. Haslett's morning tray, but she didn't sleep with it open normally. I asked that too."

"Thank you," Monk said dryly.

Evan pushed the window all the way up and looked outside.

"There's creeper of some sort here, sir; and it's broken in several places where it looks as if someone put his weight on it, some pieces crushed and leaves gone." He leaned out a little farther. "And there's a good ledge goes along as far as the drainpipe down. An agile man could climb it without too much difficulty."

Monk went over and stood beside him. "Wonder why not the next room?" he said aloud. "That's closer to the drainpipe, easier, and less chance of being seen."

"Maybe it's a man's room?" Evan suggested. "No jewelry—or at least not much—a few silver-backed brushes, maybe, and studs, but nothing like a woman's."

Monk was annoyed with himself for not having thought of the same thing. He pulled his head back in and turned to the doctor.

"Is there anything else you can tell us?"

"Not a thing, sorry." He looked harassed and unhappy. "I'll write it out for you, if you want. But now I've got live patients to see. Must be going. Good day to you."

"Good day." Monk came back to the landing door with him. "Evan, go and see the maid that found her, and get her ladies' maid and go over the room to see if anything's missing, jewelry in particular. We can try the pawnbrokers and fences. I'm going to speak to some of the family who sleep on this floor."

The next room turned out to be that of Cyprian Moidore, the dead woman's elder brother, and Monk saw him in the morning room. It was overfurnished, but agreeably warm;

8

presumably the downstairs maids had cleaned the grate, sanded and swept the carpets and lit the fires long before quarter to eight, when the upstairs maids had gone to waken the family.

Cyprian Moidore resembled his father in build and stance. His features were similar—the short, powerful nose, the broad mouth with the extraordinary mobility which might so easily become loose in a weaker man. His eyes were softer and his hair still dark.

Now he looked profoundly shaken.

"Good morning, sir," Monk said as he came into the room and closed the door.

Cyprian did not reply.

"May I ask you, sir, is it correct that you occupy the bedroom next to Mrs. Haslett's?"

"Yes." Cyprian met his eyes squarely; there was no belligerence in them, only shock.

"What time did you retire, Mr. Moidore?"

Cyprian frowned. "About eleven, or a few minutes after. I didn't hear anything, if that is what you are going to ask."

"And were you in your room all night, sir?" Monk tried to phrase it without being offensive, but it was impossible.

Cyprian smiled very faintly.

"I was last night. My wife's room is next to mine, the first as you leave the stair head." He put his hands into his pockets. "My son has the room opposite, and my daughters the one next to that. But I thought we had established that whoever it was broke into Octavia's room through the window."

"It looks most likely, sir," Monk agreed. "But it may not be the only room they tried. And of course it is possible they came in elsewhere and went *out* through her window. We know only that the creeper was broken. Was Mrs. Haslett a light sleeper?"

"No—" At first he was absolutely certain, then doubt flickered in his face. He took his hands out of his pockets. "At least I think not. But what difference does it make now? Isn't this really rather a waste of time?" He moved a step closer to the fire. "It is indisputable someone broke in and she discovered him, and instead of simply running, the wretch stabbed her." His face darkened. "You should be out there looking for him, not in here asking irrelevant questions! Perhaps she was awake anyway. People do sometimes waken in the night."

9

Monk bit back the reply that rose instinctively.

"I was hoping to establish the time," he continued levelly. "It would help when we come to question the closest constable on the beat, and any other people who might have been around at that hour. And of course it would help when we catch anyone, if he could prove he was elsewhere."

"If he was elsewhere, then you wouldn't have the right person, would you!" Cyprian said acidly.

"If we didn't know the relevant time, sir, we might think we had!" Monk replied immediately. "I'm sure you don't want the wrong man hanged!"

Cyprian did not bother to answer.

The three women of the immediate family were waiting together in the withdrawing room, all close to the fire: Lady Moidore stiff-backed, white-faced on the sofa; her surviving daughter, Araminta, in one of the large chairs to her right, hollow-eyed as if she had not slept in days; and her daughter-in-law, Romola, standing behind her, her face reflecting horror and confusion.

"Good morning, ma'am." Monk inclined his head to Lady Moidore, then acknowledged the others.

None of them replied. Perhaps they did not consider it necessary to observe such niceties in the circumstances.

"I am deeply sorry to have to disturb you at such a tragic time," he said with difficulty. He hated having to express condolences to someone whose grief was so new and devastating. He was a stranger intruding into their home, and all he could offer were words, stilted and predictable. But to have said nothing would be grossly uncaring.

"I offer you my deepest sympathy, ma'am."

Lady Moidore moved her head very slightly in indication that she had heard him, but she did not speak.

He knew who the two younger women were because one of them shared the remarkable hair of her mother, a vivid shade of golden red which in the dark room seemed almost as alive as the flames of the fire. Cyprian's wife, on the other hand, was much darker, her eyes brown and her hair almost black. He turned to address her.

"Mrs. Moidore?"

"Yes?" She stared at him in alarm.

10

"Your bedroom window is between Mrs. Haslett's and the main drainpipe, which it seems the intruder climbed. Did you hear any unaccustomed sounds during the night, any disturbances at all?"

She looked very pale. Obviously the thought of the murderer passing her window had not occurred to her before. Her hands gripped the back of Araminta's chair.

"No—nothing. I do not customarily sleep well, but last night I did." She closed her eyes. "How fearful!"

Araminta was of a harder mettle. She sat rigid and slender, almost bony under the light fabric of her morning gown—no one had thought of changing into black yet. Her face was thin, wide-eyed, her mouth curiously asymmetrical. She would have been beautiful but for a certain sharpness, something brittle beneath the surface.

"We cannot help you, Inspector." She addressed him with candor, neither avoiding his eyes nor making any apology. "We saw Octavia before she retired last night, at about eleven o'clock, or a few minutes before. I saw her on the landing, then she went to my mother's room to wish her good-night, and then to her own room. We went to ours. My husband will tell you the same. We were awoken this morning by the maid, Annie, crying and calling out that something terrible had happened. I was the first to open the door after Annie. I saw straight away that Octavia was dead and we could not help her. I took Annie out and sent her to Mrs. Willis; she is the house-keeper. The poor child was looking very sick. Then I found my father, who was about to assemble the servants for morning prayers, and told him what had happened. He sent one of the footmen for the police. There really isn't anything more to say."

"Thank you, ma'am." Monk looked at Lady Moidore. She had the broad brow and short, strong nose her son had inherited, but a far more delicate face, and a sensitive, almost ascetic mouth. When she spoke, even drained by grief as she was, there was a beauty of vitality and imagination in her.

"I can add nothing, Inspector," she said very quietly. "My room is in the other wing of the house, and I was unaware of any tragedy or intrusion until my maid, Mary, woke me and then my son told me what had . . . happened."

"Thank you, my lady. I hope it will not be necessary to

11

disturb you again." He had not expected to learn anything; it was really only a formality that he asked, but to overlook it would have been careless. He excused himself and went to find Evan back in the servants' quarters.

However Evan had discovered nothing of moment either, except a list of the missing jewelry compiled by the ladies' maid: two rings, a necklace and a bracelet, and, oddly, a small silver vase.

A little before noon they left the Moidore house, now with its blinds drawn and black crepe on the door. Already, out of respect for the dead, the grooms were spreading straw on the roadway to deaden the sharp sound of horses' hooves.

"What now?" Evan asked as they stepped out into the footpath. "The bootboy said there was a party at the east end, on the corner of Chandos Street. One of the coachmen or footmen may have seen something." He raised his eyebrows hopefully.

"And there'll be a duty constable somewhere around," Monk added. "I'll find him, you take the party. Corner house, you said?"

"Yes sir—people called Bentley."

"Report back to the station when you've finished."

"Yes sir." And Evan turned on his heel and walked rapidly away, more gracefully than his lean, rather bony body would have led one to expect.

Monk took a hansom back to the station to find the home address of the constable who would have been patrolling the area during the night.

An hour later he was sitting in the small, chilly front parlor in a house off Euston Road, sipping a mug of tea opposite a sleepy, unshaven constable who was very ill at ease. It was some five minutes into the conversation before Monk began to realize that the man had known him before and that his anxiety was not based on any omission or failure of duty last night but on something that had occurred in their previous meeting, of which Monk had no memory at all.

He found himself searching the man's face, trying without success to bring any feature of it back to recollection, and twice he missed what was said.

"I'm sorry, Miller; what was that?" he apologized the second time.

Miller looked embarrassed, uncertain whether this was an

acknowledgment of inattention or some implied criticism that his statement was unbelievable.

"I said I passed by Queen Anne Street on the west side, down Wimpole Street an' up again along 'Arley Street, every twenty minutes last night, sir. I never missed, 'cause there wasn't no disturbances and I didn't 'ave ter stop fer anythin'."

Monk frowned. "You didn't see anybody about? No one at all?"

"Oh I saw plenty o' people—but no one as there shouldn't 'a bin," Miller replied. "There was a big party up the other corner o' Chandos Street where it turns inter Cavendish Square. Coachmen and footmen an' all sorts 'angin' around till past three in the mornin', but they wasn't making no nuisance an' they certainly wasn't climbing up no drainpipes to get in no winders." He screwed up his face as if he were about to add something, then changed his mind.

"Yes?" Monk pressed.

But Miller would not be drawn. Again Monk wondered if it was because of their past association, and if Miller would have spoken for someone else. There was so much he did not know! Ignorance about police procedures, underworld connections, the vast store of knowledge a good detective kept. Not knowing was hampering him at every turn, making it necessary for him to work twice as hard in order to hide his vulnerability; but it did not end the deep fear caused by ignorance about himself. What manner of man was the self that stretched for years behind him, to that boy who had left Northumberland full of an ambition so consuming he had not written regularly to his only relative, his younger sister who had loved him so loyally in spite of his silence? He had found her letters in his rooms—sweet, gentle letters full of references to what should have been familiar.

Now he sat here in this small, neat house and tried to get answers from a man who was obviously frightened of him. Why? It was impossible to ask.

"Anyone else?" he said hopefully.

"Yes sir," Miller said straightaway, eager to please and beginning to master his nervousness. "There was a doctor paid a call near the corner of 'Arley Street and Queen Anne Street. I saw 'im leave, but I din't see 'im get there."

"Do you know his name?"

"No sir." Miller bristled, his body tightening again as if to defend himself. "But I saw 'im leave an' the front door was open an' the master o' the 'ouse was seein' 'im out. 'Alf the lights was on, and 'e weren't there uninvited!"

Monk considered apologizing for the unintended slight, then changed his mind. It would be more productive for Miller to be kept up to the mark.

"Do you remember which house?"

"About the third or fourth one along, on the south side of 'Arley Street, sir."

"Thank you. I'll ask them; they may have seen something." Then he wondered why he had offered an explanation; it was not necessary. He stood up and thanked Miller and left, walking back towards the main street where there would be cabs. He should have left this to Evan, who knew his underworld contacts, but it was too late now. He behaved from instinct and intelligence, forgetting how much of his memory was trapped in that shadowy world before the night his carriage had turned over, breaking his ribs and arm, and blotting out his identity and everything that bonded him to the past.

Who else might have been out in the night around Queen Anne Street? A year ago he would have known where to find the footpads, the cracksmen, the lookouts, but now he had nothing but guesswork and plodding deduction, which would betray him to Runcorn, who was so obviously waiting for every chance to trap him. Enough mistakes, and Runcorn would work out the incredible, delicious truth, and find the excuses he had sought for years to fire Monk and feel safe at last; no more hard, ambitious lieutenant dangerously close on his heels.

Finding the doctor was not difficult, merely a matter of returning to Harley Street and calling at the houses along the south side until he came to the right one, and then asking.

"Indeed," he was told in some surprise when he was received somewhat coolly by the master of the house, looking tired and harassed. "Although what interest it can be to the police I cannot imagine."

"A young woman was murdered in Queen Anne Street last night," Monk replied. The evening paper would carry it and it would be common knowledge in an hour or two. "The doctor may have seen someone loitering."

"He would hardly know by sight the sort of person who murders young women in the street!"

"Not in the street, sir, in Sir Basil Moidore's house," Monk corrected, although the difference was immaterial. "It is a matter of learning the time, and perhaps which direction he was going, although you're right, that is of little help."

"I suppose you know your business," the man said doubtfully, too weary and engaged in his own concerns to care. "But servants keep some funny company these days. I'd look to someone she let in herself, some disreputable follower."

"The victim was Sir Basil's daughter, Mrs. Haslett," Monk said with bitter satisfaction.

"Good God! How appalling!" The man's expression changed instantly. In a single sentence the danger had moved from affecting someone distant, not part of his world, to being a close and alarming threat. The chill hand of violence had touched his own class and in so doing had become real. "This is dreadful!" The blood fled from his tired face and his voice cracked for an instant. "What are you doing about it? We need more police in the streets, more patrols! Where did the man come from? What is he doing here?"

Monk smiled sourly to see the alteration in him. If the victim was a servant, she had brought it upon herself by keeping loose company; but now it was a lady, then police patrols must be doubled and the criminal caught forthwith.

"Well?" the man demanded, seeing what to him was a sneer on Monk's face.

"As soon as we find him, we will discover what he was doing," Monk replied smoothly. "In the meantime, if you will give me your physician's name, I will question him to see if he observed anything as he came or went."

The man wrote the name on a piece of paper and handed it to him.

"Thank you, sir. Good day."

But the doctor had seen nothing, being intent upon his own art, and could offer no help. He had not even noticed Miller on his beat. All he could do was confirm his own time of arrival and departure with an exactitude.

By mid-afternoon Monk was back in the police station, where Evan was waiting for him with the news that it would have been quite impossible for anyone at all to have passed by

15

the west end of Queen Anne Street and not have been seen by several of the servants waiting for their masters outside the house where the party was being held. There had been a sufficient number of guests, including late arrivals and early departures, to fill the mews at the back with carriages and overflow into the street at the front.

"With that many footmen and coachmen around, would an extra person be noticed?" Monk queried.

"Yes." Evan had no doubts at all. "Apart from the fact that a lot of them know each other, they were all in livery. Anyone dressed differently would have been as obvious as a horse in a field of cows."

Monk smiled at Evan's rural imagery. Evan was the son of a country parson, and every now and again some memory or mannerism showed through. It was one of the many things Monk found pleasing in him.

"None of them?" he said doubtfully. He sat down behind his desk.

Evan shook his head. "Too much conversation going on, and a lot of horseplay, chatting to the maids, flirting, carriage lamps all over the place. If anyone had shinned up a drainpipe to go over the roofs he'd have been seen in a trice. And no one walked off up the road alone, they're sure of that."

Monk did not press it any further. He did not believe it was a chance burglary by some footman which had gone wrong. Footmen were chosen for their height and elegance, and were superbly dressed. They were not equipped to climb drainpipes and cling to the sides of buildings two and three floors up, balancing along ledges in the dark. That was a practiced art which one came dressed to indulge.

"Must have come the other way," he concluded. "From the Wimpole Street end, in between Miller's going down that way and coming back up Harley Street. What about the back, from Harley Mews?"

"No way over the roof, sir," Evan replied. "I had a good look there. And a pretty good chance of waking the Moidores' coachman and grooms who sleep over the stables. Not a good burglar who disturbs horses, either. No sir, much better chance coming in the front, the way the drainpipe is and the broken creeper, which seems to be the way he did come. He must

16

have nipped between Miller's rounds, as you say. Easy enough to watch for him.''

Monk hesitated. He loathed betraying his vulnerability, even though he knew Evan was perfectly aware of it, and if he had been tempted to let it slip to Runcorn, he would have done it weeks ago during the Grey case, when he was confused, frightened and at his wit's end, terrified of the apparitions his intelligence conjured out of the scraps of recollection which recurred like nightmare forms. Evan and Hester Latterly were the two people in the world he could trust absolutely. And Hester he would prefer not to think about. She was not an appealing woman. Again Imogen Latterly's face came sweet to his mind, eyes soft and frightened as she had been when she asked him for help, her voice low, her skirts rustling like leaves as she walked past him. But she was Hester's brother's wife, and might as well have been a princess for anything she could be to Monk.

"Shall I ask a few questions at the Grinning Rat?" Evan interrupted his thoughts. "If anyone tries to get rid of the necklace and earrings they'll turn up with a fence, but word of a murder gets out pretty quickly, especially one the police won't let rest. The regular cracksmen will want to be well out of this."

"Yes—" Monk grasped at it quickly. "I'll try the fences and pawnbrokers, you go to the Grinning Rat and see what you can pick up." He fished in his pocket and brought out his very handsome gold watch. He must have saved a long time for this particular vanity, but he could not remember either the going without or the exultancy of the purchase. Now his fingers played over its smooth surface, and he felt an emptiness that all its flavor and memory were gone for him. He opened it with a flick.

"It's a good time to do that. I'll see you here tomorrow morning."

Evan went home and changed his clothes before assaying on the journey to find his hard-won contacts on the fringes of the criminal underworld. His present rather respectable, trim-fitting coat and clean shirt might be taken for the garb of a confidence trickster, but far more likely the genuine clothes of a socially aspiring clerk or minor tradesman.

When he left his lodgings an hour after speaking to Monk,

17

he looked entirely different. His fair brown hair with its wide wave was pulled through with grease and a little dirt, his face was similarly marred, he wore an old shirt without a collar and a jacket that hung off his lean shoulders. He also had for the occasion a pair of boots he had salvaged from a beggar who had found better. They rubbed his feet, but an extra pair of socks made them adequate for walking in, and thus attired he set off for the Grinning Rat in Pudding Lane, and an evening of cider, eel pie and listening.

There was an enormous variety of public houses in London, from the large, highly respectable ones which catered banquets for the well-bred and well-financed; through the comfortable, less ostentatious ones which served as meeting and business places for all manner of professions from lawyers and medical students, actors and would-be politicians; down through those that were embryo music halls, gathering spots for reformers and agitators and pamphleteers, street corner philosophers and working men's movements; right down to those that were filled with gamblers, opportunists, drunkards and the fringes of the criminal world. The Grinning Rat belonged to the last order, which was why Evan had chosen it several years ago; and he was now, if not liked there, at least tolerated.

From outside in the street he could see the lights gleaming through the windows across the dirty pavement and the gutter. Half a dozen men and several women lounged around outside the doorway, all dressed in colors so dark and drab with wear they seemed only a variation of densities in the barred light filtering out. Even when someone opened the door in a gale of laughter and a man and woman staggered down the steps, arm in arm, nothing showed but browns and duns and a flicker of dull red. The man backed away, and a woman half sitting in the gutter shouted something lewd after them. They ignored her and disappeared up Pudding Lane towards East Cheap.

Evan ignored her likewise and went inside to the warmth and the babble and the smell of ale and sawdust and smoke. He jostled his way past a group of men playing dice and another boasting the merits of fighting dogs, a temperance believer crying his creed in vain, and an ex-pugilist, his battered face good-natured and bleary-eyed.

" 'Evening, Tom," he said pleasantly.

18

" 'Evenin'," the pugilist said benignly, knowing the face was familiar but unable to recall a name for it.

"Seen Willie Durkins?" Evan asked casually. He saw the man's nearly empty mug. "I'm having a pint of cider—can I get you one?"

Tom did not hesitate but nodded cheerfully and drank the last of his ale so his mug was suitably empty.

Evan took it, made his way to the bar and purchased two ciders, passing the time of evening with the bartender who fetched him his mug from among the many swinging on hooks above his head. Each regular customer had his own mug. Evan returned to where Tom was waiting hopefully and passed him his cider, and when Tom had drunk half of it, with a huge thirst, Evan began his unobtrusive inquiry.

"Seen Willie?" he said again.

"Not tonight, sir." Tom added the "sir" by way of acknowledging the pint. He still could not think of a name. "Wot was yer wantin' 'im fer? Mebbe I can 'elp?"

"Want to warn him," Evan lied, not watching Tom's face but looking down into his mug.

"Wot abaht?"

"Bad business up west," Evan answered. "Got to find somebody for it, and I know Willie." He looked up suddenly and smiled, a lovely dazzling gesture, full of innocence and good humor. "I don't want him put away—I'd miss him."

Tom gurgled his appreciation. He was not absolutely sure, but he rather thought this agreeable young fellow might be either a rozzer or someone who fed the rozzers judicious bits of information. He would not be above doing that himself, if he had any—for a reasonable consideration, of course. Nothing about ordinary thievery, which was a way of life, but about strangers on the patch, or nasty things that were likely to bring a lot of unwelcome police attention, like murders, or arson, or major forgery, which always upset important gents up in the City. It made things hard for the small business of local burglary, street robbery, petty forgery of money and legal letters or papers. It was difficult to fence stolen goods with too many police about, or sell illegal liquors. Small-time smuggling up the river suffered—and gambling, card sharping, petty fraud and confidence tricks connected with sport, bare knuckle pugilism, and of course prostitution. Had Evan asked about any of these Tom would have been affronted and told him so. The underworld conducted these types of business all the time, and no one expected to root them out.

But there were things one did not do. It was foolish, and very inconsiderate to those who had their living to make with as little disturbance as possible.

"Wot bad business is that, sir?"

"Murder," Evan replied seriously. "Very important man's daughter, stabbed in her own bedroom, by a burglar. Stupid—"

"I never 'eard." Tom was indignant. "W'en was that, then? Nobody said!"

"Last night," Evan answered, drinking more of his cider. Somewhere over to their left there was a roar of laughter and someone shouted the odds against a certain horse winning a race.

"I never 'eard," Tom repeated dolefully. "Wot 'e want ter go an' do that fer? Stupid, I calls it. W'y kill a lady? Knock 'er one, if yer 'ave ter, like if she wakes up and starts ter 'oller. But it's a daft geezer wot makes enough row ter wake people anyway."

"And stabbing." Evan shook his head. "Why couldn't he hit her, as you said. Needn't have killed her. Now half the top police in the West End will be all over the place!" A total exaggeration, at least so far, but it served his purpose. "More cider?"

Again Tom indicated his reply by shoving his mug over wordlessly, and Evan rose to oblige.

"Willie wouldn't do anything like that," Tom said when Evan returned. " 'E in't stupid."

"If I thought he had I wouldn't want to warn him," Evan answered. "I'd let him swing."

"Yeah," Tom agreed gloomily. "But w'en, eh? Not before the crushers 'as bin all over the place, an' everybody's bin upset and business ruined for all sorts!"

"Exactly." Evan hid his face in his mug. "So where's Willie?"

This time Tom did not equivocate. "Mincing Lane," he said dourly. "If'n yer wait there an hour or so 'e'll come by the pie stand there some time ternight. An' I daresay if'n yer tells 'im abaht this 'e'll be grateful, like." He knew Evan,

20

whoever he was, would want something in return. That was the way of life.

"Thank you." Evan left his mug half empty; Tom would be only too pleased to finish it for him. "I daresay I'll try that. G'night."

"G'night." Tom appropriated the half mug before any over-zealous barman could remove it.

Evan went out into the rapidly chilling evening and walked briskly, collar turned up, looking neither to right nor left, until he turned into Mincing Lane and past the groups of idlers huddled in doorways. He found the eel pie seller with his barrow, a thin man with a stovepipe hat askew on his head, an apron around his waist, and a delicious smell issuing from the inside of containers balanced in front of him.

Evan bought a pie and ate it with enjoyment, the hot pastry crunching and flaking and the eel flesh delicate on his tongue.

"Seen Willie Durkins?" he said presently.

"Not ternight." The man was careful: it did not do to give information for nothing, and without knowing to whom.

Evan had no idea whether to believe him or not, but he had no better plan, and he settled back in the shadows, chilly and bored, and waited. A street patterer came by, singing a ballad about a current scandal involving a clergyman who had seduced a schoolmistress and then abandoned her and her child. Evan recalled the case in the sensational press a few months ago, but this version was much more colorful, and in less than fifteen minutes the patterer, and the eel stand, had collected a dozen or more customers, all of whom bought pies and stood around to listen. For which service the patterer got his supper free—and a good audience.

A narrow man with a cheerful face came out of the gloom to the south and bought himself a pie, which he ate with evident enjoyment, then bought a second and treated a scruffy child to it with evident pleasure.

"Good night then, Tosher?" the pie man asked knowingly.

"Best this month," Tosher replied. "Found a gold watch! Don't get many o' them."

The pie man laughed. "Some flash gent'll be cursin' 'is luck!" He grinned. "Shame—eh?"

"Oh, terrible shame," Tosher agreed with a chuckle.

Evan knew enough of street life to understand. "Tosher"

21

was the name for men who searched the sewers for lost articles. As far as he was concerned, they, and the mudlarks along the river, were more than welcome to what they found; it was hard won enough.

Other people came and went: costers, off duty at last; a cab driver; a couple of boatmen up from the river steps; a prostitute; and then, when Evan was stiff with cold and lack of movement and about to give up, Willie Durkins.

He recognized Evan after only a brief glance, and his round face became careful.

" 'Allo, Mr. Evan. Wot you want, then? This in't your patch."

Evan did not bother to lie; it would serve no purpose and evidence bad faith.

"Last night's murder up west, in Queen Anne Street."

"Wot murder was that?" Willie was confused, and it showed in his guarded expression, narrowed eyes, a trifle squinting in the streetlight over the pie stall.

"Sir Basil Moidore's daughter, stabbed in her own bedroom—by a burglar."

"Go on—Basil Moidore, eh?" Willie looked dubious. " 'E must be worth a mint, but 'is 'ouse'd be crawlin' with servants! Wot cracksman'd do that? It's fair stupid! Damn fool!"

"Best get it sorted." Evan pushed out his lip and shook his head a little.

"Dunno nuffin'," Willie denied out of habit.

"Maybe. But you know the house thieves who work that area," Evan argued.

"It wouldn't be one o' them," Willie said quickly.

Evan pulled a face. "And of course they wouldn't know a stranger on the patch," he said sarcastically.

Willie squinted at him, considering. Evan looked gullible; his was a dreamer's face; it should have belonged to a gentleman, not a sergeant in the rozzers. Nothing like Monk; now there was someone not to mess about with, an ambitious man with a devious mind and a hard tongue. You knew from the set of his bones and the gray eyes that never wavered that it would be dangerous to play games with him.

"Sir Basil Moidore's daughter," Evan said almost to himself. "They'll hang someone—have to. Shake up a lot of people before they find the right man—if it becomes necessary."

"O'right!" Willie said grudgingly. "O'right! Chinese Paddy was up there last night. 'E din't do nothin'—din't 'ave the chance, so yer can't bust 'im. Clean as a w'istle, 'e is. But ask 'im. If 'e can't 'elp yer, then no one can. Now let me be—yer'll gimme a bad name, 'anging 'round 'ere wi' the likes o' you."

"Where do I find Chinese Paddy?" Evan caught hold of the man's arm, fingers hard till Willie squeaked.

"Leggo o' me! Wanna break me arm?"

Evan tightened his grip.

"Dark 'Ouse Lane, Billingsgate—termorrer mornin', w'en the market opens. Yer'll know 'im easy, 'e's got black 'air like a chimney brush, an' eyes like a Chinaman. Now le' go o' me!"

Evan obliged, and in a minute Willie disappeared down Mincing Lane towards the river and the ferry steps.

Evan went straight home to his rooms, washed off the worst surface dirt in a bowl of tepid water, and slipped into bed.

At five in the morning he rose again, put on the same clothes and crept out of the house and took a series of public omnibuses to Billingsgate, and by quarter past six in the dawn light he was in the crush of costers' barrows, fishmongers' high carts and dray wagons at the entrance to Dark House Lane itself. It was so narrow that the houses reared up like cliff walls on either side, the advertisement boards for fresh ice actually stretching across from one side to the other. Along both sides were stacked mountains of fresh, wet, slithering fish of every description, piled on benches, and behind them stood the salesmen crying their wares, white aprons gleaming like the fish bellies, and white hats pale against the dark stones behind them.

A fish porter with a basket full of haddock on his head could barely squeeze past the double row of shoppers crowding the thin passageway down the middle. At the far end Evan could just see the tangled rigging of oyster boats on the water and the occasional red worsted cap of a sailor.

The smell was overpowering; red herrings, every kind of white fish from sprats to turbot, lobsters, whelks, and over all a salty, seaweedy odor as if one were actually on a beach. It brought back a sudden jolt of childhood excursions to the sea, the coldness of the water and the sight of a crab running sideways across the sand.

But this was utterly different. All around him was not the soft slurp of the waves but the cacophony of a hundred voices: "Ye-o-o! Ye-o-o! 'Ere's yer fine Yarmouth bloaters! Whiting! Turbot—all alive! Beautiful lobsters! Fine cock crabs—alive O! Splendid skate—alive—all cheap! Best in the market! Fresh 'addock! Nice glass o' peppermint this cold morning! Ha'penny a glass! 'Ere yer are, sir! Currant and meat puddings, a ha'penny each! 'Ere ma'am! Smelt! Finny 'addock! Plaice—all alive O. Whelks—mussels—now or never! Shrimps! Eels! Flounder! Winkles! Waterproof capes—a shilling apiece! Keep out the wet!''

And a news vendor cried out: "I sell food for the mind! Come an' read all abaht it! Terrible murder in Queen Anne Street! Lord's daughter stabbed ter death in 'er bed!''

Evan pushed his way slowly through the crowd of costers, fishmongers and housewives till he saw a brawny fish seller with a distinctly Oriental appearance.

"Are you Chinese Paddy?'' he asked as discreetly as he could above the babble and still be heard.

"Sure I am. Will you be wantin' some nice fresh cod, now? Best in the market!''

"I want some information. It'll cost you nothing, and I'm prepared to pay for it—if it's right," Evan replied, standing very upright and looking at the fish as if he were considering buying it.

"And why would I be selling information at a fish market, mister? What is it you want to know—times o' the tides, is it?'' Chinese Paddy raised his straight black eyebrows sarcastically. "I don't know you—''

"Metropolitan police," Evan said quietly. "Your name was given me by a very reliable fellow I know—down in Pudding Lane. Now do I have to do this in an unpleasant fashion, or can we trade like gentlemen, and you can stay here selling your fish when I leave and go about my business?'' He said it courteously, but just once he looked up and met Chinese Paddy's eyes in a hard, straight stare.

Paddy hesitated.

"The alternative is I arrest you and take you to Mr. Monk

and he can ask you again." Evan knew Monk's reputation, even though Monk himself was still learning it.

Paddy made his decision.

"What is it you're wanting to know?"

"The murder in Queen Anne Street. You were up there last night—"

" 'Ere—fresh fish—fine cod!" Paddy called out. "So I was," he went on in a quiet, hard tone. "But I never stole nuffin', an' I sure as death and the bailiffs never killed that woman!" Ignoring Evan for a moment, he sold three large cod to a woman and took a shilling and sixpence.

"I know that," Evan agreed. "But I want to know what you saw!"

"A bleedin' rozzer goin' up 'Arley Street an' down Wimpole Street every twenty minutes reg'lar," Paddy replied, looking one moment at his fish, and the next at the crowd as it passed. "You're ruinin' me trade, mister! People is wonderin' why you don't buy!"

"What else?" Evan pressed. "The sooner you tell me, the sooner I'll buy a fish and be gone."

"A quack coming to the third 'ouse up on 'Arley Street, an' a maid out on the tiles with 'er follower. The place was like bleedin' Piccadilly! I never got a chance to do anything."

"Which house did you come for?" Evan asked, picking up a fish and examining it.

"Corner o' Queen Anne Street and Wimpole Street, southwest corner."

"And where were you waiting, exactly?" Evan felt a curious prickle of apprehension, a kind of excitement and horror at once. "And what time?"

" 'Alf the ruddy night!" Paddy said indignantly. "From ten o'clock till near four. Welbeck Street end o' Queen Anne Street. That way I could see the 'ole length o' Queen Anne Street right down to Chandos Street. Bit of a party goin' on t'other end—footmen all over the place."

"Why didn't you pack up and go somewhere else? Why stick around there all night if it was so busy?"

" 'Ere, fresh cod—all alive—best in the market!" Paddy called over Evan's head. 'Ere missus! Right it is—that'll be one and eight pence—there y'are." His voice dropped again. "Because I 'ad the layout of a good place, o' course—an' I

25

don't go in unprepared. I in't a bleedin' amacher. I kept thinkin' they'd go. But that perishin' maid was 'alf the night in the areaway like a damn cat. No morals at all."

"So who came and went up Queen Anne Street?" Evan could hardly keep the anticipation out of his voice. Whoever killed Octavia Haslett had not passed the footmen and coachmen at the other end, nor climbed over from the mews—he must have come this way, and if Chinese Paddy was telling the truth, he must have seen him. A thin shiver of excitement rippled through Evan.

"No one passed me, 'cept the quack an' the maid," Paddy repeated with irritation. "I 'ad me eyes peeled all bleedin' night—just waitin' me chance—an' it never came. The 'ouse where the quack went 'ad all its lights on an' the door open and closed, open and closed—I didn't dare go past. Then the ruddy girl with 'er man. No one went past me—I'd swear to that on me life, I would. An' Mr. Monk can do any damn thing 'e can think of—it won't change it. 'Oever scragged that poor woman, 'e was already in the 'ouse, that's for certain positive. An' good luck to you findin' 'im, 'cos I can't 'elp yer. Now take one o' them fish and pay me twice wot it's worth, and get out of 'ere. You're holdin' up trade terrible, you are."

Evan took the fish and handed over three shillings. Chinese Paddy was a contact worth keeping favor with.

"Already in the house." The words rang in his head. Of course he would have to check with the courting maid as well, but if she could be persuaded, on pain of his telling her mistress if she was reluctant, then Chinese Paddy was right—whoever killed Octavia Haslett was someone who already lived there, no stranger caught in the act of burglary but a premeditated murderer who disguised his act afterwards.

Evan turned sideways to push his way between a high fishmonger's cart and a coster's barrow and out into the street.

He could imagine Monk's face when he learned—and Runcorn's. This was a completely different thing, a very dangerous and very ugly thing.

HESTER LATTERLY straightened up from the fire she had been sweeping and stoking and looked at the long, cramped ward of the infirmary. The narrow beds were a few feet apart from each other and set down both sides of the dim room with its high, smoke-darkened ceiling and sparse windows. Adults and children lay huddled under the gray blankets in all conditions of illness and distress.

At least there was enough coal and she could keep the place tolerably warm, even though the dust and fine ash from it seemed to get into everything. The women in the beds closest to the fire were too hot, and kept complaining about the grit getting into their bandages, and Hester was forever dusting the table in the center of the room and the few wooden chairs where patients well enough occasionally sat. This was Dr. Pomeroy's ward, and he was a surgeon, so all the cases were either awaiting operations or recovering from them—or, in over half the instances, not recovering but in some stage of hospital fever or gangrene.

At the far end a child began to cry again. He was only five and had a tubercular abscess in the joint of his shoulder. He had been there three months already, waiting to have it operated on, and each time he had been taken along to the theater, his legs shaking, his teeth gritted, his young face white with fear, he had sat in the anteroom for over two hours, only to be told some other case had been treated today and he was to return to his bed.

To Hester's fury, Dr. Pomeroy had never explained either to the child or to her why this had been done. But then Pomeroy regarded nurses in the same light as most other doctors did: they were necessary only to do the menial tasks—washing, sweeping, scrubbing, disposing of soiled bandages, and rolling, storing and passing out new ones. The most senior were also to keep discipline, particularly moral discipline, among the patients well enough to misbehave or become disorderly.

Hester straightened her skirt and smoothed her apron, more from habit than for any purpose, and hurried down to the child. She could not ease his pain—he had already been given all he should have for that, she had seen to it—but she could at least offer him the comfort of arms around him and a gentle word.

He was curled up on his left side with his aching right shoulder high, crying softly into the pillow. It was a desolate, hopeless sound as if he expected nothing, simply could not contain his misery any longer.

She sat down on the bed and very carefully, not to jolt the shoulder, gathered him up in her arms. He was thin and light and not difficult to support. She laid his head against her and stroked his hair. It was not what she was there for; she was a skilled nurse with battlefield experience in horrific wounds and emergency surgery and care of men suffering from cholera, typhus and gangrene. She had returned home after the war hoping to help reform the backward and tradition-bound hospitals in England, as had so many other of the women who had nursed in the Crimea; but it had proved far more difficult than she expected even to find a post, let alone to exert any influence.

Of course Florence Nightingale was a national heroine. The popular press was full of praise for her, and the public adored her. She was perhaps the only person to emerge from the whole sorry campaign covered with glory. There were stories of the hectic, insane, misdirected charge of the Light Brigade right into the mouths of the Russian guns, and scarcely a military family in the country had not lost either a son or a friend in the carnage that followed. Hester herself had watched it helplessly from the heights above. She could still see in her mind's eye Lord Raglan sitting ramrod stiff on his horse as if he had been riding in some English park, and indeed he had said afterwards that his mind had been on his wife at home. It certainly could not have been on the matter at hand, or he could never have given such a suicidal command, however it was worded—and there had been enough argument about it afterwards. Lord Raglan had said one thing—Lieutenant Nolan had conveyed another to Lords Lucan and Cardigan. Nolan was killed, torn to pieces by a splinter from a Russian shell as he dashed in front of Cardigan waving his sword and shouting. Perhaps he had intended to tell Cardigan he was charging the manned guns—not the abandoned position the order intended. No one would ever know.

Hundreds were crippled or slain, the flower of the cavalry a scatter of mangled corpses in Balaclava. For courage and supreme sacrifice to duty the charge had been a high-water mark of history—militarily it was useless.

And there had been the glory of the thin red line at the Alma, the Heavy Brigade who had stood on foot, their scarlet uniforms a wavering line holding back the enemy, clearly visible even from the far distance where the women waited. As one man fell, another took his place, and the line never gave. The heroism would be remembered as long as stories of war and courage were told, but who even now remembered the maimed and the dead, except those who were bereaved, or caring for them?

She held the child a little closer. He was no longer crying, and it comforted her in some deep, wordless place in her own spirit. The sheer, blinding incompetence of the campaign had infuriated her, the conditions in the hospital in Scutari were so appalling she thought if she survived that, kept her sanity and some remnant of humor, then she would find anything in England a relief and encouragement. At least here there would be no cartloads of wounded, no raging epidemic fevers, no men brought in with frostbitten limbs to be amputated, or bodies frozen to death on the heights above Sebastopol. There would be ordinary dirt, lice and vermin, but nothing like the armies of rats that had hung on the walls and fallen like rotting fruit, the sounds of the fat bodies plopping on beds and floors sickening her dreams even now. And there would be the normal waste to clean, but not hospital floors running with pools of excrement and blood from hundreds of men too ill to move, and rats, but not by the thousands.

But that horror had brought out the strength in her, as it had in so many other women. It was the endless pomposity, rule-bound, paper shuffling self-importance, and refusal to change that crippled her spirit now. The authorities regarded initiative as both arrogant and dangerous, and in women it was so totally misplaced as to be against nature.

The Queen might turn out to greet Florence Nightingale, but the medical establishment was not about to welcome young women with ideas of reform, and Hester had found this out through numerous infuriating, doomed confrontations.

It was all the more distressing because surgery had made such giant steps forward. It was ten years, to the month, since ether had been used successfully in America to anesthetize a patient during an operation. It was a marvelous discovery. Now all sorts of things could be done which had been impossible before. Of course a brilliant surgeon could amputate a limb; saw through flesh, arteries, muscle and bone; cauterize the stump and sew as necessary in a matter of forty or fifty seconds. Indeed Robert Liston, one of the fastest, had been known to saw through a thigh bone and amputate the leg, two of his assistant's fingers, and the tail of an onlooker's coat in twenty-nine seconds.

But the shock to the patient in such operations was appalling, and internal operations were out of the question because no one, with all the thongs and ropes in the world, could tie someone down securely enough for the knife to be wielded with any accuracy. Surgery had never been regarded as a calling of dignity or status. In fact, surgeons were coupled with barbers, more renowned for strong hands and speed of movement than for great knowledge.

Now, with anesthetic, all sorts of more complicated operations could be assayed, such as the removal of infected organs from patients diseased rather than wounded, frostbitten or gangrened; like this child she held in her arms, now close to sleep at last, his face flushed, his body curled around but eased to lie still.

She was holding him, rocking very gently, when Dr. Pomeroy came in. He was dressed for operating, in dark trousers, well worn and stained with blood, a shirt with a torn collar, and his usual waistcoat and old jacket, also badly soiled. It made little sense to ruin good clothes; any other surgeon would have worn much the same.

"Good morning, Dr. Pomeroy," Hester said quickly. She caught his attention because she wished to press him to operate on this child within the next day or two, best of all this afternoon. She knew his chances of recovery were only very moderate—forty percent of surgical patients died of postoperative infection—but he would get no better as he was, and his pain was becoming worse, and therefore his condition weaker. She endeavored to be civil, which was difficult because although she knew his skill with the knife was high, she despised him personally.

"Good morning, Miss—er—eh—" He still managed to look surprised, in spite of the fact that she had been there a month and they had conversed frequently, most often with opposing views. They were not exchanges he was likely to forget. But he did not approve of nurses who spoke before they were addressed, and it caught him awry every time.

"Latterly," she supplied, and forbore from adding, "I have not changed it since yesterday—nor indeed at all," which was on the edge of her tongue. She cared more about the child.

"Yes, Miss Latterly, what is it?" He did not look at her, but at the old woman on the bed opposite, who was lying on her back with her mouth open.

"John Airdrie is in considerable pain, and his condition is not improving," she said with careful civility, keeping her voice much softer than the feeling inside her. Unconsciously she held the child closer to her. "I believe if you will operate quickly it will be his best chance."

"John Airdrie?" He turned back to look at her, a frown between his brows. He was a small man with gingery hair and a very neatly trimmed beard.

"The child," she said with gritted teeth. "He has a tubercular abscess in the joint of his shoulder. You are to excise it."

"Indeed?" he said coldly. "And where did you take your medical degree, Miss Latterly? You are very free with your advice to me. I have had occasion to remark on it a number of times!"

"In the Crimea, sir," she said immediately and without lowering her eyes.

"Oh yes?" He pushed his hands into his trouser pockets. "Did you treat many children with tubercular shoulders there, Miss Latterly? I know it was a hard campaign, but were we really reduced to drafting sickly five-year-olds to do our fighting for us?" His smile was thin and pleased with itself. He spoiled his barb by adding to it. "If they were also reduced to permitting young women to study medicine, it was a far harder time than we here in England were led to believe."

"I think you in England were led to believe quite a lot that was not true," she retorted, remembering all the comfortable lies and concealments that the press had printed to save the faces of government and army command. "They were actually very glad of us, as has been well demonstrated since." She was referring to Florence Nightingale again, and they both knew it; names were not necessary.

He winced. He resented all this fuss and adulation for one woman by common and uninformed people who knew no better. Medicine was a matter of skill, judgment and intelligence, not of wandering around interfering with established knowledge and practice.

"Nevertheless, Miss Latterly, Miss Nightingale and all her helpers, including you, are amateurs and will remain so. There is no medical school in this country which admits women, or is ever likely to. Good heavens! The best universities do not even admit religious nonconformists! Females would be unimaginable. And who, pray, would allow them to practice? Now will you keep your opinions to yourself and attend to the duties for which we pay you? Take off Mrs. Warburton's bandages and dispose of them—" His face creased with anger as she did not move. "And put that child down! If you wish for children to hold, then get married and have some, but do not sit here like a wet nurse. Bring me clean bandages so I can redress Mrs. Warburton's wound. Then you may see if she will take a little ice. She looks feverish."

Hester was so furious she was rooted to the spot. His statements were monstrously irrelevant, patronizing and complacent, and she had no weapons she dared use against him. She could tell him all the incompetent, self-preserving, inadequate things she thought he was, but it would only defeat her purposes and make an even more bitter enemy of him than he was now. And perhaps John Airdrie would suffer.

With a monumental effort she bit back the scalding contempt and the words remained inside her.

"When are you going to operate on the child?" she repeated, staring at him.

He colored very faintly. There was something in her eyes that discomfited him.

"I had already decided to operate this afternoon, Miss Latterly. Your comments were quite unnecessary," he lied—and she knew it, but kept it from her face.

"I am sure your judgment is excellent," she lied back.

"Well what are you waiting for?" he demanded, taking his hands out of his pockets. "Put that child down and get on with it! Do you not know how to do what I asked? Surely your competence stretches that far?" He indulged in sarcasm again; he still had a great deal of status to recoup. "The bandages are in the cupboard at the end of the ward, and no doubt you have the key."

Hester was too angry to speak. She laid the child down gently, rose to her feet.

"Is that not it, hanging at your waist?" he demanded.

She strode past him, swinging the keys so wide and hard they clipped his coattails as she passed, and marched along the length of the ward to fetch the bandages.

Hester had been on duty since dawn, and by four o'clock in the afternoon she was emotionally exhausted. Physically, her back ached, her legs were stiff, her feet hurt and her boots felt tight. And the pins in her hair were digging into her head. She was in no mood to continue her running battle with the matron over the type of woman who should be recruited into nursing. She wished particularly to see it become a profession which was respected and remunerated accordingly, so women of character and intelligence would be attracted. Mrs. Stansfield had grown up with the rough-and-ready women who expected to do no more than scrub, sweep, stoke fires and carry coals, launder, clean out slops and waste, and pass bandages. Senior nurses like herself kept discipline rigid and spirits high. She had no desire, as Hester had, to exercise medical judgment, change dressings herself and give medicines when the surgeon was absent, and certainly not to assist in operations. She considered these young women who had come back from the Cri-

33

mea to overrate themselves greatly and be a disruptive and highly unwelcome influence, and she said so.

This evening Hester simply wished her good-night and walked out, leaving her surprised, and the lecture on morals and duty pent up unspoken inside her. It was very unsatisfying. It would be different tomorrow.

It was not a long journey from the infirmary to the lodging house where Hester had taken rooms. Previously she had lived with her brother, Charles, and his wife, Imogen, but since the financial ruin and death of their parents, it would be quite unfair to expect Charles to support her for longer than the first few months after she returned from the Crimea early in order to be with the family in its time of bereavement and distress. After the resolution of the Grey case she had accepted the help of Lady Callandra Daviot to obtain the post at the infirmary, where she could earn sufficient to maintain herself and could exercise the talents she possessed in administration and nursing.

During the war she had also learned a good deal about war correspondence from her friend Alan Russell, and when he died in the hospital in Scutari, she had sent his last dispatch to his newspaper in London. Later, when his death had not been realized in the thousands of others, she did not amend the error but wrote the letters herself, and was deeply satisfied when they were printed. She could no longer use his name now she was home again, but she wrote now and then, and signed herself simply as one of Miss Nightingale's volunteers. It paid only a few shillings, but money was not her primary motive; it was the desire to express the opinions she held with such intensity, and to move people to press for reform.

When she reached her lodgings, her landlady, a spare, hardworking woman with a sick husband and too many children, greeted her with the news that she had a visitor awaiting her in the parlor.

"A visitor?" Hester was surprised, and too weary to be pleased, even if it was Imogen, who was the only person she could think of. "Who is it, Mrs. Horne?"

"A Mrs. Daviot," the landlady replied without interest. She was too busy to be bothered with anything beyond her duties. "Said she'd wait for you."

"Thank you." Hester felt an unexpected lift, both because

she liked Callandra Daviot as well as anyone she knew, and because characteristically she had omitted to use her title, a modesty exercised by very few.

Callandra was sitting in the small, well-worn parlor by the meager fire, but she had not kept on her coat, even though the room was chill. Her interesting, individual face lit up when Hester came in. Her hair was as wild as always, and she was dressed with more regard for comfort than style.

"Hester, my dear, you look appallingly tired. Come and sit down. I'm sure you need a cup of tea. So do I. I asked that woman, poor creature—what is her name?—if she would bring one."

"Mrs. Horne." Hester sat down and unbuttoned her boots. She slipped them off under her skirt with an exquisite relief and adjusted the worst of the pins in her hair.

Callandra smiled. She was the widow of an army surgeon, now very much past her later middle years, and she had known Hester some time before the Grey case had caused their paths to cross again. She had been born Callandra Grey, the daughter of the late Lord Shelburne, and was the aunt of the present Lord Shelburne and of his younger brother.

Hester knew she would not have come simply to visit, not at the end of a hard day when she was aware Hester would be tired and not in the best frame of mind for company. It was too late for genteel afternoon calling, and far too early for dinner. Hester waited expectantly.

"Menard Grey comes to trial the day after tomorrow," Callandra said quietly. "We must testify on his behalf—I presume you are still willing?"

"Of course!" There was not even a second's doubt.

"Then we had better go and meet with the lawyer I have employed to conduct his defense. He will have some counsel for us concerning our testimony. I have arranged to see him in his rooms this evening. I am sorry it is so hasty, but he is extremely busy and had no other opportunity. We may have dinner first, or later, as you please. My carriage will return in half an hour; I thought it unsuitable to leave it outside." She smiled wryly; explanation was not necessary.

"Of course." Hester sank deeper into her chair and thought of Mrs. Horne's cup of tea. She would have that well before

35

she thought of changing her clothes, putting her boots on again, and traipsing out to see some lawyer.

But Oliver Rathbone was not "some lawyer"; he was the most brilliant advocate practicing at the bar, and he knew it. He was a lean man of no more than average height, neatly but unremarkably dressed, until one looked closely and saw the quality of the fabric and, after a little while, the excellence of the cut, which fitted him perfectly and seemed always to hang without strain or crease. His hair was fair and his face narrow with a long nose and a sensitive, beautifully shaped mouth. But the overriding impression was one of controlled emotion and brilliant, all-pervading intelligence.

His rooms were quiet and full of light from the chandelier which hung from the center of an ornately plastered ceiling. In the daylight they would have been equally well illuminated by three large sash windows, curtained in dark green velvet and bound by simple cords. The desk was mahogany and the chairs appeared extremely comfortable.

He ushered them in and bade them be seated. At first Hester was unimpressed, finding him a little too concerned for their ease than for the purpose of their visit, but this misapprehension vanished as soon as he addressed the matter of the trial. His voice was pleasing enough, but the preciseness of his diction made it memorable so that even his exact intonation remained with her long afterwards.

"Now, Miss Latterly," he said, "we must discuss the testimony you are to give. You understand it will not simply be a matter of reciting what you know and then being permitted to leave?"

She had not considered it, and when she did now, that was precisely what she had assumed. She was about to deny it, and saw in his face that he had read her thoughts, so she changed them.

"I was awaiting your instructions, Mr. Rathbone. I had not judged the matter one way or the other."

He smiled, a delicate, charming movement of the lips.

"Quite so." He leaned against the edge of his desk and regarded her gravely. "I will question you first. You are my witness, you understand? I shall ask you to tell the events of your family's tragedy, simply, from your own point of view. I do not wish you to tell me anything that you did not experience

36

yourself. If you do, the judge will instruct the jury to disregard it, and every time he stops you and disallows what you say, the less credence the jury will give to what remains. They may easily forget which is which.''

"I understand," she assured him. "I will say only what I know for myself.''

"You may easily be tempted, Miss Latterly. It is a matter in which your feelings must be very deep." He looked at her with brilliant, humorous eyes. "It will not be as simple as you may expect.''

"What chance is there that Menard Grey will not be hanged?'' she asked gravely. She chose deliberately the harshest words. Rathbone was not a man with whom to use euphemisms.

"We will do the best we can," he replied, the light fading from his face. "But I am not at all sure that we will succeed.''

"And what would be success, Mr. Rathbone?''

"Success? Success would be transportation to Australia, where he would have some chance to make a new life for himself—in time. But they stopped most transportation three years ago, except for cases warranting sentences over fourteen years—'' He paused.

"And failure?'' she said almost under her breath. "Hanging?''

"No," he said, leaning forward a little. "The rest of his life somewhere like the Coldbath Fields. I'd rather be hanged, myself.''

She sat silent; there was nothing to say to such a reality, and trite words would be so crass as to be painful. Callandra, sitting in the corner of the room, remained motionless.

"What can we do that will be best?'' Hester said after a moment or two. "Please advise me, Mr. Rathbone.''

"Answer only what I ask you, Miss Latterly," he replied. "Do not offer anything, even if you believe it will be helpful. We will discuss everything now, and I will judge what will suit our case and what, in the jury's minds, may damage it. They did not live through the events; many things that are perfectly clear to you may be obscure to them." He smiled with a bleak, personal humor that lit his eyes and curved the corners of his abstemious mouth. "And their knowledge of the war may be very different from yours. They may well consider all officers, especially wounded ones, to be heroes. And if we try too clumsily to persuade them otherwise, they may resent the destruction of far more of their dreams than we are aware of. Like Lady Fabia Grey, they may need to believe as they do."

Hester had a sudden sharp recollection of sitting in the bedroom at Shelburne Hall with Fabia Grey, her crumpled face aged in a single blow as half a lifetime's treasures withered and died in front of her.

"With loss very often comes hatred." Rathbone spoke as if he had felt her thoughts as vividly as she had herself. "We need someone to blame when we cannot cope with the pain except through anger, which is so much easier, at least to begin with."

Instinctively she looked up and met his gaze, and was startled by its penetration. It was both assuring and discomfiting. He was not a man to whom she could ever lie. Thank heaven it would not be necessary!

"You do not need to explain to me, Mr. Rathbone," she said with a faint answering smile. "I have been home long enough to be quite aware that a great many people require their illusions more than the bits and pieces of truth I can tell them. The ugliness needs to have the real heroism along with it to become bearable—the day after day of suffering without complaint, the dedication to duty when all purpose seems gone, the laughter when you feel like weeping. I don't think it can be told—only felt by those who were there."

His smile was sudden and like a flash of light.

"You have more wisdom than I had been led to suppose, Miss Latterly. I begin to hope."

She found herself blushing and was furious. Afterwards she must confront Callandra and ask what she had said of her that he had such an opinion. But then more likely it was that miserable policeman, Monk, who had given Rathbone this impression. For all their cooperation at the end, and their few blazing moments of complete understanding, they had quarreled most of the time, and he had certainly made no secret of the fact that he considered her opinionated, meddlesome and thoroughly unappealing.

Not that she had not expressed her views of his conduct and character very forthrightly first!

Rathbone discussed all that he would ask her, the arguments the prosecuting counsel would raise, and the issues with which he would be most likely to attempt to trap her. He warned her against appearing to have any emotional involvement which would give him the opportunity to suggest she was biased or unreliable.

By the time he showed them out into the street at quarter to eight she was so tired her mind was dazed, and she was suddenly aware again of the ache in her back and the pinching of her boots. The idea of testifying for Menard Grey was no longer the simple and unfearful thing it had seemed when she had promised with such fierce commitment to do it.

"A little daunting, is he not?" Callandra said when they were seated in her carriage and beginning the journey back to dinner.

"Let us hope he daunts them as much," Hester replied, wriggling her feet uncomfortably. "I cannot imagine his being easily deceived." This was such an understatement she felt self-conscious making it, and turned away so Callandra would not see more than the outline of her face against the light of the carriage lamps.

Callandra laughed, a deep, rich sound full of amusement.

"My dear, you are not the first young woman not to know how to express your opinion of Oliver Rathbone."

"Perspicacity and an authoritative manner will not be enough to save Menard Grey!" Hester said with more sharpness than she had intended. Perhaps Callandra would recognize that Hester spoke from a great deal of apprehension for the day after tomorrow, and a growing fear that they would not succeed.

It was the following day that she read in the newspapers of the murder of Octavia Haslett in Queen Anne Street, but since the name of the police officer investigating was not considered of any public interest, and therefore was not mentioned, it did not bring Monk to her mind any more than he already was each time she remembered the tragedy of the Greys—and of her own family.

Dr. Pomeroy was in two minds as to how to treat her request for leave in order to testify. At her insistence he had operated on John Airdrie, and the child seemed to be recovering well;

a little longer and he might not have—he had been weaker than Pomeroy realized. Nevertheless he resented her absence, and yet since he had frequently told her that she was eminently dispensable, he could hardly make too much of an issue of the inconvenience it would cause. His dilemma gave her some much needed amusement, even if it was bitterly flavored.

The trial of Menard Grey was held in the Central Criminal Court at the Old Bailey, and since the case had been sensational, involving the brutal death of an ex-officer of the Crimean War, the public seats were crowded and every newspaper distributed within a hundred miles had sent its reporters. Outside, the streets were crammed with newsboys waving the latest editions, cabbies depositing passengers, costers' barrows piled high with all manner of goods, pie and sandwich sellers crying their wares, and hot pea soup carts. Running patterers recounted the whole case, with much detail added, for the benefit of the ignorant—or any who simply wished to hear it all again. More people pressed in up Ludgate Hill, along Old Bailey itself, and along Newgate. Had they not been witnesses, Hester and Callandra would have found it impossible to gain entry.

Inside the court the atmosphere was different, darker and with an inexorable formality that forced one to be aware that this was the majesty of the law, that here all individual whim was ironed out and blind, impersonal justice ruled.

Police in dark uniform, top hat, shining buttons and belt; clerks in striped trousers; lawyers wigged and gowned, and bailiffs scurrying to shepherd people here and there. Hester and Callandra were shown into the room where they were to wait until they were called. They were not permitted into the courtroom in case they overheard evidence which might affect their own.

Hester sat silently, acutely uncomfortable. A dozen times she drew breath to speak, then knew that what she was going to say was pointless, and only to break the tension. Half an hour had gone by in stiff awkwardness when the outer door opened, and even before he entered she recognized the outline of the man's shoulders as he stood with his back to them, talking to someone beyond in the corridor. She felt a prickle of awareness, not quite apprehension, and certainly not excitement.

"Good morning, Lady Callandra, Miss Latterly." The man turned at last and came in, closing the door behind him.

"Good morning, Mr. Monk," Callandra replied, inclining her head politely.

"Good morning, Mr. Monk," Hester echoed, with exactly the same gesture. Seeing his smooth-boned face again with its hard, level gray eyes, broad aquiline nose and mouth with its faint scar, brought back all the memories of the Grey case: the anger, confusion, intense pity and fear, the brief moments of understanding each other more vividly than she had ever experienced with anyone else, and sharing a purpose with an intensity that was consuming.

Now they were merely two people who irritated each other and were brought together by their desire to save Menard Grey from further pain—and perhaps a sense of responsibility in some vague way because they had been the ones who had discovered the truth.

"Pray sit down, Mr. Monk," she instructed rather than offered. "Please be comfortable."

He remained standing.

For several moments there was silence. Deliberately she filled her mind with thoughts of how she would testify, the questions Rathbone had warned her the prosecution's lawyer would ask, and how to avoid damaging answers and being led to say more than she intended.

"Has Mr. Rathbone advised you?" she said without thinking.

His eyebrows rose. "I have testified in court before, Miss Latterly." His voice was heavy with sarcasm. "Even occasionally in cases of considerable importance. I am aware of the procedure."

She was annoyed with herself for having left herself open to such a remark, and with him for making it. Instinctively she dealt back the hardest blow that she could.

"I see a great deal of your recollection must have returned since we last met. I had not realized, or of course I should not have commented. I was endeavoring to be helpful, but it seems you do not require it."

The color drained from his face leaving two bright spots of

pink on his cheekbones. His mind was racing for an equal barb to return.

"I have forgotten much, Miss Latterly, but that still leaves me with an advantage over those who never knew anything in the beginning!" he said tartly, turning away.

Callandra smiled and did not interfere.

"It was not my assistance I was suggesting, Mr. Monk," Hester snapped back. "It was Mr. Rathbone's. But if you believe you know better than he does, I can only hope you are right and indeed you do—not for your sake, which is immaterial, but for Menard Grey's. I trust you have not lost sight of our purpose in being here?"

She had won that exchange, and she knew it.

"Of course I haven't," he said coldly, standing with his back to her, hands in his pockets. "I have left my present investigation to Sergeant Evan and come early in case Mr. Rathbone wished to see me, but I have no intention of disturbing him if he does not."

"He may not know you are here to be seen," she argued.

He turned around to face her. "Miss Latterly, can you not for one moment refrain from meddling in other people's affairs and assume we are capable of managing without your direction? I informed his clerk as I came in."

"Then all civility required you do was say so when I asked you!" she replied, stung by the charge of interfering, which was totally unjust—or anyway largely—or to some extent! "But you do not seem to be capable of ordinary civility."

"You are not an ordinary person, Miss Latterly." His eyes were very wide, his face tight. "You are overbearing, dictatorial, and seem bent to treat everyone as if they were incapable of managing without your instruction. You combine the worst elements of a governess with the ruthlessness of a workhouse matron. You should have stayed in the army—you are eminently suited for it."

That was the perfect thrust; he knew how she despised the army command for its sheer arrogant incompetence, which had driven so many men to needless and appalling deaths. She was so furious she choked for words.

"I am not," she gasped. "The army is made up of men— and those in command of it are mostly stubborn and stupid— like you. They haven't the faintest idea what they are doing, but they would rather blunder along, no matter who is killed by it, than admit their ignorance and accept help.'' She drew breath again and went on. ''They would rather die than take counsel from a woman—which in itself wouldn't matter a toss. It's their letting other people die that is unforgivable.''

He was prevented from having to think of a reply by the bailiff coming to the door and requesting Hester to prepare herself to enter the courtroom. She rose with great dignity and swept out past him, catching her skirt in the doorway and having to stop and tweak it out, which was most irksome. She flashed a smile at Callandra over her other shoulder, then with fluttering stomach followed the bailiff along the passageway and into the court.

The chamber was large, high ceilinged, paneled in wood and so crowded with people they seemed to press in on her from every side. She could feel a heat from their bodies as they jostled and craned to see her come in, and there was a rustle and hiss of breath and a shuffle of feet as people fought to maintain balance. In the press benches pencils flew, scratching notes on paper, making outlines of faces and hats.

She stared straight ahead and walked up the cleared way to the witness box, angry that her legs were trembling. She stumbled on the step, and the bailiff put out his hand to steady her. She looked around for Oliver Rathbone, and saw him immediately, but with his white lawyer's wig on he looked different, very remote. He regarded her with the distant politeness he would a stranger, and it was surprisingly chilling.

She could hardly feel worse. There was nothing to be lost by reminding herself why she was here. She allowed her eyes to meet Menard Grey's in the dock. He was pale, all the fresh color gone from his skin. He looked white, tired and very frightened. It was enough to give her all the courage she needed. What was her brief, rather childish moment of loneliness in comparison?

She was passed the Bible and swore to her name and that she would tell the truth, her voice firm and positive.

Rathbone came towards her a couple of steps and began quietly.

''Miss Latterly, I believe you were one of the several well-born young women who answered the call of Miss Florence

43

Nightingale, and left your home and family and sailed to the Crimea to nurse our soldiers out there, in the conflict?"

The judge, a very elderly man with a broad, fragile tempered face, leaned forward.

"I am sure Miss Latterly is an admirable young lady, Mr. Rathbone, but is her nursing experience of any relevance to this case? The accused did not serve in the Crimea, nor did the crime occur over there."

"Miss Latterly knew the victim in the hospital in Scutari, my lord. The roots of the crime begin there, and on the battlefields of Balaclava and Sebastopol."

"Do they indeed? I had rather thought from the prosecution that they began in the nursery at Shelburne Hall. Still—continue, please." He leaned back again in his high seat and stared gloomily at Rathbone.

"Miss Latterly," Rathbone prompted briskly.

Carefully, measuring each word to begin with, then gradually gathering confidence as the emotion of memory overtook her, she told the court about the hospital in which she had served, and the men she had come to know slightly, but as well as their injuries made possible. And as she spoke she became aware of a cessation of the jostling among the crowd. More faces were quickened in interest; even Menard Grey had raised his head and was staring at her.

Rathbone came out from behind his table and paced back and forth across the floor, not waving his arms or moving quickly to distract attention from her, but rather prowling, keeping the jury from becoming too involved in the story and forgetting it all had to do with a crime here in London, and a man on trial for his life.

He had been through her receipt of her brother's heartbroken letter recounting her parents' death, and her return home to the shame and the despair, and the financial restriction. He elicited the details without ever allowing her to repeat herself or sound self-pitying. She followed his direction with more and more appreciation for the skill with which he was building a picture of mounting and inevitable tragedy. Already the faces of the men in the jury were becoming strained with pity, and she knew how their anger would explode when the last piece was fitted into the picture and they understood the truth.

She did not dare to look at Fabia Grey in the front row, still dressed in black, or at her son Lovel and his wife, Rosamond, beside her. Each time her eyes roamed unintentionally towards them she averted them sharply, and looked either at Rathbone himself or at any anonymous face in the crowd beyond him.

In answer to his careful questions she told him of her visit to Callandra at Shelburne Hall, of her first meeting with Monk, and of all that had ensued. She made some slips, had to be corrected, but never once did she offer anything beyond a simple answer.

By the time he had come to the tragic and terrible conclusion, the faces of the jury were stunned with amazement and anger, and for the first time they were able to look at Menard Grey, because they understood what he had done, and why. Perhaps some even felt they might, had fortune been so cruel to them, have done the same.

When at last Rathbone stepped back and thanked her with a sudden, dazzling smile, she found her body was aching with the tension of clenched muscles and her hands were sore where her nails had unconsciously dug into the palms.

The counsel for the prosecution rose to his feet and smiled bleakly. "Please remain where you are, Miss Latterly. You will not mind if we put to the test this extremely moving story of yours?" It was a rhetorical question; he had no intention whatsoever of permitting such a testimony as hers had been to stand, and she felt the sweat break out on her skin as she looked at his face. At this moment he was losing, and such a thing was not only a shock to him in this instance, but of a pain so deep as to be almost physical.

"Now Miss Latterly, you admit you were—indeed still are— a woman rather past her first youth, without significant background, and in drastically impoverished circumstances—and you accepted an invitation to visit Shelburne Hall, the country home of the Grey family?"

"I accepted an invitation to visit Lady Callandra Daviot," Hester corrected.

"At Shelburne Hall," he said sharply. "Yes?"

"Yes."

"Thank you. And during that visit you spent some time with the accused, Menard Grey?"

She drew breath to say "Not alone," and just in time caught

45

Rathbone's eye, and let out her breath again. She smiled at the prosecutor as if the implication had missed her.

"Of course. It is impossible to stay with a family and not meet all the members who are in residence, and to spend time with them." She was sorely tempted to add that perhaps he did not know such things, and forebore carefully. It would be a cheap laugh, and perhaps bought very dearly. This was an adversary to whom she could give no ground.

"I believe you now have a position in one of the London infirmaries, is that so?"

"Yes."

"Obtained for you by the same Lady Callandra Daviot?"

"Obtained with her recommendation, but I believe on my own merit."

"Be that as it may—with her influence? No; please do not look to Mr. Rathbone for guidance. Just answer me, Miss Latterly."

"I do not require Mr. Rathbone's assistance," she said, swallowing hard. "I cannot answer you, with or without it. I do not know what passed between Lady Callandra and the governors of the infirmary. She suggested I apply there, and when I did, they were satisfied with my references, which are considerable, and they employed me. Not many of Miss Nightingale's nurses find it difficult to obtain a position, should they desire it."

"No indeed, Miss Latterly." He smiled thinly. "But not many of them do desire it, as you do—do they? In fact, Miss Nightingale herself comes from an excellent family who could provide for her for the rest of her life."

"That my family could not, and that my parents are both dead, is the foundation of the case that brings us here, sir," she said with a hard note of victory in her voice. Whatever he thought or felt, she knew the jury understood that, and it was they who decided, after all each counsel could say.

"Indeed," he said with a flicker of irritation. Then he proceeded to ask her again how well she had known the victim, and to imply very subtly but unmistakably that she had fallen in love with him, succumbed to his now well-established charm, and because he had rejected her, wished to blacken his name. Indeed he skirted close to suggesting she might have collaborated to conceal the crime, and now to defend Menard Grey.

She was horrified and embarrassed, but when the temptation to explode in fury came too close, she looked across at Menard Grey's face and remembered what was truly important.

"No, that is untrue," she said quietly. She thought of accusing him of sordidness, but caught Rathbone's eye again and refrained.

Only once did she see Monk. She felt a tingle of pleasure, even sweetness, to recognize the outrage in his expression as he glared at the counsel for the prosecution.

When the prosecution suddenly changed his mind and gave up, she was permitted to remain in the courtroom, since she was no longer of importance, and she found room to sit and listen while Callandra testified. She too was first questioned by Rathbone and then, with more politeness than he had used before, by the counsel for the prosecution. He judged the jury rightly that they would not view with sympathy any attempt to bully or insult an army surgeon's widow—and a lady. Hester did not watch Callandra, she had no fear for her; she concentrated on the faces of the jurymen. She saw the emotions flicker and change: anger, pity, confusion, respect, contempt.

Next Monk was called and sworn. She had not noticed in the waiting room how well he was dressed. His jacket was of excellent cut, and only the best woolen broadcloth hung in quite that way. What vanity. How, on police pay, did he manage such a thing? Then she thought with a flicker of pity that probably he did not know himself—not now. Had he wondered? Had he perhaps been afraid of the vanity or the ruthlessness the answer might reveal? How terrible it must be to look at the bare evidence of yourself, the completed acts, and know none of the reasons that made them human, explainable in terms of fear and hopes, things misunderstood, small sacrifices made, wounds compensated for—always to see only what resulted, never what was meant. This extravagant coat might be pure vanity, money grasped for—or it might be the mark of achievement after long years of saving and working, putting in extra duty when others were relaxing at home or laughing in some music hall or public house.

Rathbone began to question him, talking smoothly, knowing the words were powerful enough and emotion from him would heap the impact too high, too soon. He had called his witnesses in this order so he might build his story as it had happened, first the Crimea, then Hester's parents' death, then the crime. Detail by detail he drew from Monk the description of the flat in Mecklenburg Square, the marks of struggle and death, his own slow discovery piece by piece of the truth.

Most of the time Rathbone had his back to her, facing either Monk or the jury, but she found his voice compelling, every word as clear as a cut stone, insistent in the mind, unfolding an irresistible tragedy.

And she watched Monk and saw the respect and once or twice the momentary flicker of dislike cross his face as he answered. Rathbone was not treating him as a favored witness, rather as someone half an enemy. His phrases had a sharp turn to them, an element of antagonism. Only watching the jury did she understand why. They were utterly absorbed. Even a woman shrieking in the crowd and being revived by a neighbor did not break their attention. Monk's sympathy for Menard Grey appeared to be dragged from him reluctantly, although Hester knew it was acutely real. She could remember how Monk had looked at the time, the anger in him, the twisting pain of pity, and the helplessness to alter anything. It had been in that moment she had liked him with absolute completeness, an inner peace that shared, without reservation, and a knowledge that the communication was total.

When the court rose at the end of the afternoon, Hester went with the crowd that pushed and shoved on every side, onlookers rushing home in the jam of carts, wagons and carriages in the streets, newspaper writers hurrying to get the copy in before the presses started to roll for the first editions in the morning, running patterers to compose the next verse of their songs and pass the news along the streets.

She was outside on the steps in the sharp evening wind and the bright gas lamps looking for Callandra, from whom she had become separated, when she saw Monk. She hesitated, uncertain whether to speak to him or not. Hearing the evidence over again, recounting it herself, she had felt all the turmoil of emotions renewed, and her anger with him had been swept away.

But perhaps he still felt just as contemptuous of her? She

48

stood, unable to decide whether to commit herself and unwilling to leave.

He took the matter out of her hands by walking over, a slight pucker between his brows.

"Well, Miss Latterly, do you believe your friend Mr. Rathbone is equal to the task?"

She looked at his eyes and saw the anxiety in him. The sharp retort died away, the irrelevancies as to whether Rathbone was her friend or not. Sarcasm was only a defense against the fear that they would hang Menard Grey.

"I think so," she said quietly. "I was watching the jurors' faces while you were testifying. Of course I do not know what is yet to come, but up until now, I believe they were more deeply horrified by the injustices of what happened, and our helplessness to prevent it, than by the murder itself. If Mr. Rathbone can keep this mood until they go to consider their verdict, it may be favorable. At least—" She stopped, realizing that no matter what the jurors believed in blame, the fact remained undeniable. They could not return a verdict of not guilty, regardless of any provocation on earth. The weighing lay with the judge, not with them.

Monk had perceived it before her. The bleak understanding was in his eyes.

"Let us trust he is equally successful with his lordship," he said dryly. "Life in Coldbath Fields would be worse than the rope."

"Will you come again tomorrow?" she asked him.

"Yes—in the afternoon. The verdict will not be in till then. Will you?"

"Yes—" She thought what Pomeroy would have to say. "But I will not come until late either, if you really do not believe the verdict will come in early. I do not wish to ask for time from the infirmary without good reason."

"And will they consider your desire to hear the verdict to be a good reason?" he said dryly.

She pulled a small face, not quite a smile. "No. I shall not phrase my request in quite those terms."

"Is it what you wished—the infirmary?" Again he was as frank and direct as she recalled, and his understanding as comfortable.

"No—" She did not think of prevaricating. "It is full of

49

incompetence, unnecessary suffering, ridiculous ways of doing things which could so easily be reorganized, if only they would give up their petty self-importances and think of the end and not the means." She warmed to the subject and his interest. "A great deal of the trouble lies with their whole belief of nursing and the nature of people who should work in it. They pay only six shillings a week, and some of that is given in small beer. Many of the nurses are drunk half the time. But now the hospital provides their food, which is better than their eating the patients' food, which they used to. You may imagine what type of men and women it attracts! Most of them can neither read nor write." She shrugged expressively. "They sleep just off the wards, there are far too few basins or towels for them, and nothing more than a little Conde's fluid and now and again soap to wash themselves—even their hands after cleaning up waste."

His smile became wider and thinner, but there was a gleam of sympathy in his eyes.

"And you?" she asked. "Are you still working for Mr. Runcorn?" She did not ask if he had remembered more about himself, that was too sensitive and she would not probe. The subject of Runcorn was raw enough.

"Yes." He pulled a face.

"And with Sergeant Evan?" She found herself smiling.

"Yes, Evan too." He hesitated. He seemed about to add something when Oliver Rathbone came down the steps dressed for the street and without his wig and robes. He looked very trim and well pleased.

Monk's eyes narrowed, but he refused to comment.

"Do you think we may be hopeful, Mr. Rathbone?" Hester asked eagerly.

"Hopeful, Miss Latterly," he replied guardedly. "But still far from certain."

"Don't forget it is the judge you are playing to, Rathbone," Monk said tartly, buttoning his jacket higher. "And not Miss Latterly, or the gallery—or even the jury. Your performance before them may be brilliant, but it is dressing and not substance." And before Rathbone could reply he bowed fractionally to Hester, turned on his heel, and strode off down the darkening street.

"A man somewhat lacking in charm," Rathbone said

50

sourly. "But I suppose his calling requires little enough. May I take you somewhere in my carriage, Miss Latterly?"

"I think charm is a very dubious quality," she said with deliberation. "The Grey case is surely the finest example of excessive charm we are likely ever to see!"

"I can well believe that you do not rate it highly, Miss Latterly," he retorted, his eyes perfectly steady but gleaming with laughter.

"Oh—" She longed to be equally barbed, as subtly rude, and could think of nothing whatsoever to say. She was completely unsure whether the amusement in him was at her, at himself, or at Monk—or even whether it contained unkindness or not. "No—" She fumbled for words. "No. I find it unworthy of trust, a spurious quality, all show and no substance, glitter without warmth. No thank you; I am returning with Lady Callandra—but it is most courteous of you to offer. Good day, Mr. Rathbone."

"Good day, Miss Latterly." He bowed, still smiling.

Sir Basil Moidore stared at Monk across the carpeted expanse of the morning room floor. His face was pale but there was no vacillation in it, no lack of composure, only amazement and disbelief.

"I beg your pardon?" he said coldly.

"No one broke into your house on Monday night, sir," Monk repeated. "The street was well observed all night long, at both ends—"

"By whom?" Moidore's dark eyebrows rose, making his eyes the more startlingly sharp.

Monk could feel his temper prickling already. He resented being disbelieved more than almost anything else. It suggested he was incompetent. He controlled his voice with considerable effort.

"By the policeman on the beat, Sir Basil, a householder who was up half the night with a sick wife, the doctor who visited him." He did not mention Chinese Paddy; he did not think Moidore would be inclined to take his evidence well. "And by a large number of liveried footmen and coachmen waiting on their employers to leave a party at the corner of Chandos Street."

"Then obviously the man came from the mews," Basil responded irritably.

"Your own groom and coachmen sleep above your stables, sir," Monk pointed out. "And anyone climbing over there would be highly unlikely to get across that roof without disturbing at least the horses. Then he would have to get right over the house roof and down the other side. Almost impossible to do, unless he was a mountaineer with ropes and climbing equipment, and—"

"There is no call to be sarcastic," Basil snapped. "I take your point. Then he must have come in the front some time between your policeman's patrols. There is no other answer. He certainly was not hiding in the house all evening! And neither did he leave after the servants were up."

Monk was forced to mention Chinese Paddy.

"I am sorry, but that is not so. We also found a housebreaker who was watching the Harley Street end all night, hoping to get a chance to break in farther along. He got no opportunity because there were people about who would have observed him if he had. But he was watching all night from eleven until four—which covers the relevant time. I am sorry."

Sir Basil swung around from the table he had been facing, his eyes black, his mouth drawn down in anger. "Then why in God's name haven't you arrested him? He must be the one! On his own admission he is a housebreaker. What more do you want?" He glared at Monk. "He broke in here and poor Octavia heard him—and he killed her. What is the matter with you, standing here like a fool?"

Monk felt his body tighten with fury, the more biting because it was impotent. He needed to succeed in his profession, and he would fail completely if he were as rude as he wished, and were thrown out. How Runcorn would love that! It would be not only professional disgrace but social as well.

"Because his story is true," he replied with a level, harsh voice. "Substantiated by Mr. Bentley, his doctor and a maid who has no interest in the matter and no idea what her testimony means." He did not meet Sir Basil's eyes because he dared not let him see the anger in them, and he hated the submission of it. "The housebreaker did not pass along the street," he went on. "He did not rob anyone, because he did not have the chance, and he can prove it. I wish it were so simple; we should be very pleased to solve the case as neatly—sir."

Basil leaned forward across the table.

"Then if no one broke in, and no one was concealed here, you have created an impossible situation—unless you are suggesting—'' He stopped, the color drained out of his face and slowly a very real horror replaced the irritation and impatience. He stood stock-still. "Are you?" he said very quietly.

"Yes, Sir Basil," Monk answered him.

"That's—'' Basil stopped. For several seconds he remained in absolute silence, his thoughts apparently inward, racing, ideas grasped and rejected. Finally he came to some realization he could not cast aside. "I see," he said at last. "I cannot think of any imaginable reason, but we must face the inevitable. It seems preposterous, and I still believe that you will find some flaw in your reasoning, or that your evidence is faulty. But until then we must proceed on your assumption." He frowned very slightly. "What do you require next? I assure you we have no violent quarrels or conflicts in the house and no one has behaved in any way out of their usual custom." He regarded Monk with something between dislike and a bitter humor. "And we do not have personal relationships with our servants, let alone of the sort which would occasion this." He put his hands in his pockets. "It is absurd—but I do not wish to obstruct you."

"I agree a quarrel seems unlikely." Monk measured his words, both to keep his own dignity and to show Basil there was some sense to the argument. "Especially in the middle of the night when all the household was in bed. But it is not impossible Mrs. Haslett was privy to some secret, albeit unintentionally, that someone feared she might expose—'' It was not only possible, it excluded her from all blame. He saw Basil's face lose some of its anxiety, and a flicker of hope appeared in his eyes. His shoulder eased as he breathed out and let his arms drop.

"Poor Octavia." He looked at one of the soft landscape paintings on the wall. "That does sound possible. I apologize. I spoke hastily. You had better pursue your inquiries. What do you wish to do first?"

Monk respected him for his ability to admit both haste and discourtesy. It was more than he had expected, and something he would have found hard himself. The measure of the man was larger than he thought.

"I would like to speak to the family first, sir. They may have observed something, or Mrs. Haslett may have confided in one of them."

"The family?" Basil's mouth twitched, but whether it was from fear or a dark, inward humor Monk could not even guess. "Very well." He reached for the bell pull and tugged it. When the butler appeared he sent him to bring Cyprian Moidore to the morning room.

Monk waited in silence until he came.

Cyprian closed the door behind him and looked at his father. Seeing them almost side by side the resemblance was striking: the same shape of head; the dark, almost black eyes; and the broad mouth with its extraordinary mobility. And yet the expressions were so different the whole bearing was altered. Basil was more aware of his own power and was quicker tempered, the flash of humor more deeply covered. Cyprian was less certain, as if his strength was untried and he feared it might not prove adequate. Was the softer side of him compassion, or simply caution because he was still vulnerable and he knew it?

"The police have discerned that no one broke in to kill Octavia," Basil explained briefly and without preamble. He did not watch his son's face; apparently he was not concerned how the news affected him, nor did he explain Monk's reasoning of possible motive. "The only solution left seems to be that it was someone already living here. Obviously not the family—therefore, we must presume, one of the servants. Inspector Monk wishes to speak to all of us to see what we observed—if indeed we observed anything."

Cyprian stared at his father, then swung around to look at Monk as if he had been some monster brought in from a foreign land.

"I am sorry, sir." Monk put in the apology Basil had omitted. "I am aware that it must be distressing, but if you could tell me what you did on Monday, and what you can recall of anything Mrs. Haslett may have said, especially if at any time she confided a concern to you, or some matter she may have discovered that could be seen as dangerous to anyone else."

Cyprian frowned, concentration coming slowly to his face as thought took over from astonishment. He turned his back on his father.

"You think Octavia was killed because she knew someone's secret about—" He shrugged. "What? What could one of our servants have done that—" He stopped. It was apparent from

55

his eyes that his question was answered in his imagination and he preferred not to speak it. "Tavie said nothing to me. But then I was out most of the day. I wrote a few letters in the morning, then about eleven I went to my club in Piccadilly for luncheon and spent the afternoon with Lord Ainslie, talking about cattle, mostly. He has some stock, and I considered buying some. We keep a large estate in Hertfordshire."

Monk had a rapid impression that Cyprian was lying, not about the meeting but about the subject of it.

"Damned Owenite politician!" Basil said with a flash of temper. "Have us all living in communities like farm animals."

"Not at all!" Cyprian retorted. "His thoughts are—"

"You were here at dinner," Basil overrode him curtly before he could form his argument. "Didn't you see Octavia then?"

"Only at table," Cyprian said with an edge to his voice. "And if you recall, Tavie barely spoke—to me, or to anyone else."

Basil turned from the fireplace and looked at Monk.

"My daughter was not always in the best of health. I think on that occasion she was feeling unwell. She certainly was extremely quiet and seemed in some distress." He put his hands back in his pockets. "I assumed at the time she had a headache, but looking back now, perhaps she was aware of some ugly secret and it consumed her thoughts. Although she can hardly have realized the danger it represented."

"I wish to God she had told someone," Cyprian said with sudden passion. There was no need to add all the tumult of feelings that lay behind it, the regret and the sense of having failed. It lay heavy in his voice and in the strain in his features.

Before the elder Moidore replied there was a knock on the door.

"Come in!" he said, raising his head sharply, irked by the intrusion.

Monk wondered for a moment who the woman was, then as Cyprian's expression changed, he remembered meeting her in the withdrawing room the first morning: Romola Moidore. This time she looked less drained with shock; her skin had a bloom to it and her complexion was flawless. Her features were regular, her eyes wide and her hair thick. The only thing which prevented her from being a beauty was a suggestion of sulkiness about the mouth, a feeling that her good temper was not to be relied on. She looked at Monk with surprise. Obviously she did not remember him.

"Inspector Monk," Cyprian supplied. Then, when her face did not clear: "Of the police." He glanced at Monk, and for a moment there was a bright intelligence in his eyes. He was leaving Monk to make whatever impact he chose.

Basil immediately spoiled it by explaining.

"Whoever killed Octavia is someone who lives in this house. That means one of the servants." His eyes were on her face, his voice careful. "The only reason that makes any sense is if one of them has a secret so shameful they would rather commit murder than have it revealed. Either Octavia knew this secret or they believed she did."

Romola sat down sharply, the color fading from her cheeks, and she put her hand to her mouth, but her eyes did not leave Basil's face. Never once did she look to her husband.

Cyprian glared at his father, who looked back at him boldly—and with something that Monk thought might well be dislike. He wished he could remember his own father, but rack his memory as he might, nothing came back but a faint blur, an impression of size and the smell of salt and tobacco, and the touch of beard, and skin softer than he expected. Nothing returned of the man, his voice, his words, a face. Monk had no real idea, only a few sentences from his sister, and a smile as if there were something familiar and precious.

Romola was speaking, her voice scratchy with fear.

"Here in the house?" She looked at Monk, although she was speaking to Cyprian. "One of the servants?"

"There doesn't seem to be any other explanation," Cyprian replied. "Did Tavie say anything to you—think carefully—anything about any of the servants?"

"No," she said almost immediately. "This is terrible. The very thought of it makes me feel ill."

A shadow passed over Cyprian's face, and for a moment it seemed as if he were about to speak, but he was aware of his father's eyes on him.

"Did Octavia speak to you alone that day?" Basil asked her without change of tone.

"No—no," she denied quickly. "I interviewed governesses

57

all morning. None of them seemed suitable. I don't know what I'm going to do."

"See some more!" Basil snapped. "If you pay a requisite salary you will find someone who will do."

She shot him a look of repressed dislike, guarded enough that to a casual eye it could have been anxiety.

"I was at home all day." She turned back to Monk, her hands still clenched. "I received friends in the afternoon, but Tavie went out. I have no idea where; she said nothing when she came in. In fact she passed by me in the hall as if she had not seen me there at all."

"Was she distressed?" Cyprian asked quickly. "Did she seem frightened, or upset about anything?"

Basil watched them, waiting.

"Yes," Romola said with a moment's thought. "Yes she did. I assumed she had had an unpleasant afternoon, perhaps friends who were disagreeable, but maybe it was more than that?"

"What did she say?" Cyprian pursued.

"Nothing. I told you, she barely seemed aware she had passed me. If you remember, she said very little at dinner, and we presumed she was not well."

They all looked at Monk, waiting for him to resolve some answer from the facts.

"Perhaps she confided in her sister?" he suggested.

"Unlikely," Basil said tersely. "But Minta is an observant woman." He turned to Romola. "Thank you, my dear. You may return to your tasks. Do not forget what I have counseled you. Perhaps you would be good enough to ask Araminta to join us here."

"Yes, Papa-in-law," she said obediently, and left without looking at Cyprian or Monk again.

Araminta Kellard was not a woman Monk could have forgotten as he had her sister-in-law. From her vivid fire-gold hair, her curiously asymmetrical features, to her slender, stiff body, she was unique. When she came into the room she looked first at her father, ignored Cyprian and faced Monk with guarded interest, then turned back to her father.

"Papa?"

"Did Tavie say anything to you about learning something

58

shocking or distressing recently?'' Basil asked her. ''Particularly the day before she died?''

Araminta sat down and considered very carefully for several moments, without looking at anyone else in the room. ''No,'' she said at last. She regarded Monk with steady, amber-hazel eyes. ''Nothing specific. But I was aware that she was extremely concerned about something which she learned that afternoon. I am sorry, I have no idea what it was. Do you believe that is why she was killed?''

Monk looked at her with more interest than he had for anyone else he had yet seen in this house. There was an almost mesmeric intensity in her, and yet she was utterly composed. Her thin hands were tight in her lap, but her gaze was unwavering and penetratingly intelligent. Monk had no idea what wounds tore at the fabric of her emotions beneath, and he did not imagine he would easily frame any questions, no matter how subtle, which would cause her to betray them.

''It is possible, Mrs. Kellard,'' he answered. ''But if you can think of any other motive anyone might have to wish her harm, or fear her, please let me know. It is only a matter of deduction. There is no evidence as yet, except that no one broke in.''

''From which you conclude that it was someone already here,'' she said very quietly. ''Someone who lives in this house.''

''It seems inescapable.''

''I suppose it does.''

''What kind of a woman was your sister, Mrs. Kellard? Was she inquisitive, interested in other people's problems? Was she observant? An astute judge of character?''

She smiled, a twisted gesture with half her face.

''Not more than most women, Mr. Monk. In fact I think rather less. If she did discover anything, it will have been by chance, not because she went seeking it. You ask what kind of woman she was. The kind who walks into events, whose emotions lead her and she follows without regard to the price. She was the kind of woman who lurches into disaster without having foreseen it or understanding it once she is there.''

Monk looked across at Basil and saw the intense concentration in his face, his eyes fixed on Araminta. There was no reflection in his expression of any other emotion, no grief, no curiosity.

Monk turned to Cyprian. In him was the terrible hurt of memory and the knowledge of loss. His face was hard etched with pain, the realization of all the words that could not now be said, the affections unexpressed.

"Thank you, Mrs. Kellard," Monk said slowly. "If you think of anything else I should be obliged if you would tell me. How did you spend Monday?"

"At home in the morning," she answered. "I went calling in the afternoon, and I dined at home with the family. I spoke to Octavia several times during the evening, but I did not attach any particular importance to anything we said. It seemed totally trivial at the time."

"Thank you, ma'am."

She rose to her feet, inclined her head very slightly, and walked out without looking behind her.

"Do you wish to see Mr. Kellard?" Basil asked with raised eyebrows, an air of contempt in his stance.

The very fact that Basil questioned it made Monk accept.

"If you please."

Basil's face tightened, but he did not argue. He summoned Phillips and dispatched him to fetch Myles Kellard.

"Octavia would not have confided in Myles," Cyprian said to Monk.

"Why not?" Monk asked.

A look of distaste flickered across Basil's face at the intrusive indelicacy of such a question, and he answered before Cyprian could. "Because they did not care for each other," he replied tersely. "They were civil, of course." His dark eyes regarded Monk quickly to make sure he understood that people of quality did not squabble like riffraff. "It seems most probable the poor girl spoke to no one about whatever she learned so disastrously, and we may never learn what it was."

"And whoever killed her will go unpunished," Cyprian challenged. "That is monstrous."

"Of course not!" Basil was furious; his eyes blazed and the deep lines in his face altered to become harsh. "Do you imagine I am going to live the rest of my life in this house with someone who murdered my daughter? What is the matter with you? Good God, don't you know me better than that?"

Cyprian looked as if he had been struck, and Monk felt a sharp, unexpected twinge of embarrassment. This was a scene he should not have witnessed, these were emotions that had nothing to do with Octavia Haslett's death; a viciousness between father and son stemming from no sudden act but years of resentment and failure to understand.

"If Monk—" Basil jerked his head towards the policeman—"is incapable of finding him, whoever it is, I shall have the commissioner send someone else." He moved restlessly from the ornate mantel back to the center of the floor. "Where the hell is Myles? This morning at least, he should make himself available when I send for him!"

At that moment the door opened, without a prefacing knock, and Myles Kellard answered his summons. He was tall and slender, but in every other respect the opposite of the Moidores. His hair was brown with streaks in it and waved in a sweep back from his forehead. His face was long and narrow with an aristocratic nose and a sensuous, moody mouth. It was at once the face of a dreamer and a libertine.

Monk hesitated from politeness, and before he could speak Basil asked Myles the questions that Monk would have, but without explanation as to their purpose or the need for them. He was correct in his assumption; Myles could tell them nothing of use. He had risen late and gone out in the morning for luncheon, where he did not say, and spent the afternoon at the merchant bank where he was a director. He too had dined at home, but had not seen Octavia, except at table in the company of everyone else. He had noticed nothing remarkable.

When he had left Monk asked if there was anyone else, apart from Lady Moidore, to whom he should speak.

"Aunt Fenella and Uncle Septimus." Cyprian answered this time, cutting his father off. "We would be obliged if you could keep your questions to Mama as brief as possible. In fact it would be better if we could ask her and relay her answers to you, if they are of any relevance."

Basil looked at his son coldly, but whether for the suggestion or simply because Cyprian stole his prerogative by making it first, Monk did not know: he guessed the latter. At this point it was an easy concession to make; there would be time enough later to see Lady Moidore, when he had something better than routine and very general questions to ask her.

"Certainly," he allowed. "But perhaps your aunt and uncle? One sometimes confides in aunts especially, when no one else seems as appropriate."

Basil let out his breath in a sharp round of contempt and turned away towards the window.

"Not Aunt Fenella." Cyprian half sat on the back of one of the leather-upholstered chairs. "But she is very observant—and inquisitive. She may have noticed something the rest of us did not—if she hasn't forgotten it."

"Has she a short memory?" Monk inquired.

"Erratic," Cyprian replied with an oblique smile. He reached for the bell, but when the butler arrived it was Basil who instructed him to fetch first Mrs. Sandeman, and then Mr. Thirsk.

Fenella Sandeman bore an extraordinary resemblance to Basil. She had the same dark eyes and short, straight nose, her mouth was similarly wide and mobile, but her whole head was narrower and the lines were smoothed out. In her youth she must have had an exotic charm close to real beauty, now it was merely extraordinary. Monk did not need to ask the relationship; it was too plain to miss. She was of approximately the same age as Basil, perhaps nearer sixty than fifty, but she fought against time with every artifice imagination could conceive. Monk did not know enough of women to realize precisely what tricks they were, but he knew their presence. If he had ever understood them it was forgotten, with so much else. But he saw an artificiality in her face: the color of the skin was unnatural, the line of her brows harsh, her hair stiff and too dark.

She looked at Monk with great interest and refused Basil's invitation to sit down.

"How do you do," she said with a charming husky voice, just a fraction blurred at the edges.

"Fenella, he's a policeman, not a social acquaintance," Basil snapped. "He is investigating Octavia's death. It seems she was killed by someone here in the house, presumably one of the servants."

"One of the servants?" Fenella's black-painted eyebrows rose startlingly. "My dear, how appalling." She did not look in the least alarmed; in fact, if it were not absurd, Monk would have thought she found a kind of excitement in it.

62

Basil caught the inflection also.

"Remember your conduct!" he said tartly. "You are here because it begins to appear that Octavia may have discovered some secret, albeit accidentally, for which she was killed. Inspector Monk wonders if she may have confided such a thing to you. Did she?"

"Oh my goodness." She did not even glance at her brother; her eyes were intent on Monk. Had it not been socially ridiculous, and she at the very least twenty years his senior, he would have thought she considered flirting with him. "I shall have to think about it," she said softly. "I'm sure I cannot recall all that she said over the last few days. Poor child. Her life was full of tragedy. Losing her husband in the war, so soon after her marriage. How awful that she should be murdered over some wretched secret." She shivered and hunched her shoulders. "Whatever could it be?" Her eyes widened dramatically. "An illegitimate child, do you think? No—yes! It would lose a servant her position—but could it really have been a woman? Surely not?" She came a step closer to Monk. "Anyway, none of our servants has had a child—we would all know about it." She made a sound deep in her throat, almost a giggle. "One can hardly keep such a thing secret, can one? A crime of passion—that's it. There has been a fateful passion, which no one else knows about, and Tavie stumbled on it by chance—and they killed her—poor child. How can we help, Inspector?"

"Please be careful, Mrs. Sandeman," Monk replied with a grim face. He was very uncertain how seriously to regard her, but he felt compelled to warn her against jeopardizing her own safety. "You may discover the secret yourself, or allow the person concerned to fear you may. You would be wise to observe in silence."

She took a step backward, drew in her breath, and her eyes grew even wider. For the first time he wondered, even though it was mid-morning, if she were entirely sober.

Basil must have had the same thought. He extended his hand perfunctorily and guided her to the door.

"Just think about it, Fenella, and if you remember anything, tell me, and I will call Mr. Monk. Now go and have breakfast, or write letters or something."

For an instant the glamour and excitement vanished from

63

her face and she looked at him with intense dislike; then as quickly it was gone, and she accepted his dismissal, closing the door behind her softly.

Basil looked at Monk, searching to judge his perception, but Monk left his face blank and polite.

The last person to come in had an equally apparent relationship to the family. He had the same wide blue eyes as Lady Moidore, and although his hair was now gray, his skin was fair with the pinkness that would have been natural with light auburn hair, and his features echoed the sensitivity and fine bones of hers. However he was obviously older than she, and the years had treated him harshly. His shoulders were stooped and there was an indelible weariness in him as of the flavor of many defeats, small perhaps, but sharp.

"Septimus Thirsk." He announced himself with a remnant of military precision, as if an old memory had unaccountably slipped through and prompted him. "What can I do for you, sir?" He ignored his brother-in-law, in whose house he apparently lived, and Cyprian, who had retreated to the window embrasure.

"Were you at home on Monday, the day before Mrs. Haslett was killed, sir?" Monk asked politely.

"I was out, sir, in the morning and for luncheon," Septimus answered, still standing almost to attention. "I spent the afternoon here, in my quarters most of the time. Dined out." A shadow of concern crossed his face. "Why does that interest you, sir? I neither saw nor heard any intruder, or I should have reported it."

"Mrs. Haslett was killed by someone already in the house, Uncle Septimus," Cyprian explained. "We thought Tavie might have said something to you which would give us some idea why. We're asking everyone."

"Said something?" Septimus blinked.

Basil's face darkened with irritation. "For heaven's sake, man, the question is simple enough! Did Octavia say or do anything that led you to suppose she had stumbled on a secret unpleasant enough to cause someone to fear her! It's hardly likely, but it is necessary to ask!"

"Yes she did!" Septimus said instantly, two spots of color burning on his pale cheeks. "When she came in in the late afternoon she said a whole world had been opened up to her

64

and it was quite hideous. She said she had one more thing to discover to prove it finally. I asked her what it was, but she refused to say."

Basil was stunned and Cyprian stood paralyzed on the spot.

"Where had she been, Mr. Thirsk?" Monk asked quietly. "You said she was coming in."

"I have no idea," Septimus replied with the grief replacing anger in his eyes. "I asked her, but she would not tell me, except that one day I would understand, better than anyone else. That was all she would say."

"Ask the coachman," Cyprian said immediately. "He'll know."

"She didn't go in our coaches." Septimus caught Basil's eye. "I mean your coaches," he corrected pointedly. "She walked in. I presume she either walked all the way or found a hansom."

Cyprian swore under his breath. Basil looked confused, and yet his shoulders eased under the black cloth of his jacket and he stared beyond them all out of the window. He spoke with his back to Monk.

"It seems, Inspector, as if the poor girl did hear something that day. It will be your task to discover what it was—and if you cannot do that, to deduce in some other way who it was who killed her. It is possible we may never discover why, and it hardly matters." He hesitated, for a moment more absorbed in his own thoughts. No one intruded.

"If there is any further help the family can give you, we shall of course do so," he continued. "Now it is past midday and I can think of no purpose in which we can assist you at present. Either you or your juniors are free to question the servants at any time you wish, without disturbing the family. I shall instruct Phillips to that effect. Thank you for your courtesy so far. I trust it will continue. You may report any progress you make to me, or if I am not present, to my son. I would prefer you did not distress Lady Moidore."

"Yes, Sir Basil." He turned to Cyprian. "Thank you for your assistance, Mr. Moidore." Monk excused himself, and was shown out, not by the butler this time but by a very striking footman with bold eyes and a face whose handsomeness was spoiled only by a small, clever mouth.

In the hallway he saw Lady Moidore and had every intention

65

of passing her with no more than a polite acknowledgment, but she came towards him, dismissing the footman with a wave of her hand, and he had no option but to stop and speak with her.

"Good day, Lady Moidore."

It was hard to tell how much the pallor of her face was natural, an accompaniment to her remarkable hair, but the wide eyes and the nervous movements were unmistakable.

"Good morning, Mr. Monk. My sister-in-law tells me you believe there was no intruder in the house. Is that so?"

He could save her nothing by lying. The news would be no easier coming from someone else, and the mere fact that he had lied would make it impossible for her to believe him in future. It would add another confusion to those already inevitable.

"Yes ma'am. I am sorry."

She stood motionless. He could not even see the slight motion of her breathing.

"Then it was one of us who killed Tavie," she said. She surprised him by not flinching from it or dressing it in evasive words. She was the only one in the family to make no pretense that it must have been one of the servants, and he admired her intensely for the courage that must have cost.

"Did you see Mrs. Haslett after she came in that afternoon, ma'am?" he asked more gently.

"Yes. Why?"

"It seems she learned something while she was out which distressed her, and according to Mr. Thirsk, she intended to pursue it and discover a final proof of the matter. Did she confide anything of it to you?"

"No." Her eyes were so wide she seemed to stare at something so close to her she could not blink. "No. She was very quiet during dinner, and there was some slight unpleasantness with—" She frowned. "With both Cyprian and her father. But I assumed she had one of her headaches again. People are occasionally unpleasant with each other, especially when they live in the same house day in and day out. She did come and say good-night to me immediately before she went to bed. Her dressing robe was torn. I offered to mend it for her—she was never very good with a needle—" Her voice broke for just a moment. Memory must have been unbearably sharp, and so

66

very close. Her child was dead. The loss was not yet wholly grasped. Life had only just slipped into the past.

He hated having to press her, but he had to know.

"What did she say to you, ma'am? Even a word may help."

"Nothing but 'good night,' " she said quietly. "She was very gentle, I remember that, very gentle indeed, and she kissed me. It was almost as if she knew we should not meet again." She put her hands up to her face, pushing the long, slender fingers till they held the skin tight across her cheekbones. He had the powerful impression it was not grief which shook her most but the realization that it was someone in her own family who had committed murder.

She was a remarkable woman, possessed of an honesty which he greatly respected. It cut his emotion, and his pride, that he was socially so inferior he could offer her no comfort at all, only a stiff courtesy that was devoid of any individual expression.

"You have my deep sympathy, ma'am," he said awkwardly. "I wish it were not necessary to pursue it—" He did not add the rest. She understood without tedious explanation.

She withdrew her hands.

"Of course," she said almost under her breath.

"Good day, ma'am."

"Good day, Mr. Monk. Percival, please see Mr. Monk to the door."

The footman reappeared, and to Monk's surprise he was shown out of the front door and down the steps into Queen Anne Street, feeling a mixture of pity, intellectual stimulation, and growing involvement which was familiar, and yet he could remember no individual occasion. He must have done this a hundred times before, begun with a crime, then learned experience by experience to know the people and their lives, their tragedies.

How many of them had marked him, touched him deeply enough to change anything inside him? Whom had he loved— or pitied? What had made him angry?

He had been shown out of the front door, so it was necessary to go around to the back areaway to find Evan, whom he had detailed to speak to the servants and to make at least some search for the knife. Since the murderer was still in the house, and had not left it that night, the weapon must be there too, unless he had disposed of it since. But there would be many knives in any ordinary kitchen of such a size, and several of them used for cutting meat. It would be a simple thing to have wiped it and replaced it. Even blood found in the joint of the handle would mean little.

He saw Evan coming up the steps. Perhaps word had reached him of Monk's departure, and he had left at the same time intentionally. Monk looked at Evan's face as he ran up, feet light, head high.

"Well?"

"I had P.C. Lawley help me. We went right through the house, especially servants' quarters, but didn't find the missing jewelry. Not that I really expected to."

Monk had not expected it either. He had never thought robbery the motive. The jewelry was probably flushed down the drain, and the silver vase merely mislaid. "What about the knife?"

"Kitchen full of knives," Evan said, falling into step beside him. "Wicked-looking things. Cook says there's nothing missing. If it was one of them, it was replaced. Couldn't find anything else. Do you think it was one of the servants? Why?" He screwed up his face doubtfully. "A jealous ladies' maid? A footman with amorous notions?"

Monk snorted. "More likely a secret of some sort that she discovered." And he told Evan what he had learned so far.

Monk was at the Old Bailey by half past three, and it took him another half hour and the exertion of considerable bribery and veiled threats to get inside the courtroom where the trial of Menard Grey was winding to its conclusion. Rathbone was making his final speech. It was not an impassioned oration as Monk had expected—after all he could see that the man was an exhibitionist, vain, pedantic and above all an actor. Instead Rathbone spoke quite quietly, his words precise, his logic exact. He made no attempt to dazzle the jurors or to appeal to their emotions. Either he had given up or he had at last realized that there could be only one verdict and it was the judge to whom he must look for any compassion.

The victim had been a gentleman of high breeding and noble heritage. But so was Menard Grey. He had struggled long with his burden of knowledge and terrible, continuing injustice which would afflict more and more innocent people if he did not act.

Monk saw the jury's faces and knew they would ask for clemency. But would that be enough?

Without realizing it he was searching the crowd for Hester Latterly. She had said she would be there. He could never think of the Grey case, or any part of it, without remembering her. She should be here now to see its close.

Callandra Daviot was here, sitting in the first row behind the lawyers, next to her sister-in-law, Fabia Grey, the dowager Lady Shelburne. Lovel Grey was beside his mother at the farther end, pale, composed, not afraid to look at his brother in the dock. The tragedy seemed to have added a stature to him, a certainty of his own convictions he had lacked before. He was not more than a yard away from his mother, and yet the distance between them was a gulf which he never once looked at her to cross.

Fabia sat like stone, white, cold and relentless. The wound of disillusion had destroyed her. There was nothing left now but hatred. The delicate face which had once been beautiful was sharpened by the violence of her emotions, and the lines around her mouth were ugly, her chin pointed, her neck thin and ropey. If she had not destroyed so many others with her dreams, Monk would have pitied her, but as it was all he could feel was a chill of fear. She had lost the son she idolized to a shocking death. With him had gone all the excitement and glamour from her life. It was Joscelin who had made her laugh, flattered her, told her she was lovely and charming and gay. It was hard enough that he should have had to go to war in the Crimea and return wounded, but when he had been battered to death in his flat in Mecklenburg Square it was more than she could bear. Neither Lovel nor Menard could take his place, and she would not let them try—or accept from them such love or warmth as they would have given.

Monk's bitter solution of the case had crushed her totally, and it was something she would never forgive.

Rosamond, Lovel's wife, sat to her mother-in-law's left, composed and solitary.

The judge spoke his brief summation and the jury retired. The crowd remained in its seats, fearful lest they lose their places and miss the climax of the drama.

Monk wondered how often before he had attended the trial of someone he had arrested. The case notes he had searched so painstakingly to discover himself had stopped short with the unmasking of the criminal. They had shown him a careful man who left no detail to chance, an intuitive man who could leap from bare evidence to complicated structures of motive and opportunity, sometimes brilliantly, leaving others plodding behind, mystified. It also showed relentless ambition, a career built step by step, both by dedicated work and hard hours and by maneuvering others so he was in the place, at the time, when he could seize the advantage over less able colleagues. He made very few mistakes and forgave none in others. He had many admirers, but no one apart from Evan seemed to like him. And looking at the man who emerged from the pages he was not surprised. He did not like him himself.

Evan had met him only after the accident. The Grey case had been their first together.

He stood waiting for another fifteen minutes, thinking about the shreds he knew of himself, trying to picture the rest, and unsure whether he would find it familiar, easy to understand, therefore to forgive—or a nature he neither liked nor respected. Of the man before, or apart from his work, there was nothing, not a letter or memento that had meaning.

The jury was returning, their faces tense, eyes anxious. The buzz of voices ceased, there was no sound but the rustle of fabric and squeak of boots.

The judge asked if they had reached a verdict, and if it had been the verdict of them all.

They answered that they had. He asked the foreman what it was, and he replied: "Guilty—but we plead for clemency, my lord. Most sincerely, we ask that you give all the mercy allowed you, within the law—sir."

Monk found himself standing to attention, breathing very slowly as if the very sound of it in his ears might lose him some fraction of what was said. Beside him someone coughed, and he could have hit the man for his intrusion.

Was Hester here? Was she waiting as he was?

He looked at Menard Grey, who had risen to his feet and appeared, for all the crowd around him, as alone as a man could be. Every person in this entire paneled and vaulted hall was here to see judgment upon him, his life, or death. Beside

70

him Rathbone, slimmer, and at least three inches shorter, put out a hand to steady him, or perhaps simply to let him feel a touch and know someone else was at least aware.

"Menard Grey," the judge said very slowly, his face creased with sadness and something that looked like both pity and frustration. "You have been found guilty of murder by this court. Indeed, you have wisely not pleaded otherwise. That is to your credit. Your counsel has made much of the provocation offered you, and the emotional distress you suffered at the hands of the victim. The court cannot regard that as an excuse. If every man who felt himself ill used were to resort to violence our civilization would end."

There was a ripple of anger around the room, a letting out of breath in a soft hiss.

"However," the judge said sharply, "the fact that great wrongs were done, and you sought ways to prevent them, and could not find them within the law, and therefore committed this crime to prevent the continuation of these wrongs to other innocent persons, has been taken into account when considering sentence. You are a misguided man, but it is my judgment that you are not a wicked one. I sentence you to be transported to the land of Australia, where you will remain for a period of twenty-five years in Her Majesty's colony of Western Australia." He picked up his gavel to signal the end of the matter, but the sound of it was drowned in the cheering and stamping of feet and the scramble as the press charged to report the decision.

Monk did not find a chance to speak to Hester, but he did see her once, over the heads of a score of people. Her eyes were shining, and the tiredness suggested by her severe hairstyle, and the plain stuff of her dress, was wiped away by the glow of triumph—and utter relief. In that instant she was almost beautiful. Their eyes met and the moment was shared. Then she was carried along and he lost sight of her.

He also saw Fabia Grey as she was leaving, her body stiff, her face bleak and white with hatred. She walked alone, refusing to allow her daughter-in-law to help her, and her eldest and only remaining son chose to walk behind, head erect, a faint, tiny smile touching his mouth. Callandra Daviot would be with Rathbone. It was she, not Menard's own family, who had employed him, and she who would settle the account.

He did not see Rathbone, but he could imagine his triumph, and although it was what Monk also wanted most and had worked for, he found himself resenting Rathbone's success, the smugness he could so clearly envision in the lawyer's face and the gleam of another victory in his eyes.

He went straight from the Old Bailey back to the police station and up to Runcorn's office to report his progress to date in the Queen Anne Street case.

Runcorn looked at Monk's extremely smart jacket and his eyes narrowed and a flick of temper twitched in his high, narrow cheeks.

"I've been waiting for you for two days," he said as soon as Monk was through the door. "I assume you are working hard, but I require to be informed of precisely what you have learned—if anything! Have you seen the newspapers? Sir Basil Moidore is an extremely influential man. You don't seem to realize who we are dealing with, and he has friends in very high circles—cabinet ministers, foreign ambassadors, even princes."

"He also has enemies within his own house," Monk replied with more flippancy than was wise, but he knew the case was going to become uglier and far more difficult than it was already. Runcorn would hate it. He was terrified of offending authority, or people he thought of as socially important, and the Home Office would press for a quick solution because the public was outraged. At the same time he would be sick with fear lest he offend Moidore. Monk would be caught in the middle, and Runcorn would be only too delighted, if the results at last gave him the opportunity, to crush Monk's pretensions and make his failure public.

Monk could see it all ahead, and it infuriated him that even foreknowledge could not help him escape.

"I am not amused by riddles," Runcorn snapped. "If you have discovered nothing and the case is too difficult for you, say so, and I shall put someone else on it."

Monk smiled, showing his teeth. "An excellent idea—sir," he answered. "Thank you."

"Don't be impertinent!" Runcorn was thoroughly out of countenance. It was the last response he had expected. "If you are giving me your resignation, do it properly, man, not

72

with a casual word like this. Are you resigning?'' For a brief moment hope gleamed in his round eyes.

"No sir.'' Monk could not keep the lift in his voice. The victory was only a single thrust; the whole battle was already lost. "I thought you were offering to replace me on the Moidore case.''

"No I am not. Why?'' Runcorn's short, straight eyebrows rose. "Is it too much for your skills? You used to be the best detective on the force—at least that was what you told everyone!'' His voice grated with sour satisfaction. "But you've certainly lost your sharpness since your accident. You didn't do badly with the Grey case, but it took you long enough. I expect they'll hang Grey.'' He looked at Monk with satisfaction. He was sharp enough to have read Monk's feelings correctly, his sympathy for Menard.

"No they won't,'' Monk retorted. "They brought in the verdict this afternoon. Deportation for twenty-five years.'' He smiled, letting his triumph show. "He could make quite a decent life for himself in Australia.''

"If he doesn't die of fever,'' Runcorn said spitefully. "Or get killed in a riot, or starve.''

"That could happen in London.'' Monk kept his face expressionless.

"Well, don't stand there like a fool.'' Runcorn sat down behind his desk. "Why are you afraid of the Moidore case? You think it is beyond your ability?''

"It was someone in the house,'' Monk answered.

"Of course it was someone in the house.'' Runcorn glared at him. "What's the matter with you, Monk? Have you lost your wits? She was killed in the bedroom—someone broke in. No one suggested she was dragged out into the street.''

Monk took malicious pleasure in disabusing him.

"They were suggesting a burglar broke in,'' he said, framing each word carefully and precisely, as if to someone slow of understanding. He leaned a little forward. "I am saying that no one broke in and whoever murdered Sir Basil's daughter, he—or she—was in the house already—and is still in the house. Social tact supposes one of the servants; common sense says it is far more probably one of the family.''

Runcorn stared at him aghast, the blood draining from his

73

long face as the full implication came home to him. He saw the satisfaction in Monk's eyes.

"Preposterous," he said with a dry throat, the sound robbed of its force by his tongue sticking to the roof of his mouth. "What's the matter with you, Monk? Do you have some personal hatred against the aristocracy that you keep on accusing them of such monstrosity? Wasn't the Grey case enough for you? Have you finally taken leave of your senses?"

"The evidence is incontrovertible." Monk's pleasure was only in seeing the horror in Runcorn. The inspector would immeasurably rather have looked for an intruder turned violent, acutely difficult as it would be to trace such a one in the labyrinths of petty crime and poverty in the rookeries, as the worst slum tenements were known, whole areas where the police dared not intrude, still less maintain any rule of law. Even so it would be less fraught with personal danger than accusing, even by implication, a member of a family like the Moidores.

Runcorn opened his mouth, then closed it again.

"Yes sir?" Monk prompted, his eyes wide.

A succession of emotions chased each other over Runcorn's face: terror of the political repercussions if Monk offended people, behaved clumsily, could not back up with proof every single allegation he made; and then the double-edged hope that Monk might precipitate some disaster great enough to ruin him, and rid Runcorn of his footsteps forever at his heels.

"Get out," Runcorn said between his teeth. "And God help you if you make a mistake in this. You can be certain I shan't!"

"I never imagined you would—*sir*." And Monk stood at attention for a second—in mockery, not respect—then turned for the door.

He despaired Runcorn, and it was not until he was almost back to his rooms in Grafton Street that it occurred to him to wonder what Runcorn had been like when they first met, before Monk had threatened him with his ambition, his greater agility of mind, his quick, cruel wit. It was an unpleasant thought, and it took the warmth out of his feeling of superiority. He had almost certainly contributed to what the man had become. That Runcorn had always been weak, vain, less able, was a thin excuse, and any honesty at all evaporated it. The more flawed a man was, the shoddier it was to take advantage of his inadequacies to destroy him. If the strong were irresponsible and self-serving, what could the weak hope for?

Monk went to bed early and lay awake staring at the ceiling, disgusted with himself.

The funeral of Octavia Haslett was attended by half the aristocracy in London. The carriages stretched up and down Langham Place, stopping the normal traffic, black horses whenever possible, black plumes tossing, coachmen and footmen in livery, black crepe fluttering, harnesses polished like mirrors, but not a single piece that jingled or made a sound. An ambitious person might have recognized the crests of many noble families, not only of Britain but of France and the states of Germany as well. The mourners wore black, immaculate, devastatingly fashionable, enormous skirts hooped and petticoated, ribboned bonnets, gleaming top hats and polished boots.

Everything was done in silence, muffled hooves, well-oiled heels, whispering voices. The few passersby slowed down and bowed their heads in respect.

From his position like a waiting servant on the steps of All Saints Church, Monk saw the family arrive, first Sir Basil Moidore with his remaining daughter, Araminta, not even a black veil able to hide the blazing color of her hair or the whiteness of her face. They climbed the steps together, she holding his arm, although she seemed to support him as much as he her.

Next came Beatrice Moidore, very definitely upheld by Cyprian. She walked uprightly, but was so heavily veiled no expression was visible, but her back and shoulders were stiff and twice she stumbled and he helped her gently, speaking with his head close to hers.

Some distance behind, having come in a separate carriage, Myles Kellard and Romola Moidore came side by side, but not seeming to offer each other anything more than a formal accompaniment. Romola moved as if she was tired; her step was heavy and her shoulders a little bowed. She too wore a veil so her face was invisible. A few feet to her right Myles Kellard looked bleak, or perhaps it was boredom. He climbed the steps slowly, almost absently, and only when they reached the top did he offer her a hand at her elbow, more as a courtesy than a support.

Lastly came Fenella Sandeman in overdramatic black, a hat with too much decoration on it for a funeral, but undoubtedly handsome. Her waist was nipped in so she looked fragile, at a few yards' distance giving an impression of girlishness, then as she came closer one saw the too-dark hair and the faint withering of the skin. Monk did not know whether to pity her ridiculousness or admire her bravado.

Close behind her, and murmuring to her every now and again, was Septimus Thirsk. The hard gray daylight showed the weariness in his face and his sense of having been beaten, finding his moments of happiness in very small victories, the great ones having long ago been abandoned.

Monk did not go inside the church yet, but waited while the reverent, the grieving and the envious made their way past him. He overheard snatches of conversation, expressions of pity, but far more of outrage. What was the world coming to? Where was the much vaunted new Metropolitan Police Force while all this was going on? What was the purpose in paying to have them if people like the Moidores could be murdered in their own beds? One must speak to the Home Secretary and demand something be done!

Monk could imagine the outrage, the fear and the excuses that would take place over the next days or weeks. Whitehall would be spurred by complaints. Explanations would be offered, polite refusals given, and then when their lordships had left, Runcorn would be sent for and reports requested with icy disfavor hiding a hot panic.

And Runcorn would break out in a sweat of humiliation and anxiety. He hated failure and had no idea how to stand his ground. And he in turn would pass on his fears, disguised as official anger, to Monk.

Basil Moidore would be at the beginning of the chain—and at the end, when Monk returned to his house to tear apart the comfort and safe beliefs of his family, all their assumptions about one another and the dead woman they were burying with such a fashionable funeral now.

A newsboy strolled past as Monk turned to go inside.

" 'Orrible murder!'' the boy shouted out, regardless of

standing beside the church steps. "Police baffled! Read all about it!"

The service was very formal, sonorous voices intoning all the well-known words, organ music swelling somberly, everything jewel colors of stained glass, gray masses of stone, light on a hundred textures of black, the shuffle of feet and rustle of fabric. Someone sniffed. Footsteps were loud as ushers moved down the aisles. Boots squeaked.

Monk waited at the back, and as they left to go after the coffin to the family vault he followed as closely as he dared.

During the interment he stood behind them, next to a large man with a bald head, his few strands of hair fluttering in the sharpening November wind.

Beatrice Moidore was immediately in front of him, close to her husband now.

"Did you see that policeman here?" she asked him very quietly. "Standing at the back behind the Lewises."

"Of course," he replied. "Thank God at least he is discreet and he looks like a mourner."

"His suit is beautifully cut," she said with a lift of surprise in her voice. "They must pay them more than I thought. He almost looks like a gentleman."

"He does not," Basil said sharply. "Don't be ridiculous, Beatrice."

"He'll be back, you know." She ignored his criticism.

"Of course he'll be back," he said between his teeth. "He'll be back every day until he gives up—or discovers who it was."

"Why did you say 'give up' first?" she asked. "Don't you think he will find out?"

"I've no idea."

"Basil?"

"What?"

"What will we do if he doesn't?"

His voice was resigned. "Nothing. There is nothing to do."

"I don't think I can live the rest of my life not knowing."

He lifted his shoulders fractionally. "You will have to, my dear. There will be no alternative. Many cases are unsolved. We shall have to remember her as she was, grieve for her, and then continue our lives."

"Are you being willfully deaf to me, Basil?" Her voice shook only at the last word.

"I have heard every word you said, Beatrice—and replied to it," he said impatiently. Both of them remained looking ahead all the time, as if their full attention were on the interment. Opposite them Fenella was leaning heavily on Septimus. He propped her up automatically, his mind obviously elsewhere. From the look of sadness not only in his face but in the whole attitude of his body, he was thinking of Octavia.

"It was not an intruder," Beatrice went on with quiet anger. "Every day we shall look 'round at faces, listen to inflections of voices and hear double meanings in everything that is said, and wonder if it was that person, or if not, if they know who it was."

"You are being hysterical," Basil snapped, his voice hard in spite of its very quietness. "If it will help you to keep control of yourself, I'll dismiss all the servants and we'll hire a new staff. Now for God's sake pay attention to the service!"

"Dismiss the servants." Her words were strangled in her throat. "Oh, Basil! How will that help?"

He stood still, his body rigid under the black broadcloth, his shoulders high.

"Are you saying you think it was one of the family?" he said at last, all expression ironed out of his voice.

She lifted her head a little higher. "Wasn't it?"

"Do you know something, Beatrice?"

"Only what we all know—and what common sense tells me." Unconsciously she turned her head a fraction towards Myles Kellard on the far side of the crypt.

Beside him Araminta was staring back at her mother. She could not possibly have heard anything of what had passed between her parents, but her hands tightened in front of her, holding a small handkerchief and tearing it apart.

The interment was over. The vicar intoned the last amen, and the company turned to depart. Cyprian and his wife, Araminta with several feet between herself and her husband, Septimus militarily upright and Fenella staggering a trifle, lastly Sir Basil and Lady Moidore side by side.

Monk watched them go with pity, anger and a growing sense of darkness.

4

"DO YOU WANT ME to keep on looking for the jewelry?" Evan asked, his face puckered with doubt. Obviously he believed there was no purpose to it at all.

Monk agreed with him. In all probability it had been thrown away, or even destroyed. Whatever the motive had been for the death of Octavia Haslett, he was sure it was not robbery, not even a greedy servant sneaking into her room to steal. It would be too stupid to do it at the one time he, or she, could be absolutely sure Octavia would be there, when there was all day to do such a thing undisturbed.

"No," he said decisively. "Much better use your time questioning the servants." He smiled, baring his teeth, and Evan made a grimace back again. He had already been twice to the Moidore house, each time asking the same things and receiving much the same brief, nervous answers. He could not deduce guilt from their fear. Nearly all servants were afraid of the police; the sheer embarrassment of it was enough to shadow their reputations, let alone suspicion of having any knowledge of a murder. "Someone in that house killed her," he added.

Evan raised his eyebrows. "One of the servants?" He kept most of the surprise out of his voice, but there was still a lift of doubt there, and the innocence of his gaze only added to it.

"A far more comfortable thought," Monk replied. "We shall certainly find more favor with the powers in the land if we can arrest someone below stairs. But I think that is a gift we cannot reasonably look for. No, I was hoping that by talk-

79

ing with the servants enough we might learn something about the family. Servants notice a great deal, and although they're trained not to repeat any of it, they might unintentionally, if their own lives are in jeopardy." They were standing in Monk's office, smaller and darker than Runcorn's, even in this bright, sharp, late autumn morning. The plain wooden table was piled with papers, the old carpet worn in a track from door to chair. "You've seen most of them," he went on. "Any impressions so far?"

"Usual sort of complement," Evan said slowly. "Maids are mostly young—on the surface they look flighty, given to giggles and triviality." The sunlight came through the dusty window and picked out the fine lines on his face, throwing his expression into sharp relief. "And yet they earn their livings in a rigid world, full of obedience and among people who care little for them personally. They know a kind of reality that is harsher than mine. Some of the girls are only children." He looked up at Monk. "In another year or two I'll be old enough to be their father." The thought seemed to startle him, and he frowned. "The between-stairs maid is only twelve. I haven't discovered yet if they know anything of use, but I can't believe it was one of them."

"Maids?" Monk tried to clarify.

"Yes—older ones I suppose are possible." Evan looked dubious. "Can't think why they would, though."

"Men?"

"Can't imagine the butler." Evan smiled with a little twist. "He's a dry old stick, very formal, very military. If a person ever stirred passion of any sort in him I think it was so long ago even the memory of it has gone now. And why on earth would an excruciatingly respectable butler stab his mistress's daughter in her bedroom? What could he possibly be doing there in the middle of the night anyway?"

Monk smiled in spite of himself. "You don't read enough of the more lurid press, Evan. Listen to the running patterers some time."

"Rubbish," Evan said heartily. "Not Phillips."

"Footmen—grooms—bootboy?" Monk pressed. "And what about the older women?"

Evan was half leaning, half sitting on the windowsill.

"Grooms are in the stables and the back door is locked at

night,'' Evan replied. "Bootboy possibly, but he's only four-teen. Can't think of a motive for him. Older women—I sup-pose it is imaginable, some jealous or slight perhaps, but it would have to be a very violent one to provoke murder. None of them looks raving mad, or has ever shown the remotest inclination to violence. And they'd have to be mad to do such a thing. Anyway, passions in servants are far more often against each other. They are used to being spoken to in all manner of ways by the family.'' He looked at Monk with gravity beneath the wry amusement. "It's each other they take exception to. There's a rigid hierarchy, and there's been blood spilled before now over what job is whose.''

He saw Monk's expression.

"Oh—not murder. Just a few hard bruises and the occa-sional broken head,'' he explained. "But I think downstairs emotions concern others downstairs.''

"What about if Mrs. Haslett knew something about them, some past sin of thieving or immorality?'' Monk suggested. "That would lose them a very comfortable position. Without references they'd not get another—and a servant who can't get a place has nowhere to go but the sweatshops or the street.''

"Could be,'' Evan agreed. "Or the footmen. There are two—Harold and Percival. Both seem fairly ordinary so far. I should say Percival is the more intelligent, and perhaps am-bitious.''

"What does a footman aspire to be?'' Monk said a little waspishly.

"A butler, I imagine,'' Evan replied with a faint smile. "Don't look like that, sir. Butler is a comfortable, responsible and very respected position. Butlers consider themselves so-cially far superior to the police. They live in fine houses, eat the best, and drink it. I've seen butlers who drink better claret than their masters—''

"Do their masters know that?''

"Some masters don't have the palate to know claret from cooking wine.'' Evan shrugged. "All the same, it's a little kingdom that many men would find most attractive.''

Monk raised his eyebrows sarcastically. "And how would knifing the master's daughter get him any closer to this enjoy-able position?''

"It wouldn't—unless she knew something about him that would get him dismissed without a reference."

That was plausible, and Monk knew it.

"Then you had better go back and see what you can learn," he directed. "I'm going to speak to the family again, which I still think, unfortunately, is far more likely. I want to see them alone, away from Sir Basil." His face tightened. "He orchestrated the last time as if I had hardly been there."

"Master in his house." Evan hitched himself off the windowsill. "You can hardly be surprised."

"That is why I intend to see them away from Queen Anne Street, if I can," Monk replied tersely. "I daresay it will take me all week."

Evan rolled his eyes upward briefly, and without speaking again went out; Monk heard his footsteps down the stairs.

It did take Monk most of the week. He began straightaway with great success, almost immediately finding Romola Moidore walking in a leisurely fashion in Green Park. She started along the grass parallel with Constitution Row, gazing at the trees beyond by Buckingham Palace. The footman Percival had informed Monk she would be there, having ridden in the carriage with Mr. Cyprian, who was taking luncheon at his club in nearby Piccadilly.

She was expecting to meet a Mrs. Ketteridge, but Monk caught up with her while she was still alone. She was dressed entirely in black, as befitted a woman whose family was in mourning, but she still looked extremely smart. Her wide skirts were tiered and trimmed with velvet, the pergola sleeves of her dress were lined with black silk, her bonnet was small and worn low on the back of the head, and her hair was in the very fashionable style turned under at the ears into a lowset knot.

She was startled to see him, and not at all pleased. However there was nowhere for her to go to avoid him without being obvious, and perhaps she bore in mind her father-in-law's strictures that they were all to be helpful. He had not said so in so many words in Monk's hearing, but his implication was obvious.

"Good morning, Mr. Monk," she said coolly, standing quite still and facing him as if he were a stray dog that had approached too close and should be warded off with the fringed umbrella which she held firmly in her right hand, its point a little above the ground, ready to jab at him.

"Good morning, Mrs. Moidore," he replied, inclining his head a little in politeness.

"I really don't know anything of use to you." She tried to avoid the issue even now, as if he might go away. "I have no idea at all what can have happened. I still think you must have made a mistake—or been misled—"

"Were you fond of your sister-in-law, Mrs. Moidore?" he asked conversationally.

She tried to remain facing him, then decided she might as well walk, since it seemed he was determined to. She resented promenading with a policeman, as though he were a social acquaintance, and it showed in her face; although no one else would have known his station, certainly his clothes were almost as well cut and as fashionable as hers, and his bearing every bit as assured.

"Of course I was," she retorted hotly. "If I knew anything, I should not defend her attacker for an instant. I simply do not know."

"I do not doubt your honesty—or your indignation, ma'am," he said, although it was not entirely true. He trusted no one so far. "I was thinking that if you were fond of her, then you will have known her well. What kind of person was she?"

Romola was taken by surprise; the question was not what she had been expecting.

"I—well—it is very hard to say," she protested. "Really, that is a most unfair question. Poor Octavia is dead. It is most indecent to speak of the dead in anything but the kindest of terms, especially when they have died so terribly."

"I commend your delicacy, Mrs. Moidore," he replied with forced patience, measuring his step to hers. "But I believe at the moment truth, however tasteless, would serve her better. And since it seems an unavoidable conclusion that whoever murdered her is still in your house, you could be excused for placing your own safety, and that of your children, to the forefront of your thoughts."

That stopped her as if she had walked straight into one of the trees along the border. She drew in her breath sharply and almost cried out, then remembered the other passersby just in time and bit her knuckles instead.

"What kind of person was Mrs. Haslett?" Monk asked again.

She resumed her slow pace along the path, her face very pale, her skirts brushing the gravel.

"She was very emotional, very impulsive," she replied after only the briefest thought. "When she fell in love with Harry Haslett her family disapproved, but she was absolutely determined. She refused to consider anyone else. I have always been surprised that Sir Basil permitted it, but I suppose it was a perfectly acceptable match, and Lady Moidore approved. His family was excellent, and he had reasonable prospects for the future—" She shrugged. "Somewhat distant, but Octavia was a younger daughter, who could reasonably expect to have to wait."

"Had he an unfortunate reputation?" Monk asked.

"Not that I ever heard."

"Then why was Sir Basil so against the match? If he was of good family and had expectations, surely he would be agreeable?"

"I think it was a matter of personality. I know Sir Basil had been at school with his father and did not care for him. He was a year or two older, and a most successful person." She shrugged very slightly. "Sir Basil never said so, of course, but perhaps he cheated? Or in some other way that a gentleman would not mention, behaved dishonorably?" She looked straight ahead of her. A party of ladies and gentlemen was approaching and she nodded at them but did not make any sign of welcome. She was annoyed by the circumstance. Monk saw the color rise in her cheeks and guessed her dilemma. She did not wish them to speculate as to who he was that Romola walked alone with him in the park, and yet still less did she wish to introduce a policeman to her acquaintances.

He smiled sourly, a touch of mockery at himself, because it stung him, as well as at her. He despised her that appearances mattered so much, and himself because it caught him with a raw smart too, and for the same reasons.

"He was uncouth, brash?" he prompted with a trace of asperity.

"Not at all," she replied with satisfaction at contradicting

84

him. "He was charming, friendly, full of good humor, but like Octavia, determined to have his own way."

"Not easily governed," he said wryly, liking Harry Haslett more with each discovery.

"No—" There was a touch of envy in her now, and a real sadness that came through the polite, expected grief. "He was always kind for one's comfort, but he never pretended to an opinion he did not have."

"He sounds a most excellent man."

"He was. Octavia was devastated when he was killed—in the Crimea, you know. I can remember the day the news came. I thought she would never recover—" She tightened her lips and blinked hard, as if tears threatened to rob her of composure. "I am not sure she ever did," she added very quietly. "She loved him very much. I believe no one else in the family realized quite how much until then."

They had been gradually slowing their pace; now conscious again of the cold wind, they quickened.

"I am very sorry," he said, and meant it.

They were passed by a nurserymaid wheeling a perambulator—a brand-new invention which was much better than the old pulling carts, and which was causing something of a stir—and accompanied by a small, self-conscious boy with a hoop.

"She never even considered remarrying," Romola went on without being asked, and having regarded the perambulator with due interest. "Of course it was only a little over two years, but Sir Basil did approach the subject. She was a young woman, and still without children. It would not be unseemly."

Monk remembered the dead face he had seen that first morning. Even through the stiffness and the pallor he had imagined something of what she must have been like: the emotions, the hungers and the dreams. It was a face of passion and will.

"She was very comely?" He made it a question, although there was no doubt in his mind.

Romola hesitated, but there was no meanness in it, only a genuine doubt.

"She was handsome," she said slowly. "But her chief quality was her vividness, and her complete individuality. After Harry died she became very moody and suffered"—she avoided his eyes—"suffered a lot of poor health. When she

85

was well she was quite delightful, everyone found her so. But when she was . . ." Again she stopped momentarily and searched for the word. "When she was poorly she spoke little—and made no effort to charm."

Monk had a brief vision of what it must be like to be a woman on her own, obliged to work at pleasing people because your acceptance, perhaps even your financial survival, depended upon it. There must be hundreds—thousands—of petty accommodations, suppressions of your own beliefs and opinions because they would not be what someone else wished to hear. What a constant humiliation, like a burning blister on the heel which hurt with every step.

And on the other hand, what a desperate loneliness for a man if he ever realized he was always being told not what she really thought or felt but what she believed he wanted to hear. Would he then ever trust anything as real, or of value?

"Mr. Monk."

She was speaking, and his concentration had left her totally.

"Yes ma'am—I apologize—"

"You asked me about Octavia. I was endeavoring to tell you." She was irritated that he was so inattentive. "She was most appealing, at her best, and many men had called upon her, but she gave none of them the slightest encouragement. Whoever it was who killed her, I do not think you will find the slightest clue to their identity along that line of inquiry."

"No, I imagine you are right. And Mr. Haslett died in the Crimea?"

"Captain Haslett. Yes." She hesitated, looking away from him again. "Mr. Monk."

"Yes ma'am?"

"It occurs to me that some people—some men—have strange ideas about women who are widowed—" She was obviously most uncomfortable about what it was she was attempting to say.

"Indeed," he said encouragingly.

The wind caught at her bonnet, pulling it a little sideways, but she disregarded it. He wondered if she was trying to find a way to say what Sir Basil had prompted, and if the words would be his or her own.

Two little girls in frilled dresses passed by with their governess, walking very stiffly, eyes ahead as if unaware of the soldier coming the other way.

"It is not impossible that one of the servants, one of the men, entertained such—such ludicrous ideas—and became overfamiliar."

They had almost stopped. Romola poked at the ground with the ferrule of her umbrella.

"If—if that happened, and she rebuffed him soundly—possibly he became angry—incensed—I mean . . ." She tailed off miserably, still avoiding looking at him.

"In the middle of the night?" he said dubiously. "He was certainly extremely bold to go to her bedroom and try such a thing."

The color burned up her cheeks.

"Someone did," she pointed out with a catch in her voice, still staring at the ground. "I know it seems preposterous. Were she not dead, I should laugh at it myself."

"You are right," he said reluctantly. "Or it may be that she discovered some secret that could have ruined a servant had she told it, and they killed her to prevent that."

She looked up at him, her eyes wide. "Oh—yes, I suppose that sounds . . . possible. What kind of a secret? You mean dishonesty—immorality? But how would Tavie have learned of it?"

"I don't know. Have you no idea where she went that afternoon?" He began to walk again, and she accompanied him.

"No, none at all. She barely spoke to us that evening, except a silly argument over dinner, but nothing new was said."

"What was the argument about?"

"Nothing in particular—just frayed tempers." She looked straight ahead of her. "It was certainly nothing about where she went that afternoon, and nothing about any secret."

"Thank you, Mrs. Moidore. You have been very courteous." He stopped and she stopped also, relaxing a little as she sensed he was leaving.

"I wish I could help, Mr. Monk," she said with her face suddenly pinched and sad. For a moment grief overtook anxiety for herself and fear for the future. "If I recall anything—"

"Tell me—or Mr. Evan. Good day, ma'am."

"Good day." And she turned and walked away, but when

she had gone ten or fifteen yards she looked back again, not to say anything, simply to watch him leave the path and go back towards Piccadilly.

Monk knew that Cyprian Moidore was at his club, but he did not wish to ask for entry and interview him there because he felt it highly likely that he would be refused, and the humiliation would burn. Instead he waited outside on the pavement, kicking his heels, turning over in his mind what he would ask Cyprian when he finally came out.

Monk had been waiting about a quarter of an hour when two men passed him walking up towards Half Moon Street. There was something in the gait of one of them that struck a sharp chord in his memory, so vivid that he started forward to accost him. He had actually gone half a dozen steps before he realized that he had no idea who the man was, simply that for a moment he had seemed intimately familiar, and that there was both hope and sadness in him in that instant—and a terrible foreboding of pain to come.

He stood for another thirty minutes in the wind and fitful sun trying to bring back the face that had flashed on his recollection so briefly: a handsome, aristocratic face of a man at least sixty. And he knew the voice was light, very civilized, even a little affected—and knew it had been a major force in his life and the realization of ambition. He had copied him, his dress, his manner, even his inflection, in trying to lose his own unsophisticated Northumberland accent.

But all he recaptured were fragments, gone as soon as they were there, a feeling of success which was empty of flavor, a recurring pain as of some loss and some responsibility unfulfilled.

He was still standing undecided when Cyprian Moidore came down the steps of his club and along the street, only noticing Monk when he all but bumped into him.

"Oh—Monk." He stopped short. "Are you looking for me?"

Monk recalled himself to the present with a jolt.

"Yes—if you please, sir."

Cyprian looked anxious. "Have you—have you learned something?"

88

"No sir, I merely wanted to ask you more about your family."

"Oh." Cyprian started to walk again and Monk fell in beside him, back towards the park. Cyprian was dressed extremely fashionably, his concession to mourning in his dark coat over the jacket above the modern short waistcoat with its shawl collar, and his top hat was tall and straight sided. "Couldn't it have waited until I got home?" he asked with a frown.

"I just spoke to Mrs. Moidore, sir; in Green Park."

Cyprian seemed surprised, even a trifle discomfited. "I doubt she can tell you much. What exactly is it you wish to ask?"

Monk was obliged to walk smartly to keep up with him. "How long has your aunt, Mrs. Sandeman, lived in your father's house, sir?"

Cyprian winced very slightly, only a shadow across his face.

"Since shortly after her husband died," he replied brusquely.

Monk lengthened his own stride to match, avoiding bumping into the people moving less rapidly or passing in the opposite direction.

"Are she and your father very close?" He knew they were not; he had not forgotten the look on Fenella's face as she had left the morning room in Queen Anne Street.

Cyprian hesitated, then decided the lie would be transparent, if not now, then later.

"No. Aunt Fenella found herself in very reduced circumstances." His face was tight; he hated exposing such vulnerability. "Papa offered her a home. It is a natural family responsibility."

Monk tried to imagine it, the personal sense of obligation, the duty of gratitude, the implicit requirement of certain forms of obedience. He would like to know what affection there was beneath the duties, but he knew Cyprian would respond little to an open inquiry.

A carriage passed them too close to the curb, and its wheels sent up a spray of muddy water. Monk leaped inwards to preserve his trousers.

"It must have been very distressing for her to find herself suddenly thrown upon the resources of others," he said sympathetically. It was not feigned. He could imagine Fenella's shock—and profound resentment.

"Most," Cyprian agreed taciturnly. "But death frequently leaves widows in altered circumstances. One must expect it."

"Did she expect it?" Monk absently brushed the water off his coat.

Cyprian smiled, possibly at Monk's unconscious vanity.

"I have no idea, Mr. Monk. I did not ask her. It would have been both impertinent and intrusive. It was not my place, nor is it yours. It happened many years ago, twelve to be precise, and has no bearing on our present tragedy."

"Is Mr. Thirsk in the same unfortunate position?" Monk kept exactly level with him along the pavement, brushing past three fashionable ladies taking the air and a couple dallying in polite flirtation in spite of the cold.

"He resides with us because of misfortune," Cyprian snapped. "If that is what you mean. Obviously he was not widowed." He smiled briefly in a sarcasm that had more bitterness than amusement.

"How long has he lived in Queen Anne Street?"

"About ten years, as far as I recall."

"And he is your mother's brother?"

"You are already aware of that." He dodged a group of gentlemen ambling along deep in conversation and oblivious of the obstruction they caused. "Really, if this is a sample of your attempts at detection, I am surprised you maintain employment. Uncle Septimus occasionally drinks a little more than you may consider prudent, and he is certainly not wealthy, but he is a kind and decent man whose misfortune has nothing whatever to do with my sister's death, and you will learn nothing useful by prying into it!"

Monk admired him for his defense, true or not. And he determined to discover what the misfortune was, and if Octavia had learned something about him that might have robbed him of this double-edged but much needed hospitality had she told her father.

"Does he gamble, sir?" he said aloud.

"What?" But there was a flush of color on Cyprian's cheeks, and he knocked against an elderly gentleman in his path and was obliged to apologize.

A coster's cart came by, its owner crying his wares in a loud, singsong voice.

"I wondered if Mr. Thirsk gambled," Monk repeated. "It is a pastime many gentlemen indulge in, especially if their lives offer little other change or excitement—and any extra finance would be welcome."

Cyprian's face remained carefully expressionless, but the color in his cheeks did not fade, and Monk guessed he had touched a nerve, whether on Septimus's account or Cyprian's own.

"Does he belong to the same club as you do, sir?" Monk turned and faced him.

"No," Cyprian replied, resuming walking after only a momentary hesitation. "No, Uncle Septimus has his own club."

"Not to his taste?" Monk made it sound very casual.

"No," Cyprian agreed quickly. "He prefers more men his own age—and experience, I suppose."

They crossed Hamilton Place, hesitating for a carriage and dodging a hansom.

"What would that be?" Monk asked when they were on the pavement again.

Cyprian said nothing.

"Is Sir Basil aware that Mr. Thirsk gambles from time to time?" Monk pursued.

Cyprian drew in his breath, then let it out slowly before answering. Monk knew he had considered denying it, then put loyalty to Septimus before loyalty to his father. It was another judgment Monk approved.

"Probably not," Cyprian said. "I would appreciate it if you did not find it necessary to inform him."

"I can think of no circumstance in which it would be necessary," Monk agreed. He made an educated guess, based on the nature of the club from which Cyprian had emerged. "Similarly your own gambling, sir."

Cyprian stopped and swiveled to face him, his eyes wide. Then he saw Monk's expression and relaxed, a faint smile on his lips, before resuming his stride.

"Was Mrs. Haslett aware of this?" Monk asked him. "Could that be what she meant when she said Mr. Thirsk would understand what she had discovered?"

"I have no idea." Cyprian looked miserable.

91

"What else have they particularly in common?" Monk went on. "What interests or experiences that would make his sympathy the sharper? Is Mr. Thirsk a widower?"

"No—no, he never married."

"And yet he did not always live in Queen Anne Street. Where did he live before that?"

Cyprian walked in silence. They crossed Hyde Park Corner, taking several minutes to avoid carriages, hansoms, a dray with four fine Clydesdales drawing it, several costers' carts and a crossing sweeper darting in and out like a minnow trying to clear a path and catch his odd penny rewards at the same time. Monk was pleased to see Cyprian toss him a coin, and added another to it himself.

On the far side they went past the beginning of Rotten Row and strolled across the grass towards the Serpentine. A troop of gentlemen in immaculate habits rode along the Row, their horses' hooves thudding on the damp earth. Two of them laughed loudly and broke into a canter, harness jingling. Ahead of them three women turned back to look.

Cyprian made up his mind at last.

"Uncle Septimus was in the army. He was cashiered. That is why he has no means. Father took him in. He was a younger son so he inherited nothing. There was nowhere else for him."

"How distressing." Monk meant it. He could imagine quite sharply the sudden reduction from the finance, power and status of an officer to the ignominy and poverty, and the utter friendlessness, of being cashiered, stripped of everything—and to your friends, ceasing to exist.

"It wasn't dishonesty or cowardice," Cyprian went on, now that he was started, his voice urgent, concerned that Monk should know the truth. "He fell in love, and his love was very much returned. He says he did nothing about it—no affair, but that hardly makes it any better—"

Monk was startled. There was no sense in it. Officers were permitted to marry, and many did.

Cyprian's face was full of pity—and wry, deprecating humor.

"I see you don't understand. You will. She was the colonel's wife."

"Oh—" There was nothing more to add. It was an offense that would be inexcusable. Honor was touched, and even more, vanity. A colonel so mortified would have no retaliation except to use his office. "I see."

"Yes. Poor Septimus. He never loved anyone else. He was well in his forties at that time, a major with an excellent record." He stopped speaking and they passed a man and a woman, apparently acquaintances from their polite nods. He tipped his hat and resumed only when they were out of earshot. "He could have been a colonel himself, if his family could have afforded it—but commissions aren't cheap these days. And the higher you go—" He shrugged. "Anyway, that was the end of it. Septimus found himself middle-aged, despised and penniless. Naturally he appealed to Mama, and then came to live with us. If he gambles now and then, who's to blame him? There's little enough pleasure in his life."

"But your father would not approve?"

"No he would not." Cyprian's face took on a sudden anger. "Especially since Uncle Septimus usually wins!"

Monk took a blind guess. "Whereas you more usually lose?"

"Not always, and nothing I can't afford. Sometimes I win."

"Did Mrs. Haslett know this—of either of you?"

"I never discussed it with her—but I think she probably knew, or guessed about Uncle Septimus. He used to bring her presents when he won." His face looked suddenly bleak again. "He was very fond of her. She was easy to like, very—" He looked for the word and could not find it. "She had weaknesses that made her comfortable to talk to. She was hurt easily, but for other people, not a matter of her taking offense—Tavie never took offense."

The pain deepened in his face and he looked intensely vulnerable. He stared straight ahead into the cold wind. "She laughed when things were funny. Nobody could tell her who to like and who not to; she made up her own mind. She cried when she was upset, but she never sulked. Lately she drank a little more than was becoming to a lady—" His mouth twisted as he self-consciously used such a euphemism. "And she was disastrously honest." He fell silent, staring across at the wind ripples whipping the water of the Serpentine. Had it not been totally impossible that a gentleman should weep in a public place, Monk thought at that moment Cyprian might have.

Whatever Cyprian knew or guessed about her death, he grieved acutely for his sister.

Monk did not intrude.

Another couple walked past them, the man in the uniform of the Hussars, the woman's skirt fashionably fringed and fussy.

Finally Cyprian regained his self-control.

"It would have been something despicable," he continued. "And probably still a danger to someone before Tavie would have told another person's secret, Inspector." He spoke with conviction. "If some servant had had an illegitimate child, or a passionate affair, Tavie was the last person who would have betrayed them to Papa—or anyone else. I don't honestly think she would have reported a theft, unless it had been something of immense value."

"So the secret she discovered that afternoon was no trivial one, but something of profound ugliness," Monk said in reply.

Cyprian's face closed. "It would seem so. I'm sorry I cannot help you any further, but I really have no idea what such a thing could be, or about whom."

"You have made the picture much clearer with your candor. Thank you, sir." Monk bowed very slightly, and after Cyprian's acknowledgment, took his leave. He walked back along the Serpentine to Hyde Park Corner, but this time going briskly up Constitution Hill towards Buckingham Palace and St. James's.

It was the middle of the afternoon when he met Sir Basil, who was coming across the Horse Guards Parade from Whitehall. He looked startled to see Monk.

"Have you something to report?" he said rather abruptly. He was dressed in dark city trousers and a frock coat seamed at the waist as was the latest cut. His top hat was tall and straight sided, and worn elegantly a little to one side on his head.

"Not yet, sir," Monk answered, wondering what he had expected so soon. "I have a few questions to ask."

Basil frowned. "That could not have waited until I was at home? I do not appreciate being accosted in the street, Inspector."

Monk made no apology. "Some information about the servants which I cannot obtain from the butler."

"There is none," Basil said frostily. "It is the butler's job to employ the servants and to interview them and evaluate their references. If I did not believe he was competent to do it, I should replace him."

"Indeed." Already Monk was stung by his tone of voice and the sharp, chilly look in his eyes, as if Monk's ignorance were no more than he expected. "But were there any disciplining to do, would you not be made aware of it?"

"I doubt it, unless it concerned a member of the family—which, I presume, is what you are suggesting?" Basil replied. "Mere impertinences or tardiness would be dealt with by Phillips, or in the female servants' case, by the housekeeper, or the cook. Dishonesty or moral laxity would incur dismissal, and Phillips would engage a replacement. I would know about that. But surely you did not follow me to Westminster to ask me such paltry things, which you could have asked the butler—or anyone else in the house!"

"I cannot expect the same degree of truth from anyone else in the house, sir," Monk snapped back tartly. "Since one of them is responsible for Mrs. Haslett's death, they may be somewhat partisan in the matter."

Basil glared at him, the wind catching at the tails of his jacket and sending them flapping. He took his high hat off to save the indignity of having it blown askew.

"What do you imagine they would lie about to you and have the remotest chance of getting by with it?" he said with an edge of sarcasm.

Monk ignored the question.

"Any personal relationships between your staff, sir?" he asked instead. "Footmen and maids, for example? The butler and one of the ladies' maids—bootboy and scullery maid?"

Basil's black eyes widened in disbelief.

"Good God! Do you imagine I have the slightest idea—or any interest in the romantic daydreams of my servants, Inspector? You seem to live in a quite different world from the one I inhabit—or men like me."

Monk was furious and he did not even attempt to curb his tongue.

"Do I take it, Sir Basil, that you would have no concern if your male and female servants have liaisons with each other," he said sarcastically. "In twos—or threes—or whatever? You are quite right—it *is* a different world. The middle classes are obsessed with preventing such a thing.''

The insolence was palpable, and for a moment Sir Basil's temper flashed close to violence, but he was apparently aware that he had invited such a comment, because he moderated his reply uncharacteristically. It was merely contemptuous.

''I find it hard to believe you can maintain your position, such as it is, and be as stupid as you pretend. Of course I should forbid anything of the sort, and dismiss any staff so involved instantly and without reference.''

''And if there were such an involvement, presumably it is possible Mrs. Haslett might have become aware of it?'' Monk asked blandly, aware of their mutual dislike and both their reasons for masking it.

He was surprised how quickly Basil's expression lightened, something almost like a smile coming to his lips.

''I suppose she might,'' he agreed, grasping the idea. ''Yes, women are observant of such things. They notice inflections we are inclined to miss. Romance and its intrigue form a much greater part in their lives than they do of ours. It would be natural.''

Monk appeared as innocent as he was capable.

''What do you suppose she might have discovered on her trip in the afternoon that affected her so deeply she spoke to Mr. Thirsk of it?'' he asked. ''Was there a servant for whom she had a particular regard?''

Basil was temporarily confused. He struggled for an answer that would fit all the facts they knew.

''Her ladies' maid, I imagine. That is usual. Otherwise I am aware of no special regard,'' he said carefully. ''And it seems she did not tell anyone where she went.''

''What time off do the servants have?'' Monk pursued. ''Away from the house.''

''Half a day every other week,'' Basil replied immediately. ''That is customary.''

''Not a great deal for indulging in romance,'' Monk observed. ''It would seem more probable that whatever it was took place in Queen Anne Street.''

Sir Basil's black eyes were hard, and he slapped at his fluttering coattails irritably.

''If you are trying to say that there was something very

serious taking place in my house, of which I was unaware, indeed still am unaware, Inspector, then you have succeeded. Now if you can be as efficient in doing what you are paid for—and discover what it was—we shall all be most obliged. If there is nothing further, good day to you!''

Monk smiled. He had alarmed him, which was what he intended. Now Basil would go home and start demanding a lot of pertinent and inconvenient answers.

''Good day, Sir Basil.'' Monk tipped his hat very slightly, and turning on his heel, marched on towards Horse Guards Parade, leaving Basil standing on the grass with a face heavy with anger and hardening resolution.

Monk attempted to see Myles Kellard at the merchant bank where he held a position, but he had already left for the day. And he had no desire to see any of the household in Queen Anne Street, where he would be most unlikely to be uninterrupted by Sir Basil or Cyprian.

Instead he made a few inquiries of the doorman of Cyprian's club and learned almost nothing, except that he visited it frequently, and certainly gentlemen did have a flutter on cards or horses from time to time. He really could not say how much; it was hardly anyone else's concern. Gentlemen always settled their debts of honor, or they would be blackballed instantly, not only here but in all probability by every other club in town as well. No, he did not know Mr. Septimus Thirsk; indeed he had not heard that gentleman's name before.

Monk found Evan back at the police station and they compared the results of their day. Evan was tired, and although he had expected to learn little he was still discouraged that that was what had happened. There was a bubble of hope in him that always regarded the best of possibilities.

''Nothing you would call a romance,'' he said dispiritedly, sitting on the broad ledge of the windowsill in Monk's office. ''I gather from one of the laundrymaids, Lizzie, that she thinks the bootboy had a yearning toward Dinah, the parlormaid, who is tall and fair with skin like cream and a waist you could put your hands 'round.'' His eyes widened as he visualized her in his memory. ''And she's not yet had so much attention paid her that she's full of airs. But then that seems hardly worthy of comment. Both footmen and both grooms also admire her very heartily. I must admit, so did I.'' He smiled, robbing the remark of any seriousness. "Dinah is as yet un-moved in return. General opinion is that she will set her cap a good deal higher."

"Is that all?" Monk asked with a wry expression. "You spent all day below stairs to learn that? Nothing about the family?"

"Not yet," Evan apologized. "But I am still trying. The other laundrymaid, Rose, is a pretty thing, very small and dark with eyes like cornflowers—and an excellent mimic, by the way. She has a dislike for the footman Percival, which sounds to me as if it may be rooted in having once been something much warmer—"

"Evan!"

Evan opened his eyes wide in innocence. "Based on much observation by the upstairs maid Maggie and the ladies' maid Mary, who has a high regard for other people's romances, moving them along wherever she can. And the other upstairs maid, Annie, has a sharp dislike for poor Percival, although she wouldn't say why."

"Very enlightening," Monk said sarcastically. "Get an in-stant conviction before any jury with that."

"Don't dismiss it too lightly, sir," Evan said quite seri-ously, hitching himself off the sill. "Young girls like that, with little else to occupy their minds, can be very observant. A lot of it is superficial, but underneath the giggles they see a great deal."

"I suppose so," Monk said dubiously. "But we'll need to do much better than that to satisfy either Runcorn or the law."

Evan shrugged. "I'll go back tomorrow, but I don't know what else to ask anyone."

Monk found Septimus the following lunchtime in the public house which he frequented regularly. It was a small, cheerful place just off the Strand, known for its patronage by actors and law students. Groups of young men stood around talking ea-gerly, gesticulating, flinging arms in the air and poking fingers at an imaginary audience, but whether it was envisioned in a theater or a courtroom was impossible even to guess. There was a smell of sawdust and ale, and at this time of the day, a pleasant steam of vegetables, gravy and thick pastry.

He had been there only a few minutes, with a glass of cider, when he saw Septimus alone on a leather-upholstered seat in the corner, drinking. He walked over and sat down opposite him.

"Good day, Inspector." Septimus put down his mug, and it was a moment before Monk realized how he had seen him while he was still drinking. The mug's bottom was glass, an old-fashioned custom so a drinker might not be taken by surprise in the days when men carried swords and coaching inn brawls were not uncommon.

"Good day, Mr. Thirsk," Monk replied, and he admired the mug with Septimus's name engraved on it.

"I cannot tell you anything more," Septimus said with a sad little smile. "If I knew who killed Tavie, or had the faintest idea why, I would have come to you without your bothering to follow me here."

Monk sipped his cider.

"I came because I thought it would be easier to speak without interruption here than it would in Queen Anne Street."

Septimus's faded blue eyes lit with a moment's humor. "You mean without Basil's reminding me of my obligation, my duty to be discreet and behave like a gentleman, even if I cannot afford to be one, except now and again, by his grace and favor."

Monk did not insult him by evasion. "Something like that," he agreed. He glanced sideways as a young man with a fair face, not unlike Evan, lurched close to them in mock despair, clutching his heart, then began a dramatic monologue directed at his fellows at a neighboring table. Even after a full minute or two, Monk was not sure whether he was an aspiring actor or a would-be lawyer defending a client. He thought briefly and satirically of Oliver Rathbone, and pictured him as a callow youth at some public house like this.

"I see no military men," he remarked, looking back at Septimus.

Septimus smiled down into his ale. "Someone has told you my story."

"Mr. Cyprian," Monk admitted. "With great sympathy."

"He would." Septimus pulled a face. "Now if you had asked Myles you would have had quite a different tale, meaner, grubbier, less flattering to women. And dear Fenella . . ." He took another deep draft of his ale. "Hers would have been

99

more lurid, far more dramatic; the tragedy would have become grotesque, the love a frenzied passion, the whole thing rather gaudy; the real feeling, and the real pain, lost in effect—like the colored lights of a stage."

"And yet you like to come to a public house full of actors of one sort or another," Monk pointed out.

Septimus looked across the tables and his eye fell on a man of perhaps thirty-five, lean and oddly dressed, his face animated, but under the mask a weariness of disappointed hopes.

"I like it here," he said gently. "I like the people. They have imagination to take them out of the commonplace, to forget the defeats of reality and feed on the triumphs of dreams." His face was softened, its tired lines lifted by tolerance and affection. "They can evoke any mood they want into their faces and make themselves believe it for an hour or two. That takes courage, Mr. Monk; it takes a rare inner strength. The world, people like Basil, find it ridiculous—but I find it very heartening."

There was a roar of laughter from one of the other tables, and for a moment he glanced towards it before turning back to Monk again. "If we can still surmount what is natural and believe what we wish to believe, in spite of the force of evidence, then for a while at least we are masters of our fate, and we can paint the world we want. I had rather do it with actors than with too much wine or a pipe full of opium."

Someone climbed on a chair and began an oration to a few catcalls and a smattering of applause.

"And I like their humor," Septimus went on. "They know how to laugh at themselves and each other—they like to laugh, they don't see any sin in it, or any danger to their dignity. They like to argue. They don't feel it a mortal wound if anyone queries what they say, indeed they expect to be questioned." He smiled ruefully. "And if they are forced to a new idea, they turn it over like a child with a toy. They may be vain, Mr. Monk; indeed they assuredly are vain, like a garden full of peacocks forever fanning their tails and squawking." He looked at Monk without perception or double meaning. "And they are ambitious, self-absorbed, quarrelsome and often supremely trivial."

Monk felt a pang of guilt, as if an arrow had brushed by his cheek and missed its mark.

100

"But they amuse me," Septimus said gently. "And they listen to me without condemnation, and never once has one of them tried to convince me I have some moral or social obligation to be different. No, Mr. Monk, I enjoy myself here. I feel comfortable."

"You have explained yourself excellently, sir." Monk smiled at him, for once without guile. "I understand why. Tell me something about Mr. Kellard."

The pleasure vanished out of Septimus's face. "Why? Do you think he had something to do with Tavie's death?"

"Is it likely, do you think?"

Septimus shrugged and set down his mug.

"I don't know. I don't like the man. My opinion is of no use to you."

"Why do you not like him, Mr. Thirsk?"

But the old military code of honor was too strong. Septimus smiled dryly, full of self-mockery. "A matter of instinct, Mr. Monk," he lied, and Monk knew he was lying. "We have nothing in common in our natures or our interests. He is a banker, I was a soldier, and now I am a time server, enjoying the company of young men who playact and tell stories about crime and passion and the criminal world. And I laugh at all the wrong things, and drink too much now and again. I ruined my life over the love of a woman." He turned the mug in his hand, fingers caressing it. "Myles despises that. I think it is absurd—but not contemptible. At least I was capable of such a feeling. There is something to be said for that."

"There is everything to be said for it." Monk surprised himself; he had no memory of ever having loved, let alone to such cost, and yet he knew without question that to care for any person or issue enough to sacrifice greatly for it was the surest sign of being wholly alive. What a waste of the essence of a man that he should never give enough of himself to any cause, that he should always hear that passive, cowardly voice uppermost which counts the cost and puts caution first. One would grow old and die with the power of one's soul untasted.

And yet there was something. Even as the thoughts passed through his mind a memory stirred of intense emotions, outrage and grief for someone else, a passion to fight at all costs, not for himself but for others—and for one in particular. He knew loyalty and gratitude, he simply could not force it back into his mind for whom.

Septimus was looking at him curiously.

Monk smiled. "Perhaps he envies you, Mr. Thirsk," he said spontaneously.

Septimus's eyebrows rose in amazement. He looked at Monk's face, seeking sarcasm, and found none.

Monk explained himself. "Without realizing it," he added. "Maybe Mr. Kellard lacks the depth, or the courage, to feel anything deeply enough to pay for it. To suspect yourself a coward is a very bitter thing indeed."

Very slowly Septimus smiled, with great sweetness.

"Thank you, Mr. Monk. That is the finest thing anyone has said to me in years." Then he bit his lip. "I am sorry. I still cannot tell you anything about Myles. All I know is suspicion, and it is not my wound to expose. Perhaps there is no wound at all, and he is merely a bored man with too much time on his hands and an imagination that works too hard."

Monk did not press him. He knew it would serve no purpose. Septimus was quite capable of keeping silence if he felt honor required it, and taking whatever consequences there were.

Monk finished his cider. "I'll go and see Mr. Kellard myself. But if you do think of anything that suggests what Mrs. Haslett had discovered that last day, what it was she thought you would understand better than others, please let me know. It may well be that this secret was what caused her death."

"I have thought," Septimus replied, screwing up his face. "I have gone over and over in my mind everything we have in common, or that she might have believed we had, and I have found very little. We neither of us cared for Myles—but that seems very trivial. He has never injured me in any way—nor her, that I am aware of. We were both financially dependent upon Basil—but then so is everyone else in the house!"

"Is Mr. Kellard not remunerated for his work at the bank?" Monk was surprised.

Septimus looked at him with mild scorn, not unkindly.

"Certainly. But not to the extent that will support him in the way to which he would like to be accustomed—and definitely not Araminta as well. Also there are social implications to be considered; there are benefits to being Basil Moidore's

102

daughter which do not accrue to being merely Myles Kellard's wife, not least of them living in Queen Anne Street.''

Monk had not expected to feel any sympathy for Myles Kellard, but that single sentence, with its wealth of implications, gave him a sudden very sharp change of perception.

''Perhaps you are not aware of the level of entertaining that is conducted there,'' Septimus continued, ''when the house is not in mourning? We regularly dined diplomats and cabinet ministers, ambassadors and foreign princes, industrial moguls, patrons of the arts and sciences, and on occasion even minor members of our own royalty. Not a few duchesses and dozens of society called in the afternoons. And of course there were all the invitations in return. I should think there are few of the great houses that have not received the Moidores at one time or another.''

''Did Mrs. Haslett feel the same way?'' Monk asked.

Septimus smiled with a rueful turning down of the lips. ''She had no choice. She and Haslett were to have moved into a house of their own, but he went into the army before it could be accomplished, and of course Tavie remained in Queen Anne Street. And then Harry, the poor beggar, was killed at Inkermann. One of the saddest things I know. He was the devil of a nice fellow.'' He stared into the bottom of his mug, not at the ale dregs but into old grief that still hurt. ''Tavie never got over it. She loved him—more than the rest of the family ever understood.''

''I'm sorry,'' Monk said gently. ''You were very fond of Mrs. Haslett—''

Septimus looked up. ''Yes, yes I was. She used to listen to me as if what I said mattered to her. She would let me ramble on—sometimes we drank a little too much together. She was kinder than Fenella—'' He stopped, realizing he was on the verge of behaving like less than a gentleman. He stiffened his back painfully and lifted his chin. ''If I can help, Inspector, you may be assured that I will.''

''I am assured, Mr. Thirsk.'' Monk rose to his feet. ''Thank you for your time.''

''I have more of it than I need.'' Septimus smiled, but it did not reach his eyes. Then he tipped up his mug and drank the dregs, and Monk could see his face distorted through the glass bottom.

* * *

Monk found Fenella Sandeman the next day at the end of a long late-morning ride, standing by her horse at the Kensington Gardens end of Rotten Row. She was superbly dressed in a black riding habit with gleaming boots and immaculate black Mousquetaire hat. Only her high-necked blouse and stock were vivid white. Her dark hair was neatly arranged, and her face with its unnatural color and painted eyebrows looked rakish and artificial in the cool November daylight.

"Why, Mr. Monk," she said in amazement, looking him up and down and evidently approving what she saw. "Whatever brings you walking in the park?" She gave a girlish giggle. "Shouldn't you be questioning the servants or something? How does one detect?"

She ignored her horse, leaving the rein loosely over her arm as if that were sufficient.

"In a large number of ways, ma'am." He tried to be courteous and at the same time not play to her mood of levity. "Before I speak to the servants I would like to gain a clearer impression from the family, so that when I do ask questions they are the right ones."

"So you've come to interrogate me." She shivered melodramatically. "Well, Inspector, ask me anything. I shall give you what answers I consider wisest." She was a small woman, and she looked up at him through half-closed lashes.

Surely she could not be drunk this early in the day? She must be amusing herself at his expense. He affected not to notice her flippancy and kept a perfectly sober face, as if they were engaged in a serious conversation which might yield important information.

"Thank you, Mrs. Sandeman. I am informed you have lived in Queen Anne Street since shortly after the death of your husband some eleven or twelve years ago—"

"You have been delving into my past!" Her voice was husky, and far from being annoyed, she sounded flattered by the thought.

"Into everyone's, ma'am," he said coldly. "If you have been there such a time, you will have had frequent opportunity to observe both the family and the staff. You must know them all quite well."

She swung the riding crop, startling the horse and narrowly

104

missing its head. She seemed quite oblivious of the animal, and fortunately it was sufficiently well schooled. It remained close to her, measuring its pace obediently to hers as she moved very slowly along the path.

"Of course," she agreed jauntily. "Who do you wish to know about?" She shrugged her beautifully clothed shoulders. "Myles is fun, but quite worthless—but then some of the most attractive men are, don't you think?" She turned sideways to look at him. Her eyes must have been marvelous once, very large and dark. Now the rest of her face had so altered they were grotesque.

He smiled very slightly. "I think my interest in them is probably very different from yours, Mrs. Sandeman."

She laughed uproariously for several moments, causing half a dozen people within earshot to turn curiously to find the cause of such mirth. When she had regained her composure she was still openly amused.

Monk was discomfited. He disliked being stared at as a matter of ribaldry.

"Don't you find pious women very tedious, Mr. Monk?" She opened her eyes very wide. "Be honest with me."

"Are there pious women in your family, Mrs. Sandeman?" His voice was cooler than he intended, but if she was aware she gave no sign.

"It's full of them." She sighed. "Absolutely prickling like fleas on a hedgehog. My mother was one, may heaven rest her soul. My sister-in-law is another, may heaven preserve me—I live in her house. You have no idea how hard it is to have any privacy! Pious women are so good at minding other people's business—I suppose it is so much more interesting than their own." She laughed again with a rich, gurgling sound.

He was becoming increasingly aware that she found him attractive, and it made him intensely uncomfortable.

"And Araminta is worse, poor creature," she continued, walking with grace and swinging her stick. The horse plodded obediently at her heels, its rein trailing loosely over her arm. "I suppose she has to be, with Myles. I told you he was worthless, didn't I? Of course Tavie was all right." She looked straight ahead of her along the Row towards a fashionable group riding slowly in their direction. "She drank, you know?" She glanced at him, then away again. "All that tom-

105

myrot about ill health and headaches! She was drunk—or suffering the aftereffects. She took it from the kitchen.'' She shrugged. ''I daresay one of the servants gave it to her. They all liked her because she was generous. Took advantage, if you ask me. Treat servants above their station, and they forget who they are and take liberties.''

Then she swung around and stared at him, her eyes exaggeratedly wide. ''Oh, my goodness! Oh, my dear, how perfectly awful. Do you suppose that was what happened to her?'' Her very small, elegantly gloved hand flew to her mouth. ''She was overfamiliar with one of the servants? He ran away with the wrong idea—or, heaven help us, the right one,'' she said breathlessly. ''And then she fought him off—and he killed her in the heat of his passion? Oh, how perfectly frightful. What a scandal!'' She gulped. ''Ha-ha-ha. Basil will never get over it. Just imagine what his friends will say.''

Monk was unaccountably revolted, not by the thought, which was pedestrian enough, but by her excitement at it. He controlled his disgust with difficulty, unconsciously taking a step backwards.

''Do you think that is what happened, ma'am?''

She heard nothing in his tone to dampen her titillation.

''Oh, it is quite possible,'' she went on, painting the picture for herself, turning away and beginning to walk again. ''I know just the man to have done it. Percival—one of the footmen. Fine-looking man—but then all footmen are, don't you think?'' She glanced sideways, then away again. ''No, perhaps you don't. I daresay you've never had much occasion. Not many footmen in your line of work.'' She laughed again and hunched her shoulders without looking at him. ''Percival has that kind of face—far too intelligent to be a good servant. Ambitious. And such a marvelously cruel mouth. A man with a mouth like that could do anything.'' She shuddered, wriggling her body as if shedding some encumbrance—or feeling something delicious against her skin. It occurred to Monk to wonder if perhaps she herself had encouraged the young footman into a relationship above and outside his station. But looking at her immaculate, artificial face the thought was peculiarly repellent. As close as he was to her now, in the hard daylight, it was clear that she must be nearer sixty than fifty, and Percival not more than thirty at the very outside.

"Have you any grounds for that idea, Mrs. Sandeman, other than what you observe in his face?" he asked her.

"Oh—you are angry." She turned her limpid gaze up at him. "I have offended your sense of propriety. You are a trifle pious yourself, aren't you, Inspector?"

Was he? He had no idea. He knew his instinctive reaction now: the gentle, vulnerable faces like Imogen Latterly's that stirred his emotions; the passionate, intelligent ones like Hester's which both pleased and irritated him; the calculating, predatorily female ones like Fenella Sandeman's which he found alien and distasteful. But he had no memory of any actual relationship. Was he a prig, a cold man, selfish and incapable of commitment, even short-lived?

"No, Mrs. Sandeman, but I am offended by the idea of a footman who takes liberties with his mistress's daughter and then knifes her to death," he said ruthlessly. "Are you not?"

Still she was not angry. Her boredom cut him more deeply than any subtle insult or mere aloofness.

"Oh, how sordid. Yes of course I am. You do have a crass way with words, Inspector. One could not have you in the withdrawing room. Such a shame. You have a—" She regarded him with a frank appreciation which he found very unnerving. "An air of danger about you." Her eyes were very bright and she stared at him invitingly.

He knew what the euphemism stood for, and found himself backing away.

"Most people find police intrusive, ma'am; I am used to it. Thank you for your time, you have been most helpful." And he bowed very slightly and turned on his heel, leaving her standing beside her horse with her crop in one hand and the rein still over her arm. Before he had reached the edge of the grass she was speaking to a middle-aged gentleman who had just dismounted from a large gray and was flattering her shamelessly.

He found the idea of an amorous footman both unpleasant and unlikely, but it could not be dismissed. He had put off interviewing the servants himself for too long. He hailed a hansom along the Knightsbridge Road and directed it to take him to Queen Anne Street, where he paid the driver and went down the areaway steps to the back door.

107

Inside the kitchen was warm and busy and full of the odors of roasting meat, baking pastry and fresh apples. Coils of peel lay on the table, and Mrs. Boden, the cook, was up to her elbows in flour. Her face was red with exertion and heat, but she had an agreeable expression and was still a handsome woman, even though the veins were beginning to break on her skin and when she smiled her teeth were discolored and would not last much longer.

"If you're wanting your Mr. Evan, he's in the housekeeper's sitting room," she greeted Monk. "And if you're looking for a cup o' tea you're too soon. Come back in half an hour. And don't get under my feet. I've dinner to think of; even in mourning they've still got to eat—and so have all of us."

"Us" were the servants, and he noted the distinction immediately.

"Yes ma'am. Thank you, I'd like to speak to your footmen, if you please, privately."

"Would you now." She wiped her hands on her apron. "Sal. Put those potatoes down and go and get Harold—then when 'e's done, tell Percival to come. Well don't stand there, you great pudding. Go an' do as you're told!" She sighed and began to mix the pastry with water to the right consistency. "Girls these days! Eats enough for a working navvy, she does, and look at her. Moves like treacle in winter. Shoo. Get on with you, girl."

With a flash of temper the red-haired kitchen maid swung out of the room and along the corridor, her heels clicking on the uncarpeted floor.

"And don't you sonse out of here like that!" the cook called after her. "Cheeky piece. Eyes on the footman next door, that's 'er trouble. Lazy baggage." She turned back to Monk. "Now if you 'aven't anything more to ask me, you get out of my way too. You can talk to the footmen in Mr. Phillips's pantry. He's busy down in the cellar and won't be disturbing you."

Monk obeyed and was shown by Willie the bootboy into the pantry, the room where the butler kept all his keys, his accounts, and the silver that was used regularly, and also spent much of his time when not on duty. It was warm and extremely comfortably, if serviceably, furnished.

Harold, the junior footman, was a thickset, fair-haired

young man, in no way a pair to Percival, except in height. He must possess some other virtue, less visible to the first glance, or Monk guessed his days here would be numbered. He questioned him, probably just as Evan had already done, and Harold produced his now well-practiced replies. Monk could not imagine him the philanderer Fenella Sandeman had thought up.

Percival was a different matter, more assured, more belligerent, and quite ready to defend himself. When Monk pressed him he sensed a personal danger, and he answered with bold eyes and a ready tongue.

"Yes sir, I know it was someone in the house who killed Mrs. Haslett. That doesn't mean it was one of us servants. Why should we? Nothing to gain, and everything to lose. Anyway, she was a very pleasant lady, no occasion to wish her anything but good."

"You liked her?"

Percival smiled. He had read Monk's implication long before he replied, but whether from uneasy conscience or astute sense it was impossible to say.

"I said she was pleasant enough, sir. I wasn't familiar, if that's what you mean!"

"You jumped to that very quickly," Monk retorted. "What made you think that was what I meant?"

"Because you are trying to accuse one of us below stairs so you don't have the embarrassment of accusing someone above," Percival said baldly. "Just because I wear livery and say 'yes sir, no ma'am' doesn't mean I'm stupid. You're a policeman, no better than I am—"

Monk winced.

"And you know what it'll cost you if you charge one of the family," Percival finished.

"I'll charge one of the family if I find any evidence against them," Monk replied tartly. "So far I haven't."

"Then maybe you're too careful where you look." Percival's contempt was plain. "You won't find it if you don't want to—and it surely wouldn't suit you, would it?"

"I'll look anywhere I think there's something to find," Monk said. "You're in the house all day and all night. You tell me where to look."

"Well, Mr. Thirsk steals from the cellar—taken half the

best port wine over the last few years. Don't know how he isn't drunk half the time."

"Is that a reason to kill Mrs. Haslett?"

"Might be—if she knew and ratted on him to Sir Basil. Sir Basil would take it very hard. Might throw the old boy out into the street."

"Then why does he take it?"

Percival shrugged very slightly. It was not a servant's gesture.

"I don't know—but he does. Seen him sneaking down the steps many a time—and back up with a bottle under his coat."

"I'm not very impressed."

"Then look at Mrs. Sandeman." Percival's face tightened, a shadow of viciousness about his mouth. "Look at some of the company she keeps. I've been out in the carriage sometimes and taken her to some very odd places. Parading up and down that Rotten Row like a sixpenny whore, and reads stuff Sir Basil would burn if he saw it—scandal sheets, sensational press. Mr. Phillips would dismiss any of the maids if he caught them with that kind of thing."

"It's hardly relevant. Mr. Phillips cannot dismiss Mrs. Sandeman, no matter what she reads," Monk pointed out.

"Sir Basil could."

"But would he? She is his sister, not a servant."

Percival smiled. "She might just as well be. She has to come and go when he says, wear what he approves of, speak to whoever he likes and entertain his friends. Can't have her own here, unless he approves them—or she doesn't get her allowance. None of them do."

He was a young man with a malicious tongue and a great deal of personal knowledge of the family, Monk thought, very possibly a frightened young man. Perhaps his fear was justified. The Moidores would not easily allow one of their own to be charged if suspicion could be diverted to a servant. Percival knew that; maybe he was only the first person downstairs to see just how sharp the danger was. In time no doubt others would also; the tales would get uglier as the fear closed in.

"Thank you, Percival," Monk said wearily. "You can go—for now."

Percival opened his mouth to add something, then changed his mind and went out. He moved gracefully—well trained.

110

Monk returned to the kitchen and had the cup of tea Mrs. Boden had previously offered, but even listening carefully he learned nothing of further use, and he left by the same way he had arrived and took a hansom from Harley Street down to the City. This time he was more fortunate in finding Myles Kellard in his office at the bank.

"I can't think what to tell you." Myles looked at Monk curiously, his long face lit with a faint humor as if he found the whole meeting a trifle ridiculous. He sat elegantly on one of the Chippendale armchairs in his exquisitely carpeted room, crossing his legs with ease. "There are all sorts of family tensions, of course. There are in any family. But none of them seems a motive for murder to anyone, except a lunatic."

Monk waited.

"I would find it a lot easier to understand if Basil had been the victim," Myles went on, an edge of sharpness in his voice. "Cyprian could follow his own political interests instead of his father's, and pay all his debts, which would make life a great deal easier for him—and for the fair Romola. She finds living in someone else's house very hard to take. Ideas of being mistress of Queen Anne Street shine in her eyes rather often. But she'll be a dutiful daughter-in-law until that day comes. It's worth waiting for."

"And then you will also presumably move elsewhere?" Monk said quickly.

"Ah." Myles pulled a face. "How uncivil of you, Inspector. Yes, no doubt we shall. But old Basil looks healthy enough for another twenty years. Anyway, it was poor Tavie who was killed, so that line of thought leads you nowhere."

"Did Mrs. Haslett know of her brother's debts?"

Myles's eyebrows shot up, giving his face a quizzical look. "I shouldn't think so—but it's a possibility. She certainly knew he was interested in the philosophies of the appalling Mr. Owen and his notions of dismantling the family." He smiled with a raw, twisted humor. "I don't suppose you've read Owen, Inspector? No—very radical—believes the patriarchal system is responsible for all sorts of greed, oppression and abuse—an opinion which Basil is hardly likely to share."

"Hardly," Monk agreed. "Are these debts of Mr. Cyprian's generally known?"

"Certainly not!"

"But he confided in you?"

Myles lifted his shoulders a fraction.

"No—not exactly. I am a banker, Inspector. I learn various bits of information that are not public property." He colored faintly. "I told you that because you are investigating a murder in my family. It is not to be generally discussed. I hope you understand that."

He had breached a confidence. Monk perceived that readily enough. Fenella's words about him came back, and her arch look as she said them.

Myles hurried on. "I should think it was probably some stupid wrangle with a servant who got above himself." He was looking very directly at Monk. "Octavia was a widow, and young. She wouldn't get her excitement from scandal sheets like Aunt Fenella. I daresay one of the footmen admired her and she didn't put him in his place swiftly enough."

"Is that really what you think happened, Mr. Kellard?" Monk searched his face, the hazel eyes under their fair brows, the long, fluted nose and the mouth which could so easily be imaginative or slack, depending on his mood.

"It seems far more likely than Cyprian, whom she cared for, killing her because she might have told their father, of whom she was not fond, about his debts—or Fenella, in case Octavia told Basil about the company she keeps, which is pretty ragged."

"I gathered Mrs. Haslett was still missing her husband," Monk said slowly, hoping Myles would read the less delicate implication behind his words.

Myles laughed outright. "Good God, no. What a prude you are." He leaned back in his chair. "She mourned Haslett— but she's a woman. She'd have gone on making a parade of sorrow, of course. It's expected. But she's a woman like any other. I daresay Percival, at any rate, knows that. He'd take a little protestation of reluctance, a few smiles through the eyelashes and modest glances for what they were worth."

Monk felt the muscles in his neck and scalp tightening in anger, but he tried to keep his emotion out of his voice.

"Which, if you are right, was apparently a great deal. She meant exactly what she said."

"Oh—" Myles sighed and shrugged. "I daresay she

112

changed her mind when she remembered he was a footman, by which time he had lost his head."

"Have you any reason for suggesting this, Mr. Kellard, other than your belief that it seems likely to you?"

"Observation," he said with a shadow of irritation across his face. "Percival is something of a ladies' man, had considerable flirtations with one or two of the maids. It's to be expected, you know." A look of obscure satisfaction flickered across his face. "Can't keep people together in a house day in, day out and not have something happen now and again. He's an ambitious little beggar. Go and look there, Inspector. Now if you'll excuse me, there really is nothing I can tell you, except to use your common sense and whatever knowledge of women you have. Now I wish you good-day."

Monk returned to Queen Anne Street with a sense of darkness inside. He should have been encouraged by his interview with Myles Kellard. He had given an acceptable motive for one of the servants to have killed Octavia Haslett, and that would surely be the least unpleasant answer. Runcorn would be delighted. Sir Basil would be satisfied. Monk would arrest the footman and claim a victory. The press would praise him for his rapid and successful solution, which would annoy Runcorn, but he would be immensely relieved that the danger of scandal was removed and a prominent case had been closed satisfactorily.

But his interview with Myles had left him with a vague feeling of depression. Myles had a contempt for both Octavia and the footman Percival. His suggestions were born of a kind of malice. There was no gentleness in him.

Monk pulled his coat collar a little higher against the cold rain blowing down the pavement as he turned into Leadenhall Street and walked up towards Cornhill. Was he anything like Myles Kellard? He had seen few signs of compassion in the records he had found of himself. His judgments were sharp. Were they equally cynical? It was a frightening thought. He would be an empty man inside if it were so. In the months since he had awoken in the hospital, he had found no one who cared for him deeply, no one who felt gratitude or love for him, except his sister, Beth, and her love was born of loyalty, memory rather than knowledge. Was there no one else? No

113

woman? Where were his relationships, the debts and the dependencies, the trusts, the memories?

He hailed a hansom and told the driver to take him back to Queen Anne Street, then sat back and tried to put his own life out of his mind and think of the footman Percival—and the possibility of a stupid physical flirtation that had run out of control and ended in violence.

He arrived and entered by the kitchen door again, and asked to speak to Percival. He faced him in the housekeeper's sitting room this time. The footman was pale-faced now, feeling the net closing around him, cold and a great deal tighter. He stood stiffly, his muscles shaking a little under his livery, his hands knotted in front of him, a fine beading of sweat on his brow and lip. He stared at Monk with fixed eyes, waiting for the attack so he could parry it.

The moment Monk spoke, he knew he would find no way to frame a question that would be subtle. Percival had already guessed the line of his thought and leaped ahead.

"There's a great deal you don't know about this house," he said with a harsh, jittery voice. "Ask Mr. Kellard about his relationship with Mrs. Haslett."

"What was it, Percival?" Monk asked quietly. "All I have heard suggests they were not particularly agreeable."

"Not openly, no." There was a slight sneer in Percival's thin mouth. "She never did like him much, but he lusted after her—"

"Indeed?" Monk said with raised brows. "They seem to have hidden it remarkably well. Do you think Mr. Kellard tried to force his attentions on her, and when she refused, he became violent and killed her? There was no struggle."

Percival looked at him with withering disgust.

"No I don't. I think he lusted after her, and even if he never did anything about it at all, Mrs. Kellard still discovered it—and boiled with the kind of jealousy that only a spurned woman can. She hated her sister enough to kill her." He saw the widening of Monk's eyes and the tightening of his hands. He knew he had startled the policeman and at least for a time confused him.

A tiny smile touched the corner of Percival's mouth.

"Will that be all, sir?"

114

"Yes—yes it will," Monk said after a hesitation. "For the moment."

"Thank you, sir." And Percival turned and walked out, a lift in his step now and a slight swing in his shoulders.

5

Hester did not find the infirmary any easier to bear as days went by. The outcome of the trial had given her a sense of bitter struggle and achievement. She had been brought face-to-face again with a dramatic adversarial conflict, and for all its darkness and the pain she knew accompanied it, she had been on the side which had won. She had seen Fabia Grey's terrible face as she left the courtroom, and she knew the hate that now shriveled her life. But she also had seen the new freedom in Lovel Grey, as if ghosts had faded forever, leaving a beginning of light. And she chose to believe that Menard would make a life for himself in Australia, a land about which she knew almost nothing, but insofar as it was not England, there would be hope for him; and it was the best for which they could have striven.

She was not sure whether she liked Oliver Rathbone or not, but he was unquestionably exhilarating. She had tasted battle again, and it had whetted her appetite for more. She found Pomeroy even harder to endure than previously, his insufferable complacency, the smug excuses with which he accepted losses as inevitable, when she was convinced that with greater effort and attention and more courage, better nurses, more initiative by juniors, they need not have been lost at all. But whether that was true or not—he should fight. To be beaten was one thing, to surrender was another—and intolerable.

At least John Airdrie had been operated on, and now as she stood in the ward on a dark, wet November morning she could see him asleep in his cot at the far end, breathing fitfully. She walked down closer to him to find if he was feverish. She straightened his blankets and moved her lamp to look at his face. It was flushed and, when she touched it, it was hot. This was to be expected after an operation, and yet it was what she dreaded. It might be just the normal reaction, or it might be the first stage of infection, for which they knew no cure. They could only hope the body's own strength would outlast the disease.

Hester had met French surgeons in the Crimea and learned of treatments practiced in the Napoleonic Wars a generation earlier. In 1640 the wife of the governor of Peru had been cured of fever by the administration of a distillation from tree bark, first known as Poudre de la Comtesse, then Poudre de Jesuites. Now it was known as loxa quinine. It was possible Pomeroy might prescribe such a thing for the child, but he might not; he was extremely conservative—and he was also not due to make his rounds for another five hours.

The child stirred again. She leaned over and touched him gently, to soothe as much as anything. But he did not regain his senses, rather he seemed on the border of falling into delirium.

She made up her mind without hesitation. This was a battle she would not surrender. Since the Crimea she had carried a few basic medicines herself, things she thought she would be unable to obtain readily in England. A mixture of theriac, loxa quinine and Hoffman's liquor was among them. She kept them in a small leather case with an excellent lock which she left with her cloak and bonnet in a small outer room provided for such a purpose.

Now, the decision made, she glanced around the ward one more time to make sure no one was in distress, and when all seemed well, she hurried out and along the passage to the outer room, and pulled her case from where it was half hidden under the folds of her cloak. She fished for the key on its chain from her pocket and put it in the lock. It turned easily and she opened the lid. Under the clean apron and two freshly laundered linen caps were the medicines. The theriac and quinine mixture was easy to see. She took it out and slipped it into her pocket, then closed and locked the case again, sliding it back under her cloak.

117

Back in the ward she found a bottle of the ale the nurses frequently drank. The mixer was supposed to be Bordeaux wine, but since she had none, this would have to serve. She poured a little into a cup and added a very small dose of the quinine, stirring it thoroughly. She knew the taste was extremely bitter.

She went over to the bed and lifted the child gently, resting his head against her. She gave him two teaspoonfuls, putting them gently between his lips. He seemed unaware of what was happening, and swallowed only in reaction. She wiped his mouth with a napkin and laid him back again, smoothing the hair off his brow and covering him with the sheet.

Two hours later she gave him two more teaspoonfuls, and then a third time just before Pomeroy came.

"Very pleasing," he said, looking closely at the boy, his freckled face full of satisfaction. "He seems to be doing remarkably well, Miss Latterly. You see I was quite right to leave the operation till I did. There was no such urgency as you supposed." He looked at her with a tight smile. "You panic too easily." And he straightened up and went to the next bed.

Hester refrained from comment with difficulty. But if she told him of the fever the boy had been sinking into only five hours ago, she would also have to tell him of the medication she had given. His reaction to that she could only guess at, but it would not be agreeable. She would tell him, if she had to, when the child was recovered. Perhaps discretion would be best.

However circumstances did not permit her such latitude. By the middle of the week John Airdrie was sitting up with no hectic color in his cheeks and taking with pleasure a little light food. But the woman three beds along who had had an operation on her abdomen was sinking rapidly, and Pomeroy was looking at her with grave anxiety and recommending ice and frequent cool baths. There was no hope in his voice, only resignation and pity.

Hester could not keep silent. She looked at the woman's pain-suffused face, and spoke.

"Dr. Pomeroy, have you considered the possibility of giving her loxa quinine in a mixture of wine, theriac and Hoffman's mineral liquor? It might ease her fever."

He looked at her with incredulity turning slowly into anger

as he realized exactly what she had said, his face pink, his beard bristling.

"Miss Latterly, I have had occasion to speak to you before about your attempts to practice an art for which you have no training and no mandate. I will give Mrs. Begley what is best for her, and you will obey my instructions. Is that understood?"

Hester swallowed hard. "Is that your instruction, Dr. Pomeroy, that I give Mrs. Begley some loxa quinine to ease her fever?"

"No it is not!" he snapped. "That is for tropical fevers, not for the normal recovery from an operation. It would do no good. We will have none of that foreign rubbish here!"

Part of Hester's mind still struggled with the decision, but her tongue was already embarked on the course her conscience would inevitably choose.

"I have seen it given with success by a French surgeon, sir, for fever following amputation, and it is recorded as far back as the Napoleonic campaigns before Waterloo."

His face darkened with angry color. "I do not take my instructions from the French, Miss Latterly! They are a dirty and ignorant race who only a short time ago were bent on conquering these islands and subjecting them, along with the rest of Europe! And I would remind you, since you seem apt to forget it, that you take your instructions from me—and from me alone!" He turned to leave the unfortunate woman, and Hester stepped almost in front of him.

"She is delirious, Doctor! We cannot leave her! Please permit me to try a little quinine; it cannot harm and it may help. I will give only a teaspoonful at a time, every two or three hours, and if it does not ease her I will desist."

"And where do you propose I obtain such a medication, were I disposed to do as you say?"

She took a deep breath and only just avoided betraying herself.

"From the fever hospital, sir. We could send a hansom over. I will go myself, if you wish."

His face was bright pink.

"Miss Latterly! I thought I had already made myself clear on the subject—nurses keep patients clean and cool from excessive temperature, they administer ice at the doctor's directions and drinks as have been prescribed." His voice was rising and getting louder, and he stood on the balls of his feet, rocking a little. "They fetch and carry and pass bandages and instruments as required. They keep the ward clean and tidy; they stoke fires and serve food. They empty and dispose of waste and attend to the bodily requirements of patients."

He thrust his hands into his pockets and rocked on his feet a little more rapidly. "They keep order and lift the spirits. That is all! Do you understand me, Miss Latterly? They are unskilled in medicine, except of the most rudimentary sort. They do not in any circumstances whatever exercise their own judgment!"

"But if you are not present!" she protested.

"Then you wait!" His voice was getting increasingly shrill.

She could not swallow her anger. "But patients may die! Or at best become sufficiently worse that they cannot easily be saved!"

"Then you will send for me urgently! But you will do nothing beyond your remit, and when I come I will decide what is best to do. That is all."

"But if I know what to do—"

"You do not know!" His hands flew out of his pockets into the air. "For God's sake, woman, you are not medically trained! You know nothing but bits of gossip and practical experience you have picked up from foreigners in some campaign hospital in the Crimea! You are not a physician and never will be!"

"All medicine is only a matter of learning and observation!" Her voice was rising considerably now, and even the farther patients were beginning to take notice. "There are no rules except that if it works it is good, and if it does not then try something else." She was exasperated almost beyond endurance with his stubborn stupidity. "If we never experiment we will never discover anything better than we have now, and people will go on dying when perhaps we could have cured them!"

"And far more probably killed them with our ignorance!" he retaliated with finality. "You have no right to conduct experiments. You are an unskilled and willful woman, and if there is one more word of insubordination out of you, you will be dismissed. Do you understand me?"

120

She hesitated a moment, meeting his eyes. There was no uncertainty in them, no slightest flexibility in his determination. If she kept silent now there was just the possibility he might come back later, when she was off duty, and give Mrs. Begley the quinine.

"Yes, I understand." She forced the words out, her hands clenched in the folds of her apron and skirt at her sides.

But once again he could not leave well enough alone even after he had seemingly won.

"Quinine does not work for postoperative fever infections, Miss Latterly," he went on with mounting condescension. "It is for tropical fevers. And even then it is not always successful. You will dose the patient with ice and wash her regularly in cool water."

Hester breathed in and out very slowly. His complacency was insufferable.

"Do you hear me?" he demanded.

Before she could reply this time, one of the patients on the far side of the ward sat up, his face twisted in concentration.

"She gave something to that child at the end when he had a fever after his operation," he said clearly. "He was in a bad way, like to go into delirium. And after she did it four or five times he recovered. He's cool as you like now. She knows what she's doing—she's right."

There was a moment's awful silence. He had no idea what he had done.

Pomeroy was stunned.

"You gave loxa quinine to John Airdrie!" he accused, realization flooding into him. "You did it behind my back!" His voice rose, shrill with outrage and betrayal, not only by her but, even worse, by the patient.

Then a new thought struck him.

"Where did you get it from? Answer me, Miss Latterly! I demand you tell me where you obtained it! Did you have the audacity to send to the fever hospital in my name?"

"No, Dr. Pomeroy. I have some quinine of my own—a very small amount," she added hastily, "against fever. I gave him some of that."

He was trembling with rage. "You are dismissed, Miss Latterly. You have been a troublemaker since you arrived. You were employed on the recommendation of a lady who no doubt owed some favor to your family and had little knowledge of your irresponsible and willful nature. You will leave this establishment today! Whatever possessions you have here, take them with you. And there is no purpose in your asking for a recommendation. I can give you none!''

There was silence in the ward. Someone rustled bedclothes.

"But she cured the boy!" the patient protested. "She was right! 'E's alive because of 'er!" The man's voice was thick with distress, at last understanding what he had done. He looked at Pomeroy, then at Hester. "She was right!" he said again.

Hester could at last afford the luxury of ceasing to care in the slightest what Pomeroy thought of her. She had nothing to lose now.

"Of course I shall go," she acknowledged. "But don't let your pride prevent you from helping Mrs. Begley. She doesn't deserve to die to save your face because a nurse told you what to do." She took a deep breath. "And since everyone in this room is aware of it, you will find it difficult to excuse."

"Why you—you—!" Pomeroy spluttered, scarlet in the face but lost for words violent enough to satisfy his outrage and at the same time not expose his weakness. "You—"

Hester gave him one withering look, then turned away and went over to the patient who had defended her, now sitting with the bedclothes in a heap around him and a pale face full of shame.

"There is no need to blame yourself," she said to him very gently, but clearly enough for everyone else in the ward to hear her. He needed his excusing to be known. "It was bound to happen that one day I should fall out with Dr. Pomeroy sufficiently for this to happen. At least you have spoken up for what you know, and perhaps you will have saved Mrs. Begley a great deal of pain, maybe even her life. Please do not criticize yourself for it or feel you have done me a disfavor. You have done no more than choose the time for what was inevitable."

"Are you sure, miss? I feel that badly!" He looked at her anxiously, searching her face for belief.

"Of course I'm sure." She forced herself to smile at him. "Have you not watched me long enough to judge that for yourself? Dr. Pomeroy and I have been on a course that was destined for collision from the beginning. And it was never possible that I should have the better of it." She began to

straighten the sheet around him. "Now take care of yourself—
and may God heal you!" She took his hand briefly, then moved
away again. "In spite of Pomeroy," she added under her
breath.

When she had reached her rooms, and the heat of temper
had worn off a little, she began to realize what she had done.
She was not only without an occupation to fill her time, and
financial means with which to support herself, she had also
betrayed Callandra Daviot's confidence in her and the recommendation to which she had given her name.

She had a late-afternoon meal alone, eating only because
she did not want to offend her landlady. It tasted of nothing.
By five o'clock it was growing dark, and after the gas lamps
were lit and the curtains were drawn the room seemed to narrow and close her in in enforced idleness and complete isolation. What should she do tomorrow? There was no infirmary,
no patients to care for. She was completely unnecessary and
without purpose to anyone. It was a wretched thought, and if
pursued for long would undermine her to the point where she
would wish to crawl into bed and remain there.

There was also the extremely sobering thought that after a
week or two she would have no money and be obliged to leave
here and return to beg her brother, Charles, to provide a roof
over her head until she could—what? It would be extremely
difficult, probably impossible to gain another position in nursing. Pomeroy would see to that.

She felt herself on the edge of tears, which she despised.
She must do something. Anything was better than sitting here
in this shabby room listening to the gas hissing in the silence
and feeling sorry for herself. One unpleasant task to be done
was explaining herself to Callandra. She owed her that, and it
would be a great deal better done face-to-face than in a letter.
Why not get that over with? It could hardly be worse than
sitting here alone thinking about it and waiting for time to pass
until she could find it reasonable to go to bed, and sleep would
not be merely a running away.

She put on her best coat—she had only two, but one was
definitely more flattering and less serviceable than the other—
and a good hat, and went out into the street to find a hansom
and give the driver Callandra Daviot's address.

She arrived a few minutes before seven, and was relieved to find that Callandra was at home and not entertaining company, a contingency which she had not even thought of when she set out. She asked if she might see Lady Callandra and was admitted without comment by the maid.

Callandra came down the stairs within a few minutes, dressed in what she no doubt considered fashionable, but which was actually two years out of date and not the most flattering of colors. Her hair was already beginning to come out of its pins, although she must have left her dressing room no more than a moment ago, but the whole effect was redeemed by the intelligence and vitality in her face—and her evident pleasure in seeing Hester, even at this hour, and unannounced. It did not take her more than one glance to realize that something was wrong.

"What is it, my dear?" she said on reaching the bottom stair. "What has happened?"

There was no purpose in being evasive, least of all with Callandra.

"I treated a child without the doctor's permission—he was not there. The child seems to be recovering nicely—but I have been dismissed." It was out. She searched Callandra's face.

"Indeed." Callandra's eyebrows rose only slightly. "And the child was ill, I presume?"

"Feverish and becoming delirious."

"With what did you treat it?"

"Loxa quinine, theriac, Hoffman's mineral liquor—and a little ale to make it palatable."

"Seems very reasonable." Callandra led the way to the withdrawing room. "But outside your authority, of course."

"Yes," Hester agreed quietly.

Callandra closed the door behind them. "And you are not sorry," she added. "I assume you would do the same again?"

"I—"

"Do not lie to me, my dear. I am quite sure you would. It is a great pity they do not permit women to study medicine. You would make a fine doctor. You have intelligence, judgment and courage without bravado. But you are a woman, and that is an end of it." She sat down on a large and extremely comfortable sofa and signaled Hester to do the same. "And what do you intend to do now?"

"I have no idea."

"I thought not. Well perhaps you should begin by coming with me to the theater. You have had an extremely trying day and something in the realm of fantasy will be a satisfactory contrast. Then we will discuss what you are to do next. Forgive me for such an indelicate question, but have you sufficient funds to settle your accommodation for another week or two?"

Hester found herself smiling at such mundane practicality, so far from the moral outrage and portent of social disaster she might have expected from anyone else.

"Yes—yes I have."

"I hope that is the truth." Callandra's wild eyebrows rose inquiringly. "Good. Then that gives us a little time. If not, you would be welcome to stay with me until you obtain something more suitable."

It was better to tell it all now.

"I exceeded my authority," Hester confessed. "Pomeroy was extremely angry and will not give me any kind of reference. In fact I would be surprised if he did not inform all his colleagues of my behavior."

"I imagine he will," Callandra agreed. "If he is asked. But so long as the child recovers and survives he will be unlikely to raise the subject if he does not have to." She regarded Hester critically. "Oh dear, you are not exactly dressed for an evening out, are you? Still, it is too late to do a great deal now; you must come as you are. Perhaps my maid could dress your hair? That at least would help. Go upstairs and tell her I request it."

Hester hesitated; it had all been so rapid.

"Well don't stand there!" Callandra encouraged. "Have you eaten? We can have some refreshment there, but it will not be a proper meal."

"Yes—yes I have. Thank you—"

"Then go and have your hair dressed—be quick!"

Hester obeyed because she had no better idea.

The theater was crowded with people bent on enjoying themselves, women fashionably dressed in crinoline skirts full of flounces and flowers, lace, velvet, fringes and ribbons and all manner of femininity. Hester felt outstandingly plain and not in the least like laughing, and the thought of flirting with

125

some trivial and idiotic young man was enough to make her lose what little of her temper was left. It was only her debt, and her fondness for Callandra, that kept any curb on her tongue at all.

Since Callandra had a box there was no difficulty about seats, and they were not placed close to anyone else. The play was one of the dozens popular at the moment, concerning the fall from virtue of a young woman, tempted by the weakness of the flesh, seduced by a worthless man, and only in the end, when it was too late, desiring to return to her upright husband.

"Pompous, opinionated fool!" Hester said under her breath, her tolerance at last stretched beyond bearing. "I wonder if the police ever charged a man with boring a woman to death?"

"It is not a sin, my dear," Callandra whispered back. "Women are not supposed to be interested."

Hester used a word she had heard in the Crimea among the soldiers, and Callandra pretended not to have heard it, although she had in fact heard it many times, and even knew what it meant.

When the play was finished the curtain came down to enthusiastic applause. Callandra rose, and Hester, after a brief glance down at the audience, rose also and followed her out into the wide foyer, now rapidly filling with men and women chattering about the play, each other and any trivialities or gossip that came to mind.

Hester and Callandra stepped among them, and within a few minutes and half a dozen exchanges of polite words, they came face-to-face with Oliver Rathbone and a dark young woman with a demure expression on her extremely pretty face.

"Good evening, Lady Callandra." He bowed very slightly and then turned to Hester, smiling. "Miss Latterly. May I present Miss Newhouse?"

They exchanged formal greetings in the approved fashion.

"Wasn't it a delightful play?" Miss Newhouse said politely. "So moving, don't you think?"

"Very," Callandra agreed. "The theme seems to be most popular these days."

Hester said nothing. She was aware of Rathbone looking at her with the same inquisitive amusement he had at their first meeting, before the trial. She was not in the mood for small talk, but she was Callandra's guest and she must endure it with some grace.

"I could not but feel sorry for the heroine," Miss Newhouse continued. "In spite of her weaknesses." She looked down for a moment. "Oh, I know of course that she brought her ruin upon herself. That was the playwright's skill, was it not, that one deplored her behavior and yet wept for her at the same time?" She turned to Hester. "Do you not think so, Miss Latterly?"

"I fear I had rather more sympathy with her than was intended," Hester said with an apologetic smile.

"Oh?" Miss Newhouse looked confused.

Hester felt compelled to explain further. She was acutely aware of Rathbone watching her.

"I thought her husband so extremely tedious I could well understand why she . . . lost interest."

"That hardly excuses her betrayal of her vows." Miss Newhouse was shocked. "It shows how easily we women can be led astray by a few flattering words," she said earnestly. "We see a handsome face and a little surface glamour, instead of true worth!"

Hester spoke before thinking. The heroine had been very pretty, and it seemed the husband had bothered to learn very little else about her. "I do not need anyone to lead me astray! I am perfectly capable of going on my own!"

Miss Newhouse stared at her, nonplussed.

Callandra coughed hard into her handkerchief.

"But not as much fun, going astray alone, is it?" Rathbone said with brilliant eyes and lips barely refraining from a smile. "Hardly worth the journey!"

Hester swung around and met his gaze. "I may go alone, Mr. Rathbone, but I am perfectly sure I would not find the ground uninhabited when I got there!"

His smile broadened, showing surprisingly beautiful teeth. He held out his arm in invitation.

"May I? Just to your carriage," he said with an expressionless face.

She was unable to stop laughing, and the fact that Miss Newhouse obviously did not know what was funny only added to her enjoyment.

* * *

127

The following day Callandra sent her footman to the police station with a note requesting that Monk wait upon her at his earliest convenience. She gave no explanation for her desire to see him and she certainly did not offer any information that would be of interest or use.

Nevertheless in the late morning he presented himself at her door and was duly shown in. He had a deep regard for her, of which she was aware.

"Good morning, Mr. Monk," she said courteously. "Please be seated and make yourself comfortable. May I offer you refreshment of some kind? Perhaps a hot chocolate? The morning is seasonably unpleasant."

"Thank you," he accepted, his face rather evidently showing his puzzlement as to why he had been sent for.

She rang for the maid, and when she appeared, requested the hot chocolate. Then she turned to Monk with a charming smile.

"How is your case progressing?" She had no idea which case he was engaged on, but she had no doubt there would be one.

He hesitated just long enough to decide whether the question was a mere politeness until the chocolate should arrive or whether she really wished to know. He decided the latter.

"Little bits and pieces of evidence all over the place," he replied. "Which do not as yet seem to add up to anything."

"Is that frequent?"

A flash of humor crossed his face. "It is not unknown, but these seem unusually erratic. And with a family like Sir Basil Moidore's, one does not press as one might with less socially eminent people."

She had the information she needed.

"Of course not. It must be very difficult indeed. And the public, by way of the newspapers, and the authorities also, will naturally be pressing very hard for a solution."

The chocolate came and she served them both, permitting the maid to leave immediately. The beverage was hot, creamy and delicious, and she saw the satisfaction in Monk's face as soon as his lips touched it.

"And you are at a disadvantage that you can never observe them except under the most artificial of circumstances," she went on, seeing his rueful agreement. "How can you possibly

128

ask them the questions you really wish, when they are so fore-warned by your mere presence that all their answers are guarded and designed to protect? You can only hope their lies become so convoluted as to trap some truth.''

''Are you acquainted with the Moidores?'' He was seeking for her interest in the matter.

She waved a hand airily. ''Only socially. London is very small, you know, and most good families are connected with each other. That is the purpose of a great many marriages. I have a cousin of sorts who is related to one of Beatrice's brothers. How is she taking the tragedy? It must be a most grievous time for her.''

He set down his chocolate cup for a moment. ''Very hard,'' he replied, concentrating on a memory which puzzled him. ''To begin with she seemed to be bearing it very well, with great calm and inner strength. Now quite suddenly she has collapsed and withdrawn to her bedroom. I am told she is ill, but I have not seen her myself.''

''Poor creature,'' Callandra sympathized. ''But most unhelpful to your inquiries. Do you imagine she knows something?''

He looked at her acutely. He had remarkable eyes, very dark clear gray, with an undeviating gaze that would have quelled quite a few people, but Callandra could have outstared a basilisk.

''It occurs to me,'' he said carefully.

''What you need is someone inside the house whom the family and servants would consider of no importance,'' she said as if the idea had just occurred to her. ''And of course quite unrelated to the investigation—someone who has an acute sense of people's behavior and could observe them without their giving any thought to it, and then recount to you what was said and done in private times, the nuances of tone and expression.''

''A miracle,'' he said dryly.

''Not at all,'' she replied with equally straight-faced aridity. ''A woman would suffice.''

''We do not have women officers in the police.'' He picked up his cup again and looked at her over the rim. ''And if we did, we could hardly place one in the house.''

''Did you not say Lady Moidore had taken to her bed?''

129

"That is of some help?" He looked wide-eyed.

"Perhaps she would benefit from having a nurse in the house? She is quite naturally ill with distress at her daughter's death by murder. It seems very possible she has some realization of who was responsible. No wonder she is unwell, poor creature. Any woman would be. I think a nurse would be an excellent thing for her."

He stopped drinking his chocolate and stared at her.

With some difficulty she kept her face blank and perfectly innocent.

"Hester Latterly is at present without employment, and she is an excellent nurse, one of Miss Nightingale's young ladies. I can recommend her highly. And she would be perfectly prepared to undertake such an engagement, I believe. She is most observant, as you know, and not without personal courage. The fact that a murder has taken place in the house would not deter her."

"What about the infirmary?" he said slowly, a brilliant light coming into his eyes.

"She is no longer there." Her expression was blandly innocent.

He looked startled.

"A difference of opinion with the doctor," she explained.

"Oh!"

"Who is a fool," she added.

"Of course." His smile was very slight, but went all the way to his eyes.

"I am sure if you were to approach her," she went on, "with some tact she would be prepared to apply for a temporary position with Sir Basil Moidore, to care for Lady Moidore until such time as she is herself again. I will be most happy to supply a reference. I would not speak to the hospital, if I were you. And it might be desirable not to mention my name to Hester—unless it is necessary to avoid untruth."

Now his smile was quite open. "Quite so, Lady Callandra. An excellent idea. I am most obliged to you."

"Not at all," she said innocently. "Not at all. I shall also speak to my cousin Valentina, who will be pleased to suggest such a thing to Beatrice and at the same time recommend Miss Latterly."

* * *

Hester was so surprised to see Monk she did not even think to wonder how he knew her address.

"Good morning," she said in amazement. "Has something—" she stopped, not sure what it was she was asking.

He knew how to be circumspect when it was in his own interest. He had learned it with some difficulty, but his ambition overrode his temper, even his pride, and it had come in time.

"Good morning," he replied agreeably. "No, nothing alarming has happened. I have a favor I wish of you, if you are willing."

"Of me?" She was still astonished and half disbelieving.

"If you will? May I sit down?"

"Oh—of course." They were in Mrs. Horne's parlor, and she waved to the seat nearest the thin fire.

He accepted, and began on the purpose of his visit before trivial conversation should lead him into betraying Callandra Daviot.

"I am engaged in the Queen Anne Street case, the murder of Sir Basil Moidore's daughter."

"I wondered if you would be," she answered politely, her eyes bright with expectation. "The newspapers are still full of it. But I have never met any of the family, nor do I know anything about them. Have they any connection with the Crimea?"

"Only peripheral."

"Then what can I—" She stopped, waiting for him to answer.

"It was someone in the house who killed her," he said. "Very probably one of the family—"

"Oh—" Understanding began in her eyes, not of her own part in the case, but of the difficulties facing him. "How can you investigate that?"

"Carefully." He smiled with a downward turn of his lips. "Lady Moidore has taken to her bed. I am not sure how much of it is grief—she was very composed to begin with—and how much of it may be because she has learned something which points to one of the family and she cannot bear it."

"What can I do?" He had all her attention now.

"Would you consider taking a position as nurse to Lady

131

Moidore, and observing the family, and if possible learning what she fears so much?"

She looked uncomfortable. "They may require better references than I could supply."

"Would not Miss Nightingale speak well of you?"

"Oh, certainly—but the infirmary would not."

"Indeed. Then we shall hope they do not ask them. I think the main thing will be if Lady Moidore finds you agreeable—"

"I imagine Lady Callandra would also speak for me."

He relaxed back into his chair. "That should surely be sufficient. Then you will do it?"

She laughed very slightly. "If they advertise for such a person, I shall surely apply—but I can hardly turn up at the door and inquire if they need a nurse!"

"Of course not. I shall do what I can to arrange it." He did not tell her of Callandra Daviot's cousin, and hurried on to avoid difficult explanations. "It will be done by word of mouth, as these things are in the best families. If you will permit yourself to be mentioned? Good—"

"Tell me something of the household."

"I think it would be better if I left you to discover it yourself—and certainly your opinions would be of more use to me." He frowned curiously. "What happened at the infirmary?"

Ruefully she told him.

Valentina Burke-Heppenstall was prevailed upon to call in person at Queen Anne Street to convey her sympathies, and when Beatrice did not receive her, she commiserated with her friend's distress and suggested to Araminta that perhaps a nurse would be helpful in the circumstances and be able to offer assistance a busy ladies' maid could not.

After a few moments' consideration, Araminta was disposed to agree. It would indeed remove from the rest of the household the responsibility for a task they were not really equipped to handle.

Valentina could suggest someone, if it would not be viewed as impertinent? Miss Nightingale's young ladies were the very best, and very rare indeed among nurses; they were well-bred, not at all the sort of person one would mind having in one's house.

132

Araminta was obliged. She would interview this person at the first opportunity.

Accordingly Hester put on her best uniform and rode in a hansom cab to Queen Anne Street, where she presented herself for Araminta's inspection.

"I have Lady Burke-Heppenstall's recommendation of your work," Araminta said gravely. She was dressed in black taffeta which rustled with every movement, and the enormous skirt kept touching table legs and corners of sofas and chairs as Araminta walked in the overfurnished room. The somberness of the gown and the black crepes set over pictures and doors in recognition of death made her hair by contrast seem like a pool of light, hotter and more vivid than gold.

She looked at Hester's gray stuff dress and severe appearance with satisfaction.

"Why are you currently seeking employment, Miss Latterly?" She made no attempt at courtesy. This was a business interview, not a social one.

Hester had already prepared her excuse, with Callandra's help. It was frequently the desire of an ambitious servant to work for someone of title. They were greater snobs than many of their mistresses, and the manners and grammar of other servants were of intense importance to them.

"Now that I am home in England, Mrs. Kellard, I should prefer nursing in a private house of well-bred people to working in a public hospital."

"That is quite understandable," Araminta accepted without a flicker. "My mother is not ill, Miss Latterly; she has had a bereavement under most distressing circumstances. We do not wish her to fall into a melancholy. It would be easy enough. She will require agreeable company—and care that she sleeps well and eats sufficiently to maintain her health. Is this a position you would be willing to fill, Miss Latterly?"

"Yes, Mrs. Kellard, I should be happy to, if you feel I would suit?" Hester forced herself to be appropriately humble only by remembering Monk's face—and her real purpose here.

"Very well, you may consider yourself engaged. You may bring such belongings as are necessary, and begin tomorrow. Good day to you."

"Good day, ma'am—thank you."

Accordingly, the following day Hester arrived at Queen

Anne Street with her few belongings in a trunk and presented herself at the back door to be shown her room and her duties. It was an extraordinary position, rather more than a servant, but a great deal less than a guest. She was considered skilled, but she was not part of the ordinary staff, nor yet a professional person such as a doctor. She was a member of the household, therefore she must come and go as she was ordered and conduct herself in all ways as was acceptable to her mistress. *Mistress*—the word set her teeth on edge.

But why should it? She had no possessions and no prospects, and since she took it upon herself to administer to John Airdrie without Pomeroy's permission, she had no other employment either. And of course there was not only caring for Lady Moidore to consider and do well, there was the subtler and more interesting and dangerous job to do for Monk.

She was given an agreeable room on the floor immediately above the main family bedrooms and with a connecting bell so she could come at a moment's notice should she be required. In her time off duty, if there should be any, she might read or write letters in the ladies' maids' sitting room. She was told quite unequivocally what her duties would be, and what would remain those of the ladies' maid, Mary, a dark, slender girl in her twenties with a face full of character and a ready tongue. She was also told the province of the upstairs maid, Annie, who was about sixteen and full of curiosity, quick-witted and far too opinionated for her own good.

She was shown the kitchen and introduced to the cook, Mrs. Boden, the kitchen maid Sal, the scullery maid May, the bootboy Willie, and then to the laundrymaids Lizzie and Rose, who would attend to her linens. The other ladies' maid, Gladys, she only saw on the landing; she looked after Mrs. Cyprian Moidore and Miss Araminta. Similarly the upstairs maid Maggie, the between maid Nellie, and the handsome parlormaid Dinah were outside her responsibility. The tiny, fierce housekeeper, Mrs. Willis, did not have jurisdiction over nurses, and that was a bad beginning to their relationship. She was used to power and resented a female servant who was not answerable to her. Her small, neat face showed it in instant disapproval. She reminded Hester of a particularly efficient hospital matron, and the comparison was not a fortunate one.

"You will eat in the servants' hall with everyone else,"

Mrs. Willis informed her tartly. "Unless your duties make that impossible. After breakfast at eight o'clock we all," she said the word pointedly, and looked Hester in the eye, "gather for Sir Basil to lead us in prayers. I assume, Miss Latterly, that you are a member of the Church of England?"

"Oh yes, Mrs. Willis," Hester said immediately, although by inclination she was no such thing, her nature was all nonconformist.

"Good." Mrs. Willis nodded. "Quite so. We take dinner between twelve and one, while the family takes luncheon. There will be supper at whatever time the evening suits. When there are large dinner parties that may be very late." Her eyebrows rose very high. "We give some of the largest dinner parties in London here, and very fine cuisine indeed. But since we are in mourning at present there will be no entertaining, and by the time we resume I imagine your duties will be long past. I expect you will have half a day off a fortnight, like everyone else. But if that does not suit her ladyship, then you won't."

Since it was not a permanent position Hester was not yet concerned with time off, so long as she had opportunity to see Monk when necessary, to report to him any knowledge she had gained.

"Yes, Mrs. Willis," she replied, since a reply seemed to be awaited.

"You will have little or no occasion to go into the withdrawing room, but if you do I presume you know better than to knock?" Her eyes were sharp on Hester's face. "It is extremely vulgar ever to knock on a withdrawing room door."

"Of course, Mrs. Willis," Hester said hastily. She had never given the matter any thought, but it would not do to admit it.

"The maid will care for your room, of course," the housekeeper went on, looking at Hester critically. "But you will iron your own aprons. The laundrymaids have enough to do, and the ladies' maids are certainly not waiting on you! If anyone sends you letters—you have a family?" This last was something in the nature of a challenge. People without families lacked respectability; they might be anyone.

"Yes, Mrs. Willis, I do," Hester said firmly. "Unfortunately my parents died recently, and one of my brothers was

135

killed in the Crimea, but I have a surviving brother, and I am very fond both of him and of his wife."

Mrs. Willis was satisfied. "Good. I am sorry about your brother who died in the Crimea, but many fine young men were lost in that conflict. To die for one's Queen and country is an honorable thing and to be borne with such fortitude as one can. My own father was a soldier—a very fine man, a man to look up to. Family is very important, Miss Latterly. All the staff here are most respectable."

With great difficulty Hester bit her tongue and forbore from saying what she felt about the Crimean War and its political motives or the utter incompetence of its conduct. She controlled herself with merely lowering her eyes as if in modest consent.

"Mary will show you the female servants' staircase." Mrs. Willis had finished the subject of personal lives and was back to business.

"I beg your pardon?" Hester was momentarily confused.

"The female servants' staircase," Mrs. Willis said sharply. "You will have to go up and down stairs, girl! This is a decent household—you don't imagine you are going to use the male servants' stairs, do you? Whatever next? I hope you don't have any ideas of that sort."

"Certainly not, ma'am." Hester collected her wits quickly and invented an explanation. "I am just unused to such spaciousness. I am not long returned from the Crimea." This in case Mrs. Willis had heard only the reputation of nurses in England, which was far from savory. "We had no menservants where I was."

"Indeed." Mrs. Willis was totally ignorant in the matter, but unwilling to say so. "Well, we have five outside menservants here, whom you are unlikely to meet, and inside we have Mr. Phillips, the butler; Rhodes, Sir Basil's valet; Harold and Percival, the footmen; and Willie, the bootboy. You will have no occasion to have dealings with any of them."

"No ma'am."

Mrs. Willis sniffed. "Very well. You had best go and present yourself to Lady Moidore and see if there is anything you can do for her, poor creature." She smoothed her apron fiercely and her keys jangled. "As if it wasn't enough to be bereaved of a daughter, without police creeping all over the house and pestering people with questions. I don't know what the world is coming to! If they were doing their job in the first place all this would never have happened.''

Since she was not supposed to know it, Hester refrained from saying it was a bit unreasonable to expect police, no matter how diligent, to prevent a domestic murder.

''Thank you, Mrs. Willis,'' she said in compromise, and turned to go upstairs and meet Beatrice Moidore.

She tapped on the bedroom door, and when there was no answer, went in anyway. It was a charming room, very feminine, full of flowered brocades, oval framed pictures and mirrors, and three light, comfortable dressing chairs set about to be both ornamental and useful. The curtains were wide open and the room full of cold sunlight.

Beatrice herself was lying on the bed in a satin peignoir, her ankles crossed and her arms behind her head, her eyes wide, staring at the ceiling. She took no notice when Hester came in.

Hester was an army nurse used to caring for men sorely wounded or desperately ill, but she had a small experience of the shock and then deep depression and fear following an amputation, and the feeling of utter helplessness that overwhelms every other emotion. What she thought she saw in Beatrice Moidore was fear, and the frozen attitude of an animal that dares not move in case it draws attention to itself and does not know which way to run.

''Lady Moidore,'' she said quietly.

Beatrice realized it was a voice she did not know, and an unaccustomed tone, firmer and not tentative like a maid's. She turned her head and stared.

''Lady Moidore, I am Hester Latterly. I am a nurse, and I have come to look after you until you feel better.''

Beatrice sat up slowly on her elbows. ''A nurse?'' she said with a faint, slightly twisted smile. ''I'm not—'' Then she changed her mind and lay back again. ''There has been a murder in my family—that is not an illness.''

So Araminta had not even told her of the arrangements, let alone consulted her—unless, of course, she had forgotten?

''No,'' Hester agreed aloud. ''I would consider it more in the nature of an injury. But I learned most of my nursing in the Crimea, so I am used to injury and the shock and distress it causes. One can take some time even to desire to recover.''

"In the Crimea? How useful.''

Hester was surprised. It was an odd comment to make. She looked more carefully at Beatrice's sensitive, intelligent face with its wide eyes, jutting nose and fine lips. She was far from a classic beauty, nor did she have the rather heavy, sulky look that was currently much admired. She appeared far too spirited to appeal to many men, who might care for something a great deal more domestic seeming. And yet today her aspect completely denied the nature implicit in her features.

"Yes,'' Hester agreed. "And now that my family are dead and were not able to leave me provided for, I require to remain useful.''

Beatrice sat up again. "It must be very satisfying to be useful. My children are adult and married themselves. We do a great deal of entertaining—at least we did—but my daughter Araminta is highly skilled at preparing guest lists that will be interesting and amusing, my cook is the envy of half of London, and my butler knows where to hire any extra help we might need. All my staff are highly trained, and I have an extremely efficient housekeeper who does not appreciate my meddling in her affairs.''

Hester smiled. "Yes, I can imagine. I have met her. Have you taken luncheon today?''

"I am not hungry.''

"Then you should take a little soup, and some fruit. It can give you very unpleasant effects if you do not drink. Internal distress will not help you at all.''

Beatrice looked as surprised as her indifference would allow.

"You are very blunt.''

"I do not wish to be misunderstood.''

Beatrice smiled in spite of herself. "I doubt you very often are.''

Hester kept her composure. She must not forget that her primary duty was to care for a woman suffering deeply.

"May I bring you a little soup, and some fruit tart, or a custard?''

"I imagine you will bring it anyway—and I daresay you are hungry yourself?''

Hester smiled, glanced around the room once more, and went to begin her duties in the kitchen.

It was that evening that Hester made her next acquaintance with Araminta. She had come downstairs to the library to fetch a book which she thought would interest Beatrice and possibly help her to sleep, and she was searching along the shelves past weighty histories, and even weightier philosophies, until she should come to poetries and novels. She was bent over on her knees with her skirts around her when Araminta came in.

"Have you mislaid something, Miss Latterly?" she asked with faint disapproval. It was an undignified position, and too much at home for someone who was more or less a servant.

Hester rose to her feet and straightened her clothes. They were much of a height and looked at each other across a small reading table. Araminta was dressed in black silk trimmed with velvet with tiny silk ribbons on the bodice and her hair was as vivid as marigolds in the sun. Hester was dressed in blue-gray with a white apron, and her hair was a very ordinary brown with faint touches of honey or auburn in it in the sun, but excessively dull compared with Araminta's.

"No, Mrs. Kellard," she replied gravely. "I came to find something for Lady Moidore to read before she retires, so it might help her to sleep."

"Indeed? I would think a little laudanum would serve better?"

"It is a last resort, ma'am," Hester said levelly. "It tends to form a dependency, and can make one feel unwell afterwards."

"I imagine you know that my sister was murdered in this house less than three weeks ago?" Araminta stood very straight, her eyes unwavering. Hester admired her moral courage to be so blunt on a subject many would consider too shocking to speak of at all.

"Yes I am," she said gravely. "It is not surprising that your mother is extremely distressed, especially since I understand the police are still here quite often asking questions. I thought a book might take her mind off present grief, at least long enough to fall asleep, without causing the heaviness of drugs. It will not serve her to evade the pain forever. I don't mean to sound harsh. I have lost my own parents and a brother; I am acquainted with bereavement."

"Presumably that is why Lady Burke-Heppenstall recommended you. I think it will be most beneficial if you can keep my mother's mind from dwelling upon Octavia, my sister, or upon who might have been responsible for her death." Araminta's eyes did not flinch or evade in the slightest. "I am glad you are not afraid to be in the house. You have no need to be." She raised her shoulders very slightly. It was a cold gesture. "It is highly possible it was some mistaken relationship which ended in tragedy. If you conduct yourself with propriety, and do not encourage any attentions whatever, nor give the appearance of meddling or being inquisitive—"

The door opened and Myles Kellard came in. Hester's first thought was that he was an extraordinarily handsome man with a quite individual air to him, a man who might laugh or sing, or tell wild and entertaining stories. If his mouth was a trifle self-indulgent, perhaps it was only that of a dreamer.

"—you will find no trouble at all." Araminta finished without turning to look at him or acknowledge his presence.

"Are you warning Miss Latterly about our intrusive and rather arrogant policeman?" Myles asked curiously. He turned and smiled at Hester, an easy and charming expression. "Ignore him, Miss Latterly. And if he is overpersistent, report him to me, and I shall be glad to dispatch him for you forthwith. Whomever else he suspects—" His eyes surveyed her with mild interest, and she felt a sudden pang of regret that she was so ungenerously endowed and dressed so very plainly. It would have been most agreeable to see a spark of interest light in such a man's eyes as he looked at her.

"He will not suspect Miss Latterly," Araminta said for him. "Principally because she was not here at the time."

"Of course not," he agreed, putting out his arm towards his wife. With a delicate, almost imperceptible gesture she moved away from him so he did not touch her.

He froze, changed direction and reached instead to straighten a picture which was sitting on the desk.

"Otherwise he might," Araminta continued coolly, stiffening her back. "He seems to suspect everyone else, even the family."

"Rubbish!" Myles attempted to sound impatient, but Hester thought he was more uncomfortable. There was a sudden pinkness to his skin and his eyes moved restlessly from one object to another, avoiding their faces. "That is absurd! None of us could have the slightest reason for such a fearful thing, nor would we if we had. Really, Minta, you will be frightening Miss Latterly."

"I did not say one of us had done it, Myles, merely that Inspector Monk believed it of us—I think it must have been something Percival said about you." She watched the color ebb from his skin, then turned away and continued deliberately. "He is most irresponsible. If I were quite sure I should have him dismissed." She spoke very clearly. Her tone suggested she was musing aloud, intent upon her thoughts for themselves, not for any effect upon others, but her body inside its beautiful gown was as stiff as a twig in the still air, and her voice was penetrating. "I think it is the suspicion of what Percival said that has made Mama take to her bed. Perhaps if you were to avoid her, Myles, it might be better for her. She may be afraid of you—" She turned suddenly and smiled at him, dazzling and brittle. "Which is perfectly absurd, I know—but fear is at times irrational. We can have the wildest ideas about people, and no one can convince us they are unfounded."

She cocked her head a little to one side. "After all, whatever reason could you possibly have to have quarreled so violently with Octavia?" She hesitated. "And yet she is sure you have. I hope she does not tell Mr. Monk so, as it would be most distressing for us." She swiveled around to Hester. "Do see if you can help her to take a rather firmer hold on reality, Miss Latterly. We shall all be eternally grateful to you. Now I must go and see how poor Romola is. She has a headache, and Cyprian never knows what to do for her." She swept her skirts around her and walked out, graceful and rigid.

Hester found herself surprisingly embarrassed. It was perfectly clear that Araminta was aware she had frightened her husband, and that she took a calculated pleasure in it. Hester bent to the bookshelf again, not wishing Myles to see the knowledge in her eyes.

He moved to stand behind her, no more than a yard away, and she was acutely conscious of his presence.

"There is no need to be concerned, Miss Latterly," he said

141

with a very slight huskiness in his voice. "Lady Moidore has rather an active imagination. Like a lot of ladies. She gets her facts muddled, and frequently does not mean what she says. I am sure you understand that?" His tone implied that Hester would be the same, and her words were to be taken lightly.

She rose to her feet and met his eyes, so close she could see the shadow of his remarkable eyelashes on his cheeks, but she refused to step backwards.

"No I do not understand it, Mr. Kellard." She chose her words carefully. "I very seldom say what I do not mean, and if I do, it is accidental, a misuse of words, not a confusion in my mind."

"Of course, Miss Latterly." He smiled. "I am sure you are at heart just like all women—"

"Perhaps if Mrs. Moidore has a headache, I should see if I can help her?" she said quickly, to prevent herself from giving the retort in her mind.

"I doubt you can," he replied, moving aside a step. "It is not your attention she wishes for. But by all means try, if you like. It should be a nice diversion."

She chose to misunderstand him. "If one is suffering a headache, surely whose attention it is is immaterial."

"Possibly," he conceded. "I've never had one—at least not of Romola's sort. Only women do."

Hester seized the first book to her hand, and holding it with its face towards her so its title was hidden, brushed her way past him.

"If you will excuse me, I must return to see how Lady Moidore is feeling."

"Of course," he murmured. "Although I doubt it will be much different from when you left her!"

It was during the day after that she came to realize more fully what Myles had meant about Romola's headache. She was coming in from the conservatory with a few flowers for Beatrice's room when she came upon Romola and Cyprian standing with their backs to her, and too engaged in their conversation to be aware of her presence.

"It would make me very happy if you would," Romola said with a note of pleading in her voice, but dragged out, a little plaintive, as though she had asked many times before.

Hester stopped and took a step backwards behind the curtain, from where she could see Romola's back and Cyprian's face. He looked tired and harassed, shadows under his eyes and a hunched attitude to his shoulders as though half waiting for a blow.

"You know that it would be fruitless at the moment," he replied with careful patience. "It would not make matters any better."

"Oh, Cyprian!" She turned very petulantly, her whole body expressing disappointment and disillusion. "I really think for my sake you should try. It would make all the difference in the world to me."

"I have already explained to you—" he began, then abandoned the attempt. "I know you wish it," he said sharply, exasperation breaking through. "And if I could persuade him I would."

"Would you? Sometimes I wonder how important my happiness is to you."

"Romola—I—"

At this point Hester could bear it no longer. She resented people who by moral pressure made others responsible for their happiness. Perhaps because no one had ever taken responsibility for hers, but without knowing the circumstances, she was still utterly on Cyprian's side. She bumped noisily into the curtain, rattling the rings, let out a gasp of surprise and mock irritation, and then when they both turned to look at her, smiled apologetically and excused herself, sailing past them with a bunch of pink daisies in her hand. The gardener had called them something quite different, but *daisies* would do.

She settled in to Queen Anne Street with some difficulty. Physically it was extremely comfortable. It was always warm enough, except in the servants' rooms on the third and fourth floors, and the food was by far the best she had ever eaten—and the quantities were enormous. There was meat, river fish and sea fish, game, poultry, oysters, lobster, venison, jugged hare, pies, pastries, vegetables, fruit, cakes, tarts and flans, puddings and desserts. And the servants frequently ate what was returned from the dining room as well as what was cooked especially for them.

She learned the hierarchy of the servants' hall, exactly whose domain was where and who deferred to whom, which was extremely important. No one intruded upon anyone else's duties, which were either above them or beneath them, and they guarded their own with jealous exactitude. Heaven forbid a senior housemaid should be asked to do what was the under housemaid's job, or worse still, that a footman should take a liberty in the kitchen and offend the cook.

Rather more interestingly she learned where the fondnesses lay, and the rivalries, who had taken offense at whom, and quite often why.

Everyone was in awe of Mrs. Willis, and Mr. Phillips was considered more the master in any practical terms than Sir Basil, whom many of the staff never actually saw. There was a certain amount of joking and irreverence about his military mannerisms, and more than one reference to sergeant majors, but never within his hearing.

Mrs. Boden, the cook, ruled with a rod of iron in the kitchen, but it was more by skill, dazzling smiles and a very hot temper than by the sheer freezing awe of the housekeeper or the butler. Mrs. Boden was also fond of Cyprian and Romola's children, the fair-haired, eight-year-old Julia and her elder brother, Arthur, who was just ten. She was given to spoiling them with treats from the kitchen whenever opportunity arose, which was frequently, because although they ate in the nursery, Mrs. Boden oversaw the preparation of the tray that was sent up.

Dinah the parlormaid was a trifle superior, but it was in good part her position rather than her nature. Parlormaids were selected for their appearance and were required to sail in and out of the front reception rooms heads high, skirts swishing, to open the front door in the afternoons and carry visitors' cards in on a silver tray. Hester actually found her very approachable, and keen to talk about her family and how good they had been to her, providing her with every opportunity to better herself.

Sal, the kitchen maid, remarked that Dinah had never been seen to receive a letter from them, but she was ignored. And Dinah took all her permitted time off duty, and once a year returned to her home village, which was somewhere in Kent.

Lizzie, the senior laundrymaid, on the other hand, was very

superior indeed, and ran the laundry with an unbending discipline. Rose, and the women who came in to do some of the heavy ironing, were never seen to disobey, whatever their private feelings. It was an entertaining observation of nature, but little of it seemed of value in learning who had murdered Octavia Haslett.

Of course the subject was discussed below stairs. One could not possibly have a murder in the house and expect people not to speak of it, most particularly when they were all suspected—and one of them had to be guilty.

Mrs. Boden refused even to think about it, or to permit anyone else to.

"Not in my kitchen," she said briskly, whisking half a dozen eggs so sharply they all but flew out of the bowl. "I'll not have gossip in here. You've got more than enough to do without wasting your time in silly chatter. Sal—you do them potatoes by the time I've finished this, or I'll know the reason why! May! May! What about the floor, then? I won't have a dirty floor in here."

Phillips stalked from one room to another, grand and grim. Mrs. Boden said the poor man had taken it very hard that such a thing should happen in his household. Since it was obviously not one of the family, to which no one replied, obviously it must be one of the servants—which automatically meant someone he had hired.

Mrs. Willis's icy look stopped any speculation she overheard. It was indecent and complete nonsense. The police were quite incompetent, or they would know perfectly well it couldn't be anyone in the house. To discuss such a thing would only frighten the younger girls and was quite irresponsible. Anyone overheard being so foolish would be disciplined appropriately.

Of course this stopped no one who was minded to indulge in a little gossip, which was all the maids, to the endless patronizing comments of the male staff, who had quite as much to say but were less candid about it. It reached a peak at tea time in the servants' hall.

"I think it was Mr. Thirsk, when 'e was drunk," Sal said with a toss of her head. "I know 'e takes port from the cellar, an' no good sayin' 'e doesn't!"

"Lot o' nonsense," Lizzie dismissed with scorn. "He's

ever such a gentleman. And what would he do such a thing for, may I ask?"

"Sometimes I wonder where you grew up." Gladys glanced over her shoulder to make sure Mrs. Boden was nowhere in earshot. She leaned forward over the table, her cup of tea at her elbow. "Don't you know anything?"

"She works downstairs!" Mary hissed back at her. "Downstairs people never know half what upstairs people do."

"Go on then," Rose challenged. "Who do you think did it?"

"Mrs. Sandeman, in a fit o' jealous rage," Mary replied with conviction. "You should see some o' the outfits she wears—and d'you know where Harold says he takes her sometimes?"

They all stopped eating or drinking in breathless anticipation of the answer.

"Well?" Maggie demanded.

"You're too young." Mary shook her head.

"Oh, go on," Maggie pleaded. "Tell us!"

"She doesn't know 'erself," Sal said with a grin. "She's 'avin us on."

"I do so!" Mary retorted. "He takes her to streets where decent women don't go—down by the Haymarket."

"What—over some admirer?" Gladys savored the possibility. "Go on! Really?"

"You got a better idea, then?" Mary asked.

Willie the bootboy appeared from the kitchen doorway, where he had been keeping cavey in case Mrs. Boden should appear.

"Well I think it was Mr. Kellard!" he said with a backward glance over his shoulder. "May I have that piece o' cake? I'm starvin' 'ungry."

"That's only because you don't like 'im." Mary pushed the cake towards him, and he took it and bit into it ravenously.

"Pig," Sal said without rancor.

"I think it was Mrs. Moidore," May the scullery maid said suddenly.

"Why?" Gladys demanded with offended dignity. Romola was her charge, and she was personally offended by the suggestion.

146

"Go on with you!" Mary dismissed it. "You've never even seen Mrs. Moidore!"

"I 'ave too," May retorted. "She came down 'ere when young Miss Julia was sick that time! A good mother, she is. I reckon she's too good to be true—all that peaches-an'-cream skin and 'andsome face. She done married Mr. Cyprian for 'is money."

" 'E don't 'ave any," William said with his mouth full. " 'E's always borrowin' off folks. Least that's what Percival says."

"Then Percival's speakin' out of turn," Annie criticized. "Not that I'm saying Mrs. Moidore didn't do it. But I reckon it was more likely Mrs. Kellard. Sisters can hate something 'orrible."

"What about?" Maggie asked. "Why should Mrs. Kellard hate poor Miss Octavia?"

"Well Percival said Mr. Kellard fancied Miss Octavia something rotten," Annie explained. "Not that I take any notice of what Percival says. He's got a wicked tongue, that one."

At that moment Mrs. Boden came in.

"Enough gossiping," she said sharply. "And don't you talk with your mouth full, Annie Latimer. Get on about your business. Sal. There's carrots you 'aven't scraped yet, and cabbage for tonight's dinner. You 'aven't time to sit chatterin' over cups o' tea."

The last suggestion was the only one Hester thought suitable to report to Monk when he called and insisted on interviewing all the staff again, including the new nurse, even though it was pointed out to him that she had not been present at the time of the crime.

"Forget the kitchen gossip. What is your own opinion?" he asked her, his voice low so no servants passing beyond the housekeeper's sitting room door might overhear them. She frowned and hesitated, trying to find words to convey the extraordinary feeling of embarrassment and unease she had experienced in the library as Araminta swept out.

"Hester?"

"I am not sure," she said slowly. "Mr. Kellard was frightened, that I have no doubt of, but I could not even guess whether it was guilt over having murdered Octavia or simply

147

having made some improper advance towards her—or even just fear because it was quite apparent that his wife took a certain pleasure in the whole possibility that he might be suspected quite gravely—even accused. She was—" She thought again before using the word, it was too melodramatic, then could find none more appropriate. "She was torturing him. Of course," she hurried on, "I do not know how she would react if you were to charge him. She might simply be doing this as some punishment for a private quarrel, and she may defend him to the death from outsiders."

"Do you think she believes him guilty?" He stood against the mantel shelf, hands in his pockets, face puckered with concentration.

She had thought hard about this ever since the incident, and her reply was ready on her lips.

"She is not afraid of him, of that I am certain. But there is a deep emotion there which has a bitterness to it, and I think he is more afraid of her—but I don't know if that has anything to do with Octavia's death or is simply that she has the power to hurt him."

She took a deep breath. "It must be extremely difficult for him, living in his father-in-law's house and in a very real way being under his jurisdiction and constantly obliged to please him or face very considerable unpleasantness. And Sir Basil does seem to rule with a heavy hand, from what I have seen." She sat sideways on the arm of one of the chairs, an attitude which would have sent Mrs. Willis into a rage, both for its unladylike pose and for the harm she was sure it would do to the chair.

"I have not seen much of Mr. Thirsk or Mrs. Sandeman yet. She leads quite a busy life, and perhaps I am maligning her, but I am sure she drinks. I have seen enough of it in the war to recognize the signs, even in highly unlikely people. I saw her yesterday morning with a fearful headache which, from the pattern of her recovery, was not any ordinary illness. But I may be hasty; I only met her on the landing as I was going in to Lady Moidore."

He smiled very slightly. "And what do you think of Lady Moidore?"

Every vestige of humor vanished from her face. "I think she is very frightened. She knows or believes something which

148

is so appalling that she dare not confront it, yet neither can she put it from her mind—"

"That it was Myles Kellard who killed Octavia?" he asked, stepping forward a pace. "Hester—be careful!" He took her arm and held it hard, the pressure of his fingers so strong as to be almost painful. "Watch and listen as your opportunities allow, but do not ask anything! Do you hear me?"

She backed away, rubbing her arm. "Of course I hear you. You requested me to help—I am doing so. I have no intention of asking any questions—they would not answer them anyway but would dismiss me for being impertinent and intrusive. I am a servant here."

"What about the servants?" He did not move away but remained close to her. "Be careful of the menservants, Hester, particularly the footmen. It is quite likely one of them had amorous ideas about Octavia, and misunderstood"—he shrugged—"or even understood correctly, and she got tired of the affair—"

"Good heavens. You are no better than Myles Kellard," she snapped at him. "He all but implied Octavia was a trollop."

"It is only a possibility!" he hissed sharply. "Keep your voice down. For all we know there may be a row of eavesdroppers at the door. Does your bedroom have a lock?"

"No."

"Then put a chair behind the handle."

"I hardly think—" Then she remembered that Octavia Haslett had been murdered in her bedroom in the middle of the night, and she found she was shaking in spite of herself.

"It is someone in this house!" Monk repeated, watching her closely.

"Yes," she said obediently. "Yes, I know that. We all know that—that is what is so terrible."

149

6

HESTER LEFT her interview with Monk considerably chastened. Seeing him again had reminded her that this was not an ordinary household, and the difference of opinion, the quarrels, which seemed a trivial nastiness, in one case had been so deep they had led to violent and treacherous death. One of those people she looked at across the meal table, or passed on the stairs, had stabbed Octavia in the night and left her to bleed.

It made her a little sick as she returned to Beatrice's bedroom and knocked on the door before entering. Beatrice was standing by the window staring out into the remains of the autumn garden and watching the gardener's boy sweeping up the fallen leaves and pulling a few last weeds from around the Michaelmas daisies. Arthur, his hair blowing in the wind, was helping with the solemnity of a ten-year-old. Beatrice turned as Hester came in, her face pale, her eyes wide and anxious.

"You look distressed," she said, staring at Hester. She walked over to the dressing chair but did not sit, as if the chair would imprison her and she desired the freedom to move suddenly. "Why did the police want to see you? You weren't here when—when Tavie was killed."

"No, Lady Moidore." Hester's mind raced for a reason which would be believed, and perhaps which might even prompt Beatrice to yield something of the fear Hester was sure so troubled her. "I am not entirely certain, but I believe he thought I might have observed something since I came. And I

150

have no cause for prevaricating, insofar as I could not fear he might accuse me.''

"Who do you think is lying?'' Beatrice asked.

Hester hesitated very slightly and moved to tidy the bed, plump up the pillows and generally appear to be working. "I don't know, but it is quite certain that someone must be.''

Beatrice looked startled, as though it were not an answer she had foreseen.

"You mean someone is protecting the murderer? Why? Who would do such a thing and why? What reason could they have?''

Hester tried to excuse herself. "I meant merely that since it is someone in the house, that person is lying to protect himself.'' Then she realized the opportunity she had very nearly lost. "Although when you mention it, you are quite right, it seems most unlikely that no one else has any idea who it is, or why. I daresay several people are evading the truth, one way or another.'' She glanced up from the bed at Beatrice. "Wouldn't you, Lady Moidore?''

Beatrice hesitated. "I fear so,'' she said very quietly.

"If you ask me who,'' Hester went on, disregarding the fact that no one had asked her, "I have formed very few opinions. I can easily imagine why some people would hide a truth they knew, or suspected, in order to protect someone they cared for—'' She watched Beatrice's face and saw the muscles tighten as if pain had caught her unaware. "I would hesitate to say something,'' Hester continued, "which might cause an unjustified suspicion—and therefore a great deal of distress. For example, an affection that might have been misunderstood—''

Beatrice stared back at her, wide-eyed. "Did you say that to Mr. Monk?''

"Oh no,'' Hester replied demurely. "He might have thought I had someone in particular in mind.''

Beatrice smiled very slightly. She walked back towards the bed and lay on it, weary not in body but in mind, and Hester gently pulled the covers over her, trying to hide her own impatience. She was convinced Beatrice knew something, and every day that passed in silence was adding to the danger that it might never be discovered but that the whole household would close in on itself in corroding suspicion and concealed

151

accusations. And would her silence be enough to protect her indefinitely from the murderer?

"Are you comfortable?" she asked gently.

"Yes thank you," Beatrice said absently. "Hester?"

"Yes?"

"Were you frightened in the Crimea? It must have been dangerous at times. Did you not fear for yourself—and for those of whom you had grown fond?"

"Yes of course." Hester's mind flew back to the times when she had lain in her cot with horror creeping over her skin and the sick knowledge of what pain awaited the men she had seen so shortly before, the numbing cold in the heights above Sebastopol, the mutilation of wounds, the carnage of battle, bodies broken and so mangled as to be almost unrecognizable as human, only as bleeding flesh, once alive and capable of unimaginable pain. It was seldom herself for whom she had been frightened; only sometimes, when she was so tired she felt ill, did the sudden specter of typhoid or cholera so terrify her as to cause her stomach to lurch and the sweat to break out and stand cold on her body.

Beatrice was looking at her, for once her eyes sharp with real interest—there was nothing polite or feigned in it.

Hester smiled. "Yes I was afraid sometimes, but not often. Mostly I was too busy. When you can do something about even the smallest part of it, the overwhelming sick horror goes. You stop seeing the whole thing and see only the tiny part you are dealing with, and the fact that you can do something calms you. Even if all you accomplish is easing one person's distress or helping someone to endure with hope instead of despair. Sometimes it is just tidying up that helps, getting a kind of order out of the chaos."

Only when she had finished and saw the understanding in Beatrice's face did she realize the additional meanings of what she had said. If anyone had asked her earlier if she would have changed her life for Beatrice's, married and secure in status and well-being with family and friends, she would have accepted it as a woman's most ideal role, as if it were a stupid thing even to doubt.

Perhaps Beatrice would just as quickly have refused. Now they had both changed their views with a surprise which was still growing inside them. Beatrice was safe from material misfortune, but she was also withering inside with boredom and lack of accomplishment. Pain appalled her because she had no part in addressing it. She endured passively, without knowledge or weapon with which to fight it, either in herself or in those she loved or pitied. It was a kind of distress Hester had seen before, but never more than casually, and never with so sharp and wounding an understanding.

Now it would be clumsy to try to put into words what was far too subtle, and which they both needed time to face in their own perceptions. Hester wanted to say something that would offer comfort, but anything that came to her mind sounded patronizing and would have shattered the delicate empathy between them.

"What would you like for luncheon?" she asked.

"Does it matter?" Beatrice smiled and shrugged, sensing the subtlety of moving from one subject to another quite different, and painlessly trivial.

"Not in the least." Hester smiled ruefully. "But you might as well please yourself, rather than the cook."

"Well not egg custard or rice pudding!" Beatrice said with feeling. "It reminds me of the nursery. It is like being a child again."

Hester had only just returned with the tray of cold mutton, fresh pickle, and bread and butter and a large slice of fruit flan with cream, to Beatrice's obvious approval, when there was a sharp rap on the door and Basil came in. He walked past Hester as if he had not seen her and sat down in one of the dressing chairs close to the bed, crossing his legs and making himself comfortable.

Hester was uncertain whether to leave or not. She had few tasks to do here, and yet she was extremely curious to know more of the relationship between Beatrice and her husband, a relationship which left the woman with such a feeling of isolation that she retreated to her room instead of running towards him, either for him to protect her or the better to battle it together. After all the affliction must lie in the area of family, emotions; there must be in it grief, love, hate, probably jealousy—all surely a woman's province, the area in which her skills mattered and her strength could be used?

Now Beatrice sat propped up against her pillows and ate the cold mutton with pleasure.

Basil looked at it disapprovingly. "Is that not rather heavy for an invalid? Let me send for something better, my dear—" He reached for the bell without waiting for her answer.

"I like it," she said with a flash of anger. "There is nothing wrong with my digestion. Hester got it for me and it is not Mrs. Boden's fault. She'd have sent me more rice pudding if I had let her."

"Hester?" He frowned. "Oh—the nurse." He spoke as if she were not there, or could not hear him. "Well—I suppose if you wish it."

"I do." She ate a few more mouthfuls before speaking again. "I assume Mr. Monk is still coming?"

"Of course. But he seems to be accomplishing singularly little—indeed I have seen no signs that he has achieved anything at all. He keeps questioning the servants. We shall be fortunate if they do not all give notice when this is over." He rested his elbows on the arms of the chair and put his fingertips together. "I have no idea how he hopes to come to any resolution. I think, my dear, you may have to prepare yourself for facing the fact that we may never know who it was." He was watching her and saw the sudden tightening, the hunch of her shoulders and the knuckles white where she held the knife. "Of course I have certain ideas," he went on. "I cannot imagine it was any of the female staff—"

"Why not?" she asked. "Why not, Basil? It is perfectly possible for a woman to stab someone with a knife. It doesn't take a great deal of strength. And Octavia would be far less likely to fear a woman in her room in the middle of the night than a man."

A flicker of irritation crossed his face. "Really, Beatrice, don't you think it is time to accept a few truths about Octavia? She had been widowed nearly two years. She was a young woman in the prime of her life—"

"So she had an affair with the footman!" Beatrice said furiously, her eyes wide, her voice cutting in its scorn. "Is that what you think of your daughter, Basil? If anyone in this house is reduced to finding their pleasure with a servant, it is far more likely to be Fenella! Except that I doubt she would ever have inspired a passion which drove anyone to murder—unless it was to murder her. Nor would she have changed her mind

154

and resisted at the last moment. I doubt Fenella ever declined anyone—'' Her face twisted in distaste and incomprehension.

His expression mirrored an equal disgust, mixed with an anger that was no sudden flash but came from deep within him.

"Vulgarity is most unbecoming, Beatrice, and even this tragedy is no excuse for it. I shall admonish Fenella if I think the occasion warrants it. I take it you are not suggesting Fenella killed Octavia in a fit of jealousy over the attentions of the footman?''

It was obviously intended as sarcasm, but she took it literally.

"I was not suggesting it," she agreed. "But now that you raise the thought, it does not seem impossible. Percival is a good-looking young man, and I have observed Fenella regarding him with appreciation." Her face puckered and she shuddered very slightly. "I know it is revolting—" She stared beyond him to the dressing table with its cut glass containers and silver-topped bottles neatly arranged. "But there is a streak of viciousness in Fenella—"

He stood up and turned his back to her, looking out of the window, still apparently oblivious of Hester standing in the dressing room doorway with a peignoir over her arm and a clothes brush in her hand.

"You are a great deal more fastidious than most women, Beatrice," he said flatly. "I think sometimes you do not know the difference between restraint and abstemiousness."

"I know the difference between a footman and a gentleman," she said quietly, and then stopped and frowned, a curious little twitch of humor on her lips. "That's a lie—I have no idea at all. I have no familiarity with footmen whatsoever—"

He swung around, unaware of the slightest humor in her remark or in the situation, only anger and acute insult.

"This tragedy has unhinged your mind," he said coldly, his black eyes flat, seeming expressionless in the lamplight. "You have lost your sense of what is fitting and what is not. I think it will be better if you remain here until you can compose yourself. I suppose it is to be expected, you are not strong. Let Miss—what is her name—care for you. Araminta will see to the household until you are better. We shall not be entertaining, naturally. There is no need for you to concern yourself; we shall manage very well." And without saying anything further he walked out and closed the door very quietly behind him, letting the latch fall home with a thud.

Beatrice pushed her unfinished tray away from her and turned over, burying her face in the pillows, and Hester could see from the quivering of her shoulders that she was weeping, although she made no sound.

Hester took the tray and put it on the side table, then wrung out a cloth in warm water from the ewer and returned to the bed. Very gently she put her arms around the other woman and held her until she was quiet, then, with great care, smoothed the hair off her brow and wiped her eyes and cheeks with the cloth.

It was the beginning of the afternoon when she was returning from the laundry with her clean aprons that Hester half accidentally overheard an exchange between the footman Percival and the laundrymaid Rose. Rose was folding a pile of embroidered linen pillowcases and had just given Lizzie, who was her elder sister, the parlormaid's lace-edged aprons. She was standing very upright, her back rigid, her shoulders squared and her chin high. She was tiny, with a waist even Hester could almost have put her hands around, and small, square hands with amazing strength in them. Her cornflower-blue eyes were enormous in her pretty face, not spoiled by a rather long nose and overgenerous mouth.

"What do you want in here?" she asked, but her words were belied by her voice. It was phrased as a demand, but it sounded like an invitation.

"Mr. Kellard's shirts," Percival said noncommittally.

"I didn't know that was your job. You'll have Mr. Rhodes after you if you step out of your duties!"

"Rhodes asked me to do it for him," he replied.

"Though you'd like to be a valet, wouldn't you? Get to travel with Mr. Kellard when he goes to stay at these big houses for parties and the like—" Her voice caressed the idea, and listening, Hester could envision her eyes shining, her lips parted in anticipation, all the excitement and delights imagined, new people, an elegant servants' hall, food, music, late nights, wine, laughter and gossip.

156

"It'd be all right," Percival agreed, for the first time a lift of warmth in his voice also. "Although I get to some interesting places now." That was the tone of the braggart, and Hester knew it.

It seemed Rose did too. "But not inside," she pointed out. "You have to wait in the mews with the carriages."

"Oh no I don't." There was a note of sharpness in his voice, and Hester could imagine the glitter in his eyes and the little curl of his lips. She had seen it several times as he walked through the kitchen past the maids. "I quite often go inside."

"The kitchen," Rose said dismissively. "If you were a valet you'd get upstairs as well. Valet is better than a footman."

They were all acutely conscious of hierarchy.

"Butler's better still," he pointed out.

"But less fun. Look at poor old Mr. Phillips." She giggled. "He hasn't had any fun in twenty years—and he looks as if 'e's forgotten that."

"Don't think 'e ever wanted any of your sort o' fun." Percival sounded serious again, remote and a trifle pompous. Suddenly he was talking of men's business, and putting a woman in her place. "He had an ambition to be in the army, but they wouldn't take him because of 'is feet. Can't have been that good a footman either, with his legs. Never wear livery without padding his stocking."

Hester knew Percival did not have to add any artificial enhancement to his calves.

"His feet?" Rose was incredulous. "What's wrong with 'is feet?"

This time there was derision in Percival's voice. "Haven't you ever watched 'im walk? Like someone broke a glass on the floor and 'e was picking 'is way over it and treading on half of it. Corns, bunions, I don't know."

"Pity," she said dryly. "He'd 'ave made a great sergeant major—cut out for it, 'e was. Mind, I suppose butler's the next best thing—the way 'e does it. And he does have a wonderful turn for putting some visitors in their place. He can size up anyone coming to call at a glance. Dinah says he never makes a mistake, and you should see his face if he thinks someone is less than a gentleman—or a lady—or if they're mean with their little appreciations. He can be so rude, just with his eye-

157

brows. Dinah says she's seen people ready to curl up and die with mortification. It's not every butler as can do that.''

"Any good servant can tell quality from riffraff, or they're not worth their position," Percival said haughtily. "I'm sure I can—and I know how to keep people in their places. There's dozens of ways—you can affect not to hear the bell, you can forget to stoke the fire, you can simply look at them like they were something the wind blew in, and then greet the person behind them like they was royalty. I can do that just as well as Mr. Phillips.''

Rose was unimpressed. She returned to her first subject. "Anyway, Percy, you'd be out from under him if you were a valet—''

Hester knew why she wanted him to change. Valets worked far more closely with laundrymaids, and Hester had watched Rose's cornflower eyes following Percival in the few days she had been here, and knew well enough what lay behind the innocence, the casual comments, the big bows on her apron waist and the extra flick of her skirts and wriggle of her shoulders. She had been attracted to men often enough herself and would have behaved just the same had she Rose's confidence and her feminine skill.

"Maybe.'' Percival was ostentatiously uninterested. "Not sure I want to stay in this house anyway.''

Hester knew that was a calculated rebuff, but she did not dare peer around the corner in case the movement was noticed. She stood still, leaning back against the piles of sheets on the shelf behind her and holding her aprons tightly. She could imagine the sudden cold feeling inside Rose. She remembered something much the same in the hospital in Scutari. There had been a doctor whom she admired, no, more than that, about whom she indulged in daydreams, imagined foolishness. And one day he had shattered them all with a dismissive word. For weeks afterwards she had turned it over and over in her mind, trying to decide whether he had meant it, even done it on purpose, bruising her feelings. That thought had sent waves of hot shame over her. Or had he been quite unaware and simply betrayed a side of his nature which had been there all the time—and which was better seen before she had committed herself too far. She would never know, and now it hardly mattered.

Rose said nothing. Hester did not even hear an indrawn breath.

"After all," Percival went on, adding to it, justifying himself, "this isn't the best house right now—police coming and going, asking questions. All London knows there's been a murder. And what's more, someone here did it. They won't stop till they find them, you know."

"Well if they don't, they won't let you go—will they?" Rose said spitefully. "After all—it might be you."

That must have been a thrust which struck home. For several seconds Percival was silent, then when he did speak his voice was sharp with a distinct edge, a crack of nervousness.

"Don't be stupid! What would any of us do that for? It must have been one of the family. The police aren't that easily fooled. That's why they're still here."

"Oh yes? And questioning us?" Rose retorted. "If that's so, what do they think we're going to tell them?"

"It's just an excuse." The certainty was coming back now. "They have to pretend it's us. Can you imagine what Sir Basil would say if they let on they suspected the family?"

"Nothing 'e could say!" She was still angry. "Police can go anywhere they want."

"Of course it's one of the family." Now he was contemptuous. "And I've got a few ideas who—and why. I know a few things—but I'd best say nothing; the police'll find out one of these days. Now I've got work to do, and so 'ave you." And he pushed on past her and around the corner. Hester stepped into the doorway so she was not discovered overhearing.

"Oh yes," Mary said, her eyes flashing as she flipped out a pillowcase and folded it. "Rose has a rare fancy for Percival. Stupid girl." She reached for another pillow slip and examined the lace to make sure it was intact before folding it to iron and put away. "He's nice enough looking, but what's that worth? He'd make a terrible husband, vain as a cockerel and always looking to his own advantage. Like enough leave her after a year or two. Roving eye, that one, and spiteful. Now Harold's a much better man—but then he wouldn't look at Rose; he never sees anyone but Dinah. Been eating his heart out for her for the last year and a half, poor boy." She put the pillow slip away and started on a pile of lace-edged petticoats, wide

159

enough to fall over the huge hoops that kept skirts in the ungainly but very flattering crinoline shape. At least that shape was considered charming by those who liked to look dainty and a little childlike. Personally Hester would have preferred something very much more practical, and more natural in shape. But she was out of step with fashion—not for the first time.

"And Dinah's got her eye on next door's footman," Mary went on, straightening the ruffles automatically. "Although I can't see anything in him, excepting he's tall, which is nice, seein' as Dinah's so tall herself. But height's no comfort on a cold night. It doesn't keep you warm, and it can't make you laugh. I expect you met some fine soldiers when you were in the army?"

Hester knew the question was kindly meant, and she answered it in the same manner.

"Oh several." She smiled. "Unfortunately they were a trifle incapacitated at the time."

"Oh." Mary laughed and shook her head as she came to the end of her mistress's clothes from this wash. "I suppose they would be. Never mind. If you work in houses like this, there's no telling who you might meet." And with that hopeful remark she picked up the bundle and carried it out, walking jauntily towards the stairs with a sway of her hips.

Hester smiled and finished her own task, then went to the kitchen to prepare a tisane for Beatrice. She was taking the tray back upstairs when she passed Septimus coming out of the cellar door, one arm folded rather awkwardly across his chest as though he were carrying something concealed inside his jacket.

"Good afternoon, Mr. Thirsk," Hester said cheerfully, as if he had every business in the cellar.

"Er—good afternoon, Miss—er—er . . ."

"Latterly," she supplied. "Lady Moidore's nurse."

"Oh yes—of course." He blinked his washed-out blue eyes. "I do beg your pardon. Good afternoon, Miss Latterly." He moved to get away from the cellar door, still looking extremely uncomfortable.

Annie, one of the upstairs maids, came past and gave Septimus a knowing look and smiled at Hester. She was tall and slender, like Dinah. She would have made a good parlormaid, but she was too young at the moment and raw at fifteen, and she might always be too opinionated. Hester had caught her and Maggie giggling together more than once in the maids' room on the first landing, where the morning tea was prepared, or in the linen cupboard bent double over a penny dreadful book, their eyes out like organ stops as they pored over the scenes of breathless romance and wild dangers. Heaven knew what was in their imaginations. Some of their speculations over the murder had been more colorful than credible.

"Nice child, that," Septimus said absently. "Her mother's a pastry cook over in Portman Square, but I don't think you'll ever make a cook out of her. Daydreamer." There was affection in his voice. "Likes to listen to stories about the army." He shrugged and nearly let slip the bottle under his arm. He blushed and grabbed at it.

Hester smiled at him. "I know. She's asked me lots of questions. Actually I think both she and Maggie would make good nurses. They're just the sort of girls we need, intelligent and quick, and with minds of their own."

Septimus looked taken aback, and Hester guessed he was used to the kind of army medical care that had prevailed before Florence Nightingale, and all these new ideas were outside his experience.

"Maggie's a good girl too," he said with a frown of puzzlement. "A lot more common sense. Her mother's a laundress somewhere in the country. Welsh, I think. Accounts for the temper. Very quick temper, that girl, but any amount of patience when it's needed. Sat up all night looking after the gardener's cat when it was sick, though, so I suppose you're right, she'd be a good enough nurse. But it seems a pity to put two decent girls into that trade." He wriggled discreetly to move the bottle under his jacket high enough for it not to be noticed, and knew that he had failed. He was totally unaware of having insulted her profession; he was speaking frankly from the reputation he knew and had not even thought of her as being part of it.

Hester was torn between saving him embarrassment and learning all she could. Saving him won. She looked away from the lump under his jacket and continued as if she had not observed it.

161

"Thank you. Perhaps I shall suggest it to them one day. Of course I had rather you did not mention my idea to the house-keeper."

His face twitched in half-mock, half-serious alarm.

"Believe me, Miss Latterly, I wouldn't dream of it. I am too old a soldier to mount an unnecessary charge."

"Quite," she agreed. "And I have cleared up after too many."

For an instant his face was perfectly sober, his blue eyes very clear, the lines of anxiety ironed out, and they shared a complete understanding. Both had seen the carnage of the battlefield and the long torture of wounds afterwards and the maimed lives. They knew the price of incompetence and bravado. It was an alien life from this house and its civilized routine and iron discipline of trivia, the maids rising at five to clean the fires, black the grates, throw damp tea leaves on the carpets and sweep them up, air the rooms, empty the slops, dust, sweep, polish, turn the beds, launder, iron dozens of yards of linens, petticoats, laces and ribbons, stitch, fetch and carry till at last they were excused at nine, ten or eleven in the evening.

"You tell them about nursing," he said at last, and quite openly took out the bottle and repositioned it more comfortably, then turned and left, walking with a lift in his step and a very slight swagger.

Upstairs Hester had just brought the tray for Beatrice and set it down, and was about to leave when Araminta came in.

"Good afternoon, Mama," she said briskly. "How are you feeling?" Like her father she seemed to find Hester invisible. She went and kissed her mother's cheek and then sat down on the nearest dressing chair, her skirts overflowing in mounds of darkest gray muslin with a lilac fichu, dainty and intensely flattering, and yet still just acceptable for mourning. Her hair was the same bright flame as always, her face its delicate, lean asymmetry.

"Exactly the same, thank you," Beatrice answered without real interest. She turned slightly to look at Araminta, a pucker of confusion around her mouth. There was no sense of affection between them, and Hester was uncertain whether she should leave or not. She had a curious sense that in some way she was not intruding because the tension between the two women, the lack of knowing what to say to each other, already excluded her. She was a servant, someone whose opinion was of no importance whatever, indeed someone not really of existence.

"Well I suppose it is to be expected." Araminta smiled, but the warmth did not reach her eyes. "I am afraid the police do not seem to be achieving anything. I have spoken to the sergeant—Evan, I think his name is—but he either knows nothing or he is determined not to tell me." She glanced absently at the frill of the chair arm. "Will you speak to them, if they wish to ask you anything?"

Beatrice looked up at the chandelier above the center of the room. It was unlit this early in the afternoon, but the last rays of the lowering sun caught one or two of its crystals.

"I can hardly refuse. It would seem as if I did not wish to help them."

"They would certainly think so," Araminta agreed, watching her mother intently. "And they could not be criticized for it." She hesitated, her voice hard-edged, slow and very quiet, every word distinct. "After all, we know it was someone in the house, and while it may be one of the servants—my own opinion is that it was probably Percival—"

"Percival?" Beatrice stiffened and turned to look at her daughter. "Why?"

Araminta did not meet her mother's eyes but stared somewhere an inch or two to the left. "Mama, this is hardly the time for comfortable pretenses. It is too late."

"I don't know what you mean," Beatrice answered miserably, hunching up her knees.

"Of course you do." Araminta was impatient. "Percival is an arrogant and presumptuous creature who has the normal appetites of a man and considerable delusions as to where he may exercise them. And you may choose not to see it, but Octavia was flattered by his admiration of her—and not above encouraging him now and then—"

Beatrice winced with revulsion. "Really, Minta."

"I know it is sordid," Araminta said more gently, assurance gathering in her voice. "But it seems that someone in this house killed her—which is very hard, Mama, but we won't alter it by pretending. It will only get worse, until the police find whoever it is."

163

Beatrice narrowed her shoulders and leaned forward, hugging her legs, staring straight ahead of her.

"Mama?" Araminta said very carefully. "Mama—do you know something?"

Beatrice said nothing, but held herself even more tightly. It was an attitude of absorption with inner pain which Hester had seen often before.

Araminta leaned closer. "Mama—are you trying to protect me . . . because of Myles?"

Slowly Beatrice looked up, stiff, silent, the back of her bright head towards Hester, so similar in color to her daughter's.

Araminta was ashen, her features set, her eyes bright and hard.

"Mama, I know he found Tavie attractive, and that he was not above"—she drew in her breath and let it out slowly—"above going to her room. I like to believe that because I am her sister, she refused him. But I don't know. It is possible he went again—and she rebuffed him. He doesn't take refusal well—as I know."

Beatrice stared at her daughter, slowly stretched out her hand in a gesture of shared pain. But Araminta moved no closer, and she let her hand fall. She said nothing. Perhaps there were no words for what she either knew or dreaded.

"Is that what you are hiding from, Mama?" Araminta asked relentlessly. "Are you afraid someone will ask you if that is what happened?"

Beatrice lay back and straightened the covers around herself before replying. Araminta made no move to help her. "It would be a waste of time to ask me. I don't know, and I certainly should not say anything of that sort." She looked up. "Please, Minta, surely you know that?"

At last Araminta leaned forward and touched her mother, putting her thin, strong hand over hers. "Mama, if it were Myles, then we cannot hide the truth. Please God it was not— and they will find it was someone else . . . soon—" She stopped, her face full of concern, hope struggling with fear, and a desperate concentration.

Beatrice tried to say something comforting, something to dismiss the horror on the edge of both their minds, but in the face of Araminta's courage and unyielding desire for truth, she failed, and remained wordless.

Araminta stood up, leaned over and kissed her very lightly, a mere brushing of the lips on her brow, and left the room.

Beatrice sat still for several minutes, then slowly sank farther down in the bed.

"You can take the tray away, Hester; I don't think I want any tea after all."

So she had not forgotten her nurse was there. Hester did not know whether to be grateful her status gave her such opportunity to observe or insulted that she was of such total unimportance that no one cared what she saw or heard. It was the first time in her life she had been so utterly disregarded, and it stung.

"Yes, Lady Moidore," she said coolly, and picked up the tray, leaving Beatrice alone with her thoughts.

That evening she had a little time to herself, and she spent it in the library. She had dined in the servants' hall. Actually it was one of the best meals she had ever eaten, far richer and more varied than she had experienced in her own home, even when her father's circumstances were very favorable. He had never served more than six courses, the heaviest usually either mutton or beef. Tonight there had been a choice of three meats, and eight courses in all.

She found a book on the peninsular campaigns of the Duke of Wellington, and was deeply engrossed in it when the door opened and Cyprian Moidore came in. He seemed surprised to see her, but not unpleasantly so.

"I am sorry to disturb you, Miss Latterly." He glanced at her book. "I am sure you have well deserved a little time to yourself, but I wanted you to tell me candidly what you think of my mother's health." He looked concerned, his face marked with anxiety and his eyes unwavering.

She closed the book and he saw the title.

"Good heavens. Couldn't you find anything more interesting than that? We have plenty of novels, and some poetry— farther along to the right, I think."

"Yes I know, thank you. I chose this intentionally." She saw his doubt, then as he realized she was not joking, his puzzlement. "I think Lady Moidore is deeply concerned over the death of your sister," she hurried on. "And of course having the police in the house is unpleasant. But I don't think her health is in any danger of breakdown. Grief always takes a time to run its course. It is natural to be angry, and bewildered, especially when the loss is so unexpected. With an illness at least there is some time to prepare—"

He looked down at the table between them.

"Has she said anything about who she thinks to be responsible?"

"No—but I have not discussed the subject with her—except, of course, I should listen to anything she wished to tell me, if I thought it would relieve her anxiety."

He looked up, a sudden smile on his face. Given another place, away from his family and the oppressive atmosphere of suspicion and defense, and away from her position as a servant, she would have liked him. There was a humor in him, and an intelligence beneath the careful manners.

"You do not think we should call in a doctor?" he pressed.

"I don't believe a doctor could help," she said frankly. She debated whether to tell him the truth of what she believed, or if it would only cause him greater concern and betray that she remembered and weighed what she overheard.

"What is it?" He caught her indecision and knew there was something more. "Please, Miss Latterly?"

She found herself responding from instinct rather than judgment, and a liking for him that was far from a rational decision.

"I think she is afraid she may know who it is who killed Mrs. Haslett, and that it will bring great distress to Mrs. Kellard," she answered. "I think she would rather retreat and keep silent than risk speaking to the police and having them somehow detect what she is thinking." She waited, watching his face.

"Damn Myles!" he said furiously, standing up and turning away. His voice was filled with anger, but there was remarkably little surprise in it. "Papa should have thrown *him* out, not Harry Haslett!" He swung back to face her. "I'm sorry, Miss Latterly. I beg your pardon for my language. I—"

"Please, Mr. Moidore, do not feel the need to apologize," she said quickly. "The circumstances are enough to make anyone with any feeling lose his temper. The constant presence of the police and the interminable wondering, whether it is spoken or not, would be intensely trying to anyone but a fool who had no understanding."

"You are very kind." It was a simple enough word, and yet she knew he meant it as no easy compliment.

"I imagine the newspapers are still writing about it?" she went on, more to fill the silence than because it mattered.

He sat down on the arm of the chair near her. "Every day," he said ruefully. "The better ones are castigating the police, which is unfair; they are no doubt doing all they can. They can hardly subject us to a Spanish Inquisition and torture us until someone confesses—" He laughed jerkily, betraying all his raw pain. "And the press would be the first to complain if they did. In fact it seems they are caught either way in a situation like this. If they are harsh with us they will be accused of forgetting their place and victimizing the gentry, and if they are lenient they will be charged with indifference and incompetence." He drew in his breath and let it out in a sigh. "I should imagine the poor devil curses the day he was clever enough to prove it had to be someone in the house. But he doesn't look like a man who takes the easy path—"

"No, indeed," Hester agreed with more memory and heart than Cyprian could know.

"And the sensational ones are speculating on every sordid possibility they can think up," he went on with distaste puckering his mouth and bringing a look of hurt to his eyes.

Suddenly Hester caught a glimpse of how deeply the whole intrusion was affecting him, the ugliness of it all pervading his life like a foul smell. He was keeping the pain within, as he had been taught since the nursery. Little boys are expected to be brave, never to complain, and above all never, never to cry. That was effeminate and a sign of weakness to be despised.

"I'm so sorry," she said gently. She reached out her hand and put it over his, closing her fingers, before she remembered she was not a nurse comforting a wounded man in hospital, she was a servant and a woman, putting her hand over her employer's in the privacy of his own library.

But if she withdrew it and apologized now she would only draw attention to the act and make it necessary for him to respond. They would both be embarrassed, and it would rob the moment of its understanding and create of it a lie.

Instead she sat back slowly with a very slight smile.

She was prevented from having to think what to say next by the library door opening and Romola coming in. She glanced at them together and instantly her face darkened.

"Should you not be with Lady Moidore?" she said sharply.

Her tone stung Hester, who kept her temper with an effort. Had she been free to, she would have replied with equal acerbity.

"No, Mrs. Moidore, her ladyship said I might have the evening to do as I chose. She decided to retire early."

"Then she must be unwell," Romola returned immediately. "You should be where she can call you if she needs you. Perhaps you could read in your bedroom, or write letters. Don't you have friends or family who will be expecting to hear from you?"

Cyprian stood up. "I'm sure Miss Latterly is quite capable of organizing her own correspondence, Romola. And she cannot read without first coming to the library to choose a book."

Romola's eyebrows rose sarcastically. "Is that what you were doing, Miss Latterly? Forgive me, that was not what appearances suggested."

"I was answering Mr. Moidore's questions concerning his mother's health," Hester said very levelly.

"Indeed? Well if he is now satisfied you may return to your room and do whatever it is you wish."

Cyprian drew breath to reply, but his father came in, glanced at their faces, and looked inquiringly at his son.

"Miss Latterly believes that Mama is not seriously ill," Cyprian said with embarrassment, obviously fishing for a palatable excuse.

"Did anyone imagine she was?" Basil asked dryly, coming into the middle of the room.

"I did not," Romola said quickly. "She is suffering, of course—but so are we all. I know I haven't slept properly since it happened."

"Perhaps Miss Latterly would give you something that would help?" Cyprian suggested with a glance at Hester—and the shadow of a smile.

"Thank you, I shall manage by myself," Romola snapped. "And I intend to go and visit Lady Killin tomorrow afternoon."

"It is too soon," Basil said before Cyprian could speak. "I

think you should remain at home for another month at least. By all means receive her if she calls here.''

"She won't call," Romola said angrily. "She will certainly feel uncomfortable and uncertain what to say—and one can hardly blame her for that."

"That is not material." Basil had already dismissed the matter.

"Then I shall call on her," Romola repeated, watching her father-in-law, not her husband.

Cyprian turned to speak to her, remonstrate with her, but again Basil overrode him.

"You are tired," he said coldly. "You had better retire to your room—and spend a quiet day tomorrow." There was no mistaking that it was an order. Romola stood as if undecided for a moment, but there was never any doubt in the issue. She would do as she was told, both tonight and tomorrow. Cyprian and his opinions were irrelevant.

Hester was acutely embarrassed, not for Romola, who had behaved childishly and deserved to be reproved, but for Cyprian, who had been disregarded totally. She turned to Basil.

"If you will excuse me, sir, I will retire also. Mrs. Moidore made the suggestion that I should be in my room, in case Lady Moidore should need me." And with a brief nod at Cyprian, hardly meeting his eyes so she did not see his humiliation, and clutching her book, Hester went out across the hall and up the stairs.

Sunday was quite unlike any other day in the Moidore house, as indeed was the case the length and breadth of England. The ordinary duties of cleaning grates and lighting and stoking fires had to be done, and of course breakfast was served. Prayers were briefer than usual because all those who could would be going to church at least once in the day.

Beatrice chose not to be well enough, and no one argued with her, but she insisted that Hester should ride with the family and attend services. It was preferable to her going in the evening with the upper servants, when Beatrice might well need her.

Luncheon was a very sober affair with little conversation, according to Dinah's report, and the afternoon was spent in letter writing, or in Basil's case, he put on his smoking jacket

169

and retired to the smoking room to think or perhaps to doze. Books and newspapers were forbidden as unfitting the sabbath, and the children were not allowed to play with their toys or to read, except Scripture, or to indulge in any games. Even musical practice was deemed inappropriate.

Supper was to be cold, to permit Mrs. Boden and the other upper servants to attend church. Afterwards the evening would be occupied by Bible reading, presided over by Sir Basil. It was a day in which no one seemed to find pleasure.

It brought childhood flooding back to Hester, although her father at his most pompous had never been so unrelievedly joyless. Since leaving home for the Crimea, although it was not so very long ago, she had forgotten how rigorously such rules were enforced. War did not allow such indulgences, and caring for the sick did not stop even for the darkness of night, let alone a set day of the week.

Hester spent the afternoon in the study writing letters. She would have been permitted to use the ladies' maids' sitting room, had she wished, but Beatrice did not need her, having decided to sleep, and it would be easier to write away from Mary's and Gladys's chatter.

She had written to Charles and Imogen, and to several of her friends from Crimean days, when Cyprian came in. He did not seem surprised to see her, and apologized only perfunctorily for the intrusion.

"You have a large family, Miss Latterly?" he said, noticing the pile of letters.

"Oh no, only a brother," she said. "The rest are to friends with whom I nursed during the war."

"You formed such friendships?" he asked curiously, interest quickening in his face. "Do you not find it difficult to settle back into life in England after such violent and disturbing experiences?"

She smiled, in mockery at herself rather than at him.

"Yes I do," she admitted candidly. "One had so much more responsibility; there was little time for artifice or standing upon ceremony. It was a time of so many things: terror, exhaustion, freedom, friendship that crossed all the normal barriers, honesty such as one cannot normally afford—"

He sat facing her, balancing on the arm of one of the easy chairs.

"I have read a little of the war in the newspapers," he said with a pucker between his brows. "But one never knows how accurate the accounts are. I fear they tell us very much what they wish us to believe. I don't suppose you have read any—no, of course not."

"Yes I have!" she contradicted immediately, forgetting in the heat of the discourse how improper it was for well-bred women to have access to anything but the social pages of a newspaper.

But he was not shocked, only the more interested.

"Indeed, one of the bravest and most admirable men I nursed was a war correspondent with one of London's best newspapers," she went on. "When he was too ill to write himself, he would dictate to me, and I sent his dispatches for him."

"Good gracious. You do impress me, Miss Latterly," he said sincerely. "If you can spare time, I should be most interested to hear some of your opinions upon what you saw. I have heard rumors of great incompetence and a terrible number of unnecessary deaths, but then others say such stories are spread by the disaffected and the troublemakers wishing to advance their own cause at the expense of others."

"Oh, there is some of that too," she agreed, setting her quill and paper aside. He seemed so genuinely concerned it gave her a distinct pleasure to recount to him both some of what she had seen and experienced and the conclusions she had drawn from it.

He listened with total attention, and his few questions were perceptive and made with both pity and a wry humor she found most attractive. Away from the influence of his family, and for an hour forgetting his sister's death and all the misery and suspicion it brought in its wake, he was a man of individual ideas, some quite innovative with regard to social conditions and the terms of agreement and service between the governed and the governing.

They were deep in discussion and the shadows outside were lengthening when Romola came in, and although they were both aware of her, it was several minutes before they let go of the topic of argument and acknowledged her presence.

"Papa wishes to speak to you," she said with a frown. "He is waiting in the withdrawing room."

Reluctantly Cyprian rose to his feet and excused himself from Hester as if she had been a much regarded friend, not a semiservant.

When he had gone Romola looked at Hester with perplexed concern in her smooth face. Her complexion really was very lovely and her features perfectly proportioned, all except her lower lip, which was a trifle full and drooped at the corners sometimes, giving her a discontented look in repose, especially when she was tired.

"Really, Miss Latterly, I don't know how to express myself without seeming critical, or how to offer advice where it may not be desired. But if you wish to obtain a husband, and surely all natural women must, then you will have to learn to master this intellectual and argumentative side of your nature. Men do not find it in the least attractive in a woman. It makes them uncomfortable. It is not restful and does not make a man feel at his ease or as if you give proper deference to his judgment. One does not wish to appear opinionated! That would be quite dreadful."

She moved a stray hair back into its pins with a skilled hand.

"I can remember my mama advising me when I was a girl— it is most unbecoming in a woman to be agitated about anything. Almost all men dislike agitation and anything that detracts from a woman's image as serene, dependable, innocent of all vulgarity or meanness, never critical of anything except slovenliness or unchastity, and above all never contradictory towards a man, even if you should think him mistaken. Learn how to run your household, how to eat elegantly, how to dress well and deport yourself with dignity and charm, the correct form of address for everyone in society, and a little painting or drawing, as much music as you can master, especially singing if you have any gift at all, some needlework, an elegant hand with a pen, and a pleasing turn of phrase for a letter—and above all how to be obedient and control your temper no matter how you may be provoked.

"If you do all these things, Miss Latterly, you will marry as well as your comeliness and your station in life allow, and you will make your husband happy. Therefore you also will be happy." She shook her head very slightly. "I fear you have quite a way to go."

Hester achieved the last of these admonitions instantly, and kept her temper in spite of monstrous provocation.

"Thank you, Mrs. Moidore," she said after taking a deep breath. "I fear perhaps I am destined to remain single, but I shall not forget your advice."

"Oh, I hope not," Romola said with deep sympathy. "It is a most unnatural state for a woman. Learn to bridle your tongue, Miss Latterly, and never give up hope."

Fortunately, upon that final piece of counsel she went back to the withdrawing room, leaving Hester boiling with words unsaid. And yet she was curiously perplexed, and her temper crippled by a sense of pity that did not yet know its object, only that there was confusion and unhappiness and she was sharply aware of it.

Hester took the opportunity to rise early the following day and find herself small tasks around the kitchen and laundry in the hope of improving her acquaintance with some of the other servants—and whatever knowledge they might have. Even if the pieces seemed to them to be meaningless, to Monk they might fit with other scraps to form a picture.

Annie and Maggie were chasing each other up the stairs and falling over in giggles, stuffing their aprons in their mouths to stop the sound from carrying along the landing.

"What's entertained you so early?" Hester asked with a smile.

They both looked at her, wide-eyed and shaking with laughter.

"Well?" Hester said, without criticism in her tone. "Can't you share it? I could use a joke myself."

"Mrs. Sandeman," Maggie volunteered, pushing her fair hair out of her eyes. "It's those papers she's got, miss. You never seen anything like it, honest, such tales as'd curdle your blood—and goings-on between men and women as'd make a street girl blush."

"Indeed?" Hester raised her eyebrows. "Mrs. Sandeman has some very colorful reading?"

"Mostly purple, I'd say." Annie grinned.

"Scarlet," Maggie corrected, and burst into giggles again.

"Where did you get this?" Hester asked her, holding the paper and trying to keep a sober face.

"Out of her room when we cleaned it," Annie replied with transparent innocence.

"At this time in the morning?" Hester said doubtfully. "It's only half past six. Don't tell me Mrs. Sandeman is up already?"

"Oh no. 'Course not. She doesn't get up till lunchtime," Maggie said quickly. "Sleeping it off, I shouldn't wonder."

"Sleeping what off?" Hester was not going to let it go. "She wasn't out yesterday evening."

"She gets tiddly in her room," Annie replied. "Mr. Thirsk brings it to her from the cellar. I dunno why; I never thought he liked her. But I suppose he must do, to pinch port wine for her—and the best stuff too."

"He takes it because he hates Sir Basil, stupid!" Maggie said sharply. "That's why he takes the best. One of these days Sir Basil's going to send Mr. Phillips for a bottle of old port, and there isn't going to be any left. Mrs. Sandeman's drunk it all."

"I still don't think he likes her," Annie insisted. "Have you seen the way his eyes are when he looks at her?"

"Perhaps he had a fancy for her?" Maggie said hopefully, a whole new vista of speculation opening up before her imagination. "And she turned him down, so now he hates her."

"No." Annie was quite sure. "No, I think he despises her. He used to be a pretty good soldier, you know—I mean something special—before he had a tragic love affair."

"How do you know?" Hester demanded. "I'm sure he didn't tell you."

" 'Course not. I heard 'er ladyship talking about it to Mr. Cyprian. I think he thinks she's disgusting—not like a lady should be at all." Her eyes grew wider. "What if she made an improper advance to him, and he was revolted and turned her down?"

"Then she should hate him," Hester pointed out.

"Oh, she does," Annie said instantly. "One of these days she'll tell Sir Basil about him taking the port, you'll see. Only maybe she'll be so squiffy by then he won't believe her."

Hester seized the opportunity, and was half ashamed of doing it.

"Who do you think killed Mrs. Haslett?"

Their smiles vanished.

174

"Well, Mr. Cyprian's much too nice, an' why would he anyway?" Annie dismissed him. "Mrs. Moidore never takes that much notice of anyone else to hate them. Nor does Mrs. Sandeman—"

"Unless Mrs. Haslett knew something disgraceful about her?" Maggie offered. "That's probably it. I reckon Mrs. Sandeman would stick a knife into you if you threatened to split on her."

"True," Annie agreed. Then her face sobered and she lost all the imagination and the banter. "Honestly, miss, we think it's likely Percival, who has airs about himself in that department, and fancied Mrs. Haslett. Thinks he's one dickens of a fellow, he does."

"Thinks God made him as a special gift for women." Maggie sniffed with scorn. " 'Course there's some daft enough to let him. Then God doesn't know much about women, is all I can say."

"And Rose," Annie went on. "She's got a real thing for Percival. Really taken bad with him—the more fool her."

"Then why would she kill Mrs. Haslett?" Hester asked.

"Jealousy, of course." They both looked at her as if she were slow-witted.

Hester was surprised. "Did Percival really have that much of a fancy for Mrs. Haslett? But he's a footman, for goodness' sake."

"Tell him that," Annie said with deep disgust.

Nellie, the little tweeny maid, came scurrying up the stairs with a broom in one hand and a pail of cold tea leaves in the other, ready to scatter them on the carpets to lay the dust.

"Why aren't you sweeping?" she demanded, looking at the two older girls. "If Mrs. Willis catches me at eight and we 'aven't done this it'll be trouble. I don't want to go to bed without me tea."

The housekeeper's name was enough to galvanize both the girls into instant action, and they left Hester on the landing while they ran downstairs for their own brooms and dusters.

In the kitchen an hour later, Hester prepared a breakfast tray for Beatrice, just tea, toast, butter and apricot preserve. She was thanking the gardener for one of the very last of the late roses for the silver vase when she passed Sal, the red-haired kitchen maid, laughing loudly and nudging the footman from

175

next door, who had sneaked over, ostensibly with a message from his cook for hers. The two of them were flirting with a lot of poking and slapping on the doorstep, and Sal's loud voice could be heard up the scullery steps and along the passage to the kitchen.

"That girl's no better than she should be," Mrs. Boden said with a shake of her head. "You mark my words—she's a trollop, if ever I saw one. Sal!" she shouted. "Come back in here and get on with your work!" She looked at Hester again. "She's an idle piece. It's a wonder how I put up with her. I don't know what the world's coming to." She picked up the meat knife and tested it with her finger. Hester looked at the blade and swallowed with a shiver when she thought that maybe it was the knife someone had held in his hands creeping up the stairs in the night to stab Octavia Haslett to death.

Mrs. Boden found the edge satisfactory and pulled over the slab of steak to begin slicing it ready for the pie.

"What with Miss Octavia's death, and now policemen creeping all over the house, everyone scared o' their own shadows, 'er ladyship took to 'er bed, and a good-for-nothing baggage like Sal in my kitchen—it's enough to make a decent woman give up."

"I'm sure you won't," Hester said, trying to soothe her. If she was going to be responsible for luring two housemaids away, she did not want to add to the domestic chaos by encouraging the cook to desert as well. "The police will go in time, the whole matter will be settled, her ladyship will recover, and you are quite capable of disciplining Sal. She cannot be the first wayward kitchen maid you've trained into being thoroughly competent—in time."

"Well now, you're right about that," Mrs. Boden agreed. "I 'ave a good 'and with girls, if I do say so myself. But I surely wish the police would find out who did it and arrest them. I don't sleep safe in my bed, wondering. I just can't believe anyone in the family would do such a thing. I've been in this house since before Mr. Cyprian was born, never mind Miss Octavia and Miss Araminta. I never did care a great deal for Mr. Kellard, but I expect he has his qualities, and he is a gentleman, after all."

"You think it was one of the servants?" Hester affected

176

surprise, and considerable respect, as though Mrs. Boden's opinion on such matters weighed heavily with her.

"Stands to reason, don't it?" Mrs. Boden said quietly, slicing the steak with expert strokes, quick, light and extremely powerful. "And it wouldn't be any of the girls—apart from anything else, why would they?"

"Jealousy?" Hester suggested innocently.

"Nonsense." Mrs. Boden reached for the kidneys. "They wouldn't be so daft. Sal never goes upstairs. Lizzie is a bossy piece and wouldn't give a halfpenny to a blind man, but she knows right from wrong, and sticks by it whatever. Rose is a willful creature, always wants what she can't 'ave, and I wouldn't put it past her to do something wild, but not that." She shook her head. "Not murder. Too afraid of what'd happen to her, apart from anything else. Fond of 'er own skin, that one."

"And not the upstairs girls," Hester added instinctively, then wished she had waited for Mrs. Boden to speak.

"They can be silly bits of things," Mrs. Boden agreed. "But no harm in them, none at all. And Dinah's far too mild to do anything so passionate. Nice girl, but bland as a cup of tea. Comes from a nice family in the country somewhere. Too pretty maybe, but that's parlormaids for you. And Mary and Gladys—well, that Mary's got a temper, but it's all flash and no heat. She wouldn't harm anyone—and wouldn't have any call to. Very fond of Miss Octavia, she was, very fond—and Miss Octavia of her too. Gladys is a sourpuss, puts on airs—but that's ladies' maids. No viciousness in her, least not that much. Wouldn't 'ave the courage either."

"Harold?" Hester asked. She did not even bother to mention Mr. Phillips, not because he could not have done it, but because Mrs. Boden's natural loyalties to a servant she considered of her own seniority would prevent her from entertaining the possibility with any open-mindedness.

Mrs. Boden gave her an old-fashioned look. "And what for, may I ask? What would Harold be doing in Miss Octavia's room in the middle of the night? He can't see any girl but Dinah, the poor boy, not but it'll do him a ha'porth of good."

"Percival?" Hester said the inevitable.

"Must be." Mrs. Boden pushed away the last of the kidney and reached for the mixing bowl full of pastry dough. She tipped the dough out onto the board, floured it thoroughly and began to roll it out with the wooden pin, brisk, sharp strokes first one way, then turned it with a single movement and started in the other direction. "Always had ideas above himself, that one, but never thought it would go this far. Got a sight more money than I can account for," she added viciously. "Nasty streak in him. Seen it a few times. Now your kettle's boiling, don't let it fill my kitchen with steam."

"Thank you." Hester turned and went to the range, picking the kettle off the hob with a potholder and first scalding the teapot, then swilling it out and making the tea with the rest of the water.

Monk returned to Queen Anne Street because he and Evan had exhausted every other avenue of possible inquiry. They had not found the missing jewelry, nor had they expected to, but it was obligatory that they pursue it to the end, even if only to satisfy Runcorn. They had also taken the character references of every servant in the Moidore house and checked with all their previous employers, and found no blemish of character that was in the slightest way indicative of violence of emotion or action to come. There were no dark love affairs, no accusations of theft or immorality, nothing but very ordinary lives of domesticity and work.

Now there was nowhere to look except back in Queen Anne Street among the servants yet again. Monk stood in the housekeeper's sitting room waiting impatiently for Hester. He had again given Mrs. Willis no reason for asking to see the nurse, a woman who was not even present at the time of the crime. He was aware of her surprise and considerable criticism. He would have to think of some excuse before he saw her again.

There was a knock on the door.

"Come," he ordered.

Hester came in and closed the door behind her. She looked neat and professional, her hair tied back severely and her dress plain gray-blue stuff and undecorated, her apron crisp white. Her costume was both serviceable and more than a little prudish.

"Good morning," she said levelly.

"Good morning," he replied, and without preamble started to ask her about the days since he had last seen her, his manner

178

more curt than he would have chosen, simply because she was so similar to her sister-in-law, Imogen, and yet so different, so lacking in mystery and feminine grace.

She was recounting her duties and all that she had seen or overheard.

"All of which tells me only that Percival is not particularly well liked," he said tartly. "Or simply that everyone is afraid and he seems the most likely scapegoat."

"Quite," she agreed briskly. "Have you a better idea?"

Her very reasonableness caught him on a raw nerve. He was acutely aware of his failure to date, and that he had nowhere else to look but here.

"Yes!" he snapped back. "Take a better look at the family. Find out more about Fenella Sandeman, for one. Have you any idea where she goes to indulge her disreputable tastes, if they really are disreputable? She stands to lose a lot if Sir Basil throws her out. Octavia might have found out that afternoon. Maybe that was what she was referring to when she spoke to Septimus. And see if you can find out whether Myles Kellard really did have an affair with Octavia, or if it is just malicious gossip among servants with idle tongues and busy imaginations. It seems they don't lack for either."

"Don't give me orders, Mr. Monk." She looked at him frostily. "I am not your sergeant."

"Constable, ma'am," he corrected with a sour smile. "You have promoted yourself unwarrantably. You are not my constable."

She stiffened, her shoulders square, almost military, her face angry.

"Whatever the rank I do not hold, Mr. Monk, I think the main reason for suggesting that Percival may have killed Octavia is the belief that he either was having an affair with her or was attempting to."

"And he killed her for that?" He raised his eyebrows in sarcastic inquiry.

"No," she said patiently. "Because she grew tired of him, and they quarreled, I suppose. Or possibly the laundrymaid Rose did, in jealousy. She is in love with Percival—or perhaps *love* is not the right word—something rather cruder and more immediate, I think, would be more accurate. Although I don't know how you can prove it."

179

"Good. For a moment I was afraid you were about to instruct me."

"I would not presume—not until I am at least a sergeant."
And with a swing of her skirt she turned and went out.

It was ridiculous. It was not the way he had intended the interview to go, but something about her so frequently annoyed him, an arbitrariness. A large part of his anger was because she was in some degree correct, and she knew it. He had no idea how to prove Percival's guilt—if indeed he was guilty.

Evan was busy talking to the grooms, not that he had anything else specific to ask them. Monk spoke to Phillips, learning nothing, then sent for Percival.

This time the footman looked far more nervous. Monk had seen the tense shoulders tight and a little high, the hands that were never quite still, the fine beading of sweat on the lips, and the wary eyes. It meant nothing, except that Percival had enough intelligence to know the circle was closing and he was not liked. They were all frightened for themselves, and the sooner someone was charged, the sooner life could begin to settle to normality again, and safety. The police would go, and the awful, sick suspicion would die away. They could look each other straight in the eye again.

"You're a handsome fellow." Monk looked him up and down with anything but approval. "I gather footmen are often picked for their looks."

Percival met his eyes boldly, but Monk could almost smell his fear.

"Yes sir."

"I imagine quite a few women are enamored of you, in one way or another. Women are often attracted by good looks."

A flicker of a smirk crossed Percival's dark face and died away.

"Yes sir, from time to time."

"You must have experienced it?"

Percival relaxed a fraction, his body easing under his livery jacket.

"That's true."

"Is it ever an embarrassment?"

"Not often. You get used to it."

Conceited swine, Monk thought, but perhaps not without

180

cause. He had a suppressed vitality and a sort of insolence Monk imagined many women might find exciting.

"You must have to be very discreet?" he said aloud.

"Yes sir." Percival was quite amused now, off his guard, pleased with himself as memories came to mind.

"Especially if it's a lady, not merely one of the maids?" Monk went on. "Must be awkward for you if a visiting lady is . . . interested?"

"Yes sir—have to be careful."

"I imagine men get jealous?"

Percival was puzzled; he had not forgotten why he was here. Monk could see the thoughts flicker across his face, and none of them provided explanation.

"I suppose they might," he said carefully.

"Might?" Monk raised his eyebrows. His voice was patronizing, sarcastic. "Come, Percival, if you were a gentleman, wouldn't you be jealous as the grave if your fine lady preferred the attentions of the footman to yours?"

This time the smirk was unmistakable, the thought was too sweet, the most delicious of all superiorities, better, closer to the essence of a man than even money or rank.

"Yes sir—I imagine I would be."

"Especially over a woman as comely as Mrs. Haslett?"

Now Percival was confused. "She was a widow, sir. Captain Haslett died in the war." He shifted his weight uncomfortably. "And she didn't have any admirers that were serious. She wouldn't look at anyone—still grieving over the captain."

"But she was a young woman, used to married life, and handsome," Monk pressed.

The light was back in Percival's face. "Oh yes," he agreed. "But she didn't want to marry again." He sobered quickly. "And anyway, nobody's threatened me—it was her that was killed. And there wasn't anyone close enough to be that jealous. Anyhow, even if there was, there wasn't anyone else in the house that night."

"But if there had been, would they have had cause to be jealous?" Monk screwed up his face as if the answer mattered and he had found some precious clue.

"Well—" Percival's lips curled in a satisfied smile. "Yes—

181

I suppose they would." His eyes widened hopefully. "Was there someone here, sir?"

"No." Monk's expression changed and all the lightness vanished. "No. I simply wanted to know if you had had an affair with Mrs. Haslett."

Suddenly Percival understood and the blood fled from his skin, leaving him sickly pale. He struggled for words and could only make strangled sounds in his throat.

Monk knew the moment of victory and the instinct to kill; it was as familiar as pain, or rest, or the sudden shock of cold water, a memory in his flesh as well as his mind. And he despised himself for it. This was the old self surfacing through the cloud of forgetting since the accident; this was the man the records showed, who was admired and feared, who had no friends.

And yet this arrogant little footman might have murdered Octavia Haslett in a fit of lust and male conceit. Monk could not afford to indulge his own conscience at the cost of letting him go.

"Did she change her mind?" he asked with all the old edge to his voice, a world of biting contempt. "Suddenly saw the ridiculous vulgarity of an amorous adventure with a footman?"

Percival called him something obscene under his breath, then his chin came up and his eyes blazed.

"Not at all," he said cockily, his terror mastered at least on the surface. His voice shook, but his speech was perfectly clear. "If it was anything to do with me, it'd be Rose, the laundrymaid. She's infatuated with me, and jealous as death. She might have gone upstairs in the night with a kitchen knife and killed Mrs. Haslett. She had reason to—I hadn't."

"You are a real gentleman." Monk curled his lip with disgust, but it was a possibility he could not ignore, and Percival knew it. The sweat of relief was glistening on the footman's brow.

"All right." Monk dismissed him. "You can go for now."

"Do you want me to send Rose in?" he asked at the door.

"No I don't. And if you want to survive here, you'll do well not to tell anyone of this conversation. Lovers who suggest their mistresses for murder are not well favored by other people."

Percival made no reply, but he did not look guilty, just relieved—and careful.

Swine, Monk thought, but he could not blame him entirely. The man was cornered, and too many other hands were turning against him, not necessarily because they thought he was guilty, but someone was, and that person was afraid.

At the end of another day of interviews, all except that with Percival proving fruitless, Monk started off towards the police station to report to Runcorn, not that he had anything conclusive to say, simply that Runcorn had demanded it.

He was walking the last mile in the crisp late-autumn afternoon, trying to formulate in his mind what he would say, when he passed a funeral going very slowly north up Tottenham Court Road towards the Euston Road. The hearse was drawn by four black horses with black plumes, and through the glass he could see the coffin was covered with flowers. There must have been pounds and pounds worth. He could imagine the perfume of them, and the care that had gone into raising them in a hothouse at this time of the year.

Behind the hearse were three other carriages packed full with mourners, all in black, and again there was a sudden stab of familiarity. He knew why they were crammed elbow to elbow, and the harnesses so shiny, no crests on the carriage doors. It was a poor man's funeral; the carriages were hired, but no expense had been spared. There would be black horses, no browns or bays would do. There would be flowers from everyone, even if there was nothing to eat for the rest of the week and they sat by cold hearths in the evening. Death must have its due, and the neighborhood must not be let down by a poor show, a hint of meanness. Poverty must be concealed at all costs. They would mourn properly as a last tribute.

He stood on the pavement with his hat off and watched them go past with a feeling close to tears, not for the unknown corpse, or even for those who were bereaved, but for everyone who cared so desperately what others thought of them, and for the shadows and flickers of his own past that he saw in it. Whatever his dreams, he was part of these people, not of those in Queen Anne Street or their like. He had fine clothes now, ate well enough and owned no house and had no family, but his roots were in close streets where everyone knew each other, weddings and funerals involved them all, they knew every birth or sickness, the hopes and the losses, there was no privacy and no loneliness.

Who was it whose face had come so clearly for an instant as he waited outside the club Piccadilly, and why had he wanted so intensely to emulate him, not only his intellect, but even his accent of speech and his manner of dress and gait in walking?

He looked again at the mourners, seeking some sense of identity with them, and as the last carriage passed slowly by he caught a glimpse of a woman's face, very plain, nose too broad, mouth wide and eyebrows low and level, and it struck a familiarity in him so sharp it left him gasping, and another homely face came back to his mind and then was gone again, an ugly woman with tears on her cheeks and hands so lovely he never tired of looking at them, or lost his intense pleasure in their delicacy and grace. And he was wounded with an old guilt, and he had no idea why, or how long ago it had been.

7

Araminta was very composed as she stood in front of Monk in the boudoir, that room of ease and comfort especially for the women of the house. It was ornately decorated with lush French Louis XVI furniture, all scrolls and curlicues, gilt and velvet. The curtains were brocade and the wallpaper pink embossed in gold. It was an almost oppressively feminine room, and Araminta looked out of place in it, not for her appearance, which was slender and delicately boned with a flame of hair, but for her stance. It was almost aggressive. There was nothing yielding in her, nothing soft to compliment all the sweetness of the pink room.

"I regret having to tell you this, Mr. Monk." She looked at him unflinchingly. "My sister's reputation is naturally dear to me, but in our present stress and tragedy I believe only the truth will serve. Those of us who are hurt by it will have to endure the best we may."

He opened his mouth to try to say something at once soothing and encouraging, but apparently she did not need any word from him. She continued, her face so controlled there was no apparent tension, no quiver to the lips or voice.

"My sister, Octavia, was a very charming person, and very affectionate." She was choosing her words with great care; this was a speech which had been rehearsed before he came. "Like most people who are pleasing to others, she enjoyed admiration, indeed she had a hunger for it. When her husband, Captain Haslett, was killed in the Crimea she was, of course, deeply grieved. But that was nearly two years ago, and that is a long time for a young woman of Octavia's nature to be alone.''

This time he did not interrupt, but waited for her to continue, only showing his total attention by his unwavering gaze.

The only way her inner feelings showed was a curious stillness, as if something inside her dared not move.

''What I am endeavoring to say, Mr. Monk, much as it pains me, and all my family, is that Octavia from time to time would encourage from the footman an admiration that was personal, and of a more familiar nature than it should have been.''

''Which footman, ma'am?'' He would not put Percival's name in her mouth.

A flash of irritation tweaked her mouth. ''Percival of course. Do not affect to be a fool with me, Mr. Monk. Does Harold look like a man to have airs above his station? Besides which, you have been in this house quite long enough to have observed that Harold is taken with the parlormaid and not likely to see anyone else in that light—for all the good it will do him.'' She jerked her shoulders sharply, as if to shrug off the distasteful idea. ''Still, she is very likely not the charming creature he imagines, and he may well be better served by dreams than he would be by the disillusion of reality.'' For the first time she looked away from him. ''I daresay she is very bland and tedious once you are tired of looking at her pretty face.''

Had Araminta been a plain woman Monk might have suspected her of envy, but since she was in her own way quite remarkably fine it could not be so.

''Impossible dreams always end in awakening,'' he agreed. ''But he may grow out of his obsession before he meets with any reality. Let us hope so.''

''It is hardly important,'' she said, swinging back to face him and recall him to the subject that mattered. ''I have come to inform you of my sister's relationship with Percival, not Harold's moonings after the parlormaid. Since it seems inescapable that someone in this house murdered Octavia, it is relevant that you should know she was overfamiliar with the footman.''

''Very relevant,'' he agreed quietly. ''Why did you not mention it before, Mrs. Kellard?''

''Because I hoped it would not be necessary, of course,''

186

she replied immediately. "It is hardly a pleasant thing to have to admit—least of all to the police."

Whether that was because of the implication for crime, or the indignity of discussing it with someone of the social standing of the police, she did not say, but Monk thought from the lopsided suggestion of a sneer on her mouth that it was the latter.

"Thank you for mentioning it now." He ironed out the anger from his expression as well as he could, and was rewarded, and insulted, that she seemed to notice nothing at all. "I shall investigate the possibility," he concluded.

"Naturally." Her fine golden eyebrows rose. "I did not put myself to the discomfort of telling you for you merely to acknowledge it and do nothing."

He bit back any further comment and contented himself with opening the door for her and bidding her good-day.

He had no alternative but to face Percival, because he had already drawn from everyone else the fragments of knowledge, speculation and judgment of character on the subject. Nothing added now would be proof of anything, only the words of fear, opportunism or malice. And undoubtedly Percival was disliked by some of his fellow servants, for greater or lesser reason. He was arrogant and abrasive and he had played with at least one woman's affections, which produced volatile and unreliable testimony, at best.

When Percival appeared this time his attitude was different; the all-permeating fear was there, but far less powerfully. There was a return of the old confidence in the tilt of his head and the brash directness of his stare. Monk knew immediately there would be no point in even hoping to panic him into confession of anything.

"Sir?" Percival waited expectantly, bristlingly aware of tricks and verbal traps.

"Perhaps discretion kept you from saying so before." Monk did not bother to prevaricate. "But Mrs. Haslett was one of the ladies who had more than an employer's regard for you, was she not?" He smiled with bared teeth. "You need not permit modesty to direct your answer. It has come to me from another source."

Percival's mouth relaxed in something of a smirk, but he did not forget himself.

187

"Yes sir. Mrs. Haslett was . . . very appreciative."

Monk was suddenly infuriated by the man's complacence, his insufferable conceit. He thought of Octavia lying dead with the blood dark down her robe. She had seemed so vulnerable, so helpless to protect herself—which was ridiculous, since she was the one person in all of this tragedy who was now beyond pain or the petty fancies of dignity. But he bitterly resented this grubby little man's ease of reference to her, his self-satisfaction, even his thoughts.

"How gratifying for you," he said acidly. "If occasionally embarrassing."

"No sir," Percival said quickly, but there was a smugness to his face. "She was very discreet."

"But of course," Monk agreed, loathing Percival the more. "She was, after all, a lady, even if she occasionally forgot it."

Percival's narrow mouth twitched with irritation. Monk's contempt had reached him. He did not like being reminded that it was beneath a lady to admire a footman in that way.

"I don't expect you to understand," Percival said with a sneer. He looked Monk up and down and stood a little straighter himself, his opinion in his eyes.

Monk had no idea what ladies of whatever rank might similarly have admired him; his memory was blank but his temper burned.

"I can imagine," he replied viciously. "I've arrested a few whores from time to time."

Percival's cheeks flamed but he dared not say what came to his mind. He stared back with brilliant eyes.

"Indeed sir? I expect your job brings you into company of a great many people I have no experience of at all. Very regrettable." Now his eyes were perfectly level and hard. "But like cleaning the drains, someone has to do it."

"Precarious," Monk said with deliberate edge. "Being admired by a lady. Never know where you are. One minute you are the servant, dutiful and respectfully inferior, the next the lover, with hints of being stronger, masterful." He smiled with a sneer like Percival's own. "Then before you know where you are, back to being the footman again, 'Yes ma'am,' 'No ma'am,' and dismissed to your own room whenever my lady is bored or has had enough. Very difficult not to make a mistake—" He was watching Percival's face and the succession

188

of emotions racing across it. "Very hard to keep your temper—"

There it was—the first shadow of real fear, the quick beading of sweat on the lip, the catching of breath.

"I didn't lose my temper," Percival said, his voice cracking and loathing in his eyes. "I don't know who killed her—but it wasn't me!"

"No?" Monk raised his eyebrows very high. "Who else had a reason? She didn't 'admire' anyone else, did she? She didn't leave any money. We cannot find anything to suggest she knew something shameful about anyone. We can't find anyone who hated her—"

"Because you aren't very clever, are you." Percival's dark eyes were narrow and bright. "I already told you Rose hated her, because she was jealous as a cat over me. And what about Mr. Kellard? Or are you too well trained to dare accuse one of the gentry if you can pin it on a servant?"

"No doubt you would like me to ask why Mr. Kellard should kill Mrs. Haslett." Monk was equally angry, but would not reply to the jibe because that would be to admit it hurt. He would as soon have charged one of the family as a servant, but he knew what Runcorn would feel, and try to drive him to do, and his frustration was equally with him as with Percival. "And you will tell me whether I ask or not, to divert my attention from you."

That robbed Percival of a great deal of his satisfaction, which was what Monk had intended. Nevertheless he could not afford to remain silent.

"Because he had a fancy for Mrs. Haslett," Percival said in a hard, quiet voice. "And the more she declined him, the hotter it got—that's how it is."

"And so he killed her?" Monk said, baring his teeth in something less than a smile. "Seems an odd way of persuading her. Would put her out of his reach permanently, wouldn't it? Or are you supposing a touch of necrophilia?"

"What?"

"Gross relationship with the dead," Monk explained.

"Disgusting." Percival's lip curled.

"Or perhaps he was so infatuated he decided if he could not have her then no one should?" Monk suggested sarcastically.

It was not the sort of passion either of them thought Myles Kellard capable of, and he knew it.

"You're playing the fool on purpose," Percival said through thin lips. "You may not be very bright—and the way you've gone about this case surely shows it—but you're not that stupid. Mr. Kellard wanted to lie with her, nothing more. But he's one that won't accept a refusal." He lifted one shoulder. "And if he fancied her and she said she'd tell everyone he'd have to kill her. He couldn't cover that up the way he did with poor Martha. It's one thing to rape a maid, no one cares—but you can't rape your wife's sister and get away with it. Her father won't hide that up for you!"

Monk stared at him. Percival had won his attention without shadow this time, and he knew it; the victory was shining in his narrowed eyes.

"Who is Martha?" Resent it as he might, Monk had no option but to ask.

Percival smiled slowly. He had small, even teeth.

"Was," he corrected. "God knows where she is now—workhouse, if she's alive at all."

"All right, who was she?"

He looked at Monk with a level, jubilant stare.

"Parlormaid before Dinah. Pretty thing, neat and slender, walked like a princess. He took a fancy to her, and wouldn't be told no. Didn't believe she meant it. Raped her."

"How do you know this?" Monk was skeptical, but not totally disbelieving. Percival was too sure of himself for it to be simply a malicious invention, nor was there the sweat of desperation on his skin. He stood easily, his body relaxed, almost excited.

"Servants are invisible," Percival replied, eyes wide. "Don't you know that? Part of the furniture. I overheard Sir Basil when he made some of the arrangements. Poor little bitch was dismissed for being of loose tongue and even looser morals. He got her out of the house before she could tell anyone else. She made the mistake of going to him about it, because she was afraid she was with child—which she was. Funny thing is he didn't even doubt her—he knew she was telling the truth. But he said she must have encouraged him—it was her fault. Threw her out without a reference." He shrugged. "God knows what happened to her."

Monk thought Percival's anger was outrage for his own class rather than pity for the girl, and was ashamed of himself for his judgment. It was harsh and without proof, and yet he did not change it.

"And you don't know where she is now?"

Percival snorted. "A maid without a position or a character, alone in London, and with child? What do you think? Sweatshops wouldn't have her with a child, whorehouses wouldn't either for the same reason. Workhouse, I should think—or the grave."

"What was her full name?"

"Martha Rivett."

"How old was she?"

"Seventeen."

Monk was not surprised, but he felt an almost uncontrollable rage and a ridiculous desire to weep. He did not know why; it was surely more than pity for this one girl whom he had not even met. He must have seen hundreds of others, simple, abused, thrown out without a twinge of guilt. He must have seen their defeated faces, the hope and the death of hope, and he must have seen their bodies dead of hunger, violence and disease.

Why did it hurt? Why was there no skin of callousness grown over it? Was there something, someone who had touched him more closely? Pity—guilt? Perhaps he would never know again. It was gone, like almost everything else.

"Who else knew about it?" he asked, his voice thick with emotion which could have been taken for any of a dozen feelings.

"Only Lady Moidore, so far as I know." A quick spark flashed in Percival's eyes. "But maybe that was what Mrs. Haslett found out." He lifted his shoulders a fraction. "And she threatened to tell Mrs. Kellard? And for that matter maybe she did tell her, that night. . . ." He left it hanging. He did not need to add that Araminta might have killed her sister in a fit of fury and shame to keep her from telling the whole household. The possibilities were many, and all ugly, and nothing to do with Percival or any of the other servants.

"And you told no one?" Monk said with grating unbelief. "You had this extraordinary piece of information, and you kept it the secret the family would wish? You were discreet and obedient. Why, for heaven's sake?'' He allowed into his voice an exact mockery of Percival's own contempt for him a few moments earlier. ''Knowledge like that is power—you expect me to believe you didn't use it?''

Percival was not discomfited. ''I don't know what you mean, sir.''

Monk knew he was lying.

''No reason to tell anyone,'' Percival went on. ''Not in my interest.'' The sneer returned. ''Sir Basil wouldn't like it, and then I might find myself in the workhouse. It's different now. This is a matter of duty that any other employer would understand. When it's a matter of concealing a crime—''

''So suddenly rape has become a crime?'' Monk was disgusted. ''When did that happen? When your own neck was in danger?''

If Percival was frightened or embarrassed there was no trace of it in his expression.

''Not rape, sir—murder. That has always been the crime.'' Again his shoulders lifted expressively. ''If it's actually called murder, not justice, privilege, or some such thing.''

''Like rape of a servant, for example.'' Monk for one instant agreed with him. He hated it. ''All right, you can go.''

''Shall I tell Sir Basil you want to see him?''

''If you want to keep your position, you'd better not put it like that.''

Percival did not bother to reply, but went out, moving easily, even gracefully, his body relaxed.

Monk was too concerned, too angry at the appalling injustice and suffering, and apprehensive of his interview with Basil Moidore to spare any emotion for contempt of Percival.

It was nearly a quarter of an hour before Harold came back to tell him that Sir Basil would see him in the library.

''Good morning, Monk. You wanted to see me?'' Basil stood near the window with the armchair and the table forcing a distance between them. He looked harassed and his face creased in lines of temper. Monk irritated him by his questions, his stance, the very shape of his face.

''Good morning, sir,'' Monk replied. ''Yes, some new information has come to me this morning. I would like to ask you if it is true, and if it is, to tell me what you know of the matter.''

Basil did not seem concerned, and was only moderately interested. He was still dressed in black, but elegant, self-consciously smart black. It was not the mourning of someone bowed down with grief.

"What matter is this, Inspector?"

"A maid that worked here two years ago, by the name of Martha Rivett."

Basil's face tightened, and he moved from the window and stood straighter.

"What can she possibly have to do with my daughter's death?"

"Was she raped, Sir Basil?"

Basil's eyes widened. Distaste registered sharply in his face, then another, more thoughtful expression. "I have no idea!"

Monk controlled himself with great difficulty. "Did she come to you and say that she was?"

A slight smile moved Basil's mouth, and his hand at his side curled and uncurled.

"Inspector, if you had ever kept a house with a large staff, many of them young, imaginative and excitable women, you would hear a great many stories of all sorts of entanglements, charges and countercharges of wrongs. Certainly she came and said she had been molested—but I have no way of knowing whether she really had or whether she had got herself with child and was trying to lay the blame on someone else—and get us to look after her. Possibly one of the male servants forced his attentions—" His hands uncurled, and he shrugged very faintly.

Monk bit his tongue and stared at Basil with hard eyes.

"Is that what you believe, sir? You spoke with the girl. I believe she charged that it was Mr. Kellard who assaulted her. Presumably you also spoke with Mr. Kellard. Did he tell you he had never had anything to do with her?"

"Is that your business, Inspector?" Basil said coldly.

"If Mr. Kellard raped this girl, yes, Sir Basil, it is. It may well be the root of this present crime."

"Indeed? I fail to see how." But there was no conciliation in his voice, and no outrage.

"Then I will explain it," Monk said between his teeth. "If Mr. Kellard raped this unfortunate girl, the fact was concealed and the girl dismissed to whatever fate she could find, then

193

that says a great deal about Mr. Kellard's nature and his belief that he is free to force his attentions upon women, regardless of their feelings. It seems highly probable that he admired Mrs. Haslett, and may have tried to force his attentions upon her also.''

"And murdered her?'' Basil was considering it. There was caution in his voice, the beginning of a new thought, but still heavily tinged with doubt. "Martha never suggested he threatened her with any weapon, and she perfectly obviously had not been injured—''

"You had her examined?'' Monk asked baldly.

Temper flashed in Basil's face. "Of course I didn't. Whatever for? She made no claim of violence—I told you that.''

"I daresay she considered it of no purpose—and she was right. She charged rape, and was dismissed without a character to live or die in the streets.'' As soon as he had said it he knew his words were the result of temper, not judgment.

Basil's cheeks darkened with anger. "Some chit of a maid gets with child and accuses my daughter's husband of raping her! For God's sake, man, do you expect me to keep her in the house? Or recommend her to the houses of my friends?'' Still he remained at the far side of the room, glaring at Monk across the table and the chair. "I have a duty both to my family, especially my daughter and her happiness, and to my acquaintances. To give any recommendation to a young woman with a character that would charge such a thing of her employer would be completely irresponsible.''

Monk wanted to ask him about his duty toward Martha Rivett, but knew that such an affront would very probably cause him just the sort of complaint that Runcorn would delight in, and would give Runcorn an excuse for censure, perhaps even removal from the case.

"You did not believe her, sir?'' He was civil with difficulty. "Mr. Kellard denied having any relationship with her?''

"No he didn't,'' Basil said sharply. "He said she had led him on and was perfectly willing; it was only later when she discovered she was with child she made this charge to protect herself—and I daresay to try and force us to care for her, to stop her spreading about such a story. The girl was obviously of loose character and out to take a chance to profit from it if she could.''

194

"So you put an end to it. I assume you believed Mr. Kellard's account?"

Basil looked at him coldly. "No, as a matter of fact I did not. I think it very probable he forced his attentions on the girl, but that is hardly important now. Men have natural appetites, always have had. I daresay she flirted with him and he mistook her. Are you suggesting he tried the same with my daughter Octavia?"

"It seems possible."

Basil frowned. "And if he did, why should that lead to murder, which is what you seem to be suggesting? If she had struck at him, that would be understandable, but why should he kill her?"

"If she intended telling people," Monk replied. "To rape a maid is apparently acceptable, but would you have viewed it with the same leniency had he raped your daughter? And would Mrs. Kellard, if she knew?"

Basil's face was scored with deep lines, now all dragged downward with distaste and anxiety.

"She does not know," he said slowly, meeting Monk's eyes. "I trust I make myself plain, Inspector? For her to be aware of Myles's indiscretion would distress her, and serve no purpose. He is her husband and will remain so. I don't know what women do in your walk of life, but in ours they bear their difficulties with dignity and silence. Do you understand me?"

"Of course I do," Monk said tartly. "If she does not know now, I shall not tell her unless it becomes necessary—by which time I imagine it will be common knowledge. Similarly may I ask you, sir, not to forewarn Mr. Kellard of my knowledge in the matter. I can hardly expect him to confess to anything, but I may learn quite a lot from his first reaction when I speak to him about it."

"You expect me to . . ." Basil began indignantly, then his voice faded away as he realized what he was saying.

"I do," Monk agreed with a downward turn of his mouth. "Apart from the ends of justice towards Mrs. Haslett, you and I both know that it was someone in this house. If you protect Mr. Kellard to save scandal—and Mrs. Kellard's feelings—you only prolong the investigation, the suspicion, Lady Moidore's distress—and it will still come down to someone in the house in the end."

For a moment their eyes met, and there was intense dislike—and complete understanding.

"If Mrs. Kellard needs to know, I will be the one to tell her," Basil stated.

"If you wish," Monk agreed. "Although I would not leave it too long. If I can learn of it, so may she—"

Basil jerked upward. "Who told you? It damned well wasn't Myles! Was it Lady Moidore?"

"No, I have not spoken to Lady Moidore."

"Well, don't stand there, man! Who was it?"

"I prefer not to say, sir."

"I don't give a damn what you prefer! Who was it?"

"If you force me, sir—I decline to say."

"You—you what?" He tried to outstare Monk, and then realized he could not intimidate him without a specific threat and that he was not prepared at this point to make one. He looked down again; he was not used to being defied, and he had no ready reaction. "Well pursue your investigation for the moment, but I will know in the end, I promise you."

Monk did not force his victory; it was too tenuous and the temper between them too volatile.

"Yes sir, very possibly. Since she is the only other person you are aware of having known of this, may I speak with Lady Moidore, please?"

"I doubt she can tell you anything. I dealt with the affair."

"I'm sure you did, sir. But she knew of it, and may have observed emotions in people that you did not. She would have opportunities not afforded you, domestic occasions; and women are more sensitive to such things, on the whole."

Basil hesitated.

Monk thought of several arguments: the quick ending of the case, some justice for Octavia—and then caution argued that Octavia was dead and Basil might well think that saving the reputations of those alive was more important. He could do nothing for Octavia now, but he could still protect Araminta from deep shame and hurt. Monk ended by saying nothing.

"Very well," Basil agreed reluctantly. "But have the nurse present, and if Lady Moidore is distressed, you will cease immediately. Is that understood?"

"Yes sir," Monk said instantly. To have Hester's impressions also was an advantage he had not thought to look for. "Thank you."

Again he was required to wait while Beatrice dressed appropriately for receiving the police, and some half an hour later it was Hester herself who came to the morning room to collect him and take him to the withdrawing room.

"Shut the door," he ordered as soon as she was inside.

She obeyed, watching him curiously. "Do you know something?" she asked, her tone guarded, as though whatever it was she would find it only partly welcome.

He waited until the latch was fast and she had returned to the center of the floor.

"There was a maid here about two years ago who charged that Myles Kellard raped her, and she was promptly dismissed without a character."

"Oh—" She looked startled. Obviously she had heard nothing of it from the servants. Then, as amazement dissolved, she was furiously angry, the hot color in her cheeks. "You mean they threw her out? What happened to Myles?"

"Nothing," he said dryly. "What did you expect?"

She stood stiffly, shoulders back, chin high, and stared at him. Then gradually she realized the inevitability of what he had said and that her first thought of justice and open judgment was never a reality.

"Who knows about it?" she asked instead.

"Only Sir Basil and Lady Moidore, so far as I am aware," he replied. "That is what Sir Basil believes, anyway."

"Who told you? Not Sir Basil, surely?"

He smiled with a hard, twisted grimace. "Percival, when he thought I was closing in on him. He certainly won't go docilely into the darkness for them, whatever poor Martha Rivett did. If Percival goes down, he'll do his best to take as many of the rest of them with him as he can."

"I don't like him," she said quietly, looking down. "But I can't blame him for fighting. I think I would. I might suffer injustice for someone I loved—but not for these people, who are only too willing to see him take the blame to get it away from them. What are you going to ask Lady Moidore? You know it's true—"

"I don't," he contradicted. "Myles Kellard says she was a trollop who invited it—Basil doesn't care whether that is true

197

or not. She couldn't stay here after she'd accused Kellard—apart from the fact she was with child. All Basil cared about was clearing up the mess here and protecting Araminta."

The surprise was evident in her face. "She doesn't know?"

"You think she does?" he said quickly.

"She hates him for something. It may not be that—"

"Could be anything," he agreed. "Even so, I can't see how knowing that would be a reason for anyone to murder Octavia—even if the rape was what Octavia found out the day before she was killed."

"Neither do I," she admitted. "There's something very important we don't know yet."

"And I don't suppose I'll learn it from Lady Moidore. Still, I had better go and see her now. I don't want them to suspect we discuss them or they will not speak so freely in front of you. Come."

Obediently she opened the door again and led him across the wide hallway and into the withdrawing room. It was cold and windy outside, and the first drops of heavy rain were beating against the long windows. There was a roaring fire in the hearth, and its glow spread across the red Aubusson carpet and even touched the velvet of the curtains that hung from huge swathed pelmets in swags and rich falls to the fringed sashes, spreading their skirts on the floor.

Beatrice Moidore was seated in the largest chair, dressed in unrelieved black, as if to remind them of her bereaved state. She looked very pale, in spite of her marvelous hair, or perhaps because of it, but her eyes were bright and her manner attentive.

"Good morning, Mr. Monk. Please be seated. I understand you wish to ask me about something?"

"Good morning, Lady Moidore. Yes, if you please. Sir Basil asked that Miss Latterly should remain, in case you feel unwell and need any assistance." He sat down as he had been invited, opposite her in one of the other armchairs. Hester remained standing as suited her station.

A half smile touched Beatrice's lips, as though something he could not understand amused her.

"Most thoughtful," she said expressionlessly. "What is it you would like to ask? I know nothing that I did not know when we last spoke."

"But I do, ma'am."

"Indeed?" This time there was a flicker of fear in her, a shadow across the eyes, a tightness in the white hands in her lap.

Who was it she was frightened for? Not herself. Who else did she care about so much that even without knowing what he had learned she feared for them? Who would she protect? Her children, surely—no one else.

"Are you going to tell me, Mr. Monk?" Her voice was brittle, her eyes very clear.

"Yes ma'am. I apologize for raising what must be a most painful subject, but Sir Basil confirmed that about two years ago one of your maids, a girl called Martha Rivett, claimed that Mr. Kellard raped her." He watched her expression and saw the muscles tighten in her neck and across the high, delicate brows. Her lips pulled crooked in distaste.

"I don't see what that can have to do with my daughter's death. It happened two years ago, and it concerned her in no way at all. She did not even know of it."

"Is it true, ma'am? Did Mr. Kellard rape the parlormaid?"

"I don't know. My husband dismissed her, so I assume she was at least in great part to blame for whatever happened. It is quite possible." She took a deep breath and swallowed. He saw the constricted movement of her throat. "It is quite possible she had another relationship and became with child, and then lied to save herself by blaming one of the family—hoping that we should feel responsible and look after her. Such things, unfortunately, do happen."

"I expect they do," he agreed, keeping his voice noncommittal with a great effort. He was sharply aware of Hester standing behind the chair, and knowing what she would feel. "But if that is what she hoped in this instance, then she was sorely disappointed, wasn't she?"

Beatrice's face paled and her head moved fractionally backwards, as if she had been struck but elected to ignore the blow. "It is a terrible thing, Mr. Monk, to charge a person wrongfully with such a gross offense."

"Is it?" he asked sardonically. "It does not appear to have done Mr. Kellard any damage whatever."

She ignored his manner. "Only because we did not believe her!"

"Really?" he pursued. "I rather thought that Sir Basil did believe her, from what he said to me."

She swallowed hard and seemed to sit a little lower in the chair.

"What is it you want of me, Mr. Monk? Even if she was right, and Myles did assault her—in that way—what has it to do with my daughter's death?"

Now he was sorry he had asked her with so little gentleness. Her loss was deep, and she had answered him without evasion or antagonism.

"It would prove that Mr. Kellard has an appetite which he is prepared to satisfy," he explained quietly, "regardless of the personal cost to someone else, and that his past experience has shown him he can do it with impunity."

Now she was as pale as the cambric handkerchief between her clenched fingers.

"Are you suggesting that Myles tried to force himself upon Octavia?" The idea appalled her. Now the horror touched her other daughter as well. Monk felt a stab of guilt for forcing her to think of it—and yet he had no alternative that was honest.

"Is it impossible, ma'am? I believe she was most attractive, and that he had previously been known to admire her."

"But—but she was not—I mean . . ." Her voice died away; she was unable to bring herself to speak the words aloud.

"No. No, she was not molested in that way," he assured her. "But it is possible she had some forewarning he would come and was prepared to defend herself, and in the struggle it was she who was killed, and not he."

"That is—grotesque!" she protested, her eyes wide. "To assault a maid is one thing—to go deliberately and cold-bloodedly to your sister-in-law's bedroom at night, intent upon the same thing, against her will—is—is quite different, and appalling. It is quite wicked!"

"Is it such a great step from one to the other?" He leaned a little closer to her, his voice quiet and urgent. "Do you really believe that Martha Rivett was not equally unwilling? Just not as well prepared to defend herself—younger, more afraid, and more vulnerable since she was a servant in this house and could look for little protection."

She was so ashen now that it was not only Hester who was

afraid she might collapse; Monk himself was concerned that he had been too brutal. Hester took a step forward, but remained silent, staring at Beatrice.

"That is terrible!" Beatrice's voice was dry, difficult to force from her throat. "You are saying that we do not care for our servants properly—that we offer them no—no decency—that we are immoral!"

He could not apologize. That was exactly what he had said.

"Not all of you, ma'am—only Mr. Kellard, and that perhaps to spare your daughter the shame and the distress of knowing what her husband had done, you concealed the offense from her—which effectively meant getting rid of the girl and allowing no one else to know of it either."

She put the hands up to her face and pushed them over her cheeks and upward till her fingers ran through her hair, disarranging its neatness. After a moment's painful silence she lowered them and stared at him.

"What would you have us do, Mr. Monk? If Araminta knew it would ruin her life. She could not live with him, and she could not divorce him—he has not deserted her. Adultery is no grounds for separation, unless it is the woman who commits it. If it is the man that means nothing at all. You must know that. All a woman can do is conceal it, so she is not publicly ruined and becomes a creature of pity for the kindly—and of contempt for the others. She is not to blame for any of it, and she is my child. Would you not protect your own child, Mr. Monk?"

He had no answer. He did not know the fierce, consuming love for a child, the tenderness and the bond, and the responsibility. He had no child—he had only a sister, Beth, and he could recall very little about her, only how she had followed him, her wide eyes full of admiration, and the white pinafore she wore, frilled on the edges, and how often she fell over as she tried to run after him, to keep up. He could remember holding her soft, damp little hand in his as they walked down on the shore together, he half lifting her over the rocks till they reached the smooth sand. A wave of feeling came back to him, a mixture of impatient exasperation and fierce, consuming protectiveness.

"Perhaps I would, ma'am. But then if I had a daughter she would more likely be a parlormaid like Martha Rivett," he said ruthlessly, leaving all that that meant hanging in the air between them, and watched the pain, and the guilt, in her face.

The door opened and Araminta came in, the evening's menu in her hand. She stopped, surprised to see Monk, then turned and looked at her mother's face. She ignored Hester as she would any other servant doing her duty.

"Mama, you look ill. What has happened?" She swung around to Monk, her eyes brilliant with accusation. "My mother is unwell, Inspector. Have you not the common courtesy to leave her alone? She can tell you nothing she has not already said. Miss Latterly will open the door for you and the footman will show you out." She turned to Hester, her voice tense with irritation. "Then, Miss Latterly, you had better fetch Mama a tisane and some smelling salts. I cannot think what possessed you to allow this. You should take your duties a great deal more seriously, or we shall be obliged to find someone else who will."

"I am here with Sir Basil's permission, Mrs. Kellard," Monk said tartly. "We are all quite aware the discussion is painful, but postponing it will only prolong the distress. There has been murder in this house, and Lady Moidore wishes to discover who was responsible as much as anyone."

"Mama?" Araminta challenged.

"Of course I do," Beatrice said very quietly. "I think—"

Araminta's eyes widened. "You think? Oh—" And suddenly some realization struck her with a force so obvious it was like a physical blow. She turned very slowly to Monk. "What were your questions about, Mr. Monk?"

Beatrice drew in her breath and held it, not daring to let it out until Monk should have spoken.

"Lady Moidore has already answered them," Monk replied. "Thank you for your offer, but it concerns a matter of which you have no knowledge."

"It was not an offer." Araminta did not look at her mother but kept her hard, straight gaze level at Monk's eyes. "I wished to be informed for my own sake."

"I apologize," Monk said with a thin thread of sarcasm. "I thought you were trying to assist."

"Are you refusing to tell me?"

He could no longer evade. "If you wish to phrase it so, ma'am, then yes, I am."

Very slowly a curious expression of pain, acceptance, almost a subtle pleasure, came into her eyes.

"Because it is to do with my husband." She turned fractionally towards Beatrice. This time the fear was palpable between them. "Are you trying to protect me, Mama? You know something which implicates Myles." The rage of emotions inside her was thick in her voice. Beatrice half reached towards her, then dropped her hands.

"I don't think it does," she said almost under her breath. "I see no reason to think of Myles. . . ." She trailed off, her disbelief heavy in the air.

Araminta swung back to Monk.

"And what do you think, Mr. Monk?" she said levelly. "That is what matters, isn't it?"

"I don't know yet, ma'am. It is impossible to say until I have learned more about it."

"But it does concern my husband?" she insisted.

"I am not going to discuss the matter until I know much more of the truth," he replied. "It would be unjust—and mischief making."

Her curious, asymmetrical smile was hard. She looked from him to her mother again. "Correct me if I am unjust, Mama." There was a cruel mimicry of Monk's tone in her voice. "But does this concern Myles's attraction towards Octavia, and the thought that he might have forced his attentions upon her, and as a result of her refusal killed her?"

"You are unjust," Beatrice said in little more than a whisper. "You have no reason to think such a thing of him."

"But you have," Araminta said without hesitation, the words hard and slow, as if she were cutting her own flesh. "Mama, I do not deserve to be lied to."

Beatrice gave up; she had no heart left to go on trying to deceive. Her fear was too great; it could be felt like an electric presage of storm in the room. She sat unnaturally motionless, her eyes unfocused, her hands knotted together in her lap.

"Martha Rivett charged that Myles forced himself upon her," she said in a level voice, drained of passion. "That is why she left. Your father dismissed her. She was—" She stopped. To have added the child was an unnecessary blow. Araminta had never borne a child. Monk knew what Beatrice had been going to say as surely as if she had said it. "She was

203

irresponsible," she finished lamely. "We could not keep her in the house saying things like that."

"I see." Araminta's face was ashen white with two high spots of color in her cheeks.

The door opened again and Romola came in, saw the frozen tableau in front of her, Beatrice sitting upright on the sofa, Araminta stiff as a twig, her face set and teeth clenched tight, Hester still standing behind the other large armchair, not knowing what to do, and Monk sitting uncomfortably leaning forward. She glanced at the menu in Araminta's hand, then ignored it. It was apparent even to her that she had interrupted something acutely painful, and dinner was of little importance.

"What is wrong?" she demanded, looking from one to another of them. "Do you know who killed Octavia?"

"No we don't!" Beatrice turned toward her and spoke surprisingly sharply. "We were discussing the parlormaid who was dismissed two years ago."

"Whatever for?" Romola's voice was heavy with disbelief. "Surely that can hardly matter now?"

"Probably not," Beatrice agreed.

"Then why are you wasting time discussing it?" Romola came over to the center of the room and sat down in one of the smaller chairs, arranging her skirts gracefully. "You all look as if it were fearful. Has something happened to her?"

"I have no idea," Beatrice snapped, her temper broken at last. "I should think it is not unlikely."

"Why should it?" Romola was confused and frightened; this was all too much for her. "Didn't you give her a character? Why did you dismiss her anyway?" She twisted around to look at Araminta, her eyebrows raised.

"No, I did not give her a character," Beatrice said flatly.

"Well why not?" Romola looked at Araminta and away again. "Was she dishonest? Did she steal something? No one told me!"

"It was none of your concern," Araminta said brusquely.

"It was if she was a thief! She might have taken something of mine!"

"Hardly. She charged that she had been raped!" Araminta glared at her.

"Raped?" Romola was amazed, her expression changed

204

from fear to total incredulity. "You mean—*raped*? Good gracious!" Relief flooded her, the color returning to her beautiful skin. "Well if she was of loose morals of course you had to dismiss her. No one would argue with that. I daresay she took to the streets; women of that sort do. Why on earth are we concerned about it now? There is nothing we can do about it, and probably there never was."

Hester could contain herself no longer.

"She was raped, Mrs. Moidore—taken by force by someone heavier and stronger than herself. That does not stem from immorality. It could happen to any woman."

Romola stared at her as if she had grown horns. "Of course it stems from immorality! Decent women don't get violated—they don't lay themselves open to it—they don't invite it—or frequent such places in such company. I don't know what kind of society you come from that you could suggest such a thing." She shook her head a little. "I daresay your experiences as a nurse have robbed you of any finer feelings—I beg your pardon for saying such a thing, but you force the issue. Nurses have a reputation for loose conduct which is well known—and scarcely to be envied. Respectable women who behave moderately and dress with decorum do not excite the sort of passions you are speaking of, nor do they find themselves in situations where such a thing could occur. The very idea is quite preposterous—and repulsive."

"It is not preposterous," Hester contradicted flatly. "It is frightening, certainly. It would be very comfortable to suppose that if you behave discreetly you are in no danger of ever being assaulted or having unwelcome attentions forced upon you." She drew in her breath. "It would also be completely untrue, and a quite false sense of safety—and of being morally superior and detached from the pain and the humiliation of it. We would all like to think it could not happen to us, or anyone we know—but it would be wrong." She stopped, seeing Romola's incredulity turning to outrage, Beatrice's surprise and a first spark of respect, and Araminta's extraordinary interest and something that looked almost like a momentary flicker of warmth.

"You forget yourself!" Romola said. "And you forget who we are. Or perhaps you never knew? I am not aware what manner of person you nursed before you came here, but I assure you we do not associate with the sort of people who assault women."

"You are a fool," Araminta said witheringly. "Sometimes I wonder what world it is you live in."

"Minta," Beatrice warned, her voice on edge, her hands clenched together again. "I think we have discussed the matter enough. Mr. Monk will pursue whatever course he deems appropriate. There is nothing more we can offer at the moment. Hester, will you please help me upstairs? I wish to retire. I will not be down for dinner, nor do I wish to see anyone until I feel better."

"How convenient," Araminta said coldly. "But I am sure we shall manage. There is nothing you are needed for. I shall, see to everything, and inform Papa." She swung around to Monk. "Good day, Mr. Monk. You must have enough to keep you busy for some time—although whether it will serve any purpose other than to make you appear diligent, I doubt. I don't see how you can prove anything, whatever you suspect."

"Suspect?" Romola looked first at Monk, then at her sister-in-law, her voice rising with fear again. "Suspect of what? What has this to do with Octavia?"

But Araminta ignored her and walked past her out of the door.

Monk stood up and excused himself to Beatrice, inclined his head to Hester, then held the door open for them as they left, Romola behind them, agitated and annoyed, but helpless to do anything about it.

As soon as Monk stepped inside the police station the sergeant looked up from the desk, his face sober, his eyes gleaming.

"Mr. Runcorn wants to see you, sir. Immediate, like."

"Does he," Monk replied dourly. "Well I doubt he'll get much joy of it, but I'll give him what there is."

"He's in his room, sir."

"Thank you," Monk said. "Mr. Evan in?"

"No sir. He came in, and then he went out again. Didn't say where."

Monk acknowledged the reply and went up the stairs to Runcorn's office. He knocked on the door and at the command went in. Runcorn was sitting behind his large, highly polished desk, two elegant envelopes and half a dozen sheets of fine notepaper written on and half folded lying next to them. The other surfaces were covered with four or five newspapers, some open, some folded.

He looked up, his face dark with anger and his eyes narrow and bright.

"Well. Have you seen the newspapers, eh? Have you seen what they are saying about us?" He held one up and Monk saw the black headlines halfway down the page: QUEEN ANNE STREET MURDERER STILL LOOSE. POLICE BAFFLED. And then the writer went on to question the usefulness of the new police force, and was it money well spent or now an unworkable idea.

"Well?" Runcorn demanded.

"I hadn't seen that one," Monk answered. "I haven't spent much time reading newspapers."

"I don't want you reading the newspapers, damn it," Runcorn exploded. "I want you doing something so they don't write rubbish like this. Or this." He snatched up the next one. "Or this." He threw them away, disregarding the mess as they slid on the polished surface and fell onto the floor in a rattling heap. He grasped one of the letters. "From the Home Office." His fingers closed on it, knuckles white. "I'm getting asked some very embarrassing questions, Monk, and I can't answer them. I'm not prepared to defend you indefinitely—I can't. What in hell's name are you doing, man? If someone in that house killed the wretched woman, then you haven't far to look, have you? Why can't you get this thing settled? For heaven's sake, how many suspects can you have? Four or five at the most. What's the matter with you that you can't finish it up?"

"Because four or five suspects is three or four too many—sir. Unless, of course, you can prove a conspiracy?" Monk said sarcastically.

Runcorn slammed his fist on the table. "Don't be impertinent, damn you! A smart tongue won't get you out of this. Who are your suspects? This footman, what's his name—Percival. Who else? As far as I can see, that's it. Why can't you settle it, Monk? You're beginning to look incompetent." His anger turned to a sneer. "You used to be the best detective we had, but you've certainly lost your touch lately. Why can't you arrest this damned footman?"

"Because I have no proof he did anything," Monk replied succinctly.

"Well who else could it be? Think clearly. You used to be the sharpest and most rational man we had." His lip curled. "Before that accident you were as logical as a piece of algebra—and about as charming—but you knew your job. Now I'm beginning to wonder."

Monk kept his temper with difficulty. "As well as Percival, sir," he said heavily, "it could be one of the laundrymaids—"

"What?" Runcorn's mouth opened in disbelief close to derision. "Did you say one of the laundrymaids? Don't be absurd. Whatever for? If that's the best you can do, I'd better put someone else on the case. Laundrymaid. What in heaven's name would make a laundrymaid get out of her bed in the middle of the night and creep down to her mistress's bedroom and stab her to death? Unless the girl is raving mad. Is she raving mad, Monk? Don't say you couldn't recognize a lunatic if you saw one."

"No, she is not raving mad; she is extremely jealous," Monk answered him.

"Jealous? Of her mistress? That's ludicrous. How can a laundrymaid compare herself with her mistress? That needs some explaining, Monk. You are reaching for straws."

"The laundrymaid is in love with the footman—not a particularly difficult circumstance to understand," Monk said with elaborate, hard-edged patience. "The footman has airs above his station and imagines the mistress admired him—which may or may not be true. Certainly he had allowed the laundrymaid to suppose so."

Runcorn frowned. "Then it was the laundrymaid? Can't you arrest her?"

"For what?"

Runcorn glared at him. "All right, who are your other suspects? You said four or five. So far you have only mentioned two."

"Myles Kellard, the other daughter's husband—"

"What for?" Runcorn was worried now. "You haven't made any accusations, have you?" The blood was pink in his narrow cheeks. "This is a very delicate situation. We can't go around charging people like Sir Basil Moidore and his family. For God's sake, where's your judgment?"

Monk looked at him with contempt.

"That is exactly why I am not charging anyone, sir," he said coldly. "Myles Kellard apparently was strongly attracted by his sister-in-law, which his wife knew about—"

"That's no reason for him to kill her," Runcorn protested. "If he'd killed his wife, maybe. For heaven's sake, think clearly, Monk!"

Monk refrained from telling him about Martha Rivett until he should find the girl, if he could, and hear her side of the story and make some judgment himself as to whom he could believe.

"If he forced his attentions on her," Monk said with continued patience, "and she defended herself, then there may have been a struggle, in which she was knifed—"

"With a carving knife?" Runcorn's eyebrows went up. "Which she just conveniently chanced to have in her bedroom?"

"I don't imagine it was chance," Monk bit back savagely. "If she had reason to think he was coming she probably took it there on purpose."

Runcorn grunted.

"Or it may have been Mrs. Kellard," Monk continued. "She would have good reason to hate her sister."

"Something of an immoral woman, this Mrs. Haslett." Runcorn's lips curled in distaste. "First the footman, now her sister's husband."

"There is no proof she encouraged the footman," Monk said crossly. "And she certainly did not encourage Kellard. Unless you think it's immoral to be beautiful, I don't see how you can find fault with her for either case."

"You always did have some strange ideas of right." Runcorn was disgusted—and confused. The ugly headlines in the newspapers threatened public opinion. The letters from the Home Office lay stiff and white on his desk, polite but cold, warning that it would be little appreciated if he did not find a way to end this case soon, and satisfactorily.

"Well don't stand there," he said to Monk. "Get about finding out which of your suspects is guilty. For heaven's sake, you've only got five; you know it has to be one of them. It's a matter of exclusion. You can stop thinking about Mrs. Kellard, to begin with. She might have a quarrel, but I doubt she'd knife her sister in the night. That's cold-blooded. She couldn't expect to get away with it."

"She couldn't know about Chinese Paddy in the street," Monk pointed out.

"What? Oh—well, neither could the footman. I'd look for a man in this—or the laundrymaid, I suppose. Either way, get on with it. Don't stand here in front of my fire talking."

"You sent for me."

"Yes—well now I'm sending you out again. Close the door as you go—it's cold in the passage."

Monk spent the next two and a half days searching the workhouses, riding in endless cabs through narrow streets, pavements gleaming in the lamplight and the rain, amid the rattle of carts and the noise of street cries, carriage wheels, and the clatter of hooves on the cobbles. He began to the east of Queen Anne Street with the Clerkenwell Workhouse in Farringdon Road, then Holborn Workhouse on the Grey's Inn Road. The second day he moved westward and tried the St. George's Workhouse on Mount Street, then the St. Marylebone Workhouse on Northumberland Street. On the third morning he came to the Westminster Workhouse on Poland Street, and he was beginning to get discouraged. The atmosphere depressed him more than any other place he knew. There was some deeply ingrained fear that touched him at the very name, and when he saw the flat, drab sides of the building rearing up he felt its misery enter into him, and a coldness that had nothing to do with the sharp November wind that whined along the street and rattled an old newspaper in the gutter.

He knocked at the door, and when it was opened by a thin man with lank dark hair and a lugubrious expression, he stated immediately who he was and his profession, so there should be no mistaking his purpose in being here. He would not allow them even for an instant to suppose he was seeking shelter, or the poor relief such places were built and maintained to give.

"You'd better come in. I'll ask if the master'll see yer," the man said without interest. "But if yer want 'elp, yer'd best not lie," he added as an afterthought.

Monk was about to snap at him that he did not, when he caught sight of one of the "outdoor poor" who did, who were reduced by circumstance to seeking charity to survive from one of these grim institutions which robbed them of decision, dignity, individuality, even of dress or personal appearance; which fed them bread and potatoes, separated families, men from women, children from parents, housed them in dormitories, clothed them in uniforms and worked them from dawn until dusk. A man had to be reduced to despair before he begged to be admitted to such a place. But who would willingly let his wife or his children perish?

Monk found the hot denial sticking in his throat. It would humiliate the man further, to no purpose. He contented himself with thanking the doorkeeper and following him obediently.

The workhouse master took nearly a quarter of an hour to come to the small room overlooking the labor yard where rows of men sat on the ground with hammers, chisels and piles of rocks.

He was a pallid man, his gray hair clipped close to his head, his eyes startlingly dark and ringed around with hollow circles as if he never slept.

"What's wrong, Inspector?" he said wearily. "Surely you don't think we harbor criminals here? He'd have to be desperate indeed to seek this asylum—and a very unsuccessful scoundrel."

"I'm looking for a woman who may have been the victim of rape," Monk replied, a dark, savage edge to his voice. "I want to hear her side of the story."

"You new to the job?" the workhouse master said doubtfully, looking him up and down, seeing the maturity in his face, the smooth lines and powerful nose, the confidence and the anger. "No." He answered his own question. "Then what good do you imagine that will do? You're not going to try and prosecute on the word of a pauper, are you?"

"No—it's just corroborative evidence."

"What?"

"Just to confirm what we already know—or suspect."

"What's her name?"

"Martha Rivett. Probably came about two years ago—with child. I daresay the child would be born about seven months later, if she didn't lose it."

"Martha Rivett—Martha Rivett. Would she be a tall girl with fairish hair, about nineteen or twenty?"

"Seventeen—and I'm afraid I don't know what she looked like—except she was a parlormaid, so I expect she was handsome, and possibly tall."

"We've got a Martha about that age, with a baby. Can't remember her other name, but I'll send for her. You can ask her," the master offered.

"Couldn't you take me to her?" Monk suggested. "Don't want to make her feel—" He stopped, uncertain what word to choose.

The workhouse master smiled wryly. "More likely she'll feel like talking away from the other women. But whatever you like."

Monk was happy to concede. He had no desire to see more of the workhouse than he had to. Already the smell of the place—overboiled cabbage, dust and blocked drains—was clinging in his nose, and the misery choked him.

"Yes—thank you. I don't doubt you're right."

The workhouse master disappeared and returned fifteen minutes later with a thin girl with stooped shoulders and a pale, waxen face. Her brown hair was thick but dull, and her wide blue eyes had no life in them. It was not hard to imagine that two years ago she might have been beautiful, but now she was apathetic and she stared at Monk with neither intelligence nor interest, her arms folded under the bib of her uniform apron, her gray stuff dress ill fitting and harsh.

"Yes sir?" she said obediently.

"Martha." Monk spoke very gently. The pity he felt was like a pain in his stomach, churning and sick. "Martha, did you work for Sir Basil Moidore about two years ago?"

"I didn't take anything." There was no protest in her voice, simply a statement of fact.

"No, I know you didn't," he said quickly. "What I want to know is did Mr. Kellard pay you any attention that was more than you wished?" What a mealymouthed way of expressing himself, but he was afraid of being misunderstood, of having her think he was accusing her of lying, troublemaking, raking up old and useless accusations no one would believe, and perhaps being further punished for slander. He watched her face closely, but he saw no deep emotion in it, only a flicker, too slight for him to know what it meant. "Did he, Martha?"

She was undecided, staring at him mutely. Misfortune and workhouse life had robbed her of any will to fight.

"Martha," he said very softly. "He may have forced himself on someone else, not a maid this time, but a lady. I need to know if you were willing or not—and I need to know if it was him or if it was really someone else?"

She looked at him silently, but this time there was a spark in her eyes, a little life.

He waited.

"Does she say that?" she said at last. "Does she say she weren't willing?"

"She doesn't say anything—she's dead."

Her eyes grew huge with horror—and dawning realization, as memory became sharp and focused again.

"He killed her?"

"I don't know," he said frankly. "Was he rough with you?"

She nodded, the memory of pain sharp in her face and fear rekindling as she thought of it again. "Yes."

"Did you tell anyone that?"

"What's the point? They didn't even believe me I was unwilling. They said I was loose-tongued, a troublemaker and no better than I should be. They dismissed me without a character. I couldn't get another position. No one would take me on with no character. An' I was with child—" Her eyes hazed over with tears, and suddenly there was life there again, passion and tenderness.

"Your child?" he asked, although he was afraid to know. He felt himself cringe inside as if waiting for the blow.

"She's here, with the other babes," she said quietly. "I get to see her now and again, but she's not strong. How could she be, born and raised here?"

Monk determined to speak to Callandra Daviot. Surely she could use another servant for something? Martha Rivett was one among tens of thousands, but even one saved from this was better than nothing.

"He was violent with you?" he repeated. "And you made it quite plain you didn't want his attentions?"

"He didn't believe me—he didn't think any woman meant it when she said no," she replied with a faint, twisted smile. "Even Miss Araminta. He said she liked to be took—but I don't believe that. I was there when she married him—an' she really loved him then. You should have seen her face, all shining and soft. Then after her wedding night she changed. She looked like a sparkling fire the night before, all dressed in cherry pink and bright as you like. The morning after she looked like cold ashes in the grate. I never saw that softness back in her as long as I was there.''

"I see," Monk said very quietly. "Thank you, Martha. You have been a great help to me. I shall try to be as much help to you. Don't give up hope."

A fraction of her old dignity returned, but there was no life in her smile.

"There's nothing to hope for, sir. Nobody'd marry me. I never see anyone except people that haven't a farthing of their own, or they'd not be here. And nobody looks for servants in a workhouse, and I wouldn't leave Emmie anyway. And even if she doesn't live, no one takes on a maid without a character, and my looks have gone too."

"They'll come back. Just please—don't give up," he urged her.

"Thank you, sir, but you don't know what you're saying."

"Yes I do."

She smiled patiently at his ignorance and took her leave, going back to the labor yard to scrub and mend.

Monk thanked the workhouse master and left also, not to the police station to tell Runcorn he had a better suspect than Percival. That could wait. First he would go to Callandra Daviot.

8

MONK'S SENSE OF ELATION was short-lived. When he returned to Queen Anne Street the next day he was greeted in the kitchen by Mrs. Boden, looking grim and anxious, her face very pink and her hair poking in wild angles out of her white cap.

"Good morning, Mr. Monk. I am glad you've come!"

"What is it, Mrs. Boden?" His heart sank, although he could think of nothing specific he feared. "What has happened?"

"One of my big kitchen carving knives is missing, Mr. Monk." She wiped her hands on her apron. "I could have sworn I had it last time we had a roast o' beef, but Sal says she thinks as it was the other one I used, the old one, an' now I reckon she must be right." She poked her hair back under her cap and wiped her face agitatedly. "No one else can remember, and May gets sick at the thought. I admit it fair turns my stomach when I think it could've been the one that stabbed poor Miss Octavia."

Monk was cautious. "When did this thought come to you, Mrs. Boden?" he asked guardedly.

"Yesterday, in the evening." She sniffed. "Miss Araminta sent down for a little thin-cut beef for Sir Basil. He'd come in late and wanted a bite to eat." Her voice was rising and there was a note of hysteria in it. "I went to get my best knife, an' it weren't there. That's when I started to look for it, thinking as it had been misplaced. And it in't here—not anywhere."

"And you haven't seen it since Mrs. Haslett's death?"

"I don't know, Mr. Monk!" Her hands jerked up in the air. "I thought I 'ad, but Sal and May tell me as they 'aven't, and when I last cut beef I did it with the old one. I was so upset I can't recall what I did, and that's the truth."

"Then I suppose we'd better see if we can find it," Monk agreed. "I'll get Sergeant Evan to organize a search. Who else knows about this?"

Her face was blank; she understood no implication.

"Who else, Mrs. Boden?" he repeated calmly.

"Well I don't know, Mr. Monk. I don't know who I might have asked. I looked for it, naturally, and asked everyone if they'd seen it."

"Who do you mean by 'everyone,' Mrs. Boden? Who else apart from the kitchen staff?"

"Well—I'm sure I can't think." She was beginning to panic because she could see the urgency in him and she did not understand. "Dinah. I asked Dinah because sometimes things get moved through to the pantry. And I may have mentioned it to 'Arold. Why? They don't know where it is, or they'd 'ave said."

"Someone wouldn't have," he pointed out.

It was several seconds before she grasped what he meant, then her hand flew to her mouth and she let out a stifled shriek.

"I had better inform Sir Basil." That was a euphemism for asking Sir Basil's permission for the search. Without a warrant he could not proceed, and it would probably cost him his job if he were to try against Sir Basil's wishes. He left Mrs. Boden in the kitchen sitting in the chair and May running for smelling salts—and almost certainly a strong nip of brandy.

He was surprised to find himself shown to the library and left barely five minutes before Basil came in looking tense, his face creased, his eyes very dark.

"What is it, Monk? Have you learned anything at last? My God, it is past time you did!"

"The cook reports one of her kitchen carving knives missing, sir. I would like your permission to search the house for it."

"Well of course search for it!" Basil said. "Do you expect me to look for it for you?"

"It was necessary to have your permission, Sir Basil,"

Monk said between his teeth. "I cannot go through your belongings without a warrant, unless you permit me to."

"My belongings." He was startled, his eyes wide with disbelief.

"Is not everything in the house yours, sir, apart from what is Mr. Cyprian's, or Mr. Kellard's—and perhaps Mr. Thirsk's?"

Basil smiled bleakly, merely a slight movement of the corner of the lips. "Mrs. Sandeman's personal belongings are her own, but otherwise, yes, they are mine. Of course you have my permission to search anywhere you please. You will need assistance, no doubt. You may send one of my grooms in the small carriage to fetch whomever you wish—your sergeant . . ." He shrugged, but his shoulders under the black barathea of his coat were tense. "Constables?"

"Thank you," Monk acknowledged. "That is most considerate. I shall do that immediately."

"Perhaps you should wait for them at the head of the male servants' staircase?" Basil raised his voice a little. "If whoever has the knife gets word of this they may be tempted to move it before you can begin your task. From there you can see the far end of the passage where the female servants' staircase emerges." He was explaining himself more than usual. It was the first real crack in his composure that Monk had seen. "That is the best position I can offer. I imagine there is little point in having any one of the servants stand guard—they must all be suspect." He watched Monk's face.

"Thank you," Monk said again. "That is most perceptive of you. May I also have one of the upstairs maids stay on the main landing? They would observe anyone coming or going on other than an ordinary duty—which they would be used to. Perhaps the laundrymaids and other domestic staff could remain downstairs until this is over—and the footmen of course?"

"By all means." Basil was regaining his command. "And the valet as well."

"Thank you, sir. That is most helpful of you."

Basil's eyebrows rose. "What on earth did you expect me to do, man? It was my daughter who was murdered." His control was complete again.

There was nothing Monk could reply to that, except to express a brief sympathy again and take his leave to go down-stairs, write a note to Evan at the police station, and dispatch the groom to fetch him and another constable.

The search, begun forty-five minutes later, started with the rooms of the maids at the far end of the attic, small, cold garrets looking over the gray slates towards their own mews, and the roofs of Harley Mews beyond. They each contained an iron bedstead with mattress, pillow and covers, a wooden hard-backed chair, and a plain wood dresser with a glass on the wall above. No maid would be permitted to present herself for work untidy or in an ill-kept uniform. There was also a cupboard for clothes and a ewer and basin for washing. The rooms were distinguished one from another only by the patterns of the knotted rag rugs on the floor and by the few pictures that belonged to each inhabitant, a sketch of family, in one case a silhouette, a religious text or reproduction of a famous painting.

Neither Monk nor Evan found a knife. The constable, under detailed instructions, was searching the outside property, simply because it was the only other area to which the servants had access without leaving the premises, and thus their duty.

"Of course if it was a member of the family they've all been over half London by now," Evan observed with a crooked smile. "It could be at the bottom of the river, or in any of a million gutters or rubbish bins."

"I know that." Monk did not stop his work. "And Myles Kellard looks by far the most likely, at the moment. Or Araminta, if she knew. But can you think of a better thing to be doing?"

"No," Evan admitted glumly. "I've spent the last week and a half chasing my shadow around London looking for jewelry I'll lay any odds you like was destroyed the night it was taken—or trying to find out the past history of servants whose records are exemplary and deadly monotonous." He was busy turning out drawers of neat, serviceable feminine clothes as he spoke, his long fingers touching them carefully, his face pulled into an expression of distaste at his intrusion. "I begin to think employers don't see people at all, simply aprons and uniform stuff dresses and a lace cap," he went on. "Whose head it is on is all the same, providing the tea is hot, the table is laid, the fires are blacked and laid and stoked, the meal is cooked and served and cleared away, and every time the bell is rung, someone answers it to do whatever you want." He folded the clothes neatly and replaced them. "Oh—and of course the house is always clean and there are always clean clothes in the dresser. Who does it is largely immaterial."

"You are becoming cynical, Evan!"

Evan flashed a smile. "I'm learning, sir."

After the maids' rooms they came down the stairs to the second floor up from the main house. At one end of the landing were the rooms of the housekeeper and the cook and the ladies' maids, and now of course Hester; and at the other the rooms of the butler, the two footmen, the bootboy and the valet.

"Shall we begin with Percival?" Evan asked, looking at Monk apprehensively.

"We may as well take them in order," Monk answered. "The first is Harold."

But they found nothing beyond the private possessions of a very ordinary young man in service in a large house: one suit of clothes for the rare times off duty, letters from his family, several from his mother, a few mementoes of childhood, a picture of a pleasant-faced woman of middle years with the same fair hair and mild features as himself, presumably his mother, and a feminine handkerchief of inexpensive cambric, carefully pressed and placed in his Bible—perhaps Dinah's?

Percival's room was as different from Harold's as the one man was from the other. Here there were books, some poetry, some philosophy of social conditions and change, one or two novels. There were no letters, no sign of family or other ties. He had two suits of his own clothes in the cupboard for his times off duty, and some very smart boots, several neckties and handkerchiefs, and a surprising number of shirts and some extremely handsome cuff links and collar studs. He must have looked quite a dandy when he chose. Monk felt a stab of familiarity as he moved the personal belongings of this other young man who strove to dress and deport himself out of his station in life. Had he himself begun like this—living in someone else's house, aping their manners trying to improve himself? It was also a matter of some curiosity as to where Percival got the money for such things—they cost a great deal more than a footman's wages, even if carefully saved over several years.

"Sir!"

He jerked up and stared at Evan, who was standing white-faced, the whole drawer of the dresser on the floor at his feet, pulled out completely, and in his hand a long garment of ivory silk, stained brown in smears, and a thin, cruel blade poking through, patched and blotched with the rusty red of dried blood.

Monk stared at it, stunned. He had expected an exercise in futility, merely something to demonstrate that he was doing all he could—and now Evan held in his hand what was obviously the weapon, wrapped in a woman's peignoir, and it had been concealed in Percival's room. It was a conclusion so startling he found it hard to grasp.

"So much for Myles Kellard," Evan said, swallowing hard and laying the knife and the silk down carefully on the end of the bed, withdrawing his hand quickly as if desiring to be away from it.

Monk replaced the things he had been looking through in the cupboard and stood up straight, hands in his pockets.

"But why would he leave it here?" he said slowly. "It's damning!"

Evan frowned. "Well, I suppose he didn't want to leave the knife in her room, and he couldn't risk carrying it openly, with blood on it, in case he met someone—"

"Who, for heaven's sake?"

Evan's fair face was intensely troubled, his eyes dark, his lips pulled in distaste that was far deeper than anything physical.

"I don't know! Anyone else on the landing in the night—"

"How would he explain his presence—with or without a knife?" Monk demanded.

"I don't know!" Evan shook his head. "What do footmen do? Maybe he'd say he heard a noise—intruders—the front door—I don't know. But it would be better if he didn't have a knife in his hands—especially a bloodstained one."

"Better still if he had left it there in her room," Monk argued.

"Perhaps he took it out without thinking." He looked up and met Monk's eyes. "Just had it in his hand and kept hold

220

of it? Panicked? Then when he got outside and halfway along the corridor he didn't dare go back?''

"Then why the peignoir?" Monk said. "He wrapped it in that to take it, by the look of it. That's not the kind of panic you're talking about. Now why on earth should he want the knife? It doesn't make sense.''

"Not to us," Evan agreed slowly, staring at the crumpled silk in his hand. "But it must have to him—there it is!"

"And he never had the opportunity to get rid of it between then and now?" Monk screwed up his face. "He couldn't possibly have forgotten it!''

"What other explanation is there?" Evan looked helpless. "It's here!''

"Yes—but was Percival the one who put it here? And why didn't we find it when we looked for the jewelry?''

Evan blushed. "Well I didn't pull out drawers and look under them for anything. I daresay the constable didn't either. Honestly I was pretty sure we wouldn't find it anyway—and the silver vase wouldn't have fitted." He looked uncomfortable.

Monk pulled a face. "Even if we had, it might not have been there then—I suppose. I don't know, Evan. It just seems so . . . stupid! And Percival is arrogant, abrasive, contemptuous of other people, especially women, and he's got a hell of a lot of money from somewhere, to judge from his wardrobe, but he's not stupid. Why should he leave something as damning as this hidden in his room?''

"Arrogance?" Evan suggested tentatively. "Maybe he just thinks we are not efficient enough for him to be afraid of? Up until today he was right.''

"But he was afraid," Monk insisted, remembering Percival's white face and the sweat on his skin. "I had him in the housekeeper's room and I could see the fear in him, smell it! He fought to get out of it, spreading blame everywhere else he could—on the laundrymaid, and Kellard—even Araminta.''

"I don't know!" Evan shook his head, his eyes puzzled. "But Mrs. Boden will tell us if this is her knife—and Mrs. Kellard will tell us if that is her sister's—what did you call it?''

"Peignoir," Monk replied. "Dressing robe.''

"Right—peignoir. I suppose we had better tell Sir Basil we've found it!''

"Yes." Monk picked up the knife, folding the silk over the blade, and carried it out of the room, Evan coming after him.

"Are you going to arrest him?" Evan asked, coming down the stairs a step behind.

Monk hesitated. "I'm not happy it's enough," he said thoughtfully. "Anyone could have put these in his room—and only a fool would leave them there."

"They were fairly well hidden."

"But why keep them?" Monk insisted. "It's stupid—Percival's far too sly for that."

"Then what?" Evan was not argumentative so much as puzzled and disturbed by a series of ugly discoveries in which he saw no sense. "The laundrymaid? Is she really jealous enough to murder Octavia and hide the weapon and the gown in Percival's room?"

They had reached the main landing, where Maggie and Annie were standing together, wide-eyed, staring at them.

"All right girls, you've done a good job. Thank you," Monk said to them with a tight smile. "You can go about your own duties now."

"You've got something!" Annie stared at the silk in his hand, her face pale, and she looked frightened. Maggie stood very close to her, equal fear in her features.

There was no point in lying; they would find out soon enough.

"Yes," he admitted. "We've got the knife. Now get about your duties, or you'll have Mrs. Willis after you."

Mrs. Willis's name was enough to break the spell. They scuttled off to fetch carpet beaters and brushes, and he saw their long gray skirts whisk around the corner into the broom cupboard in a huddle together, whispering breathlessly.

Basil was waiting for the two police in his study, sitting at his desk. He admitted them immediately and looked up from the papers he had been writing on, his face angry, his brow dark.

"Yes?"

Monk closed the door behind him.

"We found a knife, sir; and a silk garment which I believe is a peignoir. Both are stained with blood."

Basil let out his breath slowly, his face barely changed, just a shadow as if some final reality had come home.

"I see. And where did you find these things?"

"Behind a drawer in the dresser in Percival's room," Monk answered, watching him closely.

If Basil was surprised it did not show in his expression. His heavy face with its short, broad nose and mouth wreathed in lines remained careful and tired. Perhaps one could not expect it of him. His family had endured bereavement and suspicion for weeks. That it should finally be ended and the burden lifted from his immediate family must be an overwhelming relief. He could not be blamed if that were paramount. However repugnant the thought, he cannot have helped wondering if his son-in-law might be responsible, and Monk had already seen that he and Araminta had a deeper affection than many a father and child. She was the only one who had his inner strength, his command and determination, his dignity and almost total self-control. Although that might be an unfair judgment, since Monk had never seen Octavia alive; but she had apparently been flawed by the weakness of drink and the vulnerability of loving her husband too much to recover from his death—if indeed that were a flaw. Perhaps it was to Basil and Araminta, who had disapproved of Harry Haslett in the first place.

"I assume you are going to arrest him." It was barely a question.

"Not yet," Monk said slowly. "The fact that they were found in his room does not prove it was he who put them there."

"What?" Basil's face darkened with angry color and he leaned forward over the desk. Another man might have risen to his feet, but he did not stand to servants, or police, who were in his mind the same. "For God's sake, man, what more do you want? The very knife that stabbed her, and her clothes found in his possession!"

"Found in his room, sir," Monk corrected. "The door was not locked; anyone in the house could have put them there."

"Don't be absurd!" Basil said savagely. "Who in the devil's name would put such things there?"

"Anyone wishing to implicate him—and thus remove suspicion from themselves," Monk replied. "A natural act of self-preservation."

"Who, for example?" Basil said with a sneer. "You have every evidence that it was Percival. He had the motive, heaven

223

help us. Poor Octavia was weak in her choice of men. I was her father, but I can admit that. Percival is an arrogant and presumptuous creature. When she rebuffed him and threatened to have him thrown out, he panicked. He had gone too far.'' His voice was shaking, and deeply as he disliked him, Monk had a moment's pity for him. Octavia had been his daughter, whatever he had thought of her marriage, or tried to deny her; the thought of her violation must have wounded him inwardly more than he could show, especially in front of an inferior like Monk.

He mastered himself with difficulty and continued. "Or perhaps she took the knife with her," he said quietly, "fearing he might come, and when he did, she tried to defend herself, poor child." He swallowed. "And he overpowered her and it was she who was stabbed." At last he turned, leaving his back towards Monk. "He panicked," he went on. "And left, taking the knife with him, and then hid it because he had no opportunity to dispose of it." He moved away towards the window, hiding his face. He breathed in deeply and let it out in a sigh. "What an abominable tragedy. You will arrest him immediately and get him out of my house. I will tell my family that you have solved the crime of Octavia's death. I thank you for your diligence—and your discretion."

"No sir," Monk said levelly, part of him wishing he could agree. "I cannot arrest him on this evidence. It is not sufficient—unless he confesses. If he denies it, and says someone else put these things in his room—"

Basil swung around, his eyes hard and very black. "Who?"

"Possibly Rose," Monk replied.

Basil stared at him. "What?"

"The laundrymaid who is infatuated with him, and might have been jealous enough to kill Mrs. Haslett and then implicate Percival. That way she would be revenged upon them both."

Basil's eyebrows rose. "Are you suggesting, Inspector, that my daughter was in rivalry with a laundrymaid for the love of a footman? Do you imagine anyone at all will believe you?"

How easy it would be to do what they all wanted and arrest Percival. Runcorn would be torn between relief and frustration. Monk could leave Queen Anne Street and take a new case. Except that he did not believe this one was over—not yet.

"I am suggesting, Sir Basil, that the footman in question is something of a braggart," he said aloud. "And he may well have tried to make the laundrymaid jealous by telling her that that was the case. And she may have been gullible enough to believe him."

"Oh." Basil gave up. Suddenly the anger drained out of him. "Well it is your job to find out which is the truth. I don't much care. Either way, arrest the appropriate person and take them away. I will dismiss the other anyway—without a character. Just attend to it."

"Or, on the other hand," Monk said coldly, "it might have been Mr. Kellard. It now seems undeniable that he resorts to violence when his desire is refused."

Basil looked up. "Does it? I don't recall telling you anything of the sort. I said that she made some such charge and that my son-in-law denied it."

"I found the girl," Monk told him with a hard stare, all his dislike flooding back. The man was callous, almost brutal in his indifference. "I heard her account of the event, and I believe it." He did not mention what Martha Rivett had said about Araminta and her wedding night, but it explained very precisely the emotions Hester had seen in her and her continuous, underlying bitterness towards her husband. If Basil did not know, there was no purpose in telling him so private and painful a piece of information.

"Do you indeed?" Basil's face was bleak. "Well fortunately judgment does not rest with you. Nor will any court accept the unsubstantiated word of an immoral servant girl against that of a gentleman of unblemished reputation."

"And what anyone believes is irrelevant," Monk said stiffly. "I cannot prove that Percival is guilty—but more urgent than that, I do not yet know that he is."

"Then get out and find out!" Basil said, losing his temper at last. "For God's sake do your job!"

"Sir." Monk was too angry to add anything further. He swung on his heel and went out, shutting the door hard behind him. Evan was standing miserably in the hall, waiting, the peignoir and the knife in his hand.

"Well?" Monk demanded.

225

"It's the kitchen knife Mrs. Boden was missing," Evan answered. "I haven't asked anyone about this yet." He held up the peignoir, his face betraying the distress he felt for death, loneliness and indignity. "But I requested to see Mrs. Kellard."

"Good. I'll take it. Where is she?"

"I don't know. I asked Dinah and she told me to wait."

Monk swore. He hated being left in the hall like a mendicant, but he had no alternative. It was a further quarter of an hour before Dinah returned and conducted them to the boudoir, where Araminta was standing in the center of the floor, her face strained and grim but perfectly composed.

"What is it, Mr. Monk?" she said quietly, ignoring Evan, who waited silently by the door. "I believe you have found the knife—in one of the servants' bedrooms. Is that so?"

"Yes, Mrs. Kellard." He did not know how she would react to this visual and so tangible evidence of death. So far everything had been words, ideas—terrible, but all in the mind. This was real, her sister's clothes, her sister's blood. The iron resolution might break. He could not feel a warmth towards her, she was too distant, but he could feel both pity and admiration. "We also found a silk peignoir stained with blood. I am sorry to have to ask you to identify such a distressing thing, but we need to know if it belonged to your sister." He had been holding it low, half behind him, and he knew she had not noticed it.

She seemed very tense, as if it were important rather than painful. He thought that perhaps it was her way of keeping her control.

"Indeed?" She swallowed. "You may show it to me, Mr. Monk. I am quite prepared and will do all I can."

He brought the peignoir forward and held it up, concealing as much of the blood as he could. It was only spatters, as if it had been open when she was stabbed; the stains had come largely from being wrapped around the blade.

She was very pale, but she did not flinch from looking at it.

"Yes," she said quietly and slowly. "That is Octavia's. She was wearing it the night she was killed. I spoke to her on the landing just before she went in to say good-night to Mama. I remember it very clearly—the lace lilies. I always admired it."

She took a deep breath. "May I ask you where you found it?" Now she was as white as the silk in Monk's hand.

"Behind a drawer in Percival's bedroom," he answered.

She stood quite still. "Oh. I see."

He waited for her to continue, but she did not.

"I have not yet asked him for an explanation," he went on, watching her face.

"Explanation?" She swallowed again, so painfully hard he could see the constriction in her throat. "How could he possibly explain such a thing?" She looked confused, but there was no observable anger in her, no rage or revenge. Not yet. "Is not the only answer that he hid it there after he had killed her, and had not found an opportunity to dispose of it?"

Monk wished he could help her, but he could not.

"Knowing something of Percival, Mrs. Kellard, would you expect him to hide it in his own room, such a damning thing; or in some place less likely to incriminate him?" he asked.

The shadow of a smile crossed her face. Even now she could see a bitter humor in the suggestion. "In the middle of the night, Inspector, I should expect him to put it in the one place where his presence would arouse no suspicion—his own room. Perhaps he intended to put it somewhere else later, but never found the opportunity." She took a deep breath and her eyebrows arched high. "One requires to be quite certain of being unobserved for such an act, I should imagine?"

"Of course." He could not disagree.

"Then it is surely time you questioned him? Have you sufficient force with you, should he prove violent, or shall I send for one of the grooms to assist you?"

How practical.

"Thank you," he declined. "But I think Sergeant Evan and I can manage. Thank you for your assistance. I regret having to ask you such questions, or that you should need to see the peignoir." He would have added something less formal, but she was not a woman to whom one offered anything as close or gentle as pity. Respect, and an understanding of courage, was all she would accept.

"It was necessary, Inspector," she acknowledged with stiff grace.

"Ma'am." He inclined his head, excusing himself, and with

Evan a step behind him, went to the butler's pantry to ask Phillips if he might see Percival.

"Of course," Phillips said gravely. "May I ask, sir, if you have discovered something in your search? One of the upstairs maids said that you had, but they are young, and inclined to be overimaginative."

"Yes we have," Monk replied. "We found Mrs. Boden's missing knife and a peignoir belonging to Mrs. Haslett. It appears to have been the knife used to kill her."

Phillips looked very white and Monk was afraid for a moment he was going to collapse, but he stood rigid like a soldier on parade.

"May I ask where you found it?" There was no "sir." Phillips was a butler, and considered himself socially very superior to a policeman. Even these desperate circumstances did not alter that.

"I think it would be better at the moment if that were a confidential matter," Monk replied coolly. "It is indicative of who hid them there, but not conclusive."

"I see." Phillips felt the rebuff; it was there in his pale face and rigid manner. He was in charge of the servants, used to command, and he resented a mere policeman intruding upon his field of responsibility. Everything beyond the green baize door was his preserve. "And what is it you wish of me? I shall be pleased to assist, of course." It was a formality; he had no choice, but he would keep up the charade.

"I'm obliged," Monk said, hiding his flash of humor. Phillips would not appreciate being laughed at. "I would like to see the menservants one at a time—beginning with Harold, and then Rhodes the valet, then Percival."

"Of course. You may use Mrs. Willis's sitting room if you wish to."

"Thank you, that would be convenient."

He had nothing to say to either Harold or Rhodes, but to keep up appearances he asked them about their whereabouts during the day and if their rooms were locked. Their answers told him nothing he did not already know.

When Percival came he already knew something was deeply wrong. He had far more intelligence than either of the other two, and perhaps something in Phillips's manner forewarned him, as did the knowledge that something had been found in the servants' rooms. He knew the family members were increasingly frightened. He saw them every day, heard the sharpened tempers, saw the suspicion in their eyes, the altered relationships, the crumbling belief. Indeed he had tried to turn Monk towards Myles Kellard himself. He must know they would be doing the same thing, feeding every scrap of information they could to turn the police to the servants' hall. He came in with the air of fear about him, his body tense, his eyes wide, a small nerve ticking in the side of his face.

Evan moved silently to stand between him and the door.

"Yes sir?" Percival said without waiting for Monk to speak, although his eyes flickered as he became aware of Evan's change of position—and its meaning.

Monk had been holding the silk and the knife behind him. Now he brought them forward and held them up, the knife in his left hand, the peignoir hanging, the spattered blood dark and ugly. He watched Percival's face minutely, every shade of expression. He saw surprise, a shadow of puzzlement as if it were confusing to him, but no blanching of new fear. In fact there was even a quick lift of hope, as if a moment of sun had shone through clouds. It was not the reaction he had expected from a guilty man. At that instant he believed Percival did not know where they had been found.

"Have you seen these before?" he said. The answer would be of little value to him, but he had to begin somewhere.

Percival was very pale, but more composed than when he came in. He thought he knew what the threat was now, and it disturbed him less than the unknown.

"Maybe. The knife looks like several in the kitchen. The silk could be any of those I've passed in the laundry. But I certainly haven't seen them like that. Is that what killed Mrs. Haslett?"

"It certainly looks like it, doesn't it?"

"Yes sir."

"Don't you want to know where we found them?" Monk glanced past him to Evan and saw the doubt in his face also, an exact reflection of what he was feeling himself. If Percival knew they had found these things in his room, he was a superb actor and a man of self-control worthy of anyone's admiration—and an incredible fool not to have found some way of disposing of them before now.

Percival lifted his shoulders a fraction but said nothing.

"Behind the bottom drawer in the dresser in your bedroom."

This time Percival was horrified. There was no mistaking the sudden rush of blood from his skin, the dilation of his eyes and the sweat standing out on his lip and brow.

He drew breath to speak, and his voice failed him.

In that moment Monk had a sudden sick conviction that Percival had not killed Octavia Haslett. He was arrogant, selfish, and had probably misused her, and perhaps Rose, and he had money that would take some explaining, but he was not guilty of murder. Monk looked at Evan again and saw the same thoughts, even to the shock of unhappiness, mirrored in his eyes.

Monk looked back at Percival.

"I assume you cannot tell me how they got there?"

Percival swallowed convulsively. "No—no I can't."

"I thought not."

"I can't!" Percival's voice rose an octave to a squeak, cracking with fear. "Before God, I didn't kill her! I've never seen them before—not like that!" The muscles of his body were so knotted he was shaking. "Look—I exaggerated. I said she admired me—I was bragging. I never had an affair with her." He started to move agitatedly. "She was never interested in anyone but Captain Haslett. Look—I was polite to her, no more than that. And I never went to her room except to carry trays or flowers or messages, which is my job." His hands moved convulsively. "I don't know who killed her—but it wasn't me! Anyone could have put these things in my room—why would I keep them there?" His words were falling over each other. "I'm not a fool. Why wouldn't I clean the knife and put it back in its place in the kitchen—and burn the silk? Why wouldn't I?" He swallowed hard and turned to Evan. "I wouldn't leave them there for you to find."

"No, I don't think you would," Monk agreed. "Unless you were so sure of yourself you thought we wouldn't search? You've tried to direct us to Rose, and to Mr. Kellard, or even Mrs. Kellard. Perhaps you thought you had succeeded—and you were keeping them to implicate someone else?"

Percival licked his dry lips. "Then why didn't I do that? I can go in and out of bedrooms easily enough; I've only got to

230

get something from the laundry to carry and no one would question me. I wouldn't leave them in my own room, I'd have hidden them in someone else's—Mr. Kellard's—for you to find!"

"You didn't know we were going to search today," Monk pointed out, pushing the argument to the end, although he had no belief in it. "Perhaps you planned to do that—but we were too quick?"

"You've been here for weeks," Percival protested. "I'd have done it before now—and said something to you to make you search. It'd have been easy enough to say I'd seen something, or to get Mrs. Boden to check her knives to find one gone. Come on—don't you think I could do that?"

"Yes," Monk agreed. "I do."

Percival swallowed and choked. "Well?" he said when he regained his voice.

"You can go for now."

Percival stared wide-eyed for a long moment, then turned on his heel and went out, almost bumping into Evan and leaving the door open.

Monk looked at Evan.

"I don't think he did it," Evan said very quietly. "It doesn't make sense."

"No—neither do I," Monk agreed.

"Mightn't he run?" Evan asked anxiously.

Monk shook his head. "We'd know within an hour—and it'd send half the police in London after him. He knows that."

"Then who did it?" Evan asked. "Kellard?"

"Or did Rose believe that Percival really was having an affair, and she did it in jealousy?" Monk thought aloud.

"Or somebody we haven't even thought of?" Evan added with a downward little smile, devoid of humor. "I wonder what Miss Latterly thinks?"

Monk was prevented from answering by Harold putting his head around the door, his face pale, his blue eyes wide and anxious.

"Mr. Phillips says are you all right, sir?"

"Yes, thank you. Please tell Mr. Phillips we haven't reached any conclusion so far, and will you ask Miss Latterly to come here."

"The nurse, sir? Are you unwell, sir? Or are you going to . . ." He trailed off, his imagination ahead of propriety.

Monk smiled sourly. "No, I'm not going to say anything to make anyone faint. I merely want to ask her opinion about something. Will you send for her please?"

"Yes sir. I—yes sir." And he withdrew in haste, glad to be out of a situation beyond him.

"Sir Basil won't be pleased," Evan said dryly.

"No, I imagine not," Monk agreed. "Nor will anyone else. They all seemed keen that poor Percival should be arrested and the matter dealt with, and us out of the way."

"And someone who will be even angrier," Evan pulled a face, "will be Runcorn."

"Yes," Monk said slowly with some satisfaction. "Yes— he will, won't he!"

Evan sat down on the arm of one of Mrs. Willis's best chairs, swinging his legs a little. "I wonder if your not arresting Percival will prompt whoever it is to try something more dramatic?"

Monk grunted and smiled very slightly. "That's a very comfortable thought."

There was a knock on the door and as Evan opened it Hester came in, looking puzzled and curious.

Evan closed the door and leaned against it.

Monk told her briefly what had happened, adding his own feelings and Evan's in explanation.

"One of the family," she said quietly.

"What makes you say that?"

She lifted her shoulders very slightly, not quite a shrug, and her brow wrinkled in thought. "Lady Moidore is afraid of something, not something that has happened, but something she is afraid may yet happen. Arresting a footman wouldn't trouble her; it would be a relief." Her gray eyes were very direct. "Then you would go away, the public and the newspapers would forget about it, and they could begin to recover. They would stop suspecting one another and trying to pretend they are not."

"Myles Kellard?" he asked.

She frowned, finding words slowly. "If he did, I think it would be in panic. He doesn't seem to me to have the nerve to cover for himself as coolly as this. I mean keeping the knife

232

and the peignoir and hiding it in Percival's room." She hesitated. "I think if he killed her, then someone else is hiding it for him—perhaps Araminta? Maybe that is why he is afraid of her—and I think he is."

"And Lady Moidore knows this—or suspects it?"

"Perhaps."

"Or Araminta killed her sister when she found her husband in her room?" Evan suggested suddenly. "That is something that might happen. Perhaps she went along in the night and found them together and killed her sister and left her husband to take the blame?"

Monk looked at him with considerable respect. It was a solution he had not yet thought of himself, and now it was there in words. "Eminently possible," he said aloud. "Far more likely than Percival going to her room, being rejected and knifing her. For one thing, he would hardly go for a seduction armed with a kitchen knife, and unless she was expecting him, neither would she." He leaned comfortably against one of Mrs. Willis's chairs. "And if she were expecting him," he went on, "surely there were better ways of defending herself, simply by informing her father that the footman had overstepped himself and should be dismissed. Basil had already proved himself more than willing to dismiss a servant who was innocently involved with one of the family, how much more easily one who was not innocent."

He saw their immediate comprehension.

"Are you going to tell Sir Basil?" Evan asked.

"I have no choice. He's expecting me to arrest Percival."

"And Runcorn?" Evan persisted.

"I'll have to tell him too. Sir Basil will—"

Evan smiled, but no answer was necessary.

Monk turned to Hester. "Be careful," he warned. "Whoever it is wants us to arrest Percival. They will be upset that we haven't and may do something rash."

"I will," she said quite calmly.

Her composure irritated him. "You don't appear to understand the risk." His voice was sharp. "There would be a physical danger to you."

"I am acquainted with physical danger." She met his eyes levelly with a glint of amusement. "I have seen a great deal more death than you have, and been closer to my own than I am ever likely to be in London."

His reply was futile, and he forbore from making it. This time she was perfectly right—he had forgotten. Dryly he excused himself and reported to the front of the house and an irate Sir Basil.

"In God's name, what more do you need?" he shouted, banging his fist on his desk and making the ornaments jump. "You find the weapon and my daughter's bloodstained clothes in the man's bedroom! Do you expect a confession?"

Monk explained with as much clarity and patience as he could exactly why he felt it was not yet sufficient evidence, but Basil was angry and dismissed him with less than courtesy, at the same time calling for Harold to attend him instantly and take a letter.

By the time Monk had returned to the kitchen and collected Evan, walked along to Regent Street and picked up a hansom to the police station to report to Runcorn, Harold, with Sir Basil's letter, was ahead of him.

"What in the devil's name are you doing, Monk?" Runcorn demanded, leaning across his desk, the paper clenched in his fist. "You've got enough evidence to hang the man twice over. What are you playing at, man, telling Sir Basil you aren't going to arrest him? Go back and do it right now!"

"I don't think he's guilty," Monk said flatly.

Runcorn was nonplussed. His long face fell into an expression of disbelief. "You what?"

"I don't think he's guilty," Monk repeated clearly and with a sharper edge to his voice.

The color rose in Runcorn's cheeks, beginning to mottle his skin.

"Don't be ridiculous. Of course he's guilty!" he shouted. "Good God man, didn't you find the knife and her bloodstained clothes in his room? What more do you want? What innocent explanation could there possibly be?"

"That he didn't put them there." Monk kept his own voice low. "Only a fool would have left things like that where they might be found."

"But you didn't find them, did you?" Runcorn said furiously, on his feet now. "Not until the cook told you her knife

234

was missing. This damn footman can't have known she'd notice it after this time. He didn't know you'd search the place."

"We already searched it once for the missing jewelry," Monk pointed out.

"Well you didn't search it very well, did you?" Runcorn accused with satisfaction lacing through his words even now. "You didn't expect to find it, so you didn't make a proper job of it. Slipshod—think you're cleverer than anybody else and leap to conclusions." He leaned forward over the desk, his hands resting on the surface, splay fingered. "Well you were wrong this time, weren't you—in fact I'd say downright incompetent. If you'd done your job and searched properly in the beginning, you'd have found the knife and the clothes and spared the family a great deal of distress, and the police a lot of time and effort."

He waved the letter. "If I thought I could, I'd take all the rest of the police wages out of yours, to cover the hours wasted by your incompetence! You're losing your touch, Monk, losing your touch. Now try to make up for it in some degree by going back to Queen Anne Street, apologizing to Sir Basil, and arresting the damned footman."

"It wasn't there when we looked the first time," Monk repeated. He was not going to allow Evan to be blamed, and he believed that what he said was almost certainly true.

Runcorn blinked. "Well all that means is that he had it somewhere else then—and put it in the drawer afterwards." Runcorn's voice was getting louder in spite of himself. "Get back to Queen Anne Street and arrest that footman—do I make myself clear? I don't know what simpler words to put it in. Get out, Monk—arrest Percival for murder."

"No sir. I don't think he did it."

"Nobody gives a fig what you think, damn it! Just do as you are told." Runcorn's face was deepening in color and his hands were clenching on the desk top.

Monk forced himself to keep his temper sufficiently to argue the case. He would like simply to have told Runcorn he was a fool and left.

"It doesn't make sense," he began with an effort. "If he had the chance to get rid of the jewelry, why didn't he get rid of the knife and the peignoir at the same time?"

"He probably didn't get rid of the jewelry," Runcorn said

with a sudden flash of satisfaction. "I expect it's still there, and if you searched properly you'd find it—stuffed inside an old boot, or sewn in a pocket or something. After all, you were looking for a knife this time; you wouldn't look anywhere too small to conceal one."

"We were looking for jewelry the first time," Monk pointed out with a touch of sarcasm he could not conceal. "We could hardly have missed a carving knife and a silk dressing robe."

"No you couldn't, if you'd been doing your job," Runcorn agreed. "Which means you weren't—doesn't it, Monk?"

"Either that or it wasn't there then," Monk agreed, staring back at him without a flicker. "Which is what I said before. Only a fool would keep things like that, when he could clean the knife and put it back in the kitchen without any difficulty at all. Nobody would be surprised to see a footman in the kitchen; they're in and out all the time on errands. And they are frequently the last to go to bed at night because they lock up."

Runcorn opened his mouth to argue, but Monk overrode him.

"Nobody would be surprised to see Percival about at midnight or later. He could explain his presence anywhere in the house, except someone else's bedroom, simply by saying he had heard a window rattle, or feared a door was unlocked. They would simply commend him for his diligence."

"A position you might well envy," Runcorn said. "Even your most fervent admirer could hardly recommend you for yours."

"And he could as easily have put the peignoir on the back of the kitchen range and closed the lid, and it would be burned without a trace," Monk went on, disregarding the interruption. "Now if it were the jewelry we found, that would make more sense. I could understand someone keeping that, in the hope that some time they would be able to sell it, or even give it away or trade it for something. But why keep a knife?"

"I don't know, Monk," Runcorn said between his teeth. "I don't have the mind of a homicidal footman. But he did keep it, didn't he, damn it. You found it."

"We found it, yes," Monk agreed with elaborate patience which brought the blood dark and heavy to Runcorn's cheeks. "But that is the point I am trying to make, sir. There is no

236

proof that it was Percival who kept it—or that it was he who put it there. Anyone could have. His room is not locked."

Runcorn's eyebrows shot up.

"Oh indeed? You have just been at great pains to point out to me that no one would keep such a thing as a bloodstained knife! Now you say someone else did—but not Percival. You contradict yourself, Monk." He leaned even farther across the desk, staring at Monk's face. "You are talking like a fool. The knife was there, so someone did keep it—for all your convoluted arguments—and it was found in Percival's room. Get out and arrest him."

"Someone kept it deliberately to put it in Percival's room and make him seem guilty." Monk forgot his temper and began to raise his voice in exasperation, refusing to back away either physically or intellectually. "It only makes sense if it was kept to be used."

Runcorn blinked. "By whom, for God's sake? This laundrymaid of yours? You've no proof against her." He waved his hand, dismissing her. "None at all. What's the matter with you, Monk? Why are you so dead against arresting Percival? What's he done for you? Surely you can't be so damned perverse that you make trouble simply out of habit?" His eyes narrowed and his face was only a few feet from Monk's.

Monk still refused to step backward.

"Why are you so determined to try to blame one of the family?" Runcorn said between his teeth. "Good God, wasn't the Grey case enough for you, dragging the family into that? Have you got it into your mind that it was this Myles Kellard, simply because he took advantage of a parlormaid? Do you want to punish him for that—is that what this is about?"

"Raped," Monk corrected very distinctly. His diction became more perfect as Runcorn lost his control and slurred his words in rage.

"All right, raped, if you prefer—don't be pedantic," Runcorn shouted. "Forcing yourself on a parlormaid is not the next step before murdering your sister-in-law."

"Raping. Raping a seventeen-year-old maid who is a servant in your house, a dependent, who dare not say much to you, or defend herself, is not such a long way from going to your sister-in-law's room in the night with the intention of forcing yourself on her and, if need be, raping her." Monk used the word loudly and very clearly, giving each letter its value. "If she says no to you, and you think she really means yes, what is the difference between one woman and another on that point?"

"If you don't know the difference between a lady and a parlormaid, Monk, that says more about your ignorance than you would like." Runcorn's face was twisted with all the pent-up hatred and fear of their long relationship. "It shows that for all your arrogance and ambition, you're just the uncouth provincial clod you always were. Your fine clothes and your assumed accent don't make a gentleman of you—the boor is still underneath and it will always come out." His eyes shone with a kind of wild, bitter triumph. He had said at last what had been seething inside him for years, and there was an uncontrollable joy in its release.

"You've been trying to find the courage to say that ever since you first felt me treading on your heels, haven't you?" Monk sneered. "What a pity you haven't enough courage to face the newspapers and the gentlemen of the Home Office that scare the wits out of you. If you were man enough you'd tell them you won't arrest anyone, even a footman, until you have reasonable evidence that he's guilty. But you aren't, are you? You're a weakling. You'll turn the other way and pretend not to see what their lordships don't like. You'll arrest Percival because he's convenient. Nobody cares about him! Sir Basil will be satisfied and you can wrap it up without offending anyone who frightens you. You can present it to your superiors as a case closed—true or not, just or not—hang the poor bastard and close the file on it."

He stared at Runcorn with ineffable contempt. "The public will applaud you, and the gentlemen will say what a good and obedient servant you are. Good God, Percival may be a selfish and arrogant little swine, but he's not a craven lickspittle like you—and I will not arrest him until I think he's guilty."

Runcorn's face was blotched with purple and his fists were clenched on the desk. His whole body shook, his muscles so tight his shoulders strained against the fabric of his coat.

"I am not asking, Monk, I am ordering you. Go and arrest Percival—now!"

"No."

"No?" A strange light flickered in Runcorn's eyes: fear, disbelief and exultancy. "Are you refusing, Monk?"

Monk swallowed, knowing what he was doing.

"Yes. You are wrong, and I am refusing."

"You are dismissed!" He flung his arm out at the door. "You are no longer employed by the Metropolitan Police Force." He thrust out one heavy hand. "Give me your official identification. As of this moment you have no office, no position, do you understand me? You are dismissed! Now get out!"

Monk fished in his pocket and found his papers. His hands were stiff and he was furious that he fumbled. He threw them on the desk and turned on his heel and strode out, leaving the door open.

Out in the passage he almost pushed past two constables and a sergeant with a pile of papers, all standing together frozen in disbelief and a kind of awed excitement. They were witnessing history, the fall of a giant, and there was regret and triumph in their faces, and a kind of guilt because such vulnerability was unexpected. They felt both superior and afraid.

Monk passed them too quickly for them to pretend they had not been listening, but he was too wrapped in his own emotions to heed their embarrassment.

By the time he was downstairs the duty constable had composed himself and retired to his desk. He opened his mouth to say something, but Monk did not listen, and he was relieved of the necessity.

It was not until Monk was out in the street in the rain that he felt the first chill of realization that he had thrown away not only his career but his livelihood. Fifteen minutes ago he had been an admired and sometimes feared senior policeman, good at his job, secure in his reputation and his skill. Now he was a man without work, without position, and in a short while he would be without money. And over Percival.

No—over the hatred between Runcorn and himself over the years, the rivalry, the fear, the misunderstandings.

Or perhaps over innocence and guilt?

9

Monk slept poorly and woke late and heavy-headed. He rose and was half dressed before he remembered that he had nowhere to go. Not only was he off the Queen Anne Street case, he was no longer a policeman. In fact he was nothing. His profession was what had given him purpose, position in the community, occupation for his time, and now suddenly desperately important, his income. He would be all right for a few weeks, at least for his lodgings and his food. There would be no other expenditures, no clothes, no meals out, no new books or rare, wonderful visits to theater or gallery in his steps towards being a gentleman.

But those things were trivial. The center of his life had fallen out. The ambition he had nourished and sacrificed for, disciplined himself towards for all the lifetime he could remember or piece together from records and other people's words, that was gone. He had no other relationships, nothing else he knew to do with his time, no one else who valued him, even if it was with admiration and fear, not love. He remembered sharply the faces of the men outside Runcorn's door. There was confusion in them, embarrassment, anxiety—but not sympathy. He had earned their respect, but not their affection.

He felt more bitterly alone, confused, and wretched than at any time since the climax of the Grey case. He had no appetite for the breakfast Mrs. Worley brought him and ate only a rasher of bacon and two slices of toast. He was still looking at the crumb-scattered plate when there was a sharp rap on the door and Evan came in without waiting to be invited. He stared at Monk and sat down astride the other hard-backed chair and said nothing, his face full of anxiety and something so painfully gentle it could only be called compassion.

"Don't look like that!" Monk said sharply. "I shall survive. There is life outside the police force, even for me."

Evan said nothing.

"Have you arrested Percival?" Monk asked him.

"No. He sent Tarrant."

Monk smiled sourly. "Perhaps he was afraid you wouldn't do it. Fool!"

Evan winced.

"I'm sorry," Monk apologized quickly. "But your resigning as well would hardly help—either Percival or me."

"I suppose not," Evan conceded ruefully, a shadow of guilt still lingering in his eyes. Monk seldom remembered how young he was, but now he looked every inch the country parson's son with his correct casual clothes and his slightly different manner concealing an inner certainty Monk himself would never have. Evan might be more sensitive, less arrogant or forceful in his judgment, but he would always have a kind of ease because he was born a minor gentleman, and he knew it, if not on the surface of his mind, then in the deeper layer from which instinct springs. "What are you going to do now, have you thought? The newspapers are full of it this morning."

"They would be," Monk acknowledged. "Rejoicing everywhere, I expect? The Home Office will be praising the police, the aristocracy will be congratulating itself it is not at fault—it may have hired a bad footman, but that kind of misjudgment is bound to happen from time to time." He heard the bitterness in his voice and despised it, but he could not remove it, it was too high in him. "Any honest gentleman can think too well of someone. Moidore's family is exonerated. And the public at large can sleep safe in its beds again."

"About right," Evan conceded, pulling a face. "There's a long editorial in the *Times* on the efficiency of the new police force, even in the most trying and sensitive of cases, to wit— in the very home of one of London's most eminent gentlemen. Runcorn is mentioned several times as being in charge of the investigation. You aren't mentioned at all." He shrugged. "Neither am I."

Monk smiled for the first time, at Evan's innocence.

"There's also a piece by someone regretting the rising arrogance of the working classes," Evan went on. "And predicting the downfall of the social order as we know it and the general decline of Christian morals."

"Naturally," Monk said tersely. "There always is. I think someone writes a pile of them and sends one in every time he thinks the occasion excuses it. What else? Does anyone speculate as to whether Percival is actually guilty or not?"

Evan looked very young. Monk could see the shadow of the boy in him so clearly behind the man, the vulnerability in the mouth, the innocence in the eyes.

"None that I saw. Everyone wants him hanged," Evan said miserably. "There seems to be general relief all 'round, and everyone is very happy to call the case closed and put an end to it. The running patterers have already started composing songs about it, and I passed one selling it by the yard on the Tottenham Court Road." His words were sophisticated, but his expression belied them. "Very lurid, and not much resemblance to the truth as we saw it—or thought we did. All twopenny dreadful stuff, innocent widow and lust in the pantry, going to bed with a carving knife to defend her virtue, and the evil footman afire with unholy passions creeping up the stairs to have his way with her." He looked up at Monk. "They want to bring back drawing and quartering. Bloodthirsty swine!"

"They've been frightened," Monk said without pity. "An ugly thing, fear."

Evan frowned. "Do you think that's what it was—in Queen Anne Street? Everyone afraid, and just wanted to put it onto someone, anyone, to get us out of the house, and to stop thinking about each other and learning more than they wanted to know?"

Monk leaned forward, pushing the plates away, and rested his elbows on the table wearily.

"Perhaps." He sighed. "God—I've made a mess of it! The worst thing is that Percival will hang. He's an arrogant and selfish sod, but he doesn't deserve to die for that. But nearly as bad is that whoever did kill him is still in that house, and is going to get away with it. And try as they might to ignore things, forget things, at least one of them has a fair idea who it is." He looked up. "Can you imagine it, Evan? Living the rest of your life with someone you know committed murder and let another man swing for it? Passing them on the stairs, sitting opposite them at the dinner table, watching them smile and tell jokes as if it had never happened?"

"What are you going to do?" Evan was watching him with intelligent, troubled eyes.

"What in hell's name can I do?" Monk exploded. "Runcorn's arrested Percival and will send him to trial. I haven't any evidence I've not already given him, and I'm not only off the case, I'm off the force. I don't even know how I'm going to keep a roof over my head, damn it. I'm the last person to help Percival—I can't even help myself."

"You're the only one who can help him," Evan said quietly. There was friendship in his face and understanding, but no moderation of the truth. "Except perhaps Miss Latterly," he added. "Anyway, apart from us, there's no one else who's going to try." He stood up from the chair, uncoiling his legs. "I'll go and tell her what happened. She'll know about Percival, of course, and the fact that it was Tarrant and not you will have told her something was wrong, but she won't know whether it's illness, another case, or what." He smiled with a wry twist of his lips. "Unless of course she knows you well enough to have guessed you lost your temper with Runcorn?"

Monk was about to deny that as ridiculous, then he remembered Hester and the doctor in the infirmary, and had a sudden blossoming of fellow-feeling, a warmth inside evaporating a little of the chill in him.

"She might," he conceded.

"I'll go to Queen Anne Street and tell her." Evan straightened his jacket, unconsciously elegant even now. "Before I'm thrown off the case too and I've no excuse to go back there."

Monk looked up at him. "Thank you—"

Evan made a little salute, with more courage in it than hope, and went out, leaving Monk alone with the remnants of his breakfast.

He stared at the table for several minutes longer, his mind half searching for something further, then suddenly a shaft of memory returned so vividly it stunned him. At some other time he had sat at a polished dining table in a room filled with gracious furniture and mirrors framed in gilt and a bowl of flowers. He had felt the same grief, and the overwhelming burden of guilt because he could not help.

It was the home of the mentor of whom he had been reminded so sharply on the pavement in Piccadilly outside Cyprian's club. There had been a financial disaster, a scandal in which he had been ruined. The woman in the funeral carriage whose ugly, grieving face had struck him so powerfully—it was his mentor's wife he had seen in her place, she whose beautiful hands he recalled; it was her distress he had ached to relieve, and been helpless. The whole tragedy had played itself out relentlessly, leaving the victims in its wake.

He remembered the passion and the impotence seething inside him as he had sat on that other table, and the resolve then to learn some skill that would give him weapons to fight injustice, uncover the dark frauds that seemed so inaccessible. That was when he had changed his mind from commerce and its rewards and chosen the police.

Police. He had been arrogant, dedicated, brilliant—and earned himself promotion—and dislike; and now he had nothing left, not even memory of his original skills.

"He what?" Hester demanded as she faced Evan in Mrs. Willis's sitting room. Its dark, Spartan furnishings and religious texts on the walls were sharply familiar to her now, but this news was a blow she could barely comprehend. "What did you say?"

"He refused to arrest Percival, and told Runcorn what he thought of him," Evan elaborated. "With the result, of course, that Runcorn threw him off the force."

"What is he going to do?" She was appalled. The sense of fear and helplessness was too close in her own memory to need imagination, and her position at Queen Anne Street was only temporary. Beatrice was not ill, and now that Percival had been arrested she would in all probability recover in a matter of days, as long as she believed he was guilty. Hester looked at Evan. "Where will he find employment? Has he any family?"

Evan looked at the floor, then up at her again.

"Not here in London, and I don't think he would go to them anyway. I don't know what he'll do," he said unhappily. "It's all he knows, and I think all he cares about. It's his natural skill.''

"Does anybody employ detectives, apart from the police?'' she asked.

He smiled, and there was a flash of hope in his eyes, then it faded. "But if he hired out his skills privately, he would need means to live until he developed a reputation—it would be too difficult.''

"Perhaps,'' she said reluctantly, not yet prepared to consider the idea. "In the meantime, what can we do about Percival?''

"Can you meet Monk somewhere to discuss it? He can't come here now. Will Lady Moidore give you half an afternoon free?''

"I haven't had any time since I came here. I shall ask. If she permits me, where will he be?''

"It's cold outside." He glanced beyond her to the single, narrow window facing onto a small square of grass and two laurel bushes. "How about the chocolate house in Regent Street?''

"Excellent. I will go and ask Lady Moidore now.''

"What will you say?'' he asked quickly.

"I shall lie,'' she answered without hesitation. "I shall say a family emergency has arisen and I need to speak with them.'' She pulled a harsh, humorous face. "She should understand a family emergency, if anyone does!''

"A family emergency.'' Beatrice turned from staring out of the window at the sky and looked at Hester with consternation. "I'm sorry. Is it illness? I can recommend a doctor, if you do not already have one, but I imagine you do—you must have several.''

"Thank you, that is most thoughtful.'' Hester felt distinctly guilty. "But as far as I know there is no ill health; it is a matter of losing a position, which may cause a considerable amount of hardship.''

Beatrice was fully dressed for the first time in several days, but she had not yet ventured into the main rooms of the house, nor had she joined in the life of the household, except to spend a little time with her grandchildren, Julia and Arthur. She looked very pale and her features were drawn. If she felt any relief at Percival's arrest it did not show in her expression. Her body was tense and she stood awkwardly, ill at ease. She forced a smile, bright and unnatural.

"I am so sorry. I hope you will be able to help, even if it is only with comfort and good advice. Sometimes that is all we have for each other—don't you think?" She swung around and stared at Hester as if the answer were of intense importance to her. Then before Hester could reply she walked away and started fishing in one of her dressing table drawers searching for something.

"Of course you know the police arrested Percival and took him away last night. Mary said it wasn't Mr. Monk. I wonder why. Do you know, Hester?"

There was no possible way Hester could have known the truth except by being privy to police affairs that she could not share.

"I have no idea, your ladyship. Perhaps he has become involved in another matter, and someone else was delegated to do this. After all, the detection has been completed—I suppose."

Beatrice's fingers froze and she stood perfectly still.

"You suppose? You mean it might not? What else could they want? Percival is guilty, isn't he?"

"I don't know." Hester kept her voice quite light. "I assume they must believe so, or they would not have arrested him; though we cannot say beyond any possible doubt until he has been tried."

Beatrice drew more tightly into herself. "They'll hang him, won't they?"

Hester felt a trifle sick. "Yes," she agreed very quietly. Then she felt compelled to persist. "Does that distress you?"

"It shouldn't—should it?" Beatrice sounded surprised at herself. "He murdered my daughter."

"But it does?" Hester allowed nothing to slip by. "It is very final, isn't it? I mean—it allows for no mistakes, no time for second thoughts on anything."

Still Beatrice stood motionless on the spot, her hands plunged in the silks, chiffons and laces in the drawer.

"Second thoughts? What do you mean?"

Now Hester retreated. "I'm not sure. I suppose another way

246

of looking at the evidence—perhaps if someone were lying—or remembered inaccurately—"

"You are saying that the murderer is still here—among us, Hester." There was no panic in Beatrice's voice, just cold pain. "And whoever it is, is calmly watching Percival go to his death on—on false evidence."

Hester swallowed hard and found her voice difficult to force into her throat.

"I suppose whoever it is must be very frightened. Perhaps it was an accident at first—I mean it was a struggle that was not meant to end in death. Don't you think?"

At last Beatrice turned around, her hands empty.

"You mean Myles?" she said slowly and distinctly. "You think it was Myles who went to her room and she fought with him and he took the knife from her and stabbed her, because by then he had too much to lose if she should speak against him and told everyone what had happened?" She leaned a little against the chest. "That is what they are saying happened with Percival, you know. Yes, of course you know. You are in the servants' hall more than I am. That's what Mary says."

She looked down at her hands. "And it is what Romola believes. She is terribly relieved, you know. She thinks it is all over now. We can stop suspecting one another. She thought it was Septimus, you know, that Tavie discovered something about him! Which is ridiculous—she always knew his story!" She tried to laugh at the idea, and failed. "Now she imagines we will forget it all and go on just as before. We'll forget everything we've learned about each other—and ourselves: the shallowness, the self-deception, how quick we are to blame someone else when we are afraid. Anything to protect ourselves. As if nothing would be different, except that Tavie won't be here." She smiled, a dazzling, nervous gesture without warmth. "Sometimes I think Romola is the stupidest woman I've ever met."

"It won't be the same," Hester agreed, torn between wanting to comfort her and the need to follow every shade or inflection of truth she could. "But in time we may at least forgive, and some things can be forgotten."

"Can they?" Beatrice looked not at her but out of the window again. "Will Minta ever forget that Myles raped that wretched girl? Whatever rape is. What is rape, Hester? If you

247

do your duty within marriage, that is lawful and right. You would be condemned for doing anything less. How different is it outside marriage that it should be regarded as such a despicable crime?''

"Is it?'' Hester allowed some of her anger to come through. "It seems to me very few people were upset about Mr. Kellard's rape of the maid, in fact they were angrier with her for speaking of it than they were with him for having done it. It all hangs upon who is involved.''

"I suppose so. But that is small comfort if it is your husband. I can see the hurt of it in her face. Not often—but sometimes in repose, when she does not think of anyone looking at her, I see pain under the composure.'' She turned back, frowning, a slow troubled expression not intended for Hester. "And sometimes I think a terrible anger.''

"But Mr. Kellard is unhurt,'' Hester said very gently, longing to be able to comfort her and knowing now beyond doubt that Percival's arrest was by no means the beginning of healing. "Surely if Mrs. Kellard were thinking any violence it would be him she would direct it against? It is only natural to be angry, but in time she may forget the sharpness of it, and even think of the fact less and less often.'' She nearly added that if Myles were to be tender enough with her, and generous, then it would eventually cease to matter. But thinking of Myles she could not believe it, and to speak such an ephemeral hope aloud might only add to the wound. Beatrice must see him at least as clearly as Hester, who knew him such a short while.

"Yes,'' Beatrice said without conviction. "Of course, you are right. And please, take what time you need this afternoon.''

"Thank you.''

As she turned to leave, Basil came in, having knocked so perfunctorily that neither of them heard him. He walked past Hester, barely noticing her, his eyes on Beatrice.

"Good,'' he said briskly. "I see you are dressed today. Naturally you are feeling much better.''

"No—'' Beatrice began, but he cut her off.

"Of course you are.'' His smile was businesslike. "I'm delighted, my dear. This fearful tragedy has naturally affected your health, but the worst of it is already over, and you will gain strength every day.''

"Over." She faced him with incredulity. "Do you really believe it is over, Basil?"

"Of course it is." He did not look at her but walked around the room slowly, looking at the dressing table, then straightening one of the pictures. "There will be the trial, of course; but you do not need to attend."

"I wish to!"

"If it will help you to feel the matter is dealt with, I can understand it, although I think it would be better if you accepted my account."

"It is not over, Basil! Just because they have arrested Percival . . ."

He swung around to face her, impatience in his eyes and mouth.

"All of it is over that needs to concern you, Beatrice. If it will help you to see justice done, then go to the trial by all means, otherwise I advise you to remain at home. Either way, the investigation is closed and you may cease to think about it. You are much better, and I am delighted to see it." She accepted the futility of arguing and looked away, her hands fiddling with the lace handkerchief from her pocket.

"I have decided to help Cyprian to obtain a seat in Parliament," Basil went on, satisfied her concern was over. "He has been interested in politics for some time, and it would be an excellent thing for him to do. I have connections that will make a safe Tory seat available to him by the next general election."

"Tory?" Beatrice was surprised. "But his beliefs are radical!"

"Nonsense!" He dismissed it with a laugh. "He reads some very odd literature, I know; but he doesn't take it seriously."

"I think he does."

"Rubbish. You have to consider such stuff to know how to fight against it, that is all."

"Basil—I—"

"Absolute nonsense, my dear. It will do him excellently. You will see the change in him. Now I am due in Whitehall in half an hour. I will see you for dinner." And with a perfunctory kiss on her cheek he left, again walking past Hester as if she were invisible.

* * *

Hester walked into the chocolate house in Regent Street and saw Monk immediately, sitting at one of the small tables, leaning forward staring into the dregs of a glass cup, his face smooth and bleak. She had seen that expression before, when he had thought the Grey case catastrophic.

She sailed in with a swish of skirts, albeit only blue stuff and not satin, and sat down on the chair opposite him prepared to be angry even before he spoke. His defeatism reached her emotions the more easily because she had no idea how to fight any further herself.

He looked up, saw the accusation in her eyes, and instantly his face hardened.

"I see you have managed to escape the sickroom this afternoon," he said with a heavy trace of sarcasm. "I presume now that the 'illness' is at an end, her ladyship will recover rapidly?"

"Is the illness at an end?" she said with elaborate surprise. "I thought from Sergeant Evan that it was far from over; in fact it appears to have suffered a serious relapse, which may even prove fatal."

"For the footman, yes—but hardly her ladyship and her family," he said without trying to hide his bitterness.

"But for you." She regarded him without the sympathy she felt. He was in danger of sinking into self-pity, and she believed most people were far better bullied out of it than catered to. Real compassion should be reserved for the helplessly suffering, of whom she had seen immeasurably too many. "So you have apparently given up your career in the police—"

"I have not given it up," he contradicted angrily. "You speak as if I did it with deliberate intent. I refused to arrest a man I did not believe guilty, and Runcorn dismissed me for it."

"Very noble," she agreed tersely. "But totally foreseeable. You cannot have imagined for a second that he would do anything else."

"Then you will have an excellent fellow-feeling," he returned savagely. "Since you can hardly have supposed Dr. Pomeroy would permit you to remain at the infirmary after prescribing the dispensing medicine yourself!" He was apparently unaware of having raised his voice, or of the couple at the next table turning to stare at them. "Unfortunately I doubt you can find me private employment detecting as a free-lance, as you can with nursing," he finished.

"It was your suggestion to Callandra." Not that she was surprised; it was the only answer that made sense.

"Of course." His smile was without humor. "Perhaps you can go and ask her if she has any wealthy friends who need a little uncovering of secrets, or tracing of lost heirs?"

"Certainly—that is an excellent idea."

"Don't you dare!" He was furious, offended and patronized. "I forbid it!"

The waiter was standing at his elbow to accept their order, but Monk ignored him.

"I shall do as I please," Hester said instantly. "You will not dictate to me what I shall say to Callandra. I should like a cup of chocolate, if you would be so good."

The waiter opened his mouth, and then when no one took any notice of him, closed it again.

"You are an arrogant and opinionated woman," Monk said fiercely. "And quite the most overbearing I have ever met. And you will not start organizing my life as if you were some damned governess. I am not helpless nor lying in a hospital bed at your mercy."

"Not helpless?" Her eyebrows shot up and she looked at him with all the frustration and impotent anger boiling up inside her, the fury at the blindness, complacency, cowardice and petty malice that had conspired to have Percival arrested and Monk dismissed, and the rest of them unable to see any way to begin to redress the situation. "You have managed to find evidence to have the wretched footman taken away in manacles, but not enough to proceed any further. You are without employment or prospects of any, and have covered yourself with dislike. You are sitting in a chocolate house staring at the dregs of an empty cup. And you have the luxury to refuse help?"

Now the people at all the tables in the immediate vicinity had stopped eating or drinking and were staring at them.

"I refuse your condescending interference," he said. "You should marry some poor devil and concentrate your managerial skills on one man and leave the rest of us in peace."

She knew precisely what was hurting him, the fear of the future when he had not even the experience of the past to draw

251

on, the specter of hunger and homelessness ahead, the sense of failure. She struck where it would wound the most surely, and perhaps eventually do the most good.

"Self-pity does not become you, nor does it serve any purpose," she said quietly, aware now of the people around them. "And please lower your voice. If you expect me to be sorry for you, you are wasting your time. Your situation is of your own making, and not markedly worse than mine—which was also of my own making, I am aware." She stopped, seeing the overwhelming fury in his face. She was afraid for a moment she had really gone too far.

"You—" he began. Then very slowly the rage died away and was replaced by a sharp humor, so hard as to be almost sweet, like a clean wind off the sea. "You have a genius for saying the worst possible thing in any given situation," he finished. "I should imagine a good many patients have taken up their beds and walked, simply to be free of your ministrations and go where they could suffer in peace."

"That is very cruel," she said a little huffily. "I have never been harsh to someone I believed to be genuinely in distress—"

"Oh." His eyebrows rose dramatically. "You think my predicament is not real?"

"Of course your predicament is real," she said. "But your anguish over it is unhelpful. You have talents, in spite of the Queen Anne Street case. You must find a way to use them for remuneration." She warmed to the subject. "Surely there are cases the police cannot solve—either they are too difficult or they do not fall within their scope to handle? Are there not miscarriages of justice—" That thought brought her back to Percival again, and without waiting for his reply she hurried on. "What are we going to do about Percival? I am even more sure after speaking to Lady Moidore this morning that there is grave doubt as to whether he had anything to do with Octavia's death."

At last the waiter managed to intrude, and Monk ordered chocolate for her, insisting on paying for it, overriding her protest with more haste than courtesy.

"Continue to look for proof, I suppose," he said when the matter was settled and she began to sip at the steaming liquid.

"Although if I knew where or what I should have looked already."

"I suppose it must be Myles," she said thoughtfully. "Or Araminta—if Octavia were not as reluctant as we have been led to suppose. She might have known they had an assignation and taken the kitchen knife along, deliberately meaning to kill her."

"Then presumably Myles Kellard would know it," Monk argued. "Or have a very strong suspicion. And from what you said he is more afraid of her than she of him."

She smiled. "If my wife had just killed my mistress with a carving knife I would be more than a trifle nervous, wouldn't you?" But she did not mean it, and she saw from his face that he knew it as well as she. "Or perhaps it was Fenella?" she went on. "I think she has the stomach for such a thing, if she had the motive."

"Well, not out of lust for the footman," Monk replied. "And I doubt Octavia knew anything about her so shocking that Basil would have thrown her out for it. Unless there is a whole avenue we have not explored."

Hester drank the last of her chocolate and set the glass down on its saucer. "Well I am still in Queen Anne Street, and Lady Moidore certainly does not seem recovered yet, or likely to be in the next few days. I shall have a little longer to observe. Is there anything you would like me to pursue?"

"No," he said sharply. Then he looked down at his own glass on the table in front of him. "It is possible that Percival is guilty; it is simply that I do not feel that what we have is proof. We should respect not only the facts but the law. If we do not, then we lay ourselves open to every man's judgment of what may be true or false; and a belief of guilt will become the same thing as proof. There must be something above individual judgment, however passionately felt, or we become barbarous again."

"Of course he may be guilty," she said very quietly. "I have always known that. But I shall not let it go by default as long as I can remain in Queen Anne Street and learn anything at all. If I do find anything, I shall have to write to you, because neither you nor Sergeant Evan will be there. Where may I send a letter, so that the rest of the household will not know it is to you?"

He looked puzzled for a moment.

"I do not post my own mail," she said with a flicker of impatience. "I seldom leave the house. I shall merely put it on the hall table and the footman or the bootboy will take it."

"Oh—of course. Send it to Mr.—" He hesitated, a shadow of a smile crossing his face. "Send it to Mr. Butler—let us move up a rung on the social ladder. At my address in Grafton Street. I shall be there for a few weeks yet."

She met his eyes for a moment of clear and total understanding, then rose and took her leave. She did not tell him she was going to make use of the rest of the afternoon to see Callandra Daviot. He might have thought she was going to ask for help for him, which was exactly what she intended to do, but not with his knowledge. He would refuse beforehand, out of pride; when it was a fait accompli he would be obliged to accept.

"He what?" Callandra was appalled, then she began to laugh in spite of her anger. "Not very practical—but I admire his sentiment, if not his judgment."

They were in her withdrawing room by the fire, the sharp winter sun streaming in through the windows. The new parlormaid, replacing the newly married Daisy, a thin waif of a girl with an amazing smile and apparently named Martha, had brought their tea and hot crumpets with butter. These were less ladylike than cucumber sandwiches, but far nicer on a cold day.

"What could he have accomplished if he had obeyed and arrested Percival?" Hester defended Monk quickly. "Mr. Runcorn would still consider the case closed, and Sir Basil would not permit him to ask any further questions or pursue any investigation. He could hardly even look for more evidence of Percival's guilt. Everyone else seems to consider the knife and the peignoir sufficient."

"Perhaps you are right," Callandra admitted. "But he is a hot-headed creature. First the Grey case, and now this. He seems to have little more sense than you have." She took another crumpet. "You have both taken matters into your own hands and lost your livelihoods. What does he propose to do next?"

"I don't know!" Hester threw her hands wide. "I don't know what I am to do myself when Lady Moidore is sufficiently well not to need me. I have no desire whatever to spend my time as a paid companion, fetching and carrying and pandering to imaginary illnesses and fits of the vapors." Suddenly she was overtaken by a profound sense of failure. "Callandra, what happened to me? I came home from the Crimea with such a zeal to work hard, to throw myself into reform and accomplish so much. I was going to see our hospitals cleaner—and of so much greater comfort for the sick." Those dreams seemed utterly out of reach now, part of a golden and lost realm. "I was going to teach people that nursing is a noble profession, fit for fine and dedicated women to serve in, women of sobriety and good character who wished to minister to the sick with skill—not just to keep a bare standard of removing the slops and fetching and carrying for the surgeons. How did I throw all that away?"

"You didn't throw it away, my dear," Callandra said gently. "You came home afire with your accomplishments in wartime, and did not realize the monumental inertia of peace, and the English passion to keep things as they are, whatever they are. People speak of this as being an age of immense change, and so it is. We have never been so inventive, so wealthy, so free in our ideas good and bad." She shook her head. "But there is still an immeasurable amount that is determined to stay the same, unless it is forced, screaming and fighting, to advance with the times. One of those things is the belief that women should learn amusing arts of pleasing a husband, bearing children, and if you cannot afford the servants to do it for you, of raising them, and of visiting the deserving poor at appropriate times and well accompanied by your own kind."

A fleeting smile of wry pity touched her lips.

"Never, in any circumstance, should you raise your voice, or try to assert your opinions in the hearing of gentlemen, and do not attempt to appear clever or strong-minded; it is dangerous, and makes them extremely uncomfortable."

"You are laughing at me," Hester accused her.

"Only slightly, my dear. You will find another position nursing privately, if we cannot find a hospital to take you. I shall write to Miss Nightingale and see what she can advise." Her face darkened. "In the meantime, I think Mr. Monk's situation is rather more pressing. Has he any skills other than those connected with detecting?"

Hester thought for a moment.

"I don't believe so."

"Then he will have to detect. In spite of this fiasco, I believe he is gifted at it, and it is a crime for a person to spend his life without using the talents God gave him." She pushed the crumpet plate towards Hester and Hester took another.

"If he cannot do it publicly in the police force, then he will have to do it privately." She warmed to the subject. "He will have to advertise in all the newspapers and periodicals. There must be people who have lost relatives, I mean mislaid them. There are certainly robberies the police do not solve satisfactorily—and in time he will earn a reputation and perhaps be given cases where there has been injustice or the police are baffled." Her face brightened conspicuously. "Or perhaps cases where the police do not realize there has been a crime, but someone does, and is desirous to have it proved. And regrettably there will be cases where an innocent person is accused and wishes to clear his name."

"But how will he survive until he has sufficient of these cases to earn himself a living?" Hester said anxiously, wiping her fingers on the napkin to remove the butter.

Callandra thought hard for several moments, then came to some inner decision which clearly pleased her.

"I have always wished to involve myself in something a trifle more exciting than good works, however necessary or worthy. Visiting friends and struggling for hospital, prison or workhouse reform is most important, but we must have a little color from time to time. I shall go into partnership with Mr. Monk." She took another crumpet. "I will provide the money, to begin with, sufficient for his needs and for the administration of such offices as he has to have. In return I shall take some of the profits, when there are any. I shall do my best to acquire contacts and clients—he will do the work. And I shall be told all that I care about what happens." She frowned ferociously. "Do you think he will be agreeable?"

Hester tried to keep a totally sober face, but inside she felt a wild upsurge of happiness.

"I imagine he will have very little choice. In his position I should leap at such a chance."

"Excellent. Now I shall call upon him and make him a proposition along these lines. Which does not answer the question of the Queen Anne Street case. What are we to do about that? It is all very unsatisfactory.''

However it was another fortnight before Hester came to a conclusion as to what she was going to do. She had returned to Queen Anne Street, where Beatrice was still tense, one minute struggling to put everything to do with Octavia's death out of her mind, the next still concerned that she might yet discover some hideous secret not yet more than guessed at.

Other people seemed to have settled into patterns of life more closely approximating normal. Basil went into the City on most days, and did whatever it was he usually did. Hester asked Beatrice in a polite, rather vague way, but Beatrice knew very little about it. It was not considered necessary as part of her realm of interest, so Sir Basil had dismissed her past inquiries with a smile.

Romola was obliged to forgo her social activities, as were they all, because the house was in mourning. But she seemed to believe that the shadow of investigation had passed completely, and she was relentlessly cheerful about the house, when she was not in the schoolroom supervising the new governess. Only rarely did an underlying unhappiness and uncertainty show through, and it had to do with Cyprian, not any suspicion of murder. She was totally satisfied that Percival was the guilty one and no one else was implicated.

Cyprian spent more time speaking with Hester, asking her opinions or experiences in all manner of areas, and seemed most interested in her answers. She liked him, and found his attention flattering. She looked forward to her meetings with him on the few occasions when they were alone and might speak frankly, not in the customary platitudes.

Septimus looked anxious and continued to take port wine from Basil's cellar, and Fenella continued to drink it, make outrageous remarks, and absent herself from the house as often as she dared without incurring Basil's displeasure. Where she went to no one knew, although many guesses were hazarded, most of them unkind.

Araminta ran the house very efficiently, even with some flair, which in the circumstances of mourning was an achievement, but her attitude towards Myles was cold with suspicion, and his towards her was casually indifferent. Now that Percival was arrested, he had nothing to fear, and mere displeasure did not seem to concern him.

Below stairs the mood was somber and businesslike. No one spoke of Percival, except by accident, and then immediately fell silent or tried to cover the gaffe with more words.

In that time Hester received a letter from Monk, passed to her by the new footman, Robert, and she took it upstairs to her room to open it.

December 19th, 1856

Dear Hester,

I have received a most unexpected visit from Lady Callandra with a business proposition which was quite extraordinary. Were she a woman of less remarkable character I would suspect your hand in it. As it is I am still uncertain. She did not learn of my dismissal from the police force out of the newspapers; they do not concern themselves with such things. They are far too busy rejoicing in the solution of the Queen Anne Street case and calling for the rapid hanging of footmen with overweening ideas in general, and Percival in particular.

The Home Office is congratulating itself on such a fortunate solution, Sir Basil is the object of everyone's sympathy and respect, and Runcorn is poised for promotion. Only Percival languishes in Newgate awaiting trial. And maybe he is guilty? But I do not believe it.

Lady Callandra's proposition (in case you do not know!) is that I should become a private investigating detective, which she will finance, and promote as she can. In return for which I will work, and share such profits as there may be—? And all she requires of me is that I keep her informed as to my cases, what I learn, and something of the process of detection. I hope she finds it as interesting as she expects!

I shall accept—I see no better alternative. I have done all I can to explain to her the unlikelihood of there being much financial return. Police are not paid on results, and private agents would be—or at least if results were not satisfactory a very large proportion of the time, they would cease to find clients. Also the victims of injustice are very often not in a position to pay anything at all. However she insists that she has money beyond her needs, and this will be her form of philanthropy—and she is convinced she will find it both more satisfying than donating her means to museums or galleries or homes for the deserving poor; and more entertaining. I shall do all I can to prove her right.

You write that Lady Moidore is still deeply concerned, and that Fenella is less than honest, but you are not certain yet whether it is anything to do with Octavia's death. This is interesting, but does not do more than increase our conviction that the case is not yet solved. Please be careful in your pursuit, and above all, remember that if you do appear to be close to discovering anything of significance, the murderer will then turn his, or her, attention towards you.

I am still in touch with Evan and he informs me how the police case is being prepared. They have not bothered to seek anything further. He is as sure as he can be that there is more to learn, but neither of us knows how to go about it. Even Lady Callandra has no ideas on that subject.

Again, please take the utmost care,

I remain, yours sincerely,
William Monk

She closed it with her decision already made. There was nothing else she could hope to learn in Queen Anne Street herself, and Monk was effectively prevented from investigating anything to do with the case. The trial was Percival's only hope. There was one person who could perhaps give her advice on that—Oliver Rathbone. She could not ask Callandra again; if she had been willing to do such a thing she would have suggested it when they met previously and Hester told her of the situation. Rathbone was for hire. There was no reason why she should not go to his offices and purchase half an hour of his time, which was very probably all she could afford.

First she asked Beatrice for permission to take an afternoon off duty to attend to her family matter, which was granted with no difficulty. Then she wrote a brief letter to Oliver Rathbone explaining that she required legal counsel in a matter of some delicacy and that she had only Tuesday afternoon on which to present herself at his offices, if he would make that available to her. She had previously purchased several postage stamps so she could send the letter, and she asked the bootboy if he would put it in the mailbox for her, which he was pleased to do.

She received her answer the following noon, there being several deliveries of post each day, and tore it open as soon as she had a moment unobserved.

December 20th, 1856

Dear Miss Latterly,

I shall be pleased to receive you at my offices in Vere Street, which is just off Lincoln's Inn Fields, on the afternoon on Tuesday 23rd of December, at three in the afternoon. I hope at that time to be of assistance to you in whatever matter at present concerns you.

Until that time, I remain yours sincerely,

Oliver Rathbone

It was brief and to the point. It would have been absurd to expect more, and yet its very efficiency reminded her that she would be paying for each minute she was there and she must not incur a charge she could not meet. There must be no wasted words, no time for pleasantries or euphemisms.

She had no appealing clothes, no silk and velvet dresses like Araminta's or Romola's, no embroidered snoods or bonnets, and no lace gloves such as ladies habitually wore. They were not suitable for those in service, however skilled. Her only dresses, purchased since her family's financial ruin, were gray or blue, and made on modest and serviceable lines and of stuff fabric. Her bonnet was of a pleasing deep pink, but that was about the best that could be said for it. It also was not new.

Still, Rathbone would not be interested in her appearance; she was going to consult his legal ability, not enjoy a social occasion.

She regarded herself in the mirror without pleasure. She was too thin, and taller than she would have liked. Her hair was thick, but almost straight, and required more time and skill than she possessed to form it into fashionable ringlets. And although her eyes were dark blue-gray, and extremely well set, they had too level and plain a stare, it made people uncomfortable; and her features generally were too bold.

But there was nothing she, or anyone, could do about it, except make the best of a very indifferent job. She could at

260

least endeavor to be charming, and that she would do. Her mother had frequently told her she would never be beautiful, but if she smiled she might make up for a great deal.

It was an overcast day with a hard, driving wind, and most unpleasant.

She took a hansom from Queen Anne Street to Vere Street, and alighted a few minutes before three. At three o'clock precisely she was sitting in the spare, elegant room outside Oliver Rathbone's office and becoming impatient to get the matter begun.

She was about to stand and make some inquiry when the door opened and Rathbone came out. He was as immaculately dressed as she remembered from last time, and immediately she was conscious of being shabby and unfeminine.

"Good afternoon, Mr. Rathbone." Her resolve to be charming was already a little thinner. "It is good of you to see me at such short notice."

"It is a pleasure, Miss Latterly." He smiled, a very sweet smile, showing excellent teeth, but his eyes were dark and she was aware only of their wit and intelligence. "Please come into my office and be comfortable." He held the door open for her, and she accepted rapidly, aware that from the moment he had greeted her, no doubt her half hour was ticking away.

The room was not large, but it was furnished very sparsely, in a fashion reminiscent more of William IV than of the present Queen, and the very leanness of it gave an impression of light and space. The colors were cool and the woodwork white. There was a picture on the farthest wall which reminded her of a Joshua Reynolds, a portrait of a gentleman in eighteenth-century dress against a romantic landscape.

All of which was irrelevant; she must address the matter in hand.

She sat down on one of the easy chairs and left him to sit on the other and cross his legs after neatly hitching his trousers so as not to lose their line.

"Mr. Rathbone, I apologize for being so blunt, but to do otherwise would be dishonest. I can afford only half an hour's worth of your time. Please do not permit me to detain you longer than that." She saw the spark of humor in his eyes, but his reply was completely sober.

"I shall not, Miss Latterly. You may trust me to attend the

clock. You may concentrate your mind on informing me how I may be of assistance to you."

"Thank you," she said. "It is concerning the murder in Queen Anne Street. Are you familiar with any of the circumstances?"

"I have read of it in the newspapers. Are you acquainted with the Moidore family?"

"No—at least not socially. Please do not interrupt me, Mr. Rathbone. If I digress, I shall not have sufficient time to tell you what is important."

"I apologize." Again there was that flash of amusement. She suppressed her desire to be irritated and forgot to be charming.

"Sir Basil Moidore's daughter, Octavia Haslett, was found stabbed in her bedroom." She had practiced what she intended to say, and now she concentrated earnestly on remembering every word in the exact order she had rehearsed, for clarity and brevity. "At first it was presumed an intruder had disturbed her during the night and murdered her. Then it was proved by the police that no one could have entered, either by the front or from the back of the house, therefore she was killed by someone already there—either a servant or one of her own family."

He nodded and did not speak.

"Lady Moidore was very distressed by the whole affair and became ill. My connection with the family is as her nurse."

"I thought you were at the infirmary?" His eyes widened and his brows rose in surprise.

"I was," she said briskly. "I am not now."

"But you were so enthusiastic about hospital reform."

"Unfortunately they were not. Please, Mr. Rathbone, do not interrupt me! This is of the utmost importance, or a fearful injustice may be done."

"The wrong person has been charged," he said.

"Quite." She hid her surprise only because there was not time for it. "The footman, Percival, who is not an appealing character—he is vain, ambitious, selfish and something of a lothario—"

"Not appealing," he agreed, sitting a little farther back in his chair and regarding her steadily.

"The theory of the police," she continued, "is that he was

enamored of Mrs. Haslett, and with or without her encouragement, he went up to her bedroom in the night, tried to force his attentions upon her, and she, being forewarned and having taken a kitchen knife upstairs with her"—she ignored his look of amazement—"against just such an eventuality, attempted to save her virtue, and in the struggle it was she, not he, who was stabbed—fatally."

He looked at her thoughtfully, his fingertips together.

"How do you know all this, Miss Latterly? Or should I say, how do the police deduce it?"

"Because on hearing, some considerable time into the investigation—in fact, several weeks—that the cook believed one of her kitchen knives to be missing," she explained, "they instituted a second and very thorough search of the house, and in the bedroom of the footman in question, stuffed behind the back of a drawer in his dresser, between the drawer itself and the outer wooden casing, they found the knife, bloodstained, and a silk peignoir belonging to Mrs. Haslett, also bloodstained."

"Why do you not believe him guilty?" he asked with interest.

Put so bluntly it was hard to be succinct and lucid in reply.

"He may be, but I do not believe it has been proved," she began, now less certain. "There is no real evidence other than the knife and the peignoir, and anyone could have placed them there. Why would he keep such things instead of destroying them? He could very easily have wiped the knife clean and replaced it, and put the peignoir in the range. It would have burned completely."

"Some gloating in the crime?" Rathbone suggested, but there was no conviction in his voice.

"That would be stupid, and he is not stupid," she said immediately. "The only reason for keeping them that makes sense is to use them to implicate someone else—"

"Then why did he not do so? Was it not known that the cook had discovered the loss of her knife, which must surely provoke a search?" He shook his head fractionally. "That would be a most unusual kitchen."

"Of course it was known," she said. "That is why whoever had them was able to hide them in Percival's room."

His brows furrowed and he looked puzzled, his interest more acutely engaged.

"What I find most pertinent," he said, looking at her over the tops of his fingers, "is why the police did not find these items in the first place. Surely they were not so remiss as not to have searched at the time of the crime—or at least when they deduced it was not an intruder but someone resident?"

"Those things were not in Percival's room then," she said eagerly. "They were placed there, without his knowledge, precisely so someone would find them—as they did."

"Yes, my dear Miss Latterly, that may well be so, but you have not taken my point. One presumes the police searched everywhere in the beginning, not merely the unfortunate Percival's room. Wherever they were, they should have been found."

"Oh!" Suddenly she saw what he meant. "You mean they were removed from the house, and then brought back. How unspeakably cold-blooded! They were preserved specifically to implicate someone, should the need arise."

"It would seem so. But one wonders why they chose that time, and not sooner. Or perhaps the cook was dilatory in noticing that her knife was gone. They may well have acted several days before her attention was drawn to it. It might be of interest to learn how she did observe it, whether it was a remark of someone else's, and if so, whose."

"I can endeavor to do that."

He smiled. "I presume that the servants do not get more than the usual time off, and that they do not leave the house during their hours of duty?"

"No. We—" How odd that word was in connection with servants. It rankled especially in front of Rathbone, but this was no time for self-indulgence. "We have half a day every second week, circumstances permitting."

"So the servants would have little or no opportunity to remove the knife and the peignoir immediately after the murder, and to fetch it from its hiding place and return it between the time the cook reported her knife missing and the police conducted their search," he concluded.

"You are right." It was a victory, small, but of great meaning. Hope soared inside her and she rose to her feet and walked quickly over to the mantel shelf and turned. "You are perfectly right. Runcorn never thought of that. When it is put to him he will have to reconsider—"

"I doubt it," Rathbone said gravely. "It is an excellent point of logic, but I would be pleasantly surprised if logic is now what is governing the police's procedure, if, as you say, they have already arrested and charged the wretched Percival. Is your friend Mr. Monk involved in the affair?"

"He was. He resigned rather than arrest Percival on what he believed to be inadequate evidence."

"Very noble," Rathbone said sourly. "If impractical."

"I believe it was temper," Hester said, then instantly felt a traitor. "Which I cannot afford to criticize. I was dismissed from the infirmary for taking matters into my own hands when I had no authority to do so."

"Indeed?" His eyebrows shot up and his face was alive with interest. "Please tell me what happened."

"I cannot afford your time, Mr. Rathbone." She smiled to soften her words—and because what she was about to say was impertinent. "If you wish to know sufficiently, then you may have half an hour of my time, and I shall tell you with pleasure."

"I should be delighted," he accepted. "Must it be here, or may I invite you to dine with me? What is your time worth?" His expression was wry and full of humor. "Perhaps I cannot afford it? Or shall we come to an accommodation? Half an hour of your time for an additional half an hour of mine? That way you may tell me the rest of the tale of Percival and the Moidores, and I shall give you what advice I can, and you shall then tell me the tale of the infirmary."

It was a singularly appealing offer, not only for Percival's sake but because she found Rathbone's company both stimulating and agreeable.

"If it can be within the time Lady Moidore permits me, I should be very pleased," she accepted, then felt unaccountably shy.

He rose to his feet in one graceful gesture.

"Excellent. We shall adjourn to the coaching house around the corner, where they will serve us at any hour. It will be less reputable than the house of a mutual friend, but since we have none, nor the time to make any, it will have to do. It will not mar your reputation beyond recall."

265

"I think I may already have done that in any sense that matters to me," she replied with a moment of self-mockery. "Dr. Pomeroy will see to it that I do not find employment in any hospital in London. He was very angry indeed."

"Were you right in your treatment?" he asked, picking up his hat and opening the door for her.

"Yes, it seemed so."

"Then you are correct, it was unforgivable." He led the way out of the offices into the icy street. He walked on the outside of the pavement, guiding her along the street, across the corner, dodging the traffic and the crossing sweeper, and at the far side, into the entrance of a fine coaching inn built in the high day when post coaches were the only way of travel from one city to another, before the coming of the steam railway.

The inside was beautifully appointed, and she would have been interested to take greater notice of pictures, notices, the copper and pewter plates and the post horns, had there been more time. The patrons also caught her attention, well-to-do men of business, rosy faced, well clothed against the winter chill, and most of all in obvious good spirits.

But Rathbone was welcomed by the host the moment they were through the door, and was immediately offered a table advantageously placed in a good corner and advised as to the specialty dishes of the day.

He consulted Hester as to her preference, then ordered, and the host himself set about seeing that only the best was provided. Rathbone accepted it as if it were pleasing, but no more than was his custom. He was gracious in his manner, but kept the appropriate distance between gentleman and innkeeper.

Over the meal, which was neither luncheon nor dinner, but was excellent, she told him the rest of the case in Queen Anne Street, so far as she knew it, including Myles Kellard's attested rape of Martha Rivett and her subsequent dismissal, and more interestingly, her opinion of Beatrice's emotions, her fear, which was obviously not removed by Percival's arrest, and Septimus's remarks that Octavia had said she heard something the afternoon before her death which was shocking and distressing, but of which she still lacked any proof.

She also told him of John Airdrie, Dr. Pomeroy and the loxa quinine.

266

By that time she had used an hour and a half of his time and he had used twenty-five minutes of hers, but she forgot to count it until she woke in the night in her room in Queen Anne Street.

"What do you advise me?" she said seriously, leaning a little across the table. "What can be done to prevent Percival being convicted without proper proof?"

"You have not said who is to defend him," he replied with equal gravity.

"I don't know. He has no money."

"Naturally. If he had he would be suspect for that alone." He smiled with a harsh twist. "I do occasionally take cases without payment, Miss Latterly, in the public good." His smile broadened. "And recoup by charging exorbitantly next time I am employed by someone who can afford it. I will inquire into it and do what I can, give you my word."

"I am very obliged to you," she said, smiling in return. "Now would you be kind enough to tell me what I owe you for your counsel?"

"We agreed upon half a guinea, Miss Latterly."

She opened her reticule and produced a gold half guinea, the last she had left, and offered it to him.

He took it with courteous thanks and slid it into his pocket.

He rose, pulled her chair out for her, and she left the coaching inn with an intense feeling of satisfaction quite unwarranted by the circumstances, and sailed out into the street for him to hail her a hansom and direct it back to Queen Anne Street.

The trial of Percival Garrod commenced in mid-January 1857, and since Beatrice Moidore was still suffering occasional moods of deep distress and anxiety, Hester was not yet released from caring for her. She complied with this arrangement eagerly, because she had not yet found other means of earning her living, but more importantly because it meant she could remain in the house at Queen Anne Street and observe the Moidore family. Not that she was aware of having learned anything helpful, but she never lost hope.

The whole family attended the trial at the Old Bailey. Basil had wished the women to remain at home and give their evidence in writing, but Araminta refused to consider obedience to such an instruction, and on the rare occasions when she and Basil clashed, it was she who prevailed. Beatrice did not confront him on the issue; she simply dressed in quiet, unadorned black, heavily veiled, and gave Robert instructions to fetch her carriage. Hester offered to go with her as a matter of service, and was delighted when the offer was accepted.

Fenella Sandeman laughed at the very idea that she should forgo such a marvelously dramatic occasion, and swept out of the room, a little high on alcohol, wearing a long black silk kerchief and flinging it in the air with one white arm, delicately mittened in black lace.

Basil swore, but it was to no avail whatever. If she even heard him, it passed over her head harmlessly.

Romola refused to be the only one left at home, and no one bothered to argue with her.

The courtroom was crammed with spectators, and since this time Hester was not required to give any evidence, she was able to sit in the public gallery throughout.

The prosecution was conducted by a Mr. F. J. O'Hare, a flamboyant gentleman who had made his name in a few sensational cases—and many less publicized ones which had earned him a great deal of money. He was well respected by his professional peers and adored by the public, who were entertained and impressed by his quiet, intense manner and sudden explosions into drama. He was of average height but stocky build, short neck and fine silver hair, heavily waved. Had he permitted it to be longer it would have been a leonine mane, but he apparently preferred to appear sleek. He had a musical lilt to his voice which Hester could not place, and the slightest of lisps.

Percival was defended by Oliver Rathbone, and as soon as she saw him Hester felt a wild, singing hope inside her like a bird rising on the wind. It was not only that justice might be done after all, but that Rathbone had been prepared to fight, simply for the cause, not for its reward.

The first witness called was the upstairs maid, Annie, who had found Octavia Haslett's body. She looked very sober, dressed in her best off-duty blue stuff dress and a bonnet that hid her hair and made her look curiously younger, both aggressive and vulnerable at the same time.

Percival stood in the dock, upright and staring in front of

him. He might lack humility, compassion or honor, but he was not without courage. He looked smaller than Hester remembered him, narrower across the shoulders and not as tall. But then he was motionless; the swagger that was part of him could not be used, nor the vitality. He was helpless to fight back. It was all in Rathbone's hands now.

The doctor was called next, and gave his evidence briefly. Octavia Haslett had been stabbed to death during the night, with not more than two blows to the lower chest, beneath the ribs.

The third witness was William Monk, and his evidence lasted the rest of the morning and all the afternoon. He was abrasive, sarcastic, and punctiliously accurate, refusing to draw even the most obvious conclusions from anything.

F. J. O'Hare was patient to begin with and scrupulously polite, waiting his chance to score a deciding thrust. It did not come until close to the end, when he was passed a note by his junior, apparently reminding him of the Grey case.

"It would seem to me, Mr. Monk—it is Mr. now, not Inspector, is that so?" His lisp was very slight indeed.

"It is so," Monk conceded without a flicker of expression.

"It would seem to me, Mr. Monk, that from your testimony you do not consider Percival Garrod to be guilty."

"Is that a question, Mr. O'Hare?"

"It is, Mr. Monk, indeed it is!"

"I do not consider it to be proved by the evidence to hand so far," Monk replied. "That is not the same thing."

"Is it materially different, Mr. Monk? Correct me if I am in error, but were you not sincerely unwilling to convict the offender in your last case as well? One Menard Grey, as I recall!"

"No," Monk instantly contradicted. "I was perfectly willing to convict him—in fact, I was eager to. I was unwilling to see him hanged."

"Oh, yes—mitigating circumstances," O'Hare agreed. "But you could find none in the case of Percival Garrod murdering his master's daughter—it would strain even your ingenuity, I imagine? So you maintain the proof of the murder weapon and the bloodstained garment of the victim hidden in his room, which you have told us you discovered, is not enough to satisfy you? What do you require, Mr. Monk, an eyewitness?"

"Only if I considered their veracity beyond question," Monk replied wolfishly and without humor. "I would prefer some evidence that made sense."

"For example, Mr. Monk?" O'Hare invited. He glanced at Rathbone to see if he would object. The judge frowned and waited also. Rathbone smiled benignly back and said nothing.

"A motive for Percival to have kept such—" Monk hesitated and avoided the word *damning*, catching O'Hare's eye and knowing a sudden victory, brief and pointless. "Such a useless and damaging piece of material," he said instead, "which he could so easily have destroyed, and a knife which he could simply have wiped and returned to the cook's rack."

"Perhaps he wished to incriminate someone else?" O'Hare raised his voice with a life of something close to humor, as if the idea were obvious.

"Then he was singularly unsuccessful," Monk replied. "And he had the opportunity. He should have gone upstairs and put it where he wished as soon as he knew the cook had missed the knife."

"Perhaps he intended to, but did not have the chance? What an agony of impotence for him. Can you imagine it?" O'Hare turned to the jury and raised his hands, palms upward. "What a rich irony! It was a man hoist with his own petard! And who would so richly deserve it?"

This time Rathbone rose and objected.

"My lord, Mr. O'Hare is assuming something which has yet to be proved. Even with all his well-vaunted gifts of persuasion, he has not so far shown us anything to indicate who put those objects in Percival's room. He is arguing his conclusion from his premise, and his premise from his conclusion!"

"You will have to do better, Mr. O'Hare," the judge cautioned.

"Oh, I will, my lord," O'Hare promised. "You may be assured, I will!"

The second day O'Hare began with the physical evidence so dramatically discovered. He called Mrs. Boden, who took the stand looking homely and flustered, very much out of her element. She was used to being able to exercise her judgment

270

and her prodigious physical skills. Her art spoke for her. Now she was faced with standing motionless, every exchange to be verbal, and she was ill at ease.

When it was shown her, she looked at the knife with revulsion, but agreed that it was hers, from her kitchen. She recognized various nicks and scratches on the handle, and an irregularity in the blade. She knew the tools of her art. However she became severely rattled when Rathbone pressed her closely about exactly when she had last used it. He took her through the meals of each day, asking her which knives she had used in the preparation, and finally she became so confused he must have realized he was alienating the entire courtroom by pressing her over something for which no one else could see a purpose.

O'Hare rose, smiling and smooth, to call the ladies' maid Mary to testify that the bloodstained peignoir was indeed Octavia's. She looked very pale, her usually rich olive complexion without a shred of its blushing cheeks, her voice uncharacteristically subdued. But she swore it was her mistress's. She had seen her wear it often enough, and ironed its satin and smoothed out its lace.

Rathbone did not bother her. There was nothing to contend.

Next O'Hare called the butler. Phillips looked positively cadaverous as he stepped into the witness box. His balding head shone in the light through his thin hair, his eyebrows appeared more ferocious than ever, but his expression was one of dignified wretchedness, a soldier on parade before an unruly mob and robbed of the weapons to defend himself.

O'Hare was far too practiced to insult him by discourtesy or condescension. After establishing Phillips' position and his considerable credentials, he asked him about his seniority over the other servants in the house. This also established, for the jury and the crowd, he proceeded to draw him a highly unfavorable picture of Percival as a man, without ever impugning his abilities as a servant. Never once did he force Phillips into appearing malicious or negligent in his own duty. It was a masterly performance. There was almost nothing Rathbone could do except ask Phillips if he had had the slightest idea that this objectionable and arrogant young man had raised his eyes as far as his master's daughter. To which Phillips replied with a horrified denial. But then no one would have expected him to admit such a thought—not now.

The only other servant O'Hare called was Rose.

She was dressed most becomingly. Black suited her, with her fair complexion and almost luminous blue eyes. The situation impressed her, but she was not overwhelmed, and her voice was steady and strong, crowded with emotion. With very little prompting she told O'Hare, who was oozing solicitude, how Percival had at first been friendly towards her, openly admiring but perfectly proper in his manner. Then gradually he had given her to believe his affections were engaged, and finally had made it quite plain that he desired to marry her.

All this she recounted with a modest manner and gentle tone. Then her chin hardened and she stood very rigid in the box; her voice darkened, thickening with emotion, and she told O'Hare, never looking at the jury or the spectators, how Percival's attentions had ceased and he had more and more frequently mentioned Miss Octavia, and how she had complimented him, sent for him for the most trivial duties as if she desired his company, how she had dressed more alluringly recently, and often remarked on his own dignity and appearance.

"Was this perhaps to make you jealous, Miss Watkins?" O'Hare asked innocently.

She remembered her decorum, lowered her eyes and answered meekly, the venom disappearing from her and injury returning.

"Jealous, sir? How could I be jealous of a lady like Miss Octavia?" she said demurely. "She was beautiful. She had all the manner and the learning, all the lovely gowns. What was there I could do against that?"

She hesitated a moment, and then went on. "And she would never have married him, that would be stupid even to think of it. If I were going to be jealous it would be of another maid like myself, someone who could have given him real love, and a home, and maybe a family in time." She looked down at her small, strong hands, and then up again suddenly. "No sir, she flattered him, and his head was turned. I thought that sort of thing only happened to parlormaids and the like, who got used by masters with no morals. I never thought of a footman being so daft. Or a lady—well . . ." She lowered her eyes.

"Are you saying that that is what you believe happened, Miss Watkins?" O'Hare asked.

Her eyes flew wide open again. "Oh no sir. I don't suppose for a moment Miss Octavia ever did anything like that! I think Percival was a vain and silly man who imagined it might. And then when he realized what a fool he'd made of himself—well—his conceit couldn't take it and he lost his temper."

"Did he have a temper, Miss Watkins?"

"Oh yes sir—I'm afraid so."

The last witness to be called regarding Percival's character, and its flaws, was Fenella Sandeman. She swept into the courtroom in a glory of black taffeta and lace, a large bonnet set well back, framing her face with its unnatural pallor, jet-black hair and rosy lips. At the distance from which most of the public saw her she was a startling and most effective sight, exuding glamour and the drama of grief—and extreme femininity sore pressed by dire circumstances.

To Hester, when a man was being tried for his life, it was at once pathetic and grotesque.

O'Hare rose and was almost exaggeratedly polite to her, as though she had been fragile and in need of all his tenderness.

"Mrs. Sandeman, I believe you are a widow, living in the house of your brother, Sir Basil Moidore?"

"I am," she conceded, hovering for a moment on the edge of an air of suffering bravely, and opting instead for a gallant kind of gaiety, a dazzling smile and a lift of her pointed chin.

"You have been there for"—he hesitated as if recalling with difficulty what to ask—"something like twelve years?"

"I have," she agreed.

"Then you will doubtless know the members of the household fairly well, having seen them in all their moods, their happiness and their misfortune, for a considerable time," he concluded. "You must have formed many opinions, based upon your observations."

"Indeed—one cannot help it." She gazed at him and a wry, slight smile hovered about her lips. There was a huskiness in her voice. Hester wanted to slide down in her seat and become invisible, but she was beside Beatrice, who was not to be called to testify, so there was nothing she could do but endure it. She looked sideways at Beatrice's face, but her veil was so heavy Hester could see nothing of her expression.

"Women are very sensitive to people," Fenella went on. "We have to be; people are our lives—"

"Exactly so." O'Hare smiled back at her. "In your own establishment you employed servants, before your husband . . . passed on?"

"Of course."

"So you are quite accustomed to judging their character and their worth," O'Hare concluded with a sidelong glance at Rathbone. "What did you observe of Percival Garrod, Mrs. Sandeman? What is your estimate of him?" He held up his pale hand as if to forestall any objection Rathbone might have. "Based, of course, upon what you saw of him during your time in Queen Anne Street?"

She lowered her eyes and a greater hush settled over the room.

"He was very competent at his work, Mr. O'Hare, but he was an arrogant man, and greedy. He liked his fine things in dress and food," she said softly but very clearly. "He had ideas and aspirations far beyond his station, and there was something of an anger in him that he should be limited to that walk of life in which God had seen fit to place him. He played with the affections of the poor girl Rose Watkins, and then when he imagined he could—" She looked up at him with a devastating stare and her voice grew even huskier. "I really don't know how to phrase this delicately. I would be so much obliged if you would assist me."

Beside Hester, Beatrice drew in her breath sharply, and in her lap her hands clenched in their kid gloves.

O'Hare came to Fenella's defense. "Are you wishing to say, ma'am, that he entertained amorous ideas about a member of the family, perhaps?"

"Yes," she said with exaggerated demureness. "That is unfortunately exactly what I—I am obliged to say. More than once I caught him speaking boldly about my niece Octavia, and I saw an expression on his face which a woman cannot misunderstand."

"I see. How distressing for you."

"Indeed," she assented.

"What did you do about it, ma'am?"

"Do?" She stared at him, blinking. "Why my dear Mr.

274

O'Hare, there was nothing I could do. If Octavia herself did not object, what was there I could say to her, or to anyone?''

"And she did not object?" O'Hare's voice rose in amazement, and for an instant he glared around the crowd, then swung back to her. "Are you quite sure, Mrs. Sandeman?"

"Oh quite, Mr. O'Hare. I regret very deeply having to say this, and in such a very public place." Her voice had a slight catch in it now, and Beatrice was so tense Hester was afraid she was going to cry out. "But poor Octavia appeared to be flattered by his attentions," Fenella went on relentlessly. "Of course she could have no idea that he meant more than words—and neither had I, or I should have taken the matter to her father, of course, regardless of what she thought of me for it!''

"Naturally," O'Hare conceded soothingly. "I am sure we all understand that had you foreseen the tragic outcome of the infatuation you would have done all you could to prevent it. However your testimony now of your observations is most helpful in seeing justice for Mrs. Haslett, and we all appreciate how distressing it must be for you to come here and tell us.''
Then he pressed her for individual instances of behavior from Percival which bore out her judgment, which she duly gave in some detail. He then asked for the same regarding Octavia's encouragement of him, and she recounted them as well.

"Oh—just before you leave, Mrs. Sandeman." O'Hare looked up as if he had almost forgotten. "You said Percival was greedy. In what way?"

"Money, of course," she replied softly, her eyes bright and spiteful. "He liked fine things he could not afford on a footman's wages.''

"How do you know this, ma'am?"

"He was a braggart," she said clearly. "He told me once how he got—little—extras.''

"Indeed? And how was that?" O'Hare asked as innocently as if the reply might have been honorable and worthy of anyone.

"He knew things about people," she replied with a small, vicious smile. "Small things, trivial to most of us, just little vanities, but ones people would rather their fellows did not know about.''

She shrugged delicately. "The parlormaid Dinah boasts about her family—actually she is a foundling and has no one at all. Her airs annoyed Percival, and he let her know he knew. The senior laundrymaid, Lizzie, is a bossy creature, very superior, but she had an affair once. He knew about that too, maybe from Rose, I don't know. Small things like that. The cook's brother is a drunkard; the kitchen maid has a sister who is a cretin.''

O'Hare hid his distaste only partially, but whether it was entirely for Percival or included Fenella for betraying such small domestic tragedies it was impossible to tell.

"A most unpleasant man," he said aloud. "And how did he know all these things, Mrs. Sandeman?"

Fenella seemed unaware of the chill in him.

"I imagine he steamed open letters," she said with a shrug. "It was one of his duties to bring in the post."

"I see."

He thanked her again, and Oliver Rathbone rose to his feet and walked forward with almost feline grace.

"Mrs. Sandeman, your memory is much to be commended, and we owe a great deal to your accuracy and sensitivity."

She gazed at him with sharpened interest. There was an element in him which was more elusive, more challenging and more powerful than O'Hare, and she responded immediately.

"You are most kind."

"Not at all, Mrs. Sandeman." He waved his hand. "I assure you I am not. Did this amorous, greedy and conceited footman ever admire other ladies in the house? Mrs. Cyprian Moidore, for instance? Or Mrs. Kellard?"

"I have no idea." She was surprised.

"Or yourself, perhaps?"

"Well—" She lowered her eyelashes modestly.

"Please, Mrs. Sandeman," he urged. "This is not a time for self-effacement."

"Yes, he did step beyond the bounds of what is—merely courteous."

Several members of the jury looked expectant. One middle-aged man with side whiskers was obviously embarrassed.

"He expressed an amorous regard for you?" Rathbone pressed.

"Yes."

"What did you do about it, ma'am?"

Her eyes flew open and she glared at him. "I put him in his

place, Mr. Rathbone. I am perfectly competent to deal with a servant who has got above himself.''

Beside Hester, Beatrice stiffened in her seat.

"I am sure you are." Rathbone's voice was laden with meaning. "And at no danger to yourself. You did not find it necessary to go to bed carrying a carving knife?''

She paled visibly, and her mittened hands tightened on the rail of the box in front of her.

"Don't be absurd. Of course I didn't!''

"And yet you never felt constrained to counsel your niece in this very necessary art?''

"I—er—" Now she was acutely uncomfortable.

"You were aware that Percival was entertaining amorous intentions towards her." Rathbone moved very slightly, a graceful stride as he might use in a withdrawing room. He spoke softly, the sting in his incredulous contempt. "And you allowed her to be so alone in her fear that she resorted to taking a knife from the kitchen and carrying it to bed to defend herself, in case Percival should enter her room at night.''

The jury was patently disturbed, and their expressions betrayed it.

"I had no idea he would do such a thing," she protested. "You are trying to say I deliberately allowed it to happen. That is monstrous!'' She looked at O'Hare for help.

"No, Mrs. Sandeman," Rathbone corrected. "I am questioning how it is that a lady of your experience and sensitive observation and judgment of character should see that a footman was amorously drawn towards your niece, and that she had behaved foolishly in not making her distaste quite plain to him, and yet you did not take matters into your own hands sufficiently at least to speak to some other member of the household.''

She stared at him with horror.

"Her mother, for example," he continued. "Or her sister, or even to warn Percival yourself that his behavior was observed. Any of those actions would almost certainly have prevented this tragedy. Or you might simply have taken Mrs. Haslett to one side and counseled her, as an older and wiser woman who had had to rebuff many inappropriate advances yourself, and offered her your assistance.''

Fenella was flustered now.

"Of course—if I had r-realized—" she stammered. "But I didn't. I had no idea it—it would—"

"Hadn't you?" Rathbone challenged.

"No." Her voice was becoming shrill. "Your suggestion is appalling. I had not the slightest notion!"

Beatrice let out a little groan of disgust.

"But surely, Mrs. Sandeman," Rathbone resumed, turning and walking back to his place, "if Percival had made amorous advances to you—and you had seen all his offensive behavior towards Mrs. Haslett, you must have realized how it would end? You are not without experience in the world."

"I did not, Mr. Rathbone," Fenella protested. "What you are saying is that I deliberately allowed Octavia to be raped and murdered. That is scandalous, and totally untrue."

"I believe you, Mrs. Sandeman." Rathbone smiled suddenly, without a vestige of humor.

"I should think so!" Her voice shook a little. "You owe me an apology, sir."

"It would make perfect sense that you should not have any idea," he went on. "If this observation of yours did not in fact cover any of these things you relate to us. Percival was extremely ambitious and of an arrogant nature, but he made no advances towards you, Mrs. Sandeman. You are—forgive me, ma'am—of an age to be his mother!"

Fenella blanched with fury, and the crowd drew in an audible gasp. Someone tittered. A juryman covered his face with his handkerchief and appeared to be blowing his nose.

Rathbone's face was almost expressionless.

"And you did not witness all these distasteful and impertinent scenes with Mrs. Haslett either, or you would have reported them to Sir Basil without hesitation, for the protection of his daughter, as any decent woman would."

"Well—I—I . . ." She stumbled into silence, white-faced, wretched, and Rathbone returned to his seat. There was no need to humiliate her further or add explanation for her vanity or her foolishness, or the unnecessarily vicious exposure of the small secrets of the servants' hall. It was an acutely embarrassing scene, but it was the first doubt cast on the evidence against Percival.

* * *

278

The next day the courtroom was even more tightly packed, and Araminta took the witness stand. She was no vain woman displaying herself, as Fenella had been. She was soberly dressed and her composure was perfect. She said that she had never cared for Percival, but it was her father's house, and therefore not hers to question his choice of servants. She had hitherto considered her judgments of Percival to be colored by her personal distaste. Now of course she knew differently, and deeply regretted her silence.

When pressed by O'Hare she disclosed, with what appeared to be great difficulty, that her sister had not shared her distaste for the footman, and had been unwise in her laxity towards servants in general. This, she found it painful to admit, was sometimes due to the fact that since the death of her husband, Captain Haslett, in the recent conflict in the Crimea, her sister had on a large number of occasions taken rather more wine than was wise, and her judgment had been correspondingly disturbed, her manners a good deal easier than was becoming, or as it now transpired, well advised.

Rathbone asked if her sister had confided in her a fear of Percival, or of anyone else. Araminta said she had not, or she would naturally have taken steps to protect her.

Rathbone asked her if, as sisters, they were close. Araminta regretted deeply that since the death of Captain Haslett, Octavia had changed, and they were no longer as affectionate as they had been. Rathbone could find no flaw in her account, no single word or attitude to attack. Prudently he left it alone.

Myles added little to what was already in evidence. He substantiated that indeed Octavia had changed since her widowhood. Her behavior was unfortunate; she had frequently, it pained him to admit, been emotional and lacking in judgment as a result of rather too much wine. No doubt it was on such occasions she had failed to deal adequately with Percival's advances, and then in a soberer moment realized what she had done, but had been too ashamed to seek help, instead resorted to taking a carving knife to bed with her. It was all very tragic and they were deeply grieved.

Rathbone could not shake him, and was too aware of public sympathy to attempt it.

Sir Basil himself was the last witness O'Hare called. He took the stand with immense gravity, and there was a rustle of sympathy and respect right around the room. Even the jury sat up a little straighter, and one pushed back as if to present himself more respectfully.

Basil spoke with candor of his dead daughter, her bereavement when her husband had been killed, how it had unbalanced her emotions and caused her to seek solace in wine. He found it deeply shaming to have to admit to it—there was a ripple of profound sympathy for him. Many had lost someone themselves in the carnage at Balaclava, Inkermann, the Alma, or from hunger and cold in the heights above Sebastopol, or dead of disease in the fearful hospital at Scutari. They understood grief in all its manifestations, and his frank admission of it formed a bond between them. They admired his dignity and his openness. The warmth of it could be felt even from where Hester was sitting. She was aware of Beatrice beside her, but through the veil her face was all but invisible, her emotions concealed.

O'Hare was brilliant. Hester's heart sank.

At last it was Rathbone's turn to begin what defense he could.

He started with the housekeeper, Mrs. Willis. He was courteous to her, drawing from her her credentials for her senior position, the fact that she not only ran the household upstairs but was responsible for the female staff, apart from those in the kitchen itself. Their moral welfare was her concern.

Were they permitted to have amorous dalliances?

She bristled at the very suggestion. They most certainly were not. Nor would she allow to be employed any girl who entertained such ideas. Any girl of loose behavior would be dismissed on the spot—and without a character. It was not necessary to remind anyone what would happen to such a person.

And if a girl were found to be with child?

Instant dismissal, of course. What else was there?

Of course. And Mrs. Willis took her duties in the regard most earnestly?

Naturally. She was a Christian woman.

Had any of the girls ever come to her to say, in however roundabout a manner, that any of the male staff, Percival or anyone else, had made improper advances to them?

No they had not. Percival fancied himself, to be true, and

280

he was as vain as a peacock; she had seen his clothes and boots, and wondered where he got the money.

Rathbone returned her to the subject: had anyone complained of Percival?

No, it was all a lot of lip, nothing more; and most maids were quite able to deal with that for what it was worth—which was nothing at all.

O'Hare did not try to shake her. He simply pointed out that since Octavia Haslett was not part of her charge, all this was of peripheral importance.

Rathbone rose again to say that much of the character evidence as to Percival's behavior rested on the assessment of his treatment of the maids.

The judge observed that the jury would make up their own minds.

Rathbone called Cyprian, not asking him anything about either his sister or Percival. Instead he established that his bedroom in the house was next door to Octavia's, then he asked him if he had heard any sound or disturbance on the night she was killed.

"No—none at all, or I should have gone to see if she were all right," Cyprian said with some surprise.

"Are you an extremely heavy sleeper?" Rathbone asked.

"No."

"Did you indulge in much wine that evening?"

"No—very little." Cyprian frowned. "I don't see the point in your question, sir. My sister was undoubtedly killed in the room next to me. That I did not hear the struggle seems to me to be irrelevant. Percival is much stronger than she . . ." He looked very pale and had some difficulty in keeping his voice under control. "I presume he overpowered her quickly—"

"And she did not cry out?" Rathbone looked surprised.

"Apparently not."

"But Mr. O'Hare would have us believe she took a carving knife to bed with her to ward off these unwelcome attentions of the footman," Rathbone said reasonably. "And yet when he came into her room she rose out of her bed. She was not found lying in it but on it, across from a normal position in which to sleep—we have Mr. Monk's evidence for that. She rose, put on her peignoir, pulled out the carving knife from wherever she had put it, then there was a struggle in which she attempted to defend herself—"

He shook his head and moved a little, shrugging his shoulders. "Surely she must have warned him first? She would not simply run at him with dagger drawn. He struggled and wrested the knife from her"—he held up his hands—"and in the battle that ensued, he stabbed her to death. And yet in all this neither of them uttered a cry of any sort! This whole tableau was conducted in total silence? Do you not find that hard to believe, Mr. Moidore?"

The jury fidgeted, and Beatrice drew in her breath sharply.

"Yes!" Cyprian admitted with dawning surprise. "Yes, I do. It does seem most unnatural. I cannot see why she did not simply scream."

"Nor I, Mr. Moidore," Rathbone agreed. "It would surely have been a far more effective defense; and less dangerous, and more natural to a woman than a carving knife."

O'Hare rose to his feet.

"Nevertheless, Mr. Moidore, gentlemen of the jury, the fact remains that she did have the carving knife—and she was stabbed to death with it. We may never know what bizarre, whispered conversation took place that night. But we do know beyond doubt that Octavia Haslett was stabbed to death—and the bloodstained knife, and her robe gashed and dark with her blood, were found in Percival's room. Do we need to know every word and gesture to come to a conclusion?"

There was a rustle in the crowd. The jury nodded. Beside Hester, Beatrice let out a low moan.

Septimus was called, and recounted to them how he had met Octavia returning home on the day of her death, and how she had told him that she had discovered something startling and dreadful, and that she lacked only one final proof of its truth. But under O'Hare's insistence he had to admit that no one else had overheard this conversation, nor had he repeated it to anyone. Therefore, O'Hare concluded triumphantly, there was no reason to suppose this discovery, whatever it was, had had anything to do with her death. Septimus was unhappy. He pointed out that simply because he had not told anyone did not mean that Octavia herself had not.

But it was too late. The jury had already made up its mind, and nothing Rathbone could do in his final summation could sway their conviction. They were gone only a short while, and returned white-faced, eyes set and looking anywhere but at Percival. They gave the verdict of guilty. There were no mitigating circumstances.

The judge put on his black cap and pronounced sentence. Percival would be taken to the place from whence he came, and in three weeks he would be led out to the execution yard and hanged by the neck until he was dead. May God have mercy upon his soul, there was none other to look for on earth.

10

"I AM SORRY," Rathbone said very gently, looking at Hester with intense concern. "I did everything I could, but the passion was rising too high and there was no other person whom I could suggest with a motive powerful enough."

"Maybe Kellard?" she said without hope or conviction. "Even if she was defending herself, it doesn't have to have been from Percival. In fact it would make more sense if it was Myles, then screaming wouldn't do much good. He would only say she'd cried out and he'd heard her and come to see what was wrong. He would have a far better excuse than Percival for being there. And Percival she could have crushed with a threat of having him dismissed. She could hardly do that with Myles, and she may not have wanted Araminta ever to know about his behavior."

"I know that." He was standing by the mantel in his office and she was only a few feet away from him, the defeat crushing her and making her feel vulnerable and an appalling failure. Perhaps she had misjudged, and Percival was guilty after all? Everyone else, apart from Monk, seemed to believe it. And yet there were things that made so little sense.

"Hester?"

"I'm sorry," she apologized. "My attention was wandering."

"I could not raise Myles Kellard as a suspect."

"Why not?"

He smiled very slightly. "My dear, what evidence should I

call that he had the least amorous interest in his sister-in-law? Which of his family do you imagine would testify to that? Araminta? She would become the laughingstock of London society, and she knows that. If it were rumored she might be pitied, but if she openly admits she knows of it, she will be despised. From what I have seen of her, she would find them equally intolerable."

"I doubt Beatrice would lie," Hester said, and then knew instantly it was foolish. "Well, he raped the maid Martha Rivett. Percival knew that."

"And what?" he finished for her. "The jury will believe Percival? Or I should call Martha herself? Or Sir Basil, who dismissed her?"

"No, of course not," she said miserably, turning away. "I don't know what else we can do. I'm sorry if I seem unreasonable. It is just so—" She stopped and looked across at him. "They'll hang him, won't they?"

"Yes." He was watching her, his face grave and sad. "There are no mitigating circumstances this time. What can you say in defense of a footman who lusts after his master's daughter, and when she refuses him, knifes her to death?"

"Nothing," she said very quietly. "Nothing at all, except that he is human, and by hanging him we diminish ourselves as well."

"My dear Hester." Slowly and quite deliberately, his lashes lowered but his eyes open, he leaned forward until his lips touched hers, not with passion but with utmost gentleness and long, delicate intimacy.

When he drew away she felt both more and less alone than she ever had before, and she knew at once from his face that it had caught him in some way by surprise also.

He drew breath as if to speak, then changed his mind and turned away, going over to the window and standing with his back half towards her.

"I am truly sorry I could not do better for Percival," he said again, his voice a little rough and charged with a sincerity she could not doubt. "For him, and because you trusted me."

"You have discharged that trust completely," she said quickly. "I expected you to do all you could—I did not expect a miracle. I can see how passion is rising among the public. Perhaps we never had a chance. It was simply necessary that we try everything within our power. I am sorry I spoke so foolishly. Of course you could not have suggested Myles—or Araminta. It would only have turned the jury even more against Percival; I can see that if I free my mind from frustration and apply a little intelligence.''

He smiled at her, his eyes bright. ''How very practical.''

''You are laughing at me,'' she said without resentment. ''I know it is considered unwomanly, but I see nothing attractive in behaving like a fool when you don't have to.''

His smile broadened. ''My dear Hester, neither do I. It is extremely tedious. It is more than enough to do so when we cannot help ourselves. What are you going to do now? How will you survive, once Lady Moidore no longer considers herself in need of a nurse?''

''I shall advertise for someone else who does—until I am able to search for a job in administration somewhere.''

''I am delighted. From what you say you have not abandoned your hope of reforming English medicine.''

''Certainly not—although I do not expect to do it in the lifetime your tone suggests. If I initiate anything at all I will be satisfied.''

''I am sure you will.'' His laughter vanished. ''A determination like yours will not be thwarted long, even by the Pomeroys of the world.''

''And I shall find Mr. Monk and go over the whole case again,'' she added. ''Just so I am sure there is nothing whatever we can still do.''

''If you find anything, bring it to me.'' He was very grave indeed now. ''Will you promise me that? We have three weeks in which it might still be possible to appeal.''

''I will,'' she said with a return of the hard, gray misery inside her. The moment's ineffable warmth was gone, Percival remembered. ''I will.'' And she bade him good-bye and took her leave to seek Monk.

Hester returned to Queen Anne Street light-footed, but the leaden feeling was at the edge of her mind waiting to return now that she was forced to think of reality again.

She was surprised to learn from Mary, as soon as she was in the house, that Beatrice was still confining herself to her room and would take her evening meal upstairs. She had gone into the ironing room for a clean apron, and found Mary there folding the last of her own linen.

"Is she ill?" Hester said with some concern—and a pang of guilt, not only for what might be dereliction of her duty but because she had not believed the malady was now anything but a desire to be a trifle spoilt, and to draw from her family the attention she did not otherwise. And that in itself was something of a mystery. Beatrice was not only a lovely woman but vivid and individual, not made in the placid mold of Romola. She was also intelligent, imaginative and at times capable of considerable humor. Why should such a woman not be the very heartbeat of her home?

"She looked pale," Mary replied, pulling a little face. "But then she always does. I think she's in a temper, myself—although I shouldn't say that."

Hester smiled. The fact that Mary should not say something never stopped her, in fact it never even made her hesitate.

"With whom?" Hester asked curiously.

"Everyone in general, but Sir Basil in particular."

"Do you know why?"

Mary shrugged; it was a graceful gesture. "I should think over what they said about Miss Octavia at the trial." She scowled furiously. "Wasn't that awful! They made out she was so tipsy she encouraged the footman to make advances—" She stopped and looked at Hester meaningfully. "Makes you wonder, doesn't it?"

"Was that not true?"

"Not that I ever saw." Mary was indignant. "She was tipsy, certainly, but Miss Octavia was a lady. She wouldn't have let Percival touch her if he'd been the last man alive on a desert island. Actually it's my belief she wouldn't have let any man touch her after Captain Haslett died. Which is what made Mr. Myles so furious. Now if she'd stabbed him, I'd have believed it!"

"Did he really lust after her?" Hester asked, for the first time using the right word openly.

Mary's dark eyes widened a fraction, but she did not equivocate.

"Oh yes. You should have seen it in his face. Mind, she was very pretty, you know, in a quite different way from Miss Araminta. You never saw her, but she was so alive—" Suddenly misery gripped hold of her again, and all the realization of loss flooded back, and the anger she had been trying to suppress. "That was wicked, what they said about her! Why do people say things like that?" Her chin came up and her eyes were blazing. "Fancy her saying all those wretched things about Dinah, and Mrs. Willis and all. They won't ever forgive her for that, you know. Why did she do it?"

"Spite?" Hester suggested. "Or maybe just exhibitionism. She loves to be the center of attention. If anyone is looking at her she feels alive—important."

Mary looked confused.

"There are some people like that." Hester tried to explain what she had never put into words before. "They're empty, insecure alone; they only feel real when other people listen to them and take notice."

"Admiration." Mary laughed bitterly. "It's contempt. What she did was vicious. I can tell you, no one 'round here'll forgive her for it."

"I don't suppose that'll bother her," Hester said dryly, thinking of Fenella's opinion of servants.

Mary smiled. "Oh yes it will!" she said fiercely. "She won't get a hot cup of tea in the morning anymore; it will be lukewarm. We will be ever so sorry, we won't know how it happened, but it will go on happening. Her best clothes will be mislaid in the laundry, some will get torn, and no one will know who did it. Everyone will have found it like that. Her letters will be delivered to someone else, caught between the pages, messages for her or from her will be slow in delivery. The rooms she's in will get cold because footmen will be too busy to stoke the fires, and her afternoon tea will be late. Believe me, Miss Latterly, it will bother her. And Mrs. Willis nor Cook won't put a stop to it. They'll all be just as innocent and smug as the rest of us, and not have an idea how it happens. And Mr. Phillips won't do nothing either. He may have airs like he was a duke, but he's loyal when it comes down to it. He's one of us."

Hester could not help smiling. It was all incredibly trivial, but there was a kind of justice in it.

Mary saw her expression, and her own eased into one of satisfaction and something like conspiracy. "You see?" she said.

"I see," Hester agreed. "Yes—very appropriate." And still with a smile she took her linen and left.

Upstairs Hester found Beatrice sitting alone in her room in one of the dressing chairs, staring out of the window at the rain beginning to fall steadily into the bare garden. It was January, bleak, colorless, and promising fog before dark.

"Good afternoon, Lady Moidore," Hester said gently. "I am sorry you are unwell. Can I do anything to help?"

Beatrice did not move her head.

"Can you turn the clock back?" she asked with a tiny self-mocking smile.

"If I could, I would have done it many times," Hester answered. "But do you suppose it would really make a difference?"

Beatrice did not reply for several moments, then she sighed and stood up. She was dressed in a peach-colored robe, and with her blazing hair she had all the warmth of dying summer in her.

"No—probably none at all," she said wearily. "We would still be the same people, and that is what is wrong. We would all still be pursuing comfort, looking to save our own reputations and just as willing to hurt others." She stood by the window watching the water running down the panes. "I never realized Fenella was so consumed with vanity, so ridiculously trying to hold on to the trappings of youth. If she were not so prepared to destroy other people simply to get attention, I should feel more pity for her. As it is I am embarrassed by her."

"Perhaps it is all she feels she has." Hester spoke equally softly. She too found Fenella repellent in her willingness to hurt, especially to expose the foibles of the servants—that was gratuitous. But she understood the fear behind the need for some quality that would earn her survival, some material possessions, however come by, that were independent of Basil and his conditional charity, if *charity* was the word.

Beatrice swung around to face her, her eyes level, very wide.

"You understand, don't you? You know why we do these grubby things—"

Hester did not know whether to equivocate; tact was not what Beatrice needed now.

"Yes, it isn't difficult."

Beatrice dropped her eyes. "I'd rather not have known. I guessed some of it, of course. I knew Septimus gambled, and I thought he took wine occasionally from the cellars." She smiled. "In fact it rather amused me. Basil is so pompous about his claret." Her face darkened again and the humor vanished. "I didn't know Septimus took it for Fenella, and even then I wouldn't have cared about it if it were sympathy for her—but it isn't. I think he hates her. She's everything in a woman that is different from Christabel—that is the woman he loved. That isn't a good reason for hating anyone, though, is it?"

She hesitated, but Hester did not interrupt.

"Strange how being dependent, and being reminded of it all the time, sours you," Beatrice went on. "Because you feel helpless and inferior, you try to get power again by doing just the same to someone else. God how I hate investigations! It will take us years to forget all we've learned about each other—maybe by then it will be too late."

"Maybe you can learn to forgive instead?" Hester knew she was being impertinent, but it was the only thing she could say with any truth, and Beatrice not only deserved truth, she needed it.

Beatrice turned away and traced her finger on the dry inside of the window, following the racing drops.

"How do you forgive someone for not being what you wanted them to be, or what you thought they were? Especially when they are not sorry—perhaps they don't even understand?"

"Or again, perhaps they do?" Hester suggested. "And how do they forgive us for having expected too much of them, instead of looking to see what they really were, and loving that?"

Beatrice's finger stopped.

"You are very frank, aren't you!" It was not a question. "But it isn't as easy as that, Hester. You see, I am not even sure that Percival is guilty. Am I wicked still to have doubts in my mind when the court says he is, and he's been sentenced, and the world says it is all over? I dream, and wake up with my mind torn with suspicions. I look at people and wonder, and I hear double and triple meanings behind what they say."

Again Hester was racked with indecision. It would seem so

much kinder to suggest that no one else could be guilty, that it was only the aftermath of all the fear still lingering on, and in time it would melt away. Daily life would comfort, and this extraordinary tragedy would ease until it became only the grief one feels for any loss.

But then she thought of Percival in Newgate prison, counting the few days left to him until one morning there was no more time at all.

"Well if Percival is not guilty, who else could it have been?" She heard the words spoken aloud and instantly regretted her judgment. It was brutal. She never for an instant thought Beatrice would believe it was Rose, and none of the other servants had even entered the field of possibility. But it could not be taken back. All she could do was wait for Beatrice's answer.

"I don't know." Beatrice measured each word. "I have lain in the dark each night, thinking this is my own house, where I came when I was married. I have been happy here, and wretched. I have borne five children here, and lost two, and now Octavia. I've watched them grow up, and themselves marry. I've watched their happiness and their misery. It is all as familiar as bread and butter, or the sound of carriage wheels. And yet perhaps I know only the skin of it all, and the flesh beneath is as strange to me as Japan."

She moved to the dressing table and began to take the pins from her hair and let it down in a shining stream like bright copper.

"The police came here and were full of sympathy and respectfully polite. Then they proved that no one could have broken in from outside, so whoever killed Octavia was one of us. For weeks they asked questions and forced us to find the answers—ugly answers, most of them, things about ourselves that were shabby, or selfish, or cowardly." She put the pins in a neat little pile in one of the cut glass trays and picked up the silver-backed brush.

"I had forgotten about Myles and that poor maid. That may seem incredible, but I had. I suppose I never thought about it much at the time, because Araminta didn't know." She pulled at her hair with the brush in long, hard strokes. "I am a coward, aren't I," she said very quietly. It was a statement, not a question. "I saw what I wanted to, and hid from the rest. And Cyprian, my beloved Cyprian—doing the same: never standing up to his father, just living in a dream world, gambling and idling his time instead of doing what he really wanted.'' She tugged even harder with the brush. ''He's bored with Romola, you know. It used not to matter, but now he's suddenly realized how interesting companionship can be, and conversation that's real, where people say what they think instead of playing polite games. And of course it's far too late.''

Without any forewarning Hester realized fully what she had woken in indulging her own vanity and pleasure in Cyprian's attention. She was only partly guilty, because she had not intended hurt, but it was enough. Neither had she thought, or cared, and she had sufficient intelligence that she could have.

''And poor Romola,'' Beatrice went on, still brushing fiercely. ''She has not the slightest idea what is wrong. She has done precisely what she was taught to do, and it has ceased to work.''

''It may again,'' Hester said feebly, and did not believe it.

But Beatrice was not listening for inflections of a voice. Her own thoughts clamored too loudly.

''And the police have arrested Percival and gone away, leaving us to wonder what really happened.'' She began to brush with long, even strokes. ''Why did they do that, Hester? Monk didn't believe it was Percival, I'm sure of that.'' She swiveled around on the dresser seat and looked at Hester, the brush still in her hand. ''You spoke to him. Did you think he believed it was Percival?''

Hester let out her breath slowly. ''No—no, I thought not.''

Beatrice turned back to the mirror again and regarded her hair critically. ''Then why did the police arrest him? It wasn't Monk, you know. Annie told me it was someone else, not even the young sergeant either. Was it simply expediency, do you suppose? The newspapers were making a terrible fuss about it and blaming the police for not solving it, so Cyprian told me. And Basil wrote to the Home Secretary, I know.'' Her voice sank lower. ''I imagine their superiors demanded they produce some result very quickly, but I did not think Monk would give in. I thought he was such a strong man—'' She did not add that Percival was expendable when a senior officer's career was threatened, but Hester knew she was thinking it; the anger in her mouth and the misery in her eyes were sufficient.

"And of course they would never accuse one of us, unless they had absolute proof. But I can't help wondering if Monk suspected one of us and simply could not find any mistake large enough, or tangible enough, to justify his action."

"Oh I don't think so," Hester said quickly, then wondered how on earth she would explain knowing such a thing. Beatrice was so very nearly right in her estimate of what had happened, Runcorn's expediency over Monk's judgment, the quarrels and the pressure.

"Don't you?" Beatrice said bleakly, putting down the brush at last. "I am afraid I do. Sometimes I think I would give anything at all to know which one of us, just so I could stop suspecting the others. Then I shrink back in horror from it, like a hideous sight—a severed head in a bucketful of maggots—only worse." She swiveled around on the seat again and looked at Hester. "Someone in my own family murdered my daughter. You see, they all lied. Octavia wasn't as they said, and the idea of Percival taking such a liberty, or even imagining he could, is ridiculous."

She shrugged, her slender shoulders pulling at the silk of her gown.

"I know she drank a trifle too much sometimes—but nothing like as much as Fenella does. Now if it were Fenella that would make sense. She would encourage any man." Her face darkened. "Except she picks out those who are rich because she used to accept presents from them and then pawn the gifts for money to buy clothes and perfumes and things. Then she stopped bothering with the pretenses and simply took the money outright. Basil doesn't know, of course. He'd be horrified. He'd probably throw her out."

"Was that what Octavia discovered and told to Septimus?" Hester said eagerly. "Perhaps that was what happened?" Then she realized how insensitive such enthusiasm was. After all, Fenella was still one of the family, even if she was shallow and vicious, and now, after the trial, a public embarrassment. She composed her face into gravity again.

"No," Beatrice said flatly. "Octavia knew about it ages ago. So did Minta. We didn't tell Basil because we despised it but understood. It is surprising what one will do when one has no money. We devise little ways, and usually they are not attractive, sometimes not even honorable." She started to fiddle with a perfume bottle, pulling the stopper out. "We are such cowards at times. I wish I couldn't see that, but I can. But Fenella would not encourage a footman beyond silly flattery. She's vain and cruel, and terrified of growing old, but she is not a whore. At least—I mean, she does not take men simply because she enjoys it—" She gave a convulsive little shudder and jammed the perfume stopper in so hard she could not remove it again. She swore under her breath and pushed the bottle to the back of the dressing table.

"I used to think Minta didn't know about Myles having forced himself on the maid, but perhaps she did? And perhaps she knew that Myles was more than properly attracted to Octavia. He is very vain too, you know? He imagines all women find him pleasing." She smiled with a downward curl of her mouth, a curiously expressive gesture. "Of course a great many do. He is handsome and charming. But Octavia didn't like him. He found that very hard to take. Perhaps he was determined to make her change her mind. Some men find force quite justifiable, you know?"

She looked at Hester, then shook her head. "No, of course you don't know—you are not married. Forgive me for being so coarse. I hope I have not offended you. I think it is all a matter of degree. And Myles and Tavie thought very differently about it."

She was silent for a moment, then pulled her gown closer around her and stood up.

"Hester—I am so afraid. One of my family may be guilty. And Monk has gone off and left us, and I shall probably never know. I don't know which is worse—not knowing, and imagining everything—or knowing, and never again being able to forget, but being helpless to do anything about it. And what if they know I know? Would they murder me? How can we live together day after day?"

Hester had no answer. There was no possible comfort to give, and she did not belittle the pain by trying to find something to say.

It was another three days before the servants' revenge really began to bite and Fenella was sufficiently aware of it to complain to Basil. Quite by chance Hester overheard much of the conversation. She had become as invisible as the rest of the

294

servants, and neither Basil nor Fenella was aware of her through the arch of the conservatory from the withdrawing room. She had gone there because it was the nearest she could come to a walk alone outside. She was permitted to use the ladies' maids' sitting room, which she did to read, but there was always the chance of being joined by Mary or Gladys and having to make conversation, or explain her very intellectual choice of reading.

"Basil." Fenella swept in, bristling with anger. "I really must complain to you about the servants in this house. You seem to be quite unaware of it, but ever since the trial of that wretched footman, the standards have declined appallingly. This is three days in a row my morning tea has been almost cold. That fool of a maid has lost my best lace peignoir. My bedroom fire has been allowed to go out. And now the room is like a morgue. I don't know how I am supposed to dress in it. I should catch my death."

"Appropriate for a morgue," Basil said dryly.

"Don't be a fool," she snapped. "I do not find this an occasion for humor. I don't know why on earth you tolerate it. You never used to. You used to be the most exacting person I ever knew—worse even than Papa."

From where Hester was she could see only Fenella's back, but Basil's face was clearly visible. Now his expression changed and became pinched.

"My standards are as high as his ever were," he said coldly. "I don't know what you mean, Fenella. My tea was piping hot, my fire is blazing, and I have never missed anything in the laundry all the years I have lived here."

"And my toast was stale on my breakfast tray," she went on. "My bed linen has not been changed, and when I spoke to Mrs. Willis about it, all I got was a lot of limp excuses, and she barely even listened to what I said. You have not the command of the house you should have, Basil. I wouldn't tolerate it a moment. I know you aren't the man Papa was, but I didn't imagine you would go to pieces like this and allow everything around you to fall apart as well."

"If you don't care for it here, my dear," he said with viciousness, "you may always find somewhere that suits you better, and run it according to your own standards."

"That's just the sort of thing I would expect you to say,"

she retorted. "But you can hardly throw me out in the street now—too many people are looking at you, and what would they say? The fine Sir Basil, the rich Sir Basil''—her face was twisted with contempt—"the noble Sir Basil whom everyone respects, has thrown his widowed sister out of his home. I doubt it, my dear, I doubt it. You always wanted to live up to Papa, and then you wanted to exceed him. What people think of you matters more than anything else. I imagine that's why you hated poor Harry Haslett's father so much, even at school—he did with ease what you had to work so hard for. Well you've got it now—money, reputation, honors—you won't jeopardize it by putting me out. What would it look like?" She laughed abrasively. "What would people say? Just get your servants to do their duty."

"Has it occurred to you, Fenella, that they are treating you like this because you betrayed their vulnerabilities in public from the witness stand—and brought it upon yourself?" His face was set in an expression of loathing and disgust, but there was also a touch of pleasure in it, a satisfaction that he could hurt. "You made an exhibition of yourself, and servants don't forgive that."

She stiffened, and Hester could imagine the color rising up her cheeks.

"Are you going to speak to them or not? Or do they just do as they please in this house?"

"They do as I please, Fenella," he said very quietly. "And so does everyone else. No, I am not going to speak to them. It amuses me that they should take their revenge on you. As far as I am concerned, they are free to continue. Your tea will be cold, your breakfast burnt, your fire out and your linen lost as long as they like."

She was too furious to speak. She let out a gasp of rage, swung on her heel and stormed out, head high, skirts rattling and swinging so wide they caught an ornament on the side table and sent it crashing.

Basil smiled with deep, hard, inward pleasure.

Monk had already found two small jobs since he advertised his services as a private inquiry agent prepared to undertake investigations outside police interest, or to continue with cases from which the police had withdrawn. One was a matter of property, and of very little reward other than that of a quickly satisfied customer and a few pounds to make sure of at least another week's lodging. The second, upon which he was currently engaged, was more involved and promised some variety and pursuit—and possibly the questioning of several people, the art for which his natural talents fitted him. It concerned a young woman who had married unfortunately and been cut off by her family, who now wished to find her again and heal the rift. He was prospering well, but after the outcome of the trial of Percival he was deeply depressed and angry. Not that he had for a moment expected anything different, but there was always a stubborn hope, even until the last, more particularly when he heard Oliver Rathbone was engaged. He had very mixed emotions about the man; there was a personal quality in him which Monk found intensely irritating, but he had no reservations in the admiration of his skill or the conviction of his dedication.

He had written to Hester Latterly again, to arrange a meeting in the same chocolate house in Regent Street, although he had very little idea what it might accomplish.

He was unreasonably cheered when he saw her coming in, even though her face was sober and when she saw him her smile was only momentary, a matter of recognition, no more.

He rose to pull out her chair, then sat opposite, ordering hot chocolate for her. They knew each other too honestly to need the niceties of greeting or the pretense at inquiry after health. They could approach what burdened them without prevarication.

He looked at her gravely, the question in his eyes.

"No," she answered. "I haven't learned anything that I can see is of use. But I am certain beyond doubt at all that Lady Moidore does not believe that Percival is guilty, but neither does she know who is. At moments she wants more than anything else to know, at other times she dreads it, because it would finally condemn someone and shatter all the beliefs and the love she has felt for that person until now. The uncertainty is poisoning everything for her, yet she is afraid that if one day she learns who it is, then that person may realize she knows and she herself will be in danger."

His face was tight with inner pain and the knowledge that

for all the effort and the struggle he had put forth, and the price it had cost him, he had failed.

"She is right," he said quietly. "Whoever it is has no mercy. They are prepared to allow Percival to hang. It would be a flight of fancy to suppose they will spare her if she endangers them."

"And I think she would." Now Hester's expression was pinched with anxiety. "Underneath the fashionable woman who retreated to her bedroom with grief there is someone of more courage, and a deeper horror at the cruelty and the lies."

"Then we still have something to fight for," he said simply. "If she wants to know badly enough, and the suspicion and the fear become unbearable to her, then one day she will."

The waiter appeared and set their chocolate in front of them. Monk thanked him.

"Something will fall into place in her memory," he continued to Hester. "A word, a gesture; someone's guilt will draw them into an error, and suddenly she will realize—and they will see it, because she will not possibly be able to be the same towards them—how could she?"

"Then we must find out—before she does." Hester stirred her chocolate vigorously, risking slopping it over with every round of the spoon. "She knows that almost everyone lied, in one degree or another, because Octavia was not as they described her in the trial." And she told him of everything that Beatrice had said the last time they spoke.

"Maybe." Monk was dubious. "But Octavia was her daughter; it is possible she simply did not want to see her as clearly as they did. If Octavia were indiscreet in her cups, perhaps vain, and did not keep the usual curb on her sensuality—her mother may not be prepared to accept that as true."

"What are you saying?" Hester demanded. "That what they all testified was right, and she encouraged Percival, and then changed her mind when she thought he would take her at her word? And instead of asking anyone for help, she took a carving knife to her bedroom?"

She picked up her chocolate but was too eager to finish the thought to stop. "And when Percival did intrude in the night, even though her brother was next door, she fought to the death with Percival and never cried out? I'd have screamed my lungs raw!" She sipped her chocolate. "And don't say she was em-

298

barrassed he'd say she had invited him. No one in her family would believe Percival instead of her—and it would be a lot easier to explain than either his injured body or his corpse.''

Monk smiled with a harsh humor. "Perhaps she hoped the mere sight of the knife would send him away—silently?''

She paused an instant. "Yes,'' she agreed reluctantly. "That does make some sense. It is not what I believe though.''

"Nor I,'' he assented. "There is too much else that is out of character. What we need is to discover the lies from the truths, and perhaps the reasons for the lies—that might be the most revealing.''

"In order of testimony,'' she agreed quickly. "I doubt Annie lied. For one thing she said nothing of significance, merely that she found Octavia, and we all know that is true. Similarly the doctor had no interest in anything but the best accuracy of which he was capable.'' She screwed up her face in intense concentration. "What reasons do people who are innocent of the crime have to lie? We must consider them. Then of course there is always the possibility of error that is not malicious, simply a matter of ignorance, incorrect assumption, and simple mistake.''

He smiled in spite of himself. "The cook? Do you think Mrs. Boden could be in error about her knife?''

She caught his amusement, but responded with only a moment's softening of her eyes.

"No—I cannot think how. She identified it most precisely. And anyway, what sense would there be in it being a knife from anywhere else? There was no intruder. The knife does not help us towards the identity of who took it.''

"Mary?''

Hester considered for a moment. "She is a person of most decided opinions—which is not a criticism. I cannot bear wishy-washy people who agree with whoever spoke to them last—but she might make an error out of a previously held conviction, without the slightest mal intent!''

"That it was Octavia's peignoir?''

"No of course not. Besides, she was not the only person to identify it. At the time you found it you asked Araminta as well, and she not only identified it but said that she remembered that Octavia had worn it the night of her death. And I think Lizzie the head laundrymaid identified it too. Besides, whether it was Octavia's or not, she obviously wore it when she was stabbed—poor woman.''

''Rose?''

''Ah—there is someone much more likely. She had been wooed by Percival—after a manner of speaking—and then passed over when he grew bored with her. And rightly or not, she imagined he might marry her—and he obviously had no such intention at all. She had a very powerful motive to see him in trouble. I think she might even have the passion and the hatred to want him hanged.''

''Enough to lie to bring about the end?'' He found it hard to believe such a terrible malice, even from a sexual obsession rejected. Even the stabbing of Octavia had been done in hot blood, at the moment of refusal, not carried out deliberately step by step, over weeks, even months afterwards. It was chilling to think of such a mind in a laundrymaid, a trim, pretty creature one would scarcely look at except with an absent-minded appreciation. And yet she could desire a man, and when rejected, torture him to a judicial death.

Hester saw his doubt.

''Perhaps not with such a terrible end in mind,'' she conceded. ''One lie begets another. She may have intended only to frighten him—as Araminta did with Myles—and then events took over and she could not retreat without endangering herself.'' She took another sip of chocolate; it was delicious, although she was becoming used to the best of foods. ''Or of course, she may have believed him guilty,'' she added. ''Some people do not consider it as in the least to bend the truth a little in order to bring about what they see as justice.''

''She lied about Octavia's character?'' He took up the thread. ''If Lady Moidore is right. But she may also have done that from jealousy. Very well—let us assume Rose lied. What about the butler, Phillips? He bore out what everyone else said about Percival.''

''He was probably largely right,'' she conceded. ''Percival was arrogant and ambitious. He clearly blackmailed the other servants over their little secrets—and perhaps the family as well; we shall probably never know that. He is not at all likable—but that is not the issue. If we were to hang everyone in London who is unlikable we could probably get rid of a quarter of the population.''

300

"At least," he agreed. "But Phillips may have embroidered his opinion a trifle out of obligation to his employer. This was obviously the conclusion Sir Basil wished, and he wished it speedily. Phillips is not a foolish man, and he is intensely aware of duty. He wouldn't see it as any form of untruth, simply as loyalty to his superior, a military ideal he admires. And Mrs. Willis testified for us."

"The family?" she prompted.

"Cyprian also testified for us, and so did Septimus. Romola—what is your opinion of her?"

A brief feeling of irritation troubled Hester, and one of guilt. "She enjoys the status of being Sir Basil's daughter-in-law, and of living in Queen Anne Street, but she frequently tries to persuade Cyprian to ask for more money. She is adept at making him feel guilty if she is not happy. She is confused, because he is bored by her and she does not know why. And sometimes I have been so frustrated that he does not tell her to behave like an adult and take responsibility for her own feelings. But I suppose I do not know enough about them to judge."

"But you do," he said without condemnation. He loathed women who put such a burden of emotional blackmail upon their fathers or their husbands, but he had no idea why the thought touched such a raw nerve in him.

"I suppose so," she admitted. "But it hardly matters. I think Romola would testify according to whatever she thought Sir Basil wanted. Sir Basil is the power in that house; he has the purse strings, and they all know it. He does not need to make a demand, it is implicit; all he has to do is allow them to know his wishes."

Monk let out his breath in a sharp sigh. "And he wishes the murder of Octavia to be closed as rapidly and discreetly as possible—of course. Have you seen what the newspapers are saying?"

Her eyebrows shot up. "Don't be absurd. Where in heaven's name would I see a newspaper? I am a servant—and a woman. Lady Moidore doesn't see anything but the social pages, and she is not interested in them at the moment."

"Of course—I forgot." He pulled a wry face. He had only remembered that she was a friend of a war correspondent in the Crimea, and when he had died in the hospital in Scutari, she had sent his last dispatches home and then, born out of the intensity of her feelings and observations, herself written the succeeding dispatches and sent them under his name. Since the casualty lists were unreliable, his editor had not been aware of the change.

"What are they saying?" she asked. "Anything that affects us?"

"Generally? They are bemoaning the state of the nation that a footman can murder his mistress, that servants are so above themselves that they entertain ideas of lust and depravity involving the well-born; that the social order is crumbling; that we must hang Percival and make an example of him, so that no such thing will ever happen again." He pulled his face into an expression of disgust. "And of course they are full of sympathy for Sir Basil. All his past services to the Queen and the nation have been religiously rehearsed, all his virtues paraded, and positively fulsome condolences written."

She sighed and stared into the dregs of her cup.

"All the vested interests are ranged against us," he said grimly. "Everyone wants it over quickly, society's vengeance taken as thoroughly as possible, and then the whole matter forgotten so we can pick up our lives and try to continue them as much like before as we can."

"Is there anything at all we can do?" she asked.

"I can't think of anything." He stood up and held her chair. "I shall go and see him."

She met his eyes with a quick pain, and admiration. There was no need either for her to ask or for him to answer. It was a duty, a last rite which failure did not excuse.

As soon as Monk stepped inside Newgate Prison and the doors clanged shut behind him he felt a sickening familiarity. It was the smell, the mixture of damp, mold, rank sewage and an all-pervading misery that hung in the stillness of the air. Too many men who entered here left only to go to the executioner's rope, and the terror and despair of their last days had soaked into the walls till he could feel it skin-crawling like ice as he followed the warder along the stone corridors to the appointed place where he could see Percival for the last time.

He had misrepresented himself only slightly. Apparently he had been here before, and as soon as the warder saw his face he leaped to a false conclusion about his errand, and Monk did not explain.

Percival was standing in a small stone cell with one high window to an overcast sky. He turned as the door opened and Monk was let in, the gaoler with his keys looming huge behind.

For the first moment Percival looked surprised, then his face hardened into anger.

"Come to gloat?" he said bitterly.

"Nothing to gloat about," Monk replied almost casually. "I've lost my career, and you will lose your life. I just haven't worked out who's won."

"Lost your career?" For a moment doubt flickered across Percival's face, then suspicion. "Thought you'd have been made. Gone on to something better! You solved the case to everyone's satisfaction—except mine. No ugly skeletons dragged out, no mention of Myles Kellard raping Martha, poor little bitch, no saying Aunt Fenella is a whore—just a jumped-up footman filled with lust for a drunken widow. Hang him and let's get on with our lives. What more could they ask of a dutiful policeman?"

Monk did not blame him for his rage or his hate. They were justified—only, at least in part, misdirected. It would have been fairer to blame him for incompetence.

"I had the evidence," he said slowly. "But I didn't arrest you. I refused to do it, and they threw me out."

"What?" Percival was confused, disbelieving.

Monk repeated it.

"For God's sake why?" There was no softness in Percival, no relenting. Again Monk did not blame him. He was beyond the last hope now, perhaps there was no room in him for gentleness of any sort. If he once let go of the rage he might crumble and terror would win; the darkness of the night would be unbearable without the burning of hate.

"Because I don't think you killed her," Monk replied.

Percival laughed harshly, his eyes black and accusing. But he said nothing, just stared in helpless and terrible knowledge.

"But even if I were still on the case," Monk went on very quietly, "I don't know what I should do, because I have no idea who did." It was an overwhelming admission of failure, and he was stunned as he heard himself make it to Percival of all people. But honesty was the very least of all he owed him.

"Very impressive," Percival said sarcastically, but there was a brief flicker of something in his face, rapid as the sunlight let through the trees by a turning leaf, then gone again. "But since you are not there, and everyone else is busy covering their own petty sins, serving their grievances, or else obliged to Sir Basil, we'll never know—will we?"

"Hester Latterly isn't." Instantly Monk regretted he had said it. Percival might take it for hope, which was an illusion and unspeakably cruel now.

"Hester Latterly?" For an instant Percival looked confused, then he remembered her. "Oh—the terribly efficient nurse. Daunting woman, but you're probably right. I expect she is so virtuous it is painful. I doubt she knows how to smile, let alone laugh, and I shouldn't think any man ever looked at her," he said viciously. "She's taken her vengeance on us by spending her time ministering to us when we are at our most vulnerable—and most ridiculous."

Monk felt a deep uprush of rage for the cruel and unthinking prejudice, then he looked at Percival's haggard face and remembered where he was, and why, and the rage vanished like a match flame in a sea of ice. What if Percival did need to hurt someone, however remotely? His was going to be the ultimate pain.

"She came to the house because I sent her," Monk explained. "She is a friend of mine. I hoped that someone inside the household in a position where no one would pay much regard to them might observe things I could not."

Percival's amazement was as profound as anything could be over the surface of the enormous center of him, which knew nothing but the slow, relentless clock ticking away his days to the last walk, the hood, the hangman's rope around his neck, and the sharp drop to tearing, breaking pain and oblivion.

"But she didn't learn anything, did she?" For the first time his voice cracked and he lost control of it.

Monk loathed himself for stupidly giving this knife thrust of hope, which was not hope at all.

"No," he said quickly. "Nothing that helps. All sorts of trivial and ugly little weaknesses and sins—and that Lady Moidore believes the murderer is still in the house, and almost certainly one of her family—but she has no idea who either.''

Percival turned away, hiding his face.

"What did you come for?"

"I'm not sure. Perhaps simply not to leave you alone, or to think no one believes you. I don't know if it helps, but you have the right to know. I hope it does."

Percival let out an explosion of curses, and swore over and over again until he was exhausted with repeating himself and the sheer, ugly futility of it. When he finished Monk had gone and the cell door was locked again, but through the tears and the bloodless skin, there was a very small light of gratitude, ease from one of the clenched and terrible knots inside him.

On the morning Percival was hanged Monk was working on the case of a stolen picture, more probably removed and sold by a member of the family in gambling debt. But at eight o'clock he stopped on the pavement in Cheapside and stood still in the cold wind amid the crowd of costers, street peddlers of bootlaces and matches and other fripperies, clerks on errands, a sweep, black-faced and carrying a ladder, and two women arguing over a length of cloth. The babble and clatter rolled on around him, oblivious of what was happening in Newgate Yard, but he stood motionless with a sense of finality and a wounding loss—not for Percival individually, although he felt the man's terror and rage and the snuffing out of his life. He had not liked him, but he had been acutely aware of his vitality, his intensity of feeling and thought, his identity. But his greatest loss was for justice which had failed. At the moment when the trapdoor opened and the noose jerked tight, another crime was being committed. He had been powerless to prevent it, for all the labor and thought he had put into it, but his was not the only loss, or even necessarily the main one. All London was diminished, perhaps all England, because the law which should protect had instead injured.

Hester was standing in the dining room. She had deliberately come to collect an apricot conserve from the table for Beatrice's tray at precisely this time. If she jeopardized her position, even if she lost it and were dismissed, she wanted to see the faces of the Moidores at the moment of hanging, and

305

to be sure each one of them knew precisely what moment this was.

She excused herself past Fenella, uncharacteristically up so early; apparently she intended to ride in the park. Hester spooned a little of the conserve into a small dish.

"Good morning, Mrs. Sandeman," she said levelly. "I hope you have a pleasant ride. It will be very cold in the park this early, even though the sun is up. The frost will not have melted at all. It is three minutes to eight."

"How very precise you are," Fenella said with a touch of sarcasm. "Is that because you are a nurse—everything must be done to the instant, in strict routine? Take your medicine as the clock chimes or it will not do you good. How excruciatingly tedious." She laughed very slightly, a mocking, tinkly sound.

"No, Mrs. Sandeman," Hester said very distinctly. "It is because in two minutes now they will hang Percival. I believe they are very precise—I have no idea why. It can hardly matter; it is just a ritual they keep."

Fenella choked on a mouthful of eggs and went into a spasm of coughing. No one assisted her.

"Oh God!" Septimus stared ahead of him, bleak and unblinking, his thoughts unreadable.

Cyprian shut his eyes as if he would block out the world, and all his powers were concentrated on his inner turmoil.

Araminta was sheet white, her curious face frozen.

Myles Kellard slopped his tea, which he had just raised to his lips, sending splashes all over the tablecloth, and the stain spread out in a brown, irregular pattern. He looked furious and confused.

"Oh really," Romola exploded, her face pink. "What a tasteless and insensitive thing to have said. What is the matter with you, Miss Latterly? No one wishes to know that. You had better leave the room, and for goodness' sake don't be so crass as to mention it to Mama-in-law. Really—you are too stupid."

Basil's face was very pale and there was a nervous twitch in the muscles at the side of his cheek.

"It could not be helped," he said very quietly. "Society must be preserved, and the means are sometimes very harsh. Now I think we may call the matter closed and proceed with our lives as normal. Miss Latterly, you will not speak of it again. Please take the conserve, or whatever it is you came for, and carry Lady Moidore's breakfast to her."

"Yes, Sir Basil," Hester said obediently, but their faces remained in the mirror of her mind, the misery and finality of it like a patina of darkness upon everything.

Two DAYS AFTER Percival was hanged, Septimus Thirsk developed a slight fever, not enough to fear some serious disease, but sufficient to make him feel unwell and confine him to his room. Beatrice, who had kept Hester more for her company than any genuine need of her professional skills, dispatched her immediately to care for him, obtain any medication she considered advisable, and do anything she could to ease his discomfort and aid his recovery.

Hester found Septimus lying in bed and in his large, airy room. The curtains were drawn wide open onto a fierce February day, with the sleet dashing against the windows like grapeshot and a sky so low and leaden it seemed to rest close above the rooftops. The room was cluttered with army memorabilia, engravings of soldiers in dress uniform, mounted cavalry officers, and all along the west wall in a place of honor, unflanked by anything else, a superb painting of the charge of the Royal Scots Greys at Waterloo, horses with nostrils flared, white manes flying in the clouds of smoke, and the whole sweep of battle behind them. She felt her heart lurch and her stomach knot at the sight of it. It was so real she could smell the gunsmoke and hear the thunder of hooves, the shouting and the clash of steel, and feel the sun burning her skin, and knew the warm odor of blood would fill her nose and throat afterwards.

And then there would be the silence on the grass, the dead lying waiting for burial or the carrion birds, the endless work, the helplessness and the few sudden flashes of victory when someone lived through appalling wounds or found some ease from pain. It was all so vivid in the moment she saw the picture, her body ached with the memory of exhaustion and the fear, the pity, the anger and the exhilaration.

She looked and saw Septimus's faded blue eyes on her, and knew in that instant they understood each other as no one else in that house ever could. He smiled very slowly, a sweet, almost radiant look.

She hesitated, not to break the moment, then as it passed naturally, she went over to him and began a simple nursing routine, questions, feeling his brow, then the pulse in his bony wrist, his abdomen to see if it were causing him pain, listened carefully to his rather shallow breathing and for telltale rattling in his chest.

His skin was flushed, dry and a little rough, his eyes over-bright, but beyond a chill she could find nothing gravely wrong with him. However a few days of care might do far more for him than any medication, and she was happy to give it. She liked Septimus, and felt the neglect and slight condescension he received from the rest of the family.

He looked at her, a quizzical expression on his face. She thought quite suddenly that if she had pronounced pneumonia or consumption he would not have been afraid—or even grievously shaken. He had long ago accepted that death comes to everyone, and he had seen the reality of it many times, both by violence and by disease. And he had no deep purpose in extending his life anymore. He was a passenger, a guest in his brother-in-law's house, tolerated but not needed. And he was a man born and trained to fight and to protect, to serve as a way of life.

She touched him very gently.

"A nasty chill, but if you are cared for it should pass without any lasting effect. I shall stay with you for a while, just to make sure." She saw his face brighten and realized how used he was to loneliness. It had become like the ache in the joints one moves so as to accommodate, tries to forget, but never quite succeeds. She smiled with quick, bright conspiracy. "And we shall be able to talk."

He smiled back, his eyes bright for once with pleasure and not the fever in him.

"I think you had better remain," he agreed. "In case I should take a sudden turn for the worse." And he coughed dramatically, although she could also see the real pain of a congested chest.

"Now I will go down to the kitchen and get you some milk and onion soup," she said briskly.

He pulled a face.

"It is very good for you," she assured him. "And really quite palatable. And while you eat it, I shall tell you about my experiences—and then you may tell me about yours!"

"For that," he conceded, "I will even eat milk and onion soup!"

Hester spent all that day with Septimus, bringing her own meals up on a tray and remaining quietly in the chair in the corner of the room while he slept fitfully in the afternoon, and then fetching him more soup, this time leek and celery mixed with creamed potato into a thick blend. When he had eaten it they sat through the evening and talked of things that had changed since his day on the battlefield—she telling him of the great conflicts she had witnessed from the grassy sward above, and he recounting to her the desperate cavalry battles he had fought in the Afghan War of 1839 to 1842—then in the conquest of Sind the year after, and in the later Sikh wars in the middle of the decade. They found endless emotions, sights and fears the same, and the wild pride and horror of victory, the weeping and the wounds, the beauty of courage, and the fearful, elemental indignity of dismemberment and death. And he told her something of the magnificent continent of India and its peoples.

They also remembered the laughter and the comradeship, the absurdities and the fierce sentimental moments, and the regimental rituals with their splendor, farcical at a glance, silver candelabra and full dinner service with crystal and porcelain for officers the night before battle, scarlet uniforms, gold braid, brasses like mirrors.

"You would have liked Harry Haslett," Septimus said with a sweet, sharp sadness. "He was one of the nicest men. He had all the qualities of a friend: honor without pomposity, generosity without condescension, humor without malice and courage without cruelty. And Octavia adored him. She spoke

310

of him so passionately the very day she died, as if his death were still fresh in her mind." He smiled and stared up at the ceiling, blinking a little to hide the tears in his eyes.

Hester reached for his hand and held it. It was a natural gesture, quite spontaneous, and he understood it without explanation. His bony fingers tightened on hers, and for several minutes they were silent.

"They were going to move away," he said at last, when his voice was under control. "Tavie wasn't much like Araminta. She wanted her own house; she didn't care about the social status of being Sir Basil Moidore's daughter or living in Queen Anne Street with the carriages and the staff, the ambassadors to dine, the members of Parliament, the foreign princes. Of course you haven't seen any of that because the house is in mourning for Tavie now—but before that it was quite different. There was something special almost every week."

"Is that why Myles Kellard stays?" Hester asked, understanding easily now.

"Of course," he agreed with a thin smile. "How could he possibly live in this manner on his own? He is quite well off, but nothing like the wealth or the rank of Basil. And Araminta is very close to her father. Myles never stood a chance—not that I am sure he wants it. He has much here he would never have anywhere else."

"Except the dignity of being master in his own house," Hester said. "The freedom to have his own opinions, to come and go without deference to anyone else's plans, and to choose his friends according to his own likes and emotions."

"Oh, there is a price," Septimus agreed wryly. "Sometimes I think a very high one."

Hester frowned. "What about conscience?" She said it gently, aware of the difficult road along which it would lead and the traps for both of them. "If you live on someone else's bounty, do you not risk compromising yourself so deeply with obligation that you surrender your own agency?"

He looked at her, his pale eyes sad. She had shaved him, and become aware how thin his skin was. He looked older than his years.

"You are thinking about Percival and the trial, aren't you." It was barely a question.

"Yes—they lied, didn't they?"

"Of course," he agreed. "Although perhaps they hardly saw it that way. They said what was in their best interest, for one reason or another. One would have to be very brave intentionally to defy Basil." He moved his legs a fraction to be more comfortable. "I don't suppose he would throw us out, but it would make life most unpleasant from day to day—endless restrictions, humiliations, little scratches on the sensitive skin of the mind." He looked across at the great picture. "To be dependent is to be so damned vulnerable."

"And Octavia wanted to leave?" she prompted after a moment.

He returned to the present. "Oh yes, she was all ready to, but Harry had not enough money to provide for her as she was used, which Basil pointed out to him. He was a younger son, you see. No inheritance. His father was very well-to-do. At school with Basil. In fact, I believe Basil was his fag—a junior who is sort of an amiable slave to a senior boy—but perhaps you knew that?"

"Yes," she acknowledged, thinking of her own brothers.

"Remarkable man, James Haslett," Septimus said thoughtfully. "Gifted in so many ways, and charming. Good athlete, fine musician, sort of minor poet, and a good mind. Shock of fair hair and a beautiful smile. Harry was like him. But he left his estate to his eldest son, naturally. Everyone does."

His voice took on a bitter edge. "Octavia would have forfeited a lot if she left Queen Anne Street. And should there be children, which they both wanted very much, then the restrictions upon their finances would be even greater. Octavia would suffer. Of course Harry could not accept that."

He moved again to make himself more comfortable. "Basil suggested the army as a career, and offered to buy him a commission—which he did. Harry was a natural soldier; he had the gift of command, and the men loved him. It was not what he wanted, and inevitably it meant a long separation—which I suppose was what Basil intended. He was against the marriage in the first place, because of his dislike for James Haslett."

"So Harry took the commission to obtain the finance for himself and Tavie to have their own house?" Hester could see it vividly. She had known so many young officers that she could picture Harry Haslett as a composite of a hundred she had seen in every mood, victory and defeat, courage and despair, triumph and exhaustion. It was as if she had known him and understood his dreams. Now Octavia was more real to her than Araminta downstairs in the withdrawing room with her tea and conversation, or Beatrice in her bedroom thinking and fearing, and immeasurably more than Romola with her children supervising the new governess in the schoolroom.

"Poor devil," Septimus said half to himself. "He was a brilliant officer—he earned promotion very quickly. And then he was killed at Balaclava. Octavia was never the same again, poor girl. Her whole world collapsed when the news came; the light fled out of her. It was as if she had nothing left even to hope for." He fell silent, absorbed in his memory of the day, the numbing grief and the long gray stretch of time afterwards. He looked old and very vulnerable himself.

There was nothing Hester could say to help, and she was wise enough not to try. Words of ease would only belittle his pain. Instead she set about trying to make him more physically comfortable, and spent the next several hours doing so. She fetched clean linen and remade the bed while he sat wrapped up and huddled in the dressing chair. Then she brought up hot water in the great ewer and filled the basin and helped him wash so that he felt fresh. She also brought from the laundry a clean nightshirt, and when he was back in bed again she returned to the kitchen, prepared and brought him up a light meal. After which he was quite ready to sleep for over three hours.

He woke considerably restored, and so obliged to her she was embarrassed. After all, Sir Basil was paying her for her skill, and this was the first time she had exercised the latter in the manner in which he intended.

The following day Septimus was so much better she was able to attend to him in the early morning, then seek Beatrice's permission to leave Queen Anne Street for the entire afternoon, as long as she returned in sufficient time to prepare Septimus for the night and give him some slight medication to see he rested.

In a gray wind laden with sleet, and with ice on the footpaths, she walked to Harley Street and took a cab, requesting the driver take her to the War Office. There she paid him and alighted with all the aplomb of one who knows precisely where

313

she is going, and that she will be admitted with pleasure, which was not at all the case. She intended to learn all she could about Captain Harry Haslett, without any clear idea of where it might lead, but he was the only member of the family about whom she had known almost nothing until yesterday. Septimus's account had brought him so sharply to life, and made him so likable and of such deep and abiding importance to Octavia, that Hester understood why two years after his death she still grieved with the same sharp and unendurable loneliness. Hester wished to know of his career.

Suddenly Octavia had become more than just the victim of the crime, a face Hester had never seen and therefore for whom she felt no sense of personality. Since listening to Septimus, Octavia's emotions had become real, her feelings those Hester might so easily have had herself, had she loved and been loved by any of the young officers she had known.

She climbed the steps of the War Office and addressed the man at the door with all the courtesy and charm she could muster, plus, of course, the due deference from a woman to a man of the military, and just a touch of her own authority, which was the least difficult, since it came to her quite naturally.

"Good afternoon, sir," she began with an inclination of her head and a smile of friendly openness. "I wonder if I might be permitted to speak with Major Geoffrey Tallis? If you would give him my name I believe he will know it. I was one of Miss Nightingale's nurses"—she was not above using that magic name if it would help—"and I had occasion to tend Major Tallis in Scutari when he was injured. It concerns the death of a widow of a former officer of distinction, and there is a matter to which Major Tallis may be able to assist—with information that would considerably ease the family's distress. Would you be good enough to have that message conveyed to him?"

It was apparently the right mixture of supplication, good reasoning, feminine appeal, and the authority of a nurse which draws from most well-bred men an automatic obedience.

"I will certainly have that message delivered to him, ma'am," he agreed, standing a trifle straighter. "What name shall I give?"

"Hester Latterly," she answered. "I regret seeking him at

such short notice, but I am still nursing a gentleman late of active service, and he is not well enough that I should leave him for above a few hours." That was a very elastic version of the truth, but not quite a downright lie.

"Of course." His respect increased. He wrote down the name "Hester Latterly" and added a note as to her occupation and the urgency of her call, summoned an orderly and dispatched him with the message to Major Tallis.

Hester was quite happy to wait in silence, but the doorman seemed disposed to converse, so she answered his questions on the battles she had witnessed and found they had both been present at the battle of Inkermann. They were deep in reminiscences when the orderly returned to say Major Tallis would receive Miss Latterly in ten minutes, if she would care to wait upon him in his office.

She accepted with a trifle more haste than she had meant to; it was a definite subtraction from the dignity she had tried to establish, but she thanked the doorman for his courtesy. Then she walked very uprightly behind the orderly inside the entrance hall, up the wide staircase and into the endless corridors until she was shown into a waiting room with several chairs, and left.

It was rather more than ten minutes before Major Tallis opened the inner door. A dapper lieutenant walked out past Hester, apparently without seeing her, and she was shown in.

Geoffrey Tallis was a handsome man in his late thirties, an ex–cavalry officer who had been given an administrative post after a serious injury, from which he still walked with a limp. But without Hester's care he might well have lost his leg altogether and been unable to continue a career of any sort. His face lit with pleasure when he saw her, and he held out his hand in welcome.

She gave him hers and he grasped it hard.

"My dear Miss Latterly, what a remarkable pleasure to see you again, and in so much more agreeable circumstances. I hope you are well, and that things prosper with you?"

She was quite honest, not for any purpose but because the words were spoken before she thought otherwise.

"I am very well, thank you, and things prosper only moderately. My parents died, and I am obliged to make my way, but I have the means, so I am fortunate. But I admit it is hard

315

to adjust to England again, and to peace, where everyone's preoccupations are so different—'' She left the wealth of implication unsaid: the withdrawing room manners, the stiff skirts, the emphasis on social position and manners. She could see that he read it all in her face, and his own experiences had been sufficiently alike for more explanation to be redundant.

"Oh indeed.'' He sighed, letting go of her hand. "Please be seated and tell me what I may do to be of help to you.''

She knew enough not to waste his time. The preliminaries had already been dealt with.

"What can you tell me of Captain Harry Haslett, who was killed at Balaclava? I ask because his widow has recently met a most tragic death. I am acquainted with her mother; indeed I have been nursing her through her time of bereavement, and am presently nursing her uncle, a retired officer.'' If he asked her Septimus's name she would affect not to know the circumstances of his "retirement.''

Major Tallis's face clouded over immediately.

"An excellent officer, and one of the nicest men I ever knew. He was a fine commander of men. It came to him naturally because he had courage and a sense of justice that men admired. There was humor in him, and some love of adventure, but not bravado. He never took unnecessary chances.'' He smiled with great sadness. "I think more than most men, he wanted to live. He had a great love for his wife—in fact the army was not the career he would have chosen; he entered it only to earn himself the means to support his wife in the manner he wished and to make some peace with his father-in-law, Sir Basil Moidore—who paid for his commission as a wedding gift, I believe, and watched over his career with keen interest. What an ironic tragedy.''

"Ironic?'' she said quickly.

His face creased with pain and his voice lowered instinctively, but his words were perfectly clear.

"It was Sir Basil who arranged his promotion, and thus his transfer from the regiment in which he was to Lord Cardigan's Light Brigade, and of course they led the charge at Balaclava. If he had remained a lieutenant as he was, he would very probably be alive today.''

"What happened?'' An awful possibility was opening up in front of her, so ugly she could not bear to look at it, nor yet

316

could she look away. "Do you know of whom Sir Basil asked his favor? A great deal of honor depends upon it," she pressed with all the gravity she could. "And, I am beginning to think, the truth of Octavia Haslett's death. Please, Major Tallis, tell me about Captain Haslett's promotion?"

He hesitated only a moment longer. The debt he owed her, their common memories, and his admiration and grief over Haslett's death prevailed.

"Sir Basil is a man of great power and influence, perhaps you are not aware quite how much. He has far more wealth than he displays, although that is considerable, but he also had obligations owed him, debts both of assistance and of finance from the past, and I think a great deal of knowledge—" He left the uses of that unspoken. "He would not find it difficult to accomplish the transfer of an officer from one regiment to another in order to achieve his promotion, if he wished it. A letter—sufficient money to purchase the new commission—"

"But how would Sir Basil know whom to approach in the new regiment?" she pressed, the idea taking firmer shape in her mind all the time.

"Oh—because he is quite well acquainted with Lord Cardigan, who would naturally be aware of all the possible vacancies in command."

"And of the nature of the regiment," she added.

"Of course." He looked puzzled.

"And their likely dispositions?"

"Lord Cardigan would—naturally. But Sir Basil hardly—"

"You mean Sir Basil was unaware of the course of the campaign and the personalities of the commanders?" She allowed the heavy doubt through her expression for him to see.

"Well—" He frowned, beginning to glimpse what he also found too ugly to contemplate. "Of course I am not privy to his communication with Lord Cardigan. Letters to and from the Crimea take a considerable time; even on the fastest packet boats it would not be less than ten or fourteen days. Things can change greatly in that time. Battles can be won or lost and a great deal of ground altered between opposing forces."

"But regiments do not change their natures, Major." She forced him to realism. "A competent commander knows which regiments he would choose to lead a charge, the more desperate the charge the more certain would he be to pick exactly the right man—and the right captain, who had courage, flair, and the absolute loyalty of his men. He would also choose someone tried in the field, yet uninjured so far, and not weary from defeat, or failure, or so scarred in spirit as to be uncertain of his mettle."

He stared at her without speaking.

"In fact once raised to captain, Harry Haslett would be ideal, would he not?"

"He would," he said almost under his breath.

"And Sir Basil saw to his promotion and his change of posting to Lord Cardigan's Light Brigade. Do you suppose any of the correspondence on the subject is still extant?"

"Why, Miss Latterly? What is it you are seeking?"

To lie to him would be contemptible—and also alienate his sympathies.

"The truth about Octavia Haslett's death," she answered.

He sighed heavily. "Was she not murdered by some servant or other? I seem to recollect seeing it in the newspapers. The man was just hanged, was he not?"

"Yes," she agreed with a heavy weariness of failure inside her. "But the day she died she learned something which shook her so deeply she told her uncle it was the most dreadful truth, and she wanted only one more piece of evidence to prove it. I am beginning to believe that it may have concerned the death of her husband. She was thinking of it the day of her own death. We had previously assumed that what she discovered concerned her family still living, but perhaps it did not. Major Tallis, would it be possible to learn if she came here that day—if she saw someone?"

Now he looked very troubled.

"What day was it?"

She told him.

He pulled a bell rope and a young officer appeared and snapped to attention.

"Payton, will you convey my compliments to Colonel Sidgewick and ask him if at any time around the end of November last year the widow of Captain Harry Haslett called upon his office. It is a matter of considerable importance, concerning both honor and life, and I would be most obliged if he would give me an answer of exactness as soon as may be possible. This lady, who is one of Miss Nightingale's nurses, is waiting upon the answer."

"Sir!" The junior snapped to attention once again, turned on his heel and departed.

While he was gone Major Tallis apologized for requiring Hester to spend her time in the waiting room, but he had other business obligations which he must discharge. She understood and assured him it was precisely what she expected and was perfectly content. She would write letters and otherwise occupy herself.

It was not long, a matter of fifteen or twenty minutes, before the door opened and the lieutenant returned. As soon as he left, Major Tallis called Hester in. His face was white, his eyes full of anxiety and fearful pity.

"You were perfectly correct," he said very quietly. "Octavia Haslett was here on the afternoon of her death, and she spoke with Colonel Sidgewick. She learned from him exactly what you learned from me, and from her words and expression on hearing, it appears she drew the same conclusions. I am most profoundly grieved, and I feel guilty—I am not sure for what. Perhaps that the whole matter occurred, and no one did anything to prevent it. Truly, Miss Latterly, I am deeply sorry."

"Thank you—thank you, Major Tallis." She forced a sickly smile, her mind whirling. "I am most grateful to you."

"What are you going to do?" he said urgently.

"I don't know. I'm not sure what I can do. I shall consult with the police officer on the case; I think that would be wisest."

"Please do, Miss Latterly—please be most careful. I—"

"I know," she said quickly. "I have learned much in confidence. Your name will not be mentioned, I give you my word. Now I must go. Thank you again." And without waiting for him to add anything further, she turned and left, almost running down the long corridor and making three wrong turnings before she finally came to the exit.

She found Monk at some inconvenience, and was obliged to wait at his lodgings until after dark, when he returned home. He was startled to see her.

"Hester! What has happened? You look fearful."

"Thank you," she said acidly, but she was too full of her

319

news to carry even an irritation for more than an instant. "I have just been to the War Office—at least I was this afternoon. I have been waiting here for you interminably—"

"The War Office." He took off his wet hat and overcoat, the rain falling from them in a little puddle on the floor. "From your expression I assume you learned something of interest?"

Only hesitating to draw breath when it was strictly necessary, she told him everything she had learned from Septimus, then all that had been said from the instant of entering Major Tallis's office.

"If that was where Octavia had been on the afternoon of her death," she said urgently, "if she learned what I did today, then she must have gone back to Queen Anne Street believing that her father had deliberately contrived her husband's promotion and transfer from what was a fine middle-order regiment to Lord Cardigan's Light Brigade, where he would be honor- and duty-bound to lead a charge in which casualties would be murderous." She refused to visualize it, but it crowded close at the back of her mind. "Cardigan's reputation is well known. Many would be bound to die in the first onslaught itself, but even of those who survived it, many would be so seriously wounded the field surgeons could do little to help them. They'd be transferred piled one upon another in open carts to the hospital in Scutari, and there they'd face a long convalescence where gangrene, typhus, cholera and other fevers killed even more than the sword or the cannon had."

He did not interrupt her.

"Once he was promoted," she went on, "his chances of glory, which he did not want, were very slight; his chances of death, quick or slow, were appallingly high.

"If Octavia did learn this, no wonder she went home ashen-faced and did not speak at dinner. Previously she thought it fate and the chances of war which bereaved her of the husband she loved so deeply and left her a dependent widow in her father's house, without escape." She shivered. "Trapped even more surely than before."

Monk agreed tacitly, allowing her to go on uninterrupted.

"Now she discovered it was not a blind misfortune which had taken everything from her." She leaned forward. "But a deliberate betrayal, and she was imprisoned with her betrayer, day after day, for as far as she could see into a gray future.

"Then what did she do? Perhaps when everyone else was asleep, she went to her father's study and searched his desk for letters, the communication which would prove beyond doubt the terrible truth." She stopped.

"Yes," he said very slowly. "Yes—then what? Basil purchased Harry's commission, and then when he proved a fine officer, prevailed upon his friends and purchased him a higher commission in a gallant and reckless regiment. In whose eyes would that be more than a very understandable piece of favor seeking?"

"No one's," she answered bitterly. "He would protest innocence. How could he know Harry Haslett would lead in the charge and fall?"

"Exactly," he said quickly. "These are the fortunes of war. If you marry a soldier, it is the chance you take—all women do. He would say he grieved for her, but she was wickedly ungrateful to charge him with culpability in it all. Perhaps she had taken a little too much wine with dinner—a fault which she was apt to indulge rather often lately. I can imagine Basil's face as he said it, and his expression of distaste."

She looked at Monk urgently. "That would be useless. Octavia knew her father and was the only one who had ever had the courage to defy him—and reap his revenge.

"But what defiance was left her? She had no allies. Cyprian was content to remain a prisoner in Queen Anne Street. To an extent he had a hostage to fortune in Romola, who obeyed her own instinct for survival, which would never include disobeying Basil. Fenella was uninterested in anyone but herself, Araminta seemed to be on her father's side in apparently everything. Myles Kellard was an additional problem, hardly a solution. And he too would never override Basil's wishes; certainly he would not do it for someone else!"

"Lady Moidore?" he prompted.

"She seemed driven, or else had retreated, to the periphery of things. She fought for Octavia's marriage in the first place, but after that it seems her resources were spent. Septimus might have fought for her, but he had no weapons."

"And Harry was dead." He took up the thread. "Leaving a void in her life nothing else could begin to heal. She must have felt an overwhelming despair, grief, betrayal and a sense of being trapped that were almost beyond endurance, and she was without a weapon to fight back."

"Almost?" she demanded. "Almost beyond endurance? Tired, stunned, confused and alone—what is 'almost' about it? And she did have a weapon, whether she intended it as such or not. Perhaps the thought had never entered her mind, but scandal would hurt Basil more than anything else—the fearful scandal of a suicide." Her voice became harsh with the tragedy and the irony of it. "His daughter, living in his home, under his care, so wretched, so comfortless, so un-Christian as to take her own life, not peacefully with laudanum, not even over the rejection of a lover, and it was too late to be the shock of Harry's death, but deliberately and bloodily in her own bedroom. Or perhaps even in his study with the betraying letter in her hand.

"She would be buried in unhallowed ground, with other sinners beyond forgiveness. Can you imagine what people would say? The shame of it, the looks, the whispers, the sudden silences. The invitations that would no longer come, the people one calls upon who would be unaccountably not at home, in spite of the fact that their carriages were in the mews and all the lights blazing. And where there had been admiration and envy, now there would be contempt—and worst of all, derision."

His face was very grave, the dark tragedy of it utterly apparent.

"If it had not been Annie who had found her, but someone else," he said, "one of the family, it would have been an easy thing to remove the knife, put her on the bed, tear her nightgown to make it seem as if there had been some struggle, however brief, then break the creeper outside the window and take a few ornaments and jewels. Then it would seem murder, appalling, grieving, but not shameful. There would be acute sympathy, no ostracism, no blame. It could happen to anyone.

"Then I seemed about to ruin it all by proving that no one had broken into the house, so a murderer must be found among the residents."

"So that is the crime—not the stabbing of Octavia, but the slow, judicial murder of Percival. How hideous, how immeasurably worse," she said slowly. "But how can we possibly prove it? They will go undiscovered and unpunished. They will get away with it! Whoever it is—"

"What a nightmare. But who? I still don't know. The scandal would harm them all. It could have been Cyprian and Romola, or even Cyprian alone. He is a big man, quite strong enough to carry Octavia from the study, if that was where it happened, up to her room and lay her on the bed. He would not even run much risk of disturbing anyone, since his room was next to hers."

It was a startlingly distressing thought. Cyprian's face with its imagination and capacity for humor and pain came sharply to her mind. It would be like him to want to conceal his sister's act, to save her name and see that she might be grieved for, and buried in holy ground.

But Percival had been hanged for it.

"Was Cyprian so weak he would have permitted that, knowing Percival could not be guilty?" she said aloud. She wished profoundly she could dismiss that as impossible, but Cyprian yielding to Romola's emotional pressure was too clear in her mind, as was the momentary desperation she had seen in his face when she had watched him unobserved. And he of all of them seemed to grieve most deeply for Octavia, with the most wounding pity.

"Septimus?" Monk asked.

It was the kind of reckless, compassionate act Septimus might perform.

"No," she denied vehemently. "No—he would never permit Percival to hang."

"Myles would." Monk was looking at her with intense emotion now, his face bleak and strained. "He would have done it to save the family name. His own status is tied inextricably with the Moidores'— in fact it is totally dependent on it. Araminta might have helped him—and might not."

A sharp memory returned to Hester of Araminta in the library, and of the charged emotion between her and Myles. Surely she knew he had not killed Octavia—and yet she was prepared to let Monk think he had, and watch Myles sweat with fear. That was a very peculiar kind of hatred—and power. Was it fueled by the horror of her own wedding night and its violence, or by his rape of the maid Martha—or by the fact that they were conspirators in concealing the manner of Octavia's death, and then of allowing Percival to hang for it?

"Or Basil himself?" she suggested.

"Or even Basil for reputation—and Lady Moidore for love?" he said. "In fact Fenella is the only one for whom I can find no reason and no means." His face was white, and there was a look of such grief and guilt in his eyes she felt the most intense admiration for his inner honesty, and a warmth towards the pity he was capable of but so rarely showed.

"Of course it is all only speculation," she said much more gently. "I know of no proof for any of it. Even if we had learned this before Percival was ever charged, I cannot even imagine how we might prove it. That is why I have come to you—and of course I wished to share the knowledge with you."

There was a look of profound concentration on his face. She waited, hearing the sounds of Mrs. Worley working in the kitchen and the rattle of hansoms and a dray cart passing in the street outside.

"If she killed herself," he said at last, "then someone removed the knife at the time they discovered her body, and presumably replaced it in the kitchen—or possibly kept it, but that seems unlikely. It does not seem, so far as we can see, the act of someone in panic. If they put the knife back . . . no." His face screwed up in impatience. "They certainly did not put the peignoir back. They must have hidden them both in some place we did not search. And yet we found no trace of anyone having left the house between the time of her death and the time the police constable and the doctor were called." He stared at her, as if seeking her thoughts, and yet he continued to speak. "In a house with as many staff as that, and maids up at five, it would be difficult to leave unseen—and to be sure of being unseen."

"But surely there were places in the family's rooms you did not search?" she said.

"I imagine so." His face was dark with the ugliness of it. "God! How brutal! They must have kept the knife and the peignoir, stained with her blood, just in case they were needed—to incriminate some poor devil." He shuddered involuntarily, and she felt a sudden coldness in the room that had nothing to do with the meager fire or the steady sleet outside, now turning to snow.

"Perhaps if we could find the hiding place," she said tentatively, "we might know who it was who used it?"

He laughed, a jerky, painful sound.

"The person who put it in Percival's room behind the drawers in his dresser? I don't think we can assume that the hiding place incriminates them."

She felt foolish.

"Of course not," she admitted quietly. "Then what can we look for?"

He sank into silence again for a long time, and she waited, racking her brains.

"I don't know," he said at last, with obvious difficulty. "Blood in the study might be indicative—Percival would not have killed her there. The whole premise is that he forced his way into her bedroom and she fought him off and was killed in the process—"

She stood up, suddenly full of energy now that there was something to do.

"I will look for it. It won't be difficult—"

"Be careful," he said so sharply that it was almost a bark. "Hester!"

She opened her mouth to be dismissive, full of the excitement of at last having some idea to pursue.

"Hester!" He caught her by the shoulder, his hands hard.

She winced and would have pulled away had she the strength.

"Hester—listen to me!" he said urgently. "This man—or woman—has done far more than conceal a suicide. They have committed a slow and very deliberate murder." His face was tight with distress. "Have you ever seen a man hanged? I have. And I watched Percival struggle as the net tightened around him for the weeks before—and then I visited him in Newgate. It is a terrible way to die."

She felt a little sick, but she did not retreat.

"They will have no pity for you," he went on relentlessly, "if you threaten them in even the slightest way. In fact I think now that you know this, it would be better if you were to send in your notice. Tell them by letter that you have had an accident and cannot return. No one is needing a nurse; a ladies' maid could perfectly well perform all that Lady Moidore wants."

"I will not." She stood almost chest to chest with him and

325

glared. "I am going back to Queen Anne Street to see if I can discover what really happened to Octavia—and possibly who did it and caused Percival to be hanged." She realized the enormity of what she was saying, but she had left herself no retreat.

"Hester."

"What?"

He took a deep breath and let her go. "Then I will remain in the street nearby, and shall look to see you at least every hour at a window that gives to the street. If I don't, I shall call Evan at the police station and have him enter the place—"

"You can't!" she protested.

"I can!"

"On what pretext, for heaven's sake?"

He smiled with bitter humor. "That you are wanted in connection with a domestic theft. I can always release you afterwards—with unblemished character—a case of mistaken identity."

She was more relieved than she would show.

"I am obliged to you." She tried to say it stiffly, but her emotion showed through, and for a moment they stared at each other with that perfect understanding that occasionally flashed between them. Then she excused herself, picked up her coat again and allowed him to help her into it, and took her leave.

She entered the Queen Anne Street house discreetly and avoided all but the most essential conversation, going upstairs to check that Septimus was still recovering well. He was pleased to see her and greeted her with interest. She found it hard not to tell him anything of her discoveries or conclusions, and she made excuses to escape and go to Beatrice as soon as she could without hurting his feelings.

After she had brought up her dinner she asked permission to retire early, saying she had letters to write, and Beatrice was content to acquiesce.

She slept very restlessly, and it was no difficulty to rise at a little after two in the morning and creep downstairs with a candle. She dared not turn up the gas. It would glare like the sun and be too far away for her to reach to turn it down should she hear anyone else about. She slipped down the female servants' staircase to the landing, then down the main staircase to the hall and into Sir Basil's study. With an unsteady hand she knelt down, candle close to the floor, and searched the red-and-blue Turkey carpet to find an irregularity in the pattern that might mark a bloodstain.

It took her about ten minutes, and it seemed like half the night, before she heard the clock in the hall chime and it nearly startled her into dropping the candle. As it was she spilled hot wax and had to pick it off the wool with her fingernail.

It was then she realized the irregularity was not simply the nature of the carpet maker but an ugliness, an asymmetry nowhere else balanced, and on bending closer she saw how large it was, now nearly washed out, but still quite discernible. It was behind the large oak desk, where one might naturally stand to open any of the small side drawers, only three of which had locks.

She rose slowly to her feet. Her eye went straight to the second drawer, where she could see faint scoring marks around the keyhole, as if someone had forced it open with a crude tool and a replacement lock and repolishing of the bruised wood could not completely hide it.

There was no way in which she could open it; she had neither skill nor instrument—and more than that, she did not wish to alarm the one person who would most notice a further damage to the desk. But she could easily guess what Octavia had found—a letter, or more than one, from Lord Cardigan, and perhaps even the colonel of the regiment, which had confirmed beyond doubt what she already had learned from the War Office.

Hester stood motionless, staring at the desk with its neatly laid-out dish of sand for blotting ink on a letter, sticks of scarlet wax and tapers for seals, stand of carved sardonyx and red jasper for ink and quills, and a long, exquisite paper knife in imitation of the legendary sword of King Arthur, embedded in its magical stone. It was a beautiful thing, at least ten inches long and with an engraved hilt. The stone itself which formed its stand was a single piece of yellow agate, the largest she had ever seen.

She stood, imagining Octavia in exactly the same spot, her mind whirling with misery, loneliness and the ultimate defeat. She must have stared at that beautiful thing as well.

Slowly Hester reached out her hand and took it. If she had

327

been Octavia she would not have gone to the kitchen for Mrs. Boden's carving knife; she would have used this lovely thing. She took it out slowly, feeling its balance and the sharpness of its tip. It was many seconds in the silent house, the snow falling past the uncurtained window, before she noticed the faint dark line around the joint between the blade and the hilt. She moved it to within a few inches of the candle's flame. It was brown, not the gray darkness of tarnish or inlaid dirt, but the rich, reddish brown of dried blood.

No wonder Mrs. Boden had not missed her knife until just before she told Monk of it. It had probably been there in its rack all the time; she simply confused herself with what she assumed to be the facts.

But there had been blood on the knife they found. Whose blood, if this slender paper knife was what had killed Octavia?

Not whose. It was a kitchen knife—a good cook's kitchen would have plenty of blood available from time to time. One roast, one fish to be gutted, or a chicken. Who could tell the difference between one sort of blood and another?

And if it was not Octavia's blood on the knife, was it hers on the peignoir?

Then a sudden shaft of memory caught her with a shock like cold water. Had not Beatrice said something about Octavia having torn her peignoir, the lace, and not being skilled at such fine needlework, she had accepted Beatrice's offer to mend it for her? Which would mean she had not even been wearing it when she died. But no one knew that except Beatrice—and out of sensitivity to her grief, no one had shown her the blood-soaked garment. Araminta had identified it as being the one Octavia had worn to her room that night—and so it was—at least as far as the upstairs landing. Then she had gone to say good-night to her mother and left the garment there.

Rose too could be mistaken, for the same reason. She would only know it was Octavia's, not when she had worn it.

Or would she? She would at least know when it was last laundered. It was her duty to wash and iron such things—and to mend them should it be necessary. How had she overlooked mending the lace? A laundrymaid should do better.

She would have to ask her about it in the morning.

Suddenly she was returned to the present—and the realization that she was standing in her nightgown in Sir Basil's study, in exactly the same spot where Octavia in her despair must have killed herself—holding the same blade in her hand. If anyone found her here she would have not a shred of an excuse—and if it was whoever found Octavia, they would see immediately that she also knew.

The candle was low and the bowl filling with melted wax. She replaced the knife, setting it exactly as it had been, then picked up the candle and went as quickly as she could to the door and opened it almost soundlessly. The hallway was in darkness; she could make out only the dimmest luminescence from the window that faced onto the front of the house, and the falling snow.

Silently she tiptoed across the hall, the tiles cold on her bare feet, and up the stairs, seeing only a tiny pool of light around herself, barely enough to place her feet without tripping. At the top she crossed the landing and with difficulty found the bottom of the female servants' stairway.

At last in her own room she snuffed out the candle and climbed into her cold bed. She was chilled and shaking, the perspiration wet on her body and her stomach sick.

In the morning it took all the self-control she possessed to see first to Beatrice's comfort, and her breakfast, and then to Septimus, and to leave him without seeming hasty or neglectful in her duty. It was nearly ten o'clock before she was able to make her way to the laundry and find Rose.

"Rose," she began quietly, not to catch Lizzie's attention. She would certainly want to know what was going on, to supervise if it was any kind of work, and to prevent it until a more suitable time if it was not.

"What do you want?" Rose looked pale; her skin had lost its porcelain clarity and bloom and her eyes were very dark, almost hollow. She had taken Percival's death hard. There was some part of her still intrigued by him, and perhaps she was haunted by her own evidence and the part she had played before the arrest, the petty malice and small straw of direction that might have led Monk to him.

"Rose," Hester spoke again, urgently, to draw Rose's attention away from the apron of Dinah's she was smoothing with the flatiron. "It is about Miss Octavia—"

329

"What about her?" Rose was uninterested, and her hand moved back and forth with the iron, her eyes bent on her work.

"You cared for her clothes, didn't you? Or was it Lizzie?"

"No." Still Rose did not look at her. "Lizzie usually cared for Lady Moidore's and Miss Araminta's, and sometimes Mrs. Cyprian's. I did Miss Octavia's, and the gentlemen's linens, and we split the maids' aprons and caps as the need came. Why? What does it matter now?"

"When was the last time you laundered Miss Octavia's peignoir with the lace lilies on it—before she was killed?"

Rose put down the iron at last and turned to Hester with a frown. She considered for several minutes before she answered.

"I ironed it the morning before, and took it up about noon. She wore it that night, I expect—" She took a deep breath. "And I heard she did the night after, and was killed in it."

"Was it torn?"

Rose's face tightened. "Of course not. Do you think I don't know my job?"

"If she had torn it the first night, would she have given it to you to mend?"

"More probably Mary, but then Mary might have brought it to me—she's competent, and pretty good at altering tailored things and dinner gowns, but those lilies are very fine work. Why? What does it matter now?" Her face screwed up. "Anyway, Mary must have mended it, because I didn't—and it wasn't torn when the police gave it to me to identify; the lilies and all the lace were perfect."

Hester felt a sick excitement.

"Are you sure? Are you absolutely sure—to swear someone's life on?"

Rose looked as if she had been struck; the last vestige of blood left her face.

"Who is there to swear for? Percival's already dead! You know that! What's wrong with you? Why do you care now about a piece of lace?"

"Are you?" Hester insisted. "Are you absolutely sure?"

"Yes I am." Rose was angry because she did not understand Hester's insistence and it frightened her. "It wasn't torn when the police showed it to me with the blood on it. That part of it wasn't stained, and it was perfectly all right."

"You couldn't be mistaken? Is there more than one piece of lace on it?"

"Not like that." She shook her head. "Look, Miss Latterly, whatever you may think of me, and it shows in your hoity-toity manners—I know my job and I know a shoulder from a hem of a peignoir. The lace was not torn when I sent it up from the laundry, and it was not torn when I identified it for the police—for any good that does anyone."

"It does a lot," Hester said quietly. "Now would you swear to it?"

"Why?"

"Would you?" Hester could have shaken her in sheer frustration.

"Swear to who?" Rose persisted. "What does it matter now?" Her face worked as if some tremendous emotion shook her. "You mean—" She could hardly find the words. "You mean—it wasn't Percival who killed her?"

"No—I don't think so."

Rose was very white, her skin pinched. "God! Then who?"

"I don't know—and if you've any sense at all, and any desire to keep your life, let alone your job, you'll say nothing to anyone."

"But how do you know?" Rose persisted.

"You are better not understanding—believe me!"

"What are you going to do?" Her voice was very quiet, but there was anxiety in it, and fear.

"Prove it—if I can."

At that moment Lizzie came over, her lips tight with irritation.

"If you need something laundered, Miss Latterly, please ask me and I will see it is done, but don't stand here gossiping with Rose—she has work to do."

"I'm sorry," Hester apologized, forcing a sweet smile, and fled.

She was back in the main house and halfway up the stairs to Beatrice's room before her thoughts cleared. If the peignoir was whole when Rose sent it up, and whole when it was found in Percival's room, but torn when Octavia went to say good-night to her mother, then she must have torn it some time during that day, and no one but Beatrice had noticed. She had not been wearing it when she died; it had been in Beatrice's

331

room. Some time between Octavia leaving it there and its being discovered, someone had taken it, and a knife from the kitchen, covered the knife in blood and wrapped the peignoir around it, then hidden them in Percival's room.

But who?

When had Beatrice mended it? Surely that night? Why would she bother after she knew Octavia was dead?

Then where had it been? Presumably lying in the workbasket in Beatrice's room. No one would care about it greatly after that. Or was it returned to Octavia's room? Yes, surely returned, since otherwise whoever had taken it would realize their mistake and know Octavia had not been wearing it when she went to bed.

She was on the top stair on the landing now. It had stopped raining and the sharp, pale winter sun shone in through the windows, making patterns on the carpet. She had passed no one else. The maids were all busy about their duties, the ladies' maids attending to wardrobe, the housekeeper in her linen room, the upstairs maids making beds, turning mattresses and dusting everything, the tweeny somewhere in the passageway. Dinah and the footmen were somewhere in the front of the house, the family about their morning pleasures, Romola in the schoolroom with the children, Araminta writing letters in the boudoir, the men out, Beatrice still in her bedroom.

Beatrice was the only one who knew about the torn lily, so she would not make the mistake of staining that peignoir—not that Hester had ever suspected her in the first place, or certainly not alone. She might have done it with Sir Basil, but then she was also frightened that someone had murdered Octavia, and she did not know who. Indeed she feared it might have been Myles. Hester considered for only an instant that Beatrice might have been a superb actress, then she abandoned it. To begin with, why should she? She had no idea Hester would repeat anything she said, let alone everything.

Who knew which peignoir Octavia wore that evening? She had left the withdrawing room fully dressed in a dinner gown, as did all the women. Whom had she seen after changing for the night but before retiring?

Only Araminta—and her mother.

Proud, difficult, cold Araminta. It was she who had hidden

332

her sister's suicide, and when it was inevitable that someone should be blamed for murder, contrived that it should be Percival.

But she could not have done it alone. She was thin, almost gaunt. She could never have carried Octavia's body upstairs. Who had helped her? Myles? Cyprian? Or Basil?

And how to prove it?

The only proof was Beatrice's word about the torn lace lilies. But would she swear to that when she knew what it meant?

Hester needed an ally in the house. She knew Monk was outside; she had seen his dark figure every time she had passed the window, but he could not help in this.

Septimus. He was the one person she was sure was not involved, and who might have the courage to fight. And it would take courage. Percival was dead and to everyone else the matter was closed. It would be so much easier to let it all lie.

She changed her direction and instead of going to Beatrice's room went on along the passage to Septimus's.

He was propped up on the bed reading with the book held far in front of him for his longsighted eyes. He looked up with surprise when she came in. He was so much better her attentions were more in the nature of friendship than any medical need. He saw instantly that there was something gravely concerning her.

"What has happened?" he asked anxiously. He set the book down without marking the page.

There was nothing to be served by prevarication. She closed the door and came over and sat on the bed.

"I have made a discovery about Octavia's death—in fact two."

"And they are very grave," he said earnestly. "I see that they trouble you. What are they?"

She took a deep breath. If she was mistaken, and he was implicated, or more loyal to the family, less brave than she believed, then she might be endangering herself more than she could cope with. But she would not retreat now.

"She did not die in her bedroom. I have found where she died." She watched his face. There was nothing but interest. No start of guilt. "In Sir Basil's study," she finished.

He was confused. "In Basil's study? But, my dear, that

333

doesn't make any sense! Why would Percival have gone to her there? And what was she doing there in the middle of the night anyway?'' Then slowly the light faded from his face. "Oh—you mean that she did learn something that day, and you know what it was? Something to do with Basil?''

She told him what she had learned at the War Office, and that Octavia had been there the day of her death and learned the same.

"Oh dear God!'' he said quietly. "The poor child—poor, poor child.'' For several seconds he stared at the coverlet, then at last he looked up at her, his face pinched, his eyes grim and frightened. "Are you saying that Basil killed her?''

"No. I believe she killed herself—with the paper knife there in the study.''

"Then how did she get up to the bedroom?''

"Someone found her, cleaned the knife and returned it to its stand, then carried her upstairs and broke the creeper outside the window, took a few items of jewelry and a silver vase, and left her there for Annie to discover in the morning.''

"So that it should not be seen as suicide, with all the shame and scandal—'' He drew a deep breath and his eyes widened in appalled horror. "But dear God! They let Percival hang for it!''

"I know.''

"But that's monstrous. It's murder.''

"I know that.''

"Oh—dear heaven,'' he said very quietly. "What have we sunk to? Do you know who it was?''

She told him about the peignoir.

"Araminta,'' he said very quietly. "But not alone. Who helped her? Who carried poor Octavia up the stairs?''

"I don't know. It must have been a man—but I don't know who.''

"And what are you going to do about this?''

"The only person who can prove any of it is Lady Moidore. I think she would want to. She knows it was not Percival, and I believe she might find any alternative better than the uncertainty and the fear eating away at all her relationships forever.''

"Do you?'' He thought about it for some time, his hand curling and uncurling on the bedspread. "Perhaps you are right. But whether you are or not, we cannot let it pass like this—whatever its cost."

"Then will you come with me to Lady Moidore and see if she will swear to the peignoir's being torn the night of Octavia's death and in her room all night, and then returned some time later?"

"Yes." He moved to climb to his feet, and she put out both her hands to help him. "Yes," he agreed again. "The least I can do is be there—poor Beatrice."

He had not yet fully understood.

"But will you swear to her answer, if need be before a judge? Will you strengthen her when she realizes what it means?"

He straightened up until he stood very erect, shoulders back, chest out.

"Yes, yes I will."

Beatrice was startled to see Septimus behind Hester when they entered her room. She was sitting at the dressing table brushing her hair. This was something which would ordinarily have been done by her maid, but since it was not necessary to dress it, she was going nowhere, she had chosen to do it herself.

"What is it?" she said quietly. "What has happened? Septimus, are you worse?"

"No, my dear." He moved closer to her. "I am perfectly well. But something has happened about which it is necessary that you make a decision, and I am here to lend you my support."

"A decision? What do you mean?" Already she was frightened. She looked from him to Hester. "Hester? What is it? You know something, don't you?" She drew in her breath and made as if to ask, then her voice died and no sound came. Slowly she put the hairbrush down.

"Lady Moidore," Hester began gently. It was cruel to spin it out. "On the night she died, you said Octavia came to your room to wish you good-night."

"Yes—" It was barely even a whisper.

"And that her peignoir was torn across the lace lilies on the shoulder?"

"Yes—"

"Are you absolutely sure?"

335

Beatrice was puzzled, some small fraction of her fear abating.

"Yes, of course I am. I offered to mend it for her." The tears welled up in her eyes, beyond her control. "I did—" She gulped and fought to master her emotion. "I did—that night, before I went to sleep. I mended them perfectly."

Hester wanted to touch her, to take her hands and hold them, but she was about to deal another terrible blow, and it seemed such hypocrisy, a Judas kiss.

"Would you swear to that, on your honor?"

"Of course—but who can care—now?"

"You are quite sure, Beatrice?" Septimus knelt down awkwardly in front of her, touching her with clumsy, tender hands. "You will not take that back, should it become painful in its meanings?"

She stared at him. "It is the truth—why? What are its meanings, Septimus?"

"That Octavia killed herself, my dear, and that Araminta and someone else conspired to conceal it, to protect the honor of the family." It was so easily encapsulated, all in one sentence.

"Killed herself? But why? Harry has been dead for—for two years."

"Because she learned that day how and why he died." He spared her the last, ugly details, at least for now. "It was more than she could bear."

"But Septimus." Now her mouth and throat were so dry she could scarcely force the words. "They hanged Percival for killing her!"

"I know that, my dear. That is why we must speak."

"Someone in my house—in my family—murdered Percival!"

"Yes."

"Septimus, I don't know how I can bear it!"

"There is nothing to do but bear it, Beatrice." His voice was very gentle, but there was no wavering in it. "We cannot run away. There is no way of denying it without making it immeasurably worse."

She clutched his hand and looked at Hester.

"Who was it?" she said, her voice barely trembling now, her eyes direct.

336

"Araminta," Hester replied.

"Not alone."

"No. I don't know who helped her."

Beatrice put her hands very slowly over her face. She knew—and Hester realized it when she saw her clenched knuckles and heard her gasp. But she did not ask. Instead she looked for a moment at Septimus, then turned and walked very slowly out of the room, down the main stairs, and out of the front door into the street to where Monk was standing in the rain.

Gravely, with the rain soaking her hair and her dress, oblivious of it, she told him.

Monk went straight to Evan, and Evan took it to Runcorn.

"Balderdash!" Runcorn said furiously. "Absolute balderdash! Whatever put such a farrago of total nonsense in your head? The Queen Anne Street case is closed. Now get on with your present case, and if I hear any more about this you will be in serious trouble. Do I make myself clear, Sergeant?" His long face was suffused with color. "You are a great deal too like Monk for your own good. The sooner you forget him and all his arrogance, the better chance you will have of making yourself a career in the police force."

"You won't question Lady Moidore again?" Evan persisted.

"Great guns, Evan. What is wrong with you? No I won't. Now get out of here and go and do your job."

Evan stood to attention for a moment, the words of disgust boiling up inside him, then turned on his heel and went out. But instead of returning to his new inspector, or to any part of his present case, he found a hansom cab and directed it to take him to the offices of Oliver Rathbone.

Rathbone received him as soon as he could decently dismiss his current, rather garrulous client.

"Yes?" he said with great curiosity. "What is it?"

Clearly and concisely Evan told him what Hester had done, and saw with a mixture of emotions the acute interest with which Rathbone listened, and the alternating fear and amusement in his face, the anger and the sudden gentleness. Young as Evan was, he recognized it as an involvement of more than intellectual or moral concern.

337

Then he recounted what Monk had added, and his own still smoldering experience with Runcorn.

"Indeed," Rathbone said slowly and with deep thought. "Indeed. Very slender, but it does not take a thick rope to hang a man, only a strong one—and I think this may indeed be strong enough."

"What will you do?" Evan asked. "Runcorn won't look at it."

Rathbone smiled, a neat, beautiful gesture. "Did you imagine he might?"

"No—but—" Evan shrugged.

"I shall take it to the Home Office." Rathbone crossed his legs and placed his fingers tip to tip. "Now tell me again, every detail, and let me be sure."

Obediently Evan repeated every word.

"Thank you." Rathbone rose to his feet. "Now if you will accompany me I shall do what I can—and if we are successful, you may choose yourself a constable and we shall make an arrest. I think perhaps we had better be quick." His face darkened. "From what you say, Lady Moidore at least is already aware of the tragedy to shatter her house."

Hester had told Monk all she knew. Against his wishes she had returned to the house, soaked and bedraggled and without an excuse. She met Araminta on the stairs.

"Good heavens," Araminta said with incredulity and amusement. "You look as if you have taken a bath with all your clothes on. Whatever possessed you to go out in this without your coat and bonnet?"

Hester scrambled for an excuse and found none at all.

"It was quite stupid of me," she said as if it were an apology for half-wittedness.

"Indeed it was idiotic!" Araminta agreed. "What were you thinking of?"

"I—er—"

Araminta's eyes narrowed. "Have you a follower, Miss Latterly?"

An excuse. A perfectly believable excuse. Hester breathed a prayer of gratitude and hung her head, blushing for her carelessness, not for being caught in forbidden behavior.

"Yes ma'am."

"Then you are very lucky," Araminta said tartly. "You are plain enough, and won't see twenty-five again. I should take whatever he offers you." And with that she swept past Hester and went on down the hall.

Hester swore under her breath and raced up the stairs, brushing past an astonished Cyprian without a word, and then up the next flight to her own room, where she changed every item of clothing from the skin out, and spread her wet things the best she could to dry.

Her mind raced. What would Monk do? Take it all to Evan, and thus to Runcorn. She could imagine Runcorn's fury from what Monk had told her of him. But surely now he would have no choice but to reopen the case?

She fiddled on with small duties. She dreaded returning to Beatrice after what she had done, but she had little else justification to be here, and now least of all could she afford to arouse suspicion. And she owed Beatrice something, for all the pain she was awakening, the destruction which could not now be avoided.

Heart lurching and clammy-handed, she went and knocked on Beatrice's door.

They both pretended the morning's conversation had not happened. Beatrice talked lightly of all sorts of things in the past, of her first meeting with Basil and how charmed she had been with him, and a little in awe. She spoke of her girlhood growing up in Buckinghamshire with her sisters, of her uncle's tales of Waterloo and the great eve of battle ball in Brussels, and the victory afterwards, the defeat of the emperor Napoleon and all Europe free again, the dancing, the fireworks, the laughter, the great gowns and the music and fine horses. Once as a child she had been presented to the Iron Duke himself. She recalled it with a smile and a faraway look of almost forgotten pleasure.

Then she spoke of the death of the old king, William IV, and the accession of the young Victoria. The coronation had been splendid beyond imagination. Beatrice had been in the prime of her beauty then, and without conceit she told of the celebrations she and Basil had attended, and how she had been admired.

Luncheon came and went, and tea also, and still she fought

339

off reality with increasing fierceness, the color heightening in her cheeks, her eyes more feverish.

If anyone missed them, they made no sign of it, nor came to seek them.

It was half past four, and already dark, when there was a knock on the door.

Beatrice was ashen white. She looked at Hester once, then with a massive effort said quite levelly, "Come in."

Cyprian came in, his face furrowed with anxiety and puzzlement, not yet fear.

"Mama, the police are here again, not that fellow Monk, but Sergeant Evan and a constable—and that wretched lawyer who defended Percival."

Beatrice rose to her feet; only for a moment did she sway.

"I will come down."

"I am afraid they do wish to speak to all of us, and they refuse to say why. I suppose we had better oblige them, although I cannot think what it can be about now."

"I am afraid, my dear, that it is going to be extremely unpleasant."

"Why? What can there be left to say?"

"A great deal," she replied, and took his arm so that he might support her along the corridor and down the stairs to the withdrawing room, where everyone else was assembled, including Septimus and Fenella. Standing in the doorway were Evan and a uniformed constable. In the middle of the floor was Oliver Rathbone.

"Good afternoon, Lady Moidore," he said gravely. In the circumstances it was a ridiculous form of greeting.

"Good afternoon, Mr. Rathbone," she answered with a slight quiver in her voice. "I imagine you have come to ask me about the peignoir?"

"I have," he said quietly. "I regret that I must do this, but there is no alternative. The footman Harold has permitted me to examine the carpet in the study—" He stopped, and his eyes wandered around the assembled faces. No one moved or spoke.

"I have discovered the bloodstains on the carpet and on the handle of the paper knife." Elegantly he slid the knife out of his pocket and held it, turning it very slowly so its blade caught the light.

Myles Kellard stood motionless, his brows drawn down in disbelief.

Cyprian looked profoundly unhappy.

Basil stared without blinking.

Araminta clenched her hands so hard the knuckles showed, and her skin was as white as paper.

"I suppose there is some purpose to this?" Romola said irritably. "I hate melodrama. Please explain yourself and stop play-acting."

"Oh be quiet!" Fenella snapped. "You hate anything that isn't comfortable and decently domestic. If you can't say something useful, hold your tongue."

"Octavia Haslett died in the study," Rathbone said with a level, careful voice that carried above every other rustle or murmur in the room.

"Good God!" Fenella was incredulous and almost amused. "You don't mean Octavia had an assignation with the footman on the study carpet. How totally absurd—and uncomfortable, when she has a perfectly good bed."

Beatrice swung around and slapped her so hard Fenella fell over sideways and collapsed into one of the armchairs.

"I've wanted to do that for years," Beatrice said with intense satisfaction. "That is probably the only thing that will give me any pleasure at all today. No—you fool. There was no assignation. Octavia discovered how Basil had Harry set at the head of the charge of Balaclava, where so many died, and she felt as trapped and defeated as we all do. She took her own life."

There was an appalled silence until Basil stepped forward, his face gray, his hand shaking. He made a supreme effort.

"That is quite untrue. You are unhinged with grief. Please go to your room, and I shall send for the doctor. For heaven's sake, Miss Latterly, don't stand there, do something!"

"It is true, Sir Basil." She stared at him levelly, for the first time not as a nurse to her employer but as an equal. "I went to the War Office myself, and learned what happened to Harry Haslett, and how you brought it about, and that Octavia had been there the afternoon of her death and heard the same."

Cyprian looked at his father, then at Evan, then at Rathbone.

"But then what was the knife and the peignoir in Percival's

341

room?'' he asked. ''Papa is right. Whatever Octavia learned about Harry, it doesn't make any sense. The evidence was still there. That was Octavia's peignoir, with her blood on it, wrapped around the knife.''

''It was Octavia's peignoir with blood on it,'' Rathbone agreed. ''Wrapped around a knife from the kitchen—but it was not Octavia's blood. She was killed with the paper knife in the study, and when someone found her, they carried her upstairs and put her in her own room to make it seem as if she had been murdered.'' His fastidious face showed distress and contempt. ''No doubt to save the shame of a suicide and the disgrace to the family and all it would cost socially and politically. Then they cleaned the knife and returned it to its place.''

''But the kitchen knife,'' Cyprian repeated. ''And the peignoir. It was hers. Rose identified it, and so did Mary, and more important, Minta saw her in it on the landing that night. And there is blood on it.''

''The kitchen knife could have been taken any time,'' Rathbone said patiently. ''The blood could have come from any piece of meat purchased in the course of ordering supplies for the table—a hare, a goose, a side of beef or mutton—''

''But the peignoir.''

''That is the crux of the whole matter. You see, it was sent up from the laundry the day before, in perfect order, clean and without mark or tear—''

''Of course,'' Cyprian agreed angrily. ''They wouldn't send it up in any other way. What are you talking about, man?''

''On the evening of her death''—Rathbone ignored the interruption, if anything he was even more polite—''Mrs. Haslett retired to her room and changed for the night. Unfortunately the peignoir was torn, we shall probably never know how. She met her sister, Mrs. Kellard, on the landing, and said good-night to her, as you pointed out, and as we know from Mrs. Kellard herself—'' He glanced at Araminta and saw her nod so slightly only the play of light on her glorious hair showed the movement at all. ''And then she went to say good-night to her mother. But Lady Moidore noticed the tear and offered to mend it for her—is that not so, ma'am?''

''Yes—yes it is.'' Beatrice's voice was intended to be low but it was a hoarse whisper, painful in its grief.

''Octavia took it off and gave it to her mother to mend,'

Rathbone said softly, but every word was as distinct as a separate pebble falling into iced water. "She went to bed without it—and she was without it when she went to her father's study in the middle of the night. Lady Moidore mended it, and it was returned to Octavia's room. It was from there that someone took it, knowing Octavia had worn it to bid them goodnight but not that she had left it in her mother's room—"

One by one, first Beatrice, then Cyprian, then the others, they turned to Araminta.

Araminta seemed frozen, her face haggard.

"Dear God in heaven. You let Percival hang for it," Cyprian said at last, his lips stiff, his body hunched as if he had been beaten.

Araminta said nothing; she was as pale as if she herself were dead.

"How did you get her upstairs?" Cyprian asked, his voice rising now as if anger could somehow release a fraction of the pain.

Araminta smiled a slow, ugly smile, a gesture of hate as well as hard, bitter hurt.

"I didn't—Papa did that. Sometimes I thought if it were discovered, I should say it was Myles, for what he did to me, and has done all the years we've been married. But no one would believe it." Her voice was laden with years of impotent contempt. "He hasn't the courage. And he wouldn't lie to protect the Moidores. Papa and I would do that—and Myles wouldn't protect us when it came to the end." She rose to her feet and turned to face Sir Basil. There was a thin trickle of blood running down her fingers from where her nails had gouged the skin of her palms.

"I've loved you all my life, Papa—and you married me to a man who took me by force and used me like a whore." Her bitterness and pain were overwhelming. "You wouldn't let me leave him, because Moidores don't do things like that. It would tarnish the family name, and that's all you care about—power. The power of money—the power of reputation—the power of rank."

Sir Basil stood motionless and appalled, as if he had been struck physically.

"Well, I hid Octavia's suicide to protect the Moidores," Araminta went on, staring at him as if he were the only one who could hear her. "And I helped you hang Percival for it. Well now that we're finished—a scandal—a mockery"—her voice shook on the edge of dreadful laughter—"a byword for murder and corruption—you'll come with me to the gallows for Percival. You're a Moidore, and you'll hang like one—with me!"

"I doubt it will come to that, Mrs. Kellard," Rathbone said, his voice wrung out with pity and disgust. "With a good lawyer you will probably spend the rest of your life in prison—for manslaughter, while distracted with grief—"

"I'd rather hang!" she spat out at him.

"I daresay," he agreed. "But the choice will not be yours." He swung around. "Nor yours, Sir Basil. Sergeant Evan, please do your duty."

Obediently Evan stepped forward and placed the iron manacles on Araminta's thin white wrists. The constable from the doorway did the same to Basil.

Romola began to cry, deep sobs of self-pity and utter confusion.

Cyprian ignored her and went to his mother, quietly putting his arms around her and holding her as if he had been the parent and she the child.

"Don't worry, my dear; we shall take care of you," Septimus said clearly. "I think perhaps we shall eat here tonight and make do with a little hot soup. We may wish to retire early, but I think it will be better if we spend the evening together by the fire. We need each other's company. It is not a time to be alone."

Hester smiled at him and walked over to the window and drew the curtain sufficiently to allow her to stand in the lighted alcove. She saw Monk outside in the snow, waiting, and raised her hand to him in a slight salute so that he would understand.

The front door opened and Evan and the constable led out Basil Moidore and his daughter for the last time.

DEFEND AND BETRAY

To my father

With thanks to Jonathan Manning,
B.A. (Cantab.), for advice on points of law
regarding manslaughter, perverse
verdicts, etc. in 1857.

1

H*ESTER LATTERLY ALIGHTED* from the hansom cab. A two-seater vehicle for hire by the trip, it was a recent and most useful invention enabling one to travel much more cheaply than having to hire a large carriage for the day. Fishing in her reticule, she found the appropriate coin and paid the driver, then turned and walked briskly along Brunswick Place towards Regent's Park, where the daffodils were in full bloom in gold swaths against the dark earth. So they should be; this was April the twenty-first, a full month into the spring of 1857.

She looked ahead to see if she could discern the tall, rather angular figure of Edith Sobell, whom she had come to meet, but she was not yet visible among the courting couples walking side by side, the women's wide crinoline skirts almost touching the gravel of the paths, the men elegant and swaggering very slightly. Somewhere in the distance a band was playing something brisk and martial, the notes of the brass carrying in the slight breeze.

She hoped Edith was not going to be late. It was she who had requested this meeting, and said that a walk in the open would be so much pleasanter than sitting inside in a chocolate shop, or strolling around a museum or a gallery where Edith at least might run into acquaintances and be obliged to in-

1

terrupt her conversation with Hester to exchange polite nonsense.

Edith had all day in which to do more or less as she pleased; indeed, she had said time hung heavily on her hands. But Hester was obliged to earn her living. She was presently employed as a nurse to a retired military gentleman who had fallen and broken his thigh. Since being dismissed from the hospital where she had first found a position on returning from the Crimea—for taking matters into her own hands and treating a patient in the absence of the doctor—Hester had been fortunate to find private positions. It was only her experience in Scutari with Florence Nightingale, ended barely a year since, which had made any further employment possible at all.

The gentleman, Major Tiplady, was recovering well, and had been quite amenable to her taking an afternoon off. But she was loth to spend it waiting in Regent's Park for a companion who did not keep her appointments, even on so pleasant a day. Hester had seen so much incompetence and confusion during the war, deaths that could have been avoided had pride and inefficiency been set aside, that she had a short temper where she judged such failings to exist, and a rather hasty tongue. Her mind was quick, her tastes often unbecomingly intellectual for a woman; such qualities were not admired, and her views, whether right or wrong, were held with too much conviction. Edith would need a very fine reason indeed if she were to be excused her tardiness.

Hester waited a further fifteen minutes, pacing back and forth on the path beside the daffodils, growing more and more irritated and impatient. It was most inconsiderate behavior, particularly since this spot had been chosen for Edith's convenience; she lived in Clarence Gardens, a mere half mile away. Perhaps Hester was angry out of proportion to the offense, and even as her temper rose she was aware of it, and still unable to stop her gloved fists from clenching or her step from getting more rapid and her heels from clicking sharply on the ground.

She was about to abandon the meeting altogether when at

2

last she saw the gawky, oddly pleasing figure of Edith. She was still dressed predominantly in black, still in mourning for her husband, although he had been dead nearly two years. She was hurrying along the path, her skirts swinging alarmingly and her bonnet so far on the back of her head as to be in danger of falling off altogether.

Hester started towards her, relieved that she had come at last, but still preparing in her mind a suitable reproach for the wasted time and the inconsideration. Then she saw Edith's countenance and realized something was wrong.

"What is it?" she said as soon as they met. Edith's intelligent, eccentric face, with its soft mouth and crooked, aquiline nose, was very pale. Her fair hair was poking out untidily from under her bonnet even more than would be accounted for by the breeze and her extremely hasty progress along the path. "What has happened?" Hester demanded anxiously. "Are you ill?"

"No . . ." Edith was breathless and she took Hester's arm impulsively and continued walking, pulling Hester around with her. "I think I am quite well, although I feel as if my stomach were full of little birds and I cannot collect my thoughts."

Hester stopped without disengaging her arm. "Why? Tell me, what is it?" All her irritation vanished. "Can I help?"

A rueful smile crossed Edith's mouth and disappeared.

"No—except by being a friend."

"You know I am that," Hester assured her. "What has happened?"

"My brother Thaddeus—General Carlyon—met with an accident yesterday evening, at a dinner party at the Furnivals'."

"Oh dear, I am sorry. I hope it was not serious. Is he badly hurt?"

Incredulity and confusion fought in Edith's expression. She had a remarkable face, not in any imagination beautiful, yet there was humor in the hazel eyes and sensuality in the mouth, and its lack of symmetry was more than made up for by the quickness of intelligence.

3

"He is dead," she said as if the word surprised even herself.

Hester had been about to begin walking again, but now she stood rooted to the spot. "Oh my dear! How appalling. I am so sorry. However did it happen?"

Edith frowned. "He fell down the stairs," she said slowly. "Or to be more accurate, he fell over the banister at the top and landed across a decorative suit of armor, and I gather the halberd it was holding stabbed him through the chest. . . ."

There was nothing for Hester to say except to repeat her sympathy.

In silence Edith took her arm and they turned and continued again along the path between the flower beds.

"He died immediately, they say," Edith resumed. "It was an extraordinary chance that he should fall precisely upon the wretched thing." She shook her head a little. "One would think it would be possible to fall a hundred times and simply knock it all over and be badly bruised, perhaps break a few bones, but not be speared by the halberd."

They were passed by a gentleman in military uniform, red coat, brilliant gold braid and buttons gleaming in the sun. He bowed to them and they smiled perfunctorily.

"Of course I have never been to the Furnivals' house," Edith went on. "I have no idea how high the balcony is above the hallway. I suppose it may be fifteen or twenty feet."

"People do have most fearful accidents on stairs," Hester agreed, hoping the remark was helpful and not sententious. "They can so easily be fatal. Were you very close?" She thought of her own brothers: James, the younger, the more spirited, killed in the Crimea; and Charles, now head of the family, serious, quiet and a trifle pompous.

"Not very," Edith replied with a pucker between her brows. "He was fifteen years older than I, so he had left home, as a junior cadet in the army, before I was born. I was only eight when he married. Damaris knew him better."

"Your elder sister?"

4

"Yes—she is only six years younger than he is." She stopped. "Was," she corrected.

Hester did a quick mental calculation. That would have made Thaddeus Carlyon forty-eight years old now, long before the beginning of old age, and yet still far in excess of the average span of life.

She held Edith's arm a little closer. "It was good of you to come this afternoon. If you had sent a footman with a message I would have understood completely."

"I would rather come myself," Edith answered with a slight shrug. "There is very little I can do to help, and I admit I was glad of an excuse to be out of the house. Mama is naturally terribly distressed. She shows her feelings very little. You don't know her, but I sometimes think she would have been a better soldier than either Papa or Thaddeus." She smiled to show the remark was only half meant, and even then obliquely and as an illustration of something she did not know how else to express. "She is very strong. One can only guess what emotions there are behind her dignity and her command of herself."

"And your father?" Hester asked. "Surely he will be a comfort to her."

The sun was warm and bright, and hardly a breeze stirred the dazzling flower heads. A small dog scampered between them, yapping with excitement, and chased along the path, grabbing a gentleman's cane in its teeth, much to his annoyance.

Edith drew breath to make the obvious answer to Hester's remark, then changed her mind.

"Not a lot, I should think," she said ruefully. "He is angry that the whole thing has such an element of the ridiculous. It is not exactly like falling in battle, is it?" Her mouth tightened in a sad little smile. "It lacks the heroic."

Hester had not thought of it before. She had been too aware of the reality of death and loss, having experienced the sudden and tragic deaths of her younger brother and both her parents within a year of each other. Now she visualized General Carlyon's accident and realized precisely what Edith meant. To fall over the banister at a dinner party and spear yourself on the halberd of an empty suit of armor was hardly a glorious military death. It might take a better man than his father, Colonel Carlyon, not to feel a certain resentment and sting to family pride. She said nothing of it, but she could not keep from her mind the thought that perhaps the general had been a great deal less than sober at the time.

"I imagine his wife is very shocked," she said aloud. "Had they family?"

"Oh yes, two daughters and a son. Actually, both daughters are older and married, and the younger was present at the party, which makes it so much worse." Edith sniffed sharply, and Hester could not tell if it was a sign of grief, anger, or merely the wind, which was decidedly cooler across the grass now they were out of the shelter of the trees.

"They had quarreled," Edith went on. "According to Peverell, Damaris's husband. In fact, he said it was a perfectly ghastly party. Everyone seemed to be in a fearful temper and at each other's throats half the evening. Both Alexandra, Thaddeus's wife, and Sabella, his daughter, quarreled with him both before dinner and over the table. And with Louisa Furnival, the hostess."

"It sounds very grim," Hester agreed. "But sometimes family differences can seem a great deal more serious than they really are. I know, it can make the grief afterwards much sharper, because quite naturally it is added to by guilt. Although I am sure the dead know perfectly well that we do not mean many of the things we say, and that under the surface there is a love far deeper than any momentary temper."

Edith tightened her grip in gratitude.

"I know what you are trying to say, my dear, and it is not unappreciated. One of these days I must have you meet Alexandra. I believe you would like her, and she you. She married young and had children straightaway, so she has not experienced being single, nor had any of the adventures you have. But she is of as independent a mind as her circumstances allow, and certainly not without courage or imagination."

"When it is suitable I shall be delighted," Hester agreed, although she was not in truth looking forward to spending any of her very precious free time in the company of a recent widow, however courageous. She saw more than sufficient pain and grief in the course of her profession. But it would be gratuitously unkind to say so now, and she was genuinely fond of Edith and would have done much to please her.

"Thank you." Edith looked sideways at her. "Would you think me unforgivably callous if I spoke of other things?"

"Of course not! Had you something special in mind?"

"My reason for making an appointment to meet you where we could speak without interruption, and instead of inviting you to my home," Edith explained, "is that you are the only person I can think of who will understand, and who might even be able to help. Of course in a little while I will be needed at home for the present, now this terrible thing has happened. But afterwards . . ."

"Yes?"

"Hester, Oswald has been dead for close to two years now. I have no children." A flicker of pain crossed her features, showing her vulnerable in the hard spring light, and younger than her thirty-three years. Then it was gone again, and resolve replaced it. "I am bored to distraction," she said with a firm voice, unconsciously increasing her pace as they turned on the path that led down to a small bridge over ornamental water and on towards the Royal Botanical Society Gardens. A small girl was throwing bread to the ducks.

"And I have very little money of my own," Edith went on. "Oswald left me too little to live on, in anything like the way I am accustomed, and I am dependent upon my parents—which is the only reason I still live at Carlyon House."

"I assume you have no particular thoughts on marrying again?"

Edith shot her a look of black humor, not without self-mockery.

"I think it is unlikely," she said frankly. "The marriage

7

market is drenched with girls far younger and prettier than I, and with respectable dowries. My parents are quite content that I should remain at home, a companion for my mother. They have done their duty by me in finding one suitable husband. That he was killed in the Crimea is my misfortune, and it is not incumbent upon them to find me another—for which I do not hold them in the least to blame. I think it would be an extremely difficult task, and in all probability a thankless one. I would not wish to be married again, unless I formed a profound affection for someone.''

They were side by side on the bridge. The water lay cool and cloudy green below them.

"You mean fell in love?'' Hester said.

Edith laughed. "What a romantic you are! I would never have suspected it of you.''

Hester ignored the personal reference. "I am relieved. For a fearful moment I thought you were going to ask me if I could introduce you to anyone.''

"Hardly! I imagine if you knew anyone you could whole-heartedly recommend, you would marry him yourself.''

"Do you indeed?'' Hester said a trifle sharply.

Edith smiled. "And why not? If he were good enough for me, would he not also be good enough for you?''

Hester relaxed, realizing she was being very gently teased.

"If I find two such gentlemen, I shall tell you,'' she conceded generously.

"I am delighted.''

"Then what is it I may do for you?''

They started up the gentle incline of the farther bank.

"I should like to find an occupation that would keep my interest and provide a small income so that I may have some financial independence. I realize,'' Edith put in quickly, "that I may not be able to earn sufficient to support myself, but even an increment to my present allowance would give me a great deal more freedom. But the main thing is, I cannot bear sitting at home stitching embroidery no one needs, painting pictures I have neither room nor inclination to hang,

8

and making endless idiotic conversation with Mama's callers. It is a waste of my life.''

Hester did not reply straightaway. She understood the emotion and the situation profoundly. She had gone to the Crimea because she wanted to contribute to the effort towards the war, and to relieve the appalling conditions of the men freezing, starving, and dying of wounds and disease in Sebastopol. She had returned home in haste on hearing of the deaths of both her parents in the most tragic circumstances. Very soon after, she had learned that there was no money, and although she had accepted the hospitality of her surviving brother and his wife for a short time, it could not be a permanent arrangement. They would have agreed, but Hester would have found it intolerable. She must find her own way and not be an added burden upon their strained circumstances.

She had come home on fire to reform nursing in England, as Miss Nightingale had in the Crimea. Indeed most of the women who had served with her had espoused the same cause, and with similar fervor.

However, Hester's first and only hospital appointment had ended in dismissal. The medical establishment was not eager to be reformed, least of all by opinionated young women, or indeed by women at all. And considering that no women had ever studied medicine, and such an idea was unthinkable, that was not to be wondered at. Nurses were largely unskilled, employed to wind bandages, fetch and carry, dust, sweep, stoke fires, empty slops and keep spirits high and morality above question.

''Well?'' Edith interrupted. ''Surely it is not a hopeless cause.'' There was a lightness in her voice but her eyes were earnest, full of both hope and fear, and Hester could see she cared deeply.

''Of course not,'' she said soberly. ''But it is not easy. Too many occupations, of the forms that are open to women, are of a nature where you would be subject to a kind of discipline and condescension which would be intolerable to you.''

9

"You managed," Edith pointed out.

"Not indefinitely," Hester corrected. "And the fact that you are not dependent upon it to survive will take a certain curb from your tongue which was on mine."

"Then what is left?"

They were standing on the gravel path between the flowers, a child with a hoop a dozen yards to the left, two little girls in white pinafores to the right.

"I am not sure, but I shall endeavor to find out," Hester promised. She stopped and turned to look at Edith's pale face and troubled eyes. "There will be something. You have a good hand, and you said you speak French. Yes, I remember that. I will search and enquire and let you know in a few days' time. Say a week or so. No, better make it a little longer, I would like to have as complete an answer as I can."

"A week on Saturday?" Edith suggested. "That will be May the second. Come to tea."

"Are you sure?"

"Yes of course. We shall not be entertaining socially, but you are coming as a friend. It will be quite acceptable."

"Then I shall. Thank you."

Edith's eyes widened for a moment, giving her face a brightness, then she clasped Hester's hand quickly and let it go, turning on her heel and striding along the path between the daffodils and down towards the lodge without looking back.

Hester walked for another half hour, enjoying the air before returning to the street and finding another hansom to take her back to Major Tiplady and her duties.

The major was sitting on a chaise longue, which he did under protest, considering it an effeminate piece of furniture, but he enjoyed being able to stare out of the window at passersby, and at the same time keep his injured leg supported.

"Well?" he asked as soon as she was in. "Did you have a pleasant walk? How was your friend?"

Automatically she straightened the blanket around him.

"Don't fuss!" he said sharply. "You didn't answer me.

10

How was your friend? You did go out to meet a friend, didn't you?"

"Yes I did." She gave the cushion an extra punch to plump it up, in spite of his catching her eye deliberately. It was a gentle banter they had with each other, and both enjoyed it. Provoking her had been his best entertainment since he had been restricted to either his bed or a chair, and he had developed a considerable liking for her. He was normally somewhat nervous of women, having spent most of his life in the company of men and having been taught that the gentle sex was different in every respect, requiring treatment incomprehensible to any but the most sensitive of men. He was delighted to find Hester intelligent, not given to fainting or taking offense where it was not intended, not seeking compliments at every fit and turn, never giggling, and best of all, quite interested in military tactics, a blessing he could still hardly believe.

"And how is she?" he demanded, glaring at her out of brilliant pale blue eyes, his white mustache bristling.

"In some shock," Hester replied. "Would you like tea?"

"Why?"

"Because it is teatime. And crumpets?"

"Yes I would. Why was she shocked? What did you say to her?"

"That I was very sorry," Hester smiled with her back to him, as she was about to ring the bell. It was not part of her duty to cook—fortunately, because she had little skill at it.

"Don't prevaricate with me!" he said hotly.

Hester rang the bell, then turned back to him and changed her expression to one of sobriety. "Her brother met with a fatal accident last evening," she told him. "He fell over the banister and died immediately."

"Good gracious! Are you sure?" His face was instantly grave, his pink-and-white skin as usual looking freshly scrubbed and innocent.

"Perfectly, I am afraid."

"Was he a drinking man?"

"I don't believe so. At least not to that extent."

11

The maid answered the summons and Hester requested tea and hot crumpets with butter. When the girl had gone, she continued with the story. "He fell onto a suit of armor, and tragically the halberd struck his chest."

Tiplady stared at her, still not totally sure whether she was exercising some bizarre female sense of humor at his expense. Then he realized the gravity in her face was quite real.

"Oh dear. I am very sorry." He frowned. "But you cannot blame me for not being sure you were entirely serious. It is a preposterous accident!" He hitched himself a little higher on the chaise longue. "Have you any idea how difficult it is to spear a man with a halberd? He must have fallen with tremendous force. Was he a very large man?"

"I have no idea." She had not thought about it, but now that she did, she appreciated his view. To have fallen so hard and so accurately upon the point of a halberd held by an inanimate suit of armor, in such a way that it penetrated through clothes into the flesh, and between the ribs into the body, was an extraordinary chance. The angle must have been absolutely precise, the halberd wedged very firmly in the gauntlet, and as Major Tiplady said, the force very great indeed. "Perhaps he was. I had never met him, but his sister is tall, although she is very slight. Maybe he was of a bigger build. He was a soldier."

Major Tiplady's eyebrows shot up. "Was he?"

"Yes. A general, I believe."

The major's face twitched with an amusement he found extreme difficulty in concealing, although he was perfectly aware of its unsuitability. He had recently developed a sense of the absurd which alarmed him. He thought it was a result of lying in bed with little to do but read, and too much company of a woman.

"How very unfortunate," he said, staring at the ceiling. "I hope they do not put on his epitaph that he was finally killed by impaling himself upon a weapon held by an empty suit of armor. It does seem an anticlimax to an outstanding military career, and to smack of the ridiculous. And a general too!"

"Seems not at all unlikely for a general to me," Hester said tartly, remembering some of the fiascoes of the Crimean War, such as the Battle of the Alma, where men were ordered first one way and then the other, and were finally caught in the river, hundreds dying unnecessarily; not to mention Balaclava, where the Light Brigade, the flower of the English cavalry, had charged into the mouths of the Russian guns and been mown down like grass. That was a nightmare of blood and slaughter she would never forget, nor the succeeding days and nights of sleepless labor, helplessness and pain.

Suddenly Thaddeus Carlyon's death seemed sadder, more real, and at the same time far less important.

She turned back to Major Tiplady and began straightening the blanket over his legs. He was about to protest, then he recognized the quite different quality in her expression and submitted wordlessly. She had changed from a pleasant and efficient young woman, whom he liked, into the army nurse she used to be such a short time since, seeing death every day and hideously aware of the magnitude and the futility of it.

"You said he was a general." He watched her with a pucker between his brows. "What was his name?"

"Carlyon," she replied, tucking in the ends of the blanket firmly. "Thaddeus Carlyon."

"Indian Army?" he asked, then before she could reply, "Heard of a Carlyon out there, stiff sort of fellow, but very much admired by his men. Fine reputation, never backed down in the face of the enemy. Not all that fond of generals myself, but pity he should die like that."

"It was quick," she said with a grimace. Then for several moments she busied herself around the room, doing largely unnecessary things, but the movement was automatic, as if remaining still would have been an imprisonment.

Finally the tea and crumpets came. Biting into the crisp, hot dough and trying to stop the butter from running down her chin, she relaxed and returned to the present.

She smiled at him.

"Would you like a game of chess?" she offered. She was

exactly skilled enough to give him a good game without beating him.

"Oh I would," he said happily. "Indeed I would."

Hester spent her free time for the next several days in pursuing possible opportunities for Edith Sobell, as she had promised. She did not think nursing offered any openings Edith would find either satisfying or indeed available to her. It was regarded as a trade rather than a profession, and most of the men and women employed in it were of a social class and an education, or lack of it, which resulted in their being regarded with scant respect, and paid accordingly. Those who had been with Miss Nightingale, now a national heroine only a little less admired than the Queen, were viewed differently, but it was too late for Edith to qualify for that distinction. And even though Hester herself most definitely did qualify, she was finding employment hard enough, and her opinions little valued.

But there were other fields, especially for someone like Edith, who was intelligent and well-read, not only in English literature but also in French. There might well be some gentleman who required a librarian or an assistant to research for him whatever subject held his interest. People were always writing treatises or monographs, and many needed an assistant who would perform the labor necessary to translate their ideas into a literary form.

Most women who wished a lady companion were intolerably difficult and really only wanted a dependent whom they could order around—and who could not afford to disagree with them. However, there were exceptions, people who liked to travel but did not find it pleasurable to do so alone. Some of these redoubtable women would be excellent employers, full of interest and character.

There was also the possibility of teaching; if the pupils were eager and intelligent enough it might be highly rewarding.

Hester explored all these areas, at least sufficiently to have something definite to tell Edith when she accepted the invi-

14

tation to go to Carlyon House for afternoon tea on May the second.

Major Tiplady's apartments were at the southern end of Great Titchfield Street, and therefore some distance from Clarence Gardens, where Carlyon House was situated. Although she could have walked, it would have taken her the better part of half an hour, and she would have arrived tired and overheated and untidy for such an engagement. And she admitted with a wry humor that the thought of afternoon tea with the elder Mrs. Carlyon made her more than a little nervous. She would have cared less had Edith not been her friend; then she could have been free to succeed or fail without emotional damage. As it was, she would rather have faced a night in military camp above Sebastopol than this engagement.

However there was no help for it now, so she dressed in her best muslin afternoon gown. It was not a very glamorous affair, but well cut with pointed waist and softly pleated bodice, a little out of date, though only a lady of fashion would have known it. The faults lay all in the trimmings. Nursing did not allow for luxuries. When she went to bid Major Tiplady good-bye, he regarded her with approval. He had not the least idea of fashion and very pretty women terrified him. He found Hester's face with its strong features very agreeable, and her figure, both too tall and a little too thin, to be not at all displeasing. She did not threaten him with aggressive femininity, and her intellect was closer to that of a man, which he rather liked. He had never imagined that a woman could become a friend, but he was being proved wrong, and it was not in any way an experience he disliked.

"You look very . . . tidy," he said with slightly pink cheeks.

From anyone else it would have infuriated her. She did not wish to look tidy; tidiness was for housemaids, and junior ones at that. Even parlormaids were allowed to be handsome; indeed, they were required to be. But she knew he meant it well, and it would be gratuitously cruel to take exception, however much *distinguished* or *appealing* would have been preferred. *Beautiful* was too much to hope for. Her sister-in-law, Imogen, was beautiful—and appealing. Hester had discovered that very forcefully when that disastrous policeman Monk had been so haunted by her last year during the affair in Mecklenburg Square. But Monk was an entirely different matter, and nothing to do with this afternoon.

"Thank you, Major Tiplady," she accepted with as much grace as she could. "And please be careful while I am away. If you wish for anything, I have put the bell well within your reach. Do not try to get up without calling Molly to assist you. If you should"—she looked very severe—"and you fall again, you could find yourself in bed for another six weeks!" That was a far more potent threat than the pain of another injury, and she knew it.

He winced. "Certainly not," he said with affronted dignity.

"Good!" And with that she turned and left, assured that he would remain where he was.

She hailed a hansom and rode along the length of Great Titchfield Street, turned into Bolsover Street and went along Osnaburgh Street right into Clarence Gardens—a distance of approximately a mile—and alighted a little before four o'clock. She felt ridiculously as if she were about to make the first charge in a battle. It was absurd. She must pull herself together. The very worst that could happen would be embarrassment. She ought to be able to cope with that. After all, what was it—an acute discomfort of the mind, no more. It was immeasurably better than guilt, or grief.

She sniffed hard, straightened her shoulders and marched up the front steps, reaching for the bell pull and yanking it rather too hard. She stepped back so as not to be on the very verge when the door was opened.

It happened almost immediately and a smart maid looked at her enquiringly, her pretty face otherwise suitably expressionless.

"Yes ma'am?"

16

"Miss Hester Latterly, to see Mrs. Sobell," Hester replied. "I believe she is expecting me."

"Yes of course, Miss Latterly. Please come in." The door opened all the way and the maid stepped aside to allow her past. She took Hester's bonnet and cloak.

The hallway was as impressive as she had expected it to be, paneled with oak to a height of nearly eight feet, hung with dark portraits framed in gilt with acanthus leaves and curlicues. It was gleaming in the light from the chandelier, lit so early because the oak made it dim in spite of the daylight outside.

"If you please to come this way," the maid requested, going ahead of her across the parquet. "Miss Edith is in the boudoir. Tea will be served in thirty minutes." And so saying she led Hester up the broad stairs and across the first landing to the upper sitting room, reserved solely for the use of the ladies of the house, and hence known as the boudoir. She opened the door and announced Hester.

Edith was inside staring out of the window that faced the square. She turned as soon as Hester was announced, her face lighting with pleasure. Today she was wearing a gown of purplish plum color, trimmed with black. The crinoline was very small, almost too insignificant to be termed a crinoline at all, and Hester thought instantly how much more becoming it was—and also how much more practical than having to swing around so much fabric and so many stiff hoops. She had little time to notice much of the room, except that it was predominantly pink and gold, and there was a very handsome rosewood escritoire against the far wall.

"I'm so glad you came!" Edith said quickly. "Apart from any news you might have, I desperately need to talk of normal things to someone outside the family."

"Why? Whatever has happened?" Hester could see without asking that something had occurred. Edith looked even more tense than on their previous meeting. Her body was stiff and her movements jerky, with a greater awkwardness than usual, and she was not a graceful woman at the best of times. But more telling was the weariness in her and the total absence of her usual humor.

Edith closed her eyes and then opened them wide.

"Thaddeus's death is immeasurably worse than we first supposed," she said quietly.

"Oh?" Hester was confused. How could it be worse than death?

"You don't understand." Edith was very still. "Of course you don't. I was not explaining myself at all." She took a sudden sharp breath. "They are saying it was not an accident."

"They?" Hester was stunned. "Who is saying it?"

"The police, of course." Edith blinked, her face white. "They say Thaddeus was murdered!"

Hester felt momentarily a little dizzy, as though the room with its gentle comfort had receded very far away and her vision was foggy at the edges, Edith's face sharp in the center and indelible in her mind.

"Oh my dear—how terrible! Have they any idea who it was?"

"That is the worst part," Edith confessed, for the first time moving away and sitting down on the fat pink settee.

Hester sat opposite her in the armchair.

"There were only a very few people there, and no one broke in," Edith explained. "It had to have been one of them. Apart from Mr. and Mrs. Furnival, who gave the party, the only ones there who were not my family were Dr. Hargrave and his wife." She swallowed hard and attempted to smile. It was ghastly. "Otherwise it was Thaddeus and Alexandra; their daughter Sabella and her husband, Fenton Pole; and my sister, Damaris, and my brother-in-law, Peverell Erskine. There was no one else there."

"What about the servants?" Hester said desperately. "I suppose there is no chance it could have been one of them."

"What for? Why on earth would one of the servants kill Thaddeus?"

Hester's mind raced. "Perhaps he caught them stealing?"

"Stealing what—on the first landing? He fell off the balcony of the first landing. The servants would all be downstairs at that time in the evening, except maybe a ladies' maid.''

"Jewelry?''

"How would he know they had been stealing? If they were in a bedroom he wouldn't know it. And if he saw them coming out, he would only presume they were about their duties.''

That was totally logical. Hester had no argument. She searched her mind and could think of nothing comforting to say.

"What about the doctor?'' she tried.

Edith flashed a weak smile at her, appreciating what she was attempting.

"Dr. Hargrave? I don't know if it's possible. Damaris did tell me what happened that evening, but she didn't seem very clear. In fact she was pretty devastated, and hardly coherent at all.''

"Well, where were they?'' Hester had already been involved in two murders, the first because of the deaths of her own parents, the second through her acquaintance with the policeman William Monk, who was now working privately for anyone who required relatives traced, thefts solved discreetly, and other such matters dealt with in a private capacity, where they preferred not to engage the law or where no crime had been committed. Surely if she used her intelligence and a little logic she ought to be of some assistance.

"Since they assumed at first that it was an accident,'' she said aloud, "surely he must have been alone. Where was everyone else? At a dinner party people are not wandering around the house individually.''

"That's just it,'' Edith said with increasing unhappiness. "Damaris made hardly any sense. I've never seen her so . . . so completely . . . out of control. Even Peverell couldn't calm or comfort her—she would scarcely speak to him.''

"Perhaps they had a . . .'' Hester sought for some polite way of phrasing it. "Some difference of opinion? A misunderstanding?''

19

Edith's mouth twitched with amusement. "How euphemistic of you. You mean a quarrel? I doubt it. Peverell really isn't that kind of person. He is rather sweet, and very fond of her." She swallowed, and smiled with a sudden edge of sadness, as of other things briefly remembered, perhaps other people. "He isn't weak at all," she went on. "I used to think he was. But he just has a way of dealing with her, and she usually comes 'round—in the end. Really much more satisfactory than ordering people. I admit he may not be an instant great passion, but I like him. In fact, the longer I know him the more I like him. And I rather think she feels the same." She shook her head minutely. "No, I remember the way she was when she came home that evening. I don't think Peverell had anything to do with it."

"What did she say about where people were? Thaddeus— I beg your pardon, General Carlyon—fell, or was pushed, over the banister from the first landing. Where was everyone else at the time?"

"Coming and going," Edith said hopelessly. "I haven't managed to make any sense of it. Perhaps you can. I asked Damaris to come and join us, if she remembers. But she doesn't seem to know what she's doing since that evening."

Hester had not met Edith's sister, but she had heard frequent reference to her, and it seemed that either she was emotionally volatile and somewhat undisciplined or she had been judged unkindly.

At that moment, as if to prove her a liar, the door opened and one of the most striking women Hester had ever seen stood framed by the lintel. For that first moment she seemed heroically beautiful, tall, even taller than Hester or Edith, and very lean. Her hair was dark and soft with natural curl, unlike the present severe style in which a woman's hair was worn scraped back from the face with ringlets over the ears, and she seemed to have no regard for fashion. Indeed her skirt was serviceable, designed for work, without the crinoline hoops, and yet her blouse was gorgeously embroidered and woven with white ribbon. She had a boyish air about her, neither coquettish nor demure, simply blazingly candid. Her face was long, her features so mobile and sensitive they reflected her every thought.

She came in and closed the door, leaning against it for a moment with both hands behind her and regarding Hester with a frankly interested stare.

"You are Hester Latterly?" she asked, although the question was obviously rhetorical. "Edith said you were coming this afternoon. I'm so glad. Ever since she told me you went to the Crimea with Miss Nightingale, I have been longing to meet you. You must come again, when we are more ourselves, and tell us about it." She flashed a sudden illuminating smile. "Or tell me, anyway. I'm not at all sure Papa would approve, and I'm quite certain Mama would not. Far too independent. Rocks the foundations of society when women don't know their proper place—which, of course, is at home, keeping civilization safe for the rest of us."

She walked over to a neo-rococo love seat and threw herself on it utterly casually. "Seeing we learn to clean our teeth every day," she went on. "Eat our rice pudding, speak correctly, never split infinitives, wear our gloves at all the appropriate times, keep a stiff upper lip whatever vicissitudes we may find ourselves placed in, and generally set a good example to the lower classes—who depend upon us for precisely this." She was sitting sideways over the seat. For anyone else it would have been awkward, but for her it had a kind of grace because it was so wholehearted. She did not care greatly what others thought of her. Yet even in this careless attitude there was an ill-concealed tension in her, and Hester could easily imagine the frenzied distress Edith had spoken of.

Now Damaris's face darkened again as she looked at Hester.

"I suppose Edith has told you about our tragedy—Thaddeus's death—and that they are now saying it was murder?" Her brow furrowed even more deeply. "Although I can't imagine why anyone should want to kill Thaddeus." She turned to Edith. "Can you? I mean, he was a terrible bore at times, but most men are. They think all the wrong

21

things are important. Oh—I'm sorry—I do mean most men, not all!'' Suddenly she had realized she might have offended Hester and her contrition was real.

"That is quite all right.'' Hester smiled. "I agree with you. And I daresay they feel the same about us.''

Damaris winced. "Touché. Did Edith tell you about it?''

"The dinner party? No—she said it would be better if you did, since you were there.'' She hoped she sounded concerned and not unbecomingly inquisitive.

Damaris closed her eyes and slid a little farther down on her unorthodox seat.

"It was ghastly. A fiasco almost from the beginning.'' She opened her eyes again and stared at Hester. "Do you really want to know about it?''

"Unless you find it too painful.'' That was not the truth. She wanted to know about it regardless, but decency, and compassion, prevented her from pressing too hard.

Damaris shrugged, but she did not meet Hester's eyes. "I don't mind talking about it—it is all going on inside my head anyway, repeating over and over again. Some parts of it don't even seem real anymore.''

"Begin at the beginning,'' Edith prompted, curling her feet up under her. "That is the only way we have a hope of making any sense of it. Apparently someone did kill Thaddeus, and it is going to be extremely unpleasant until we find out who.''

Damaris shivered and shot her a sour glance, then addressed Hester.

"Peverell and I were the first to arrive. You haven't met him, but you will like him when you do.'' She said it unselfconsciously and without desire for effect, simply as a comment of fact. "At that time we were both in good spirits and looking forward to the evening.'' She lifted her eyes to the ceiling. "Can you imagine that? Do you know Maxim and Louisa Furnival? No, I don't suppose you do. Edith says you don't waste time in Society.''

Hester smiled and looked down at her hands in her lap to avoid meeting Edith's eyes. That was a charmingly euphemistic way of putting it. Hester was too old to be strictly marriageable, well over twenty-five, and even twenty-five was optimistic. And since her father had lost his money before his death, she had no dowry, nor any social background worth anyone's while to pursue. Also she was of an unbecomingly direct character and both held and expressed too many opinions.

"I have no time I can afford to waste," she answered aloud.

"And I have too much," Edith added.

Hester brought them back to the subject. "Please tell me something of the Furnivals."

Damaris's face lost its momentary look of ease.

"Maxim is really quite agreeable, in a brooding, dark sort of way. He's fearfully decent, and he manages to do it without being stuffy. I often felt if I knew him better he might be quite interesting. I could easily imagine falling madly in love with him—just to know what lies underneath—if I didn't already know Peverell. But whether it would stand a close acquaintance I have no idea." She glanced at Hester to make sure she understood, then continued, staring up at the molded and painted ceiling. "Louisa is another matter altogether. She is very beautiful, in an unconventional way, like a large cat—of the jungle sort, not the domestic. She is no one's tabby. I used to envy her." She smiled ruefully. "She is very small. She can be feminine and look up at any man at all—where I look down on far more than I wish. And she is all curves in the most flattering places, which I am not. She has very high, wide cheekbones, but when I stopped being envious, and looked a little more closely, I did not care for her mouth."

"You are not saying much of what she is like, Ris," Edith prompted.

"She is like a cat," Damaris said reasonably. "Sensuous, predatory, and taking great care of her own, but utterly charming when she wishes to be."

Edith looked across at Hester. "Which tells you at least

23

that Damaris doesn't like her very much. Or that she is more than a trifle envious."

"You are interrupting," Damaris said with an aloof air. "The next to arrive were Thaddeus and Alexandra. He was just as usual, polite, pompous and rather preoccupied, but Alex looked pale and not so much preoccupied as distracted. I thought then that they must have had a disagreement over something, and of course Alex had lost."

Hester nearly asked why "of course," then realized the question was foolish. A wife would always lose, particularly in public.

"Then Sabella and Fenton came," Damaris continued. "That's Thaddeus's younger daughter and her husband," she explained to Hester. "Almost immediately Sabella was rude to Thaddeus. We all pretended we hadn't noticed, which is about all you can do when you are forced to witness a family quarrel. It was rather embarrassing, and Alex looked very . . ." she searched for the word she wanted. ". . . very brittle, as though her self-control might snap if she were pressed too hard." Her face changed swiftly, and a shadow passed over it. "The last ones to arrive were Dr. Hargrave and his wife." She altered her position slightly in the chair, with the result that she was no longer facing Hester. "It was all very polite, and trivial, and totally artificial."

"You said it was ghastly." Edith's eyebrows rose. "You don't mean you sat around through the entire evening being icily civil to each other. You told me Thaddeus and Sabella quarreled and Sabella behaved terribly, and Alex was white as a sheet, which Thaddeus either did not even notice—or else pretended not to. And that Maxim was hovering over Alex, and Louisa obviously resented it."

Damaris frowned, her shoulders tightening. "I thought so. But of course it may simply have been that it was Maxim's house and he felt responsible, so he was trying to be kind to Alex and make her feel better, and Louisa misunderstood." She glanced at Hester. "She likes to be the center of attention and wouldn't appreciate anyone being so absorbed in someone else. She was very scratchy with Alex all evening."

"You all went in to dinner?" Hester prompted, still searching for the factual elements of the crime, if the police were correct and there had been one.

"What?" Damaris knitted her brows, staring at the window. "Oh—yes, all on each other's arms as we had been directed, according to the best etiquette. Do you know, I can't even remember what we ate." She lifted her shoulders a little under the gorgeous blouse. "It could have been bread pudding for all I tasted. After the desserts we went to the withdrawing room and talked nonsense while the men passed the port, or whatever men do in the dining room when the women have gone. I've often wondered if they say anything at all worth listening to." She looked up at Hester quickly. "Haven't you?"

Hester smiled briefly. "Yes I have. But I think it may be one of those cases where the truth would be disappointing. The mystery is far better. Did the men rejoin you?"

Damaris grimaced in a strange half smile, rueful and ironic. "You mean was Thaddeus still alive then? Yes he was. Sabella went upstairs to be alone, or I think more accurately to sulk, but I can't remember when. It was before the men came in, because I thought she was avoiding Thaddeus."

"So you were all in the withdrawing room, apart from Sabella?"

"Yes. The conversation was very artificial. I mean more so than usual. It's always pretty futile. Louisa was making vicious little asides about Alex, all with a smooth smile on her face, of course. Then Louisa rose and invited Thaddeus to go up and visit Valentine—" She gave a quick little gasp as if she had choked on something, and then changed it into a cough. "Alex was furious. I can picture the look on her face as if I had only just seen it."

Hester knew Damaris was speaking of a subject about which she felt some deep emotion, but she had no idea why, or quite what emotion it was. But there was little point in pressing the matter at all if she stopped now.

"Who is Valentine?"

25

Damaris's voice was husky as she answered. "He is the Furnivals' son. He is thirteen—nearly fourteen."

"And Thaddeus was fond of him?" Hester said quietly.

"Yes—yes he was." Her tone had a kind of finality and her face a bleakness that stopped Hester from asking any more. She knew from Edith that Damaris had no children of her own, and she had enough sensitivity to imagine the feelings that might lie behind those words. She changed the subject and brought it back to the immediate.

"How long was he gone?"

Damaris smiled with a strange, wounded humor.

"Forever."

"Oh." Hester was more disconcerted than she was prepared for. She felt dismay, and for a moment she was robbed of words.

"I'm sorry," Damaris said quickly, looking at Hester with wide, dark eyes. "Actually I don't know. I was absorbed in my own thoughts. Some time. People were coming and going." She smiled as if there were some punishing humor in that thought. "Maxim went off for something, and Louisa came back alone. Alex went off too, I suppose after Thaddeus, and she came back. Then Maxim went off again, this time into the front hall—I should have said they went up the back stairs to the wing where Valentine has his room, on the third floor. It is quicker that way."

"You've been up?"

Damaris looked away. "Yes."

"Maxim went into the front hall?" Hester prompted.

"Oh—yes. And he came back looking awful and saying there had been an accident. Thaddeus had fallen over the banister and been seriously hurt—he was unconscious. Of course we know now he was dead." She was still looking at Hester, watching her face. Now she looked away again. "Charles Hargrave got up immediately and went to see. We all sat there in silence. Alex was as white as a ghost, but she had been most of the evening. Louisa was very quiet; she turned and went, saying she was fetching Sabella down, she ought to know her father had been hurt. I can't really

26

remember what else happened till Charles—Dr. Hargrave—came back to say Thaddeus was dead, and of course we would have to report it. No one should touch anything."

"Just leave him there?" Edith said indignantly. "Lying on the floor in the hallway, tangled up with the suit of armor?"

"Yes . . ."

"They would have to." Hester looked from one to the other of them. "And if he was dead it wouldn't cause him any distress. It is only what we think . . ."

Edith pulled a face, but said nothing more, curling her legs up a little higher.

"It's rather absurd, isn't it?" Damaris said very quietly. "A cavalry general who fought all over the place being killed eventually by falling over the stairs onto a halberd held by an empty suit of armor. Poor Thaddeus—he never had any sense of humor. I doubt he would have seen the funny side of it."

"I'm sure he wouldn't." Edith's voice broke for a moment, and she took a deep breath. "And neither would Papa. I wouldn't mention it again, if I were you."

"For heaven's sake!" Damaris snapped. "I'm not a complete fool. Of course I won't. But if I don't laugh I think I shall not be able to stop crying. Death is often absurd. People are absurd. I am!" She sat up properly and swiveled around straight in the seat, facing Hester.

"Someone murdered Thaddeus, and it had to be one of us who were there that evening. That's the awful thing about it all. The police say he couldn't have fallen onto the point of the halberd like that. It would never have penetrated his body—it would just have gone over. He could have broken his neck, or his back, and died. But that was not what happened. He didn't break any bones in the fall. He did knock his head, and almost certainly concuss himself, but it was the halberd through the chest that killed him—and that was driven in after he was lying on the ground."

She shivered. "Which is pretty horrible—and has not the remotest sort of humor about any part of it. Isn't it silly how we have this quite offensive desire to laugh at all the worst

27

and most tragic things? The police have already been around asking all sorts of questions. It was dreadful—sort of unreal, like being inside a magic lantern show, except that of course they don't have stories like that.''

"And they haven't come to any conclusions?'' Hester went on relentlessly, but how else could she be of any help? They did not need pity; anyone could give them that.

"No.'' Damaris looked grim. "It seems several of us would have had the opportunity, and both Sabella and Alex had obviously quarreled with him recently. Others might have. I don't know.'' Then suddenly she stood up and smiled with forced gaiety.

"Let us go in to tea. Mama will be angry if we are late, and that would spoil it all.''

Hester obeyed willingly. Apart from the fact that she thought they had exhausted the subject of the dinner party, at least for the time being, she was most interested in meeting Edith's parents, and indeed she was also ready for tea.

Edith uncurled herself, straightening her skirts, and followed them downstairs, through the big hall and into the main withdrawing room, where tea was to be served. It was a magnificent room. Hester had only a moment in which to appreciate it, since her interest, as well as her manners, required she give her attention to the occupants. She saw brocaded walls with gilt-framed pictures, an ornate ceiling, exquisitely draped curtains in claret-colored velvet with gold sashes, and a darker patterned carpet. She caught sight of two tall bronzes in highly ornate Renaissance style, and had a dim idea of terra-cotta ornaments near the mantel.

Colonel Randolf Carlyon was sitting totally relaxed, almost like a man asleep, in one of the great armchairs. He was a big man gone slack with age, his ruddy-skinned face partially concealed by white mustache and side whiskers, his pale blue eyes tired. He made an attempt to stand as they came in, but the gesture died before he was on his feet, a half bow sufficing to satisfy etiquette.

Felicia Carlyon was as different as was imaginable. She was perhaps ten years younger than her husband, no more than her mid-sixties, and although her face showed a certain strain, a tightness about the mouth and shadows around the large, deep-set eyes, there was nothing in the least passive or defeated about her. She stood in front of the walnut table on which tea was laid, her body still slender and rigidly upright with a deportment many a younger woman would have envied. Naturally she was wearing black in mourning for her son, but it was handsome, vivid black, well decorated with jet beading and trimmed with black velvet braid. Her black lace cap was similarly fashionable.

She did not move when they came in, but her glance went straight to Hester, and Hester was intensely aware of the force of her character.

"Good afternoon, Miss Latterly," Felicia said graciously, but without warmth. She reserved her judgment of people; her regard had to be earned. "How pleasant of you to come. Edith has spoken most kindly of you."

"Good afternoon, Mrs. Carlyon," Hester replied equally formally. "It is gracious of you to receive me. May I offer you my deepest sympathies for your loss."

"Thank you." Felicia's complete composure and the brevity with which she accepted made it tactless to add anything further. Obviously she did not wish to discuss the subject; it was deeply personal, and she did not share her emotions with anyone. "I am pleased you will take tea with us. Please be comfortable." She did not move her body, but the invitation was implicit.

Hester thanked her again and sat, not in the least comfortably, on the dark red sofa farthest from the fire. Edith and Damaris both seated themselves and introductions were completed, Randolf Carlyon contributing only what was required of him for civility.

They spoke of the merest trivialities until the maid came with the last of the dishes required for tea, paper-thin sandwiches of cucumber, watercress and cream cheese, and finely chopped egg. There were also French pastries and cake with cream and jam. Hester looked at it with great appreciation, and wished it were an occasion on which it would be acceptable to eat heartily, but knew unquestionably that it was not.

When tea had been poured and passed Felicia looked at her with polite enquiry.

"Edith tells me you have traveled considerably, Miss Latterly. Have you been to Italy? It is a country I should have liked to visit. Unfortunately at the time when it would have been suitable for me, we were at war, and such things were impossible. Did you enjoy it?"

Hester wondered for a frantic moment what on earth Edith could have said, but she dared not look at her now, and there was no evading an answer to Felicia Carlyon. But she must protect Edith from having appeared to speak untruthfully.

"Perhaps I was not clear enough in my conversation with Edith." She forced a slight smile. She felt like adding "ma'am," as if she were speaking to a duchess, which was absurd. This woman was socially no better than herself—or at least than her parents. "I regret my traveling was in the course of war, and anything but educational in the great arts of Italy. Although I did put in to port there briefly."

"Indeed?" Felicia's arched eyebrows rose, but it would be immeasurably beneath her to allow her good manners to be diverted. "Did war oblige you to leave your home, Miss Latterly? Regrettably we seem to have trouble in so many parts of the Empire at the moment. And they speak of unrest in India as well, although I have no idea whether that is serious or not."

Hester hesitated between equivocation and the truth, and decided truth would be safer, in the long run. Felicia Carlyon was not a woman to overlook an inconsistency or minor contradiction.

"No, I was in the Crimea, with Miss Nightingale." That magic name was sufficient to impress most people, and it was the best reference she had both as to character and worth.

"Good gracious," Felicia said, sipping her tea delicately.

"Extraordinary!" Randolf blew out through his whiskers.

"I think it is fascinating." Edith spoke for the first time

since coming into the withdrawing room. "A most worth-while thing to do with one's life."

"Traveling with Miss Nightingale is hardly a lifetime occupation, Edith," Felicia said coolly. "An adventure, per-haps, but of short duration."

"Inspired by noble motives, no doubt," Randolf added. "But extraordinary, and not entirely suitable for a—a—" He stopped.

Hester knew what he had been going to say; she had met the attitude many times before, especially in older soldiers. It was not suitable for gentlewomen. Females who followed the army were either enlisted men's wives, laundresses, ser-vants, or whores. Except the most senior officers' ladies, of course, but that was quite different. They knew Hester was not married.

"Nursing has improved immensely in the last few years," she said with a smile. "It is now a profession."

"Not for women," Felicia said flatly. "Although I am sure your work was very noble, and all England admires it. What are you doing now you are home again?"

Hester heard Edith's indrawn breath and saw Damaris swiftly lower her eyes to her plate.

"I am caring for a retired military gentleman who has broken his leg quite severely," Hester answered, forcing her-self to see the humor of the situation rather than the offense. "He requires someone more skilled in caring for the injured than a housemaid."

"Very commendable," Felicia said with a slight nod, sip-ping at her tea again.

Hester knew implicitly that what she did not add was that it was excellent only for women who were obliged to support themselves and were beyond a certain age when they might reasonably hope for marriage. She would never countenance her own daughters descending to such a pass, as long as there was a roof over their heads and a single garment to put on their backs.

Hester made her smile even sweeter.

"Thank you, Mrs. Carlyon. It is most gratifying to be of

31

use to someone, and Major Tiplady is a gentleman of good family and high reputation."

"Tiplady . . ." Randolf frowned. "Tiplady? Can't say I ever heard of him. Where'd he serve, eh?"

"India."

"Funny! Thaddeus, my son, you know, served in India for years. Outstanding man—a general, you know. Sikh Wars—'45 to '46, then again in '49. Was in the Opium Wars in China in '39 as well. Very fine man! Everyone says so. Very fine indeed, if I do say so. Son any man would be proud of. Never heard him mention anyone called Tiplady."

"Actually I believe Major Tiplady was sent to Afghanistan—the Afghan Wars of '39 and '42. He talks about it sometimes. It is most interesting."

Randolf looked at her with mild reproof, as one would a precocious child.

"Nonsense, my dear Miss Latterly. There is no need to affect interest in military matters in order to be polite. My son has very recently died"—his face clouded—"most tragically. As no doubt you are aware from Edith, but we are used to bearing our loss with fortitude. You do not need to consider our feelings in such a way."

Hester drew breath to say her interest had nothing to do with Thaddeus Carlyon and long predated her even having heard of him, then decided it would not be understood or believed, and would appear merely offensive.

She compromised.

"Stories of courage and endeavor are always interesting, Colonel Carlyon," she said with a very direct stare at him. "I am extremely sorry for your loss, but I never for a moment considered affecting an interest or a respect I did not feel."

He seemed caught off balance for a moment. His cheeks grew pinker and he blew out his breath sharply, but glancing sideways at Felicia, Hester saw a flicker of appreciation and something which might have been a dark, painful humor, but it was too brief for her to do more than wonder at it.

Before any reply was required, the door opened and a man came in. His manner seemed on the surface almost deferential, until one observed that actually he did not wait for any approval or acknowledgment; it was simply that there was no arrogance in him. Hester judged he was barely an inch taller than Damaris, but still a good height for a man, of very average build if a little round-shouldered. His face was unremarkable, dark eyed, lips hidden by his mustache, features regular, except that there was an aura of good humor about him as though he held no inner anger and optimism were a part of his life.

Damaris looked up at him quickly, her expression lightening.

"Hallo, Pev. You look cold—have some tea."

He touched her gently on the shoulder as he passed and sat down in the chair next to hers.

"Thank you," he accepted, smiling across at Hester, waiting to be introduced.

"My husband," Damaris said quickly. "Peverell Erskine. Pev, this is Hester Latterly, Edith's friend, who nursed in the Crimea with Florence Nightingale."

"How do you do, Miss Latterly." He inclined his head, his face full of interest. "I hope you are not bored by endless people asking you to tell us about your experiences. We should still be obliged if you would do it for us."

Felicia poured his tea and passed it. "Later, perhaps, if Miss Latterly should call again. Did you have a satisfactory day, Peverell?"

He took her rebuff without the least irritation, almost as if he had not noticed it. Hester would have felt patronized and retaliated. That would have been far less satisfying, and watching Peverell Erskine, she realized it with a little stab of surprise.

He took a cucumber sandwich and ate it with relish before replying.

"Yes thank you, Mama-in-law. I met a most interesting man who fought in the Maori Wars ten years ago." He looked at Hester. "That is in New Zealand, you know? Yes, of course you do. They have the most marvelous birds there. Quite unique, and so beautiful." His agreeable face was full

33

of enthusiasm. "I love birds, Miss Latterly. Such a variety. Everything from a hummingbird no bigger than my little finger, which hovers in the air to suck the nectar from a flower, right up to an albatross, which flies the oceans of the earth, with a wingspan twice the height of a man." His face was bright with the marvels he perceived, and in that instant Hester knew precisely why Damaris had remained in love with him.

She smiled back. "I will trade with you, Mr. Erskine," she offered. "I will tell you everything I know about the Crimea and Miss Nightingale if you will tell me about what you know of birds."

He laughed cheerfully. "What an excellent idea. But I assure you, I am simply an amateur."

"By far the best. I should wish to listen for love of it, not in order to become learned."

"Mr. Erskine is a lawyer, Miss Latterly," Felicia said with distinct chill. Then she turned to her son-in-law. "Did you see Alexandra?"

His expression did not alter, and Hester wondered briefly if he had avoided telling her this immediately because she had been so curt in cutting him off. It would be a good-natured and yet effective way of asserting himself so she did not overrule him completely.

"Yes I did." He addressed no one in particular, and continued sipping his tea. "I saw her this morning. She is very distressed of course, but bearing it with courage and dignity."

"I would expect that of any Carlyon," Felicia said rather sharply. "You do not need to tell me that. I beg your pardon, Miss Latterly, but this is a family matter which cannot interest you. I wish to know her affairs, Peverell. Is everything in order? Does she have what she requires? I imagine Thaddeus left everything tidy and well arranged?"

"Well enough . . ."

Her eyebrows rose. "Well enough? What on earth do you mean?"

"I mean that I have taken care of the preliminaries, and

34

so far there is nothing that cannot be satisfactorily dealt with, Mama-in-law.''

"I shall require to know more than that, at a suitable time.''

"Then you will have to ask Alexandra, because I cannot tell you,'' he said with a bland and totally uncommunicative smile.

"Don't be absurd! Of course you can.'' Her large blue eyes were hard. "You are her solicitor; you must be aware of everything there is.''

"Certainly I am aware of it.'' Peverell set down his cup and looked at her more directly. "But for precisely that reason I cannot discuss her affairs with anyone else.''

"He was my son, Peverell. Have you forgotten that?''

"Every man is someone's son, Mama-in-law,'' he said gently. "That does not invalidate his right to privacy, nor his widow's.''

Felicia's face was white. Randolf retreated farther back into his chair, as if he had not heard. Damaris sat motionless. Edith watched them all.

But Peverell was not disconcerted. He had obviously foreseen both the question and his answer to it. Her reaction could not have surprised him.

"I am sure Alexandra will discuss with you everything that is of family concern,'' he went on as if nothing had happened.

"It is all of family concern, Peverell!'' Felicia said with a tight, hard voice. "The police are involved. Ridiculous as that seems, someone in that wretched house killed Thaddeus. I assume it was Maxim Furnival. I never cared for him. I always thought he lacked self-control, in a finer sense. He paid far too much attention to Alexandra, and she had not the sense to discourage him! I sometimes thought he imagined himself in love with her—whatever that may mean to such a man.''

"I never saw him do anything undignified or hasty,'' Damaris said quickly. "He was merely fond of her.''

"Be quiet, Damaris,'' her mother ordered. "You do not

35

know what you are talking about. I am referring to his nature, not his acts—until now, of course.''

"We don't know that he has done anything now," Edith joined in reasonably.

"He married that Warburton woman; that was a lapse of taste and judgment if ever I saw one," Felicia snapped. "Emotional, uncontrolled."

"Louisa?" Edith asked, looking at Damaris, who nodded.

"Well?" Felicia turned to Peverell. "What are the police doing? When are they going to arrest him?"

"I have no idea."

Before she could respond the door opened and the butler came in looking extremely grave and not a little embarrassed, and carrying a note on a silver tray. He presented it not to Randolf but to Felicia. Possibly Randolf's eyesight was no longer good.

"Miss Alexandra's footman brought it, ma'am," he said very quietly.

"Indeed." She picked it up without speaking and read it through. The very last trace of color fled from her skin, leaving her rigid and waxy pale.

"There will be no reply," she said huskily. "You may go."

"Yes ma'am." He departed obediently, closing the door behind him.

"The police have arrested Alexandra for the murder of Thaddeus," Felicia said with a level, icily controlled voice, as soon as he was gone. "Apparently she has confessed."

Damaris started to say something and choked on her words. Immediately Peverell put his hand over hers and held it hard.

Randolf stared uncomprehendingly, his eyes wide.

"No!" Edith protested. "That's—that's impossible! Not Alex!"

Felicia rose to her feet. "There is no purpose in denying it, Edith. Apparently it is so. She has admitted it." She squared her shoulders. "Peverell, we would be obliged if

36

you would take care of the matter. It seems she has taken leave of her senses, and in a fit of madness become homicidal. Perhaps it can be dealt with privately, since she does not contest the issue.''

Her voice gained confidence. ''She can be put away in a suitable asylum. We shall have Cassian here, naturally, poor child. I shall fetch him myself. I imagine that will have to be done tonight. He cannot remain in that house without family.'' She reached for the bell, then turned to Hester. ''Miss Latterly, you have been privy to our family tragedy. You will surely appreciate that we are no longer in a position to entertain even the closest friends and sympathisers. Thank you for calling. Edith will show you to the door and bid you good-bye.''

Hester stood up. ''Of course. I am most extremely sorry.''

Felicia acknowledged her words with a look but no more. There was nothing to add. All that was possible now was to excuse herself to Randolf, Peverell and Damaris, and leave.

As soon as they were in the hall Edith clasped her arm.

''Dear God, this is terrible! We have to do something!''

Hester stopped and faced her. ''What? I think your mother's answer may be the best. If she has lost her mind and become violent—''

''Rubbish!'' Edith exploded fiercely. ''Alex is not mad. If anyone in the family killed him, it will be their daughter Sabella. She really is . . . very strange. After the birth of her child she threatened to take her own life. Oh—there isn't time to tell you now, but believe me there is a long story about Sabella.'' She was holding Hester so hard there was little choice but to stay. ''She hated Thaddeus,'' Edith went on urgently. ''She didn't want to marry; she wanted to become a nun, of all things. But Thaddeus would not hear of it. She hated him for making her marry, and still does. Poor Alex will have confessed to save her. We've got to do something to help. Can't you think of anything?''

''Well . . .'' Hester's mind raced. ''Well, I do know a private sort of policeman who works for people—but if she

37

has confessed, she will be tried, you know. I know a brilliant lawyer. But Peverell . . .''

"No," Edith said quickly. "He is a solicitor, not a barrister—he doesn't appear in court. He won't mind, I swear. He would want the best for Alex. Sometimes he appears to do whatever Mama says, but he doesn't really. He just smiles and goes his own way. Please, Hester, if there is anything you can do . . . ?''

"I will," Hester promised, clasping Edith's hand. "I will try!"

"Thank you. Now you must go before anyone else comes out and finds us here—please!"

"Of course. Keep heart."

"I will—and thank you again."

Quickly Hester turned and accepted her cloak from the waiting maid and went to the door, her mind racing, her thoughts in turmoil, and the face of Oliver Rathbone sharp in her mind.

As soon as Hester returned, Major Tiplady, who had had little to do but stare out of the window, observed from her face that something distressing had happened, and since it would soon be public knowledge in the newspapers, she did not feel she was betraying any trust by telling him. He was very aware that she had experienced something extraordinary, and to keep it secret would close him out to no purpose. It would also make it far harder to explain why she wished for yet further time away from the house.

"Oh dear," he said as soon as she told him. He sat very upright on the chaise longue. "This is quite dreadful! Do you believe that something has turned the poor woman's mind?"

"Which woman?" She tidied away his tea tray, which the maid had not yet collected, setting it on the small table to the side. "The widow or the daughter?"

"Why—" Then he realized the pertinence of the question. "I don't know. Either of them, I suppose—or even both. Poor creatures." He looked at her anxiously. "What do you propose to do? I cannot see anything to be done, but you seem to have something in mind."

She flashed him a quick, uncertain smile. "I am not sure." She closed the book he had been reading and put it on the table next to him. "I can at least do my best to find her the very best lawyer—which she will be able to afford." She tucked his shoes neatly under the chaise.

"Will her family not do that anyway?" he asked. "Oh, for heaven's sake sit down, woman! How can anyone concentrate their thoughts when you keep moving around and fussing?"

She stopped abruptly and turned to look at him.

With unusual perception he frowned at her. "You do not need to be endlessly doing something in order to justify your position. If you humor me, that will be quite sufficient. Now I require you to stand still and answer me sensibly—if you please."

"Her family would like her put away with as little fuss as possible," she replied, standing in front of him with her hands folded. "It will cause the least scandal that may be achieved after a murder."

"I imagine they would have blamed someone else if they could," he said thoughtfully. "But she has rather spoiled that by confessing. But I still do not see what you can do, my dear."

"I know a lawyer who can do the miraculous with causes which seem beyond hope."

"Indeed?" He was dubious, sitting upright and looking a little uncomfortable. "And you believe he will take this case?"

"I don't know—but I shall ask him and do my best." She stopped, a slight flush in her face. "That is—if you will permit me the time in which to see him?"

"Of course I will. But . . ." He looked vaguely self-conscious. "I would be obliged if you would allow me to know how it proceeds."

She smiled dazzlingly at him.

"Naturally. We shall be in it together."

"Indeed," he said with surprise and increasing satisfaction. "Indeed we shall."

* * *

40

Accordingly, she had no difficulty in being permitted to leave her duties once more the following day and take a hansom cab to the legal offices of Mr. Oliver Rathbone, whose acquaintance she had made at the conclusion of the Grey murder, and then resumed during the Moidore case a few months later. She had sent a letter by hand (or to be more accurate, Major Tiplady had, since he had paid the messenger), requesting that Mr. Rathbone see her on a most urgent matter, and had received an answer by return that he would be in his chambers at eleven o'clock the following day, and would see her at that hour if she wished.

Now at quarter to eleven she was traveling inside the cab with her heart racing and every jolt in the road making her gasp, trying to swallow down the nervousness rising inside her. It really was the most appalling liberty she was taking, not only on behalf of Alexandra Carlyon, whom she had never met, and who presumably had not even heard of her, but also towards Oliver Rathbone. Their relationship had been an odd one, professional in that she had twice been a witness in cases he had defended. William Monk had investigated the second one after the police force officially closed it. In both cases they had drawn Oliver Rathbone in before the conclusion.

At times the understanding between Rathbone and herself had seemed very deep, a collaboration in a cause in which they both fiercely believed. At others it had been more awkward, aware that they were a man and a woman engaged in pursuits quite outside any rules society had laid down for behavior, not lawyer and client, not employer and employee, not social friends or equals, and most certainly not a man courting a woman.

And yet their friendship was of a deeper sort than those she had shared with other men, even army surgeons in the field during the long nights in Scutari, except perhaps with Monk in the moments between their quarrels. And also there had been that one extraordinary, startling and sweet kiss, which she could still recall with a shiver of both pleasure and loneliness.

The cab was stopping and starting in the heavy traffic along High Holborn—hansoms, drays, every kind of carriage.

Please heaven Rathbone would understand this was a call most purely on business. It would be unbearable if he were to think she was pursuing him. Trying to force an acquaintance. Imagining into that moment something which they both knew he did not intend. Her face burned at the humiliation. She must be impersonal and not endeavor to exercise even the slightest undue influence, still less appear to flirt. Not that that would be difficult; she would have no idea how to flirt if her life depended upon it. Her sister-in-law had told her that countless times. If only she could be like Imogen and appeal with sweet helplessness to people, simply by her manner, so men instinctively would desire to help her. It was very nice to be efficient, but it could also be a disadvantage to be obviously so. It was also not especially attractive—either to men or to women. Men thought it unbecoming, and women found it vaguely insulting to them.

Her thoughts were interrupted by the hansom's arrival at Vere Street and Oliver Rathbone's offices, and she was obliged to descend and pay the driver. Since it was already five minutes before her appointment, she mounted the steps and presented herself to the clerk.

A few minutes later the inner door opened and Rathbone came out. He was precisely as she had remembered him; indeed she was taken aback by the vividness of her recall. He was little above average height, with fair hair graying a trifle at the temples, and dark eyes that were acutely aware of all laughter and absurdity, and yet liable to change expression to anger or pity with an instant's warning.

"How agreeable to see you again, Miss Latterly," he said with a smile. "Won't you please come into my office, where you may tell me what business it is that brings you here?" He stood back a little to allow her to pass, then followed her in and closed the door behind him. He invited her to sit in one of the large, comfortable chairs. The office was as it had been last time she was there, spacious, surprisingly free from the oppressive feeling of too many books, and with bright light from the windows as if it were a place from which to observe the world, not one in which to hide from it.

"Thank you," she accepted, arranging her skirts only minimally. She would not give the impression of a social call.

He sat down behind his desk and regarded her with interest.

"Another desperate case of injustice?" he asked, his eyes bright.

Instantly she felt defensive, and had to guard herself from allowing him to dictate the conversation. She remembered quickly that this was his profession, questioning people in such a way that they betrayed themselves in their answers.

"I would be foolish to prejudge it, Mr. Rathbone," she replied with an equally charming smile. "If you were ill, I should be irritated if you consulted me and then prescribed your own treatment."

Now his amusement was unmistakable.

"If some time I consult you, Miss Latterly, I shall keep that in mind. Although I doubt I should be so rash as ever to think of preempting your judgment. When I am ill, I am quite a pitiful object, I assure you."

"People are also frightened and vulnerable, even pitiful, when they are accused of crime and face the law without anyone to defend them—or at least anyone adequate to the occasion," she answered.

"And you think I might be adequate to this particular occasion?" he asked. "I am complimented, if not exactly flattered."

"You might be, if you understood the occasion," she said a trifle tartly.

His smile was wide and quite without guile. He had beautiful teeth.

"Bravo, Miss Latterly. I see you have not changed. Please tell me, what is this occasion?"

"Have you read of the recent death of General Thaddeus Carlyon?" She asked so as to avoid telling him that with which he was already familiar.

43

"I saw the obituary. I believe he met with an accident, did he not? A fall when he was out visiting someone. Was it not accidental?" He looked curious.

"No. It seems he could not have fallen in precisely that way, at least not so as to kill himself."

"The obituary did not describe the injury."

Memory of Damaris's words came back to her, and a wry, bitter humor. "No—they wouldn't. It has an element of the absurd. He fell over the banister from the first landing onto a suit of armor."

"And broke his neck?"

"No. Please do not keep interrupting me, Mr. Rathbone—it is not something you might reasonably guess." She ignored his look of slight surprise at her presumption. "It is too ridiculous. He fell onto the suit of armor and was apparently speared to death by the halberd it was holding. Only the police said it could not have happened by chance. He was speared deliberately after he had fallen and was lying senseless on the floor."

"I see." He was outwardly contrite. "So it was murder; that, I presume, I may safely deduce?"

"You may. The police enquired into the matter for several days, in fact two weeks. It occurred on the evening of April twentieth. Now the widow, Mrs. Alexandra Carlyon, has confessed to the crime."

"That I might reasonably have guessed, Miss Latterly. It is regrettably not an unusual circumstance, and not absurd, except as all human relationships have an element of humor or ridiculousness in them." He did not go on to guess for what reason she had come to see him, but he remained sitting very upright in his chair, giving her his total attention.

With an effort she refrained from smiling, although a certain amusement had touched her, albeit laced with tragedy.

"She may well be guilty," she said instead. "But my interest in the matter is that Edith Sobell, the sister of General Carlyon, feels most strongly that she is not. Edith is convinced that Alexandra has confessed in order to protect her

44

daughter, Sabella Pole, who is very lightly balanced, and hated her father.''

"And was present on the occasion?''

"Yes—and according to what I can learn of the affair from Damaris Erskine, the general's other sister, who was also at the ill-fated dinner party, there were several people who had the opportunity to have pushed him over the banister.''

"I cannot act for Mrs. Carlyon unless she wishes it,'' he pointed out. "No doubt the Carlyon family will have their own legal counsel.''

"Peverell Erskine, Damaris's husband, is their solicitor, and Edith assures me he would not be averse to engaging the best barrister available.''

His fine mouth twitched in the ghost of a smile.

"Thank you for the implied compliment.''

She ignored it, because she did not know what to say.

"Will you please see Alexandra Carlyon and at least consider the matter?'' she asked him earnestly, self-consciousness overridden by the urgency of the matter. "I fear she may otherwise be shuffled away into an asylum for the criminally insane, to protect the family name, and remain there until she dies.'' She leaned towards him. "Such places are the nearest we have to hell in this life—and for someone who is quite sane, simply trying to defend a daughter, it would be immeasurably worse than death.''

All the humor and light vanished from his face as if washed away. Knowledge of appalling pain filled his eyes, and there was no hesitation in him.

"I will certainly keep my mind open in the matter,'' he promised. "If you ask Mr. Erskine to instruct me, and engage my services so that I may apply to speak with Mrs. Carlyon, then I will give you my word that I will do so. Although of course whether I can persuade her to tell me the truth is another thing entirely.''

"Perhaps you could engage Mr. Monk to carry out investigations, should you—'' She stopped.

"I shall certainly consider it. You have not told me what

45

was her motive in murdering her husband. Did she give one?''

She was caught off guard. She had not thought to ask.

"I have no idea," she answered, wide-eyed in amazement at her own omission.

"It can hardly have been self-defense." He pursed his lips. "And we would find it most difficult to argue a crime of passion, not that that is considered an excuse—for a woman, and a jury would find it most . . . unbecoming." Again the black humor flickered across his face, as if he were conscious of the irony of it. It was a quality unusual in a man, and one of the many reasons she liked him.

"I believe the whole evening was disastrous," she continued, watching his face. "Apparently Alexandra was upset, even before she arrived, as though she and the general had quarreled over something. And I gather from Damaris that Mrs. Furnival, the hostess, flirted with him quite openly. But that is something which I have observed quite often, and very few people are foolish enough to take exception to it. It is one of the things one simply has to endure." She saw the faint curl of amusement at the corners of his lips, and ignored it.

"I had better wait until Mr. Erskine contacts me," he said with returning gravity. "I will be able to speak to Mrs. Carlyon herself. I promise you I will do so."

"Thank you. I am most obliged." She rose to her feet, and automatically he rose also. Now it suddenly occurred to her that she owed him for his time. He had spared her almost half an hour, and she had not come prepared to pay. His fee would be a considerable amount of money from her very slender resources. It was an idiotic and embarrassing error.

"I shall send you my account when the matter is closed," he said, apparently without having noticed her confusion. "You will understand that if Mrs. Carlyon engages me, and I accept the case, what she tells me will have to remain confidential between us, but I shall of course inform you whether I am able to defend her or not." He came around from behind the desk and moved towards the door.

46

"Of course," she said a little stiffly, overwhelmed with relief. She had been saved from making a complete fool of herself. "I shall be happy if you are able to help. I shall now go and tell Mrs. Sobell—and of course Mr. Erskine." She did not mention that so far as she was aware, Peverell Erskine knew nothing about the enquiry. "Good day, Mr. Rathbone—and thank you."

"It was a pleasure to see you again, Miss Latterly." He opened the door for her and held it while she passed through, then stood for several moments watching her leave.

Hester went immediately to Carlyon House and asked the parlormaid who answered the door if Mrs. Sobell were in.

"Yes, Miss Latterly," the girl answered quickly, and from her expression, Hester judged that Edith had forewarned her she was expected. "If you please to come to Mrs. Sobell's sitting room, ma'am," the maid went on, glancing around the hallway, then lifting her chin defiantly and walking smartly across the parquet and up the stairs, trusting Hester was behind her.

Across the first landing and in the east wing she opened the door to a small sunlit room with floral covered armchairs and sofa and soft watercolor paintings on the walls.

"Miss Latterly, ma'am," the maid said quietly, then withdrew.

Edith rose to her feet, her face eager.

"Hester! Did you see him? What did he say? Will he do it?"

Hester found herself smiling briefly, although there was little enough humor in what she had to report.

"Yes I saw him, but of course he cannot accept any case until he is requested by the solicitor of the person in question. Are you sure Peverell will be agreeable to Mr. Rathbone acting for Alexandra?"

"Oh yes—but it won't be easy, at least I fear not. Peverell may be the only one who is willing to fight on Alex's behalf. But if Peverell asks Mr. Rathbone, will he take the case? You did tell him she had confessed, didn't you?"

"Of course I did."

"Thank heaven. Hester, I really am most grateful to you for this, you know. Come and sit down." She moved back to the chairs and curled up in one and waved to the other, where Hester sat down and tucked her skirts comfortably. "Then what happens? He will go and see Alex, of course, but what if she just goes on saying she did it?"

"He will employ an investigator to enquire into it," Hester replied, trying to sound more certain than she felt.

"What can he do, if she won't tell him?"

"I don't know—but he's better than most police. Why did she do it, Edith? I mean, what does she say?"

Edith bit her lip. "That's the worst part of it. Apparently she said it was out of jealousy over Thaddeus and Louisa."

"Oh—I . . ." Hester was momentarily thrown into confusion.

"I know." Edith looked wretched. "It is very sordid, isn't it? And unpleasantly believable, if you know Alex. She is unconventional enough for something so wild and so foolish to enter her mind. Except that I really don't believe she ever loved Thaddeus with that sort of intensity, and I am quite sure she did not lately."

For a moment she looked embarrassed at such candor, then her emotions at the urgency and tragedy of it took over again. "Please, Hester, do not allow your natural repugnance for such behavior to prevent you from doing what you can to help her. I don't believe she killed him at all. I think it was far more probably Sabella—God forgive her—or perhaps I should say God help her. I think she may honestly be out of her mind." Her face tightened into a somber unhappiness. "And Alex taking the guilt for her will not help anyone. They will hang an innocent person, and Sabella in her lucid hours will suffer even more—don't you see that?"

"Yes of course I see it," Hester agreed, although in honesty she thought it not at all improbable that Alexandra Carlyon might well have killed her husband exactly as she had confessed. But it would be cruel, and serve no purpose, to say so to Edith now, when she was convinced of Alexandra's innocence, or passionately wished to be. "Have you any idea why Alexandra would feel there was some cause for jealousy over the general and Mrs. Furnival?"

Edith's eyes were bright with mockery and pain.

"You have not yet met Louisa Furnival, or you would not bother to ask. She is the sort of woman anyone might be jealous of." Her expressive face was filled with dislike, mockery, and something which could almost have been a kind of admiration. "She has a way of walking, an air to her, a smile that makes you think she has something that you have not. Even if she had done nothing whatsoever, and your husband found no interest in her at all, it would be easy to imagine he had, simply because of her manner."

"That does not sound very hopeful."

"Except that I would be amazed if Thaddeus ever gave her more than a passing glance. He really was not in the least a flirt, even with Louisa. He was . . ." She lifted her shoulders very slightly in a gesture of helplessness. "He was very much the soldier, a man's man. He was always polite to women, of course, but I don't think he was ever fearfully comfortable with us. He didn't really know what to talk about. Naturally he had learned, as any well-bred man does, but it was learned, if you know what I mean." She looked at Hester questioningly. "He was brilliant at action, brave, decisive, and nearly always right in his judgment; and he knew how to express himself to his men, and to new young men interested in the army. He used to come alight then; I've watched his eyes and seen how much he cared."

She sighed. "He always assumed women weren't interested, and that's not true. I would have been—but it hardly matters now, I suppose. What I'm trying to say is that one doesn't flirt with conversation about military strategy and the relative merits of one gun over another, least of all with someone like Louisa. And even if he did, one does not commit murder over such a thing, it is . . ." Her face puckered, and for a moment Hester wondered with sudden hurt what Oswald Sobell had been like, and what pain Edith might have suffered in their brief marriage, what wounds of jealousy she herself had known. Then the urgency of the present reasserted itself and she returned to the subject of Alexandra.

"I imagine it is probably better that the truth should be learned, whatever it is," she said aloud to Edith. "And I suppose it is possible the murderer is not either Alexandra or Sabella, but someone else. Perhaps if Louisa Furnival is a flirt, and was casting eyes at Thaddeus, her own husband might have imagined there was more to it than there was, and might finally have succumbed to jealousy himself."

Edith put her hands up and covered her face, leaning forward across her knees.

"I hate this!" she said fiercely. "Everyone involved is either family or a friend of sorts. And it has to have been one of them."

"It is wretched," Hester agreed. "That is one of the things I learned in the other crimes I have seen investigated: you come to know the people, their dreams and their griefs, their wounds—and whoever it is, it hurts you. You cannot island yourself from it and make it 'them,' and not 'us.' "

Edith removed her hands and looked up, surprise in her face, her mouth open to argue; then slowly the emotion subsided and she accepted that Hester meant exactly what she said.

"How very hard." She let her breath out slowly. "Somehow I always took it for granted there would be a barrier between me and whoever did such a thing—I mean usually. There would be a whole class of people whose hurt I could exclude . . ."

"Only with a sort of dishonesty." Hester rose to her feet and walked over to the high window above the garden. It was a sash window open at top and bottom, and the perfume of wallflowers in the sun drifted up. "I forgot to tell you last time, with all the news of the tragedy, but I have been enquiring into what sort of occupation you might find, and I think the most interesting and agreeable thing you could do would be as a librarian." She watched a gardener walk across the grass with a tray of seedlings. "Or researcher for someone who wishes to write a treatise, or a monograph or some such thing. It would pay you a small amount insufficient to support you, but it would take you away from Carlyon House during the days.''

"Not nursing?'' There was a note of disappointment in Edith's voice, in spite of her effort to conceal it, and a painful self-consciousness. Hester realized with a sudden stab of embarrassment that Edith admired her and that what she really sought was to do the same thing Hester did, but had been reluctant to say so.

With her face suddenly hot she struggled for a reply that would be honest and not clumsy. It would not be kind to equivocate.

''No. It is very hard to find a private position, even if you have the training for it. It is far better to use the skills you have.'' She did not face her; it was better Edith did not see her sudden understanding. ''There are some really very interesting people who need librarians or researchers, or someone to write up their work for them. You could find someone who writes on a subject in which you might become most interested yourself.''

''Such as what?'' There was no lightness in Edith's voice.

''Anything?'' Hester turned to face her and forced a cheerfulness into her expression. ''Archaeology . . . history . . . exploration.'' She stopped as she saw a sudden spark of real excitement in Edith's eyes. She smiled with overwhelming relief and a surge of unreasonable happiness. ''Why not? Women have begun to think of going to most marvelous places—Egypt, the Magreb, Africa even.''

''Africa! Yes . . .'' Edith said almost under her breath, her confidence returned, the wound vanished in hope. ''Yes. After all this is over I will. Thank you, Hester—thank you so much!''

She got no further because the sitting room door opened and Damaris came in. Today she looked utterly different. Gone was the contradictory but distinctly feminine air of the previous occasion. This time she was in riding habit and looked vigorous and boyish, like a handsome youth, faintly Mediterranean, and Hester knew the instant their eyes met

51

that the effect was wholly intentional, and that Damaris enjoyed it.

Hester smiled. She had dared in reality far further than Damaris into such forbidden masculine fields, seen real violence, warfare and chivalry, the honest friendship where there was no barrier between men and women, where speech was not forever dictated by social ritual rather than true thoughts and feelings, where people worked side by side for a desperate common cause and only courage and skill mattered. Very little of such social rebellion could shake her, let alone offend.

"Good afternoon, Mrs. Erskine," she said cheerfully. "I am delighted to see you looking so well, in such trying circumstances."

Damaris's face broke into a wide grin. She closed the door behind her and leaned against the handle.

"Edith said you were going to see a lawyer friend of yours who is totally brilliant—is that true?"

This time Hester was caught off guard. She had not thought Damaris was aware of Edith's request.

"Ah—yes." There was no point in prevarication. "Do you think Mr. Erskine will mind?"

"Oh no, not at all. But I cannot answer for Mama. You had better come in to luncheon and tell us about it."

Hester looked desperately at Edith, hoping she would rescue her from having to go. She had expected simply to tell Edith about Rathbone and then leave her to inform Peverell Erskine; the rest of the family would find out from him. Now it seemed she was going to have to face them all over the luncheon table.

But Edith was apparently unaware of her feelings. She stood up quickly and moved towards the door.

"Yes of course. Is Pev here?"

"Yes—now would be a perfect time." Damaris turned around and pulled the door open. "We need to act as soon as we can." She smiled brilliantly at Hester. "It really is most kind of you."

The dining room was heavily and ornately furnished, and

with a full dinner service in the new, fashionable turquoise, heavily patterned and gilded. Felicia was already seated and Randolf occupied his place at the head of the table. He looked larger and more imposing than he had lounging in the armchair at afternoon tea. His face was heavy, and set in lines of stubborn, weary immobility. Hester tried to imagine him as a young man, and what it might have been like to be in love with him. Was he dashing in uniform? Might there have been a trace of humor or wit in his face then? The years change people; there were disappointments, dreams that crumbled. And she was seeing him at the worst possible time. His only son had just been murdered, and almost certainly by a member of his own family.

"Good afternoon, Mrs. Carlyon, Colonel Carlyon," she said, swallowing hard, and trying at least temporarily to put out of her mind the confrontation which must come when Oliver Rathbone was mentioned.

"Good afternoon, Miss Latterly," Felicia said with her eyebrows arched in as much surprise as was possible with civility. "How agreeable of you to join us. To what occasion do we owe the pleasure of a second visit in so short a time?"

Randolf muttered something inaudible. He seemed to have forgotten her name, and had nothing to say beyond an acknowledgment of her presence.

Peverell looked as benign and agreeable as before, but he smiled at her without speaking.

Felicia was very obviously waiting. Apparently it was not merely a rhetorical question; she wished an answer.

Damaris strode over to her place at the table and sat down with something of a swagger, ignoring the frown which shadowed her mother's face.

"She came to see Peverell," she answered with a slight smile.

Felicia's irritation deepened.

"At luncheon?" Her voice held a chill incredulity. "Surely if it were Peverell she wished to see she would have made an appointment with him in his offices, like anyone else. She would hardly wish to conduct her private business in our company, and over a meal. You must be mistaken, Damaris. Or is this your idea of humor? If it is, it is most misplaced, and I must require you to apologize, and not do such a thing again.''

"Not humorous at all, Mama," she said with instant sobriety. "It is in order to help Alex, so it is entirely appropriate that it should be discussed here, with us present. After all, it does concern the whole family, in a way."

"Indeed?" Felicia kept her eyes on Damaris's face. "And what can Miss Latterly possibly do to help Alexandra? It is our tragedy that Alexandra would seem to have lost her sanity." The skin across her cheekbones tightened as if she were expecting a blow. "Even the best doctors have no cure for such things—and not even God can undo what has already happened."

"But we don't know what has happened, Mama," Damaris pointed out.

"We know that Alexandra confessed that she murdered Thaddeus," Felicia said icily, concealing from them all whatever wells of pain lay beneath the bare words. "You should not have asked Miss Latterly for her help; there is nothing whatsoever that she, or anyone else, can do about the tragedy. We are quite able to find our own doctors who will take care of her disposition to a suitable place of confinement, for her own good, and that of society." She turned to Hester for the first time since the subject had been raised. "Do you care to take soup, Miss Latterly?"

"Thank you." Hester could think of nothing else to say, no excuse or explanation to offer for herself. The whole affair was even worse than she had foreseen. She should have declined the invitation and excused herself. She could have told Edith all she needed to know quite simply and left the rest to Peverell. But it was too late now.

Felicia nodded to the maid and the tureen was brought in and the soup served in silence.

After taking several sips Randolf turned to Hester.

"Well—if it is not a doctor you are counseling us about, Miss Latterly, perhaps we had better know what it is."

Felicia looked at him sharply, but he chose to ignore her.

Hester would like to have told him it was between her and Peverell, but she did not dare. No words came to her that could have been even remotely civil. She looked back at his rather baleful stare and felt acutely uncomfortable.

There was silence around the table. No one came to her rescue, as if their courage had suddenly deserted them also.

"I—" She took a deep breath and began again. "I have the acquaintance of a most excellent barrister who has previously fought and won seemingly impossible cases. I thought—I thought Mr. Erskine might wish to consider his services for Mrs. Carlyon."

Felicia's nostrils flared and a spark of cold anger lit her face.

"Thank you, Miss Latterly, but as I think I have already pointed out, a barrister is not required. My daughter-in-law has already confessed to the crime; there is no case to be argued. It is only a matter of arranging for her to be put away as discreetly as possible in the place best suited to care for her in her state."

"She may not be guilty, Mama," Edith said tentatively, the force and enthusiasm gone out of her voice.

"Then why would she admit to it, Edith?" Felicia asked without bothering to look at her.

Edith's face tightened. "To protect Sabella. Alex isn't insane, we all know that. But Sabella may well be . . ."

"Nonsense!" Felicia said sharply. "She was a trifle emotional after her child was born. It happens from time to time. It passes." She broke a little brown bread on the plate to her left, her fingers powerful. "Women have been known to kill their children sometimes, in such fits of melancholia, but not their fathers. You should not offer opinions in matters you know nothing about."

"She hated Thaddeus!" Edith persisted, two spots of color in her cheeks, and it came to Hester sharply that the reference to Edith's ignorance of childbirth had been a deliberate cruelty.

"Don't be ridiculous!" Felicia said to her sharply. "She

was unruly and very self-willed. Alexandra should have been much firmer with her. But that is hardly the same thing as being homicidal.''

Peverell smiled charmingly. "It really doesn't matter, Mama-in-law, because Alexandra will give me whatever instructions she wishes, and I shall be obliged to act accordingly. After she has thought about it awhile, and realized that it will not simply be a matter of being shut away in some agreeable nursing establishment, but of being hanged . . .'' He ignored Felicia's indrawn breath and wince of distaste at the grossness of his choice of words. ''. . . then she may change her plea and wish to be defended.'' He took another sip from his spoon. "And of course I shall have to put all the alternatives before her.''

Felicia's face darkened. "For goodness sake, Peverell, are you not competent to get the matter taken care of decently and with some discretion?'' she said with exasperated contempt. "Poor Alexandra's mind has snapped. She has taken leave of her wits and allowed her jealous fancies to provoke her into a moment of insane rage. It can help no one to expose her to public ridicule and hatred. It is the most absurd of crimes. What would happen if every woman who imagined her husband paid more attention to another woman than he should—which must be half London!—were to resort to murder? Society would fall apart, and everything that goes with it.'' She took a deep breath and began again, more gently, as if explaining to a child. "Can you not put it to her, when you see her, that even if she has no feeling left for herself, or for us, that she must consider her family, especially her son, who is a child? Think what the scandal will do to him! If she makes public this jealousy of hers, and goodness knows there was no ground for it except in her poor mad brain, then she will ruin Cassian's future and at the very least be a source of embarrassment to her daughters.''

Peverell seemed unmoved, except by politeness and a certain outward sympathy for Felicia.

"I will point out all the possible courses to her, Mama-in-law, and the results, as I believe them, of any action she might make." He dabbed his lips with his napkin and his face retained so smooth an expression he might have been discussing the transfer of a few acres of farmland, with no real perception of the passions and tragedies of which they were speaking.

Damaris watched him with wide eyes. Edith was silent. Randolf continued with his soup.

Felicia was so angry with him she had great difficulty in controlling her expression, and on the edge of the table her fingers were knotted around her napkin. But she would not permit him to see that he had beaten her.

Randolf put his spoon down. "I suppose you know what you are doing," he said with a scowl. "But it sounds very unsatisfactory to me."

"Well the army is rather different from the law." Peverell's expression was still one of interest and unbroken patience. "It's still war, of course; conflict, adversarial system. But weapons are different and rules have to be obeyed. All in the brain." He smiled as if inwardly pleased with something the rest of them could not see, not a secret pleasure so much as a private one. "We also deal in life and death, and the taking of property and land—but the weapons are words and the arena is in the mind."

Randolf muttered something inaudible, but there was acute dislike in his heavy face.

"Sometimes you make yourself sound overly important, Peverell," Felicia said acidly.

"Yes." Peverell was not put out of countenance in the least. He smiled at the ceiling. "Damaris says I am pompous." He turned to look at Hester. "Who is your barrister, Miss Latterly?"

"Oliver Rathbone, of Vere Street, just off Lincoln's Inn Fields," Hester replied immediately.

"Really?" His eyes were wide. "He is quite brilliant. I remember him in the Grey case. What an extraordinary verdict! And do you really think he would be prepared to act for Alexandra?"

"If she wishes him to." Hester felt a surge of self-consciousness that took her by surprise. She found herself unable to meet anyone's eyes, even Peverell's, not because he was critical but because he was so remarkably perceptive.

"How excellent," he said quietly. "How absolutely excellent. It is very good of you, Miss Latterly. I am sufficiently aware of Mr. Rathbone's reputation to be most obliged. I shall inform Mrs. Carlyon."

"But you will not allow her to entertain any false notions as to her choices in the matter," Felicia said grimly. "No matter how brilliant"—she said the word with a peculiar curl of her lip as though it were a quality to be held in contempt—"this Mr. Rathbone may be, he cannot twist or defy the law, nor would it be desirable that he should." She took a deep breath and let it out in an inaudible sigh, her mouth suddenly tight with pain. "Thaddeus is dead, and the law will require that someone answer for it."

"Everyone is entitled to defend themselves in their own way, whatever they believe is in their interest, Mama-in-law," Peverell said clearly.

"Possibly, but society also has rights, surely—it must!" She stared at him defiantly. "Alexandra's ideas will not be allowed to override those of the rest of us. I will not permit it." She turned to Hester. "Perhaps now you will tell us something of your experiences with Miss Nightingale, Miss Latterly. It would be most inspiring. She is truly a remarkable woman."

Hester was speechless with amazement for a moment, then a reluctant admiration for Felicia's sheer command overtook her.

"Yes—by—by all means . . ." And she began with the tales she felt would be most acceptable to them and least likely to provoke any further dissension: the long nights in the hospital at Scutari, the weariness, the patience, the endless work of cleaning to be done, the courage. She forbore from speaking of the filth, the rats, the sheer blinding incompetence, or the horrifying figures of the casualties that could have been avoided by foresight, adequate provisions, transport and sanitation.

* * *

That afternoon Peverell went first to see Alexandra Carlyon, then to Vere Street to speak to Oliver Rathbone. The day after, May 6, Rathbone presented himself at the prison gates and requested, as Mrs. Carlyon's solicitor, if he might speak with her. He knew he would not be refused.

It was foolish to create in one's mind a picture of what a client would be like, her appearance, or even her personality, and yet as he followed the turnkey along the gray passages he already had a picture formed of Alexandra Carlyon. He saw her as dark-haired, lush of figure and dramatic and emotional of temperament. After all, she had apparently killed her husband in a rage of jealousy—or if Edith Sobell were correct, had confessed it falsely in order to shield her daughter.

But when the turnkey, a big woman with iron-gray hair screwed into a knot at the back of her head, finally unlocked the door and swung it open, he stepped into the cell and saw a woman of little more than average height. She was very slender—too slender for fashion—her fair hair had a heavy natural curl, and her face was highly individual, full of wit and imagination. Her cheekbones were broad, her nose short and aquiline, her mouth beautiful but far too wide, and at once passionate and humorous. She was not lovely in any traditional sense, and yet she was startlingly attractive, even exhausted and frightened as she was, and dressed in plainest white and gray.

She looked up at him without interest, because she had no hope. She was defeated and he knew it even before she spoke.

"How do you do, Mrs. Carlyon," he said formally. "I am Oliver Rathbone. I believe your brother-in-law, Mr. Erskine, has told you that I am willing to represent you, should you wish it?"

She smiled, but it was a ghost of a gesture, an effort dragged up out of an attempt at good manners rather than anything she felt.

"How do you do, Mr. Rathbone. Yes, Peverell did tell

59

me, but I am afraid you have wasted a journey. You cannot help me."

Rathbone looked at the turnkey.

"Thank you—you may leave us. I will call when I want to be let out again."

"Very well," said the woman, and she retreated, locking the door behind her with a loud click as the lever turned and fell into place.

Alexandra remained sitting on the cot and Rathbone lowered himself to sit on the far end of it. To continue standing would be to give the impression he was about to leave, and he would not surrender without a fight.

"Possibly not, Mrs. Carlyon, but please do not dismiss me before permitting me to try. I shall not prejudge you." He smiled, knowing his own charm because it was part of his trade. "Please do not prejudge me either."

This time her answering smile was in her eyes only, and there was sadness in it, and mockery.

"Of course I will listen to you, Mr. Rathbone; for Peverell's sake as well as in good manners. But the truth remains that you cannot help me." Her hesitation was so minute as to be almost indiscernible. "I killed my husband. The law will require payment for that."

He noticed that she did not use the word *hang*, and he knew in that moment that she was too afraid of it yet to say it aloud. Perhaps she had not even said it to herself in her own mind. Already his pity was engaged. He thrust it away. It was no basis on which to defend a case. His brain was what was needed.

"Tell me what happened, Mrs. Carlyon; everything that you feel to be relevant to your husband's death, starting wherever you wish."

She looked away from him. Her voice was flat.

"There is very little to tell. My husband had paid a great deal of attention to Louisa Furnival for some time. She is very beautiful, and has a kind of manner about her which men admire a great deal. She flirted with him. I think she flirted with most men. I was jealous. That's all . . ."

60

"Your husband flirted with Mrs. Furnival at a dinner party, so you left the room and followed him upstairs, pushed him over the banister," he said expressionlessly, "and when he fell you went down the stairs after him, and as he lay senseless on the floor you picked up the halberd and drove it through his chest? I assume this was the first time in your twenty-three years of marriage that he had so offended you?"

She swung around and looked at him with anger. Phrased like that and repeated blindly it sounded preposterous. It was the first spark of real emotion he had seen in her, and as such the very beginning of hope.

"No of course not," she said coldly. "He was more than merely flirting with her. He had been having an affair with her and they were flaunting it in my face—and in front of my own daughter and her husband. It would have been enough to anger any woman."

He watched her face closely, the remarkable features, the sleeplessness, the shock and the fear. He did see anger there also, but it was on the surface, a flare of temper, shallow and without heat, the flame of a match, not the searing heat of a furnace. Was that because she was lying about the flirting, the affair, or because she was too exhausted, too spent to feel any passion now? The object of her rage was dead and she was in the shadow of the noose herself.

"And yet many women must have endured it," he replied, still watching her.

She lifted her shoulders very slightly and he realized again how thin she was. The white blouse and gray unhooped skirt made her look almost waiflike, except for the power in her face. She was not a childlike woman at all; that broad brow and short, round jaw were too willful to be demure, except by deliberate artifice, and it would be a deception short-lived.

"Tell me how it happened, Mrs. Carlyon," he tried again. "Start that evening. Of course the affair with Mrs. Furnival had been continuing for some time. By the way, when did you first realize they were enamored of each other?"

"I don't remember." Still she did not look at him. There was no urgency in her at all. It was quite obvious she did not care whether he believed her or not. The emotion was gone again. She shrugged very faintly. "A few weeks, I suppose. One doesn't know what one doesn't want to." Now suddenly there was real passion in her, harsh and desperately painful. Something hurt her so deeply it was tangible in the small room.

He was confused. One moment she felt so profoundly he could almost sense the pulse of it himself; the next she was numb, as if she were speaking of total trivialities that mattered to no one.

"And this particular evening brought it to a climax?" he said gently.

"Yes . . ." Her voice was husky anyway, with a pleasing depth to it unusual in a woman. Now it was little above a whisper.

"You must tell me what happened, event by event as you recall it, Mrs. Carlyon, if I am to . . . understand." He had nearly said *to help*, when he remembered the hopelessness in her face and in her bearing, and knew that she had no belief in help. The promise would be without meaning to her, and she would reject him again for using it.

As it was she still kept her face turned away and her voice was tight with emotion.

"Understanding will not achieve anything, Mr. Rathbone. I killed him. That is all the law will know or care about. And that is unarguable."

He smiled wryly. "Nothing is ever unarguable in law, Mrs. Carlyon. That is how I make my living, and believe me I am good at it. I don't always win, but I do far more often than I lose."

She swung around to face him and for the first time there was real humor in her face, lighting it and showing a trace of the delightful woman she might be in other circumstances.

"A true lawyer's reply," she said quietly. "But I am afraid I would be one of those few."

"Oh please. Don't defeat me before I begin!" He allowed an answering trace of lightness into his tone also. "I prefer to be beaten than to surrender."

"It is not your battle, Mr. Rathbone. It is mine."

"I would like to make it mine. And you do need a barrister of some kind to plead your case. You cannot do it yourself."

"All you can do is repeat my confession," she said again.

"Mrs. Carlyon, I dislike intensely any form of cruelty, especially that which is unnecessary, but I have to tell you the truth. If you are found guilty, without any mitigating circumstances, then you will hang."

She closed her eyes very slowly and took a long, deep breath, her skin ashen white. As he had thought earlier, she had already touched this in her mind, but some defense, some hope had kept it just beyond her grasp. Now it was there in words and she could no longer pretend. He felt brutal watching her, and yet to have allowed her to cling to a delusion would have been far worse, immeasurably dangerous.

He must judge exactly, precisely all the intangible measures of fear and strength, honesty and love or hate which made her emotional balance at this moment if he were to guide her through this morass which he himself could only guess at. Public opinion would have no pity for a woman who murdered out of jealousy. In fact there would be little pity for a woman who murdered her husband whatever the reason. Anything short of life-threatening physical brutality was expected to be endured. Obscene or unnatural demands, of course, would be abhorred, but so would anyone crass enough to mention such things. What hell anyone endured in the bedroom was something people preferred not to speak of, like fatal diseases and death itself. It was not decent.

"Mrs. Carlyon . . ."

"I know," she whispered. "They will . . ." She still could not bring herself to say the words, and he did not force her. He knew they were there in her mind.

"I can do a great deal more than simply repeat your confession, if you will tell me the truth," he went on. "You did not simply push your husband over the banister and then stab him with the halberd because he was overfamiliar with Mrs. Furnival. Did you speak to him about it? Did you quarrel?"

"No."

"Why not?"

She turned to look at him, her blue eyes uncomprehending.

"What?"

"Why did you not speak to him?" he repeated patiently. "Surely at some time you must have told him his behavior was distressing you?"

"Oh . . . I—yes." She looked surprised. "Of course . . . I asked him to be—discreet . . ."

"Is that all? You loved him so much you were prepared to stab him to death rather than allow another woman to have him—and yet all you did was to ask—" He stopped. He could see in her face that she had not even thought of that sort of love. The very idea of a consuming sexual passion which culminated in murder was something that had not occurred to her with regard to herself and the general. She seemed to have been speaking of something else.

Their eyes met, and she realized that to continue with that pretense would be useless.

"No." She looked away and her voice changed again. "It was the betrayal. I did not love him in that way." The very faintest smile tugged at the corners of her wide mouth. "We had been married twenty-three years, Mr. Rathbone. Such a long-lived passion is not impossible, I suppose, but it would be rare."

"Then what, Mrs. Carlyon?" he demanded. "Why did you kill him as he lay there in front of you, senseless? And do not tell me you were afraid he would attack you for having pushed him, either physically or in words. The last thing he would have done was allow the rest of the dinner party to know that his wife had pushed him downstairs. It has far too much of the ridiculous."

She drew breath, and let it out again without speaking.

"Had he ever beaten you?" he asked. "Seriously?"

She did not look at him. "No," she said very quietly. "It would help if he had, wouldn't it? I should have said yes."

"Not if it is untrue. Your word alone would not be greatly helpful anyway. Many husbands beat their wives. It is not a legal offense unless you feared for your life. And for such a profound charge you would need a great deal of corroborative evidence."

"He didn't beat me. He was a—a very civilized man—a hero." Her lips curled in a harsh, wounding humor as she said it, as if there were some dark joke behind the words.

He knew she was not yet prepared to share it, and he avoided rebuff by not asking.

"So why did you kill him, Mrs. Carlyon? You were not passionately jealous. He had not threatened you. What then?"

"He was having an affair with Louisa Furnival—publicly—in front of my friends and family," she repeated flatly.

He was back to the beginning. He did not believe her; at least he did not believe that was all. There was something raw and deep that she was concealing. All this was surface, and laced with lies and evasions. "What about your daughter?" he asked.

She turned back to him, frowning. "My daughter?"

"Your daughter, Sabella. Had she a good relationship with her father?"

Again the shadow of a smile curled her mouth.

"You have heard she quarreled with him. Yes she did, very unpleasantly. She did not get on well with him. She had wished to take the veil, and he thought it was not in her best interest. Instead he arranged for her to marry Fenton Pole, a very agreeable young man who has treated her well."

"But she has still not forgiven her father, even after this time?"

"No."

"Why not? Such a grudge seems excessive."

"She—she was very ill," she said defensively. "Very disturbed—after the birth of her child. It sometimes happens." She stared at him, her head high. "That was when she began to be angry again. It has largely passed."

"Mrs. Carlyon—was it your daughter, and not you, who killed your husband?"

She swung around to him, her eyes wide, very blue. She

65

really did have a most unusual face. Now it was full of anger and fear, ready to fight in an instant.

"No—Sabella had nothing to do with it! I have already told you, Mr. Rathbone, it was I who killed him. I absolutely forbid you to bring her into it, do you understand me? She is totally innocent. I shall discharge you if you suggest for a moment anything else!"

And that was all he could achieve. She would say nothing more. He rose to his feet.

"I will see you again, Mrs. Carlyon. In the meantime speak of this to no one, except with my authority. Do you understand?" He did not know why he bothered to say this. All his instincts told him to decline the case. He could do very little to help a woman who deliberately killed her husband without acceptable reason, and a flirtation at a dinner party was not an acceptable reason to anyone at all. Had she found him in bed with another woman it might be mitigating, especially if it were in her own house, and with a close friend. But even that was not much. Many a woman had found her husband in bed with a maid and been obliged to accept in silence, indeed to keep a smile on her face. Society would be more likely to criticize her for being clumsy enough to find them, when with a little discretion she could have avoided placing herself—and him—in such a situation.

"If that is what you wish," she said without interest. "Thank you for coming, Mr. Rathbone." She did not even ask who had sent him.

"It is what I wish," he answered. "Good day, Mrs. Carlyon." What an absurd parting. How could she possibly have a good anything?

Rathbone left the prison in a turmoil of mind. Every judgment of intelligence decreed that he decline the case. And yet when he hailed a hansom he gave the driver instructions to go to Grafton Street, where William Monk had his rooms, and not to High Holborn and Peverell Erskine's offices, where he could tell him politely that he felt unable to be of any real assistance to Alexandra Carlyon.

All the way riding along in the cab at a steady trot his mind was finding ways of refusing the case, and the most excellent reasons why he should. Any competent barrister could go through the motions of pleading for her, and for half the sum. There was really nothing to say. It might well be more merciful not to offer her hope, or to drag out the proceedings, which would only prolong the pain of what was in the end inevitable.

And yet he did not reach forward and tap on the window to redirect the cabby. He did not even move in his seat until they stopped at Grafton Street and he climbed down and paid the man. He even watched him move away along towards the Tottenham Court Road and turn the corner without calling him back.

A running patterer came along the footpath, a long lean man with fair hair flopping over his brow, his singsong voice reciting in easy rhymes some domestic drama ending in betrayal and murder. He stopped a few yards from Rathbone, and immediately a couple of idle passersby hesitated to hear the end of his tale. One threw him a threepenny piece.

A costermonger walked up the middle of the street with his barrow, crying his wares, and a cripple with a tray of matches hobbled up from Whitfield Street.

There was no purpose in standing on the paving stones. Rathbone went up and knocked on the door. It was a lodging house, quite respectable and spacious, very suitable for a single man of business or a minor profession. Monk would have no need of a house. From what he could remember of him, and he remembered him very vividly, Monk preferred to spend his money on expensive and very well-cut clothes. Apparently he had been a vain and highly ambitious man, professionally and socially. At least he had been, before the accident which had robbed him of his memory, at first so totally that even his name and his face were strange to him. All his life had had to be detected little by little, pieced together from fragments of evidence, letters, records of his police cases when he was still one of the most brilliant detectives London had seen, and from the reactions of others and their emotions towards him.

Then had come his resignation over the Moidore case, both on principle and in fury, because he would not be ordered against his judgment. Now he struggled to make a living by doing private work for those who, for one reason or another, found the police unsuitable or unavailable to them.

The buxom landlady opened the door and then, seeing Rathbone's immaculate figure, her eyes widened with surprise. Some deep instinct told her the difference between the air of a superior tradesman, or a man of the commercial classes, and this almost indefinably different lawyer with his slightly more discreet gray coat and silver-topped cane.

"Yes sir?" she enquired.

"Is Mr. Monk at home?"

"Yes sir. May I tell 'im 'o's calling?"

"Oliver Rathbone."

"Yes sir, Mr. Rathbone. Will you come in, sir, an' I'll fetch 'im down for yer."

"Thank you." Obediently he followed her into the chilly morning room, with its dark colors, clean antimacassars and arrangement of dried flowers, presumably set aside for such purposes.

She left him, and a few minutes later the door opened again and Monk came in. Immediately he saw Monk, all the old emotions returned in Rathbone: the instinctive mixture of liking and dislike; the conviction in his mind that a man with such a face was ruthless, unpredictable, clever, wildly humorous and quick tongued, and yet also vindictive, fiercely emotional, honest regardless of whom it hurt, himself included, and moved by the oddest of pity. It was not a handsome face; the bones were strong and finely proportioned, the nose aquiline and yet broad, the eyes startling, but the mouth was too wide and thin and there was a scar on the lower lip.

"Morning Monk," Rathbone said dryly. "I have a thankless case which needs some investigation."

Monk's eyebrows rose sharply. "So naturally you came to

me? Should I be obliged?'' Humor flashed across his face and vanished. ''I presume it is not also moneyless? You certainly do not work for the love of it.'' His voice was excellent. He had trained himself to lose his original lilting provincial Northumbrian accent, and had replaced it with perfectly modulated Queen's English.

''No.'' Rathbone kept his temper without difficulty. Monk might irritate him, but he was damned if he would allow him to dictate the interview or its tone. ''The family has money, which naturally I shall use in what I deem to be the client's best interest. That may be to employ you to investigate the case—but I fear there will be little to find that will be of use to her.''

''You are quite right,'' Monk agreed. ''It does sound thankless. But since you are here, I presume you want me to do it anyway.'' It was not a question but a conclusion. ''You had better tell me about it.''

With difficulty Rathbone kept his equanimity. He would not permit Monk to maneuver him into defensiveness. He smiled deliberately.

''Have you read of the recent death of General Thaddeus Carlyon?''

''Naturally.''

''His wife has confessed to killing him.''

Monk's eyebrows rose and there was sarcasm in his face, but he said nothing.

''There has to be more than she has told me,'' Rathbone went on levelly, with some effort. ''I need to know what it is before I go into court.''

''Why does she say she did it?'' Monk sat down astride one of the two wooden chairs, facing Rathbone over the back of it. ''Does she accuse him of anything as a provocation?''

''Having an affair with the hostess of the dinner party at which it happened.'' This time it was Rathbone who smiled bleakly.

Monk saw it and the light flickered in his eyes. ''A crime of passion,'' he observed.

''I think not,'' Rathbone answered. ''But I don't know

why. She seems to have a depth of feeling in inappropriate places for that.''

"Could she have a lover herself?" Monk asked. "There would be a great deal less latitude for that than for anything he might do in such a field.''

"Possibly." Rathbone found the thought distasteful, but he could not reason it away. "I shall need to know.''

"Did she do it?''

Rathbone thought for several moments before answering.

"I don't know. Apparently her sister-in-law believes it was the younger daughter, who is seemingly very lightly balanced and has been emotionally ill after the birth of her child. She quarreled with her father both before the night of his death and at the dinner party that evening.''

"And the mother confessed to protect her?" Monk suggested.

"That is what the sister-in-law says she believes.''

"And what do you believe?''

"Me? I don't know.''

There was a moment's silence while Monk hesitated.

"You will be remunerated by the day," Rathbone remarked almost casually, surprised by his own generosity. "At double police pay, since it is temporary work." He did not need to add that if results were poor, or hours artificially extended, Monk would not be used again.

Monk's smile was thin but wide.

"Then you had better tell me the rest of the details, so I can begin, thankless or not. Can I see Mrs. Carlyon? I imagine she is in prison?''

"Yes. I will arrange permission for you, as my associate.''

"You said it happened at a dinner party . . .''

"At the house of Maxim and Louisa Furnival, in Albany Street, off Regent's Park. The other guests were Fenton and Sabella Pole, Sabella being the daughter; Peverell and Damaris Erskine, the victim's sister and brother-in-law; and a Dr. Charles Hargrave and his wife—and of course General and Mrs. Carlyon.''

"And the medical evidence? Was that provided by this Dr. Hargrave or someone else?"

"Hargrave."

A look of bitter amusement flickered in Monk's eyes.

"And the police? Who is on the case?"

Rathbone understood, and for once felt entirely with Monk. A pompous fool who was prepared to allow others to suffer to save his pride infuriated him more than almost anything else.

"I imagine it will fall under Runcorn's command," he said, meeting Monk's eyes with understanding.

"Then there is no time to be wasted," Monk said, straightening up and rising from his seat. He squared his shoulders. "The poor devils haven't a chance without us. God knows who else they will arrest—and hang!" he added bitterly.

Rathbone made no answer, but he was aware of the quick stab of memory, and he felt Monk's anger and pain as if it were his own.

"I'm going to see them now," he said instead. "Tell me what you learn." He rose to his feet as well and took his leave, passing the landlady on the way out and thanking her.

At the police station Rathbone was greeted with civility and some concern. The desk sergeant knew his reputation, and remembered him as being associated with Monk, whose name still called forth both respect and fear not only in the station but throughout the force.

"Good afternoon, sir," the sergeant said carefully. "And what can I do for you?"

"I should like to see the officer in charge of the Carlyon case, if you please."

"That'll be Mr. Evan, sir. Or will you be wanting to see Mr. Runcorn?" His blue eyes were wide and almost innocent.

"No thank you," Rathbone said tartly. "Not at this stage, I think. It is merely a matter of certain physical details I should like to clarify."

"Right sir. I'll see if 'e's in. If 'e in't, will you call again, sir, or will you see Mr. Runcorn anyway?"

"I suppose I had better see Mr. Runcorn."

"Yes sir." And the desk sergeant turned and disappeared up the stairs. Three minutes later he came back and told Rathbone that if he went up Mr. Runcorn would give him five minutes.

Reluctantly Rathbone obeyed. He would much rather have seen Sergeant Evan, whose imagination and loyalty to Monk had been so evident in the Moidore case, and in the Grey case before that.

Instead he knocked on the door and went in to see Superintendent Runcorn sitting behind his large, leather-inlaid desk, his long, ruddy-skinned face expectant and suspicious.

"Yes, Mr. Rathbone? The desk sergeant says you want to know about the Carlyon case. Very sad." He shook his head and pursed his lips. "Very sad indeed. Poor woman took leave of her senses and killed her husband. Confessed to it." He looked at Rathbone with narrowed eyes.

"So I heard," Rathbone agreed. "But I assume you did look into the possibility of the daughter having killed him and Mrs. Carlyon confessing in order to protect her?"

Runcorn's face tightened. "Of course."

Rathbone thought he was lying, but he kept the contempt from his face.

"And it could not be so?"

"It could be," Runcorn said carefully. "But there is nothing to suggest that it is. Mrs. Carlyon has confessed, and everything we have found supports that." He leaned back a little in his chair, sniffing. "And before you ask, there is no way that it could possibly have been an accident. He might have fallen over by accident, but he could not possibly have speared himself on the halberd. Someone either followed him down or found him there, and picked up the halberd and drove it into his chest." He shook his head. "You'll not defend her, Mr. Rathbone, not from the law. I know you're a very clever man, but no one can deny this. A jury is ordinary men, sensible men, and they'll hang her—whatever you say."

"Possibly," Rathbone agreed with a feeling of defeat. "But this is only the beginning. We have a long way to go yet. Thank you, Mr. Runcorn. May I see the medical report?"

"If you like. It will do you no good."

"I'll see it anyway."

Runcorn smiled. "As you wish, Mr. Rathbone. As you wish."

3

Monk ACCEPTED THE CASE of Alexandra Carlyon initially because it was Rathbone who brought it to him, and he would never allow Rathbone to think any case daunted him too much even to try. He did not dislike Rathbone; indeed there was much in him he both admired and felt instinctively drawn towards. His wit always appealed to Monk no matter how cutting, or against whom it was directed, and Rathbone was not cruel. He also admired the lawyer's brain. Monk had a swift and easy intelligence himself, and had always felt success enough in his own powers not to resent brilliance in others—or to fear it, as Runcorn did.

Before the accident he had felt himself equal to any man, and superior to most. All the evidence he had uncovered since, both of his actual achievements and of the attitudes of others towards him, indicated his opinion was not merely arrogance but a reasonably well-founded judgment.

Then one night of torrential rain, less than a year ago, the carriage in which he was riding had overturned, killing the cabby and knocking Monk senseless. When he awoke in hospital he knew nothing, not even his name. Over the succeeding months he had learned his own nature slowly, often unpleasantly, seeing himself from the outside, not understanding his reasons, only his acts. The picture was of a ruthless man, ambitious, dedicated to the pursuit of justice greater than merely the law, but a man without friendships or family ties. His only sister he had seemed to write seldom and not to have visited for years, in spite of her regular, gentle letters to him.

His subordinates admired and feared him. His seniors resented him and were frightened of his footsteps on their heels—most especially Runcorn. What injuries he had done any of them he still could only guess.

There was also the fleeting memory of some gentleness, but he could put no face to it, and certainly no name. Hester Latterly's sister-in-law, Imogen, had first woken in him such a sweetness it was momentarily almost numbing, robbing him of the present and tantalizing him with some indefinable comfort and hope. And then before he could force anything into clarity, it was gone again.

And there were also memories of an older man, a man who had taught him much, and around whom there was a sense of loss, a failure to protect at a time when his mentor desperately needed it. But this picture too was incomplete. Only fragments came into his mind, a face imperfectly, an older woman sitting by a dining room table, her face filled with grief, a woman who could weep without distorting her features. And he knew he had cared for her.

Then he had left the force in a rage over the Moidore case, without even thinking what he could do to survive without his profession. It had been hard. Private cases were few. He had only begun a couple of months ago, and the support of Lady Callandra Daviot had been necessary to avoid being put out of his rooms onto the street. All that remarkable woman had asked in return for being a financial backer in his new venture was that she be included in any story that was of interest. He had been delighted to agree to such terms, although so far he had dealt only with three missing people, two of whom he had found successfully; half a dozen minor thefts; and one debt collection, which he would not have taken had he not known the defaulter was well able to pay. As far as Monk was concerned, debtors in poverty were welcome to escape. He certainly was not going to hunt them down.

But he was very glad indeed of a well-paying job now funded by a lawyer's office, and possibly offering interest for Callandra Daviot as well, insofar as it contained more passion and need for help than anything he had worked on since leaving his position.

It was too late that afternoon to accomplish anything; already the shadows were lengthening and the evening traffic was filling the streets. But the following morning he set out early for Albany Street and the house of Maxim and Louisa Furnival, where the death had occurred. He would see the scene of the crime for himself, and hear their account of the evening. As Rathbone had said, it appeared on the surface a thankless task, since Alexandra Carlyon had confessed; but then the sister-in-law might be right, and she had done so only to protect her daughter. What they did with the truth was Alexandra Carlyon's decision, or Rathbone's, but the first thing was to find it. And he certainly did not trust Runcorn to have done so.

It was not very far from Grafton Street to Albany Street, and since it was a brisk, sunny morning he walked. It gave him time to order in his mind what he would look for, what questions to ask. He turned up Whitfield Street, along Warren Street and into the Euston Road, busy with all manner of carts and carriages about their business or their trade. A brewer's dray passed by him, great shire horses gleaming in the sun, decked in shining harness and with manes braided. Behind them were berlines and landaus and of course the ever-present hansoms.

He crossed the road opposite the Trinity Church and turned right into Albany Street, running parallel to the park, and set his mind to think as he strode the length of it to the Furnivals' house. He brushed past other pedestrians without noticing them: ladies flirting, gossiping; gentlemen taking the air, discussing sport or business; servants about errands, dressed in livery; the occasional peddler or newsboy. Carriages bowled past in both directions.

He looked a gentleman, and he had every intention of behaving as if he were one. When he arrived at Albany Street he presented himself at the front door of the Furnivals' house and asked the maid who answered it if he might speak with Mrs. Louisa Furnival. He also presented her with his card, which stated only his name and address, not his occupation.

"It concerns a legal matter in which Mrs. Furnival's assistance is required," he told her, seeing her very understandable indecision. She knew he had not called before, and in all probability her mistress did not know him. Still, he was very presentable . . .

"Yes sir. If you'll come in I'll find out if Mrs. Furnival's at home."

"Thank you," he accepted, not questioning the euphemism. "May I wait here?" he asked when they were in the hall.

"Yes sir, if you'd rather." She seemed to see nothing to object to, and as soon as she was gone he looked around. The stairway was very beautiful, sweeping down the right-hand wall as he stood facing it. The balcony stretched the full width of the landing above, a distance of about thirty-five feet as far as he could judge, and at least twenty feet above the hall. It would be an unpleasant fall, but not by any means necessarily a fatal one. In fact it would be quite possible to have overbalanced across the banister and dropped the distance without serious injury at all.

And the suit of armor was still there below the corner where the banister turned to come down. One would have had to fall over the very corner of it to land on the armor. It was a fine piece, although a trifle ostentatious, perhaps, in a London house. It belonged in a baronial hall with interior stonework and great open fireplaces, but it was extremely decorative here, and an excellent conversation piece, making the house one to remain in the memory, which was presumably the purpose of it. It was full late medieval knight's armor, covering the entire body, and the right-hand gauntlet was held as if to grasp a spear or pike of some sort, but was empty now. No doubt the police would have the halberd as evidence to be presented at Alexandra Carlyon's trial.

He looked around to see the disposition of the rest of the reception rooms. There was a door to his right, just beyond the foot of the stairs. If that were the withdrawing room, surely anyone in it must have heard that suit of armor fall to the ground, even though the hall was well scattered with carpets, either Bokhara or a good imitation. The metal pieces would crash against each other, even on cushions.

There was another door to the right, under the high point of the stairs, but that was more likely a library or billiard room. One did not often have a main reception room entrance so masked.

To the left was a very handsome double door. He went across and opened it softly. Since the maid had not gone to it, but towards the back of the house, he trusted it was empty at the moment.

He looked in. It was a very large, lavishly appointed dining room, with an oak table big enough to seat at least a dozen people. He pulled the door closed again quickly and stepped back. They could not have been dining when Thaddeus Carlyon fell onto the armor. Here too they could not have failed to hear it.

He had resumed his place in the center of the hall only just in time as the maid reappeared.

"Mrs. Furnival will see you, sir, if you like to come this way," she said demurely.

She led him to a wide corridor towards the back of the house, past another doorway, straight ahead to the withdrawing room, which opened onto the garden, as far as possible from the hall.

There was no time to look at the furnishings, except to get the briefest impression of crowding with overstuffed sofas and chairs in hot pinks and reds, rich curtains, some rather ordinary pictures, and at least two gilt-framed mirrors.

The woman who commanded his attention was actually physically quite small, but of such striking personality that she dominated the room. Her bones were slender, yet his

78

overriding impression was of voluptuousness. She had a mass of dark hair, much fuller around her face than the current fashion; but it was also far more flattering to her broad, high cheekbones and long eyes, which were so narrow he could not at first be sure of their color, whether they were green or brown. She was not at all like a real cat, and yet there was an intensely feline quality in her, a grace and a detachment that made him think of small, fierce wild animals.

She would have been beautiful, in a sensuous and highly individual way, had not a meanness in her upper lip sent a tingling jar through him, like a warning.

"Good afternoon, Mr. Monk." Her voice was excellent, strong and level, much more immediate than he had expected, more candid. From such a woman he had expected something self-consciously childlike and artificially sweet. This was a most pleasant surprise. "How may I help you with a legal matter? I presume it is to do with poor General Carlyon?"

So she was both intelligent and forthright. He instantly altered what he had been going to say. He had imagined a sillier woman, a flirt. He was wrong. Louisa Furnival was much more powerful than he had supposed. And that made Alexandra Carlyon easier to understand. This woman in front of him was a rival to fear, not a casual pastime for an evening that might well have been heavy without a little frivolity.

"Yes," he agreed with equal frankness. "I am employed by Mr. Oliver Rathbone, counsel to Mrs. Carlyon, to make sure that we have understood correctly exactly what happened that evening."

She smiled only slightly, but there was humor in it, and her eyes were very bright.

"I appreciate your honesty, Mr. Monk. I do not mind interesting lies, but boring ones annoy me. What is it you wish to know?"

He smiled. He was not flirting with her—such a thing would not have entered his mind for himself—but he saw the spark of interest in her face, and instinctively used it.

"As much as you can remember of what happened that

evening, Mrs. Furnival,'' he replied. "And later, all you know, and are prepared to tell me, of General and Mrs. Carlyon and their relationship.''

She lowered her gaze. "How very thorough of you, Mr. Monk. Although I fear thoroughness may be all you will be able to offer her, poor creature. But you must go through the motions, I understand. Where shall I begin? When they arrived?''

"If you please.''

"Then sit down, Mr. Monk,'' she invited, indicating the overstuffed pink sofa. He obeyed, and she walked, with more swagger and sensuality than pure grace, over towards the window where the light fell on her, and turned to face him. In that moment he realized she knew her own power to an exactness, and enjoyed it.

He leaned back, waiting for her to begin.

She was wearing a rose-colored crinoline gown, cut low at the bosom, and against the lushly pink curtains she was strikingly dramatic to look at, and she smiled as she began her account.

"I cannot remember the order in which they arrived, but I recall their moods very clearly indeed.'' Her eyes never left his face, but even in the brilliance from the window he still could not see what color they were. "But I don't suppose times matter very much at that point, do they?'' Her fine eyebrows rose.

"Not at all, Mrs. Furnival,'' he assured her.

"The Erskines were just as usual,'' she went on. "I suppose you know who they are? Yes, of course you do.'' She smoothed the fabric of her skirt almost unconsciously. "So was Fenton Pole, but Sabella was in quite a temper, and as soon as she was through the door she was rude to her father—oh! Which means he must already have been here, doesn't it?'' She shrugged. "I think the last to arrive were Dr. and Mrs. Hargrave. Have you spoken to him?''

"No, you are the first.''

She seemed about to comment on that, then changed her

mind. Her glance wandered away and she stared into the distance as if visualizing in her mind.

"Thaddeus—that is, the general—seemed as usual." A tiny smile flickered over her mouth, full of meaning and amusement. He noticed it, and thought it betrayed more of her than of the general or their relationship. "He was a very masculine man, very much the soldier. He had seen some very interesting action, you know?" This time she did look at Monk, her eyebrows high, her face full of vitality. "He spoke to me about it sometimes. We were friends, you know? Yes, I daresay you do. Alexandra was jealous, but she had no cause. I mean, it was not in the least improper." She hesitated for only an instant. She was far too sophisticated to wait for the obvious compliment, and he did not pay it, but it entered his mind. If General Carlyon had not entertained a few improper ideas about Louisa Furnival, then he was a very slow-blooded man indeed.

"But Alexandra seemed in something of an ill temper right from the beginning," she went on. "She did not smile at all, except briefly as was required by civility, and she avoided speaking to Thaddeus altogether. To tell you the truth, Mr. Monk, it strained my abilities as a hostess to keep the occasion from becoming embarrassing for my other guests. A family quarrel is a very ugly thing to have to witness and makes people most uncomfortable. I gather this one must have been very bitter, because all evening Alexandra was holding in an anger which no observant person could miss."

"But one-sided, you say?"

"I beg your pardon?"

"One-sided," he repeated. "According to you, the general was not angry with Mrs. Carlyon; he behaved as normal."

"Yes—that is true," she acknowledged with something like surprise. "Perhaps he had forbidden her something, or made a decision she did not like, and she was still smarting over it. But that is hardly reason to kill anyone, is it?"

"What would be reason to kill, Mrs. Furnival?"

She drew in her breath quickly, then shot him a bright, sharp smile.

"What unexpected things you say, Mr. Monk! I have no idea. I have never thought of killing anyone. That is not how I fight my battles."

He met her eyes without a flicker. "How do you fight them, Mrs. Furnival?"

This time the smile was wider. "Discreetly, Mr. Monk, and without forewarning people."

"And do you win?"

"Yes I do." Too late she wished to take it back. "Well, usually," she amended. "Of course if I did not, I should not . . ." She tailed off, realizing that to justify herself would be clumsy. He had not accused her; in fact he had not even allowed the thought to come through his words. She had raised it herself.

She continued with the story, looking up at the far wall again. "Then we all went in to dinner. Sabella was still making occasional bitter remarks, Damaris Erskine was behaving appallingly to poor Maxim, and Alex spoke to everyone except Thaddeus—oh, and very little to me. She seemed to feel I was on his side, which was foolish. Of course I was on no one's side, I was simply doing my duty as hostess."

"And after dinner?"

"Oh, as usual the gentlemen stayed at the table for port, and we went to the withdrawing room where we sat and gossiped for a while." She lifted her beautiful shoulders in an expression of both humor and boredom. "Sabella went upstairs, as I recall, something about a headache. She has not been entirely well since the birth of her child."

"Did you gossip about anything in particular?"

"I really cannot remember. It was rather difficult, as I said. Damaris Erskine had been behaving like a complete fool all evening. I have no idea why. Usually she is quite a sensible woman, but that evening she seemed on the point of hysteria ever since just before dinner. I don't know if she had quarreled with her husband, or something. They are very close, and she did seem to be avoiding him on this occasion, which is unusual. I really wondered once or twice if she had had rather too much wine before she came. I can't think what else would account for her manner, or why poor Maxim should be the principal victim. She is rather eccentric, but this was really too much!''

"I'll enquire into it," he remarked. "Then what happened? At some point the general must have left the room.''

"Yes he did. I took him up to see my son, Valentine, who was at home because he has just recovered from the measles, poor boy. They were very fond of each other, you know. Thaddeus has always taken an interest in him, and of course Valentine, like any boy looking towards manhood, has a great admiration for the military and exploration and foreign travel." She looked at him very directly. "He loved to hear Thaddeus's tales of India and the Far East. I am afraid my husband does not go in very much for that sort of thing.''

"You took General Carlyon upstairs to see your son. Did you remain with him?''

"No. My husband came up to find me, because the party needed some considerable management. As I said before, several people were behaving badly. Fenton Pole and Mrs. Hargrave were struggling to keep some sort of civilized conversation going. At least that is what Maxim said.''

"So you came down, leaving the general with Valentine?''

"Yes, that's right." Her face tightened. "That is the last time I saw him.''

"And your husband?''

She shifted her position very slightly, but still stood against the rich swath of the curtain.

"He stayed upstairs. And almost as soon as I got back down here again, Alexandra went up. She looked furious, white-faced and so tense I thought she was intending to have a terrible quarrel, but there was nothing any of us could do to stop her. I didn't know what it was about—and I still don't.''

He looked at her without any humor at all, directly and blankly.

"Mrs. Carlyon said she killed him because he was having an affair with you, and everyone knew it.''

Her eyes widened and she looked at him with complete incredulity, as if he had said something absurd, so ridiculous as to be funny rather than offensive.

"Oh really! That is too foolish! She couldn't possibly believe such a thing! It is not only untrue, it is not even remotely credible. We have been agreeable friends, no more. Nor would it ever have appeared to anyone that we were more—I assure you, no one else thought so. Ask them! I am an amusing and entertaining woman, I hope, and capable of friendship, but I am not irresponsible."

He smiled, still refusing to pay the implicit compliment, except with his eyes. "Can you think of any reason why Mrs. Carlyon would believe it?"

"No—none at all. None that are sane." She smiled at him, her eyes bright and steady. They were hazel after all. "Really, Mr. Monk, I think there must be some other reason for whatever she did—some quarrel we know nothing of. And honestly, I cannot see why it matters. If she killed him, and it seems inescapable that she did, then what difference does it make why?"

"It might make a difference to the judge, when he comes to sentence her, if and when she is convicted," he replied, watching her face for pity, anger, grief, any emotions he could read. He saw nothing but cool intelligence.

"I am not familiar with the law, except the obvious." She smiled. "I would have thought they would hang her regardless."

"Indeed they may," he conceded. "You left the story with your husband and the general upstairs, and Mrs. Carlyon just going up. What happened then?"

"Maxim came down, and then a little later, maybe ten minutes, Alexandra came down, looking dreadful. Shortly after that Maxim went out into the front hall—we had all used the back stairs as it is quicker to go up to Valentine's rooms that way—and almost immediately he came back to say Thaddeus had had an accident and was seriously hurt. Charles—that is, Dr. Hargrave, went to see if he could help.

84

He came back after the briefest time to say Thaddeus was dead and we should call the police.''

"Which you did?''

"Of course. A Sergeant Evan came, and they asked us all sorts of questions. It was the worst night I can ever remember.''

"So it is possible that Mrs. Carlyon, your husband, Sabella or yourself could have killed him—as far as opportunity is concerned?''

She looked surprised. "Yes—I suppose so. But why should we?''

"I don't know yet, Mrs. Furnival. When did Sabella Pole come downstairs?''

She thought for a moment. "After Charles said Thaddeus was dead. I cannot remember who went up for her. Her mother, I expect. I realize you are employed to help Alexandra, but I cannot see how you can. Neither my husband nor I had anything to do with Thaddeus's death. I know Sabella is very emotional, but I don't believe she killed her father—and no one else could have, apart from having no possible reason.''

"Is your son still at home, Mrs. Furnival?''

"Yes.''

"May I speak with him?''

There was a guarded look to her face which he found most natural in the circumstances.

"Why?'' she asked.

"He may have seen or heard something which precipitated the quarrel resulting in the general's death.''

"He didn't. I asked him that myself.''

"I would still like to hear from him, if I may. After all, if Mrs. Carlyon murdered the general a few minutes afterwards, there must have been some indication of it then. If he is an intelligent boy, he must have been aware of something.''

She hesitated for several moments. He thought she was weighing up the possible distress to her son, the justification for denying his request, and the light it would cast on her own motives and on Alexandra Carlyon's guilt.

"I am sure you would like this whole affair cleared up as soon as possible," he said carefully. "It cannot be pleasant for you to have it unresolved."

Her eyes did not waver from his face.

"It is resolved, Mr. Monk. Alexandra has confessed."

"But that is not the end," he argued. "It is merely the end of the first phase. May I see your son?"

"If you find it important. I shall take you up."

He followed her out of the withdrawing room, walking behind and watching her slight swagger, the elegant, feminine line of her shoulders, and the confident way she managed the big skirt with its stiff hoops. She led him along the passage, then instead of going up the main stairs, she turned right and went up the second staircase to the landing of the north wing. Valentine's rooms were separated from the main bedrooms by a guest suite, presently unused.

She knocked briefly but opened the door without waiting for a reply. Inside the large airy room was furnished as a schoolroom with tables, a large blackboard and several bookcases and a schoolteacher's desk. The windows opened onto other roofs, and the green boughs of a great tree. Inside, sitting on the bench by the window, was a slender dark boy of perhaps thirteen or fourteen years of age. His features were regular, with a long nose, heavy eyelids and clear blue eyes. He stood up as soon as he saw Monk. He was far taller than Monk expected, very close to six feet, and his shoulders were already broadening, foreshadowing the man he would become. He towered over his mother. Presumably Maxim Furnival was a tall man.

"Valentine, this is Mr. Monk. He works for Mrs. Carlyon's lawyer. He would like to ask you some questions about the evening the general died." Louisa was as direct as Monk would have expected. There was no attempt at evasion in her, no protection of him from reality.

The boy was tense, his face wary, and even as Louisa

spoke Monk saw a tension in his body, an anxiety narrowing his eyes, but he did not look away.

"Yes sir?" he said slowly. "I didn't see anything, or I would have told the police. They asked me."

"I'm sure." Monk made a conscious effort to be gentler than he would with an adult. The boy's face was pale and there were marks of tiredness around his eyes. If he had been fond of the general, admired him as both a friend and a hero, then this must have been a brutal shock as well as a bereavement. "Your mother brought the general up to see you?"

Valentine's body tightened and there was a bleakness in his face as if he had been dealt a blow deep inside him where the pain was hidden, only betraying itself as a change in his muscles, a dulling in his eyes.

"Yes."

"You were friends?"

Again the look was guarded. "Yes."

"So it was not unusual that he should call on you?"

"No, I've—I've known him a long time. In fact, all my life."

Monk wished to express some sympathy, but was uncertain what words to use. The relationship between a boy and his hero is a delicate thing, and at times very private, composed in part of dreams.

"His death must be a great blow to you. I'm sorry." He was uncharacteristically awkward. "Did you see your mother or your father at that time?"

"No. I—the general was—alone here. We were talking . . ." He glanced at his mother for an instant so brief Monk almost missed it.

"About what?" he asked.

"Er . . ." Valentine shrugged. "I don't remember now. Army—army life . . ."

"Did you see Mrs. Carlyon?"

Valentine looked very white. "Yes—yes, she came in."

"She came into your rooms here?"

"Yes." He swallowed hard. "Yes she did."

Monk was not surprised he was pale. He had seen a murderer and her victim a few minutes before the crime. He had almost certainly been the last one to see General Carlyon alive, except for Alexandra. It was a thought sufficient to chill anyone.

"How was she?" he asked very quietly. "Tell me what you can remember—and please be careful not to let your knowledge of what happened afterwards color what you say, if you can help it."

"No sir." Valentine looked squarely at him; his eyes were wide and vividly blue. "Mrs. Carlyon seemed very upset indeed, very angry. In fact she was shaking and she seemed to find it difficult to speak. I've seen someone drunk once, and it was rather like that, as if her tongue and her lips would not do what she wished."

"Can you remember what she said?"

Valentine frowned. "Not exactly. It was more or less that he should come downstairs, and that she had to speak to him—or that she had spoken, I don't remember which. I thought they had had a quarrel over something and it looked as if she wanted to start it up again. Sir?"

"Yes?"

This time he avoided his mother's eyes deliberately. "Can you do anything to help Mrs. Carlyon?"

Monk was startled. He had expected the opposite.

"I don't know yet. I have only just begun." He wanted to ask why Valentine should wish her helped, but he knew it would be clumsy in front of Louisa.

Valentine turned to the window. "Of course. I'm sorry."

"Not at all," Monk said quietly. "It is very decent of you to ask."

Valentine looked at him quickly, then away again, but in that instant Monk saw the flash of gratitude.

"Did the general seem upset?" he asked.

"No, not really."

"So you think he had no idea she was in such a fury?"

"No, I don't think so. Well if he had known, he wouldn't have turned his back on her, would he? He's a lot bigger than she is and he would have to have been caught by surprise . . ."

"You are quite right. It's a good point."

Valentine smiled unhappily.

Louisa interrupted for the first time.

"I don't think he can tell you anything more, Mr. Monk."

"No. Thank you." He spoke to Valentine. "I am grateful for your forbearance."

"You're welcome, sir."

They were back downstairs in the hall and Monk was ready to take his leave when Maxim Furnival came in, handing his hat and stick to the maid. He was a tall, slender man with hair almost black and deep-set dark brown eyes. He was very nearly handsome, except his lower lip was a trifle too full, and when he smiled there was a gap between his front teeth. It was a moody face, emotional, intelligent and without cruelty.

Louisa explained Monk's presence quickly. "Mr. Monk is working for Alexandra Carlyon's lawyer."

"Good afternoon, Mr. Furnival." Monk inclined his head. He needed this man's help. "I appreciate your courtesy."

Maxim's face darkened immediately, but it was with pity rather than irritation.

"I wish there was something we could do. But it's too late now." His voice was constricted, as though his distress were startlingly deep and full of anger. "We should have done it weeks ago." He moved towards the passage leading to the withdrawing room. "What is there now, Mr. Monk?"

"Only information," Monk answered. "Is there anything you remember of that evening that might explain things better?"

A flash of ironic humor crossed Maxim's face, and something that looked like self-blame. "Believe me, Mr. Monk, I've racked my brain trying to think of an explanation, and I know nothing now I didn't know then. It's a complete mystery to me. I know, of course, that Alex and Thaddeus had differences of opinion. In fact, to be honest, I know they did not get on particularly well; but that is true of a great many people, if not most, at some time or another. It does not excuse one breaking the marriage vows, and it certainly doesn't result in their killing each other."

"Mrs. Carlyon says she did it out of jealousy over her husband's attention towards Mrs. Furnival . . ."

Maxim's eyes widened in surprise. "That's absurd! They've been friends for years, in fact since before—before Valentine was born. Nothing has happened suddenly to make her jealous, nothing has changed at all." He looked genuinely confused. If he were an actor he was superb. It had crossed Monk's mind to wonder if it might have been he and not Alexandra who was the jealous spouse, or even for a wild moment if the general was Valentine's father. But he could think of no reason why Alexandra should confess to protect Maxim, unless they were lovers—in which case he had little cause to be jealous over the general and Louisa. In fact, it was in his interest it should continue.

"But Mrs. Carlyon was distressed that evening?" he asked aloud.

"Oh yes." Maxim poked his hands deep into his pockets and frowned. "Very. But I don't know what about, except that Thaddeus rather ignored her, but that is hardly cause for violence. Anyway, everyone seemed rather excitable that evening. Damaris Erskine was almost to the point of frenzy." He did not mention that she had singled him out for her abuse. "And I have no idea why about that either." He looked bewildered. "Nor had poor Peverell, to judge by his face. And Sabella was very overwrought as well—but then she has been rather often lately." His expression was rueful and more than a little embarrassed. "Altogether it was a pretty dreadful evening."

"But nothing happened to make you think it would end in murder?"

"Good God, no! No, nothing at all. It was just . . ." He stopped, his face bleak, lost for any words adequate to explain his feelings.

"Thank you, Mr. Furnival." Monk could think of nothing further to ask at this point. He thanked Louisa also and took his leave, going out into the patchy sunshine of Albany Street with his mind crowded with thoughts and impressions: Louisa's arrogant walk and her confident, inviting face with

90

an element of coldness in it in repose; Valentine's hidden pain; and Maxim's innocence.

Next Monk visited Alexandra Carlyon's younger daughter, Sabella. The elder daughter lived in Bath, and was no part of this tragedy, except as it deprived her of her father, and almost certainly in due course of the law, of her mother also. But Sabella might well be at the heart of it, either the true motive for Alexandra's crime or even the murderer herself.

The Poles' house was on George Street, only a short walk away, the other side of the Hampstead Road, and it took him ten minutes on foot to reach the step. When the door opened he explained to the parlormaid that he was engaged to do all he could to assist Mrs. Carlyon, and he would be obliged if he might speak to Mr. or Mrs. Pole to that end.

He was shown into the morning room, a small, chilly place even in the bright, gusty winds of May with a sudden rain squall battering against the heavily curtained windows. And to be fair, they were very newly in mourning for Sabella's father.

It was not Sabella who came, but Fenton Pole, a pleasant, unremarkable young man with strawberry fair hair and an earnest face, regular features and china-blue eyes. He was fashionably dressed in a shawl-collared waistcoat, very white shirt and somber suit. He closed the door behind him and regarded Monk with misgiving.

"I am sorry to disturb you in a time of such family grief," Monk began straightaway. "But the matter of helping Mrs. Carlyon cannot wait."

Fenton Pole's frown became deeper and he moved towards Monk with a candid expression, as if he would confide something, then stopped a few feet away.

"I cannot think what anyone can do to help her," he said anxiously. "Least of all my wife or I. We were present that evening, but anything I saw or heard only adds to her troubles. I think, Mr. Monk, that the least damage we can do would be to say as little as possible and let the end be as mercifully rapid as may be." He looked down at his shoes, then up at Monk with a frown. "My wife is not well, and I refuse to add anymore to her distress. She has lost both father and mother, in the most dreadful circumstances. I am sure you appreciate that?"

"I do, Mr. Pole," Monk conceded. "It would be hard to imagine anything worse than what appears to have happened. But so far it is only an appearance. We owe it to her, as well as ourselves, to see if there are other explanations, or mitigating circumstances. I am sure your wife, in love for her mother, would wish that too."

"My wife is not well . . ." Pole repeated rather sharply.

"I regret it profoundly," Monk interrupted. "But events will make no allowance for individual illness or grief." Then before Pole could protest again, "But perhaps if you would tell me what you recall of the evening, I will have to disturb your wife very little—only to see if she can add anything you do not know."

"I don't see that it can help." Pole's jaw hardened and there was a stubborn light in his blue eyes.

"Neither do I, until I hear what you have to say." Monk was beginning to grow irritated, and he concealed it with difficulty. He did not suffer foolishness, prejudice or complacency with any grace, and this man was exhibiting at least two of these faults. "But it is my profession to learn such things, and I have been employed by Mrs. Carlyon's barrister to discover what I can."

Pole regarded him without answering.

Deliberately Monk sat down on one of the higher chairs as if he intended to be there for some time.

"The dinner party, Mr. Pole," he insisted. "I understand your wife quarreled with her father almost as soon as she arrived at the Furnivals' house. Do you know what was the cause of that difference?"

Pole looked discomfited. "I cannot see what that has to do with the general's death, but since you ask, I don't know what the cause was. I imagine it was some old misunderstanding and nothing new or of any importance."

92

Monk looked at him with disbelief as civil as he could make it.

"Surely something was said? It is impossible to have a quarrel without mentioning what it is about, at least nominally, even if what is spoken of is not the real cause."

Pole's blond eyebrows rose. He pushed his hands even deeper into his pockets and turned away irritably. "If that is what you want. I thought from what you were saying that you wished to know the real cause—although it can hardly matter now."

Monk felt his anger rising. His muscles were tight and his voice was harsh when he replied.

"What did they say to each other, Mr. Pole?"

Pole sat down and crossed his legs. He looked at Monk coldly.

"The general made some observation about the army in India, and Sabella said she had heard there was a very tense situation there. The general told her it was nothing. In fact he was rather dismissive of her opinions, and it angered her. She felt he was being condescending and told him so. Sabella imagines that she knows something about India—and I am afraid that perhaps I have indulged her. At that point Maxim Furnival intervened and tried to turn the subject to something else, not entirely successfully. It was not anything remarkable, Mr. Monk. And it certainly had no bearing upon Mrs. Carlyon's quarrel with him."

"What was that about?"

"I have no idea!" he snapped. "I simply assume there was one, because she could not possibly have killed him unless there was a most violent difference between them. But none of us were aware of anything of the sort, or naturally we should have done something to prevent it." He looked annoyed, as if he could not believe Monk was so stupid intentionally.

Before Monk could reply the door opened and a lovely but disheveled young woman stood facing them, her fair hair over her shoulders, her gown wrapped around by a shawl.

She held it with one slender, pale hand grasped close to her throat. She stared at Monk, disregarding Pole.

"Who are you? Polly said you are trying to help Mama. How can you do that?"

Monk rose to his feet. "William Monk, Mrs. Pole. I am employed by your mother's barrister, Mr. Rathbone, to see if I can learn something to mitigate her case."

She stared at him in silence. Her eyes were very wide and fixed, and there was a hectic color in her cheeks.

Pole had risen when she came in, and now he turned to her gently. "Sabella, my dear, there is no cause to let this concern you. I think you should go back and lie down . . ."

She pushed him away angrily and came towards Monk. Pole put his hand on her arm and she snatched it away from him.

"Mr. Monk, is it possible you can do something to help my mother? You said 'mitigation.' Does that mean the law might take into account what manner of man he was? How he bullied us, forced us to his will regardless of our own desires?"

"Sabella . . ." Pole said urgently. He glared at Monk. "Really, Mr. Monk, this is all irrelevant and I—"

"It is not irrelevant!" Sabella said angrily, cutting across him. "Will you be good enough to answer me, Mr. Monk?"

He heard the rising hysteria in her voice and it was quite obvious she was on the edge of losing control altogether. It was hardly remarkable. Her family had been shattered by the most appalling double tragedy. She had effectively lost both her parents in a scandal which would ruin their reputations and tear her family life apart and expose it to public ignominy. What could he say to her that would not either make it worse or be totally meaningless? He forced his dislike of Pole out of his mind.

"I don't know, Mrs. Pole," he said very gently. "I hope so. I believe she must have had some reason to do such a thing—if indeed it was she who did it. I need to learn what the reason was: it may be grounds for some sort of defense."

"For God's sake, man!" Pole exploded furiously, his face

94

tight with rage. "Have you no sense of decency at all? My wife is ill—can you not see that? I am sorry, but Mrs. Carlyon's defense, if indeed there can be any, lies with her solicitors, not with us. You must do what you can and not involve my wife. Now I must ask you to leave, without causing any more distress than you already have." He stood, holding his position rather than moving towards Monk, but his threat was plain. He was a very angry man, and Monk thought he was also frightened, although his fear might well be for his wife's mental state and nothing more. Indeed she did look on the border of complete collapse.

Monk no longer had authority to insist, as he had when a policeman. He had no choice but to leave, and do it with as much dignity as possible. Being asked to leave was galling enough, being thrown out would be a total humiliation, which he would not endure. He turned from Pole to Sabella, but before he could collect his own excuses, she spoke.

"I have the deepest affection for my mother, Mr. Monk, and regardless of what my husband says, if there is anything at all I can do . . ." She stood rigidly, her body shaking, very deliberately ignoring Pole. "I shall do it! You may feel free to call upon me at any time. I shall instruct the servants that you are to be allowed in, and I am to be told."

"Sabella!" Pole was exasperated. "I forbid it! You really have no idea what you are saying—"

Before he could finish she swung around on him in fury, her face spotted with color, her eyes brilliant, lips twisted.

"How dare you forbid me to help my mother! You are just like Papa—arrogant, tyrannical, telling me what I may and may not do, regardless of my feelings or what I know to be right." Her voice was getting higher and more and more shrill. "I will not be dictated to—I—"

"Sabella! Keep your voice down!" he said furiously. "Remember who you are—and to whom you speak. I am your husband, and you owe me your obedience, not to mention your loyalty."

"Owe you?" She was shouting now. "I do not *owe* you

95

anything! I married you because my father commanded me and I had no choice."

"You are hysterical!" Pole's face was scarlet with fury and embarrassment. "Go to your room! That is an order, Sabella, and I will not be defied!" He waved his arm towards the door. "Your father's death has unhinged you, which is understandable, but I will not have you behave like this in front of a—a—" He was lost for words to describe Monk.

As if she had just remembered his presence, Sabella looked back at Monk, and at last realized the enormity of her behavior. Her color paled and with shuddering breath she turned and went out of the room without speaking again, leaving the door swinging.

Pole looked at Monk with blazing eyes, as if it were Monk's fault he had witnessed the scene.

"As you can see, Mr. Monk," he said stiffly, "my wife is in a very distressed state. It will be perfectly clear to you that nothing she says can be of any use to Mrs. Carlyon, or to anyone else." His face was hard, closed to all entreaty. "I must ask you not to call again. In spite of what she says, you will not be permitted in. I regret I cannot help, but it must be plain to anyone that we are in no state to do so. Good day to you. The maid will show you to the door." And so saying he turned around on his heel and went out, leaving Monk alone.

There was nothing to do but leave also, his mind filled with images and doubts. Surely Sabella Pole was passionate enough, and lightly balanced enough as Edith Sobell had apparently believed, to have pushed her father downstairs and then lifted that halberd and speared him to death. And she certainly seemed to have no idea at all of propriety, or what her station required of her, or perhaps even of sanity.

Monk met Hester Latterly, by arrangement, the following day. It was not that he entirely wanted to—his emotions were very mixed—but she was an excellent ally. She had acute observation, an understanding of women he would never achieve simply because he was a man. Also she was born of a different social class, and so would perceive and interpret nuances he might easily misunderstand. And of course in this instance she knew Edith Sobell, and had access to the Carlyon family, which might be invaluable if the case proved worth fighting and there was any weapon to use.

He had first met her in the Grey case nearly a year ago. She had been staying at Shelburne Court, the Grey country seat, and he had bumped into her when out walking on the estate. She had been conceited, opinionated, extremely bossy, far too outspoken, and as far as he was concerned, in no way attractive. She had proved to be resourceful, courageous, determined, and her candid tongue had at times been a blessing. She had bullied him out of defeat with her rudeness and her blind refusal to accept despair.

In fact there had been moments when he had felt a kind of friendship for her more totally honest than he had for anyone else, even John Evan. She saw him without any deluding mists of admiration, self-interest or fear for her own position, and there was something extraordinarily sweet and comfortable about a friend who knows you and accepts you at your worst, your most bitter, or defeated, who sees your emotional ugliness naked and is not afraid to call it by name, and yet does not turn from you or allow you to cease to struggle, who wills your survival as precious.

Therefore he went out in the early afternoon to meet Hester just outside Major Tiplady's apartment in Great Titchfield Street, and walk with her down to Oxford Street, where they could find an agreeable place to take tea or hot chocolate. Perhaps her company would even be pleasant.

He had barely arrived at Tiplady's house when she came down the steps, head high, back stiff as if she were on parade. It reminded him sharply of the first occasion on which they had met; she had a very individual way of carrying herself. It both jarred on him for its assurance and sense of purpose, not a feminine characteristic at all, rather more like a soldier; and also was oddly comforting because of its familiarity. It evoked most sharply the way she alone had been willing to fight the Grey case and had not recoiled from him in horror or disappointment when his part in it all had looked not only hopeless but inexcusable.

97

"Good afternoon, Mr. Monk," she said rather stiffly. She made no concession to ordinary civilities and the small trifles that most people indulged in as a preamble to more serious conversation. "Have you begun on the Carlyon case? I imagine it is not easy. I admit, from what Edith Sobell says, there can be little chance of a happy outcome. Still, to send the wrong person to the gallows would be even worse—as, I presume, we are agreed?" She shot him a sharp, very candid glance.

There was no need to make any comment; memory was a blade pointed between them, full of pain, but there was no blame in it, only shared emotion.

"I haven't seen Mrs. Carlyon herself yet." He set a smart pace and she kept up with him without difficulty. "I shall do that tomorrow. Rathbone has arranged it for me in the morning. Do you know her?"

"No—I know only the general's family, and that very slightly."

"What is your opinion?"

"That is a very large question." She hesitated, uncertain what her considered judgment was.

He looked at her with unconcealed scorn.

"You have become uncharacteristically genteel, Miss Latterly. You were never backwards in expressing your opinions of people in the past." He smiled wryly. "But of course that was when your opinion was unasked for. The fact that I am interested seems to have frozen your tongue."

"I thought you wanted a considered opinion," she retorted brusquely. "Not something merely given on the spur of the moment and without reflection."

"Assuming your opinions in the past have been on the spur of the moment, perhaps a considered opinion would be better," he agreed with a tight smile.

They came to the curb, hesitated while a carriage went past, harness gleaming, horses stepping high, then crossed Margaret Street into Market Place. Oxford Street was clearly visible ahead of them, crowded with traffic, all manner of vehicles of fashion, business, leisure and trade, pedestrians, idlers and street sellers of every sort.

"Mrs. Randolf Carlyon seems to be the most powerful member of the family," Hester answered when they reached the farther pavement. "A very forceful person, I should judge, ten years younger than her husband, and perhaps in better health—"

"It is unlike you to be so diplomatic," he interrupted. "Do you mean the old man is senile?"

"I—I'm not sure."

He glanced at her with surprise. "It is unlike you not to say what you mean. You used to err on the side of being far too frank. Have you suddenly become tactful, Hester? Why, for heaven's sake?"

"I am not tactful," she snapped back. "I am trying to be accurate—which is not at all the same thing." She lengthened her stride a fraction. "I am not sure whether he is senile or not. I have not seen him at sufficient length to judge. It is my opinion so far that he is definitely losing his vitality but that she was always the stronger personality of the two."

"Bravo," he said with slightly sarcastic approval. "And Mrs. Sobell, who seems to think her sister-in-law innocent? Is she a rose-gathering optimist? It seems, in the face of a confession, about the only sort of person who could still imagine there is anything to be done for Mrs. Carlyon, apart from pray for her soul."

"No she isn't," she replied with considerable acerbity. "She is a clear-sighted widow of considerable good sense. She thinks it far more likely Sabella Pole, the general's daughter, is the one who killed him."

"Not unreasonable," he conceded. "I have just met Sabella, and she is very highly emotional, if not outright hysterical."

"Is she?" Hester said quickly, turning to look at him, interest dismissing all her irritation. "What was your judgment of her? Might she have killed her father? I know from Damaris Erskine, who was at the party, that she had the opportunity."

They were at the corner of Market Street and Oxford Street, and turned into the thoroughfare, walking side by side along the footpath. He took her arm, largely to make sure they remained together and were not divided by passersby bustling in the opposite direction.

"I have no idea," he replied after a moment or two. "I form my opinions on evidence, not intuition."

"No you don't," she contradicted. "You cannot possibly be so stupid, or so pompous, as to disregard your intuitive judgment. Whatever you have forgotten, you remember enough of past experiences with people to know something of them merely by their faces and the way they behave to each other, and when you speak to them."

He smiled dryly. "Then I think Fenton Pole believes she could have done it," he replied. "And that is indicative."

"Then perhaps there is some hope?" Unconsciously she straightened up and lifted her chin a little.

"Hope of what? Is that any better an answer?"

She stopped so abruptly a gentleman behind bumped into her and growled under his breath, tripping over his cane and going around her with ill grace.

"I beg your pardon, sir?" Monk said loudly. "I did not catch your remark. I presume you apologized to the lady for jostling her?"

The man colored and shot him a furious glance.

"Of course I did!" he snapped, then glowered at Hester. "I beg your pardon, ma'am!" Then he turned on his heel and strode off.

"Clumsy fool," Monk said between his teeth.

"He was only a trifle awkward-footed," she said reasonably.

"Not him—you." He took her by the arm and moved her forward again. "Now attend to what we are doing, before you cause another accident. It can hardly be better that Sabella Pole should be guilty—but if it is the truth, then we must discover it. Do you wish for a cup of coffee?"

Monk entered the prison with a sharp stab of memory, not from the time before his accident, although surely he must have been in places like this on countless occasions, probably

100

even this prison itself. The emotion that was so powerful now was from only a few months back, the case which had caused him to leave the police force, throw away all the long years of learning and labor, and the sacrifices to ambition.

He followed the turnkey along the grim passages, a chill on his skin. He still had little idea what he would say to Alexandra Carlyon, or indeed what kind of woman she would be—presumably something like Sabella.

They came to the cell and the turnkey opened the door.

"Call w'en yer want ter come aht," she said laconically. Making no further comment, she turned around without interest, and as soon as Monk was inside, slammed the door shut and locked it.

The cell was bare but for a single cot with straw pallet and gray blankets. On it was sitting a slender woman, pale-skinned, with fair hair tied loosely and pinned in a knot at the back of her head. As she turned to look at him he saw her face. It was not at all what he had expected; the features were nothing like Sabella's, far from being ordinarily pretty. She had a short, aquiline nose, very blue eyes and a mouth far too wide, too generous and full of sensuality and humor. Now she gazed at him almost expressionlessly and he knew in that single moment that she had no hope of reprieve of any sort. He did not bother with civilities, which could serve no purpose. He too had been mortally afraid and he knew its taste too well.

"I am William Monk. I expect Mr. Rathbone told you I would come."

"Yes," she said tonelessly. "But there is nothing you can do. Nothing you could discover would make any difference."

"Confessions alone are not sufficient evidence, Mrs. Carlyon." He remained standing in the center of the floor looking down at her. She did not bother to rise. "If you now wish to retract it for any reason," he went on, "the prosecution will still have to prove the case. Although admittedly it will be harder to defend you after your saying you had done it. Unless, of course, there is a good reason." He did not

101

make it a question. He did not think her hopelessness was due to a feeling that her confession condemned her so much as to some facts he as yet did not fully understand. But this was a place to begin.

She smiled briefly, without light or happiness. "The best of reasons, Mr. Monk. I am guilty. I killed my husband." Her voice was remarkably pleasing, low-pitched and a trifle husky, her diction very clear.

Without any warning he had an overwhelming sense of having done this before. Violent emotions overwhelmed him: fear, anger, love. And then as quickly it was gone again, leaving him breathless and confused. He was staring at Alexandra Carlyon as if he had only just seen her, the details of her face sharp and surprising, not what he expected.

"I beg your pardon?" He had missed whatever she had said.

"I killed my husband, Mr. Monk," she repeated.

"Yes—yes, I heard that. What did you say next?" He shook his head as if to clear it.

"Nothing." She frowned very slightly, puzzled now.

With a great effort he brought his mind back to the murder of General Carlyon.

"I have been to see Mr. and Mrs. Furnival."

This time her smile was quite different; there was sharp bitterness in it, and self-mockery.

"I wish I thought you could discover Louisa Furnival was guilty, but you cannot." There was a catch in her voice which at any other time he could have taken for laughter. "If Thaddeus had rejected her she might have been angry, even violently so, but I doubt she ever loved anyone enough to care greatly if he loved her or not. The only person I could imagine her killing would be another woman—a really beautiful woman, perhaps, who rivaled her or threatened her well-being." Her eyes widened as thoughts raced through her imagination. "Maybe if Maxim fell so deeply in love with someone he could not hide it—then people would know Louisa had been bested. Then she might kill."

"And Maxim was not fond of you?" he asked.

102

There was very faint color in her cheeks, so slight he noticed it only because she was facing the small high window and the light fell directly on her.

"Yes—yes, he was, in the past—but never to the degree where he could have left Louisa. Maxim is a very moral man. And anyway, I am alive. It is Thaddeus who is dead." She said the last words without feeling, certainly without any shred of regret. At least there was no playacting, no hypocrisy in her, and no attempt to gain sympathy. For that he liked her.

"I saw the balcony, and the banister where he went over." She winced.

"I assume he fell backwards?"

"Yes." Her voice was unsteady, little more than a whisper.

"Onto the suit of armor?"

"Yes."

"That must have made a considerable noise."

"Of course. I expected people to come and see what had happened—but no one did."

"The withdrawing room is at the back of the house. You knew that."

"Of course I did. I thought one of the servants might hear."

"Then what? You followed him down and saw he was struck senseless with the fall—and no one had come. So you picked up the halberd and drove it into his body?"

She was white-faced, her eyes like dark holes. This time her voice would hardly come at all.

"Yes."

"His chest? He was lying on his back. You did say he went over backwards?"

"Yes." She gulped. "Do we have to go over this? It cannot serve any purpose."

"You must have hated him very much."

"I didn't—" She stopped, drew in her breath and went on, her eyes down, away from his. "I already told Mr. Rathbone. He was having an affair with Louisa Furnival. I was . . . jealous."

He did not believe her.

"I also saw your daughter."

She froze, sitting totally immobile.

"She was very concerned for you." He knew he was being cruel, but he saw no alternative. He had to find the truth. With lies and defenses Rathbone might only make matters worse in court. "I am afraid my presence seemed to precipitate a quarrel between her and her husband."

She glared at him fiercely. For the first time there was real, violent emotion in her.

"You had no right to go to her! She is ill—and she has just lost her father. Whatever he was to me, he was her father. You . . ." She stopped, perhaps aware of the absurdity of her position, if indeed it was she who had killed the general.

"She did not seem greatly distressed by his death," he said deliberately, watching not only her face but also the tension in her body, the tight shoulders under the cotton blouse, and her hands clenched on her knees. "In fact, she made no secret that she had quarreled bitterly with him, and would do all she could to aid you—even at the cost of her husband's anger."

Alexandra said nothing, but he could feel her emotion as if it were an electric charge in the room.

"She said he was arbitrary and dictatorial—that he had forced her into a marriage against her will," he went on.

She stood up and turned away from him.

Then again he had a sudden jolt of memory so sharp it was like a physical blow. He had been here before, stood in a cell with a small fanlight like this, and watched another slender woman with fair hair that curled at her neck. She too had been charged with killing her husband, and he had cared about it desperately.

Who was she?

The image was gone and all he could recapture was a shaft of dim light on hair, the angle of a shoulder, and a gray dress, skirts too long, sweeping the floor. He could recall no more, no voice, certainly no faintest echo of a face, nothing—eyes, lips—nothing at all.

104

But the emotion was there. It had mattered to him so fiercely he had thrown all his mind and will into defending her.

But why? Who was she?

Had he succeeded? Or had she been hanged?

Was she innocent—or guilty?

Alexandra was talking, answering him at last.

"What?"

She swung around, her eyes bright and hard.

"You come in here with a cruel tongue and no—no gentleness, no—no sensibility at all. You ask the harshest questions." Her voice caught in her throat, gasping for breath. "You remind me of my daughter whom I shall probably never see again, except across the rail of a courtroom dock—and then you haven't even the honor to listen to my answers! What manner of man are you? What do you really want here?"

"I am sorry!" he said with genuine shame. "My thoughts were absent for only a moment—a memory . . . a—a painful one—of another time like this."

The anger drained out of her. She shrugged her shoulders, turning away again.

"It doesn't matter. None of it makes any difference."

He pulled his thoughts together with an effort.

"Your daughter quarreled with her father that evening . . ."

Instantly she was on guard again, her body rigid, her eyes wary.

"She has a very fierce temper, Mrs. Carlyon—she seemed to be on the edge of hysteria when I was there. In fact I gathered that her husband was anxious for her."

"I already told you." Her voice was low and hard. "She has not been well since the birth of her child. It happens sometimes. It is one of the perils of bearing children. Ask anyone who is familiar with childbirth—and . . ."

"I know that," he agreed. "Women quite often become temporarily deranged—"

"No! Sabella was ill—that's all." She came forward, so close he thought she was going to grasp his arm, then she stood still with her hands by her sides. "If you are trying to say that it was Sabella who killed Thaddeus, and not I, then you are wrong! I will confess it in court, and will certainly hang"—she said the word plainly and deliberately, like pushing her hand into a wound—"rather than allow my daughter to take the blame for my act. Do you understand me, Mr. Monk?"

There was no jar of memory, nothing even faintly familiar. The echo was as far away now as if he had never heard it.

"Yes, Mrs. Carlyon. It is what I would have expected you to say."

"It is the truth." Her voice rose and there was a note of desperation in it, almost of pleading. "You must not accuse Sabella! If you are employed by Mr. Rathbone—Mr. Rathbone is my lawyer. He cannot say what I forbid him to."

It was half a statement, half a reassurance to herself.

"He is also an officer of the court, Mrs. Carlyon," he said with sudden gentleness. "He cannot say something which he knows beyond question to be untrue."

She stared at him without speaking.

Could his memory have something to do with that older woman who wept without distorting her face? She had been the wife of the man who had taught him so much, upon whom he had modeled himself when he first came south from Northumberland. It was he who had been ruined, cheated in some way, and Monk had tried so hard to save him, and failed.

But the image that had come to him today was of a young woman, another woman like Alexandra, charged with murdering her husband. And he had come here, like this, to help her.

Had he failed? Was that why she no longer knew him? There was no record of her among his possessions, no letters, no pictures, not even a name written down. Why? Why had he ceased to know her?

The answers crowded in on him: because he had failed, she had gone to the gallows . . .

"I shall do what I can to help, Mrs. Carlyon," he said quietly. "To find the truth—and then you and Mr. Rathbone must do with it whatever you wish."

4

At mid-morning on May 11, Hester received an urgent invitation from Edith to call upon her at Carlyon House. It was hand-written and delivered by a messenger, a small boy with a cap pulled over his ears and a broken front tooth. It requested Hester to come at her earliest convenience, and that she would be most welcome to stay for luncheon if she wished.

"By all means," Major Tiplady said graciously. He was feeling better with every day, and was now quite well enough to be ferociously bored with his immobility, to have read all he wished of both daily newspapers and books from his own collection and those he requested from the libraries of friends. He enjoyed Hester's conversation, but he longed for some new event or circumstance to intrude into his life.

"Go and see the Carlyons," he urged. "Learn something of what is progressing in that wretched case. Poor woman! Although I don't know why I should say that." His white eyebrows rose, making him look both belligerent and bemused. "I suppose some part of me refuses to believe she should kill her husband—especially in such a way. Not a woman's method. Women use something subtler, like poison—don't you think?" He looked at Hester's faintly surprised expression and did not wait for an answer. "Anyway, why should she kill him at all?'' He frowned. ''What could he have done to her to cause her to resort to such a—a—fatal and inexcusable violence?''

''I don't know,'' Hester admitted, putting aside the mending she had been doing. ''And rather more to the point, why does she not tell us? Why does she persist in this lie about jealousy? I fear it may be because she is afraid it is her daughter who is guilty, and she would rather hang than see her child perish.''

''You must do something,'' Tiplady said with intense feeling. ''You cannot allow her to sacrifice herself. At least . . .'' He hesitated, pity twisting his emotions so plainly his face reflected every thought that passed through his mind: the doubt, the sudden understanding and the confusion again. ''Oh, my dear Miss Latterly, what a terrible dilemma. Do we have the right to take from this poor creature her sacrifice for her child? If we prove her innocent, and her daughter guilty, surely that is the last thing she would wish? Do we then not rob her of the only precious thing she has left?''

''I don't know,'' Hester answered very quietly, folding the linen and putting the needle and thimble back in their case. ''But what if it was not either of them? What if she is confessing to protect Sabella, because she fears she is guilty, but in fact she is not? What hideous irony if we know, only when it is too late, that it was someone else altogether?''

He shut his eyes. ''How perfectly appalling. Surely this friend of yours, Mr. Monk, can prevent such a thing? You say he is very clever, most particularly in this field.''

A flood of memory and sadness washed over her. ''Cleverness is not always enough . . .''

''Then you had better go and see what you can learn for yourself,'' he said decisively. ''Find out what you can about this wretched General Carlyon. Someone must have hated him very dearly indeed. Go to luncheon with his family. Watch and listen, ask questions, do whatever it is detectives do. Go on!''

''I suppose you don't know anything about him?'' she asked without hope, looking around the room a last time before going to her own quarters to prepare herself. Everything he might need seemed to be available for him, the maid would serve his meal, and she should be back by mid-afternoon herself.

"Well, as I said before, I know him by repute," Tiplady replied somberly. "One cannot serve as long as I have and not know at least the names of all the generals of any note—and those of none."

She smiled wryly. "And which was he?" Her own opinion of generals was not high.

"Ah . . ." He breathed out, looking at her with a twisted smile. "I don't know for myself, but he had a name as a soldier's soldier, a good-enough leader, inspiring, personally heroic, but outside uniform not a colorful man, tactically neither a hero nor a disaster."

"He did not fight in the Crimea, then?" she said too quickly for thought or consideration to guard her tongue. "They were all one or the other—mostly the other."

A smile puckered his lips against his will. He knew the army's weaknesses, but they were a closed subject, like family faults, not to be exposed or even admitted to outsiders—least of all women.

"No," he said guardedly. "As I understand it he served most of his active time in India—and then spent a lot of years here at home, in high command, training younger officers and the like."

"What was his personal reputation? What did people think of him?" She straightened his blanket yet again, quite unnecessarily but from habit.

"I've no idea." He seemed surprised to be asked. "Never heard anything at all. I told you—he was not personally a colorful man. For heaven's sake, do go and see Mrs. Sobell. You have to discover the truth in the matter and save poor Mrs. Carlyon—or the daughter."

"Yes, Major. I am about to go." And without adding anything further except a farewell, she left him alone to think and imagine until she should return.

* * *

109

Edith met her with a quick, anxious interest, rising from the chair where she had been sitting awkwardly, one leg folded under her. She looked tired and too pale for her dark mourning dress to flatter her. Her long fair hair was already pulled untidy, as if she had been running her hand over her head and had caught the strands of it absentmindedly.

"Ah, Hester. I am so glad you could come. The major did not mind? How good of him. Have you learned anything? What has Mr. Rathbone discovered? Oh, please, do come and sit down—here." She indicated the place opposite where she had been, and resumed her own seat.

Hester obeyed, not bothering to arrange her skirts.

"I am afraid very little so far," she answered, responding to the last question, knowing it was the only one which mattered. "And of course there will be limits to what he could tell me anyway, since I have no standing in the case."

Edith looked momentarily confused, then quite suddenly she understood.

"Oh yes—of course." Her face was bleak, as if the different nature of things lent a grimmer reality to it. "But he is working on it?"

"Of course. Mr. Monk is investigating. I expect he will come here in due course."

"They won't tell him anything." Edith's brows rose in surprise.

Hester smiled. "Not intentionally, I know. But he is already engaged with the possibility that it was not Alexandra who killed the general, and certainly not for the reason she said. Edith . . ."

Edith stared at her, waiting, her eyes intent.

"Edith, it may be that it was Sabella after all—but is that going to be an answer that Alexandra will want? Should we be doing her any service to prove it? She has chosen to give her life to save Sabella—if indeed Sabella is guilty." She leaned forward earnestly. "But what if it was neither of them? If Alexandra simply thinks it is Sabella and she is confessing to protect her . . ."

110

"Yes," Edith said eagerly. "That would be marvelous! Hester, do you think it could be true?"

"Perhaps—but then who? Louisa? Maxim Furnival?"

"Ah." The light died out of Edith's eyes. "Honestly, I wish it could be Louisa, but I doubt it. Why should she?"

"Might she really have been having an affair with the general, and he threw her over—told her it was all finished? You said she was not a woman to take rejection lightly."

Edith's face reflected a curious mixture of emotions: amusement in her eyes, sadness in her mouth, even a shadow of guilt.

"You never knew Thaddeus, or you wouldn't seriously think of such a thing. He was . . ." She hesitated, her mind reaching for ideas and framing them into words. "He was . . . remote. Whatever passion there was in him was private, and chilly, not something to be shared. I never saw him deeply moved by anything."

A quick smile touched her mouth, imagination, pity and regret in it. "Except stories of heroism, loyalty and sacrifice. I remember him reading 'Sohrab and Rustum' when it was first published four years ago." She glanced at Hester and saw her incomprehension. "It's a tragic poem by Arnold." The smile returned, bleak and sad. "It's a complicated story; the point is they are father and son, both great military heroes, and they kill each other without knowing who they are, because they have wound up on opposite sides in a war. It's very moving."

"And Thaddeus liked it?"

"And the stories of the great heroes of the past—ours and other people's. The Spartans combing their hair before Thermopylae—they all died, you know, three hundred of them, but they saved Greece. And Horatius on the bridge . . ."

"I know," Hester said quickly. "Macaulay's 'Lays of Ancient Rome.' I begin to understand. There were the passions he could identify with: honor, duty, courage, loyalty—not bad things. I'm sorry . . ."

Edith gave her a look of sudden warmth. It was the first time they had spoken of Thaddeus as a person they could

111

care about rather than merely as the center of a tragedy. "But I think he was a man of thought rather than feeling," she went on, returning to the business of it. "Usually he was very controlled, very civilized. I suppose in some ways he was not unlike Mama. He had an absolute commitment to what is right, and I never knew him to step outside it—in his speech or his acts."

She screwed up her face and shook her head a little. "If he had some secret passion for Louisa he hid it completely, and honestly I cannot imagine him so involved in it as to indulge himself in what he would consider a betrayal, not so much of Alexandra as of himself. You see, to him adultery would be wrong, against the sanctity of home and the values by which he lived. None of his heroes would do such a thing. It would be unimaginable."

She lifted her shoulders high in an exaggerated shrug. "But suppose if he had, and then grown tired of her, or had an attack of conscience. I really believe that Louisa—whom I don't much care for, but I must be honest, I think is quite clever enough to have seen it coming long before he said anything—would have preempted him by leaving him herself. She would choose to be the one to end it; she would never allow him to."

"But if she loved him?" Hester pressed. "And some women do love the unattainable with a passion they never achieve for what is in their reach. Might she not be reluctant to believe he would never respond—and care so much she would rather kill him than . . ."

Edith laughed jerkily. "Oh Hester. Don't be absurd! What a romantic you are. You live in a world of grand passions, undying love and devotion, and burning jealousy. Neither of them were remotely like that. Thaddeus was heroic, but he was also pompous, stuffy, very rigid in his views, and cold to talk to. One cannot always be reading epic poetry, you know. Most of the time he was a guarded, ungiving man. And Louisa is passionate only about herself. She likes to be loved, admired, envied—especially envied—and to be comfortable, to be the center of everyone's attention. She would never put involvement with anyone else before her own self-image. Added to that, she dresses gorgeously, parades around and flirts with her eyes, but Maxim is very proper about morality, you know? And he has the money. If Louisa went too far he wouldn't stand for it." She bit her soft lower lip. "He loved Alex very much, you know, but he denied himself anything with her. He wouldn't let Louisa play fast and loose now."

Hester watched Edith's face carefully; she did not wish to hurt, but the thoughts were high in her mind. "But Thaddeus had money surely? If Louisa married him, she wouldn't need Maxim's money?"

Edith laughed outright. "Don't be absurd! She'd be ruined if Maxim divorced her—and Thaddeus certainly wouldn't get involved in anything like that. The scandal would ruin him too."

"Yes, I suppose it would," Hester agreed sensibly. She sat silently for several minutes, thoughts churning around in her head.

"I hate even to think of this at all," Hester said with a shudder of memory. "But what if it were someone else altogether? Not any one of the guests, but one of the servants? Did he go to the Furnivals' house often?"

"Yes, I believe so, but why on earth should a servant want to kill him? That's too unlikely. I know you want to find something—but . . ."

"I don't know. Something in the past? He was a general—he must have made both friends and enemies. Perhaps the motive for his death lies in his career, and is nothing to do with his personal life."

Edith's face lit up. "Oh Hester. That's brilliant of you! You mean some incident on the battlefield, or in the barracks, that has at long last been revenged? We must find out all we can about the Furnivals' servants. You must tell him—Monk, did you say? Yes, Mr. Monk. You must tell him what we have thought of, and set him about it immediately!"

Hester smiled at the thought of so instructing Monk, but she acquiesced, and before Edith could continue with her ideas, the maid came to announce that luncheon was served and they were expected at table.

Apparently Edith had already informed the family that Hester was expected. No remarks were passed on her presence, except a cool acknowledgment of her arrival and an invitation to be seated at the specified place, and a rather perfunctory wish that she should enjoy her meal.

She thanked Felicia and took her seat otherwise in silence.

"I imagine you have seen the newspapers?" Randolf said, glancing around the table. He looked even wearier today than the last time Hester had seen him, but certainly had Monk asked her now if she thought him senile, she would have denied it without doubt. There was an angry intelligence in his eyes, and any querulousness around his mouth or droop to his features was set there by character as much as the mere passage of time.

"Naturally I have seen the headlines," Felicia said sharply. "I do not care for the rest. There is nothing we can do about it, but we do not have to discuss this with one another. It is like all evil speaking and distasteful speculation: one sets one's mind against it and refuses to be distressed. Would you be so good as to pass me the condiments, Peverell?"

Peverell did as he was bidden, and smiled from the corner of his vision at Hester. There was the same gentleness in his eyes, a mild awareness of humor, as she had observed before. He was an ordinary man—and yet far from ordinary. She could not imagine that Damaris had entertained romantic notions about Maxim Furnival; she was not foolish enough to destroy what she had for a cheap moment of entertainment. For all her flamboyance, she was not a stupid or shallow woman.

"I have not seen the newspapers," Edith said suddenly, looking at her mother.

"Of course you haven't." Felicia stared at her with wide eyes. "Nor shall you."

"What are they saying of Alexandra?" Edith persisted, apparently deaf to the warning note in Felicia's voice.

"Precisely what you would expect," Felicia answered. "Ignore it."

"You say that as if we could." Damaris's tone was sharp, almost an accusation. "Don't think about it, and it is of no importance. Just like that—it is dealt with."

"You have a great deal yet to learn, my dear," Felicia said with chill, looking at her daughter in something close to exasperation. "Where is Cassian? He is late. A certain amount of latitude may be allowed, but one must exercise discipline as well." She reached out her hand and rang the little silver bell.

Almost immediately a footman appeared.

"Go and fetch Master Cassian, James. Tell him he is required at luncheon."

"Yes ma'am." And obediently he left.

Randolf grunted, but spoke no words, and addressed himself again to his food.

"I imagine the newspapers write well of General Carlyon." Hester heard her own voice loud in the silence, sounding clumsy and terribly contrived. But how else was she to serve any purpose here? She could not hope any of them would say or do something in which she could find meaning, simply eating their luncheon. "He had a brilliant career," she went on. "They are bound to have written of it."

Randolf looked at her, his heavy face puckered.

"He did," he agreed. "He was an outstanding man, an ornament to his generation and his family. Although what you can possibly know about it, Miss Latterly, I fail to see. I daresay your remark is well meant, and intended as a kindness, and for your civility, I thank you." He looked anything but grateful.

Hester felt as if she had trespassed by praising him, as though they felt he was their particular property and only they might speak of him.

"I have spent a considerable time in the army myself, Colonel Carlyon," she said in defense.

"Army!" he snorted with quite open contempt. "Non-

115

sense, young woman! You were a nurse, a skivvy to tend to the slops for the surgeons. Hardly the same thing!"

Her temper frayed raw, and she forgot Monk, Rathbone and Alexandra Carlyon.

"I don't know how you know anything about it," she said, mimicking his tone savagely and precisely. "You were not there. Or you would be aware that army nursing has changed a great deal. I have watched battles and walked the field afterwards. I have helped surgeons in field hospitals, and I daresay I have known as many soldiers in the space of a few years as you have."

His face was turning a rich plum color and his eyes were bulging.

"And I did not hear General Carlyon's name mentioned by anyone," she added coldly. "But I now work nursing a Major Tiplady, and he knew of General Carlyon, because he had also served in India, and he spoke of him in some detail. I did not speak without some knowledge. Was I misinformed?"

Randolf was torn between the desire to be thoroughly rude to her and the need to defend his son, his family pride, and to be at least reasonably civil to a guest, even one he had not invited. Family pride won.

"Of course not," he said grudgingly. "Thaddeus was exceptional. A man not only of military brilliance, but a man without a stain of dishonor on his name."

Felicia kept her eyes on her plate, her jaw tight. Hester wondered what inner grief tore at her at the loss of her only son, grief she would keep hidden with that same rigid discipline which had no doubt sustained her all her life, through the loneliness of long separations, perhaps service abroad in unfamiliar places, harsh climate, fear of injury and disease; and now scandal and devastating loss. On the courage and duty of such women had the soldiers of the Empire leaned.

The door opened and a small boy with fair hair and a thin, pale face came into the room; his first glance was to Randolf, then to Felicia.

"I'm sorry, Grandmama," he said very quietly.

"You are excused," Felicia replied formally. "Do not make a habit of it, Cassian. It is impolite to be late to meals. Please take your place, and James will bring your luncheon."

"Yes, Grandmama." He skirted wide around his grandfather's chair, around Peverell without looking at him, then sat in the empty seat next to Damaris.

Hester resumed eating her meal, but discreetly she looked at him as he kept his eyes down on his plate and without relish began his main course. Since he was too late for soup he was not to be spoiled by being permitted to catch up. He was a handsome child, with honey fair hair and fair skin with a dusting of freckles lending tone to his pallor. His brow was broad, his nose short and already beginning to show an aquiline curve. His mouth was wide and generous, still soft with childhood, but there was a sulkiness to it, an air of secrecy. Even when he looked up at Edith as she spoke to him, and to request the water or the condiments, there was something in his aspect that struck Hester as closed, more careful than she would have expected a child to be.

Then she remembered the appalling events of the last month, which must have scarred his senses with a pain too overwhelming to take in. In one evening his father was dead and his mother distraught and filled with her own terrors and griefs, and within a fortnight she was arrested and forcibly taken from him. Did he even know why yet? Had anyone told him the full extent of the tragedy? Or did he believe it was an accident, and his mother might yet be returned to him?

Looking at his careful, wary face it was impossible to know, but he did not look terrified and there were no glances of appeal at anyone, even though he was with his family, and presumably knew all of them moderately well.

Had anyone taken him in their arms and let him weep? Had anyone explained to him what was happening? Or was he wandering in a silent confusion, full of imaginings and fears? Did they expect him to shoulder his grief like a full-grown man, be stoic and continue his new and utterly

117

changed life as if it needed no answers and no time for emotion? Was his adult air merely an attempt to be what they expected of him?

Or had they not even thought about it at all? Were food and clothes, warmth and a room of his own, considered to be all a boy his age required?

The conversation continued desultorily and Hester learned nothing from it. They spoke of trivialities of one sort or another, acquaintances Hester did not know, society in general, government, the current events and public opinion of the scandals and tragedies of the day.

The last course had been cleared away and Felicia was taking a mint from the silver tray when Damaris at last returned to the original subject.

"I passed a newsboy this morning, shouting about Alex," she said unhappily. "He was saying some awful things. Why are people so—so vicious? They don't even know yet if she did anything or not!"

"Shouldn't have been listening," Randolf muttered grimly. "Your mother's told you that before."

"I didn't know you were going out." Felicia looked across the table at her irritably. "Where did you go?"

"To the dressmakers'," Damaris replied with a flicker of annoyance. "I have to have another black dress. I'm sure you wouldn't wish me to mourn in purple."

"Purple is half mourning." Felicia's large, deep-set eyes rested on her daughter with disfavor. "Your brother is only just buried. You will maintain black as long as it is decent to do so. I know the funeral is over, but if I find you outside the house in lavender or purple before Michaelmas, I shall be most displeased."

The thought of black all summer was plain in Damaris's face, but she said nothing.

"Anyway, you did not need to go out," Felicia went on. "You should have sent for the dressmaker to come to you." A host of thoughts was plain in Damaris's face, most especially the desire to escape the house and its environs.

"What did they say?" Edith asked curiously, referring to the newspapers again.

"They seemed to have judged already that she was guilty," Damaris replied. "But it isn't that, it was the—the viciousness of it."

"What do you expect?" Felicia frowned. "She has confessed to the world that she has done something quite beyond understanding. It defies the order of everyone's lives, like madness. Of course people will be . . . angry. I think *vicious* is the wrong word to choose. You don't seem to understand the enormity of it." She pushed her salmon mousse to the side of her plate and abandoned it. "Can you imagine what would happen to the country if every woman whose husband flirted with someone else were to murder him? Really, Damaris, sometimes I wonder where your wits are. Society would disintegrate. There would be no safety, no decency or certainty in anything. Life would fall to pieces and we would be in the jungle."

She signaled peremptorily for the footman to remove the plate. "Heaven knows, Alexandra had nothing untoward to have to endure, but if she had then she should have done so, like thousands of other women before her, and no doubt after. No relationships are without their difficulties and sacrifices."

It was something of an exaggeration, and Hester looked around at their faces to see if anyone was going to reason with her. But Edith kept her eyes on her plate; Randolf nodded as if he agreed totally; and Damaris glanced up, her eyes on Hester, but she said nothing either. Cassian looked very grave, but no one seemed to bother that the allusions to his parents were made in front of him, and he showed no emotions at all.

It was Peverell who spoke.

"Fear, my dear," he said, looking at Edith with a sad smile. "People are frequently at their ugliest when they are afraid. Violence from garroters we expect, from the working classes among themselves, even now and then from gentlemen—a matter of insult and honor over a woman, or—in very bad taste, but it happens—over money.''

The footman removed all the fish plates and served the meat course.

''But when women start using violence,'' Peverell went on, ''to dictate how men shall behave in the matter of morals or their appetites, then that threatens not only their freedom but the sanctity of their homes. And it strikes real terror into people, because it is the basic safety at the core of things, the refuge that all like to imagine we can retreat to from whatever forays into conflict we may make in the course of the day or the week.''

''I don't know why you use the word *imagine*.'' Felicia fixed him with a stony stare. ''The home is the center of peace, morality, unquestioning loyalty, which is the refuge and the strength to all who must labor, or battle in an increasingly changing world.'' She waved away the meat course, and the footman withdrew to serve Hester. ''Without it what would there be worth living for?'' she demanded. ''If the center and the heart give way, then everything else is lost. Can you wonder that people are frightened, and appalled, when a woman who has everything given her turns 'round and kills the very man who protected and provided for her? Of course they react displeased. One cannot expect anything else. You must ignore it. If you had sent for the dressmaker, as you should have, then you would not have witnessed it.''

Nothing further was said in the matter, and half an hour later when the meal was finished, Edith and Hester excused themselves. Shortly after that, Hester took her leave, having told Edith all she knew of progress so far, and promising to continue with every bit of the very small ability she possessed, and trying to assure her, in spite of her own misgivings, that there was indeed some hope.

Major Tiplady was staring towards the window waiting for her when she returned home, and immediately enquired to know the outcome of her visit.

''I don't know that it is anything really useful,'' she answered, taking off her cloak and bonnet and laying them on the chair for Molly to hang up. "But I learned quite a lot more about the general. I am not sure that I should have liked him, but at least I can feel some pity that he is dead."

"That is not very productive," Tiplady said critically. He regarded her narrowly, sitting very upright. "Could this Louisa woman have killed him?"

Hester came over and sat on the chair beside him.

"It looks very doubtful," she confessed. "He seems a man far more capable of friendship than romances; and Louisa apparently had too much to lose, both in reputation and finance, to have risked more than a flirtation." She felt suddenly depressed. "In fact it does seem as if Alexandra was the one—or else poor Sabella—if she really is deranged."

"Oh dear." Tiplady looked crushed. "Then where do we go from here?"

"Perhaps it was one of the servants," she said with sudden hope again.

"One of the servants?" he said incredulously. "Whatever for?"

"I don't know. Some old military matter?"

He looked doubtful.

"Well, I shall pursue it!" she said firmly. "Now, have you had tea yet? What about supper? What would you care for for supper?"

Two days later she took an afternoon off, at Major Tiplady's insistence, and went to visit Lady Callandra Daviot in order to enlist her help in learning more of General Carlyon's military career. Callandra had helped her with both counsel and friendship when she first returned from the Crimea, and it was with her good offices that she had obtained her hospital post. It was extremely gracious of Callandra not to have been a good deal harsher in her comments when Hester had then lost it through overstepping the bounds of her authority.

Callandra's late husband, Colonel Daviot, had been an army surgeon of some distinction; a quick-tempered, charming, stubborn, witty and somewhat arbitrary man. He had had a vast acquaintance and might well have known something of General Carlyon. Callandra, still with connections to the Army Medical Corps, might be able either to recall hearing of the general, or to institute discreet enquiries and learn something of his career and, more importantly, of his reputation. She might be able to find information about the unofficial events which just might lead to another motive for murder, either someone seeking revenge for a wrong, a betrayal on the field, or a promotion obtained unfairly—or imagined to be so, or even some scandal exposed or too harshly pursued. The possibilities were considerable.

They were sitting in Callandra's room, which could hardly be called a withdrawing room, since she would have received no formal visitors there. It was full of bright sunlight, desperately unfashionable, cluttered with books and papers, cushions thrown about for comfort, two discarded shawls and a sleeping cat which should have been white but was liberally dusted with soot.

Callandra herself, well into middle age, gray hair flying all over the place as if she were struggling against a high wind, her curious intelligent face long-nosed, full of humor, and quite out of fashion also, was sitting in the sunlight, which if it were habit might account for her indelicate complexion. She regarded Hester with amusement.

"My dear girl, do you not imagine Monk has already told me of the case? That was our bargain, if you recall. And quite naturally I have made considerable efforts to learn what I can of General Carlyon. And of his father. One may learn much of a man by knowing something of his parents—or of a woman, of course." She scowled ferociously. "Really, that cat is quite perverse. God intended him to be white, so what does he do but climb up chimneys! It quite sets my teeth on edge when I think that sooner or later he will lick all that out of his coat. I feel as if my own mouth were full of soot. But I can hardly bathe him, although I have thought of it—and told him so."

"I should think a great deal of it will come off on your

furniture,'' Hester said without disquiet. She was used to Callandra, and she had quite an affection for the animal anyway.

"Probably," Callandra agreed. "He is a refugee from the kitchen at the moment, and I must give the poor beast asylum."

"Why? I thought his job was in the kitchen, to keep the mice down."

"It is—but he is overfond of eggs."

"Can the cook not spare him an egg now and again?"

"Of course. But when she doesn't he is apt to help himself. He has just looped his paw 'round half a dozen this morning and sent them all to the floor, where quite naturally they broke, and he was able to eat his fill. We shall not now be having soufflé for dinner." She rearranged herself rather more comfortably and the cat moved itself gently in its sleep and began to purr. "I presume you wish to know what I have heard about General Carlyon?" Callandra asked.

"Of course."

"It is not very interesting. Indeed he was a remarkably uninteresting man, correct to a degree which amounts to complete boredom—for me. His father purchased his commission in the Guards. He was able and obeyed the letter of the law, very popular with his fellows, most of them, and in due course obtained promotion, no doubt a great deal to do with family influence and a certain natural ability with a weapon. He knew how to command his men's absolute loyalty—and that counts for a lot. He was an excellent horseman, which also helped."

"And his private reputation?" Hester said hopefully.

Callandra looked apologetic. "A complete blank," she confessed. "He married Alexandra FitzWilliam after a brief courtship. It was most suitable and both families were happy with the arrangement, which since they were the ones who were largely responsible for it, is not surprising. They had one daughter, Sabella, and many years later, their only son, Cassian. The general was posted to the Indian army, and remained abroad for many years, mostly in Bengal, and I have spoken to a friend of mine who served there also, but he had never heard anything the least bit disreputable about Carlyon, either his military duties or his personal life. His men respected him, indeed some intensely so.

"I did hear one small story which seems to indicate the character of the man. One young lieutenant, only been in India a few weeks, made an awful mess of a patrol, got himself lost and half of his men wounded. Carlyon, a major at the time, rode out with a couple of volunteers to look for this young fellow, at considerable risk to himself, found him, looked after the wounded and fought off an attack of some sort. He got nearly all of them safely back to the post. Tore the young fellow to shreds himself, but lied like a trooper to save him from coming up on a charge for total incompetence. Which all seems very unselfish, until you realize how it enhances his own reputation, and how his men admired him for it. He seems to have counted the hero worship of his men more than his own preferment, although that came too."

"Very human," Hester said thoughtfully. "Not entirely admirable, but not hard to understand."

"Not at all admirable," Callandra said grimly. "Not in a military leader. A general should be above all trusted; that is a far calmer emotion than hero worship, and far more to be relied on when the going is really hard."

"I suppose so—yes, of course." Hester reasserted her common sense. It was the same with any great leader. Florence Nightingale was not an especially lovable woman, being far too autocratic, insensitive to the vanities and foibles of others, intolerant of weakness and yet highly eccentric herself. But she was a leader even those who most loathed her would still follow, and the men she served regarded her as a saint—but then perhaps most saints were not easy people.

"I asked with some hope if he had gambled excessively," Callandra continued. "Been too rigid with discipline, espoused any barbaric sects of belief, earned any personal enemies, or had friendships that might lay him open to question—if you see what I mean?'' She looked at Hester dubiously.

"Yes, I see what you mean," Hester acknowledged with a wry smile. It was not a thought which had occurred to her, but it was a good one. What if the general's lover was not a woman, but a man? But it seemed that was not to be fruitful either. "What a pity—that would be a powerful motive.''

"Indeed.'' Callandra's face tightened. "But I could find no evidence whatsoever. And the person to whom I spoke was one who would not have minced words and pretended he would not have heard of such things. I am afraid, my dear, that General Carlyon was of totally traditional behavior in every way—and not a man who seems to have given anyone cause to hate him or to fear him.''

Hester sighed. "Nor his father?''

"Much the same—very much the same, simply less successful. He served in the Peninsular War under the Duke of Wellington, and saw Waterloo—which one would think might make him interesting, but apparently it did not. The only difference between father and son seems to be that the colonel had his son first and his two daughters afterwards, whereas the general did it the other way 'round. And he reached a higher rank, no doubt because he had a father of influence to aid him. I'm sorry my enquiries have turned up so very little. It is most disappointing.''

And on that note, their conversation became more general, and they spent a most agreeable afternoon together until Hester rose to take her leave and return to Major Tiplady and her duties.

At the same time as Hester was dining with the Carlyon family, Monk was paying his first visit to Dr. Charles Hargrave, both as someone unrelated to the Carlyon family who had attended the party that evening and as the medical officer who had first seen the body of the general.

He had made an appointment in order not to find the doctor out on a call when he came, and therefore he approached with confidence, even at the unsuitable hour of half past eight in the evening. He was admitted by the maid and shown immediately to a pleasant and conventional study where he was received by Hargrave, an unusually tall man, lean and elegant of build, broad shouldered, and yet not athletic in manner. His coloring was nondescript fair, his eyes a little hooded and greenish blue in shade, his nose long and pointed, but not quite straight, as if at some time it had been broken and ill set. His mouth was small, his teeth when he smiled very regular. It was a highly individual face, and he seemed a man very much at his ease.

"Good evening, Mr. Monk. I doubt I can be of any assistance, but of course I shall do everything I can, although I have already spoken to the police—naturally."

"Thank you, sir," Monk accepted. "That is most generous of you."

"Not at all. A wretched business." Hargrave waved towards one of the large leather-covered chairs beside the fireplace, and as Monk sat in one, he sat in the other. "What can I tell you? I assume you already know the course of events that evening."

"I have several accounts, none seriously at variance with another," Monk replied. "But there remain some unanswered questions. For example, do you know what so distressed Mrs. Erskine?"

Hargrave smiled suddenly, a charming and candid gesture. "No idea at all. Quarrel with Louisa, I should think, but I haven't the faintest notion about what. Although it did seem to me she was quite uncharacteristically beastly to poor Maxim. Sorry not to be more helpful. And before you ask, neither do I know why Thaddeus and Alexandra quarreled."

"Could that also have been about Mrs. Furnival?" Monk asked.

Hargrave considered for a moment or two before replying, placing his fingers together in a steeple and looking at Monk over the point of them.

"I thought at first that it was unlikely, but on consideration perhaps it is not. Rivalry is a strange thing. People may fight passionately over something, not so much because they de-

126

sire it for itself but because they wish to win the struggle, and be seen to win it—or at least not to lose." He regarded Monk closely, searching his face, his expression grave. "What I was going to say is that although Alexandra was not deeply in love with the general, it may be that her pride was very precious to her, and to have her friends and family see him giving his attention to someone else may have been more than she was prepared to endure." He saw Monk's doubt, or imagined it. "I realize murder is a very extreme reaction to that." He frowned, biting his lips. "And solves nothing at all. But then it is absurd to imagine it would solve anything else either—but the general was undoubtedly murdered."

"Was he?" Monk did not ask the question with skepticism so much as enquiry for clarification. "You examined the body; you did not perceive it as murder immediately, did you?"

Hargrave smiled wryly. "No," he admitted. "I would not have said anything that evening, whatever I had thought. I confess, I was considerably shaken when Maxim came back and said Thaddeus had had an accident, and then of course when I saw him I knew immediately that he was dead. It was a very nasty wound. My first thoughts, after it was obvious I could do nothing for him, were to break it as gently as possible to his family, many of whom were present, especially his wife. Of course I had no idea then that she was involved in it, and already knew better than any of us what had happened."

"What had happened, Dr. Hargrave, in your medical opinion?"

Hargrave pursed his lips.

"Exactly," Monk added.

"Perhaps I had better describe the scene as I found it." Hargrave crossed his legs and stared at the low fire in the hearth, lit against the evening chill. "The general was lying sprawled on the floor below the curve of the banister," he began. "The suit of armor was on the floor beside him. As I remember, it had come to pieces, presumably from the impact of his body on it. It can have been held together only by rather perished leather straps, and a certain amount of sheer balance and weight of itself. One gauntlet was under his body, the other close to his head. The helmet had rolled away about eighteen inches.''

''Was the general on his back or his face?'' Monk asked.

''His back,'' Hargrave said immediately. ''The halberd was sticking out of his chest. I assumed he had gone over sideways, overbalanced and then twisted in the air in his effort to save himself, so that the point of the halberd had gone through his chest. Then when he hit the armor, it had deflected him and he had landed on his back. Awkward, I can see that now, but I wasn't thinking of murder at the time—only of what I could do to help.''

''And you saw immediately that he was dead?''

A bleak, rueful expression crossed Hargrave's face. ''The first thing I did was to bend and reach for a pulse. Automatic, I assume. Pretty futile, in the circumstances. When I found none, I looked more closely at the wound. The halberd was still in it.'' He did not shiver, but the muscles of his body tightened and he seemed to draw into himself. ''When I saw how far it had penetrated, I knew he could not possibly live more than a few moments with such an injury. It had sunk more than eight inches into his body. In fact when we moved him later we could see the mark where the point had scarred the floor underneath. She must have . . .'' His voice caught. He took a breath. ''Death must have been more or less instantaneous.''

He swallowed and looked at Monk apologetically. ''I've seen a lot of corpses, but mostly from age and disease. I haven't had to deal with violent death very often.''

''Of course not,'' Monk acknowledged with a softer tone. ''Did you move him?''

''No. No, it was obvious it was going to require the police. Even an accident of that violence would have to be reported and investigated.''

''So you went back into the room and informed them he was dead? Can you recall their individual reactions?''

''Yes!'' Hargrave looked surprised, his eyes widening.

"They were shocked, naturally. As far as I can remember, Maxim and Peverell were the most stunned—and my wife. Damaris Erskine had been preoccupied with her own emotions most of the evening, and I think it was some time before she really took in what I said. Sabella was not there. She had gone upstairs—I think honestly to avoid being in the room with her father, whom she loathed—"

"Do you know why?" Monk interrupted.

"Oh yes." Hargrave smiled tolerantly. "Since she was about twelve or thirteen she had had some idea of becoming a nun—sort of romantic idea some girls get." He shrugged, a shadow of humor across his face. "Most of them grow out of it—she didn't. Naturally her father wouldn't hear of such a thing. He insisted she marry and settle down, like any other young woman. And Fenton Pole is a nice enough man, well-bred, well-mannered, with more than sufficient means to keep her in comfort."

He leaned forward and poked the fire, steadying one of the logs with the poker. "To begin with it looked as if she had accepted things. Then she had a very difficult confinement and afterwards seemed not to regain her balance—mentally, that is. Physically she is perfectly well, and the child too. It can happen. Most unfortunate. Poor Alexandra had a very difficult time with her—not to mention Fenton."

"How did she take her father's death?"

"I'm afraid I really don't know. I was too preoccupied with Alexandra, and with sending for the police. You'll have to ask Maxim or Louisa."

"You were occupied with Mrs. Carlyon? Did she take the news very hard?"

Hargrave's eyes were wide and there was a grim humor there. "You mean was she surprised? It is impossible to tell. She sat frozen as if she could hardly comprehend what was happening. It might have been that she already knew—or equally easily it might have been shock. And even if she knew, or suspected murder, it may have been fear that it was Sabella who had done it. I have thought it was many times since then, and I have no more certainty now than I did at the time."

"And Mrs. Furnival?"

Hargrave leaned back and crossed his legs.

"There I am on much surer ground. I am almost positive that she was taken totally by surprise. The evening had been very tense and not at all pleasant due to Alexandra's very evident quarrel with her husband, Sabella's continued rage with him, which she made almost no effort to conceal, in spite of the obvious embarrassment it caused everybody, and Damaris Erskine's quite unexplainable almost hysteria, and her rudeness to Maxim. She seemed to be so consumed with her own emotions she was hardly aware of what was going on with the rest of us."

He shook his head. "Peverell was naturally concerned with her, and embarrassed. Fenton Pole was annoyed with Sabella because she had made something of a habit of this recently. Indeed the poor man had every cause to find the situation almost intolerable.

"Louisa was, I confess, taking up the general's attention in a manner many wives would have found difficult to accommodate—but then women have their own resources with which to deal with these things. And Alexandra was neither a plain woman nor a stupid one. In the past Maxim Furnival paid more than a little attention to her—quite as much as the general was giving Louisa that evening—and I have a suspicion it was rooted in a far less superficial feeling. But that is only a notion; I know nothing."

Monk smiled, acknowledging the confidence.

"Dr. Hargrave, what is your opinion of the mental state of Sabella Pole? In your judgment, is it possible that she killed her father and that Alexandra has confessed to protect her?"

Hargrave leaned back very slowly, pursing his lips, his eyes on Monk's face.

"Yes, I think it is possible, but you will need a great deal more than a possibility before the police will take any notice of it. And I certainly cannot say she definitely did anything,

130

or that her behavior betrays more than an emotional imbalance, which is quite well known in women who have recently given birth. Such melancholia sometimes takes the form of violence, but towards the child, not towards their own fathers.''

"And you also were the medical consultant to Mrs. Carlyon?''

"Yes, for what that is worth, which I fear is nothing in this instance.'' Again he shook his head. "I can offer no evidence of her sanity or the unlikelihood that she committed this crime. I really am sorry, Mr. Monk, but I believe you are fighting a lost cause.''

"Can you think of any other reason whatever why she should have killed her husband?''

"No.'' Hargrave was totally serious. "And I have tried. So far as I am aware, he was never violent to her or overtly cruel in any way. I appreciate that you are seeking any mitigating circumstances—but I am truly sorry, I know of none. The general was a normal, healthy man, and as sane as any man alive. A trifle pompous, perhaps, and outside military matters, a bore—but that is not a capital sin.''

Monk did not know what he had been hoping for; still he felt a deep sense of disappointment. The possibilities were narrowing, the chances to discover something of meaning were fading one by one, and each was so inconclusive.

"Thank you, Dr. Hargrave.'' Monk rose to his feet. "You have been very patient.''

"Not at all.'' Hargrave stood up and moved towards the door. "I'm only sorry I could be of no assistance. What will you do now?''

"Retrace my steps,'' Monk said wearily. "Go back over police records of the investigation, recheck the evidence, times, places, answers to questions.''

"I am afraid you are in for a disappointing time,'' Hargrave said ruefully. "I have very little idea why she should suddenly leave all sanity and self-interest, but I fear you will find in the end that Alexandra Carlyon killed her husband.''

131

"Possibly," Monk conceded, opening the door. "But I have not given up yet!"

Monk had not so far been to the police about the case, and he would not go to Runcorn. The relationship between them had always been difficult, strained by Monk's ambition forever treading on Runcorn's heels, hungry for his rank, and making no secret that he believed he could do the job better. And Runcorn, afraid in his heart that that was true, had feared him, and out of fear had come resentment, bitterness, and then hatred.

Finally Monk had resigned in rage, refusing to obey an order he considered profoundly incompetent and morally mistaken. Runcorn had been delighted, free at last of his most dangerous subordinate. The fact that Monk had proved to be correct, as had happened so often before, had robbed him of victory, but not of the exquisite release from Monk's footsteps at his back and his shadow forever darkening his prospects.

John Evan was a totally different matter. He had not known Monk before the accident and had been assigned to work as his sergeant on his return from convalescence, when he began the Grey case. He had found a man discovering himself through evidence, the views and emotions of others, records of past cases, and not at all certain that he liked what he saw. Evan had learned Monk's vulnerability, and eventually guessed how little he knew of himself, and that he fought to keep his job because to lose it would be to lose not just his means of livelihood but the only certainty he possessed. Even at the very worst times, when Monk had doubted himself, not merely his competence but even his honor and his morality, Evan had never once betrayed him, to Runcorn or to anyone else. Evan and Hester Latterly had saved him when he himself had given it up as impossible.

John Evan was an unusual policeman, the son of a country parson, not quite a gentleman but certainly not a laborer or an artisan. Consequently Evan had an ease of manner that Monk admired and that irritated Runcorn, since both of them

132

in their very different ways had aspirations to social advancement.

Monk did not wish to return to the police station to see Evan. It held too many memories of his own prowess and authority, and his final leaving, when juniors of all sorts had gathered, spellbound and awestruck, ears to the keyhole, to hear that last blazing quarrel, and then had scattered like rabbits when Monk threw open the door and strode out, leaving Runcorn scarlet-faced but victorious.

Instead he chose to seek him in the public house where Evan most frequently took his luncheon, if time and opportunity afforded. It was a small place, crowded with the good-natured chatter of street sellers, newsmen, petty clerks and the entrepreneurs on the edge of the underworld. The smells of ale and cider, sawdust, hot food and jostling bodies were pervasive and not unpleasant. Monk took a position where he could see the door, and nursed a pint of cider until Evan came in. Then he forced his way to the counter and pushed till he was beside him.

Evan swung around with surprise, and pleasure lit his face immediately. He was a lean young man with a long, aquiline nose, hazel eyes and an expression of gentle, lugubrious humor. Now he was quite openly delighted.

"Mr. Monk!" He had never lost the sense that Monk was his superior and must be treated with a certain dignity. "How are you? Are you looking for me?" There was a definite note of hope in his voice.

"I am," Monk confessed, more pleased at Evan's eagerness than he would willingly have expected, or conceded.

Evan ordered a pint of cider and a thick mutton-and-pickle sandwich, made with two crusty slices, and another pint for Monk, then made his way over to a corner where they could be relatively private.

"Yes?" he said as soon as they were seated. "Have you a case?"

Monk half hid his smile. "I'm not sure. But you have."

Evan's eyebrows shot up. "I have?"

"General Carlyon."

133

Evan's disappointment was apparent. "Oh—not much of a case there, I'm afraid. Poor woman did it. Jealousy is a cruel thing. Ruined a good many lives." His face puckered. "But how are you involved in it?" He took a large bite from his sandwich.

"Rathbone is defending her," Monk answered. "He hired me to try and find out if there are any mitigating circumstances—and even if it is possible that it was not she who killed him but someone else."

"She confessed," Evan said, holding his sandwich in both hands to keep the pickle from sliding out.

"Could be to protect the daughter," Monk suggested. "Wouldn't be the first time a person confessed in order to take the blame for someone they loved very deeply."

"No." Evan spoke with his mouth full, but even so his doubt was obvious. He swallowed and took a sip of his cider, his eyes still on Monk. "But it doesn't look like it in this case. We found no one who saw the daughter come downstairs."

"But could she have?"

"Can't prove that she didn't—just no cause to think she did. Anyway, why should she kill her father? It couldn't possibly gain her anything, as far as she was concerned; the harm was already done. She is married and had a child—she couldn't go back to being a nun now. If she'd killed him, then . . ."

"She'd have very little chance indeed of becoming a nun," Monk said dryly. "Not at all a good start to a life of holy contemplation."

"It was your idea, not mine." Evan defended himself, but there was an answering flick of humor in his eyes. "And as for anyone else—who? I can't see Mrs. Carlyon confessing to save Louisa Furnival from the gallows, can you?"

"Not intentionally, no, only unintentionally, if she thought it was Sabella." Monk took a long pull from his cider.

Evan frowned. "We thought it was Sabella to begin with," he conceded. "Mrs. Carlyon only confessed when it must have seemed to her we were going to arrest Sabella."

"Or Maxim Furnival," Monk went on. "Perhaps he was jealous. It looks as if he had more cause. It was Louisa who was doing the flirting, setting the pace. General Carlyon was merely responding."

Evan continued with his sandwich, and spoke with his mouth full again.

"Mrs. Furnival is the sort of woman who always flirts. It's her manner with most men. She even flirted with me, in a sort of way." He blushed very slightly, not at the memory— he was a most personable young man, and he had been flirted with before—but at reciting it to Monk. It sounded so unbecomingly immodest. "This can't have been the first time she made a public spectacle of exercising her powers. Why, if he put up with it all these years—the son is thirteen so they have been married fourteen years at least, and actually I gather quite a lot longer—why would Maxim Furnival suddenly lose his head so completely as to murder the general? From what I gather of him, General Carlyon was hardly a romantic threat to him. He was a highly respectable, rather pompous soldier well past his prime, stiff, not much sense of humor and not especially handsome. He had money, but so has Furnival."

Monk said nothing, and began to wish he had ordered a sandwich as well.

"Sorry," Evan said sincerely. "I really don't think there is anything you can do for Mrs. Carlyon. Society will not see any excuses for murdering a husband out of jealousy because he flirted. In fact, even if he had a full-blown affair and flaunted it publicly, she would still be expected to turn the other way, affect not to have seen anything amiss, and behave with dignity." He looked apologetic and his eyes were full of regret. "As long as she was provided for financially, and had the protection of his name, she would be considered to have a quite satisfactory portion in life, and must do her duty to keep the sanctity and stability of the home—whether he wished to return to it or not."

Monk knew he was right, and whatever his private thoughts of the morality of it, that was how she would be judged. And

135

of course any jury would be entirely composed of men, and men of property at that. They would identify with the general. After all, what would happen to them if women were given the idea that if their husbands flirted they could get away with killing them? She would find very short shrift there.

"I can tell you the evidence as we found it if you like, but it won't do any good," Evan said ruefully. "There's nothing interesting in it; in fact nothing you couldn't have deduced for yourself."

"Tell me anyway," Monk said without hope.

Evan obliged, and as he had said, there was nothing of any use at all, nothing that offered even a thread to follow.

Monk went back to the bar and ordered a sandwich and two more pints of cider, then after a few more minutes of conversation about other things, bade Evan farewell and left the public house. He went out into the busy street with a sense of the warmth of friendship which was still a flavor to be relished with a lingering surprise, but even less hope for Alexandra Carlyon than before.

Monk would not go back to Rathbone and admit defeat. It was not proved. Really he had no more than Rathbone had told him in the beginning. A crime had three principal elements, and he cited them in his mind as he walked along the street between costermongers' barrows, young children of no more than six or seven years selling ribbons and matches. Sad-faced women held bags of old clothes; indigent and disabled men offered toys, small handmade articles, some carved of bone or wood, bottles of this and that, patent medicines. He passed by news vendors, singing patterers and every other inhabitant of the London streets. And he knew beneath them in the sewers there would be others hunting and scavenging a living, and along the river shore seeking the refuse and the lost treasures of the wealthier denizens of the great city.

Motive had failed him. Alexandra had a motive, even if it was a self-defeating and short-sighted one. She had not

136

looked like a woman torn by a murderously jealous rage. But that might be because it had been satisfied by his death, and now she could see the folly, and the price of it.

Sabella had motive, but it was equally self-defeating, and she had not confessed. Indeed she seemed genuinely concerned for her mother. Could it be she had committed the crime, in a fit of madness, and did not even remember it? From her husband's anxiety, it seemed not impossible he thought so.

Maxim Furnival? Not out of jealousy over Louisa, unless the affair were a great deal deeper than anyone had so far discovered. Or was Louisa so in love with the general she would have caused a public scandal and left her husband for him? On the evidence so far that was absurd.

Louisa herself? Because the general had flirted with her and then rejected her? There was no evidence whatsoever to suggest he had rejected her at all. On the contrary, there was every indication he was still quite definitely interested—although to what degree it was impossible to say.

Means. They all had the means. All it required was a simple push when the general was standing at the turn of the stairs with his back to the banister, as he might if he had stopped to speak to someone. He would naturally face them. And the halberd was there for anyone to use. It did not require strength or skill. Any person of adult height could have used his or her body's weight to force that blade through a man's chest, although it might take an overtowering passion to sink it to the floor.

Opportunity. That was his only course left. If the events of the dinner party had been retold accurately (and to imagine them all lying was too remote and forced an idea to entertain), then there were four people who could have done it, the four he had already considered: Alexandra, Sabella, Louisa and Maxim.

Who else was in the house and not at the party? All the servants—and young Valentine Furnival. But Valentine was little more than a child, and by all accounts very fond of the general. That left the servants. He must make one last effort to account for their whereabouts that evening. If nothing else, it might establish beyond question whether Sabella Pole could have come downstairs and killed her father.

He took a hansom—after all, Rathbone was paying for it—and presented himself at the Furnivals' front door. Although he wanted to speak to the servants, he must obtain permission first.

Maxim, home early, was startled to see him, and even more to hear his request, but with a smile that conveyed both surprise and pity he granted it without argument. Apparently Louisa was out taking tea with someone or other, and Monk was glad of it. She was far more acute in her suspicion, and might well have hindered him.

He began with the butler, a very composed individual well into his late sixties, with a broad nose and a tight, satisfied mouth.

"Dinner was served at nine o'clock." He was uncertain whether to add the "sir" or not. Precisely who was this person making enquiries? His master had been unclear.

"Which staff were on duty?" Monk asked.

The butler's eyes opened wide to convey his surprise at such an ignorant question.

"The kitchen and dining room staff, sir." His voice implied "of course."

"How many?" Monk kept his patience with difficulty.

"Myself and the two footmen," the butler replied levelly. "The parlormaid and the downstairs maid who serves sometimes if we have company. In the kitchen there were the cook, two kitchen maids and a scullery maid—and the bootboy. He carries things if he's needed and does the occasional errand."

"In all parts of the house?" Monk asked quickly.

"That is not usually required," the butler replied somberly.

"And on this occasion?"

"He was in disgrace, sent to the scullery."

"What time in the evening was that?" Monk persisted.

138

"Long before the general's death—about nine o'clock, I gather."

"That would be after the guests arrived," Monk observed.

"It would," the butler agreed grimly.

It was only idle curiosity which made him ask, "What happened?"

"Stupid boy was carrying a pile of clean linen upstairs for one of the maids, who was busy, and he bumped into the general coming out of the cloakroom. Wasn't looking where he was going, I suppose—daydreaming—and he dropped the whole lot. Then instead of apologizing and picking them up, like any sensible person, he just turned on his heel and fled. The laundress had a few hard words to say to him, I can promise you! He spent the rest of the evening in the scullery. Didn't leave it."

"I see. What about the rest of the staff?"

"The housekeeper was in her sitting room in the servants' wing. The tweenies would be in their bedroom, the upstairs maids in theirs, the stillroom maid had an evening off to go and visit her mother, who's been took poorly. Mrs. Furnival's ladies' maid would be upstairs and Mr. Furnival's valet likewise."

"And the outside staff?"

"Outside, sir." The butler looked at him with open contempt.

"They have no access to the house?"

"No sir, they have no need."

Monk gritted his teeth. "And none of you heard the general fall onto the suit of armor, or the whole thing come crashing down?"

The butler's face paled, but his eyes were steady.

"No sir. I already told the police person who enquired. We were about our duties, and they did not necessitate any of us coming through the hall. As you may have observed, the withdrawing room is to the rear of the house, and by that time dinner was well finished. We had no cause to pass in that direction."

"After dinner were you all in the kitchen or the pantry clearing away?"

"Yes sir, naturally."

"No one left?"

"What would anyone leave for? We had more than sufficient to keep us busy if we were to get to bed before one."

"Doing what, precisely?" It galled Monk to have to persist in the face of such dignified but subtly apparent scorn. But he would not explain to the man.

Because his master had required it, the butler patiently answered these exceedingly tedious and foolish questions.

"I saw to the silver and the wine, with the assistance of the first footman. The second footman tidied up the dining room and set everything straight ready for morning, and fetched more coal up in case it was required—"

"The dining room," Monk interrupted. "The second footman was in the dining room. Surely he would have heard the armor go over?"

The butler flushed with annoyance. He had been caught out.

"Yes sir, I suppose he would," he said grudgingly. "If he'd been in the dining room when it happened."

"And you said he fetched up coal. Where from?"

"The coal cellar, sir."

"Where is the door to it?"

"Back of the scullery . . . sir." The "sir" was heavy with irony.

"Which rooms would he bring coal for?"

"I . . ." The butler stopped. "I don't know, sir." His face betrayed that he had realized the possibilities. For the dining room, the morning room, the library or billiard room the footman would have crossed the hall.

"May I speak with him?" Monk did not say please; the request was only a formality. He had every intention of speaking with the man regardless.

The butler was not going to put himself in the position of being wrong again.

"I'll send him to you." And before Monk could argue

140

that he would go to the man, which would give him an opportunity to see the servants' area, the butler was gone.

A few minutes later a very nervous young man came in, dressed in ordinary daytime livery of black trousers, shirt and striped waistcoat. He was in his early twenties, fair haired and fair skinned, and at the moment he was extremely ill at ease. Monk guessed the butler had reasserted his authority over the situation by frightening his immediate junior.

Out of perversity Monk decided to be thoroughly pleasant with the young man.

"Good morning," he said with a disarming smile—at least that was how it was intended. "I apologize for taking you from your duties, but I think you may be able to help me."

"Me sir?" His surprise was patent. " 'Ow can I do that, sir?"

"By telling me, as clearly as you can remember, everything you did the evening General Carlyon died, starting after dinner when the guests went to the withdrawing room."

The footman screwed up his face in painfully earnest concentration and recounted his usual routine.

"Then what?" Monk prompted.

"The withdrawing room bell rang," the footman answered. "And since I was passing right by there, I answered it. They wanted the fire stoked, so I did it."

"Who was there then?"

"The master wasn't there, and the mistress came in just as I was leaving."

"And then?"

"Then I—er . . ."

"Had another word with the kitchen maid?" Monk took a guess. He smiled as he said it.

The footman colored, his eyes downcast. "Yes sir."

"Did you fetch the coal buckets for the library?"

"Yes sir—but I don't remember how many minutes later it was." He looked unhappy. Monk guessed it was probably quite some time.

"And crossed the hall to do it?"

"Yes sir. The armor was still all right then."

So whoever it was, it was not Louisa. Not that he had held any real hope that it might be.

"Any other rooms you took coal for? What about upstairs?"

The footman blushed hotly and lowered his eyes.

"You were supposed to, and didn't?" Monk guessed.

The footman looked up quickly. "Yes I did, sir! Mrs. Furnival's room. The master doesn't care for a fire at this time o' the year."

"Did you see someone, or something, when you were upstairs?"

"No sir!"

What was the man lying about? There was something; it was there in his pink face, his downcast eyes, his awkward hands and feet. He was riddled with guilt.

"Where did you go upstairs? What rooms did you pass? Did you hear something, an argument?"

"No sir." He bit his lip and still avoided Monk's eyes.

"Well?" Monk demanded.

"I went up the front stairs—sir . . ."

Suddenly Monk understood. "Oh, I see—with the coal buckets?"

"Yes sir. Please sir . . ."

"I shan't tell the butler," Monk promised quickly.

"Thank you, sir! I—thank you sir." He swallowed. "The armor was still there, sir; and I didn't see the general—or anyone else, except the upstairs maid."

"I see. Thank you. You have helped me considerably."

"Have I sir?" He was doubtful, but relieved to be excused.

Next Monk went upstairs to find the off-duty housemaids. It was his last hope that one of them had seen Sabella.

The first maid offered no hope at all. The second was a bright girl of about sixteen with a mass of auburn hair. She seemed to grasp the significance of his questions, and answered readily enough, although with wary eyes, and he caught a sense of eagerness that suggested to him she had

142

something to hide as well as something to reveal. Presumably she was the one the footman had seen.

"Yes, I saw Mrs. Pole," she said candidly. "She wasn't feeling well, so she lay down for a while in the green room."

"When was that?"

"I—I dunno, sir."

"Was it long after dinner?"

"Oh, yes sir. We 'as our dinner at six o'clock!"

Monk realized his mistake and tried to undo it.

"Did you see anyone else while you were on the landing?"

The color came to her face and suddenly the picture was clearer.

"I shan't report what you say, unless I have to. But if you lie, you may go to prison, because an innocent person could be hanged. You wouldn't want that, would you?"

Now she was ashen white, so frightened as to be robbed momentarily of words.

"So who did you see?"

"John." Her voice was a whisper.

"The footman who was filling the coal buckets?"

"Yes sir—but I didn't speak to him—honest! I jus' came to the top o' the stairs, like. Mrs. Pole were in the green room, 'cause I passed the door and it was open, an' I seen 'er like."

"You came all the way down from your own room at the top of the house?"

She nodded, guilt over her attempt to see the footman outweighing every other thought. She had no idea of the significance of what she was saying.

"How did you know when he was going to be there?"

"I . . ." She bit her lip. "I waited on the landing."

"Did you see Mrs. Carlyon go upstairs to Master Valentine's room?"

"Yes sir."

"Did you see Mrs. Carlyon come down again?"

"No sir, nor the general, sir—I swear to God!"

"Then what did you do?"

143

"I went as far as the top o' the stairs and looked for John, sir. I knew that was about the time 'e'd be fillin' the coal buckets."

"Did you see him?"

"No. I reckon I were too late. I 'ad to 'ang around cos of all the people comin' and goin'. I 'ad ter wait for the master ter go down again."

"You saw Mr. Furnival go down again?"

"Yes sir."

"When you were at the top of the stairs, looking for John—think very carefully, you may have to swear to this in court, before a judge, so tell the truth, as you know it . . ."

She gulped. "Yes sir?"

"Did you look down at the hallway below you?"

"Yes sir. I were looking for John."

"To come from the back of the house?"

"Yes sir—with the coal buckets."

"Was the suit of armor standing where it usually does?"

"I think so."

"It wasn't knocked over?"

"No—o' course it weren't, or I'd 'ave seen it. It'd be right between me and the corridor to the back."

"Then where did you go, after waiting for John and realizing you were too late?"

"Back upstairs again."

He saw the flicker in her eyes, barely discernible, just a tremor.

"Tell me the truth: did you pass anyone?"

Her eyes were downcast, the blush came again. "I heard someone comin', I don't know who. I didn't want to be caught there, so I went into Mrs. Pole's room to see if she needed anything. I was goin' ter say I thought I'd 'eard 'er call out, if anyone asked me."

"And the people passed, going along the passage to the front stairs?"

"Yes sir."

"When was that?"

"I dunno, sir. God help me, I don't! I swear it!"

144

"That's all right, I believe you." Alexandra and the general, minutes before she killed him.

"Did you hear anything?"

"No sir."

"You didn't hear voices?"

"No sir."

"Or the suit of armor crashing over?"

"No sir. The green room is a long way from the top o' the stairs, sir." She did not bother to swear—it was easily verifiable.

"Thank you," he said honestly.

So only Alexandra had the opportunity after all. It was murder.

"You've been a great help." He forced the words out. "A very great help. That's all—you can go." And Alexandra was guilty. Louisa and Maxim had already gone up and come down again, and the general was alive.

"Yes sir. Thank you, sir." And she turned on her heel and fled.

5

O*LIVER* R*ATHBONE* A*WAITED* the arrival of Monk
with some hope, in spite of his reason telling him that it was
extremely unlikely he had been able to find any worthwhile
evidence that it was not after all Alexandra Carlyon who had
killed the general. He shared Monk's contempt for Runcorn
personally, but he had a considerable respect for the police
in general, and had found that when they brought a case to
trial, they were seldom fundamentally in error. But he did
hope that Monk might have turned up a stronger and more
sympathetic motive than jealousy. And if he were honest,
there was a lingering corner in his mind which cherished a
vague idea that it might indeed have been someone else—
although how it would be any better had it been Sabella, he
had no idea, except that so far Sabella was not his client.

As well as Monk, he had invited Hester Latterly. He had
hesitated before doing so. She had no official part in the case,
nor indeed had she had in any other case. But she had opportunities for observation of the Carlyon family that neither
he nor Monk possessed. And it had been she who had brought
him the case in the first place and enlisted his help. She was
owed some information as to the conclusion—if indeed there
was a conclusion. Monk had sent him a message that he had

146

incontrovertible evidence which he must share, so it was unquestionably a decisive point.

Apart from that, he felt a wish that she should be included, and he chose not to examine the cause of it. Therefore at ten minutes before eight on the evening of May 14, he was awaiting their arrival with uncharacteristic nervousness. He was sure he was concealing it perfectly, and yet it was there, once or twice a flutter in his stomach, a very slight tightening of his throat, and several changed decisions as to what he intended to say. He had chosen to receive them in his home rather than his office, because in the office time was precious and he would feel compelled simply to hear the bare outlines of what Monk had learned, and not to question him more deeply and to explore his understanding and his instinct. At home there was all evening, and no sense of haste, or of time being money.

And also, since it was in all probability a miserable tale, perhaps he owed Monk something more generous than simply a word of thanks and dismissal, and his money. And if she had heard from Monk directly what his discoveries were, it would be far easier for Hester to accept Rathbone's declining the case, if that were the only reasonable choice left to him. That was all most logical, nevertheless he found himself repeating it over and over, as if it required justification.

Although he was expecting them, their arrival caught him by surprise. He had not heard them come, presumably by hansom since neither of them had a carriage of their own. He was startled by the butler, Eames, announcing their presence, and a moment later they were in the room, Monk as beautifully tailored as usual. His suit must have cost as much as Rathbone's own, obviously bought in his police days when he had money for such luxuries. The waistcoat was modishly short with a shawl collar, and he wore a pointed, standing collar with a lavish bow tie.

Hester was dressed much more reservedly, in a cool teal-green gown with pointed waist and pagoda sleeves with separate gathered undersleeves of white broderie anglaise. There was no glamour to it, and yet he found it remarkably pleas-

147

ing. It was both simple and subtle, and the shade accentuated the slight flush in her cheeks.

They greeted each other very formally, even stiffly, and he invited them to be seated. He noticed Hester's eyes glancing around the room, and suddenly it seemed to him less satisfactory than it had. It was bare of feminine touches. It was his, not inherited from his family, and there had been no woman resident in it since he came, some eleven years ago. His housekeeper and his cook he did not count. They maintained what he had, but introduced nothing new, nothing of their own taste.

He saw Hester look at the forest-green carpet and upholstery, and the plain white walls, the mahogany woodwork. It was very bare for current fashion, which favored oak, ornate carving and highly decorative china and ornaments. It was on the tip of his tongue to make some comment to her, but he could think of nothing that did not sound as if he were seeking a compliment, so he remained silent.

"Do you wish for my findings before dinner, or after?" Monk asked. "If you care what I say, I think you may prefer them after."

"I cannot but leap to the conclusion that they are unpleasant," Rathbone replied with a twisted smile. "In which case, do not let us spoil our meal."

"A wise decision," Monk conceded.

Eames returned with a decanter of sherry, long-stemmed glasses and a tray of savory tidbits. They accepted them and made trivial conversation about current political events, the possibility of war in India, until they were informed that dinner awaited them.

The dining room was in the same deep green, a far smaller room than that in the Furnivals' house; obviously Rathbone seldom entertained more than half a dozen people at the most. The china was imported from France, a delicately gold-rimmed pattern of extreme severity. The only concession to flamboyance was a magnificent Sevres urn covered in a profusion of roses and other flowers in blazing reds, pinks, golds and greens. Rathbone saw Hester look at it several times,

148

but forbore from asking her opinion. If she praised it he would think it mere politeness; if not then he would be hurt, because he feared it was ostentatious, but he loved it.

Throughout the meal conversation centered on subjects of politics and social concern, which he would not personally have imagined discussing in front of a woman. He was well versed in the fashion and graces of Society, but Hester was different. She was not a woman in the customary sense of someone separate from the business of life outside the home, a person to be protected from the affairs or the emotions that involved the mind.

After the final course they returned to the withdrawing room and at last there was no reason any longer to put off the matter of the Carlyon case.

Rathbone looked across at Monk, his eyes wide.

"A crime contains three elements," Monk said, leaning back in his chair, a dour, ironic smile on his face. He was perfectly sure that Rathbone knew this, and quite possibly Hester did also, but he was going to tell them in his own fashion.

Rathbone could feel an irritation rising inside him already. He had a profound respect for Monk, and part of him liked the man, but there was also a quality in him which abraded the nerves like fine sandpaper, an awareness that at any time he might lash out with the unforeseeable, the suddenly disturbing, cutting away comforts and safely held ideas.

"The means were there to hand for anyone," Monk went on. "To wit, the halberd held by the suit of armor. They all had access to it, and they all knew it was there because any person entering the hall had to see it. That was its function—to impress."

"We knew they all could have done it," Rathbone said tersely. His irritation with Monk had provoked him into haste. "It does not take a powerful person to push a man over a banister, if he is standing next to it and is taken by surprise. And the halberd could have been used by anyone of average build—according to the medical report—although to penetrate the body and scar the floor beneath it must have been

149

driven with extraordinary violence." He winced very slightly, and felt a chill pass through him at such a passion of hate. "At least four of them were upstairs," he hurried on. "Or otherwise out of the withdrawing room and unobserved during the time the general went upstairs until Maxim Furnival came in and said he had found him on the floor of the hall."

"Opportunity," Monk said somewhat officiously. "Not quite true, I'm afraid. That is the painful part. Apparently the police questioned the guests and Mr. and Mrs. Furnival at some length, but they only corroborated with the servants what they already knew."

"One of the servants was involved?" Hester said slowly. There was no real hope in her face, because of his warning that the news was not good. "I wondered that before, if one of them had a military experience, or was related to someone who had. The motive might be quite different, something in his professional life and nothing personal at all . . ." She looked at Monk.

There was a flicker in Monk's face, and Rathbone knew in that instant that he had not thought of that himself. Why not? Inefficiency—or had he reached some unarguable conclusion before he got that far?

"No." Monk glanced at him, then away again. "They did not question the movements of the servants closely enough. The butler said they had all been about their duties and noticed nothing at all, and since their duties were in the kitchen and servants' quarters, it was not surprising they had not heard the suit of armor fall. But on questioning him more closely, he admitted one footman tidied the dining room, which was not in the time period we are interested in. He was told to fill the coal scuttles for the rest of the house, including the morning room and the library, which are off the front hall."

Hester turned her head to watch him. Rathbone sat up a little straighter.

Monk continued impassively, only the faintest of smiles touching the corners of his mouth.

150

"The footman's observations as to the armor, and he could hardly have missed it had it been lying on the floor in pieces with the body of the general across it and the halberd sticking six feet out of his chest like a flagpole—"

"We take your point," Rathbone said sharply. "That reduces the opportunities of the suspects. I assume that is what you are eventually going to tell us?"

A flush of annoyance crossed Monk's face, then vanished and was replaced by satisfaction, not at the outcome, but at his own competence in proving it.

"That, and the romantic inclinations of the upstairs maid, and the fact that the footman had a lazy streak, and preferred to carry the scuttles up the front stairs instead of the back, for Mrs. Furnival's bedroom, make it impossible that anyone but Alexandra could have killed him. I'm sorry."

"Not Sabella?" Hester asked with a frown, leaning a little forward in her seat.

"No." He turned to her, his face softening for an instant. "The upstairs maid was waiting around the stair head to catch the footman, and when she realized she had missed him, and heard someone coming, she darted into the room where Sabella was resting, just off the first landing, on the pretext that she thought she had heard her call. And when she came out again the people had passed, and she went on back up to the servants' back stairs, and her own room. The people who passed her must have been Alexandra and the general, because after the footman had finished, he went down the back stairs, just in time to meet the news that General Carlyon had had an accident, and the butler had been told to keep the hall clear, and to send for the police."

Rathbone let out his breath in a sigh. He did not ask Monk if he were sure; he knew he would not have said it if there were the slightest doubt.

Monk bit his lip, glanced at Hester, who looked crushed, then back at Rathbone.

"The third element is motive," he said.

Rathbone's attention jerked back. Suddenly there was hope again. If not, why would Monk have bothered to mention it?

Damn the man for his theatricality! It was too late to pretend he was indifferent, Monk had seen his change of expression. To affect a casual air now would make himself ridiculous.

"I presume your discovery there is more useful to us?" he said aloud.

Monk's satisfaction evaporated.

"I don't know," he confessed. "One could speculate all sorts of motives for the others, but for her there seems only jealousy—and yet that was not the reason."

Rathbone and Hester stared at him. There was no sound in the quiet room but a leaf tapping against the window in the spring breeze.

Monk pulled a dubious face. "It was never easy to believe, in spite of one or two people accepting it, albeit reluctantly. I believed it myself for a while." He saw the sudden start of interest in their faces, and continued blindly. "Louisa Furnival is certainly a woman who would inspire uncertainty, self-doubt and then jealousy in another woman—and must have done so many times. And there is the possibility that Alexandra could have hated her not because she was so in love with the general but simply because she could not abide publicly being beaten by Louisa, being seen to be second best in the rivalry which cuts deepest to a person's self-esteem, most especially a woman's."

"But . . ." Hester could not contain herself. "But what? Why don't you believe it now?"

"Because Louisa was not having an affair with the general, and Alexandra must have known he was not."

"Are you sure?" Rathbone leaned forward keenly. "How do you know?"

"Maxim has money, which is important to Louisa," Monk replied, watching their faces carefully. "But even more important is her security and her reputation. Apparently some time ago Maxim was in love with Alexandra." He glanced up as Hester leaned forward, nodding quickly. "You knew that too?"

"Yes—yes, Edith told me. But he would not do anything

about it because he is very moral, and believes profoundly in his marriage vows, regardless of emotions afterwards."

"Precisely," Monk agreed. "And Alexandra must have known that, because she was so immediately concerned. Louisa is not a woman to throw away anything—money, honor, home, Society's acceptance—for the love of a man, especially one she knew would not marry her. And the general would not; he would lose his own reputation and career, not to mention the son he adored. In fact I doubt Louisa ever threw away anything intentionally. Alexandra knew her, and knew the situation. If Louisa had been caught in an affair with the general, Maxim would have made life extremely hard for her. After all, he had already made a great sacrifice in order to sustain his marriage. He would demand the same of her. And all this Alexandra knew . . ." He left the rest unsaid, and sat staring at them, his face somber.

Rathbone sat back with a feeling of confusion and incompleteness in his mind. There must be so much more to this story they had not even guessed at. They had only pieces, and the most important one that held it all together was missing.

"It doesn't make sense," he said guardedly. He looked across at Hester, wondering what she thought, and was pleased to see the same doubt reflected in her face. Better than that, the attention in her eyes betrayed that she was still acutely involved in the matter. In no way had she resigned interest merely because the answer eluded them but left the guilt undeniable.

"And you have no idea what the real motive was?" he said to Monk, searching his face to see if he concealed yet another surprise, some final piece held back for a last self-satisfying dramatic effect. But there was nothing. Monk's face was perfectly candid.

"I've tried to think," he said frankly. "But there is nothing to suggest he used her badly in any way, nor has anyone else suggested anything." He also glanced at Hester.

Rathbone looked at her. "Hester? If you were in her place,

can you think of anything which would make you kill such a man?''

"Several things," she admitted with a twisted smile, then bit her lip as she realized what they might think of her for such feelings.

Rathbone grinned in sudden amusement. "For example?" he asked.

"The first thing that comes to mind is if I loved someone else."

"And the second?"

"If he loved someone else." Her eyebrows rose. "Frankly I should be delighted to let him go. He sounds so—so restricting. But if I could not bear the social shame of it, what my friends would say, or my enemies, the laughter behind my back, and above all the pity—and the other woman's victory . . ."

"But he was not having an affair with Louisa," Monk pointed out. "Oh—you mean another woman entirely? Someone we have not even thought of? But why that night?"

Hester shrugged. "Why not? Perhaps he taunted her. Perhaps that was the night he told her about it. We shall probably never know what they said to one another."

"What else?"

The butler returned discreetly and enquired if there was anything more required. After asking his guests, Rathbone thanked him and bade him good-night.

Hester sighed. "Money?" she answered as the door closed. "Perhaps she overspent, or gambled, and he refused to pay her debts. Maybe she was frightened her creditors would shame her publicly. The only thing . . ." She frowned, looking first at one, then the other of them. Somewhere outside a dog barked. Beyond the windows it was almost dark. "The thing is, why did she say she had done it out of jealousy of Louisa? Jealousy is an ugly thing, and in no way an excuse—is it?" She turned to Rathbone again. "Will the law take any account of that?"

"None at all," he answered grimly. "They will hang her,

154

if they find her guilty, and on this evidence they will have no choice."

"Then what can we do?" Hester's face was full of anxiety. Her eyes held Rathbone's and there was a sharp pity in them. He wondered at it. She alone of them had never met Alexandra Carlyon. His own dragging void of pity he could understand; he had seen the woman. She was a real living being like himself. He had been touched by her hopelessness and her fear. Her death would be the extinguishing of someone he knew. For Monk it must be the same, and for all his sometime ruthlessness, Rathbone had no doubt Monk was just as capable of compassion as he was himself.

But for Hester she was still a creature of the imagination, a name and a set of circumstances, no more.

"What are we going to do?" Hester repeated urgently.

"I don't know," he replied. "If she doesn't tell us the truth, I don't know what there is that I can do."

"Then ask her," Hester retorted. "Go to her and tell her what you know, and ask her what the truth is. It may be better. It may offer some . . ." Her voice tailed off. "Some mitigation," she finished lamely.

"None of your suggestions were any mitigation at all," Monk pointed out. "She would hang just as surely as if it had been what she claims."

"What do you want to do, give up?" Hester snapped.

"What I want is immaterial," Monk replied. "I cannot afford the luxury of meddling in other people's affairs for entertainment."

"I'll go and see her again," Rathbone declared. "At least I will ask her."

Alexandra looked up as he came into the cell. For an instant her face lit with hope, then knowledge prevailed and fear took its place.

"Mr. Rathbone?" She swallowed with difficulty, as though there were some constriction in her throat. "What is it?"

The door clanged shut behind him and they both heard the

155

lock fall and then the silence. He longed to be able to comfort her, at least to be gentle, but there was no time, no place for evasion.

"I should not have doubted you, Mrs. Carlyon," he answered, looking straight at her remarkable blue eyes. "I thought perhaps you had confessed in order to shield your daughter. But Monk has proved beyond any question at all that it was, as you say, you who killed your husband. However, it was not because he was having an affair with Louisa Furnival. He was not—and you knew he was not."

She stared at him, white-faced. He felt as if he had struck her, but she did not flinch. She was an extraordinary woman, and the feeling renewed in him that he must know the truth behind the surface facts. Why in heaven's name had she resorted to such hopeless and foredoomed violence? Could she ever have imagined she would get away with it?

"Why did you kill him, Mrs. Carlyon?" he said urgently, leaning towards her. It was raining outside and the cell was dim, the air clammy.

She did not look away, but closed her eyes to avoid seeing him.

"I have told you! I was jealous of Louisa!"

"That is not true!"

"Yes it is." Still her eyes were closed.

"They will hang you," he said deliberately. He saw her wince, but she still kept her face towards his, eyes tight shut. "Unless we can find some circumstance that will at least in part explain what you did, they will hang you, Mrs. Carlyon! For heaven's sake, tell me why you did it." His voice was low, grating and insistent. How could he get through the shield of denial? What could he say to reach her mind with reality? He wanted to touch her, take her by those slender arms and shake sense into her. But it would be such a breach of all possible etiquette, it would shatter the mood and become more important, for the moment, than the issue that would save or lose her life.

"Why did you kill him?" he repeated desperately.

"Whatever you say, you cannot make it worse than it is already."

"I killed him because he was having an affair with Louisa," she repeated flatly. "At least I thought he was."

And he could get nothing further from her. She refused to add anything, or take anything from what she had said.

Reluctantly, temporarily defeated, he took his leave. She remained sitting on the cot, immobile, ashen-faced.

Outside in the street the rain was a steady downpour, the gutter filling, people hurrying by with collars up. He passed a newsboy shouting the latest headlines. It was something to do with a financial scandal and the boy caressed the words with relish, seeing the faces of passersby as they turned. "Scandal, scandal in the City! Financier absconds with fortune. Secret love nest! Scandal in the City!"

Rathbone quickened his pace to get away from it. They had temporarily forgotten Alexandra and the murder of General Carlyon, but as soon as the trial began it would be all over every front page and every newsboy would be crying out each day's revelations and turning them over with delight, poring over the details, imagining, condemning.

And they would condemn. He had no delusion that there would be any pity for her. Society would protect itself from threat and disruption. They would close ranks, and even the few who might feel some twinge of pity for her would not dare to admit it. Any woman who was in the same situation, or imagined herself so, would have even less compassion. If she herself had to endure it, why should Alexandra be able to escape? And no man whose eyes or thoughts had ever wandered, or who considered they might in the future, would countenance the notion that a wife could take such terrible revenge for a brief and relatively harmless indulgence of his very natural appetites. Carlyon's offense of flirtation, not even proved to be adultery, would be utterly lost in her immeasurably deeper offense of murder.

Was there anything at all Rathbone could do to help her? She had robbed him of every possible weapon he might have

157

used. The only thing still left to him was time. But time to do what?

He passed an acquaintance, but was too absorbed in thought to recognize him until he was twenty yards farther along the pavement. By then it was too late to retrieve his steps and apologize for having ignored his greeting.

The rain was easing into merely a spring squall. Bright shafts of sunlight shone fitfully on the wet pavement.

If he went into court with all he had at present he would lose. There would be no doubt of it. He could imagine it vividly, the feeling of helplessness as the prosecution demolished his case effortlessly, the derision of the spectators, the quiet and detached concern of the judge that there should be some semblance of a defense, the crowds in the gallery, eager for details and ultimately for the drama of conviction, the black cap and the sentence of death. Worse than those, he could picture the jury, earnest men, overawed by the situation, disturbed by the story and the inevitability of its end, and Alexandra herself, with the same white hopelessness he had seen in her face in the cell.

And afterwards his colleagues would ask him why on earth he had given such a poor account of himself. What ailed him to have taken so foregone a case? Had he lost his skills? His reputation would suffer. Even his junior would laugh and ask questions behind his back.

He hailed a cab and rode the rest of the way to Vere Street in a dark mood, almost resolved to decline the case and tell Alexandra Carlyon that if she would not tell him the truth then he was sorry but he could not help her.

At his offices he alighted, paid the driver and went in to be greeted by his clerk, who informed him that Miss Latterly was awaiting him.

Good. That would give him the opportunity to tell her now that he had seen Alexandra, and failed to elicit from her a single thing more than the idiotic insistence of the story they all knew to be untrue. Perhaps Peverell Erskine could persuade her to speak, but if even he could not, then the case was at an end as far as he was concerned.

Hester stood up as soon as he was inside, her face curious, full of questions.

He felt a flicker of doubt. His certainty wavered. Before he saw her he had been resolved to decline the case. Now her eagerness confounded him.

"Did you see her?" She made no apology for having come. The matter was too important to her, and she judged to him also, for her to pretend indifference or make excuses.

"Yes, I have just come from the prison . . ." he began.

"Oh." She read from his expression, the weariness in him, that he had failed. "She would not tell you." For a moment she was taken aback; disappointment filled her. Then she took a deep breath and lifted her head a little. A momentary compassion for him was replaced by anxiety again. "Then the reason must be very deep—something she would rather die than reveal." She shuddered and her face pulled into an expression of pain. "It had to be something very terrible—and I cannot help believing it must concern some other person."

"Then please sit down," he asked, moving to the large chair behind the desk himself.

She obeyed, taking the upright chair opposite him. When she was unconscious of herself she was curiously graceful. He brought his mind back to the case.

"Or be so ugly that it would only make her situation worse," he went on reasonably, then wished he had not. "I'm sorry," he said quickly. "But Hester—we must be honest."

She did not even seem to notice his use of her Christian name. Indeed it seemed very natural to her.

"As it is there is nothing I can do for her. I have to tell Erskine that. I would be defrauding him if I allowed him to think I could say anything more than the merest novice barrister could."

If she suspected fear for his reputation, the dread of losing, it did not show in her face, and he felt a twinge of shame that the thoughts had been there in his own mind.

"We have to find it!" she said uncertainly, convincing herself as well as him. "There is still time, isn't there?"

"Till the trial? Yes, some weeks. But what good will it do, and where do we begin?"

"I don't know, but Monk will." Her eyes never wavered from his face. She saw the shadow in his expression at mention of Monk's name, and wished she had been less clumsy. "We cannot give up now," she went on. There was no time for self-indulgence. "Whatever it is, surely we must find out if she is protecting someone else. Oh I know she did it—the proof is beyond argument. But why? Why was she prepared to kill him, and then to confess to it, and if necessary face the gallows? It has to be something—something beyond bearing. Something so terrible that prison, trial and the rope are better!"

"Not necessarily, my dear," he said gently. "Sometimes people commit even the most terrible crimes for the most trivial of reasons. Men have killed for a few shillings, or in a rage over a petty insult . . . ."

"Not Alexandra Carlyon," she insisted, leaning across the desk towards him. "You have met her! Did she? Do you believe she sacrificed all she had—her husband, her family, her home, her position, even her life—over something trivial?" She shook her head impatiently. "And what woman cares about an insult? Men fight duels of honor—women don't! We are perfectly used to being insulted; the best defense is to pretend you haven't noticed—then you need not reply. Anyway, with a mother-in-law like Felicia Carlyon, I imagine Alexandra had sufficient practice at being insulted to be mistress of anything. She is not a fool, is she?"

"No."

"Or a drunkard?"

"No."

"Then we must find out why she did it! If you are thinking of the worst, what has she to lose? What better way to spend her money than to try to save her life?"

"I doubt I can . . ." he began. Then not only Hester's face but memory of Alexandra herself, the remarkable eyes,

160

the strong, intelligent features and sensuous mouth, the possibility of humor came back to him. He wanted to know; it would hurt him as long as he did not.

"I'll try," he conceded, and felt a surprising stab of pleasure as her eyes softened and she smiled, relaxing at last.

"Thank you."

"But it may do no good," he warned her, hating to curb her hope, and afraid of the darker despair and anger with him if he misled her.

"Of course," she assured him. "I understand. But at least we shall try."

"For what it may be worth . . ."

"Shall you tell Monk?"

"Yes—yes, I shall instruct him to continue his search."

She smiled, a sudden brilliant gesture lighting her face.

"Thank you—thank you very much."

Monk was surprised that Rathbone should request him to continue in the case. As a matter of personal curiosity he would like to have known the real reason why Alexandra Carlyon had killed her husband. But he could afford neither the time nor the finance to seek an answer when it could scarcely affect the outcome of any trial, and would almost certainly be a long and exhausting task.

But Rathbone had pointed out that if Erskine wished it, as her solicitor and acting in her best interest, then that was possibly the best use for her money. Certainly there was no other use that could serve her more. And presumably her heirs and the general's were all cared for.

Perhaps that was a place to begin—money? He doubted it would show anything of use, but if nothing else, it must be eliminated, and since he had not even a guess as to what the answer might be, this was as good a place as any. He might be fortunately surprised.

It was not difficult to trace the Carlyon estate, since wills were a matter of public record. Thaddeus George Randolf Carlyon had died possessed of a very considerable wealth. His family had invested fortunately in the past. Although his father was still alive, Thaddeus had always had a generous allowance, which he in turn had spent sparingly and invested on excellent advice, largely in various parts of the Empire: India, southern Africa and the Anglo-Egyptian Sudan, in export business which had brought him a more than handsome return. And he had lived comfortably, but at very moderate expense in view of his means.

It occurred to Monk while reading the financial outlines that he had not yet seen Carlyon's house, and that was an omission which must be rectified. One occasionally learned a great deal about people from their choice of books, furnishings, pictures, and the small items on which they did or did not spend their money.

He turned his attention to the disposition the general had chosen for his estate. The house was Alexandra's to live in for the duration of her life, then it passed to their only son, Cassian. He also bequeathed her sufficient income to ensure the upkeep of the house and a reasonable style of living for the duration of her life, adequately, but certainly not extravagantly, and there was no provision made should she wish to undertake any greater expense. She would not be able to purchase any new horses or carriages without considerable savings on other things, nor would she be able to take any extended journeys, such as a tour of Italy or Greece or any other sunny climate.

There were small bequests to his daughters, and personal mementos to his two sisters and to Maxim and Louisa Furnival, to Valentine Furnival, and to Dr. Charles Hargrave. But the vast bulk of his estate, both real and financial, went to Cassian, during his minority to be held in trust for him by a firm of solicitors, and administered by them. Alexandra had no say in the matter and there was no stipulation that she should even be consulted.

It was an inescapable conclusion that she had been far better off while Thaddeus was alive. The only question was, had she been aware of that prior to his death, or had she expected to become a wealthy woman?

Was there any purpose in asking the solicitors who had

drawn the will, and who were to administer the estate? They might tell him, in the interests of justice. There was no point to be served by hiding such a thing now.

An hour later he presented himself at Messrs. Goodbody, Pemberton and Lightfoot. He found Mr. Lightfoot, the only surviving original partner, to be quite agreeable to informing him that on hearing of the general's death—such a sad affair, heaven only knew what the world was coming to when respectable women like Mrs. Carlyon sank to such depths—of course he could not believe it at the time. When he had called upon her to acquaint her with her position and assure her of his best services, she showed no surprise or distress at the news. Indeed she had seemed scarcely to be interested. He had taken it then to be shock and grief at the death of her husband. Now, of course! He shook his head, and wondered again what had happened to civilized society that such things came to pass.

It was on the edge of Monk's tongue to tell him that she had not yet been tried, let alone convicted of anything, but he knew it would be a waste of time. She had confessed, and as far as Mr. Lightfoot was concerned, that was the end of the matter. And indeed, he might well be right. Monk had no reasonable argument to offer.

He was hurrying along Threadneedle Street, past the Bank of England, and turned left down Bartholomew Lane, then suddenly did not know where he was going. He stopped, momentarily confused. He had turned the corner with absolute confidence, and now he did not know where he was. He looked around. It was familiar. There was an office opposite him; the name meant nothing, but the stone doorway with a brass plate in it woke in him a sense of anxiety and profound failure.

Why? When had he been here before, and for whom? Was it something to do with that other woman he had remembered briefly and so painfully in the prison with Alexandra Carlyon? He racked his mind for any link of memory that might have to do with her: prison, courtroom, police station, a house, a street . . . Nothing came—nothing at all.

An elderly gentleman passed him, walking briskly with a silver-topped cane in his hand. For an instant Monk thought he knew him, then the impression faded and he realized the set of the shoulder was wrong, the breadth of the man. Only the gait and the silver-topped cane were somehow familiar.

Of course. It was nothing to do with the woman that tugged at his mind. It was the man who had helped him in his youth, his mentor, the man whose wife wept silently, stricken with a grief he had shared, and had had helpless inability to prevent.

What had happened? Why was—was . . . Walbrook!

With singing triumph he knew the name quite clearly and without doubt. Walbrook—that had been his name. Frederick Walbrook . . . banker—commercial banker. Why did he have this terrible feeling of failure? What had his part been in the disaster that had struck?

He had no idea.

He gave up for the moment and retraced his steps back to Threadneedle Street, and then Cheapside and up towards Newgate.

He must bring back his mind to Alexandra Carlyon. What he could learn might be her only chance. She had begged him to help her, save her from the gallows and clear her name. He quickened his pace, visualizing her anguished face and the terror in her, her dark eyes . . .

He cared about it more intensely than anything he had ever known before. The emotion surging up inside him was so urgent he was hardly even aware of his feet on the pavement or the people passing by him. He was jostled by bankers and clerks, errand runners, peddlers and newsboys without even being aware of them. Everything hung on this.

He suddenly recalled a pair of eyes so clearly, wide and golden brown—but the rest of her face was a blank—no lips, no cheeks, no chin, just the golden eyes.

He stopped and the man behind him bumped into him, apologized bitterly, and moved on. Blue eyes. He could picture Alexandra Carlyon's face in his mind quite clearly, and it was not what his inner eye had seen: wide mouth full of humor and passion, short aquiline nose, high cheekbones and blue eyes, very blue. And she had not begged him to help, in fact she seemed almost indifferent about it, as if she knew his efforts were doomed.

He had met her only once, and he was pursuing the case because Oliver Rathbone asked him, not because he cared about her, more than a general compassion because she was in desperate trouble.

Who was it that came so vividly to his mind, and with such a powerful emotion, filling him with urgency, and terror of failure?

It must be someone from that past which haunted him and which he so ached to retrieve. It was certainly nothing since his accident. And it was not Imogen Latterly. Her face he could recall without any effort at all, and knew his relationship with her had been simply her trust in him to help clear her father's name—which he had failed to do.

Had he failed to help this other woman also? Had she hanged for a murder she did not commit? Or did she?

He started to walk rapidly again. At least he would do everything humanly possible to help Alexandra Carlyon—with her help or without it. There must be some passionate reason why she had pushed the general over the stairs, and then followed him down and as he lay senseless at her feet, picked up the halberd and driven it through his body.

It seemed money could not have been the cause, because she had known she would be less well off with him dead than she had been when he was alive. And socially she would be a widow, which would mean at least a year of mourning, then in all probability several more years of dark gowns, modest behavior and few if any social engagements. Apart from the requirements of mourning, she would be invited very infrequently to parties. Widows were something of a disadvantage, having no husband to escort them; except wealthy and eligible widows, which Alexandra was not, nor had she expected to be.

He must enquire into her life and habits as her friends knew her. To be of any value, those enquiries should be with

165

those who were as unbiased as possible and would give a fair view. Perhaps Edith Sobell would be the person most likely to help. After all, it was she who had sought Hester's aid, convinced that Alexandra was innocent.

Edith proved more than willing to help, and after an enforced idleness on Sunday, for the next two days Monk pursued various friends and acquaintances who all gave much the same observations. Alexandra was a good friend, agreeable in nature but not intrusive, humorous but never vulgar. She appeared to have no vices except a slight tendency to mockery at times, a tongue a little sharp, and an interest in subjects not entirely suitable for ladies of good breeding, or indeed for women at all. She had been seen reading political periodicals, which she had very rapidly hidden when disturbed. She was impatient with those of slower wit and could be very abrupt when questions were inquisitive or she felt pressed to an opinion she preferred not to give. She was overfond of strawberries and loud band music, and she liked to walk alone—and speak to unsuitable strangers. And yes— she had on occasion been seen going into a Roman Catholic church! Most odd. Was she of that faith? Certainly not!

Was she extravagant?

Occasionally, with clothes. She loved color and form.

With anything else? Did she gamble, like new carriages, fine horses, furniture, silver, ornate jewelry?

Not that anyone had remarked. Certainly she did not gamble.

Did she flirt?

No more than anyone.

Did she owe money?

Definitely not.

Did she spend inordinate periods of time alone, or where no one knew where she was?

Yes—that was true. She liked solitude, the more especially in the last year or so.

Where did she go?

To the park.

Alone?

Apparently. No one had observed her with someone else.

All the answers seemed frank and without guile; the women who gave them bemused, sad, troubled—but honest. And all were unprofitable.

As he went from one smart house to another, echoes of memory drifted across his mind, like wraiths of mist, and as insubstantial. As soon as he grasped them they became nothing. Only the echo of emotion remained, fierce and painful, love, fear, terrible anxiety and a dread of failure.

Had Alexandra gone to seek counsel or comfort from a Roman Catholic priest? Possibly. But there was no point in looking for such a man; his secrets were inviolable. But it must surely have been something profound to have driven her to find a priest of a different faith, a stranger in whom to confide.

There were two other outstanding possibilities to investigate. First, that Alexandra had been jealous not of Louisa Furnival but of some other woman, and in this case justifiably so. From what he had learned of him, Monk could not see the general as an amorous adventurer, or even as a man likely to fall passionately in love to a degree where he would throw away his career and his reputation by abandoning his wife and his only son, still a child. And a mere affair was not cause for most wives to resort to murder. If Alexandra had loved her husband so possessively as to prefer him dead rather than in the arms of another woman, then she was a superb actress. She appeared intelligent and somewhat indifferent to the fact that her husband was dead. She was stunned, but not racked with grief; frightened for herself, but even more frightened for her secret being discovered. Surely a woman who had just killed a man she loved in such a fashion would show some traces of such a consuming love—and the devastation of grief.

And why hide it? Why pretend it was Louisa if it was not? It made no sense.

Nevertheless he would investigate it. Every possibility must be explored, no matter how remote, or seemingly nonsensical.

The other possibility—and it seemed more likely—was that Alexandra herself had a lover; and now that she was a widow, she intended in due course to marry whoever it was. That made far more sense. It would be understandable, in those circumstances, if she hid the facts. If Thaddeus had betrayed her with another woman, she was at least the injured party. She might have, in some wild hope, imagined society would excuse her.

But if she wished to betray him with a lover of her own, and had murdered him to free herself, no one on earth would excuse that.

In fact the more Monk thought about it, the more did it seem the only solution that fitted all they knew. It was an exceedingly ugly thought—but imperative he learn if it were the truth.

He decided to begin at Alexandra Carlyon's home, which she had shared with the general for the last ten years of his life, since his return from active service abroad. Since Monk was indirectly in Mrs. Carlyon's employ, and she had so far not been convicted of any crime, he felt certain he would find a civil, even friendly reception.

The house on Portland Place was closed and forbidding in appearance, the blinds drawn in mourning and a black wreath on the door. For the first time he could recall, he presented himself at the servants' entrance, as if he had been hawking household goods or was calling to visit some relative in service.

The back door was opened by a bootboy of perhaps twelve years, round-faced, snub-nosed and wary.

"Yes sir?" he said guardedly. Monk imagined he had probably been told by the butler to be very careful of inquisitive strangers, most especially if they might be from the newspapers. Had he been butler he would have said something of the sort.

"Wotcher want?" the boy added as Monk said nothing.

"To speak with your butler, and if he is not available, with your housekeeper," Monk replied. He hoped fervently that Alexandra had been a considerate mistress, and her staff were loyal enough to her to wish her well now and give what assistance they might to someone seeking to aid her cause, and that they would have sufficient understanding to accept that that was indeed his aim.

"Woffor?" The boy was not so easily beguiled. He looked Monk up and down, the quality of his suit, his stiff-collared white shirt and immaculate boots. " 'Oo are yer, mister?"

"William Monk, employed by Mrs. Carlyon's barrister."

The boy scowled. "Wot's a barrister?"

"Lawyer—who speaks for her in court."

"Oh—well, yer'd better come in. I'll get Mr. 'Agger." And he opened the door wider and permitted Monk into the back kitchen. He was left to stand there while the boy went for the butler, who was in charge of the house now that both master and mistress were gone, until either Mrs. Carlyon should be acquitted or the executors should dispose of the estate.

Monk stared about him. He could see through the open doorway into the laundry room, where the dolly tub was standing with its wooden dolly for moving, lifting and turning the clothes, the mangle for squeezing out the water, and the long shelf with jars of various substances for washing the different kinds of cloth: boiled bran for sponging chintz; clean horses' hoof parings for woollens; turpentine and ground sheep's trotters, or chalk, to remove oil and grease; lemon or onion juice for ink; warm cows' milk for wine or vinegar stains; stale bread for gold, silver or silken fabrics; and of course some soap.

There were also jars of bleach, a large tub of borax for heavy starching, and a board and knife for cutting up old potatoes to soak for articles to be more lightly starched.

Monk recognized them all from dim memories, habit, and recollections of more recent investigations which had taken him into kitchens and laundry rooms. This was apparently a well-run household, with all the attentions to detail one would expect from an efficient staff.

Sharply he recalled his mother with the luxury of home made soap from fat and wood ash. For the laundry, like other poorer women, she used lye, the liquid made from wood ash collected from furnaces and open fires and then mixed with water. Sometimes urine, fowl dung or bran were added to make it more effective. In 1853 the tax had been taken off soap, but that was long after he left home. She would have been overwhelmed by all this abundance.

He turned his attention to the room he was in, but had little time to see more than the racks piled with brussels sprouts, asparagus, cabbage and strings of stored onions and potatoes kept from last autumn, when the butler appeared, clad in total black and looking grim. He was a man in his middle years, short, sandy-haired, with mustache, thick side whiskers, and balding on top. His voice when he spoke was very precise.

"Yes, Mr.—er, Monk? What can we do for you? Any way in which we can help the mistress, of course we will. But you understand I shall need some proof of your identity and your purpose in coming here?" He clicked his teeth. "I don't mean to be uncivil, sir, but you must understand we have had some charlatans here, pretending to be who they were not, and out to deceive us for their own purposes."

"Of course." Monk produced his card, and a letter from Rathbone, and one from Peverell Erskine. "Very prudent of you, Mr. Hagger. You are to be commended."

Hagger closed his eyes again, but the pink in his cheeks indicated that he had heard the compliment, and appreciated it.

"Well, sir, what can we do for you?" he said after he had read the letters and handed them back. "Perhaps you would care to come into the pantry where we can be private?"

"Thank you, that would be excellent," Monk accepted, and followed him into the small room, taking the offered seat. Hagger sat opposite him and looked enquiringly.

As a matter of principle, Monk told him as little as possible. One could always add more later; one could not retract.

He must begin slowly, and hope to elicit the kind of information he wanted, disguised among more trivial details.

170

"Perhaps you would begin by telling me something of the running of the house, Mr. Hagger? How many staff have you? How long have they been here, and if you please, something of what you know of them—where they were before here, and so on."

"If you wish, sir." Hagger looked dubious. "Although I cannot see how that can possibly help."

"Nor I—yet," Monk conceded. "But it is a place to begin."

Dutifully Hagger named the staff, their positions in the household and what their references said of them. Then at Monk's prompting he began to outline a normal week's events.

Monk stopped him once or twice to ask for more detail about a dinner party, the guests, the menu, the general's attitude, how Mrs. Carlyon had behaved, and on occasions when she and the general had gone out, whom they had visited.

"Did Mr. and Mrs. Pole dine here often?" he asked as artlessly as he could.

"No sir, very seldom," Hagger replied. "Mrs. Pole only came when the general was away from home." His face clouded. "I am afraid, sir, that there was some ill feeling there, owing to an event in the past, before Miss Sabella's marriage."

"Yes, I am aware of it. Mrs. Carlyon told me." It was an extension of the truth. Alexandra had told Edith Sobell, who had told Hester, who in turn had told him. "But Mrs. Carlyon and her daughter remained close?"

"Oh yes sir." Hagger's face lightened a little. "Mrs. Carlyon was always most fond of all her children, and relations were excellent—" He broke off with a frown so slight Monk was not sure if he had imagined it.

"But . . ." he said aloud.

Hagger shook his head. "Nothing, sir. They were always excellent."

"You were going to add something."

"Well, only that she seemed a trifle closer to her daugh-

171

ters, but I imagine that is natural in a woman. Master Cassian was very fond of his father, poor child. Thought the world o' the general, he did. Very natural 'e should. General took a lot o' care with 'im; spent time, which is more than many a man will with 'is son, 'specially a man as busy as the general, and as important. Admired him for that, I did.''

"A fine trait," Monk agreed. "One many a son might envy. I assume from what you say that these times did not include Mrs. Carlyon's presence?"

"No, sir, I can't recall as they ever did. I suppose they spoke of man's affairs, not suitable for ladies—the army, acts o' heroism and fighting, adventures, exploration and the like." Hagger shifted in his seat a trifle. "The boy used to come downstairs with stars in his eyes, poor child—and a smile on his lips." He shook his head. "I can't think what he must be feeling, fair stunned and lost, I shouldn't wonder."

For the first time since seeing Alexandra Carlyon in prison Monk felt an overwhelming anger against her, crowding out pity and divorcing him utterly from the other woman who haunted the periphery of his mind, and whose innocence he had struggled so intensely to prove. She had had no child—of that he was quite certain. And younger—yes, she had been younger. He did not know why he was so sure of that, but it was a certainty inside him like the knowledge one has in dreams, without knowing where it came from.

He forced himself back to the present. Hagger was staring at him, a flicker of anxiety returning to his face.

"Where is he?" Monk asked aloud.

"With his grandparents, sir, Colonel and Mrs. Carlyon. They sent for him as soon as 'is mother was took."

"Did you know Mrs. Furnival?"

"I have seen her, sir. She and Mr. Furnival dined here on occasion, but that's all I could say—not exactly 'know.' She didn't come 'ere very often."

"I thought the general was a good friend of the Furnivals'?"

"Yes sir, so 'e was. But far more often 'e went there."

172

"How often?"

Hagger looked harassed and tired, but there was no guilt in his expression and no evasion. "Well, as I understand it from Holmes, that's 'is valet, about once or twice a week. But if you're thinking it was anything improper, sir, all I can say is I most sincerely think as you're mistaken. The general 'ad business with Mr. Furnival, and 'e went there to 'elp the gentleman. And most obliged Mr. Furnival was too, from what I hear."

Monk asked the question he had been leading towards, the one that mattered most, and whose answer now he curiously dreaded.

"Who were Mrs. Carlyon's friends, if not Mrs. Furnival? I imagine she had friends, people she called upon and who came here, people with whom she attended parties, dances, the theater and so on?"

"Oh yes, sir, naturally."

"Who are they?"

Hagger listed a dozen or so names, most of them married couples.

"Mr. Oundel?" Monk asked. "Was there no Mrs. Oundel?" He felt surprisingly miserable as he asked it. He did not want the answer.

"No sir, she died some time ago. Very lonely, he was, poor gentleman. Used to come 'ere often."

"I see. Mrs. Carlyon was fond of him?"

"Yes sir, I think she was. Sorry for 'im, I should say. 'E used to call in the afternoons sometimes, and they'd sit in the garden and talk for ages. Went 'ome fairly lifted in spirits." He smiled as he said it, and looked at Monk with a sudden sadness in his eyes. "Very good to 'im, she was."

Monk felt a little sick.

"What is Mr. Oundel's occupation? Or is he a gentleman of leisure?"

"Bless you, sir, 'e's retired. Must be eighty if 'e's a day, poor old gentleman."

"Oh." Monk felt such an overwhelming relief it was absurd. He wanted to smile, to say something wild and happy.

173

Hagger would think he had taken leave of his wits—or at the very least his manners. "Yes—yes, I see. Thank you very much. You have been most helpful. Perhaps I should speak to her ladies' maid? She is still in the house?"

"Oh yes sir, we wouldn't presume to let any of the staff go until—I mean . . ." Hagger stopped awkwardly.

"Of course," Monk agreed. "I understand. Let us hope it doesn't come to that." He rose to his feet.

Hagger also rose to his feet, his face tightened, and he fumbled awkwardly. "Is there any hope, sir, that . . ."

"I don't know," Monk said candidly. "What I need to know, Mr. Hagger, is what reason Mrs. Carlyon could possibly have for wishing her husband dead."

"Oh—I'm sure I can't think of any! Can't you—I mean, I wish . . ."

"No," Monk cut off hope instantly. "I am afraid she is definitely responsible; there can be no doubt."

Hagger's face fell. "I see. I had hoped—I mean . . . someone else . . . and she was protecting them."

"Is that the sort of person she was?"

"Yes sir, I believe so—a great deal of courage, stood up to anyone to protect 'er own . . ."

"Miss Sabella?"

"Yes sir—but . . ." Hagger was caught in a dilemma, his face pink, his body stiff.

"It's all right," Monk assured him. "Miss Sabella was not responsible. That is beyond question."

Hagger relaxed a little. "I don't know 'ow to 'elp," he said miserably. "There isn't any reason why a decent woman kills her husband—unless he threatened her life."

"Was the general ever violent towards her?"

Hagger looked shocked. "Oh no sir! Most certainly not."

"Would you know, if he had been?"

"I believe so, sir. But you can ask Ginny, what's Mrs. Carlyon's maid. She'd know beyond question."

"I'll do that, Mr. Hagger, if you will be so good as to allow me to go upstairs and find her?"

"I'll 'ave 'er sent for."

174

"No—I should prefer to speak to her in her normal place of work, if you please. Make her less nervous, you understand?" Actually that was not the reason. Monk wished to see Alexandra's bedroom and if possible her dressing room and something of her wardrobe. It would furnish him a better picture of the woman. All he had seen her wearing was a dark skirt and plain blouse; far from her usual dress, he imagined.

"By all means," Hagger concurred. "If you'll follow me, sir." And he led the way through a surprisingly busy kitchen, where the cook was presiding over the first preparation for a large dinner. The scullery maid had apparently already prepared the vegetables, the kitchen maid was carrying dirty pots and pans to the sink for the scullery maid to wash, and the cook herself was chopping large quantities of meat ready to put into a pie dish, lined with pastry, and the crust ready rolled to go on when she had finished.

A packet of Purcel's portable jelly mixture, newly available since the Great Exhibition of 1851, was lying ready to make for a later course, along with cold apple pie, cream and fresh cheese. It looked as if the meal would feed a dozen.

Then of course Monk remembered that even when all the family were at home, they only added three more to the household, which was predominantly staff, and with upstairs and downstairs, indoor and outdoor, must have numbered at least twelve, and they continued regardless of the death of the general or the imprisonment of Mrs. Carlyon, at least for the moment.

Along the corridor they passed the pantry, where a footman was cleaning the knives with India rubber, a buff leather knife board and a green-and-red tin of Wellington knife polish. Then past the housekeeper's sitting room with door closed, the butler's sitting room similarly, and through the green baize door to the main house. Of course most of the cleaning work would normally be done before the family rose for breakfast, but at present there was hardly any need, so the maids had an extra hour in bed, and were now occupied in sweeping, beating carpets, polishing floors with melted

175

candle ends and turpentine, cleaning brass with boiling vinegar.

Up the stairs and along the landing Monk followed Hagger until they came to the master bedroom, apparently the general's, past his dressing room next door, and on to a very fine sunny and spacious room which he announced as being Mrs. Carlyon's. Opening off it to the left was a dressing room where cupboard doors stood open and a ladies' maid was busy brushing down a blue-gray outdoor cape which must have suited Alexandra's fair coloring excellently.

The girl looked up in surprise as she saw Hagger, and Monk behind him. Monk judged her to be in her mid-twenties, thin and dark, but with a remarkably pleasant countenance.

Hagger wasted no time. "Ginny, this is Mr. Monk. He is working for the mistress's lawyers, trying to find out something that will help her. He wants to ask you some questions, and you will answer him as much as you can—anything 'e wants to know. Understand?"

"Yes, Mr. Hagger." She looked very puzzled, but not unwilling.

"Right." Hagger turned to Monk. "You come down when you're ready, an' if there's ought else as can 'elp, let me know."

"I will, thank you, Mr. Hagger. You have been most obliging," Monk accepted. Then as soon as Hagger had departed and closed the door, he turned to the maid.

"Go on with what you are doing," he requested. "I shall be some time."

"I'm sure I don't know what I can tell you," Ginny said, obediently continuing to brush the cape. "She was always a very good mistress to me."

"In what way good?"

She looked surprised. "Well . . . considerate, like. She apologized if she got anything extra dirty, or if she kept me up extra late. She gave me things as she didn't want no more, and always asked after me family, and the like."

"You were fond of her?"

176

"Very fond of 'er, Mr.—"

"Monk."

"Mr. Monk, can you 'elp 'er now? I mean, after she said as she done it?" Her face was puckered with anxiety.

"I don't know," Monk admitted. "If there were some reason why, that people could understand, it might help."

"What would anybody understand, as why a lady should kill 'er 'usband?" Ginny put away the cape and brought out a gown of a most unusual deep mulberry shade. She shook it and a perfume came from its folds that caught Monk with a jolt of memory so violent he saw a whole scene of a woman in pink, standing with her back to him, weeping softly. He had no idea what her face was like, except he found it beautiful, and he recalled none of her words. But the feeling was intense, an emotion that shook him and filled his being, an urgency amounting to passion that he must find the truth, and free her from a terrible danger, one that would destroy her life and her reputation.

But who was she? Surely she had nothing to do with Walbrook? No—one thing seemed to resolve in his mind. When Walbrook was ruined, and Monk's own career in commerce came to an end, he had not at that point even thought of becoming a policeman. That was what had decided him—his total inability to either help Walbrook and his wife, or even to avenge them and put his enemy out of business.

The woman in pink had turned to him because he was a policeman. It was his job to find the truth.

But he could not bring her face to mind, nor anything to do with the case, except that she was suspected of murder—murdering her husband—like Alexandra Carlyon.

Had he succeeded? He did not even know that. Or for that matter, if she was innocent or guilty. And why had he cared with such personal anguish? What had been their relationship? Had she cared for him as deeply, or was she simply turning to him because she was desperate and terrified?

"Sir?" Ginny was staring at him. "Are you all right, sir?"

"Oh—oh yes, thank you. What did you say?"

"What would folks reckon was a reason why it might be all right for a lady to kill 'er 'usband? I don't know of none."

"Why do you think she did it?" Monk asked baldly, his wits still too scattered to be subtle. "Was she jealous of Mrs. Furnival?"

"Oh no sir." Ginny dismissed it out of hand. "I don't like to speak ill of me betters, but Mrs. Furnival weren't the kind o' person to—well, sir, I don't rightly know 'ow to put it—"

"Simply." Monk's attention was entirely on her now, the memory dismissed for the time being. "Just in your own words. Don't worry if it sounds ill—you can always take it back, if you want."

"Thank you, sir, I'm sure."

"Mrs. Furnival."

"Well, sir, she's what my granny used to call a flighty piece, sir, beggin' yer pardon, all smiles and nods and eyes all over the place. Likes the taste o' power, but not one to fall what you'd call in love, not to care for anyone."

"But the general might have cared for her? Was he a good judge of women?"

"Lord, sir, he didn't hardly know one kind o' woman from another, if you take my meaning. He wasn't no ladies' man."

"Isn't that just the sort that gets taken in by the likes of anyone such as Mrs. Furnival?"

"No sir, because 'e weren't susceptible like. I seen 'er when she was 'ere to dinner, and he weren't interested 'ceptin' business and casual talking like to a friend. And Mrs. Carlyon, she knew that, sir. There weren't no cause for 'er to be jealous, and she never imagined there were. Besides . . ." She stopped, the pink color up her cheeks.

"Besides what, Ginny?"

Still she hesitated.

"Ginny, Mrs. Carlyon's life is at stake. As it is, if we don't find some good reason, she'll hang! Surely you don't think she did it without a good reason, do you?"

"Oh no sir! Never!"

178

"Well then . . ."

"Well, sir, Mrs. Carlyon weren't that fond o' the general anyway, as to mind all that terrible if occasionally 'e took 'is pleasures elsewhere, if you know what I mean?"

"Yes, I know what you mean. Quite a common enough arrangement, when a couple have been married a long time, no doubt. And did Mrs. Carlyon—have other interests?"

She colored very faintly, but did not evade the subject.

"Some time ago, sir, I did rather think as she favored a Mr. Ives, but it was only a little flattery, and enjoying his company, like. And there was Mr. McLaren, who was obviously very taken with 'er, but I don't think she more than passing liked him. And of course she was always fond of Mr. Furnival, and at one time . . ." She lowered her eyes. "But that was four years ago now. And if you ask if she ever did anything improper, I can tell you as she didn't. And bein' 'er maid, like, an' seein' all 'er most private things, I would know, I'll be bound."

"Yes, I imagine you would," Monk said. He was inclined to believe her, in spite of the fact that she could only be biased. "Well, if the general was not overly fond of Mrs. Furnival, is it possible he was fond of someone else, another lady, perhaps?"

"Well, if he was, sir, 'e hid it powerful well," she said vehemently. "Holmes, that's his valet, didn't know about it—an' I reckon he'd have at least an idea. No sir, I'm sorry, I can't 'elp you at all. I truly believe as the general was an exemplary man in that respect. Everything in loyalty an' honor a woman would want."

"And in other respects?" Monk persisted. He glanced along the row of cupboards. "It doesn't look as if he kept her short of money?"

"Oh no, sir. I don't think 'e was very interested in what the mistress wore, but 'e weren't never mean about it one bit. Always 'ad all she wanted, an' more."

"Sounds like a model husband," Monk said dispiritedly.

"Well, yes, I suppose so—for a lady, that is," she conceded, watching his face.

179

"But not what you would like?" he asked.

"Me? Well—well sir, I think as I'd want someone who—maybe this sounds silly, you bein' a gentleman an' all—but I'd want someone as I could 'ave fun with—talk to, like. A man who'd . . ." She colored fiercely now. "Who'd give me a bit of affection—if you see what I mean, sir."

"Yes, I see what you mean." Monk smiled at her without knowing quite why. Some old memory of warmth came back to him, the kitchen in his mother's house in Northumberland, her standing there at the table with her sleeves rolled up, and cuffing him gently around the ear for being cheeky, but it was more a caress than a discipline. She had been proud of him. He knew that beyond doubt in that moment. He had written regularly from London, letting her know how he was doing, of his career and what he hoped to achieve. And she had written back, short, oddly spelled letters in a round hand, but full of pride. He had sent money when he could, which was quite often. It pleased him to help her, after all the lean, sacrificing years, and it was a mark of his success.

Then after Walbrook's ruin, there had been no more money. And in embarrassment he had ceased to write. What utter stupidity! As if that would have mattered to her. What a pride he had. What an ugly, selfish pride.

"Of course I know what you mean," he said again to the maid. "Perhaps Mrs. Carlyon felt the same way, do you suppose?"

"Oh I wouldn't know, sir. Ladies is different. They don't— well . . ."

"They didn't share a room?"

"Oh no, sir—not since I been here. And I 'eard from Lucy, as I took over from, not before that neither. But then gentry don't, do they? They got bigger 'ouses than the likes of my ma and pa."

"Or mine," Monk agreed. "Was she happy?"

Ginny frowned, looking at him guardedly. "No sir, I don't think as she were."

"Did she change lately in any way?"

"She's been awful worried over something lately. An' she

180

and the general 'ad a terrible row six months ago—but there's no use askin' me what about, because I don't know. She shut the doors and sent me away. I just know because o' the way she was all white-faced and spoke to no one, and the way she looked like she seen death face-to-face. But that was six months ago, an' I thought it was all settled again.''

"Did he ever hurt her physically, Ginny?''

"Great 'eaven's, no!'' She shook her head, looking at him with deep distress. "I can't 'elp you, sir, nor 'er. I really don't know of anything at all as why she should 'ave killed 'im. He were cold, and terrible tedious, but 'e were generous with 'is money, faithful to 'er, well-spoken, didn't drink too much nor gamble nor keep fast company. And although 'e were terrible 'ard to Miss Sabella over that going into a nunnery business, he were the best father to young master Cassian as a boy could ask. And terrible fond of 'im Master Cassian were, poor little thing. If it weren't that I know as she wasn't a wicked woman, I'd think—well, I'd think as she were.''

"Yes,'' Monk said miserably. "Yes—I am afraid I would too. Thank you for your time, Ginny. I'll take myself downstairs.''

It was not until Monk had fruitlessly interviewed the rest of the staff, who bore out what Hagger and Ginny had said, partaken of luncheon in the servants' hall, and was outside in the street that he realized just how much of his own life had come back to him unbidden: his training in commerce, his letters home, Walbrook's ruin and his own consequent change of fortune—but not the face of the woman who so haunted him, who she was, or why he cared so intensely . . . or what had happened to her.

181

6

WITH MAJOR TIPLADY'S ENTHUSIASTIC PERMISSION,
Hester accepted an invitation to dine with Oliver Rathbone
in the very proper circumstances of taking a hansom to the
home in Primrose Hill of Rathbone's father, who proved to
be an elderly gentleman of charm and distinction.

Hester, determined not to be late, actually arrived before
Rathbone himself, who had been held up by a jury taking far
longer to return than foreseen. She alighted at the address
given her, and when she was admitted by the manservant,
found herself in a small sitting room. It opened onto a garden
in which late daffodils were blowing in the shade under the
trees and a massive honeysuckle vine all but drowned the
gate in the wall leading into a very small, overgrown orchard
whose apples, in full blossom, she could just see over the
top.

The room itself was crowded with books of various shapes
and sizes, obviously positioned according to subject matter
and not to please the eye. On the walls were several paintings
in watercolors, one which she noticed immediately because
it held a place of honor above the mantel. It was of a youth
in costume of leather doublet and apron, sitting on the base
of a pillar. The whole work was in soft earth colors, ochers
and sepia, except for the dark red of his cap, and it was

unfinished; the lower half of his body, and a small dog he reached out to stroke, were still in sketch form.

"You like it?" Henry Rathbone asked her. He was taller than his son, and very lean, shoulders stooped as from many years of intensive study. His face was aquiline, all nose and jaw, and yet there was a serenity in it, a mildness that set her at ease the moment she saw him. His gray hair was very sparse, and he looked at her with shortsighted blue eyes.

"Yes I do, very much," she answered honestly. "The more I look at it, the more it pleases me."

"It is my favorite," he agreed. "Perhaps because it is unfinished. Completed it might have been harder, more final. This leaves room for the imagination, almost a sense of collaboration with the artist."

She knew precisely what he meant, and found herself smiling at him.

They moved on to discuss other things, and she questioned him shamelessly because she was so interested, and because she was so comfortable with him. He had traveled in many foreign places, and indeed spoke the German language fluently. He seemed not to have been enraptured with scenery, totally unlike herself, but he had met and fallen into conversations with all manner of unlikely people in little old shops which he loved rummaging through. No one was too outwardly ordinary to excite his interest, or for him to have discovered some aspect of their lives which was unique.

She barely noticed that Rathbone was an hour late, and when he came in in a flurry of apologies, she was amused to see the consternation in his face that no one had missed him, except the cook, whose preparations were discommoded.

"Never mind," Henry Rathbone said easily, rising to his feet. "It is not worth being upset about. It cannot be helped. Miss Latterly, please come into the dining room; we shall do the best we can with what there is."

"You should have started without me," Oliver said with a flash of irritation across his face. "Then you would have had it at its best."

"There is no need to feel guilty," his father replied. He

indicated where Hester was to sit, and the manservant held her chair for her. "We know you were detained unavoidably. And I believe we were enjoying ourselves."

"Indeed I was," Hester said sincerely, and took her place.

The meal was served. The soup was excellent, and Rathbone made no comment; to do so now would be so obviously ungracious. When the fish was brought, a little dry from having had to wait, he bit into it and met Hester's eye, but refrained from comment.

"I spoke with Monk yesterday," he said at length. "I am afraid we have made almost no progress."

Hester was disappointed, yet the mere fact that he had kept from mentioning the subject for so long had forewarned her that the news would be poor.

"That only means that we have not yet discovered the reason," she said doggedly. "We shall have to look harder."

"Or persuade her to tell us," Oliver added, placing his knife and fork together and indicating to the manservant that he might remove the plates.

The vegetables were a trifle overdone by any standard, but the cold saddle of mutton was perfect, and the array of pickles and chutneys with it rich and full of variety and interest.

"Are you acquainted with the case, Mr. Rathbone?" Hester turned to Henry enquiringly, not wishing him to be excluded from the conversation.

"Oliver has mentioned it," he replied, helping himself liberally to a dark chutney. "What is it you hope to find?"

"The true reason why she killed him. Unfortunately it is beyond question that she did."

"What reason has she given you?"

"Jealousy of her hostess of that evening, but we know that is not true. She said she believed her husband was having an affair with this woman, Louisa Furnival, but we know that he was not, and that she knew that."

"But she will not tell you the truth?"

"No."

He frowned, cutting off a piece of meat and spreading it liberally with the chutney and mashed potato.

"Let us be logical about it," he said thoughtfully. "Did she plan this murder before she committed it?"

"We don't know. There is nothing to indicate whether she did or not."

"So it might have been a spur-of-the-moment act—lacking forethought, and possibly not considering the consequences either."

"But she is not a foolish woman," Hester protested. "She cannot have failed to know she would be hanged."

"If she was caught!" he argued. "It is possible an overwhelming fury possessed her and she acted unreasonably."

Hester frowned.

"My dear, it is a mistake to imagine we are all reasonable all of the time," he said gently. "People act from all sorts of impulses, sometimes quite contrary to their own interests, had they stopped to think. But so often we don't, we do what our emotions drive us to. If we are frightened we either run or freeze motionless, or we lash out, according to our nature and past experience."

He ignored his food, looking at her with concentration. "I think most tragedies happen when people have had too little time to think or weigh one course against another, or perhaps even to assess the real situation. They leap in before they have seen or understood. And then it is too late." Absentmindedly he pushed the pickle toward Oliver. "We are full of preconceptions; we judge from our own viewpoint. We believe what we have to, to keep the whole edifice of our views of things to be as they are. A new idea is still the most dangerous thing in the world. A new idea about something close to ourselves, coming quite suddenly and without warning, can make us so disconcerted, so frightened at the idea of all our beliefs about ourselves and those around us crumbling about our ears that we reach to strike at the one who has introduced this explosion into our lives—to deny it, violently if need be."

"Perhaps we don't know nearly enough about Alexandra Carlyon," she said thoughtfully, staring at her plate.

"We know a great deal more now than we did a week

185

ago,'' Oliver said quietly. ''Monk has been to her house and spoken with her servants, but the picture that emerges of both her and the general does nothing to set her in a better light, or explain why she should kill him. He was chilly, and possibly a bore, but he was faithful to her, generous with his money, had an excellent reputation, indeed almost perfect—and he was a devoted father to his son, and not unreasonable to his daughters.''

''He refused to allow Sabella to devote herself to the Church,'' Hester said hotly. ''And forced her to marry Fenton Pole.''

Oliver smiled. ''Not unreasonable, really. I think most fathers might well do the same. And Pole seems a decent enough man.''

''He still ordered her against her will,'' she protested.

''That is a father's prerogative, especially where daughters are concerned.''

She drew in her breath sharply, longing to remonstrate, even to accuse him of injustice, but she did not want to appear abrasive and ungracious to Henry Rathbone. It was an inappropriate time to pursue her own causes, however justifiable. She liked him more than she had expected, and his ill opinion of her would hurt. He was utterly unlike her own father, who had been very conventional, not greatly given to discussion; and yet in his company she was reminded, with comfort and a stab of pain, of all the wealth of belonging, the ease of family. Her own loneliness was sharpened by the sudden awareness. She had forgotten, perhaps deliberately, how good it had been when her parents were alive, in spite of the restrictions, the discipline and the staid and old-fashioned views. She had chosen to forget, to accommodate her grief.

Now, unaccountably, with Henry Rathbone the best of it returned.

Henry interrupted her thoughts, jerking her back to the present and the Carlyon case. ''But that all happened some time ago. The daughter is married already, from what you say?''

"Yes. They have a child," she said hastily.

"So this may rankle still, but it will not be the motive for murder so long after?"

"No."

"Let us suggest a hypothesis," Henry said thoughtfully, his meal almost forgotten. "The crime seems to have been committed on the spur of the moment. Alexandra saw the opportunity and took it—rather clumsily, as it turns out. Which means, if we are correct, either that she learned something that evening which so distressed her that she lost all sense of reason or self-preservation, or that she already wished to kill him but had not previously found an opportunity to do it." He looked at Hester. "Miss Latterly, in your judgment, what might shake a woman so? In other words, what would a woman hold so dear that she would kill to protect it?"

Oliver stopped eating, his fork in the air.

"We haven't looked at it that way," he said, turning to her. "Hester?"

She thought, wishing to give the most careful and intelligent answer she could.

"Well, I suppose the thing that would make me most likely to act without thinking, even of the risk to myself, would be some threat to the people I loved most—which in Alexandra's case would surely be her children." She allowed herself a half smile. "Regrettably it was obviously not her husband. To me it would have been my parents and brothers, but all of them except Charles are dead anyway." She said it because it was high in her mind, not to seek sympathy, then immediately wished she had not. She went on before they could offer any. "But let us say family—and in the case where there are children, I imagine one's home as well. There are some homes that go back for generations, even centuries. I would imagine one might care about them so extremely as to kill to preserve them, or to keep them from falling into the possession of others. But that does not apply here."

"Not according to Monk," Oliver agreed, watching with

dark, intent eyes. "And anyway, the house is his, not hers—and not an ancestral home in any way. What else?"

Hester smiled wryly, very aware of him. "Well, if I were beautiful, I suppose my looks would also be precious to me. Is Alexandra beautiful?"

He thought for a moment, his face reflecting a curious mixture of humor and pain. "Not beautiful, strictly speaking. But she is most memorable, and perhaps that is better. She has a face of distinct character."

"So far you have only mentioned one thing which she might care about sufficiently," Henry Rathbone pointed out. "What about her reputation?"

"Oh yes," Hester agreed quickly. "If one's honor is sufficiently threatened, if one were to be accused of something wrongfully, that could make one lose one's temper and control and every bit of good sense. It is one of the things I hate above all else. That is a distinct possibility. Or the honor of someone I loved—that would cut equally deeply."

"Who threatened her honor?" Oliver asked with a frown. "We have heard nothing at all to suggest anyone did. And if it were so, why should she not tell us? Or could it have been someone else's honor? Who? Not his, surely?"

"Blackmail," Hester said immediately. "A person blackmailed would naturally not tell—or it would reveal the very subject she had killed to hide."

"By her husband?" Oliver said skeptically. "That would be robbing one pocket to pay the other."

"Not for money," she said quickly, leaning forward over the table. "Of course that would make no sense. For something else—perhaps simply power over her."

"But who would he tell, my dear Hester? Any scandal about her would reflect just as badly upon him. Usually if a woman has disgraced herself, it is the husband whom the blackmailer would tell."

"Oh." She saw the point of what he was saying and it made excellent sense. "Yes." She looked at his eyes, expecting criticism, and saw a gentleness and a humor that for an instant robbed her of her concentration. She was far too

188

comfortable here with the two of them she liked so much. It would be so easy to wish to stay, to wish to belong. She recalled herself rapidly to the subject.

"It doesn't make sense as it is," she said quietly, lowering her eyes and looking away from him. "You said he was an excellent father, with the exception a couple of years ago of forcing Sabella to marry instead of taking the veil."

"Then if it doesn't make sense as it is," Henry said thoughtfully, "it means that either there is some element which you have not thought of, or else you are seeing something wrongly."

Hester looked at his mild, ascetic face and realized what intelligence there was in his eyes. It was the cleverest face she had seen that held absolutely nothing spiteful or ungenerous whatever. She found herself smiling, without any specific reason.

"Then we had better go back and look at it again," she resolved aloud. "I think perhaps it is the second of those two cases, and we are seeing something wrongly."

"Are you sure it is worth it?" Henry asked her gently. "Even if you do discover why she killed him, will it alter anything? Oliver?"

"I don't know. Quite possibly not," Oliver confessed. "But I cannot go into court with no more than I know now."

"That is your pride," Henry said frankly. "What about her interests? Surely if she wished you to defend her with the truth, she would have told it you?"

"I suppose so," he conceded. "But I should be the judge of what is her best defense in law, not she."

"I think you simply don't wish to be beaten," his father said, returning to his plate. "But I fear you may find the victory very small, even if you can obtain it. Who will it serve? It may merely demonstrate that Oliver Rathbone can discover the truth and lay it bare for all to see, even if the wretched accused would rather be hanged than reveal it herself."

"I shan't reveal it if she does not give me permission," Oliver said quickly, his face pink, his dark eyes wide. "For heaven's sake, what do you take me for?"

"Occasionally hotheaded, my dear boy," Henry replied. "And possessed of an intellectual arrogance and curiosity, which I fear you have inherited from me."

They continued the evening very pleasantly speaking of any number of things other than the Carlyon case. They discussed music, of which all were fond. Henry Rathbone was quite knowledgeable, having a great love of Beethoven's late quartets, composed when Beethoven himself was already severely deaf. They had a darkness and a complexity he found endlessly satisfying, and a beauty wrought out of pain which excited his pity but also reached a deeper level of his nature and fed a hunger there.

They also spoke of political events, the news from India and the growing unrest there. They touched only once on the Crimean War, but Henry Rathbone was so infuriated by the incompetence and the unnecessary deaths that after a quick glance at each other, Hester and Oliver changed the subject and did not hark back to it again.

Before leaving Hester and Oliver took a slow stroll around the garden and down to the honeysuckle hedge at the border of the orchard. The smell of the first flowers was close and sweet in the hazy darkness and she could see only the outline of the longest upflung branches against the starlit sky. For once they did not talk of the case.

"The news from India is very dark," she said, staring across at the pale blur of the apple blossoms. "It is so peaceful here it seems doubly painful to think of mutiny and battle. I feel guilty to have such beauty . . ."

He was standing very close to her and she was aware of the warmth of him. It was an acutely pleasant feeling.

"There is no need for guilt," he replied. She knew he was smiling although she had her back to him, and could scarcely have seen him in the dark anyway. "You could not help them," he went on, "by not appreciating what you have. That would merely be ungrateful."

"Of course you are right," she agreed. "It is self-indulgent for the sake of conscience, but actually achieves nothing at all, except ingratitude, as you say. I used to walk near the battlefields sometimes, in the Crimea, and knew what had happened so close by, and yet I needed the silence and the flowers, or I could not have gone on. If you don't keep your strength, both physical and spiritual, you are of no help to those who need you. All my intelligence knows that."

He took her elbow gently and they walked towards the herbaceous border, lupin spears just visible against the pale stones of the wall and the dusky outline of a climbing rose.

"Do you find hard cases affect you like that?" she asked presently. "Or are you more practical? I don't know—do you often lose?"

"Certainly not." There was laughter in his voice.

"You must lose sometimes!"

The laughter vanished. "Yes, of course I do. And yes—I find myself lying awake imagining how the prisoner must feel, tormenting myself in case I did not do everything I could have, and I was lying in my warm bed, and will do the next night, and the next . . . and that poor devil who depended on me will soon lie in the cold earth of an unhallowed grave."

"Oliver!" She swung around and stared at him, without thinking, reaching for both his hands.

He clasped her gently, fingers closing over hers.

"Don't your patients die sometimes, my dear?"

"Yes, of course."

"And don't you wonder if you were to blame? Even if you could not have saved them, could not have eased their pain, their fear?"

"Yes. But you have to let it go, or you would cripple yourself, and then be of no more use to the next patient."

"Of course." He raised her hands and touched his lips to them, first the left, and then the right. "And we shall both continue to do so, all we can. And we shall both also look at the moonlight on the apple trees, and be glad of it without guilt that no one else can see it precisely as we do. Promise me?"

191

"I promise," she said softly. "And the stars and the honeysuckle as well."

"Oh, don't worry about the stars," he said with laughter back in his voice. "They are universal. But the honeysuckle on the orchard fence and the lupins against the wall belong peculiarly to an English garden. This is ours."

Together they walked back to where Henry was standing by the French doors of the sitting room just as the clear song of a nightingale trilled through the night once and vanished.

Half an hour later Hester left. It was remarkably late, and she had enjoyed the evening more than any other she could recall for a very long time indeed.

It was now May 28, and more than a month since the murder of Thaddeus Carlyon and since Edith had come to Hester asking her assistance in finding some occupation that would use her talents and fill her time more rewardingly than the endless round of domestic pleasantries which now occupied her. And so far Hester had achieved nothing in that direction.

And quite apart from Edith Sobell, Major Tiplady was progressing extremely well and in a very short time would have no need of her services, and she would have to look for another position herself. And while for Edith it was a matter of finding something to use her time to more purpose, for Hester it was necessary to earn her living.

"You are looking much concerned, Miss Latterly," Major Tiplady said anxiously. "Is something wrong?"

"No—oh no. Not at all," she said quickly. "Your leg is healing beautifully. There is no infection now, and in a week or two at the outside, I think you may begin putting your weight on it again."

"And when is the unfortunate Carlyon woman coming to trial?"

"I'm not sure, precisely. Some time in the middle of June."

"Then I doubt I shall be able to dispense with you in two

192

weeks." There was a faint flush in his cheeks as he said it, but his china-blue eyes did not waver.

She smiled at him. "I would be less than honest if I remained here once you are perfectly well. Then how could you recommend me, should anyone ask?"

"I shall give you the very highest recommendation," he promised. "When the time comes—but it is not yet. And what about your friend who wishes for a position? What have you found for her?"

"Nothing so far. That is why I was looking concerned just now." It was at least partially true, if not the whole truth.

"Well, you had better look a little harder," he said seriously. "What manner of person is she?"

"A soldier's widow, well-bred, intelligent." She looked at his innocent face. "And I should think most unlikely to take kindly to being given orders."

"Awkward," he agreed with a tiny smile. "You will not find it an easy task."

"I am sure there must be something." She busied herself tidying away three books he had been reading, without asking him if he were finished or not.

"And you haven't done very well with Mrs. Carlyon either, have you," he went on.

"No—not at all. We must have missed something." She had related much of her discussions to him to while away the long evenings, and to help put it all in order in her own mind.

"Then you had better go back and see the people again," he advised her solemnly, looking very pink and white in his dressing robe with his face scrubbed clean and his hair a trifle on end. "I can spare you in the afternoons. You have left it all to the men. Surely you have some observations to offer? Take a look at the Furnival woman. She sounds appalling!"

He was getting very brave in offering his opinions, and she knew that if Monk and Rathbone were right, Louisa Furnival was the sort of woman who would terrify Major Tiplady into a paralyzed silence. Still, he was quite correct.

193

She had left it very much to other people's judgment. She could at least have seen Louisa Furnival herself.

"That is an excellent idea, Major," she concluded. "But what excuse can I give for calling upon a woman I have never met? She will show me the door instantly—and quite understandably."

He thought very gravely for several minutes, and she disappeared to consult the cook about dinner. In fact the subject was not raised again until she was preparing to leave him for the night.

"She is wealthy?" the major said suddenly as she was assisting him into bed.

"I beg your pardon?" She had no idea what he was talking about.

"Mrs. Furnival," he said impatiently. "She is wealthy?"

"I believe so—yes. Apparently her husband does very well out of military contracts. Why?"

"Well go and ask her for some money," he said reasonably, sitting rigidly and refusing to be assisted under the blankets. "For crippled soldiers from the Crimea, or for a military hospital or something. And if by any chance she gives you anything, you can pass it on to an appropriate organization. But I doubt she will. Or ask her to give her time and be a patron of such a place."

"Oh no," Hester said instinctively, still half pushing at him. "She would throw me out as a medicant."

He resisted her stubbornly. "Does it matter? She will speak to you first. Go in Miss Nightingale's name. No self-respecting person would insult her—she is revered next to the Queen. You do want to see her, don't you, this Furnival woman?"

"Yes," Hester agreed cautiously. "But . . ."

"Where's your courage, woman? You saw the charge of the Light Brigade." He faced her defiantly. "You've told me about it! You survived the siege of Sebastopol. Are you afraid of one miserable woman who flirts?"

"Like many a good soldier before me." Hester grinned. "Aren't you?"

He winced. "That's a foul blow."

"But it hit the mark," she said triumphantly. "Get into bed."

"Irrelevant! I cannot go—so you must!" He still sat perched on the edge. "You must fight whatever the battle is. This time the enemy has picked the ground, so you must gird yourself, choose your weapons well, and attack when he least expects it." Finally he swung his feet up and she pulled the blankets over him. He finished with fervor. "Courage."

She grimaced at him, but he gave no quarter. He lay back in the bed while she tucked the sheets around him, and smiled at her seraphically.

"Tomorrow late afternoon, when her husband may be home also," he said relentlessly. "You should see him too."

She glared at him. "Good night."

However the following afternoon at a little before five, dressed in a blue-gray gown of great sobriety, no pagoda sleeves, no white broderie, and looking as if she had indeed just come off duty in Miss Nightingale's presence, Hester swallowed her pride and her nerves, telling herself it was a good cause, and knocked on Louisa Furnival's front door. She hoped profoundly the maid would tell her Mrs. Furnival was out.

However she was not so fortunate. She was conducted into the hall after only the briefest of pauses while the maid announced her name and business. She barely had time to register the doors in the hallway and the handsome banister sweeping across the balcony at the far end and down the stairs. The suit of armor had been replaced; however, without the halberd. Alexandra must have stood with the general at the top on the landing, perhaps silently, perhaps in the last, bitter quarrel, and then she had lunged forward and he had gone over. He must have landed with an almighty crash. However had they not heard him?

The floor was carpeted, a pale Chinese rug with heavy pile. That would have softened the noise to some extent. Even so . . .

She got no further. The maid returned to say that Mrs.

Furnival would be pleased to receive her, and led her through the long corridor to the back of the house and the withdrawing room opening onto the garden.

She did not even bother to look at the sunlight on the grass, or the mass of flowering bushes. All her attention was on the woman who awaited her with unconcealed curiosity. She assumed in that instant that she had gained admittance so easily because Louisa was bored.

"Good afternoon, Miss Latterly. The Florence Nightingale Hospital? How interesting. In what way can I possibly be of help to you?"

Hester regarded her with equal curiosity. She might have only a few moments in which to form an opinion before she was asked to leave. The woman in front of her standing by the mantel wore a full crinoline skirt, emphasizing the extreme femininity of her form. It was up to the minute in fashion: pointed waist, pleated bodice, floral trimmings. She looked both voluptuous and fragile, with her tawny skin and mass of fine dark hair, dressed immaculately but far fuller than the fashion dictated. She was one of those few women who can defy the current mode and make her own style seem the right one, and all others ordinary and unimaginative. Self-confidence surrounded her, making Hester already feel dowdy, unfeminine, and remarkably foolish. She knew immediately why Alexandra Carlyon had expected people to believe in a passionate jealousy. It must have happened dozens of times, whatever the reality of any relationship.

She changed her mind as to what she had been going to say. She was horrified as she heard her own voice. It was bravado, and it was totally untrue. Something in Louisa Furnival's insolence provoked her.

"We learned a great deal in the Crimea about just how much good nursing can save the lives of soldiers," she said briskly. "Of course you are probably aware of this already." She widened her eyes innocently. "But perhaps you have not had occasion to think on the details of the matter. Miss Nightingale herself, as you well know, is a woman of excellent family, her father is well known and respected, and Miss Nightingale is highly educated. She chose nursing as a way of dedicating her life and her talents to the service of others—"

"We all agree that she is a most excellent woman, Miss Latterly," Louisa interrupted impatiently. Praise of other women did not appeal to her. "What has this to do with you, or me?"

"I will come immediately to the point." Hester looked at Louisa's long, slanting eyes, saw the fire of intelligence in them. To take her for a fool because she was a flirt would be a profound mistake. "If nursing is to become the force for saving life that it could be, we must attract into its service more well-bred and well-educated young women."

Louisa laughed, a rippling, self-conscious sound, made from amusement but tailored over years to have exactly the right effect. Had any man been listening he might well have found her wild, exotic, fascinating, elusive—all the things Hester was not. With a flash of doubt she wondered what Oliver Rathbone would have made of her.

"Really, Miss Latterly. You surely cannot imagine I would be interested in taking up a career in nursing?" Louisa said with something close to laughter. "That is ridiculous. I am a married woman!"

Hester bit back her temper with considerable difficulty. She could very easily dislike this woman.

"Of course I did not imagine you would be." She wished she could add her opinion of the likelihood of Louisa's having the courage, the skill, the unselfishness or the stamina to do anything of the sort. But this was not the time. It would defeat her own ends. "But you are the sort of woman that other women wish to model themselves upon." She squirmed inwardly as she said it. It was blatant flattery, and yet Louisa did not seem to find it excessive.

"How kind of you," she said with a smile, but her eyes did not leave Hester's.

"Such a woman, who is both well known and widely . . ." She hesitated. "And widely envied, would find that her words were listened to with more attention, and given more weight, than most other people's." She did not flinch from Louisa's brown-hazel eyes. She was speaking the truth now, and would dare anyone with it. "If you were to let it be known that you thought nursing a fine career for a young woman, not unfeminine or in any way degraded, then I believe more young women, hesitating about choosing it, might make their decisions in favor. It is only a matter of words, Mrs. Furnival, but they might make a great deal of difference."

"You are very persuasive, Miss Latterly." Louisa moved gracefully and arrogantly to the window, swinging her skirts as if she were walking outside along an open path. She might play at the coquette, but Hester judged there was nothing yielding or submissive in her. If she ever pretended it, it would be short-lived and to serve some purpose of her own.

Hester watched her, and remained seated where she was, silently.

Louisa was looking out of the window at the sun on the grass. The light on her face betrayed no age lines yet, but there was a hardness to the expression she could not have noticed, or she would not have stood so. And there was a meanness in her thin upper lip.

"You wish me to allow it to be known in those social circles I frequent that I admire nursing as an occupation for a woman, and might have followed it myself, were I not married?" she asked. The humor of it still appealed to her, the amusement was there in her face.

"Indeed," Hester agreed. "Since quite obviously you could not do it now, no one can expect you to prove what you say by offering your services, only your support."

Laughter flickered over Louisa's mouth. "And you think they would believe me, Miss Latterly? It seems to me you imagine them a little gullible."

"Do you often find yourself disbelieved, Mrs. Furnival?" Hester asked as politely as she could, given such a choice of words.

Louisa's smile hardened.

"No—no, I cannot say I can recall ever having done so. But I have never claimed to admire nursing before."

Hester raised her eyebrows. "Nor anything else that was an . . . an extending—of the truth?"

Louisa turned to face her.

"Don't be mealymouthed, Miss Latterly. I have lied outright, and been utterly believed. But the circumstances were different."

"I am sure."

"However, if you wish, I shall do as you suggest," Louisa cut her off. "It would be quite entertaining—and certainly different. Yes, the more I think of it, the more it appeals to me." She swung around from the window and walked back across towards the mantel. "I shall begin a quiet crusade to have young women of breeding and intelligence join the nurses. I can imagine how my acquaintances will view my new cause." She turned swiftly and came back over to Hester, standing in front of her and staring down. "And now, if I am to speak so well of this wonderful career, you had better tell me something about it. I don't wish to appear ignorant. Would you care for some refreshment while we talk?"

"Indeed, that would be most agreeable," Hester accepted.

"By the way, who else are you approaching?"

"You are the only one, so far," Hester said with absolute veracity. "I haven't spoken to anyone else as yet. I don't wish to be blatant."

"Yes—I think this could be most entertaining." Louisa reached for the bell and rang it vigorously.

Hester was still busy recounting everything she could to make nursing seem dramatic and glamorous when Maxim Furnival came home. He was a tall, slender man with a dark face, emotional, and made in lines that could as easily sulk or be dazzlingly bright. He smiled at Hester and enquired after her health in the normal manner of politeness, and when Louisa explained who Hester was, and her purpose in coming, he seemed genuinely interested.

They made polite conversation for some little time, Maxim charming, Louisa cool, Hester talking more about her experiences in the Crimea. Only half her attention was upon her answers. She was busy wondering how deeply Maxim had loved Alexandra, or if he had been jealous over Louisa and the ease with which she flirted, her total self-confidence. She did not imagine Louisa being gentle, yielding with pleasure to other than the purely physical. She seemed a woman who must always retain the emotional power. Had Maxim found that cold, a lonely thing when the initial passion had worn off, and then sought a gentler woman, one who could give as well as take? Alexandra Carlyon?

She had no idea. She realized again with a jolt of surprise that she had never seen Alexandra. All she knew of her was Monk's description, and Rathbone's.

Her attention was beginning to flag and she was repeating herself. She saw it in Louisa's face. She must be careful.

But before she could add much more the door opened and a youth of about thirteen came in, very tall and gangling as if he had outgrown his strength. His hair was dark but his eyes were heavy-lidded and clear blue, his nose long. In manner he was unusually diffident, hanging back half behind his father, and looking at Hester with shy curiosity.

"Ah, Valentine." Maxim ushered him forward. "My son, Valentine, Miss Latterly. Miss Latterly was in the Crimea with Miss Nightingale, Val. She has come to persuade Mama to encourage other young women of good family and education to take up nursing."

"How interesting. How do you do, Miss Latterly," Valentine said quietly.

"How do you do," Hester replied, looking at his face and trying to decide whether the gravity in his eyes was fear or a natural reticence. There was no quickening of interest in his face, and he looked at her with a sort of weary care. The spontaneity she would have expected from someone of his years was absent. She had looked to see an emotion, even if it was boredom or irritation at being introduced to someone in whom he had no interest. Instead he seemed guarded.

Was that a result of there having been a murder in his house so recently, and by all accounts of a man of whom he was very fond? It did not seem unreasonable. He was suffering from shock. Fate had dealt him an extraordinary blow, unseen in its coming, and having no reasonable explanation. Perhaps he no longer trusted fate to be either kind or sensible. Hester's pity was quickened, and again she wished intensely that she understood Alexandra's crime, even if there were no mitigation for it.

They said little more. Louisa was growing impatient and Hester had exhausted all that she could say on the subject, and after a few more polite trivialities she thanked them for their forbearance and took her leave.

"Well?" Major Tiplady demanded as soon as she reached Great Titchfield Street again. "Did you form any opinion? What is she like, this Mrs. Furnival? Would you have been jealous of her?"

Hester was barely through the door and had not yet taken off her cloak or bonnet.

"You were quite right," she conceded, placing her bonnet on the side table and undoing the button of her cloak and placing it on the hook. "It was definitely a good idea to meet her, and it went surprisingly well." She smiled at him. "In fact I was astoundingly bold. You would have been proud of me. I charged the enemy to the face, and carried the day, I think."

"Well don't stand there smirking, girl." He was thoroughly excited and the pink color rose in his cheeks. "What did you say, and what was she like?"

"I told her"—Hester blushed at the recollection—"that since all women admire her, her influence would be very powerful in encouraging young ladies of breeding and education to take up nursing—and would she use her good offices to that end."

"Great heavens. You said that?" The major closed his eyes as if to digest this startling piece of news. Then he opened them again, bright blue and wide. "And she believed you?"

"Certainly." She came over and sat on the chair opposite him. "She is a dashing and very dominant personality, very sure of herself, and quite aware that men admire her and women envy her. I could flatter her absurdly, and she would believe me, as long as I stayed within the bounds of her own field of influence. I might have been disbelieved had I told her she was virtuous or learned—but not that she was capable of influencing people.''

''Oh dear.'' He sighed, not in unhappiness, but mystification. The ways of women were something he would never understand. Just when he thought he had begun to grasp them, Hester went and did something completely incomprehensible, and he was back to the beginning again. ''And did you come to any conclusions about her?''

''Are you hungry?'' she asked him.

''Yes I am. But first tell me what you concluded!''

''I am not certain, except I am quite sure she was not in love with the general. She is not a woman who has had to change her plans, or has been deeply bereaved. Actually the only person who seemed really shaken was her son, Valentine. The poor boy looked quite stunned.''

Major Tiplady's face registered a sudden bleak pity, as if mention of Valentine had brought the reality of loss back to him, and it ceased to be a puzzle for the intellect and became a tragedy of people again, and their pain and confusion.

Hester said no more. Her mind was still busy trying to make a deeper sense out of her impressions of the Furnivals, hoping against experience to see something which she had missed before, something Monk had missed—and Rathbone.

The following morning she was surprised when at about eleven o'clock the maid announced that she had a visitor.

''I have?'' she asked dubiously. ''You mean the major has?''

''No, Miss Latterly, ma'am. It's a lady to see you, a Mrs. Sobell.''

''Oh! Oh yes.'' She glanced at Major Tiplady. He nodded, his eyes alive with interest. She turned back to the maid. ''Yes, please ask her to come in.''

A moment later Edith came in, dressed in a deep lilac silk gown with a wide skirt and looking surprisingly attractive.

There was only sufficient black to pay lip service to mourning, and the rich color enhanced her somewhat sallow skin. For once her hair was beautifully done and apparently she had come by carriage, because the wind had not pulled any of it loose.

Hester introduced her to the major, who flushed with pleasure—and annoyance at still being confined to his chaise longue and unable to stand to greet her.

"How do you do, Major Tiplady," Edith said with courtesy. "It is very gracious of you to receive me."

"How do you do, Mrs. Sobell. I am delighted you have called. May I extend my condolences on the death of your brother. I knew him by repute. A fine man."

"Oh thank you. Yes—it was a tragedy altogether, in every respect."

"Indeed. I hope the solution may yet prove less awful than we fear."

She looked at him curiously, and he colored under her gaze.

"Oh dear," he said hastily. "I fear I have been intrusive. I am so sorry. I know of it only because Miss Latterly has been so concerned on your behalf. Believe me, Mrs. Sobell, I did not mean to sound—er . . ." He faltered, not sure what word to use.

Edith smiled at him suddenly, a radiant, utterly natural expression. Under its warmth he became even pinker, stammered without saying anything at all, then slowly relaxed and smiled hesitantly back.

"I know Hester is doing all she can to help," Edith went on, looking at the major, not at Hester, who was busy taking her bonnet and shawl and giving them to the maid. "And indeed she has obtained for Alexandra the most excellent barrister, who in his turn has employed a detective. But I fear they have not yet discovered anything which will alter what appears to be a total tragedy."

"Do not give up hope yet, my dear Mrs. Sobell," Major Tiplady said eagerly. "Never give up until you are beaten and have no other course open to you. Miss Latterly went only yesterday afternoon to see Mrs. Furnival and form some opinion of her own as to her character.''

"Did you?'' Edith turned to Hester with a lift in her voice. "What did you think of her?''

Hester smiled ruefully. "Nothing helpful, I'm afraid. Would you like tea? It would be no trouble at all.''

Edith glanced at the major. It was not a usual hour for tea, and yet she very much wished to have an excuse to stay awhile.

"Of course,'' the major said hastily. "Unless you are able to remain for luncheon? That would be delightful.'' He stopped, realizing he was being too forward. "But you probably have other things to do—people to call on. I did not mean to be . . .''

Edith turned back to him. "I should be delighted, if it is not an imposition?''

Major Tiplady beamed with relief. "Not at all—not at all. Please sit down, Mrs. Sobell. I believe that chair is quite comfortable. Hester, please tell Molly we shall be three for luncheon.''

"Thank you,'' Edith accepted, sitting on the big chair with uncharacteristic grace, her back straight, her hands folded, both feet on the floor.

Hester departed obediently.

Edith glanced at the major's elevated leg on the chaise longue.

"I hope you are recovering well?''

"Oh excellently, thank you.'' He winced, but not with pain at any injury, rather at his incapacity, and the disadvantage at which it placed him. "I am very tired of sitting here, you know. I feel so . . .'' He hesitated again, not wishing to burden her with his complaints. After all, she had merely asked in general politeness, not requiring a detailed answer. The color swept up his cheeks again.

"Of course,'' she agreed with a quick smile. "You must be terribly . . . caged. I am used to spending all my time in one house, and I feel as if I were imprisoned. How much worse must you feel, when you are a soldier and used to

204

traveling all over the world and doing something useful all the time." She leaned forward a little, and unconsciously made herself more comfortable. "You must have been to some marvelous places."

"Well . . ." The pink spots in his cheeks grew deeper. "Well, I had not thought of it quite like that, but yes, I suppose I have. India, you know?"

"No, I don't know," she said frankly. "I wish I did."

"Do you really?" He looked surprised and hopeful.

"Of course!" She regarded him as if he had asked a truly odd question. "Where in India have you been? What is it like?"

"Oh it was all the usual thing, you know," he said modestly. "Scores of other people have been there too—officers' wives, and so on, and written letters home, full of descriptions. It isn't very new, I'm afraid." He hesitated, looking down at the blanket over his knees, and his rather bony hands spread across them. "But I did go to Africa a couple of times."

"Africa! How marvelous!" She was not being polite; eagerness rang in her voice like music. "Where in Africa? To the south?"

He watched her face keenly to make sure he was not saying too much.

"At first. Then I went north to Matabeleland, and Mashonaland . . ."

"Did you?" Her eyes were wide. "What is it like? Is that where Dr. Livingstone is?"

"No—the missionary there is a Dr. Robert Moffatt, a most remarkable person, as is his wife, Mary." His face lit with memory, as if the vividness of it were but a day or two since. "Indeed I think perhaps she is one of the most admirable of women. Such courage to travel with the word of God and to carry it to a savage people in an unknown land."

Edith leaned towards him eagerly. "What is the land like, Major Tiplady? Is it very hot? Is it quite different from England? What are the animals like, and the flowers?"

"You have never seen so many different kinds of beasts in all your life," he said expressively, still watching her. "Elephants, lions, giraffes, rhinos, and so many species of deer and antelope you cannot imagine it, and zebras and buffalo. Why, I have seen herds so vast they darkened the ground." He leaned towards her unconsciously, and she moved a fraction closer.

"And when something frightens them," he went on, "like a grass fire, and they stampede, then the earth shakes and roars under tens of thousands of hooves, and the little creatures dart in every direction before them, as before a tidal wave. Which reminds me, most of the ground there is red—a rich, brilliant soil. Oh, and the trees." He shrugged his shoulders. "Of course most of the veldt is just grassland and acacia trees, with flat tops—but there are flowering trees to dazzle the eyes so you scarcely can believe what they see. And—" He stopped suddenly as Hester came back into the room. "Oh dear—I am afraid I am monopolizing the conversation. You are too generous, Mrs. Sobell."

Hester stopped abruptly, then a slow smile spread over her face and she continued in.

"Not at all," Edith denied immediately. "Hester, has Major Tiplady ever told you about his adventures in Mashonaland and Matabeleland?"

"No," Hester said with some surprise, looking at the major. "I thought you served in India."

"Oh yes. But he has been to Africa too," Edith said quickly. "Major"—she faced him again eagerly—"you should write down everything about all these places you have been to, so we all may hear about them. Most of us don't even leave our miserable little parts of London, let alone see wild and exotic places such as you describe. Think how many people could while away a winter afternoon with imagination on fire with what you could tell them."

He looked profoundly abashed, and yet there was an eagerness in him he could not hide.

"Do you really think so, Mrs. Sobell?"

"Oh yes! Indeed I do," Edith said urgently. "It is quite apparent that you can recall it most clearly, and you recount it so extraordinarily well."

Major Tiplady colored with pleasure, and opened his

mouth to deny it, as modesty required. Then apparently he could think of nothing that did not sound ungracious, and so remained silent.

"An excellent idea," Hester agreed, delighted for the major and for Edith, and able to endorse it with some honesty as well. "There is so much rubbish written, it would be marvelous that true adventures should be recorded not only for the present day, but for the future as well. People will always want to know the explorations of such a country, whatever may happen there."

"Oh—oh." Major Tiplady looked very pleased. "Perhaps you are right. However, there are more pressing matters which I can see you need to discuss, my dear Mrs. Sobell. Please do not let your good manners prevent you from doing so. And if you wish to do so in private . . ."

"Not at all," Edith assured him. "But you are right, of course. We must consider the case." She turned to Hester again, her brightness of expression vanished, the pain replacing it. "Hester, Mr. Rathbone has spoken to Peverell about the trial. The date is set for Monday, June twenty-second, and we still have nothing to say but the same miserable lie with which we began. Alexandra did not do it"—she avoided using the word *kill*—"because of anything to do with Louisa Furnival. Thaddeus did not beat her, or leave her short of money. She had no other lover that we can find trace of. I cannot easily believe she is simply mad—and yet what else is there?" She sighed and the distress in her face deepened. "Perhaps Mama is right." She dragged her mouth down, as if even putting form to the thought was difficult, and made it worse.

"No, my dear, you must not give up," Major Tiplady said gently. "We shall think of something." He stopped, aware that it was not his concern. He knew of it only by virtue of his injured leg, and Hester's presence to nurse him. "I'm sorry," he apologized, embarrassed that he had intruded again, a cardinal sin in his own view. No gentleman intruded into another person's private affairs, especially a woman's.

"Don't apologize," Edith said with a hasty smile. "You

207

are quite right. I was disheartened, but that is when courage counts, isn't it? Anyone can keep going when all is easy."

"We must use logic." Hester sat down on the remaining chair. "We have been busy running 'round gathering facts and impressions, and not applying our brains sufficiently."

Edith looked puzzled, but did not argue. Major Tiplady sat up a little straighter on the chaise longue, his attention total.

"Let us suppose," Hester continued, "that Alexandra is perfectly sane, and has done this thing from some powerful motive which she is not prepared to share with anyone. Then she must have a reason for keeping silent. I was speaking with someone the other day who suggested she might be protecting someone or something she valued more than life."

"She is protecting someone else," Edith said slowly. "But who? We have ruled out Sabella. Mr. Monk proved she could not have killed her father."

"She could not have killed her father," Hester agreed quickly. "But we have not ruled out that there may be some other reason why she was in danger, of some sort, and Alexandra killed Thaddeus to save her from it."

"For example?"

"I don't know. Perhaps she has done something very odd, if childbirth has turned her mind, and Thaddeus was going to have her committed to an asylum."

"No, Thaddeus wouldn't do that," Edith argued. "She is Fenton's wife—he would have to do it."

"Well maybe he would have—if Thaddeus had told him to." Hester was not very happy with the idea, but it was a start. "Or it might be something quite different, but still to do with Sabella. Alexandra would kill to protect Sabella, wouldn't she?"

"Yes, I believe so. All right—that is one reason. What else?"

"Because she is so ashamed of the reason she does not wish anyone to know," Hester said. "I'm sorry—I realize that is a distasteful thought. But it is a possibility."

Edith nodded.

"Or," suggested Major Tiplady, looking from one to the other of them, "it is some reason which she believes will not make her case any better than it is now, and she would prefer that her real motive remain private if it cannot save her."

They both looked at him.

"You are right," Edith said slowly. "That also would be a reason." She turned to Hester. "Would any of that help?"

"I don't know," Hester said grimly. "Perhaps all we can look for now is sense. At least sense would stop it hurting quite so much." She shrugged. "I cannot get young Valentine Furnival's face out of my mind's eye; the poor boy looked so wounded. As if everything the adult world had led him to believe only confused him and left him with nowhere to turn!"

Edith sighed. "Cassian is the same. And he is only eight, poor child, and he's lost both his parents in one blow, as it were. I have tried to comfort him, or at least not to say anything which would belittle his loss, that would be absurd, but to spend time with him, talk to him and make him feel less alone." She shook her head and a troubled expression crossed her face. "But it hasn't done any good. I think he doesn't really like me very much. The only person he really seems to like is Peverell."

"I suppose he misses his father very much," Hester said unhappily. "And he may have heard whispers, no matter how much people try to keep it from him, that it was his mother who killed him. He may view all women with a certain mistrust."

Edith sighed and bent her head, putting her hands over her face as if she could shut out not only the light but some of what her mind could see as well.

"I suppose so," she said very quietly. "Poor little soul— I feel so totally helpless. I think that is the worst part of all this—there is nothing whatever we can do."

"We will just have to hope." Major Tiplady reached out a hand as if to touch Edith's arm, then suddenly realized what he was doing and withdrew it. "Until something occurs to us," he finished quietly.

But nearly a week later, on June 4, nothing had occurred.

209

Monk was nowhere to be seen. Oliver Rathbone was working silently in his office in Vere Street, and Major Tiplady was almost recovered, although loth to admit it.

Hester received a message from Clarence Gardens in Edith's rather sprawling script asking her to come to luncheon the following day. She was to come, not as a formal guest so much as Edith's friend, with a view to persuading her parents that it would not be unseemly for Edith to become a librarian to some discreet gentleman of unspotted reputation, should such a position be found.

"I cannot endure this idleness any longer," she had written. "Merely to sit here day after day, waiting for the trial and unable to lift a finger to assist anyone, is more than I can bear, and keep a reasonable temper or frame of mind."

Hester was also concerned about where she herself would find her next position. She had hoped Major Tiplady might know of some other soldier recently wounded or in frail health who would need her services, but he had been extremely unforthcoming. In fact all his attention lately seemed to be on the Carlyons and the case of the general's death.

However, he made no demur at all when she asked him if he would be agreeable to her taking luncheon with Edith the following day; in fact he seemed quite eager that she should.

Accordingly noon on the fifth saw her in Edith's sitting room discussing with her the possibilities of employment, not only as librarian but as companion if a lady of suitable occupation and temperament could be found. Even teaching foreign languages was not beyond consideration if the worse came to the worst.

They were still arguing the possibilities and seeking for more when luncheon was announced and they went downstairs to find Dr. Charles Hargrave in the withdrawing room. He was lean, very tall, and even more elegant than Hester had imagined from Edith's brief description of him. Introductions were performed by Felicia, and a moment later Randolf came in with a fair, handsome boy with a face still soft with the bloom of childhood, his hair curling back from his brow, his blue eyes wary and a careful, closed expression.

He was introduced, although Hester knew he was Cassian Carlyon, Alexandra's son.

"Good morning, Cassian," Hargrave said courteously, smiling at the boy.

Cassian dropped his shoulder and wriggled his left foot up his right ankle. He smiled back. "Good morning, sir."

Hargrave looked directly at him, ignoring the adults in the room and speaking as if they were alone, man to man.

"How are you getting on? Are you quite well? I hear your grandfather has given you a fine set of lead soldiers."

"Yes sir, Wellington's army at Waterloo," the boy answered with a flicker of enthusiasm at last touching his pale face. "Grandpapa was at Waterloo, you know? He actually saw it, isn't that tremendous?"

"Absolutely," Hargrave agreed quickly. "I should think he has some splendid stories he can tell you."

"Oh yes sir! He saw the emperor of the French, you know. And he was a funny little man with a cocked hat, and quite short when he wasn't on his white horse. He said the Iron Duke was magnificent. I would love to have been there." He dropped his shoulder again and smiled tentatively, his eyes never leaving Hargrave's face. "Wouldn't you, sir?"

"Indeed I would," Hargrave agreed. "But I daresay there will be other battles in the future, marvelous ones where you can fight, and see great events that turn history, and great men who win or lose nations in a day."

"Do you think so, sir?" For a moment his eyes were wide and full of unclouded excitement as the vision spread before his mind.

"Why not?" Hargrave said casually. "The whole world lies in front of us, and the Empire gets bigger and more exciting every year. There's all of Australia, New Zealand, Canada. And in Africa there's Gambia, Sierra Leone, the Gold Coast, South Africa; and in India there's the Northwest Province, Bengal, Oudh, Assam, Arakan, Mysore, and all the south, including Ceylon and islands in every ocean on earth."

"I'm not sure I even know where all those places are, sir," Cassian said with wonderment.

"Well then I had better show you, hadn't I?" Hargrave said, smiling broadly. He looked at Felicia. "Do you still have a schoolroom here?"

"It has been closed a long time, but we intend to open it again for Cassian's use, as soon as this unsettled time is over. We will engage a suitable tutor for him of course. I think a complete change is advisable, don't you?"

"A good idea," Hargrave agreed. "Nothing to remind him of things best put away." He turned back to Cassian. "Then this afternoon I shall take you up to the old school-room and we shall find a globe, and you shall show me all those places in the Empire that you know, and I shall show you all the ones you don't. Does that appeal to you?"

"Yes sir—thank you sir," Cassian accepted quickly. Then he glanced at his grandmother, saw the approval in her eyes, and moved around so that his back was to his grandfather, studiously avoiding looking at him.

Hester found herself smiling and a little prickle of warmth coming into her for the first time on behalf of the child. It seemed he had at least one friend who was going to treat him as a person and give him the uncritical, undemanding companionship he so desperately needed. And from what he said, his grandfather too was offering him some thoughts and tales that bore no relationship to his own tragedy. It was a generosity she would not have expected from Randolf, and she was obliged to view him with a greater liking than before. From Peverell she had expected it anyway, but he was out on business most of the day, when Cassian had his long hours alone.

They were about to go into the dining room when Peverell himself came in, apologized for being late and said he hoped he had not delayed them. He greeted Hester and Hargrave, then looked around for Damaris.

"Late again," Felicia said with tight lips. "Well we certainly cannot wait for her. She will have to join us wherever we are at the time she gets here. If she misses her meal it is her own doing." She turned around and without looking at any of them led the way into the dining room.

212

They were seated and the maid had come with soup when Damaris opened the door and stood on the threshold. She was dressed in a very slender gown, almost without hoops they were so small, the whole outfit in black and dove-gray, her hair pulled back from her long, thoughtful face with its lovely bones and emotional mouth.

For a moment there was silence, and the maid stopped with the soup ladle in the air.

"Sorry I'm late," she said with a tiny smile curling her lips, her eyes going first to Peverell, then to Edith and Hester, finally to her mother. She was leaning against the lintel.

"Your apologies are wearing a little thin!" Felicia said tartly. "This is the fifth time this fortnight that you have been late for a meal. Please continue to serve, Marigold."

The maid resumed her duty.

Damaris straightened up and was about to move forward and take her seat when she noticed Charles Hargrave for the first time. He had been partly shielded by Randolf. Her whole body froze and the blood drained from her skin. She swayed as if dizzy, and put both hands onto the door lintel to save herself.

Peverell rose to his feet immediately, scraping his chair back.

"What is it, Ris? Are you ill? Here, sit down, my dear." He half dragged her to his own abandoned chair and eased her into it. "What has happened? Are you faint?"

Edith pushed across her glass of water and he seized it and held it up to Damaris's lips.

Hargrave rose and came forward to kneel beside her, looking at her with a professional calm.

"Oh really," Randolf said irritably, and continued with his soup.

"Did you have any breakfast?" Hargrave asked, frowning at Damaris. "Or were you late for that also? Fasting can be dangerous, you know, make you light-headed."

She lifted her face and met his eyes slowly. For seconds they stared at each other in a strange, frozen immobility, he with concern, she with a look of bewilderment as if she barely knew where she was.

213

"Yes," she said at last, her voice husky. "That must be what it is. I apologize for making such a nuisance of myself." She swallowed awkwardly. "Thank you for the water Pev— Edith. I am sure I shall be perfectly all right now."

"Ridiculous!" Felicia said furiously, glaring at her daughter. "Not only are you late, but you come in here making an entrance like an operatic diva and then half swoon all over the place. Really, Damaris, your sense of the melodramatic is both absurd and offensive, and it is time you stopped drawing attention to yourself by any and every means you can think of!"

Hester was acutely uncomfortable; it was the sort of scene an outsider should not be privy to.

Peverell looked up, his face suddenly filled with anger.

"You are being unjust, Mama-in-law. Damaris had no intention of making herself ill. And I think if you have some criticism to make, it would be more fitting if you were to do it in private, when neither Miss Latterly nor Dr. Hargrave would be embarrassed by our family differences."

It was a speech delivered in a gentle tone of voice, but it contained the most cutting criticism that could be imagined. He accused her of behaving without dignity, without loyalty to her family's honor, and perhaps worst of all, of embarrassing her guests, sins which were socially and morally unforgivable.

She blushed scarlet, and then the blood fled, leaving her ashen. She opened her mouth to retaliate with something equally vicious, and was lost to find it.

Peverell turned from his mother-in-law to his wife. "I think it would be better if you were to lie down, my dear. I will have Gertrude bring you up a tray."

"I . . ." Damaris sat upright again, turning away from Hargrave. "I really . . ."

"You will feel better if you do," Peverell assured her, but there was a steel in his voice that brooked no argument. "I will see you to the stairs. Come!"

Obediently, leaning a little on his arm, she left, muttering "Excuse me" over her shoulder.

Edith began eating again and gradually the table returned

to normal. A few moments later Peverell came back and made no comment as to Damaris, and the episode was not referred to again.

They were beginning dessert of baked apple and caramel sauce when Edith caused the second violent disruption.

"I am going to find a position as a librarian, or possibly a companion to someone," she announced, looking ahead at the centerpiece of the table. It was an elaborate arrangement of irises, full-blown lupins from some sheltered area of the garden, and half-open white lilac.

Felicia choked on her apple.

"You are what?" Randolf demanded.

Hargrave stared at her, his face puckered, his eyes curious.

"I am going to seek a position as a librarian," Edith said again. "Or as a companion, or even a teacher of French, if all else fails."

"You always had an unreliable sense of humor," Felicia said coldly. "As if it were not enough that Damaris has to make a fool of herself, you have to follow her with idiotic remarks. What is the matter with you? Your brother's death seems to have deprived all of you of your wits. Not to mention your sense of what is fitting. I forbid you to mention it again. We are in a house of mourning, and you will remember that, and behave accordingly." Her face was bleak and a wave of misery passed over it, leaving her suddenly older and more vulnerable, the brave aspect that she showed to the world patently a veneer. "Your brother was a fine man, a brilliant man, robbed of the prime of his life by a wife who lost her reason. Our nation is the poorer for his loss. You will not make our suffering worse by behaving in an irresponsible manner and making wild and extremely trying remarks. Do I make myself clear?"

Edith opened her mouth to protest, but the argument died out of her. She saw the grief in her mother's face, and pity and guilt overrode her own wishes, and all the reasons she had been so certain of an hour ago talking to Hester in her own sitting room.

"Yes, Mama, I . . ." She let out her breath in a sigh.

"Good!" Felicia resumed eating, forcing herself to swallow with difficulty.

"I apologize, Hargrave," Randolf said with a frown. "Family's hit hard, you know. Grief does funny things to women—at least most women. Felicia's different—remarkable strength—a most outstanding woman, if I do say so."

"Most remarkable." Hargrave nodded towards Felicia and smiled. "You have my greatest respect, ma'am; you always have had."

Felicia colored very slightly and accepted the compliment with an inclination of her head.

The meal continued in silence, except for the most trivial and contrived of small talk.

When it was over and they had left the table and Hester had thanked Felicia and bidden them farewell, she and Edith went upstairs to the sitting room. Edith was thoroughly dejected; her shoulders were hunched and her feet heavy on the stairs.

Hester was extremely sorry for her. She understood why she had offered no argument. The sight of her mother's face so stripped, for an instant, of all its armor, had left her feeling brutal, and she was unable to strike another blow, least of all in front of others who had already seen her wounded once.

But it was no comfort to Edith, and offered only a long, bleak prospect ahead of endless meals the same, filled with little more than duty. The world of endeavor and reward was closed off as if it were a view through a window, and someone had drawn the curtains.

They were on the first landing when they were passed, almost at a run, by an elderly woman with crackling black skirts. She was very lean, almost gaunt, at least as tall as Hester. Her hair had once been auburn but now was almost white; only the tone of her skin gave away her original coloring. Her dark gray eyes were intent and her brows drawn down. Her thin face, highly individual, was creased with temper.

"Hallo, Buckie," Edith said cheerfully. "Where are you off to in such a rush? Been fighting with Cook again?"

"I don't fight with Cook, Miss Edith," she said briskly. "I simply tell her what she ought to know already. She takes it ill, even though I am right, and loses her temper. I cannot abide a woman who cannot control her temper—especially when she's in service."

Edith hid a smile. "Buckie, you don't know my friend, Hester Latterly. Miss Latterly was in the Crimea, with Florence Nightingale. Hester, this is Miss Buchan, my governess, long ago."

"How do you do, Miss Buchan," Hester said with interest.

"How do you do, Miss Latterly," Miss Buchan replied, screwing up her face and staring at Hester. "The Crimea, eh? Well, well. I'll have to have Edith tell me all about it. Right now I'm off up to see Master Cassian in the schoolroom."

"You're not going to teach him, are you, Buckie?" Edith said in surprise. "I thought you gave up that sort of thing years ago!"

"Of course I did," Miss Buchan said tartly. "Think I'm going to take up lessons again at my age? I'm sixty-six, as you well know. I taught you to count, myself, and your brother and sister before you!"

"Didn't Dr. Hargrave go up with him, to show him the globe?"

Miss Buchan's face hardened, a curious look of anger in her eyes and around her mouth.

"Indeed he did. I'll go and find out if he's there, and make sure nothing gets broken. Now if you will excuse me, Miss Edith, I'll be on my way. Miss Latterly." And without waiting to hear anything further she almost pushed past them, and walked very briskly, her heels clicking on the floor, and took the second flight of stairs to the schoolroom at something inelegantly close to a dash.

7

MONK WAS FINDING THE CARLYON CASE, as Rathbone had said, a thankless one. But he had given his word that he would do all he could for as long as it was asked of him. There were over two weeks yet until the trial, and so far he had found nothing that could be of use in helping even to mitigate the case against Alexandra, let alone answer it. It was a matter of pride not to give up now, and his own curiosity was piqued. He did not like to be beaten. He had not been beaten on a serious case since the accident, and he thought seldom before it.

And there was also the perfectly practical fact that Rathbone was still paying him, and he had no other case pending.

In the afternoon Monk went again to see Charles Hargrave. He had been the Carlyon family doctor for many years. If anyone knew the truth, or the elements from which the truth could be deduced, it would be he.

He was received courteously, and as soon as he explained why he believed Hargrave could help, he was led through into the same pleasing room as before. Hargrave instructed the servants he was not to be interrupted except for an emergency, and then offered Monk a seat and made himself available to answer any questions he was free to.

''I cannot tell you any personal facts about Mrs. Carlyon,

you understand," he said with an apologetic smile. "She is still my patient, and I have to assume that she is innocent until the law says otherwise, in spite of that being patently ridiculous. But I admit, if I thought there was anything at all that would be of help in your case, I should break that confidence and give you all the information I had." He lifted his shoulders a trifle. "But there is nothing. She has had only the very ordinary ailments that most women have. Her confinements were without incident. Her children were born normally, and thrived. She herself recovered her health as soon and as happily as most women do. There is really nothing to tell."

"Not like Sabella?"

His face shadowed. "No—no, I am afraid Sabella was one of those few who suffer profoundly. No one knows why it happens, but occasionally a woman will have a difficult time carrying a child, during confinement, or afterwards. Sabella was quite well right up until the last week. Her confinement was long and extremely painful. At one time I was fearful lest we lose her."

"Her mother would be most distressed."

"Of course. But then death in childbirth is quite common, Mr. Monk. It is a risk all women take, and they are aware of it."

"Was that why Sabella did not wish to marry?"

Hargrave looked surprised. "Not that I know of. I believe she genuinely wished to devote her life to the Church." Again he raised his shoulders very slightly. "It is not unknown among girls of a certain age. Usually they grow out of it. It is a sort of romance, an escape for a young and overheated imagination. Some simply fall in love with an ideal of man, a figure from literature or whatever, some with the most ideal of all—the Son of God. And after all"—he smiled with a gentle amusement touched only fractionally with bitterness—"it is the one love which can never fall short of our dreams, never disillusion us, because it lies in illusion anyway." He sighed. "No, forgive me, that is not quite right. I

219

mean it is mystical, its fulfillment does not rest with any real person but in the mind of the lover."

"And after the confinement and the birth of her child?" Monk prompted.

"Oh—yes, I'm afraid she suffered a melancholia that occasionally occurs at such times. She became quite deranged, did not want her child, repelled any comfort or offer of help, any friendship; indeed any company except that of her mother." He spread his hands expressively. "But it passed. These things do. Sometimes they take several years, but usually it is only a matter of a month or two, or at most four or five."

"There was no question of her being incarcerated as insane?"

"No!" Hargrave was startled. "None at all. Her husband was very patient, and they had a wet nurse for the child. Why?"

Monk sighed. "It was a possibility."

"Alexandra? Don't see how. What are you looking for, Mr. Monk? What is it you hope to find? If I knew, perhaps I could save your time, and tell you if it exists at all."

"I don't know myself," Monk confessed. Also he did not wish to confide in Hargrave, or anyone else, because the whole idea involved some other person who was a threat to Alexandra. And who better than her doctor, who must know so many intimate things?

"What about the general?" he said aloud. "He is dead and cannot care who knows about him, and his medical history may contain some answer as to why he was killed."

Hargrave frowned. "I cannot think what. It is very ordinary indeed. Of course I did not attend him for the various injuries he received in action." He smiled. "In fact I think the only time I attended him at all was for a cut he received on his upper leg—a rather foolish accident."

"Oh? It must have been severe for him to send for you."

"Yes, it was a very nasty gash, ragged and quite deep. It was necessary to clean it, stop the bleeding with packs, then to stitch it closed. I went back several times to make quite sure it healed properly, without infection."

"How did it happen?" A wild thought occurred to Monk

220

that it might have been a previous attack by Alexandra, which the general had warded off, sustaining only a thigh injury.

A look of puzzlement crossed Hargrave's face.

"He said he had been cleaning an ornamental weapon, an Indian knife he had brought home as a souvenir, and taken it to give to young Valentine Furnival. It had stuck in its scabbard, and in forcing it out it slipped from his grasp and gashed him on the leg. He was attempting to clean it, or something of the sort."

"Valentine Furnival? Was Valentine visiting him?"

"No—no, it happened at the Furnivals' house. I was sent there."

"Did you see the weapon?" Monk asked.

"No—I didn't bother. He assured me the blade itself was clean, and that since it was such a dangerous thing he had disposed of it. I saw no reason to pursue it, because even in the unlikely event it was not self-inflicted, but a domestic quarrel, it was none of my affair, so long as he did not ask me to interfere. And he never did. In fact he did not mention it again as long as I knew him." He smiled slightly. "If you are thinking it was Alexandra, I must say I think you are mistaken, but even if so, he forgave her for it. And nothing like it ever occurred again."

"Alexandra was at the Furnivals' house?"

"I've no idea. I didn't see her."

"I see. Thank you, Dr. Hargrave."

And although he stayed another forty-five minutes, Monk learned nothing else that was of use to him. In fact he could find no thread to follow that might lead him to the reason why Alexandra had killed her husband, and still less why she should remain silent rather than admit it, even to him.

He left in the late afternoon, disappointed and puzzled.

He must ask Rathbone to arrange for him to see the woman again, but while that was in hand, he would go back to her daughter, Sabella Pole. The answer as to why Alexandra had killed her husband must lie somewhere in her nature, or in

221

her circumstances. The only course that he could see left to him was to learn still more about her.

Accordingly, eleven o'clock in the morning saw him at Fenton Pole's house in Albany Street, again knocking on the door and requesting to see Mrs. Pole, if she would receive him, and handing the maid his card.

He had chosen his time carefully. Fenton Pole was out on business, and as he had hoped, Sabella received him eagerly. As soon as he came into the morning room where she was she rose from the green sofa and came towards him, her eyes wide and hopeful, her hair framing her face with its soft, fair curls. Her skirts were very wide, the crinoline hoops settling themselves straight as she rose and the taffeta rustling against itself with a soft, whispering sound.

Without any warning he felt a stab of memory that erased his present surroundings of conventional green and placed him in a gaslit room with mirrors reflecting a chandelier, and a woman talking. But before he could focus on anything it was gone, leaving nothing behind but confusion, a sense of being in two places at once, and a desperate need to recapture it and grasp the whole of it.

"Mr. Monk," Sabella said hastily. "I am so glad you came again. I was afraid after my husband was so abrupt to you that you would not return. How is Mama? Have you seen her? Can you help? No one will tell me anything, and I am going nearly frantic with fear for her."

The sunlight in the bright room seemed unreal, as if he were detached from it and seeing it in a reflection rather than reality. His mind was struggling after gaslight, dim corners and brilliant splinters of light on crystal.

Sabella stood in front of him, her lovely oval face strained and her eyes full of anxiety. He must pull his wits together and give her his attention. Every decency demanded it. What had she said? Concentrate!

"I have requested permission to see her again as soon as possible, Mrs. Pole," he replied, his words sounding far away. "As to whether I can help, I am afraid I don't know yet. So far I have learned little that seems of any use."

She closed her eyes as if the pain were physical, and stepped back from him.

"I need to know more about her," he went on, memory abandoned for the moment. "Please, Mrs. Pole, if you can help me, do so. She will not tell us anything, except that she killed him. She will not tell us any reason but the one we know is not true. I have searched for any evidence of another cause, and I can find none. It must be in her nature, or in your father's. Or in some event which as yet we know nothing of. Please—tell me about them!"

She opened her eyes and stared at him; slowly a little of the color came back into her face.

"What sort of thing do you wish to know, Mr. Monk? I will tell you anything I can. Just ask me—instruct me!" She sat down and waved to a seat for him.

He obeyed, sinking into the deep upholstery and finding it more comfortable than he had expected.

"It may be painful," he warned. "If it distresses you please say so. I do not wish to make you ill." He was gentler with her than he had expected to be, or was his habit. Perhaps it was because she was too concerned with her mother to think of being afraid of him for herself. Fear brought out a pursuing instinct in him, a kind of anger because he thought it was unwarranted. He admired courage.

"Mr. Monk, my mother's life is in jeopardy," she replied with a very direct gaze. "I do not think a little distress is beyond my bearing."

He smiled at her for the first time, a quick, generous gesture that came quite spontaneously.

"Thank you. Did you ever hear your parents quarreling, say, in the last two or three years?"

She smiled back at him, only a ghost, and then was gone.

"I have tried to think of that myself," she said seriously. "And I am afraid I have not. Papa was not the sort of man to quarrel. He was a general, you know. Generals don't quarrel." She pulled a little face. "I suppose that is because the only person who would dare to quarrel with a general would be another general, and you so seldom get two in any one

223

place. There is presumably a whole army between one general and the next."

She was watching his face. "Except in the Crimea, so I hear. And then of course they did quarrel—and the results were catastrophic. At least that is what Maxim Furnival says, although everybody else denies it and says our men were fearfully brave and the generals were all very clever. But I believe Maxim . . ."

"So do I," he agreed. "I believe some were clever, most were brave enough, but far too many were disastrously ignorant and inexcusably stupid!"

"Oh do you think so?" The fleeting smile crossed her face again. "Not many people will dare to say that generals are stupid, especially so close to a war. But my father was a general, and so I know how they can be. They know some things, but others they have no idea of at all, the most ordinary things about people. Half the people in the world are women, you know?" She said it as if the fact surprised even herself.

He found himself liking her. "Was your father like that?" he asked, not only because it mattered, but because he was interested.

"Very much." She lifted her head and pushed back a stray strand of hair. The gesture was startlingly familiar to him, bringing back not a sight or a sound, but an emotion of tenderness rare and startling to him, and a longing to protect her as if she were a vulnerable child; and yet he knew beyond question that the urgency he felt was not that which he might have towards any child, but only towards a woman.

But which woman? What had happened between them, and why did he not know her now? Was she dead? Had he failed to protect her, as he had failed with the Walbrooks? Or had they quarreled over something; had he been too precipitate with his feelings? Did she love someone else?

If only he knew more of himself, he might know the answer to that. All he had learned up until now showed him that he was not a gentle man, not used to bridling his tongue to protect other people's feelings, or to stifling his own wants, needs, or opinions. He could be cruel with words. Too many cautious and bruised inferiors had borne witness to that. He recalled with increasing discomfort the wariness with which they had greeted him when he returned from the hospital after the accident. They admired him, certainly, respected his professional ability and judgment, his honesty, skill, dedication and courage. But they were also afraid of him—and not only if they were lax in duty or less than honest, but even if they were in the right. Which meant that a number of times he must have been unjust, his sarcastic wit directed against the weak as well as the strong. It was not a pleasant knowledge to live with.

"Tell me about him." He looked at Sabella. "Tell me about his nature, his interests, what you liked best about him, and what you disliked."

"Liked best about him?" She concentrated hard. "I think I liked . . ."

He was not listening to her. The woman he had loved—yes, *loved* was the word—why had he not married her? Had she refused him? But if he had cared so much, why could he not now even recall her face, her name, anything about her beyond these sharp and confusing flashes?

Or had she been guilty of the crime after all? Was that why he had tried to expunge her from his mind? And she returned now only because he had forgotten the circumstances, the guilt, the dreadful end of the affair? Could he have been so mistaken in his judgment? Surely not. It was his profession to detect truth from lies—he could not have been such a fool!

". . . and I liked the way he always spoke gently," Sabella was saying. "I can't recall that I ever heard him shout, or use language unbecoming for us to hear. He had a lovely voice." She was looking up at the ceiling, her face softer, the anger gone from it, which he had only dimly registered when she must have been speaking of some of the things she disliked in her father. "He used to read to us from the Bible—the Book of Isaiah especially," she went on. "I don't remember what he said, but I loved listening to him because

225

his voice wrapped all 'round us and made it all seem important and good.''

"And your greatest dislike?" he prompted, hoping she had not already specified it when he was not listening.

"I think the way he would withdraw into himself and not even seem to notice that I was there—sometimes for days," she replied without hesitation. Then a look of sorrow came into her eyes, and a self-conscious pain. "And he never laughed with me, as if—as if he were not altogether comfortable in my company." Her fair brows puckered as she concentrated on Monk. "Do you know what I mean?"

Then as quickly she looked away. "I'm sorry, that is a foolish question, and embarrassing. I fear I am being no help at all—and I wish I could." This last was said with such intense feeling that Monk ached to be able to reach across the bright space between them and touch her slender wrist, to assure her with some more immediate warmth than words, that he did understand. But to do so would be intrusive, and open to all manner of misconstruction. All he could think of was to continue with questions that might lead to some fragment of useful knowledge. He did not often feel so awkward.

"I believe he had been friends with Mr. and Mrs. Furnival for a long time?"

She looked up, recalling herself to the matter in hand and putting away memory and thought of her own wounds.

"Yes—about sixteen or seventeen years, I think, something like that. They had been much closer over the last seven or eight years. I believe he used to visit them once or twice a week when he was at home." She looked at him with a slight frown. "But he was friends with both of them, you know. It would be easy to believe he was having an affair with Louisa—I mean easy as far as his death is concerned, but I really do not think he was. Maxim was very fond of Mama, you know? Sometimes I used to think—but that is another thing, and of no use to us now.

"Maxim is in the business of dealing in foodstuffs, you know, and Papa put a very great deal of army contracts his way. A cavalry regiment can use a marvelous amount of corn, hay, oats and so on. I think he also was an agent for saddlery and other things of that sort. I don't know the details, but I know Maxim profited greatly because of it, and has become a very respected power in the trade, among his fellows. I think he must be very good at it."

"Indeed." Monk turned it over in his mind; it was an interesting piece of information, but he could not see how it was of any use to Alexandra Carlyon. It did not sound in any way corrupt; presumably a general might suggest to his quartermaster that he obtain his stores from one merchant rather than another, if the price were fair. But even had it not been, why should that cause Alexandra any anger or distress—still less drive her to murder?

But it was another thread leading back to the Furnivals.

"Do you remember the incident where your father was stabbed with the ornamental knife? It happened at the Furnivals' house. It was quite a deep injury."

"He wasn't stabbed," she said with a tiny smile. "He slipped and did it himself. He was cleaning the knife, or something. I can't imagine why. It wasn't even used."

"But you remember it?"

"Yes of course. Poor Valentine was terribly upset. I think he saw it happen. He was only about eleven or twelve, poor child."

"Was your mother there?"

"At the Furnivals'? Yes, I think so. I really don't remember. Louisa was there. She sent for Dr. Hargrave to come immediately because it was bleeding pretty badly. They had to put a lot of bandages on it, and he could barely get his trousers back on, even with Maxim's valet to help him. When he came down the stairs, assisted by the valet and the footman, I could see the great bulges under the cloth of his trousers. He looked awfully pale and he went straight home in the carriage."

Monk tried to visualize it. A clumsy accident. But was it relevant? Could it conceivably have been an earlier attempt to kill him? Surely not—not in the Furnivals' house and so long ago. But why not in the Furnivals' house? She had finally killed him there. But why no attempt between then and now?

Sabella had said she saw the swell of the bandages under his trousers. Not the bloodstained tear where the knife had gone through! Was it possible Alexandra had found him in bed with Louisa and taken the knife to him in a fit of jealous rage? And they had conspired to conceal it—and the scandal? There was no point in asking Sabella. She would naturally deny it, to protect her mother.

He stayed a further half hour, drawing from her memories of her parents, some quite varied, but not showing him anything he had not already learned from his talk with the servants in Alexandra's own home. She and the general had been reasonably content in their relationship. It was cool but not intolerable. He had not abused her in any way, he had been generous, even-tempered, and had no apparent vices; he was simply an unemotional man who preferred his own interests and his own company. Surely that was the position of many married women, and nothing to warrant serious complaint, let alone violence.

He thanked her, promised her again that he would not cease to do all he could for her mother, right to the last possible moment, then took his leave with a deep regret that he could offer her no real comfort.

He was outside on the warm pavement in the sun when the sudden fragrance of lilac in bloom made him stop so abruptly a messenger boy moving along the curb nearly fell over him. The smell, the brightness of the light and the warmth of the paving stones woke in him a feeling of such intense loneliness, as if he had just this moment lost something, or realized it was beyond his reach when he had thought it his, that he found his heart pounding and his breath caught in his throat.

But why? Who? Whose closeness, whose friendship or love had he lost? How? Had they betrayed him—or he them? He had a terrible fear that it was he who had betrayed them!

One answer he knew already, as soon as the question formed in his mind—it was the woman whom he had tried to defend from a charge of killing her husband. The woman with the fair hair and dark amber eyes. That was certain: but only that—no more.

He must find out! If he had investigated the case then there would be police records of it: names, dates, places—conclusions. He would find out who the woman was and what had happened to her, if possible what they had felt for each other, and why it had ended.

He moved forward with a fresh, determined stride. Now he had purpose. At the end of Albany Street he turned into the Euston Road and within a few minutes had hailed a cab. There was only one course open. He would find Evan and get him to search through the records for the case.

But it was not so easy. He was not able to contact Evan until early in the evening, when he came back tired and dispirited from a fruitless chase after a man who had embezzled a fortune and fled with it across the Channel. Now began the burdensome business of contacting the French police to apprehend him.

When Monk caught up with Evan leaving the police station on his way home, Evan was sufficiently generous of spirit to be pleased to see him, but he was obviously tired and discouraged. For once Monk put his own concern out of his immediate mind, and simply walked in step with Evan for some distance, listening to his affairs, until Evan, knowing him well, eventually asked why he had come.

Monk pulled a face.

"For help," he acknowledged, skirting his way around an old woman haggling with a coster.

"The Carlyon case?" Evan asked, stepping back onto the pavement.

"No—quite different. Have you eaten?"

"No. Given up on the Carlyon case? It must be coming to trial soon."

"Care to have dinner with me? There's a good chophouse 'round the corner."

Evan smiled, suddenly illuminating his face. "I'd love to. What is it you want, if it's not the Carlyons?"

"I haven't given up on it, I'm still looking. But this is a case in the past, something I worked on before the accident."

Evan was startled, his eyes widened. "You remember!"

"No—oh, I remember more, certainly. Bits and pieces keep coming back. But I can remember a woman charged with murdering her husband, and I was trying to solve the case, or to be more precise, I was trying to clear her."

They turned the corner into Goodge Street and halfway along came to the chophouse. Inside was warm and busy, crowded with clerks and businessmen, traders and men of the minor professions, all talking together and eating, a clatter of knives, forks, chink of plates and the pleasant steam of hot food.

Monk and Evans were conducted to a table and took their seats, giving their orders without reference to a menu. For a moment an old comfort settled over Monk. It was like the best of the past, and for all the pleasure of being rid of Runcorn, he realized how lonely he was without the comradeship of Evan, and how anxious he was lurching from one private case to another, with never the certainty of anything further, and only a week or two's money in hand.

"What is it?" Evan asked, his young face full of interest and concern. "Do you need to find the case because of Mrs. Carlyon?"

"No." Monk did not even think of being dishonest with him, and yet he was self-conscious about exposing his vulnerability. "I keep getting moments of memory so sharp, I know I cared about it profoundly. It is simply for myself; I need to know who she was, and what happened to her." He watched Evan's face for pity, dreading it.

"Her?" Evan said casually.

"The woman." Monk looked down at the white tablecloth. "She keeps coming back into my mind, obscuring what I am thinking of at the time. It is my past, part of my life I need to reclaim. I must find the case."

"Of course." If Evan felt any curiosity or compassion he hid it, and Monk was profoundly grateful.

Their meals arrived and they began to eat, Monk with indifference, Evan hungrily.

"All right," Evan said after a few moments, when the edge of his appetite had been blunted. "What do you want me to do?"

Monk had already thought of this carefully. He did not want to ask more of Evan than he had to, or to place him in an intolerable position.

"Look through the files of my past cases and see which ones fit the possibilities. Then give me what information you can, and I'll retrace my steps. Find whatever witnesses there still are available, and I'll find her."

Evan put some meat in his mouth and chewed thought-fully. He did not point out that he was not permitted to do this, or what Runcorn would say if he found out, or even that it would be necessary to practice a certain amount of deception to his colleagues in order to obtain such files. They both knew it. Monk was asking a very considerable favor. It would be indelicate to make it obvious, and Evan was not an unkind man, but a small smile did curl the corners of his sensitive mouth, and Monk saw it and understood. His resentment died even as it was born. It was grossly unfair.

Evan swallowed.

"What do you know about her?" he asked, reaching for his glass of cider.

"She was young," Monk began, saw the flash of humor in Evan's face, and went on as if he had not. "Fair hair, brown eyes. She was accused of murdering her husband, and I was investigating the case. That's all. Except I must have spent some time on it, because I knew her quite well—and I cared about her."

Evan's laughter died completely, replaced by a complexity of expression which Monk knew was an attempt to hide his sympathy. It was ridiculous, and sensitive, and admirable. And from anyone else Monk would have loathed it.

"I'll find all the cases that answer these criteria," Evan promised. "I can't bring the files, but I'll write down the details that matter and tell you the outline."

"When?"

"Monday evening. That will be my first chance. Can't tell you what time. This chop is very good." He grinned. "You can give me dinner here again, and I'll tell you what I know."

"I'm obliged," Monk said with a very faint trace of sarcasm, but he meant it more than it was easy for him to say.

"There's the first," Evan said the following Monday evening, passing a folded piece of paper across the table to Monk. They were sitting in the cheerful hubbub of the chophouse with waiters, diners and steaming food all around them. "Margery Worth, accused of murdering her husband by poison in order to run off with a younger man." Evan pulled a face. "I'm afraid I don't know what the result of the trial was. Our records only show that the evidence you collected was pretty good, but not conclusive. I'm sorry."

"You said the first." Monk took the paper. "There are others?"

"Two more. I only had the time to copy one of them, and that is only the bare outline, you know. Phyllis Dexter. She was accused of killing her husband with a carving knife." He shrugged expressively. "She claimed it was self-defense. From what you have in your notes there is no way of telling whether it was or not, nor what you thought of it. Your feelings are plain enough; you sympathized with her and thought he deserved all he got. But that doesn't mean that she told the truth."

"Any notes on the verdict?" Monk tried to keep the excitement out of his voice. This sounded as if it could be the case about which he cared so much, if only by reading his notes from the file Evan could sense the emotion through it. "What happened to her? How long ago was it?"

"No idea what happened to her," Evan replied with a rueful smile. "Your notes didn't say, and I didn't dare ask anyone in case they realized what I was doing. I had no reason to know."

"Of course. But when did it happen? It must have been dated."

"1853."

"And the other one, Margery Worth?"

"1854." Evan passed over the second piece of paper. "There is everything in there I could copy in the time. All the places and principal people you interviewed."

"Thank you." Monk meant it and did not know how to say it without being clumsy, and embarrassing Evan. "I . . ."

"Good," Evan said quickly with a grin. "So you should. What about getting me another mug of cider?"

The next morning, with an unusual mixture of excitement and fear, Monk set off on the train for Suffolk and the village of Yoxford. It was a brilliant day, sky with white towers of cloud in the sunlight, fields rolling in green waves from the carriage windows, hedges burgeoning with drifts of hawthorn blossoms. He wished he could be out to walk among it and smell the wild, sweet odor of it, instead of in this steaming, belching, clanking monster roaring through the countryside on a late spring morning.

But he was driven by a compulsion, and the only thatched village nestling against the folded downs or half hidden by its trees which held any interest for him was the one which might yield up his past, and the woman who haunted him.

He had read Evan's notes as soon as he got to his rooms the previous evening. He tried this one first simply because it was the closer of the two. The second lay in Shrewsbury, and would be a full day's journey away, and since Shrewsbury was a far larger town, might be harder to trace now it was three years old.

The notes on Margery Worth told a simple story. She was a handsome young woman, married some eight years to a man nearly twice her age. One October morning she had reported to the local doctor that her husband had died in the night, she knew not how. He had made no disturbance and she was a heavy sleeper and had been in the next room since she had taken a chill and did not wish to waken him with her sneezing.

The doctor duly called around with expressions of sympathy, and pronounced that Jack Worth was indeed dead, but he was unsatisfied as to the cause. The body was removed and a second opinion called for. The second opinion, from a doctor in Saxmundham, some four and a half miles away, was of the view that Jack Worth had not died naturally but of some poison. However he could not be certain, he could not name the poison, nor could he state positively when it had been administered, and still less by whom.

The local police had been called in, and confessed themselves confused. Margery was Jack Worth's second wife, and he had two grown sons by the first who stood to inherit the farm, which was of considerable size, and extremely fertile. Margery was to have the house for the duration of her life, or until she remarried, and a small income, barely sufficient to survive.

Scotland Yard was sent for. Monk had arrived on November 1, 1854. He had immediately seen the local police, then had interviewed Margery herself, the first doctor, the second doctor, both the surviving sons, and several other neighbors and shopkeepers. Evan had not been able to make copies of any of his questions, or their answers, only the names, but it would be sufficient to retrace his steps, and the villagers would doubtless remember a great deal about a celebrated murder only three years old.

The journey took him rather more than two hours, and he alighted at the small station and walked the road some three quarters of a mile back to the village. There was one main street stretching westward, with shops and a public house, and as far as he could see only one side street off it. It was a little early for luncheon, but not at all inappropriate to go to the public house and have a glass of cider.

He was greeted with silent curiosity and it was ten minutes before the landlord finally spoke to him.

"Mornin', Mr. Monk. What be you doin' back 'ere, then? We in't 'ad no more murders you know."

"I'm glad to hear it," Monk said conversationally. "I'm sure one is enough."

"More'n so," the landlord agreed.

Another few minutes passed in silence. Two more men came in, hot and thirsty, bare arms brown from the wind and sun, eyes blinking in the interior darkness after the brilliance outside. No one left.

"So what you 'ere for then?" the landlord said at last.

"Tidying up a few things," Monk replied casually.

The landlord eyed him suspiciously. "Like wot, then? Poor Margery 'anged. Wot else is there to do?"

That was the last question answered first, and brutally. Monk felt a sick chill, as if something had slipped out of his grasp already. And yet the name meant nothing to him. He could vaguely recall this street, but what use was that? There was no question that he had been here; the question was, was Margery Worth the woman he had cared about so intensely? How could he find out? Only her form, her face would tell him, and they were destroyed with her life on the gallows rope.

"A few questions must be asked," he said as noncommittally as he could, but his throat was tight and his heart raced, and yet he felt cold. Was that why he could not remember—bitter dreadful failure? Was it pride that had blocked it out, and the woman who had died with it?

"I want to retrace some of my steps and be sure I recall it rightly." His voice was husky and the excuse sounded lame even as he said it.

" 'Oo's asking?" The landlord was wary.

Monk compromised the truth. "Their lordships in London. That's all I can say. Now if you'll excuse me, I'll go and see if the doctor's still about."

" 'E's still about." The landlord shook his head. "But ol' Doc Sillitoe from Saxmundham's dead now. Fell off 'is 'orse and cracked 'is 'ead wide open."

"I'm sorry to hear it." Monk went out and turned left along the road, trusting memory and good luck would find the right house for him. Everyone knew where the doctor lived.

He spent that day and the following one in Yoxford. He spoke to the doctor and to both Jack Worth's sons, now in possession of his farm; the police constable, who greeted him with fear and embarrassment, eager to please him even now;

and to his landlord for the night. He learned much about his first investigation which was not recorded in his notes, but none of it struck any chord in memory except a vague familiarity with a house or a view along a street, a great tree against the sky or the wave of the land. There was nothing sharp, no emotion except a sort of peace at the beauty of the place, the calm skies filled with great clouds sailing across the width of heaven in towers like splashed and ruffled snow, the green of the land, deep huddled oaks and elms, the hedges wide, tangled with wild roses and dappled with cow parsley that some of the locals called ladies' lace. The may blossom was heavy and its rich scent reached out and clung around him. The flowering chestnuts raised myriad candles to the sun, and already the corn was springing green and strong.

But it was utterly impersonal. He felt no lurch of emotion, no tearing inside that loss or drowning loneliness was ahead.

His retraced footsteps taught him that he had been hard on the local constable, critical of the inability to collect evidence and deduce facts from it. He rued his harsh words but it was too late to undo them now. He did not know exactly what he had said; only the man's nervousness and his repeated apologies, his eagerness to please made the past obvious. Why had he been so harsh? He might have been accurate, but it was unnecessary, and had not made the man a better detective, only hurt him. What did he need to be a detective for, here in a tiny village where the worst he would deal with would be a few drunken quarrels, a little poaching, the occasional petty theft? But to apologize now would be absurd, and do no good. The harm was done. He could not ease his conscience with belated patronage.

It was from the local doctor, unprepared to see him back, and full of respect, that he learned how unremitting had been his pursuit of the case and how his attention to detail, his observation of mannerisms and subtle, intuitive guesses had finally learned the poison used, the unsuspected lover who had driven Margery to rid herself of her husband, and sent her to her own early death.

"Brilliant," the doctor had said again, shaking his head.

"Brilliant, you were, and no mistake. Never used to 'ave time for Lunnon folk myself, before that. But you surely showed us a thing or two." He eyed Monk with interest untouched by liking. "And bought that picture from Squire Leadbetter for a pretty penny. Spent your money like you 'ad no end of it, you did. Folks still talk about it."

"Bought the picture . . . ?" Monk frowned, trying to recall. There was no picture of any great beauty among his things. Had he given it to the woman?

"Lord bless me, don't you remember?" The doctor looked amazed, his sandy eyebrows raised in incredulity. "Cost more'n I make in a month, it did, an' no mistake. I suppose you were that pleased with yourself in your case. An' it was a clever piece o' work, I'll give you that. We all knew no one else could 'ave done it, an' p'raps the poor creature got all she deserved, God forgive 'er."

And that was the final seal on his disappointment. If he had gone out and committed some extravagance, of which he now had no trace, to celebrate his success in the case, he could hardly have anguished over Margery Worth's death. This was another ruthlessly brilliant case for Inspector Monk, but it was no clue to the woman who trespassed again and again into his mind these days, who intruded when he thought of Alexandra Carlyon, and who stirred in him such memories of loneliness, of hope, and of having struggled so hard to help her, and not knowing now whether he had failed or succeeded, or how—or even why.

It was late. He thanked the doctor, stayed one more night, and on the morning of Thursday the eleventh, caught the earliest train back to London. He was tired not by physical effort, but by disappointment and a crowding sense of guilt, because he had less than two weeks left before the trial, and he had wasted over two days pursuing a wild goose of his own. Now he still had no idea why Alexandra had killed the general, or what he could tell Oliver Rathbone to help him.

In the afternoon he used the permission Rathbone had obtained for him and went again to the prison to see Alexandra. Even as he was going in the vast gates and the gray walls towered over him, he had little idea what he could say to her beyond what he or Rathbone had already said, but he had to try at least one more time. It was June 11, and on June 22 the trial was to begin.

Was this history repeating itself—another fruitless attempt with time running out, scrambling for evidence to save a woman from her own acts?

He found her in the same attitude, sitting on the cot, shoulders hunched, staring at the wall but seeing something in her own mind. He wished he knew what it was.

"Mrs. Carlyon . . ."

The door slammed behind him and they were alone.

She looked up, a slight flicker of surprise over her face as she recognized him. If she had expected anyone, it must have been Rathbone. She was thinner than last time, wearing the same blouse, but the fabric of it pulled tighter, showing the bones of her shoulders. Her face was very pale. She did not speak.

"Mrs. Carlyon, we have only a short time left. It is too late to deal in pleasantries and evasions. Only the truth will serve now."

"There is only one truth that matters, Mr. Monk," she said wearily. "And that is that I killed my husband. There are no other truths they will care about. Please don't pretend otherwise. It is absurd—and doesn't help."

He stood still in the middle of the small stone floor, staring down at her.

"They might care why you did it!" he said with a hard edge to his voice, "if you stopped lying about it. You are not mad. There was some reason behind it. Either you had a quarrel there at the top of the stairs, and you lunged at him and pushed him over backwards, and then when he fell you were still so possessed with rage you ran down the stairs after him and as he lay on the floor, tangled in the suit of armor in its pieces, you picked up the halberd and finished him off." He watched her face and saw her eyes widen and her mouth wince, but she did not look away from him. "Or else you planned it beforehand and led him to the stairs deliberately, intending to push him over. Perhaps you hoped he would break his neck in the fall, and you went down after him to make sure he had. Then when you found he was relatively unhurt, you used the halberd to do what the fall had failed to.''

"You are wrong,'' she said flatly. "I didn't think of it until we were standing at the top of the stairs—oh, I wanted to find a way. I meant to kill him some time, I just hadn't thought of the stairs until then. And when he stood there at the top, with his back to the banister and that drop behind him, and I knew he would never . . .'' She stopped and the flicker of light which had been in her blue eyes died. She looked away from him.

"I pushed him,'' she went on. "And when he went over and hit the armor I thought he was dead. I went down quite slowly. I thought it was the end, all finished. I expected people to come, because of the noise of the armor going over. I was going to say he fell—overbalanced.'' Her face showed a momentary surprise. "But no one came. Not even any of the servants, so I suppose no one heard after all. When I looked at him, he was senseless, but he was still alive. His breathing was quite normal.'' She sighed and the muscles of her jaw tightened. "So I picked up the halberd and ended it. I knew I would never have a better chance. But you are wrong if you think I planned it. I didn't—not then or in that way.''

He believed her. He had no doubt that what she said was the truth.

"But why?'' he said again. "It wasn't over Louisa Furnival, or any other woman, was it?''

She stood up and turned her back to him, staring at the tiny single window, high in the wall and barred against the sky.

"It doesn't matter.''

"Have you ever seen anyone hanged, Mrs. Carlyon?'' It was brutal, but if he could not reason her into telling him, then there was little left but fear. He hated doing it. He saw her body tighten and the hands by her sides clench. Had he done this before? It brought no memory. Everything in his mind was Alexandra, the present, the death of Thaddeus Carlyon and no one else, no other time or place. "It's an ugly thing. They don't always die immediately. They take you from the cell to the yard where the noose is . . ." He swallowed hard. Execution repelled him more than any other act he knew of, because it was sanctioned by law. People would contemplate it, commit it, watch it and feel justified. They would gather together in groups and congratulate each other on its completion and say that they upheld civilization.

She stood without moving, thin and slight, her body painfully rigid.

"They lay the rope 'round your neck, after they have put a hood over your head, so you can't see it—that's what they say it is for. Actually I think it is so they cannot see you. Perhaps if they could look at your face, your eyes, they couldn't do it themselves."

"Stop it!" she said between her teeth. "I know I will hang. Do you have to tell me every step to the gallows rope so I do it more than once in my mind?"

He wanted to shake her, to reach out and take her by the arms, force her to turn around and face him, look at him. But it would only be an assault, pointless and stupid, perhaps closing the last door through which he might yet find something to help her.

"Did you try to stab him once before?" he asked suddenly.

She looked startled. "No! Whatever makes you think that?"

"The knife wound in his thigh."

"Oh that. No—he did that himself, showing off for Valentine Furnival."

"I see."

She said nothing.

"Is it blackmail?" he said quietly. "Is there someone who holds some threat over you?"

"No."

"Tell me! Perhaps we can stop them. At least let me try."

"There is no one. What more could anyone do to me than the law will already do?"

"Nothing to you—but to someone you love? Sabella?"

"No." There was a lift in her voice, almost like a bitter laugh, had she the strength left for it.

He did not believe her. Was this it at last? She was prepared to die to protect Sabella, in some way they had not yet imagined.

He looked at her stiff back and knew she would not tell him. He would still have to find out, if he could. There were twelve days left before the trial.

"I won't stop trying," he said gently. "You'll not hang if I can prevent it—whether you wish me to or not. Good day, Mrs. Carlyon."

"Good-bye, Mr. Monk."

That evening Monk dined with Evan again and told him of his abortive trip to Suffolk, and Evan gave him notes of one more case which might have been the woman he had tried so hard to save. But tonight his mind was still on Alexandra, and the incomprehensible puzzle she presented.

The following day he went to Vere Street and told Oliver Rathbone of his interview in the prison, and his new thoughts. Rathbone was surprised, and then after a moment's hesitation, more hopeful than he had been for some time. It was at least an idea which made some sense.

That evening he opened the second set of notes Evan had given him and looked at them. This was the case about Phyllis Dexter, of Shrewsbury, who had knifed her husband to death. The Shrewsbury police had had no trouble establishing the facts. Adam Dexter was a large man, a heavy drinker and known to get into the occasional brawl, but no one had heard that he had beaten his wife, or in any other way treated her more roughly than most men. Indeed, he seemed in his own way quite fond of her.

On his death the local police had been puzzled as to how they might prove, one way or the other, whether Phyllis was speaking the truth. All their efforts, expended over the first week, had left them no wiser than at the beginning. They had sent for Scotland Yard, and Runcorn had dispatched Monk.

The notes were plain that Monk had interviewed Phyllis herself, immediate neighbors who might have heard a quarrel or threat, the doctor who had examined the body, and of course the local police.

Apparently he had remained in Shrewsbury for three weeks, going relentlessly over and over the same ground until he found a weakness here, a change of emphasis there, the possibility of a different interpretation or a shred of new evidence. Runcorn had sent for him to come back; everything they had indicated guilt, and justice should be allowed to take its course, but Monk had defied him and remained.

Eventually he had pieced together a story, with the most delicate of proof, that Phyllis Dexter had had three miscarriages and two stillbirths, and had eventually refused her husband's attentions because she could no longer bear the pain it caused her. In a drunken fury at her rejection, as if it were of him, not of her pain, he had attempted to force her. On this occasion his sense of outrage had driven him to assault her with the broken end of a bottle, and she had defended herself with the carving knife. In his clumsiness he had got the worst of the brief battle, and within moments of his first charge, he lay dead on the floor, the knife in his chest and the broken bottle shattered—a scatter of shards over the floor.

There was no note as to the outcome of the case. Whether the Shrewsbury police had accepted Monk's deduction or not was not noted. Nor was there any record as to a trial.

There was nothing for Monk to do but purchase a ticket and take the train to Shrewsbury. The people there at least would remember such a case, even if few others did.

On the late afternoon of the thirteenth, in golden sunlight, Monk alighted at Shrewsbury station and made his way through the ancient town with its narrow streets and magnificent Elizabethan half-timbered houses to the police station.

The desk sergeant's look of polite enquiry turned to one of wary self-defense, and Monk knew he had been recognized, and not with pleasure. He felt himself harden inside, but he could not justify himself because he had no memory of what he had done. It was a stranger with his face who had been here four years before.

"Well, Mr. Monk, I'm sure I don't know," the desk sergeant said to his enquiry. "That case is all over and done with. We thought as she was guilty, but you proved as she weren't! It's not for us to say, but it don't do for a woman to go murderin' 'er 'usband because she takes it into 'er 'ead as to refuse 'im what's 'is by right. Puts ideas of all sorts in women's 'eads. We'll have them murderin' their 'usbands all over the place!"

"You're quite right," Monk said tartly.

The desk sergeant looked surprised, and pleased.

"It's not for you to say," Monk finished.

The sergeant's face tightened and his skin flushed red.

"Well I don't know what you'll be wanting from us. If you'd be so good as to tell me, I'll mebbe see what I can do for you."

"Do you know where Phyllis Dexter is now?" Monk asked.

The sergeant's eyes lit with satisfaction.

"Yes I do. She left these parts right after the trial. Acquitted, she was; walked out o' the courtroom and packed 'er things that night."

"Do you know where she went?" Monk kept his temper with difficulty. He would like to wipe the smug smile off the man's face.

The man's satisfaction wavered. He met Monk's eyes and his courage drained away.

"Yes sir. I heard as it were somewhere in France. I don't rightly know where, but there's them in the town as can tell you, I expect. At least where she went to from 'ere. As to where she is now, I expect being the detective you are, you'll be able to learn that when you get there."

There was nothing more to be learned here, so Monk duly thanked him and took his leave.

He spent the evening at the Bull Inn and in the morning went to find the doctor who had been concerned in the case. He went with some trepidation. Apparently he had made himself unpopular here; the desk sergeant's aggression had been born of those weeks of fear and probably some humiliation as well. Monk knew his own behavior at his station in London under Runcorn, his sarcastic tongue, his impatience with men of less ability than himself. He was not proud of it.

He walked down the street where the doctor's house was and found with a sharp sense of satisfaction that he knew it. The particular pattern of beams and plastering was familiar. There was no need to look for the name or a number; he could remember being here before.

With excitement catching in his throat he knocked on the door. It seemed an age before it was answered by an aged man with a game leg. Monk could hear it dragging on the floor. His white hair was thinly plastered across his skull and his teeth were broken, but his face lit with pleasure as soon as his eyes focused on Monk.

"My, if it in't Mr. Monk back again!" he said in a cracked falsetto voice. "Well bless my soul! What brings you back to these parts? We in't 'ad no more murders! Least, not that I knows of. 'Ave we?"

"No Mr. Wraggs, I don't think so." Monk was elated to an absurd degree that the old man was so pleased to see him, and that he in turn could recall his name. "I'm here on a private matter, to see the doctor, if I may?"

"Ah no, sir." Wraggs's face fell. "You're never poorly, are you, sir? Come in and set yourself down, then. I'll get you a drop o' summink!"

"No, no, Mr. Wraggs, I'm very well, thank you," Monk said hastily. "I just want to see him as a friend, not professionally."

"Ah, well." The old man breathed a sigh of relief. "That's all right then! Still, come on in just the same. Doctor's out on a call right now, but 'e'll be back by an' by. Now what can I get you, Mr. Monk? You just name it, and if we got it, it's yours."

It would have been churlish to refuse so generous an offer.

"Well, I'll have a glass of cider, and a slice of bread and cheese, if you've got it," he accepted.

" 'Course we got it!" Wraggs said delightedly, and led the way in, hobbling lopsidedly ahead of Monk into the parlor.

Monk wondered with a silent blessing what kindness he had shown this old man that he was so welcome here, but he could not ask. He hoped profoundly it was not simply the old man's nature that was so blithely giving, and he was glad he could not put it to the test. Instead he accepted the hospitality and sat talking with him for well over an hour until the doctor returned. Actually in that space he learned from him almost all he wished to know. Phyllis Dexter had been a very pretty woman with soft honey-brown hair and golden brown eyes, a gentle manner and a nice wit. Opinion in the town had been violently divided about her innocence or guilt. The police had felt her guilty, as had the mayor and many of the gentry. The doctor and the parson had taken her side, so had the innkeeper, who had had more than enough of Adam Dexter's temper and sullen complaints. Wraggs was emphatic that Monk himself had pursued his enquiries night and day, bullying, exhorting, pleading with witnesses, driving himself to exhaustion, sitting up into the small hours of the morning poring over the statements and the evidence till his eyes were red.

"She owes 'er life to you, Mr. Monk, and no mistake," Wraggs said with wide eyes. "A rare fighter you were. No woman, nor man neither, ever had a better champion in their cause, I'll swear to that on my Bible oath, I will."

"Where did she go to, Mr. Wraggs, when she left here?"

"Ah, that she didn't tell no one, poor soul!" Wraggs shook his head. "An' who can blame 'er, I ask you, after what some folk said."

Monk's heart sank. After the hope, the warmth of Wraggs's welcome and the sudden sight of some better part of himself, it had all slipped away again.

"You've no idea?" He was horrified to hear a catch in his voice.

"No sir, none at all." Wraggs peered at him with anxiety

and sorrow in his old eyes. "Thanked you with tears, she did, an' then just packed 'er things and went. Funny, you know, but I thought as you knew where she'd gone, 'cause I 'ad a feeling as you 'elped her go! But there, I suppose I must a' bin wrong."

"France—the desk sergeant in the police station said he thought it was France."

"Well I shouldn't wonder." Wraggs nodded his head. "Poor lady would want to be out o' England, now wouldn't she, after all what folks said about 'er!"

"If she went south, who would know where she was?" Monk said reasonably. "She would take a new name and be lost in the crowd."

"Ah no sir, not hardly. Not with the pictures of her in the newspapers! An' 'andsome as she was, people'd soon see the likeness. No, better she go abroad. And I for one hopes she's found a place for 'erself."

"Pictures?"

"Yes sir—all in the illustrated news they was. Here, don't you remember? I'll get it for you. We kept them all." And without waiting for Monk he scrambled to his feet and went over to the desk in the corner. He rummaged around for several minutes, then came back proudly holding a piece of paper which he put in front of Monk.

It was a clear picture of a remarkably pretty woman of perhaps twenty-five or twenty-six, with wide eyes and a long, delicate face. Seeing it he remembered her quite clearly. Emotion came back: pity, some admiration, anger at the pain she had endured and at people's ignorance and refusal to understand it, determination that he would see her acquitted, intense relief when he had succeeded, and a quiet happiness. But nothing more; no love, no despair—no haunting, persistent memory.

8

By JUNE 15 there was a bare week to go before the trial commenced and the newspapers had again taken up the subject. There was much speculation as to what would be revealed, surprise witnesses for the defense, for the prosecution, revelations about character. Thaddeus Carlyon had been a hero, and his murder in such circumstances shocked people profoundly. There must be some explanation which would provide an answer and restore the balance of their beliefs.

Hester dined again at the Carlyon house, not because she was considered a close enough friend of the family to be welcome even at such a time, but because it was she who had recommended Oliver Rathbone, and they all now wished to know something more about him and what he was likely to do to try and defend Alexandra.

It was an uncomfortable meal. Hester had accepted although she could not tell them anything of Rathbone, except his integrity and his past success, which presumably at least Peverell already knew. But she still hoped she might learn some tiny shred of fact which would, together with other things, lead to Alexandra's true motive. Anything about the general surely ought to be useful in some fashion?

"I wish I knew more about this man Rathbone," Randolf

said morosely, staring down the length of the table at no one in particular. "Who is he? Where does he come from?"

"What on earth does that matter, Papa?" Edith said, blinking at him. "He's the best there is. If anyone can help Alexandra, he will."

"Help Alexandra!" He faced her angrily, his eyes wide, his brows furrowed. "My dear girl, Alexandra murdered your brother because she had some insane idea he was amorously involved with another woman. If he had been, she should have borne it like a lady and kept her silence, but as we all know, he was not." His voice was thick with distress. "There is nothing in the world more unbecoming in a woman than jealousy. It has been the curse of many an otherwise more than acceptable character. That she should carry it to the extreme of murder, and against one of the finest men of his generation, is a complete tragedy."

"What we need to know," Felicia said very quietly, "is what kind of implications and suggestions he is likely to make to try and defend her." She turned to Hester. "You are familiar with the man, Miss Latterly." She caught Damaris's eye. "I beg your pardon," she said stiffly. "*Familiar* was an unfortunate choice of word. That was not what I intended." She blinked; her wide eyes were cold and direct. "You are sufficiently acquainted with him to have recommended him to us. To what degree can you answer for his . . . his moral decency? Can you assure us that he will not attempt to slander our son's character in order to make there seem to be some justification for his wife having murdered him?"

Hester was taken aback. This was not what she had expected, but after only an instant's thought she appreciated their view. It was not a foolish question.

"I am not answerable for his conduct in any way, Mrs. Carlyon," she replied gravely. "He is not employed by any of us here, but by Alexandra herself." She was acutely conscious of Felicia's grief. The fact that she could not like her did not lessen her awareness of its reality, or her pity for it. "But it would not be in her interest to make any charge against the general that could not be substantiated with proof," she went on. "I believe it would predispose the jury against her. But quite apart from that, had the general been the most totally wretched, inconsiderate, coarse and vile man, unless he threatened her life, or that of her child, it would be pointless to raise it, because it would be no excuse for killing him."

Felicia sat back in her chair, her face calmer.

"That is good, and I presume in the circumstances, certainly all we can hope for. If he has any sense, he will claim she is insane and throw her on the mercy of the court." She swallowed hard and her chin lifted; her eyes were wide and very blue. She looked ahead of her, at no one. "Thaddeus was a considerate man, a gentleman in every way." Her voice was harsh with emotion. "He never raised a hand against her, even when at times she sorely provoked him. And I know she did. She has been flighty, inconsiderate, and refused to understand the necessity of his leaving her when his career took him abroad in the life to which he dedicated himself for the service of his Queen and country."

"You should see some of the letters of condolence we have received," Randolf added with a sigh. "Only this morning one came from a sergeant who used to be in the Indian army with him. Just heard, poor fellow. Devastated. Said Thaddeus was the finest officer he ever served with. Spoke of his courage, his inspiration to the men." He blinked hard and his head sank a little lower. His voice became thicker, and Hester was not sure whether it was purely from grief or grief mixed with self-pity. "Said how he had kept all the men cheerful when they were pinned down by a bunch of savages, howling like demons." He was staring into the distance as if he saw not the sideboard with the elaborate Coalport china on it, but some baking plain under an Indian sun. "Almost out of ammunition, they were, and waiting to die. Said Thaddeus gave them heart, made them proud to be British and give their lives for the Queen." He sighed again.

Peverell smiled sadly. Edith pulled a face, partly sorrow, partly embarrassment.

"That must be a great comfort to you," Hester said, then

found it sounded hollow the moment her words were out. "I mean to know that he was so admired."

"We knew it anyway," Felicia said without looking at her. "Everyone admired Thaddeus. He was a leader among men. His officers thought he was a hero, his troops would follow him anywhere. Had the gift of command, you see?" She looked at Hester, eyes wide. "He knew how to inspire loyalty because he was always fair. He punished cowardice and dishonesty; he praised courage and honor, and duty. He never denied a man his right, and never charged a man unless he was sure that man was guilty. He kept total discipline, but the men loved him for it."

"Have to in the army," Randolf added, glaring at Hester. "Do you know what happens when there is no discipline, girl? Army falls to pieces under fire. Every man for himself. Un-British! Frightful! A soldier must obey his superior at all times—instantly."

"Yes I do know," Hester said without thinking, but from the depth of her own feeling. "Sometimes it's glorious, and sometimes it's unmitigated disaster."

Randolf's face darkened. "What the devil do you mean, girl? What on earth do you know about it? Damned impertinence! I'll have you know I fought in the Peninsular War, and at Waterloo against the emperor of the French, and beat him too."

"Yes, Colonel Carlyon." She met his eyes without flinching. She felt a pity for him as a man; he was old, bereaved, muddle-headed and becoming more than a little maudlin. But soldierlike she stood her ground. "And magnificent campaigns they were, none more brilliant in all our history. But times have changed. And some of our commanders have not changed with them. They fought the Crimea with the same tactics, and they were not good enough. A soldier's blind obedience is only as good as his commander's knowledge of the situation and skill in combat."

"Thaddeus was brilliant," Felicia said icily. "He never lost a major campaign and no soldier forfeited his life because of any incompetence of his."

"Certainly not," Randolf added, and slid a fraction farther down in his seat, hiccuping.

"We all know he was a very good soldier, Papa," Edith said quietly. "And I am glad that men who served with him have written to say how grieved they are he is gone. It is a wonderful thing to have been so admired."

"He was more than admired," Felicia said quickly. "He was also loved."

"The obituaries have been excellent," Peverell put in. "Few men have had their passing marked by such respect."

"It is appalling that this whole disaster was ever allowed to progress this far," Felicia said with a tight expression in her face, blinking as if to avoid tears.

"I don't know what you mean." Damaris looked at her perplexedly. "Progress to what?"

"To trial, of course." Felicia's face puckered with anger and distress. "It should have been dealt with long before it ever got so far." She turned to Peverell. "I blame you for that. I expected you to cope with it and see that Thaddeus's memory was not subjected to vulgar speculation; and that Alexandra's madness, and it must be said, wickedness, was not made a public sensation for the worst elements of humanity to revel in. As a lawyer, you should have been able to do it, and as a member of this family, I would have thought your loyalty to us would have seen that you did."

"That's unfair," Damaris said immediately, her face hot and her eyes bright. "Just because one is a lawyer does not mean one can do anything one likes with the law. In fact just the opposite. Peverell has a trust towards the law, an obligation, which none of the rest of us have. I don't know what you think he could have done!"

"I think he could have certified Alexandra as insane and unfit to stand trial," Felicia snapped. "Instead of encouraging her to get a lawyer who will drag all our lives before the public and expose all our most private emotions to the gaze of the common people so they can decide something we all know anyway—that Alexandra murdered Thaddeus. For God's sake, she doesn't deny it!"

251

Cassian sat white-faced, his eyes on his grandmother.

"Why?" he said, a very small voice in the silence.

Hester and Felicia spoke at once.

"We don't know," Hester said.

"Because she is sick," Felicia cut across her. She turned to Cassian. "There are sicknesses of the body and sicknesses of the mind. Your mother is ill in her brain, and it caused her to do a very dreadful thing. It is best you try not to think of it, ever again." She reached out towards him tentatively, then changed her mind. "Of course it will be difficult, but you are a Carlyon, and you are brave. Think of your father, what a great man he was and how proud he was of you. Grow up to be like him." For a moment her voice caught, too thick with tears to continue. Then she mastered herself with an effort so profound it was painfully visible. "You can do that. We shall help you, your grandfather and I, and your aunts."

Cassian said nothing, but turned and looked very carefully at his grandfather, his eyes somber. Then slowly he smiled, a shy, uncertain smile, and his eyes filled with tears. He sniffed hard, swallowed, and everyone turned away from him so as not to intrude.

"Will they call him at the trial?" Damaris asked anxiously.

"Of course not." Felicia dismissed the idea as absurd. "What on earth could he know?"

Damaris turned to Peverell, her eyes questioning.

"I don't know," he answered. "But I doubt it."

Felicia stared at him. "Well for heaven's sake do something useful! Prevent it! He is only eight years old!"

"I cannot prevent it, Mama-in-law," he said patiently. "If either the prosecution or the defense wishes to call him, then the judge will decide whether Cassian is competent to give evidence or not. If the judge decides he is, then Cassian will do so."

"You shouldn't have allowed it to come to trial," she repeated furiously. "She has confessed. What good can it do anyone to parade the whole wretched affair before a court? They will hang her anyway." Her eyes hardened and she

252

glanced across the table. "And don't look at me like that, Damaris! The poor child will have to know one day. Perhaps it is better we don't lie to him, and he knows now. But if Peverell had seen to it that she was put away in Bedlam, it wouldn't be necessary to face the problem at all."

"How could he do that?" Damaris demanded. "He isn't a doctor."

"I don't think she is mad anyway," Edith interrupted.

"Be quiet," Felicia snapped. "Nobody wants to know what you think. Why would a sane woman murder your brother?"

"I don't know," Edith admitted. "But she has a right to defend herself. And Peverell, or anyone else, ought to wish that she gets it . . ."

"Your brother should be your first concern," Felicia said grimly. "And the honor of your family your next. I realize you were very young when he first left home and went into the army, but you knew him. You were aware what a brave and honorable man he was." Her voice quivered for the first time in Hester's hearing. "Have you no love in you? Does his memory mean no more to you than some smart intellectual exercise in what is legally this or that? Where is your natural feeling, girl?"

Edith flushed hotly, her eyes miserable.

"I cannot help Thaddeus now, Mama."

"Well you certainly cannot help Alexandra," Felicia added.

"We know Thaddeus was a good man," Damaris said gently. "Of course Edith knows it. But she is a lot younger, and she never knew him as I did. He was always just a strange young man in a soldier's uniform whom everyone praised. But I know how kind he could be, and how understanding. And although he disciplined his men in the army, and made no allowances or bent any rules, with other people he could be quite different, I know. He was . . ." Suddenly she stopped, gave a funny little half smile, half sigh, and bit her lip. There was intense pain in her face. She avoided Peverell's eyes.

"We are aware of your appreciation of your brother, Damaris," Felicia said very quietly. "But I think you have said enough. That particular episode is far better not discussed—I'm sure you agree?"

Randolf looked confused. He started to speak, then stopped again. No one was listening to him anyway.

Edith looked from Damaris to her mother and back again.

Peverell made as if to say something to his wife, but she looked everywhere but at him, and he changed his mind.

Damaris stared at her mother as if some realization almost beyond belief had touched her. She blinked, frowned, and remained staring.

Felicia met her gaze with a small, wry smile, quite unwavering.

Gradually the amazement waned and another even more powerful emotion filled Damaris's long, sensitive, turbulent face, and Hester was almost sure it was fear.

"Ris?" Edith said tentatively. She was confused as to the reason, but aware that her sister was suffering in some fierce, lonely way, and she wanted to help.

"Of course," Damaris said slowly, still staring at her mother. "I wasn't going to discuss it." She swallowed hard. "I was just remembering that Thaddeus could be . . . very kind. It seemed . . . it seemed an appropriate time to—think of it."

"You have thought of it," Felicia pointed out. "It would have been better had you done so silently, but since you have not, I should consider the matter closed, if I were you. We all appreciate your words on your brother's virtues."

"I don't know what you are talking about," Randolf said sulkily.

"Kindness." Felicia looked at him with weary patience. "Damaris is saying that Thaddeus was on occasion extremely kind. It is not always remembered of him, when we are busy saying what a brave soldier he was." Then again without warning emotion flooded her face. "All a man's good qualities should be remembered, not just the public ones," she finished huskily.

"Of course." He frowned at her, aware that he had been sidetracked, but not sure how, still less why. "No one denies it."

Felicia considered the matter sufficiently explained. If he did not understand, it was quite obvious she did not intend to enlighten him. She turned to Hester, her emotion gone, her expression perfectly controlled.

"Miss Latterly. Since, as my husband has said, jealousy is one of the ugliest and least sympathetic of all human emotions, and becomes a woman even less than a man, can you tell us what manner of defense this Mr. Rathbone intends to put forward?" She looked at Hester with the same cool, brave face she might have presented to the judge himself. "I imagine he is not going to be rash enough to attempt to lay the blame elsewhere, and say she did not do it at all?"

"That would be pointless," Hester answered, aware that Cassian was watching her with a guarded, almost hostile expression. "She has confessed, and there is unarguable proof that she did it. The defense must rest in the circumstances, the reason why."

"Indeed." Felicia's eyebrows rose very high. "And just what sort of a reason does this Mr. Rathbone believe would excuse such an act? And how does he propose to prove it?"

"I don't know." Hester faced her pretending a confidence far from anything she felt. "It is not my prerogative to know, Mrs. Carlyon. I have no part in this tragedy, other than as a friend of Edith's, and I hope of yours. I mentioned Mr. Rathbone's name to you before I knew that there was no question that Alexandra was guilty of the act. But even had I known it, I would still have told you, because she needs a lawyer to speak for her, whatever her situation."

"She does not need someone to persuade her to fight a hopeless cause," Felicia said acidly. "Or lead her to imagine that she can avoid her fate. That is an unnecessary cruelty, Miss Latterly, tormenting some poor creature and stringing out its death in order to entertain the crowd!"

Hester blushed hotly, but there was far too much guilt in her for her to find any denial.

255

It was Peverell who came to her rescue.

"Would you have every accused person put to death quickly, Mama-in-law, to save them the pain of struggle? I doubt that that is what they would choose."

"And how would you know that?" she demanded. "It might well have been exactly what Alexandra would choose. Only you have all taken that opportunity away from her with your interference."

"We offered her a lawyer," Peverell replied, refusing to back away. "We have not told her how to plead."

"Then you should have. Perhaps if she had pleaded guilty then this whole sorry business would be over with. Now we shall have to go into court and conduct ourselves with all the dignity we can muster. I presume you will be testifying, since you were there at that wretched party?"

"Yes. I have no choice."

"For the prosecution?" she enquired.

"Yes."

"Well at least if you go, one imagines Damaris will be spared. That is something. I don't know what you can possibly tell them that will be of use." There was half a question in her voice, and Hester knew, watching her tense face and brilliant eyes, that she was both asking Peverell what he intended saying, and warning him of family loyalties, trusts, unspoken ties that were deeper than any single occasion could test or break.

"Neither do I, Mama-in-law," he agreed. "Presumably only my observations as to who was where at any particular time. And maybe the fact that Alex and Thaddeus did seem to be at odds with each other. And Louisa Furnival took Thaddeus upstairs alone, and Alex seemed extraordinarily upset about it."

"You'll tell them that?" Edith said, horrified.

"I shall have to, if they ask me," he said apologetically. "That is what I saw."

"But Pev—"

He leaned forward. "My dear, they already know it.

Maxim and Louisa were there, and they will say that. And Fenton Pole, and Charles and Sarah Hargrave . . .''

Damaris was very pale. Edith buried her face in her hands.

"This is going to be awful."

"Of course it is going to be awful," Felicia said thickly. "That is the reason why we must think carefully what we are going to say beforehand, speak only the truth, say nothing malicious or undignified, whatever we may feel, answer only what we are asked, exactly and precisely, and at all times remember who we are!"

Damaris swallowed convulsively.

Cassian stared at her with huge eyes, his lips parted.

Randolf sat up a trifle straighter.

"Offer no opinions," Felicia continued. "Remember that the vulgar press will write down everything you say, and quite probably distort it. That you cannot help. But you can most certainly help your deportment, your diction, and the fact that you do not lie, prevaricate, giggle, faint, weep or otherwise disgrace yourself by being less than the ladies you are—or the gentlemen, as the case is. Alexandra is the one who is accused, but the whole family will be on trial."

"Thank you, my dear." Randolf looked at her with a mixture of obligation, gratitude and an awe which for one ridiculous moment Hester imagined was akin to fear. "As always you have done what is necessary."

Felicia said nothing. A flicker of pain passed across her rigid features, but it was gone again almost as soon as it was there. She did not indulge in such things; she could not afford to.

"Yes, Mama," Damaris said obediently. "We will all do our best to acquit ourselves with dignity and honesty."

"You will not be required," Felicia said, but there was a slight melting in her tone, and their eyes met for a moment. "But of course if you choose to attend, you will be noticed, and no doubt some busybody will recognize you as a Carlyon."

"Will I go, Grandmama?" Cassian asked, his face troubled.

"No, my dear, you will certainly not go. You will remain here with Miss Buchan."

"Won't Mama expect me to be there?"

"No, she will wish you to be here where you can be comfortable. You will be told all you need to know." She turned away from him to Peverell again and continued to discuss the general's last will and testament. It was a somewhat simple document that needed little explanation, but presumably she chose to argue it as a final closing of any other subject.

Everyone bent to continue with the meal, hitherto eaten entirely mechanically. Indeed Hester had no idea what any of the courses had been or even how many there were.

Now her mind turned to Damaris, and the intense, almost passionate emotion she had seen in her face, the swift play from sorrow to amazement to fear, and then the deep pain.

And according to Monk, several people had said she had behaved in a highly emotional manner on the evening of the general's death, bordering on the edge of hysteria, and been extremely offensive to Maxim Furnival.

Why? Peverell seemed to know nothing of its cause, nor had he been able to comfort her or offer any help at all.

Was it conceivable that she knew there was going to be violence, even murder? Or had she seen it? No—no one else had seen it, and Damaris had been distracted with some deep torment of her own long before Alexandra had followed Thaddeus upstairs. And why the rage at Maxim?

But then if the motive for the murder was something other than the stupid jealousy Alexandra had seized on, perhaps Damaris knew what it was? And knowing it, she might have foreseen it would end as it did.

Why had she said nothing? Why had she not trusted that Peverell and she together might have prevented it? It was perfectly obvious Peverell had no idea what troubled her; the expression in his eyes as he looked at her, the way he half spoke, and then fell silent, were all eloquent witness of that.

Was it the same horror, force, or fear that kept Alexandra silent even in the shadow of the hangman's rope?

In something of a daze Hester left the table and together

with Edith went slowly upstairs to her sitting room. Damaris and Peverell had their own wing of the house, and frequently chose to be there rather than in the main rooms with the rest of the family. Hester thought it was extremely long-suffering of Peverell to live in Carlyon House at all, but possibly he could not afford to keep Damaris in this style, or anything like it, otherwise. It was a curious side to Damaris's character that she did not prefer independence and privacy, at the relatively small price of a modest household, instead of this very lavish one. But then Hester had never been used to luxury, so she did not know how easy it was to become dependent upon it.

As soon as the door was closed in the sitting room Edith threw herself onto the largest sofa and pulled her legs up under her, regardless of the inelegance of the position and the ruination of her skirt. She stared at Hester, her curious face with its aquiline nose and gentle mouth filled with consternation.

"Hester—it's going to be terrible!"

"Of course it is," Hester agreed quietly. "Whatever the result, the trial is going to be ghastly. Someone was murdered. That can only ever be a tragedy, whoever did it, or why."

"Why . . ." Edith hugged her knees and stared at the floor. "We don't even know that, do we." It was not a question.

"We don't," Hester said thoughtfully, watching Edith's face. "But do you think Damaris might?"

Edith jerked up, her eyes wide. "Damaris? Why? How would she? Why do you say that?"

"She knew something that evening. She was almost distracted with emotion—on the verge of hysteria, they said."

"Who said? Pev didn't tell us."

"It doesn't seem as if he knew why," Hester replied. "But according to what Monk was able to find out, from quite early in the evening, long before the general was killed, Damaris was so frantic about something she could barely keep control of herself. I don't know why I didn't think of it before, but maybe she knew why Alexandra did it. Perhaps she even feared it would happen, before it did."

"But if she knew . . ." Edith said slowly, her face filled with distress and dawning horror. "No—she would have stopped it. Are you—are you saying Damaris was part of it?"

"No. No, certainly not," Hester denied quickly. "I mean she may have feared it would happen, because perhaps what caused her to be so terribly upset was the knowledge of why Alexandra would do such a thing. And if it is something so secret that Alexandra would rather hang than tell anyone, then I believe Damaris will honor her feelings and keep the secret for her."

"Yes," Edith agreed slowly, her face very white. "Yes, she would. It would be her sense of honor. But what could it be? I can't think of anything so—so terrible, so dark that . . ." She tailed off, unable to find words for the thought.

"Neither can I," Hester agreed. "But it exists—it must— or why will Alexandra not tell us why she killed the general?"

"I don't know." Edith bent her head to her knees.

There was a knock on the door, nervous and urgent.

Edith looked up, surprised. Servants did not knock.

"Yes?" She unwound herself and put her feet down. "Come in."

The door opened and Cassian stood there, his face pale, his eyes frightened.

"Aunt Edith, Miss Buchan and Cook are fighting again!" His voice was ragged and a little high. "Cook has a carving knife!"

"Oh—" Edith stifled an unladylike word and rose. Cassian took a step towards her and she put an arm around him. "Don't worry, I'll take care of it. You stay here. Hester . . ."

Hester was on her feet.

"Come with me, if you don't mind," Edith said urgently. "It may take two of us, if it's as bad as Cass says. Stay here, Cass! It will be all right, I promise!" And without waiting any further she led the way out of the sitting room, along

260

towards the back landing. Before they had reached the servants' stairs it was only too apparent that Cassian was right.

"You've no place 'ere, yer miserable old biddy! You should a' bin put out ter grass like the dried-up old mare yer are!"

"And you should have been left in the sty in the first place, you fat sow," came back the stinging reply.

"Fat indeed, is it? And what man'd look at you, yer withered old bag o' bones? No wonder yer spend yer life looking after other folks' children! Nobody'd ever get any on you!"

"And where are yours, then? Litters of them. One every season—running around on all fours in the byre, I shouldn't wonder. With snouts for noses and trotters for feet."

"I'll cut yer gizzard out, yer sour old fool! Ah!"

There was a shriek, then laughter.

"Oh damnation!" Edith said exasperatedly. "This sounds worse than usual."

"Missed!" came the crow of delight. "You drunken sot! Couldn't hit a barn door if it was in front of you—you cross-eyed pig!"

"Ah!"

Then a shriek from the kitchen maid and a shout from the footman.

Edith scrambled down the last of the stairs, Hester behind her. Almost immediately they saw them, the upright figure of Miss Buchan coming towards them, half sideways, half backwards, and a couple of yards away the rotund, red-faced cook, brandishing a carving knife in her hand.

"Vinegar bitch!" the cook shouted furiously, brandishing the knife at considerable risk to the footman, who was trying to get close enough to restrain her.

"Wine belly," Miss Buchan retorted, leaning forward.

"Stop it!" Edith shouted sternly. "Stop it at once!"

"Yer want to get rid of 'er." The cook stared at Edith but waved the knife at Miss Buchan. "She's no good for that poor boy. Poor little child."

Behind them the kitchen maid wailed again and stuffed the corners of her apron into her mouth.

"You don't know what you're talking about, you fat fool,"

Miss Buchan shouted back at her, her thin, sharp face full of fury. "All you do is stuff him full of cakes—as if that solved anything."

"Be quiet," Edith said loudly. "Both of you, be quiet at once!"

"And all you do is follow him around, you dried-up old witch!" The cook ignored Edith completely and went on shouting at Miss Buchan. "Never leave the poor little mite alone. I don't know what's the matter with you."

"Don't know," Miss Buchan yelled back at her. "Don't know. Of course you don't know, you stupid old glutton. You don't know anything. You never did."

"Neither do you, you miserable old baggage!" She waved the knife again, and the footman darted backwards, missing his step and overbalancing. "Sit up there all by yourself dreaming evil thoughts," the cook went on, oblivious of the other servants gathering in the passage. "And then come down here to decent folk, thinking you know something." She was well into her stride and Edith might as well not have been there. "You should 'ave bin born an 'undred years ago—then they'd 'ave burned you, they would. And served you right too. Poor little child. They shouldn't allow you anywhere near 'im."

"Ignorant you are," Miss Buchan cried back at her. "Ignorant as the pigs you look like—nothing but snuffle around all day eating and drinking. All you think about is your belly. You know nothing. Think if a child's got food on his plate he's got everything, and if he eats it he's well. Ha!" She looked around for something to throw, and since she was standing on the stairs, nothing came to hand. "Think you know everything, and you know nothing at all."

"Buckie, be quiet!" Edith shrieked.

"That's right, Miss Edith," the cook said, cheering her on. "You tell 'er to keep 'er wicked mouth closed! You should get rid of 'er! Put 'er out! Daft, she is. All them years with other folks' children have turned 'er wits. She's no good for that poor child. Lost 'is father and 'is mother, poor little mite, and now 'e 'as to put up with that old witch. It's enough

262

to drive 'im mad. D'yer know what she's bin tellin' 'im? Do yer?''

"No—nor do I want to," Edith said sharply. "You just be quiet!"

"Well you should know!" The cook's eyes were blazing and her hair was flying out of nearly all its pins. "An' if nobody else'll tell yer, I will! Got the poor little child so confused 'e don't know anything anymore. One minute 'is grandmama tells 'im 'is papa's dead and 'e's gotter ferget 'is mama because she's a madwoman what killed 'is papa an' will be 'anged for it. Which God 'elp us is the truth."

The footman had rearmed himself and approached her again. She backhanded him almost unconsciously.

"Then along comes that wizened-up ol' bag o' bones," she continued regardless, "an' tells 'im 'is mama loves 'im very much and in't a wicked woman at all. Wot's 'e to think?" Her voice was rising all the time. "Don't know whether 'e's comin' or goin', nor 'oo's good nor bad, nor what's the truth about anything." She finally took the damp dish towel out of her apron pocket and hurled it at Miss Buchan.

It hit Miss Buchan in the chest and slid to the floor. She ignored it completely. Her face was pale, her eyes glittering. Her thin, bony hands were knotted into fists.

"You ugly, interfering old fool," she shouted back. "You know nothing about it. You should stay with your pots and pans in the kitchen where you belong. Cleaning out the slop pots is your place. Scrubbing the pans, slicing the vegetables, food, food, food! Keep their stomachs full—you leave their minds to me."

"Buckie, what have you been saying to Master Cassian?" Edith asked her.

Miss Buchan went very white. "Only that his mother's not a wicked woman, Miss Edith. No child should be told his mother's wicked and doesn't love him."

"She murdered his father, you daft old bat!" the cook yelled at her. "They'll hang her for it! How's 'e goin' to understand that, if he doesn't know she's wicked, poor little creature?"

"We'll see," Miss Buchan said. "She's got the best lawyer in London. It's not over yet."

" 'Course it's over," the cook said, scenting victory. "They'll 'ang 'er, and so they should. What's the city coming to if women can murder their 'usbands any time they take a fancy to—and walk away with it?"

"There's worse things than killing people," Miss Buchan said darkly. "And you know nothing."

"That's enough!" Edith slipped between the two of them. "Cook, you are to go back to the kitchen and do your own job. Do you hear me?"

"She should be got rid of," the cook repeated, looking over Edith's shoulder at Miss Buchan. "You mark my words, Miss Edith, she's a—"

"That's enough." Edith took the cook by the arm and physically turned her around, pushing her down the stairs.

"Miss Buchan," Hester said quickly, "I think we should leave them. If there is to be any dinner in the house, the cook should get back to her duties."

Miss Buchan stared at her.

"And anyway," Hester went on, "I don't think there's really any point in telling her, do you? She isn't listening, and honestly I don't think she'd understand even if she were."

Miss Buchan hesitated, looking at her with slow consideration, then back at the retreating cook, now clasped firmly by Edith, then at Hester again.

"Come on," Hester urged. "How long have you known the cook? Has she ever listened to you, or understood what you were talking about?"

Miss Buchan sighed and the rigidity went out of her. She turned and walked back up the stairs with Hester. "Never," she said wearily. "Idiot," she said again under her breath.

They reached the landing and went on up again to the schoolroom floor and Miss Buchan's sitting room. Hester followed her in and closed the door. Miss Buchan went to the dormer window and stared out of it across the roof and into the branches of the trees, leaves moving in the wind against the sky.

Hester was not sure how to begin. It must be done very carefully, and perhaps so subtly that the actual words were never said. But perhaps, just perhaps, the truth was at last within her grasp.

"I'm glad you told Cassian not to think his mother was wicked," she said quietly, almost casually. She saw Miss Buchan's back stiffen. She must go very carefully. There was no retreat left now, nothing must be said in haste or unguardedly. Even in fury she had betrayed nothing, still less would she here, and to a stranger. "It is an unbearable thing for a child to think."

"It is," Miss Buchan agreed, still staring out of the window.

"Even though, as I understand it, he was closer to his father."

Miss Buchan said nothing.

"It is very generous of you to speak well of Mrs. Carlyon to him," Hester went on, hoping desperately that she was saying the right thing. "You must have had a special affection for the general—after all, you must have known him since his childhood." Please heaven her guess was right. Miss Buchan had been their governess, hadn't she?

"I had," Miss Buchan agreed quietly. "Just like Master Cassian, he was."

"Was he?" Hester sat down as if she intended to stay some time. Miss Buchan remained at the window. "You remember him very clearly? Was he fair, like Cassian?" A new thought came into her mind, unformed, indefinite. "Sometimes people seem to resemble each other even though their coloring or their features are not alike. It is a matter of gesture, mannerism, tone of voice . . ."

"Yes," Miss Buchan agreed, turning towards Hester, a half smile on her lips. "Thaddeus had just the same way of looking at you, careful, as if he were measuring you in his mind."

"Was he fond of his father too?" Hester tried to picture Randolf as a young man, proud of his only son, spending time with him, telling him about his great campaigns, and the boy's face lighting up with the glamour and the danger and the heroism of it.

"Just the same," Miss Buchan said with a strange, sad expression in her face, and a flicker of anger coming and going so rapidly Hester only just caught it.

"And to his mother?" Hester asked, not knowing what to say next.

Miss Buchan looked at her, then away again and out of the window, her face puckered with pain.

"Miss Felicia was different from Miss Alexandra," she said with something like a sob in her voice. "Poor creature. May God forgive her."

"And yet you find it in your heart to be sorry for her?" Hester said gently, and with respect.

"Of course," Miss Buchan replied with a sad little smile. "You know what you are taught, what everyone tells you is so. You are all alone. Who is there to ask? You do what you think—you weigh what you value most. Unity: one face to the outside world. Too much to lose, you see. She lacked the courage . . ."

Hester did not understand. She groped after threads of it, and the moment she had them the next piece made no sense. But how much dare she ask without risking Miss Buchan's rebuffing her and ceasing to talk at all? One word or gesture of seeming intrusion, a hint of curiosity, and she might withdraw altogether.

"It seems she had everything to lose, poor woman," she said tentatively.

"Not now," Miss Buchan replied with sudden bitterness. "It's all too late now. It's over—the harm is all done."

"You don't think the trial might make a difference?" Hester said with fading hope. "You sounded before as if you did."

Miss Buchan was silent for several minutes. Outside a gardener dropped a rake and the sound of the wood on the path came up through the open window.

"It might help Miss Alexandra," Miss Buchan said at last. "Please God it will, although I don't see how. But what will it do to the child? And God knows, it can't alter the past for anyone else. What's done is done."

Hester had a curious sensation, almost like a tingling in the brain. Suddenly shards of a pattern fell together, incomplete, vague, but with a tiny, hideous thread of sense.

"That is why she won't tell us," she said very slowly. "To protect the child?"

"Tell you?" Miss Buchan faced Hester, a pucker of confusion between her brows.

"Tell us the real reason why she killed the general."

"No—of course not," she said slowly. "How could she? But how did you know? No one told you."

"I guessed."

"She'll not admit it. God help her, she thinks that is all there is to it—just the one." Her eyes filled with tears of pity and helplessness, and she turned away again. "But I know there are others, of course there are. I knew it from his face, from the way he smiles, and tells lies, and cries at night." She spoke very quietly, her voice full of old pain. "He's frightened, and excited, and grown up, and a tiny child, and desperately, sickeningly alone, all at the same time like his father before him, God damn him!" Miss Buchan took a long, shuddering breath, so deep it seemed to rack her whole, thin body. "Can you save her, Miss Latterly?"

"I don't know," Hester said honestly. All the pity in the world now would not permit a lie. It was not the time. "But I will do everything I can—that I swear to you."

Without saying anything else she stood up and left the room, closing the door behind her and walking away towards the rest of the small rooms in the wing. She was looking for Cassian.

She found him standing in the corridor outside the door to his bedroom, staring up at her, his face pale, his eyes careful.

"You did the right thing to get Edith to stop the fight," she said matter-of-factly. "Do you like Miss Buchan?"

He continued to stare at her without speaking, his eyelids heavy, his face watchful and uncertain.

"Shall we go into your room?" she suggested. She was

not sure how she was going to approach the subject, but nothing now would make her turn back. The truth was almost reached, at least this part of it.

Wordlessly he turned around and opened the door. She followed him in. Suddenly she was furious that the burden of so much tragedy, guilt and death should rest on the narrow, fragile shoulders of such a child.

He walked over to the window; the light on his face showed the marks of tears on his soft, blemishless skin. His bones were still not fully formed, his nose just beginning to strengthen and lose its childish outline, his brows to darken.

"Cassian," she began quietly.

"Yes ma'am?" He looked at her, turning his head slowly.

"Miss Buchan was right, you know. Your mother is not a wicked person, and she does love you very much."

"Then why did she kill my papa?" His lip trembled and with great difficulty he stopped himself from crying.

"You loved your papa very much?"

He nodded, his hand going up to his mouth.

The rage inside her made her tremble.

"You had some special secrets with your papa, didn't you?"

His right shoulder came up and for an instant a half smile brushed over his mouth. Then there was fear in his eyes, a guarded look.

"I'm not going to ask you about it," she said gently. "Not if he told you not to tell anyone. Did he make you promise?"

He nodded again.

"That must have been very difficult for you?"

"Yes."

"Because you couldn't tell Mama?"

He looked frightened and backed away half a step.

"Was that important, not to tell Mama?"

He nodded slowly, his eyes on her face.

"Did you want to tell her, at first?"

He stood quite still.

Hester waited. Far outside she heard faint murmurs from the street, carriage wheels, a horse's hooves. Beyond the window the leaves flickered in the wind and threw patterns of light across the glass.

Slowly he nodded.

"Did it hurt?"

Again the long hesitation, then he nodded.

"But it was a very grown-up thing to do, and being a man of honor, you didn't tell anyone?"

He shook his head.

"I understand."

"Are you going to tell Mama? Papa said if she ever knew she'd hate me—she wouldn't love me anymore, she wouldn't understand, and she'd send me away. Is that what happened?" His eyes were very large, full of fear and defeat, as if in his heart he had already accepted it was true.

"No." She swallowed hard. "She went because they took her, not because of you at all. And I'm not going to tell her, but I think perhaps she knows already—and she doesn't hate you. She'll never hate you."

"Yes she will! Papa said so!" His voice rose in panic and he backed away from her.

"No she won't! She loves you very much indeed. So much she is prepared to do anything she can for you."

"Then why has she gone away? She killed Papa, Grandmama told me—and Grandpapa said so too. And they'll take her away and she'll never come back. Grandmama said so. She said I've got to forget her, not think about her anymore! She's never coming back!"

"Is that what you want to do—forget her?"

There was a long silence.

His hand came up to his mouth again. "I don't know."

"Of course you don't, I'm sorry. I should not have asked. Are you glad now no one is doing that to you anymore—what Papa did?"

His eyelids lowered again and he hunched his right shoulder and looked at the ground.

Hester felt sick.

"Someone is. Who?"

He swallowed hard and said nothing.

269

"Someone is. You don't have to tell me who—not if it's secret."

He looked up at her.

"Someone is?" she repeated.

Very slowly he nodded.

"Just one person?"

He looked down again, frightened.

"All right—it's your secret. But if you want any help any time, or someone to talk to, you go to Miss Buchan. She's very good at secrets, and she understands. Do you hear me?"

He nodded.

"And remember, your mama loves you very much, and I am going to try to do everything I can to see that she comes back to you. I promise you."

He looked at her with steady blue eyes, slowly filling with tears.

"I promise," she repeated. "I'm going to start right now. Remember, if you want to be with somebody, talk to them, you go to Miss Buchan. She's here all the time, and she understands secrets—promise me?"

Again he nodded, and turned away as his eyes brimmed over.

She longed to go over and put her arms around him, let him weep, but if he did he might not be able to regain the composure, the dignity and self-reliance he must have in order to survive the next few days or weeks.

Reluctantly she turned and went out of the door, closing it softly behind her.

Hester excused herself to Edith as hastily as possible and without any explanation, then as soon as she was on the pavement she began to walk briskly towards William Street. She hailed the very first hansom she saw and requested the driver to take her to Vere Street, off Lincoln's Inn Fields, then she sat back to compose herself until she should arrive at Rathbone's office.

Once there she alighted, paid the driver and went in. The clerk greeted her civilly, but with some surprise.

"I have no appointment," she said quickly. "But I must see Mr. Rathbone as soon as possible. I have discovered the motive in the Carlyon case, and as you must know, there is no time to be lost."

He rose from his seat, setting down his quill and closing the ledger.

"Indeed, ma'am. Then I will inform Mr. Rathbone. He is with a client at the moment, but I am sure he will be most obliged if you are able to wait until he is free."

"Certainly." She sat down and with the greatest difficulty watched the hands on the clock go around infinitely slowly until twenty-five minutes later the inner office door opened. A large gentleman came out, his gold watch chain across an extensive stomach. He glanced at her without speaking, wished the clerk good-day, and went out.

The clerk went in to Rathbone immediately, and within a moment was out again.

"If you please, Miss Latterly?" He stood back, inviting her in.

"Thank you." She barely glanced at him as she passed.

Oliver Rathbone was sitting at his desk and he rose to his feet before she was across the threshold.

"Hester?"

She closed the door behind her and leaned against it, suddenly breathless.

"I know why Alexandra killed the general!" She swallowed hard, an ache in her throat. "And my God, I think I would have done it too. And gone to the gallows before I would have told anyone why."

"Why?" His voice was husky, little more than a whisper. "For God's sake why?"

"Because he was having carnal knowledge of his own son!"

"Dear heaven! Are you sure?" He sat down suddenly as though all the strength had gone out of him. "General Carlyon—was . . . ? Hester . . . ?"

"Yes—and not only he, but probably the old colonel as well—and God knows who else."

271

Rathbone shut his eyes and his face was ashen.

"No wonder she killed him," he said very quietly.

Hester came over and sat down on the chair opposite the desk. There was no need to spell it out. They both knew the helplessness of a woman who wanted to leave her husband without his agreement, and that even if she did, all children were legally his, not hers. By law she would forfeit all right to them, even nursing babies, let alone an eight-year-old son.

"What else could she do?" Hester said blankly. "There was no one to turn to—I don't suppose anyone would have believed her. They'd lock her up for slander, or insanity, if she tried to say such a thing about a pillar of the military establishment like the general."

"His parents?" he said, then laughed bitterly. "I don't suppose they'd ever believe it, even if they saw the act."

"I don't know," she admitted. "The old colonel does it too—so he would be no help. Presumably Felicia never knew? I don't know how Alexandra did; the child certainly didn't tell her. He was sworn to secrecy, and terrified. He'd been told his mother wouldn't love him anymore, that she'd hate him and send him away if she ever found out."

His face was pale, the skin drawn tight.

"How do you know?"

Detail by detail she related to him the events of the afternoon. The clerk knocked on the door and said that the next client was here. Rathbone told him to go away again.

"Oh God," he said quietly when she had finished. He turned from the window where he had moved when she was halfway through. His face was twisted with pity, and anger for the pain and loneliness and the fear of it. "Hester . . ."

"You can help her, can't you?" she pleaded. "She'll hang for it, if you don't, and he'll have no one. He'll be left in that house—for it to go on."

"I know!" He turned away and looked out of the window. "I'll do what I can. Let me think. Come back tomorrow, with Monk." His hands clenched by his sides. "We have no proof."

She wanted to cry out that there must be, but she knew he

did not speak lightly, or from defeat, only from the need to be exact. She rose to her feet and stood a little behind him.

"You've done what seemed impossible before," she said tentatively.

He looked back at her, smiling, his eyes very soft.

"My dear Hester . . ."

She did not flinch or ease the demand in her face.

"I'll try," he said quietly. "I promise you I will try."

She smiled quickly, reached up her hand and brushed his cheek, without knowing why, then turned and left, going out into the clerk's office with her head high.

The following day, late in the morning, Rathbone, Monk and Hester sat in the office in Vere Street with all doors closed and all other business suspended until they should have reached a decision. It was June 16.

Monk had just heard from Hester what she had learned at the Carlyon house. He sat pale-faced, his lips tight, his knuckles clenched. It marred his opinion of himself that he was shocked, but he was, too deeply to conceal it. It had not occurred to him that someone of the breeding and reputation of General Carlyon should indulge in such a devastating abuse. He was too angry even to resent the fact that it had not occurred to him to look for such an answer. All his thoughts were outward, to Alexandra, to Cassian, and to what was to come.

"Is it a defense?" he demanded of Rathbone. "Will the judge dismiss it?"

"No," Rathbone said quietly. He was very grave this morning and his long face was marked by lines of tiredness; even his eyes looked weary. "I have been reading cases all night, checking every point of law I can find on the subject, and I come back each time to what is, I think, our only chance, and that is a defense of provocation. The law states that if a person receives extraordinary provocation, and that may take many forms, then the charge of murder may be reduced to manslaughter."

"That's not good enough," Monk interrupted, his voice

273

rising with his emotion. "This was justifiable. For God's sake, what else could she do? Her husband was committing incest and sodomy against her child. She had not only a right but a duty to protect him. The law gave her nothing—she has no rights in her son. In law it is his child, but the law never intended he should be free to do that to him."

"Of course not," Rathbone agreed quietly, the effort of restraint trembling behind it. "Nevertheless, the law gives a woman no rights in her child. She has no means to support it, and no freedom to leave her husband if he does not wish her to, and certainly no way to take her child with her."

"Then what else can she do but kill him?" Monk's face was white. "How can we tolerate a law which affords no possible justice? And the injustice is unspeakable."

"We change it, we don't break it," Rathbone replied.

Monk swore briefly and violently.

"I agree," Rathbone said with a tight smile. "Now may we proceed with what is practical?"

Monk and Hester stared at him wordlessly.

"Manslaughter is the best we can hope for, and that will be extremely difficult to prove. But if we succeed, the sentence is largely at the discretion of the judge. It can be as little as a matter of months, or as great as ten years."

Both Hester and Monk relaxed a little. Hester smiled bleakly.

"But we must prove it," Rathbone went on. "And that will be very hard to do. General Carlyon is a hero. People do not like their heroes tarnished, let alone utterly destroyed." He leaned back a little, sliding his hands into his pockets. "And we have had more than enough of that with the war. We have a tendency to see people as good or evil; it is so much easier both on the brain and on the emotions, but especially the emotions, to place people into one or the other category. Black or white. It is a painful adjustment to have to recognize and accommodate into our thinking the fact that people with great qualities which we have admired may also have ugly and profoundly repellent flaws."

He did not look at either of them, but at a space on the

farther wall. "One then has to learn to understand, which is difficult and painful, unless one is to swing completely 'round, tear up one's admiration, and turn it into hate—which is also painful, and wrong, but so much easier. The wound of disillusion turns to rage because one has been let down. One's own sense of betrayal outweighs all else."

His delicate mouth registered wry pity.

"Disillusion is one of the most difficult of all emotions to wear gracefully, and with any honor. I am afraid we will not find many who will do it. People will be very reluctant to believe anything so disturbing. And we have had far too much disturbance to our settled and comfortable world lately as it is—first the war, and all the ugly whispers there are of inefficiency and needless death, and now wind of mutiny in India. God knows how bad that will turn out to be."

He slid a little farther down in his chair. "We need our heroes. We don't want them proved to be weak and ugly, to practice vices we can barely even bring ourselves to name—let alone against their own children."

"I don't care a damn whether people like it or not," Monk said violently. "It is true. We must force them to see it. Would they rather we hang an innocent woman, before we oblige them to see a truth which is disgusting?"

"Some of them well might." Rathbone looked at him with a faint smile. "But I don't intend to allow them that luxury."

"If they would, then there is not much hope for our society," Hester said in a small voice. "When we are happy to turn from evil because it is ugly, and causes us distress, then we condone it and become party to its continuance. Little by little, we become as guilty of it as those who commit the act—because we have told them by our silence that it is acceptable."

Rathbone glanced at her, his eyes bright and soft.

"Then we must prove it," Monk said between his teeth. "We must make it impossible for anyone to deny or evade."

"I will try." Rathbone looked at Hester, then at Monk. "But we haven't enough here yet. I'll need more. Ideally I need to name the other members of the ring, if there is one, and from what you say"—he turned to Hester—"there may be several members. And of course I dare not name anyone without proof. Cassian is only eight. I may be able to call him; that will depend upon the judge. But his testimony alone will certainly not be sufficient."

"I think Damaris might know," Hester said thoughtfully. "I'm not certain, but she undoubtedly discovered something at the party that evening, and it shook her so desperately she was hardly able to keep control of herself."

"We have several people's testimony to that," Monk added.

"If she will admit it, that will go a long way towards belief," Rathbone said guardedly. "But it will not be easy to make her. She is called as a witness for the prosecution."

"Damaris is?" Hester was incredulous. "But why? I thought she was on our side."

Rathbone smiled without pleasure. "She has no choice. The prosecution has called her, and she must come, or risk being charged with contempt of court. So must Peverell Erskine, Fenton and Sabella Pole, Maxim and Louisa Furnival, Dr. Hargrave, Sergeant Evan, and Randolf Carlyon."

"But that's everyone." Hester was horrified. Suddenly hope was being snatched away again. "What about us? That's unjust. Can't they testify for us too?"

"No, a witness can be called by only one side. But I shall have an opportunity to cross-examine them," Rathbone replied. "It will not be as easy as if they were my witnesses. But it is not everyone. We can call Felicia Carlyon—although I am not sure if I will. I have not subpoenaed her, but if she is there I may call her at the last moment—when she has had an opportunity to hear the other testimony."

"She won't tell us anything," Hester said furiously. "Even if she could. And I don't suppose she knows. But if she did, can you imagine her standing up in court and admitting that any member of her family committed incest and sodomy, let alone her heroic son, the general!"

"Not willingly." Rathbone's face was grim, but there was a faint, cold light in his eyes. "But it is my art, my dear, to make people admit what they do not wish to, and had not intended to.''

"You had better be damnably good at it," Monk said angrily.

"I am." Rathbone met his eyes and for a moment they stared at each other in silence.

"And Edith," Hester said urgently. "You can call Edith. She will help all she can."

"What does she know?" Monk swung around to her. "Willingness won't help if she doesn't know anything."

Hester ignored him. "And Miss Buchan. She knows."

"A servant." Rathbone bit his lip. "A very elderly woman with a hot temper and a family loyalty . . . If she turns against them they won't forgive her. She will be thrown out without a roof over her head or food to eat, and too old to work anymore. Not an enviable position."

Hester felt hopelessness wash over her anger. A black defeat threatened to crush her.

"Then what can we do?"

"Find some more evidence," Rathbone replied. "Find out who else is involved."

Monk thought for a few moments, his hands knotted hard in his lap.

"That should be possible: either they came to the house or the child was taken to them. The servants will know who called. The footmen ought to know where the boy went." His face pinched with anger. "Poor little devil!" He looked at Rathbone critically. "But even if you prove other men used him, will that prove that his father did, and that Alexandra knew it?"

"You give me the evidence," Rathbone replied. "Everything you get, whether you think it is relevant or not. I'll decide how to use it."

Monk rose to his feet, scraping back his chair, his whole body hard with anger.

"Then we have no time to lose. God knows there is little enough."

"And I shall go to try and persuade Alexandra Carlyon to

allow us to use the truth," Rathbone said with a tight little smile. "Without her consent we have nothing."

"Oliver." Hester was aghast.

He turned to her, touching her very gently.

"Don't worry, my dear. You have done superbly. You have discovered the truth. Now leave me to do my part."

She met his eyes, dark and brilliant, took a deep breath and let it out slowly, forcing herself to relax.

"Of course. I'm sorry. Go and see Alexandra. I shall go and tell Callandra. She will be as appalled as we are."

Alexandra Carlyon turned from the place where she had been standing, staring up at the small square of light of the cell window. She was surprised to see Rathbone.

The door swung shut with a hollow sound of metal on metal, and they were alone.

"You are wasting your time, Mr. Rathbone," she said huskily. "I cannot tell you anything more."

"You don't need to, Mrs. Carlyon," he said very gently. "I know why you killed your husband—and God help me, had I been in your place I might have done the same."

She stared at him uncomprehendingly.

"To save your son from further unnatural abuse . . ."

What little color there was left fled from her face. Her eyes were wide, so hollow as to seem black in the dim light.

"You—know . . ." She sank onto the cot. "You can't. Please . . ."

He sat on the bottom of the cot, facing her.

"My dear, I understand that you were prepared to go to the gallows rather than expose your son to the world's knowledge of his suffering. But I have something very dreadful to tell you, which must change your mind."

Very slowly she raised her head and looked at him.

"Your husband was not the only one to use him in that way."

Her breath caught in her throat, and she seemed unable to find it again. He thought she was going to faint.

"You must fight," he said softly but with intense urgency.

278

"It seems most probable that his grandfather is another—and there is at least a third, if not more. You must use all the courage you have and tell the truth about what happened, and why. We must destroy them, so they can never harm Cassian again, or any other child."

She shook her head, still struggling to breathe.

"You must!" He took both her hands. At first they were limp, then slowly tightened until they clung onto him as if she were drowning. "You must! Otherwise Cassian will go to his grandparents, and the whole tragedy will continue. You will have killed your husband for nothing. And you yourself will hang—for nothing."

"I can't." The words barely passed her lips.

"Yes you can! You are not alone. There are people who will be with you, people as horrified and appalled as you are, who know the truth and will help us fight to prove it. For your son's sake, you must not give up now. Tell the truth, and I will fight to see that it is believed—and understood."

"Can you?"

He took a deep breath and met her eyes.

"Yes—I can."

She stared at him, exhausted beyond emotion.

"I can," he repeated.

9

THE TRIAL OF ALEXANDRA CARLYON began on the morning of Monday, June 22. Major Tiplady had intended to be present, not out of cheap curiosity; normally he shunned such proceedings as he would have an accident had a horse bolted in the street and thrown and trampled its rider. It was a vulgar intrusion into another person's embarrassment and distress. But in this case he felt a deep and personal concern for the outcome, and he wished to demonstrate his support for Alexandra, and for the Carlyon family, or if he were honest, for Edith; not that he would have admitted it, even to himself.

When he put his foot to the ground he was well able to bear his weight on it. It seemed the leg had healed perfectly. However, when he attempted to bend it to climb the step up into a hansom, he found, to his humiliation, that it would not support him as he mounted. And he knew dismounting at the other end might well be even worse. He was both abashed and infuriated, but he was powerless to do anything about it. It obviously needed at least another week, and trying to force the issue would only make it worse.

Therefore he deputed Hester to report to him, since she was still in his employ and must do what she could for his comfort. He insisted this was crucial to it. She was to report to him everything that happened, not only the evidence that was given by each witness but their manner and bearing, and whether in her best judgment they were telling the truth or not. Also she was to observe the attitudes of everyone else who appeared for the prosecution and for the defense, and most particularly the jury. Naturally she should also mark well all other members of the family she might see. To this end she should equip herself with a large notebook and several sharp pencils.

"Yes Major," she said obediently, hoping she would be able to fulfil so demanding an assignment adequately. He asked a great deal, but his earnestness and his concern were so genuine she did not even try to point out the difficulties involved.

"I wish to know your opinions as well as the facts," he said for the umpteenth time. "It is a matter of feelings, you know? People are not always rational, especially in matters like this."

"Yes, I know," she said with magnificent understatement. "I will watch expressions and listen to tones of voice—I promise you."

"Good." His cheeks pinkened a trifle. "I am most obliged." He looked down. "I am aware it is not customarily part of a nurse's duties . . ."

She hid a smile with great difficulty.

"And it will not be pleasant," he added.

"It is merely a reversal of roles," she said, allowing her smile to be seen.

"What?" He looked at her quickly, not understanding. He saw her amusement, but did not know what caused it.

"Had you been able to go, then I should have had to ask you to repeat it all to me. I have no authority to require it of you. This is far more convenient."

"Oh—I see." His eyes filled with perception and amusement as well. "Yes—well, you had better go, or you might be late and not obtain a satisfactory seat."

"Yes Major. I shall be back when I am quite sure I have

281

observed everything. Molly has your luncheon prepared, and . . .''

''Never mind.'' He waved his hands impatiently. ''Go on, woman.''

''Yes Major.''

She was early, as she had said; even so the crowds were eager and she only just got a seat from which she could see all the proceedings, and that was because Monk had saved it for her.

The courtroom was smaller than she had expected, and higher-ceilinged, more like a theater with the public gallery far above the dock, which itself was twelve or fifteen feet above the floor where the barristers and court officials had their leather-padded seats at right angles to the dock.

The jury was on two benches, one behind the other, on the left of the gallery, several steps up from the floor, and with a row of windows behind them. On the farther end of the same wall was the witness box, a curious affair up several steps, placing it high above the arena, very exposed.

At the farther wall, opposite the gallery and the dock, was the red-upholstered seat on which the judge sat. To the right was a further gallery for onlookers, newsmen and other interested parties.

There was a great amount of wooden paneling around the dock and witness box, and on the walls behind the jury and above the dock to the gallery rail. It was all very imposing and as little like an ordinary room as possible, and at the present was so crowded with people one was able to move only with the greatest difficulty.

''Where have you been?'' Monk demanded furiously. ''You're late.''

She was torn between snapping back and gratitude to him for thinking of her. The first would be pointless and only precipitate a quarrel when she least wanted one, so she chose the latter, which surprised and amused him.

The Bill of Indictment before the Grand Jury had already

been brought at an earlier date, and a true case found and Alexandra charged.

"What about the jury?" she asked him. "Have they been chosen?"

"Friday," he answered. "Poor devils."

"Why poor?"

"Because I wouldn't like to have to decide this case," Monk answered. "I don't think the verdict I want to bring in is open to me."

"No," she agreed, more to herself than to him. "What are they like?"

"The jury? Ordinary, worried, taking themselves very seriously," he replied, not looking at her but straight ahead at the judge's bench and the lawyers' tables below.

"All middle-aged, I suppose? And all men of course."

"Not all middle-aged," he contradicted. "One or two are youngish, and one very old. You have to be between twenty-one and sixty, and have a guaranteed income from rents or lands, or live in a house with not less than fifteen windows—"

"What?"

"Not less than fifteen windows," he repeated with a sardonic smile, looking sideways at her. "And of course they are all men. That question is not worthy of you. Women are not considered capable of such decisions, for heaven's sake. You don't make any legal decisions at all. You don't own property, you don't expect to be able to decide a man's fate before the law, do you?"

"If one is entitled to be tried before a jury of one's peers, I expect to be able to decide a woman's fate," she said sharply. "And rather more to the point, I expect if I come to trial to have women on the jury. How else could I be judged fairly?"

"I don't think you'd do any better with women," he said, pulling his face into a bitter expression and looking at the fat woman in front of them. "Not that it would make the slightest difference if you did."

She knew it was irrelevant. They must fight the case with

283

the jury as it was. She turned around to look at others in the crowd. They seemed to be all manner of people, every age and social condition, and nearly as many women as men. The only thing they had in common was a restless excitement, a murmuring to one another, a shifting from foot to foot where they were standing, or a craning forward if they were seated, a peering around in case they were to miss something.

"Of course I really shouldn't be 'ere," a woman said just behind Hester. "It won't do me nerves any good at all. Wickedest thing I ever 'eard of, an' 'er a lady too. You expec' better from them as ought ter know 'ow ter be'ave theirselves."

"I know," her companion agreed. "If gentry murders each other, wot can yer expec' of the lower orders? I ask yer."

"Wonder wot she's like? Vulgar, I shouldn't wonder. Of course they'll 'ang 'er."

"O' course. Don't be daft. Wot else could they do?"

"Right and proper thing too."

" 'Course it is. My 'usband don't always control 'isself, but I don't go murderin' 'im."

" 'Course you don't. No one does. What would 'appen to the world if we did?"

"Shockin'. And they're sayin' as there's mutiny in India too. People killin' an' murderin' all over the place. I tell yer, we live in terrible times. God 'isself only knows what'll be next!"

"An' that's true for sure," her companion agreed, sagely nodding her head.

Hester longed to tell them not to be so stupid, that there had always been virtue and tragedy—and laughter, discovery and hope—but the clerk called the court to order. There was a rustle of excitement as the counsel for the prosecution came in dressed in traditional wig and black gown, followed by his junior. Wilberforce Lovat-Smith was not a large man, but he had a walk which was confident, even a trifle arrogant, and full of vitality, so that everyone was immediately aware of him. He was unusually dark of complexion and under the white horsehair wig very black hair was easily visible. Even at this distance, Hester could see with surprise as he turned that his eyes were cold gray-blue. He was certainly not a handsome man, but there was something compelling in his features: sharp nose, humorous mouth and heavy-lidded eyes which suggested sensuality. It was the face of a man who had succeeded in the past, and expected to again.

He had barely taken his place when there was another murmur of excitement as Rathbone came in, also gowned and wigged and followed by a junior. He looked unfamiliar to Hester, lately used to seeing him in ordinary clothes and informal in his manner. Now he was quite obviously thinking only of the contest ahead on which depended not only Alexandra's life but perhaps the quality of Cassian's also. Hester and Monk had done all they could; now it lay with Rathbone. He was a lone gladiator in the arena, and the crowd was hungering for blood. As he turned she saw the familiar profile with its long nose and delicate mouth so ready to change from pity to anger, and back to wry, quick humor again.

"It's going to begin," someone whispered behind her. "That's the defense. It's Rathbone—I wonder what he's going to say?"

"Nothing 'e can say," came the reply from a man somewhere to her left. "Don't know why 'e bothers. They should 'ang 'er, save the government the money."

"Save us, more like."

"Ssh!"

"Ssh yerself!"

Monk swung around, his voice vicious. "If you don't want a trial you should vacate the seat and allow someone who does to sit in it. There are plenty of slaughterhouses in London if all you want is blood."

There was a gasp of fury.

" 'Ow dare you speak to my wife like that?" the man demanded.

"I was speaking to you, sir," Monk retorted. "I expect you to be responsible for your own opinions."

"Hold your tongue," someone else said furiously. "Or we'll all be thrown out! The judge is coming."

And indeed he was, splendid in robes touched with scarlet, white wig only slightly fuller than those of the lawyers. He was a tallish man with a broad brow and fine strong nose, short jaw and good mouth, but he was far younger than Hester had expected, and for no reason that she understood, her heart sank. In some way she had imagined a fatherly man might have more compassion, a grandfatherly man even more again. She found herself sitting forward on the edge of the hard bench, her hands clenched, her shoulders tight.

There was a rising wave of excitement, then a sudden silence as the prisoner was brought in, a craning forward and turning of heads on the benches behind the lawyers, of all except one woman dressed entirely in black, and veiled. Beneath the gallery in the dock the prisoner had been brought in.

Even the jury, seemingly against their will, found their eyes moving towards her.

Hester cursed the arrangement which made it impossible to see the dock from the gallery.

"We should have got seats down there," she said to Monk, nodding her head towards the few benches behind the lawyers' seats.

"We?" he said acidly. "If it weren't for me you'd be standing outside."

"I know—and I'm grateful. All the same, we should still try to get a seat down there."

"Then come an hour earlier next time."

"I will. But it doesn't help now."

"What do you want to do?" he whispered sarcastically. "Lose these seats and go out and try to get in downstairs?"

"Yes," she hissed back. "Of course I do. Come on!"

"Don't be ridiculous. You'll end up with nothing."

"You can do as you please. I'm going."

The woman in front swung around. "Be quiet," she said furiously.

"Mind your own business, madam," Monk said, freezing calm, then grasped Hester by the elbow and propelled her out past the row of protesting onlookers. Up the aisle and outside in the hallway he maintained silence. They went down the stairs, and at the door of the lower court he let go of her.

"All right," he said with a scathing stare. "Now what do you propose to do?"

She gulped, glared back at him, then swung around and marched to the doors.

A bailiff appeared and barred the way. "I'm sorry. You can't go in there, miss. It's all full up. You should 'a come earlier. You'll 'ave ter read about it in the papers."

"That will not be satisfactory," she said with all the dignity she could muster. "We are involved in the case, retained by Mr. Rathbone, counsel for the defense. This is Mr. Monk," she inclined her head slightly. "He is working with Mr. Rathbone, and Mr. Rathbone may need to consult with him during the course of the evidence. I am with him."

The bailiff looked over her head at Monk. "Is that true, sir?"

"Certainly it is," Monk said without a flicker, producing a card from his vest pocket.

"Then you'd better go in," the bailiff agreed cautiously. "But next time, get in 'ere a bit sooner, will you."

"Of course. We apologize," Monk said tactfully. "A little late business, you understand."

And without arguing the point any further, he pushed Hester inside and allowed the bailiff to close the doors.

The court looked different from this level, the judge's seat higher and more imposing, the witness box oddly more vulnerable, and the dock very enclosed, like a wide cage with wooden walls, very high up.

"Sit down," Monk said sharply.

Hester obeyed, perching on the end of the nearest bench and forcing the present occupants to move up uncomfortably close to each other. Monk was obliged to stand, until someone graciously changed places to the next row and gave him space.

For the first time, with something of a start, Hester saw the haggard face of Alexandra Carlyon, who was permitted to sit because the proceedings were expected to take several days. It was not the face she had envisioned at all; it was far too immediate and individual, even pale and exhausted as it was. There was too much capacity for intelligence and pain in it; she was acutely aware that they were dealing with the agonies and desires of a unique person, not merely a tragic set of circumstances.

She looked away again, feeling intrusive to be caught staring. She already knew more of her much too intimate suffering than anyone had a right to.

The proceedings began almost straightaway. The charge had already been made and answered. The opening speeches were brief. Lovat-Smith said the facts of the case were only too apparent, and he would prove step by step how the accused had deliberately, out of unfounded jealousy, murdered her husband, General Thaddeus Carlyon, and attempted to pass off her crime as an accident.

Rathbone said simply that he would answer with such a story that would shed a new and terrible light on all they knew, a light in which no answer would be as they now thought, and to look carefully into both their hearts and their consciences before they returned a verdict.

Lovat-Smith called his first witness, Louisa Mary Furnival. There was a rustle of excitement, and then as she appeared a swift indrawing of breath and whisper of fabric against fabric as people craned forward to see her. And indeed she presented a spectacle worth their effort. She was dressed in the darkest purple touched with amethyst, dignified, subdued in actual tones, and yet so fashionably and flamboyantly cut with a tiny waist and gorgeous sleeves. Her bonnet was perched so rakishly on her wide brushed dark hair as to be absolutely dashing. Her expression should have been demure, that of an elegant woman mourning the shocking death of a friend, and yet there was so much vitality in her, such awareness of her own beauty and magnetism, that no one thought of such an emotion for more than the first superficial instant.

She crossed the space of floor in front of the lawyers and climbed the flight of steps up into the witness box, negotiating her skirts through the narrow rails with considerable skill, then turned to face Lovat-Smith.

She swore as to her name and residence in a low, husky voice, looking down at him with shining eyes.

"Mrs. Furnival"—he moved forward towards her, hands in his pockets under his gown—"will you tell the court what you can recall of the events of that dreadful evening when General Carlyon met his death? Begin with the arrival of your guests, if you please."

Louisa looked perfectly composed. If the occasion intimidated her in any way, there was not the slightest sign of it in her face or her bearing. Even her hands on the witness box railing were quite relaxed.

"The first to arrive were Mr. and Mrs. Erskine," she started. "The next were General Carlyon and Alexandra." She did not glance at the dock as she said it.

Lovat-Smith was talking to Louisa.

Alexandra might not have been present for any emotional impact Louisa showed.

"At that time, Mrs. Furnival," Lovat-Smith was saying, "what was the attitude between General and Mrs. Carlyon? Did you notice?"

"The general seemed as usual," Louisa replied levelly. "I thought Alexandra very tense, and I was aware that the evening might become difficult." She allowed the ghost of a smile to cross her face. "As hostess, I was concerned that the party should be a success."

There was a ripple of laughter around the court, dying away again immediately.

Hester glanced up at Alexandra, but her face was expressionless.

"Who arrived next?" Lovat-Smith asked.

"Sabella Pole and her husband, Fenton Pole. She was immediately rude to her father, the general." Louisa's face shadowed very slightly but she forbore from more than the vaguest of implied criticism. She knew it was ugly and above all she would avoid that. "Of course she has not been well," she added. "So one forgave her readily. It was an embarrassment, no more."

"You did not fear it indicated any dangerous ill will?" Lovat-Smith asked with apparent concern.

"Not at all." Louisa dismissed it with a gesture.

"Who else arrived at this dinner of yours?"

"Dr. Charles Hargrave and Mrs. Hargrave; they were the last."

"And no one else called that evening?"

"No one."

"Can you tell us something of the course of events, Mrs. Furnival?"

She shrugged very delicately and half smiled.

Hester watched the jury. They were fascinated with her and Hester had no doubt she knew it.

"We spent some time in the withdrawing room," Louisa said casually. "We talked of this and that, as we will on such occasions. I cannot recall what we said, only that Mrs. Carlyon picked a quarrel with the general, which he did all he could to avoid, but she seemed determined to bring the matter to an open dispute."

"Do you know what it was about?"

"No, it seemed to be very nebulous, just a longstanding ill feeling, so far as I could judge. Of course I did not overhear it all . . ." She left it hanging delicately, not to rule out the possibility of a raging jealousy.

"And at dinner, Mrs. Furnival," Lovat-Smith prompted. "Was the ill feeling between General and Mrs. Carlyon still apparent?"

"Yes, I am afraid it was. Of course at that time I had no idea it was anything serious . . ." For an instant she looked contrite, abashed at her own blindness. There was a murmur of sympathy around the courtroom. People turned to look at the dock. One of the jurors nodded sagely.

"And after dinner?" Lovat-Smith asked.

"The ladies withdrew and left the men to take port and cigars," Louisa continued. "In the withdrawing room we simply spoke of trivial things again, a little gossip, and a few opinions of fashion and so on. Then when the men rejoined us I took General Carlyon upstairs to visit my son, who admired him greatly, and to whom he had been a good friend." A spasm of pain passed over her immaculate features and again there was a buzz of sympathy and anger around the room.

Hester looked at Alexandra in the dock, and saw hurt and puzzlement in her face.

The judge lifted his eyes and stared over the heads of the counsel to the body of the court. The sound subsided.

"Continue, Mr. Lovat-Smith," he ordered.

Lovat-Smith turned to Louisa. "Did this occasion any response that you observed, Mrs. Furnival?"

Louisa looked downwards modestly, as if embarrassed to admit it now.

"Yes. I am afraid Mrs. Carlyon was extremely angry. I thought at the time it was just a fit of pique. Of course I realize now that it was immeasurably deeper than that."

Oliver Rathbone rose to his feet.

"I object, my lord. The witness—"

"Sustained," the judge interrupted him. "Mrs. Furnival, we wish to know only what you observed at the time, not what later events may have led you to conclude, correctly or incorrectly. It is for the jury to interpret, not for you. At this time you felt it to be a fit of pique—that is all."

Louisa's face tightened with annoyance, but she would not argue with him.

"My lord," Lovat-Smith acknowledged the rebuke. He turned back to Louisa. "Mrs. Furnival, you took General Carlyon upstairs to visit with your son, whose age is thirteen, is that correct? Good. When did you come downstairs again?"

"When my husband came up to tell me that Alexandra—Mrs. Carlyon—was extremely upset and the party was becoming very tense and rather unpleasant. He wished me to return to try to improve the atmosphere. Naturally I did so."

"Leaving General Carlyon still upstairs with your son?"

"Yes."

"And what happened next?"

"Mrs. Carlyon went upstairs."

"What was her manner, Mrs. Furnival, from your own observation?" He glanced at the judge, who made no comment.

"She was white-faced," Louisa replied. Still she ignored Alexandra as if the dock had been empty and she were speaking of someone absent. "She appeared to be in a rage greater than any I have ever seen before, or since. There was nothing I could do to stop her, but I still imagined that it was some private quarrel and would be settled when they got home."

Lovat-Smith smiled. "We assume you did not believe it would lead to violence, Mrs. Furnival, or you would naturally have taken steps to prevent it. But did you still have no idea as to its cause? You did not, for example, think it was jealousy over some imagined relationship between the general and yourself?"

She smiled, a fleeting, enigmatic expression. For the first time she glanced at Alexandra, but so quickly their eyes barely met. "A trifle, perhaps," she said gravely. "But not serious. Our relationship was purely one of friendship—quite platonic—as it had been for years. I thought she knew that, as did everyone else." Her smile widened. "Had it been more, my husband would hardly have been the friend to the general he was. I did not think she was . . . obsessive about it. A little envious, maybe—friendship can be very precious. Especially if you feel you do not have it."

"Exactly so." He smiled at her. "And then?" he asked, moving a little to one side and putting his hands deeper into his pockets.

Louisa took up the thread. "Then Mrs. Carlyon came downstairs, alone."

"Had her manner changed?"

"I was not aware of it . . ." She looked as if she were

waiting for him to lead her, but as he remained silent, she continued unasked. "Then my husband went out into the hall." She stopped for dramatic effect. "That is the front hall, not the back one, which we had been using to go up to my son's room—and he came back within a moment, looking very shaken, and told us that General Carlyon had had an accident and was seriously hurt."

"Seriously hurt," Lovat-Smith interrupted. "Not dead?"

"I think he was too shocked to have looked at him closely," she answered, a faint, sad smile touching her mouth. "I imagine he wanted Charles to come as soon as possible. That is what I would have done."

"Of course. And Dr. Hargrave went?"

"Yes—after a few moments he was back to say that Thaddeus was dead and we should call the police—because it was an accident that needed explaining, not because any of us suspected murder then."

"Naturally," Lovat-Smith agreed. "Thank you, Mrs. Furnival. Would you please remain there, in case my learned friend has any questions to ask you." He bowed very slightly and turned to Rathbone.

Rathbone rose, acknowledged him with a nod, and moved forward towards the witness box. His manner was cautious, but there was no deference in it and he looked up at Louisa very directly.

"Thank you for a most clear description of the events of that tragic evening, Mrs. Furnival," he began, his voice smooth and beautifully modulated. As soon as she smiled he continued gravely. "But I think perhaps you have omitted one or two events which may turn out to be relevant. We can hardly overlook anything, can we?" He smiled back at her, but there was no lightness in the gesture, and it died instantly, leaving no trace in his eyes. "Did anyone else go up to see your son, Valentine?"

"I . . ." She stopped, as if uncertain.

"Mrs. Erskine, for example?"

Lovat-Smith stirred, half rose as if to interrupt, then changed his mind.

293

"I believe so," Louisa conceded, her expression making it plain she thought it irrelevant.

"And how was her manner when she came down?" Rathbone said softly.

Louisa hesitated. "She seemed . . . upset."

"Just upset?" Rathbone sounded surprised. "Not distressed, unable to keep her mind on a conversation, distracted by some inner pain?"

"Well . . ." Louisa lifted her shoulder delicately. "She was in a very strange mood, yes. I thought perhaps she was not entirely well."

"Did she give any explanation for the sudden change from her usual manner to such a distracted, offensive, near-frenzied mood?"

Lovat-Smith rose to his feet.

"Objection, my lord! The witness did not say Mrs. Erskine was offensive or near frenzied, only that she was distressed and unable to command her attention to the conversation."

The judge looked at Rathbone. "Mr. Lovat-Smith is correct. What is your point, Mr. Rathbone? I confess, I fail to see it."

"It will emerge later, my lord," Rathbone said, and Hester had a strong feeling he was bluffing, hoping that by the time Damaris was called, they would have learned precisely what it was that she had discovered. Surely it must have to do with the general.

"Very well. Proceed," the judge directed.

"Did you find the cause of Mrs. Erskine's distress, Mrs. Furnival?" Rathbone resumed.

"No."

"Nor of Mrs. Carlyon's distress either? Is it an assumption that it had to do with you, and your relationship with the general?"

Louisa frowned.

"Is that not so, Mrs. Furnival? Did Mrs. Carlyon ever say anything either to you, or in your hearing, to suggest that she was distressed because of a jealousy of you and your friendship with her husband? Please be exact.''

Louisa drew in her breath deeply, her face shadowed, but still she did not glance towards the dock or the motionless woman in it.

"No."

Rathbone smiled, showing his teeth.

"Indeed, you have testified that she had nothing of which to be jealous. Your friendship with the general was perfectly proper, and a sensible woman might conceivably have regarded it as enviable that you could have such a comfortable regard, perhaps, but not cause for distress, let alone a passionate jealousy or hatred. Indeed there seems no reason for it at all. Is that not so?''

"Yes." It was not a flattering description, and certainly not glamorous, or the image Hester had seen Louisa project. Hester smiled to herself and glanced at Monk, but Monk had not caught the inflection. He was watching the jury.

"And this friendship between yourself and the general had existed for many years, some thirteen or fourteen years, in fact?''

"Yes."

"With the full knowledge and consent of your husband?''

"Of course.''

"And of Mrs. Carlyon?''

"Yes."

"Did she at any time at all approach you on the matter, or let you know that she was displeased about it?''

"No." Louisa raised her eyebrows. "This came without any warning at all.''

"What came, Mrs. Furnival?''

"Why the . . . the murder, of course.'' She looked a little disconcerted, not entirely sure whether he was very simple or very clever.

He smiled blandly, a slight curling of the lips. "Then on what evidence do you suppose that jealousy of you was the cause?''

She breathed in slowly, giving herself time, and her expression hardened.

"I—I did not think it, until she herself claimed it to be so. But I have experienced unreasonable jealousies before, and it was not hard to believe. Why should she lie about it? It is not a quality one would wish to claim—it is hardly attractive."

"A profound question, Mrs. Furnival, which in time I will answer. Thank you." He half turned away. "That is all I have to ask you. Please remain there, in case my learned friend has any questions to redirect to you."

Lovat-Smith rose, smiling, a small, satisfied gesture.

"No thank you, I think Mrs. Furnival by her very appearance makes the motive of jealousy more than understandable."

Louisa flushed, but it was quite obviously with pleasure, even a vindication. She shot a hard glance at Rathbone as she very carefully came down the steps, negotiating the hoops of her wide skirts with a swaggering grace, and walked across the small space of the floor.

There was a rustle of movement in the crowd and a few clearly audible shouts of admiration and approval. Louisa sailed out with her head high and an increasing satisfaction in her face.

Hester found her muscles clenching and a totally unreasonable anger boiling up inside her. It was completely unfair. Louisa could not know the truth, and in all likelihood she believed that Alexandra had murdered the general out of exactly the sudden and violent jealousy she envisioned. But Hester's anger remained exactly the same.

She looked up at the dock and saw Alexandra's pale face. She could see no hatred in it, no easy contempt. There was nothing there but tiredness and fear.

The next witness to be called was Maxim Furnival. He took the stand very gravely, his face pale. He was stronger than Hester had remembered, with more gravity and power to his features, more honest emotion. He had not testified yet, but she found herself disposed towards him. She glanced up at Alexandra again, and saw a momentary breaking of her self-control, a sudden softening, as if memories, and perhaps a sweetness, came through with bitter contrast. Then it was gone again, and the present reasserted itself.

Maxim was sworn in, and Lovat-Smith rose to address him.

"Of course you were also at this unfortunate dinner party, Mr. Furnival?"

Maxim looked wretched; he had none of Louisa's panache or flair for appearing before an audience. His bearing, the look in his face, suggested his mind was filled with memory of the tragedy, an awareness of the murder that still lay upon them. He had looked at Alexandra once, painfully, without evasion and without anger or blame. Whatever he thought of her, or believed, it was not harsh.

"Yes," he replied.

"Naturally," Lovat-Smith agreed. "Will you please tell us what you remember of that evening, from the time your first guests arrived."

In a quiet voice, but without hesitation, Maxim recounted exactly the same events as Louisa had, only his choice of words was different, laden with his knowledge of what had later occurred. Lovat-Smith did not interrupt him until he came to the point where Alexandra returned from upstairs, alone.

"What was her manner, Mr. Furnival? You did not mention it, and yet your wife said that it was worthy of remark." He glanced at Rathbone; he had forestalled objection, and Rathbone smiled back.

"I did not notice," Maxim replied, and it was so obviously a lie there was a little gasp from the crowd and the judge glanced at him a second time in surprise.

"Try your memory a little harder, Mr. Furnival," Lovat-Smith said gravely. "I think you will find it comes to you." Deliberately he kept his back to Rathbone.

Maxim frowned. "She had not been herself all evening." He met Lovat-Smith's eyes directly. "I was concerned for her, but not more so when she came down than earlier."

Lovat-Smith seemed on the edge of asking yet again, but heard Rathbone rise from his seat to object and changed his mind.

"What happened next?" he said instead.

"I went to the front hall, I forget what for now, and I saw Thaddeus lying on the floor with the suit of armor in pieces all around him—and the halberd in his chest." He hesitated only to compose himself, and Lovat-Smith did not prompt him. "It was quite obvious he had been very seriously hurt, far too seriously for me to do anything useful to help him, so I went back to the withdrawing room to get Charles Hargrave—the doctor . . ."

"Yes, naturally. Was Mrs. Carlyon there?"

"Yes."

"How did she take the news that her husband had had a serious, possibly even fatal accident, Mr. Furnival?"

"She was very shocked, very pale indeed and I think a trifle faint, what do you imagine? It is a fearful thing to have to tell any woman."

Lovat-Smith smiled and looked down at the floor, pushing his hands into his pockets again.

Hester looked at the jury. She could see from the puckered brows, the careful mouths, that their minds were crowded with all manner of questions, sharper and more serious for being unspoken. She had the first intimation of Lovat-Smith's skill.

"Of course," Lovat-Smith said at last. "Fearful indeed. And I expect you were deeply distressed on her behalf." He turned and looked up at Maxim suddenly. "Tell me, Mr. Furnival, did you at any time suspect that your wife was having an affair with General Carlyon?"

Maxim's face was pale, and he stiffened as if the question were distasteful, but not unexpected.

"No, I did not. If I said I trusted my wife, you would no doubt find that of no value, but I had known General Carlyon for many years, and I knew that he was not a man to enter into such a relationship. He had been a friend to both of us for some fifteen years. Had I at any time suspected there to be anything improper I should not have allowed it to continue. That surely you can believe?"

"Of course, Mr. Furnival. Would it be true then to say that you would find Mrs. Carlyon's jealousy in that area to be unfounded, not an understandable passion rooted in a cause that anyone might sympathize with?"

Maxim looked unhappy, his eyes downcast, avoiding Lovat-Smith.

"I find it hard to believe she truly thought there was an affair," he said very quietly. "I cannot explain it."

"Your wife is a very beautiful woman, sir; jealousy is not always a rational emotion. Unreasonable suspicion can—"

Rathbone was on his feet.

"My lord, my honorable friend's speculations on the nature of jealousy are irrelevant to this case, and may prejudice the jury's opinions, since they are being presented as belonging to Mrs. Carlyon in this instance."

"Your objection is sustained," the judge said without hesitation, then turned to Lovat-Smith. "Mr. Lovat-Smith, you know better than that. Prove your point, do not philosophize."

"I apologize, my lord. Thank you, Mr. Furnival, that is all."

"Mr. Rathbone?" the judge invited.

Rathbone rose to his feet and faced the witness box.

"Mr. Furnival, may I take you back to earlier in the evening; to be precise, when Mrs. Erskine went upstairs to see your son. Do you recall that?"

"Yes." Maxim looked puzzled.

"Did she tell you, either then or later, what transpired when she was upstairs?"

Maxim frowned. "No."

"Did anyone else—for example, your son, Valentine?"

"No."

"Both you and Mrs. Furnival have testified that when Mrs. Erskine came down again she was extremely distressed, so much so that she was unable to behave normally for the rest of the evening. Is that correct?"

"Yes." Maxim looked embarrassed. Hester guessed not for himself but for Damaris. It was indelicate to refer to someone's emotional behavior in public, particularly a woman, and a friend. Gentlemen did not speak of such things.

Rathbone flashed him a brief smile.

"Thank you. Now back to the vexing question of whether Mrs. Furnival and General Carlyon were having any nature of relationship which was improper. You have sworn that at no time during the fifteen years or so of their friendship did you have any cause to believe it was not perfectly open and seemly, and all that either you as Mrs. Furnival's husband, or the accused as the general's wife, would have agreed to—as indeed you did agree. Do I understand you correctly, sir?"

Several of the jurors were looking sideways up at Alexandra, their faces curious.

"Yes, you do. At no time did I have any cause whatsoever to believe it was anything but a perfectly proper friendship," Maxim said stiffly, his eyes on Rathbone, his brows drawn down in concentration.

Hester glanced at the jury and saw one or two of them nodding. They believed him; his honesty was transparent, as was his discomfort.

"Did you suppose Mrs. Carlyon to feel the same?"

"Yes! Yes I did!" Maxim's face became animated for the first time since the subject had been raised. "I—I still find it hard—"

"Indeed," Rathbone cut him off. "Did she ever say anything in your hearing, or do anything at all, to indicate that she thought otherwise? Please—please be quite specific. I do not wish for speculation or interpretation in the light of later events. Did she ever express anger or jealousy of Mrs. Furnival with regard to her husband and their relationship?"

"No—never," Maxim said without hesitation. "Nothing at all." He had avoided looking across at Alexandra, as if afraid the jury might misinterpret his motives or doubt his honesty, but now he could not stop his eyes from flickering for a moment towards her.

"You are quite certain?" Rathbone insisted.

"Quite."

The judge frowned, looking closely at Rathbone. He leaned forward as if to say something, then changed his mind.

Lovat-Smith frowned also.

"Thank you, Mr. Furnival." Rathbone smiled at him. "You have been very frank, and it is much appreciated. It is distasteful to all of us to have to ask such questions and open up to public speculation what should remain private, but the force of circumstances leaves us no alternative. Now unless Mr. Lovat-Smith has some further questions for you, you may leave the stand."

"No—thank you," Lovat-Smith replied, half rising to his feet. "None at all."

Maxim left, going down the steps slowly, and the next witness was called, Sabella Carlyon Pole. There was a ripple of expectation around the court, murmurs of excitement, rustles of fabric against fabric as people shifted position, craned forward in the gallery, jostling each other.

"That's the daughter," someone said to Hester's left. "Mad, so they say. 'Ated her father."

"I 'ate my father," came the reply. "That don't make me mad!"

"Sssh," someone else hissed angrily.

Sabella came into the court and walked across the floor, head high, back stiff, and took the stand. She was very pale, but her face was set in an expression of defiance, and she looked straight at her mother in the dock and forced herself to smile.

For the first time since the trial had begun, Alexandra looked as if her composure would break. Her mouth quivered, the steady gaze softened, she blinked several times. Hester could not bear to watch her; she looked away, and felt a coward, and yet had she not turned, she would have felt intrusive. She did not know which was worse.

Sabella swore to her name and place of residence, and to her relationship with the accused.

"I realize this must be painful for you, Mrs. Pole," Lovat-Smith began courteously. "I wish it were possible for me to

301

spare you it, but I regret it is not. However I will try to be brief. Do you recall the evening of the dinner party at which your father met his death?''

"Of course! It is not the sort of thing one forgets."

"Naturally." Lovat-Smith was a trifle taken aback. He had been expecting a woman a little tearful, even afraid of him, or at the very least awed by the situation. "I understand that as soon as you arrived you had a disagreement with your father, is that correct?''

"Yes, perfectly."

"What was that about, Mrs. Pole?"

"He was patronizing about my views that there was going to be trouble in the army in India. As it turns out, I was correct."

There was a murmur of sympathy around the room, and another sharper one of irritation that she should presume to disagree with a military hero, a man, and her father—and someone who was dead and could not answer for himself; still worse, that the appalling news coming in on the India and China mail ships should prove her right.

"Is that all?" Lovat-Smith raised his eyebrows.

"Yes. It was a few sharp words, no more."

"Did your mother quarrel with him that evening?"

Hester looked sideways at the dock. Alexandra's face was tense, filled with anxiety, but Hester believed it was fear for Sabella, not for herself.

"I don't know. Not in my hearing," Sabella answered levelly.

"Have you ever heard your parents quarrel?"

"Of course."

"On what subject, in the last six months, let us say?"

"Particularly, over whether my brother Cassian should be sent away to boarding school or remain at home and have a tutor. He is eight years old."

"Your parents disagreed?"

"Yes."

"Passionately?" Lovat-Smith looked curious and surprised.

"Yes," she said tartly. "Apparently they felt passionately about it."

"Your mother wished him to remain at home with her, and your father wished him to begin his training for adulthood?"

"Not at all. It was Father who wanted him at home. Mama wanted him to go away to school."

Several jurors looked startled, and more than one turned to look at Alexandra.

"Indeed!" Lovat-Smith also sounded surprised, but uninterested in such details, although he had asked for them. "What else?"

"I don't know. I have my own home, Mr. Lovat-Smith. I visited my parents very infrequently. I did not have a close relationship with my father, as I am sure you know. My mother visited me in my home often. My father did not."

"I see. But you were aware that the relationship between your parents was strained, and on the evening of the unfortunate dinner party, particularly so?"

Sabella hesitated, and in so doing betrayed her partiality. Hester saw the jury's faces harden, as if something inside had closed; from now on they would interpret a difference in her answers. One man turned curiously and looked at Alexandra, then away again, as if caught peeping. It too was a betraying gesture.

"Mrs. Pole?" Lovat-Smith prompted her.

"Yes, of course I was aware of it. Everyone was."

"And the cause? Think carefully: knowing your mother, as close to you as she was, did she say anything which allowed you to understand the cause of her anger?"

Rathbone half rose to his feet, then as the judge glanced at him, changed his mind and sank back again. The jury saw it and their faces lit with expectancy.

Sabella spoke very quietly. "When people are unhappy with each other, there is not necessarily a specific cause for each disagreement. My father was very arbitrary at times, very dictatorial. The only subject of quarrel I know of was over Cassian and his schooling."

"Surely you are not suggesting your mother murdered your father because of his choice of education for his son, Mrs. Pole?" Lovat-Smith's voice, charming and distinctive, was filled with incredulity only just short of the offensive.

In the dock Alexandra moved forward impulsively, and the wardress beside her moved also, as if it were even conceivable she should leap over the edge. The gallery could not see it, but the jurors started in their seats.

Sabella said nothing. Her soft oval face hardened and she stared at him, not knowing what to say and reluctant to commit an error.

"Thank you, Mrs. Pole. We quite understand." Lovat-Smith smiled and sat down again, leaving the floor to Rathbone.

Sabella looked at Rathbone guardedly, her cheeks flushed, her eyes wary and miserable.

Rathbone smiled at her. "Mrs. Pole, have you known Mrs. Furnival for some time, several years in fact?"

"Yes."

"Did you believe that she was having an affair with your father?"

There was a gasp of indrawn breath around the courtroom. At last someone was getting to the crux of the situation. Excitement rippled through them.

"No," Sabella said hotly. Then she looked at Rathbone's expression and repeated it with more composure. "No, I did not. I never saw or heard anything to make me think so."

"Did your mother ever say anything to you to indicate that she thought so, or that the relationship gave her any anxiety or distress of any sort?"

"No—no, I cannot recall that she ever mentioned it at all."

"Never?" Rathbone said with surprise. "And yet you were very close, were you not?"

For the first time Sabella quite openly looked up towards the dock.

"Yes, we were—we are close."

"And she never mentioned the subject?"

"No."

"Thank you." He turned back to Lovat-Smith with a smile.

Lovat-Smith rose.

"Mrs. Pole, did you kill your father?"

The judge held up his hand to prevent Sabella from replying, and looked at Rathbone, inviting him to object. It was an improper question, since it had not been part of the examination in chief, and also she should be warned of the possibility of incriminating herself.

Rathbone shrugged.

The judge sighed and lowered his hand, frowning at Lovat-Smith.

"You do not need to answer that question unless you wish to," he said to Sabella.

"No, I did not," Sabella said huskily, her voice little more than a whisper.

"Thank you." Lovat-Smith inclined his head; it was all he had required.

The judge leaned forward. "You may go, Mrs. Pole," he said gently. "There is nothing further."

"Oh," she said, as if a little lost and wishing to find something more to say, something to help. Reluctantly she came down, assisted for the last two steps by the clerk of the court, and disappeared into the crowd, the light catching for a moment on her pale hair before she was gone.

There was an adjournment for luncheon. Monk and Hester found a man with a sandwich cart, purchased a sandwich each and ate them in great haste before returning to find their seats again.

As soon as the court reassembled and came to order the next witness was summoned.

"Fenton Pole!" the bailiff said loudly. "Calling Fenton Pole!"

Fenton Pole climbed up the stairs to the stand, his face set, his jaw hard in lines of utter disapproval. He answered Lovat-Smith tersely but very much as though he believed his mother-in-law to be guilty, but insane. Never even for an instant did he turn his head and look up at her. Twice Lovat-

Smith had to stop him from expressing his view in so many words, as if it excused the family from any connection. After all madness was like a disease, a tragedy which might strike anyone, therefore they were not accountable. His resentment of the whole matter was apparent.

There were murmurs of sympathy from the crowd, even one quite audible word of agreement; but looking at the jury again Hester could see at least one man's face cloud over and a certain disapproval touch him. He seemed to take his duty very seriously, and had probably been told much about not judging the case before all the evidence was in. And for all he sought impartiality, he did not admire disloyalty. He shot Fenton Pole a look of deep dislike. For an instant Hester felt unreasonably comforted. It was silly, and her wiser self knew it, and yet it was a straw in the wind, a sign that at least one man had not yet condemned Alexandra outright.

Rathbone asked Fenton Pole very little, only if he had any precise and incontrovertible evidence that his father-in-law was having an affair with Louisa Furnival.

Pole's face darkened with contempt for such vulgarity, and with offense that the matter should have been raised at all.

"Certainly not," he said vigorously. "General Carlyon was not an immoral man. To suppose that he indulged in such adulterous behavior is quite unbalanced, not rational at all, and without any foundation in fact."

"Quite so," Rathbone agreed. "And have you any cause, Mr. Pole, to suppose that your mother-in-law, Mrs. Carlyon, believed him to be so deceiving her, and betraying his vows?"

Pole's lips tightened.

"I would have thought our presence here today was tragically sufficient proof of that."

"Oh no, Mr. Pole, not at all," Rathbone replied with a harsh sibilance to his voice. "It is proof only that General Carlyon is dead, by violence, and that the police have some cause, rightly or wrongly, to bring a case against Mrs. Carlyon."

There was a rustle of movement in the jury. Someone sat up a trifle straighter.

Fenton Pole looked confused. He did not argue, although the rebuttal was plain in his face.

"You have not answered my question, Mr. Pole," Rathbone pressed him. "Did you see or hear anything to prove to you that Mrs. Carlyon believed there to be anything improper in the relationship between Mrs. Furnival and the general?"

"Ah—well . . . said like that, I suppose not. I don't know what you have in mind."

"Nothing, Mr. Pole. And it would be quite improper for me to suggest anything to you, as I am sure his lordship would inform you."

Fenton Pole did not even glance at the judge.

He was excused.

Lovat-Smith called the footman, John Barton. He was overawed by the occasion, and his fair face was flushed hot with embarrassment. He stuttered as he took the oath and gave his name, occupation and residence. Lovat-Smith was extremely gentle with him and never once condescended or treated him with less courtesy than he had Fenton Pole or Maxim Furnival. To the most absolute silence from the court and the rapt attention of the jury, he elicited from him the whole story of the clearing away after the dinner party, the carrying of the coal buckets up the front stairs, the observation of the suit of armor still standing on its plinth, who was in the withdrawing room, his meeting with the maid, and the final inevitable conclusion that only either Sabella or Alexandra could possibly have killed Thaddeus Carlyon.

There was a slow letting out of a sigh around the courtroom, like the first chill air of a coming storm.

Rathbone rose amid a crackling silence. Not a juryman moved.

"I have no questions to ask this witness, my lord."

There was a gasp of amazement. Jurors swiveled around to look at one another in disbelief.

The judge leaned forward. "Are you sure, Mr. Rathbone? This witness's evidence is very serious for your client."

"I am quite sure, thank you, my lord."

307

The judge frowned. "Very well." He turned to John. "You are excused."

Lovat-Smith called the upstairs maid with the red hair, and sealed beyond doubt the incontestable fact that it could only have been Alexandra who pushed the general over the stairs, and then followed him down and plunged the halberd into his body.

"I don't know why this has to go on," a man said behind Monk. "Waste o' time."

"Waste o' money," his companion agreed. "Should just call it done, 'ang 'er now. Nothing anyone can say to that."

Monk swung around, his face tight, hard, eyes blazing.

"Because Englishmen don't hang people without giving them a chance to explain," he said between his teeth. "It's a quaint custom, but we give everyone a hearing, whatever we think of them. If that doesn't suit you, then you'd better go somewhere else, because there's no place for you here!"

" 'Ere! 'Oo are you callin' foreign? I'm as English as you are! An' I pay me taxes, but not for the likes of 'er to play fast an' loose wi' the law. I believe in the law, I do. Can't 'ave women going 'round murderin' their 'usbands every time they get a fit o' jealousy. No one in England'd be safe!"

"You don't believe in the law." Monk accused bitterly. "You believe in the rope, and mob rule, you just said so."

"I never did. You lyin' bastard!"

"You said forget the trial, overthrow the courts, hang her now, without waiting for a verdict." Monk glared at him. "You want to do away with judge and jury and be both yourself."

"I never said that!"

Monk gave him a look of total disgust, and turned to Hester, as they rose on adjournment, taking her a trifle roughly by the elbow, and steering her out through the noisy, shoving crowd.

There was nothing to say. It was what they could have expected: a crowd who knew no more than the newspapers had led them to believe; a judge who was fair, impartial and unable to help; a prosecuting counsel who was skilled and would be

308

duped or misled by no one. The evidence proved that Alexandra had murdered her husband. That should not depress them or make them the least discouraged. It was not in question.

Monk was pushing his way through the people who jostled and talked, swirling around like dead leaves in an eddy of wind, infuriating him because he had purpose and was trying to force his way out as if somehow haste could help them to escape what was in their minds.

They were out in Old Bailey and turning onto Ludgate Hill when at last he spoke.

"I hope to God he knows what he is doing."

"That is a stupid thing to say," she replied angrily, because she was frightened herself, and stung for Rathbone. "He's doing his best—what we all agreed on. And anyway, what alternative is there? There isn't any other plan. She did do it. It would be pointless to try to deny it. There's nothing else to say, except the reason why."

"No," he agreed grimly. "No, there isn't. Damn, but it's cold. June shouldn't be this cold."

She managed to smile. "Shouldn't it? It frequently is."

He glared at her wordlessly.

"It'll get better." She shrugged and pulled her cloak higher. "Thank you for saving me a seat. I'll be here tomorrow."

She parted from him and set off into the chill air. She took a hansom, in spite of the expense, to Callandra Daviot's house.

"What has happened?" Callandra asked immediately, rising from her chair, her face anxious as she regarded Hester, seeing her tiredness, the droop of her shoulders and the fear in her eyes. "Come sit down—tell me."

Hester sat obediently. "Only what we expected, I suppose. But they all seem so very rational and set in their ideas. They know she did it—Lovat-Smith has proved that already. I just feel as if no matter what we say, they'll never believe he was anything but a fine man, a soldier and a hero. How can we prove he sodomized his own son?" Deliberately she used the hardest word she could find, and was perversely

309

annoyed when Callandra did not flinch. "They'll only hate her the more fiercely that we could say such a thing about such a fine man." She spoke with heavy sarcasm. "They'll hang her higher for the insult."

"Find the others," Callandra said levelly, her gray eyes sad and hard. "The alternative is giving up. Are you prepared to do that?"

"No, of course not. But I'm trying to think, if we are realistic, we should be prepared to be beaten."

Callandra stared at her, waiting, refusing to speak.

Hester met her look silently, then gradually began to think.

"The general's father abused him." She was fumbling towards something, a thread to begin pulling. "I don't suppose he started doing it himself suddenly, do you?"

"I have no idea—but sense would suggest not."

"There must be something to find in the past, if only we knew where to look," she went on, trying to make herself believe. "We've got to find the others; the other people who do this abysmal thing. But where? It's no use saying the old colonel did—we'll never prove that. He'll deny it, so will everyone else, and the general is dead."

She leaned back slowly. "Anyway, what would be the use? Even if we proved someone else did, that would not prove it of the general, or that Alexandra knew. I don't know where to begin. And time is so short." She stared at Callandra miserably. "Oliver has to start the defense in a couple of days, at the outside. Lovat-Smith is proving his case to the hilt. We haven't said a single thing worth anything yet—only that there was no evidence Alexandra was jealous."

"Not the others who abuse," Callandra said quietly. "The other victims. We must search the military records again."

"There's no time," Hester said desperately. "It would take months. And there might be nothing anyway."

"If he did that in the army, there will be something to find." Callandra's voice had no uncertainty in it, no quaver of doubt. "You stay at the trial. I'll search for some slip he's made, some drummer boy or cadet who's been hurt enough for it to show."

310

"Do you think . . . ?" Hester felt a quick leap of hope, foolish, quite unreasonable.

"Calm down, order your mind," Callandra commanded. "Tell me again everything that we know about the whole affair!"

Hester obeyed.

When the court was adjourned Oliver Rathbone was on his way out when Lovat-Smith caught up with him, his dark face sharp with curiosity. There was no avoiding him, and Rathbone was only half certain he wanted to. He had a need to speak with him, as one is sometimes compelled to probe a wound to see just how deep or how painful it is.

"What in the devil's name made you take this one?" Lovat-Smith demanded, his eyes meeting Rathbone's, brilliant with intelligence. There was a light in the back of them which might have been a wry kind of pity, or any of a dozen other things, all equally uncomfortable. "What are you playing at? You don't even seem to be trying. There are no miracles in this, you know. She did it!"

Somehow the goad lifted Rathbone's spirits; it gave him something to fight against. He looked back at Lovat-Smith, a man he respected, and if he were to know him better, might even like. They had much in common.

"I know she did," he said with a dry, close little smile. "Have I worried you, Wilberforce?"

Lovat-Smith smiled with answering tightness, his eyes bright. "Concerned me, Oliver, concerned me. I should not like to see you lose your touch. Your skill hitherto has been one of the ornaments of our profession. It would be . . . disconcerting"—he chose the word deliberately—"to have you crumble to pieces. What certitude then would there be for any of us?"

"How kind of you," Rathbone murmured sarcastically. "But easy victories pall after a while. If one always wins, perhaps one is attempting only what is well within one's capabilities—and there lies a kind of death, don't you think?

That which does not grow may well be showing the first signs of atrophy.''

They were passed by two lawyers, heads close together. They both turned to look at Rathbone, curiosity in their faces, before they resumed their conversation.

"All probably true," Lovat-Smith conceded, his eyes never leaving Rathbone's, a smile curling his mouth. "But though it is fine philosophy, it has nothing to do with the Carlyon case. Are you going to try for diminished responsibility? You've left it rather late—the judge will not take kindly to your not having said so at the beginning. You should have pleaded guilty but insane. I would have been prepared to consider meeting you somewhere on that.''

"Do you think she's insane?" Rathbone enquired with raised eyebrows, disbelief in his voice.

Lovat-Smith pulled a face. "She didn't seem so. But in view of your masterly proof that no one thought there was an affair between Mrs. Furnival and the general, not even Mrs. Carlyon herself, by all accounts, what else is there? Isn't that what you are leading to: her assumption was groundless, and mad?''

Rathbone's smile broadened into a grin. "Come along, Wilberforce. You know better than that! You'll hear my defense when the rest of the court does.''

Lovat-Smith shook his head, a furrow between his black eyebrows.

Rathbone gave him a tiny mock salute with more bravado than he felt, and took his leave. Lovat-Smith stood on the spot on the great courtroom steps, deep in thought, seemingly unaware of the coming and going around him, the crush of people, the chatter of voices.

Instead of going home, which perhaps he ought to have done, Rathbone took a hansom and went out to Primrose Hill to take supper with his father. He found Henry Rathbone standing in the garden looking at the young moon pale in the sky above the orchard trees, and half listening to the birdsong as the late starlings swirled across the sky and here and there a thrush or a chaffinch gave a warning cry.

For several moments they both stood in silence, letting the peace of the evening smooth out the smallest of the frets and wrinkles of the day. The bigger things, the pains and disappointments, took a firmer shape, less angry. Temper drained away.

"Well?" Henry Rathbone said eventually, half turning to look at Oliver.

"I suppose as well as could be expected," Oliver replied. "Lovat-Smith thinks I have lost my grip in taking the case at all. He may be right. In the cold light of the courtroom it seems a pretty wild attempt. Sometimes I even wonder if I believe in it myself. The public image of General Thaddeus Carlyon is impeccable, and the private one almost as good." He remembered vividly his father's anger and dismay, his imagination of pain, when he had told him of the abuse. He did not look at him now.

"Who testified today?" Henry asked quietly.

"The Furnivals. Lord, I loathe Louisa Furnival!" he said with sudden vehemence. "She is the total antithesis of everything I find attractive in a woman. Devious, manipulative, cocksure of herself, humorless, materialistic and completely unemotional. But I cannot fault her in the witness box." His face tightened. "And how I wanted to. I would take the greatest possible pleasure in tearing her to shreds!"

"How is Hester Latterly?"

"What?"

"How is Hester?" Henry repeated.

"What made you ask that?" Oliver screwed up his face.

"The opposite of everything you find attractive in a woman," Henry replied with a quiet smile.

Oliver blushed, a thing he did not do often. "I didn't see her," he said, feeling ridiculously evasive although it was the absolute truth.

Henry said nothing further, and perversely Oliver felt worse than if he had pursued the matter and allowed him to argue.

313

Beyond the orchard wall another cloud of starlings rose chattering into the pale sky and circled around, dark specks against the last flush of the sun. The honeysuckle was coming into bloom and the perfume of it was so strong the breeze carried it across the lawn to where they were standing. Oliver felt a rush of emotion, a sweetness, a longing to hold the beauty and keep it, which was impossible and always would be, a loneliness because he ached to share it, and pity, confusion and piercing hope all at once. He remained silent because silence was the only space large enough to hold it without crushing or bruising the heart of it.

The following morning he went to see Alexandra before court began. He did not know what he could say to her, but to leave her alone would be inexcusable. She was in the police cell, and as soon as she heard his step she swung around, her eyes wide, her face drained of all color. He could feel the fear in her touching him like a palpable thing.

"They hate me," she said simply, her voice betraying the tears so close to the surface. "They have already made up their minds. They aren't even listening. I heard one woman call out 'Hang her!' " She struggled to keep her control and almost failed. She blinked hard. "If women feel like that, what hope is there for me with the jury, who are all men?"

"More hope," he said very gently, and was amazed at the certainty in his own voice. Without thinking he took her hands in his, at first quite unresisting, like those of someone too ill to respond. "More hope," he said again with even greater assurance. "The woman you heard was frightened because you threaten her own status if you are allowed to go free and Society accepts you. Her only value in her own eyes is the certainty of her unquestionable purity. She has nothing else marketable, no talent, no beauty, no wealth or social position, but she has her impeccable virtue. Therefore virtue must keep its unassailable value. She does not understand virtue as a positive thing—generosity, patience, courage, kindness—only as the freedom from taint. That is so much easier to cope with."

314

She smiled bleakly. "You make it sound so very reasonable, and I don't feel it is at all. I feel it as hate." Her voice quivered.

"Of course it is hate, because it is fear, which is one of the ugliest of emotions. But later, when they have the truth, it will swing 'round like the wind, and blow just as hard from the other direction."

"Do you think so?" There was no belief in her and no lightness in her eyes.

"Yes," he said with more certainty than he was sure of. "Then it will be compassion and outrage—and fear lest such a thing happen to those they love, their own children. We are capable of great ugliness and stupidity," he said gently. "But you will find many of the same people just as capable of courage and pity as well. We must tell them the truth so they can have the chance."

She shivered and half turned away.

"We are singing in the dark, Mr. Rathbone. They aren't going to believe you, for the very reasons you talk about. Thaddeus was a hero, the sort of hero they need to believe in, because there are hundreds like him in the army, and they are what keep us safe and build our Empire." She hunched a little farther into herself. "They protect us from the real armies outside, and from the armies of doubt inside. If you destroy the British soldier in his red coat, the men who stood against all Europe and defeated Napoleon, saved England from the French, acquired Africa, India, Canada, quarter of the world, what have you left? No one is going to do that for one woman who is a criminal anyway."

"All you are saying is that the odds are heavy against us." He deliberately made his voice harder, suppressing the emotion he felt. "That same redcoat would not have turned away from battle because he was not sure of winning. You haven't read his history if you can entertain that thought for a second. His finest victories have been when outnumbered and against the odds."

"Like the charge of the Light Brigade?" she said with sudden sarcasm. "Do you know how many of them died? And for nothing at all!"

"Yes, one man in six of the entire Brigade—God knows how many were injured," he replied flatly, aware of a dull heat in his cheeks. "I was thinking more of the 'thin red line'—which if you recall stood a single man deep, and repulsed the enemy and held its ground till the charge broke and failed."

There was a smile on her wide mouth, and tears in her eyes, and no belief.

"Is that what you intend?"

"Certainly."

He could see she was still frightened, he could almost taste it in the air, but she had lost the will to fight him anymore. She turned away; it was surrender, and dismissal. She needed her time alone to prepare for the fear and the embarrassment, and the helplessness of the day.

The first witness was Charles Hargrave, called by Lovat-Smith to confirm the events of the dinner party already given, but primarily to retell his finding of the body of the general, with its terrible wound.

"Mr. Furnival came back into the room and said that the general had had an accident, is that correct?" Lovat-Smith asked.

Hargrave looked very serious, his face reflecting both his professional gravity and personal distress. The jury listened to him with a respect they reserved for the more distinguished members of certain professions: medicine, the Church, and lawyers who dealt with the bequests of the dead.

"Quite correct," Hargrave replied with a flicker of a smile across his rakish, rather elegant sandy face. "I presume he phrased it that way because he did not want to alarm people or cause more distress than necessary."

"Why do you say that, Doctor?"

"Because as soon as I went into the hallway myself and saw the body it was perfectly apparent that he was dead. Even a person with no medical training at all must have been aware of it."

"Could you describe his injuries—in full, please, Dr. Hargrave?"

The jury all shifted fractionally in their seats, attention and unhappiness vying in their expressions.

A shadow crossed Hargrave's face, but he was too practiced to need any explanation as to the necessity for such a thing.

"Of course," he agreed. "At the time I found him he was lying on his back with his left arm flung out, more or less level with one shoulder, but bent at the elbow. The right arm was only a short distance from his side, the hand twelve or fourteen inches from his hip. His legs were bent, the right folded awkwardly under him, and I judged it to be broken below the knee, his left leg severely twisted. These guesses later turned out to be correct." An expression crossed his face it was impossible to name, but it did not seem to be complacency. His eyes remained always on Lovat-Smith, never once straying upwards towards Alexandra in the dock opposite him.

"The injuries?" Lovat-Smith prompted.

"At the time all that was visible was bruising to the head, bleeding from the scalp at the left temple where he had struck the ground. There was a certain amount of blood, but not a great deal."

People in the gallery were craning their necks to stare up at Alexandra. There was a hiss of indrawn breath and a muttering.

"Let me understand you, Doctor." Lovat-Smith held up his hand, strong, short-fingered and slender. "There was only one injury to the head that you could see?"

"That is correct."

"As a medical man, what do you deduce from that?"

Hargrave lifted his wide shoulders very slightly. "That he fell straight over the banister and struck his head only once."

Lovat-Smith touched his left temple.

"Here?"

"Yes, within an inch or so."

"And yet he was lying on his back, did you not say?"

"I did," Hargrave said very quietly.

"Dr. Hargrave, Mr. Furnival has told us that the halberd was protruding from his chest." Lovat-Smith paced across

317

the floor and swung around, staring up at Hargrave on the witness box, his face creased in concentration. "How could a man fall from a balcony onto a weapon held upright in the hands of a suit of armour, piercing his chest, and land in such a way as to bruise himself on the front of his temple?"

The judge glanced at Rathbone.

Rathbone pursed his lips. He had no objections. He did not contest that Alexandra had murdered the general. This was all necessary, but beside the point of the real issue.

Lovat-Smith seemed surprised there was no interruption. Far from making it easier for him, it seemed to throw him a trifle off his stride.

"Dr. Hargrave," he said, shifting his balance from one foot to the other.

A juror fidgeted. Another scratched his nose and frowned.

"I have no idea," Hargrave replied. "It would seem to me as if the only explanation must be that he fell backwards, as one would naturally, and in some way twisted in the air after—" He stopped.

Lovat-Smith's black eyebrows rose curiously.

"You were saying, Doctor?" He spread his arms out. "He fell over backwards, turned in the air to allow the halberd to pierce his chest, and then somehow turned again so he could strike the floor with his temple? All without breaking the halberd or tearing it out of the wound. And then he rolled over to lie on his back with one leg folded under the other? You amaze me."

"Of course not," Hargrave said seriously, his temper unruffled, only a deep concern reflected in his face.

Rathbone glanced at the jury and knew they liked Hargrave, and Lovat-Smith had annoyed them. He also knew it was intentional. Hargrave was his witness, he wished him to be not only liked but profoundly believed.

"Then what are you saying, Dr. Hargrave?"

Hargrave was very serious. He looked at no one but Lovat-Smith, as if the two of them were discussing some tragedy in their gentlemen's club. There were faint mutters of approval from the crowd.

318

"That he must have fallen and struck his head, and then spun, the halberd been driven into his body when he was lying on the ground. Perhaps he was moved, but not necessarily. He could quite naturally have struck his head and then rolled a little to lie on his back. His head was at an odd angle—but his neck was not broken. I looked for that, and I am sure it was not so."

"You are saying it could not have been an accident, Dr. Hargrave?"

Hargrave's face tightened. "I am."

"How long did it take you to come to this tragic conclusion?"

"From the time I first saw the body, about—about one or two minutes, I imagine." A ghost of a smile moved his lips. "Time is a peculiar commodity on such an occasion. It seems both to stretch out endlessly, like a road before and behind with no turning, and at the same time to crush in on you and have no size at all. To say one or two minutes is only a guess, made afterwards using intelligence. It was one of the most dreadful moments I can recall."

"Why? Because you knew someone in that house, one of your personal friends, had murdered General Thaddeus Carlyon?"

Again the judge glanced at Rathbone, and Rathbone made no move. A frown crossed the judge's face, and still Rathbone did not object.

"Yes," Hargrave said almost inaudibly. "I regret it, but it was inescapable. I am sorry." For the first and only time he looked up at Alexandra.

"Just so," Lovat-Smith agreed solemnly. "And accordingly you informed the police?"

"I did."

"Thank you."

Rathbone looked at the jury again. Not one of them looked at the dock. She sat there motionless, her blue eyes on Rathbone, without anger, without surprise, and without hope.

He smiled at her, and felt ridiculous.

319

10

MONK LISTENED TO LOVAT-SMITH questioning
Charles Hargrave with a mounting anxiety. Hargrave was
creating an excellent impression with the jury; he could see
their grave, attentive faces. He not only had their respect but
their belief. Whatever he said about the Carlyons they would
accept.

There was nothing Rathbone could do yet, and Monk's
intelligence knew it; nevertheless he fretted at the helplessness and the anger rose in him, clenching his hands and
hardening the muscles of his body.

Lovat-Smith stood in front of the witness box, not elegantly (it was not in him), but with a vitality that held attention more effectively, and his voice was fine, resonant and
individual, an actor's instrument.

"Dr. Hargrave, you have known the Carlyon family for
many years, and indeed been their medical adviser for most
of that time, is that not so?"

"It is."

"You must be in a position to have observed their characters, their relationships with one another."

Rathbone stiffened, but did not yet interrupt.

Lovat-Smith smiled, glanced at Rathbone, then back up at
Hargrave.

"Please be careful to answer only from your own observation," he warned. "Nothing that you were told by someone else, unless it is to account for their own behavior; and please do not give us your personal judgment, only the grounds upon which you base it."

"I understand," Hargrave acknowledged with the bleakest of smiles. "I have given evidence before, Mr. Lovat-Smith. What is it you wish to know?"

With extreme care as to the rules of evidence, all morning and well into the afternoon Lovat-Smith drew from Hargrave a picture of Thaddeus Carlyon as honorable and upright, a military hero, a fine leader to his men, an example to that youth which looked to courage, discipline and honor as their goals. He had been an excellent husband who had never ill-used his wife with physical violence or cruelty, nor made excessive demands of her in the marriage bed, but on the other hand had given her three fine children, to whom he had been a father of devotion beyond the normal. His son adored him, and rightly so, since he had spent much time with the boy and taken great care in the determination of his future. There was no evidence whatsoever that he had ever been unfaithful to his wife, nor drunk to excess, gambled, kept her short of money, insulted her, slighted her in public, or in any other way treated her less than extremely well.

Had he ever exhibited any signs whatever of mental or emotional instability?

None at all; the idea would be laughable, were it not so offensive.

What about the accused, who was also his patient?

That, tragically, was different. She had, in the last year or so, become agitated without apparent cause, been subject to deep moods of melancholy, had fits of weeping for which she would give no reason, had absented herself from her home without telling anyone where she was going, and had quarreled violently with her husband.

The jury were looking at Alexandra, but with embarrassment now, as if she were someone it was vulgar to observe, like someone naked, or caught in an intimate act.

"And how do you know this, Dr. Hargrave?" Lovat-Smith enquired.

Still Rathbone sat silently.

"Of course I did not hear the quarrels," Hargrave said, biting his lip. "But the weeping and the melancholy I saw, and the absences were apparent to everyone. I called more than once and found unexplainably that she was not there. I am afraid the agitation, for which she would never give me a reason, was painfully obvious each time she saw me in consultation. She was so disturbed as to be hysterical—I use the word intentionally. But she never gave me any reason, only wild hints and accusations."

"Of what?" Lovat-Smith frowned. His voice rose dramatically with interest, as if he did not know what the answer would be, although Monk, sitting almost in the same seat as on the previous day, assumed he must. Surely he was far too skilled to have asked the question without first knowing the answer. Although it was just possible his case was so strong, and proceeding without challenge, that he might have thought he could take the risk.

The jury leaned forward a trifle; there was a tiny rustle of movement. Beside Monk on the bench Hester stiffened. The spectators near them felt no such restraints of delicacy as the jury. They stared at Alexandra quite openly, faces agog.

"Accusations of unfaithfulness on the general's part?" Lovat-Smith prompted.

The judge looked at Rathbone. Lovat-Smith was leading the witness. Rathbone said nothing. The judge's face tightened, but he did not interrupt.

"No," Hargrave said reluctantly. He drew in his breath. "At least, they were unspecific, I was not sure. I think she was merely speaking wildly, lashing out at anyone. She was hysterical; it made no sense."

"I see. Thank you." Lovat-Smith inclined his head. "That is all, Doctor. Please remain where you are, in case my learned friend wishes to question you."

"Oh indeed, I do." Rathbone rose to his feet, his voice purring, his movements tigerlike. "You spoke most frankly about the Carlyon family, and I accept that you have told us all you know, trivial as that is." He looked up at Hargrave in the high, pulpitlike witness stand. "Am I correct, Dr. Hargrave, in supposing that your friendship with them dates back some fifteen or sixteen years?"

"Yes, you are." Hargrave was puzzled; he had already said this to Lovat-Smith.

"In fact as a friendship with the family, rather than General Carlyon, it ceased some fourteen years ago, and you have seen little of them since then?"

"I—suppose so." Hargrave was reluctant, but not disturbed; his sandy face held no disquiet. It seemed a minor point.

"So in fact you cannot speak with any authority on the character of, for example, Mrs. Felicia Carlyon? Or Colonel Carlyon?"

Hargrave shrugged. It was an oddly graceful gesture. "If you like. It hardly seems to matter; they are not on trial."

Rathbone smiled, showing all his teeth.

"But you mentioned your friendship with General Carlyon?"

"Yes. I was his physician, as well as that of his wife and family."

"Indeed, I am coming to that. You say that Mrs. Carlyon, the accused, began to exhibit signs of extreme distress—indeed you used the word *hysteria*?"

"Yes—I regret to say she did," Hargrave agreed.

"What did she do, precisely, Doctor?"

Hargrave looked uncomfortable. He glanced at the judge, who met his eyes without response.

"The question disturbs you?" Rathbone remarked.

"It seems unnecessarily—exposing—of a patient's vulnerability," Hargrave replied, but his eyes remained on Rathbone; Alexandra herself might have been absent for all the awareness he showed of her.

"You may leave Mrs. Carlyon's interest in my hands," Rathbone assured him. "I am here to represent her. Please answer my question. Describe her behavior. Did she scream?'' He leaned back a little to stare up at Hargrave, his eyes very wide. "Did she faint, take a fit?'' He spread his hands wide. "Throw herself about, have hallucinations? In what way was she hysterical?''

Hargrave sighed impatiently. "You exhibit a layman's idea of hysteria, if you pardon my saying so. Hysteria is a state of mind where control is lost, not necessarily a matter of uncontrolled physical behavior.''

"How did you know her mind was out of control, Dr. Hargrave?'' Rathbone was very polite. Watching him, Monk longed for him to be thoroughly rude, to tear Hargrave to pieces in front of the jury. But his better sense knew it would forfeit their sympathy, which in the end was what would win or lose them the case—and Alexandra's life.

Hargrave thought for a moment before beginning.

"She could not keep still,'' he said at length. "She kept moving from one position to another, at times unable even to remain seated. Her whole body shook and when she picked up something, I forget what, it slipped through her fingers. Her voice was trembling and she fumbled her words. She wept uncontrollably.''

"But no deliriums, hallucinations, fainting, screaming?'' Rathbone pressed.

"No. I have told you not.'' Hargrave was impatient and he glanced at the jury, knowing he had their sympathy.

"Tell us, Dr. Hargrave, how would this behavior differ from that of someone who had just received a severe shock and was extremely distressed, even agonized, by her experience?''

Hargrave thought for several seconds.

"I cannot think that it would,'' he said at last. "Except that she did not speak of any shock, or discovery.''

Rathbone opened his eyes wide, as if mildly surprised. "She did not even hint that she had learned her husband had betrayed her with another woman?''

He leaned a little forward over the rail of the witness box. "No—no, she did not. I think I have already said, Mr. Rathbone, that she could have made no such dramatic discovery, because it was not so. This affair, if you wish to call it that, was all in her imagination."

"Or yours, Doctor," Rathbone said, his voice suddenly gritted between his teeth.

Hargrave flushed, but with embarrassment and anger rather than guilt. His eyes remained fixed on Rathbone and there was no evasion in them.

"I answered your question, Mr. Rathbone," he said bitterly. "You are putting words into my mouth. I did not say there was an affair, indeed I said there was not!"

"Just so," Rathbone agreed, turning back to the body of the court again. "There was no affair, and Mrs. Carlyon at no time mentioned it to you, or suggested that it was the cause of her extreme distress."

"That is . . ." Hargrave hesitated, as if he would add something, then found no words and remained silent.

"But she was extremely distressed by something, you are positive about that?"

"Of course."

"Thank you. When did this occur, your first observation of her state of mind?"

"I have not a precise date, but it was in July of last year."

"Approximately nine months before the general's death?"

"That is right." Hargrave smiled. It was a trivial calculation.

"And you have no idea of any event at this time which could have precipitated it?"

"No idea at all."

"You were General Carlyon's physician?"

"I have already said so."

"Indeed. And you have recounted the few occasions on which you were called to treat him professionally. He seems to have been a man in excellent health, and those injuries he sustained in action were quite naturally treated by the army surgeons in the field."

"You are stating the obvious," Hargrave said with tight lips.

"Perhaps it is obvious to you why you did not mention the

one wound that you did treat, but it escapes me," Rathbone said with the smallest of smiles.

For the first time Hargrave was visibly discomfited. He opened his mouth, said nothing, and closed it again. His hands on the rail were white at the knuckles.

There was silence in the courtroom.

Rathbone walked across the floor a pace or two and turned back.

There was a sudden lifting of interest throughout the court. The jury shifted on their benches almost imperceptibly.

Hargrave's face tightened, but he could not avoid an answer, and he knew it.

"It was a domestic accident, and all rather foolish," he said, lifting his shoulder a little as if to dismiss it, and at the same time explain its omission. "He was cleaning an ornamental dagger and it slipped and cut him in the upper leg."

"You observed this happen?" Rathbone asked casually.

"Ah—no. I was called to the house because the wound was bleeding quite badly, and naturally I asked him what had happened. He told me."

"Then it is hearsay?" Rathbone raised his eyebrows. "Not satisfactory, Doctor. It may have been the truth—equally it may not."

Lovat-Smith came to his feet.

"Is any of this relevant, my lord? I can understand my learned friend's desire to distract the jury's minds from Dr. Hargrave's evidence, indeed to try and discredit him in some way, but this is wasting the court's time and serving no purpose at all."

The judge looked at Rathbone.

"Mr. Rathbone, do you have some object in view? If not, I shall have to order you to move on."

"Oh yes, my lord," Rathbone said with more confidence than Monk thought he could feel. "I believe the injury may be of crucial importance to the case."

Lovat-Smith swung around with an expressive gesture, raising his hands palm upwards.

Someone in the courtroom tittered with laughter, and it was instantly suppressed.

Hargrave sighed.

"Please describe the injury, Doctor," Rathbone continued.

"It was a deep gash to the thigh, in the front and slightly to the inside, precisely where a knife might have slipped from one's hand while cleaning it."

"Deep? An inch? Two inches? And how long, Doctor?"

"About an inch and a half at its deepest, and some five inches long," Hargrave replied with wry, obvious weariness.

"Quite a serious injury. And pointing in which direction?" Rathbone asked with elaborate innocence.

Hargrave stood silent, his face pale.

In the dock Alexandra leaned a fraction forward for the first time, as if at last something had been said which she had not expected.

"Please answer the question, Dr. Hargrave," the judge instructed.

"Ah—er—it was . . . upwards," Hargrave said awkwardly.

"Upwards?" Rathbone blinked and even from behind his elegant shoulders expressed incredulity, as if he could not have heard correctly. "You mean—from the knee up towards the groin, Dr. Hargrave?"

"Yes," Hargrave said almost inaudibly.

"I beg your pardon? Would you please repeat that so the jury can hear you?"

"Yes," Hargrave said grimly.

The jury was puzzled. Two leaned forward. One shifted in his seat, another frowned in deep concentration. They did not know what relevance it could possibly have, but they knew duress when they saw it, and felt Hargrave's reluctance and the sudden change in tension.

Even the crowd was silent.

A lesser man than Lovat-Smith would have interrupted again, but he knew it would only betray his own uncertainty.

"Tell us, Dr. Hargrave," Rathbone went on quietly, "how

327

a man cleaning a knife could have it slip from his hand so as to stab himself upwards, from knee to groin?'' He turned on the spot, very slowly. ''In fact, perhaps you would oblige us by showing us exactly what motion you had in mind when you—er—believed this account of his? I presume you know why a military man of his experience, a general indeed, should be clumsy enough to clean a knife so incompetently? I would have expected better from the rank and file.'' He frowned. ''In fact, ordinary man as I am, I have no ornamental knives, but I do not clean my own silver, or my own boots.''

''I have no idea why he cleaned it,'' Hargrave replied, leaning forward over the rail of the witness box, his hands gripping the edge. ''But since it was he who had the accident with it, I was quite ready to believe him. Perhaps it was because he did not normally clean it that he was clumsy.''

He had made a mistake, and he knew it immediately. He should not have tried to justify it.

''You cannot know it was he who had the accident, if indeed it was an accident,'' Rathbone said with excessive politeness. ''Surely what you mean is that it was he who had the wound?''

''If you wish,'' Hargrave replied tersely. ''It seems a quibble to me.''

''And the manner in which he was holding it to sustain such a wound as you describe so clearly for us?'' Rathbone raised his hand as if gripping a knife, and bent his body experimentally into various contortions to slip and gash himself upwards. It was perfectly impossible, and the court began to titter with nervous laughter. Rathbone looked up enquiringly at Hargrave.

''All right!'' Hargrave snapped. ''It cannot have happened as he said. What are you suggesting? That Alexandra tried to stab him? Surely you are supposed to be here defending her, not making doubly sure she is hanged!''

The judge leaned forward, his face angry, his voice sharp.

''Dr. Hargrave, your remarks are out of order, and grossly prejudicial. You will withdraw them immediately.''

"Of course. I'm sorry. But I think it is Mr. Rathbone you should caution. He is incompetent in his defense of Mrs. Carlyon."

"I doubt it. I have known Mr. Rathbone for many years, but if he should prove to be so, then the accused may appeal on that ground." He looked towards Rathbone. "Please continue."

"Thank you, my lord." Rathbone bowed very slightly. "No, Dr. Hargrave, I was not suggesting that Mrs. Carlyon stabbed her husband, I was pointing out that he must have lied to you as to the cause of this wound, and that it seemed undeniable that someone stabbed him. I shall make my suggestions as to who, and why, at a later time."

There was another rustle of interest, and the first shadow of doubt across the faces of the jury. It was the only time they had been given any cause to question the case as Lovat-Smith had presented it. It was a very small shadow, no more than a flicker, but it was there.

Hargrave turned to step down.

"Just one more thing, Dr. Hargrave," Rathbone said quickly. "What was General Carlyon wearing when you were called to tend this most unpleasant wound?"

"I beg your pardon?" Hargrave looked incredulous.

"What was General Carlyon wearing?" Rathbone repeated. "In what was he dressed?"

"I have no idea. For God's sake! What does it matter?"

"Please answer my question," Rathbone insisted. "Surely you noticed, when you had to cut it away to reach the wound?"

Hargrave made as if to speak, then stopped, his face pale.

"Yes?" Rathbone said very softly.

"He wasn't." Hargrave seemed to regather himself. "It had already been removed. He had on simply his underwear."

"I see. No—no blood-soaked trousers?" Rathbone shrugged eloquently. "Someone had already at least partially treated him? Were these garments lying close to hand?"

"No—I don't think so. I didn't notice."

Rathbone frowned, a look of suddenly renewed interest crossing his face.

"Where did this—accident—take place, Dr. Hargrave?"

Hargrave hesitated. "I—I'm not sure."

Lovat-Smith rose from his seat and the judge looked at him and shook his head fractionally.

"If you are about to object that it is irrelevant, Mr. Lovat-Smith, I will save you the trouble. It is not. I myself wish to know the answer to this. Dr. Hargrave? You must have some idea. He cannot have moved far with a wound such as you describe. Where did you see him when you attended it?"

Hargrave was pale, his face drawn.

"In the home of Mr. and Mrs. Furnival, my lord."

There was a rustle of excitement around the room, a letting out of breath. At least half the jurors turned to look up at Alexandra, but her face registered only complete incomprehension.

"Did you say in the house of Mr. and Mrs. Furnival, Dr. Rathbone?" the judge said with undisguised surprise.

"Yes, my lord," Hargrave replied unhappily.

"Mr. Rathbone," the judge instructed, "please continue."

"Yes, my lord." Rathbone looked anything but shaken; indeed he appeared quite calm. He turned back to Hargrave. "So the general was cleaning this ornamental knife in the Furnivals' house?"

"I believe so. I was told he was showing it to young Valentine Furnival. It was something of a curio. I daresay he was demonstrating its use—or something of the sort . . ."

There was a nervous titter around the room. Rathbone's face registered a wild and fleeting humor, but he forbore from making the obvious remark. Indeed he turned to something utterly different, which took them all by surprise.

"Tell me, Dr. Hargrave, what was the general wearing when he left to go back to his own house?"

"The clothes in which he came, of course."

Rathbone's eyebrows shot up, and too late Hargrave realized his error.

"Indeed?" Rathbone said with amazement. "Including those torn and bloodstained trousers?"

Hargrave said nothing.

"Shall I recall Mrs. Sabella Pole, who remembers the incident quite clearly?"

"No—no." Hargrave was thoroughly annoyed, his lips in a thin line, his face pale and set. "The trousers were quite intact—and not stained. I cannot explain it, and did not seek to. It is not my affair. I simply treated the wound."

"Indeed," Rathbone agreed with a small, unreadable smile. "Thank you, Dr. Hargrave. I have no further questions for you."

The next witness was Evan, for the police. His testimony was exactly what most would have foreseen and presented no interest for Monk. He watched Evan's sensitive, unhappy face as he recounted being called to the Furnivals' house, seeing the body and drawing the inevitable conclusions, then the questioning of all the people concerned. It obviously pained him.

Monk found his attention wandering. Rathbone could not provide a defense out of what he had, no matter how brilliant his cross-examination. It would be ridiculous to hope he could trick or force from any one of the Carlyons the admission that they knew the general was abusing his son. He had seen them outside in the hallway, sitting upright, dressed in black, faces set in quiet, dignified grief, totally unified. Even Edith Sobell was with them and now and again looked with concern at her father. But Felicia was in the courtroom, since she had not been subpoenaed to give evidence, and therefore was permitted inside the court. She was very pale behind her veil, and rigid as a plastic figure.

It was imperative they had to find out who else was involved in the pederasty, apart from the general and his father. Cassian had said "others," not merely his grandfather. Who? Who had access to the boy in a place sufficiently private? That was important; it had to be utterly private. One would hardly undertake such an activity where there was the slightest risk of interruption.

The interrogations went on and Monk was almost unaware of them.

Family again? Peverell Erskine? Was that what Damaris had discovered that night which had driven her nearly frantic with distress, so much so that she had been unable to control herself? After seeing Valentine Furnival she had come downstairs in a state bordering on hysteria. Why? Had she learned that her husband was sodomizing his nephew? But what could possibly have taken place up there that would tell her such a thing? Peverell himself had remained downstairs. Everyone had sworn to that. So she could not have seen anything. And Cassian was not even in the Furnivals' house.

But she had seen or heard something. Surely it could not be a coincidence that it had been the night of the murder? But what? What had she discovered?

Fenton Pole had been present. Was he the other one who abused Cassian, and in some way the cause of Sabella's hatred?

Or was it Maxim Furnival? Was the relationship between the general and Maxim not only one of mutual business interest but the indulgence of a mutual vice as well? Was that the reason for his frequent visits to the Furnival house, and nothing to do with Louisa? That would be a nice irony. No wonder Alexandra found a bitter and terrible humor in it.

But she had not known there was anyone else. She had thought that in killing the general she had ended it, freed Cassian from the abuse. She knew of no one else, not even the old colonel.

Evan was still testifying, this time answering Rathbone, but the questions were superfluous, only clarifying points already made, that Evan had found nothing to prove the jealousy Alexandra had denied, and he found it hard to believe in himself.

Monk's thoughts wandered away again. That wound on the General's leg. Surely it had been Cassian who had inflicted that? From what Hester had said of her interview with the boy, and her observation of him, he was ambivalent about the abuse, uncertain whether it was right or wrong, afraid to lose his mother's love, secretive, flattered, frightened, but not entirely hating it. There was a frisson of excitement in him even when he mentioned it, the thrill of inclusion in the adult world, knowing something that others did not.

Had he ever been taken to the Furnivals' house? They should have asked about that. It was an omission.

"Did the general ever take Cassian to the Furnivals' house?" he whispered to Hester next to him.

"Not that I know of," she replied. "Why?"

"The other pederast," he replied almost under his breath. "We have to know who it is."

"Maxim Furnival?" she said in amazement, raising her voice without realizing it.

"Be quiet," someone said angrily.

"Why not?" he answered, leaning forward so he could whisper. "It's got to be someone who saw the boy regularly, and privately—and where Alexandra didn't know about it."

"Maxim?" she repeated, frowning at him.

"Why not? It's someone. Who stabbed the general? Does Rathbone know, or is he just hoping we'll find out before he's finished?"

"Just hoping," she said unhappily.

"Ssh!" a man hissed behind them, tapping Monk on the shoulder with his forefinger.

The reprimand infuriated Monk, but he could think of no satisfactory rejoinder. His face blazed with temper, but he said nothing.

"Valentine," Hester said suddenly.

"Be quiet!" The man in front swung around, his face pinched with anger. "If you don't want to listen, then go outside!"

Monk disregarded him. Of course—Valentine. He was only a few years older than Cassian. He would be an ideal victim first. And everyone had said how fond he had been of the general, or at least how fond the general had been of him. He had visited the boy regularly. Perhaps Valentine, terrified, confused, revolted by the general and by himself, had finally fought back.

How to be certain? And how to prove it?

He turned to look at Hester, and saw the same thoughts reflected in her eyes.

Her lips formed the words *It is worth trying*. Then her eyes darkened with anxiety. "But be careful," she whispered urgently. "If you're clumsy you could ruin it forever."

It was on the tip of his tongue to retaliate, then the reality of its importance overtook all vanity and irritation.

"I will." He promised so softly it was barely audible even to her. "I'll be 'round about. I'll try to get proof first." And he stood up, much to the fury of the person on his other side, and wriggled past the whole row, stepping on toes, banging knees and nearly losing his footing as he found his way out. The first thing was to learn what was physically possible. If Fenton Pole had never been alone with Cassian or Valentine, then he was not worth pursuing as a suspect. Servants would know, particularly footmen; footmen knew where their masters went in the family carriage, and they usually knew who visited the house. If Pole had been careful enough to travel to some other place to meet there, and go by hansom, then it would be a far harder task to trace him, and perhaps pointless.

He must begin with the obvious. He hailed a cab and gave the driver the address of Fenton and Sabella Pole's house.

All the remainder of the afternoon he questioned the servants. At first they were somewhat reluctant to answer him, feeling that in the absence of knowledge, silence was the wisest and safest course. But one maid in particular had come with Sabella on her marriage, and her loyalties were to Alexandra, because that was where her mistress's loyalties were. She was more than willing to answer anything Monk wished to know, and she was quite capable of discovering from the footman, groom and parlormaid every detail he needed.

Certainly Mr. Pole had known the general before he met Miss Sabella. It was the general who had introduced them, that she knew herself; she had been there at the time. Yes, they had got along very well with each other, better than with Mrs. Carlyon, unfortunately. The reason? She had no idea, except that poor Miss Sabella had not wished to marry, but to go into the Church. There was nothing anyone could say against Mr. Pole. He was always a gentleman.

Did he know Mr. and Mrs. Furnival well?

Not very, the acquaintance seemed to be recent.

Did Mr. Pole often visit the general at his home?

No, hardly ever. The general came here.

Did he often bring young Master Cassian?

She had never known it to happen. When Master Cassian came it was with his mother, to visit Miss Sabella during the daytime, when Mr. Pole was out.

Monk thanked her and excused himself. It seemed Fenton Pole was not a suspect, on the grounds of physical impossibility. The opportunity was simply not there.

He walked in the clear evening back to Great Titchfield Street, passing open carriages as people took the air, fashionably dressed in bonnets with ribbons and gowns trimmed with flowers; couples out strolling arm in arm, gossiping, flirting; a man walking his dog. He arrived a few moments after Hester returned from the court. She looked tired and anxious, and Major Tiplady, sitting up on an ordinary chair now, appeared concerned for her.

"Come in, come in, Mr. Monk," he said quickly. "I fear the news is not encouraging, but please be seated and we shall hear it together. Molly will bring us a cup of tea. And perhaps you would like supper? Poor Hester looks in need of some refreshment. Please—be seated!" He waved his arm in invitation, but his eyes were still on Hester's face.

Monk sat down, primarily to encourage Hester to speak, but he accepted the invitation to supper.

"Excuse me." Tiplady rose to his feet and limped to the door. "I shall see about it with Molly and Cook."

"What is it?" Monk demanded. "What has happened?"

"Very little," Hester said wearily. "Only what we expected. Evan recounted how Alexandra had confessed."

"We knew that would come," Monk pointed out, angry that she was so discouraged. He needed her to have hope, because he too was afraid. It was a ridiculous task they had set themselves, and they had no right to have given Alexandra hope. There was none, none at all of any sense.

"Of course," she said a little sharply, betraying her own fragile emotions. "But you asked me what had happened."

He looked at her and met her eyes. There was a moment of complete understanding, all the pity, the outrage, all the delicate shades of fear and self-doubt for their own part in it. They said nothing, because words were unnecessary, and too clumsy an instrument anyway.

"I started to look at physical possibilities," he said after a moment or two. "I don't think Fenton Pole can be the other abuser. There doesn't seem to have been enough opportunity for him to be alone with either Cassian or Valentine."

"So where are you going next?"

"The Furnivals', I think."

"To Louisa?" she said with a flash of bitter amusement.

"To the servants." He understood precisely what she meant, with all its undertones. "Of course she would protect Maxim, but since it hasn't been mentioned yet, she won't have any idea that we are looking for abuse of children. She'll be thinking of herself, and the old charge about the general."

Hester said nothing.

"Then I'll go to the Carlyons'."

"The Carlyons'?" Now she was surprised. "You'll not find anything there, but even if you did, what good would it do? They'll all lie to protect him, and we know about him anyway! It's the other person we need to find—with proof."

"Not the colonel—Peverell Erskine."

She was stunned, her face filled with amazement and disbelief. "Peverell! Oh no! You can't think it was him!"

"Why not? Because we like him?" He was hurting himself as well as her and they both understood it. "Do you think it has to be someone who looks like a monster? There was no violence used, no hate or greed—just a man who has never grown up enough to find an appropriate closeness with an adult woman, a man who only feels safe with a child who won't judge him or demand a commitment or the ability to

336

give, who won't see the flaws in his character or the clumsiness or inadequacy of his acts."

"You sound as if you want me to feel sorry for him," she said with tight, hard disgust, but he did not know whether that disgust was at him, at the abuses, or only at the situation—or even if it was so hard because underneath it was the wrench of real pity.

"I don't care what you feel," he lied back. "Only what you think. Just because Peverell Erskine is an agreeable man and his wife loves him doesn't mean he can't have weaknesses that destroy him—and others."

"I don't believe it of Peverell," she said stubbornly, but she gave no reason.

"That's just stupid," he snapped at her, aware of the anger inside himself to which he chose to give no name. "You're hardly much use if you are working on that level of intelligence."

"I said I don't believe it," she retorted equally violently. "I didn't say I wouldn't investigate the possibility."

"Oh yes?" He raised his eyebrows sarcastically. "How?"

"Through Damaris, of course," she said with stinging contempt. "She discovered something that night—something that upset her beyond bearing. Had you forgotten that? Or did you just think I had?"

Monk stared at her, and was about to make an equally acid reply when the door opened again and Major Tiplady returned, immediately followed by the maid with a tray of tea, announcing that supper would be ready in a little over half an hour. It was the perfect opportunity to change his tone altogether, and be suddenly charming, to enquire after Major Tiplady's recovery, appreciate the tea, and even to speak courteously to Hester. They talked of other things: the news from India, the ugly rumors of opium war in China, the Persian War, and unrest in the government at home. All the subjects were distressing, but they were far away, and he found the brief half hour most agreeable, a relief from responsibility and the urgent present.

* * *

The following day Lovat-Smith called further witnesses as to the unblemished character of the general, his fine nature and heroic military record. Once again Hester went to court to watch and listen on Major Tiplady's behalf, and Monk went first to the house of Callandra Daviot, where he learned from her, to his chagrin, that she had been unable to find anything beyond the merest whisper to indicate that General Carlyon had ever formed any relationships that were anything but the most proper and correct. However, she did have extensive lists of names of all youths who had served with his regiment, both in England and in India, and she produced it with an apology.

"Don't worry," he said with sudden gentleness. "This may be all we need."

She looked at him with something close to a squint, disbelief plain in her face.

He scanned down the list rapidly to see if the name of the Furnivals' bootboy was there. It was on the second page, Robert Andrews, honorable discharge, owing to wounds received in action. He looked up, smiling at her.

"Well?" she demanded.

"Maybe," he answered. "I'm going to find out."

"Monk!"

"Yes." He looked at her with a sudden awareness of how much she had done for him. "I think this may be the Furnivals' bootboy," he explained with a lift of hope in his voice. "The one who dropped all the laundry when he came face-to-face with the general on the night of the murder. I'm going to the Furnivals' house now to find out. Thank you."

"Ah," she said with a touch of satisfaction creeping into her expression at last. "Ah—well . . . good."

He thanked her again and bade her good-bye with a graceful kiss to the air, then hurried out to find a hansom to take him back to the Furnivals' house.

He reached it at a quarter to ten, in time to see Maxim leave, presumably to go into the City. He waited almost an hour and a half, and was rewarded by seeing Louisa, glamorous and quite unmistakable in a richly flowered bonnet and skirts so wide it took very great skill for her to negotiate the carriage doors.

As soon as she was well out of sight, Monk went to the back door and knocked. It was opened by the bootboy, looking expectant. His expression changed utterly when he saw Monk; apparently he had been anticipating someone else.

"Yes?" he said with a not unfriendly frown. He was a smart lad and stood very straight, but there was a watchfulness in his eyes, a knowledge of hurt.

"I was here before, speaking to Mrs. Furnival," Monk began carefully, but already he felt a kind of excitement. "And she was kind enough to help me in enquiring into the tragedy of General Carlyon's death."

The boy's expression darkened, an almost imperceptible tightening of the skin around his eyes and mouth, a narrowing of the lips.

"If you want Mrs. Furnival, you should 'ave gone to the front door," he said warily.

"I don't, this time." Monk smiled at him. "There are just a few details about other people who have called at the house in the past, and perhaps Master Valentine could help me. But I need to speak with one of your footmen, perhaps John."

"Well you'd better come in," the bootboy said cautiously. "An' I'll ask Mr. Diggins, 'e's the butler. I can't let you do that meself."

"Of course not." Monk followed him in graciously.

"Wot's your name, then?" the boy asked.

"Monk—William Monk. What is yours?"

"Who, me?" The boy was startled.

"Yes—what is your name?" Monk made it casual.

"Robert Andrews, sir. You wait 'ere, an' I'll see Mr. Diggins for yer." And the boy straightened his shoulders again and walked out very uprightly, as if he were a soldier on parade. Monk was left in the scullery, pulse racing, thoughts teeming in his mind, longing to question the boy and knowing how infinitely delicate it was, and that a word or a look that was clumsy might make him keep silence forever.

"What is it this time, Mr. Monk?" the butler asked when he returned a few minutes later. "I'm sure we've all told you all we know about that night. Now we'd just like to forget it and get on with our work. I'll not 'ave you upsetting all our maids again!"

"I don't need to see the maids," Monk said placatingly. "Just a footman would be quite sufficient, and possibly the bootboy. It is only about who called here frequently."

"Robert said something about Master Valentine." The butler looked at Monk closely. "I can't let you see him, not without the master's or the mistress's permission, and they're both out at the present."

"I understand." Monk chose not to fight when he knew he could not win. That would have to wait for another time. "I daresay you know everything that goes on in the house anyway. If you can spare the time?"

The butler considered for a moment. He was not immune to flattery, if it were disguised well enough, and he certainly liked what was his due.

"What is it you wish to know, in particular, Mr. Monk?" He turned and led the way towards his own sitting room, where they could be private, in case the matter should be in any way delicate. And regardless of that, it created the right impression in front of the other staff. It did not do to stand around discussing presumably private business in full view of everyone.

"How often did General Carlyon come here to visit, either Mrs. Furnival or Master Valentine?"

"Well, Mr. Monk, he used to come more often in the past, before he had his accident, sir. After that he came a lot less."

"Accident?"

"Yes sir—when he injured his leg, sir."

"That would be when he was hurt with the knife. Cleaning the knife, and it slipped and gashed him in the thigh," Monk said as levelly as he could.

"Yes sir."

"Where did that happen? In what room?"

"I'm afraid I don't know, sir. Somewhere upstairs, I be-

340

lieve. Possibly in the schoolroom. There is an ornamental knife up there. At least there was. I haven't seen it since then. May I ask why you need to know, sir?''

"No reason in particular—just that it was a nasty thing to happen. Did anyone else visit Master Valentine regularly? Mr. Pole, for example?''

"No sir, never that I know of.'' The first question remained in the butler's face.

"Or Mr. Erskine?''

"No sir, not as far as I know of. What would that have to do with the general's death, Mr. Monk?''

"I'm not sure,'' Monk said candidly. "I think it's possible that someone may have . . . exerted certain . . . pressures on Master Valentine.''

"Pressures, sir?''

"I don't want to say anything more until I know for certain. It could malign someone quite without foundation.''

"I understand, sir.'' The butler nodded sagely.

"Did Master Valentine visit the Carlyon house, to your knowledge?''

"Not so far as I am aware, sir. I do not believe that either Mr. or Mrs. Furnival is acquainted with Colonel and Mrs. Carlyon, and their acquaintance with Mr. and Mrs. Erskine is not close.''

"I see. Thank you.'' Monk was not sure whether he was relieved or disappointed. He did not want it to be Peverell Erskine. But he needed to find out who it was, and time was getting desperately short. Perhaps it was Maxim after all— the most obvious, when one thought about it. He was here all the time. Another father abusing his son. He found his stomach clenching and his teeth ached with the tightness of his jaw. It was the first time he had felt even the briefest moment of pity for Louisa.

"Is there anything else, sir?'' the butler said helpfully.

"I don't think so.'' What was there to ask that could be addressed to this man and yield an answer leading to the identity of whoever had so used Valentine? But however slender the chance of hearing any admission of a secret so desperately painful, and he loathed the idea of forcing the boy or tricking him, still he must at least attempt to learn something. "Have you any idea what made your bootboy behave so badly the night the general was killed?" he asked, watching the man's face. "He looked like a smart and responsible sort of lad, not given to indiscipline."

"No sir, I don't, and that's a fact." Diggins shook his head. Monk could see no evasion or embarrassment in him. "He's been a very good boy, has young Robert," he went on. "Always on time, diligent, respectful, quick to learn. Nothing to explain except that one episode. You had it right there, sir, he's a fine lad. Used to be in the army, you know— a drummer boy. Got wounded somewhere out in India. Honorable discharge from the service. Come 'ere very highly recommended. Can't think what got into him. Not like him at all. Training to be a footman, 'e is, and very likely make a good one. Although 'e's been a bit odd since that night. But then so 'ave we all—can't 'old that against 'im."

"You don't think he saw something to do with the murder, do you?" Monk asked as casually as he could.

Diggins shook his head. "I can't think what that might be, sir, that he wouldn't have repeated it, like it would be his duty to. Anyway, it was long before the murder. It was early in the evening, before they even went in to dinner. Nothing untoward had happened then."

"Was it before Mrs. Erskine went upstairs?"

"Now that I wouldn't know, sir. I only know young Robert came out of the kitchen and was on his way up the back stairs on an errand for Mrs. Braithwaite, she's the housekeeper, when he crossed the passage and near bumped into General Carlyon, and stood there like a creature paralyzed and let all the linens he'd fetched fall in a heap on the floor, and turned on his heel and went back into the kitchen like the devil was after him. All the linens had to be sorted out and some o' them ironed again. The laundress wasn't best pleased, I can tell you." He shrugged. "And he wouldn't say a word to anyone, just went white and very quiet. Perhaps he was took ill, or something. Young people can be very odd."

"A drummer boy, you said?" Monk confirmed. "He'd be used to seeing some terrible things, no doubt . . ."

"I daresay. I never bin in the army myself, sir, but I should imagine so. But good training. Given him his obedience, and the respect for his elders. He's a good lad. He won't never do that again, I'm sure."

"No. No, 'course not." Thoughts raced through his mind as to how he could approach the boy—what he could say— the denials, the desperate embarrassment and the boy's shame. With sickening doubt as to the wisdom of it, where his duty or his honor lay, he made up his mind. "Thank you very much, Mr. Diggins. You have been most helpful, I appreciate it."

"No more than my duty, Mr. Monk."

Monk found himself outside in the street a few moments later, still torn with indecision. A drummer boy who had served with Carlyon, and then come face-to-face with him in the Furnivals' house on the night of the murder, and fled in— what? Terror, panic, shame? Or just clumsiness?

No—he had been a soldier, although then little more than a child. He would not have dropped his laundry and fled simply because he bumped into a guest.

Should Monk have pursued it? To what end? So Rathbone could get him on the stand and strip his shame bare before the court? What would it prove? Only that Carlyon was indeed an abuser of children. Could they not do that anyway, without destroying this child and making him relive the abuse in words—and in public? It was something Alexandra knew nothing of anyway, and could not have affected her actions.

It was the other abuser they needed to find, and to prove. Was it Maxim Furnival? Or Peverell Erskine? Both thoughts were repulsive to him.

He increased his pace, walking along Albany Street, and within moments was at Carlyon House. He had no excitement in the chase, only an empty, sick feeling in his stomach.

All the family were at the trial, either waiting to give evidence or in the gallery watching the proceedings. He went to the back door and asked if he might speak to Miss Buchan. It stuck in his throat to say it, but he sent a message that he was a friend of Miss Hester Latterly's and had come on an errand for her.

After only ten minutes kicking his heels in the laundry room he was finally admitted to the main house and conducted up three flights of stairs to Miss Buchan's small sitting room with its dormer windows over the roofs.

"Yes, Mr. Monk?" she said dubiously.

He looked at her with interest. She was nearer seventy than sixty, very thin, with a sharp, intelligent face, long nose, quick faded eyes, and the fine fresh complexion that goes with auburn hair, although it was now gray, almost white. She was a hot-tempered woman of great courage, and it showed in her face. He found it easy to believe she had acted as Hester had told him.

"I am a friend of Miss Latterly's," he said again, establishing himself before he launched into his difficult mission.

"So you told Agnes," she said skeptically, looking him up and down, from his polished leather boots and his long straight legs to his beautifully cut jacket and his smooth, hard-boned face with its gray eyes and sarcastic mouth. She did not try to impress him. She knew from his look, something in his bearing, that he had not had a governess himself. There was no nursery respect in him, no memories of another woman like her who had ruled his childhood.

He found himself coloring, knowing his ordinary roots were as visible to her as if he had never lost his provincial accent and his working-class manners. Ironically, his very lack of fear had betrayed him. His invulnerability had made him vulnerable. All his careful self-improvement hid nothing.

"Well?" she said impatiently. "What do you want? You haven't come this far just to stand here staring at me!"

"No." He collected himself rapidly. "No, Miss Buchan. I'm a detective. I'm trying to help Mrs. Alexandra Carlyon." He watched her face to see how she reacted.

344

"You're wasting your time," she said bleakly, sudden pain obliterating both her curiosity and her humor. "There's nothing anyone can do for her, poor soul."

"Or for Cassian?" he asked.

Her eyes narrowed; she looked at him in silence for several seconds. He did not turn away but met her gaze squarely.

"What would you be trying to do for him?" she said at last.

"See it doesn't happen to him anymore."

She stood still, her shoulders stiff, her eyes on his.

"You can't," she said at last. "He'll remain in this house, with his grandfather. He has no one else now."

"He has his sisters."

She pursed her lips slowly, a new thought turning over in her mind.

"He could go to Sabella," he suggested tentatively.

"You'd never prove it," she said almost under her breath, her eyes wide. They both knew what she was referring to; there was no need to speak the words. The old colonel was in their vision as powerfully as if some aura of him were there, like a pungent smoke after a man and his cigar or pipe have passed by.

"I might," he said slowly. "Can I speak to Cassian?"

"I don't know. Depends what you want to say. I'll not let you upset him—God knows the poor child has enough to bear, and worse to come."

"I won't do more than I have to," Monk pressed. "And you will be there all the time."

"I most certainly will," she said darkly. "Well, come on then, don't stand there wasting time. What has to be done had best be done quickly."

Cassian was alone in his own room. There were no schoolbooks visible, nor any other improving kind of occupation, and Monk judged Miss Buchan had weighed the relative merits of forced effort to occupy his mind and those of allowing him to think as he wished and permit the thoughts which had to lie below the surface to come through and claim the attention they would sooner or later have to have. Monk approved her decision.

Cassian looked around from the window where he was gazing. His face was pale but he looked perfectly composed. One could only guess what emotions were tearing at him beneath. Clutched in his fingers was a small gold watch fob. Monk could just see the yellow glint as he turned his hand.

"Mr. Monk would like to talk to you for a while," Miss Buchan said in a matter-of-fact voice. "I don't know what he has to say, but it might be important for your mother, so pay him attention and tell him all the truth you know."

"Yes, Miss Buchan," the boy said obediently, his eyes on Monk, solemn but not yet frightened. Perhaps all his fear was centered in the courtroom at the Old Bailey and the secrets and the pain which would be torn apart and exposed there, and the decisions that would be made. His voice was flat and he looked at Monk warily.

Monk was not used to children, except the occasional urchin or working child his normal routine brought him into contact with. He did not know how to treat Cassian, who had so much of childhood in his protected, privileged daily life, and nothing at all in his innermost person.

"Do you know Mr. Furnival?" he asked bluntly, and felt clumsy in asking, but small conversation was not his milieu or his skill, even with adults.

"No sir," Cassian answered straightaway.

"You have never met him?" Monk was surprised.

"No sir." Cassian swallowed. "I know Mrs. Furnival."

It seemed irrelevant. "Do you." Monk acknowledged it only as a courtesy. He looked at Miss Buchan. "Do you know Mr. Furnival?"

"No I do not."

Monk turned back to Cassian. "But you know your sister Sabella's husband, Mr. Pole?" he persisted, although he doubted Fenton Pole was the man he needed.

"Yes sir." There was no change in Cassian's expression except for a slight curiosity, perhaps because the questions seemed so pointless.

Monk looked at the boy's hands, still grasping the piece of gold.

"What is that?"

Cassian's fingers closed more tightly on it and there was a faint pink color fresh in his cheeks. Very slowly he held it out for Monk to take.

Monk picked it up. The watch fob opened up to be a tiny pair of scales, such as the blind figure of Justice carries. A chill touched him inside.

"That's very handsome," he said aloud. "A present?"

Cassian swallowed and said nothing.

"From your uncle Peverell?" Monk asked as casually as he could.

For a moment no one moved or spoke, then very slowly Cassian nodded.

"When did he give it to you?" Monk turned it over as if admiring it further.

"I don't remember," Cassian replied, and Monk knew he was lying.

Monk handed it back and Cassian took it quickly, closing his hand over it again and then putting it out of sight in his pocket.

Monk pretended to forget it, walking away from the window towards the small table where, from the ruler, block of paper, and jar of pencils, it was obvious Cassian did his schoolwork since coming to Carlyon House. He felt Miss Buchan watching him, waiting to intervene if he trespassed too far, and he also felt Cassian tense and his eyes follow him. A moment later he came over and stood at Monk's elbow, his face wary, eyes troubled.

Monk looked at the table again, at the other items. There was a pocket dictionary, a small book of mathematical tables, a French grammar and a neat folding knife. At first he thought it was for sharpening pencils, then he saw what an elegant thing it was, far too sophisticated for a child. He reached out for it, out of the corner of his eye saw Cassian tense, his hand jerk upward, as if to stop him, then freeze motionless.

347

Monk picked up the knife and opened it. It was fine-bladed, almost like a razor, the sort a man uses to cut a quill to repair the nib. The initials P.E. were engraved on the handle.

"Very nice," Monk said with a half smile, turning to Cassian. "Another gift from Mr. Erskine?"

"Yes—no!" Cassian stopped. "Yes." His chin tightened, his lower lip came forward, as if to defy argument.

"Very generous of him," Monk commented, feeling sick inside. "Anything else he gave you?"

"No." But his eyes swiveled for an instant to his jacket, hanging on the hook behind the door, and Monk could just see the end of a colored silk handkerchief poking out from an inside pocket.

"He must be very fond of you," he said, hating himself for the hypocrisy.

Cassian said nothing.

Monk turned back to Miss Buchan.

"Thank you," he said wearily. "There isn't a great deal more to ask."

She looked doubtful. It was plain she did not see any meaning to the questions about the gifts; it had not occurred to her to suspect Peverell Erskine. Perhaps it was just as well. He stayed a few moments longer, asking other things as they came to his mind, times and people, journeys, visitors, nothing that mattered, but it disguised the gifts and their meaning.

Then he said good-bye to the child, thanked Miss Buchan, and left Carlyon House, his knowledge giving him no pleasure. The sunlight and noise of the street seemed far away, the laughter of two women in pink-and-white frills, parasols twirling, sounding tinny in his ears, the horses' hooves loud, the hiss of carriage wheels sibilant, the cry of a peddler a faraway irritant, like the buzzing of a bluebottle fly.

Hester arrived home from the trial weary and with very little to tell Major Tiplady. The day's evidence had been largely what anyone might have foreseen, first Peverell Erskine saying, with something that looked vaguely like reluctance, what an excellent man Thaddeus Carlyon had been.

Rathbone had not tried to shake him, nor to question his veracity nor the accuracy of his observations.

Next Damaris Erskine had been asked about her brother, and had echoed her husband's sentiments and seconded his observations. Rathbone had not asked her anything else at all, but had reserved the right to recall her at a later time, should that prove to be in the interests of the defense.

There had been no revelations. The crowd was growing more intense in their anger towards Alexandra. The general was the kind of man they most liked to admire—heroic, upright, a man of action with no dangerous ideas or unnerving sense of humor, no opinions they would have to disapprove of or feel guilty about understanding, a good family man whose wife had most hideously turned on him for no sane reason. Such a woman should be hanged, to discourage all other women from such violence, and the sooner the better. It was murmured all through the day, and said aloud when finally the court rose for the weekend.

It was a discouraging day, and she came back to Great Titchfield Street tired and frightened by the inevitability of events, and the hatred and incomprehension in the air. By the time she had recounted it all to Major Tiplady she was close to tears. Even he could find no hope in the situation; the best he could offer was an exhortation to courage, the greatest of all courage, to continue to fight with all one has even when victory seems beyond possibility.

The following day a crisp wind blew from the east but the sky was sharp blue and flowers were fluttering in the wind. It was Saturday, and there was no court sitting, so there was brief respite. Hester woke with a sense not of ease but of greater tension because she would rather have continued with it now that it was begun. This was only prolonging the pain and the helplessness. It would have been a blessing were there anything more she could do, but although she had been awake, turning and twisting, thrashing it over and over in her mind, she could think of nothing. They knew the truth of what had happened to Alexandra, what she had done, and why—exactly, passionately and irrevocably why. She had not known there was another man, let alone two others, or who they were.

There was little point in trying to prove it was old Randolf Carlyon; he would never admit it, and his family would close around him like a wall of iron. To accuse him would only prejudice the crowd and the jury still more deeply against Alexandra. She would appear a wild and vicious woman with a vile mind, depraved and obsessed with perversions.

They must find the third man, with either irrefutable proof or sufficient accusations not to be denied. And that would mean the help of Cassian, Valentine Furnival, if he were also a victim, and anyone else who knew about it or suspected—Miss Buchan, for example.

And Miss Buchan would risk everything if she made such a charge. The Carlyons would throw her out and she would be destitute. And who else would take her in, a woman too old to work, who made charges of incest and sodomy against the employers who had fed and housed her in her old age?

No, there was little comfort in a long, useless weekend. She wished she could curl over and go back to sleep, but it was broad daylight; through a chink in the curtain the sun was bright, and she must get up and see how Major Tiplady was. Not that he was unable to care for himself now, but she might as well do her duty as fully as possible to the end.

Perhaps the morning could be usefully spent in beginning to look for a new post. This one could not last beyond the confusion of the trial. She could afford a couple of weeks without a position, but not more. And it would have to be one where she lived in the house of the patient. She had given up her lodgings, since the expense of keeping a room when she did not need one was foolish, and beyond her present resources. She pushed dreams of any other sort of employment firmly out of her mind. They were fanciful, and without foundation, the maunderings of a silly woman.

After breakfast she asked Major Tiplady if he would excuse her for the day so she might go out and begin to enquire at various establishments that catered to such needs if there were any people who required a nurse such as herself. Unfortunately midwifery was something about which she knew almost nothing, nor about the care of infant children. There was a much wider need for that type of nursing.

Reluctantly he agreed, not because he needed her help in anything, simply because he had grown used to her company and liked it. But he could see the reasoning, and accepted it.

She thanked him, and half an hour later was about to leave when the maid came in with a surprised look on her face to announce that Mrs. Sobell was at the door.

"Oh!" The major looked startled and a little pink. "To see Miss Latterly, no doubt? Please show her in, Molly! Don't leave the poor lady standing in the hall!"

"No sir. Yes sir." Molly's surprise deepened, but she did as she was bidden, and a moment later Edith came in, dressed in half-mourning of a rich shade of pink lilac. Hester thought privately she would have termed it quarter-mourning, if asked. It was actually very pretty, and the only indications it had anything to do with death were the black lace trimmings and black satin ribbons both on the shawl and on the bonnet. Nothing would change the individuality of her features, the aquiline nose that looked almost as if it had been broken, very slightly crooked, and far too flat, the heavy-lidded eyes and the soft mouth, but Edith looked remarkably gentle and feminine today, in spite of her obvious unhappiness.

The major climbed to his feet, utterly disregarding his leg, which was now almost healed but still capable of giving him pain. He stood almost to attention.

"Good morning, Mrs. Sobell. How very nice to see you. I hope you are well, in spite of . . ." He stopped, looking at her more closely. "I'm sorry, what a foolish thing to say. Of course you are distressed by all that is happening. What may we do to comfort you? Please come in and sit down; at least make yourself comfortable. No doubt you wish to speak to Miss Latterly. I shall find myself some occupation."

"No, no! Please," Edith said quickly and a little awkwardly.

"I should be most uncomfortable if you were to leave on my account. I have nothing in particular to say. I—I simply . . ." Now she too colored very pink. "I—I simply wished to be out of the house, away from my family—and . . ."

"Of course," he said quickly. "You wished to be able to speak your mind without fear of causing offense or distress to those you love."

Her face flooded with relief. "You are extraordinarily perceptive, Major Tiplady."

Now his cheeks were very red and he had no idea where to look.

"Oh please sit down," Hester interrupted, acting to stop the awkwardness, or at least to give it respite. "Edith."

"Thank you," Edith accepted, and for the first time in Hester's acquaintance with her, she arranged her skirts elegantly and sat upright on the edge of the seat, as a lady should. In spite of the grimness of the situation Hester was obliged to hide a smile.

Edith sighed. "Hester, what is happening? I have never been to a trial before, and I don't understand. Mr. Rathbone is supposed to be so brilliant, and yet from what I hear it seems he is doing nothing at all. I could do as much. So far all he has achieved is to persuade us all that Thaddeus was quite innocent of any affair, either with Louisa Furnival or anyone else. And to add that Alexandra knew it too. What possible good can that do?" Her face was screwed up with incomprehension, her eyes dark and urgent. "It makes Alexandra look even worse in a way, because it takes from her any possible reason that one could attempt to understand, if not forgive. Why? She has already confessed that she did do it, and it has been proved. He didn't challenge that. In fact if anything he reconfirmed it. Why, Hester? What is he doing?"

Hester had told Edith nothing of their appalling discoveries, and now she hesitated, wondering if she should, or if by so doing she might foil Rathbone's plans for examination in the witness box. Was it possible that in spite of the outrage she would undoubtedly feel, Edith's family loyalty would be powerful enough for her to conceal the shame of it? Might she even disbelieve it?

Hester dare not put it to the test. It was not her prerogative to decide, not her life in the balance, nor her child whose future lay in the judgment.

She sat down in the chair opposite Edith.

"I don't know," she lied, meeting her friend's eyes and hating the deceit. "At least I have only guesses, and it would be unfair to him and to you to give you those." She saw Edith's face tighten as if she had been struck, and the fear deepened in her eyes. "But I do know he has a strategy," she hurried on, leaning forward a little, only dimly aware of Major Tiplady looking anxiously from one to the other of them.

"Does he?" Edith said softly. "Please don't try to give me hope, Hester, if there really isn't any. It is not a kindness."

The major drew breath to speak, and both turned to look at him. Then he changed his mind and remained silent and unhappy, facing Hester.

"There is hope," Hester said firmly. "But I don't know how great it is. It all depends on convincing the jury that—"

"What?" Edith said quickly. "What can he convince them of? She did it! Even Rathbone himself has proved that! What else is there?"

Hester hesitated. She was glad Major Tiplady was there, although there was nothing he could do, but his mere presence was a kind of comfort.

Edith went on with a faint, bitter smile. "He can hardly persuade them she was justified. Thaddeus was painfully virtuous—all the things that count to other people." She frowned suddenly. "Actually we still don't know why she did do it. Is he going to say she is mad? Is that it? I don't think she is." She glanced at the major. "And they have subpoenaed me to give evidence. What shall I do?"

"Give evidence," Hester answered. "There's nothing else you can do. Just answer the questions they ask and no more. But be honest. Don't try to guess what they want. It is up to

Rathbone to draw it from you. If you look as if you are trying to help it will show and the jury won't believe you. Just don't lie—about anything he asks you."

"But what can he ask me? I don't know anything."

"I don't know what he will ask you," Hester said exasperatedly. "He wouldn't tell me, even if I were to ask him. I have no right to know. And far better I don't. But I do know he has a strategy—and it could win. Please believe me, and don't press me to give you answers I don't have."

"I'm sorry." Edith was suddenly penitent. She rose to her feet quickly and walked over to the window, less graceful than usual because she was self-conscious. "When this trial is over I am still going to look for a position of some sort. I know Mama will be furious, but I feel suffocated there. I spend all my life doing nothing whatsoever that matters at all. I stitch embroidery no one needs, and paint pictures even I don't like much. I play the piano badly and no one listens except out of politeness. I make duty calls on people and take them pots of conserve and give bowls of soup to the deserving poor, and feel like such a hypocrite because it does hardly any good, and we go with such an air of virtue, and come away as if we've solved all their problems, and we've hardly touched them." Her voice caught for an instant. "I'm thirty-three, and I'm behaving like an old woman. Hester, I'm terrified that one day I'm going to wake up and I will be old—and I'll have done nothing at all that was worth doing. I'll never have accomplished anything, served any purpose, helped anyone more than was purely convenient, never felt anything really deeply once Oswald died—been no real use at all." She kept her back to them, and stood very straight and still.

"Then you must find work of some sort to do," Hester said firmly. "Even if it is hard or dirty, paid or unpaid, even thankless—it would be better than waking up every morning to a wasted day and going to bed at night knowing you wasted it. I have heard it said that most of what we regret is not what we did but what we did not do. I think on the whole that is

354

correct. You have your health. It would be better to wait on others than do nothing at all.''

"You mean go into service?'' Edith was incredulous and there was a frail, slightly hysterical giggle under the surface of her voice.

"No, nothing quite so demanding—it would really be more than your mother deserves. I meant helping some poor creature who is too ill or too mithered to help herself.'' She stopped. "Of course that would be unpaid, and that might not work . . .''

"It wouldn't. Mama would not permit it, so I would have to find lodgings of my own, and that requires money—which I don't have.''

Major Tiplady cleared his throat.

"Are you still interested in Africa, Mrs. Sobell?''

She turned around, her eyes wide.

"Go to Africa? How could I do that? I don't know anything about it. I hardly think I should be of any use to anyone. I wish I were!''

"No, not go there.'' His face was bright pink now. "I—er—well, I'm not sure, of course . . .''

Hester refused to help him, although with a sweet surge of pleasure she knew what he wanted to say.

He threw an agonized glance at her, and she smiled back charmingly.

Edith waited.

"Er . . .'' He cleared his throat again. "I thought—I thought I might . . . I mean if you are serious about people's interest? I thought I might write my memoirs of Mashonaland, and I—er . . .''

Edith's face flooded with understanding—and delight.

"Need a scribe. Oh yes, I should be delighted. I can think of nothing I should like better! *My Adventures in Mashonaland,* by Major—Major Tiplady. What is your given name?''

He blushed crimson and looked everywhere but at her.

Hester knew the initial was *H,* but no more. He had signed his letter employing her only with that initial and his surname.

"You have to have a name," Edith insisted. "I can see it, bound in morocco or calf—nice gold lettering. It will be marvelous! I shall count it such a privilege and enjoy every word. It will be almost as good as going there myself—and in such splendid company. What is your name, Major? How will it be styled?"

"Hercules," he said very quietly, and shot her a look of total pleading not to laugh.

"How very fine," she said gently. *My Adventures in Mashonaland,* by Major Hercules Tiplady. May we begin as soon as this terrible business is over? It is the nicest thing that has happened to me in years."

"And to me," Major Tiplady said happily, his face still very pink.

Hester rose to her feet and went to the door to ask the maid to prepare luncheon for them, and so that she could give rein to her giggles where she could hurt no one—but it was laughter of relief and a sudden bright hope, at least for Edith and the major, whom she had grown to like remarkably. It was the only good thing at the moment, but it was totally good.

11

MONK BEGAN THE WEEKEND with an equal feeling of gloom, not because he had no hope of finding the third man but because the discovery was so painful. He had liked Peverell Erskine, and now it looked inevitable it was he. Why else would he have given a child such highly personal and useless gifts? Cassian had no use for a quill knife, except that it was pretty and belonged to Peverell—as for a silk handkerchief, children did not use or wear such things. It was a keepsake. The watch fob also was too precious for an eight-year-old to wear, and it was personal to Peverell's profession, nothing like the Carlyons', which would have been something military, a regimental crest, perhaps.

He had told Rathbone, and seen the same acceptance and unhappiness in him. He had mentioned the bootboy also, but told Rathbone that there was no proof Carlyon had abused him, and that that was the reason the boy had turned and fled in the Furnival house the night of the murder. He did not know if Rathbone had understood his own action, what were the reasons he accepted without demur, or if he felt his strategy did not require the boy.

Monk stood at the window and stared out at the pavement of Grafton Street, the sharp wind sending a loose sheet of newspaper bowling along the stones. On the corner a peddler was selling bootlaces. A couple crossed the street, arm in arm, the man walking elegantly, leaning over a little towards the woman, she laughing. They looked comfortable together, and it shot a pang of loneliness through him that took him by surprise, a feeling of exclusion, as if he saw the whole of life that mattered, the sweeter parts, through glass, and from a distance.

Evan's last case file lay on the desk unopened. In it might lie the answer to the mystery that teased him. Who was the woman that plucked at his thoughts with such insistence and such powerful emotion, stirring feelings of guilt, urgency, fear of loss, and over all, confusion? He was afraid to discover, and yet not to was worse. Part of him held back, simply because once he had uncovered it there would be nothing left to offer hope of finding something sweet, a better side of himself, a gentleness or a generosity he had failed in so far. It was foolish, and he knew it, even cowardly—and that was the one criticism strong enough to move him. He walked over to the table and opened the cover.

He read the first page still standing. The case was not especially complex. Hermione Ward had been married to a wealthy and neglectful husband, some years older than herself. She was his second wife and it seemed he had treated her with coolness, keeping her short of funds, giving her very little social life and expecting her to manage his house and care for the two children of his first wife.

The house had been broken into during the night, and Albert Ward had apparently heard the burglar and gone downstairs to confront him. There had been a struggle and he had been struck on the head and died of the wound.

Monk pulled around a chair and sat down. He continued with the second page.

The local police in Guildford had investigated, and found several circumstances which roused their suspicions. The glass from the broken window was outside, not in, where one might have expected it to fall. The widow could name nothing which had been stolen, nor did she ever amend her opinion in the cooler light of the following week. Nothing was found in pawnshops or sold to any of the usual dealers known to the police. The resident servants, of whom there were six, heard nothing in the night, no sound, no disturbance. No footprints or any other marks of intruders were seen.

The police arrested Hermione Ward and charged her with having murdered her husband. Scotland Yard was sent for. Runcorn dispatched Monk to Guildford. The rest of the record presumably lay with the Guildford police.

The only way he could find out would be to go there. It was a short journey and easily made by train. But this was Saturday. It might be awkward. Perhaps the officer he needed would not be there. And the Carlyon trial would be resumed on Monday, and he must be present. What could he do in two days? Maybe not enough.

They were excuses because he was afraid to find out.

He despised cowardice; it was the root of all the weaknesses he hated most. Anger he could understand, thoughtlessness, impatience, greed, even though they were ugly enough—but without courage what was there to fire or to preserve any virtue, honor or integrity? Without the courage to sustain it, not even love was safe.

He moved over to the window again and stared at the buildings opposite and the roofs shining in the sun. There was not even any point in evading it. It would hurt him until he found out what had happened, who she was and why he had felt so passionately, and yet walked away from it, and from her. Why were there no mementos in his room that reminded him of her, no pictures, no letters, nothing at all? Presumably the idea of her was one thing too painful to wish to remember. The reality was quite different. This would go on hurting. He would wake in the night with scalding disillusion—and terrible loneliness. For once he could easily, terribly easily, understand those who ran away.

And yet it was also too important to forget, because his mind would not let him bury it. Echoes kept tugging at him, half glimpses of her face, a gesture, a color she wore, the way she walked, the softness of her hair, her perfume, the

359

rustle of silk. For heaven's sake, why not her name? Why not all her face?

There was nothing he could do here over the weekend. The trial was adjourned and he had nowhere else to search for the third man. It was up to Rathbone now.

He turned from the window and strode over to the coat stand, snatching a jacket and his hat and going out of the door, only just saving it from slamming behind him.

"I'm going to Guildford," he informed his landlady, Mrs. Worley. "I may not be back until tomorrow."

"But you'll be back then?" she said firmly, wiping her hands on her apron. She was an ample woman, friendly and businesslike. "You'll be at the trial of that woman again?"

He was surprised. He had not thought she knew.

"Yes—I will."

She shook her head. "I don't know what you want to be on cases like that for, I'm sure. You've come a long way down, Mr. Monk, since you was in the police. Then you'd 'a bin chasin' after people like that, not tryin' to 'elp them."

"You'd have killed him too, in her place, if you'd had the courage, Mrs. Worley," he said bitingly. "So would any woman who gave a damn."

"I would not," she retorted fiercely. "Love o' no man's ever goin' to make me into a murderess!"

"You know nothing about it. It wasn't love of a man."

"You watch your tongue, Mr. Monk," she said briskly. "I know what I read in the newspapers as comes 'round the vegetables, and they're plain enough."

"They know nothing, either," he replied. "And fancy you reading the newspapers, Mrs. Worley. What would Mr. Worley say to that? And sensational stories, too." He grinned at her, baring his teeth.

She straightened her skirts with a tweak and glared at him.

"That isn't your affair, Mr. Monk. What I read is between me and Mr. Worley."

"It's between you and your conscience, Mrs. Worley—it's no one else's concern at all. But they still know nothing. Wait till the end of the trial—then tell me what you think."

"Ha!" she said sharply, and turned on her heel to go back to the kitchen.

He caught the train and alighted at Guildford in the middle of the morning. It was a matter of another quarter of an hour before a hansom deposited him outside the police station and he went up the steps to the duty sergeant at the desk.

"Yes sir?" The man's face registered dawning recognition. "Mr. Monk? 'Ow are you, sir?" There was respect in his voice, even awe, but Monk did not catch any fear. Please God at least here he had not been unjust.

"I'm very well, thank you, Sergeant," he replied courteously. "And yourself?"

The sergeant was not used to being asked how he was, and his face showed his surprise, but he answered levelly enough.

"I'm well, thank you sir. What can I do for you? Mr. Markham's in, if it was 'im you was wanting to see? I ain't 'eard about another case as we're needin' you for; it must be very new." He was puzzled. It seemed impossible there could be a crime so complicated they needed to call in Scotland Yard and yet it had not crossed his desk. Only something highly sensitive and dangerous could be so classed, a political assassination, or a murder involving a member of the aristocracy.

"I'm not with the police anymore," Monk explained. There was little to be gained and everything to be risked by lying. "I've gone private." He saw the man's incredulity and smiled. "A difference of opinion over a case—a wrongful arrest, I thought."

The man's face lightened with intelligence. "That'd be the Moidore case," he said with triumph.

"That's right!" It was Monk's turn to be surprised. "How did you know about that?"

"Read it, sir. Know as you was right." He nodded with satisfaction, even if it was a trifle after the event. "What can we do for you now, Mr. Monk?"

Again honesty was the wisest. So far the man was a friend,

361

for whatever reason, but that could easily slip away if he lied to him and were caught.

"I've forgotten some of the details of the case I came here for, and I'd like to remind myself. I wondered if it would be possible to speak with someone. I realize it's Saturday, and those who worked with me might be off duty, but today was the only day I could leave the City. I'm on a big case."

"No difficulty, sir. Mr. Markham's right 'ere in the station, an' I expect as 'e'd be 'appy to tell you anything you wanted. It was 'is biggest case, an' 'e's always 'appy to talk about it again." He moved his head in the direction of the door leading off to the right. "If you go through there, sir, you'll find 'im at the back, like always. Tell 'im I sent you."

"Thank you, Sergeant," Monk accepted, and before it became obvious that he did not remember the man's name, he went through the door and through the passageway. Fortunately the direction was obvious, because he remembered none of it.

Sergeant Markham was standing with his back to Monk, and as soon as Monk saw him there was something in the angle of his shoulders and the shape of his head, the set of his arms, that woke a memory and suddenly he was back investigating the case, full of anxiety and hard, urgent fear.

Then Markham turned and looked at him, and the moment vanished. He was in the present again, standing in a strange police duty room facing a man who knew him, and yet about whom he knew nothing except that they had worked together in the past. His features were only vaguely familiar; his eyes were blue like a million Englishmen, his skin fair and pale so early in the season, his hair still thick, bleached by sun a little at the front.

"Yes sir?" he enquired, seeing first of all Monk's civilian clothes. Then he looked more closely at his face, and recognition came flooding back. "Why, it's Mr. Monk." The eagerness was tempered. There was admiration in his eyes, but caution as well. " 'Ow are you, sir? Got another case?" The interest was well modified with other emotions less sanguine.

"No, the same as before." Monk wondered whether to smile, or if it would be so uncharacteristic as to be ridiculous. The decision was quickly made; it was false and it would freeze on his face. "I've forgotten some of the details and for reasons I can't explain, I need to remind myself, or to be exact, I need your help to remind me. You still have the records?"

"Yes sir." Markham was obviously surprised, and there was acceptance in his expression as habit. He was used to obeying Monk and it was instinctive, but there was no comprehension.

"I'm not on the force anymore." He dared not deceive Markham.

Now Markham was totally incredulous.

"Not on the force." His whole being registered his amazement. "Not—not—on the force?" He looked as if he did not understand the words themselves.

"Gone private," Monk explained, meeting his eyes. "I've got to be back in the Old Bailey on Monday, for the Carlyon case, but I want to get these details today, if I can."

"What for, sir?" Markham had a great respect for Monk, but he had also learned from him, and knew enough to accept no one's word without substantiation, or to take an order from a man with no authority. Monk would have criticized him unmercifully for it in the past.

"My own private satisfaction," Monk replied as calmly as he could. "I want to be sure I did all I could, and that I was right. And I want to find the woman again, if I can." Too late he realized how he had betrayed himself. Markham would think him witless, or making an obscure joke. He felt hot all over, sweat breaking out on his body and then turning cold.

"Mrs. Ward?" Markham asked with surprise.

"Yes, Mrs. Ward!" Monk gulped hard. She must be alive, or Markham would not have phrased it that way. He could still find her!

"You didn't keep in touch, sir?" Markham frowned.

Monk was so overwhelmed with relief his voice caught in

his throat. "No." He swallowed and coughed. "No—did you expect me to?"

"Well, sir." Markham colored faintly. "I know you worked on the case so hard as a matter of justice, of course, but I couldn't help but see as you were very fond of the lady too—and she of you, it looked like. I 'alf thought, we all thought . . ." His color deepened. "Well, no matter. Beggin' your pardon, sir. It don't do to get ideas about people and what they feel or don't feel. Like as not you'll be wrong. I can't show you the files, sir; seein' as you're not on the force any longer. But I ain't forgot much. I can tell you just about all of it. I'm on duty right now. But I get an hour for luncheon, leastways I can take an hour, and I'm sure the duty sergeant'll come for me. An' if you like to meet me at the Three Feathers I'll tell you all I can remember."

"Thank you, Markham, that's very obliging of you. I hope you'll let me stand you to a meal?"

"Yes, sir, that's handsome of you."

And so midday saw Monk and Sergeant Markham sitting at a small round table in the clink and chatter of the Three Feathers, each with a plate piled full of hot boiled mutton and horseradish sauce, potatoes, spring cabbage, mashed turnips and butter; a glass of cider at the elbow; and steamed treacle pudding to follow.

Markham was as good as his word, meticulously so. He had brought no papers with him, but his memory was excellent. Perhaps he had refreshed it discreetly for the occasion, or maybe it was sufficiently sharp he had no need. He began as soon as he had taken the edge off his appetite with half a dozen mouthfuls.

"The first thing you did, after reading the evidence, was go back over the ground as we'd already done ourselves." He left out the "sir" he would have used last time and Monk noted it with harsh amusement.

"That was, go to the scene o' the crime and see the broken window," Markham went on. "O' course the glass was all cleaned up, like, but we showed you where it 'ad lain. Then we questioned the servants again, and Mrs. Ward 'erself. Do you want to know what I can remember o' that?''

''Only roughly,'' Monk replied. ''If there was anything of note? Not otherwise.''

Markham continued, outlining a very routine and thorough investigation, at the end of which any competent policeman would have been obliged to arrest Hermione Ward. The evidence was very heavy against her. The great difference between her and Alexandra Carlyon was that she had everything to gain from the crime: freedom from a domineering husband and the daughters of a previous wife, and the inheritance of at least half of his very considerable wealth. Whereas, on the surface at least, Alexandra had everything to lose: social position, a devoted father for her son, and all but a small interest in his money. And yet Alexandra had confessed very early on, and Hermione had never wavered in protesting her total innocence.

''Go on!'' Monk urged.

Markham continued, after only a few more mouthfuls. Monk knew he was being unfair to the man in not allowing him to eat, and he did not stop himself.

''You wouldn't let it rest at that,'' Markham said with admiration still in his voice at the memory of it. ''I don't know why, but you believed 'er. I suppose that's the difference between a good policeman and a really great one. The great ones 'ave an instinct for innocence and guilt that goes beyond what the eye can see. Anyway, you worked night and day; I never saw anyone work so 'ard. I don't know when you ever slept, an' that's the truth. An' you drove us till we didn't know whether we was comin' or goin'.''

''Was I unreasonable?'' Monk asked, then instantly wished he had not. It was an idiotic question. What could this man answer? And yet he heard his own voice going on. ''Was I . . . offensive?''

Markham hesitated, looking first at his plate, then up at Monk, trying to judge from his eyes whether he wanted a candid answer or flattery. Monk knew what the decision would have to be; he liked flattery, but he had never in his

365

life sought it. His pride would not have permitted him. And Markham was a man of some courage. He liked him now. He hoped he had had the honesty and the good judgment to like him before, and to show it.

"Yes," Markham said at last. "Although I wouldn't 'ave said so much offensive. Offense depends on who takes it. I don't take it. Can't say as I always liked you—too 'ard on some people because they didn't meet your standards, when they couldn't 'elp it. Different men 'as different strengths, and you weren't always prepared to see that."

Monk smiled to himself, a trifle bitterly. Now that he was no longer on the force, Markham had shown a considerable temerity and put tongue to thoughts he would not have dared entertain even as ideas in his mind a year ago. But he was honest. That he would not have dared say such things before was no credit to Monk, rather the reverse.

"I'm sorry, Mr. Monk." Markham saw his face. "But you did drive us terrible 'ard, and tore strips off them as couldn't match your quickness." He took another mouthful and ate it before adding, "But then you was right. It took us a long time, and tore to shreds a few folk on the way, as was lying for one reason or another; but in the end you proved as it weren't Mrs. Ward at all. It was 'er ladies' maid and the butler together. They were 'avin' an affair, the two o' them, and 'ad planned to rob their master, but 'e came down in the night and found them, so they 'ad to kill 'im or face a life in gaol. And personally I'd rather 'ang than spend forty years in the Coldbath Fields or the like—an' so would most folk."

So it was he who had proved it—he had saved her from the gallows. Not circumstance, not inevitability.

Markham was watching him, his face pinched with curiosity and puzzlement. He must find him extraordinary. Monk was asking questions that would be odd from any policeman, and from a ruthless and totally assured man like himself, beyond comprehension.

Instinctively he bent his head to slice his mutton, and kept at least his eyes hidden. He felt ridiculously vulnerable. This was absurd. He had saved Hermione, her honor and her life.

Why did he no longer even know her? He might have been keen for justice, as he was for Alexandra Carlyon—even passionate for it—but the emotion that boiled up in him at the memory of Hermione was far more than a hunger for the right solution to a case. It was deep and wholly personal. She haunted him as she could have only if he loved her. The ache was boundless for a companionship that had been immeasurably sweet, a gentleness, a gateway to his better self, the softer, generous, tender part of him.

Why? Why had they parted? Why had he not married her? He had no idea what the reason was, and it frightened him. Perhaps he should leave the wound unopened. Let it heal.

But it was not healing. It still hurt, like a skin grown over a place that suppurated yet.

Markham was looking at him.

"You still want to find Mrs. Ward?" he asked.

"Yes—yes I do."

"Well she left The Grange. I suppose she had too many memories from there. And folk still talked, for all it was proved she 'ad nothing to do with it. But you know 'ow it is—in an investigation all sorts o' things come out, that maybe 'ave nothing to do with the crime but still are better not known. I reckon there's no one as 'asn't got something they'd sooner keep quiet."

"No, I shouldn't think so," Monk agreed. "Where did she go, do you know?"

"Yes—yes, she bought a little 'ouse over Milton way. Next to the vicarage, if I remember rightly. There's a train, if you've a mind to get there."

"Thank you." He ate the treacle pudding with a dry mouth, washed it down with the cider, and thanked Markham again.

It was Sunday just after midday when he stood on the step of the Georgian stone house next to the vicarage, immaculately kept, weedless graveled path, roses beginning to bloom in the sun. Finally he summoned courage to knock on the door. It was a mechanical action, done with a decision of the mind, but almost without volition. If he permitted his emotions through he would never do it.

It seemed an age of waiting. There was a bird singing somewhere behind him in the garden, and the sound of wind in the young leaves in the apple trees beyond the wall around the vicarage. Somewhere in the distance a lamb bleated and a ewe answered it.

Then without warning the door opened. He had not heard the feet coming to the other side. A pert, pretty maid stood expectantly, her starched apron crisp, her hair half hidden by a lace cap.

His voice dried in his throat and he had to cough to force out the words.

"Good morning, er—good afternoon. I—I'm sorry to trouble you at this—this hour—but I have come from London—yesterday . . ." He was making an extraordinary mess of this. When had he ever been so inarticulate? "May I speak with Mrs. Ward, please? It is a matter of some importance." He handed her a card with his name, but no occupation printed.

She looked a little doubtful, but regarded him closely, his boots polished and very nearly new, his trousers with a little dust on the ankles from his walk up from the station, but why not on such a pleasant day? His coat was excellently cut and his shirt collar and cuffs very white. Lastly she looked at his face, normally with the confidence of a man of authority but now a facade, and a poor one. She made her decision.

"I'll ask." Something like amusement flickered in her smile and her eyes definitely had laughter in them. "If you'll come to the parlor and wait, please, sir."

He stepped inside and was shown to the front parlor. Apparently it was a room not frequently used; probably there was a less formal sitting room to the rear of the house.

The maid left him and he had time to look. There was a tall upright clock against the nearest wall, its case elaborately carved. The soft chairs were golden brown, a color he found vaguely oppressive, even in this predominantly gentle room

368

with patterned carpet and curtains, all subdued and comfortable. Over the mantelpiece was a landscape, very traditional, probably somewhere in the Lake District—too many blues for his taste. He thought it would have been subtler and more beautiful with a limited palette of grays and muted browns.

Then his eyes went to the backs of the chairs and he felt a wild lurch of familiarity clutch at him and his muscles tightened convulsively. The antimacassars were embroidered with a design of white heather and purple ribbons. He knew every stitch of it, every bell of the flowers and curl of scroll.

It was absurd. He already knew that this was the woman. He knew it from what Markham had told him. He did not need this wrench of the emotional memory to confirm it. And yet this was knowledge of quite a different nature, not expectation but feeling. It was what he had come for—at last.

There was a quick, light step outside the door and the handle turned.

He almost choked on his own breath.

She came in. There was never any doubt it was her. From the crown of her head, with its softly curling fair hair; her honey-brown eyes, wide-set, long-lashed; her full, delicate lips; her slender figure; she was completely familiar.

When she saw him her recognition was instant also. The color drained out of her skin, leaving her ashen, then it flooded back in a rich blush.

"William!" She gasped, then collected her own wits and closed the door behind her. "William—what on earth are you doing here? I didn't think I should ever—I mean—that we should meet again." She came towards him very slowly, her eyes searching his face.

He wanted to speak, but suddenly he had no idea what to say. All sorts of emotions crowded inside him: relief because she was so exactly what all his memories told him, all the gentleness, the beauty, the intelligence were there; fear now that the moment of testing was here and there was no more time to prepare. What did she think of him, what were her feelings, why had he ever left her? Incredulity at himself.

369

How little he knew the man he used to be. Why had he gone? Selfishness, unwillingness to commit himself to a wife and possibly a family? Cowardice? Surely not that—selfishness, pride, he could believe. That was the man he was discovering.

"William?" Now she was even more deeply puzzled. She did not understand silence from him. "William, what has happened?"

He did not know how to explain. He could not say, I have found you again, but I cannot remember why I ever lost you!

"I—I wanted to see how you are," he said. It sounded weak, but he could think of nothing better.

"I—I am well. And you?" She was still confused. "What brings you to . . . ? Another case?"

"No—no." He swallowed. "I came to see you."

"Why?"

"Why!" The question seemed preposterous. Because he loved her. Because he should never have left. Because she was all the gentleness, the patience, the generosity, the peace that was the better side of him, and he longed for it as a drowning man for air. How did she not know that? "Hermione!" The need burst from him with the passion he had been trying to suppress, violent and explosive.

She backed away, her face pale again, her hands moving up to her bosom.

"William! Please . . ."

Suddenly he felt sick. Had he asked her before, told her his feelings, and she had rejected him? Had he forgotten that, because it was too painful—and only remembered that he loved her, not that she did not love him?

He stood motionless, overcome with misery and appalling, desolating loneliness.

"William, you promised," she said almost under her breath, looking not at him but at the floor. "I can't. I told you before—you frighten me. I don't feel that—I can't. I don't want to. I don't want to care so much about anything, or anyone. You work too hard, you get too angry, too involved in other people's tragedies or injustices. You fight too

370

hard for what you want, you are prepared to pay more than I—for anything. And you hurt too much if you lose.'' She gulped and looked up, her eyes full of pleading. ''I don't *want* to feel all that. It frightens me. I don't like it. You frighten me. I don't love that way—and I don't want you to love me like that—I can't live up to it—and I would hate trying to. I want . . .'' She bit her lip. ''I want peace—I want to be comfortable.''

Comfortable! God Almighty!

''William? Don't be angry—I can't help it—I told you all that before. I thought you understood. Why have you come back? You'll only upset things. I'm married to Gerald now, and he's good to me. But I don't think he would care for you coming back. He's grateful you proved my innocence, of course he is—'' She was speaking even more rapidly now, and he knew she was afraid. ''And of course I shall never cease to be grateful. You saved my life—and my reputation— I know that. But please—I just can't . . .'' She stopped, dismayed by his silence, not knowing what else to add.

For the sake of his own dignity, some salve to his self-respect, he must assure her he would go quietly, not cause her any embarrassment. There was no purpose whatever in staying anyway. It was all too obvious why he had left in the first place. She had no passion to match his. She was a beautiful vessel, gentle at least outwardly, but it was born from fear of unpleasantness, not of compassion, such as a deeper woman might have felt—but she was a shallower vessel than he, incapable of answering him. She wanted to be comfortable; there was something innately selfish in her.

''I am glad you are happy,'' he said, his voice dry, catching in his throat. ''There is no need to be frightened. I shall not stay. I came across from Guildford. I have to be in London tomorrow morning anyway—a big trial. She—the woman accused—made me think of you. I wanted to see you—know how you are. Now I do; it is enough.''

''Thank you.'' The relief flooded her face. ''I—I would rather Gerald did not know you were here. He—he wouldn't like it.''

"Then don't tell him," he said simply. "And if the maid mentions it, I was merely an old friend, calling by to enquire after your health, and to wish you happiness."

"I am well—and happy. Thank you, William." Now she was embarrassed. Perhaps she realized how shallow she sounded; but it was at least past, and she had no intention of apologizing for it or trying to ameliorate its truth.

Nor did she offer him refreshment. She wanted him to leave before her husband returned from wherever he was—perhaps church.

There was nothing of any dignity or worth to be gained by remaining—only a petty selfishness, a desire for a small revenge, and he would despise it afterwards.

"Then I shall walk to the station and catch the next train towards London." He went to the door, and she opened it for him hastily, thanking him once again.

He bade her good-bye and two minutes later was walking along the lane under the trees with the wind-swung leaves dancing across the sunlight, birds singing. Here and there was a splash of white hawthorn blossom in the hedges, its perfume so sweet in the air that quite suddenly it brought him close to unexpected tears, not of self-pity because he had lost a love, but because what he had truly hungered for with such terrible depth had never existed—not in her. He had painted on her lovely face and gentle manner a mask of what he longed for—which was every bit as unfair to her as it was to him.

He blinked, and quickened his pace. He was a hard man, often cruel, demanding, brilliant, unflinching from labor or truth—at least he had been—but by God he had courage. And with all the changes he meant to wreak in himself, that at least he would never change.

Hester spent Sunday, with Edith's unintentional help, visiting Damaris. This time she did not see Randolf or Felicia Carlyon, but went instead to the gate and the door of the wing where Damaris and Peverell lived and, when they chose, had a certain amount of privacy. She had nothing to say to

Felicia, and would be grateful not to be faced with the duty of having to try to find something civil and noncommittal to fill the silences there would inevitably be. And she also felt a trifle guilty for what she intended to do, and what she knew it would cost them.

She wished to see Damaris alone, absolutely alone, without fear of interruption from anyone (least of all Felicia), so she could confront her with the terrible facts that Monk had found, and perhaps wring from her the truth about the night of the murder.

Without knowing why, Edith had agreed to distract Peverell and keep him from home, on whatever pretext came to her mind. Hester had told her only that she needed to see Damaris, and that it was delicate and likely to be painful, but that it concerned a truth they had to learn. Hester felt abominably guilty that she had not told Edith what it was, but knowledge would also bring the obligation to choose, and that was a burden she dared not place on Edith in case she chose the wrong way, and love for her sister outweighed pursuit of truth. And if the truth were as ugly as they feared, it would be easier for Edith afterwards if she had had no conscious hand in exposing it.

She repeated this over to herself as she sat in Damaris's elegant, luxurious sitting room waiting for her to come, and finding sparse comfort in it.

She looked around the room. It was typical of Damaris, the conventional and the outrageous side by side, the comfort of wealth and exquisite taste, the safety of the established order—and next to it the wildly rebellious, the excitement of indiscipline. Idealistic landscapes hung on one side of the room, on the other were reproductions of two of William Blake's wilder, more passionate drawings of the human figure. Religion, philosophy and daring voyages into new politics sat on the same bookshelf. Artifacts were romantic or blasphemous, expensive or tawdry, practical or useless, personal taste side by side with the desire to shock. It was the room of two totally different people, or one person seeking to have the best of opposing worlds, to make daring voyages of exploration and at the same time keep hold of comfort and the safety of the long known.

When Damaris came in she was dressed in a gown which was obviously new, but so old in style it harked back to lines of the French Empire. It was startling, but as soon as Hester got over the surprise of it, she realized it was also extremely becoming, the line so much more natural than all the current layers of stiff petticoats and hooped skirts. It was also certainly far more comfortable to wear. Although she thought Damaris almost certainly chose it for effect, not comfort.

"How nice to see you," Damaris said warmly. Her face was pale and there were shadows of sleeplessness around her eyes. "Edith said you wanted to speak to me about the case. I don't know what I can tell you. It's a disaster, isn't it." She flopped down on the sofa and without thinking tucked her feet up to be comfortable. She smiled at Hester rather wanly. "I'm afraid your Mr. Rathbone is out of his depth—he isn't clever enough to get Alexandra out of this." She pulled a face. "But from what I have seen, he doesn't even appear to be trying. Anyone could do all that he has so far. What's that matter, Hester? Doesn't he believe it is worth it?"

"Oh yes," Hester said quickly, stung for Rathbone as well as for the truth. She sat down opposite Damaris. "It isn't time yet—his turn comes next."

"But it will be too late. The jury have already made up their minds. Couldn't you see that in their faces? I did."

"No it isn't. There are facts to come out that will change everything, believe me."

"Are there?" Damaris screwed up her face dubiously. "I can't imagine that."

"Can't you?"

Damaris squinted at her. "You say that with extra meaning—as if you thought I could. I can't think of anything at all that would alter what the jury think now."

There was no alternative, no matter how Hester hated it, and she did hate it. She felt brutal, worse than that, treacherous.

"You were at the Furnivals' house the night of the murder,'' she began, although it was stating what they both knew and had never argued.

"I don't know anything," Damaris said with absolute candor. "For heaven's sake, if I did I would have said so before now."

"Would you? No matter how terrible it was?"

Damaris frowned. "Terrible? Alexandra pushed Thaddeus over the banister, then followed him down and picked up the halberd and drove it into his body as he lay unconscious at her feet! That's pretty terrible. What could be worse?"

Hester swallowed but did not look away from Damaris's eyes.

"Whatever you found out when you went upstairs to Valentine Furnival's room before dinner—long before Thaddeus was killed."

The blood fled from Damaris's face, leaving her looking ill and vulnerable, and suddenly far younger than she was.

"That has nothing to do with what happened to Thaddeus," she said very quietly. "Absolutely nothing. It was something else—something . . ." She hunched her shoulders and her voice trailed off. She pulled her feet a little higher.

"I think it has." Hester could not afford to be lenient.

The ghost of a smile crossed Damaris's mouth and vanished. It was self-mockery and there was no shred of happiness in it.

"You are wrong. You will have to accept my word of honor for that."

"I can't. I accept that you believe it. I don't accept you are right."

Damaris's face pinched. "You don't know what it was, and I shall not tell you. I'm sorry, but it won't help Alexandra, and it is my—my grief, not hers."

Hester felt knotted up inside with shame and pity.

"Do you know why Alexandra killed him?"

"No."

"I do."

Damaris's head jerked up, her eyes wide.

"Why?" she said huskily.

Hester took a deep breath.

"Because he was committing sodomy and incest with his own son," she said very quietly. Her voice sounded obscenely matter-of-fact in the silent room, as if she had made some banal remark that would be forgotten in a few moments, instead of something so dreadful they would both remember it as long as they lived.

Damaris did not shriek or faint. She did not even look away, but her skin was whiter than before, and her eyes hollower.

Hester realized with an increasing sickness inside that, far from disbelieving her, Damaris was not even surprised. It was as if it were a long-expected blow, coming at last. So Monk had been right. She had discovered that evening that Peverell was involved. Hester could have wept for her, for the pain. She longed to touch her, to take her in her arms as she would a weeping child, but it was useless. Nothing could reach or fold that wound.

"You knew, didn't you?" she said aloud. "You knew it that night!"

"No I didn't." Damaris's voice was flat, almost without expression, as if something in her were already destroyed.

"Yes you did. You knew Peverell was doing it too, and to Valentine Furnival. That's why you came down almost beside yourself with horror. You were close to hysterical. I don't know how you kept any control at all. I wouldn't have— I don't think—"

"Oh God—no!" Damaris was moved to utter horror at last. "No!" She uncurled herself so violently she half-fell off the settee, landing awkwardly on the ground. "No. No, I didn't. Not Pev. How could you even think such a thing? It's—it's—wild—insane. Not Pev!"

"But you knew." For the first time Hester doubted. "Wasn't that what you discovered when you went up to Valentine's room?"

"No." Damaris was on the floor in front of her, splayed

376

out like a colt, her long legs at angles, and yet she was absolutely natural. "No! Hester—dear heaven, please believe me, it wasn't."

Hester struggled with herself. Could it be the truth?

"Then what was it?" She frowned, racking her mind. "You came down from Valentine's room looking as if you'd seen the wrath of heaven. Why? What else could you possibly have found out? It was nothing to do with Alexandra or Thaddeus—or Peverell, then what?"

"I can't tell you!"

"Then I can't believe you. Rathbone is going to call you to the stand. Cassian was abused by his father, his grandfather—I'm sorry—and someone else. We have to know who that other person was, and prove it. Or Alexandra will hang."

Damaris was so pale her skin looked gray, as if she had aged in moments.

"I can't. It—it would destroy Pev." She saw Hester's face. "No. No, it isn't that. I swear by God—it isn't."

"No one will believe you," Hester said very quietly, although even as she said it, she knew it was a lie—she believed it. "What else could it be?"

Damaris bowed her head in her hands and began to speak very quietly, her voice aching with unshed tears.

"When I was younger, before I met Pev, I fell in love with someone else. For a long time I did nothing. I loved him with . . . chastity. Then—I thought I was losing him. I—I loved him wildly . . . at least I thought I did. Then . . ."

"You made love," Hester said the obvious. She was not shocked. In the same circumstances she might have done the same, had she Damaris's beauty, and wild beliefs. Even without them had she loved enough . . .

"Yes." Damaris's voice choked. "I didn't keep his love . . . in fact I think in a way that ended it."

Hester waited. Obviously there was more. By itself it was hardly worth repeating.

Damaris went on, her voice catching as she strove to control it, and only just succeeding. "I learned I was with child. It was Thaddeus who helped me. That was what I was talking

377

about when I said he could be kind. I had no idea Mama knew anything about it. Thaddeus arranged for me to go away for a while, and for the child to be adopted. It was a boy. I held him once—he was beautiful." At last she could keep the tears back no longer and she bent her head and wept, sobs shaking her body and long despairing cries tearing her beyond her strength to conceal.

Hester slid down onto the floor and put both her arms around her, holding her close, stroking her head and letting the storm burn itself out and exhaust her, all the grief and guilt of years bursting its bounds at last.

It was many minutes later when Damaris was still, and Hester spoke again.

"And what did you learn that night?"

"I learned where he was." Damaris sniffed fiercely and sat up, reaching for a handkerchief, an idiotic piece of lace and cambric not large enough to do anything at all.

Hester stood up and went to the cloakroom and wrung out a hand towel in cold water and brought it back, and also a large piece of soft linen she found in the cupboard beside the basin. Without saying anything she handed them to Damaris.

"Well?" she asked after another moment or two.

"Thank you." Damaris remained sitting on the floor. "I learned where he was," she said, her composure back again. She was too worn out for any violent emotion anymore. "I learned what Thaddeus had done. Who he had . . . given him to."

Hester waited, resuming her seat.

"The Furnivals," Damaris said with a small, very sad smile. "Valentine Furnival is my son. I knew that when I saw him. I hadn't seen Valentine for years, you see, not since he was a small child—about Cassian's age, or even less. Actually I so dislike Louisa, and I didn't go there very often, and when I did he was always away at school, or when he was younger, already in bed. That evening he was at home because he'd had measles. But this time, when I saw him, he'd changed so much—grown up—and . . . ." She took a deep, rather shaky breath. "He was so like his father when he was younger, I knew . . ."

"Like his father?" Hester searched her brains, which was stupid. There was no reason in the world why it should be anyone she had even heard of, much less met; in fact, there was every reason why it should not. Yet there was something tugging at the corners of her mind, a gesture, something about the eyes, the color of hair, the heavy lids . . .

"Charles Hargrave," Damaris said very quietly, and instantly Hester knew it was the truth: the eyes, the height, the way of standing, the angle of the shoulders.

Then another, ugly thought pulled at the edge of her mind, insistent, refusing to be silenced.

"But why did that upset you so terribly? You were frantic when you came down again, not quiet shaken, but frantic. Why? Even if Peverell found out Valentine was Hargrave's son—and I assume he doesn't know—even if he saw the resemblance between Valentine and Dr. Hargrave, there is no reason why he should connect it with you."

Damaris shut her eyes and again her voice was sharp with pain.

"I didn't know Thaddeus abused Cassian, believe me, I really didn't. But I knew Papa abused him—when he was a child. I knew the look in his eyes, that mixture of fear and excitement, the pain, the confusion, and the kind of secret pleasure. I suppose if I'd ever really looked at Cass lately I'd have seen it there too—but I didn't look. And since the murder I just thought it was part of his grief. Not that I've spent much time with him anyway—I should have, but I haven't. I know about Thaddeus, because I saw it once . . . and ever after it was in my mind."

Hester drew breath to say something—and nothing seemed adequate.

Damaris closed her eyes.

"I saw the same look in Valentine's face." Her voice was tight, as if her throat were burned inside. "I knew he was being abused too. I thought it was Maxim—I hated him so much I would have killed him. It never occurred to me it was

379

Thaddeus. Oh God. Poor Alex." She gulped. "No wonder she killed him. I would have too—in her place. In fact if I'd known it was he who abused Valentine, I would have anyway. I just didn't know. I suppose I assumed it was always fathers." She laughed harshly, a tiny thread of hysteria creeping back into her voice. "You should have suspected me. I would have been just as guilty as Alexandra—in thought and intent, if not in deed. It was only inability that stopped me—nothing else."

"Many of us are innocent only through lack of chance—or of means," Hester said very softly. "Don't blame yourself. You'll never know whether you would have or not if the chance had been there."

"I would." There was no doubt in Damaris's voice, none at all. She looked up at Hester. "What can we do for Alex? It would be monstrous if she were hanged for that. Any mother worth a damn would have done the same!"

"Testify," Hester answered without hesitation. "Tell the truth. We've got to persuade the jury that she did the only thing she could to protect her child."

Damaris looked away, her eyes filling with tears.

"Do I have to tell about Valentine? Peverell doesn't know! Please . . ."

"Tell him yourself," Hester said very quietly. "He loves you—and he must know you love him."

"But men don't forgive easily—not things like that." The despair was back in Damaris's voice.

Hester felt wretched, still hoping against all likelihood that it was not Peverell.

"Peverell isn't 'men,' " she said chokingly. "Don't judge him by others. Give him the chance to be all—all that he could be." Did she sound as desperate and as hollow as she felt? "Give him a chance to forgive—and love you for what you really are, not what you think he wants you to be. It was a mistake, a sin if you like—but we all sin one way or another. What matters is that you become kinder and wiser because of it, that you become gentler with others, and that you have never repeated it!"

"Do you think he will see it like that? He might if it were anyone else—but it's different when it's your own wife."

"For heaven's sake—try him."

"But if he doesn't, I'll lose him!"

"And if you lie, Alexandra will lose her life. What would Peverell think of that?"

"I know." Damaris stood up slowly, suddenly all her grace returning. "I've got to tell him. God knows I wish I hadn't done it. And Charles Hargrave, of all people. I can hardly bear to look at him now. I know. Don't tell me again, I do know. I've got to tell Pev. There isn't any way out of it—lying would only make it worse."

"Yes it would." Hester put out her hand and touched Damaris's arm. "I'm sorry—but I had no choice either."

"I know." Damaris smiled with something of the old charm, although the effort it cost her was apparent. "Only if I do this, you'd better save Alex. I don't want to say all this for nothing."

"Everything I can. I'll leave nothing untried—I promise."

12

ALEXANDRA SAT ON THE WOODEN BENCH in the small cell, her face white and almost expressionless. She was exhausted, and the marks of sleeplessness were plain around her eyes. She was far thinner than when Rathbone had first seen her and her hair had lost its sheen.

"I can't go on," she said wearily. "There isn't any point. It will only damage Cassian—terribly." She took a deep breath. He could see the rise of her breast under the thin gray muslin of her blouse. "They won't believe me. Why should they? There's no proof, there never could be. How could you prove such a thing? People don't do it where they can be seen."

"You know," Rathbone said quietly, sitting opposite her and looking at her so intensely that in time she would have to raise her head and meet his eyes.

She smiled bitterly. "And who's going to believe me?"

"That wasn't my point," he said patiently. "If you could know, then it is possible others could also. Thaddeus himself was abused as a child."

She jerked her head up, her eyes full of pity and surprise.

"You didn't know?" He looked at her gently. "I thought not."

"I'm sorry," she whispered. "But if he was, how could

382

he, of all people, abuse his own son?'' Her incomprehension was full of confusion and pain. "Surely if—why? I don't understand.''

"Neither do I," he answered frankly. "But then I have never walked that path myself. I had quite another reason for telling you, one of very much more urgent relevance." He stopped, not fully sure if she was listening to him.

"Have you?" she said dully.

"Yes. Can you imagine how he suffered? His lifelong shame, and the fear of being discovered? Even some dim sense of what he was committing upon his own child—and yet, the need was so overwhelming, so consuming it still drove him—"

"Stop it," she said furiously, jerking her head up. "I'm sorry! Of course I'm sorry! Do you think I enjoyed it?" Her voice was thick, choking with indescribable anguish. "I racked my brain for any other way. I begged him to stop, to send Cassian away to boarding school—anything at all to put him beyond reach. I offered him myself, for any practice he wanted!" She stared at him with helpless fury. "I used to love him. Not passionately, but love just the same. He was the father of my children and I had covenanted to be loyal to him all my life. I don't think he ever loved me, not really, but he gave me all he was capable of.''

She sank lower on the bench and dropped her head forward, covering her face with her hands. "Don't you think I see his body on that floor every time I lie in the dark? I dream about it—I've redone that deed in my nightmares, and woken up cold as ice, with the sweat standing out on my skin. I'm terrified God will judge me and condemn my soul forever.''

She huddled a little lower into herself. "But I *couldn't* let that happen to my child and do nothing—just let it go on. You don't know how he changed. The laughter went out of him—all the innocence. He became sly. He was afraid of me—of me! He didn't trust me anymore, and he started telling lies—stupid lies—and he became frightened all the time, and suspicious of people. And always there was the sort of . . . secret glee in him . . . a—a—guilty pleasure. And yet he cried at night—curled up like a baby, and crying in his sleep. I couldn't let it go on!''

Rathbone broke his own rules and reached out and took her thin shoulders in his hands and held her gently.

''Of course you couldn't! And you can't now! If the truth is not told, and this abuse is not stopped, then his grandfather—and the other man—will go on just as his father did, and it will all have been for nothing.'' Unconsciously his fingers tightened. ''We think we know who the other man is, and believe me he will have the same chances as the general had: any day, any night, to go on exactly the same.''

She began to weep softly, without sobbing, just the quiet tears of utter despair. He held her gently, leaning forward a little, his head close to hers. He could smell the faint odor of her hair, washed with prison soap, and feel the warmth of her skin.

''Thaddeus was abused as a child,'' he went on relentlessly, because it mattered. ''His sister knew it. She saw it happen once, by his father—and she saw the reflection of the same emotion in the eyes again in Valentine Furnival. That was what drove her to distraction that evening. She will swear to it.''

Alexandra said nothing, but he could feel her stiffen with surprise, and the weeping stopped. She was utterly still.

''And Miss Buchan knew about Thaddeus and his father—and about Cassian now.''

Alexandra took a shaky breath, still hiding her face.

''She won't testify,'' she said with a long sniff. ''She can't. If she does they'll dismiss her—and she has nowhere to go. You mustn't ask her. She'll have to deny it, and that will only make it worse.''

He smiled bleakly. ''Don't worry about that. I never ask questions unless I already know the answer—or, to be more precise, unless I know what the witness will say, true or untrue.''

''You can't expect her to ruin herself.''

''What she chooses to do is not your decision.''

"But you can't," she protested, pulling away from him and lifting her head to face him. "She'd starve."

"And what will happen to Cassian? Not to mention you." She said nothing.

"Cassian will grow up to repeat the pattern of his father," he said ruthlessly, because it was the only thing he knew which would be more than she could bear, regardless of Miss Buchan's fate. "Will you permit that? The shame and guilt all over again—and another wretched, humiliated child, another woman suffering as you do now?"

"I can't fight you," she said so quietly he could barely hear her. She sat huddled over herself, as if the pain were deep in the center of her and somehow she could fold herself around it.

"You are not fighting me," he said urgently. "You don't need to do anything now but sit in the dock, looking as you do, and remembering, as well as your guilt, the love of your child—and *why* you did it. I will tell the jury your feelings, trust me!"

"Do whatever you will, Mr. Rathbone. I don't think I have strength left to make judgments anymore."

"You don't need it, my dear." He stood up at last, exhausted himself, and it was only Monday, June 29. The second week of the trial had commenced. He must begin the defense.

The first witness for the defense was Edith Sobell. Lovat-Smith was sitting back in his chair, legs crossed over casually, head tilted, as if he were interested only as a matter of curiosity. He had made a case that seemed unarguable, and looking around the crowded courtroom, there was not a single face which registered doubt. They were there only to watch Alexandra and the Carlyon family sitting in their row at the front, the women dressed in black and Felicia veiled, rigid and square-shouldered, Randolf unhappy but entirely composed.

Edith took the stand and stumbled once or twice when swearing the oath, her tongue clumsy in her nervousness.

385

And yet there was a bloom to her skin, a color that belied the situation, and she stood erect with nothing of the defensiveness or the weight of grief which lay on her mother.

"Mrs. Sobell," Rathbone began courteously, "you are the sister of the victim of this crime, and the sister-in-law of the accused?"

"I am."

"Did you know your brother well, Mrs. Sobell?"

"Moderately. He was several years older than I, and he left home to go into the army when I was a child. But of course when he returned from service abroad and settled down I learned to know him again. He lived not far from Carlyon House, where I still live, since my husband's death."

"Would you tell me something of your brother's personality, as you observed it?"

Lovat-Smith shifted restlessly in his seat, and the crowd had already lost interest, all but a few who hoped there might be some completely new and shocking revelation. After all, this witness was for the defense.

Lovat-Smith rose to his feet.

"My lord, this appears to be quite irrelevant. We have already very fully established the nature of the dead man. He was honorable, hardworking, a military hero of considerable repute, faithful to his wife, financially prudent and generous. His only failings seem to have been that he was somewhat pompous and perhaps did not flatter or amuse his wife as much as he might." He smiled dryly, looking around so the jury could see his face. "A weakness we might all be guilty of, from time to time."

"I don't doubt it," Rathbone said acerbically. "And if Mrs. Sobell agrees with your estimation, I will be happy to save the court's time by avoiding having her repeat it. Mrs. Sobell?"

"I agree," Edith said with a look first at Rathbone, then at Lovat-Smith. "He also spent a great deal of time with his son, Cassian. He seemed to be an excellent and devoted father."

"Quite: he seemed to be an excellent and devoted father,"

he repeated her precise words. "And yet, Mrs. Sobell, when you became aware of the tragedy of his death, and that your sister-in-law had been charged with causing it, what did you do?"

"My lord, that too is surely quite irrelevant?" Lovat-Smith protested. "I appreciate that my learned friend is somewhat desperate, but this cannot be allowed!"

The judge looked at Rathbone.

"Mr. Rathbone, I will permit you some leniency, so that you may present the best defense you can, in extremely difficult circumstances, but I will not permit you to waste the court's time. See to it that the answers you draw are to some point!"

Rathbone looked again at Edith.

"Mrs. Sobell?"

"I . . ." Edith swallowed hard and lifted her chin, looking away from where her mother and father sat upright in their row in the front of the gallery, now no longer witnesses. For an instant her eyes met Alexandra's in the dock. Then she continued speaking. "I contacted a friend of mine, a Miss Hester Latterly, and asked her help to find a good lawyer to defend Alexandra—Mrs. Carlyon."

"Indeed?" Rathbone's eyebrows shot up as if he were surprised, although surely almost everyone in the room must know he had planned this most carefully. "Why? She was charged with murdering your brother, this model man."

"At first—at first I thought she could not be guilty." Edith's voice trembled a little but she gained control again. "Then when it was proved to me beyond question that she was . . . that she had committed the act . . . I still thought there must be some better reason than the one she gave."

Lovat-Smith rose again.

"My lord! I hope Mr. Rathbone is not going to ask the witness to draw some conclusion? Her faith in her sister-in-law is very touching, but it is not evidence of anything except her own gentle—and, forgive me, rather gullible—nature!"

"My learned friend is leaping to conclusions, as I am afraid he is prone to do," Rathbone said with a tiny smile.

"I do not wish Mrs. Sobell to draw any conclusions at all, simply to lay a foundation for her subsequent actions, so the court will understand what she did, and why."

"Proceed, Mr. Rathbone," the judge instructed.

"Thank you, my lord. Mrs. Sobell, have you spent much time with your nephew, Cassian Carlyon, since his father's death?"

"Yes of course. He is staying in our house."

"How has he taken his father's death?"

"Irrelevant!" Lovat-Smith interrupted again. "How can a child's grief possibly be pertinent to the accused's guilt or innocence? We cannot turn a blind eye to murder because if we hanged the guilty person then a child would be robbed of both his parents—tragic as that is. And we all pity him . . ."

"He does not need your pity, Mr. Lovat-Smith," Rathbone said irritably. "He needs you to hold your tongue and let me proceed with uncovering the truth."

"Mr. Rathbone," the judge said tartly. "We sympathize with your predicament, and your frustration, but your language is discourteous, and I will not allow it. Nevertheless, Mr. Lovat-Smith, it is good counsel, and you will please observe it until you have an objection of substance. If you interrupt as often as this, we shall not reach a verdict before Michaelmas."

Lovat-Smith sat down with a broad smile.

Rathbone bowed, then turned back to Edith.

"I think you are now permitted to continue, Mrs. Sobell. If you please. What was your observation of Cassian's manner?"

Edith frowned in concentration.

"It was very hard to understand," she replied, thinking carefully. "He grieved for his father, but it seemed to be very—very adult. He did not cry, and at times he seemed very composed, almost relieved."

Lovat-Smith rose to his feet, and the judge waved him to sit down again. Rathbone turned to Edith.

"Mrs. Sobell, will you please explain that curious word *relieved*. Try not to give us any conclusions you may have

388

come to in your own mind, simply your observations of fact. Not what he seemed, but what he said, or did. Do you understand the difference?''

"Yes, my lord. I'm sorry." Again her nervousness betrayed itself in clenched hands on the witness box rail, and a catch in her voice. "I saw him alone on several occasions, through a window, or from a doorway when he did not know I was there. He was quite at ease, sitting smiling. I asked him if he was happy by himself, thinking he might be lonely, but he told me he liked it. Sometimes he went to my father—his grandfather—"

"Colonel Carlyon?" Rathbone interrupted.

"Yes. Then other times he seemed to go out of his way to avoid him. He was afraid of my mother." As if involuntarily, she glanced at Felicia, then back to Rathbone again. "He said so. And he was very upset about his own mother. He told me she did not love him—that his father had told him so."

In the dock Alexandra closed her eyes and seemed to sway as if in physical pain. A gasp escaped her in spite of all her effort at self-control.

"Hearsay," Lovat-Smith said loudly, rising to his feet. "My lord . . ."

"That is not permitted," the judge apologized to Edith. "I think we have gathered from your testimony that the child was in a state of considerable confusion. Is that what you wished to establish, Mr. Rathbone?"

"More than that, my lord: the nature of his confusion. And that he developed close, and ambivalent, relationships with other people."

Lovat-Smith let out a loud moan and raised his hands in the air.

"Then you had better proceed and do so, Mr. Rathbone," the judge said with a tight smile. "If you can. Although you have not shown us yet why this has any relevance to the case, and I advise that you do that within a very short time."

"I promise you that it will become apparent in later testimony, my lord," Rathbone said, his voice still calculatedly light. But he abandoned the course for the present, knowing he had left it imprinted on the jury's minds, and that was all that mattered. He could build on it later. He turned back to Edith.

"Mrs. Sobell, did you recently observe a very heated quarrel between Miss Buchan, an elderly member of your household staff, and your cook, Mrs. Emery?"

A ghost of amusement crossed Edith's face, curving her mouth momentarily.

"I have observed several, more than I can count," she conceded. "Cook and Miss Buchan have been enemies for years."

"Quite so. But the quarrel I am referring to happened within the last three weeks, on the back stairs of Carlyon House. You were called to assist."

"That's right. Cassian came to fetch me because he was afraid. Cook had a knife. I'm sure she did not intend to do anything with it but make an exhibition, but he didn't know that."

"What was the quarrel about, Mrs. Sobell?"

Lovat-Smith groaned audibly.

Rathbone ignored it.

"About?" Edith looked slightly puzzled. He had not told her he was going to pursue this. He wanted her obvious unawareness to be seen by the jury. This case depended upon emotions as much as upon facts.

"Yes. What was the subject of the difference?"

Lovat-Smith groaned even more loudly. "Really, my lord," he protested.

Rathbone resumed facing the judge. "My learned friend seems to be in some distress," he said unctuously.

There was a loud titter of amusement, nervous, like a ripple of wind through a field before thunder.

"The case," Lovat-Smith said loudly. "Get on with the case, man!"

"Then bear your agony a little less vocally, old chap," Rathbone replied equally loudly, "and allow me to." He swung around. "Mrs. Sobell—to remind you, the question was, would you please tell the court the subject of the quarrel between the governess, Miss Buchan, and the cook?''

"Yes—yes, if you wish, although I cannot see—"

"We none of us can," Lovat-Smith interrupted again.

"Mr. Lovat-Smith," the judge said sharply. "Mrs. Sobell, answer the question. If it proves irrelevant I will control Mr. Rathbone's wanderings."

"Yes, my lord. Cook accused Miss Buchan of being incompetent to care for Cassian. She said Miss Buchan was . . . there was a great deal of personal abuse, my lord. I would rather not repeat it."

Rathbone thought of permitting her to do so. A jury liked to be amused, but they would lose respect for Miss Buchan, which might be what would win or lose the case. A little laughter now would be too dearly bought.

"Please spare us," he said aloud. "The subject of the difference will be sufficient—the fact that there was abuse may indicate the depth of their feelings."

Again Edith smiled hurriedly, and then continued.

"Cook said that Miss Buchan was following him around everywhere and confusing him by telling him his mother loved him, and was not a wicked woman." She swallowed hard, her eyes troubled. That she did not understand what he wanted was painfully obvious. The jury were utterly silent, their faces staring at her. Suddenly the drama was back again, the concentration total. The crowd did not whisper or move. Even Alexandra herself seemed momentarily forgotten.

"And the cook?" Rathbone prompted.

"Cook said Alexandra should be hanged." Edith seemed to find the word difficult. "And of course she was wicked. Cassian had to know it and come to terms with it."

"And Miss Buchan's reply?"

"That Cook didn't know anything about it, she was an ignorant woman and should stay in the kitchen where she belonged."

"Did you know to what Miss Buchan referred?" Rathbone asked, his voice low and clear, without any theatrics.

"No."

"Was a Miss Hester Latterly present at this exchange?"

"Yes."

"When you had parted the two protagonists, did Miss Latterly go upstairs with Miss Buchan?"

"Yes."

"And afterwards leave in some haste, and without explanation to you as to why?"

"Yes, but we did not quarrel," Edith said quickly. "She seemed to have something most urgent to do."

"Indeed I know it, Mrs. Sobell. She came immediately to see me. Thank you. That is all. Please remain there, in case my learned friend has something to ask you."

There was a rustle and a sigh around the court. A dozen people nudged each other. The expected revelation had not come . . . not yet.

Lovat-Smith rose and sauntered over to Edith, hands in his pockets.

"Mrs. Sobell, tell me honestly, much as you may sympathize with your sister-in-law, has any of what you have said the slightest bearing on the tragedy of your brother's death?"

She hesitated, glancing at Rathbone.

"No, Mrs. Sobell," Lovat-Smith cautioned sharply. "Answer for yourself, please! Can you tell me any relation between what you have said about your nephew's very natural confusion and distress over his father's murder, and his mother's confession and arrest, and this diverting but totally irrelevant quarrel between two of your domestics?" He waved his hands airily, dismissing it, "And the cause at trial: namely whether Alexandra Carlyon is guilty or not guilty of murdering her husband, your brother? I remind you, in case after all this tarradiddle you, like the rest of us, are close to forgetting."

He had gone too far. He had trivialized the tragedy.

"I don't know, Mr. Lovat-Smith," she said with a sudden return of composure, her voice now grim and with a hard edge. "As you have just said, we are here to discover the truth, not to assess it beforehand. I don't know why Alexandra did what she did, and I wish to know. It has to matter."

"Indeed." Lovat-Smith gave in gracefully. He had sufficient instinct to recognize an error and cease it immediately. "It does not alter facts, but of course it matters, Mrs. Sobell. I have no further questions. Thank you."

"Mr. Rathbone?" the judge asked.

"I have no further questions, thank you, my lord."

"Thank you, Mrs. Sobell, you may go."

Rathbone stood in the center of the very small open space in front of the witness box.

"I call Miss Catriona Buchan."

Miss Buchan came to the witness box looking very pale, her face even more gaunt than before, her thin back stiff and her eyes straight forward, as if she were a French aristocrat passing through the old women knitting at the foot of the guillotine. She mounted the stairs unaided, holding her skirts in from the sides, and at the top turned and faced the court. She swore to tell the truth, and regarded Rathbone as though he were an executioner.

Rathbone found himself admiring her as much as anyone he had ever faced across that small space of floor.

"Miss Buchan, I realize what this is going to cost you, and I am not unmindful of your sacrifice, nevertheless I hope you understand that in the cause of justice I have no alternative?"

"Of course I do," she agreed with a crisp voice. The strain in it did not cause her to falter, only to sound a little more clipped than usual, a little higher in pitch, as if her throat were tight. "I would not answer did I not understand that!"

"Indeed. Do you remember quarreling with the cook at Carlyon House some three weeks ago?"

"I do. She is a good enough cook, but a stupid woman."

"In what way stupid, Miss Buchan?"

"She imagines all ills can be treated with good regular meals and that if you only eat right everything else will sort itself out."

"A shortsighted view. What did you quarrel about on that occasion, Miss Buchan?"

Her chin lifted a little higher.

"Master Cassian. She said I was confusing the child by telling him his mother was not a wicked woman, and that she still loved him."

In the dock Alexandra was so still it seemed she could not even be breathing. Her eyes never left Miss Buchan's face and she barely blinked.

"Is that all?" Rathbone asked.

Miss Buchan took a deep breath, her thin chest rising and falling. "No—she also said I followed the boy around too much, not leaving him alone."

"Did you follow the boy around, Miss Buchan?"

She hesitated only a moment. "Yes."

"Why?" He kept his voice level, as if the question were not especially important.

"To do what I could to prevent him being abused anymore."

"Abused? Was someone mistreating him? In what way?"

"I believe the word is sodomy, Mr. Rathbone," she said with only the slightest tremor.

There was a gasp in the court as hundreds of throats drew in breath.

Alexandra covered her face with her hands.

The jury froze in their seats, eyes wide, faces aghast.

In the front row of the gallery Randolf Carlyon sat immobile as stone. Felicia's veiled head jerked up and her knuckles were white on the rail in front of her. Edith, now sitting beside them, looked as if she had been struck.

Even the judge stiffened and turned to look up at Alexandra. Lovat-Smith stared at Rathbone, his face slack with amazement.

Rathbone waited several seconds before he spoke.

"Someone in the house was sodomizing the child?" He said it very quietly, but the peculiar quality of his voice and his exquisite diction made every word audible even at the very back of the gallery.

"Yes," Miss Buchan answered, looking at no one but him.

"How do you know that, Miss Buchan? Did you see it happen?"

"I did not see it this time—but I have in the past, when Thaddeus Carlyon himself was a child," she said. "And I knew the signs. I knew the look in a child's face, the sly pleasure, the fear mixed with exultancy, the flirting and the shame, the self-possession one minute, then the terror of losing his mother's love if she knew, the hatred of having to keep it a secret, and the pride of having a secret—and then crying in the night, and not being able to tell anyone why— and the total and overwhelming loneliness . . ."

Alexandra had lifted her face. She looked ashen, her body rigid with anguish.

The jury sat immobile, eyes horrified, skin suddenly pale.

The judge looked at Lovat-Smith, but for once he did not exercise his right to object to the vividness of her evidence, unsupported by any provable fact. His dark face looked blurred with shock.

"Miss Buchan," Rathbone continued softly. "You seem to have a vivid appreciation of what it is like. How is that?"

"Because I saw it in Thaddeus—General Carlyon—when he was a child. His father abused him."

There was such a gasp of horror around the room, a clamor of voices in amazement and protest, that she was obliged to stop.

In the gallery newspaper runners tripped over legs and caught their feet in onlookers' skirts as they scrambled to get out and seize a hansom to report the incredible news.

"Order!" the judge commanded, banging his gavel violently on his bench. "Order! Or I shall clear the court!"

Very slowly the room subsided. The jury had all turned to look at Randolf. Now again they faced Miss Buchan.

"That is a desperately serious thing to charge, Miss Buchan," Rathbone said quietly. "You must be very certain that what you say is true?"

"Of course I am." She answered him with the first and only trace of bitterness in her voice. "I have served the Carlyon family since I was twenty-four, when I came to look after Master Thaddeus. That is over forty years. There is nowhere else I can go now—and they will hardly give me a roof over my head in my old age after this. Does anyone imagine I do it lightly?"

Rathbone glanced for only a second at the jury's faces, and saw there the conflict of horror, disgust, anger, pity, and confusion that he had expected. She was a woman caught between betraying her employers, with its irreparable consequences to her, or betraying her conscience, and a child who had no one else to speak for him. The jurors were of a servant-keeping class, or they would not be jurors. Yet few of them were of position sufficient to have governesses. They were torn in loyalties, social ambition, and tearing pity.

"I know that, Miss Buchan," Rathbone said with a ghost of a smile. "I want to be sure that the court appreciates it also. Please continue. You were aware of the sodomy committed by Colonel Randolf Carlyon upon his son, Thaddeus. You saw the same signs of abuse in young Cassian Carlyon, and you were afraid for him. Is that correct?"

"Yes."

"And did you know who had been abusing him? Please be careful to be precise, Miss Buchan. I do mean *know*, supposition or deduction will not do."

"I am aware of that, sir," she said stiffly. "No, I did not know. But since he normally lived at his own home, not in Carlyon House, I supposed that it was his father, Thaddeus, perpetuating on his son what he himself endured as a child. And I assumed that that was what Alexandra Carlyon discovered, and why she did what she did. No one told me so."

"And that abuse ceased after the general's death? Then why did you think it necessary to protect him still?"

"I saw the relationship between him and his grandfather, the looks, the touching, the shame and the excitement. It was exactly the same as before—in the past. I was afraid it was happening again."

There was utter silence in the room. One could almost hear the creak of corsets as women breathed.

"I see," Rathbone said quietly. "So you did your best to protect the boy. Why did you not tell someone? That would seem to be a far more effective solution."

A smile of derision crossed her face and vanished.

"And who would believe me?" For an instant her eyes moved up to the gallery and the motionless forms of Felicia and Randolf, then she looked back at Rathbone. "I'm a domestic servant, accusing a famous and respected gentleman of one of the most vile of crimes. I would be thrown out, and then I wouldn't be able to do anything at all."

"What about Mrs. Felicia Carlyon, the boy's grandmother?" he pressed, but his voice was gentle. "Wouldn't she have to have some idea? Could you not have told her?"

"You are naive, Mr. Rathbone," she said wearily. "If she had no idea, she would be furious, and throw me out instantly—and see to it I starved. She couldn't afford to have me find employment ever again, in case I repeated the charge to her social equals, even to friends. And if she knew herself—then she had decided not to expose it and ruin the family with the shame of it. She'd not allow me to. If she had to live with that, then she'd do everything in her power to keep what she had paid such a price to preserve."

"I see." Rathbone glanced at the jury, many of them craning up at the gallery, faces dark with disgust, then at Lovat-Smith, now sitting upright and silent, deep in concentration. "So you stayed in Carlyon House," Rathbone continued, "saying nothing, but doing what you could for the child. I think we may all understand your position—and admire you for having the courage to come forward now. Thank you, Miss Buchan."

Lovat-Smith rose to his feet, looking profoundly unhappy.

"Miss Buchan, I regret this," he said with such sincerity it was palpable. "But I must press you a little more harshly than my learned friend has. The accusation you make is abominable. It cannot be allowed to stand without challenge. It will ruin the lives of an entire family." He inclined his head towards the gallery, where now there was the occasional murmur of anger. "A family known and admired in this city, a family which has dedicated itself to the service of the Queen and her subjects, not only here but in the farthest parts of the Empire as well."

Miss Buchan said nothing, but faced him, her thin body erect, hands folded. She looked fragile, and suddenly very old. Rathbone ached to be able to protect her, but he was impotent to do anything now, as he had known he would be, and she knew it too.

"Miss Buchan," Lovat-Smith went on, still courteously. "I assume you know what sodomy is, and you do not use the term loosely?"

She blushed, but did not evade his look.

"Yes sir, I know what it is. I will describe it for you, if you force me."

He shook his head. "No—I do not force you, Miss Buchan. How do you know this unspeakable act was committed on General Carlyon when he was a child? And I do mean knowledge, Miss Buchan, not supposition, no matter how well reasoned, in your opinion." He looked up at her, waiting.

"I am a servant, Mr. Lovat-Smith," she replied with dignity. "We have a peculiar position—not quite people, not quite furniture. We are often party to extraordinary scenes because we are ignored in the house, as if we had not eyes or brains. People do not mind us knowing things, seeing things they would be mortified to have their friends see."

One of the jurors looked startled, suddenly thoughtful.

"One day I had occasion to return to the nursery unexpectedly," Miss Buchan resumed. "Colonel Carlyon had neglected to lock the door, and I saw him in the act with his son. He did not know I saw. I was transfixed with horror—although I should not have been. I knew there was something very seriously wrong, but I did not understand what—until then. I stood there for several seconds, but I left as soundlessly as I had come. My knowledge is very real, sir."

"You witnessed this gross act, and yet you did nothing?" Lovat-Smith's voice rose in disbelief. "I find that hard to credit, Miss Buchan. Was not your first duty clearly towards your charge, the child, Thaddeus Carlyon?"

She did not flinch.

"I have already told you, there was nothing I could do."

"Not tell his mother?" He waved an arm up towards the

gallery where Felicia sat like stone. "Would she not have been horrified? Would she not have protected her child? You seem, by implication, to be expecting us to believe that Alexandra Carlyon," he indicated her with another expansive gesture, "a generation later, was so violently distressed by the same fact that she murdered her husband rather than allow it to continue! And yet you say that Mrs. Felicia Carlyon would have done nothing!"

Miss Buchan did not speak.

"You hesitate," Lovat-Smith challenged, his voice rising. "Why, Miss Buchan? Are you suddenly not so certain of answers? Not so easy?"

Miss Buchan was strong. She had already risked, and no doubt lost, everything. She had no stake left, nothing else could be taken from her but her self-esteem.

"You are too facile, young man," she said with all the ineffable authority of a good governess. "Women may be as immeasurably different from each other as men. Their loyalties and values may be different also, as may be the times and circumstances in which they live. What can a woman do, in such a position? Who will believe her, if she accused a publicly loved man of such a crime?" She did not once betray that she even knew Felicia was there in the room with them, much less that she cared what Felicia thought or felt. "People do not wish to believe it of their heroes, and both Randolf and Thaddeus Carlyon were heroes, in their own ways. Society would have crucified her as a wicked woman if they did not believe her, as a venally indiscreet one if they did. She would know that, and she chose to preserve what she had. Miss Alexandra chose to save her child, or to try to. It remains to be seen whether or not she has sacrificed herself in vain."

Lovat-Smith opened his mouth to argue, attack her again, and then looked at the jury and decided better of it.

"You are a remarkable woman, Miss Buchan," he said with a minute bow. "It remains to be seen whether any further facts bear out your extraordinary vision of events, but

399

no doubt you believe you speak the truth. I have nothing further to ask you.''

Rathbone declined to reexamine. He knew better than to gild the lily.

The court rose for the luncheon adjournment in an uproar.

The first witness of the afternoon was Damaris Erskine. She too looked pale, with dark circles under her eyes as if she had wept herself into exhaustion but had found little sleep. All the time her eyes kept straying to Peverell. He was sitting very upright in his seat next to Felicia and Randolf in the front of the gallery, but as apart from them in spirit as if they were in different rooms. He ignored them totally and stared without movement at Damaris, his eyes puckered in concern, his lips undecided on a smile, as if he feared it might be taken for levity rather than encouragement.

Monk sat two rows behind Hester, in the body of the court behind the lawyers. He did not wish to sit beside her. His emotions were too raw from his confrontation with Hermione. He wanted a long time alone, but circumstances made that impossible; however, there was a certain aloneness in the crowd of a courtroom, and in centering his mind and all his feelings he could on the tragedy being played out in front of him.

Rathbone began very gently, with the softly cautious voice Monk knew he adopted when he was about to deliver a mortal blow and loathed doing it, but had weighed all the facts, and the decision was irrevocable.

"Mrs. Erskine, you were present at the home of Mr. and Mrs. Furnival on the night your brother was killed, and you have already told us of the order of events as you recall them.''

"Yes,'' she said almost inaudibly.

"But I think you have omitted what most undoubtedly was for you the most devastating part of the evening, that is until Dr. Hargrave said that your brother had not died by accident, but been murdered.''

Lovat-Smith leaned forward, frowning, but he did not interrupt.

400

"Several people have testified," Rathbone went on, "that when you came down the stairs from seeing young Valentine Furnival, you were in a state of distress bordering on hysteria. Would you please tell us what happened up there to cause this change in you?"

Damaris studiously avoided looking towards Felicia and Randolf, nor did she look at Alexandra, sitting pale-faced and rigid in the dock. She took one or two moments to steel herself, and Rathbone waited without prompting her.

"I recognized—Valentine . . ." she said at last, her voice husky.

"Recognized him?" Rathbone repeated the word. "What a curious expression, Mrs. Erskine. Was there ever any doubt in your mind as to who he was? I accept that you did not see him often, indeed had not seen him for some years while he was away at boarding school, since you infrequently visited the house. But surely there was only one boy present?"

She swallowed convulsively and shot him a look of pleading so profound there was a murmur of anger around the room and Felicia jerked forward, then sat up again as Randolf's hand closed over her arm.

Almost imperceptibly Peverell nodded.

Damaris raised her chin.

"He is not the Furnivals' natural child: he is adopted. Before my marriage fourteen years ago, I had a child. Now that he is—is of nearly adult height—a young man, not a boy, he . . ." For a moment more she had to fight to keep control.

Opposite her in the gallery, Charles Hargrave leaned forward a little, his face tense, sandy brows drawn down. Beside him, Sarah Hargrave looked puzzled and a flicker of anxiety touched her face.

"He resembles his father," Damaris said huskily. "So much, I knew he was my son. You see, at the time the only person I could trust to help me was my brother, Thaddeus. He took me away from London, and he saw to the child's being adopted. Suddenly, when I saw Valentine, it all made sense. I knew what Thaddeus had done with my child."

"Were you angry with your brother, Mrs. Erskine? Did

401

you resent it that he had given your son to the Furnivals to raise?''

"No! No—not at all. They had . . ." She shook her head, the tears running down her cheeks, and her voice cracking at last.

The judge leaned forward earnestly, his face full of concern.

Lovat-Smith rose, all the brilliant confidence drained away from him, only horror left.

"I hope my learned friend is not going to try to cloud the issue and cause this poor woman quite pointless distress?" He turned from Rathbone to Damaris. "The physical facts of the case place it beyond question that only Alexandra Carlyon had the opportunity to murder the general. Whatever Mrs. Erskine's motive, if indeed there were any, she did not commit the act." He turned around so that half his appeal was to the crowd. "Surely this exposure of a private grief is cruelly unnecessary?"

"I would not do it if it were," Rathbone said between his teeth, his eyes blazing. He swiveled around on his heel, presenting his back to Lovat-Smith. "Mrs. Erskine, you have just said you did not resent your brother's having given your son to the Furnivals. And yet when you came downstairs you were in a state of distress almost beyond your ability to control, and quite suddenly you exhibited a rage towards Maxim Furnival which was close to murderous in nature! You seem to be contradicting yourself!"

"I—I—saw . . ." Damaris closed her eyes so tightly it screwed up her face.

Peverell half rose in his seat.

Edith held both her hands to her face, knuckles clenched.

Alexandra was frozen.

Monk glanced up at the gallery and saw Maxim Furnival sitting rigid, his dark face puckered in puzzlement and ever-increasing apprehension. Beside him, Louisa was quite plainly furious.

Monk looked along at Hester, and saw the intense concentration in her as she turned sideways, her eyes fixed on

Damaris and her expression one of such wrenching pity that it jolted him at once with its familiarity and its strangeness. He tried to picture Hermione, and found the memory blurred. He found it hard to remember her eyes at all, and when he did, they were bland and bright, without capability of pain.

Rathbone moved a step closer to Damaris.

"I regret this profoundly, Mrs. Erskine, but too much depends upon it for me to allow any compassion for you to override my duty to Mrs. Carlyon—and to Cassian."

Damaris raised her head. "I understand. I knew that my brother Thaddeus was abused as a child. Like Buckie—Miss Buchan—I saw it once, by accident. I never forgot the look in his eyes, the way he behaved. I saw the same look in Valentine's face, and I knew he was abused too. I supposed at that time that it was his father—his adopted father—Maxim Furnival, who was doing it."

There was a gasp around the room and a rustle like leaves in the wind.

"Oh God! No!" Maxim shot to his feet, his face shock-white, his voice half strangled in his throat.

Louisa sat like stone.

Maxim swung around, staring at her, but she continued to look as if she had been transfixed.

"You have my utmost sympathy, Mr. Furnival," the judge said over the rising level of horror and anger from the crowd. "But you must refrain from interruption, nevertheless. But I would suggest to you that you consider obtaining legal counsel to deal with whatever may occur here. Now please sit down, or I shall be obliged to have the bailiff remove you."

Slowly, looking bemused and beaten, Maxim sat down again, turning helplessly to Louisa, who still sat immobile, as though too horrified to respond.

Up in the gallery Charles Hargrave grasped the rail as if he would break it with his hands.

Rathbone returned his attention to Damaris.

"You spoke in the past tense, Mrs. Erskine. You thought at the time it was Maxim Furnival. Has something happened to change your view?"

"Yes." A faint echo of the old flair returned, and the ghost of a smile touched her mouth and vanished. "My sister-in-law murdered my brother. And I believe it was because she discovered that he was abusing her son—and I believe mine also—although I have no reason to think she knew of that."

Lovat-Smith looked up at Alexandra, then rose to his feet as though reluctantly.

"That is a conclusion of the witness, my lord, and not a fact."

"That is true, Mr. Rathbone," the judge said gravely. "The jury will ignore that last statement of Mrs. Erskine's. It was her belief, and no more. She may conceivably have been mistaken; you cannot assume it is fact. And Mr. Rathbone, you deliberately led your witness into making that observation. You know better."

"I apologize, my lord."

"Proceed, Mr. Rathbone, and keep it relevant."

Rathbone inclined his head in acknowledgment, then with curious grace turned back to Damaris.

"Mrs. Erskine, do you *know* who abused Valentine Furnival?"

"No."

"You did not ask him?"

"No! No, of course not!"

"Did you speak of it to your brother?"

"No! No I didn't. I didn't speak of it to anyone."

"Not to your mother—or your father?"

"No—not to anyone."

"Were you aware that your nephew, Cassian Carlyon, was being abused?"

She flushed with shame and her voice was low and tight in her throat. "No. I should have been, but I thought it was just his grief at losing his father—and fear that his mother was responsible and he would lose her too." She looked up once at Alexandra with anguish. "I didn't spend as much time with him as I should have. I am ashamed of that. He seemed to prefer to be alone with his grandfather, or with my husband. I thought—I thought that was because it was his mother who killed his father, and he felt women . . ." She trailed off unhappily.

"Understandable," Rathbone said quietly. "But if you had spent time with him, you might have seen whether he too was abused—"

"Objection," Lovat-Smith said quickly. "All this speech of abuse is only conjecture: We do not know that it is anything beyond the sick imaginings of a spinster servant and a young girl in puberty, who both may have misunderstood things they saw, and whose fevered and ignorant minds leaped to hideous conclusions—quite erroneously."

The judge sighed. "Mr. Lovat-Smith's objection is literally correct, Mr. Rathbone." His heavy tone made it more than obvious he did not share the prosecutor's view for an instant. "Please be more careful in your use of words. You are quite capable of conducting your examination of Mrs. Erskine without such error."

Rathbone inclined his head in acceptance, and turned back to Damaris.

"Did your husband, Peverell Erskine, spend much time with Cassian after he came to stay at Carlyon House?"

"Yes—yes, he did." Her face was very white and her voice little more than a whisper.

"Thank you, Mrs. Erskine. I have no more questions for you, but please remain there. Mr. Lovat-Smith may have something to ask you."

Damaris turned to Lovat-Smith.

"Thank you," Lovat-Smith acknowledged. "Did you murder your brother, Mrs. Erskine?"

There was a ripple of shock around the room. The judge frowned sharply. A juror coughed. Someone in the gallery stood up.

Damaris was startled. "No—of course I didn't!"

"Did your sister-in-law mention this alleged fearful abuse to you, at any time, either before or after the death of your brother?"

"No."

"Have you any reason to suppose that such a thing had

ever entered her mind; other, of course, than the suggestion made to you by my learned friend, Mr. Rathbone?"

"Yes—Hester Latterly knew of it."

Lovat-Smith was taken by surprise.

There was a rustle and murmur of amazement around the court. Felicia Carlyon leaned forward over the gallery railing to stare down at where Hester was sitting upright, white-faced. Even Alexandra turned.

"I beg your pardon?" Lovat-Smith said, collecting his wits rapidly. "And who is Hester Latterly? Is that a name that has arisen once before in this case? Is she a relative—or a servant perhaps? Oh—I recall: she is the person to whom Mrs. Sobell enquired for a lawyer for the accused. Pray tell us, how did this Miss Latterly know of this deadly secret of your family, of which not even your mother was aware?"

Damaris stared straight back at him.

"I don't know. I did not ask her."

"But you accepted it as true?" Lovat-Smith was incredulous and he allowed his whole body to express his disbelief. "Is she an expert in the field, that you take her word, unsubstantiated by any fact at *all*, simply a blind statement, over your own knowledge and love and loyalty to your own family? That is truly remarkable, Mrs. Erskine."

There was a low rumble of anger from the court. Someone called out "Traitor!"

"Silence!" the judge ordered, his face hard. He leaned forward towards the witness stand. "Mrs. Erskine? It does call for some explanation. Who is this Miss Latterly that you take her unexplained word for such an abominable charge?"

Damaris was very pale and she looked across at Peverell before answering, and when she spoke it was to the jury, not to Lovat-Smith or the judge.

"Miss Latterly is a good friend who wishes to find the truth of this case, and she came to me with the knowledge, which has never been disputed, that I discovered something the evening of my brother's death which distressed me almost beyond bearing. She assumed it was something else, something which would have done a great injury to another person—so I was obliged, in justice, to tell her the truth. Since she was correct in her assumption of abuse to Cassian, I did not argue with her, nor did I ask her how she knew. I was too concerned to allay her other suspicion even to think of it."

She straightened up a little more, for the first time perhaps, unconsciously looking heroic. "And as for loyalty to my family, are you suggesting I should lie, here, in this place, and under oath to God, in order to protect them from the law—and the consequence of their acts towards a desperately vulnerable child? And that I should conceal truths which may help you bring justice to Alexandra?" There was a ring of challenge in her voice and her eyes were bright. Not once had she looked towards the gallery.

There was nothing for Lovat-Smith to do but retreat, and he did it gracefully.

"Of course not, Mrs. Erskine. All we required was that you should explain, and you have done so. Thank you—I have no more questions to ask you."

Rathbone half rose. "Nor I, my lord."

The judge released her. "You are excused, Mrs. Erskine."

The entire courtroom watched as she stepped down from the witness box, walked across the tiny space to the body of the court and up the steps through the seated crowd and took her place beside Peverell, who quite automatically rose to his feet to greet her.

There was a long sigh right around the room as she sat down.

Felicia deliberately ignored her. Randolf seemed beyond reaction. Edith reached a hand across and clasped hers gently.

The judge looked at the clock.

"Have you many questions for your next witness, Mr. Rathbone?"

"Yes, my lord; it is evidence on which a great deal may turn."

"Then we shall adjourn until tomorrow."

Monk left the court, pushing his way through the jostling, excited crowds, journalists racing to find the first hansoms

407

to take them to their papers, those who had been unable to find room inside shouting questions, people standing around in huddles, everyone talking.

Then outside on the steps he was uncertain whether to search for Hester or to avoid her. He had nothing to say, and yet he would have found her company pleasing. Or perhaps he would not. She would be full of the trial, of Rathbone's brilliance. Of course that was right, he was brilliant. It was even conceivable he would win the case, whatever winning might be. She had become increasingly fond of Rathbone lately. He realized it now with some surprise. He had not even thought about it before; it was something he had seen without its touching the conscious part of his mind.

Now he was startled and angry that it hurt.

He walked down the steps into the street with a sudden burst of energy. Everywhere there were people, newsboys, costermongers, flower sellers, men with barrows of sandwiches, pies, sweets, peppermint water, and a dozen other kinds of food. People pushed and shouted, calling for cabs.

This was absurd. He liked both Hester and Rathbone—he should be happy for them.

Without realizing what he was doing he bumped into a smart man in black with an ivory-topped cane, and stepped into a hansom ahead of him. He did not even hear the man's bellow of fury.

"Grafton Street," he commanded.

Then why was there such a heaviness inside him, a sense of loss all over again?

It must be Hermione. The disillusion over her would surely hurt for a long time; that was only natural. He had thought he had found love, gentleness, sweetness— Damn! Don't be idiotic! He did not want sweetness. It stuck in his teeth and cloyed his tongue. God in heaven! How far he must have forgotten his own nature to have imagined Hermione was his happiness. And now he was further betraying himself by becoming maudlin over it.

But by the time the cab set him down in Grafton Street some better, more honest self admitted there was a place for tenderness, the love that overlooks error, that cherishes weakness and protects it, that thinks of self last, and gives even when the thanks are slow in coming or do not come at all, for generosity of spirit, laughter without cruelty or victory. And he still had little idea where to find it—even in himself.

The first witness of the next day was Valentine Furnival. For all his height, and already broadening shoulders, he looked very young and his high head could not hide his fear.

The crowd buzzed with excitement as he climbed the steps of the witness stand and turned to face the court. Hester felt a lurch almost like sickness as she saw his face and recognized in it exactly what Damaris must have seen—an echo of Charles Hargrave.

Instinctively she turned her head to see if Hargrave was in the gallery again, and if he had seen the same thing, knowing now that Damaris was the boy's mother. As soon as she saw him, his skin white, his eyes shocked, almost unfocused, she knew beyond question that he understood. Beside him, Sarah Hargrave sat a little apart, facing first Valentine on the stand, then her husband next to her. She did not even try to seek Damaris Erskine.

In spite of herself, Hester was moved to pity; for Sarah it was easy, but for Hargrave it twisted and hurt, because it was touched with anger.

The judge began by questioning Valentine for a few moments about his understanding of the oath, then turned to Rathbone and told him to commence.

"Did you know General Thaddeus Carlyon, Valentine?" he asked quite conversationally, as if they had been alone in some withdrawing room, not in the polished wood of a courtroom with hundreds of people listening, craning to catch every word and every inflexion.

Valentine swallowed on a dry throat.

"Yes."

"Did you know him well?"

A slight hesitation. "Yes."

"For a long time? Do you know how long?"

"Yes, since I was about six: seven years or more."

"So you must have known him when he sustained the knife injury to his thigh? Which happened in your home."

Not one person in the entire court moved or spoke. The silence was total.

"Yes."

Rathbone took a step closer to him.

"How did it happen, Valentine? Or perhaps I should say, why?"

Valentine stared at him, mute, his face so pale it occurred to Monk, watching him, that he might faint.

In the gallery Damaris leaned over the rail, her eyes desperate. Peverell put his hand over hers.

"If you tell the truth," Rathbone said gently, "there is no need to be afraid. The court will protect you."

The judge drew a breath, as if about to protest, then apparently changed his mind.

Lovat-Smith said nothing.

The jury were motionless to a man.

"I stabbed him," Valentine said almost in a whisper.

In the second row from the front Maxim Furnival covered his face with his hands. Beside him Louisa bit her nails. Alexandra put her hands over her mouth as if to stifle a cry.

"You must have had a very profound reason for such an act," Rathbone prompted. "It was a deep wound. He could have bled to death, if it had severed an artery."

"I—" Valentine gasped.

Rathbone had miscalculated. He had frightened him too much. He saw it immediately.

"But of course you did not," he said quickly. "It was merely embarrassing—and I'm sure painful."

Valentine looked wretched.

"Why did you do it, Valentine?" Rathbone said very gently. "You must have had a compelling reason—something that justified striking out in such a way."

Valentine was on the edge of tears and it took him some moments to regain his composure.

Monk ached for him, remembering his own youth, the

410

desperate dignity of thirteen, the manhood which was so close, and yet so far away.

"Mrs. Carlyon's life may depend upon what you say," Rathbone urged.

For once neither Lovat-Smith nor the judge reproved him for such a breach.

"I couldn't bear it any longer," Valentine replied in a husky voice, so low the jury had to strain to hear him. "I begged him, but he wouldn't stop!"

"So in desperation you defended yourself?" Rathbone asked. His clear, precise voice carried in the silence, even though it was as low as if they were alone in a small room.

"Yes."

"Stop doing what?"

Valentine said nothing. His face was suddenly painfully hot as the blood rushed up, suffusing his skin.

"If it hurts too much to say, may I say it for you?" Rathbone asked him. "Was the general sodomizing you?"

Valentine nodded very slightly, just a bare inch or two movement of the head.

Maxim Furnival let out a stifled cry.

The judge turned to Valentine.

"You must speak, so that there can be no error in our understanding," he said with great gentleness. "Simply yes or no will do. Is Mr. Rathbone correct?"

"Yes sir." It was a whisper.

"I see. Thank you. I assure you, there will be no action taken against you for the injury to General Carlyon. It was self-defense and no crime in any sense. A person is allowed to defend their lives, or their virtue, with no fault attached whatever. You have the sympathy of all present here. We are outraged on your behalf."

"How old were you when this began?" Rathbone went on, after a brief glance at the judge, and a nod from him.

"Six—I think," Valentine answered. There was a long sigh around the room, and an electric shiver of rage. Damaris sobbed and Peverell held her. There was a swelling rumble of fury around the gallery and a juror groaned.

Rathbone was silent for a moment; it seemed he was too appalled to continue immediately.

"Six years old," Rathbone repeated, in case anyone had failed to hear. "And did it continue after you stabbed the general?"

"No—no, he stopped."

"And at that time his own son would be . . . how old?"

"Cassian?" Valentine swayed and caught hold of the railing. He was ashen.

"About six?" Rathbone asked, his voice hoarse.

Valentine nodded.

This time no one asked him to speak. Even the judge was white-faced.

Rathbone turned away and walked a pace or two, his hands in his pockets, before swinging around and looking up at Valentine again.

"Tell me, Valentine, why did you not appeal to your parents over this appalling abuse? Why did you not tell your mother? Surely that is the most natural thing for a small child to do when he is hurt and frightened? Why did you not do that in the beginning, instead of suffering all those years?"

Valentine looked down, his eyes full of misery.

"Could your mother not have helped you?" Rathbone persisted. "After all, the general was not your father. It would have cost them his friendship, but what was that worth, compared with you, her son? She could have forbidden him the house. Surely your father would have horsewhipped a man for such a thing?"

Valentine looked up at the judge, his eyes brimming with tears.

"You must answer," the judge said gravely. "Did your father abuse you also?"

"No!" There was no mistaking the amazement and the honesty in his voice and his startled face. "No! Never!"

The judge took a deep breath and leaned back a little, the shadow of a smile over his mouth.

"Then why did you not tell him, appeal to him to protect

you? Or to your mother. Surely she would have protected you."

The tears brimmed over and ran down Valentine's cheeks unchecked.

"She knew." He choked and struggled for breath. "She told me not to tell anyone, especially Papa. She said it would . . . embarrass him—and cost him his position."

There was a roar of rage around the room and a cry of "Hang her!"

The judge called for order, banging his gavel, and it was several minutes before he could continue. "His position?" He frowned at Rathbone, uncomprehending. "What position?"

"He earns a great deal of money from army contracts," Valentine explained.

"Supplied by General Carlyon?"

"Yes sir."

"That is what your mother said? Be very sure you speak accurately, Valentine."

"Yes—she told me."

"And you are quite sure that your mother knew exactly what the general was doing to you? You did not fail to tell her the truth?"

"No! I did tell her!" He gulped, but his tears were beyond his control anymore.

The anger in the room was now so ugly it was palpable in the air.

Maxim Furnival sat upright, his face like a dead man's. Beside him, Louisa was motionless, her eyes stone-hard and hot, her mouth a thin line of hate.

"Bailiff," the judge said in a low voice. "You will take Louisa Furnival in charge. Appropriate dispositions will be made to care for Valentine in the future. For the moment perhaps it would be best he remain to comfort his father."

Obediently a large bailiff appeared, buttons gleaming, and forced his way through the rows to where Louisa still sat, face blazing white. With no ceremony, no graciousness at all, he half pulled her to her feet and took her, stumbling and catching her skirts, back along the row and up the passageway out of the court.

Maxim started to his feet, then realized the futility of doing anything at all. It was an empty gesture anyway. His whole body registered his horror of her and the destruction of everything he had thought he possessed. His only concern was for Valentine.

The judge sighed. "Mr. Rathbone, have you anything further you feel it imperative you ask this witness?"

"No, my lord."

"Mr. Lovat-Smith?"

"No, my lord."

"Thank you. Valentine, the court thanks you for your honesty and your courage, and regrets having to subject you to this ordeal. You are free to go back to your father, and be of whatever comfort to each other you may."

Silently Valentine stepped down amid rustles and murmurs of compassion, and made his way to the stricken figure of Maxim.

"Mr. Rathbone, have you further witnesses to call?" the judge asked.

"Yes, my lord. I can call the bootboy at the Furnival house, who was at one point a drummer in the Indian army. He will explain why he dropped his linen and fled when coming face-to-face with General Carlyon in the Furnival house on the evening of the murder . . . if you believe it is necessary? But I would prefer not to—I imagine the court will understand."

"We do, Mr. Rathbone," the judge assured him. "Do not call him. We may safely draw the conclusion that he was startled and distressed. Is that sufficient for your purpose?"

"Yes, thank you, my lord."

"Mr. Lovat-Smith, have you objection to that? Do you wish the boy called so that you may draw from him a precise explanation, other than that which will naturally occur to the jury?"

"No, my lord," Lovat-Smith said immediately. "If the defense will stipulate that the boy in question can be proved to have served with General Thaddeus Carlyon?"

"Mr. Rathbone?"

"Yes, my lord. The boy's military record has been traced, and he did serve in the same immediate unit with General Carlyon."

"Then you have no need to call him, and subject him to what must be acutely painful. Proceed with your next witness."

"I crave the court's permission to call Cassian Carlyon. He is eight years old, my lord, and I believe he is of considerable intelligence and aware of the difference between truth and falsehood."

Alexandra shot to her feet. "No," she cried out. "No—you can't!"

The judge looked at her with grim pity.

"Sit down, Mrs. Carlyon. As the accused you are entitled to be present, as long as you conduct yourself appropriately. But if you interrupt the proceedings I will have to order your removal. I should regret that; please do not make it necessary."

Gradually she sank back again, her body shaking. On either side of her two gray-dressed wardresses took her arms, but to assist, not to restrain.

"Call him, Mr. Rathbone. I will decide whether he is competent to testify, and the jury will put upon his testimony what value they deem appropriate."

An official of the court escorted Cassian as far as the edge of the room, but he crossed the small open space alone. He was about four feet tall, very frail and thin, his fair hair neatly brushed, his face white. He climbed up to the witness box and peered over the railing at Rathbone, then at the judge.

There was a low mutter and sigh of breath around the court. Several of the jurors turned to look where Alexandra sat in the dock, as if transfixed.

"What is your name?" the judge asked Cassian quietly.

"Cassian James Thaddeus Randolf Carlyon, sir."

"Do you know why we are here, Cassian?"

"Yes sir, to hang my mother."

Alexandra bit her knuckles and the tears ran down her cheeks.

A juror gasped.

In the crowd a woman sobbed aloud.

The judge caught his breath and paled.

"No, Cassian, we are not! We are here to discover what happened the night your father died, and why it happened—and then to do what the law requires of us to deal justly with it."

"Are you?" Cassian looked surprised. "Grandma said you were going to hang my mother, because she is wicked. My father was a very good man, and she killed him."

The judge's face tightened. "Well just for now you must forget what your grandmother says, or anyone else, and tell us only what you know for yourself to be true. Do you understand the difference between truth and lies, Cassian?"

"Yes of course I do. Lying is saying what is not true, and it is a dishonorable thing to do. Gentlemen don't lie, and officers never do."

"Even to protect someone they love?"

"No sir. It is an officer's duty to tell the truth, or remain silent, if it is the enemy who asks."

"Who told you that?"

"My father, sir."

"He was perfectly correct. Now when you have taken the oath and promised to God that you will tell us the truth, I wish you either to speak exactly what you know to be true, or to remain silent. Will you do that?"

"Yes sir."

"Very well, Mr. Rathbone, you may swear your witness."

It was duly done, and Rathbone began his questions, standing close to the witness box and looking up.

"Cassian, you were very close to your father, were you not?"

"Yes sir," he answered with complete composure.

"Is it true that about two years ago he began to show his love for you in a new and different way, a very private way?"

416

Cassian blinked. He looked only at Rathbone. Never once had he looked up, either at his mother in the dock opposite, or at his grandparents in the gallery above.

"It cannot hurt him now for you to tell the truth," Rathbone said quite casually, as if it were of no particular importance. "And it is most urgent for your mother that you should be honest with us."

"Yes sir."

"Did he show his love for you in a new and very physical way, about two years ago?"

"Yes sir."

"A very private way?"

A hesitation. "Yes sir."

A sound of weeping came from the gallery. A man blasphemed with passionate anger.

"Did it hurt?" Rathbone asked very gravely.

"Only at first."

"I see. Did your mother know about this?"

"No sir."

"Why not?"

"Papa told me it was something women didn't understand, and I should never tell her." He took a deep breath and suddenly his composure dissolved.

"Why not?"

He sniffed. "He said she would stop loving me if she knew. But Buckie said she still loved me."

"Oh, Buckie is quite right," Rathbone said quickly, his own voice husky. "No woman could love her child more; I know that myself."

"Do you?" Cassian kept his eyes fixed on Rathbone, as if to prevent himself from knowing his mother was there, in case he looked at her and saw what he dreaded.

"Oh yes. I know your mother quite well. She has told me she would rather die than have you hurt. Look at her, and you will know it yourself."

Lovat-Smith started up from his seat, then changed his mind and subsided into it again.

417

Very slowly Cassian turned for the first time and looked at Alexandra.

A ghost of a smile forced itself across her features, but the pain in her face was fearful.

Cassian looked back at Rathbone.

"Yes sir."

"Did your father go on doing this—this new thing, right up until just before he died?"

"Yes sir."

"Did anyone else, any other man, ever do this to you?"

There was total silence except for a low sigh from somewhere at the back of the gallery.

"We know from other people that this is so, Cassian," Rathbone said. "You have been very brave and very honest so far. Please do not lie to us now. Did anyone else do this to you?"

"Yes sir."

"Who else, Cassian?"

He glanced at the judge, then back at Rathbone.

"I can't say, sir. I was sworn to secrecy, and a gentleman doesn't betray."

"Indeed," Rathbone said with a note of temporary defeat in his voice. "Very well. We shall leave the subject for now. Thank you. Mr. Lovat-Smith?"

Lovat-Smith rose and took Rathbone's place in front of the witness stand. He spoke to Cassian candidly, quietly, man to man.

"You kept this secret from your mother, you said?"

"Yes sir."

"You never told her, not even a little bit?"

"No sir."

"Do you think she knew about it anyway?"

"No sir, I never told her. I promised not to!" He watched Lovat-Smith as he had watched Rathbone.

"I see. Was that difficult to do, keep this secret from her?"

"Yes sir—but I did."

"And she never said anything to you about it, you are quite sure?"

418

"No sir, never."

"Thank you. Now about this other man. Was it one, or more than one? I am not asking you to give me names, just a number. That would not betray anyone."

Hester glanced up at Peverell in the gallery, and saw guilt in his face, and a fearful pity. But was the guilt for complicity, or merely for not having known? She felt sick in case it were complicity.

Cassian thought for a moment or two before replying.

"Two, sir."

"Two others?"

"Yes sir."

"Thank you. That is all. Rathbone?"

"No more, thank you, for now. But I reserve the right to recall him, if it will help discover who these other men are."

"I will permit that," the judge said quickly. "Thank you, Cassian. For the moment you may go."

Carefully, his legs shaking, Cassian climbed down the steps, only stumbling a little once, and then walked across the floor and disappeared out of the door with the bailiff. There was a movement around the court, murmurs of outrage and compassion. Someone called out to him. The judge started forward, but it was already done, and the words had been of encouragement. It was pointless to call order or have the offender searched for.

"I call Felicia Carlyon," Rathbone said loudly.

Lovat-Smith made no objection, even though she had not been in Rathbone's original list of witnesses and hence had been in the court all through the other testimony.

There was a rustle of response and anticipation. But the mood of the crowd had changed entirely. It was no longer pity which moved them towards her, but pending judgment.

She took the stand head high, body stiff, eyes angry and proud. The judge required that she unveil her face, and she did so with disdainful obedience. She swore the oath in a clear, ringing voice.

"Mrs. Carlyon," Rathbone began, standing in front of

her, "you appear here on subpoena. You are aware of the testimony that has been given so far."

"I am. It is wicked and malicious lies. Miss Buchan is an old woman who has served in my family's house for forty years, and has become deranged in her old age. I cannot think where a spinster woman gets such vile fancies." She made a gesture of disgust. "All I can suppose is that her natural instincts for womanhood have been warped and she has turned on men, who rejected her, and this is the outcome."

"And Valentine Furnival?" Rathbone asked. "He is hardly an elderly and rejected spinster. Nor a servant, old and dependent, who dare not speak ill of an employer."

"A boy with a boy's carnal fantasies," she replied. "We all know that growing children have feverish imaginations. Presumably someone did use him as he says, for which I have the natural pity anyone would. But it is wicked and irresponsible of him to say it was my son. I daresay it was his own father, and he wishes to protect him, and so charges another man, a dead man, who cannot defend himself."

"And Cassian?" Rathbone enquired with a dangerous edge to his voice.

"Cassian," she said, full of contempt. "A harassed and frightened eight-year-old. Good God, man! The father he adored has been murdered, his mother is like to be hanged for it—you put him on the stand in court, and you expect him to be able to tell you the truth about his father's love for him. Are you half-witted, man? He will say anything you force out of him. I would not condemn a cat on that."

"Presumably your husband is equally innocent?" Rathbone said with sarcasm.

"It is unnecessary even to say such a thing!"

"But you do say it?"

"I do."

"Mrs. Carlyon, why do you suppose Valentine Furnival stabbed your son in the upper thigh?"

"God alone knows. The boy is deranged. If his father has abused him for years, he might well be so."

"Possibly," Rathbone agreed. "It would change many

people. Why was your son in the boy's bedroom without his trousers on?''

"I beg your pardon?" Her face froze.

"Do you wish me to repeat the question?"

"No. It is preposterous. If Valentine says so, then he is lying. Why is not my concern."

"But Mrs. Carlyon, the wound the general sustained in his upper inside leg bled copiously. It was a deep wound, and yet his trousers were neither torn nor marked with blood. They cannot have been on him at the time."

She stared at him, her expression icy, her lips closed.

There was a murmur through the crowd, a movement, a whisper of anger suddenly suppressed, and then silence again.

Still she did not speak.

"Let us turn to the question of your husband, Colonel Randolf Carlyon," Rathbone continued. "He was a fine soldier, was he not? A man to be proud of. And he had great ambitions for his son: he also should be a hero, if possible of even higher rank—a general, in fact. And he achieved that."

"He did." She lifted her chin and stared down at him with wide, dark blue eyes. "He was loved and admired by all who knew him. He would have achieved even greater things had he not been murdered in his prime. Murdered by a jealous woman."

"Jealous of whom, her own son?"

"Don't be absurd—and vulgar," she spat.

"Yes it is vulgar, isn't it," he agreed. "But true. Your daughter Damaris knew it. She accidentally found them one day . . ."

"Nonsense!"

"And recognized it again in her own son, Valentine. Is she lying also? And Miss Buchan? And Cassian? Or are they all suffering from the same frenzied and perverted delusion—each without knowing the other, and in their own private hell?"

She hesitated. It was manifestly ridiculous.

"And you did not know, Mrs. Carlyon? Your husband abused your son for all those years, presumably until you

421

sent him as a boy cadet into the army. Was that why you sent him so young, to escape your husband's appetite?''

The atmosphere in the court was electric. The jury had expressions like a row of hangmen. Charles Hargrave looked ill. Sarah Hargrave sat next to him in body, but her heart was obviously elsewhere. Edith and Damaris sat side by side with Peverell.

Felicia's face was hard, her eyes glittering.

''Boys do go into the army young, Mr. Rathbone. Perhaps you do not know that?''

''What did your husband do then, Mrs. Carlyon? Weren't you afraid he would do what your son did, abuse the child of some friend?''

She stared at him in frozen silence.

''Or did you procure some other child for him, some boot-boy, perhaps,'' he went on ruthlessly, ''who would be unable to retaliate—safe. Safe from scandal—and—'' He stopped, staring at her. She had gone so white as to appear on the edge of collapse. She gripped the railing in front of her and her body swayed. There was a long hiss from the crowd, an ugly sound, full of hate.

Lovat-Smith rose to his feet.

Randolf Carlyon let out a cry which strangled in his throat, and his face went purple. He gasped for breath and people on either side of him moved away, horrified and without compassion. A bailiff moved forward to him and loosened his tie roughly.

Rathbone would not let the moment go by.

''That is what you did, isn't it, Mrs. Carlyon?'' he pressed. ''You procured another child for your husband. Perhaps a succession of children—until you judged him too old to be a danger anymore. But you didn't protect your own grandson. You allowed him to be used as well. Why, Mrs. Carlyon? Why? Was your reputation really worth all that sacrifice, so many children's terrified, shamed and pitiful lives?''

She leaned forward over the rail, hate blazing in her eyes.

''Yes! Yes, Mr. Rathbone, it was! What would you expect me to do? Betray him to public humiliation? Ruin a great career: a man who taught others bravery in the face of the enemy, who went to battle with head high, never counting the odds against him. A man who inspired others to greatness—for what? An appetite? Men have appetites, they always have had. What was I to do—tell people?" Her voice was thick with passionate contempt. She utterly ignored the snarls and hisses behind her.

"Tell whom? Who would have believed me? Who could I go to? A woman has no rights to her children, Mr. Rathbone. And no money. We belong to our husbands. We cannot even leave their houses without their permission, and he would never have given me that. Still less would he have allowed me to take my son."

The judge banged his gavel and called for order.

Felicia's voice was shrill with rage and bitterness. "Or would you have had me murder him—like Alexandra? Is that what you approve of? Every woman who suffers a betrayal or an indignity at her husband's hands, or whose child is hurt, belittled or humiliated by his father, should murder him?"

She leaned over the rail towards him, her voice strident, her face twisted. "Believe me, there are a lot of other cruelties. My husband was gentle with his son, spent time with him, never beat him or sent him to bed without food. He gave him a fine education and started him on a great career. He had the love and respect of the world. Would you have me forfeit all that by making a wild, vile accusation no one would have believed anyway? Or end up in the dock—and on the rope's end—like her?"

"Was there nothing in between, Mrs. Carlyon?" Rathbone said very softly. "No more moderate course—nothing between condoning the abuse and murder?"

She stood silent, gray-faced and suddenly very old.

"Thank you," he said with a bleak smile, a baring of the teeth. "That was my own conclusion too. Mr. Lovat-Smith?"

There was a sigh around the room, a long expelling of breath. The jury looked exhausted.

Lovat-Smith stood up slowly, as if he were now too tired to have any purpose in continuing. He walked over to the

423

witness box, regarding Felicia long and carefully, then lowered his eyes.

"I have nothing to ask this witness, my lord."

"You are excused, Mrs. Carlyon," the judge said coldly. He opened his mouth as if to add something, then changed his mind.

Felicia came down the steps clumsily, like an old woman, and walked away towards the doors, followed by a silent and total condemnation.

The judge looked at Rathbone.

"Have you any further evidence to call, Mr. Rathbone?"

"I would like to recall Cassian Carlyon, my lord, if you please?"

"Is it necessary, Mr. Rathbone? You have proved your point."

"Not all of it, my lord. This child was abused by his father, and his grandfather, and by one other. I believe we must know who that other man was as well."

"If you can discover that, Mr. Rathbone, please do so. But I shall prevent you the moment you cause the child unnecessary distress. Do I make myself plain?"

"Yes, my lord, quite plain."

Cassian was recalled, small and pale, but again entirely composed.

Rathbone stepped forward.

"Cassian—your grandmother has just given evidence which makes it quite clear that your grandfather also abused you in the same manner. We do not need to ask you to testify on that point. However there was one other man, and we need to know who he is."

"No sir, I cannot tell you."

"I understand your reasons." Rathbone fished in his pocket and brought out an elegant quill knife with a black-enameled handle. He held it up. "Do you have a quill knife, something like this?"

Cassian stared at it, a pink flush staining his cheeks.

Hester glanced up at the gallery and saw Peverell look puzzled, but no more.

"Remember the importance of the truth," Rathbone warned. "Do you have such a knife?"

"Yes sir," Cassian answered uncertainly.

"And perhaps a watch fob? A gold one, with the scales of justice on it?"

Cassian swallowed. "Yes sir."

Rathbone pulled out a silk handkerchief from his pocket also. "And a silk handkerchief too?"

Cassian was very pale. "Yes sir."

"Where did you get them, Cassian?"

"I . . ." He shut his eyes, blinking hard.

"May I help you? Did your uncle Peverell Erskine give them to you?"

Peverell rose to his feet, and Damaris pulled him back so violently he lost his balance.

Cassian said nothing.

"He did—didn't he?" Rathbone insisted. "And did he make you promise not to tell anyone?"

Still Cassian said nothing, but the tears brimmed over his eyes and rolled down his cheeks.

"Cassian—is he the other man who made love to you?"

There was a gasp from the gallery.

"No!" Cassian's voice was high and desperate, shrill with pain. "No! No, he isn't. I took those things! I stole them—because—because I wanted them."

In the dock Alexandra sobbed, and the wardress beside her held her shoulder with sudden, awkward gentleness.

"Because they are pretty?" Rathbone said with disbelief.

"No. No." Cassian's voice was still hard with anguish. "Because he was kind to me," Cassian cried. "He was the only one—who—who didn't do that to me. He was just—just my friend! I . . ." He sobbed helplessly. "He was my friend."

"Oh?" Rathbone affected disbelief still, although his own voice was harsh with pain. "Then if it was not Peverell Erskine, who was it? Tell me and I will believe you!"

"Dr. Hargrave!" Cassian sobbed, crumpling up and sliding down into the box in uncontrolled weeping at last. "Dr.

Hargrave! He did! He did it! I hate him! He did it! Don't let him go on! Don't let him! Uncle Pev, make them stop!''

There was a bellow of rage from the gallery. Two men seized Hargrave and held him before the bailiff could even move.

Rathbone strode over to the witness box and up the steps to help the child to his feet and put his arms around him. He half carried him out, and met Peverell Erskine down from the gallery and forcing his way past the bailiff and marching over the space in front of the lawyers' benches.

''Take him, and for God's sake look after him,'' Rathbone said passionately.

Peverell lifted the boy up and carried him out past the bailiffs and the crowd, Damaris at his heels. The door closed behind them to a great sigh from the crowd. Then immediately utter stillness fell again.

Rathbone turned to the judge.

''That is my case, my lord.''

The clock went unregarded. No one cared what time it was, morning, luncheon or afternoon. No one was moving from their seats.

''Of course people must not take the life of another human being,'' Rathbone said as he rose to make his last plea, ''no matter what the injury or the injustice. And yet what else was this poor woman to do? She has seen the pattern perpetuate itself in her father-in-law, her husband—and now her son. She could not endure it. The law, society—*we*—have given her no alternative but to allow it to continue—down the generations in never-ending humiliation and suffering—or to take the law into her own hands.'' He spoke not only to the jury, but to the judge as well, his voice thick with the certainty of his plea.

''She pleaded with her husband to stop. She begged him—and he disregarded her. Perhaps he could not help himself. Who knows? But you have seen how many people's lives have been ruined by this—this abomination: an appetite exercised with utter disregard for others.''

He stared in front of him, looking at their pale, intent faces.

''She did not do it lightly. She agonized—she has nightmares that border on the visions of hell. She will never cease

426

to pay within herself for her act. She fears the damnation of God for it, but she will suffer that to save her beloved child from the torment of his innocence now—and the shame and despair, the guilt and terror of an adulthood like his father's—destroying his own life, and that of his future children—down the generations till God knows when!

"Ask yourselves, gentlemen, what would you have her do? Take the easier course, like her mother-in-law? Is that what you admire? Let it go on, and on, and on? Protect herself, and live a comfortable life, because the man also had good qualities? God almighty . . ." He stopped, controlling himself with difficulty. "Let the next generation suffer as she does? Or find the courage and make the abominable sacrifice of herself, and end it now?

"I do not envy you your appalling task, gentlemen. It is a decision no man should be asked to make. But you are—and I cannot relieve you of it. Go and make it. Make it with prayer, with pity, and with honor!

"Thank you."

Lovat-Smith came forward and addressed the jury, quiet, stating the law. His voice was subdued, wrung with pity, but the law must be upheld, or there would be anarchy. People must not seek murder as a solution, no matter what the injury.

It was left only for the judge to sum up, which he did gravely, using few words, and dismissing them to deliberate.

The jury returned a little after five in the evening, haggard, spent of all emotion, white-faced.

Hester and Monk stood side by side at the back of the crowded courtroom. Almost without being aware of it, he reached out and held her hand, and felt her fingers curl around his.

"Have you reached a verdict upon which you are agreed?" the judge asked.

"We have," the foreman replied, his voice awed.

"And is it the verdict of you all?"

"It is, my lord."

"And what is your verdict?"

He stood absolutely upright, his chin high, his eyes direct. "We find the accused, Alexandra Carlyon, not guilty of murder, my lord—but guilty of manslaughter. And we ask, may it please you, my lord, that she serve the least sentence the law allows.''

The gallery erupted in cheers and cries of jubilation. Someone cheered for Rathbone, and a woman threw roses.

In the front row Edith and Damaris hugged each other, and then as one turned to Miss Buchan beside them and flung their arms around her. For a moment she was too startled to react, then her face curved into a smile and she held them equally close.

The judge raised his eyebrows very slightly. It was a perverse verdict. She had quite plainly committed murder, in the heat of the moment, but legally murder.

But a jury cannot be denied. It was the verdict of them all, and they each one faced forward and looked at him without blinking.

''Thank you,'' he said very quietly indeed. ''You are discharged of your duty.'' He turned to Alexandra.

''Alexandra Elizabeth Carlyon, a jury of your peers has found you not guilty of murder, but of manslaughter—and has appealed for mercy on your behalf. It is a perverse verdict, but one with which I have the utmost sympathy. I hereby sentence you to six months' imprisonment; and the forfeit of all your goods and properties, which the law requires. However, since the bulk of your husband's estate goes to your son, that is of little moment to you. May God have mercy on you, and may you one day find peace.''

Alexandra stood in the dock, her body thin, ravaged by emotion, and the tears at last spilled over and ran in sweet, hot release down her face.

Rathbone stood with his own eyes brimming over, unable to speak.

Lovat-Smith rose and shook him by the hand.

At the back of the courtroom Monk moved a little closer to Hester.

Now in bookstores . . .

A SUDDEN, FEARFUL DEATH

Another Inspector Monk Novel
by

Anne Perry

Here are the opening pages of
A SUDDEN,
FEARFUL DEATH. . . .

1

WHEN SHE FIRST came into the room, Monk thought it would simply be another case of domestic petty theft, or investigating the character prospects of some suitor. Not that he would have refused such a task; he could not afford to. Lady Callandra Daviot, his benefactress, would provide sufficient means to see that he kept his lodgings and ate at least two meals a day, but both honor and pride necessitated that he take every opportunity that offered itself to earn his own way.

This new client was well dressed, her bonnet neat and pretty. Her wide crinoline skirts accentuated her waist and slender shoulders, and made her look fragile and very young, although she was close to thirty. Of course the current fashion tended to do that for all women, but the illusion was powerful, and it still woke in most men a desire to protect and a certain rather satisfying feeling of gallantry.

"Mr. Monk?" she inquired tentatively. "Mr. William Monk?"

He was used to people's nervousness when first approaching him. It was not easy to engage an inquiry agent. Most matters about which one would wish such steps taken were of their very nature essentially private.

Monk rose to his feet and tried to compose his face into

an expression of friendliness without overfamiliarity. It was not easy for him; neither his features nor his personality lent itself to it.

"Yes ma'am. Please be seated." He indicated one of the two armchairs, a suggestion to the decor of his rooms made by Hester Latterly, his sometimes friend, sometimes antagonist, and frequent assistant, whether he wished it or not. However, this particular idea, he was obliged to admit, had been a good one.

Still gripping her shawl about her shoulders, the woman sat down on the very edge of the chair, her back ramrod straight, her fair face tense with anxiety. Her narrow, beautiful hazel eyes never left his.

"How may I help you?" He sat on the chair opposite her, leaning back and crossing his legs comfortably. He had been in the police force until a violent difference of opinion had precipitated his departure. Brilliant, acerbic and at times ruthless, Monk was not used to setting people at their ease or courting their custom. It was an art he was learning with great difficulty, and only necessity had made him attempt it at all.

She bit her lip and took a deep breath before plunging in.

"My name is Julia Penrose, or I should say more correctly, Mrs. Audley Penrose. I live with my husband and my younger sister just south of the Euston Road . . ." She stopped, as if his knowledge of the area might matter and she had to assure herself of it.

"A very pleasant neighborhood." He nodded. It meant she probably had a house of moderate size, a garden of some sort, and kept at least two or three servants. No doubt it was a domestic theft, or a suitor for the sister about whom she entertained doubts.

She looked down at her hands, small and strong in their neat gloves. For several seconds she struggled for words.

His patience broke.

"What is it that concerns you, Mrs. Penrose? Unless you tell me, I cannot help."

"Yes, yes I know that," she said very quietly. "It is not

easy for me, Mr. Monk. I realize I am wasting your time, and I apologize. . . .''

"Not at all," he said grudgingly.

She looked up, her face pale but a flash of humor in her eyes. She made a tremendous effort. "My sister has been . . . molested, Mr. Monk. I wish to know who was responsible."

So it was not a petty matter after all.

"I'm sorry," he said gently, and he meant it. He did not need to ask why she had not called the police. The thought of making such a thing public would crush most people beyond bearing. Society's judgment of a woman who had been sexually assaulted, to whatever degree, was anything from prurient curiosity to the conviction that in some way she must have warranted such a fate. Even the woman herself, regardless of the circumstances, frequently felt that in some unknown way she was to blame, and that such things did not happen to the inncoent. Perhaps it was people's way of coping with the horror it engendered, the fear that they might become similar victims. If it were in some way the woman's own fault, then it could be avoided by the just and the careful. The answer was simple.

"I wish you to find out who it was, Mr. Monk," she said again, looking at him earnestly.

"And if I do, Mrs. Penrose?" he asked. "Have you thought what you will do then? I assume from the fact that you have not called the police that you do not wish to prosecute?"

The fair skin of her face became even paler. "No, of course not," she said huskily. "You must be aware of what such a court case would be like. I think it might be even worse than the—the event, terrible as that must have been." She shook her head. "No—absolutely not! Have you any idea how people can be about. . . .''

"Yes," he said quickly. "And also the chances of a conviction are not very good, unless there is considerable injury. Was your sister injured, Mrs. Penrose?"

Her eyes dropped and a faint flush crept up her cheeks.

"No, no, she was not—not in any way that can now be proved." Her voice sank even lower. "If you understand me? I prefer not to . . . discuss—it would be indelicate . . ."

"I see." And indeed he did. He was not sure whether he believed the young woman in question had been assaulted, or if she had told her sister that she had in order to explain a lapse in her own standards of mortality. But already he felt a definite sympathy with the woman here in front of him. Whatever had happened, she now faced a budding tragedy.

She looked at him with hope and uncertainty. "Can you help us, Mr. Monk? 'Least—at least as long as my money lasts? I have saved a little from my dress allowance, and I can pay you up to twenty pounds in total." She did not wish to insult him, and embarrass herself, and she did not know how to avoid either.

He felt an uncharacteristic lurch of pity. It was not a feeling which came to him easily. He had seen so much suffering, almost all of it more violent and physical than Julia Penrose's, and he had long ago exhausted his emotions and built around himself a shell of anger which preserved his sanity. Anger drove him to action; it could be exorcised and leave him drained at the end of the day, and able to sleep.

"Yes, that will be quite sufficient," he said to her. "I should be able either to discover who it is or tell you that it is not possible. I assume you have asked your sister, and she has been unable to tell you?"

"Yes indeed," she responded. "And naturally she finds it difficult to recall the event—nature assists us in putting from our minds that which is too dreadful to bear."

"I know," he said with a harsh, biting humor she would never comprehend. It was barely a year ago, in the summer of 1856, just at the close of the war in the Crimea, that he had been involved in a coaching accident and woken in the narrow gray cot of a hospital, cold with terror that it might be the workhouse and knowing nothing of himself at all, not even his name. Certainly it was the crack to his head which had brought it on, but as fragments of memory had returned, snatches here and there, there was still a black horror which held most of it from him, a dread of learning the unbearable. Piece by piece he had rediscovered something of himself. Still, most of it was unknown, guessed at, not remembered. Much of it had hurt him. The man who emerged was not easy to like and he still felt a dark fear about things he might yet discover: acts of ruthlessness, ambition, brilliance without mercy. Yes, he knew all about the need to forget what the mind or the heart could not cope with.

She was staring at him, her face creased with puzzlement and growing concern.

He recalled himself hastily. "Yes of course, Mrs. Penrose. It is quite natural that your sister should have blanked from her memory an event so distressing. Did you tell her you intended coming to see me?"

"Oh yes," she said quickly. "It would be quite pointless to attempt to do it behind her back, so to speak. She was not pleased, but she appreciates that it is by far the best way." She leaned a little farther forward. "To be frank, Mr. Monk, I believe she was so relieved I did not call the police that she accepted it without the slightest demur."

It was not entirely flattering, but catering to his self-esteem was something he had not been able to afford for some time.

"Then she will not refuse to see me?" he said aloud.

"Oh no, although I would ask you to be as considerate as possible." She colored faintly, raising her eyes to look at him very directly. There was a curiously firm set to her slender jaw. It was a very feminine face, very slight-boned, but by no means weak. "You see, Mr. Monk, that is the great difference between you and the police. Forgive my discourtesy in saying so, but the police are public servants and the law lays down what they must do about the investigation. You, on the other hand, are paid by me, and I can request you to stop at any time I feel it the best moral decision, or the least likely to cause profound hurt. I hope you are not angry that I should mark that distinction?"

Far from it. Inwardly he was smiling. It was the first time he felt a spark of quite genuine respect for Julia Penrose.

"I take your point very nicely, ma'am," he answered,

rising to his feet. "I have a duty both moral and legal to report a crime if I have proof of one, but in the case of rape— I apologize for such an ugly word, but I assume it is rape we are speaking of?"

"Yes," she said almost inaudibly, her discomfort only too apparent.

"For that crime it is necessary for the victim to make a complaint and to testify, so the matter will rest entirely with your sister. Whatever facts I learn will be at her disposal."

"Excellent." She stood up also and the hoops of her huge skirt settled into place, making her once more look fragile. "I assume you will begin immediately?"

"This afternoon, if it will be convenient to see your sister then? You did not tell me her name."

"Marianne—Marianne Gillespie. Yes, this afternoon will be convenient."

"You said that you had saved from your dress allowance what seems to be a considerable sum. Did this happen some time ago?"

"Ten days," she replied quickly. "My allowance is paid quarterly. I had been circumspect, as it happens, and most of it was left from the last due date."

"Thank you, but you do not owe me an accounting, Mrs. Penrose. I merely needed to know how recent was the offense."

"Of course I do not. But I wish you to know that I am telling you the absolute truth, Mr. Monk. Otherwise I cannot expect you to help me. I trust you, and I require that you should trust me."

He smiled suddenly, a gesture which lit his face with charm because it was so rare, and so totally genuine. He found himself liking Julia Penrose more than he had anticipated from her rather prim and exceedingly predictable appearance—the huge hooped skirts so awkward to move in and so unfunctional, the neat bonnet which he loathed, the white gloves and demure manner. It had been a hasty judgment, a practice which he despised in others and even more in himself.

"Your address?" he said quickly.

"Number fourteen, Hastings Street," she replied.

"One more question. Since you are making these arrangements yourself, am I to assume that your husband is unaware of them?"

She bit her lip and the color in her cheeks heightened. "You are. I should be obliged if you would be as discreet as possible."

"How shall I account for my presence, if he should ask?"

"Oh." For a moment she was disconcerted. "Will it not be possible to call when he is out? He attends his business every weekday from nine in the morning until, at the earliest, half past four. He is an architect. Sometimes he is out considerably later."

"It will be, I expect, but I would prefer to have a story ready in case we are caught out. We must at least agree on our explanations."

She closed her eyes for a moment. "You make it sound so . . . deceitful, Mr. Monk. I have no wish to lie to Mr. Penrose. It is simply that the matter is so distressing, it would be so much pleasanter for Marianne if he did not know. She has to continue living in his house, you see?" She stared up at him suddenly with fierce intensity. "She has already suffered the attack. Her only chance of recovering her emotions, her peace of mind, and any happiness at all, will lie in putting it all behind her. How can she do that if every time she sits down at the table she knows that the man opposite her is fully aware of her shame? It would be intolerable for her!"

"But you know, Mrs. Penrose," he pointed out, although even as he said it he knew that was entirely different.

A smile flickered across her mouth. "I am a woman, Mr. Monk. Need I explain to you that that brings us closer in a way you cannot know. Marianne will not mind me. With Audley it would be quite different, for all his gentleness. He is a man, and nothing can alter that."

There was no possible comment to make on such a statement.

437

"What would you like to tell him to explain my presence?" he asked.

"I—I am not sure." She was momentarily confused, but she gathered her wits rapidly. She looked him up and down: his lean, smooth-boned face with its penetrating eyes and wide mouth, his elegant and expensively dressed figure. He still had the fine clothes he had bought when he was a senior inspector in the Metropolitan Police with no one to support but himself, before his last and most dreadful quarrel with Runcorn.

He waited with a dry amusement.

Evidently she approved what she saw. "You may say we have a mutual friend and you are calling to pay your respects to us," she replied decisively.

"And the friend?" He raised his eyebrows. "We should be agreed upon that."

"My cousin Albert Finnister. He is short and fat and lives in Halifax where he owns a woolen mill. My husband has never met him, nor is ever likely to. That you may not know Yorkshire is beside the point. You may have met him anywhere you choose, except London. Audley would wonder why he had not visited us."

"I have some knowledge of Yorkshire," Monk replied, hiding his smile. "Halifax will do. I shall see you this afternoon, Mrs. Penrose."

"Thank you. Good day, Mr. Monk." And with a slight inflection of her head she waited while he opened the door for her, then took her leave, walking straight-backed, head high, out into Fitzroy Street and north towards the square, and in a hundred yards or so, the Euston Road.

Monk closed the door and went back to his office room. He had lately moved here from his old lodgings around the corner in Grafton Street. He had resented Hester's interference in suggesting the move in her usual high-handed manner, but when she had explained her reasons, he was obliged to agree. In Grafton Street his rooms were up a flight of stairs and to the back. His landlady had been a motherly soul, but not used to the idea of his being in private practice and un-

438

willing to show prospective clients up. Also they were obliged to pass the doors of other residents, and occasionally to meet them on the stairs or the hall or landing. This arrangement was much better. Here a maid answered the door without making her own inquiries as to people's business and simply showed them in to Monk's very agreeable ground-floor sitting room. Grudgingly at first, he conceded it was a marked improvement.

Now to prepare to investigate the rape of Miss Marianne Gillespie, a delicate and challenging matter, far more worthy of his mettle then petty theft or the reputation of an employee or suitor.